Syllabus and notes

Anatiposi

R. L. Dabney

Syllabus and notes

Reprint of the original, first published in 1871.

1st Edition 2023 | ISBN: 978-3-38211-744-3

Anatiposi Verlag is an imprint of Outlook Verlagsgesellschaft mbH.

Verlag (Publisher): Outlook Verlag GmbH, Zeilweg 44, 60439 Frankfurt, Deutschland
Vertretungsberechtigt (Authorized to represent): E. Roepke, Zeilweg 44, 60439 Frankfurt, Deutschland
Druck (Print): Books on Demand GmbH, In de Tarpen 42, 22848 Norderstedt, Deutschland

SYLLABUS AND NOTES

OF

THE COURSE

OF

SYSTEMATIC AND POLEMIC THEOLOGY

TAUGHT IN

Union Theological Seminary, Virginia.

BY

R. L. DABNEY, D. D.

PUBLISHED BY THE STUDENTS.

RICHMOND:
SHEPPERSON & GRAVES, PRINTERS.
1871.

CONTENTS.

PART I.

Natural Theology.

Revealed Theology.

PART II.

TABLE OF ERRATA.

NOTE.—Owing to the circumstances under which these lectures were printed, it has been impossible to prevent a number of mistakes from appearing in the text, some of which are quite serious. An attempt (necessarily a hurried one) has been made to collect most of them in the table given below. Many, however, which are purely typographical, and some others which can be readily corrected by the reader, are not included. It is possible that some have been omitted which should have been inserted, but it is hoped that these will not occasion serious inconvenience to the reader:

Page 18, 10th line from bottom, for divine, read *diverse.*
" 28, 9th " bottom, for seccession, read *succession.*
" 35, 9th " top, for prelations, read *relations.*
" 35, 5th " bottom, for long, read *bony.*
" 39, 12th " top, for posteriori, read *fortiori.*
" 56, 2d " top, for "I do not assert," read *I do assert.*
" 57, 16th " bottom, for origidal, read *original.*
" 76, 4th " top, for resalted, read *resulted.*
" 80, 26th " bottom, for anomis, read *anomia.*
" 82, 8th " top, for hings, read *things.*
" 86, 9th " bottom, for Jew Pater, read *Jupiter.*
" 93, 8th " bottom, for Paul's, read *God's.*
" 93, bottom line, for promise, read *premise.*
" 95, 16th line from top, for affect, read *effect.*
" 102, 7th " bottom, for Ps. lxlii, read *Ps. xcvii.*
" 102, 6th " bottom, for cxlv : 16, read *cxlv :* 17.
" 103, 11th " bottom, for Ps. lxliv, read *xciv.*
" 108, 11th " top, for His, read *of His.*
" 111, 10th " top, for katisma katismatos, read *ktisma ktismatos.*
" 113, 10th " bottom, for min-, read *mine.*
" 118, 5th " top, place comma after *Logos.*
" 120, 2d " bottom, for xix, read *xviii.*
" 122, 10th " bottom, for sames, read *names.*
" 123, 19th " bottom, for Acrians, read *Arians.*
" 134, 21st " top, for incita, read *insita.*
" 157, 16th " bottom, insert 2. before *It.*
" 164, 1st line, for prospon, read *prosapon.*
" 176, 14th line from bottom, for summers, read *centuries.*
" 180, 13th " bottom, for "is the death," read *is not the death.*

" 186, 18th " top, for "sinful head," read *sinful men*.
" 187, 6th " bottom, for Theleniadzomenoi, read *Seleniadzomenoi*.
" 189, 8th " top, for reasons, read *seasons*.
" 190, 12th " top, for prodesis, read *prothesis*.
" 195, 22d " top, for complimentary, read *complementary*.
" 199, 25th " top, for "ox yux," read *efflux*.
" 202, 2d " top, for "and modified," read "and *not* modified."
" 202, 16th " bottom, for equality, read *equally*.
" 209, 20th " top, after Adam's, insert *descendants*.
" 210, 2d " top, for "9, § 3," read "10, § 1."
" 210, 13th " top, for insperable, read *inseparable*.
" 221, 23d " top, for Fabriciu, read *Fabricius*.
" 234, 3d " top, for improved, read *unproved*.
" 237, 13th " bottom, for ill-starved, read *ill-starred*.
" 240, 10th " bottom, after "when" insert *we*.
☞ After page 240, eight pages are numbered 225–232, for 241–248.
Page 246, 28th line from bottom, for edoulensate, read *edouleusate*.
" 256, top line, for expicit, read *explicit*.
" 290, 1st line, for xxxi, read *xxxii*.
" 296, 18th line from bottom, for line read *hire*.
" 297, middle of page, for xxxii, read *xxxiii*.

PART II.

The first Lecture should be No. XXXIV, and all the following changed accordingly.

Page 1, 17th line from top, for "Dick Lect. 49," read *Dick Lect*. 48.
" 3, 25th " bottom, for kames, read *kaine*.
" 9, 6th " top, for Racorian, read *Racovian*.
" 9, 21st " top, for Knaap, read *Knapp*.
" 10, last word of second line, for "of," read *no*.
" 10, 7th line from top, for modum, read *nodum*.
" 15, 14th " bottom, for "to," read *is, that*.
" 17, 24th " bottom, for liberal, read *literal*.
" 23, 28th " bottom, for resumed, read *assumed*.
" 26, 3d " top, for Mopuestia, read *Mopsuestia*.
" 26, 7th " top, for Theodoret, read *Theodore*.
" 26, 2d and 25th lines from bottom, for Enosis, read *henosis*.
" 32, 3d line from top, for Decrteum, read *decretum*.
" 32, 18th " for second, read *first*.
" 34, 11th line from bottom, for reasons, read *seasons*.
" 36, 25th " top, for notus, read *nodus*.
" 36, 16th " bottom, after "Socinians," insert the parenthesis just preceding.
" 36, 16th " bottom, for Eph. read *Pet*.
" 40, 25th " top, for primitive, read *punitive*.
" 43, 18th " bottom, for axcated, read *exacted*.
" 46, 15th " " for "it might be generous," read *generous it might be*.

ERRATA.

" 52, 15th " " for "may seem," read may *be seen*.
" 52, 12th " " for Dutram, read *Outram*.
" 53, 9th " " for quality, read *quantity*.
" 54, 12th " top, for distinguished, read *extinguished*.
" 66, 4th " top, for "on," read *of*.
" 69, 16th " bottom, for converse, read *contrary*.
" 69, 11th " " for 12, read 18.
" 69, 10th " " for Tim. read *Cor*.
" 71, 20th " " for raetus, read *reatus*.
" 72, 1st line, for satisfaction, read *sanctification*.
" 75, 23d line from top, for xv: 10, read *xvi:* 8.
" 75, 22d " bottom, for 400, read 500.
" 76, 22d " top, after "does," dele *not*.
" 77, 13th " top, for masked, read *asked*.
" 100, 19th " top, for perceptively, read *preceptively*.
" 116, 17th " bottom, for rauo, read *muo*.
" 118, 9th " top, for synaphcia, read *sunapheia*.
" 121, 14th " bottom, for liv, read li.
" 122, 6th " bottom, for imitation, read *initiation*.
" 125, 12th " bottom, for tertum, read *tertium*.
" 128. From this point, the Lectures are correctly numbered.
" 135, 10th line from top, for 6, read 16.
" 136, 12th " " for Philem. xviii, read *Philem*. 18.
" 169, 5th " " for 61, read 16.
" 197, 17th " " for "of," read *or*.
" 200, 14th " " for 302, read 198.
" 209, 20th " bottom, for union, read *ruin*.

NOTE TO THE READER.

AD LECTOREM.—Our preceptor in Theology having given to the classes the course of lectures which he had delivered to previous ones, to be used by us in any manner we found most convenient for our assistance in this study, we have printed them in this form for private circulation among ourselves, our predecessors and successors in the Seminary. Our reasons for doing so are the following: We found these lectures useful, so far as we had proceeded, in assisting our comprehension of the text-books. As Dr. Dabney announced a change in the method of his instruction, in which he would cease to deliver the lectures orally, from his chair; and placed them in MS. at the disposal of the students, we desired to continue to avail ourselves of their assistance. To provide ourselves with copies, and to extend their use to subsequent fellow-students, the most convenient and obvious mode was to print them. This has been done at the expense of the students of 1870; and a small number of copies, beyond our own need, has been struck off.

A few explanations may be necessary for the understanding of the method of study, of which these notes form a part. The system consists of recitations on lessons from text-books, chiefly the Confession of Faith and Turrettin's Elenchtic Theology, oral instructions and explanations of the Professor, the preparation and reading Theses by the students upon the topics under discussion, and finally review recitations upon the whole. The design is to combine, as far as may be, the assistance of the living teacher, with the cultivation of the powers of memory, comparison, judgment, reasoning and expression, by the researches of the students themselves, and to fix the knowledge acquired, by repeated views of it. When a "head" of divinity is approached, the first step which our Professor takes, is to propound to us, upon the black-board, a short, comprehensive *syllabus*, of its discussion, in the form of questions; the whole prefaced by a suitable lesson in the text-book. Our first business is to master and recite this lesson. Having thus gotten, from our standard author, a trustworthy outline of the discussion, we proceed next, to investigate the same subject, as time allows, in other writers, both friendly and hostile, preliminary to the composition of a thesis. It is to guide this research, that the *syllabus*, with its numerous references to books, has been given us. These have been carefully selected by the Professor, so as to direct to the ablest and most thorough accessible authors, who defend and impugn the truth. The references may, in many cases, be far more numerous than any Seminary-student can possibly read, at the time, with the duties of the other departments upon his hands. To guide his selection, therefore, the most important authority is named first, under each question, (it may be from our text-book, or from some other,) then the next in value, and last, those others which the student may consult with profit at his greater leisure. This *syllabus* with its references we find one of the most valuable features of our course; it guides not only our first investigations, but those of subsequent years, when the exigencies of our pastoral work may require us to return and make a wider research into the same subject. It directs our inquiries intelligently, and rescues us from the drudgery of wading through masses of literary rubbish to find the opinions of the really influential minds, by giving us some of the experience of one older than ourselves, whose duty it has been made to examine many books upon theology and its kindred sciences.

After the results of our own research have been presented, it has been Dr. Dabney's usage to declare his own view of the whole subject; and these lectures form the mass of what is printed below. They take the form therefore of *resumes* of the discussion already seen in the books; oftentimes reciting in plainer or fresher shape even the arguments of the text-book itself, when the previous examination has revealed the fact that the class have had difficulty in grasping them, and often reproducing the views to which the other references of the syllabus had already directed us. It needs hardly to be added that the Professor of course made no pretense of originality, save in the mode of connecting, harmonizing, or refuting some of the statements passed in review. Indeed, it seemed ever to be his aim to show us how to get for ourselves, in advance of his help, all the things to which in his final lecture he assisted us. These lectures being henceforth in the hands of the classes, will take the place of a subordinate text-book, along with the others; and the time formerly devoted to their oral delivery will be applied to giving us the fruits of other researches in advance of the existing course.

It only remains that we indicate the order of subjects. This is chiefly that observed in the Confession of Faith. But the course begins with Natural Theology, which is then followed by a brief review of the doctrines of psychology and ethicks, which are most involved in the study of theology. This being done, the lectures proceed to revealed theology, assuming, as a postulate established by another department in the Seminary, the inspiration and infallibility of the Scriptures.

The form in which the Lectures are presented to our comrades is dictated by the necessity of having them issued from the press weekly, in order to meet our immediate wants in the progress of the course. It needs only be said in conclusion that this printing is done by Dr. Dabney's consent.

COMMITTEE OF PRINTING.

LECTURES.

NATURAL THEOLOGY.

LECTURE I.

PREFATORY, AND EXISTENCE OF GOD.

SYLLABUS.

1. What is Theology, and what its divisions? Prove that there is a science of *Natural* Theology.
   Consult Turrettin, Loc. I, Que. 2, 3. Dick, Lect. 1.
2. What the two lines of argument to prove the existence of a God? What the *a priori* arguments? Are they valid?
   Stillingfleet, Origines Sacræ, Bk. III, ch. 1. Dr. Samuel Clarke, Discourse of the Being and Attributes of God, § 1 to 12. Chalmer's Nat. Theol., Lect. 3. Dick, Lect. 16. Cudworth's Intellect. System.
3. State the argument of Clarke. Of Howe. Are they sound? Are they a priori?
   Locke's Essay, Bk, IV, ch. 10. Dr. S. Clarke, as above. Howe's Living Temple, Ch. II, § 9 to end.
4. State the arguments of Breckinridge's Theology. Is it valid?
   Knowledge of God. Objective, Bk. I, Ch. 5.
5. Give an outline of the argument from design.
   Paley's Natural Theology, Ch. 1, 2, 3. Xenophon's *Memorabilia*, Lib. I, ch. 4. Cicero, de Natura Deorum, Lib. II, § 2-8. Turrettin, Loc. III, Que. 1. Theological treatises generally.

Theology, What?—It is justly said: Every science should begin by defining its terms, in order to shun verbal fallacies. The word *Theology*, (theou logos), has undergone peculiar mutations, in the history of science. The Greeks often used it for their theories of theogony and cosmogony. Aristotle uses it in a more general form, as equivalent to all metaphisics: dividing theoretical philosophy into physical, mathematical, and theological. Many of the early Christian fathers used it in the restricted sense of the doctrine of Christ's divinity: (scil. Ioannes 'o theologos). But it has now come to be used commonly, to describe the *whole science of God's being and nature, and relations to the creature.* The name is appropriate: 'Science of God.' Th. Aquinas: "*Theologia a Deo docetur, Deum docet, ad Deum ducit.*" God its author, its subject, its end.

Its Divisions.—The distribution of Theology into didactic, polemic, and practical is sufficiently known. Now, all didactic inculcation of truth is indirect refutation of the opposite error. Polemic Theology has been defined as direct refutation of error. The advantage of this has been supposed to be, that the way for easiest and most thorough refutation is to systematize the error, with reference to its first principle, or PROTON PSEUDOS. But the attempt to form a science of polemics, different from Didactic Theology fails; because error never has true method. Confusion is its characteristic. The system of discussion, formed on its false method, cannot be scientific. Hence, separate treatises on polemics have usually slidden into the methods of didactics; or they have been confused. Again: Indirect refutation is often more effectual than direct. There is therefore, in this course, no separate polemic; but what is said against errors is divided between the historical, and didactic.

IS THERE A NATURAL THEOLOGY?—Theology is divided into natural and revealed, according to the sources of our knowledge of it: from natural reason; from revelation. What is *science?* Knowledge demonstrated and methodized. That *there is* a science of Natural Theology of at least some certain and connected propositions, although limited, and insufficient for salvation at best, is well argued from Scripture, e. g. Ps. xix: 1–7. Acts xiv: 15; or xvii: 23. Rom. i: 19; ii: 14, &c.; and from the fact that nearly all heathens have religious ideas, and rites of worship. Not that religious ideas are innate; but the capacity to establish some such ideas, from natural data, is innate. Consider further: Is not this capacity implied in man's capacity to receive a revealed theology? Does revelation demonstrate God's existence; or assume it? Does it rest the first truths on pure dogmatism, or on evidence which man apprehends? The latter; and then man is assumed to have some natural capacity for such apprehension. But if nature reflects any light concerning God, (as Scripture asserts,) then man is capable of deriving some theology from nature.

WHY DENIED?—Some old divines were wont to deny that there was any science of Natural Theology, and to say that without revelation man would not naturally learn its first truth. They attribute the grains of truth mixed with the various polytheisms to the remnants of tradition descending from Noah's family. They urge that some secluded tribes, Hottentots, Australians, have no religious ideas; that some men are sincere atheists after reflection; and that there is the wildest variety, yea contradiction, between the different schools of heathens. These divines seem to fear lest, by granting a Natural Theology, they should grant too much to natural reason; a fear ungrounded and extreme. They are in danger of a worse consequence; reducing man's capacity for receiving divine verities so low, that the rational skeptick will be able to turn upon them, and say: "Then, by so inept a creature, the guarantees of a true revelation cannot be certainly apprehended."

PROOF.—To reply more in detail; I grant much influence to primeval traditions, (a subject of great interest learnedly discussed in Theo. Gale's Court of the Gentiles.) But that so inconstant a cause is able to perpetuate in men these fixed convictions of the invisible, shows in man a natural religious capacity. That there have been atheistic persons and tribes, is inconclusive. Some tribes deduce no science of geometry, statics, or even numbers; but this does not prove man non-logical. Some profess to disbelieve axioms, as Hume that of causation, but this is far from proving man incapable of a natural science of induction. Besides, the atheism of these tribes is doubtful; savages are shrewd, suspicious, and fond of befooling inquisitive strangers by assumed stupidity. And last; the differences of Natural Theology among polytheists are a diversity in unity; all involve the prime truths; a single first cause, responsibility, guilt, a future life, future rewards and punishments.

Existence of God.—2. The first truth of theology is the existence of God. Divines have attempted to prove this rationally by two modes of argument, the *à priori* and *à posteriori*. The latter infers a God by reasoning backwards from effects to cause. The former should accordingly mean reasoning downwards from cause to effect; the meaning attached to the phrase by Aristotle and his followers. But now the term *à priori* reasoning is used, in this connexion, to denote conclusions gained without the aid of experience, from the primary judgments, and especially, *the attempt to infer the truth of a notion, directly from its nature or condition in the mind.*

A Priori Argument. What, and by Whom Urged?—It appears to be common among recent writers (as Dick, Chalmers' Natural Theology) to charge Dr. Samuel Clarke as the chief assertor of the *à priori* argument among Englishmen. This is erroneous. It may be more correctly said to have been first intimated by *Epicurus* (whose atomic theory excluded the *à posteriori* argument;) as appears from a curious passage in *Cicero, de natura Deorum*, Lib. I, c. 16. It was more articulately stated by the celebrated *Des Cartes* in his Meditations; and naturalized to the English mind rather by Bishop Stillingfleet, than by Dr. Clarke. The student may find a very distinct statement of it in the *Origines Sacræ* of the former, book III, chapter I, § 14; while Dr. Clarke, § 8 of his Discourse, expressly says that the personal intelligence of God must be proved *à posteriori*, and not *à priori*. But *Des Cartes* having founded his psychology on the two positions: 1st. *Cogito; ergo sum;* and 2nd, The *Ego* is spirit, not matter; proceeds to ask: Among all the ideas in the consciousness, how shall the true be distinguished from the false, seeing all are obviously, not consistent? As to primary ideas, his answer is; by the clearness with which they commend themselves to our consciousness as immediate truths. Now, among our ideas, no other is so clear and unique as that of a *first Cause*, eternal and infinite. Hence we may immediately accept it as consciously true. Moreover, that we have this idea of a God proves there must be a God; because were there none, the rise of His idea in our thought could not be accounted for; just as the idea of triangles implies the existence of some triangle. Now the *à priori* argument of Stillingfleet is but a specific application of *Des Cartes'* method. We find, says he, that in thinking a God we must think Him as eternal, self-existent, and necessarily existent. But since we indisputably do think a God, it is impossible but that God is. Since necessary existence is unavoidably involved in our idea of a God, therefore His existence must necessarily be granted.

Its Defect.—Now, surely this process is not necessarily inconclusive, because it is *à priori;* there are processes, in which we validly determine the truth of a notion by simple inspection of its contents and conditions. But the defect of Stillingfleet's reasoning is, that it does not give the correct account of our thought. If the student will inspect the two propositions, which form an enthymeme, he will see that the conclusion depends on this assumption, as its major premise: That we can have no idea in our consciousness, for which there is not an answering objective reality. (This is, obviously, the assumed major: because without it the enthymeme can only contain the conditional conclusion, that God, if there is one, necessarily exists.) But that major premise is, notoriously, not universally true.

A Posteriori Argument of Dr. S. Clarke.—Now, instead of saying that Dr. Clarke's method in the Discourse of the Being, &c., of God, is the *à priori*, it is more correct to say (with Hamilton's Reid) that it is an *à posteriori* argument, inferring the existence of God from His effects; but disfigured at one or two points by useless Cartesian elements. His first position is: Since something now exists, something has existed from eternity. This, you will find, is the starting-point of the argument, with all reasoners; and it is solid. For if, at any time in the past eternity, there had been absolutely nothing, since nothing cannot be a cause of existence, time and space must have remained forever blank of existence. Hence, 2d., argues Dr. Clarke: there has been, from eternity, some immutable and independent Being: because an eternal succession of dependent beings, without independent first cause, is impossible. 3d. This Being, as independent eternally, must be self-existent, that is, necessarily existing. For its eternal independence shows that the spring, or causative source of its existence could not be outside of itself; it is therefore within itself forever. But the only true idea of such self-existence is, that the idea of its non-existence would be an express contradiction. And here, Dr. Clarke very needlessly adds: our notion that the existence is necessary proves that it cannot but exist. He reasons also: our conceptions of infinite time and infinite space are necessary: we cannot but think them. But they are not substance: they are only modes of substance. Unless some substance exists of which they are modes, they cannot exist, and so, would not be thought. Hence, there must be an infinite and eternal substance. 4th. The substance of this Being is not comprehensible by us: but this does not make the evidence for its existence less certain. For, 5th. Several of its attributes are demonstrable; as that it must be. 6th. Infinite and omnipresent. 7th. That it must be One. And 8th. That it must be intelligent and free, &c. The conclusion is, that this Being must be Creator and God, unless the universe can itself fulfil the conditions of eternity, necessary self-existence, infinitude, and intelligence and free choice. This is Pantheism: which he shows cannot be true.

Clarke's Argument valid, because in the main a posteriori.—On this argument as a whole, I remark, that it is in the main valid, because it is in the main *à posteriori*: it appeals to the intuitive judgment of cause, to infer from finite effects an infinite first Cause. The Cartesian features attached to the 3d proposition are excrescences: but we may remove them, and leave the chain adamantine. We will prune them away, not for the reasons urged by Dr. Chalmers, which are in several particulars as invalid as Dr. Clarke; but for the reason already explained on page 7. I only add, it seems to me inaccurate to argue that time and space can only be conceived by us as modes of substance; and therefore infinite and eternal substance must exist. The truth here is: that we cannot conceive of finite substance or events, without placing it in time and space; a different proposition from Dr. Clarke's.

HOWE'S DEMONSTRATION.—3. I think we have the metaphysical argument for the being of a God, stated in a method free from these objections, by the great Puritan divine, *John Howe.* He flourished about 1650, A. D., and prior to Dr. Clarke. See his Living Temple, chapter II. He begins thus: 1. Since we now exist, something has existed from eternity. 2. Hence, at least, some *uncaused* Being, for the eternal has nothing prior to it. 3. Hence some *independent* Being. 4. Hence that Being exists *necessarily*; for its independent, eternal, inward spring of existence cannot be conceived as possibly at any time inoperative. 5. This Being must be *self-active*; active; because if other beings did not spring from its action, they must all be eternal, and so independent, and necessary, which things are impossible for beings variously organized and changeable; and *self*-active, because in eternity nothing was before Him to prompt His action. 6. This Being is *living;* for self-prompted activity is our very idea of life. 7. He is of boundless intelligence, power, freedom, &c.

WHAT NEEDED TO COMPLETE IT?—This argument is in all parts well knit. But it is obviously *à posteriori*; for all depends from a simple deduction, from a universe of effects, back to their cause; and in the same way are inferred the properties of that cause. The only place where the argument needs completion, is at the fifth step. So far forth, the proof is perfect, that *some* eternal, uncaused, necessary being exists. But how do we prove that this One created all other beings? The answer is: these others must all be either eternal or temporal. If they are all eternal, then all are uncaused, independent, self-existent, and necessary. This we shall see is *Pantheism.* If the rest are temporal, then they were all caused, but by what? Either by the one uncaused, eternal Being; or by other similar temporal beings generating them. But the latter is the theory of an *infinite, independent series of finite organisms each one dependent.* When therefore, we shall have stopped these two breaches, by refuting Pantheism and the hypothesis of infinite series, the demonstration will be perfect.

VIEW OF PLATO.—Now Platonism held that *all substance* is uncaused and eternal, as to its being. All finite rational spirits are, said this theology, emanations of the TO 'ON, the eternal intelligence; and all matter has been from eternity, in the state of inert, passive, chaotic 'ULE. It referred all organization, fashioning the only *creation* it admitted, and change, however, either directly or indirectly, to the intelligent first Cause. This scheme does not seem easily refuted by natural reason. Let it be urged that the very notion of the first Cause implies its *singleness;* and more solidly, that the unity of plan and working seen in nature points to only a single ultimate cause; Plato could reply, that he made only one first Cause; for 'ULE is inert; and only the *recipient* of causation. Let that rule be urged, which Hamilton calls his "law of parsimony;" that hypotheses must include nothing more than is necessary to account for the *phenomena*; Plato could say: No; the reason as much demands the supposition of a material pre-existing, as of an almighty Workman; for even omnipotence cannot work, with *nothing to work on.* Indeed, so far as I know, all human systems, Plato's, Epicurus,' Zeno's, Pythagoras,' the Peripatetic, had this common feature; that it is self-evident, substance cannot rise out of *nihil* into *esse*; that *ex nihilo nihil fit.* And we shall see how obstinate is the tendency of philosophy to relapse to this maxim, in the instances of Spinoza's Pantheism, and Kant's and Hamilton's theory of causation. Indeed it may be doubted whether the human mind, unaided by revelation, would ever have advanced farther than this. It was from an accurate knowledge of the history of philosophy, that the apostle declared, (Hebrews xi: 3) the doctrine of an almighty creation out of nothing is one of pure faith.

Can the Platonic Doctrine of the Eternity of all Substances be refuted by reason?—Dr. Clarke, as you saw, does indeed attempt a rational argument that the eternity of matter is impossible. The eternal must be necessary; hence an eternal cause must necessarily be. So, that which can possibly be thought as existing and yet not necessary, cannot be eternal. Such is his logic. I think inspection will show you a double defect. The first enthymeme, as we saw (p. 8) is not conclusive; and the second, even if the first were true, would be only inferring the converse; which is not necessarily conclusive.

Howe states a more plausible argument, at which Dr. Clarke also glances. Were matter eternal, it must needs be necessary. But then it must be ubiquitious, homogeneous, immutable, like God's substance; because this inward eternal necessity of being cannot but act always and everywhere alike. Whereas we see matter diverse, changing and only in parts of space. I doubt whether this is solid; or whether from the mere postulate of necessary existence, we can infer anything more than Spinoza does; that eternal matter can possibly exist in no other organisms and sequences of change, than those in which it actually exists. Our surest refutation of this feature of Platonism is God's word. This heathen theology is certainly nearest of any to the Christian, here, and less repugnant than any other, to the human reason and God's honour.

Breckinridge's Demonstration.—4. Dr. R. J. Breckinridge, (vol. I, p. 56, &c.,) constructs what he assures us, is an argument of his own, for the being of a God. A brief inspection of it will illustrate the subject. 1. Because something now is—at least the mind that reasons—therefore something eternal is. 2. All known substance is matter or spirit. 3. Hence only three possible alternatives; either, a.) some matter is eternal; and the source of all spirit and all other matter. Or, b.) some being combined of matter and spirit is the eternal one, and source of all other matter and spirit. Or, c.) some spirit is eternal, and produced all other spirit and matter. The third hypothesis must be the true one; not the second; because we are matter and spirit combined, and consciously, cannot create; and moreover the first Cause must be single. Not the first, because matter is inferior to mind; and the inferior does not produce the superior.

Its Defects.—The objections to this structure begin at the second part, where the author leaves the established forms of Howe and Clarke. First: the argument cannot apply, in the mind of a pure idealist, or of a materialist. Second: it is not rigidly demonstrated that there can be no substance but matter and spirit; all that can be done is to say negatively, that no other is known to us. Third: the three alternative propositions do not exhaust the case; the Pantheists and the Peripatetic, of eternal organization, show us that others are conceivable, as obviously does Platonic. Fourth: that we, combined of matter and spirit, consciously cannot create, is short of proof that some higher being thus constituted cannot. Christ could create, if He pleased; He is thus constituted. Last: it is unfortunate that an argument, which aims to be so experimental, should have the analogy of our natural experience so much against it. For we only witness human spirits producing effects, when incorporate. As soon as they are disembodied, (at death,) they totally cease to be observed causes of any effects.

TELEOLOGICAL ARGUMENT.—5. The teleological argument for the being and attributes of a God has been so well stated by Paley, in his Natural Theology, that though as old as Job and Socrates, it is usually mentioned as Paley's argument. I refer you especially to his first three chapters. Beginning from the instance of a peasant finding a watch on a common, and although not knowing how it came there, concluding that some intelligent agent constructed it; he applies the same argument, with great beauty and power, to show that man and the universe have a Maker. For we see everywhere intelligent arrangements; as the eye for seeing, the ear for hearing, &c., &c. Nor is the peasant's reasoning to a watch-maker weakened, because he never saw one at work, or even heard of one; nor because a part of the structure is not understood; nor because some of the adjustments are seen to be imperfect; nor, if you showed the peasant, in the watch a set of wheels for reproducing its kind, would he be satisfied that there was no watchmaker? for he would see that this reproductive mechanism could not produce the intelligent arrangements. Nor would he be satisfied with a "law of nature," or a physical principle of order, as the sole cause.

ARE THE TWO RIVAL LINES OF PROOF?—It is a fact somewhat curious, that the metaphysical and the teleological arguments have each had their exclusive advocates in modern times. The applauders of Paley join Dr. Thomas Brown in scouting the former as shadowy and inconclusive. The supporters of the metaphysical divines depreciate Paley, as leading us to nothing above a mere *Demiurgus*. In truth both lines of reasoning are valid, and each needs the other. Dr. Brown, for instance, in carrying Paley's argument to its higher conclusions, must tacitly borrow some of the very metaphysics which he professes to disdain. Otherwise it remains incomplete, and leads to no more than a sort of *Artifex Mundi*, whose existence is run back merely to a date prior to human experience, and whose being, power and wisdom are demonstrated to extend only so far as man's inquiries have gone. But that He is eternal, immutable, independent, immense, infinite in power or wisdom, it can never assure us. True, in viewing the argument, your mind did leap to the conclusion that the artificer of nature's contrivances is the Being of "eternal power and godhead;" but it was only because you passed, almost unconsciously perhaps, through that metaphysical deduction of which Howe gives us the exact description. Howe's is the comprehensive, Paley's the partial (but very lucid) display of the *à posteriori* argument. Paley's premise; that every contrivance must have an intelligent contriver, is but an instance under the more general one, that every effect must have a cause. The inadequacy of Paley's argument may be illustrated in this; that he seems to think the peasant's discovery of a stone, instead of a watch, could not have led his mind to the same conclusion, whereas a pebble as really, though not so impressively, suggests a cause, as an organized thing. For even the pebble should make us think either that it is such as can have the ground of its existence in its present form in itself; and so, can be eternal, self-existent, and necessary; or else that it had a Producer, who does possesss these attributes.

VALUE OF THE TELEOLOGICAL ARGUMENT.—But, on the other hand, this argument from contrivance has great value, for these reasons. It is plain and popular. It enables us to evince the unity of the first causes through the unity of purpose and convergence of the consequences of creation. It aids us in showing the personality of God, as a being of intelligence and will; and it greatly strengthens the assault we shall be enabled to make on Pantheism, by showing, unless there is a personal and divine first Cause prior to the universe, this must itself be, not only measured, eternal, independent, necessarily existent, but endued with intelligence.

LECTURE II.

SYLLABUS.

EXISTENCE OF GOD. (continued.)

1. Show, in a few instances, how the argument from design may be drawn from *animal organisms*, from *man's mental and emotional structure*, and from the *adaptation* of *matter* to our mental faculties. See Paley, Natural Theology, bk. iv, ch. 3. 16.
Chalmer's Natural Theology, bk. iv, ch. 1, 2. Bk. iv, ch. 5.
2. Can the being of God be argued from the existence of conscience? Turrettin, Loc. iii. Que. 1. §14, 15. Alexander's Moral Science, ch. 12. Chalmer's Natural Theology, bk. iii, ch. 2. Charnock, Attr. Discourse i, § 3.
3. Can any sound argument be drawn from the *Consensus Populorum*? Turretin, Loc. iii, Que. 1, §16--18. Dick, Lec. 17. Cicero de Natura Deorum, lib. i. Charnock on Attr., Discourse i, §1.
4. Refute the evasion of Hume that the universe is a *singular effect*. Alexander's Moral Science, ch. 28. Chalmer's Natural Theology, bk. i. ch. 4. Watson's Theolgical Inst. Pt. ii, ch. 1.
5. Can the universe be accounted for, without a Creator, as an infinite series of temporal effects? Turrettin, Loc. iii, Que. 1, § 6, 7. Alexander's Moral Science, ch. 28. Dr. S. Clarke, Discouse, § 2.
6. Refute the pantheistic scheme of the universe. Alexander's Moral Science, ch. 28. Chalmers' Natural Theology, bk. i, ch. 5. Dr. S. Clarke, Discourse, § 3, 7, 9, &c.

1. INSTANCES OF CONTRIVANCE TO AN END.—To resume: A single instance of intelligent contrivance in the works of creation would prove an intelligent Creator. Yet, it is well to multiply these proofs, even

largely: for they give us then a *wider foundation* of deduction, stronger views of the *extent* of the creative wisdom and power; and better evidence of God's unity.

FROM ORGANS OF ANIMALS.—Hence, as instances, showing how the argument is constructed: If the design is to produce the physical part of the sensation of vision; *the eye* is obviously an optical instrument, contrived with *lenses* to refract, expedients for obtaining an *achromatic spectrum*, adjustments for distance and quantity of light, and protection of the eye, by situation, bony socket, brow, lids, lubricating fluids; and in birds, the nicticating membrane. Different creatures also have eyes adapted to their lives and media of vision; as birds, cats, owls, fishes. So, *the ear* is an auditory apparatus, with a concha to converge the sound-waves, a tube, a tympanum to transmit vibration, the three bones (*malleus, stipes and incus*) in instable equilibrium, to convey it to the *sensorium*, &c.

FROM SPIRITUAL STRUCTURE OF MAN.—The world of *spirit* is just as full of *evident contrivances*. See (e. g.) the laws of *habit* and *imitation*, exactly adjusted to educate, and to form the character; and the faculties of memory, association, taste, &c. The evidences of contrivance are, if possible, still more beautiful in our emotional structure; e. g. in the instincts of parental love, sympathy, resentment and its natural limits, sexual love, and its natural check, modesty; and above all, conscience, with its self-approval and remorse. All these are adadjusted to obvious ends.

IN ARRANGEMENTS FOR COMPENSATING DEFECTS.—We see marks of more recondite design, in the natural *compensations* for necessary defects. The elephant's short neck is made up by a lithe proboscis. Bird's heads cannot carry teeth: but they have a gizzard. Insects with fixed heads, have a number of eyes to see around them. Brutes have less reason, but more instinct; &c., &c.

FROM DESIGNED ADAPTATIONS.—The *adaptations* of one department of nature to another show at once contrivance, selecting will, and *unity* of mind. Thus, the *media* and the *organs* of sense are made for each other. The forms and colours of natural objects are so related to taste; the degree of fertility imparted to the earth, to man's necessity for labour; the stability of physical law, to the necessary judgments of the reason thereabout. So all *nature*, material and spiritual, animal, vegetable, inorganic, on our planet, in the starry skies, are full of wise contrivance.

2. CONSCIENCE PROVES THERE IS A GOD.—The moral phenomena of conscience present a twofold evidence for the being of a God, worthy of fuller illustration than space allows. This faculty is a most ingenious spiritual contrivance, adjusted to a beneficent end: viz., the promotion of virtuous acts, and repression of wicked. As such, it proves a contriver, just as any organic adjustment does. But second: we shall find, later in the course, that our moral judgments are intuitive, primitive, and necessary; the most inevitable functions of the reason. Now, the idea of our acts which have *rightness* is unavoidably attended with the judgment that they are *obligatory*. Obligation must imply an *obliger*. This is not always any known creature: hence, the Creator. Again, our conscience of wrong doing unavoidably suggests *fear;* but

fear implies an avenger. The secret sinner, the imperial sinner above all creature-power, shares this dread. Now, one may object, that this process is not valid, unless we hold God's *mere* will the sole source of moral distinctions; which we do not teach, since an atheist is reasonably compelled to hold them. But the objection is not just. The primitive law of the reason must be accepted as valid to us, whatever its source. For parallel: The intuitive belief in causation is found on inspection, to contain the propostion, 'There is a first Cause.' But in order for the validity of this proposition, it is not necessary for us to say that this intuition is God's arbitrary implantation. It is intrinsically true to the nature of things; and the argument to a first Cause therefore only the more valid.

This moral argument to the being of a God, as it is immediate and strictly logical, is doubtless far the most practical. Its force is seen in this, that theoretical atheists, in danger and death, usually at the awakening of remorse, acknowledge God.

3. Argument from Universal Consent.—You find the argument from the Consensus Populorum, much elaborated by your authorities. I conclude that it gives a strong probable evidence for the being of a God, thus: The truth is abstract; its belief would not have been so nearly universal, nor so obviously essential to man's social existence did not a valid ground for it exist in man's laws of thought. For it can be accounted for neither by fear, policy nor self-interest.

4. Objected, that Contrivance betrays Limitation.—From the affirmative argument, we return to evasions. An objection is urged, that the argument from design, if valid, proves only a creator of *limited powers.* For contrivance is the expedient of weakness. E. g. one constructs a derrick, because he is too weak to lift the mass as a Sampson. If the Creator has eternal power and godhead, why did he not go straight to His ends, without means, as in Ps. 33: 9? I answer, design proves a designer, though in part unintelligible. 2nd. It would not be unworthy of the Almighty to choose this manner of working, in order to leave His signature on it for *man to read.* 3d. Chiefly: Had God employed no means to ends, he must have remained the only agent; there would have been no organized nature; but only the one supernatural agent.

Hume Objects that the World is a Singular Effect.—Hume strives to undermine the argument from the creation to a Creator, by urging, that since experience only teaches us the uniformity of the tie between effect and cause, it is unwarranted to apply it farther than experience goes with us. But no one has had any experience of a *world-maker*, as we have of making implements in the arts. The universe, if an effect at all, is one wholly singular; the only one anybody has known, and from the earliest human experience, substantially as it is now. Hence the empirical induction to its first Cause is unauthorized.

Dr. Alexander's Answer.—Note first: this is from the same mint with his argument against miracles. Creation is simply the first miracle; the same objection is in substance brought; viz: no testimony can be weighty enough to prove against universal experience, that a miracle has occurred. Next, Dr. Alexander, to rebut, resorts to an illustraraion; a country boy who had seen only ploughs and horse-carts, is shown a steam-frigate; yet he immediately infers a mechanic for it. The fact will be so; but it will not give us the whole analysis. True the frigate is greatly larger and more complicated than a horse-cart; (as the universe is than any human machine). But still Hume might urge that the boy would see a thousand *empirical* marks, cognizable to his experiences, (timber with marks of the plane on it, as on his plough-beam, the cable as evidently twisted of hemp, as his plough-lines; the huge anchor with as evident dints of the hammer, as his plough-share,) which taught him that the wonderful ship was also a produced mechanism. Astonishing as it is to him, compared with the plough, it is experimentally seen to be *not natural*, like the universe.

CHALMERS' ANSWER.—Chalmers, in a chapter full of contradictions, seems to grant that experience alone teaches us the law of causation, and asserts that still the universe is not "a singular effect." To show this, he supposes with Paley, the peasant from a watch inferring a watch-maker: and then by a series of abstractions, he shows that the logical basis of the inference is not anything peculiar to that watch, as that it is a gold, or a silver, a large, a small, or a good watch, or a machine to measure time at all; but simply the fact that it is a manifest contrivance for an end. The effect then, is no longer singular; yet the inference to some adequate agent holds. To this ingenious process Hume would object, that it is experience alone which guides in making those successive abstactions, by which we separate the accidental from the essential effect and cause. This, Chalmers himself admits. Hence, as we have no experience of world-making, no such abstraction is here allowable, to reduce the world to the class of common effects. Besides; has Hume admitted that it is an effect at all? In fine, he might urge this difference, that the world is *native*, while the watch, the plough, the ship bears, to the most unsophisticated observer, empirical marks of being made, and not native.

TRUE ANSWER.—Let us not then refute Hume from his own premises; for they are false. *It is not experience* which teaches us, that every effect has its cause, but the *à priori* reason. (This Chalmers first asserts, and then unwisely surrenders.) Neither child nor man believes that maxim to be true in the hundredth case, because he has experienced its truth in ninty-nine; he instinctively believed it in the first case. It is not a true canon of inductive logic, that the tie of cause and effect can be asserted only so far as experience proves its presence. If it were, *would induction ever teach us anything we did not know before?* Would there be any inductive science? Away with the nonsense! Grant that the world is "a singular effect." It is a phenomenon, it could not be without a cause of its being, either extrinsic, or intrinsic. And this we know, not by experience, but by one of those primitive judgments of the reason, which alone make experience intelligible and valid.

CAN THE PRESENT UNIVERSE BE THE RESULT OF AN INFINITE SERIES OF ORGANISMS? 5.—But may not this universe have the ground of its being in *itself?* This is another evasion of the atheists. Grant, they say, that nothing cannot produce something. Theists go outside the universe to seek its cause; and when they suppose they have found it in a God, they are unavoidably driven to represent Him as uncaused from without, eternal, self-existent, and necessary. Now it is a simpler hopythesis, just to suppose that the universe which we see, is the uncaused, eternal, self-existent, necessary Being. Why may we not adopt it? Seeing we must run back to the mystery of some uncaused, eternal being, why may we not accept the obvious teaching of nature and experience, and conclude that this is it? Since the organisms which adorn this universe are all temporal, and since the earth and other stars move in temporal cycles, we shall then have to suppose that the infinite past eternity, through which this self-existent universe has existed, was made up of an infinite succession of these organisms and cycles, each previous one producing the next: as the infinite future eternity which will be. But what is absurd in such a hypothesis?

Metaphysical Answers Invalid.—Now I will not reply, with Dr. Clarke and others, that if the universe is eternal it must be necessary; and this necessity must make its substance homogeneous and unchangeable throughout infinite time and space. It might be plausibly retorted, that this tendency to regular, finite organisms, which we see, was the very necessity of nature inherent in matter. Nor does it seem to me solid to say, with Robert Hall in his sermon, Turrettin, and others, that an eternal series of finite durations is impossible; because if each particular part had a beginning, while the series had none, we should have the series existing before its first member; the chain stretching farther back than its farthest link. The very supposition was, that the series had *no first* member. Is a past eternity any more impossible to be made up of the addition of an infinite number of finite parts, than an abstract infinite future? Surely not. Now there is to be just such an infinite future: namely, your and my immortality, which, although it may not be measured by solar days and years, will undoubtedly be composed of parts of successive time infinitely multiplied. But to this future eternity, it would be exactly parallel to object, that we make each link in it have an end, while the whole is endless; which would involve the same absudity, of a chain extended forward after the last link was ended. The answer again is: that according to the supposition, there is *no* last link, the number thereof being infinite. In a word, what mathematician does not know that infinitude may be generated by the addition of finites repeated an infinite number of times; and that two proper infinites may be unequal? These simple remarks, I think, suggest the refutation of Turrettin's useless metaphysics (S. 7–9.) on this subject.

True Answers.—The true answers to the atheistic hypothesis are these:

(1.) Take any line of generative organisms, for instance: (oak trees bearing acorns, and those acorns rearing oaks, e. g.) the being of each individual in the series demands an adequate cause. When we push the inquiry back one step, and ask the cause of the parent which (seemingly) caused it, we find precisely the same difficulty unanswered. Whatever distance we run back along the line, we clearly see no approach is made towards finding the adequate cause of the series, or of the earliest individual considered. Hence it is wholly unreasonable to suppose that the introduction of infinitude into the series helps to give us an adequate cause. We only impose on ourselves with an undefined idea. Paley's illustration here is as just as beautiful. Two straight parrallel lines pursued ever so far, make no approximation; they will never meet though infinitely extended.

(2.) An adequate cause existing at the time the phenomenon arises, must be assigned for every effect. For a cause not present at the rise of the effect is no cause. Now then; when a given oak was sprouted all the previous oaks and acorns of its line save one or two had perished. Was this acorn, even with its parent oak, the adequate cause of the whole structure of the young tree, including the ingenious contrivances thereof? Surely not. But the previous dead oaks and acorns are no cause; for they are not there. An absent cause is no cause. The original cause of this oak is not in the series at all.

(3.) Even if we permit ourselves to be dazzled with the notion that somehow the infinitude of the series can account for its self-productive power; this maxim is obvious: that in a series of transmitted causes the whole power of the cause must be successively in each member of the series. For each one could only transmit what power it received from its immediate predecessor; and if at any stage, any portion of the causative power were lost, all subsequent stages must be without it. But evidently no one generation of acorns ever had power or intelligence to create the subtle contrivances of vegetable life in their progeny; and to suppose that all did, is but multiplying the absurdity.

(4.) This question should be treated according to the atheist's point of view, scientifically: science always accepts testimony in preference to hypothesis. Now there is a testimony, that of the Mosaic Scripture, as supported by universal tradition, which says that all series of organisms began in the creative act of an intelligent first Cause. The atheist may object, that men, as creatures themselves, have no right of their own knowledge, to utter such traditionary testimony; for they could not be present before the organisms existed, to witness how they were brought into existence. The only pretext for such tradition would be that some prior superhuman Being, who did witness man's production, revealed to him how he was produced; but whether any such prior Being existed, is the very thing in debate, and so may not be taken for granted.

True; but the *existence* of the testimony must be granted; for it is a fact that it exists, and it must be accounted for. And the question is, whether the only good account is not, that the universe did have an intelligent Cause, and that this Cause taught primeval man whence he originated. Otherwise, not only is the universe left unaccounted for, but the universal tradition.

(5.) Science exalts experience above hypothesis even more than testimony. Now, the whole state of the world bears the appearance of *recency*. The recent discovery of new continents, the great progress of new arts since the historic era began, and the partial population of the earth by man, all belie the eternity of the human race. But stronger still, geology proves the creation, in time, of race after race of animals, and the comparatively recent origin of man, by her fossil records. These show the absolute beginning of *genera*. And the attempt to account for them by the development theory (Chambers or Darwin) is utterly repudiated by even the better irreligious philosophers; for if there is anything that Natural History has established, it is that organic life is separated from inorganic forces, mechanical, chemical, electrical, or other, by inexorable bounds; and that *genera* may begin or end, but never transmute themselves into other *genera*.

6. PANTHEISM.—As I pointed out, there are but two hypotheses by which the demonstration of an eternal, intelligent, personal first Cause can be evaded. The one has just been discussed; the other is the pantheistic. No separate first Cause of the universe need be assigned, it says, because the universe is God. The first Cause, and the whole creation are supposed to be *one substance*, world-god, possessing all the attributes of both. As extremes often meet, pantheism leads to the same practical results with atheism.

PERIPATETIC PANTHEISM.—The ancient form of pantheism, probably peripatetic in its source, admitted that matter, dead, senseless, divisible, cannot be the proper seat of intelligence and choice, which are indivisible; and that the universe is full of marks of intelligent design, so that an *Anima Mundi*, an intelligent Principle, must be admitted in the universe. Yes, I reply, it must, and that *personal*. Because it obviously has intelligence, choice, and will; and how can personality be better defined? Nor can it inhabit the universe as a soul its body, not being limited to it in time or space, nor bearing that relation to it. Not in time: because, being eternal, it existed a whole past eternity before it; for we have proved the latter temporal. Not in space; for we have seen this Intelligence eternal ages not holding its *ubi* in space by means of body; and there is not a single reason for supposing that it is now limited to the part of space which bodies occupy. It is not connected with matter by any tie of animality; because immensely the larger part of matter is inanimate.

PANTHEISM OF SPINOZA.—Modern pantheism appears either in the hypothesis of Spinoza the Jew, or in that of the later German idealists. Both see that even the material universe teems with intelligent contrivances; and more, that the nobler part, that known by consciousness, and so, most immediately known, is a world of thought and feeling in human breasts. Hence intelligence and will must be accounted for, as well as matter. Now, Spinoza's 1st position is: There can be no real substance, except it be self-existent, and so, eternal. That is: it is incredible that any true substance can pass from *nihil* into *esse*. 2d. All the self-existent must be one; this is unavoidable from the unity of its characteristic attribute. 3d. The one real substance must therefore be eternal, infinite, and necessarily existent. Hence, 4th. All other seeming beings are not real substance, but modes of existence of this sole Being, the TO PAN. 5th. All possible attributes, however seemingly divine, must be modes, nearer or remote, of this Being; and it is necessary therefore to get rid of the prejudice, that modes of thought and will, and modes of extension, cannot be referred to the same substance. Hence this is the true account of the universe. All material bodies (so called) are but different *modes of extension*, in which the necessary substance projects himself; and all personal spirits (so called) are but modes of thought and will, in which the same TO PAN pulsates.

Now you see that the whole structure rests on two unproved and preposterous asssumptions: that real substance cannot be except it be self-existent; and that the self-existent can be but one. The human mind is incapable of demonstrating either.

PANTHEISM OF THE MODERN IDEALIST.—Says the modern idealist: Let the mind take nothing for granted, except the demonstrated; and it will find that it really *knows nothing save its consciousnesses.* Of what is it conscious? Only of its own subjective states. Men fancy that these must be referred to a *subject*, called mind, spirit, self; as the substance of which they are states. So they fancy that they find objective sources for their sensations, and objective limits to their volitions; but if it fancies it knows either, it is only by a subjective consciousness. These, after all, are its only real possessions. Hence, it has no right to assert either substantive self, or objective matter; it only knows, in fact, a series of self-consciousnesses. Hence; our thinking and willing, *constitute our being.* Hence, too, the whole seeming objective world is only educed from a non-existence as it is thought by us. The total *residuum* then, is an impersonal power of thought, only existing as it exerts its self-consciousness in the various beings of the universe, (if there is a universe) and in God. Its subjective consciousnesses constitute spiritual substance (so called,) self, fellow-man, God; and its objective, the seeming objective material bodies of the universe.

REFUTATION. 1. INTUITION MUST BE ACCEPTED AS VALID.—Against both these forms of pantheism I present the following outline of a refutation. (1st.) If the mind may not trust the intuition which refers all attributes and affections to their substances, and which gives real objective sources for sensations, it may not believe in its intuitive self-consciousness, nor in that intuition of cause for every phenomenon, on which Spinoza founds the belief in his One Substance. *Falsus in uno; falsus in omnibus.* There is an end of all thinking. That the intuitions above asserted, are necessary and primary, I prove by this: that every man, including the idealist, unavoidably makes them.

CONSCIOUSNESS IMPLIES MY PERSONALITY.—(2.) We are each one, *conscious of our personality.* You cannot renounce the world's "self," *Ego*, self-consciousness; but that you have implied it. Hence, if we think according to our own subjective law, we cannot think another intelligence and will, without imputing to it a personality. Least of all the supreme intelligence and will. To deny this is to claim to be more perfect than God. But worse yet; if I am not a person, my nature is a lie, and thinking is at an end. If I am a person, and as the pantheist says, I am God, and God is I, then he is a person; and the pantheistic system is still self-contradicted.

EXTENSION AND THOUGHT CANNOT BE REFERRED TO A COMMON SUBSTANCE.—(3.) Modes of extension, and modes of thought and will cannot be attributes of one substance. Matter is divisible; neither consciousness, nor thought, nor feeling is; therefore the substance which thinks is indivisible. Matter is extended; has form; has relative bulk and weight. All these properties are impossible to be thought of any function of spirit, as relevant to them. Who can conceive of a thought triturated into many parts, as a stone into grains of sand; of a resentment split into halves; of a conception which is so many fractions of an inch longer or thicker than another; of an emotion triangular or circular, of the top and bottom of a volition?

IF SPINOZA TRUE, THE TO PAN CANNOT VARY.—(4.) If there is but one substance, TO PAN, the eternal, self-existent, necessary; then it must be homogeneous and indivisible. This is at least a just *argumentum ad hominem* for Spinoza. Did he not infer the necessary unity of all real substance, from the force of its one characteristic attribute, self and necessary existence? Now, this immanent necessity, which is so imperative as to exclude plurality; must it not also exclude diversity; or at least contrariety? How then can this one, unchangable substance exist at the same time in different and even contradictory states; motion and rest; heat and cold; attraction and repulsion? How can it, in its modes of thought and will, at the same time love in one man, and hate in another, the same object? How believe and disbelieve the same thing?

NO EVIL NOR GOOD.—(5.) On this scheme there can be no responsibility, moral good or evil, guilt, reward, righteous penalty, or moral government of the world. All states of feeling, and all volitions are those of TO PAN. Satan's wrong volitions are but God willing, and his transgressions, God acting. By what pretext can the Divine Will be held up as a moral standard? Anything which a creature wills, is God's will.

FATALISTIC.—(6.) And this because, next, pantheism is a scheme of stark necessity. Necessity of this kind is inconsistent with reponsibility. But again; it contradicts our consciousness of free-agency. We know, by our consciousness, that in many things we act freely, we do what we do, because we choose; we are conscious that our souls determine themselves. But if Pantheism were true, every volition, as well as every other event, would be ruled by an iron fate. So avowed stoicism, the pantheism of the Old World; so admits Spinoza. And consistently; for the TO PAN, impersonal, developing himself according to an imminent eternal necessity, must inevitably pass through all those modifications of thought and extension, which this necessity dictates, and no others; and the acts of God are as fated as ours.

GOD WOULD HAVE ALL SIN AND WOE. (7.) I retort upon the pantheist that picture which he so much delights to unfold in fanciful and glowing guise. Pantheism, says he, by deifying nature, clothes everything which is sweet or grand with the immediate glory of divinity, and ennobles us by placing us perpetually in literal contact with God. Do we look without on the beauties of the lanscape? Its loveliness is but one beam of the multiform smile upon His face. The glory of the sun is the flash of His eye. The heavings of the restless sea are but the throbs of the divine bosom, and the innumerable stars are but the sparkles of His eternal brightness. And when we look within us, we recognize in every emotion which ennobles or warms our breasts, the aspirations, the loves, the gratitudes which bless our being, the pulses of God's own heart beating through us. Nay, but, say I, are the manifestations of the universal Being, all lovely and good? If pantheism is true, must we not equally regard all that is abhorrent in nature, the rending thunder, and the rushing tornado, the desolating earthquake and volcanos, the frantic sea lashing helpless navies into wreck, as the throes of disorder or ruin in God? And when we picture the scenes of sin and woe, which darken humanity, the remorse of the villain's privacy, the orgies of crime and cruelty hidden beneath the veil of night, the despairing death-beds, the horrors of battle fields, the wails of nations growing pale before the pestilence, the din of burning and ravaged cities, and all the world of eternal despair itself, we see in the whole but the agony and crime of the divine Substance. Would it then be best called Devil or God? Since suffering and sin are so prevalent in this world, we may call it Pan-diabolism, with more propriety than pantheism. Nor is it any relief to this abhorrent conclusion to say, that pain and evil are necessitated, and are only seeming evils. Consciousness declares them real.

LECTURE III.

SYLLABUS.

DIVINE ATTRIBUTES.

1. How much can reason infer of the attributes of God? His *eternity?* How?
   Turrettin, Loc. iii, Que. 10. Dick, Lec. 17. Dr. S. Clarke, Discourse, &c., § 1, 2, 5. Charnock on Attr. vol. i, 5th Discourse.
2. His *unity?* How?
   Turrettin, Que. 3. Paley, Natural Theology. Dick, Lec. 18. Dr. S. Clarke, Discourse, &c., § 7.
3. *His spirituality and simplicity? How?*
   Turrettin, Que. 7. Dick, Lec. 17. Dr. S. Clarke, Discourse, § 8. Rev. Ro. Hall, Sermon i, vol. 3. Charnock, vol. i, Discourse 3.
4. His *infinitude*, and especially his *immensity?* How?
   Turrettin, Que. 8 and 9. Dick, Lec. 19. Dr. S. Clarke, § 6. Charnock, vol. i, Discourse 7.
5. His *immutability?*
   Turrettin, Que. 11. Dick, Lec. 20. Dr. S. Clarke, § 2. Charnock, vol. i, Discourse 6.

Traditionary Knowledge not to be separated from Rational, here.—It is exceedingly hard for us to return an exact answer to the question, How much reason can infer of the attributes of God? Shall we say: "So much as the wisest pagans, like Plato, discovered of them?" It still remains doubtful how much unacknowledged aid he may not have received from Hebrew sources. Many think that Plato received much, through Pythagoras and his Egyptian and Mesopotamain researches. Or if we seek to find how far our own minds can go on this subject, without drawing upon the Scriptures, we are not sure of the answer; because when results have been given to us, it is much easier to discover the logical tie between them and their premises, than to detect unaided both proofs and results. Euclid having told us that the square of the hypothenuse equals the squares of the two remaining sides of every right angled triangle, it becomes much easier to hunt up a synthetic argument to prove it, than it would have been to detect this great relation by analysis. But when we approach Natural Theology, we cannot forget the attributes which the Scriptures ascribe to God.

1. GOD'S ETERNITY.—Yet some things are as clear as God's being. The first and and most obvious of these attributes is, that He has *no beginning*, and *no end*. By God's eternity divines also intend a third thing: His *existence without succession*. These three propositions express their definition of His eternity: *existence not related to time*. For the first: His being never had a beginning: for had there ever been a time when the First Cause was not, nothing could ever have existed. So natural reason indicates that His being will never end, by this, that all pagans and philosophers make their gods immortal. The account of this conclusion seems to be, that it follows from God's independence, self-existence, and necessary existence. These show that there can be *no cause* to make *God's being end*. The immortality of the First Cause then is certain, unless we ascribe to it the power and wish of self-annihilation. But neither of these is possible. What should ever prompt God's will to such a volition? His simplicity of substance (to be separately proved anon) does not permit the act; for the only kind of destruction of which the universe has any experience, is by disintegration. The *necessity* of God's existence proves it can never end. The ground of His existence, intrinsic in Himself, is such that it cannot but be operative; witness the fact that, had it been, at any moment of the past infinite duration, inoperative, God and the universe would have been from that moment, forever impossible.

IS IT UNSUCCESSIVE?—But that God's existence is without succession, does not seem so clear to natural reason. It is urged by Turrettin that "God is immense. But if His existence were measured by parts of duration it would not be incommensurable." This is illogical. Do not the schoolmen themselves say, that *essentia* and *esse* are not the same? To measure the continuance of God's *esse* by successive parts of time, is not to measure His essence thereby. A similar distinction shows the weakness of Turrettin's second argument: "That because simple and immutable, He cannot exist in succession, for the flux of being from past to present, and present to future would be change, and even change of composition." I reply, it is God's *substance* which is simple and immutable; that its *subsistence* should be a continuance in sucession does not imply a change in substance. Nor is it correct metaphysics to say that a subsistence in succession is *compounded*, namely of the essence and the successive *momenta* of time through which it is transmitted. (See here, Kant.)

Nor is Dr. Dick's argument even so plausible: That God's being in a past eternity must be unsuccessive, because an infinite past, composed of successive parts, is impossible; and whatever God's mode of subsistence was, that it is, and will be. An infinite future made up of a succession of infinitely numerous finite parts is possible, as Dick admits; and so an infinite past thus constituted is equally as possible. Neither is *comprehensible* to our minds. If Turrettin or Charnock only meant that God's subsistence is not a succession marked off by *changes* in His essence or states, their reasonings would prove it. But if it is meant that the divine consciousness of its own existence has no relation to successive duration, I think it unproved, and incapable of proof to us. Is not the whole plausibility of the notion hence; that divines, following that analysis of our idea of our own duration into the succession of our own consciousnesses, [which Locke made so popular in his war against innate ideas,] infer: Since all God's thoughts and acts are ever equally present with Him, He can have no succession in His consciousnesses; and so, no relation to successive time. But the analysis is false (see Lecture VI, p. 68,) and would not prove the conclusion as to God, if correct. Though the creature's consciousnesses constituted an unsuccessive unit act, as God's do, it would not prove that the consciousness of the former was unrelated to duration. But 2d. In all the acts and changes of creatures, the relation of succession is actual and true. Now, although God's knowledge of these as it is subjective to Himself, is unsuccessive, yet it is doubtless *correct*, i. e., *true to the objective facts.* But these have actual succession. So that the idea of successive duration must be in God's thinking. Has He not all the ideas we have; and infinitely more? But if God in thinking the objective, ever thinks successive duration, can we be sure that His own consciousness of His own subsistence is unrelated to succession in time? The thing is too high for us. The attempt to debate it will only produce one of those "antinomies" which emerge, when we strive to comprehend the incomprehensible.

2. Unity of God.—Does reason show the First Cause to be *one?* or plural? If the first, whence the strong tendency to *polytheism?* This may be explained by the craving of the mind for concrete ideas: by the variety and seeming contrariety of effects in the world; by conscious *guilt*, craving a daysman higher than man, yet less awful than the Supreme, and by the apotheosis of famous men. Reason does pronounce God *one*. But here again, I repudiate weak supports. Argues Turrettin: If there are more than one, *all equal*, neither is God: if unequal, only the highest is God. This idea of *exclusive supremacy* is doubtless, essential to religious trust: Has it, thus far, been shown essential to the conception of a First Cause? Were there two or more independent eternal beings, neither of them would be an *infallible object of trust.* But has it been proved, *as yet*, that we are entitled to expect such a one? Again, Dr. S. Clarke urges: The First Cause exists necessarily: but a.) This necessity must operate forever, and everywhere alike, and, b.) This absolute sameness must make oneness. Does not this savour of Spinosism? Search and see. As to the former proposition: all that we can infer from necessary existence is, that it cannot but be just what it is. *What* it is, whether singular, dual, plural; that is just the question. As to the 2d proposition, *sameness* of operation does not necessarily imply *oneness* of effect. Have two successive nails from the same machine, necessarily numerical identity? Others argue again: We must ascribe to God every conceivable perfection, because, if not, another more perfect might be conceived; and then he would be the God. I reply: Yes, *if he existed.* It is no reasoning to make the capacity of our imaginations the test of the substantive existence of objective things. Again, it is argued, more justly, that, if we can show that the eternal, self-existent Cause must

be absolute and infinite in essence, then His exclusive unity follows: for that which is infinite is all-embracing as to that essence. Covering, so to speak, all *that kind* of being, it leaves no room for anything of its kind coördinate with itself. Just as after defining a *universe*, we cannot place any creature outside of it: so, if God is infinite, there can be but one. Whether He is infinite we will inquire.

Argued from inter-dependence of all His Effects.—The valid and practical argument, however, for God's unity, is the *convergency* of design and inter-dependency of all His works. All dualists, indeed, from Zoroaster to Manes, find their pretext in the numerous cross-effects in nature, seeming to show cross-purposes—e. g. One set of causes educe a fruitful crop: when it is just about to gladden the reaper, it is beaten into the mire by hail, through another set of atmospheric causes. Everywhere poisons are set against food, evil against good, death against life. Are there not two antagonist wills in Nature? Now it is a poor reply, especially to the mind aroused by the vast and solemn question of the origin of evil, or to the heart wrung by irresistible calamity, to say with Paley, that we see *similarity* of contrivance in all nature. Two hostile kings may wage internecine war, by precisely the same means and appliances. The true answer is, that, question nature as we may, through all her kingdoms, animal, inorganic, celestial, from the minutest disclosures of the microscope, up to the grandest revelations of the telescope, *second causes are all inter-dependent;* and *the designs convergent* so far as comprehended. So that each effect depends, more or less directly, on all the others. Thus, in the first instance: The genial showers and suns gave, and the hail destroyed, the grain. But look deeper: They are all parts of *one and the same* meteorologic system. The same cause exhaled the vapour which made the genial rain and the ruthless hail. Nay, more; the pneumatic currents which precipitated the hail, were constituent parts of a system which, *at the same moment,* were doing somewhere a work of blessing. Nature is one machine, moved by one mind. Should you see a great mill, at one place delivering its meal to the suffering poor, and at another crushing a sportive child between its iron wheels, it would be hasty to say, "Surely, these must be deeds of opposite agents." For, on searching, you find that there is but one water-wheel, and not a single smaller part which does not inosculate, nearly or remotely, with that. This instance suggests also, that dualism is an inapplicable hypothesis. Is *Ormusd* stronger than *Ahriman?* Then he will be victor. Are both equal in power? Then the one would not allow the other to work with his machinery; and the true result, instead of being a mixture of cross-effects, would be a sort of "dead lock" of the wheels of nature.

3. God a Spirit.—We only know substance by its properties; but our reason intuitively compels us to refer the sensible properties to a *subjectum*, a *substratum* of true being, or *substantia*. We thus know, first, spiritual substance, as that which is conscious, thinks, feels, and wills; and then material substance, as that which is unconscious, thoughtless, lifeless, inert. To all the latter we are compelled to give some of the attributes of extension; to the former it is impossible to ascribe any of them. Now, therefore, if this first Cause is to be referred to any

class of substance known to us, it must be to one of these two. Should it be conceived that there is a third class, unknown to us, to which the first Cause may possibly belong, it would follow, supposing we had been compelled to refer the first Cause to the class of spirits, (as we shall see anon, that we must,) that to this third class must also belong all creature spirits, as *species* to a *genus*. For we know the attributes, those of thought and will, common between God and them; it would be the *differentia*, which would be unknown. Is the first Cause, then, to be referred to the class, spirits? Yes; because we find it possessed, in the highest possible degree, of every one of the attributes by which we recognize spirit. *It thinks;* as we know by two signs. It produced us, who think; and there cannot be more in the effect than was in the cause. It has filled the universe with contrivances, the results of thought. It chooses; for this selection of contrivances implies choice. And again, whence do creatures derive the power of choice, if not from it? It is the first Cause of *life;* but this is obviously an attribute of spirit, because we find full life nowhere, except we see signs of spirit along with it. The first Cause is the source of *force*, and of motion. But matter shows us, in no form, any power to originate motion. Inertia is its normal condition. We shall find God's power and presence penetrating and inhabiting all material bodies; but matter has a displacing power, as to all other matter. That which is impenetrable obviously is not ubiquitous.

But may not God be like us, matter and spirit in one person? I answer, No. Because this would be to be organized; but organization can neither be eternal, nor immutable. Again, if He is material, why is it that He is never cognizable to any sense? We know that He is all about us always, yet never visible, audible, nor palpable. And last, He would no longer be penetrable to all other matter, nor ubiquitous.

SIMPLICITY OF GOD'S SUBSTANCE—Divines are accustomed to assert of the divine substance an absolute *simplicity*. If by this it is meant that He is uncompounded, that His substance is ineffably homogeneous, that it does not exist by assemblage of atoms, and is not discerptible, it is true. For all this is clear from His true spirituality and eternity. We must conceive of spiritual substance as existing thus; because all the acts, states, and consciousnesses of spirits, demand a simple, uncompounded substance. The same view is probably drawn from His eternity and independence. For the only sort of construction or creation, of which we see anything in our experience, is that made by some aggregation of parts, or composition of substance; and the only kind of death we know is by disintegration. Hence, that which has neither beginning nor end is uncompounded.

But that God is more simple than finite spirits in this, that in Him substance and attribute are one and the same, as they are not in them, I know nothing. The argument is, that as God is immutably what He is, without succession, His essence does not like ours pass from mode to mode of being, and from act to act, but is always all modes, and exerting all acts; hence His modes and His acts are Himself. God's thought is God. He is not active, but activity. I reply, that if this means more than is true of a man's soul, viz: that its thought is no entity, save *the soul thinking;* that its thought, as abstracted from the soul that thinks it, is only an abstraction and not a thing; it is undoubtedly false. For then we should have reached the pantheistic notion, that God has no other being than the infinite series of His own consciousnesses and acts. Nor would we be far off from the other result of this fell theory; that *all that is, is God*. For he who has identified God's acts thus with His being, will next identify the effects thereof, the existence of the creatures therewith.

4. GOD IMMENSE.—*Infinitude* means the absolutely limitless character of God's *essence*. *Immensity* means the absolutely limitless being of His *substance*. His being, as eternal, is in no sense circumscribed by *time;* as immense, in no wise circumscribed by *space*. But let us not conceive of this as a repletion of infinite space by diffusion of particles: like e. g. an elastic gas released *in vacuo*. The scholastic formula was, 'The *whole* substance, in its whole essence, is simultaneously present in every point of infinite space, yet without multiplication of itself. This is unintelligible; (but so is His immensity;) it may assist to exclude the idea of material extension. God's *omnipresence* is His similar presence in all the space of the universe.

Now, to me, it is no proof of His immensity to say, the necessity of His nature must operate everywhere, because absolute from all limitation. The inference does not hold. Nor to say that our minds impel us to ascribe all perfection to God; whereas exclusion from any space would be a limitation; for this is not conclusive of existences without us. Nor to say, that God must be everywhere, because His action and knowledge are everywhere, and these are but His essence acting and knowing. Were the latter true, it would only prove God's omnipresence. But so far as reason apprehends His immensity, it seems to my mind to be a deduction from His omnipresence. The latter we deduce from His simultaneous action and knowledge, everywhere and perpetually, throughout His universe. Now, let us not say that God is nothing else than His acts. Let us not rely on the dogma of the mediæval physicks: 'That substance cannot act save where it is present.' But God, being the first Cause, is the source of all force. He is also pure spirit. Now we may admit that the sun (by its attraction of gravitation) may act upon parts of the solar system removed from it by many millions of miles; and that, without resorting to the hypothesis of an elastic ether by which to propogate its impulse. It may be asked: if the sun's action throughout the solar system fails to prove His presence throughout it, how does God's universal action prove His omnipresence? The answer is in the facts above stated. There is no force originally inherent in matter. The power which is deposited in them must come from the first Cause, and must work uuder His perpetual superintendence. His, not theirs, is the recollection, intelligence, and purpose which guide. Now, as we are conscious that our intelligence only acts where it is present, and where it perceives, this view of Providence necessarrily impels us to impute omnipresence to this *universal cause*. For the powers of the cause must be where the effect is.

But now, having traced His being up to the extent of the universe, which is to us practically immense, why limit it there? Can the mind avoid the inference that it extends farther? If we stood on the boundary of the universe, and some angel should tell us that this was "the edge of the divine substance," would it not strike us as contradictory? Such a Spirit, already seen to be omnipresent, has no bounding outline.

Again, we see God doing and regulating so many things, over so vast an area, and with such absolute sovereignty, that we must believe His resources and power are absolute *within* the universe. But it is practically boundless to us. To succeed always inside of it, God must command such a multitude of relations, that we are practically impelled to the conclusion, that there are no relations, and nothing to be related outside His universe. But if His power is exclusive of all other, in all infinite space, we can scarcely avoid the conclusion that His substance is in all space.

God Infinite.—By passing from one to another of God's attributes, and discovering their boundless character, we shall at last establish the infinitude of His essence or nature. It is an induction from the several parts.

5. By God's immutability, we mean that He is incapable of change. As to His attributes, His nature, His purposes, He remains the same from eternity to eternity. Creation, and other acts of God in time, imply no change in Him; for the purpose to do those acts at that given time was always in Him, just as when He effected them. This attribute follows from His necessary existence; which is such that He cannot be any other than just what He is. It follows from His self-existence and independence; there being none to change Him. It follows from His simplicity: for how can change take place, when there is no composition to be changed? It follows from His perfection; for being infinite, He cannot change for the better; and will not change for the worse. Scarcely any attribute is more clearly manifested to the reason than God's immutability.

LECTURE IV.

SYLLABUS.

DIVINE ATTRIBUTES. (Continued.)

1. Can reason infer God's *omnipotence*? How?
   Turretin Loc. iii, Que. 211. Dr. S. Clarke's Discourse, Prop. X. Dick, Lect. 211, 22. Charnock, Discourse X.
2. His *omniscience*? How?
   Turrettin, Que. 12. Dr. Clarke, Prop. viii and xi. Dick, Lect. 21, 22. Charnock, Discourse 8, § 2.
3. His *righteousness*? How?
   Turrettin, Que. 19. Dr. Clarke, Prop. xii. Dick, Lect. 25. Chalmers Nat. Theology, Bk. iii, ch. 2.
4. *His goodness*? How?
   Turrettin, Que. 20. Dr. Clarke, Ubi supra. Charnock, Discourse xii, § 4. Chalmer's Natural Theol., Bk. iv, ch. 2. Leibnitz, *Theodicee Abrigee.*
5. Does reason show that man bears *moral relations* to God? What are they, and what the natural duties deduced?
   Butler's Analogy, Pt. I, Ch. 2-5. Howe's Living Temple, Pt. I, Ch. 6. Dr. Clarke's Discourse, 2nd vol., Prop. I to IV.

1. God all Powerful.—When we enquire after God's power, we mean

here, not His *potestas*, or EXOUSIA or authority, but His *potentia* or DUNAMIS. When we say: He can do all things, we do not mean that He can suffer, or be changed, or be hurt; for the passive capacity of these things is not power, but weakness or defect. We ascribe to God no passive power. When we say God's power is omnipotence, we mean that its object is only the *possible*, not the absolutely impossible. Here, however, we must again define, that by the absolutely impossible, we do not mean the physically impossible. For we see God do many things above nature, (PHUSIS;) that is, above what material, or human, or angelic nature can effect. But we mean the doing of that which implies an *inevitable contradiction*. Some, e. g. Lutherans of older school, say it is a derogation from God's omnipotence, to limit it by the inevitable self-contradiction: [that He is able to confer actual ubiquity on Christ's material body.] But we object: Popularly God's omnipotence may be defined as His ability to do *all things*. Now of two incompatibles, both cannot become entities together; for, by the terms of the case, the entity of the one destroys that of the other. But if they are not, and cannot be both *things*, the power of doing all things does not embrace the doing of incompatibles. But 2d, more conclusively; if even omnipotence could effect both of two contradictories, then the self-contradictory would become the true; which is impossible for man to believe. Hence, 3d, the assertion would infringe the foundation principle of all truth; that a thing cannot be thus, and not thus, in the same sense, and at the same time.

But between these limits we believe God is omnipotent: That is, His power is *absolute as to all being*. In proof, note: He obviously has great power; He has enough to produce all the effects in the universe. *Cause* implies power: He is the universal first Cause. 2d. His power is at least equal to the aggragate of all the forces in the universe, of every kind; because all sprang from Him at first. A mechanic constructs a machine far stronger than himself; it is because he *borrows* the forces of nature. There was no source whence God could borrow: He must needs produce all those forces of nature Himself; and He sustains them. 3d. God is *one*, and all the rest is produced by Him; so, since all the forces that exist, except His own, depend on Him, they cannot limit His force. Hence, it is absolutely unlimited, save by its own nature. And now, the exhibition of it already made in creation is so vast and varied, embracing (probably) the very existence of matter, and certainly its whole organization, the very existence of finite spirits, and all their attributes, and the government of the whole, that this power is practically to us immense. 4th. We have found God immutable. Whatever He once did, He can do again. He is as able to go on making universes such as this indefinitely, as to make this. 5th. He does not exist by seccession; and hence He is able to make two or more at once, as well as successively. It is hard to conceive how power can be more infinite than this.

GOD'S POWER IMMEDIATE.—Once more, God's power must be conceived of as primarily immediate; i. e. His simple volition is its effectuation; and no means interpose between the will and the effect. Our wills operate on the whole external world through our members; and they, often, through implements, still more external. But God has no members; so that we must conceive of His will as producing its effects on the objects thereof, as immediately as our wills do on our bodily members. Moreover, the first exertion of God's power must have been immediate; for at first *nothing existed to be means.* God's immutability assures us that the power of so acting is not lost to Him. The attribution of such immediate power to God does not deny that He also acts through "second causes."

2. WISDOM DISTINGUISHED FOR KNOWLEDGE. None who believe in God have ever denied to Him *knowledge* and *wisdom.* Wisdom is the employment of things known, with judicious reference to proper ends. Now; God is Spirit; but to think, to know, to choose, are the very powers of spirits. The universe is full of beautiful contrivances. These exhibit knowledge, wisdom, and choice, coëxtensive with the aggregate of the whole.

GOD'S KNOWLEDGE OF TWO KINDS.—But I had best pause and explain the usual distinctions made in God's knowledge. His *scientia visionis,* or *libera,* is His knowledge of whatever has existence before His view; that is, of all that is, has been, or is decreed to be. His *scientia intelligentiae,* or *simplex* (uncompounded with any volition) is His infinite conception of all the possible, which He does not purpose to effectuate. Others add a *scientia media,* which they suppose to be His knowledge of the future free and responsible acts of free agents. They call it mediate, because they suppose God foreknows these acts only inferentially, by means of His knowledge of their characters and circumstances. But Calvinists regard all this as God's *scientia visionis.* Let us see whether, in all these directions, God's knowledge is not without limit.

PROVED FROM GOD'S WILL.—First, I begin from the simple fact that He is spiritual and omnipotent First Cause. All being save His own is the offspring of His will. Grant a God, and the doctrine of a providence is almost self-evident to the reason. This refers not only phenomena of specific creation, but *all phenomena,* to God's will. If any thing or event has actuality, it is because He has willed it. But now, can volition be conceived, in a rational spirit, except as conditioned on cognition *à priori* to itself? Hence, 1st, a knowledge is implied in God, *à priori* to and coëxtensive with His *whole purpose.* But because this purpose (that of universal, almighty First Cause) includes the whole that has been, is, and shall be; and since volition does not obscure, but fix the cognition which is the object thereof, God has a *scientia visionis,* embracing all the actual. 2nd. Will implies *selection:* there must be more in the *à priori* cognition than is in the volition. Hence God's scientia simplex, or knowledge of the possible, is wider than his *scientia visionis.* This view will be found to have settled the question between us and Arminians, whether God purposes the acts of free agents because He has foreseen their certain futurition, or whether their futurition is certain because He has purposed them. Look and see.

KNOWLEDGE AND WISDOM SEEN IN HIS WORKS.—But more popularly; all God's works reveal marks of His knowledge, thought and wisdom. But these works are so vast, so varied, so full of contrivance, they disclose to us a knowledge practically boundless. His infinite power implies omniscience, for "knowledge *is* power." Certain success implies full knowledge of means and effects. We saw God is omnipresent; but He is spirit. Hence He knows all that is present to Him; for it is the nature of spirit to know. A parallel argument arises from God's providence; (which reason unavoidably infers.) The *ends* which are subserved show as much knowledge and wisdom as the structure of the beings used—so that we see evidence of complete knowledge of all second causes, including reasonable agents and their acts. For so intimate is the connexion of cause with cause, that perfect knowledge of the whole alone, can certify results from any. Here also we learn, God's knowledge of past and future is as perfect as of present things; for the completion of far-reaching plans, surely evolved from their remote causes, implies the retention by God of all the past, and the clear anticipation of all the future. Nay, what ground of certain futurition is there, save that God purposes it? His omnipotence here shows that He has a complete foreknowledge; because that which is to be is no other that what He purposes. God's immutability proves also His perfect knowledge of past, present, and future. Did He discover new things, these might become bases for new purposes, or occasions of new volitions, and God would no longer be the same in will. God's omniscience is implied also in all His moral attributes; for if He does not perform His acts understandingly, He is not praiseworthy in them. Last, our consciences reveal an intuition of God's infinite knowledge; for our fears recognize Him as seeing our most secret, as well as our public acts. His unfading knowledge of the past is especially pointed out by conscience; for whenever she remembers, she takes it for granted that God does. Thus we find God's *scientia visionis* is a perfect knowledge, past, present, and future, of all beings and all their actions, including those of moral agents.

SCIENTIA SIMPLEX INFERRED.—How do we infer His knowledge of the possible? Thus: A reasonable being must first *conceive*, in order to *produce*. He cannot make, save as he first has his own idea to make by. Then, before God set about making the universe, He had in His mind the conception in all its details, of what He was to make. How long before? As God changes not, it must have been from eternity. There then was a knowledge of the possible. But was that which is now actual, the only possible before God's thought? Sovereignty implies selection; and this, two or more things to choose among. And unless God had before Him the ideas of all possible universes, He may not have chosen the one which, had He known more, would have pleased Him best; His power was limited. In conclusion, the infallibility of all God's knowledge is implied in His power. Ordinarily, He chooses to work only through regular second causes. But causes and effects are so linked, that any uncertainty in one, jeopadizes all the subsequent. But we see that God is possessed of some way of effectuating all His will. Therefore He infallibly knows all causes; but each effect is in turn a cause.

GOD'S KNOWLEDGE ALL PRIMITIVE.—We must also believe that God knows all things intuitively, and not deductively. A deduction is a discovery. To discover something implies previous imperfection of knowledge. God's knowledge, moreover, is not successive, as ours is, but simultaneous. Inference implies succession; for conclusion comes after premise.

3. Rectitude.—God's righteousness, as discoverable by reason, means, generally, His rectitude, and not His distributive justice. Is He a moral being? Is His will regulated by right? Reason answers, yes; by justice, by faithfulness, by goodness, by holiness.

Rectitude of God proved by Bishop Butler.—First, because this character is manifest in the order of nature which He has established. This argument cannot be better stated than in the method of Bishop Butler. 1. God is Governor over man; as appears from the fact that, in a multitude of cases, He rewards our conduct with pleasures and pains. For the order of Nature, whether maintained by God's present providence, or impressed on it at first only, is God's doing; its rewards are His rewarding. 2. The character of proper rewards, and especially of punishments, appears clearly in these traits. They follow acts, though pleasant in the doing. They sometimes tarry long, and at last fall violently. After men have gone certain lengths, repentance and reform are vain, &c. 3. The rewards and penalties of society go to confirm; because they are of God's ordaining. Second: This God's rule is *moral;* because the conduct which earns well-being is virtuous; and ill-being, sinful. True, remedial processes, such as repentance, reform, have their peculiar pains: but these are chargeable rather to the sin, than the remedy. True again, the wicked sometimes prosper; but natural reason cannot but regard this as an exception, which future awards will right. Further: Society, (which is God's ordinance,) usually rewards virtue and punishes vice. Love of approbation is instinctive; but God thus teaches men most generally to approve the right. And last: How clear the course of Nature makes God's approval of the right appear, is seen in this; that all virtuous societies tend to self-perpetuation in the long run, and all vicious ones to self-extinction. Third: Life is full of instances of probation, as seed-time for harvest, youth for old age, which indicates that man is placed under a moral probation here.

God's Rectitude argued from Conscience.—But a most powerful argument for God's rectitude is that presented by the existence of conscience in man. Its teachings are universal. Do some deny its intuitive authority, asserting it to be only a result of habit or policy? It is found to be a *universal result;* and this proves that God has laid in us some intentional foundation for the result. Now, whatever, the differences of moral opinion, the peculiar trait of conscience is, that it always enjoins that which seems to the person right. It may be disregarded; but the man must think, if he thinks at all, that in doing so, he has done wrong. The act it condemns may give pleasure; but the wickedness of the act, if felt at all, can only give pain. Conscience is the *imperative faculty.* Now if God had not conceived the moral distinctions, he could not have imprinted it on us. But is his will governed by it? Does he not from eternity know extension as an object of thought, an attribute of matter, and sin, as a quality of the rebel creature? Yet He Himself is neither extended, nor evil. The reply is: since God has from eternity had the idea of moral distinction, whence was it derived, save from His own perfection? In what being illustrated, if not in Himself? But more, conscience is God's imperative in the human soul. This is its peculiarity among rational judgments. But since God implanted conscience, its imperative is the direct expression of His will, that man shall act righteously. But when we say, that every known expression of a being's will is for the right, this is virtually to say that he wills always righteously. The King's character is disclosed in the character of his edicts.

God's truth and faithfulness are evinced by the same arguments; and by these, in addition. The structure of our senses and intelligence, and the adaptation of external nature thereto, are His handiwork. Now, when our senses and understanding are legitimately used, their informations are always found, so far as we have opportunity to test them, *correspondent to reality.* One sense affirms the correctness of another. Senses confirm reasonings, and *vice versa.* Last, unless we can postulate truth in God, there is no truth anywhere. For our laws of perception and thought being His imprint, if His truth cannot be relied on, their truth cannot, and universal skepticism is the result.

4. God's Benevolence.—"The world is full of the goodness of the Lord." I only aim to classify the evidences that God is benevolent. And 1st, generally: since God is the original Cause of all things, all the happiness amidst His works is of His doing, and therefore proves His benevolence. But more definitely; the natures of all orders of sentient beings, if not violated, are constructed, in the main, to secure their appropriate well-being. Instance the insect, the fish, the bird, the ox, the man. 3d. Many things occur in the special providence of God which show Him benevolent; such as providing remedial medicines, &c., for pain, and special interpositions in danger. 4th. God might, compatibly with justice, have satisfied Himself with so adapting external nature to man's senses and mind, as to make it minister to his being and intelligence, and thus secure the true end of his existence, without, in so doing, making them pleasant to his senses. Our food and drink might have nourished us, our senses of sight and hearing might have informed us, without making food sweet, light beautiful, and sounds melodious to us. And yet appetite might have impelled us to use our senses and take our food. Such, in a word, is God's goodness, that He turns aside to strew incidental enjoyment. The more unessential these are to His main end, the stronger the argument. 5th. God has made all the beneficent emotions, love, sympathy, benevolence, forgiveness, delightful in their exercise, and all the malevolent ones, as resentment, envy, revenge, painful to their subjects, thus teaching us, that He would have us propagate happiness and diminish pain. Last: Conscience, which is God's imperative, enjoins benevolence on us as one duty, whenever compatible with others. Benevolence is therefore God's will; and doubtless, He who wills us to be so, is benevolent Himself.

No Pagan theist ever has doubted God's *Providence.* You may refer me to the noted case of the Epicurean; they were practical atheists. Their notion that it was derogatory to the blessedness and majesty of the gods to be wearied with terrestial affairs, betrays in one word a false conception of the divine perfections. Fatigue, confusion, worry, are the results of weakness and limitation. To infinite knowledge and power the fullest activities are infinitely easy and so pleasurable. Common sense argues from the perfection of God that He does uphold and direct all things by His Providence. His wisdom and power enable Him to it. His goodness and justice certainly impel

Him to it; for it would be neither benevolent nor just, having brought sentient beings into existence, to neglect their welfare, rights and guilt. God's wisdom will certainly prosecute those suitable ends for which He made the universe, by superintending it. To have made it without an object; or, having one, to overlook that object wholly after the world was already made, would neither of them argue a wise being. The manifest dependence of the creature confirms the argument.

Existence of evil. How explained?—But there stands out the great fact of the existence of much suffering in the universe of God; and reason asks: "If God is almighty, all-wise, sovereign, why, if benevolent, did He admit *any* suffering in His world? Has He not chosen it because He is pleased with it *per se?* It is no answer to say: God makes the suffering the *means of good*, and so chooses it, not for its own sake, but for its results. If He is omnipotent and all-wise, He could have produced the same *quantum* of good by other means, leaving out the suffering. Is it replied: No, that the virtues of sympathy, forgiveness, patience, submission, could have had no existence unless suffering existed. I reply that then their absence would have been no blemish or lack in the creature's character. It is only because there is suffering, that sympathy therewith is valuable. Suppose it be said again: "All physical evil is the just penalty of moral evil," and so necessitated by God's justice? The great dificulty is only pushed one step farther back. For, while it is true, sin being admitted, punishment ought to follow, the question returns: Why did the Almighty permit *sin*, unless He be defective in holiness, as in benevolence? It is no *theodicée* to say that God cannot always exclude sin, without infringing free-agency; for I prove, despite all Pelagians, from Celestius down to Bledsoe, that God can do it, by His pledge to render elect angels and men indefectible for ever. Does God then choose sin? This is the mighty question, where a *theodicée* has been so often attempted in vain. The most plausible theory is that of the *optimist;* that God saw that this actual universe, though involving evil, is on the whole the most beneficient universe which was possible in the nature of things. For they argue, in support of that proposition: God being infinitely good and wise, cannot will to bring out of *posse* into *esse*, a universe which is, on the whole, less beneficent than any possible universe. The obvious objection to this bettistic scheme is, that it limits the powers of God. Being infinite, He *could* have made a universe, which should have had the same *quantum* of happiness with this, without the same evils.

Optimist Theory modified.—But there is a more legitimate and defensible hypothesis. It is not competent to us to say that *beneficence* of result is, or ought to be God's chief ultimate end in creation and Providence. It is one of His worthy ends; this is all we should assert. But may we not assume that doubtless there is *a set of ends*, (no man may presume to say what all the parts of that collective end are,) which God eternally sees to be the properest ends of His creation and providence? I think we safely may. Doubtless those ends are just such as they ought to be, with reference to all God's perfections; and the proper inference from those perfections is, that He is producing just such a universe, in its structure and management, as will, on the whole, most perfectly subserve that set of ends. In this sense, and no other, I am an optimist. But now, let us make this all-important remark: When the question is raised, whether a God of infinite powers can be benevolent in permitting natural, and holy in permitting moral evil, in His universe, *the burden of proving the negative rests on the doubter.* We who hold the affirmative are entitled to the presumption, *because* the contrivances of creation and providence are *beneficent so far as we comprehend them.* Even the physical and moral evils in the universe are obviously so overruled, as to bring good out of evil. (Here is the proper value in the argument, of the instances urged by the optimist: that suffering makes occasion for fortitude and sympathy, &c., &c.; and that even man's apostacy made way for the glories of Redemption.) The conclusion from all these beautiful instances is, that so far as finite minds can follow them, even the evils tend towards the good. Hence, the presumptive probability is in favour of a solution of the mystery, consistent with the infinite perfections of God. To sustain that presumption against the impugner, we have only to make the hypothesis, that for reasons we cannot see, God saw it was not possible to separate the existing evils from that system which, as a whole, satisfied His own properest ends. Now let the skeptick *disprove* that hypothesis! To do so, he must have omniscience. Do you say, I cannot demonstrate it? Very true; for neither am I omniscient. But I have proved that the reasonable presumption is in favour of the hypothesis that it may be true, although we cannot explain *how* it comes to be true.

5. Man's duties to God.—If the existence and moral perfections of God be admitted, no one will dispute that man bears moral relations to Him. This appears very simply, from the fact that man is a moral being, related to God as his Maker and providential Ruler. It is also inferrible from the marks of a *probation*, and a moral rule appearing in the course of nature. And it is emphatically pronounced by the native supremacy of conscience, commanding us to obey. Rational Deists, as well as Natural Theologians, have attempted to deduce the duties man owes his Creator. They are usually (on grounds sufficiently obvious) summed up as: 1. Love, with reverence and gratitude; 2. Obedience; 3. Penitence; 4. Worship. The rule of obedience is, of course, in natural religion, the law of nature in the conscience.

LECTURE V.

SYLLABUS.

IMMORTALITY OF SOULS, AND FUTURE REWARDS.

1. Is the soul immortal? And are the future consequences of virtue and vice in this life, everlasting?

Butler's Analogy. Pt. I, Ch. 1, 2, 5. Turrettin, Loc. i, Que. 14. Dr. S. Clarke's Discourse. Vol. ii. Prop. iv. Dr. Thomas Brown, Lect. 96, 97. Breckinridge's Theol. Vol. i, pp. 58–70. Chalmers' Nat. Theol. Bk. iii, Ch. 3.

2. Does Reason hold out any sure prospect of pardon for sins?
   Butler's Analogy, Pt. II, Ch. 5. University Lectures—Dr. Van Zandt, p. 43-51. Dr. S. Clarke, as above, Prop. vi.
3. Can Natural Theology be sufficient for man's religious welfare? How much evidence here, for the inspiration of the Bible?
   Turrettin, Loc. i, Que. 4. University Lecture by Van Zandt. Chalmers' Nat. Theol. Bk. v, Ch. 1. Dr. S. Clarke, as above. Prop. v to viii, inclusive. Leland's Necessity of Revelation at large.

1. ARE THE SOUL AND ITS MORAL PRELATIONS IMMORTAL?

THE SOUL IMMATERIAL.—Dr. Thomas Brown says that the question of the soul's immortality is involved in that of its immateriality. But there are two kinds of materialists: those who believe thinking, feeling, and willing to be simple effects of organization; and those who believe the soul to be a separate substance, and, although matter of some purer sort, yet monadic and atomic. The latter might, with some consistency, believe in its immortality. We reject both.

The great evidence of the soul's spirituality will be found, when inspected, intuitive. Man only knows by his own ideas. The very consciousness of these implies a being, a *substance which is conscious.* So that man's knowledge of himself, as conscious, thinking substance, is *a priori* to, though implicitly present in, all his other thinkings—i. e., he knows his own thinking self first, and by knowing it, knows all other things. But this thinking self is impressed from without with certain affections, called sensation, which the man is as inevitably impelled to refer to objective substance, to the *non Ego.* Now, in comparing this conviction of the Ego, and the non Ego, a certain contrast arises of their attributes: the one is that which thinks, feels, and wills, which is single and monadic; that is, the ideas of separation into parts, or of existence in parts, of shape, extension, solidity, impenetrability, resistance, momentum, &c., are so absolutely irrelevant to it as attributes, that it is impossible seriously to refer them to the *Ego*, even in thought. But the *non Ego*, made known by sensation, does exist in parts, is divisible, extended, impenetrable, inert, bounded by figure, endued with weight and *momentum.* But all attributes of thought and feeling and volition are here incompatible. The law of our reason compels us to refer this absolute contrast of attributes to a true difference of substance; so that while we name the *Ego* spirit, the objective we call matter. And especially must the substances be different; for this cause, that every particle of matter, however small, may be divided; whereas the soul and all its functions are indivisible. The thought of their top and bottom, of halving or quartering them, is preposterous. The substance which thinks is, therefore, a spiritual *monad.*

OBJECTIONS REFUTED.—Materialists have objected that material affections have this oneness to our conception; as a musical tone, the numerous series of successive vibrations of a chord divisible into parts. I reply, that the oneness is only in the perception of it. Only as it becomes our mental affection, does it assume unity. As we trace the effect from the vibration of the chord to that of the air, the *tympanum*, the long series, the aqueous humour, the fimbrated nerve, the series is still one of successive parts. It is only when we pass from the material organ to the mind, that the phenomenon is no longer a series of pulses, but a unified sensation. This very case proves most strongly, the unifying power which belongs to the mind alone. So, when an extended object produces a sensation, though the object perceived is divisible, the perception thereof, as a mental act, is indivisible.

THE SOUL IMMORTAL.—Now, the soul being another substance than the body, it is seen at once, that the body's dissolution does not *necessarily* imply that of the soul. Indeed, let us look beyond first impressions, and we shall see that the presumption is the other way. The fact that we have already passed from one to another stage of existence, from *foetus* to infant, to child, to man, implies that another stage may await us; unless there be some such evidence of the soul's dependence on the body for existence (as well as for contact with the external world,) as will destroy that presumption. But there is no such dependence; as appears from our experience in amputations, flux of bodily particles, emaciation under disease, &c. In none of these cases is the loss of the spirit proportioned to the bodily loss. This independence is proved by the fact, that in sensation even, the bodily organ is merely the soul's instrument. The eye, e. g., is but its optic glass: that in sleep the soul may be active while the body is wholly passive; and chiefly, that all the higher processes of soul, memory, conception, imagination, reasoning, are wholly independent of the body. Even if the grossest representationist scheme of perception and thought, (that, for instance, of Hartly, or of Hobbes,) were adopted, making the *phantasmata* or *species* derived through the senses, the object of perception, still the question returns, How does the soul get its conception of general notions: of time, of space, of God, of self? Herein, surely, it is independent of the body.

DOES MENTAL DISEASE IMPLY THE SOUL'S MORTALITY:—Here again, materialists have objected, that the cases of mental imbecility in infancy and dotage, and of mania or lunacy, seem to show a strict dependence of soul on body, if not an identity. In dotage, is not the mind, like the body, tottering to its extinction? If our theory of monadic spirit were true, would *mental disease* be possible? I reply, that strictly speaking, spirit is not essentially diseased. It is the bodily organ of its action, which is deranged, or weakened. Bear in mind, that though there are undoubted processes of thought independent of the body, *sensations* form the larger part of our subjects of thought and volition. Now, remember that the soul is subject to the law of *habit;* and we shall easily see that where, through the disease of the bodily organs, the larger number of the objects of its action are distorted, the balance of its working may be disturbed, and yet the soul's substance undiseased. That this is the correct explanation, is confirmed by what happens in dreams: the mind's action is wholly abnormal; it is because the absence of sensations has changed the balance of its working. Let the body awake, and the ordinary current of sensations flow aright, and the mind is at once itself. Again, in lunacy and dotage, ideas gained by the mind before the bodily disease or decline took place, are usually recalled and used by the mind correctly; while more recent ones are either distorted, or wholly evanescent. Finally, while it is inconsistent to ascribe an organic disease to that which is not organized, a functional derangement does not seem wholly out of the question.

ONLY DEATH KNOWN IS DISSOLUTION. THE SOUL SIMPLE.—It appears then, that the thinking monad is independent of the body for its existence. Impressive as are the changes of bodily dissolution, they contain no philosophic ground for denying the conclusion drawn from the experience of the soul's existence through so many moments, and so many changes. But the phenomenon of death itself suggests a powerful analogy to show that the soul will not die. What is death? It is but separation of parts. When we examine all the seemingly destructive processes of nature, combustion, decomposition, we find no atom of matter annihilated; they only change their collocations. There is no proof that God ever destroys an atom. The soul is a spiritual atom; why suppose it is destroyed? The only death is dissolution; the soul cannot dissolve. And this is my conception of its immortality; not a *self* or *nece sary* existence, but the absence of all intrinsic ground of decay, and of all purpose in its Maker to extinguish its being.

WOULD NOT BRUTES BE THUS SHOWN IMMORTAL?—But, objects the materialist: The same reasonings would prove the immortality of brutes. I reply, this is an objection *ad ignorantiam.* Where the necessary absurdity, should it be true? But remember, all the moral arguments, (the most conclusive,) are lacking to this conclusion. I confess, it is hard for me to conclude that the substance which, in my horse, has memory, association of ideas, fear, joy, volition, is not spirit. But this spirit is not a *moral* essence. What God chooses to do with it when the body dies, I know not. Ignorance here is no argument against the results of positive knowledge elsewhere.

EQUAL REWARDS REQUIRE A FUTURE EXISTENCE.—The well known argument for a future existence from God's righteousness compared with the imperfect distribution of awards here, need not be elaborated. All your books state it. It is conclusive. An objection has, indeed, been urged: That if the awards are so unequal, no evidence remains of God's perfect rectitude; and so the former premise is lost. I reply: The course of temporal providence is neither the only nor chief proof of God's rectitude. Conscience demonstrates that attribute, without the light of observation. Further, while the awards are not exact, they approximate exactness here, showing that it is God's nature to be, finally, strictly just. And last, the inequalities of awards are explained consistently with God's rectitude by this: that they give scope for man's fortitude and sympathy, and for God's long suffering.

CONSCIENCE.—Conscience, apprehending God's justice, gives us a different, and an instinctive proof of a future existence. Remorse for sins does by no means verge towards its termination, as death approaches; but recruits its fury. If the soul could apprehend this life as its only existence, at the conscious approach of death, remorse would relax its grasp; and at the expiring breath, would release the criminal, as having paid the debt of justice. We find in the dying conscience an inevitable and universal recognition of its immortality.

DOES HOPE PROVE IT?—The ancient, and some modern moralists, attached much importance to man's longing for existence, horror of extinction, and hopes in the future. I cannot but feel, with Dr. Brown, that these lack weight. Is not this horror of extinction resolvable into that love of life which we share with the animals? Hope does, indeed, ever fly before us, to the end. But is it not as much a hope of sensual or worldly good, as of spiritual? But should we infer from these premises, that a brute's or a man's animal existence will be perpetual, we should err.

MAN'S SPIRITUAL CAPACITIES FORMED FOR IMMORTALITY.—I find a more solid argument in man's capacity to know and serve God, and in his capacity of indefinite mental and moral improvement. God's motive for creating must have been from Himself; because, when He began, nothing else existed whence to draw it. He must, therefore, have sought, in creation, to satisfy and glorify His own perfections. Natural Theology tells us of no rational creatures, save men. Should there ever be a time when there are no rational creatures in the universe, there would be no recipients of God's spiritual goodness, and none to comprehend His glory. To have no eyes to behold the light, is virtually to quench it. Can we then believe that the only creature capable of knowing and enjoying Him shall perish so soon—perish, as to the majority of our race, before they understand Him at all? But again, man, unlike all other sentient creatures, is capable of indefinite improvement. The ox, the elephant, the horse, soon reaches the narrow limits of its intelligence; and these, the same fixed by the common instincts of its race, for its progenitors. The first bee built its cells as artistically as those of this "enlightened century." But man can make almost indefinite advancements. And when he has taken all the strides between a Newton or a Washington, and a naked Australian, there is no reason, save the narrow bounds of his mortal life, to limit his farther progress. Farther, it is precisely in his mental and moral powers, that the room for growth exists. His muscular strength soon reaches that standard beyond which there is no usual increase. His senses are educated up to a certain penetration; there the vast and the minute arrest them. But memory, reason, conscience, affections, habits, may be cultivated to indefinite grades of superiority. Let us now view man's terrestrial pursuits, his vanity, his disappointments, his follies, and the futilities in which the existence of most men is consumed. How utterly trivial! How unworthy of the grand endowment! If this life were all, well might we exclaim, with the Hebrew poet, "Wherefore hast Thou made all men in vain?" *We see* that God is unspeakably wise in all His comprehended works; we must conclude that He has not expended so much for naught: that these seeds of immortality will inherit their suitable growth. I see a man setting scions in his nursery a few inches apart; but I learn that they are trees which will require forty feet for their ultimate growth. If the man knows what he is about, I conclude that he intends to transplant them.

REASON DIVINES NO BODILY RESURRECTION.—For these various reasons, then, we may look across the gulf of death with the confident expectation of a future spiritual existence. I say spiritual; for the resurrection of the body is a doctrine of pure revelation, for which natural reason presents us only the faintest analogies, if any. It is the glory of the Bible, that it alone reveals the immortality of *man*, of the whole united person, which lives, hopes, fears, sins, and dies here. But in proving the immortality of the soul, a sufficient basis is laid for the larger part of the moral forces which bring our responsibility to bear aright. The essential point is to evince the *proper identity* of the being who acts here, and is rewarded hereafter. It is mental, and not personal identity, which lays this essential basis for responsibility. It is the spirit which understands, feels, and chooses, which recognizes identity in its consciousness. Hence, it is the spirit which is responsible.

FUTURE EXISTENCE MUST BE ENDLESS, AND UNDER RESPONSIBILITY. Now, if existence is continued beyond the grave, there is nothing to check the conclusion that it will be continued forever. Suppose a soul just emerged from the impressive revolution of bodily death? then it must repeat all the reasonings we have considered, and with redoubled force, that after so many changes are survived, *à posteriori*, all others will be. But if man's conscious existence is continuous and endless, few will care or dare to deny that his moral relations to God are so, likewise. For they proceed directly from the more original relation of creature to Creator. The startling evidences that this life is somehow a probation for that endless existence, the youth of that immortal manhood, have been stated by Bishop Butler with unrivalled justness. No more is needed by the student than to study him.

2. DOES REASON SEE HOPE OF PARDON? No. Conscience convinces every man that he is a sinner, and that God is just. Does natural reason infer any adequate proofs that God will, on any terms, be merciful; or is His righteousness as imperative as that conscience, which is His vicegerent within us? This is the question of most vital interest to us in natural religion. We are pointed to the abounding evidences of God's benevolence, and told that mercy is but benevolence towards the guilty. But, alas! Nature is almost equally full of evidences of His severity. Again, we are pointed to that hopeful feature in the order of His providence, which is but another expression for the regular ordering of His will, where we see remedial processes offered to man, for evading the natural consequences of his errors and faults. Does man surfeit himself? Nature offers a healing medicine, and arrests the death which his intemperance has provoked. Does the prodigal incur the penalty of want? Repentance and industry may repair his broken fortunes. So, alleviations seem to be provided on every hand, to interpose mercifully between man's sins and their natural penalties. May we not accept these as showing that there is some way in which God's mercy will arrest our final retribution? This expectation may have that slight force which will prepare us to embrace with confidence the satisfaction of Christ, when it is revealed to us in the gospel. But I assert that, without revelation, all these slight hints of a possible way of mercy are too much counterbalanced by the appearances of severity, to ground any hope or comfort in the guilty breast. What is the testimony of conscience? Does she accept any of the throes of repentance, or the natural evils inflicted on faults, as a sufficient atonement? On the contrary, after the longest series of temporal calamities, the approach of death only sharpens her lash. The last act of culminating remorse, as the trembling criminal is dismissed from his sufferings here, is to remit him to a just and more fearful doom beyond the grave. And what say conscience and experience of the atoning virtue of our repentance and reformations? They only

repair the consequences of our faults in part. The sense of guilt remains: yea, it is the very nature of repentance to renew its confession of demerit with every sigh and tear of contrition. And the genuineness of the sorrow for sin has no efficacy whatever to recall the consequences of the wrong act, and make them as though they had never been. But, above all, every palliation of natural penalty, every remedial process offered to our reach by nature, or ministered by the self-sacrifice of friends is but temporary. For, after all, death comes to every man, to the most penitent, the most genuinely reformed, the restored sinner most fenced in by the mediatorial love of his fellows, as certainly as to the most reckless profligate; and death is the terrible sum of all natural penalties. This one, universal fact, undoes every thing which more hopeful analogies had begun, and compels us to admit that the utmost reason can infer of God's mercy is, that it admits a suspension of doom.

3. Is Natural Theology sufficient?—The last question which we shall now discuss in Natural Theology, is concerning its sufficiency to lead a soul to eternal blessedness. Now, I have strenuously contended that there is some science of Natural Theology. We have seen that it teaches us clearly our own spirituality and future existence, the existence and several of the attributes of God, His righteousness and goodness and our responsibility to Him, His providential control over all His works, and our endless relation to the sanctions of His moral attributes. But man needs more than this for his soul's well-being; and we assert that Natural Theology is fatally defective in the essential points. We might evince this practically by pointing to the customary state of all gentile nations, to the darkness of their understandings and absurdities of their beliefs, the monstrous perversions of their religious worship, and the blackness of their general morals, their evil consciences during their lives, and their death-beds either apathetic or despairing. If it be said that I have chosen unfavourable examples, then I might argue the point practically again, by pointing to the brightest specimens of pagan philosophy. We see that with all the germs of truth mixed with their creeds, there were many errors, that their virtues lacked symmetry and completeness, and their own confessions of uncertainty and darkness were usually emphatic in proportion to their wisdom.

Cannot atone, nor regenerate.—But to specify. One fatal defect of Natural Theology has been already illustrated. Man knows himself a sinner in the hands of righteous Omnipotence, and has no assurance whatever of any plan of mercy. An equally fatal defect might be evinced, (far more clearly than divines have usually done,) in its lack of regenerating agency. If we knew nothing of the sad story of Adam's probation and fall, just reasoning would yet teach us, that man is a morally depraved being. The great fact stands out, that his will is invincibly arrayed against the mandates of his own conscience, on at least some points. Every man's will exhibits this tendency in some respects, with a certainty as infallible as any law of nature. Now such a tendency of will cannot be revolutionized by any system of moral suasion; for the conclusive reason that the efficacy of all objective things to act as inducements, depends on the state of the will, and therefore cannot revolutionize it. The effect cannot renew its own cause. But Natural Theology offers no moral force higher than moral suasion. Can then the creature who remains an everlasting sinner, possess everlasting well-being?

Lacks authority.—Another striking defect of Natural Theology is its lack of authority over the conscience. One would think that where the inferences of natural reason appeared conclusive, bringing the knowledge of a God to the understauding, this God would be recognized as speaking in all her distinct assertions; and the conscience and heart would bow to Him as implicitly as when He is revealed in His word. But practically it is not so. Men are but too ready to hold revealed truth in unrighteousness; and Natural Theology has ever shown a still greater lack of authority, even over hearts which avowed her truth. Perhaps the reason of this is, that every mind has indistinctly and half consciously recognized this profound metaphysical defect, which underlies nearly all her reasonings. How do we first know spirit? By our own consciousness, presenting to us the thinking *Ego*. How do we know thought, volition, power? As we are first conscious of it in ourselves. What is our first cognition of the right and the wrong? It is in the mandates of our own consciences. And the way we conceive of the infinite Spirit, with His thought, will, power, rectitude, is by projecting upon Him our self-derived conception of this essence and these attributes, freed from the limitations which belong to ourselves. Seeing, then, that God and His character are to so great an extent but ourselves objectified, elevated above our conscious defects, and made absolute from our conscious limits, how can we ever know that the correspondence of the objective reality, with this conception of it, is accurate? It is as though our self-consciousness were the mirror, in which alone we can see the *spectrum* of the great Invisible reflected. How shall we ever tell to what degree it may be magnified, distorted, coloured, by the imperfection of the reflecting surface, seeing Natural Theology can never enable us to turn around and inspect the great original, eye to eye? That something is there, a something vast, grand and real, our laws of thought forbid us to doubt; and that it has a general outline like the reflected image, we may not doubt; for else, what was it that cast the mighty *spectum* upon the disc of our reason? But reason can never clear up the vagueness and uncertainty of outline and detail, nor verify His true features. Now, when Revealed Theology comes, it enables us to make this verification; and especially when we see "God manifest in the flesh," "the brightness of the Father's glory, and express image of His person."

Why then study Natural Theology?—It may be asked, if Natural Theology cannot save, why study it? I answer: 1st. It teaches some truths; and no truth is valueless. 2d. When Revelation comes, Natural Theology gives satisfaction to the mind, by showing us two independent lines of proof for sundry great propositions? 3d. It excites the craving of the soul for a Revelation. 4th. When that comes, it assists us to verify it, because it meets the very wants which Natural Theology has discovered.

A Revelation may be expected. Finally, if Revelation is absolutely necessary for salvation, there is the strongest probability that

God has given one. This appears from God's goodness and wisdom. It is proved, second, by the admissions of the Deistical argument, which always assumes the burden of proof in the proposition: "Revelation is not necessary." It appears, third, from the general expectation and desire of a communication from the skies among Pagans. Last: when we see (as will be demonstrated at another place) that the enjoyment of infallible commmunications from the infinite Mind is the natural condition of life to all reasonable spirits, the argument will become conclusive, that God surely has given a message to man. Now, no other book save the Bible presents even a plausible claim to be that Revelation.

LECTURE VI.

SYLLABUS.

THE SOURCES OF OUR THINKING.

1. Has man any *innate* ideas?
   Locke's Essay. Book i, Ch. 2. Dugald Stuart on the Mind, Ch. 1, 3. 4. Morell, Hist. Mod. Phil., p. 76–95. Cousin Du Vrai Leçons 1re et 2me.
2. Must all thinking proceed from intuitive beliefs? Why? If unproved, why are they received as valid? What the answer to Hume's skepticism?
   Same authorities. Morell, p. 252–254. Jouffroy, Introduct. to Ethicks., vol. i, Lect. 8–10. Cousin Du Vrai. Laçon's 3me et 4me.
3. What are the tests of intuitive beliefs? Show that our belief in our own consciousness, and spiritual existence, in our identity, in the reality of the external world, and established axioms belong to this class.
   Cousin, as above. Mill's Logic, Bk, ii: Ch. 5. Southern Review of April, 1869. Positivism in England.
4. Prove especially that our belief in causation and power is intuitive.
   Same authorities. Mill, Bk. ii, Ch. 5 and 21. Dr. Thomas Brown, Lect. 6 and 7. Morell, pp. 186, 187, 254, 382, &c. Chalmer's Nat. Theol., Bk. i, Ch. 4.

Show the connexion of this doctrine with Natural Theology and all science.

Is it necessary to study the mind's powers, before all else?—Many think, with Locke, that the inquiry into the powers of the human mind should precede all other science, because one should know his instrument before he uses it. But what instrument of knowing is man to employ in the examination of his own mind? Only his own mind. Hence, it follows, that the mind's native laws of thinking must be, to some extent at least, taken upon trust, at the outset, no matter where we begin. This is the less to be regretted, because the correct use of the mind's powers depends on nature, and not on our success in analyzing them. Men syllogized before Aristotle, and generalized before Bacon. I have therefore not felt obliged to begin with these inquiries into the sources of our thinking; but have given you a short sketch of Natural Theology to familiarize your minds to your work.

WHY THEN, BEFORE THEOLOGY?—You may ask: Since every science must employ the mental powers, and yet the teacher of Chemistry, Mathematics, Mechanics, does not find it necessary to preface his instructions with inquiries into the laws and facts of psychology, why should the divine do it? One answer is, that thoroughness in theology is so much more important. Another is, experience shows that theological speculation is much more intimately concerned with a correct psychology than physical. The great English mathematicians, of the school of Newton, have usually held just views of philosophy: the French of the school of *La Place* have usually been sensualistic *Ideologues* of the lowest school. In mathematics and astronomy, they have agreed well enough; in theology, they have been as wide apart as Christianity and atheism. This is because theology and ethicks are little concerned with physical observations: much with abstract ideas and judgments. For these reasons it is necessary for the divine to attain correct views of the great facts of mental science; *while yet we do not stake the validity of theological truths on the validity of any mere psychological arguments.*

My purpose is to give by no means a complete synopsis, even, of mental science; but to settle for you correct opinions concerning those fundamental facts and laws of spirit, upon which theological questions most turn.

1. QUESTION OF INNATE IDEAS.—Of these I take up first the question, *Has the the mind any innate ideas?* The right answer is, No; but it has *innate powers*, which *à priori* dictate certain laws of thought and sensibility, whenever we gain ideas by sensitive experience. Locke, famous for exploding the doctrine of innate ideas, goes too far; teaching that we derive all our ideas (he defines an *idea*, whatever we have in our minds as the object of thought) from sensation. This he holds is a passive process; and all that the processes of reflection (the active ones) can do, is to recall, group, compare, combine, or abstract these materials. Before sensation, the mind is a *tabula rasa*, without impress in itself, passively awaiting whatever may be projected on it from without. To show that no ideas are innate, he takes up two classes, hitherto considered most clearly such, abstract ideas of space, time, identity, and infinity, &c., and axioms; assuming that if these can be explained as derived ideas, and not innate, there are none such. He teaches, then, that we only get the idea of *space*, by seeing two bodies separated thereby; of *time*, by deriving it from the succession of mental impressious; of *identity*, as remembered consciousnesses. *Axioms*, he holds to be clearly truths of derivation, because untutored minds do not believe them, as they would were they intuitive, until they see them from concrete, experimental cases, by sensation.

FATAL CONSEQUENCES OF A SENUALISTIC PSYCHOLOGY.—Consider how far this kind of vicious analysis may lead, as in the hands of Condillac, to sensationalism, and last, to materialism and atheism. If no first truth is of higher source than an inference of experience, then none can be safely postulated beyond experience. Hence, the argument for a God, the belief of all the supernatural, is invalid. Witness Hume's evasion, that the world is a "singular effect." How can sensation show us a God? Another equally logical, although a most heterogeneous consequence, is the Pyrrhonism of Bishop Berkeley. And another must be the adoption of some artificial scheme of ethicks, resolving the highest law of conscience into a deduction of self-interest, or some such wretched scheme. For if there is nothing in the mind, save what comes by sense, (*Nihil in intellectu quod non prius in sensu*,) whence the notions of right and obligation.

TRUE STATEMENT.—The great error of the analysis of Locke was in mistaking the occasional cause, sensation, for the efficient cause of abstract ideas, which is the reason itself. For example: we first develope the idea of space, when we see bodies in space; but the idea of space is implied *à priori*, in the very perception of that which is extended, not learned derivatively from it. True, our most natural conception of *time* is of that measured in our successive consciousnesses. But the word, "*succession*" once spoken, time is already conceived. That is to say, the reason, on perceiving a thing extended, intuitively places it in space; and *event*, in *time;* the sense furnishing the occasion, the reason furnishing the abstract notion, or form, for the concrete perception. So in the other cases. To the attempt to *derive* axioms, we answer that the sensitive experience of some instance is the occasion, but the intuition of the reason the efficient of these primitive and necessary judgments. For since our experiences of their truth are few and partial, how can experience tell us that they are universally true? To the objection, that they do not universally and necessarily command the assent of untutored minds, I fearlessly rejoin that this is only true in cases where the language of their enunciatien is not understood. But of this, more anon.

WHENCE NEW ABSTRACT NOTIONS?—To show the student how shallow is the analysis which traces the whole of our thinking to sense, I ask: When the "reflective" processes of comparison, e. g., have given us perception of a *relation* between two sensible objects, (as of a *ratio* between two dimensions,) is not this relation a *new idea?* Whence is it?

THE MIND ACTIVE, AND ENDUED WITH ATTRIBUTES.—In a word, you may find the simplest, and also the highest and most general refutation of this sensualistic philosophy in this fact. The mind is an *intelligent agent.* Has it any attributes? Any cognizable, permanent *essentia?* Surely. Now, then, must not those essential qualities imply *powers?* And will any one say that they are only passive powers, and yet the mind is an *agent?* Surely not. Then the mind, although not furnished with innate ideas, must have some innate powers of determining its own acts of intelligence.

It is related that when Locke's Essay on the the Human Understanding was first reported to his great cotemporary, Leibnitz, some one remarked that Locke's system of psychology was built on a literal acceptation of the old scholastic maxim, *Nihil in intellectu, quod non prius in sensu.* Leibnitz answered: *Ita; Nisi Intellectus Ipse!* These words contain the key to the whole discussion.

2. ALL OUR BELIEFS CANNOT BE PROVED.—There is a plausible temptation to deny this, and to treat all our notions and beliefs as derived. It arises from the feeling that it is more philosophical to take nothing upon trust; to require proof of everything. But does not a derived

truth imply something to derive from? If therefore primitive judgments are treated as derived, the problem is only removed one step backward to this question: Whence the truths of which these are the deductions? Primary or derived? To prove every postulate is therefore impossible; because the first proof implies some premise from which to prove. Unless then, some things are seen to be true intuitively, there can be no reasoning. And these unproved truths are the foundations of all that we prove.

METAPHYSICS. SKEPTICISM. ITS GROUNDS.—The question then arises, If these primary beliefs are unproved, how can we know that any of our thinking thence is true? I have now introduced you to the very centre of the skeptical objections of the school of Montaigne and Hume, against the certainty of all human knowledge. Let us also view the other, less radical grounds. They argue, then: 1st. That knowledge must be uncertnin as long as it is incomplete; because the discovery of the unknown related parts may change our view of those supposed to be known. And that men in all ages have believed differently with equal confidence. 2d. That perception only shows us qualities, and not substances, so that we have only the mind's inference, unproved and undemonstrable, for the existence and essence of the latter. 3d. That our organs of sense, the instruments of all perceptions, are perpetually changing their atomic structure; that they often deceive us; that the significance which we give to sensations depends on habits, knowledge and education; and that as to memory, we must take the correctness of her reproductions wholly upon trust. 4th. That our general and abstract ideas, such as those of causation, space, identity, substance, &c., have not even the uncertain evidence of sensation; but are given by the mind's own *à priori* forms of thought; so that we have no proof for them, save that nature teaches us to think so. And last: The sweeping objection is, that man only knows his own subjective states; to the outside of that charmed circle he can never pass, to compare those states with objective reality. But as there is no ground for our assuming the validity of this objective perception, except that *it is nature* to make it, we have only to suppose a different structure given to our minds, to make all seem false, which now seems true.

REFUTATION OF SKEPTICISM.—Such are the sweeping objections. To the first three of the special ones, there is one general, and perfectly valid answer. It is not proved that all the teachings of sensation, memory, reason, are untrustworthy, because they are sometimes misinterpreted, or because men differ about them sometimes. For the mind knows that it is furnished with *criteria* for verifying seeming perceptions, recollections, inferences, which *criteria* give certain results, when applicable, and when faithfully applied. *If there are no such, how did the skeptic find out the falsehood of so many of the seeming dicta of these faculties?* As to the first and radical plea, that primitive judgments must be, from their very nature, *unproved;* and that man can never know anything besides his own subjective states, I freely grant that a direct logical refutation is out of the question, from the very terms of it. But a valid indirect one lies in these facts: 1st. That the skeptic, just as much, and as necessarily, holdsthese primary beliefs as we do. Being implied in the validity of all other beliefs, they must be accepted as true, or all thinking must cease; we are no longer intelligent beings. But the skeptic *will think:* his argument against us is thinking, (erroneous.) 2d. We cannot conceive how an intelligent being could be formed at all, against whose primary beliefs the same objections would not lie, most against God's! 3d. The fact that primitive beliefs are unproved is the very glory of their certainty, and not their weakness. They admit no proof, only because they are so immediate. The perversity of the skeptic is just that of the man who, when in perfect contact with a tree, or post, should declare it impossible to ascertain whether it was near or distant, because forsooth he was so near that no measuring rule could be introduced, to measure the distance! 4th. Chiefly we apply the *argumentum ad hominem* of Pascal. If no knowledge can be certain, then the skeptic must not affirm his unbelief; for this, if admitted, would be a true proposition. The very mental processes exhibited in these objections imply many of the primary beliefs, against the validity of which the skeptic objects. If *nothing* can be proved, what right has he *to go about proving*, that nothing can be proved? Finally: Truth is intrinsic, and not a mere consequence of our mental structure.

3. Which are primitive judgments?—The test of an intutive, or primary truth established by the best writers are three. (1.) They are *primary:* (what Hamilton calls, ambiguously, *incomprehensible*, not capable of being comprehended under some more general and primary judgment, and of being explained thereby.) They are primary, because they are not derived or inferred from any other truth, prior in order of proof to them; but are seen to be true without any dependence on a premise. (2.) They are necessary—i. e., the mind not only sees that they *are* true, but must be true; sees that the negation of them would lead to a direct contradiction. (3.) They are *universal*—i. e., the mind is obliged to believe them as much true in every relevant case, as in the first; and *all people* that are sane, when the terms of their enunciation are comprehended with entire fairness, and dispassionately considered, are absolutely certain, the world over, to accept them as true. Now, our adversaries, the sensationalists, would freely admit that if the mind has any judgments which would s *and* these three tests, they are indeed immediate intuitions. The most practical way, therefore, to discuss their validity will be to do it in application to special classes of supposed intutions.

Axioms are such.—Are the propositions called axiomatic truths, immediate intuitions; or are they derived truths? Sensationalists say, the latter; because they are not primary truths; but deductions of our experience; for they say, as we have seen Locke write, no one has them till he learns them by experimental, sensational trial, and observation; and the announcement of them, instead of receiving from the untutored mind that immediate assent we claim, would, in many cases, excite only a vacant stare. We have already shown that the concrete case is only the *occasion*, not the *source*, of the axiomatic judgment. And as to the latter objection, the mind hitherto uninformed fails to assent to them, only because he does not understand the terms, or comprehend the relations connected with the proposition. Grant that the presenting of a concrete, experimental case is at first necessary to enable this mind to comprehend terms and relations; still we claim (the decisive fact) that once they are comprehended, the acceptance of the proposition is inevitable. How preposterous is this objection, that because the mind did not *see*, while the medium was obstructed, therefore the object is not visible. One might, with equal justice, say that my child had no faculty of immediate eye-sight, because he would not be willing to affirm which of "two pigs in a poke" was biggest! I argue again under this head, that several axioms are incapable of being experimentally inferred; because they never can be brought under the purview of the senses: e. g. "Divergent straight lines will never meet if produced to infinity." No one will ever inspect with his sight or touch an infinite line! But, says Mill, one forms a mental diagram of an infinite pair of lines; and by inspection of them, learns the truth. I reply, what guides and compels the mind in the formation of the infinite part of this mental diagram, so as to *ensure* its correspondence with the sensible part? Not sense, surely; for that is the part of the mental diagram, which no *eye* can ever see. It is just this a priori power of judgment, which Mill denies. My argument stands. Once more I argue on this head, that axioms *cannot* be experimentally derived; because they are universal truths; but each man's experience is partial. The first time a child ever divides an apple, he at once apprehends that the whole is larger than either of its parts. At this one illustration of it, he as much believes it of all the divided apples of the universe, as though he had spent an age in dividing millions of apples for experiment. How can a universal truth come from a *single* case? If experience were the source of the belief, the greatest multitude of cases one could try, would never be enough to demonstrate a universal proposition; for the proportion of similar cases possible in the universe, and still untried, would be infinitely preponderent still. Experience of the past can, of itself, never determine the future.

The sensationalist is inconsistent. He says axioms are learned from experience by sense; and there are no primary judgments of the pure reason. Aye! But how does the mind learn that sensational experience is true? that perceptions have any validity? Only by a primary judgment! Here then is the axiomatic truth, that *what sense gives* us experimentally is true. This, surely, is not derived! Indeed, the attempt to construct a system of cognitions with a denial of primary ideas and judgments, will be found in every case, as preposterous as the attempt to hang a chain upon nothing.

For axioms are necessary truths.—When we ask whether axiomatic truths will meet the second test, that of necessity, sensationalists say: "What is a necessary truth? Does one answer, with Whewell, that it is one, *the negation of which is* INCONCEIVABLE; then this is no test of primary truths, no test of truths at all; because our capacity of concieving things to be possible or otherwise, depends on our mental habits, associations, and acquirements, notoriously: e. g. The Guinea negro king could not conceive it possible that water could be solidified by cold, in the higher latitudes." This will be found to be a mere verbal sophism, deriving its whole plausibility from the unlucky use of a vague term, by the friends of the true theory. A truth is not necessary, because we *negatively* are not able to conceive the actual existence of the opposite thereof; but a truth is necessary when we, *positively, are* able to apprehend that the negation thereof includes an inevitable contradiction. It is not that we *cannot see how* the opposite comes to be true, but it is that we *are able to see* that the opposite cannot possibly be true. Let any man consult his consciousness: is not the proposition, "a whole is greater than its parts," seen by the *mind* in a light of necessity, totally different from this: "The natives of Guinea are generally black, of England generally white?" Yet the latter is *as* true as the former!

THEY ARE UNIVERSAL?—Last, on this head, sensationalists ring many changes on the assertion that axiomatic beliefs are not held by all men alike; that there is debate what *are* axioms, and the widest differences; and that some things long held to be necessary truths, (e. g. Ex nihilo nihil fit; Nature abhors a vacuum; a body cannot act without a medium on another with which it is not present,) are now found not only to be not axioms, but not true at all. I reply, all this proves that the human mind is an imperfect instrument, as to its primary judgments; not that it has none. The same mode of objecting would prove, with equal fairness, (or unfairness,) that derived truths have no inferential validity; for the differences about them have been still wider. Man is often incautious in his thinking, unconsciously blinded by hypothesis, habit and prejudice; and thus he has sometimes (not so very often after all) failed to apply the tests of axiomatic truth carefully. Still the fact remains, that there *are* first truths, absolutely universal in their acceptance, on which every sane mind in the world acts, and always has acted from Adam's day, with unflinching confidence. *On that fact I stand.*

OUR OWN SPIRITUAL EXISTENCE INTUITIVELY SEEN.—The remarks made in introducing my discussion of the immateriality of the soul, have already indicated the grounds on which we claim our belief in our own spiritual existence as an intuition. In the propositions, *Cogito, ergo sum*, Des Cartes meant to indicate, what is undoubtedly true, that the very consciousness of thinking implies an intuitive perception of an existing *substance that thinks*.. But what better definition of spirit, as a something instinctively contrasted with matter, than that it is substance which thinks?

IDENTITY INTUITIVELY SEEN.—Locke made our very belief of our own identity, a derived notion, the simple result of our remembered consciousnesses. It may be very true that a second consciousness succeeding a first, may be the *occasion* of the rise of our notion of identity. But it cannot be the *cause*, for the identity of the thinking being who has the two consciousnesses is implied *à priori* in those states. The word *self* cannot be comprehended by our thought, without comprehending in it the notion of identity. And it has been well remarked, that our belief in our identity cannot be a deduction, because it must be implied before hand, in our very capacity to perceive any relation between premises and conclusion. If the comprehension of the former is not felt to be the act of the same thinking subject who comprehends the latter, then of course there is no possibility of a logical dependence being perceived between them.

REALITY OF THE OBJECTIVE INTUITIVELY SEEN.—Once more, we assert against Berkeley, and all other idealists, that our reference of our sensations to an external world as their cause; and that a world of substances, to which the mind refers the qualities which alone sensation perceives, is a valid intuition. It is primary; witness the notable failures of all the attempts to analyse it into something more primary, from Aristotle to Reid. It is necessary; for the pure idealist can no more rid himself of the practical belief that is was an objective reality, and not a mere subjective notion of a pain, which caused him to feel that he had butted his head against a post. And it is universal. All minds learn it. And if we analyse the mental part of our sensation, we shall find that perception is, in its very nature, a perception of a *relation* between sensitive mind, and outward matter. Grant to the idealist even the assertion, that the mind immediately knows only its own subjective states; yet, when it is conscious of the subjective part of what we call a perception, it still knows by its consciousness, that there was an effect which it did not induce upon itself. Surely this subjectivity must include a consciousness of its own volitions. So, of the absence of a volition of its own. Then, as the mind intuitively and necessarily knows that no effect can be without a cause, it must refer this phenomenon, the subjective act of perception, consciously uncaused from within, to some real thing without.

4. Cause for every Effect intuitively believed.—But the intuition which has been most debated, and is of most fundamental importance to theologians, is our notion of causation. The doctrine of common sense here is, that when the mind sees an effect, it intuitively refers it to some *cause*, as producing its occurrence. Moreover, the antecedent something which made it to be, is intuitively apprehended as having a *power* to produce its occurrence; otherwise it would not have occurred. For the mind is impelled by its own nature to think, that if there had not been a something adequate to make the occurrence to be, it would not have been. Nothing can only result in nothing; and a thing cannot produce its own occurrence; for then it must act before it is. Hence, also, this immediate deduction that this power will always produce the same result, when applied under the same circumstances. The *occasion* of the rise of this notion of power is, no doubt, as Morell has said, with many authors, our consciousness of our own volitions. Now, the sensational psychologists, at the head of whom stands Hume in this particular, deny all this; and say that our belief that similar causes will produce like effects, is only a probable induction of our experience; (so Mill, adding that this probability rises to a practical certainty, as one induction *concurs* with another,) that the mind merely *presumes* the sequence will be repeated again, because it has been presented so often; that since the mind is entitled to no idea, save what perception gives her, and the senses perceive only the two terms of the sequence, without tie of *power* between them, the notion of this tie is baseless; and *power* in causation is naught. Dr. Thomas Brown, while he asserts the intuitive origin of our expectation, that like will produce like, and even argues it with great acuteness, still falls into the latter error, denying that the mind has any ground for a notion of *power* other than "immediate, invariable antecedence;" for this is all perception gives us.

OF NO FORCE TO SAY: POWER NOT PERCEIVED.—Now, our first remark, in defending the correct doctrine, is, that this argument is of no force to any except *pure sensationalists.* When perception furnishes the occasion, a sequence, the reason, by its innate power, furnishes the notion of *cause* in it. Perception does not show us *souls*, not even our own; but reason *compels* us to supply the notion of soul as the *subject* of perceptions and all other states. Perception does not show us substance in matter, but only a bundle of properties; reason compels us to supply the notion of substance. And such an argument is peculiarly inconsistent in the mouth of Brown, who asserts that our belief in the recurrence of causative sequences is intuitive; for it is impossible for the reason to evade the question, What except *power* in the antecedent can make the sequence immediate and invariable? *The something that makes it so*, is just our notion of the power.

THE BELIEF NOT DERIVED FROM ASSOCIATION.—Having thus rebutted objections to the true view, we return to show that the opposite one is unreasonable and absurd. The heterodox metaphysicians deny that we intuitively apprehend the fact, that every effect must have its proper cause, and *vice versa:* and the most plausible ground of denial is to say, that this presumption grows in our minds by the operation of the associating faculty. It is a law of our minds, that they are apt to repeat those sequences of thought, which they have had before in the same juxtaposition; and hence the habit grows up, of thinking of the same consequent, when we see the same antecedent; and we naturally *learn* to expect to see it. But I will show that the belief in cause is not the consequence, but the *ground* and origin of the association. For instance: man knows perfectly well that certain sequences which recur before him perpetually and regularly, as of light on darkness, are not causative; while he believes that certain others, as of light on the sun's rising, are causative. Now, if the associative habit had produced the notion of causation, it would have done it alike in both cases; for both sequences recurred with exactly the same uniformity.

NOR FROM EXPERIENCE.—I remark, farther, that no *experiences* of the fact that a given antecedent *had* produced a given consequent so far as observed, could logically produce the conviction that it would, and must do so everywhere, and in all the future, if it were not sustained by an intuitive recognition of cause and effect in the sequence. The experience of the past only proves the past; there is no logical tie which entitles us to project it on the future if we deny the intuitive one. *How many* experiences of a regular sequence entitle us to carry our expectations into the future? one hundred? 500? What then is the difference between case 499th and case 500th that the latter alone, when added to the previous past experiences, authorizes to say that now case 501st still in the future, must eventuate so and so? There is no reasonable answer. In truth, experience of a mere sequence, by itself, *generates no confidence whatever*, in its future recurrence with causative certainty. You may ask, does not a mere empirical induction (*inductio simplicis enumerationis*, Bacon,) the mere recurrence of an observed sequence, beget in our minds even a probable expectation of its recurrence in the future? I answer, yes, in certain sorts of cases; but this probable expectation proceeds from this: We know intuitively that the consequent in this sequence *must* have some producing cause, whether we have rightly detected it among the seeming antecedents, is not yet proved; and hence two facts are inferred; this seeming, visible antecedent may be the cause, seeing it has so frequently preceded; and if it be indeed the cause, then we are certain it will always be followed by the effect. But we have not yet convinced ourselves that some *unseen* antecedent may not intervene in each case observed; and, therefore, our expectation that the seeming antecedent will continue to be followed by the effect, is only probable It is, therefore, not the *number of instances experienced*, in which the sequence occurred, which begets our expectation that the sequence must recur in the future; but it is the probability the mind sees, that the seeming antecedent may be the true one, which begets that expectation. And if that probability rises to a certainty in one or two cases of the observed sequence, it may be as strong as after ten thousand cases.

Illustration of the above.—This was ingeniously (perhaps unintentionally) illustrated by some of the performances of the calculating machine constructed by the famous Babbage. The machinery could be so adjusted that it would exhibit a series of numbers in an aperture of the dial plate, having a given *ratio*, up to millions. And then, without any new adjustment by the maker, it would change the *ratio* and begin a new series, which it would again continue with perfect regularity until the spectators were weary of watching. Now, if a regular empirical induction, however long continued, could demonstrate anything, it would have done it here. But just when the observer had convinced himself that the first *ratio* expressed the necessary law of the machine, *Presto!* a change; and a different one supercedes it, without visible cause.

One instance cannot form a habit of association.—This introduces the argument, that it is not habit or experience which begets the belief in the regular connexion of cause with effect, because, in many cases, it arises in full strength after *one trial*. The child thrusts his finger in flame: the result is acute pain. He is just as certain from that moment, that the same act will produce the same feeling, as after ten thousand trials. It is because his mind compels him to think the primative judgment, "effect follows cause;" and the *singleness* of the antecedent enables him to decide that *this antecedent* is the cause. Take another case: A school boy, utterly ignorant of the explosive qualities of gunpowder, shuts himself up in a room with a portion for his boyish experiments. After finding it passive under many experiments, he at length applies fire, and there is an immediate explosion. But at the moment the tongs also fell on it; and hence it may not be yet patent which of the two antecedents (simultaneous) was *cause*. He resolves to clear up this doubt by another trial, in which the tongs shall not fall. He applies fire, excluding this time all other antecedent changes, and the explosion follows again. And now this boy is just as certain that fire will inevitably explode any gunpowder that is precisely like this, provided the conditions be precisely similar, as a million of experiments could make him. He has ascertained the tie of *cause*.

In truth, as Dr. Chalmers well says, experience is so far from *begetting* this belief in the regular efficiency of causation, that its effect is, on the oontrary, to limit and correct that belief. A little child strikes his spoon on the table; the effect is noise. At first he expects to be able to produce the same effect by striking it on the bed or carpet, and is vexed at the failure. Experience corrects his expectation: not by adding anything to his intuitive judgment of like cause, like effect; but by teaching him that in this case, the cause of noise was complex, not single, as he had before supposed, being the impact of the *spoon and* the elasticity of the thing struck.

Kant's argument.—The subtile, and yet simple reasoning, by which *Kant* (Critick of Pure Reason. Bk. ii, Ch. 2, § 3,) shows the absurdity of resolving cause and effect into mere sequence, is worthy of your attention here. He suggests two instances: In one I look *successively* at the different parts of a large house over the way. I perceive *first*, for instance, its front, and *then* its end. But do I ever think for a moment that the *being* of the end is successive upon the being of the front? Never. I know they are simultaneous. In another case, I see a vessel in the river just opposite to me; and next, I see it below me. The perceptions are *no more* successive than those of the front and end of the house. But now, can I ever think that the being of the vessel in the two positions is co-etaneous? It is impossible. Why? The only answer is, that the law of the reason has, by intuition, seen effect and dependency, in the last pair of successive perceptions, which were not in the first pair. The same vessel *has moved;* motion is an effect; its cause must precede it. And this suggests the other member of his argument; In a causative sequence, the interval of time is wholly inappreciable to the senses; the cause A and the effect B seem to come *together*. Now, why is it that the mind *alwaps refuses* to conceive the matter so as to think B leads A, and will only think that A leads B? Why do you not think that the loud sound of the blow caused the impact of the hammer, just as often as you do that the impact caused the sound? Surely there is a law of the reason regulating this! Now, that something, which determines the order of the sequence, is power.

The intuitive belief of cause necessary prior premise of all experimental induction.—Last, it is only because our judgment of cause is *à priori* and intuitive, that any process of induction, practical or scientific, can be valid or demonstrative. Bacon shows, what even J. S. Mill admits, that a merely empirical induction can never give certain expectation of future recurrence. To reach this, some canon of induction must be applied which will discriminate the *post hoc* from the *propter hoc*. Does not Mill himself teach the neceesity of such canons? Inspect any instance of their application to observed sequences, and you will find that each step proceeds upon the intuitive law of cause, as its postulate. Each step is a syllogism, in which the intuitive truth gives the major premise.

Example.—Let us take a simp'e case falling under what Mill calls his Method by Agreement. (The student will find my assertion true of either of the others.) The school boy, with his parcel of gunpowder, e. g., is searching among the antecedents for the true cause of the phenomenon of explosion, which we will call D. That cause is not detected at first, because he cannot be certain that he procures its occurrence with only a single antecedent. First he constructs an experiment, in which he contrives to exclude all antecedents save two, A and B. The result D follows; but it is not determined whether A or B, or the two jointly, caused it. He contrives a second experiment, in which B is excluded; but another antecedent event C happens along with A, and again D follows. Now we can get the truth. We reason thus: "In the first experiment, the cause of D must have been either A or B, or the two combined." But *why?* Besause the effect D *must have had some*, immediate, present cause. [But we know that no other immediate antecedent effects were present, save A and B.] *This is our à priori intuition.* Well, in the second experiment, either A or C, or the two combined, must have caused D. *Why?* The same intuition gives the only answer. But we proved, in the first experiment, C had nothing to do with producing D; and in the second, B had nothing to do with producing D; because C was absent in the first, and B in the second. Then A was the true cause all the time. Why? Why may not B have been the cause, that time when it was present? Because every effect has its own cause, which is regular, every time it is produced. The premise is still the intuition: "Like causes produce like effects."

THAT WHICH IS NECESSARY PRIOR PREMISE, CANNOT BE DEDUCTION.—It thus appears, that this intuitive belief is essential beforehand, to enable us to convert an experimental induction into a demonstrated general law. Could anything more clearly prove that the original intuition itself cannot have been an experimental induction? It passes human wit to see how a logical process can prove its own premise, when the premise is what proves the process. Yet this absurdity Mill gravely attempts to explain. His solution is, that we may trust the law of cause as a general premise, because it is "an empirical law coëxtensive with all human experience." May we conclude, then, that a man is entitled to argue from the law of cause as a valid general premise, only after he has acquired "all human experience?" This simple question dissolves the sophism into thin air. It is experimentally certain, that this is not the way in which the mind comes by the belief of the law; because no man, to the day of his death, acquires all human experience, but only a part, which, relatively to the whole, is exceedingly minute; and because every man believes the law of cause to be universal, when he begins to acquire experience. The just doctrine, therefore, is that experimental instances are only the occasions, upon which the mind's own intuitive power furnishes the self-evident law.

I have required your careful attention to this demonstration, because, as Hume's cavils have taught us, without the true doctrine of causation, we cannot demonstrate the supernatural, nor even the existence of God.

LECTURE VII.

SYLLABUS.

SOURCES OF OUR THINKING. (Contiuued.)

1. Is the Intuitional Reason a different faculty from, and of higher authority than the Logical Understanding?
   Locke's Essay, Bk. iv, Ch. ii, § 7. Moshiem Eccles. Hist., Cent. 17th, Sec. i, § 24. Morell, p. 125, pp. 161-168.
2. To ascertain the origin of moral distinctions in our minds, state and refute the Selfish System of Morals, as held by Hobbes, and others.
   Jouffroy's Introduc. to Ethicks, Lect. ii. Dr. Thos. Brown, Lect. 78, 79. Cousin, Le Vrai, &c., Leçon 12th. Morell, p. 71-75.
3. State and refute the utilitarian theory, (as held by Hume or Bentham.)
   "Crimes of Philanthrophy," in the *Land we Love*, Dec. 1866. Jouffroy, Lect. 13, 14, Brown, Lect. 77, 78. Cousin, Le Vrai, &c. Leçon, 13th. Morell, p. 215, &c.
4. State and discuss Paley's form of the Selfish System.
   Paley's Moral Phil., p. 24-60. (8vo. Ed.) Jouffroy, Ch. 15. Brown, Lect. 79, 80. Alex. Moral Science, Ch. 1, 2, 3. Cousin, Du Vrai, du Beau et du Bien, as above.
5. State and discuss the Sentimental Theory of Dr. Adam Smith.
   Jouffroy, Lect. 16-18. Brown, Lect. 80-81.

1. Transcendetalists claim primitive judgments licentiously.—After Bacon, the first analysts of the laws of thought, such as Hobbes and Locke, set out with the fascinating idea of accepting nothing upon trust, and bringing everything to the test of experimental proof. The miserable sensationalism and materialism to which this led in the hands of Priestly in England, and Condillac in France, taught men to reflect, that unless some primary judgments are allowed to start from, there can be no beginning at all; so that some truths must have a prior authority than that of proof. By what faculty, then, are they perceived? Transcendentalists, from Spinoza to the modern, have all answered, by the intuitive reason: whose sight is direct intellection, whose conclusions are super-logical, and not, therefore, amenable to logical refutation. The frightful license of dogmatizing, to which these schools have proceeded, shows the motive: it is to enjoy an emancipation from the logical obligations of *proving* dogmas. Do we say to them, Your assertions do not seem to us true, and we disprove them thus and thus; they reply, "Ah, that is by your plodding, logical understanding; intuitions of the pure reason are not amenable to it; and if you do not see that our opinion is necessarily true, in spite of objections, it is only because the reason is less developed in you." So the quarrel now stands. It seems to me obvious, therefore, that the next adjustment and improvement, which the science of mind must conceive, should be adjustment of the relations between intuitions and valid deductions.

How resisted. Now, we might practically bring the transcendentalist to reason by saying, first, that they always claim the validity of the logical understanding, when they find it convenient to use it. [The very evasion above stated is a deduction, by one step, from false premises!] Hence, consistency requires them to bow to it everywhere. Second; we might apply the established tests of a true intuition to their pretended ones, primariness, necessary truth, and universality; and thus show that, when they profess by the pure reason to see dogmas which contradict or transcend the common sense of mankind, they are but making wild hypotheses. But third: I am convinced the radical overthrow of their system will be seen to be, at length, in this position: that the mind sees the truth of a valid deduction by the *same faculty*, and with *equal authority*, as an axiom or other first truth—i. e., when major and minor premise have a conclusive relation, and that relation is fairly comprehended, the reason sees the conclusion as immediately, as necessarily, as intuitively, as authoritatively, as when it sees a primary truth.

All judgments intuitive and necessary, if valid.—To my mind, the simple and sufficient proof of this view of the logical function is in these questions. What is the human intelligence, but a function of of seeing truth? As the eye only *sees by looking*, and all looking is direct and immediate sense intuition, how else can the mind see, than by looking—i. e., by rational intuition? Whether the object of bodily eyesight be immediate or reflective, an object or its *spectrum*, it is still equally true that the eye only sees by looking—looking immediately; in the latter case the *spectrum* only is its immediate object. So the mind only sees by looking; and all its looking is intuition; if not immediate, it is not its own; it is naught. One of the earliest, Locke, concurs with one of the latest ,McGuffey, of the great English-speaking psychologists, in asserting the view I adopted before consulting either. Locke's proof of it seems to me perfectly valid. He argues, (*loco citato*,) that if the mind's perception of a valid relation between a proposition and its next premise were not immediate, then there must be, between the two, some proposition to mediate our view of it. But between a proposition and its *next premise*, there can be no other interposed.

Objections solved.—But to this view many sound philosophers, even, would probably object strenuously: That the first great mark of intuitive authority, primariness, was lacking; that the position is utterly overthrown by the wide and various *differences* of opinion on subjects of deduction; while in first truths, there must be universal agreement; and that it is inconsistent with the fact that many *derived* conclusions claim no more than a *probable* evidence. To the first, I reply, the action of the reason in seeing a deduced truth, is not indeed a primary judgment; but the fact that the truth is seen only by relation to premises, does not make the intellection less immediate and necessary. Just so truly as the first truth is seen to be necessarily true, so the deduced truth is seen to be necessarily true, the premises being as they are. Several of our intuitions are *intuitions of relations*. Why should it be thought so strange that these intellections by relations should be intuitive? To the second, propositions *called* axioms have *not* always commanded universal agreement; and we are obliged to explain this fact by misapprehension of *terms*, or ignorance of relations included in the propositions. Well, the same explanation accounts consistently for the differences men have in their deductions; and the more numerous differences in this class of propositions is accounted for by the facts, that while axioms are few, deductions are countless; and in any *one* there are *more* terms, because more propositions liable to misconception. But I do not assert, that in a valid syllogism, that if the major and minor are known to be true, and the terms are all fairly comprehended, the belief of the conclusion by the hearer is as inevitable, as necessary, as universal, as when an axiom is stated. Third; though in many deductions the evidence is but probable, the fact that *there is* probable evidence, may be as necessarily admitted, as in an intuitive and positive truth.

II. SOURCE OF OUR MORAL JUDGMENTS.—We now approach, young gentlemen, that great class of our judgments which are of supreme importance in theology, as in practical life—the class known as our moral judgments. Every sane man is conscious of acts of soul, which pronounce certain rational agents *right* or *wrong* in certain acts. With these right or wrong acts our souls unavoidably conjoin certain notions and feelings of obligation, merit, demerit, approbation or disapprobation, and desert of reward or penalty. It is this peculiar class of mental states which constitute the subject of the science of *ethicks*, or *morals.* All questions as to the nature and validity of moral judgments run into the radical question, as to their origin. Are they the results of a fundamental and intuitive law of reason? Or are they artificial, or factitious results of some other natural principles, developed into a form only apparently peculiar by habit, association, or training? In answering this all-important question, I shall pursue this method, to set aside the various false analyses, until we reach the true one.

THE SELFISH SYSTEM.—The *Selfish System*, presenting itself in many varied forms from Hobbes (natural desire of emjoyment only motive) through Meandeville (the desire of being applauded is the moral motive) down to Paley, has always this characteristic: it resolves our idea of virtue into self-interest. Its most refined form, perhaps, is that which says, since acts of benevolence, sympathy, justice, are found to be attended with an immediate inward pleasure, (self-approbation,) *that* pleasure is the motive of our moral acts. Discuss several phases together.

REFUTED. 1ST, BY INTUITIVE BELIEFS OF RIGHT AND FREE AGENCY.—I remark, that on the selfish system, the notion of *right*, duty, obligation, free agency, could never have arisen in the mind, and have no relevancy or meaning. Let man frame the proposition: "That which furthers self-interest is *right;*" the very employment of the word *right* betrays the fact that the mind *recognizes a standard other than that of self-interest.* And any analysis of the notion shows that it is utterly violated and falsified, when made *identical* with self-interest. Thus, Hobbes says, each man's natural *right* is to pursue his own natural self-interest supremely. But according to his own showing, this "right" in A implies no corresponding *duty* in him, and no obligation in his neighbour, B, to respect it, and no recognition on the part of any other. Any body has a "right" to prevent A from having his "right." Queer *right* this!

If interest is the whole motive, then, when the question arises, whether I shall do, or omit a certain action, you cannot consistently expect me to consider anything but this: whether or not the doing of it will promote my own advantage, and that in the form I happen to prefer. If I say, "This result will most gratify me," the argument is at an end; my proposed act is, for me, right; there is no longer any standard of uniform moral distinction. The same remark shows that the judgment of obligation to a given act is then baseless. Attempt to apply any of those arguments, by which Epicureanism attempts to interpose an "ought not" between a man and any natural indulgence; (as this: "This sensual pleasure will indeed promote animal, but hinder intellectual pleasure, which is higher. And since pleasure is the rational chief good, you should prefer the more to the less;") the reply is: "Animal joys are *to me* larger than intellectual;" and the ground of obligation is gone. If no indulgence is less or more *virtuous* than any other, then no possible argument of *obligation* can be constructed, in the face of an existing *preference*, for refraining from any. If the sensualistic psychology is true, from which the selfish schemes proceed, then desire for natural good, which they make the only moral motive, is a passive affection of the soul. It is no more voluntary, when the object of desire is presented, than is pain when you are struck, or a chill when you are deluged with cold water. Where, now, is that free agency which, we intuitively feel, is rudimental to all moral action and responsibility? Man is no longer self-directed by subjective rational motives, but drawn hither and thither like a puppet, by external forces. But if not a free, he cannot be a moral agent. Of course, also, there is no longer any basis for any judgment of *merit* or *demerit* in acts, or any moral obligation to punishment. Penalties become the mere *expedients* of the stronger for protecting their own selfishness. And as this is as true of the future, all religious sanctions are at an end!

2D. FROM PRECEDENCE OF INTUITIVE DESIRE TO CALCULATION.—This theory teaches that this selfish pleasure apprehended by the mind, in acquiring an object, must always be the motive for seeking it. The analysis is false; desire must be *instinctive;* otherwise man could not have his *first volition* till *after* the volition had put him on the way of *experiencing* the pleasant *result* of the fruition! Many desires are obviously instructive; e. g., curiosity. Now, since the self-pleasing cannot be the origidal element of the desire, it cannot be proved that this is our element of rightness, in classifying our desires. See now, how this analysis would assign the effect as the cause of its own cause. A does a disinterested act. The consciousness of having done disinterestedly gives to A an inward pleasure. This after-pleasure, proceeding from the consciousness that the act was unselfish, prompted to the act! Thus the effect caused its own cause! The absurdity of the scheme is further proved by this: If the fact that a disinterested act results in inward satisfaction to him who did it, proves that act selfish; then the fact that a selfish act usually results in inward *pain* to him who perpetrates it, proves that act to have been a disinterested one in motive.

3D. FROM INTUITIVE DIFFERENCE OF ADVANTAGE AND MERIT.—If the selfish theory of action were true, the adaptation of another person's conduct to confer personal advantage on us, should be synonymous with *merit* in our eyes. The villian who shared with us the reward of his misdeeds, to bribe us to aid or applaud him, would evoke the same sentiment of gratitude, as the mother who blessed us with her virtuous self-sacrifice; and there would be no generic difference between the hollow flattery of the courtier for the monster on whose bounty he fattened, and the approbation of the virtuous for patriotism or benevolence.

4TH. FROM VIVIDNESS OF UNSOPHISTICATED MORAL SENTIMENTS.—If our notion of *good acts* is nothing but a generalization of the idea of acts promotive of our self-interest, he who has most experimental knowledge of human affairs (i. e., he who is most hackneyed in this world's ways,) must have the clearest and strongest apprehensions of moral distinctions; because he would most clearly apprehend this tendency of actions. He who was wholly inexperienced, could have no moral distinctions. Is this so? Do we not find the most unsophisticated have the most vivid moral sympathies? The ignorant child in the nursery more than the hackneyed man of experience?

5TH. FROM CONSCIOUSNESS. NO MERIT WHERE SELF REIGNS.—But the crowning absurdity of the the theory appears here; that our consciousness always teaches us, the pleasure we have in well-doing depends wholly upon our feeling that the virtuous act had no reference to self; and the moment we feel that self-pleasing was our prime motive, we feel that our moral pleasure therein is wholly marred. Indeed, the best and the sufficient argument against this miserable theory would perhaps be the instinctive loathing and denial uttered against it by every man's soul, who is rightly constituted. The honest man knows, by his immediate consciousness, that when he does right, selfishness is not his motive; and that if it were, he would be utterly self-condemned. As *Cousin* nervously remarks: Our consciousness tells us, that the approbation we feel for disinterested virtue is wholly disinterested, and it is impossible for us to feel it unless we feel that the agent for whom we feel it was disinterested in this act; Thus, a thousand things in the acts, the language, and the consciousnesses of men are utterly irreconcilable with this hateful analysis, and show it to be as unphilosophical as degrading. Our crowning objection is found in its effect on our view of the divine character. That which is man's finite virtue must be conceived infinite, as constituting the virtue of God, (if there is a God.) His holiness must be only sovereign self-interest!

III. UTILITARIAN ETHICKS.—In the third place I group together three theories of the nature of virtue, which really amount to the same; that of David Hume, who taught that an act is apprehended by us as virtuous, because it is seen to be *useful to mankind;* that of Jeremy Bentham, who taught that whatever conduct is conducive to *the greatest good of the greatest* number, is right. and that of some New Englahd divines and philosophers, who teach that virtue consists in *benevolence.* The latter is practically synonymous with the two former. For the practical expression of *benevolence* is *beneficence.* This theory of virtue is a natural off-shoot of Jonathan Edward's theory of virtue, which makes it *love* of *being;* and its filiation may be seen by the remark just made above. These theories derive all the plausibility of their sophistries from three facts: It has been so often said, that "Honesty is the best policy," that men come to think the goodness of the policy is what makes it honest; to promote utility, or, in other words, to do acts of beneficence to mankind, is, in a multitude of cases, right and praisewarthy; the duties of benevolence *are* duties, and a very extensive class thereof; but not, therefore, exhaustive of all duties. Once more, in the business of legislation, *the expedient* is very much the guide; and crimes are punished chiefly in proportion to their tendency to injure the well-doing of society. This might easily deceive one who, like Bentham, was far more of a legislator than philosopher, to suppose that he had found in the beneficence of acts, the essential element of their virtue. He forgets that human laws propose as their end only the protection of human well-being in this world; and not the accurate final apportionment of merits. This is God's function alone.

1st. It is selfish, in fact.—The *utilitarian schemes* of ethicks profess to stand in contrast to the selfish, because they propose not the sefish good of the agent, but the well-being of mankind, as the element and test of virtue. But they would really involve, as Jouffroy argues, the vice of the selfish systems, if consistently carried out to their last result. For when the question is raised, "*Why* do men come to regard the *utile* as the *right?*" the answer must be, because well-being (natural enjoyment) is the properest end of man. But thence it must follow, that desire of natural good is man's properest motive of action. Thus, the *moral motive* is as effectually left out of the analysis as by Hobbes himself; and the same absurd psychology is assumed, which makes desire for natural good the result of experienced good, whereas the desire must act first, or the good would never have come to be experienced. But more; if desire for natural good is man's properest motive of action, it must follow, that his own personal good must always be the properest end of moral action; because this must always be the nearest, most immediate object of the natural desire. These schemes make *aggregate humanity* the supreme object of moral action; the true God. But the individual agent is a part of that aggregate; a part of his own God! And as he is the most attainable part—the only part for whose natural welfare he can labour effectually—I see not how the practical conclusion is to be avoided; that he is his own properest supreme end. Thus we are led back to the vilest results of the selfish system; and such, experience teaches us, is the practical tendency. While the utilitarian schemes profess great beneficence, they make their votaries supremely politic and selfish.

2d. Utility not the conscious rule of obligation.—But farther; the scheme does not correctly state the facts of our consciousness. The mind does not feel that obligation to an act is always its mere utility or beneficence, nor that the merit of the agent arises out of the advantage his act effects. How often, for instance, do questions arise, as to the obligation of *speaking truth;* where if the utility were the element of obligation, none would be felt; yet the mind would feel most guilty, had falsehood been uttered in the case. Again; were utility the element of virtue, the rightness or wrongness of an act would only be apprehended so far as experience had given us knowledge as to the beneficence or mischievousness of its effects. Is this so? Does not the conscience lash us for secret sins which leave no loss o reputation, health, or capacity behind them; and lash us all the more promptly and keenly, as we are inexperienced of crime and its wretched consequences? Farther; were this theory true, all truly useful things should affect us with similar sentiments of moral approbation, a convenient bureau, or good milch cow, as truly as a faithful friend, or a benevolent rescuer. Does Hume attempt to escape by saying that it is the *rational and voluntary useful act* which affects us with the sentiment of approbation? Then, we reply, he has given up the case; for evidently the morality of the act is not in its utility, but in its rational motive. Once more; if utility is the sole element of virtue, then the degree of utility should also be the *measure* of virtuous merit. We would always feel those acts to be most meritorious which were most conducive to natural good. But do we? e. g. Which ennobles Daniel most in our eyes: the heroism which refused to bow his conscience to an impious prohibition of his king, when the penalty was the lions' den, or the diligence which dispensed order and prosperity over one hundred and twenty provinces? And the extravagant conclusions of Godwin must be accepted—that duties must be graded by us in proportion to the public importance of the person who was their object; so that it might be the son's duty to see his own father drown, in order to save some more valuable life, who is a stranger to him.

3D IF SO, WE MIGHT "DO EVIL THAT GOOD MAY COME."—Were the utilitarian scheme true, it might be in some cases utterly impossible to convince a man that it was immoral to "do evil that good might come." If the consequences of the evil act, so far as foreseen by his mind, seemed beneficial, it would be right to do it. Nor could the claims of retributive justice in many cases be substantiated; the criminal who gave, by his penitence, sufficient guarantee that he would offend no more, could not be made, without immorality, to pay his debt of guilt. And above all, *eternal retributions* would be utterly indefensible in a God of infinite wisdom and power. How can they advantage the universe, including the sufferers, as much as their pardon and thorough conversion would benefit them, without injuring the rest?

IV. PALEY'S SCHEME.—Paley's type of the Selfish System may be said to be equally perspicuous and false. That such a specimen of impotency and sophism in philosophy should come from a mind capable of so much justice and perspicuity of reasoning as he has exhibited in the experimental field of Natural Theology is one of the most curious facts in the history of opinion. I shall first attempt to rebutt the objections which he insinuates against the originality of moral perceptions, and then criticize his own theory.

ATTACKS ORIGINALITY OF MORAL JUDGMENTS.—He first proposes to test the question, whether such distinctions are originally and intuitively perceived, by supposing a case of what we call odious filial treachery, stated to a mind perfectly untutored by human associations, example, and teaching; and asking us whether he would immediately feel its vileness, with us. We answer, of course, No. But to show how absurdly preposterous the test is, we need not, with Dr. Alexander, dwell on the *complexity* of the moral problem involved. The simple answer is, that such a mind would not have the moral sentiment, because he would not comprehend the *relations* out of which the violated obligations grew, nor the very words used, to state them. In no proper sense could the untutored mind be said to *see the case*. Now, what a paltry trick is it, to argue that a mind has not a power of comparison, because it cannot compare objects which it does not behold at all?

ATTRIBUTES THEM TO ASSOCIATION.—Paley insinuates (none of his objections to moral intuitions are stated boldly) that our notions of the moral may all be accounted for by *association and imitation*. Thus, "having noticed that certain actions produced, or tended to produce, good consequences, whenever those actions are spoken of, they suggest, by the law of association, the pleasing idea of the good they are wont to produce. What association begins, imitation strengthens; this habit of connecting a feeling of pleasure with classes of acts is confirmed by similar habits of thought and feeling around us, and we dub it the sentiment of moral approbation." (Borrowed from Hume.) Now, this analysis is shown to be worthless in this one word. The law of association does not *transmute*, but only *reproduces*, the mental states connected by it. How, then, can the feeling of pleasure, which begins from a perceived tendency in a class of acts to promote natural good, be changed by association into the pleasure of moral approbation? They are distinct enough at first. Again: How, on this scheme, could men ever come to have pain of conscience at sins which are naturally pleasurable, and attended with no more direct natural ill? And how could the fact ever be explained, that we often have the sentiment of remorse for doing something in compliance with general associations and imitation?

OBJECTS, THAT THEY ARE NOT REFERABLE TO ANY SIMPLER TYPE.—Another class of objections is drawn from the facts that man has no *innate ideas* of the abstract element of moral right; and that moralists, though asserting the instinctive origin of moral perceptions, have never been able to point to any one type, or simple abstract element, (as veracity, &c.,) into which all moral acts might be resolved. After our criticism of Locke, no farther answer will be needed to the first objection. The second, when examined, will be found to be a bald begging of the question. The question is, whether the rightness of acts is an original perception of the human reason. Now, if it be, it will of course follow that it *cannot be* referred to some more general type of perception. Can this general idea, *a truth*, be analysed? Why not? Because it is already simple and primary. Who dreams of arguing now that the human reason has no original capacity of perceiving truth in propositions, because it has no more general and abstract type, into which the sorts of truth in different classes of propositions may be referred? So, of the idea of *rightness*.

AND VARIABLE.—Paley also borrows the common argument of objectors, from the wide variety, and even contrariety of moral opinions in different ages and nations. In one nation, filial duty is supposed to consist in nursing an aged parent; in another land, in eating him, &c., &c. The answers are, that no one ever pretended any human faculty was perfect in its actings, however original. Habit and association, example, passion, have great influence in perverting any faculty. Next, as justly remarked by Dr. Alexander, many of the supposed cases of contrariety of moral judgments are fully explained by the fact, that the dictate of conscience, right in the general, is perverted by some error or ignorance of the understanding. The Christian mother feels it her duty to cherish the life of her infant; the Hindoo to drown hers in Holy Ganges! True. Yet both act on the dictate of conscience—that a mother should seek the highest good of her infant. The Hindoo has been taught by her false creed, to believe that she does this by transferring it in childhood to heaven. Once more; it is a most erroneous conclusion to infer that because men perform, in some countries, what are here regarded as odious vices, with seeming indifference and publicity, that therefore their moral sentiments about them do not agree with ours. An educated Hindoo will lie for a penny, and when detected, laugh at it as smart. A Hottentot woman will seem shameless in her lewdness. Yet we are informed that the Hindoo reverences and admires the *truthfulness* of a Christianized Briton; and that the poor Hottentot scorns the unchaste European missionary, just as any female here would. The amount of the case is, that conscience may be greatly stupefied or drowned by evil circumstances; but her general dictates, so far as heard, are infallibly uniform.

PALEY'S DEFINITION OF DUTY, &c.—Paley, having succeeded to his own satisfaction, in proving that there is no sufficient evidence of moral intuitions existing in the human soul, gives his own definition. "Virtue is doing good to mankind, according to the will of God, for the sake of everlasting happiness." And moral obligation, he defines, as nothing else than a forcible motive arising out of a command of another. That this scheme should ever have seemed plausible to Christians, can only be accounted for by the fact that we intuitively feel, when a God is properly apprehended, that His will is a perfect rule of right; and that it is moral to do all He commands. But when we raise the question, *why?* the answer is, *because His will*, like His character, *is holy*. To do His will, then, is not obligatory *merely* because an Almighty has commanded it; but *He has commanded it because it is obligatory*. The distinction of right and wrong is intrinsic.

OBJECTIONS. THE SYSTEM A SELFISH ONE.—The objections to Paley's system are patent. He himself raises the question, wherein virtue, on his definition, differs from a prudent self-love in temporal things. His answer is, the latter has regard only to this life; the former considers also future immortal well-being. Brown well observes of this, that it is but a more odious refinement upon the selfish system; defiling man's very piety, by making it a selfish trafficking for personal advantage with God, and fostering a more gigantic moral egotism, insomuch as immortality is longer than moral life. All the objections levelled against the selfish system by me, apply, therefore, justly here. This scheme of Paley is equally false to our consciousness, which tells us that when we act, in all relative duties, with least reference to self, then we are most praiseworthy.

FORCE MAY JUSTIFY SIN.—But we may add, more especially, that on Paley's scheme of obligation, it is hard to see how he could deny that there may be, in some cases, as real a moral obligation to do wrong as to do right. A company of violent men overpower me, and command me, on pain of instant death, to burn down my neighbour's dwelling. Here is "a forcible motive arising from the command of another." Why does it not constitute a moral obligation to the crime? Paley would reply, because God commands me not to burn it, on pain of eternal death; and this obligation destroys the other, because the motive is vastly more forcible. It seems, then, that in God's case, it is His *might* which make His *right*.

NO OBLIGATION WITHOUT REVELATION. AND NO VIRTUE IN GOD.—Once more. On Paley's scheme, there could be no morality, nor moral obligation, where there is no revelation from God; because neither the rule, nor motive, nor obligation of virtue exists. They do not exist indeed, Paley might reply, in the form of a revealed theology; but they are there in the teachings and evidences of Natural Theology. "The heathen which have not the law are a law unto themselves, their cansciences," &c. But if there are no authoritative intuitions given by God to man's soul, of moral distinctions, then Natural Theology has no sufficient argument whatever to prove that God is a moral being, or that He wills us to perform moral acts. Look and see. And, in fine: What can God's morality be; since there is no will of a higher being to regulate His acts, and no being greater than He to hold out the motive of eternal rewards for obeying!

V. DR. A. SMITH'S THEORY.—The ingenious scheme of Dr. Adam Smith, Theory of Mor. Sents. may be seen very perspicuously unfolded in Jouffroy. This scheme is by no means so mischievous and degrading as that of Hobbes, Hume, or Paley. But it is incorrect. Its fundamental defect is, that in each step it assumes the prior existence of the moral sentiment, in order to account for it. For instance, it says: We feel approbation for an act, when we experience a sympathetic emotion with the sentiments in the agent which prompted it. But sympathy only reproduces the same emotion; it does not transmute it; so that unless the producing sentiment in the agent were moral, it could not, by sympathy, generate a moral sentiment in us. It supposes *conscience* comes thus: We imagine an ideal man contemplating our act, conceive the kind of sentiments he feels for us, and then sympathize therewith. But how do we determine the sentiments of this ideal man looking at our act? He is but a projection of our own moral sentiments. So, in each step, Dr. S. has to assume the phenomenon, as already produced; for the production of which he would account.

LECTURE VIII.

SYLLABUS.

ETHICAL THEORIES. (Concluded.)

1. What the true theory of the moral Distinction ond Obligation? Compare it with that of *Jouffroy*. Is the moral Distinction seen by the Reason, or by a distinct faculty?

Bp. Butler's Sermons, viz: Preface, and Sermon on Rom. xii: 4, 5. Cousin, Le Vrai, Le Beau, Le Bien, Leçon 14th. Alexander's Moral Science, Ch. 2-7, inclus., and Ch. 10. Jouffroy, Introduc. to Ethics, Lect. 1 to 3.

2. Explain the moral *Emotion* involved with the moral judgment, and in connexion criticize the schemes of Hutcheson and Brown
Cousin, as above. Alex., Mor. Sc., Ch. 6 to 11. Dr. Thos. Brown, Lect. 81, 82. Jouffroy, Lect. 19, 20.
3. State the true doctrine of the supremacy and authority of conscience.
Butler's Sermon on Rom. ii: 14. Alexander, Ch. 8, 9.
4. What qualities are necessary to moral agency and responsibility?
Alexander, Ch. 13, 14, Dr. Thos. Brown, Lect. 73.

1. Moral Judgments are intuitive.—Are moral distinctions intrinsic; and are they intuitively perceived? We have now passed in review all the several theories which answer, *no;* and found them untenable. Hence, alone, we derive a strong probability that the affirmative is the true answer; e. g. All the chemists endeavour in vain to analyse a given material substance into some other known one; but fail. It is, therefore, assumed to be simple, and original.

We must assume this of the moral sentiment; or else it is unintelligible how mankind ever became possessed of the moral idea. For every *original* and simple idea, whether sensitive or rational, with which our souls are furnished, we find an appropriate original power; and without this the idea could never have been entertained by man. Had man no eye, he would have never had ideas of light and colours; no ear, he could never have had the idea of melody; no taste, he would forever have lacked the idea of beauty. So, if the idea of rightness in acts is not identical with that of truth, nor utility, nor benevolence, nor self-love, nor love of applause, nor sympathetic harmony, nor any other original sentiment: it must be received directly by an original moral power in the soul. To this, in the second place, consciousness testifies: the man who calmly and fully investigates his own mental processes, will perceive that his view and feeling of the rightness of some acts arise immediately in his mind; without any medium, except the comprehension of the real relations of the act; that their rise is unavoidable; and that their failure to rise would be immediately and necessarily apprehended by all as a fundamental defect of his soul. There is, indeed, a great diversity in the estimation of the more complex details of moral questions. And man's intuition of those distinctions is often disturbed by three causes, well stated by Dr. Brown—complexity of elements, habits of association and prevalent passion. But, allowing for these, there is just the *universal and immediate agreement in all sane human minds,* which we expect to find in the acceptance of necessary first truths. In the fundamental and simple ideas of the moral, men are agreed. And in the case of *any other* intuitions, we have to make precisely the same allowances, and to expect the same disturbing causes. These, with the remarks I made in refutatation of Paley's objections, I think suffice to sustain the true theory on that point.

Illustrated from Logical Judgments.—I hold, then, that as there is, in some *propositions,* (not in all—some are truisms, many are meaningless, and some so unknown as to be neither affirmed or denied,) the element of *truth or falsehood,* original, simple, incapable of analysis or definition in simpler terms, and ascertainable by the mind's intellection; so there is in *actions,* of the class called *moral,* an intrinsic quality of *rightness or wrongness,* equally simple, original, and incapable of analysis; and like simple truth, perceived immediately by the inspection of the reason. This quality is intrinsic: they are not right merely because God has commanded, or because He has *formed* souls to think so, or because He has established any relation of utility, beneficence, or self-interest therewith. But God has commanded them, and formed these relations to them, because they are right. Just as a *proposition* is not true because our minds are so constructed as to apprehend it such; but our minds were made by God to see it so, because it is true.

Some Moral Judgments likewise deductive.—But understand me; I do not assert that all moral distinctions in particular acts are intuitively seen, or necessarily seen. As in propositions, some have primary, and some deductive truth; some are seen to be true without premises, and some by the help of premises; so, in acts having moral quality, the rightness or wrongness of some is seen immediately, and of some deductively. In the latter, the moral relation of the agent is not immediately seen, but the moral judgment is mediated only by the knowledge of some other truths. If these truths are not known, then the moral quality of the act is not obvious. From this simple remark it very clearly follows, that if the mind's belief touching these truths, which are premises to the moral judgment, be erroneous, the moral judgment will also err. Just as in logic, so here; false premises, legitimately used, will lead to false conclusions. And here is the explanation of the discrepancies in moral judgments, which have so confused Ethicks.

II. But there are several writers of eminence, who, while they substantially, yea nobly, uphold the originality and excellence of man's moral distinctions, err, as we think, in the details of their analysis. A moment's inquiry into their several departures from my theory, will best serve to define and establish it.

The Moral Distinction seen by the Reason.—a.) Seeing that the moral distinction is intrinsic; what is the faculty of the soul by which it is apprehended? (Bear in mind a faculty is not a *limb* of mind, but only a name we give to one phase or sort of its processes.) Does it apprehend it by its reason; or by a distinct moral faculty? Says Dr. Hutcheson, an English writer: By a distinct, though rational perceptive faculty, which he names, the *moral sense;* and describes as an *internal sense*—i. e., a class of processes perceptive, and also exhibiting sensibility. Says Dr. Alexander, The perceptive part of our moral processes, is simply a *judgment of the reason.* It is but an intellection of the understanding, like any other judgment of relations, except that it immediately awakens a peculiar *emotion*, viz: the moral. Now, it might be plausibly said that the reason is concerned only with the *judgment of truth;* and we have strenuously repudiated the analysis which reduces the moral distinction to mere truth. But it should rather be said, that the proper field of the reason is the *judgment of relations;* truth existing in propositions is only one class. There seems no ground to suppose that the moral judgments, so far as merely intellective of the distinction, is other than a simple judgment of the reason; because, so far as we know, wherever reason is, there, and there only, are moral judgments. 2d. If the faculties were two, the one, we might rationally expect, might sometime convict the other of inaccuracy, as the *memory* does the reason, and *vice versa*. 3d. The identit of the two processes seems strongly indicated by the fact, that if th reason is misled by any *falsehood* of view, the moral sentiment is infa libly perverted to just the same extent. The moral motive is alway a rational one. Some rational perception of the *truth* of a propositio predicting relation, is necessary, as the occasion of its acting, an the object of a moral judgment. The *reason why* brutes have not mora ideas, is that they have not reason. In short, I see nothing gained b supposing an inward perceptive faculty called moral sense, other tha the reason itself.

b.) Next, we notice the question: at *what stage* of its perceptions c the relations of acts does the reason see the moral distinction? I each separate case, immediately, as soon as the soul is enough develope to apprehend the relations of the particular act? No; answers Jouf roy; but only after a final generalization is accomplished by the reasoı

Jouffroy's Scheme.—His theory is: 1. That in the merely ani mal stage of existence, the infant acts from direct, uncalculatin *instinct* alone. The rational idea of its own natural good is the *cons quence*, not *origin*, of the experienced pleasure following from the grat fication of instinct. 2. Thus experience presents the occasions upo which the reason gives the general idea of *personal good;* and the mc tives of *self-calculation* begin to act. But 3d. The child also observe similar instincts resulting in its fellow-men, in natural enjoyment t them; and as it forms the general idea of its own natural good (Sati faction of whole circle of instincts to greatest attainable degree) as i properest personal end, reason presents the general truth, that a sim lar personal end exists for this, that, the other, and *every* fellow-ma *Here*, then, arises a still more general idea; the *greatest attainable na ural good of all beings generally;* the "absolute good," or "univers order;" and as soon as this is reached, the reason intuitively pronounce it the moral good; to live for this is now seen to be man's proper *mor end;* and rightness in acts is their rational tendency to that end. Th is rather a subtile and ingenious generalization of the *result* of ou moral judgments, than correct account of their origin. This general zation, as made by the opening mind, might suggest the notion of sy metry, or utility as belonging to the "absolute order," but surely th of *obligatoriness* is an independent element of rational perception? I the idea of *rightness* and obligation had never connected itself in th opening mind with any one specific act having a tendency to man's natur good, how comes the mind to apprehend the *universal order* as the obliga tory moral end, when once the reason forms that abstraction? It seem to me that the element of moral judgment must be *presupposed*, to accour for the result. Again; the supposed process is inconsistent with corre idea of the generalizing process. That process does not transmut but only colligates the facts which it ranks together. The general attr butes which the mind apprehends as constituting the connotation c the general term, are precisely the attributes which it saw to be commo in all the special cases grouped together. So that if a *moral ord* had not been already apprehended by the reason in the specifi acts, the mere apprehension of the *universal order* would not prc duce the conviction of its morality. Experience would strengthe the moral idea. But usually the most unhackneyed have it mo vividly. But it is right to say, that Jouffroy, notwithstandin this peculiarity of his theory, deserves the admiration of his readers, for the beauty of his analyses, and the general elevation of his views.

SENTIMENTAL SCHEME OF DR. THOMAS BROWN.—c.) The ethical lectures of Dr. Thomas Brown, of Edinburg, are marked by great acuteness, and nobility of general tone; and he has rendered gallant service in refuting the more erroneous theories. He makes moral distinctions original and authoritative; and yet allows the reason only a secondary function in them. The *whole result* of his analysis is this: when certain actions (an action is nothing more than the agent acting) are presented, there arises *immediately* an *emotion*, called, for want of a more vivid term, moral approbation, without any previous condition of self-calculation, judgment of relation in the *reason*, &c. This *immediate emotion* constitutes our whole feeling of the rightness, obligation, meritoriousness, of the agent. As experience gathers up and recollects the successive acts which affect us with the moral emotion, reason makes the generalization of them into a class; and thus, derivatively forms the general idea of virtue. Man's moral capacity, therefore, is, strictly, not a *power of intellection*, but a *sensibility*. The reason only generalizes into a class, those acts which have the immediate power of affecting this sensibility in the same way. And Brown's system deserves yet more than Adam Smith's, which he so ably refutes, to be called *the* Sentimental System. The moral sentiment is with him strictly an *intrinsic* emotion.

Now, it does not seem to me a valid objection, to say with Jouffroy, that thus, the moral emotion is made *one among the sett* of our natural instincts: and there no longer appears any reason why it should be more dominant over the others *out of its own domain*, than they over it; (e. g., more than taste, or resentment, or appetite.) For the very nature of this moral instinct, Brown might reply, is, that it claims all other susceptibilities which have moral quality, *are in its own domain*.

OBJECTION. 1st. SOUL ALWAYS SEES, IN ORDER TO FEEL. 2d. NO VIRTUE WITHOUT RATIONAL, IMPERSONAL MOTIVE. 3d. THERE WOULD BE NO UNIFORM STANDARD.—The truer objections are: that this notion does not square with the analogies of the soul. In every case, our emotions arise out of an intellection. This is true, in a lower sense, even of our animal instincts. It is perception which awakens appetites. It is the conception of an intent to injure, which gives the signal to our resentment, even when it arises towards an agent non-moral. And in all the more intellectual emotions, as of taste, love, moral complacency, the view of the understanding and that alone, evokes the emotion in a normal way. The soul *feels*, because it has *seen*. How else *could* reason rule our emotions? Surely this is one of our most important distinctions from brutes, that our emotions are not *mere* instincts, but rational affections. Note, especially too, that if our moral sentiments had no element of judgment at their root, the fact would be inexplicable, that they *never*, like *all* other instinctive emotions, *come in collision with reason*. Again: Dr. B. has very properly shown, in overthrowing the selfish systems of human action, that our instincts are not *prompted by self-interest*. He seems, therefore, to think that when he makes the moral emotion *an instinctive sensibility*, he has done all that is needed to make it *disinterested*. But an action is *not*, the-er fore, disinterested, because it is not self-interested. Then would our very animal appetites, even in infancy, be virtues! The truth i in *instinctive* volitions, the motive is personal to the agent; but n consciously so. In *selfish* volitions the motive is personal to the agen and he knows it. Only when the *motive is impersonal, and* HE KNO *it*, is there disinterestedness, or virtue. Last; if Brown's theory we correct, moral good would only be relative to each man's sensibilit and there could be no uniform standard. An act might be good one, bad to another, just as it presented itself to his sensibility; truly as in the sense of the natural good; one man calls oysters goo and another considers oysters bad; Whereas the true doctrine is, th moral distinctions are as intrinsic in certain acts, as truth is in certa propositions: and eternal and immutable. Even God sees, and ca the right to be right, because it is so: not *vice versa*. Dr. Brown fo sees this; and in attempting to rebut it, is guilty of peculiar absurdit Why, says he, does it give any more intrinsic basis for moral distin tions in the acts (or agents acting) themselves, to suppose that o cognizance of them is by a rational judgment, than to say, with hi that it is in the way they naturally affect a sensibility in us? The c pacity of having the intuitive judgment is itself but a sort of ration sensibility to be affected in a given way; and, in either case, we ha no ground for any belief of an intrinsic permanence of the relation quality perceived; than that our Maker made us to be affected s Thus, he betrays the whole basis of morals and truth, to a sweepi skepticism. Does not intuition compel us to believe that reason is a fected with such and such judgments, *because* the grounds of them a actual and intrinsic in the objects? Dr. Brown goes to the absu length of saying, that the supposed relations ascertained by reason he elf, are not intrinsic; and exist nowhere, except in the perceiving reaso e. g., the relation of square of Hypotheneuse. Says he: were the nowhere a *perceiving mind* comprehending this relation, the relati would have no existence, no matter how many right-angled triangl existed! Is not this absolute skepticism? Is it not equivalent to sa ing that none of the perceptions of reason, (i. e., human beliefs,) ha any objective validity? There need be no stronger refutation of l theory, than that he should acknowledge himself driven by it to su an admission.

THE MORAL STATE COMPLEX ILLUSTRATED BY TASTE.—The corre view, no doubt, is this: that our simplest moral states consist of t elements: a judgment of the understanding, or rational perception the moral quality in the act; and an immediate peculiar emotio called approbation, arising thereupon, giving more or less warmth the judgment. In our moral estimates of more complex cases, just in our intellectual study of *derived* truths, the process may be mo inferential, and more complex. It has been often, and justly remarke that the parallel between the rational æsthetic functions of the sou and its moral functions, is extremely instructive. Psychology teaches that rational taste (for instance, the pleasure of literary beauty reading a fine passage,) consists of a judgment, or cluster of judgmen and a peculiar emotion immediately supervening thereon. The ph nomenon of taste is, then, complex, consisting of an action of the i telligence, and a motion of the sensibility. The former is cause; t latter is consequence. After the excitement of the sensibility h wholly waned, the judgment which aroused it remains fixed and unchanged. Now, it is thus with our moral sentiments. A rational judgment of the intrinsic rightness or wrongness of the act immediately produces an emotion of approbation or disapprobation, which is original, and peculiar. The whole vividness of the sentiment may pass away; but the rational judgment will remain as permanent as any judgment of truth in propositions. The great distinction between the æsthetic and ethical actions of the soul, is that the latter carries the practical and sacred perception of *obligation*.

III. Conscience, what? Obligation, what?—*Conscience*, as I conceive, is but the faculty of the soul just described, acting with reference to *our own* moral acts, conceived as future, done, or remembered as done. When we conceive the wrongness of an act as done by ourselves, that judgment and emotion take the form of self-blame, or *remorse;* wherein the emotion is made more pungent than in other cases of disapprobation, by our instinctive and our self-calculating self-love, one or both. So of the contrasted case. And the *merit* of an action, looked at as past, is no other than this judgment, and feeling of its rightness, which intuitively connects the idea of *title to reward* with the agent, i. e. Our ideas of merit and demerit are intuitions arising immediately upon the conception of the rightness or wrongness of the acts; connecting natural good or evil with moral good or evil, by an immediate tie. Our ideas of desert of reward or punishment, therefore, are not identical with our sentiments of the rightness or wrongness of acts, as Dr. Brown asserts, but are intuitively consequent thereon. Dr. B. also asserts, as also Dr. Alexander, that our notion of *obligation* is no other than our intuitive judgment of *rightness* in acts, regarded as prospective. Therefore, it is useless and foolish to raise the question: "Why am I *obliged*, morally, to do that which is right?" it is as though one should debate why he should believe an axiom. This is substantially correct. But when they say: *whatever is right, is obligatory*, and *vice versa*, there is evidently a partial error. For there is a limited class of acts, of which the rightness is not proportioned to the obligation to perform them; but on the contrary, the less obligation, the more admirable is the virtue of doing them gratuitously. Such are some acts of generosity to unworthy enemies: and especially God's to rebel man. That God was under *no* obligation to give His Son to die for them, is the very reason His grace in doing so is so admirable! Obligation, therefore, is not always the correlative of rightness in the act, but it is, always, the correlative of *a right* in the object. This is the distinction which has been overlooked—i. e., a multitude of our acts have a personal *object*, God, self, a man, or mankind, one or more; and the conscience in many cases apprehends, not only that the act would be *right;* but that such are the relations of ourselves to the object, that he has *a* right, a *moral title* to have it done, in such sense that not only the doing of the opposite to him, but the withholding of the act itself, would be wrong. In every such case, the notion of obligation arises. And that, stronger or weaker, whether the object's right be perfect or imperfect.

Imperative of Conscience is intuitive.—The most important thing, however, for us to observe, is that every sane mind *intuitively recognizes this moral obligation*. The judgment and emotion we cal conscience, carries this peculiarity over all other states of reason o instinct; that it contains *the imperative element.* It utters a command the rightness of which the understanding is necessitated to admit Other motives, rational or instinctive, may often (alas!) overcome i in *force;* but none of them can dispute its authority. It is as impos sible for the mind, after having given the preference to other motives to think its choice therein right, as it is to think any other intuitio untrue. Conscience is the Maker's imperative in the soul.

Must conscience misguided, be obeyed.—Hence, it must follow that the dictate of conscience must always be obeyed; or sin ensue But conscience is not infallible, *as guided by man's fallible understand ing:* it is clear, from both experience and reason, that her fiat may b misdirected. In that case, is the act innocent, or wrong? If you sa the latter, you seem involved in a glaring paradox; that to obey woul be wrong; and yet to disobey would be wrong. How can both be true If you say the former, other utter absurdities would follow. 1st. Trut would seem to be of no consequence in order to right; and the con science might just as well be left uninformed, as informed, so far a one man is personally concerned therein. 2d. Each man's view o duty would be valid for him; so that there might be as many clashin views of duty, as *men*, and each valid in itself; so that we would reac such absurdities as these: A has a *right* to a given object, which B ha an equal right to prevent his having; so that B has a *moral right* to d to A what is to him a *moral wrong!* 3d. Many of the most odiou acts in the world, reprobated by all posterity, as the persecutions of Saul, or a Dominic, would be justified, because the perpetrators be lieved they were doing God service.

Solution.—The solution of this seeming paradox is in this fact that God has not given man a conscience which is capable of mislead ing him, when lawfully and innocently used. In other words, whil *lack* of knowledge necessary to perceive our whole duty may ofte occur, (in which case it is always innocent to postpone acting,) positiv error of moral judgment only arises from guilty haste or heedlessnes or indolence, or from sinful passion or prejudice. When, therefore, man sincerely believes it right in his conscience to do what is intrinsi cally wrong, the wrongness is not in the fact that he obeyed conscience (for this abstractly is right,) but in the fact that he had before, and a the time, *perverted conscience* by sinful means.

IV. What constitutes Moral agency.—We intuitively apprehen that all agents are not proper subjects of moral approbation or disap probation. Hence, the question must be settled: what are the ele ments essential to moral responsibility? This can be settled no othe wise than by an appeal to our intuitions. For instance: we may tak an act of the *form* which would have moral quality, if done by a mora agent—e. g., inflicting causeless bodily pain; and attributing it to suc cessive sorts of agents, from lower to higher, ascertain what the element are, which confer responsibility. As we walk through a grove, a dea branch falls on our heads; we feel that resentment would be absurd much more disapprobation; the thing is dead. We walk near ou horse, he wantonly kicks or bites. There is a certain type of anger but it is not moral disapprobation; we feel still, that this would be absurd. Here, there is sensibility and will in the agent; but no conscience or reason. We walk with our friend; he treads on our corns and produces intolerable pain; but it is obviously *unintentional*. We pass through a lunatic asylum; a maniac tries to kill us. Here is sensibility, free-will, intention; but reason is dethroned. In neither of these cases would we have moral disapprobation. A stronger man takes hold of our friend, and by brute force makes him strike us; there is no anger towards our friend; he is under co-action. We learn from these various instances, that free-agency, intention, and rationality are all necessary, to constitute man a responsible moral agent.

LECTURE IX.

SYLLABUS.

FREE-AGENCY AND THE WILL.

1. Is man's conduct under a fatal necessity?
   Alexander, Moral Science, Ch. 15, 16. Cousin, Le Vrai, &c. Leçon 14. Jouffroy, Lect. 4 and 5. Morell, Hist., Mod. Phil. on Hobbes and Sensationalism, p. 74, &c., 299, &c.
2. What constitutes Free-Agency? State the theory of "Contrary Choice," or "Indifferency of Will," and the theory of certain influence of motives.
   Turrettin, Loc. x, Que. 1, Que. 3, §1-4. Alexander, Chs. 16, 18, 19. Edwards on the Will, Introduc, and p. i. Morell, p. p. 299, &c. Reid's Philosophy. Watson's Theology. Institutes.
3. Sustain the doctrine of the certain influence of motives, over volitions, and answer objections.
   Turrettin, Loc. x, Que. Edwards on the Will, Pt. iii. Alexander. Ch. 16 to 19, inclusive.

I. Man a free-agent, denied by two parties.—But is man a free-agent? Many have denied it. These may be ranked under two classes, Theological Fatalists, and *Sensualistic Necessitarians*. The former argue from the doctrine of God's foreknowledge and providence; the latter from the certainty, or, as it has unluckily been termed, *necessity* of the Will. Say the one party: God has foreknown and foreordained all that is done by rational man, as well as by irrational elements, and His almighty providence infallibly effectuates it all. Therefore, man's will is only seemingly free; he must be a machine; compelled by God (for if God had no efficacious means to compel, He could not certainly have foreknown) to do what God purposed from eternity; and, therefore, man never had any real choice; he is the slave of this divine fate. Say the other party, headed by Hobbes: man's volitions are all *effects:* following with a physical necessity upon the movement of the preponderant *desires*. But what are his desires? The soul intrinsically is passive; its attributes are nothing but certain susceptibilities of being affected in certain ways, by impressions from without. There is nothing, no thought, no feeling in the mind except what sensation produced there; indeed all inward states are but modified sensations. Hence, desire is but the *reflex* of the perception of a desirable object, resentment but the re-action from impact. Man's emotions, then, are the physical results of outward impressions, and his volitions the necessary effects of his emotions. Man's whole volitions, therefore, are causatively determined from without. While he supposes himself free, he is the *slave of circumstances;* of *fate*, if those circumstances have been fixed by fate; of blind chance, if those circumstances arise by chance.

Replies to them.—Now, in answer to all this, it would be enough to say, that our *consciousness* contradicts it. There can be no higher evidence than that of consciousness. Every man *feels conscious* that when ever he has power to do what he wills, he acts *freely.* And the validity of this uniform, immediate testimony of consciousness, as *Cousin* well remarks, on this subject, must, in a sense, supercede all other evidence of our free-agency; because all possible premises of such arguments must depend on the testimony of consciousness. But still, it is correct to argue, that man must be a free agent; because this is inevitably involved in his responsibility. Conscience tells us we are responsible for our moral acts. Reason pronounces, intuitively, that responsibility would be absurd were we not free agents. It may be well added, that when you approach revealed theology, you find the Scriptures, (which so frequently asserts God's decree and providence,) assert and imply, with equal frequency, man's free-agency. The king of Babylon (Isaiah xiv) fulfils God's purpose in capturing the sinful Jews; but he also fulfils the purpose of his own heart. But we can do more than rebut the Fatalist's views by the testimony of our consciousness; we can expose their sophistry. God's mode of effectuating His purposes as to the acts of free agents, is not by compelling their acts or wills, contrary to their preferences and dispositions; either secretly or openly; but by operating *through their dispositions.* And as to the latter argument, from the certainty of the will; we repudiate the whole philosophy of sensationalism, from which it arises. True, volitions are *effects;* but not effects of the *objects* upon which they go forth. The perception of these is but the *occasion* of their rise, not the cause. When desire attaches itself upon any external object, terminating in volition, the whole activity and power are in the mind, not in the object. The true immediate cause of volition, is the mind's own previous view and feeling; and this, again, is the result of the mind's spontaneity, as guided by its own prevalent attributes and habitudes.

II. Freedom and necessity defined. Semi-Pelaganism and Calvinists.—What constitutes man a *free agent?* Say one party: the self-determining power of the *will;* say the other: the self-determining power of the *soul.* The one asserts that our acts of volition are *uncaused* phenomena, that the will remains *in equilibrio, after* all the preliminary conditions of judgment in the understanding, and emotion of the native dispositions are fulfilled, that the act of choice is *self-determined* by the will, and not by these preliminary states of soul tending thereto; so that volitions are in every case, more or less *contingent.* The other party repudiates, indeed, the old sensational creed, of a physical tie between the external objects which are the occasions of our judgments and feelings; and attributes all action of *will* to the soul's own spontaneity as its efficient source. But it asserts that this spontaneity, like all other forces in the universe, acts *according to law*, that this law is the connexion between the soul's own states, and its own choices, the former being as much of its own spontaneity as the latter; that therefore volitions are not uncaused, but always follow the actual state of judgment and feeling, (single or complex,) at the time being; and that this connexion is not contingent, but efficient and *certain.* And *this certainty* is all that they mean by *moral necessity.*

III. Will determined by subjective Motive. Arguments.—The latter is evidently the true doctrine; because, a) Our *consciousness* says so. Every man feels that when he acts, as a thinking being, he has *a motive* for acting so: and that if he had not had, he would not have done it. The man is conscious that *he* determines himself, else, he would not be free; but he is equally conscious that it is himself judging and feeling, which determines himself choosing: b) Otherwise there would be no such thing as a recognition of *character*, or permanent *principles.* For there would be no efficient influence of the man's own principles over his actions; (and it is by his actions alone we would know his principles;) and his principles might be of a given character, and his actions of a different, or of *no character.* c) Consequently there would be no *certain* result from *human influence* over man's character and actions, in education and moral government. We might educate the *principles*, and still fail to educate the *actions* and *habits.* The fact which we all experience every day would be impossible, that we can cause our fellow-men to put forth certain volitions, that we can often do it with a foreseen certainty, and still we feel that those acts are free and responsible. d) Otherwise man might be neither a reasonable nor a moral being. Not reasonable, because his acts might be wholly uncontrolled at last by his whole understanding; not moral, because the merit of an act depends on its *motive*, and his acts would be *motiveless.* The self-determined volition has its freedom essentially in this, according to its advocates; that it is caused by no motive. Hence, no acts are free and virtuous except those which a man does without having any reason for them! Is this good sense? Does not the virtuousness of a man's acts depend upon the kind of reason which moved him to them? e) In the choice of one's *sumnum bonum*, the will is certainly not contingent. Can a rational being choose his own *misery*, apprehended as such, and eschew his own happiness, for their own sakes? Yet that choice is free; and if certainty is compatible with free-agency in this the most important case, why not in any other? f) God, angels, saints in glory, and the human nature of Jesus Christ must be certainly determined to right volitions by the holiness of their own natures, and in all but the first case by the indwelling grace, and the determinate purpose of God So, on the other hand, devils, lost souls, and those who on earth have sinned away their day of grace, must be certainly determined to evil, by their own decisive evil natures, and habits; Yet their choice is free in both cases.

g) If the will were contingent, there *could* be no *scientia media*;

and we should be compelled to the low and profane ground of the Soc'nian; that God does not certainly foreknow all things; and in the nature of things, *cannot*. For the definition of *Scientia media* is, that it is that contingent knowledge of what free agents will do in certain foreseen circumstances, arising out of God's infinite insight into their dispositions. But if the will may decide in the teeth of that foreseen disposition, there can be no certain knowledge how it will decide. Nor is the evasion suggested by modern Arminians (i. e., Mansel's Lim. of Relig. Thought) of any force; that it is incompetent for our finite unstandings to say that God cannot have this *scientia media*, because *we* cannot see *how* He is to have it. For the thing is not merely among the incomprehensibles, but the *impossibles*. If a thing is *certainly* foreseen, it must be certain to occur, or else the foreknowledge of its certain occurrence is false. h) Last, God would have no efficient means of governing free agents; things would be perpetually emerging through their contingent acts, unforeseen by God, and across His purposes; and His government would be, like man's, one of sorry expedients to patch up His failures. Nor could He bestow any certain answer to prayer, either for our own protection against temptation and wrong choice, or the evil acts of other free agents. All the predictions of Scripture concerning events in which the free moral acts of rational agents enter as second causes, are arguments against the contingency of the will. But we see striking instances in Joseph, the Assyrians, Cyrus, and especially the Jews who rejected their Lord.

j) The demonstration may be closed by the famous *Reductio ad absurdum*, which Edwards has borrowed from the scholastics. If the will is not determined to choice by motive, but determines itself, then the will must determine itself thereto by an *act of choice;* for this is the will's only function. That is, the will must choose to choose. Now, this prior choice must be held by our opponents to be self-determined. Then it must be determined by the will's act of choice—i. e., the will must choose to choose to choose. Thus we have a ridiculous and endless *regressus*.

OBJECTIONS. THAT THIS MAKES US MACHINES.—Now, the objections most confidently urged, are: a.) That our view makes man a machine, an intelligent one, indeed; but a machine in which choice follows motive by a physical tie. Ans. Man is in one sense a machine, (if you will use so inappropriate an illustration,) his spontaneous force of acting has its *regular laws*. But he is *not* a machine, in the essential point; the *motive power* is not external, but is in himself.

b.) THAT MAN ACTS AGAINST HIS OWN JUDGMENT.—It is objected that our scheme fails to account for all choices where the man acts against his own better judgment and prevalent feelings; or, in other words, that while the dictate of the understanding as to the truly preferable is one way, the will acts the other way; e. g., the drunkard breaks his own anxiously made resolutions of temperance, and drinks. I reply, No; still the man has chosen according to what was the prevalent view of his judgment and feelings as a whole, *at the time*. That drunkard does judge sobriety the preferable part in the end, and on the whole; but as to the question of *this present glass of drink*, (the only immediate object of volition,) his understanding is misinformed by strong propensity, and the delusive hope of subsequent reform, combining the advantages of present indulgence with future impunity; so that its judgment is, that the preferable good will be *this one glass*, rather than present, immediate self-denial.

c.) That Repentance implies power of contrary choice.—It is objected that our repentance for having chosen wrong, always implies the feeling that we might have chosen otherwise, had we pleased. I reply, Yes; but not unless that choice had been preceded at the time by a different view of the preferable. The thing for which the man blames himself is, that he had not those different feelings and views. d.) It is objected that our theory could never account for a man's choosing between two alternative objects, equally accessible and desirable, inasmuch as the desire for either is equal, and the will has no self-determining power. The answer is, that the equality of objects by no means implies the equality of subjective desires. For the mind is never in precisely the same state of feeling to *any* external object or objects, for two minutes together, but ever ebbing and flowing more or less. In this case, although the objects remain equal, the mind will easily make a difference, perhaps an imaginary one. And farther: the two objects being equal, the inertia of will towards choosing *a given* one of them, may be infinitesimally small; so that an infinitesimally small preponderance of subjective motive may suffice to overcome it. Remember, there is already a subjective motive in the general, to choose *some* one of them, possessing all the strength which is occasioned by the beggar's apprehension of the value of *a* golden eagle to him.

e.) That man is not responsible if necessitated.—The leading objection echoed by Arminians against the certainty of the will, is, that if man is not free from all constraint, whether of motive or coaction, it is unjust in God to hold him subject to blame, or to commands to those acts against which His will is certainly determined, or to punishments for failure. We reply, practically, that men *are* held blameable and punishable for acts to which their wills are certainly determined, both among men and before God; and all consciences approve. This is indisputable, in the case of those who are overmastered by a malignant emotion, as in Gen. xxxvii: 4, of devils and lost souls, and of those who have sinned away their day of grace. The Arminian rejoins, (Watson, vol. 2, p. 438:) Such transgressors, notwithstanding their inability of will, are justly held responsible for all subsequent failures in duty, because they sinned away the contingency of their own wills, by their own personal, free act, after they became intelligent agents. But as man is *born* in this inability of will, through an arrangement with a federal head, to which he had no opportunity to dissent, it would be unjust in God to hold him responsible, unless he had restored the contingency of will to them lost in Adam, by the common sufficient grace bestowed through Christ. But the distinction is worthless: 1st, because, then, God would have been under an obligation in righteousness, to furnish a plan of redemption: but the Scriptures represent His act therein as purely gracious. 2d. Because, then, all the guilt of the subsequent sins of those who had thrown away the contingency of their own wills, would have inhered in the acts alone by which they lost it. True; that act would have been an enormously guilty one; the man would have therein committed *moral suicide*. But it would also be true that the man was thereafter *morally dead;* and the dead cannot work. 3. The Arminian should, by parity of reason, conclude, that in any will *certainly* determined to holiness, the acts are not meritorious, unless that determination resalted from the being's own volvntary self-culture, and formation of good dispositions and habits. Therefore God's will, which has been from eternity certainly determined to good, does nothing meritorious!

But the more analytical answer to this class of objections is: that the certainty of disobedience in the sinner's will is no excuse for him, because it proceeds from a *voluntary cause*—i. e., moral disposition. As the volition is only the man willing, the motive is the man feeling; it is the *man's self.* There is no lack of the requisite capacities, if the man would use those capacities aright. Now, a man cannot plead the existence of an obstacle as his excuse, which consists purely in his own spontaneous emission of opposition.

Certainty of the Will proved by God's sovereignty.—I have indicated, both when speaking of fatalism and of the impossibility of a *scientia media* concerning a contingent will, the argument for the certainty of the will contained in the fact of God's sovereignty. If *He* is universal First Cause, then nothing is uncaused. Such is the argument; as simple as it is comprehensive. It cannot be taught that volitions are uncaused, unless you make all free agents a species of gods, independent from Jehovah's control. In other words, if His providence extends to the acts of free agents, their volitions cannot be uncaused; for providence includes control, and control implies power. The argument from God's sovereignty is, indeed, so conclusive, that the difficulty, with thinking minds is not to admit it, but to avoid being led by it to an extreme. The difficulty rather is, to see how, in the presence of this universal, absolute sovereignty, man can retain a true spontaneity. I began by defining that, while the will of man is not self-determining, his soul is. I believe that a free, rational Person does properly *originate* effects; that he is a true fountain of spontaneity, determining his own powers, from within, to new effects. This is a most glorious part of that image of God, in which he is created. This is free-agency! Now, how can this fact be reconciled with what we have seen of God as absolute First Cause?

Yet Man under Providence is free.—The reconciliation may and does transcend our comprehension, and yet be neither unreasonable nor incredible. The point where the little circle of creature volition inosculates with the immense circle of the divine will, is beyond human view. When we remember that the wisdom, power, and resources of God are infinite, it is not hard to see that there may be a way by which our spontaneity is directed, omnipotently, and yet without infringement of its reality. The sufficient proof is, that we, finite creatures, can often efficaciously direct the free will of our fellows, without infringing it. Does any one say that still, in every such case, the agent, if free as to us, has power to do the opposite of what we induce him to do? True, he has physical power. But yet the causative efficacy of our means is *certain;* witness the fact that we were able certainly to predict our success. A *perfect certainty*, such as results from God's infinitely wise and powerful providence over the creature's will, is all that we mean by *moral necessity*. We assert no other kind of necessity over the free will. More mature reflection shows us, that so far are God's sovereignty and providence from infringing man's free-agency, they are its necessary conditions. Consider: What would the power of choice be worth to us if there were no stability in the laws of nature, or no uniformity in its powers? No natural means for effectuating volitions would have any certainty, whence choice would be impotent, and motives would cease to have any reasonable weight. Could you intelligently elect to sow, if there were no ordinance of nature ensuring seed time and harvest? But now, *what* shall give that stability to nature? A mechanical, physical necessity? That results in naught but fatalism The only other answer is; it must be the intelligent purpose of an almighty, personal God.

MOTIVE, WHAT? THE INDUCEMENT NOT MOTIVE.—Most important light is thrown upon the subject, by the proper answer to the question, *what is motive?* The will not being, as we have seen, self-moved, what is it which precedes the volition, and is the true cause? I reply, by distinguishing between *motive* and *inducement*. The inducement is that external object, towards which the desire tends, in rising to choice. Thus, the gold seen by the thief is the inducement to his volition to steal. But the perception of the gold is not his *motive* to that volition. His motive is the cupidity of his own soul, projecting itself upon the gold. And this cupidity, (as in most instances of motive,) is a complex of certain conceptions of the intellect, and concupiscence of the heart; conceptions of various utilities of the gold, and concupiscence towards the pleasures which it could procure. The inducement is objective; the motive is subjective. The inducement is merely the *occasion*, the motive is the true *cause* of the resulting volition. The object which is the inducement projects no force into the thief's soul. On the contrary, it is the passive object of a force of soul projected upon it. The moral power is wholly from within outwards. The action is wholly that of the thief's soul, the inducement is only acted on. The proof of this all important view is in this case. The same purse of gold is seen, in the same circumstances of opportunity and privacy, by two men; the second is induced by it to steal: on the first it had no such power. Why the difference? The difference must be subjective in the two men, because objectively, the two cases are identical. Your good sense leads you to explain the different results by the differing characters of the two men. You say: "It is because the first man was honest, the second covetous." That is to say, the causative efficiency which dictated the two volitions was, in each case, from within the two men's souls, not from the gold. Besides, the objects of sense are inert, dead, senseless, and devoid of will. It is simply foolish to conceive of them as emitting a moral activity. The thief's *soul* is the only agent in the case.

SENSUALISTIC VIEW OF NECESSITY FALSE.—This plain view sheds a flood of light on the doctrine of the will. A volition has always a cause, which is the (subjective) motive. This cause is efficient, otherwise the effect, volition, would not follow. But the motive is subjective; i. e., it is the agent judging and desiring, just as truly as the volition is the agent choosing. And this subjective desire, causative of the choice, is a function of the agent's activity, not of his passivity. (See e. g. Hamilton, separating the conative powers from the sensibility.) The desire is as much of the agent's spontaneity (self-action) as is the choosing. Thus is corrected the monstrous view of those who deduced a doctrine of the necessity of the will from a sensualistic psychology. If volition is efficiently *caused* by desire, and if desire is but the passive reflex of objective perception, then, indeed, is man a mere machine. His seeming free-agency is wholly deceptive; and his choice is dictated from without. Then, indeed, the outcry of the semi-Pelagian against such a necessity is just. But inducement is not motive; desire is an activity, and not a passivity of our souls. Our own subjective judgments and appetencies cause our volitions.

INDUCEMENT RECEIVES ITS INFLUENCE FROM THE SUBJECTITE DISPOSITION.—On the other hand, it is equally plain, that the adaptation of any object to be an inducement to volition depends on some subjective attribute of appetency in the agent. This state of appetency is a priori to the inducement, not created by it, but conferring on the object its whole fitness to be an inducement. In other words, when we seek to propagate a volition, by holding out an inducement as occasion, or means, we always presuppose in the agent whom we address, some active propensity. No one attempts to allure a hungry horse with bacon, or a hungry man with hay. Why? Common sense recognizes in each animal an *à priori* state of appetite, which has already determined to which of them the bacon shall be inducement, and to which the hay. The same thing is true of the spiritual desires, love of applause, of power, of justice, &c. Hence, it follows, that inducement has no power whatever to revolutionize the subjective states of appetency natural to an agent. The effect cannot determine its own cause.

From this point of view may also be seen the justice of that philosophy of common sense, with which we sat out; when we remarked that every one regarded a man's free acts as *indices* of an abiding or permanent *character*. This is only because the abiding appetencies of soul decide which objects shall be, and which shall not be inducements to choice.

LECTURE X.

SYLLABUS.

THE RESPONSIBILITY AND PROVINCE OF REASON IN RELIGION.

1. Have our affections which precede our moral volitions a moral character? Turrettin, Loc. ix, Que. 2. Alex. Mor. Science, Ch. 20, 22, 23, 27. Edwards on the Will, Pt. iv, § i.

2. Is man responsible for his beliefs?
Alex., Mor. Science, Ch. 9. Univ. Lecture i. Review of Do., by Rev. C. R. Vaughan, *So. Lit. Messenger*, 1852.
3. What is the proper province of Reason in revealed Theology?
Turrettin, Loc. i, Que. 8, 9, 10. Hodge's Outlines, Ch. ii. Milner's "End of Controversy." Hill's Divinity, Bk. ii, Ch. v.

I. Is concupiscence morally evil?—Wide difference of opinion has long prevailed, as to man's responsibility for his moral dispositions, and feelings, and habits, leading to volitions. Philosophers of the Pelagian and semi-Pelagian schools say, that since responsibility is coëxtensive only with free-agency, man cannot have any moral praise or blame attached to dispositions; for that they are not voluntary is clear from the assertion that they cause volition. Hence, also, the definition of sin and holiness, as consisting only of wrong or right *acts of the soul*. But we argue that man is evidently praise, or blameworthy for his dispositions, principles and habits, as well as for his volitions. We make our appeal here to consciousness, which causes us shame and self-reproach for evil propensities not ripened into volitions, and tells us that we would feel equal resentment for evil dispositions towards us and our rights, though never formed into the overt intention of injury. 2d. Our minds intuitively judge that the moral character of an act resides in its motives. Witness the process of investigation in the charge for crime before a jury. Indeed, the act of volition, nakedly considered, is a merely natural effect, and has no more moral character than the muscular motions which follow it. For the volition which extends the hand with alms to an enemy, or with a bribe to one to commit a sin, is the same physical volition we must go back of it, to the motive by which it was caused, to settle its moral character. That element is not in the naked volition; says the Pelagian, it is not in the motives prior to volition; then it is nowhere! 3d. The notion is inconsistent with our established idea about *character*. Here is a man who is said to have a *dishonest character*. It only becomes cognizable to us by his acts. He must, then, have performed a series of acts, having the common quality of dishonesty. Now, nothing comes from nothing; there must be some *cause* for that sameness of character; and that cause is the prevalent *disposition to steal* separate from, and prior to, each theivish act. For the bad cause cannot be in the will itself; this would be peculiarly objectionable to the Pelagian. This, then, is what is meant when this man is said to have a *bad character*. Has the word *bad* here, no proper meaning? Does the family of daughters, the separate acts, bear no relationship to their mother? 4th. On the Pelagian scheme, the wickedness of *sins of omission* would be inexplicable. For in them, there is often no volition at all; and therein consists their wickedness. A man passing by the water sees an innocent child drowning; the idea of rescue is suggested to his mind; but he comes to no choice, does nothing, and while he hesitates, the child sinks to rise to more. Is he innocent? Our conscience declares that he is not. Now, we can consistently explain *wherein* he is not: viz., in the state of his selfish and indolent feelings. But the opposite party have no explanation.

Answer to objection that the involuntary cannot be sin.—Their main argument has been hinted, that nothing can be moral which is not voluntary. The answer is, that this is as true of our dispositions, in the sense essential to moral agency, as it is of our acts. Our dispositions cannot, indeed, be the *results of volition*, lying before volition; but are they not *spontaneous?* Does any external force compel us to feel them? As the volition is the soul choosing, so the disposition is the soul feeling, equally of its own accord. The matter may be tested thus. Would a disposition to a wicked act, (not yet formed into a purpose,) subsist for one instant in a *perfectly holy* breast? Would it not die in its very incipiency? just as the spark would go out in a *vacuum?* Said old General Woodson, when he quit his daily toddy of sixty years to join the temperance society: "I set my *resolution* so strong that it killed my *inclination*."

Answer to objection that Soul's essence cannot be depraved —Another objection is: that our theory of the immorality of evil dispositions would imply that the soul's essence is altered; or that depravity is a change in the substance of the soul: which would make God the author of sin, and man an unfortunate, sentient puppet. For say they, there is nothing but the soul and its acts; and if you deny that all morality resides in acts, some of it must reside in the essence of the soul itself. The sophism of this argument would be sufficiently exposed by asking, what is a moral *act*. If you make it any thing more than a mere notional object of thought, an imagination about which we think, is it any thing besides the *soul acting?* Well; in the same sense, our moral dispositions are but our souls feeling. I reply again, and yet more decisively, that immoral quality is only negative—i. e., Ε 'ΑΜΑΡΤΙΑ ΕΣΤΙ ΑΝΟΜΙΣ. It is the *lack* of conformity to God's will which constitutes sin. The negative absence of this principle of active conformity is all that is necessary to predicate. Thus, the idea of depravity's being a *substantial* change is seen to be out of the question

II. Man responsible for his beliefs.—The question whether man is responsible for his belief, is nearly connected with the one just discussed. Many modern writer have urged that he is not, because belief is the necessary and involuntary result of evidence seen by the mind. Further, it is urged; if the doctrine that man is responsible for his belief be held, then the horrible doctrine of persecution will follow; for erroneous beliefs being often very mischievous, if also criminal, it would follow that they ought to be punished by society To the first, I reply, that while the admission of demonstrative proofs *when weighed by the mind*, is necessary and involuntary, the voluntary powers have a great deal to do with the question whether they shall be weighed fairly or not. Inattention, prejudice against the truth or the advocate, heedlessness, guilty and wicked habits of perverting the soul's faculties: all these are voluntary; and I fearlessly assert, that no erroneous belief on any important moral question *can* arise in a sane mind, except through the operation of one or more of these causes. In this, then, is the guilt of false beliefs on moral subjects To the second objection, I reply, that it does not follow, because a man is responsible for his beliefs, he is responsible to his fellow-man There are abundant reasons for denying the latter, which it would be easy to show, if I were going into the subject of freedom of thought

Because Nature and Providence rule thus.—On the affirmative

side, I remark, first: that all the analogies of nature show us a Providence holding man responsible for his beliefs. If prejudice, passion, haste, inattention, prevents a man from attaching due weight to testimony or other evidence, as to the poison of a given substance, he experiences its effects just as though he had taken it of set purpose. So of all other things.

Because all wrong beliefs have a criminal cause.—Second: Conscience clearly condemns many acts, based immediately on certain beliefs, which were sincerely held at the time of acting. Now, if the belief had been innocent, the act necessarily dictated thereby could not have been blame-worthy. Witness Paul confessing the sin of his persecutions. Indeed, since belief on moral subjects ought to, and must dictate *conduct*, if man is allowed to be a rational free agent, each man's own belief must be his own guide; and hence, an act might be right to one man, and wrong to another, at the same time. A would have a right (because he believed so) to a thing which B had a right to; and so B would have a moral right to do to A what would be to him a moral wrong! And farther; since whatever a man sincerely believed, would be right to him, truth would cease to be of any essential importance.

III. Province of Reason in Revealed Religion.—The question with which we close this brief review of the nature of man's primary judgments, has ever been of fundamental importance in the Church: "What is the legitimate province of Reason, in revealed theology?" The pretended warfare between *reason and faith* has been waged by all those who wished to make a pretext for believing unreasonably and wickedly. On the one hand, it is possible so to exalt the authority of the Church, or of theology, (as is done by Rome,) as to violate the very capacity of reason to which religion appeals. On the other, it is exceedingly easy to give too much play to it, and admit thus the *virus* of Rationalism in some of its forms.

Rationalism, What?—All the different forms of rationalism, which admit a revelation as true or desirable at all, may be grouped under two classes. 1. Those who hold the proton pseudos of the Socinians; that man is to hold nothing credible in religion which he cannot *comprehend*. 2. Those who, like the modern German rationalists, make the interpretations of Scripture square with the teachings of human philosophy, instead of making their philosophy square with the plain meaning of revelation. Under the latter class must be ranked all those who, like Hugh Miller, in his Testimony of the Rocks, hold that the interpretation of the Pentateuch, concerning cosmogony, must be moulded supremely by the demands of geological theories, instead of being settled independently by its own laws of fair exegesis. Here, also, belong those who, like A. Barnes, say that the Bible must not be allowed to mean what would legitimate American slavery, because he holds that *his ethical arguments* prove it cannot be right: *Et id omne genus.*

Comprehension not the Measure of Truth.—The absurdity of the first class will be shown, more fully, when we come to deal with the Socinian theology. It is enough to say now, that reason herself repudiates such a boast as preposterous. She does not truly comprehend all of *any* thing: not the whole nature and physiology of the blade of grass which man presses with his foot: nor the *modus* of that union of body and soul which consciousness compels us to admit. Every line of knowledge which we follow, leads us to the circumference of darkness, where it is lost to our comprehension; and the more man knows, the more frequently is he compelled to stop humbly at that limit, and acknowledge his lack of comprehension. So that the most truly wise man is he who knows and believes *most hings which he does not comprehend.* Again, reason tells us that the ground of her assent is not the comprehension of all the relations of the proposition: but the view of its *evidence.* Now, if these things are just and true in all natural knowledge, how much more true in the things of the infinite God? The attempt of the Socinian to make a god altogether comprehensible, has resulted in a plan attended inevitably with more and worse incomprehensibilities, yea, impossibilities, than they reject.

On Rationalist Scheme, no Revealed Rule of Faith.—To the second class of rationalists, the simple answer which reason gives is, that such a revelation as they admit, is practically no revelation at all. That is, it is no authoritative standard of belief to any soul, on any point on which it may happen to have any opinion derived from other sources than the Bible. For each man's speculative conclusions are, to him, his philosophy; and if one man is entitled to square his Bible to his philosophy, the other must be equally so. Further, it is well known that the deductions of all philosophies are fallible. The utter inconsistency of Rationalism, with any honest adoption of a Revelation, appears thus: It is the boast of Rationalists, that human science is progressive: that our generation is far in advance of our fathers. May not our children be as far in advance of us? Things now held as scientific truth, will probably be excluded; things now not dreamed of, will probably be discovered and explained. When that time comes, it must follow, on the Rationalists' scheme, that the interpretation of the Scriptures shall receive new modifications from these new lights of reason. Propositions which we now hold as the meaning of Scripture, will then be shown by the lights of human science to be false! What is it reasonable that we should do, at this time, with those places of Scripture? Will any one say, 'Reserve your opinion on them, until the light comes?' Alas! there is now no means for us to know whereabouts in the Bible they are! No; we must attempt to construe the whole Scripture, as best we may. Will any one say that our construction is true to us, but will be false to our more scientific children? Hardly. If, therefore, the Bible is a revelation from the infallible God, reason herself clearly asserts that where the plain teachings of Scripture clash with such deductions, the latter are to be presumed to be wrong; and unless revelation carries that amount of authority, it is practically worthless. Rationalism is the wolf of infidelity sneaking under the sheep's clothing of faith.

It follows, then, that reason is not to be the *measure*, nor the *ground* of the beliefs of revealed theology.

But Revelation does not Violate Reason.—But on the other hand: 1st, the laws of thought which necessarily rule in the human soul, were established by the same God who gave the Bible. Hence, if there is a revelation from Him, and if these laws of thought are legitimately used, there must be full harmony between reason and Scripture. But man knows that he is not infallible; he knows that he almost always employs his powers of thought with imperfect accuracy. On the other hand, if revelation is admitted, its very idea implies infallible truth and authority. Hence it is clearly reasonable that opinion must always hold itself ready to stand corrected by revelation.

2nd. NECESSARY LAWS OF THOUGHT MUST BE RESPECTED BY IT.—The Scriptures always address us as rational creatures, and presuppose the authority of our native, fundamental laws of thought. If we think at all, we must do it according to those laws. Therefore, to require us to violate or ignore them fundamentally, would be to degrade us to unreasoning animals; we should then be as incapable of religion as pigs.

3rd. AUTHENTICITY OF REVELATION NOT SELF-EVIDENT.—The claim which the Scriptures address to us, to be the one authentic and authoritative revelation from God, *is addressed to our reason*. This is clear from the simple fact, that there are presented to the human race more than one professed revelation; and that they cannot be authoritative witnesses to their own authority prior to its admission. It appears also from this, that man is required not only to obey, but to believe and love the Bible. Now he cannot do this except upon evidence. The evidences of inspiration must, therefore, present themselves to man's reason; to reason to be employed impartially, humbly, and in the fear of God. He who says he believes, when he sees no proof, is but pretending, or talking without meaning.

4th. REVELATION CANNOT AUTHORIZE SELF-CONTRADICTIONS. LIMITATIONS OF THIS ADMISSION.—Among those evidences, the reason must entertain this question; whether anything asserted in revelations is inevitably contradictory with reason or with some other thing asserted in revelation. For if a book clearly contained such things, it would be proof it was not from God; because God, who first created our laws of reason, will not contradict Himself by teaching incompatibles in His works and word. And again: in demanding faith (always a sincere and intelligent faith,) of us in such contradictories, He would be requiring of us an impossibility. If I see that a thing is impossible to be true, it is impossible for me to believe it. Yet here, we must guard this concession against abuse; asserting, first, that the reason which is entitled to this judgment of contradiction concerning the Scriptures, shall be only a right, humble, and holy reason, acting in the fear and love of God; and not a reason unsanctified, hostile, and blind. Second, that the supposed contradiction must be contained in the immediate and unquestioned language of the Scripture itself, and not merely deduced therefrom by some supposed inference. And third, that the truth supposed to be overthrown by it shall be also an express statement of God's word, or some necessary, axiomatic truth, universally held by mankind. For if one should object against the Bible, that some inference he had drawn from its words were irreconcilable with some similar inference, or some supposed deduction of his human logic, we should always be entitled to reply: that his powers of thought being confessedly inaccurate, it was always more probable he had inferred erroneously, than that Scripture had spoken inconsistently.

5th. REASON AND HUMAN KNOWLEDGE ANCILLARY TO REVELATION.—Reason is also to be employed to interpret and illustrate the Scriptures. To do this, the whole range of man's natural knowledge may be taxed. The interpretation is never to presume to make reason the *measure* of belief, but the mere handmaid of Scripture. And the mode of interpretation is to be by comparing Scriptnre with Scripture according to the legitimate laws of language. The Scripture must be its own canon of hermeneutics; and that, independent of all other supposed rival sciences. For otherwise, as has been shown above, it would cease to carry a practical authority over the human mind as a rule of faith. A Bible which must wait to hear what *philosophy* may be pleased to permit it to say, and which must change its *dicta* as often as philosophy chooses to change, would be no Bible for any sensible man.

FAITH RESTS ON EVIDENCE, NOT DICTATION.—Now, the prelatic system of Church-authority stands opposed to this Protestant theory of private judgment. Prelatists claim for the reasonableness of their slavish system, this analogy: that the child, in all its primary education, has to accept things on trust as he is told. Human knowledge, say they, begins in *dogma*, not in reasoning. So should divine. The reply is, that this is a false analogy, in two vital respects. The secular knowledge which begins absolutely in dogma, is only that of signs; not of things and ultimate truths. The child must indeed learn from dogma, that a certain rafter-shaped mark inscribed on the paper is the accepted sign of the vowel-sound A. The things of God are not mere signs, but essential truths. Second, the reception of divine truth is not an infantile, but an adult work. We are required to do it in the exercise of a mature intelligence, and to be infants only in guilelessness.

DISTINGUISH THIS SYSTEM FROM RATIONALISM.—Prelatists and papists are fond of charging that the theory of private judgment amounts simply to rationalism. For, say they, "to make revelation wait on reason for the recognition of her *credentials*, virtually gives to the revealed dogma only the force of reason. 'The stream can rise no higher than its fountain.' On the Protestant scheme, revelation receives no more authority than reason may confer." The only plausibility of such objections is in the words of a false trope. Revelation it is said, 'submits its credentials to the reason,' according to us Protestants. Suppose I prefer to say (the correct trope,) we hold that revelation *imposes* its credentials upon the healthy reason. In fact, as when the eye looks at the sun, there are activities of the organ towards the result of vision, such as adjusting the axes of the two balls, directing them, refracting the rays, &c., and yet, *the light is not from the eye, but from the sun;* so in apprehending the validity of the Bible's credentials, *the light is from the Revelation;* not from the mind. Its activities about the apprehension of the evidence, are only receptive, not productive.

But the simple key to the answer is, that the question which we bring to the human reason, 'Is this book God speaking?' is one, single questions, perfectly defined, and properly within the reach of reason. The other question, which the Rationalist wishes to make reason answer, is: 'What are the things proper for God to say about Himself and religion?' This is, in fact, a multitude of questions, and mostly wholly above the reach of reason. We may illustrate the difference by the case of an ambassador. The court to which he comes is competent to entertain the question of his credentials. This is implied in the expectation that this court is to treat with him. The matter of credentials is one definite question, to be settled by one or two plain *criteri ı*, such as a signature, and the imprint of a seal. But what may be the secret will of his sovereign, is a very different set of questions. To dictate one's surmises here, and especially to annex the sovereign's authority to them, is impertinent folly. But the messages of the plenipotentiary carry all the force of the recognized signature and seal.

Moreover, we must remember that man's state is probationary. There is an intrinsic difference between truth and error, right reasoning and sophism, and the purpose of God in revelation is (necessarily) not to supplant reason, but to put man on his probation for its right use.

NO STRIFE OF REASON WITH FAITH.—Last: Let the student, from the first, discard all the false and mischievous ideas generated by the slang of the "contest between reason and faith"—of the propriety of having "reason conquer faith, or faith conquer reason." There is no such contest. The highest reason is to believe implicitly what God's word says, as soon as it is clearly ascertained to be God's word. The dictate of reason herself, is to believe; because she sees the evidences to be reasonable.

I need only add, that I hold the scriptures to be, in all its parts, of plenary inspiration; and we shall henceforward assume this, as proved by the inquiries of another department.

LECTURE XI.

SYLLABUS.

REVEALED THEOLOGY. GOD AND HIS ATTRIBUTES.

1. Give the derivation and meaning of the several *names* applied to God in the Scriptures.

Turrettin, Loc. iii, Qu. 4. Breckinridge's Theol., vol i, p 199. Concordance and Lexicons.

2. What is the meaning of the term, God's *attributes?* And what the most common classifications of them?

Turrettin, Loc, iii, Qu. 5 and 6. Dick, Lect, 21. Breckinridge's Theology, vol. 1, p. 260, &c.

3. What are the Scriptural evidences for God's *unity, spirituality* and *simpl city?*
   Turrett., Loc. iii, Qu. 3 and 7. Dick, Lect. 17 and 18.
4. What are the Bible proofs of God's *immensity?*
   Turrett., Loc. iii, Qu. 9. Dick, Lect. 19.
5. What is the Scriptural proof of God's *eternity?*
   Turrett., Loc. iii., Qu. 10. Dick, Lect. 17.
6. Prove from the Bible, that God is *immutable.*
   Turrett., Loc. iii, Qu. 11. Dick, Lect. 20. On the whole, Charnock on Attr., at appropriate places.

Infallibility of Scripture assumed.—In approaching the department of Revealed Theology, the first question is concerning the inspiration of the scriptures. This having been settled, we may proceed to assume them as inspired and infallible. Our business now is merely to ascertain and collect their teachings, to systematize them, and to show their relation to each other. The task of the student of Revealed Theology, is therefore, in the first place, mainly exegetical. Having discovered the teachings of revelation by sound exposition, and having arranged them, he is to add nothing except what follows "by good and necessary consequence." Consequently, there is no study in which the truth is more important, that "with the lowly is wisdom."

1. God's Names reveal Him.—The New Testament, and still more, the Old, presents us with an interesting subject of study, in the names and titles of God, which they employ to give our feeble mind a conception of His manifold perfections. The names Jehovah, Jah, El, Adonai, Eloah, Elohim, El, Shaddai, and Jehovah Tsebaoth, in the latter, and Theos, Kurios, Hupistos, Pantokrator, in the former, give of themselves an extensive description of His nature. For being all, according to the genius of the ancient languages, significant of some quality,they are, when rightly interpreted, proof texts to sustain several divine attributes.

Jehovah.—Jehovah, with its abbreviation Jah., (most frequently appearing in the doxology Hallelu Jah.,) has ever been considered by the Church the most distinctive and sacred, because the incommunicable name of God. The student is familiar with the somewhat superstitious reverence with which the later Hebrews regard it, never pronouncing it aloud, but substituting it in reading the Scriptures by the word Adonai. There seems little doubt that it presents the same radical with the substantive verb, hayah, in the future. [This is surprisingly confirmed in the Greek mythology, derived, as is known, from the Phœnician; and for the origin of that, compare Gen. xxii: 14, with xx: 4, where Abimẹlek the Philistine, doubtless had the true name of God. From Jehovah, we have *Jove*; (Latin, Jew Pater,) and its Greek synonym is Zeus, from Zeo, to live.] Along with this name is also to be classed the verbal from *Ehiyeh.* (Exod. iii: 14, explained by Jno. viii: 58.) In Ex. vi: 2, 3, we learn that the characteristic name by which God commissioned Moses was Jehovah. This is an additional argument to show that it means *self-existence* and independence.

This the Incommunicable Name.—Such a meaning would of itself lead us to expect that this name, with its kindred derivatives, is never applied to any but the one proper God; because no other being has the attribute which it signifies. A further proof is found in the fact that it is never applied as a proper name, to any other being in scriptures. The angel who appeared to Abraham, to Moses, and to Joshua, (Gen. xviii: 1; Exod. iii: 2–4; Josh. v: 13; vi: 3,) was evidently Jehovah Christ. When Moses named the altar Jehovah-nissi, (Ex. xvii: 15,) he evidently no more dreamed of calling *it* Jehovah, than did Abram, when he called a locality (Gen. xxii: 14,) Jehovah-jireh. And when Aaron said concerning the worship of the calf: "To-morrow is the feast of Jehovah," he evidently considered the image only as representative of the true God. But the last and crowning evidence that this name is always distinctive, is that God expressly reserves it to Himself. (See Exod. iii: 15; xv: 3; xx: 2; Ps. lxxxiii: 18; Is. xlii: 8; lxviii: 2; Amos v: 8; ix: 6.) The chief value of this fact is not only to vindicate to God exclusively the attribute of self-existence; but to greatly strengthen the argument for the divinity of Christ. When we find the incommunicable name given to Him, it is the strongest proof that He is very God.

Other Names.—*Adonai*, the Lord, a *pluralis excellentiæ*, is the equivalent of the Greek kurios. It is never applied, so far as I know, to any other than God. Its meaning is possession and dominion, expressed by the word *Dominus*, which in Vulg., is the current translation both for it and *Jehovah*.

Shaddai is also a *pluralis excellentiæ*, expressing *omnipotence*. Sometimes (as Job v. 17,) it stands by itself; sometimes (as Gen. xvii: 1,) it is connected with El. This seems to be the name by which God entered technically into covenant with Abraham. It appears in the New Testament in its Greek version Pantokrator. (Rev. i: 18.) *Elyon* is said to be a verbal adjective from 'azah, "to ascend," is rendered in Ps. ix: 8; xxi; 3, *Most High*. It signifies the exaltation of God's character.

Tzebäoth is frequently used as an epithet qualifying one of the other names of God, as Jehovah of Hosts. (*sc. exercituum.*) In this title, the heavenly bodies, orders of sentient creatures, &c., are represented as obeying God, as the bands of an army their General.

Communicable Names.—We come now to what may be called the *communicable* names of God—i. e., those used to express false gods or imaginary mighty men, &c., as well as the true. It is a striking peculiarity, that these alone are subjected to inflection by taking on the construct state, and pronominal suffixes. They are *El*, expressing the idea of *might*, and Eloah, Elohim, the singular and plural form of the same, derived from the verb eloch "to reverence." The singular is said to be used only in books of poetry. The plural (majestatis,) is the common word used by God, and translated Theos, Deus, God, expressing the simple idea of His divinity, as God of creation and providence.

Gathering up these names alone, and comprehending their conjoined force according to the genius of Oriental language, we find that they compose by themselves an extensive revelation of God's nature. They clearly show Him to be self-existent, independent, immutable and eternal; Ehyeh Jehovah, infinite in perfections, exalted in majesty, almighty in power, and of universal dominion. We shall find *all of God* implicitly, in these traits.

The scriptures give to God a number of expressive metaphorical titles (which some very inaccurately and needlessly would classify as His Metaphorical attributes, whereas they express, not attributes, but *relations*,) such as 'King,' 'Lawgiver,' 'Judge,' 'Rock,' 'Tower,' 'Deliverer,' 'Shepherd,' 'Husbandman,' 'Father,' &c. These cannot be properly called His *names*.

II. Attributes what? Identical with Essence?—God's attributes are those permanent, or essential *qualities* of His nature, which He has made known to us in His word. When we say they are *essential* qualities, we do not mean that they compose His *substance*, as parts thereof making up a whole: still less, that they are *members*, attached to God, by which He acts. They are traits qualifying His nature always, and making it the nature it is. The question whether God's attributes are *parts* of His essence, has divided not only scholastics, Socinians and orthodox, but even Mohammedans; affecting, as it does, the proper conception of His unity and simplicity. We must repudiate the gross idea that they are parts of His substance, or members attached to it; for then He would be susceptible of division, and so of destruction. His substance is a *unit*, a *unicity*. God's omniscience, e. g., is not something *attached to* His substance, whereby He knows; but only a power or quality of knowing, qualifying His infinite substance itself. To avoid this gross error, the scholastics, (including many Protestants,) used to say that God's essence, and each or every attribute, are *identical;* i. e., that His whole essence is identical with each attribute. They were accustomed to say, that God's knowing is God, God's willing is God, or that the whole God is in every act; and this they supposed to be necessary to a proper conception of His simplicity. Now, as before remarked, in Lecture iv, Natural Theology, if all this means any more than what I expressed above, it is *pantheism*. If it only mean's that God's knowledge is but the Infinite Spirit knowing, then it is merely stating in unintelligible language, what I have already stated; and what is as true in its finite measure, of the attributes of human spirits, as in its infinite sense, of God's attributes.

God is infinite, *and therefore* incomprehensible, for our minds, in His essence. (Job xi: 7–9.) Now, since our only way of knowing His essence is as we know the attributes which (in our poor shortcoming phrase) *compose it*, each of God's attributes and acts must have an element of incomprehensible about it. (See Job xxvi: 14; Ps. cxxxix: 5, 6; Is. xl: 28; Rom. xi: 33.) One of the most important attainments for you to make, therefore, is for you to rid your minds for once and all, of the notion, that you either do or can comprehend the whole of what is expressed of any of God's attributes. Yet there is solid truth in our apprehension of them up to our limited measure—i. e., our conceptions of them, if scriptural, will be not essentially false, but only defective. Of this, we have this twofold warrant: First, that God has told us we are, in our own rational and moral attributes, formed in His image, so that His infinite, are the *normae* of our finite essential qualities; and second, that God has chosen such and such *human words* (as wisdom, rectitude, knowledge,) to express these divine attributes. The Bible does not use words dishonestly.

Are the Separate Attributes of Infinite Number?—Another question has been raised by orthodox divines, (e. g., Breckinridge,) whether since God's essence is infinite, we must not conceive of it as having an infinite number of distinct attributes. That is, whatever may be the revelations of Himself made by God in word and works, and however numerous and glorious the essential attributes displayed therein, an infinite number of other attributes still remain, not dreamed of by His wisest creatures. The origin of this notion seems to be very clearly in *Spinozism*, which sought to identify the multifarious universe and God, by making all the kinds of beings, however numerous and diverse, *modes* of His attributes. Now, if the question is asked, can a finite mind *prove* that *this circle* of attributes revealed in the Scriptures which seem to us to present a God so perfect, so *totus teres et rotundus*, are the only distinct essential attributes His essence has, I shall freely answer, *no.* By the very reason that the essence is infinite and incomprehensible, it must follow that a finite mind can never know whether He has exhausted the enumeration of the distinct qualities thereof or not, any more than He can fully comprehend one of them. But if it be said that the infinitude of the essence necessitates an infinite number of distinct attributes, I again say, *no;* for would not one infinite attribute mark the essence as infinite? Man cannot reason here. But the same attribute may exhibit numberless varied acts.

Classifications of Attributes.—In most sciences, classification of special objects of study, is of prime importance, for two reasons. The study of resemblances and diversities, on which classifications proceed, aids us in learning the individuals classified more accurately. The objects are so exceedingly numerous, that unless general classes were formed, of which general propositions could be predicated, the memory would be overwhelmed, and the task of science endless. The latter reason has very slight application, in treating God's attributes; because their known number is not great. The former reason applies very fairly. Many classifications have been proposed, of which I will state the chief.

a.) Into Communicable and Incommunicable.—The old orthodox classification was into *communicable* and *incommunicable.* Thus, *omniscience* was called a communicable attribute; because God confers on angels and men, not identically His omnisciences, or a part of it, but *an* attribute of knowledge having a likeness, in its lower degree, to His. His eternity is called an incommunicable attribute, because man has, and can have nothing like it, in any finite measure even. In some of the attributes, as God's independence and self-existence, this distinction may be maintained; but in many others to which it is usually applied, it seems of little accuracy. For instance, God's eternity may be stated as *His* infinite relation to duration. Man's finite life is his finite relation to duration, and I see not but the analogy is about as close between this and God's eternity, as between man's little knowledge, and His omniscience.

b.) Into Relative and Absolute.—Another distribution, proposed by others, is into *absolute* and *relative.* God's immensity, for instance, is His absolute attribute; His omnipresence His corresponding relative attribute. The distinction happens to be pretty accurate in this case, but it would be impossible to carry it through the whole.

c.) Into Natural and Moral.—Another distribution is into *natural* and *moral* attributes; the natural being those which qualify God's being as an infinite spirit merely—e. g., omniscience, power, ubiquity; the moral being those which qualify Him as a *moral* Being, viz., righteousness, truth, goodness, and holiness. This distinction is just and accurate, but the *terms* are bungling. For God's moral attributes are as truly natural (i. e., original,) as the others.

The distribution into negative and positive, and the Cartesian, into internal (intellect and will) and external, need not be more than mentioned. Dr. Breckinridge has proposed a more numerous classification, into *primary*, viz: those belonging to God as simply *being essential*, viz: those qualifying His being as pure spirit; *natural*, viz: those constituting Him a free and intelligent spirit; *moral*, viz: those constituting Him a righteous being; and *consummate* being those perfections which belong to Him as the concurrent result of the preceding. The general objection is, that it is too artificial and complicated. It may be remarked, further, that the distinction of primary and essential attributes is unfounded. Common sense would tell us that we cannot know God as being, except as we know Him as spiritual being; and dialectics would say that the consideration of the *essentia* must *precede* that of the *esse*. Further, the subordinate distribution of attributes under the several heads is confused.

Best classification.—The distribution which I would prefer, would conform most nearly to that mentioned in the third place, into moral and non-moral. All the latter, as duration, ubiquity, knowledge, power, &c., will be found to be qualified by the consummate attribute of infinitude. All the former, truth, righteousness, goodness, will be found converging into the consummate attribute of *holiness*, the crowning perfection and glory of the divine nature.

III. Unity of God.—What we conceived to be the best rational proofs of God's *unity* and *simplicity*, were presented in a previous lecture on Natural Theology; giving the preference to that from the convergent harmony of creation. Theologians are also accustomed to argue it from the necessity of His existence (inconclusively,) from His infinitude (more solidly.) But our best proof is the Word, which asserts His *exclusive*, as well as His numerical unity. (Deut. vi: 4; 1 Kings viii: 60; Is. xliv: 6; Mark xii: 29, 32; 1 Cor. viii: 4; Eph. iv: 6; Gal. iii: 20; 1 Tim. ii: 5; Deut. xxxii: 39; Is. xliii: 10, 11; xxxvii: 16; xliv: 8, &c.

He is a Spirit.—The *spiritualtiy* of God we argued rationally, first from the fact that He is an intelligent and voluntary first cause; for our understandings are, properly speaking, unable to attribute these qualities to any other than spiritual substance. We found the same conclusion flowed necessarily from the fact, that God is the ultimate source of all force. It is implied in His immensity and omnipresence. He is Spirit, because the fountain of life. This also is confirmed by Scriptures emphatically. (See Deut. iv: 15–18; Ps. cxxxix: 7; Is. xxxi: 3; John iv: 24; 2 Cor. iii: 17.) This evidence is greatly strengthened by the fact, that not only is the Father, but the divine nature in Christ, and the Holy Ghost, also, are called again and again *Spirit.* (See for former, Rom. i: 4; Heb. ix: 14.) For latter, the title *Holy Ghost*, PNEUMA, everywhere in New Testament, and even in Old. We may add, also, all those passages which declare God, although always most intimately present, to be beyond the cognizance of all our senses. (Col. i: 15; 1 Tim. i: 17; Heb. xi: 27.)

HIS SIMPLICITY.—The *simplicity* of God, theologically defined, is not expressly asserted in the Bible. But it follows as a necessary inference, from His spirituality. Our consciousness compels us to conceive of our own spirits as absolutely simple; because the consciousness is always such, and the whole conscious subject, *ego*, is in each conscious state indivisibly. The very idea of dividing a thought, an emotion, a volition, a sensation, mechanically into parts, is wholly irrelevant to our conception of them; it is impossible. Hence, as God tells us that our spirits were formed in the image of His, and as He has employed this word, PNEUMA, to express the nature of His substance, we feel authorized to conceive of it as also simple. But there are still stronger reasons; for a.) Otherwise God's absolute unity would be lost. b.) He would not be incapable of change. c.) He might be disintegrated, and so, destroyed.

We are well aware that many representations occur in Scriptures which seem to speak of God as having a material form, e. g., in the theophanies and parts, as hands, face, &c., &c. The latter are obviously only *representations* adapted to our faculties, to set before us the different modes of God's workings. The seeming forms, angelic or human, in which He appeared to the patriarchs, were but the symbols of His presence.

IV. IMMENSITY AND OMNIPRESENCE.—The distinction between God's *immensity* and *omnipresence* has already been stated. Both are asserted in Scripture. The former in 1 Kings viii: 27, and parallel in Chron.; Is. lxvi: 1.

The latter in Ps. cxxxix: 7-10; Acts xvii: 27, 28; Jer. xxiii: 24; Heb. i: 3. It follows, also, from what is asserted of God's works of creation and providence, and of His infinite knowledge. (See Nat. Theol. Lect. III.

V. ETERNITY.—God's *eternity* has been already defined, as an existence absolutely without beginning, without end, and without succession: and the rational evidences thereof have been presented. As to the question, whether God's thoughts and purposes are absolutely unconnected with all successive duration, we saw, when treating this question in the Natural Theolog Lecture, good reason to doubt. The grounds of doubt need not be repeated. But there is a more popular sense, in which the *punctum stans*, may be predicated of the divine existence, that past and future are as *distinctly* and immutably present with the Divine Mind, as the present. This is probably indicated by the striking phrase, Is. lvii: 15, and more certainly, by Exod. iii: 14, compared with Jno. viii: 58; by Ps. xc: 4, and 2 Peter, iii: 8.

That God's Being has neither beginning nor end, is stated in repeated places—as Gen. xxi: 33; Ps. xc: 1, 2; cii: 26-28; Is. xli: 4; 1 Tim. i: 17; Heb. i: 12; Rev. i: 8.

VI. Immutability.—That God is immutable in His essence, thoughts, volitions, and all His perfections, has been already argued from His perfection itself, from His independence and sovereignty, from His simplicity and from His blessedness. This unchangeableness not only means that He is devoid of all change, decay, or increase of *substance:* but that His knowledge, His thoughts and plans, and His moral principles and volitions remain forever the same. This immutability of His knowledge and thoughts flows from its infinitude. For, being complete from eternity, there is nothing new to be added to His knowledge. His nature remaining the same, and the objects present to His mind remaining forever unchanged, it is clear that His active principles and purposes must remain forever in the same state; because there is nothing new to Him to awaken or provoke new feelings or purposes.

Our Confession says, that God hath neither *parts* nor *passions.* That He has something analogous to what are called in man *active principles,* is manifest, for He wills and acts; therefore He must feel. But these active principles must not be conceived of as *emotions*, in the sense of ebbing and flowing accesses of feeling. In other words, they lack that agitation and rush, that change from cold to hot, and hot to cold, which constitute the characteristics of passion in us. They are, in God, an ineffable, fixed, peaceful, unchangeable calm, although the springs of volition. That such principles may be, although incomprehensible to us, we may learn from this fact: That in the wisest and most sanctified *creatures,* the active principles have least of passion and agitation, and yet they by no means become inefficacious as springs of action—e. g., moral indignation in the holy and wise parent or ruler. That the above conception of the calm immutability of *God's* active principles is necessary, appears from the following: The agitations of literal passions are incompatible with His blessedness. The *objects* of those feelings are as fully present to the Divine Mind at one time as another; so that there is nothing to *cause* ebb or flow. And that ebb would constitute a change in Him. When, therefore, the Scriptures speak of God as becoming wroth, as repenting, as indulging His fury against His adversaries, in connexion with some particular event occurring in time, we must understand them *anthropopathically.* What is meant is, that the outward manifestations of His active principles were as though these feelings then arose.

God's immutability, as thus defined, is abundantly asserted in Scriptures. (Numb. xxiii: 19; Ps. cii: 26; xxxiii: 11; cx: 4; Is. xlvi: 10; Mal. iii: 6; Jas. i: 17; Heb. vi: 17; xiii: 8.)

Objections Answered.—This attribute has been supposed to be inconsistent with the incarnation of the Godhead in Christ; with God's works done in time, and especially His creation; and with His reconciliation with sinners upon their repentance. To the first, it is enough to reply, that neither was God's *substance* changed by the incarnation; for there was no confusion of natures in the person of Christ, nor was His plan modified: for He always intended and foresaw it. To the second, the purpose to create precisely all that is created, was from eternity in God, and to do it just at the time He did. Had He *not* executed that purpose when the set time arrived, there would have been the change. To the third, I reply, the change is not in God; but in the sinner. For God to change His treatment as the sinner's character changes, this is precisely what His immutability dictates.

LECTURE XII.

SYLLABUS.

DIVINE ATTRIBUTES—(Continued.)

1. What is the Scriptural account of God's *knowledge* and *wisdom?* What the meaning of His *simple*, His *free*, His *mediate* knowledge? Does God's *free* knowledge extend to the future acts of free agents?
   Turrettin, Loc. iii, Qu. 12, 13. Dick, Lect. 21, 22. Watson's Theo. Inst., Pt. II, Ch. 4 and Ch. 28, § 3. Dr. Chr. Knapp, § xxii.
2. Do the Scriptures teach God to be a *voluntary* being? What limitation, if any, on His will? Prove that He is omnipotent. Does God govern free-agents omnipotently?
   Turrettin, Loc. iii, Qu. 14, 21, 22. Dick, Lect. 23. Watson, Theo. Inst. Pt. II, Ch. 28, § 3, 4. Knapp, § xxi.
3. What is the distinction between God's *decretive* and *preceptive will?* Is it just? Between His *antecedent* and *consequent* will? Are His volitions ever conditioned on anything out of Himself?
   Turrettin, Loc. iii, Qu. 15, 16, 17. Knapp, § xxv and xxvi.
4. Is God's will the sole source of moral distinctions?
   Turrettin, Loc. iii, Qu. 18.

I. God's Knowledge and Wisdom.—The difference between knowledge and wisdom has been already defined as this: *knowledge* is the simple cognition of things; *wisdom* is the selecting and subordinating of them to an end, as means. Not only must there be the power of selecting and subordinating means to an end, to constitute wisdom; but to a *worthy end*. Wisdom therefore, is a higher attribute than knowledge, involving especially the moral perfections. For when one proceeds to the selection of an end, there is *choice;* and the moral element is introduced. Wisdom and knowledge are the attributes which characterize God as pure mind, as a being of infinite and essential intelligence. That God's knowledge is vast, we argued from His *spirituality*, from His *creation* of other minds; (Ps. xciv: 7–10,) from His work of creation in general, from His omnipresence: (Ps. cxxxix: 1–12,) and from His other perfections of *power*, (and especially) of *goodness*, *truth*, and *righteousness*, to the exercise of which knowledge is constantly essential. Of His wisdom, the great natural proof is the wonderful, manifold, and beneficent *contrivances* in His works of creation, (Ps. civ: 24,) and providence. That Paul's knowledge is distinct, and in every case intuitive, never deductive, seems to flow from its perfection. We only know substances by their attributes; God must know them in their true substance; because it was His creative wisdom which clothed each substance with its essential qualities. We only learn many things by inference from other things; God all things intuitively; because there can be no succession in His knowledge, admitting of the relation of promise and conclusion.

Omniscience.—We may show the infinite extent of God's knowledge, by viewing it under several distributions. He perfectly knows *Himself.* (1 Cor. ii: 11.) He has all the past perfectly before His Mind, so that there is no room for any work of *recollection.* (Is. xli: 22; xliii: 9.) This is also shown by the doctrine of a universal judgment. (Eccl. xii: 14; Luke viii: 17; Rom. ii: 16; iii: 6; xiv: 10; Matt. xii: 36; Ps. lvi: 8; Mal. iii: 16; Rev. xx: 12; Jer. xvii: 1.)

All the acts and thoughts of all His creatures, which occur in the present are known to Him as they occur. (Gen. xvi: 13; Prov. xv: 3; Ps. cxlvii: 4; xxxiv: 15; Zech. iv: 10; Prov. v: 21; Job xxxiv: 23; Luke xii: 6; Heb. iv: 13.) Especially do the Scriptures claim for God a full and perfect knowledge of man's thoughts, feelings and purposes—however concealed in the soul. (Job xxxiv: 21; Ps. cxxxix: 4; Jer. xvii: 10; Jno. ii: 25; Ps. xliv: 21, &c.)

God also knows, and has always known, all that shall ever occur in the future. (See Is. xlii: 9; Acts xv: 18.) Of this all God's predictions likewise, afford clear evidence. The particularity of God's foreknowledge even of the most minute things, may be seen, well defended. Turrettin, Loc. 3, Qu. 12, § 4–6.

Scientia Simplex. What?—Or, adopting another distribution, we may assert that God knows all the possible and all the actual. It is His knowledge of the former, which is called by the scholastics *scientia simplicis intelligentiæ.* Its object is not that which God has determined to effectuate, (the knowledge of which is called "*free*" or *scientia visionis;* but that which His infinite intelligence sees might be effectuated, if He saw fit to will it. The scholastics call it His knowledge of that which has *essentia,* but not *esse.*) That God has an infinite knowledge of possibles, other than those He purposes to actualize, no one can doubt, who considers the fecundity of this intelligence, as exhibited in His actual works. Can it be, that those works have exhausted all God's conceptions? Further: God's wise *selection* of means and ends, implies that conceptions existed in the divine mind, other than those He has embodied in creation or act, from among which He chose.

Theodicea thence.—The Formalist Divines of the school of Wolff, (as represented by Stapfer, Bulfinger, &c.,) make much of this distinction between God's knowledge of the possible and the actual, to build a defence of God's holiness and benevolence, in the permission of evil. Say they; *Scientia simplicis intelligentiæ,* is not *free* in God. He is impelled by a metaphysical necessity, to conceive of the possible according to truth. It is God's conception which generates its *essentia;* but about this, God exercises no voluntary, and therefore, no *moral act* of His nature. God's will is only concerned in bringing the thing out of *posse* into *esse.* But the *esse* changes nothing in the *essentia;* determines nothing about the quality of the thing actualized. Therefore God's will is not morally responsible for any evil it produces. This pretended argument scarcely needs exposure. It is Realistic in its whole structure. The plain answer is, that the thing or event only *in posse,* is non-existent, with all its evils. God's will is certainly concerned in bringing it out of *posse* into *esse.* And unless God is bound by fate, His will therein is free. (See my Rev. of Breckinridge.) It is, however, perfectly correct, to say that the object of God's *free* knowledge owes its futurition primarily to His will. Had He not purposed its production, it would never have been produced; for He is sovereign first cause. Now, if He willed it, of course He fore-knew it.

GOD KNOWS ALL ACTS OF FREE AGENTS WITH A SCIENTIA VISIONIS.—This leads us to the oft mooted question: whether acts *contingent*, and especially those of rational free-agents, are objects of God's *scientia visionis*, or of a *scientia media*. This is said to have been first invented by the Jesuit Molina, in order to sustain their semi-Pelagian doctrine of a self-determining will, and of conditional election. By *mediate* foreknowledge, they mean a kind intermediate between God's knowledge of the *possible*; for these acts are possessed of futurition, and the *scientia visionis*: for they suppose the futurition and foreknowledge of it is not the result of *God's will*, but of the contingent second cause. It is called *mediate* again: because they suppose God arrives at it, not directly by knowing His own purpose to affect it: but indirectly; by His infinite insight into the manner in which the contingent second cause will act, under given outward circumstances, foreseen or produced by God. The existence of such a species of knowledge the Calvinists usually deny *in toto*. To clear the way for this discussion, I remark;

First. That God has a perfect and universal foreknowledge of all the volitions of free-agents. The Scriptures expressly assert it. (Ezek. xi: 5; Is. xlvii: 8; Ps, cxxxix: 3, 4; 1 Sam. xxiii: 12; Jno. xxi: 18: 1 Jno. iii: 20; Acts xv: 18. It is equally implied in God's attribute of heart-searching knowledge, which He claims for Himself. (Rev. ii: 23, *et passim*.) It is altogether necessary to God's knowledge and control of all the future into which any creature's volition enters as a part of the immediate or remote causation. And this department of the future is so vast, so important in God's government, that if He could not foreknow and control it, He would be one of the most baffled, confused, and harassed of all Beings; and His government one of perpetual uncertainties, failures, and partial expedients. Last: God's predictions of such free acts of His creatures, and His including them in His decrees, in so many cases, show beyond dispute that He has some certain way to foreknow them. See every prophecy in Scripture where human or angelic acts enter. Where the prediction is positive, and proves true, the foreknowledge must have been certain. For these reasons, the impiety of early Socinians in denying God even a universal *scientia media*, is to be utterly repudiated.

NO SCIENTIA MEDIA. ITS ERROR.—In discussing the question whether God's foreknowledge of future acts of free-agents is *mediate* in the sense defined, I would beg you to note, that the theological *virus* of the proposition, is in this point: That in such cases, the *foreknowledge of the act precedes the purpose of God as to it*. i. e., They say God purposes, *because* He foresees it, instead of saying with us, that He only foresees because He purposes it. Against this point of the doctrine, Turrettin's argument is just and conclusive. Of this the sum, abating His unnecessary distinctions, is: a.) These acts are either possible, or future, so that it is impossible to withdraw them from one or the other of the two classes of God's knowledge, His simple, or His actual. b.) God cannot certainly foreknow an act, unless its futurition is certain. If His foreknowing it made it certain, then His foreknowledge involves foreordination. If the connexion with the second cause producing it made it certain, then it does not belong at all to the class of contingent events! And the causative connexion being *certain*, when God foreordained the existence of the second cause, He equally ordained that of the effect. But there are but the two sources, from which the certainty of its futurition could have come. c.) The doctrine would make God's knowledge and power dependent on contingent acts of His creatures: thus violating God's perfections and sovereignty. d.) God's election of men would have to be in every case conditioned on His foresight of their conduct, (what Semi-Pelagians are seeking here.) But in one case at least, it is unconditioned: that of His election of sinners to redemption. (Rom. ix: 16, &c.)

To God nothing is contingent.—But in a metaphysical point of view, I cannot but think that Turrettin has made unnecessary and erroneous concessions. The future acts of free agents fall under the class of *contingent effects:* i. e., as Turrettin concedes the definition, of effects such that the cause being in existence, the effect may, or may not follow. (Illustrate.) (He adopts this, to sustain his scholastic doctrine of immediate physical *concursus:* of which more when we treat the doctrine of Providence. But let me ask: Has this distinction of *contingent effects* any place at all, in God's mind? Is it not a distinction relevant only to our ignorance? An effect is in some cases, *to us* contingent; because our partial blindness prevents our foreseeing precisely what are the *present concurring* causes, promoting, or preventing, or whether the things supposed to be, are real causes, under the given circumstances. I assert that wherever the causative tie exists at all, its connexion with its effect is certain, (metaphysically necessary.) If not, it is no true cause at all. There is, therefore, to God, no such thing, in a strictness of speech, as a *contingent effect.* The contingency, (in popular phrase, *uncertainty,*) pertains not to the question whether the adequate cause will act certainly, if present; but whether it is certainly present. To God, therefore, whose knowledge is perfect, there is literally no such thing as a contingent effect. And this is true concerning the acts of free-agents, emphatically; they are *effects.* Their second cause is the agent's own *desires* as acting upon the objective inducements presented by Providence; the causative connexion is certain, in many cases, to our view; in all cases to God's. Is not this the very doctrine of Turrettin himself, concerning the will? The acts of free agents, then, arise through *second causes.*

True Distinction of this Knowledge.—The true statement of the matter, then, should be this: The objects of God's *scientia visionis,* or free knowledge, fall into two great classes: a.) Those which God effectuates *per se,* without any second cause. b.) Those which He effectuates through their natural second causes. Of the latter, many are physical—e. g., the rearing of vegetables through seeds; and to the latter belong all natural volitions of free agents, caused by the *subjective* dispositions of their nature, acting on the objective circumstances of their providential position. Now in all effects which

God produces through second causes, His foreknowledge, involving as as it does, a fore-ordination, is in a certain sense relative. That is, it embraces those second causes, as means, as well as the effects ordained through them. (And thus it is that "the liberty or contingency of second causes is not taken away, but rather established.") Further, the foreknowledge which purposes to produce a certain effect by *means of* a given second cause, must, of course, include a thorough knowledge of the nature and power of the cause. That that cause derived that nature from another part or act of God's purpose, surely is no obstacle to this. Here, then, is a proper sense, in which it may be said that God's foresight of a given effect is relative—i. e., through His knowledge of the nature and power and presence of its natural, or second cause. May not relative knowledge be intuitive and positive? Several of our axioms are truths of relation. Yet, it by no means follows, therefore, as the Semi-Pelagian would wish, that such a foreknowledge is antecedent to God's preordination concerning it. *Because God, in foreordaining the presence and action* of the natural cause, according to His knowledge of its nature, *does also efficaciously foreordain the effect.*

God's Relative Knowledge.—When, therefore, it is said that God's foreknowledge of the volitions of free-agents is relative in this sense; i. e., through His infinite insight into the way their dispositions will naturally act under given circumstances, placed around them by His intentional providence, the Calvinist should by no means flout it; but accept it, under proper limitations. But the term mediate is not accurate, to express this orthodox sense; because it seems to imply *derivation* subsequent, in the part of God's cognition said to be mediated, from the independent will of the creature. The Calvinist is the very man to accept it with consistency. For, on the theory of the Semi-Pelagian, such a foreknowledge by insight is impossible; volitions being uncaused, according to them; but on our theory it is perfectly reasonable, volitions, according to us, being certain, or necessary effects of dispositions. And I repeat, we need not feel any hyper-orthodox fear that this view will infringe the perfection of God's knowledge, or sovereignty, in His foresight of the free acts of His creatures; it is the very way to establish them, and yet leave the creature responsible. For if God is able to foresee that the causative connexion, between the second cause and its effect, is certain; then *in decreeing the presence* of the cause and the proper external conditions of its action, *He also decrees the occurrence of the effect.* And, that volitions are not contingent, but certain effects, is the very thing the Calvinist must contend for, if he would be consistent. The history of this controversy on *scientia media* presents another instance of the rule; that usually mischievous errors have in them a certain *modicum* of valuable truth. Without this, they would not have strength in them to run, and do mischief.

II. God's will and power omnipotent over free agents also. We should apprehend no real distinction between God's *will* and His power; because in our spirits, to will is identical with the putting forth of power; and because Scripture represents all God's working as being done by a simple volition. Ps. xxxiii: 9; xxxiii: 6; Gen. i:

3. That God is a free and voluntary being, we inferred plainly from the selection of contrivances to produce His ends, and of ends to be produced; for these selections are acts of choice. He is Universal *Cause*, and *Spirit*. What is volition but a spirit's causation? Of His vast power, the works of creation and providence are sufficient, standing proofs. And the successive displays brought to our knowledge have been so numerous and vast, that there seems to reason herself every probability His power is infinite. There must be an inexhaustible reserve, where so much is continually put forth. Finally, were He not omnipotent, He would not be very God. The being, whoever it is, which defies His power would be His rival. The Scriptures also repeatedly assert His omnipotence. See Gen. xvii: 1; Rev. i: 8; Jer. xxxii: 17; Matt. xix: 26; Luke i: 37; Rev. xix: 6; Matt. vi: 13. They say with equal emphasis, that God exercises full sovereignty over free agents, securing the performance by them, and upon them, of all that He pleases, yet consistently with their freedom and responsibility. Dan. iv: 35; Prov. xxi: 1; Ps. lxxvi: 10; Phil. ii: 13; Rom. ix: 19; Eph. i: 11, &c. The same truth is evinced by every prediction in which God has positively foretold what free agents should do; for had He not some way of securing the result, He would not have predicted it positively. Here may be cited the histories of Pharaoh. Exod. iv: 21; vi: 1; of Joseph, Gen. xlv: 5; of the Assyrian king, Is. x: 5–7; of Cyrus, Is. xlv: 1; of Judas, Acts ii: 23, &c., &c. It is objected by those of Pelagian tendencies, that *some* such instances of control do not prove that God has universal sovereignty over all free agents; for they may be lucky instances, in which God managed to cause them to carry out His will by some expedient. To say nothing of the texts quoted above, it may be answered, that these cases, with others that might be quoted, are too numerous, too remote, and too strong, to be thus accounted for. Further: if God could control one, He can another; there being no different powers to overcome; and there will hardly be a prouder or more stubborn case than that of Pharaoh or Nebuchadnezzor. A parallel answer may be made to the evasion from the argument for God's foreknowledge of man's volitions, from His predictions of them. Once more: if God is not sovereign over free-agents, He is of course not sovereign over any events dependent on the volitions of free agents, either simultaneous or previous. But those events make up a vast multitude, and include all the affairs of God's Government which most interest us and concern His providence. If He has not this power, He is, indeed, a poor dependence for the Christian, and prayer for His protection is little worth. The familiar objection will, of course, be suggested, that if God governs men sovereignly, then they are not free agents. The discussion of it will be postponed till we treat of Providence. Enough meantime, to say, that we have indubitable evidence of *both;* of the one from consciousness, of the other from Scripture and reason. Yet, that these agents were responsible and guilty, see Is. x: 12; Acts i: 25. Their reconciliation may transcend, but does not violate reason—witness the fact that man may often influence his fellow-man so decisively as to be able to count on it, and yet, that act be free, and responsible.

Omnipotence does not do self-contradictions.—We have seen (Natural Theology) that God's omnipotence is not to be understood, notwithstanding the emphatic assertions of Scripture, that all things are possible with Him, as a power to do contradictions. It has also been usually said by Theologians that God's will is *limited*, not only by the necessary contradiction, but by His own perfections. The meaning is correct; the phrase is incorrect. God's *will* is not limited; for those perfections as much ensure that He will never *wish*, as that He will never *do*, those incompatible things. He does absolutely *all* that He wills. But thus explained, the qualification is fully sustained by Scripture. 2 Tim. ii: 13; Tit. i: 2; Heb. vi: 18; Jas. i: 13.

III. Secret and revealed will distinguished.—I have argued that God's will is absolutely executed over all free-agents; and yet Scripture is full of declarations that sinful men and devils disobey His will! There must be, therefore, a distinction between His secret, and revealed, His decretive, and preceptive will. All God's will must be, in reality, a single, eternal, immutable act. The distinction, therefore, is one necessitated by our limitation of understanding, and relates only to the manifestation of the *parts* of this will to the creature. By God's decretive will, we mean that part of His will by which He foreordains whatever comes to pass. By His perceptive, that by which he enjoins on creatures what is right and proper for them to do. The deretive we also call His secret will; because it is for the most part (except as disclosed in some predictions and the effectuation) retained in His own breast. His perceptive we call His revealed will, because it is published to man for his guidance. Although this distinction is beset with plausible quibbles, yot every man is impelled to make it; for otherwise either alternative is odious and absurd. Say that God has no secret decretive will, and He wishes just what He commands and nothing more, and we represent Him as a Being whose desires are perpetually crossed and baffled; yea, trampled on; the most harrassed, embarrassed, and impotent Being in the universe. Deny the other part of our distinction, and you regresent God as acquiescing in all the iniquities done on earth and in hell. Again, Scripture clearly establishes the distinction. Witness all the texts already quoted to show that God's sovereignty overrules all the acts of men to His purposes. Add Rom. xi: 33, to end; Prov. xvi: 4. See also Deut. xxix: 29. Special cases are also presented, (the most emphatic possible,) in which God's decretive will differed from His preceptive will, as to the same individuals. See Exod. iv: 21–23; Ezek. iii: 7, with xviii: 31.

Objections.—The objections are, that this distinction represents God as either insincere in His precepts to His creatures, or else, as having His own volitions at war among themselves; and that, by making His secret will decretive of sinful acts as well as holy, we represent Him as unholy. The seeming inconsistency is removed by these considerations. "God's perceptive *will*." In this phrase, the word *will* is used in a different sense. For, in fact, while God *wills* the utterance of the precepts, the acts enjoined are *not objects of God's volition*, save in the cases where they are actually embraced in His decretive will. All the purposes which God carries out by permitting and overruling the evil acts of His creatures, are infinitely holy and proper for Him to carry out. It may be right for Him to permit what it would be wrong for us to do, and therefore wrong for Him to command us to do. Not only is it righteous and proper for an infinite Sovereign to withhold from His creatures, in their folly, a part of His infinite and wise designs; but it is absolutely unavoidable; for their minds being finite, it is impossible to make them comprehend God's infinite plan. Seeing, then, that He could not give them His whole immense design as the rule of their conduct, what rule was it most worthy of His goodness and holiness to reveal? Evidently, the moral law, requiring of them what is righteous and good for them. There is no insincerity in God's giving this law, although He may, in a part of the cases, secretly determine not to give unmerited grace to constrain men to keep it. Remember, also, that if even in these cases men would keep it, God would not fail to reward them according to His promise. But God, foreknowing that they would freely choose not to keep it, for wise reasons determines to leave them to their perverse choice, and overrule it to His holy designs. I freely admit that the divine nature is inscrutable; and that mystery must always attach to the divine purposes. But there is a just sense in which a wise and righteous man might say, that he sincerely wished a given subject of his would would not transgress, and yet that, foreseeing his perversity, he fully purposed to permit it, and carry out his purposes thereby. Shall not the same thing be possible for God in a higher sense?

Antecedent and Consequent Will.—There is a sense in which some parts of God's will may be said to be *antecedent* to, and some parts consequent to His foresight of man's acts—i. e., as our finite minds are compelled to conceive them. Thus: although God's will acts by one, eternal, comprehensive, simultaneous act, we cannot conceive of His determination to permit man's fall, except as a consequence of His prior purpose to create man; (because if none were created, there would be none to fall;) and of His decree to give a Redeemer, as consequent on His foresight of the fall. But the Arminian Scholastics have perverted this simple distinction thus, making the antecedent act of God's will precede the view had by God of the creature's action; and the consequent, following upon, and *produced by* that foresight; e. g., the purpose to create man was antecedent, to punish his sin consequent. I object, that this notion really violates the unity and eternity of God's volition. 2d. It derogates from the independence of Gods wilt, making it determined by, instead of determining, the creature's conduct. 3d. It overlooks the fact that all the parts of the chain, the means as well as the end, the second causes as well as consequences, are equally and as early determined by, and embraced in, God's comprehensive plan. As to a sequence and dependency between the parts of God's decree, the truth, so far as man's mind is capable of comprehending, seems to be this: That the decree is in fact *one*, in God's mind, and has no succession; but we being incapable of apprehending it save by parts, are compelled to conceive God, as having regard in one part of His eternal plan to a state of facts destined by Him to proceed out of another part of it. This remark will have no little importance when we come to view *supralapsarianism*.

God's will absolute.—God's purposes are all independent of any condition extereal to Himself in this sense; that they are not caused by anything *ab extra*. The things decreed may be conditioned on other parts of His own purpose, in that they embrace means necessary to ends. While the purposes have no *cause* outside of God, they doubtless all have wise and sufficient reasons, known to God.

IV. MORAL DISTINCTIONS ETERNAL.—I believe that the moral law is not right merely because it is commanded, but is commanded because it is right. Because: a.) God's will acts under the prompting of His own perfections—i. e., His moral volitions are not *uncaused*. His perfections, therefore, must have a rectitude antecedent, (in the order of production,) to his volitions. b.) Otherwise, it would be entirely conceivable that God might have made it *right* to do all vile things, and even to deny His Godhead! c.) No argument could be founded for the necessity of atonement; because God's purpose of mercy would have constituted the act of mercy an act of justice, without satisfaction to justice. d.) There would be no distinction at all between moral and positive precepts; whereas we know that there is a *reason* to be found why it is *morally right* to obey God's positive precepts, in the relations of Creator, Benefactor, and Redeemer, which He bears to us. e.) God's sovereignty would not be moral.

Yet our doctrine does not represent God as *under external moral authority;* because the ground of the rectitude of His volitions exists, for Him, nowhere but in His own perfections.

LECTURE XIII.

SYLLABUS.

GOD'S MORAL ATTRIBUTES.

1. Define and prove from Scripture God's *ab olute* and *relative*, His *distributive*, and *punitive justice*.
   Turrettin, Loc. iii, que. 19. Dick, Lect. 25. Ridgeley, B dy of Divinity, que. vii, p. 164. Watson's Theol. Institutes, pt. ii, ch. vii, §, (1,) Chr. Knapp, § xxx, xxxi.
2. What is God's *goodness?* What the relation of it to His *love*, His *grace*, and His *mercy?* What Scriptural proof that He possesses these attributes?
   Turrettin, Loc. iii, que. 20. Dick, Lect. 24. Ridgeley, que. vii, p. 168, &c. Charnock, Disc. xii, § 2-3, (pp. 255 to 287.) Watson's Theol. Inst., pt. ii, ch. 6. Knapp, § xxviii, 2.
3. Difine and prove God's *truth* and *faithfulness*, and defend from objections.
   Dick, Lect. 26. Ridgeley, que. vii, p. 186, &c. Watson's Theol. Inst., pt. ii, ch. vii, (ii.)

4. What is the *holiness* of God? Prove it.
   Dick, Lect. 27. Charnock, Disc. xi, § i, (pp. 135-144.) Ridgeley, que. vii, p. 160, &c.
5. Prove God's *infinitude.*
   Turrettin, Loc. iii, que. 8.

Moral attributes God's chief glory.—We have now reached that which is the most glorious, and at the same time, the most important class of God's attributes; those which qualify Him as an infinitely perfect moral Being. These are the attributes which regulate His will and are, therefore, so to speak, His practical perfections. Without these, His infinite presence, power, and wisdom would be rather objects of terror and fear, than of love and trust. Indeed, it is impossible ts conceive how the horrur of a rational being could be more thoroughly awakened, than by the idea of wicked *omnipotence* wielding all possible powers for the ruin or promotion of our dearest interests, yet uncontrolled alike by created power, and by moral restraints. The forlorn despair of the wretch who is left alone in the solitude of the ocean, to buffet its innumerable waves, would be a faint shadow of that which would settle over a universe in the hands of such a God. But blessed be His name, He is declared, by His works and word, to be a God of complete moral perfections. And this is the ground on which the Scriptures base their most frequent and strongest claims to the praise and love of His creatures. His power, His knowledge, His wisdom, His immutability are glorious; but the glory and lovliness of His moral attributes excelleth.

Enumeration.—God's distinct moral attributes may be counted as three—His *justice,* His *goodness,* and His *truth*—these three concurring in His consummate moral attribute, *holiness.*

I. Justice defined.—God's *absolute* justice is technically defined by theologians as the general rectitude of character, intrinsic in His own will. His *relative* justice is the acting out of that rectitude towards His creatures. His *distributive justice* is the quality more precisely indicated when we call Him a *just* God, which prompts Him to give to every one his due. His *punitive justice* is that phase of His distributive justice which prompts Him always to allot its due punishment to sin. No Christian theologian denies to God the quality of absolute justice, nor of relative, as far as His general dealings with His creatures go. We have seen that even reason infers it clearly from the *authority of conscience* in man; from the *instinctive pleasure* accompanying well-doing, and *pain* attached to ill-doing; from the *general tendency* which God's providence has established by which virtue usually promotes invidual and social well-being, and vice destroys them; and from many *providential retributions* where crimes are made to become their own avengers. And Scripture declares His rectitude in too many places and forms, to be disputed. e. g., Ps. lxlii: 15; Ezra ix: 15; Ps. xix: 9; cxlv: 16; Rev. xvi: 7, &c., &c., Ps. lxxxix: 14; Hab. i: 13.

Is God's punitive justice essential?—Different theories.—It is upon the *punitive* justice of God that the difference arises. As the establishing of this will establish *a fortiori,* the general righteousness of God's dealings, we shall continue the discussion on this point. The Socinians deny that retributive justice is an essential or an immutable attribute of God. They do not, indeed, deny that God punishes sin; nor that it would be right for Him to do so in all cases, if He willed it; but they deny that there is anything in His perfections to ensure His always willing it, as to every sin. Instead of believing that God's righteous character impels Him unchangeably to show His displeasure against sin in this way, they hold that, in those cases where He wills to punish it, He does it merely for the sinner's reformation, or the good of His government. The New England divines also hold that while God's purpose to punish sin is uniform and unchangeable, it is only that this form of *prevention* against the mischiefs of sin may be diligently employed, for the *good* of the universe. They hold that His law is not the expression of His essence, but the invention of His wisdom. Both these opinions have this in common; that they resolve God's justice into benevolence, or utility. The principle will be more thoroughly discussed by me in the Senior Course, in connexion with the Atonement. I only remark here, that such an account of the divine attribute of justice is attended by all the absurdities which lie against the Utilitarian System of morals among men; and by others. It is opposed to God's independence, making the creature His *end*, instead of Himself, and the carrying out of His own perfections. It violates our conscience, which teaches us that to inflict judicial suffering on one innocent for the sake of utility, would be heinous wrong, and that there is in all sin an inherent desert of punishment for its own sake. It resolves righteousness into mere prudence, and right into advantage.

Affirmative view.—Now Calvinists hold that God is immutably determined by His own eternal and essential justice, to visit every sin with punishment according to its desert. Not indeed that He is constrained, or His free-agency is bound herein; for He is immutably impelled by nothing but His own perfection. Nor do they suppose that this unchangeableness is a blind physical necessity, operating under all circumstances, like gravitation, with a mechanical regularity. It is the perfectly regular operation of a rational perfection, co-existing with His other attributes of mercy, wisdom, &c., and therefore modifying itself according to its object; as much approving, yea, demanding, the pardon of the penitent and believing sinner, for whose sins penal satisfaction is made and applied, as before, it demanded his punishment. In this sense, then: that God's retributive justice is not a mere expedient of benevolent utility, but a distinct essential attribute, I argue, by the following scriptural proofs:

Proved by Scripture.—a.) Those Scriptures where God is declared to be a just and inflexible judge. Exod. xxxiv: 7; Ps. v: 5; Gen. xviii: 25; Ps. lxliv: 2; l: 6; Is. 11: 3–4.

b.) Those Scriptures where God is declared to *hate sin*. e. g., Ps. vii: 11; Ps. v: 4–6; xlv: 7; Deut. iv: 24; Prov. xi: 20; Ps. xiv: 1; Jer. xliv: 4; Is. lxi: 8. If the Socinian, or the New England view were correct, God could not be said to hate sin, but only the consequences of it. And our own consciences tell us that a moral indifference to the intrinsic character of a bad act would of itself stamp a Being as immoral.

By the Law.—c.) From God's moral law, which is the transcript of His own essential perfections. Of this law, the penal sanction is always an essential part. See Rom. x: 5; Gal. iii: 12; Rom. v. 12.

The ceremonial law equally proves it: for the great object of all the bloody sacrifices was to hold forth the great theological truth that there is no pardon of the sinner, without the punishment of the sin in a substitute. Heb. ix: 22.

By Christ's Death.—d.) The death of Christ, a sinless being who had no guilt of His own for which to atone. We are told that "our sins were laid upon" Christ; that "He was made sin," that "He suffered the just for the unjust;" "that God might be just, and yet the justifyer of the ungodly;" that "the chastisement of our peace was upon Him," &c. Is. liii: 5 to 11; Rom. iii: 24–26; Gal. iii: 13, 14; 1 Pet. iii: 18, &c. Now, if Christ only suffered to make a governmental display of the *mischievous consequences* of sin, then *sin itself* was not punished in Him, and all the sins of the pardoned remain forever unpunished, in express contradiction to these Scriptures. Moreover, the transaction of Calvary, instead of being a sublime exhibition of God's righteousness, was only an immoral farce. And last: not only is God not immutably just, but He is capable of being positively unjust: in that the only innocent man since Adam was made to suffer most of all men!

Objection, that magistrates pardon. Answer.—The particular phase of the argument from God's rectoral justice, or moral relations to the rational universe as its *Ruler*, will be considered more appropriately when we come to the doctrine of atonement; as also, Socinian objections. One of these, however, has been raised, and is so obvious, that it must be briefly noted here. It is, that the righteousness of magistrates, parents, masters, and teachers, is not incompatible with some relaxations of punitive justice; why then should that of our Heavenly Father be so, who is infinitely benevolent; who is the God of love? The answer is: that God's government differs from theirs in three particulars. They are not the appointed, supreme retributors of crime, (Rom. xii: 19), and their punishments, while founded on retributive justice, are not chiefly guided by this motive, but by the *policy* of repressing sin, and promoting order. Second: they are not immutable, either in fact or profession; so that when they change their threats into pardons without satisfaction to the threatening, their natures are not necessarily dishonored. Third: they are not omniscient, to know all the *motives* of the offender, and all the evidences of guilt in doubtful cases, so as to be able exactly to graduate the degree and certainty of guilt. These three differences being allowed for, it would be as improper for man to pardon without satisfaction, as God.

II. God's Benevolence, &c.—God's *goodness* is, to creatures, one of His loveliest attributes; because it is from this that all the happiness which all enjoy flows, as water from a spring. Goodness is the *generic* attribute of which the love of benevolence, grace, pity, mercy forgiveness, are but specific actings, distinguished by the attitude of their *objects*, rather than by the intrinsic principle. *Goodness* is God's infinite *will to dispense well-being*, in accordance with His other attributes of wisdom, righteousness, &c., and on all orders of His creatures, according to their natures and rights. *Love* is God's active (but passionless) affection, by which He delights in His creatures, and in their well-being, and delights consequently in conferring it. It is usually distinguished into love of *complacency*, and love of *benevolence*. The former is a moral emotion, (though in God passionless), being His holy delight in holy qualities in His creatures, co-operating with His simple goodness to them as creatures. The latter is but His goodness manifesting itself, actively. *Grace* is the exercise of goodness where it is undeserved, as in bestowing *assured eternal blessedness* on the elect angels; and redemption on hell-deserving man. And because all spiritual and holy qualities in saints are bestowed by God, without desert on their part, they are called also, their graces, *charismata*. *Pity*, or simple compassion, is goodness going forth towards a suffering object, and prompting, of course, to the removal of suffering. *Mercy* is pity towards one *suffering for guilt*. But as all the suffering of God's rational creatures is for guilt, His compassion to them is always mercy. All mercy is also grace; but all grace is not mercy.

Are all the moral attributes only phases of Goodness?—Many theologians (of the Socinian, New England and Universalist schools) overstrain God's goodness, by representing it as His *one*, universally prevalent moral attribute; in such sense that His justice is but a punitive policy dictated by goodness, His truth but a politic dictate of His benevolence, &c. Their chief reliance for support of this view is on the supposed contrariety of goodness and retributive justice; and on such passages as, "God is love," &c. To the last, the answer is plain: if an exclusive sense must be forced on such a text, as makes it mean that God has no quality but benevolence, then, when Paul and Moses say, "Our God is a consuming fire," we should be taught that He has no quality but justice; and when another says, "God is light," that He is nothing but simple intelligence, without will or character. The interpretation of all must be consistent *inter se*. The supposed incompatibility of goodness and justice we utterly deny. They are two phases, or aspects of the same perfect character. God is not good to a certain extent, and then just, for the rest of the way, as it were by patches; but infinitely good and just at once, in all His character, and in all His dealings. He would not be truly good, if He were not just. The evidence is this very connexion between holiness and happiness, so intimate as to give pretext for the confusion of virtue and benevolence among moralists. God's wise goodness, so ineffably harmonized by His own wisdom and holiness, would of itself prompt Him to be divinely just; and His justice, while it does not necessitate, approves His divine goodness.

Scriptural proofs of God's Goodness.—The rational proofs of God's goodness have been already presented, drawn from the structure of man's sensitive, social, and moral nature, and from the adaptations of the material world thereto. (See Natural Theology. Lecture 4.) To this I might add, that the very act of constructing such a creation, where sentient beings are provided, in their several orders, with their respective natural good, bespeaks God a benevolent Being. For, being sufficient unto Himself, it must have been His desire to communicate His own blessedness, which prompted Him to create these recipients of it. Does any one object, that we say He made all for His own glory; and therefore, His motive was selfish, and not benevolent? I rejoin: What must be the attributes of that Being, who thus considers His own glory as most appropriately illustrated in bestowing enjoyment? The fact that God *makes beneficence His glory*, proves Him, in the most in trinsic and noble sense, benevolent.

When we approach Scripture, we find *goodness*, in all its severa phases, profusely asserted of God. Ps. cxlv: 8, 9; 1 Jno. iv: 8; Exo xxxiv: 6; Ps. xxxiii: 5; lii: 1; ciii: 8; xiii: 17; Ps. cxxxvi; Jas. v 11; 2 Pet. iii: 15, &c.

Crowning proof for Redemption.—But the crowning proof whicl the Scriptures present of God's goodness, is the redemption of sinners Rom. v: 8; Jno. iii: 16; 1 Jno. iii: 1; iv: 10. The enhancement c this amazing display are, first: that man's misery was so entirely sell procured, and the sin which procures it so unspeakably abominable t God's infinite holiness; second: that the misery from which He deliver is so immense and terrible, while the blessedness He confers is so com plete, exalted and everlasting; third: that ruined man was to Him s entirely unimportant and unnecessary, and moreover so trivial and lit tle, when compared with God; fourth: that our continued attitud towards Him throughout all this plan of mercy is one of aggravatin unthankfulness, enmity, and rebellion; fifth: that God should hav given such a *price* for such a wretched and hateful object, as the humilia tion of His own Son, and the condescending work of the Holy Ghost and last: that He should have exerted the highest wisdom known t man in any of the divine counsels, and the noblest energies of divin power, to reconcile His truth and justice with His goodness in man' redemption. Each of these features has been justly made the subjec of eloquent illustration. In this argument is the inexhaustible fund o proof for God's goodness. The work of redemption reveals a love, com passion, condescension, so strong, that nothing short of eternity wil suffice to comprehend it.

The great standing difficulty concerning the divine goodness has bee already briefly considered, in Lect. 4, § 4.

III. God's truth, and Faithfulness.—God's *Truth* may be sai to be an attribute which characterizes all God's other moral attributes and His intellectual. The word truth is so simple as to be, perhaps undefinable. It may be said to be that which is agreeable to reality o things. God's knowledge is perfectly true; being exactly correspond ent with the reality of the objects thereof. His wisdom is true; bein unbiassed by error of knowledge, prejudice, or passion. His justice i true; judging and acting always according to the real state of characte and facts. His goodness is true; being perfectly sincere, and its out goings exactly according to His own perfect knowledge of the real stat of its objects, and His justice. But in a more special sense, God' truth is the attribute which characterizes all His communications t His creatures. When those communications are promissory, or mina tory, it is called His *faithfulness*. This attribute has been manifested through two ways, to man, the testimony of our senses and intelligent faculties, and the testimony of Revelation. If our confidence in God' truth were undermined, the effect would be universally ruinous. Not only would Scripture with all its doctrines, promises, threatenings, pre cepts, and predictions, become worthless, but the basis of all confidence in our own faculties would be undermined; and universal skepticism would arrest all action. Man could neither believe his fellow-man, nor his own experience, nor senses, nor reason, nor conscience, nor consciousness, if he could not believe his God.

EVIDENCES OF IT, FROM REASON.—The evidences of God's truth and faithfulness are two-fold. We find that He deals truly in the informations which He has ordained our own senses and faculties to give us, *whenever they are legitimately used.* The grounds upon which we believe them have been briefly reviewed in my remarks upon metaphysical skepticism. God has so formed our minds that we cannot but take for granted the legitimate informations of our senses, consciousness, and intuitions. But this unavoidable trust is abundantly confirmed by subsequent experiences. The testimonies of one sense, for instance, are always confirmed by those of the others, when they are applied; e. g., when the eyes tells us a given object is present, the touch, if applied, confirms it. The expectations raised by our intuitive reason, as e. g., that like causes will produce like effects, are always verified by the occurrence of the expected *phenomena.* Thus a continual process is going on, like the "proving" of a result in arithmatic. Either the seemingly true informations of our senses are really true, or the harmonious coherency of the set of errors which they assert is perfectly miraculous.

FROM SCRIPTURE.—The second class of proofs is that of Scripture. Truth and faithfulness are often predicated of God in the most unqualified terms. 2 Cor. i: 18; Rev. iii: 7; vi: 10; xv: 3; xvi: 7; Deut. vii: 9; Heb. x: 23.

All the statements and doctrines of Scripture, so far as they come within the scope of man's consciousness and intuitions, are seen to be infallibly true; as, for instance, that "the carnal mind is enmity against God;" that we "go astray as soon as we be born, speaking lies," &c., &c. Again, Scripture presents us with a multitude of specific evidences of His truth and faithfulness, in the promises, threatenings, and predictions, which are contained there; for all have been fulfilled, so far as ripened.

The supposed exceptions, where threats have been left unfulfilled, as that of Jonah against Nineveh, are of very easy solution. A *condition* was always either implied or expressed, on which the execution of the threat was suspended.

The apparent insincerity of God's offers of mercy, and commands of obedience and penitence, held forth to those to whom He secretly intended to give no grace to comply, offers a more plausible objection. But it has been virtually exploded by what was said upon the secret and decretive, as distinguished from the revealed and preceptive will of God. I shall return to it again more particularly when I come to treat of effectual calling.

IV. GOD'S HOLINESS.—When places, Mount Zion, utensils, oils, meats, altars, days, &c., are called *holy*, the obvious meaning is, that they are consecrated—i. e., set apart to the religious service of God. This idea is also prominent, when God's priests, prophets, and professed people, are called holy. But when applied to God, the word is most evidently not used in a ceremonial, but in a spiritual sense. Most frequently it seems to express the general idea of His *moral purity*, as Levit. xi: 44; Ps. cxlv: 17; 1 Pet. i: 15, 16; sometimes it seems to express rather the idea of His majesty, not exclusive of His moral perfections, but inclusive also of His power, knowledge and wisdom, as in Ps. xxii: 3; xcviii: 1; Is. vi: 3; Rev. iv: 8. Holiness, therefore, is to be regarded, not as a distinct attribute, but as the resultant of all God's moral attributes together. And as His justice, goodness, and truth are all predicated of Him as a Being of intellect and will, and would be wholly irrelevant to anything unintelligent and involuntary, so His holiness implies a reference to the same attributes. His moral attributes are the special crown; His intelligence and will are the brow that wear it. His holiness is the collective and consummate glory His nature as an infinite, morally pure, active, and intelligent Spirit.

V. God's Infinity.—We have now gone around the august circle of the Divine attributes, so far as they are known to us. In another sense I may say that the summation of them leads us to God's other consummate attribute—His infinitude. This is an idea which can only be defined negatively. We mean by it that God's being and attributes are wholly without bounds. Some divines, indeed, of modern schools, would deny that we mean anything by the term, asserting that infinitude is an idea which the human mind cannot have at all. They employ Sir W. Hamilton's well known argument, that "the finite mind cannot think the unconditioned; because to think it is to limit it." It has always seemed to me that the plain truth on this subject is, that man's mind does *apprehend* the idea of infinitude, (else whence the word?) but that it cannot *comprehend* it. It knows *that there is* the infinite; it cannot fully know *what* it is. God's nature is absolutely without bound, as to His substance, (immense,) as to His duration, (eternal,) as to His knowledge, (omniscience,) as to His will, (omnipotence), as to His moral perfections, (holiness.) It is an infinite essence.

Supremacy.—One of the consequences which flows from these perfections of God is His absolute *sovereignty*, which is so often asserted of Him in Scripture; e. g., Dan. iv: 35; Rev. xix: 16: Rom. ix: 15–23; 1 Tim. vi: 15; Rev. iv: 11. By this we do not mean a power to do everything, as, e. g., to punish an innocent creature, contradictory to God's own perfections; but a *righteous* title to do everything, and control every creature, unconstrained by anything outside His own will, but always in harmony with His own voluntary perfections. When we call it a righteous title, we mean that it is not only a dunamis, but an exousia, not only a physical *potentia*, but a moral *potestas*. The foundations of this righteous authority are, first, God's infinite perfections; second, His creation of all His creatures out of nothing; and third, His preservation and blessing of them. This sovereignty, of course, carries with it the correlative duty of implicit obedience on our part.

But second: Another consequence which flows from the infinite perfections of God is that He is entitled not only to dispose of us and our services, for His own glory, but to receive our supreme, sincere affections. Just in degree as the hearts of His intelligent creatures are right, will they admire, revere, and love God, above all creatures, singly or collectively.

LECTURE XIV.

SYLLABUS.

THE TRINITY.

1. Explain the origin and meaning of the terms, *Trinity*, *Essence*, *Substance*, *Subsistance*, *Person*, HOMOOUSION.
   Turrettin, Loc. iii, que. 23. Hill's Divin., Bk. iii, ch. x, § 2, 3. Knapp, Section xlii, § iii, Lect. xliii, § ii. Dick, Lect. 28.
2. Give the *history of opinions* touching the *Trinity*; and especially the *Patripassian, Sabellian, and Arian*
   Knapp, Sections xlii and xliii. Hill, Bk. iii, ch. x. Dick, Lect. 29. Hagenback, Hist. of Doc. Mosheim, Com. de Reb., ante Constantinum, vol. i, § 68, vol. ii, § 32 and 33.
3. Define the doctrine of the Trinity, as held by the orthodox: and state the propositions included in it.
   Turrettin, Loc. iii, que. 25, § 1-3, and que. 27. Hill and Dick, as above. Jno. Howe, "Calm and Sober Inquiry Concerning Possibility of a Trinity."
4. What rationalistic explanations of the doctrine were attempted by the Origenists; and what by the mediaeval scholastics? Are they of any value?
   Th. Aquinas, *Summa.* Hill, as above. Neander, Ch. Hist., 2 Am. Edit., Boston, vol. ii, p. 360, &c., vol. iv, 457, &c. Moshiem, Com., vol. ii, § 27 and 31. Knapp, Section xlii. Watson, Theol, Inst., pt. ii, ch. 8, i (i.) 2.
5. Present the *general* Bible evidence for a Trinity, from the Old Testament and from the New.
   Turrettin, Loc. iii, que. 25 and 26. Dick, Lect. 28. Knapp, Sect. xxxiv, xxxv.

§ I. NOMENCLATURE.—While a part of the *terms* introduced by the Scholastics to define this doctrine are useful, others of them illustrate in a striking manner the disposition to substitute words for ideas, and to cheat themselves into the belief that they had extended the latter, by inventing the former. The Greek Fathers, like the theologians of our own country, usually make no distinction between *essence*, and *substance*, representing both by the word OUSIA, being. But the Latin Scholastics make a distinction between *essentia*, *esse*, and *substantia*. By the first, they mean that which constitutes the substance, the *kind* of thing it is: or its *nature*, if it be a thing created. By the second, they mean the state of being in existence. By the third, they mean the subject itself, which exists, and to which the essence belongs. *Subsistence* differs from *substance*, as mode differs from that of which it is the mode. To call a thing *substance* only affirms *that* it is an existing thing. Its *subsistence* marks the *mode* in which it exists. E. g., matter and spirit are both substances of different kinds. But they *subsist* very differently. The infinite spirit *exists* as a simple, indivisible substance; but it subsists as three persons. Such is perhaps the most intelligible account of the use of these two terms; but the pupil will see, if he analyses his own ideas, that they help him to no nearer or clearer conception of the personal distinction.

The word *Person*, PROSOPON, *persona*, (sometimes HUPOSTASIS, in the later Greeks), means more than the Latin idea, of a *role* sustained for the time being; but less than the popular modern sense, in which it is employed as equivalent to *individual*. Its meaning will be more fully defined below. HOMOUSIOS means of *identical substance*. The Greek Fathers also employed the word EMPERICHORESIS, intercomprehension, to signify that the personal distinction implied no *separation* of substance. But, on the contrary, there is the most intimate mutual embracing of each in each; what we should call, were the substance material, an *interpenetration*.

§ II. THREE TENDENCIES OF OPINION ON TRINITY.—The subsistence of the three persons in the Godhead was the earliest subject of general schism in the primitive Church. To pass over the primitive Gnostic and Manichaean sects, three tendencies, or schools of opinion, may be marked in the earlier ages; and in all subsequent times, the Orthodox, or Trinitarian, the Monarchian, and the Arian. The first will be expounded in its place. The tendency of mind prompting both the others may be said to be the same, and indeed, the same which has prevailed ever since, viz: a desire to evade the inscrutable mystery of three in one, by so explaining the second and third persons, as to reach an absolute unity both of person and substance, for the self-existent God. (AMONEARCHE.) Hence, it may justly be said that Arianism, and even Socinianism, are as truly monarchian theories, as that of Noëtus, to whom the title was considered as most appropriate.

PATRIPASSION.—*Noëtus*, an obscure clergyman, (if a clergyman) of Smyrna, is said to have founded a sect on the doctrine, that there is only one substance and person in the Godhead; that the names, Father, Son, and Holy Ghost, are nothing but *names* for certain phases of action or *rôles*, which God successively assumes. Christ was this *one* person, the Godhead or Father, united to a holy man, Jesus, by a proper Hypostatic union. The Holy Ghost is still this same person, the Father, acting His part as revealer and sanctifier. Hence, it is literally true, that the *Father* suffered, i. e., in that qualified sense in which the Godhead was concerned in the sufferings experienced by the humanity, in the Mediatorial Person. This theory, while doing violence to Scripture, and deranging our theology in many respects, is less fatal by far, than that of Arians, and Socinians: because it retains the proper divinity of the Messiah, and of the Holy Ghost.

SABELLIAN.—The Sabellian theory (broached by Sabellius, of Pentapolis in Lybia Cyrenaica, about A. D., 268,) has been by some represented, as though it were hardly distinguishable from the Patripassian; and as though he made the names, Father, Son, and Holy Ghost the mere titles of three modes of action which the one Godhead successively assumes. By others it has been represented as only a sort of high Socinianism, as though he had taught that the Holy Ghost was an influence emanating from the Godhead, and Christ was a holy man upon whom a similar influence had been projected. But Mosheim has shown, I think, in his *Com. de Rebus*, &c, that both are incorrect, and that the theory of Sabellius was even *more* abstruse than either of these. The term which he seems to have employed was that the Father, Son, and Holy Ghost are three *forms* (SCHEMATA) of the Godhead, which presented real portions of His substance, extended into them, as it were, by a sort of spiritual division. Thus, the Son and Holy Ghost are not parts of the Father; but all three are parts, or forms, of a more recondite *godhead*. According to this scheme, therefore, the Son and Holy Ghost are precisely as divine as the Father: but it will appear to the attentive student very questionable, whether the true godhead of all three is not vitiated.

ARIAN.—The theory of Arius is so fully stated, and well known, that though more important, it needs few words. He represents the Son, prior to His incarnation, as an infinitely exalted *creature*, produced (or generated) by God out of nothing, endued with the nearest possible approximation to His own perfections, adopted into sonship, clothed with a sort of deputized divinity, and employed by God as His glorious agent in all His works of creation and redemption. The Holy Ghost is merely a KATISMA KATISMATOS, produced by the Son.

ERROR TENDS EITHER TO OBLITERATE OR WIDEN PERSONAL DISTINCTIONS—Now, it has been well stated by Dr. Hill, that there *can* be but three schemes in substance: the orthodox, the Patripassian, and the Subordinationist. All attempts to devise some other path, have merged themselves virtually into one or the other of these errors. Either the personal distinctions are obliterated, or they are so widened as to make the Son another, and an inferior substance. Now, the refutation of the latter schemes will be sufficiently accomplished if we succeed (in the next Lecture) in establishing the proper divinity, and identity of substance of the Son.

PATRIPASSIAN SCHEME REFUTED.—The refutation of the former class of theories is effected by showing that some true and definite distinction of persons is predicated in Scripture, of the Father, Son and Holy Ghost. It will appear in so many places, asserted in so many forms, so intertwined with the very woof of the Scriptures, that its denial does fatal violence to the integrity of their language. a.) I point to those numerous passages, where one Person is said to act upon, or act through another. See, e. g., Exod. xxiii: 20; Ps. ii: 6, cx., Is. xlii: 1; liii: 12; Jno. xv: 26; xx: 21, &c., &c., where God the Father is said to *send*, to *enthrone*, to *appoint*, to sacerdotal office, to *uphold*, to reward the Son, and the Son and Father to send the Holy Ghost. b.) Consider those, in which mutual principles of affection are said to subsist between the persons. Is. xlii: 1; Jno. x: 17, 18, &c., &c. c.) There is a multitude of other passages, where voluntary principles and volitions are said to be exercised by the several persons as such, towards inferior and external objects. Exod. xxiii: 21. (The subject is the Messiah, as will be proved.) Eph. iv; 30; Rev. vi: 16, &c., &c. Yet, since these principles are all perfectly harmonious, as respects the three persons, there is no dissension of will, breach in unity of council, or difference of perfections. d.) There is a still larger multitude of texts, which assert of the persons as such, actions and agencies towards inferior, external objects. See, for instance, Jno. v: 19; 1 Cor. xii: 11, &c., &c. Now, if these personal names, of Father, Son, and Holy Ghost, meant no more than three influences or energies, or three phases of action of the same person, or three *forms* of one substance, is it not incredible that all these properties of personality, choosing, loving, hating, sending and being sent, understanding, acting, should be asserted of them? It would be the wildest abuse of language ever dreamed of.

§ III. DEFINITION OF TRINITY.—The doctrine of the Trinity, as held by the Catholic Church, cannot be better defined, than in the words of our confession. (Recite ch. II, § 3.) It embraces the following *propositions:*

1. The true *unity*, indivisibility, and simplicity of God

2. The subsistence of a threefold personal distinction, marked by a part of the properties of separate personalities, (in some inscrutable manner entirely compatible with true unity) as intelligence, active principles, volition, action.

3. Identity of substance, so that the whole godhead is truly in each person, without confusion or division, and all the essence belongs alike to all the persons.

4. The distinction of the three persons, each by its *property*, incommunicable from one person to another, and the existence consequently, of an eternal relation between them.

INSCRUTABLE; BUT NOT IMPOSSIBLE.—Now, that it is inscrutable how these things *can be*, we freely admit. Did they involve a necessary self-contradiction, we should also admit, that the understanding would be incapable of receiving them all together. But we do not hold that the persons are three in the *same sense* in which they are one. If it be asked what is the precise meaning of the phrase, *person in the Godhead?* we very freely answer, that we know only in part. You will observe that all the Socinian and Rationalist objections mentioned in your text-books against this doctrine, either proceed on the misrepresentation, that we make three equal to *one*, (as in the notorious Socinian formula; let a. b. c. represent the persons, and x. the Godhead; then a=x: b=x: c=x. Add, and we have a+b.+c=3x=x,) in the same sense; or they are *argumenta ad ignorantiam.* But is it not just what we should expect, that when God reveals something about the subsistence of His being, it should be thoroughly inscrutable to us? We must remember that the human mind has no cognizance of *substance*, in fact, except as the unknown ground, to which our intuitions impell us to refer properties. It is only the properties that we truly *know.* This is true of material substance; how much more true of spiritual substance? And more yet of the infinite? God, in revealing Himself to the natural reason, only reveals His properties or attributes—His substance remains as invisible as ever. Look back, I pray you, to that whole knowledge of God which we have acquired thus far, and you will see that it is nothing but a knowledge of attributes. Of the substance to which these properties are referred, we have only learned *that it is.* *What* it is, remains impenetrable to us. We have named it *simple spirit.* But is this, after all, more than a name, and the affirmation of an unknown fact to our understandings? For, when we proceed to examine our own conception of spirit, we find that it is a negation of material attributes only. Our very attempts to conceive of it, (even formed after we have laid down this as our prime feature of it, that it is the antithesis of *matter*,) in its substance, are still obstructed by an inability to get out of a materialistic circle of notions. We name it PNEUMA, *spiri us*, *breath;* as though it were only a gaseous and transparent form of matter; and only differed *thus* from the solid and opaque. This obstinate materialistic limit of our conceptions arises, I suppose, from the fact, that conceptions usually arise from *perceptions*, and these are only of sensible, i. e., of material ideas. This obstinate incapacity of our minds may be further illustrated by asking ourselves: What is really our conception of God's immensity? When we attempt the answer do we not catch ourselves always framing the notion of a transparent body extended beyond assignable limits Nothing more! Yet, reason compels us to hold that God's substance is *not extended* at all, neither as a vast solid, nor a measureless ocean of liquid, nor an immense volume of hydrogen gas expanded beyond limit. Extension, in all these forms, is a property wholly irrelevant to spirit. Again: (and this is most in point,) every Socinian objection which has any plausibility in it, involves this idea; that a trinity of Persons must involve a division of God's substance into three parts. But we know that divisibility is not a property of spirit at all—the dea is wholly irrelevant to it, belonging only to matter.

Objections all materialistic.—The Socinian would say here: 'Precisely so; and hence we reason against the impossibility of a trinity in unity. If divisibility is totally irrelevant to infinite Spirit, then it is *indivisible*, and so, can admit no trinity.

Inspect this carefully, and you will find that it is merely a verbal fallacy. The Socinian cheats himself with the notion that he knows something here, of the divine substance, which he does not know. By *indivisible* here, he would have us understand the *mechanical power of utterly resisting division*, like that imputed to an atom of matter. But has Spirit this material property? This is still to move in the charmed circle of material conceptions. The true idea is, not that the divine substance is *materially atomic*; but that the whole idea of parts and separation is irrelevant to its substance, in both a negative and affirmative sense. To say that Spirit is indivisible, in that material sense, is as false as to say that it is divisible. Thus the stock argument of the Socinian against the possibility of a trinity is found to be a fallacy; and it is but another instance of our incompetency to comprehend the real substance of spirit, and of the confusion which always attends our efforts to do so. We cannot disprove here, by our own reasonings, any more than we can prove; for the subject is beyond our cognition.

I pray the student to bear in mind, that I am not here attempting to *explain the Trinity*, but just the contrary: I am endeavouring to convince him that it cannot be explained. (And because it cannot be explained, it cannot be rationally rebutted.) I would show him that we must reasonably expect to find the doctrine inexplicable, *and to leave it so.* I wish to show him that all our difficulties on this doctrine arise from the vain conceit that we comprehend something of the subsistence of God's substance, when, in fact, we only apprehend something. Could men be made to see that they comprehend nothing, all the supposed impossibilities would vanish; there would remain a profound and majestic mystery.

§ IV. Rational Explanations of Greek Scholastics.—The minfrom which every attempted *rationale* of the Trinity has come, was the New Platonic; and the chief *media* of their introduction to the Christ tian Theology, Clem. Alexandrinus and Origen. Following the trinitarian scheme which the New Platonists attributed (with insufficient grounds) to Plato, of To on, Nous and Psyche; they usually represent God the Father as the intelligent substance, intrinsically and eternally active, the Nous, as the idea of self, generated from eternity by God's self-intellection; and the Psyche, as the active complacency arising upon it. The Platonizing Fathers, who called themselves orthodox, were not slow to fling the charge of *monarchianism* (MONE ARCHE) against all Patripassians and Arians alike; as reaching by diverse roads, an assertion of a single divine person. The modern student will be apt to think that their rationalism betrays the very same tendency; an unwillingness to bow the intellect to the dense mystery of a real and proper three in one; and an attempt to evade it by virtually destroying the personality of the 2d and 3d persons.

OF AQUINAS.—This attempted explanation appears, with new completeness and fullness, after the Peripatetics had modified the Platonic system, in the Latin Scholastics. Thomas Aquinas, for instance, states the matter about thus: Infinite activity of thought is the very essence of the Divine substance. But from eternity there was but a two-fold object of thought for this intellect to act on—God's *self*, and His *decree*. Now, as man is made intellectually in God's image, we cannot conceive of God's thinking, except by conceiving of our own acts of thought as the finite *type* of which His is the infinite antitype. Now, when man *thinks*, or conceives, it is only by means of a *species* or image of that which is the object of his thought, present before his mind. So, God's very act of thinking of Himself and His decree generates in the divine mind, a *species* of them; it generates them eternally; because God is eternally and necessarily active in thinking. This *species* or *idea* is therefore eternal as God, yet generated by God, it is of the same essence, for it is a non-corporeal, spiritual entity, and God's essence is pure intellection. It is one with God; for it is God's idea of *Himself*, and *His own* eternal purpose which is Himself purposing. This is the *Logos*, the 2d Person. Again, as in our souls, so in God, the presence of a moral object in conception awakens moral sentiment, and of a plan or device, approval or disapproval; so, God's contemplation of this *idea* of Himself and His decree, begets a moral complacency, and a volition to effectuate (when the fullness of time shall have come) the decree. This complacency and volition are the Spirit, the 3d or *practical* Person of the Godhead, proceeding from the Father and the *Idea*, or *Logos*.

OBJECTIONS TO IT.—This *rationale* we cannot but regard as worthless, though ingenious. *First*, the Scriptures inform us in advance, that God is *inscrutable*; and that we need not expect to explain His subsistence. Job ii: 7. *Second*: According to this explanation, both the NOUS and the PSYCHE would be compounded, the former of the two *species* of God's being, and of His decree; the latter of two feelings, His moral self-complacency, and His volition to effectuate His decree. *Third*: Neither the 2d nor 3d persons would be *substance* at all, but mere idea and feeling, which have no entity whatever, except as affections of the substance of the Father. This seems to our minds an objection so obvious and conclusive, that no doubt the student is almost incredulous that acute men should have seriously advanced a theory obnoxious to it. The answer is, that the Platonic and Peripatetic metaphysics ignored, in a manner astonishing to the modern mind, the distinction between substance and attribute. Between the two kinds of entity, they drew no generic distinction. But is not this one of the very traits of modern, trancendental Idealism, from Spinoza down? *Fourth*: On this scheme of a trinity, I see not how the conclusion could be avoided, that every intelligent free agent is as much a finite trinity in unity as God is an infinite one. Let us then attempt no explanation where explanation is impossible.

§ V. Proof of Trinity wholly of Revelation.—Having thus defined the doctrine, we proceed to its proof. That this evidence for the Trinity must be wholly a matter of revelation, would appear sufficiently from the weakness of the attempt made by the Scholastics, to find some proof or presumptive probability in the light of reason. The most plausible of these, perhaps, is that which Neander informs us, Raymund Lully employed against the Unitarian Moslems of Barbury, which is not discarded even by the great Aquinas. They say God is immutable from eternity. He exists now in a state of *active* benevolence. Hence, there must have always been, from eternity, some sense in which God had an *object* of His benevolence, in some measure extraneous; else active benevolence would have been impossible; and the result would be, that the creation of the angels (or earliest holy creatures) would have constituted an *era of change* in God. The reasoning appears unsound by this simple test. God is now actively righteous and punitive, as well as good; and a parallel argument will prove, therefore, with equal conclusiveness, the eternity of a devil. The solution of the sophism is to be found in those remarks, by which we defended God's immutability against the objection, that the *creation* of the universe constituted a change in God. It does not; because God's purpose to create, when His chosen time should have come, was unchangeably present with Him from eternity. Creation makes the change in the creature: not in God.

General Direct Proofs.—The Scripture evidence for a Trinity presents itself in two forms. The most extensive and conclusive may be called the indirect and inferential proof, which consists in these two facts when collated: 1st. That God is one. 2d. That not only the Father, but the Son and Holy Ghost, are proper God. This evidence presents itself very extensively over the Bible; and the two propositions may be said to be intertwined with its whole woop and warf. The other testimony is the *general direct testimony*, where *a plurality* in the one God is either stated or involved in some direct statement. The latter evidence is the one we present now; the former will become evident as we present the proof of the Divinity of the 2d and 3d Persons.

The text-books assigned to the students present a collection and discussion of those passages so complete, that I shall not make an unnecessary recapitulation. I shall only set down a list of those passages which I consider relevant; and conclude with a few cursive remarks on the argument in a few points. The student, then, may solidly advance the following testimonies, as cited and expounded by the Books.

From the Old Testament:

Gen. i: 2, with Ps. civ: 30; Prov. viii: 22, &c.

Gen. i: 26; iii: 22; xi: 7; Is. vi: 8.

Numb. vi: 24–26, may have some feeble weight when collated with Is. vi: 3, and 2 Cor. xiii: 14.

Hosea i: 7; Is. xliii: 16; Ps. xlv: 6.

The argument from the plural forms *Adonim*, *Elohim* it seems to me ought to be surrendered after the objections of Calvin and Buxtorff.

In the New Testament a very clear argument arises from the formula of Baptism. Matt. xxviii: 19. The only objections of any plausibility, is that from 1 Cor. x: 2—"Baptised unto Moses." In addition to the answers of Turrettin, it is surely sufficient to say, that this is a very different case from that where the names of the 2d and 3d persons are connected with that of God the Father in the same sentence and same construction.

Another indisputable argument is derived from the Apostolic benediction. 2 Cor- xiii: 14. See also Rev. i: 4, 5; 1 Cor. xii: 4-6.

The argument from the baptism of Christ seems to me possessed of some force, when the meaning of the Father's avowal, and of the Spirit's descent are understood in the light of Scripture.

The much litigated passage in 1 John v: 7, is certainly of too doubtful genuineness to be advanced, polemically, against the adversaries of the Trinity; however we may believe that the tenour of its teaching is agreeable to that of the Scriptures elsewhere.

LECTURE XV.

SYLLABUS.

DIVINITY OF CHRIST.

1. Prove that Christ is very God, from what the Scripture say of His *preexistence.*
   Turrettin, Loc. iii, que. 2-8. Hill, Bk. iii, ch. 3 and 4. Dick, Lect. 30th. Watson's Theol. Inst., pt. ii, ch. x.
2. What is the doctrine of the Old Testament concerning the proper divinity of the Messiah? And was He the person revealed in the theophanies?
   Hill's Div., Bk. iii, ch. 5. Hengstenberg's Christolegie, vol. i, ch. 3. Dick, Lect. 31. Watson, pt. ii, ch. xi.
3. Are the divine *names* ascribed to Christ?
   Turrettin, as above. Hill's Div., Bk. iii, ch. 7, § 1. Dick, Lect. 30, 31. Watson, pt. 2, ch. xii.
4. Are the divine *attributes* given to Christ?
   Turrettin, as above. Hill, as above, § 2. Dick, Lect. 31. Watson, as above, ch. xiii.
5. Are the divine *works* ascribed to Christ?
   Same authorities. Watson, as above, ch. xiv.
6. Is divine worship in the Scriptures rendered to Christ?
   Turrettin, as above. Hill, as above, § 3. Dick, Lect. 32. Watson, as above, ch. xv. See on the whole, Abbadie, on the Trinity. Wardlaw's Socinian Controversy. Moses Stuart against Channing. Evasions and objections to be argued under their appropriate heads.

A PRIME ARTICLE.—This may be called a *prime article* of revealed theology; affecting not only the subsistence of the Godhead, but the questions whether Christ is to be trusted, obeyed, and worshipped as God, the nature and efficacy of His atoning offices, the constitution of the Church, and all its rites. He who believes in the divinity of Jesus Christ is a Christian; he who does not, (whatever his professions), is a mere Deist. Without this Divinity, the Bible is, "the Drama of Ham let, with the part of Hamlet omitted."

ARGUED SCRIPTURALLY UNDER FIVE HEADS.—We have already established a trinity of persons in the Godhead; and this alone, if validly proved, would show the divinity of Jesus Christ. For where else in Revelation, than in the persons of Him and the Holy Ghost can the other persons be so naturally and plausibly found? But, not to urge this. the general strain of the language of the Old and New Testaments produces an overwhelming impression, that they mean to represent the Messiah as divine. Note the contrast between their descriptions of Him, and of Moses, the greatest of men; the fact that Jews have almost uniformly understood the New Testament as inculcating it, and thus rejected it as idolatrous; the laborious evasions to which Socinians are are obliged to resort; and the fact that the great majority of both friends and enemies have so understood it. If the Apostles did not *intend* to teach this doctrine they have certainly had the remarkable ill-luck of producing the very impression which they should have avóided, especially in a Book intended to subvert idolatry.

There is, as has been intimated, a general testimony for this truth, interwoven with the whole texture of Scripture, which cannot be adequately presented in a few propositions, because of its extent. It can only be appreciated by the extended and familiar study of the whole Bible. But the more specific arguments for the divinity of Jesus Christ have usually been digested into the five heads: of His *Pre-existence*, *Names*, *Attributes*, *Works*, and *Worship*. This distribution is sufficiently correct. My purpose will be, to employ the very limited space I can allot to so extensive an argument, first in giving you a syllabus of it, which shall possess some degree of completeness; and second, in illustrating some of the more important testimonies, so as to exhibit, in a few instances, the manner in which they apply, and exegetical evasions are to be quashed.

I. CHRIST'S PRE-EXISTENCE.—If Jesus Christ had an existence before He was born of the virgin, this at once settles the question, as Hill remarks, that He is not mere man. And if this pre-existence was characterized by eternity, independence, or divine works of Creation and Providence, it further settles the question that He was not a creature. The theophanies of a second person of the Godhead, if revealed in the Old Testament, [and if that person can be identified with Jesus Christ], as well as His works of creation, if ascribed to Him, will be parts of this argument for His pre-existence, as well as fall under other heads.

But we find a more direct testimony for His pre-existence contained in a number of passages, where Christ is said to have been "sent," to have "come from heaven," to "come into the world," to be "made flesh," &c., &c. See Jno. iii: 31; vi: 38; xvi: 28; xiii: 3; vi: 62; 1 Jno. iv: 23; Jno. i: 14; Heb. ii: 7, 9, 14, 16. Of one of us, it may be popularly said that we *came* into existence, came into the world; but these phrases could not be used with propriety, of one who then only *began* to exist.

Consult also, Jno. i: 1–17; iii: 13; viii: 58; xvii: 5; 1 Cor. xv: 47;

2 Cor. viii: 9; Heb. i: 10, 11; Rev. i: 8, 17; ii: 8; iii: 14; Jno. i: 15, 30.

Jno. i: &c.—In the passage, from Jno. i: 1–17, only two evasions seem to have a show of plausibility: 1st, to deny the personality of the Logos 2nd, to deny that His pre-existence is taught in the phrase, enarche. But the first is refuted by showing that the Logos is the creator of all: that in verse 4 He is identified with the Phos, which Phos again, verses 6, 7, was the object of John Baptist's preparatory ministry; which Phos again was rejected by the world, verses 10, 11, and this Phos, identical with the Logos, was incarnate, (verse 14), was testified unto by John Baptist, (verse 15); and is finally identified, (verse 17), with Jesus Christ, the giver of grace and truth. That the phrase, enarche, does assert His pre-existence is proved by the resemblance of it to the Septuagient rendering of Gen. i: 1. By the author's use of en, instead of egeneto, by His association with God, verse 2 showing a pre-existence similar to God's; by His creation of all things, (verse 3), and by the utter folly of the gloss which would make the Evangelist say that Jesus Christ was in existence when His ministry began. That John should have used the peculiar philosophic titles, Logos, and Phos, for Jesus Christ, is most reasonably explained by the state of opinion and theological language when He wrote His Gospel. The Chaldean Paraphrase, and the Platonizing tendencies of Philo and his sect, had familiarized the speculative Jews to these terms, as expressive of the second person; and meantime, the impious speculations of Judaizing Gnostics, represented by Cerinthus, had attempted to identify Jesus Christ with one of the *Aions* of their dreams, a sort of luminous emanation of the divine intelligence. It was to vindicate the truth from this folly, that St. John adopts the words Logos and Phos, in this emphatic assertion of the Messiah's proper divinity. See also 1 Jno. i: 1; Rev. xix: 13.

II. Divinity of Christ in Old Testament.—That the Messiah was to be *human*, was so clearly revealed in the Old Testament, that no Jew misunderstood it. He was to be the Son of David according to the flesh. It may seem somewhat incompatible with a similar disclosure of His proper divinity, that the Jewish mind should have been so obstinately closed to that doctrine. But the evidences of it in the Old Testament are so strong, that we are compelled to account for the failure of the unbelieving Jews to embrace it, by the stubbornness of prejudice, and death in sin. The Messianic predictions of the Old Testament have formed the subjects by themselves, of large volumes; I can, therefore, do little more than enumerate the most conclusive of them as to His divinity, giving the preference, of course, to those of them which are interpreted of, and applied to, Jesus Christ, by the infallible exposition of the New Testament. Compare, then, Num. xiv: 22, and xxi: 5, 6, and Ps. xcv: 9, with 1 Cor. x: 9. The tempting of the Lord of the Old Testament, is described by Paul as tempting Christ; in consequence of which they were destroyed of serpents. Ps. cii: 26, ascribes to God an immutable eternity; but Heb. i: 10, 11, applies it to Jesus Christ. In Is. vi, the prophet sees a vision of Jehovah, surrounded with every circumstance of divine majesty. But Jno. xii: 41, explains: "These things said Esaias, when he saw His glory, and spake of Him." Is. xlv; 22, 23. Jehovah says: "Look unto me, and be ye saved, all ye ends of the earth;" but Rom. xiv: 11, and 1 Cor. i: 30, evidently apply the context to Jesus Christ. Thus, also, compare Ps. lxviii: 18, with Eph. iv: 8, 9; Joel. ii: 32, with Rom. x: 13; Is. vii: 14, with Matt. i: 22; Micah. v: 2, with Matt. ii: 6, and Mal. iii: 1, with Mark i: 2, and Luke i: lxxvi. The three last pairs of references contain a proof peculiarly striking. In Is. vii: 14, the child born of a virgin is to be named *God with us*. In Matt. i: 22, a child, Jesus Christ, *is* born of a virgin, and receives, by divine injunction, through the mouth of an angel, the name *God with us;* because He was conceived of the Holy Ghost, and was to save His people from their sins. In Micah. v: 2, Bethlehem is destined to the honor of bringing forth the Ruler whose attribute was *eternity;* in Matt. ii: 6, it is declared that this prediction is fulfilled by the appearance of Jesus Christ. In Mal. iii; 1, the Angel of the Covenant is foretold. He is identified with Jesus Christ by his forerunner, John, who is expressly declared to be the person here predicted, by Luke i: 76. But that this angel is divine, is clear from his propriety in the temple ("his temple") which is God's house, and from the divine functions of Judge and heart-Searcher, which He there exercises. In Ps. cx: 1, David calls the Messiah *Adonai*, though His descendant according to the flesh. In Matt. xxii: 45, Christ Himself applies this to the Messiah ("What think ye of *Christ?* Whose Son is He?"); and challenges them (in substance) to account for it without granting His divinity. And this 110th Psalm, then proceeds to ascribe to this Being eternity of priesthood, (v. 4,) as expounded Heb. vii: 3, as having "neither beginning of days, nor end of life," supreme authority, and judgment over mankind. The Ps. 2, describes God as setting His King upon His holy hill of Zion: who is declared to be His eternal Son, (v. 7,) the Ruler of the whole earth, (v. 8,) the sovereign avenger of His opponents, (v. 9,) and the appointed object of religious trust. Surely these are divine attributes. c.) Jer. xvii: 5. But Acts iv: 25–28, attribute the whole prediction to Jesus Christ. So Ps. xlv: 6, call the king *God*, (Elohim,) and attributes to Him an everlasting throne. But Heb. i: 8, applies these words to the Son, afterwards defined to be Jesus Christ. So let the student compare for himself, (for time will fail me to go into explanation of every text,) Zech. xii: 10, with John xix: 37, Is. lxi: 1; (Speaker calls Himself I, the Lord, v. 8,) with Luke iv: 18–21. Examine, also, Is. iv: 2; ix: 5, 6, 7; xi: 4, 10; Ps. lxxii: 17, 5; Dan. vii: 13, 14. Zech. chap. xiii: 7, compared with xi: 13; xii: 10; Jer. xxiii: 5, 6.

Argument from the Theophanies and Angel of Covenant.—But a second important class of Old Testament evidences for the divinity of Christ, will appear when we inquire who was the Person who appeared in the theophanies granted to the Patriarchs. A personal distinction by which God the Father might disclose Himself to man in another person than His own, seems to be indicated by His nature. He is called the invisible God. I Tim. i: 17; Heb. xi: 27. It is declared that no man can see Him and live. Exod. xxxiii: 20; and we read, in the cases of some of the theophanies, that the persons favoured with them were amazed at their surviving the fearful privilege. Gen. xxxii: 30; Judges vi: 22, 23. But besides this concealed Person, who, though everywhere present, rarely makes Himself cognizable, and never visible to mortals, the New Testament, especially, informs us of another Person, the same in essence, whose office it has ever been, since God had a Church, to act as the mediating Messenger and Teacher of that Church, and bring man into providential and gracious relations with the inaccessible God. This function Christ has performed, both before and since His incarnation; and thus He is the Word, the Light, the visible Image to man of the invisible Godhead. See Jno. i: 9: i: 18; 1 Jno. i: 1, 2; 2 Cor. iv: 4; Heb. i: 3.

Yet this distinction cannot be pushed so far as though the Father never communicates with men, as the 1st person. Some of the very places cited to prove the divinity of the *Son*, show the *Father as such*, testifying to the Son. Ps. ii, and cx. And in Exod. xxiii: 20; xxxii: 34, language is used by *a* person, concerning another person, under the title of *angel*, which cannot possibly be identified as one; yet both are divine. It would be a great error, therefore, and would throw this whole argument into confusion, to exclude Jehovah the Father wholly from these communications to Old Testament saints, and attribute all the messages to the Son immediately. It so happens that *Moses* received these theophanies, in which we are compelled to admit the personal presence of the 1st person *per se*, as well as the 2d. May not this be the explanation, that He was honoured to be the Mesites of the Old Testament Church, in a sense in which no other mere man ever was: in that He communicated directly with the person of the Father? Exod. xxxiii: 11. Did not Jehovah Christ speak face to face to Jacob, Abraham, Manoah? &c.

Augustine's difficulty.—Another seeming difficulty presents itself (said to have been urged with confidence by St. Augustine and other Fathers) from Heb. i: 1, 2, and ii: 2, 3. The Apostle, it is urged, seems here to teach, that the Old Testament was distinguished from the New, by being *not* communicated through God, (the Son,) but through creatures, as agents. I answer, if the texts be strained into this meaning, they will then contradict the context. For the theophanies and other immediate divine communications must be imputed to a divine person, the Father, if not the Son; and then there would be no basis, on their premises, for the Apostle's argument, that the New Testament was more authoritative, because the teaching of a *divine* minister. The truth is, that the Apostle's contrast is only this: In the Old Testament the Messiah did not appear as an incarnate prophet, ministering His own message ordinarily and publickly among the people. (His theophanic *teachings* were always *private* to some one human agent.) In the New Testament He did. Nor can it be supposed that *The* Angel of Jehovah, who presented these theophanies, is explained by the di' Angellon, of Heb. ii: 2 He was wholly a different Being; their ministry was only attendant, and co-operative, at Sinai. (See Stephen, Acts vii: 53; Ps. lxviii: 17)

Instances of theophanies.—The 2d person seems to be identified in the following places: Gen. xvi: 7. *The* Angel of Jehovah found Hagar—v. 10; He promises to exert divine power—v. 11; claims to have heard her distress; and v. 13, Hagar is surprised that she survives the Divine vision. Gen. xviii, three *men* visit Abraham identified, xix: 1, as *angels*. The chief angel of these three, in xix: 14, 17, &c., makes Himself known as *Jehovah*, receives Abraham's worship, &c.

And in Gen. xlviii: 15, 16, this Jehovah is called by Jacob, "*the* Angel which redeemed me from all evil," &c., and invoked to bless Joseph's sons, a divine function. Again, in Gen. xxi: 17, *The Angel of God* speaks to Hagar, promising her, v. 18, a divine exertion of power. In Gen. xxii: 1, *Elohim* commands Abraham to take his son Isaac and sacrifice him. V. 11, when in the act of doing it, the Angel of Jehovah arrests, and says, v. 13, "Thou hast not withheld thy son from *Me;*" and, v. 14, Abraham names the place Jehovah jireh. In Gen. xxxi: 11, *the Angel of Jehovah* appears to Jacob in a dream, identified in v. 13, with God, the God of Gen. xxviii: 11–22, the God of Bethel then declared Jehovah. In Gen. xxxii: 25, Jacob wrestles with an angel, seeks his blessing, and names the place *Penuel.* This Angel is in the narrative called Elohim, and in Hosea xii: 4–6, describing the same transaction, Elohim, Angel and Jehovah of Hosts. In the same method compare Exod. iii: 2, with v. 4, 6, 14–16; Exod. xiv: 19, with v. 24; Exod. xxiii: 20, with subsequent verse; Exod. xxxii: 24, with xxxiii: 3, 4; Numb. xxii: 22, with v. 32–35; Josh. v: 14, to vi: 2; Judges ii: 1–4. Compare Judges vi: 11, with v. 14, 15, 18, 21, 22, &c. Judges xiii: 3, with v. 21. And Is. lxiii: 9; Zech. i: 12–15, compare vi: 15. Compare Zech. iii: 2, with v. 1; Ps. xxxiv: 8; xxxv: 5.

Conclusions.—Now, the amount of what has been proved in these citations is, that two Persons, both having unquestionable divine attributes, yet sometimes employing the incommunicable name in common, appear on the stage. They are distinguished by unquestioned personal distinctions of *willing, acting, feeling.* One is the Sender, the other is the Sent. (Malach.) The one usually acts with a certain reserve and invisibility, the other is called the "Angel of His countenance." Is. lxiii: 9. Compare with Col. i: 15; Heb. i: 3. To this latter the phrase, Angel of Jehovah is so often applied, that it becomes at length a proper name. And the completing link of the evidence is given by Mal. iii: 1–3. For there the "Angel of the Covenant" is, in the text itself, identified with Jehovah; and in Matt. xi: 10; Mark. i: 2; Luke i: 76; vii: 27, with Jesus Christ. Thus, these theophanies not only disclose a personal distinction in the Godhead, but show the divinity of Jesus Christ.

For objections, and theories of evasion, see Hengstenberg.

III. Names of God given to Christ.—The argument from the application of the divine *names* to Jesus Christ has been in part anticipated under the last head. To comprehend its full force, the student must recall the evidences by which we showed that Jehovah, especially, was God's *incommunicable name.* But in the New Testament this is not characteristically rendered, except by Kurios, which stands also for Adonai, and Adoni, (the latter applied to human masters.) Hence, it may be supposed that the Socinian evasion will be more damaging to all the argument from the cases in which the New Testament applies the terms Kurios, Theos, to Jesus Christ. That evasion, as you know, is that the titles, God, Lord, are applied in Bible language to Magnates, Magistrates, and Angels; and, therefore, their application to Jesus Christ proves not His proper divinity, but only His dignity. But let it be borne in mind, that if the language of the New Testament is deficient in the power of distinguishing the communicable from the incommunicable titles of God, it also lacks the usage of applying His titles to exalted creatures. There is no example of such a thing in the New Testament, except those quoted from the Septuagint. Hence, when the New Testament calls Christ Lord and God, the conclusion is fair, that it attributes to Him proper divinity.

SON.—But we argue, first, He is also called God's Son; and to show that this means more than when Angels, Church-members, &c., are called sons of God, He is called the *beloved Son*—God's *own* Son—God's *only begotten Son*. See Ps. ii: 7; Matt. iii: 17; xvii: 5; Dan. iii: 25; Matt. iv: 3; xxvi: 63; xxvii: 43, 54; Luke i: 35; Jno. iii: 18; x: 36; ix: 7; Rev. ii: 18; cf. v. 8. Here He is called Son, because He can work miracles, because begotten by the Holy Ghost. His title of Son is conceived by His enemies as a claim of proper divinity, which He dies rather than repudiate. The attempts to evade the force of the title *Only begotten* seem peculiarly impotent. One is, that He is so called, although only a man, because conceived, without Natural Father, by the Holy Ghost. Adam was still more so, having had neither Natural Father nor Mother. Yet he is never called only-begotten. Another is, that Christ is Son, because of His commission and inspiration. In this sense, Moses, Elijah, &c., were generically the same. But see Heb. iii: 1–6. The third is, that He is called God's only begotten Son, because He enjoyed the privilege of a resurrection. But the dead man of 2 Kings xiii: 21, the son of the Shunemite, and the saints who arose when Christ died, enjoyed the privilege earlier; and Enoch and Elijah enjoyed one still more glorious, a translation.

For the arguments which rebut the Socinian evasions on this head, the student must, for the rest, be referred to text Books and Comments. The following proof-texts will be found justly applicable:

Jno. i: 1, 2; x: 30; xx: 28; Acts xx: 28; (somewhat doubtful,) Rom. ix: 5; 1 Tim. iii: 16; Phil. ii: 6; Heb. i: 8; 1 Jno. v: 20.

TEXTS ADDED BY DR. MIDDLETON.—By the application of a principle of criticism asserted by Dr. Granville Sharpe and Dr. Wordsworth, of the English Church, and afterwards subjected to a most searching text, by Dr. Middleton on the Greek Article, this list of divine names applied to Jesus Christ may be much enlarged. Dr. Middleton thus states it: "When two or more attributes (i. e., adjectives, participles, descriptive substantives) joined by a copulative or copulatives, are assumed of the *same* person or thing, before the first Attributive, the Article is inserted, before the remaining ones omitted; e. g., Plutarch: ROSKIOS HO HUIOS KAI KLERONOMOS TOU TETHNEKOTOS &c., where HUIOS and KLERONOMOS, describe the one person Roscius. (Proper nouns, abstract nouns, and simple sames of substances without descriptive connotation, are exempted from this rule.) Its correctness is sustained by its consistent *rationale*, founded on the nature of the Article, by a multitude of classical examples, and by the manner in which the Greek Fathers uniformly cite the passages in question from the New Testament. They are to be presumed to be best aquainted with their own idiom. For instance, Eph. v: 5, we have EN TEI BASILEIAI TOU CHRISTOU KAI THEOU. Instead of rendering "Kingdom of Christ and of God," we should read, Kingdom of Him who is Christ and God. In Titus ii: 13, TOU MEGALOU THEOU KAI SOTEROS HEMÔN JESOU CHRISTOU, is rendered, "of the great God and (of) our Saviour Jesus Christ." It should be "of our great God and Saviour, Jesus Christ." See also 2 Pet. i: 1.

IV. ATTRIBUTES.—The names of God may not be incommunicable, and the application of them might possibly be ambiguous therefore; but when we see the incommunicable *attributes* of God given to Jesus Christ, they compose a more irresistable proof that He is very God. This is especially strong when those qualities which God reserves to Himself alone, are ascribed to Jesus Christ. We find, then:

Eternity clearly ascribed to Christ in Ps. cii: 26, as interpreted in Heb. i: 11, 12; Prov. viii: 23, &c. Is. ix: 6; Micah v: 2; Jno. i: 2; 1 Jno. i: 2; Rev. i: 7, 8, 17; iii: 14; xxii: 13; and the last three employ the very phrasology in which God asserts His eternity in Is. xliii· 10, and xliv: 6.

Immutability, the kindred attribute, and necessary corollary of eternity. Ps. cii: 26, as before; Heb. xiii: 8.

Immensity and *omnipresence*. Matt. xviii: 20; xxviii: 20; Jno. iii: 13: Col. i: 17.

Omniscience. Matt. xi: 27; Jno. ii: 24, 25; Heb. iv: 12, 13; Luke vi: 8; Jno. xvi: 30; xxi: 17; Rev. ii: 23, compared with 1 Kings viii: 39; Jer. xvii: 10. Here Christ knows the most inscrutable of all Beings, God Himself; and the human heart, which God claims it as His peculiar power to fathom.

Soveignty and *power*. Jno. v: 17; Matt. xxviii: 18; Heb. i: 3; Rev. i: 8; xi: 15–17. And, in fine, see Col. ii: 9; i: 19. The last subdivision will suggest the next head of argument, that from His divine works. But upon the whole, it may be remarked, that these ascription of divine attributes to Christ leave no evasion. For it is in the nature of things simply impossible that a finite nature should receive infinite endowments. Even Omnipotence cannot make a *part* to contain the *whole*.

V. WORKS.—Divine *works* are ascribed to Christ. Hill, with an affectation of philosophic fairness, which he sometimes carries to an unnecessry length, seems to yield the point to the Acrians, in part: that as God has endued His different orders of creatures with degrees of power so exceedingly various, He may have given to this exalted creature powers which to man appear actually boundless; and that even the proposition, that God might enable him to create a world, by filling him with His mighty power, does not appear necessarily absurd. But to my mind it seems clear, that there is a limit plain and distinct between those things which finite and dependent power can, by a vast extension, be enabled to do: and those for which all measures of created power are alike incompetent. There are many things which are superhuman, which perhaps are not superangelic. Satan may perhaps have power to move an atmospheric storm, before which man and his mightiest works would be a stubble. But Satan is as unable to create a fly out of nothing, as is man. For the performance of this kind of works, by deputation, no increase of finite power can prepare a creature. Moreover, to create a world such as ours, to direct it by a controlling providence, to judge its rational inhabitants, so as to apportion to every man according to his works; all this implies the possession of omnipressence, infinite knowledge, memory, and attention, as impossible for a creature to exercise, as infinite power. But, however this may be, Scripture always ascribes creation to God as a divine work. This is done, first, in many express passages, as Jer. x: 10–12; Ps. xcv; civ; Rev. iv: 10, 11; and second, by all those passages, as Ps. xix: 1–7, in which we are directed to read the greatness and character of God in the works of creation. If He used some other rational agent in the work, why is *Creator* so emphatically His title? And why are we so often referred to His works to learn His attributes? And once more, the most noted passages, as Jno. i: 1–3, in which creation is ascribed to the Son, contain most emphatic assertions of His partaking the divine essence; so that it is plain the divinity of the work was in the writer's mind.

The space allotted to this argument will forbid my going into the Socinian evasions of the several texts, tortuous and varied as they are. The most important of them may be seen handled with great skill by Dr. Hill, Bk. iii, ch. 3 and 4. But we clearly find the following divine works ascribed to Jesus Christ:

Creation of the world. Prov. viii: 23, 27, &c.; Jno. i: 1–3; Col. i: 15–17; Heb. i: 1–3, 10. And along with this, may be mentioned his sustentation of all things, asserted in the same passages.

Miracles, performed, not by deputed, but by autocratic power. Jno. v: 21; vi: 40; Acts iv: 7, 10; ix: 34; cf. Jno. v: 36; Mark ii: 8–11. Jno. ii: 19; x· 18: Rom. i: 4.

Forgiving sin. Mark ii: 10.

Judging men and angels. Matt. xxv: 31, 32; 2 Cor. v: 10; Rom. xiv: 10; Acts xvii: 31; Jno. v: 22. True, it is said that the Twelve shall sit on twelve thrones, judging the twelve tribes of Israel: Matt. xix: 22, and that the saints shall judge angels; but other Scriptures explain this, that they shall be merely assessors of Jesus Christ.

VI. Worship.—Last. The peculiar worship of God is given to Christ. See Matt. xxviii: 19; Luke xxiv: 52; Jno. v: 23; Acts vii: 59, 60; Jno. xiv: 1; and Ps. ii: 12, compared with Jer. xvii: 5; Acts ix: 14; 1 Cor. i: 2; Phil. ii: 10; Heb. i: 6; Rev. i: 5, 6; vii: 10; v: 13.

In connexion weigh these passages, as showing how unlikely the Scripture would be to permit such worship, (or Christ Himself,) if He were not proper God. Is. xlii 8; Matt. iv: 10; or Luke iv: 8; Mark xii: 29; Acts xiv: 14, 15; Rev. xix: 10; xxii: 9. Remember that the great object of Scripture is to reclaim the world from *idolatry*.

The Arian and Socinian evasions are well stated and refuted by Hill, Bk. iii, ch. 7, § 3.

LECTURE XVI.

SYLLABUS.

DIVINITY OF THE HOLY GHOST, AND OF THE SON.

1. What is the doctrine of the Socinians, Arians, and Orthodox concerning the Holy Ghost?
   Hagenbach, Hist. of Doctr., (Arianism.) Hill, Bk. iii, ch. 9. Turrettin, Loc. iii, que. 30.
2. Prove the *Personality* of the Holy Ghost.
   Turrettin, Loc. iii, que. 30, § 1-11. Owen on the Holy Ghost, Bk. i, ch. 2, 3. Dick, Lect. 33. Hill, as above. Dwight's Theology, (sub voce.) Knapp, Sect. xxxix.
3. Prove from the Scriptures the *divinity* of this Person.
   Turrettin, Loc. iii, que. 30, § 12-end. Dick, Hill, and Dwight, as above. Knapp, Sect. xl.
4. State the controversy between the Greek and Latin Churches, on the procession of the Holy Ghost. Which party was in the right? Why?
   Turrettin, Loc. iii, que. 31. Dick and Hill, as above.
5. Do the *offices* of the 2d and 3d persons *in Redemption* imply the possession of proper divinity by them?
   Turrettin, Loc. iii, que. 24. Dick, Lect. 32. Hill, Bk. iii, ch. 8, end.

1. History of Doctrine of Holy Ghost.—The Arian controversy was so fiercely agitated concerning the divinity of the 2d person, that the 3d Person was almost overlooked in it, by both parties. It is stated that Arius held the Holy Ghost to be a person—but a creature—the first creature namely, which the Son brought into existence by the Father's instructions, after His own creation. He was thus, ktisma ktismatos. On the other hands, few, perhaps, of the orthodox, except Athanasius, saw clearly the necessity of extending to Him likewise the same essence, (homoosion,) with the Father; and attributing to Him in the work of Redemption, proper, divine attributes. The most of them, e. g., a great anti-Arian writer, Hilary of Arles, contented themselves with saying, that He was a Person, and was spoken of in Scripture as a divine Spirit, and God's beneficent Agent in sanctification; but that farther than this, the Scriptures did not bear Him out. A little after the middle of the 4th century, *Mascedonius*, primate of Constantinople, was led by his semi-Arian views to teach that the Holy Ghost was but a name for the divine power and influences, diffused from the Father through the Son. It was this error, along with others, occasioned the revisal of the Nicene Creed, by the 2d Council of Constantinople. Yet even this, while attributing to the Holy Ghost a *procession from the Father*, and the same worship and glory attributed to the Father and Son, and while calling Him Life-giving Lord, still did not expressly ascribe to Him the phrase homoosion toi Patri. The consubstantial divinity of the Holy Ghost, however, continued to be the practical doctrine of the Church Catholic. When the Socinians, in the 16th century, sought to overthrow the doctrine of the Trinity, they represented all that is said of the Holy Ghost as mere parallel locutions for the Godhead itself, or as impersonations of the power, energy, wisdom, or general influence of the Godhead on

created souls. The words, Holy Ghost, then, are the name, not of a *Person*, but of an *abstraction*.

2. HIS PERSONALITY.—Hence, the first task which we should assume, is to learn what the Scriptures teach concerning the *personality* of this Being. We may premise, with Dick, that it is natural and reasonable that the Scriptures would say less to evince the personality and divinity of the Holy Ghost than of the Son; because in the order of the divine manifestation in Redemption, the Son is naturally and properly revealed first. The purchase precedes the application of Redemption. But after a plurality in unity was once established, it was easy to admit a trinity.

Now, we may freely admit that in several places, represented by Ps. cxxxix: 7, the word Spirit is a mere parallelism to express God's self. We may freely admit that were there no passages, except those in which the Holy Ghost is said to be shed forth, as in Is. xxxii: 15, it would not be proved that it might not mean only God's influences. But there are many others which admit of no such explanation. a.) A number of personal *acts* are attributed to the Holy Ghost as *creation*. Gen. i: 2; Ps. civ: 30, the Generation of Christ's body and soul. Matt. i: 18; Luke i: 35. *Teaching* and *revealing*. Jno. xiv; 26; xv: 25, 26. Gal. iv: 6: Rom. viii: 16; 1 Tim. iv: 1; 1 Pet. i: 11; 2 Pet. i: 21; Is. xi: 2, 3. *To search the decree* of God, 1 Cor. ii: 10. To *set apart to the ministry*, Is. lxi: 1; Acts xiii: 2; xx; 28. *To intercede*, PARAKLETOS, Jno. xvi: 7; Rom. viii; 27. *To have volitions.* 1 Cor. xii: 11. To regenerate and sanctify, Jno. iii: 6; 2 Cor. iii: 6; Eph. ii: 22, &c. Add here, as showing the personal agencies of the Holy Ghost, Luke xii: 12; Acts v: 32; xv: 28; xvi: 6; xxviii: 25; Rom. xv: 16; 1 Cor. ii: 13; Heb. ii: 4; iii: 7.

b.) The Holy Ghost is said to exercise the active feelings of a *person;* to be tempted, Acts v: 9; to be vexed, Is. lxiii: 10; to be grieved, Eph. iv: 30.

NO PROSOPOPOEIA HERE.—But here we must meet the well known evasion of the Socinian, who pleads that these are but instances of the trope of *Impersonation*, like those of Rom. vii: 11; iii: 19; 1 Cor. xiii: 7; Gen. iv: 10; Heb. xii: 24. We will not plead, with Turrettin, that the explanation is inapplicable to the Holy Ghost; because impersonations are usually of things corporeal and inanimate, as when the *blood* of Abel cried, &c.; for the case of 1 Cor. xiii: 7, proves that the Scripture does not limit the figure to this class of objects, but sometimes impersonates abstractions. The true answers are, that the Socinian explanation is inapplicable, because no candid writer uses an impersonation, without placing something in his context, or afterwards dropping the figure, so as to show unmistakably to the reader, that he meant *only* an impersonation. The force of this is only seen when the reader gathers the multitude of places in the Scriptures, where such language prevails, speaking of the Holy Ghost as though He were a person; and when he finds the utter absence of the proper qualification. b.) The explanation is impossible, because in a multitude of places the Holy Ghost is distinguished from the Godhead, whose impersonated attribute He would be on this supposition; e. g., when it is said, "charity suffereth long and is kind," the only possible meaning is, that the *charitable man* does so. When it is said God's Spirit will guide us into all truth, if the figure of impersonation were there, the meaning would be, that *God*, who is spiritual, will guide us. But in the very passage the spirit that guides is distinguished from God. "Whatsoever he shall hear, (i. e., from Father and Son,) that shall he speak." This leads us to argue:

c.) That the Holy Ghost must be a Person, because distinguished so clearly from the Father, whose quality or influence He would be if He were an abstraction; and farther, because distinguished in some places alike from the Father and Son; e. g., He is sent by both. Jno. xiv: 16; xv: 26; xvi: 7. The PNEUMA, though neuter, is construed with the masculine pronouns. Jno. xvi: 13; Eph. i: 13, 14. He concurs with the Father, and Son, in acts or honours which are to them undoubtedly personal: and, hence to Him likewise. Matt. xxviii: 19; 2 Cor. xiii: 14.

d.) His presence is represented by visible symbols, a thing which is never done for a mere abstraction elsewhere in Scripture, and is, indeed, logically preposterous. For the propriety of the material symbol depends wholly on some metaphorical resemblance between the *accidents* of the matter, and the attributes of the Being symbolized; e. g., Shekinah represents God; its brightness represents His glory. Its purity—His holiness. Its fierce heat—His jealousy, &c., &c, Now, if the dove, Matt. iii: 16, and the fiery tongues, Acts ii: 3, symbolize the Holy Ghost, and He an abstraction, the analogy has to be sought between the accidents or qualities of the dove and the fire, and the *attributes of an abstraction!* (Quid rides.) But moreover, in Matt. iii: 16, the three persons all attest their presence at once—the Father, in His voice from heaven; the Son, in His human person; the Spirit, in the descending dove. Here, surely, the dove does not personate an abstract attribute of the Father or Son, for this would be to personate *them* as possessing that attribute. But they, at the moment, had their distinct personal representation.

e.) The personality of the Holy Ghost is most plainly implied in the act of sinning against Him, committed by Ananias. Acts v: 3. Israel, Is. lxiii: 10; the Pharisees, Matt. xii: 31, 32. Some one may say: that 1 Tim. vi: 1, speaks of the sin of blasphomy against God's word and doctrine. Such an explanation is impossible in the above cases: and especially in Matt. xii: 31, 32. For if the Holy Ghost only represents an attribute of God, then to blaspheme that attribute is simply to blaspheme God. But in this case, the acts of blaspheming the Father and Son, is expressly distinguished from that of blaspheming the Holy Ghost, and have different grades of guilt assigned them.

f.) It is also implied that the Holy Ghost is a Person, by the distinction made between Him and His gifts. 1 Cor. xii: 4 and 8. If the Holy Ghost were an influence, or exertion of God's power on the creature, as He must be held to be in these places, by Socinians, then He would be virtually here, the gift of a gift! This leads us to notice a class of texts, in which the Socinian explanation appears supremely ridiculous; it is those in which the Holy Ghost is distinguished from the power of God. Now, if He be but a name for God's influences and energies upon the souls of men, the general word power, (DUNAMIS) ought to represent the idea of Him with substantial correctness.

Then, when Luke iv: 14 says: Christ returned from the desert to Galilee "in the power of the Spirit," it is equivalent to: "In the power of the power." Acts i: 8. "But ye shall receive power, after that the holy power is come upon you." I Cor. ii: 4. "And my speech and my preaching was not with enticing words of man's wisdom, but in demonstration of the power, and of power." Also Acts x: 38; Rom. xv: 13, 19.

The Holy Ghost then, is not an abstraction, nor an influence merely, but a Person, in the full sense in which that word is applied to the Father and Son, possessing will and active principles, intelligence, and action.

3. THIS PERSON IS DIVINE.—The next step is to prove His proper divinity; and this has now become comparatively easy. We follow the familiar order, showing that He has in Scripture the names, attributes, works, and worship of God. The principles upon which the argument proceeds, are the same already unfolded in the argument for the divinity of Christ. a.) We find Jehovah applied to the Spirit, by comparing Exod. xvii: 7, with Heb. iii: 9; 2 Sam. xxiii: 2, Is. vi: 9, with Act, xxviii: 25; *possibly* Jer. xxxi: 31, compared with Heb. x: 15. The name God, is by plain implication ascribed to Him in Acts v: 3, 4, &c., and 1 Cor. iii: 16, with vi: 19. The name *Highest*, seems to be given Him in Luke i: 35. b.) The *attributes* are ascribed to Him, as *omnipresence* implied by, (1 Cor. iii: 13,) and by the promises of the Holy Ghost to an innumerable multitude of Christians at once. *Omniscience*, 1 Cor. ii: 10, with v. 11; omnipresence, 1 Cor. xii: 13. The same thing appears from His agency in inspiration and prophecy. Jno. xvi: 13; 2 Pet. i: 21. *Sovereignty*, 1 Cor. xii: 11. c.) The works of God, as of creation, Gen. i: 2. Preservation, Ps. civ: 30. Miracles, Matt. xii: 28; 1 Cor. xii: 4. Regeneration and sanctification, Jno. iii: 5: 1 Cor. vi: 11; 2 Thess. ii: 13; 1 Pet. i: 2. Resurrection of the dead, Rom. viii: 11. d.) The worship of God is also attributed to Him, in the formula of Baptism, the Apostolic benediction, and the prayer of Rev. i: 4. Other passages cited seem to me of very questionable application.

OBJECTIONS ANSWERED.—Against the Spirit's personality, it has been urged that it is preposterous to speak of a Person as shed forth, poured out; as constituting the material of an anointing, as in 1 Jno. ii: 27; whereas, if the Holy Ghost is understood as only a name for God's influences, the figure is proper. The answer is, that the Holy Spirit's gifts are meant, when the giver is named, a most common and natural metonymy. The expressions are surely no harder to reconcile, than those of "putting on Christ," to be baptized into Christ. Eph. v: 30; Rom. xiii: 14; Gal. iii: 27.

To the proper divinity of the Holy Ghost it has been objected, that He is evidently subordinate, inasmuch as He is sent by the Father and the Son, and is limited in His messages by what they commit to Him. John xvi: 7, 13. The obvious answer is, that this subordination is only economical, relating to the official work to which the Divine Spirit condescends for man's redemption, and it no more proves His inferiority, than the humiliation of the Son His.

4. HISTORY OF QUESTION OF PROCESSION.—The Nicene Creed, as

settled A. D. 381, by the Council of Constantinople, had stated that the Holy Ghost proceedeth from the Father, saying nothing of any procession from the Son. But the Western Doctors, especially Augustine, leaned more and more towards the view, that His personal relation connected Him in the same inscrutable way, with the Father and the Son. As the Arian Christians of the Gothic nations, who had occupied the Western provinces of the empire, began to come into the Orthodox Catholic Church, it was judged more important, to assert the procession of the Holy Ghost from the Son equally with the Father, in order to eradicate any lingering ideas of a subordination of substance in the Son, which converts from Arianism might be supposed to feel. Hence, we are told, a provincial council in Toledo, A. D. 458, first enacted that the Latin form of the creed should receive the addition of the words, *filioque*. But this, although popular in Spain and France, was not adopted in Rome, even so late as A. D. 809, when Charlemagne endeavoured in vain to secure its adoption by the Bishop of Rome. But the Latin Christians were continually using it more extensively, to the indignation of the Greeks. This addition, as yet unwarranted, was the bone of contention (along with others,) throughout the 9th and subsequent centuries. The Latin Primate seems to have sanctioned the addition to the creed, about the 11th century, under the urgency of the celebrated Father, Vincentius of Lerins. In the great Council of Lyons, A. D. 1274, the Greeks, eager for a compromise, on account of the pressure of the Mohammedans, submitted to the Latin doctrine. But they soon returned to their old views with new violence. Again, in 1439, the kingdom of Constantinople, then tottering to its fall, submitted to a partial compromise, in order to secure Western support; and it was agreed in the Council of Florence (adjourned to Pisa,) that it should be said: the Holy Ghost proceedeth from the Father *through* the Son. But even this, the Greeks soon repudiated; and both parties have returned, ever since, to their opposition.

ARGUMENT INCONCLUSIVE.—To the dispassionate mind, the dispute cannot but appear of small importance, and the grounds of both parties uncertain. The basis on which the idea itself of an eternal and necessary relation of procession rests, seems to me scarcely sufficiently solid without the analogy of the Son. It is composed of the facts that the Holy Ghost is called the *Spirit*, (PNEUMA,) of the Father, (from PNEA,) and that in one solitary passage, (John. xv: 26,) it is said, He "proceedeth from the Father." All parties admit, that if there is such an eternal relation as procession, it is inscrutable. On the one hand, the Greeks rely on the fact that He is never said to *proceed* from the Son; and on the ancient view of the Greek scholastic fathers, that the Father alone is the ARCHE, OR PEGE THEOU. On the other hand, the Latins urge, that the Holy Ghost is stated to be related to the Son, in the Scriptures, in every way, except procession, just as He is to the Father. He is the "Spirit of the Son," as well as the Spirit of the Father, (and they suppose the very name *Spirit*, expresses His eternal relation as much as the word procession.) He is sent by the Son, and He is sent by the Father; He shows the things of the Son as much as those of the Father: for Christ says, (John xvi: 15,) "All things that the Father hath are mine." But as Dick well observes: unless it can be proved that spiration, mission, and speaking the things of Christ, exhaust the whole meaning of procession, the demonstration is not complete. And since the whole meaning of procession is not intelligible to human minds, that equality of meaning cannot be known, except by an express assertion of God Himself. Such an express word we lack; and hence, it appears to me, that this is a subject on which we should not dogmatize. Enough for us to know the blessed truth, that under the Covenant of Grace, the Divine Spirit condescends economically to commit the dispensation of His saving influences to the Son as our king, and to come at His bidding, according to the agreement, to subdue, sanctify, and save us. It may be said, that, as there is a peculiar point of view from which the grace, condescension and majesty of both the other persons are especially displayed, calling for our gratitude and reverence, so the same thing is true of the Holy Ghost. The Father condescends, in giving his Son. The Son is assuming our nature and guilt, and the Spirit in making His immediate abiding place in our guilty breasts, and there purging out the depravity, which His majesty and justice, as very God, would rather prompt Him to avenge.

5. Divinity of 2nd and 3d Persons proved by offices in Redemption.—The nature of the offices performed by the 2nd and 3d persons in redemption, imply and demand a proper divinity. This argument will require us to anticipate some truths concerning the mediatorial offices, and the doctrines of redemption; but I trust that sufficient general knowledge exists in all well-informed young Christians, to make the discussion intelligible to them. This argument is peculiarly important and interesting, although too little urged by theologians, ancient or modern. It shows that this high mystery of the Trinity has a most extensive *practical* aspect; and that the scheme of the Socinian not only impugns a mystery, but makes havoc of the Christian's most practical hopes.

Christ performs the work of our redemption in three offices, as prophet, priest, and king. The offices of the Holy Ghost, in applying redemption, connect themselves with the first in enlightening and guiding us, and with the third in converting us. I shall, therefore, couple the evidences of His divinity from those two offices, with what I have to say of the Son's under the same heads.

Christ and Holy Ghost, as Guides, must be Divine.—a.) Christ and His Spirit cannot be the *sufficient guides* of an immortal spirit, unless they have a truly infinite understanding. If our view be limited only to the preparation of a Bible for us, and all the constant, varied, endless, *inward* guidance be left out of view, then the wonder would be, how one moderate volume could be made to contain principles sufficient for an *infinite* diversity of applications. No human book does this. To draw up, select topics for, digest such a code, required omniscience.

But this is not all. We have daily inward guidance, by the Holy Ghost and providences applying the word. Now, so endlessly diversified and novel are the exigencies of *any one soul*, and so eternal and infinite the consequences connected it may be, with any one act, that it requires an infinite understanding to lead one soul, infallibly, through its mortal life, in such a way as to ensure safe consequences to all eternity. How much more to lead all Christians at once?

But this is not all. Saints will be *under duty* in heaven. They will be finite and fallible, though holy and wise. The number and diversity of moral exigencies to which each soul will be subjected in his immortality, becomes infinite. Hence, if He had only a finite wisdom to meet them, however high, the probability would at last become violent, that His wisdom would be inadequate, and he would err and fall. But Christ continues head of His people forever.

Christ, as Priest, must be Divine.—b.) As Priest, Christ must be divine. First: Unless above law, He could have no imputable active obedience. Second: Unless sustained by omnipotence, He could not have sustained the wrath of God for the sins of the world; and unless of infinite dignity, His atonement by a few years' suffering would not have been of worth enough to satisfy the law. Third: After the sacrifice comes intercession; and unless He had an infinite understanding, sleepless attention, and omnipresence, He could not attend to the petitions of so many at the same time. Here see how worthless are Popish intercessors.

Our King must be Divine.—c.) Christ, through His Holy Ghost, begins His kingly work with us, by "subduing us unto Himself." This is effected in the work of regeneration. Now we shall see, when we discuss effectual calling, that this is a *directly* almighty work. Our sanctification also demands *omniscience*. For he who would cure the ulcer, must probe it; but the heart is deceitful beyond all created ken. If the Holy Ghost, who is the practical, indwelling agent of these works, is a creature, then we have but a creature-redemption, no matter how divine the Beings that send Him. For the channel of communication to our souls being finite, the communications would be limited. If you have the whole Atlantic Ocean connected with your resorvoir by an inch pipe, you can draw but an inch of water at once. The vastness of the source does you no good, beyond the calibre of the connecting pipe.

Moreover, Christ has *all power* committed to His hand, for the church's good. It requires omniscience to comprehend this, and omnipotence to wield it. See Rom. viii: 38, 39; Eph. vi: 12.

In fine, all is enhanced, when we remember that our *stake* is the soul, our all, whose loss is irreparable. There is no comfort unless we have an infallible dependence.

LECTURE XVII.

SYLLABUS.

PERSONAL DISTINCTIONS IN THE TRINITY.

1. State the opinions of the Socinians, the Arians, and the Orthodox, concerning the *generation* and *filiation* of the Son.
   Turrettin, Loc. iii, que. 27 and 29. Hill's Divinity, Bk. iii, ch. 10, § 3, 4. Dick, Lect. 29. Knapp, Sec. xliii.

2. What were the opinions of the anti-Nicene Fathers, concerning the *subordination* of the 2d and 3d Persons, the three-fold generation of the Son, and the distinction of Logos endiathetos, and Logos Prophorikos.
The same citations. Knapp, Lect. xlii. Neander.

3. Prove the eternal generation of the Son; refute the common objections, and overthrow the Socinian and Arian explanations thereof.
Same citations. Watson's Theol. Inst., pt. ii, ch. xii, § v.

4. What is the difference between the generation of the Son, and the Procession of the Spirit? Can the latter be proved eternal?
Same citations.

I. The discussions and definitions of the more formal and scholastic Theologians, concerning the personal distinctions in the Godhead, have always seemed to me to present a striking instance of the reluctance of the human mind to confess its own weakness. For, let any one read them with the closest attention, and he will perceive that he has acquired little more than a set of *terms*, whose abstruseness serves to conceal from him their practical lack of meaning, It is debated whether the personal distinction is *real*, or *formal*, or *virtual*, or *personal*, or *modal*. Turrettin decides that it may best be called *modal*—i. e., as a distinction in the *modus subsistendi*. But what that mode of subsistence is, remains none the less inscrutable; and the chief reason why the term *modal* is least objectionable, seems to be that it is most general. After all, the mind must be content with these facts, the truth of which it may apprehend, although their full meaning cannot be comprehened by us; that there is an eternal and necessary distinction between the essence and the persons, the former being absolute, and the latter relative; that the whole essence is truly in each person, with all its attributes; that yet the essence is not divided or distributed between them, but single and indivisible; that the distinction of persons is one truly subsisting, subsisting eternally by the very necessity of the divine nature, and not merely relative to our apprehensions of it; and that the persons are not convertible the one into the other, nor the properties of the one predicable of another.

Personal Properties.—Each Person has its peculiar property, which is not indeed constitutive of, but distinctive of it. The property of the Father is *to be unbegotten;* of the Son, *generation;* and of the Spirit, *procession.* Hence, three characteristic relations—in the Father, *paternity;* in the Son, *filiation;* and in the Holy Ghost, *spiration.* That there are such properties and relations we know; *what* they are, we do not know.

2. Order of the Persons.—We find ourselves speaking almost inevitably of 1st, 2d, and 3d persons; thus implying some *order* in the persons. No orthordox Christian, of course, understands this order as relating to a priority of time, or of essential dignity. To what, then, does it relate? And is there any substantial reason for assigning such an order at all? We reply: There must be; when we find that where the three persons are mentioned by Scripture, in connexion, as in Matt. xxviii: 19, &c., &c., they are usually mentioned as Father, Son, and Holy Ghost, and not in reversed order; that in all allusions to the properties and relations of the three, the Father is always spoken of (e. g., the word *Father*) by some term or trait implying

primary rank, and the other two, by some implying secondariness; as Christ is *His* Son, the Holy Ghost *His* Spirit; they are *sent*, He the *Sender;* and in their working, there is always a sort of reference to the Father's primariness, (if I may coin a word,) as directing their operation. See also Jno. v: 26; x: 38; xiv: 11; xvii: 21; Heb. i: 3.

VIEW OF GREEK FATHERS THEREON.—But if it be asked, *what* is this primariness, the answer is not so easy. It was the usual answer of the ante-Nicene, and especially the Greek Fathers, that it indicated the order of derivation, that the personality of the Son is *from* that of the Father, not the Father's from the Son; and so of the Holy Ghost. (And so far it must be allowed, the fair force of the Scripture facts just stated, carries them properly enough.) The Father they regarded as ANAITIOS, as PEGE THEOU, or ARCHE THEOU, the Son and Holy Ghost as AITIATOI, as THEOI EK THEOU, and as deriving their personal subsistence from the eternal act of the Father in communicating the divine essence to them in those modes of subsistence. And this view was embodied in both forms of the Nicene Creed; of A. D. 325 and 381, where the Son is called "God of God, Light of Light, and very God of very God;" language never applied to the Father as to the Son. Their idea is, that the Father, the original Godhead, eternally generates the *person*, not the substance of the Son, and produces by procession the *person*, not the substance of the Holy Ghost, by inscrutably communicating the whole indivisible divine substance, essentially identical with Himself, in these two modes of subsistence; thus eternally causing the two persons, by causing the two additional modes of subsistence. This statement, they suppose, was virtually implied in the very relation of terms, Father and His Son, Father and His PNEUMA by the primariness of order always assigned to the Father, and by the distinction in the order of working. And they relied upon this view to vindicate the doctrine of the Trinity from the charge of tritheism. You will probably think, with me, that its value for this last purpose is questionable, for this reason: that the modes of subsistence of the persons being wholly inscrutable, the true answer to the charge of tritheism is to be found *for our minds*, in that fact, coupled with the Scriptural affirmation that God is *one* as truly as the persons are three. Hence, no explanation of the derivation of one subsistence from another really brings us any nearer to the secret, *How* it is one and three. But the answers, which the advocates of this Patristic view presented to objections, seem to my mind much more consistent than Dick would intimate. Was it objected, that they represented the 2d and 3d persons as *beginning* to exist, and thus robbed them of a true self-existence and eternity? These Fathers could answer with justice: No; the processes of personal derivation were *eternal immanent processes*, and the Father has a personal priority, not in time, but only in causation; e. g., the sun's rays have existed precisely as long as He has; yet the rays are *from* the sun, not the sun from the rays. And the 2d person may be *derived* as to His personality, THEOS EK THEOU, and yet self-existent God; because His essence is the one self-existent essence, and it is *only* His personality which is derived. They regard self-existence as an attribute of essence, not of person. Was it objected that these derived personalities were *unequal* to the 1st person? They answered; No;

because the Father put His whole essence in the two other modes of subsistence. Was it said, that then the personal subsistence of the 2d and 3d was dependent on the good pleasure of the 1st, and therefore revocable at His pleasure? They answered, that the generation and procession were not free, contingent acts, but necessary and essential acts, free indeed, yet necessitated by the very nature of the eternal substance. You will perceive that I have not used the word subordination, but *derivation*, to express this personal relation. If you ask me whether I *adopt* the Patristic view, thus cleared, as my own, I reply, that there seems to me nothing in it inconsistent with revealed truth; yet it seems to me rather a rational explanation of revealed facts, than a revealed fact itself. On such a subject, therefore, none should dogmatize.

Logos endiathetos, &c.—It may be well to explain, also, how the Rationalizing Fathers connected their theory of the Trinity with this generation of the Son. Attempting to comprehend the Divine essence, through the analogy of the human spirit, and according to the Platonic metaphysics, they said that the Son, or Logos, is God's Reason, or intellective action; and the Holy Ghost His Psuche, or emotive and vital activity. In the ages of eternity the Son was the Logos endiathetos or *Ratio incita*, God's reason acting only by self-comprehension, according to Prov. viii: 22; Jno. i: 2. When, in time, God began to effectuate His decree in works of creation and providence, He became the Logos prophorikos, or *ratio prolata*. When at length He was born of the flesh for man's redemption, He became the Logos ensarkikos, incarnate. Hence, the Father may be said to have made three productions of the Son—one from eternity, one when, in time, the Son was sent out as Agent of God's working, one when He was born of the Virgin.

3. Is Christ's Generation eternal.—This is the transition point, to enable us to comprehend the views of the Arians concerning Christ's generation. These heretics usually admitted the justice of the metaphysical explanation of God's immanent acts. But, said they, as the human mind has not *one*, but a numerous series of acts of intellection, noemata, so, *à fortiori*, the infinite mind of God. There is, of course, some primary noema, and this is the eternal, immanent logos of Jno. i: 2. There are other noemata in the divine mind, and some one of these is the one embodied, in time, in the creation of the *Son*, "by whom He made the worlds." Thus they endeavoured to reconcile the creation of the Son out of nothing, with the eternity of a logos. How worthless all this is, I need not say.

Scripture language thereon.—The Arians, like all others, heterodox and orthodox, find in the Scriptures ascriptions of a peculiar Sonship of Christ, needing some explanation. And we might as well array the more general of these Scripture representations here, as at a later stage of the discussion. I shall then pursue the method of bringing the several explanations of the Arian, Socinian, and orthodox, to the test of these Scriptures. The Messiah is called *the* Son of God, directly or indirectly, once in the Old Testament, and about one hundred and sixteen times in the New Testament; while no creature is ever called *the son* of God, in the singular number, except Adam.

Luke iii: 38. And there the peculiarity is accounted for by the fact that it was the Evangelist's purpose to show that Adam, like Christ, had no human father. Christ is God's beloved Son. Matt. iii: 17; xvii: 5; Mark i: 11, &c. He is the Son who alone knoweth the Father. Luke x: 22; Jno. x: 15; and who reveals Him. He claims God as "His own Father," in such a sense as to make the Jews believe that He made Himself equal with God. Jno. v: 17–19. He is a Son to be honoured as the Father is. Jno. v: 23. He doeth whatever He seeth the Father do. Jno. v: 19. He is *one* with the Father. Jno. x: 30. He is in the bosom of the Father, though incarnate. Jno. i: 18; and is the only begotten of the Father. Jno. i: 14; and PROTOTOKOS PASES KTISEOS. Col. i: 13. Here, surely, is evidence of some peculiar relation other than that borne by God's rational, or even His holy creatures generally.

ARIAN EXPOSITION.—Now, says the Arian, this Divine Creature is called *the Son*, and *only begotten*, because He is the first Creature the Father ever produced out of nothing, and the only one whom He produced immediately, by His own agency, all subsequent productions, including those of the Holy Ghost being through the agency of this Son. He is called *Son*, moreover, because He has received a peculiar adoption, is deputized God to other creatures, and a splendid creature image of the divine glory. He is also called Son, as being born by miraculous power of a virgin, and being constituted God's Messenger to fallen man. And last: He is Son, as being the Heir, by adoption, of God's throne, and glory.

SOCINIAN EXPLANATION.—The Socinian makes Jesus Christ only a holy man; and in his eyes His peculiar Sonship means nothing more than that He was born of a virgin without human father, that He was adopted by God, and endued with most eminent spiritual endowments, that He was sent forth as God's chosen mouth-piece to call a fallen race to repentence and obedience; and that He received the privilege of an immediate glorification, including His resurrection, ascension, and exaltation to God's throne.

A PECULIAR VIEW OF SOME TRINITARIANS.—But among Trinitarians themselves there are some, who give to Christ's *Sonship* a merely temporal meaning. They believe that the 2d and the 3d persons are as truly divine as we do; they believe with us, that there is a personal distinction, which has been eternal; but they do not believe that the terms generation and procession were ever intended by Scripture to express that eternal relation. On the contrary, they suppose that they merely denote the temporal functions which the persons assume for man's redemption.

SOCINIAN EXPLANATION FAILS.—Now, to begin with the lowest scheme, the Socinian: it utterly fails at the first blush of the contest. It does not explain why Christ is called *the Son*, while all other creatures are called sons in the plural only. It does not explain why He was the beloved Son, why He comprehended and revealed the Father, why He was of equal honour, and identical substance, rather than other holy creatures. It utterly fails to explain why He is *only beg tten*; for Adam was begotten by God's direct power, not only without father, but without mother. His endowments and His mission only differed in *degree* from those of other prophets, who were, therefore, in this sense, as truly *sons* as He. And last: His resurrection and glorification leave Him behind Enoch and Elijah, who were translated.

ARIAN EXPLANATION FAILS.—The Arian scheme also fails to explain how His Sonship made Him one with the Father, and of equal honour; how it capacitates Him to be the revealer and image of the Father's person and glory in a manner generically different from all other creatures; and how it proves Him *only begotten*. It leaves unsatisfied the declaration, that while they were KTISIS, He was PROTOTOKOS: and *begotten before every creature;* so that He would be produced in a totally different way from, and produced *before*, the whole creature class to which, on their scheme, He belongs! And last, like the Socinian scheme, it leaves wholly unexplained how a creature (therefore finite) *could* be competent to the exercise of *all the works he seeth the Father do*, and to a divine glorification.

ONLY AN ETERNAL GENERATION MEETS THE TEXTS.—Against the third view I would urge the general force of the passages I collected above. It may at least be said, that if it was not intended to teach that the permanent personal distinction was that of filiation, the Scriptures have been singularly unfortunate. But I shall proceed to cite other authorities, which are more decisive of the point. In doing this I shall be also adding to the overthrow of the Arian and Socinian views, by an *à fortiori* argument. For if a scheme of temporal filiation coupled with the admission of a true and eternal, though unnamed, personal distinction, will not satisfy the meaning of the texts; still less will the scheme of a temporal filiation which denies the eternity and divinity of the 2d person.

BECAUSE CHRIST IS SON, WHEN SENT.—a.) In a number of passages it is said, that God "sent." "gave," &c., *His Son:* e. g., Rom. viii: 3. "God sending His own Son, in the likeness of sinful flesh," &c. So, Jno. iii: 16; 1 Jno. iii: 8; iv: 9; Gal. iv: 4; Acts iii: 26. Now, who would dream that when God says, "He sends the Son in the flesh," He was not His Son before, but was made such by the sending?

SON, WHEN PRE-EXISTENT.—b.) The three Old Testament passages, Ps. ii: 7; Prov. viii: 22, 23; Micah v: 2, are advanced with great subtlety and force by Turrettin. He favours, for the first, the interpretation of the "to-day" ("have I begotten thee,") as the *punctum stans*, or eternal *now*, of the divine decree. The great objection is, that the idiom and usage of the Psalms does not sustain it. It is better, with Calvin and Hengstenberg, to understand the verb, "have begotten," according to a frequent Hebrew usage, as equivalent to, the manifestation, or declaration of His generation. This took place when Christ was revealed to His Church. The passage then does not prove, but neither does it disprove, the eternity of His generation. In this text, as well as Prov. viii: 22, 23, Turrettin argues the identity of the subject with Jesus Christ, with great force. In Micah v: 2; xxiv: 6, the application to Jesus Christ is indisputable, being fixed by Matt. ii: 6. The relevancy of the text to His eternal generation depends on two points—whether the phrase "going forth," MOTSAOTH, means generation or production, or only manifestation in action; and whether the phrase "from of old, from days of forever" means eternity, or only antiquity. As to the former question, we are shut up to the first meaning of generation by the usage. (Gesenius giving only "origin, descent,") and by the consideration that Christ's manifestation in action has not been eternal. As to the second question, the sense of proper eternity is certainly the most natural. The only plausible rendering besides the one giving by Turrettin is the one hinted by Gesenius: ("whose descent is from antiquity; referring to the antiquity of Christ's human lineage.) And manifestly this gives to the noun the perverted sense of *channels of descent* instead of *act of production*, its proper meaning.

Father is eternally Father.—c.) We find another argument for the eternal generation of the Son, in a number of passages, as the Baptismal formula; the Apostolic benediction; Matt. xi: 27; Luke x: 22; Jn. v: 22; x: 33–37; Rom. viii: 32; &c., &c. In all these cases the word Son is used in immediate connexion with the word Father, so that it is impossible to avoid the conclusion that the one is *reciprocal* to the other. The Son is evidently Son in a sense answering to that in which the Father is Father. But do these passages permit us to believe that the first Person here receives that term only because He has produced a human nature in which to clothe the Son, when the two first passages give an enumeration of the three divine Persons as making up the Godhead, presented in its most distinctive divine attitude, receiving the highest acts of worship, and all the others bring to view acts in which the Father and Son mutually share essentially divine acts or honours? It is plain that the paternity here means something characteristic and permanent; so, then, does the filiation.

Rom. i: 3, 4.—d.) In Rom. i: 3, 4; we read that the "Son of God was made of the seed of David according to the flesh, declared with power (horisthentos) to be the Son of God according to the Spirit of Holiness," &c. Here we not only find the evidence of head a.) that the Son was *made* flesh, and so was Son before; but the evident antithesis between the flesh and the Spirit of holiness, His divine nature compels us to read that His resurrection forcibly manifested Him to be *God's Son* as to his divine nature, even as he was David's as to his human. But if His filiation to God respects His divine nature, as contrasted with His human, the question is settled.

Christ is Son when Creating.—e.) I may group together two very similar passages, Col. i: 14–17; and Heb. i: 3–6. The Sonship is surely not merely the incarnation. when it is stated to be a begetting before every creature! The Son as Son, and not as incarnate only, is represented in both passages as performing divine functions, as representing the Father's nature and glory; whence we must infer that His Sonship is something belonging to His divinity, not His humanity merely. And in Heb, v: 5 and 6, the Apostle seem to aim explicitly to separate His Sonship from that of all others as divine and peculiar.

Objections.—It has been supposed that the following texts were repugnant to our view, by showing that the filiation had a temporal origin in Christ's incarnation and exaltation as as a mediatorial Person: Matt. xvi: 16; Luke i: 35; Jno. i: 49; seem, it is said, to imply that His Sonship is nothing else than His Messsiahship, and in Jno. x:

35, 36; it is said, He states Himself to be Son because sanctified and sent into the world by the Father. The answer is, that this argument confound the traits which *define* Him as Son with those which *constitute* Him the Son. To say that the Messiah, the Sent, is the one who is Son, is far short of saying that these offices make Him the Son. It is said that Acts xiii: 33; and Col. i: 18 refer the Sonship to his resurrection, the former of these passages especially, citing Ps. ii: 7 in support of that view. I reply, that it is only a mistranslation which seems to make Acts xiii: 33 relate to Christ's resurrection at all. We should read, in that God hath set up (as Messiah) Jesus: as it is written in the 2 Ps: "Thou art My Son: this day have I begotten Thee." Here we see a striking confirmation of the sense given above to this Ps. viz: that Christ's Sonship was declaratively manifested by His instalment as Messiah. In the Col. i: 18; Christ is said to be the PROTOTOKOS EK TON NEKRON. But evidently the concluding words should explain the meaning: "That *in all things* He might have the pre-eminence," in the resurrection of New Testament Saints, as well as in an eternal generation.

Once more it is claimed that Luke i: 35; plainly defines the incar, nation as the ground of the Sonship. The simplest reply is that the divine nature compare Rom. i: 4;) was never born of the virgint but only the humanity. This nature, thus united in the mediatorial Person, was called God's Son, because of its miraculous generation, so that the whole mediatorial person, in both natures, might be Son of God; that which is eternal, eternally Son, and that which is temporal, temporally Son.

General force of Words: Father—Son.—In fine, there is a general argument for the eternal generation of the Son, in the simple fact that Scripture has chosen this most simple and important pair of words to express a relation between the first and second Persons. There must have been a reason for the choice, there must be *something* corresponding to the well-known meaning of this pair of words, else eternal truth would not have employed them. That meaning must of course be compatible with God's immateriality and eternity, and must be stripped of all the elements arising from man's corporeal and finite nature and temporal existence. It is not corporeal generation, nor generation in time; but after stripping it of all this, do we not inevitably get this, as the *residuum* of meaning, that the personal subsistence of the Son is derivative, though eternal, and constitutes His nature the same with the Father's?

Personal Relation of Holy Ghost.—1. It is a remarkable fact, that while so many terms and traits belonging to *generation* are given to the 2d Person, not one of them is ever given in Scripture to the 3d. He is indeed "sent" as the Son is "sent;" but this is in both cases, not the modal, but merely the official term. The nature of the 3d personality is always represented by the word "breath," and his production is only called a "proceeding out." The inference seems fair, that the mode of personal subsistence, and the personal relation is therefore different from that of the Son. But as both are inscrutable, we cannot tell in what they differ. See Turrettin, Locus 3, que. 31, § 3.

Is it Eternal?—The evidence for the eternity of this personal relation between the Spirit and the other two Persons, is much more scanty than that for the eternity of the Son's filiation. In only one place Jno. xv: 26 is the Holy Ghost said to proceed from the Father. If that place stood alone, it could never be determined from it whether it was intended by our Saviour to define the mode of the eternal subsistence of the 3d person, or only to denote his official function in time. But beside the analogy of the Son's relation, we may infer with reasonable certainty that it intends an eternal relation. As his generation is not a mere commissioning in time, so the Spirits' procession is not a mere sending or an office in time. Otherwise the symmetry of the doctrine of the Trinity would be fatally broken, while the Scriptures hold out three co-ordinate Persons, eternally subsisting and related as Persons, *inter se*, we should be guilty of representing the 3d as bearing no permanent relation to the others.

LECTURE XVIII.

SYLLABUS.

DECREE OF GOD.

1. How do Theologians classify the acts of God?

Turrettin, Loc. iv, que. 1. Dick, Lect. 34.

2. What is God's Decree? Wherein different from Fate? What is the distinction between permissive and efficacious?

Conf. of Faith, ch. iii, Turrettin, *ubi supra*, and Loc. 6, que. 2, Dick, *ubi supra*, Calv. Inst. Bk. iii, ch. 21.

3. Establish the following properties of the decree, a) *Unity*, b) *Eternity*, c) *Universality*, embracing especially the future acts of free agents, d) *Efficiency*, e) *Absoluteness* from conditions f) *Freedom*, and g) *Wisdom*.

Turrett, Loc. iv, que. 2, 3 and 4. Hill Bk. iv, ch. 7, § 1-3. Dick, *ubi supra*. Watson's Theo. Inst. c . 26, § i. Knap, p. Sect. xxxii.

4. How may the objections be answered; a) That the Decree destroys free agency and responsibility; b) Supersedes the use of means, c) Makes God the author of Sin.

Turrettin, as above, Dick, Lects. 34 and 36.

I. God's acts classified.—Our study now leads us from the consideration of God's nature to His acts. Theologians have usually classified them under three sorts. The 1st are God's immanent eternal acts, which are wholly subjective. These are the generation of the Son, and procession of the Holy Ghost. 2d, are God's immanent and eternal acts having reference to objects out of Himself. This class includes His decree; and unchangeable and eternal act of God never passing over so as to cease to be His act, yet being relative to His creation. 3d, are God's transient acts towards the universe external to Himself, including all His works of creation and providence done in time.

II. Decree Proved by God's Intelligence.—"The decrees of God are His eternal purpose according to the counsel of His will, whereby, for His own glory, He hath foreordained whatsoever comes to pass."

Nature and Revelation concur to teach us that God is a Being of infinite intelligence, and of will. The eternal object of his cognition, as we saw, when investigating His omniscience, is nothing less than *the whole of the possible*; for the wisdom and selection displayed in the creation of the actual, show that there was more before the Divine Mind, than what was effectuated. But when we inquire for the *ground* of the difference between God's natural and his voluntary knowledge, we find no other than His volition. That is, the only way in which any objects can by any possibility have passed from God's vision of the possible into His foreknowledge of the actual, is by His purposing to effectuate it. God's foreknowledge embraces every being and act that shall ever be, as is proved by reason and Scripture (Acts xv: 18; Is. xlii: 9; xlvi: 10.) Hence his *purpose* must be of the same extent.

By His Power.—The same conclusion follows by a more popular reasoning from God's power; that power extends to all beings and events, and is the source of all existence. Now it is impossible for us to conceive how an intelligent Being can set about producing anything, save as He has the conception of the thing to be produced in His mind, and the intention to produce it in His will. Last of all can we attribute an unintelligent and aimless working to God. But if He is concerned in the production of all things, and had an intelligent purpose with reference to all which he produced, *there* is His decree; and His perfections, as we shall see, forbid our imputing any beginning to it. So the sovereignty of God, which regulates all the universe, the doctrine of His providence, so fully asserted in Scripture, and His concurring perfections of knowledge and wisdom, show that He must have a purpose as to all things. See Eph. i: 11; Ps. xxxiii: 11. Other passages, extending this purpose specifically to various departments of events, and especially to those concerning which the decree is most contested, will be cited in other connexions. These also are appropriate here.

Is the Decree in God Essentially?— The question whether God's decrees abide in Him essentially or accidentally, is but the same with that which we saw raised concerning the *simplicity* of the divine essence. The scholastic divines, in order to defend their metaphysical notion of this, said that God knows, feels, wills, &c., by His essence, or that God's knowledge is but His essence knowing, &c. As we then concluded concerning His knowledge, so I now say concerning his purpose. If it is meant that God's purpose is but God purposing, and as abstracted from Him, is but an abstraction, and not an existent thing, I fully concur. But in the same sense, the purpose of a human soul is but that soul purposing. The difference of the two cases is, that God's purpose is immanent and immutable, the mans' evanescent and mutable. To make the decree of God's essence in any other sense, is to give it essence; to make it a mode of the divine subsistence. And this trenches hard by the awful verge of pantheism. For if the decree is but a mode of the divine subsistence, then its effectuation in the creature's *existence* must still have the same essence, and all creatures are but modes of God, and their acts of God's acts. The decrees are not *accidents* with God, in the sense that, being the result of God's immutable perfections, they cannot change nor fail, but are as permanent as God's essence.

FATE, WHAT?—The doctrine of God's decree has been often impugned as no better than the Stoic's Fate. The modern, and indeed, the ancient interpreters of their doctrine, differ as to their meaning. Some, as Seneca, seem to represent *fate* as no other than the intelligent, eternal purpose of the Almighty. But others describe it as a physical necessity, self-existent and immanent in the links of causation themselves, by which effect is evolved out of cause according to a law eternally and necessarily existent in the Universe and all its parts. To this necessity Gods are as much subject as men. This definition is more probably the true one, because it agrees better with a pantheistic system, and such stoicism was. Now it is obvious, that this fate necessitates God as much as man, and that not by the influence of his own intelligence and perfections, but by an influence physical and despotic. Whereas our view of God's purpose makes it His most free, sovereign, wise and holy act of choice. This fate is a blind necessity; God's decree is intelligent, just, wise and benevolent. Fate was a necessity destroying man's spontaneity. God's decree, in purposing to make and keep man a free agent, first produced and then protects the exercise of it.

GOD'S DECREE EFFECTIVE OR PERMISSIVE.—God's decree "foreordains whatsoever comes to pass;" there was *no event* in the womb of the future, the futurition of which was not made certain to God by it. But we believe that this certainty is effectuated in different ways, according to the different natures of God's creatures. One class of effects God produces by His own immediate agency, (as creations, regenerations, inspirations,) and by physical causes, which are continually and immediately energized by His power. This latter subdivision is covered by what we call the laws of material nature. As to these, God's purpose is called *effective*, because He *Himself* effects the results, without the agency of other intelligent agents. The other class of effects is, the spontaneous acts of rational free agents other than God. The being and powers of these are derived from and dependent on God. But yet He has been pleased to bestow on them a spontaneity of choice, which makes them as truly agents, sources of self-determined force, in their little, dependent sphere of action, as though there were no sovereign force over them. In my theory of the will, I admitted and claimed as a great truth of our consciousness, that man's action is spontaneous, that the soul *is* self determined (though not the faculty of willing) in all its free acts, that the whole fountain of the volition is in the soul itself; and that the external object of the action is but the occasional cause of volition, Yet these spontaneous acts God has some way of directing, (only partially known to us) and these are the objects of His *permissive decree.* By calling it permissive, we do not mean that their futurition is not certain to God; or that He has not made it certain; we mean that they are such acts as He efficiently brings about by simply *leaving the spontaneity of other free agents to work of itself*, under incitements, occasions, bounds and limitations, which His wisdom and power throw around. To this class may be attributed all the acts of rational free agents, except such as are evoked by God's own grace, and especially all their sinful acts.

III. PROPERTIES—THE DECREE A UNIT.—The properties of God's decree are, 1st Unity. It is *one act* of the divine mind; and not many. This view is at least suggested by Scripture, which speak of it usually as a PROTHESIS, a "purpose," a "counsel." It follows from the nature of God. As His natural knowledge is all immediate and cotemporaneous, not successive, like ours, and His comprehension of it all infinitely complete always, His purpose founded thereon, must be a single, all-comprehensive and simultaneous act. Besides, the whole decree is eternal and immutable. All therefore must co-exist together always in God's mind. Last, God's plan is shown, in its effectuation, to be one; cause is linked with effect, and what was effect becomes cause; and influences of events on events interlace with each other, and descend in widening streams to subsequent events; so that the whole complex result is interconnected through every part. As astronomers suppose that the removal of one planet from our system would modify more or less the balance and orbits of all the rest, so the failure of one event in this plan would derange the whole, directly or indirectly. God's plan is, never to effectuate a result apart from, but always *by* its own cause. As the plan is thus a unit in its effectuation, so it must have been in its conception. Most of the errors which have arisen in the doctrine have come from the mistake of imputing to God that apprehension of His purpose in *successive parts*, to which the limitation of our minds confine us, in conceiving of it.

THE DECREE ETERNAL—OBJECTIONS.—2. The decree is eternal. One may object: that God must exist before His decree, the subject before its act. I reply, He exists before it only in the order of production, not in time. For intellection is His essential state, and His comprehension of His purpose may be as eternal as Himself. The sun's rays are from the sun, but measuring by duration, there were rays as early as there was a sun. It has been objected that some parts of the decree are consequent on other parts, and cannot therefore be equally early. I reply, the real *sequence* is only in the events as effectuated, not in the decree of them. The latter is a co-existent unit with God, and there is no sequence of parts in it, except to our feeble minds. It is said the comprehension of the possible must have gone before in the divine mind, in order that the determination to effectuate that part which commended itself to the divine wisdom, might follow. I reply: God does need to learn things deductively, or to view them piecemeal and successively; but His infinite mind sees all by immediate intuition and together; and in seeing, concludes. The most plausible objection is, that many of God's purposes must have been formed in time, because suspended on the acts of other free agents to be done in time; e g., Deut. xxviii: 2, 15; Jer xviii: 10. The answer is, that all these acts, though contingent to man, were certainly foreknown to God.

ARGUED FROM GOD'S PERFECTIONS AND SCRIPTURE.—Having thus cleared away objections, we might argue very simply: If God had an intention to act, before each act, when was that intention born? No answer will be found tenable till we run back to eternity. For, God's knowledge was always perfect, so that He finds out nothing new, to become the occasion of a new plan. His wisdom was always perfect, to give Him the same guidance in selecting means and ends. His power was always infinite, to prevent any failure or successful resistance, which would cause Him to resort to new expedients. His character is immutable; so that He will not causelessly change His own mind. There is therefore nothing to account for any addition to his original plan. But we may reason more comprehensively. It is, as we saw, only God's *purpose*, which causes a part of the possible to become the actual. As the *whole* of God's *scientia simplicis intelligentiae* was present to Him from eternity, a reason is utterly wanting in Him, why any part of the decree should be formed later than any other part.

And to this agree the Scriptures: Is. xlvi: 10; Matt. xxv: 34; 1 Cor. ii: 7; Eph. i: 4; 2 Thess. ii: 13; 2 Tim. i: 9; 1 Pet. i: 20. On these, two remarks should be made. Although they do not expressly assert the eternity of *all* God's decrees, several of them do assert the eternity of the very ones most impugned, His decrees concerning events dependent on free agent. In the language of Scripture, to say a thing was done "before the formation of the world," is to say it is from eternity, because with the creation of the universe began successive duration. All before this is the measureless eternity. In conclusion I add the express assertion of Acts xv: 18.

THE DECREE UNIVERSAL.—3. The decree is universal, embracing absolutely *all* creatures, and all their action. No nominal Christians contest this, except as to the acts of free agents, which the Arminians, but especially the Socinians, exempted from God's sovereign decree, and the latter heretics from His foreknowledge. We have seen that God's foreknowledge is founded on His foreordination. If then we prove that God has a perfect foreknowledge of all future events, we shall have virtually proved that He has foreordained them. The Socinians are more consistent than the Arminians here, in that they deny *both* to God. They define God's omniscience as His knowledge of all the *knowable*. *All* the future acts of free-agents, say they, cannot be foreknown, because a multitude of them are purely contingent; the volitions springing from a will *in equilibrio*. It is therefore no derogation to God's understanding, that He does not foreknow all of them, any more than it would be to the goodness of an eye, that it does not see what as yet does not exist. When free agents perform acts unforeseen to God, His wisdom, say they, provides Him with a multitude of resources, by which he overrules the result, and still makes them concur *substantially* (not absolutely) with His wise and good plans.

INCLUDES THE VOLITIONS OF FREE AGENTS.—Now, in opposition to all this, we have shown that the future volitions of free agents are none of them among the unknowable; because none contingent to God. We argue farther that God must have foreordained, and so foreknown all events, including these volitions: a.) Because, else, His providence would not be sovereign, and His independence, and omnipotence would be impugned. We have seen that the course of events is a chain, in which every link has a direct or remote connexion with every other. Into a multitude of physical events, the volitions of free agents enter as part causes; and if God had not a control over all these, he could not have over the dependent results. His government would be a capricious patchwork of new expedients. Because He could not control everything, He would not be absolutely sure of controlling anything, for all are inter-dependent. b.) God's knowledge would receive continual accretions, and hence His feelings and plans would change with them;

His immutability would be gone. c.) Prophecy concerning the acts of free agents would have been impossible. For unless *all* the collateral links of causation are under God's control, it may be that He will be unable to control a single result. But a multitude of the acts of the proudest, most arrogant and rebellious men were exactly and confidently predicted, of your Nebuchadnezzars, Pharoahs, Cyrus, &c., &c. To this last agree the Scriptures: Eph. i: 10, 11; Rom. xi: 33; Heb. iv: 13; Rom. ix: 15, 18; Acts xv: 18; xvii: 26; Job xiv: 5; Is. xlvi: 10. *men's volitions* especially including the evil. Eph. ii; 10; Acts ii: 23; iv: 27, 28; Ps. lxxvi; 10; Prov. xvi: 4–33; Dan. iv: 34, 35; Gen. xlv: 5; Is. x: 5–15; Josh. xi: 20; Pro. xx: 24; Is. xlv: 7; Amos iii: 6; &c. Add all those texts where the universality of God's providential control is asserted: for Providence is but the execution of the decree.

THE DECREE EFFICIENT.—4. Nearly akin to this is the remark that the decree is efficient. By this I mean that God's purpose is in every case absolutely sure to be effectuated. Nearly all the arguments adduced under the last head apply here: God's sovereignty, God's wisdom, His independence, and the dependence of all other things on Him, the "immutability of His counsel," and of His knowledge and other attributes, the certainty of His predictions, all demand that "His counsel shall stand, and He shall do all His pleasure." See Matt. xxvi: 54; Luke xxii: 22; Acts iv: 28; Prov. xvi: 33; Matt. x: 29–30. Here we see that things most minute, most contingent in our view of them, and most voluntary are yet efficaciously produced by God.

OVER FREE AGENTS ALSO.—The Arminians have too much reverence for God's perfections to limit His knowledge as to the actions of free agents. But they endeavor to evade the inevitable conclusion of the decree, and to save their favorite doctrine of conditional purposes by limiting His concern with the acts, and especially sins, of free agents, to a *mere* foreknowledge, permission, and intention to make the permitted act a condition of some part of the decree. I urge that they who concede so much, cannot consistently stop there. If the sinful act (to take the strongest case against the Calvinist,) of the free agent has been from eternity *certainly* foreseen by God, then its occurrence must be certain. But in this universe nothing comes without a cause; there must therefore be some *ground* for the certainty of its occurrence. And it is upon that ground that God's foreknowledge of it rests. Do you ask what that ground is? I reply by asking: How does God's knowledge of the possible pass into his knowledge of the actual? Only by His determining to secure the occurrence of all the latter. Conceive of God as just now about to create a free agent, according to His plan, and launch him out on his path of freedom. If God *foreknows* all that the free agent will choose to do, if created; does He not purpose the doing of all this when He creates Him? To deny this is a contradiction. We may not be able to see fully how God certainly procures the doing of such acts by free agents, still leaving them to act purely from their own spontaneity: but we cannot deny that He does, without overthowing His sovereignty and foreknowledge. Such events may be wholly contingent to man; but to God none of them can be contingent; else all the parts of His decree connected as effect with them as causes, would be in the same degree contingent. Thus God could scarcely have any eternal foreknowledge or decree at all, as to free agents or anything connected with them.

5. THE DECREE NOT CONDITIONAL.—We are now prepared to approach the proposition, that God's act in forming His decree is unconditioned on anything to be done by His creatures. In another sense, a multitude of *the things decreed* are conditional; God's whole plan is a wise unit, linking means with ends, and causes with effects. In regard to each of these effects, the occurrence of it is conditional on the presence of its cause, and is made so dependent by God's decree itself. But while the *events decreed* are conditional, God's act in forming the decree is not conditional, on anything which is to occur in time; because in the case of each dependent event, His decree as much determined the occurrence of the cause, as of its effect. And this is true equally of those events in His plan dependent on the free acts of free agents. No better illustration can be given, of the mode in which God decrees dependent or conditioned events, absolutely, by equally decreeing the conditions through which they are to be brought about, than Acts xxvii: 22 with 31. The Arminian admits that all such intermediate acts of men were eternally *foreseen* of God, and thus embraced in His plan as conditions: but not *foreordained*. We reply: if they were certainly foreseen, their occurrence was certain; if this was certain, then there must have been *something* to determine that certainty; and that something was either God's wise foreordination, or a blind physical fate. Let the Arminian choose.

But the eternity of the decree already proved shows that its formation did not depend on the creature; for all that was conditional on His contingent act must have hung in suspense in God's mind until after the act occurred. Therefore, the condition never was contingent to God, i. e., as above explained, it was also foredetermined by the same decree.

The immutability of God's decree argues the same, and in the same way. If the condition on which His results hung were truly contingent, then it might turn out in one or another of several different ways. Hence it would always be possible that God might have to change His plans.

It is equally plain that His sovereignty would no longer be entire: but God would be dependent on His creatures for ability to effectuate many of His plans; and some might fail in spite of all He could do. I have already indicated that God's foreknowledge of the conditions, and of all dependent on them, could not possibly be certain. For if a thing is not certain to occur, a certain expectation that it will occur, is an erroneous one. Hence, the Arminian is driven by consistency to the impious conclusions of the Socinian, limiting God's knowledge.

But Arminians are exceedingly fond of saying, that the dream of absolute decrees is a metaphysical invention not sustained by Scripture, and only demanded by consistency with other unhallowed human speculation. Hence I shall take pains, as on other points, to show that it is expressly the doctrine of Scripture. Here may be cited all the proofs by which I showed that the decree is *universal* and *efficacious*. For the very conception of the matter which I have inculcated is, that *events are* conditioned on events, but that the decree is not, because it embraces the conditions as efficaciously as the results. See also Ps. xlvi; 10, 11; Rom. ix: 11; Matt. xi: 25, 26; Eph. i: 5 and 11; Is. xl: 13; Rom. ix: 15–18: Acts ii: 23; iii: 18; Gen. l: 20.

His decree includes means and conditions. 2 Thess. ii: 13; 1 Pet. i: 2: Eph. i: 4; Phil. ii: 13; Eph. ii: 8; 2 Tim. ii: 25.

Does this make God the author of sin?—But against this view objections are urged with great clamour and confidence. They may be summed up into two: that absolute decrees make God the author of of sin, and that the Scriptures contradict our view by displaying many conditional threats and promises of God, e. g., Ezek. xviii: 21; Ps. lxxxi: 13, 14; &c., &c., and some cases in which decrees were actually revoked and changed in consequence of men's conduct, as 1 Sam. xiii: 13; Luk. vii: 30.

That God is not, and connot be the author of sin, is plain from express Scripture, Jas. i: 13, 7; 1 Jno. i: 5; Eccl. vii: 29; Ps. xcii: 15; from God's law, which prohibits all sin; from the holiness of His nature, which is incapable of it; and from the nature of sin itself, which must be *man's* own free activity, or else is not responsible and guilty. But I remark, 1st, that so far as the great mystery of God's permission of sin enters into this objection, our minds are incapable of a complete explanation. But this incapacity is precisely the same, whatever scheme we adopt for accounting for it, unless we deny to God complete foreknowledge and power. 2. The simple fact that God clearly foresaw every sin the creature would commit, and yet created him, is attended with all the difficulty which attaches to our view. But that foresight the Arminian admits. By determining to create the creature, foreknowing that he would sin, God obviously determined the occurrence of the sin, through the creature's free agency; for at least He could have refrained from creating him. But this is just as strong as our view of the case involves. The Arminian pleads: Yea, but God determined to create a creature who, He foresaw would sin, not for the sake of the sin, but for the sake of the good and holy ends connected there with. I reply, 3d. Well, the very same plea avails for us. We can say just as consistently: God purposed to produce these free agents, to sustain their free agency untrammeled, to surround them with outward circumstances of a given kind, to permit that free agency, moved by those circumstances as *occasional causes*, to exert itself in a multitude of acts, some sinful, not for the sake of the sin, but for the sake of some good and holy results which His infinite wisdom has seen best to connect therewith. Last, in the sinful act, the agency and choice is the sinner's alone; because the inscrutable modes God has for effectuating the certain occurrence of His volitions never cramp or control the creatures spontaneity: as conciousness testifies.

Objected that God's threats and promises are conditional.—The second class of objections Arminians also advance with great confidence; saying that unless we are willing to charge God with insincerity, His conditional promise or threat must be received by us *as an exact disclosure of His real purpose.* Let us test this in any case, such as our adversaries usually select: e. g., Is. i: 19: "If ye be willing and obedient, ye shall eat the good of the land." Did not God *know*, at the time He uttered these words that they would not be willing and obedient? See ch. vi: 10–12. Was it not His fixed intention, at that very moment to deprive them of the good of the land, in consequence of their clearly foreseen disobedience? Here then is the very same ground for the pretended charge of insincerity in God. The truth is, that God's preceptive threats and promises are *not* a disclosure of His secret purpose. But the distinction between His secret and revealed will, is one which is inevitably made by every thinking mind, and is absolutely unavoidable, unless man's mind can become as capacious as God's. And see Deut. xxix: 29. Nor does this impugn God's sincerity. The sophism of the Arminian is just that, in this case, already pointed out: counfounding conditionality of events decreed, with conditionality of God's decree. God purposed, in this case, that the event, Israel's punishment, should be conditioned on the other event, their disobedience. So that His conditional promise was perfectly truthful. But He also purposed, secretly, to withhold that undeserved constraining grace, which might have prevented Israel's disobedience, so that the condition, and the thing conditioned on it should both come to pass. Again, the idea that God has revocable decrees, is as utterly incompatible with the foreknowledge of man's free acts, as with their foreordination. When it said that the Pharisees rejected the counsel of God concerning themselves, the word counsel means but *precept*, cf. Ps. cvii: 11; Prov. i: 25, 30; Rev. iii: 18.

THE DECREE FREE.—6. The *freedom* of God's decree follows from what has been already argued. If it was eternal, then, when it was formed, there was no Being outside of Himself to constrain or be the motive of it. If absolute, then God was *induced* to it by no act of other agents, but only by His own perfections. And this leads us to remark, that when we say the decree is *free*, we do not mean God's acts in forming it, in disregard of His own perfections, *but under the guidance of His own perfections alone.* Ps. xv: 3; Eph. i: 5.

7. The *wisdom* of God's decree is manifest from the wisdom of that part of His plan which has been unfolded. Although much there is inscrutable to us, we see enough to convince us that all is wise. Rom. xi: 33, 34.

DOES THE DECREE SUPERSEDE MEANS?—IV. Of the general objections against the decree of God, to which I called your attention, two remain to be noticed. One is, that if it were true, it would supersede the use of all means. "If what is to be will be, why trouble ourselves with the useless and vain attempt either to procure or prevent it?"

This popular objection is exceedingly shallow. The answer, is that the use of the means, where free agents are concerned, is just as much included in the decree, as the result. God's *purpose* to institute and sustain the laws of causation in nature, is the very thing which gives efficacy to means, instead of taking it away. Further, both Scripture and consciousness tell us, that in using man's acts as means, God's infinite skill does it always without marring His freedom in the least.

IS IT INCONSISTENT WITH FREE AGENCY?—But it is objected, second, that if there were an absolute decree, *man could not be free*; and so, could not be responsible. But consciousness and God's word assure us we are free. I reply, the facts cannot be incompatible because Scripture most undoubtedly asserts both, and both together. See Is. x: 5 to 15;

Acts ii: 23. Second, Feeble man procures free acts from his fellow-man, by availing himself of the power of circumstances as inducements to his known dispositions, and yet he regards the agents as free and responsible, and the agent so regards himself. If man can do this sometimes, why may not an infinite God do it all the time? Third, If there is anything about absolute decrees to impinge upon man's freedom of choice, it must be in their *mode of execution*, for God's merely *having* such a purpose in His secret breast could affect man in no way. But Scripture and consciousness assure us that God executes this purpose as to man's acts, not against, but through and with man's own free will. In producing spiritually good acts, He "worketh in man *to will* and to do;" and "makes him willing in the day of his power." And in bringing about bad acts, He simply *leaves* the sinner in circumstances such that he does, of himself only, yet certainly, choose the wrong. Last, This objection implies that man's acts of choice could not be free, unless contingent and uncaused. But we have seen that this theory of the will is false, foolish, and especially destructive to rational liberty.

LECTURE XIX.

SYLLABUS.

PREDESTINATION.

1. Wherein are the terms *Predestination* and *Election* distinguished from God's *Decree*? What the usage and meaning of the original words, PROGNOSIS EKLOGE and cognates?
   Turret. Loc. iv, que. 7, Dick, Lect. 35, Conf. of F., ch. 3.
2. Prove that there is a definite election of individual men to salvation, whose number can neither be increased nor diminished.
   Turret. Loc. iv, ques. 12, 16, Conf. of F., ch. 3, Calv. Inst. Bk. iii. chs. 21, 22. Dick, Lect. 35. Hill's Div., Bk. iv, ch. 7. Burnet on 39 Articles. Art. xvii, Knapp, sect. xxxii. Watson's Theo. Inst., ch. xxvi, § 1, 2.
3. Has the decree of predestination the qualities predicated of the whole decree.
   Dick, Lect. 35.
4. Does predestination embrace angels as well as men; and with the same kind of Decree?
   Turrettin, Loc. iv, que. 8.
5. State the differences between the *Sublapsarian* and *Supralapsarian* schemes. Which is correct?
   Dick, Lect. 35. Turett. Loc. iv, ques. 9th, 14th and 18th, § 1-5. Burnet, as above.

DEFINITIONS.—I. While God's decree is His purpose as to *all* things, His *predestination* may be defined to be His purpose concerning the everlasting destiny of His rational creatures. His *election* is His purpose of saving eternally some men and angels. Election and reprobation are both included in predestination. The word PROORISMOS, the proper original for predestination does not occur in this connexion in the New Testament, but the kindred verb and participle are found in the following passages, describing God's foreordination of the religious state or acts of persons: Acts iv: 28: Rom. viii: 29, 30; Eph. i: 5; Luk. xxii: 22. That this predetermination of men's privileges and destinies by God includes the reprobation of the wicked, as well as the election of the saints, will be established more fully in the next lecture.

The word PROGNOSIS PROGINOSKO, as applied to this subject, means more than a simple inactive cognition of the future state of men by God, a positive or active selection. This is proved by the Hebraistic usage of this class of words; as in 1 Thess. v: 12; Jno. x: 14; Ps. i: 6; 2 Tim. ii: 19; and by the following passages, where the latter meaning is indisputable: Rom. xi: 2; 1 Pet. i: 20. This will appear extremely reasonable, when we remember that according to the order of God's acts, His foreknowledge is the effect of His foreordination.

EKLOGE, EKLEGO are used for various kinds of selection to office, &c., and once, by metonymy, for the body of Elect, Rom. xi: 7. When applied to God's call to religious privilege or to salvation, it is sometimes inclusive of effectual calling; as Jno. xv: 16, 19. Arminians would make this all of election: but that it means a prior and different selection is plain in Matt. xx: 16; 2 Thes. ii: 13. The words PROTHESIS, Rom. viii: 28; ix: 11; Eph. i: 11; and TASSO, Acts xiii: 48, very clearly express a foreordination of God as to man's religious state.

PROPOSITIONS.—II. "By the decree of God, for the manifestation of His own glory, some men and angels are predestinated unto everlasting life, and others foreordained to everlasting death."

"These angels and men, thus predestinated and foreordained, are particularly and unchangeably designed; and their number is so certain and definite, that it cannot be either increased or diminished.."

PREDESTINATION OF MEN PROVED. FROM DECREE.—To discuss this thesis, first, as to men. I would argue *first:* From the general doctrine of decrees. The decree is universal. If God has anything to do with the sinner's redemption, it must be embraced in that decree. But salvation is everywhere attributed to God, as His work. *He* calls. *He* justifies. *He* regenerates. *He* keeps us by faith unto salvation. *He* sanctifies. All the arguments drawn from God's attributes of wisdom, infinite knowledge, omnipotence, and immutability, in support of His eternal decree, show that His agency in saving the sinners who are saved, *is a purposed one*, and that this purpose is eternal. Ps. xxxiii: 10: Numb. xxiii: 19; Mal. iii: 6; Jas. i: 17; Heb. vi: 17.

Second. FROM ORIGINAL SIN.—The same thing follows from what Scripture and observation teach us of the heart of all men. We are by nature ungodly, hostile to God, and His law, blind in mind, and certainly determined to worldliness in preference to godliness, by a native disposition. Hence, no man cometh to Christ, except the Father who hath sent Him draw him. Unless some power above man made the difference between the believer and unbeliever, it would never vitally appear. But if God makes it, He does it of purpose, and that purpose must be eternal. Hence, no intelligent mind which admits original sin, denies election. The two doctrines stand or fall together.

Third. FROM SCRIPTURE TESTIMONIES.—A number of passages of Scripture assert God's election of individuals, in language too clear to be evaded: Matt. xxiv; 24; Jno. 15: 16; Acts xiii: 48; Rom. viii: 29, 30; ix: 11; xvi; 22–24; xi: 5, 7; Eph. i: 4; v: 11; Phil. iv: 3; 2 Tim. i: 9; 2 Tim. ii: 19. The most of these you will find commented on in your text books, in such a manner as effectually to clear them of the evasions of adversaries. *Fourth*, The Saints have their names "written in the book of life," or in "the Lamb's book," or "in Heaven." See Phil. iv: 3; Heb. xii: 23; Rev. xiii: 8.

PREDESTINATION MORE THAN SELECTION OF A CHARACTER TO BE FAVOURED.—This class of passages is peculiarly convincing; and especially against that phase of error, which makes God's election nothing else than a determination that whosoever believes and repents shall be saved, or in other words, a selection of a certain quality or trait, as the one which procures for its possessors the favour of God. This feeble notion may be farther refuted by remarking that all the language employed about predestination is personal, and the pronouns and other adjuncts indicate persons and not classes. It is "*whom* (masculine) He foreknew, them He also did predestinate." It is "As many as were ordained to eternal life, believed," (masc.) Acts xiii: 48. Again; a mere determination to bestow favour on the possessors of certain qualities, would be inert and passive as to the propagation of those qualities; whereas God's election propagates the very qualities. See Rom. ix: 11, 18, 22, 23; Eph. i: 4, 5; 2 Thess. ii: 13. "He hath chosen *us* to salvation *through*, &c." And once more: were this determination to bestow favour on faith and penitence the whole of election, no one would ever possess those qualities; for, as we have seen, all men's hearts are fully set in them to do evil, and would certainly continue impenitent did not God, out of His gracious purpose, efficaciously persuade some to come to Him. These qualties which are thus supposed to be elected, are themselves the consequences of election.

PREDESTINATION PROVED BY PROVIDENCE.—Fifth, A most convincing proof of a very practical nature may be derived from the observed course of God's providence. That providence determines sovereignly the metes and bounds of each man's outward privileges, of his life and opportunities. It determines whether he shall be born and live in a Pagan, or a Christian country, how long he shall enjoy means of grace, and of what efficacy, when and where he shall die. Now in deciding these things sovereignly, the salvation or loss of the man's soul is practically decided, for without time, means, and opportunity, he will not be saved. This is peculiarly strong as to two classes, Pagans and infants. Arminians admit a sovereign election of nations in the aggregate to religious privileges, or rejection therefrom. But it is indisputable that in so fixing their outward condition, the religious fate is virtually *fixed* forever. What chance has that man practically, for reaching Heaven, whom God caused to be born, to live, to die, in Tahiti in the Sixteenth century? Did not the casting of his lot there virtually fix his lot for eternity? In short, the sovereign election of aggregate *na-*

tions to privilege necessarily implies, with such a mind as God's, the intelligent and intentional decision of the fate of individuals, practically fixed thereby. Is not God's mind infinite? Are not his perceptions perfect? Does He like a feeble mortal, "shoot at the covey, without perceiving the individual birds?" As to infants, Arminians believe that all such, which die in infancy, are redeemed. When, therefore, God's providence determines that a given human being shall die an infant, He infallibly determines its redemption, and in this case, at least, the decision cannot have been by foresight of faith, repentance, or good works; because the little soul has none, until after its redemption. This point is especially conclusive against the Arminian, because they are so positive that all who die in infancy are saved.

Evasions of Rom. ix considered.—The declarations of the Holy Ghost in Rom. ix and xi are so decisive in our favour, that they must needs end the debate with all who revere the Divine authority, but for an evasion. The escape usually sought by Arminians (as by Watson, Inst.) is: That the Apostle in these places, teaches, not a personal election to salvation, but a national or aggregate election to privileges. My first and main objection to this is, that it is utterly irreconcileable with the *scope* of St. Paul in the passage. What is that scope? Obviously to defend his great proposition of "Justification by free grace through faith," common to Jew and Gentile, from a cavil which, from pharisaic view, was unanswerable, viz: "That if Paul's doctrine were true, then the covenant of election with Abraham was falsified." How does the Apostle answer? Obviously (and irresistibly) that this covenant was never meant to embrace all his lineage as an aggregate, Rom. ix: 6. "Not as though the word (covenant) of God had taken none effect." *For they are not all Israel, which are of Israel,*" &c. This decisive fact he then proves, by reminding the Jews that, at the very first descent, one of Abraham's sons was excluded, and the other chosen, and at the next descent, where not only the father, but the mother was the same, and the children were even twins of one birth (to make the most absolute possible identity of lineage) one was again sovereignly excluded. So, all down the line, some Hebrews of regular lineage were excluded, and some chosen. Thus, the Apostle's scope require the disintegrating of the supposed aggregates; the very line of his argument compels us to deal with individuals, instead of masses. But, according to Watson, the Apostle, in speaking of the rejection of Esau, and the selection of Jacob, and of the remaining selections of Rom. ix and xi, only employs the names of the two Patriarchs, to impersonate the two nations of Israel and Edom. He quotes in confirmation, Mal. i: 2, 3; Gen. xxv: 23. But as Calvin well remarks, the primogeniture *typified* the blessing of true redemption; so that Jacob's election to the former represented that to the latter. Let the personal histories of the two men decide this. Did not the mean, supplanting Jacob become the humble penitent saint; while the generous, dashing Esau degenerated into the reckless, Pagan, Nomad chief? The selection of the two *posterities*, the one for Church privileges, and the other for Pagan defection, was the *consequence* of the personal election and rejection of the two progenitors. The Arminian gloss violates every law of Hebrew thought and religious usage. According to these, the posterity *follow* the *status* of their progenitor. According to the Arminians, the progenitors would follow the *status* of their posterity. Farther, the whole discussion of these chapters is personal, it is individuals with whom God deals here. The election cannot be of masses to privilege, because the elect are explicitly excepted out of the masses to which they belonged ecclesiastically. See ch. ix: vv. 6, 7, 15, 23, 24; ch. xi: vv. 2, 4, 5, 7. "The election hath obtained it and *the rest were blinded.*" The discussion ranges, also, over others than Hebrews and Edomites, to Pharaoh, an individual unbeliever, &c. Last, the blessings given in this election are personal. See Rom. viii: 29; Eph. i: 5; 2 Thess. ii: 13.

III. PREDESTINATION ETERNAL, EFFICACIOUS, UNCHANGEABLE, &c.—God's decree we found possessed of the properties of unity, universality, eternity, efficiency and immutability, sovereignty, absoluteness and wisdom. Inasmuch as predestination is but a part, to our apprehension of this decree, it partakes of all those properties, as a part of the whole. And the general evidence would be the same presented on the general subject of the decree. The part of course is not universal as was the whole. But we shall find just what the general argument would have led us to expect: that the decree of predestination is,

a.) Eternal. Eph. i: 4. "He hath chosen us in Christ before the foundation of the world." 2 Thess. ii: 13. "From the beginning." 2 Tim. i: 9. "Before the world began." (See last Lect.)

b.) Immutably efficacious. There is no reason why this part of the decree should not be as much so as all the rest; for God's foreknowledge and control of the acts of all His creatures have been already established. He has no more difficulty in securing the certain occurrence of all those acts of volition, from man and devils, which are necessary to the certain redemption of the elect, than in any other department of His almighty providence. Why then, should this part of the decree be exempted from those emphatic assertions of its universal and absolute efficacy? Numb. xxiii: 19; Ps. xxxiii: 11. Is. xlvi: 10. But farther, unless God's purpose of saving each elect sinner were immutable and efficacious, Christ would have no certain warrant that He would ever see of the travail of His soul at all. For the same causes that seduced one might seduce another. Again: no sinner is saved without special and Almighty grace; for his depravity is total, and his heart wholly averse from God; so that if God has not provided, in His eternal plan, resources of gracious power, adequate to subdue unto Himself, and to sustain in grace, every sinner He attempts to save, I see no probability that any will be saved at all. For, the proneness to apostasy is such in *all*, that if God did not take efficacious care of them, the best would backslide and fail of Heaven. The efficacy of the decree of election is also proved by the fact, that God has pre-arranged *all the means* for its effectuation. See Rom. viii: 29, 30. And in fine, a multitude of Scripture confirms this precious truth: Matt. xxiv: 24; Jno. x: 28–30; 17: 6 and 12; Heb. 6: 17; 2 Tim. ii: 19.

OBJECTIONS TO EFFICIENT PREDESTINATION.—Objections against this gracious truth are almost countless, as though instead of being one of the most precious in Scripture it were oppressive and cruel. It is said that the infallibility of the elect, and their security in Christ, Matt. xxiv: 24; Jno. x: 28, only guarantee them againt such assaults as their free will may refuse to assent to; and imply nothing as to the purpose of God to permit or prevent the object of His favour from going astray of his own accord. Not to tarry on more minute answers, the simple reply to this is: that then there would be no guarantees at all; and these gracious Scriptures are mere mockeries of our hope; for it is notorious that the only way the spiritual safety of a believer *can* be injured is by the assent of his own free-will, because it is only then that there is responsibility or guilt.

Objected that the Saints warned against falling.—It is objected that this election cannot be immutably efficacious, because we read in Scripture of Saints who are warned against forfeiting it; of others who felt a wholesome fear of doing so; and of God's threats that He would, on occasion of certain sins, blot their names from His book of life, &c. Rom. xiv: 15; 1 Cor. ix: 27; Ps. lxix: 28: Rev. xxii: 19; 2 Pet. i: 10. As to the last passage, to make sure, BEBAIAN POIEISTHAI, our election, is most manifestly spoken only with reference to the believer's own apprehension of it, and comfort from it; not as to the reality of God's secret purpose. This is fully borne out by the means indicated—diligence in holy living. Such fruits being the *consequence* and not the *cause* of God's grace to us, it would be simply preposterous to propose to ensure or strengthen His secret purpose of grace, by their productions. All they can do is to strengthen our own apprehension that such a purpose exists. When the persecuted Psalmist praps, Ps. lxix: 28, that God would "blot his enemies out of the book of the living," it by no means seems clear that anything more is imprecated than their removal from this life. But grant the other meaning, as we do, in Rev. xxii: 19, the obvious explanation is that God speaks of them according to their seeming and profession. The language is adapted *ad hominem*. It is not intended to decide whether God has a secret immutable purpose of love or not, as to them, whether they were ever elected and effectually called indeed, and may yet be lost; but it only states the practical truth, that wickedness would forfeit that position in God's grace, which they professed to have. Several of the other passages are in part explained by the fact that the Christians addrested had not yet attained a comfortable assurance that they were elected. Hence they might most consistently feel all these wholesome fears, lest the partial and uncertain hope they entertained might turn out spurious. But the most general and thorough answer which covers all these cases is this: Granting that God *has* a secret purpose infallibly to save a given soul, that purpose embraces *means* as fully as ends; and those means are such as suit a rational free agent, including all reasonable appeals to hope and fear, prospect of danger, &c., &c. Now, that an elect man may fall totally *is* naturally possible, considering him in his own powers; hence when God plies this soul with fears of falling, it is by no means any proof that God intends to permit him to fall, in His secret purpose. Those fears may be the very means designed by God to keep him from it.

Selection not a caprice.—c.) God's predestination is *wise*. It is not grounded on the foreseen excellence of the elect, but it is doubtless grounded on good reasons, worthy of the Divine wisdom. See Rom. xi:-end, words spoken by Paul with especial reference to this part of the decree. The sovereignty and unconditioned nature of God's decree will be postponed till we come to discuss the Arminian views.

ANGELS ARE PREDESTINATED.—IV. There is undoubtedly a predestination of angels. They are a part of God's creation and government and if what we have asserted of the universality of His purpose is true, it must fix their destiny and foresee all their acts just as men's. His sovereignty, wisdom, infinite foreknowledge, and power necessitate the supposition. The Scripture confirms it, telling us of *elect* angels, 1 Tim. v: 21; of "*holy* angels," Matt. xxv: 31, *et passim*, as contrasted with wicked angels; that "God spared not the angels that sinned, but cast them down to hell, and delivered them into chains of darkness, *to be reserved* into judgment," 2 Pet. ii: 4. Of the "everlasting fire *prepared* for the devil and his angels," Matt. xxv: 41. Of the "angels which *kept not their first estate*, but left their own habitation, whom God *hath reserved* under darkness, in everlasting chains unto the judgment of the great day," Jud. vi, and of Michael and *his* angels, and the Dragon and *his* angels," Rev. xii: 7. Collating these passages, I think we clearly learn, that there are two kinds of spirits of that order; holy and sinful angels, servants of Christ and servants of Satan; that they were all created in an estate of holiness and happiness, and abode in the region called Heaven; (God's holiness and goodness are sufficient proof that *He* would never have created them otherwise), that the evil angels voluntarily forfeited their estate by sinning, and were then excluded forever from Heaven and holiness; that those who maintained their estate were elected thereto by God, and that their estate of holiness and blessedness is now forever assured. Now the most natural inference from these Bible facts is, that a *covenant of works* was the dispensation under which God's predestination of angels was effectuated. The fact that those who sinned fell thereby into a state of irreparable condemnation is most naturally explained by such a covenant. The fact that the elect angels received the adoption of life by maintaining their holiness for a time, seems almost to necessitate that supposition. That the probation under that covenant was temporary, is implied in the fact that some are already separated, and known as *elect*, while others are condemned. The former must be finally justified and confirmed; the latter finally reprobated.

PREDESTINATION OF ANGELS DIFFERS FROM MEN'S.—1st. Now it is manifest that these gracious and righteous dealings of God with His angels *in time*, were all foreordained by Him from eternity. Those who fell, He must have permissively ordained to fall, and those who are confirmed, He must have selected from eternity to be confirmed. But in two respects, this election of angels differs from that of men. God's predestination apprehended *men*, as all lying alike in a mass of total depravity and condemnation, and the difference He has made was in pure mercy, unprompted by any thing of good foreseen in the saints. But God's predestination apprehended angels as standing alike in innocency at first, and as left to the determination of a will which as yet had full ability to keep the law perfectly. In the election of men, while the decree is unconditional, its effectuation is dependent on the elect man's believing and repenting. So, in the case of angels, while the *decree* was unconditional the effectuation of it seems to have been conditioned on the elect angel's keeping the law perfectly for a given time. Now here is the difference of the two cases, in the elect man the ability of will to perform that condition of his salvation is inwrought in him by God's power, executing His *efficacious decree,* (see last Lect.) by His sovereign and almighty regeneration of the dead soul. In the case of the elect angel, the condition of his salvation was fulfilled in his own *natural* strength; and was ordained by God no otherwise than by His *permissive decree.* So also, the effectuating of the reprobation of the non-elect angels were dependent on their voluntary disobedience, and this too was only determined by God's permissive decree. It has been asked if all the angels were alike innocent and peccable, with full ability of will to keep the law perfectly, and yet with freedom of will to sin; how came it that the experiment did not result alike for all, that all did not fall or stand, that like causes did not produce like effects? Must there not have been a cause for the different results? And must not this cause be sought outside the angels' wills, in God's agency? The answer is: that the outward relations of no two beings to circumstances and beings other than themselves can ever be identical. In those different circumstances, were presented different *occasional causes* for volitions, sufficient to account for different volitions, from wills that were at first in similar moral states. And it was by His providential ordering of those outward relations and circumstances, that God was able permissively to determine the results. Yet the acts of the two classes of angels, good and bad, were wholly their own.

2D DIFFERENCE.—The second difference between their election and man's, is that the angels were not chosen in a mediator. They needed none, because they were not chosen out of a state of guilt, and had not arrayed God's moral attributes against them. Some have supposed that their confirming grace was and is mediated to them by Jesus Christ, quoting Col. ii: 10; i: 14, 15; 1 Pet. i: 12; Heb. i: 6; Phil. 2: 10; 1 Pet. iii: 22; Eph. i: 10; Col. i: 20.

These passages doubtless teach that the Son was, in the beginning, the immediate agent of *creation* for these, as for all other beings; and that the God-man now includes angels in His mediatorial kingdom, in the same sense in which He includes the rest of the universe, besides the saints. But that He is not a *mediator* for angels is clear, from the fact that, while He is never called such, He is so emphatically called the Mediator between God and man," 1 Tim. ii: 5, Second. He has assumed no community of nature with angels. Last, It is expressly denied in Heb. ii: 16, 17. (Greek.)

V. All who call themselves Calvinists admit that God's decree is, in His mind, a cotemporaneous unit. Yet the attempt to assign an order to its relative parts, has led to three different schemes of predestination: that of the *Supralapsarian*, of the Sublapsarian, and of the Hypothetic Universalist.

SUPRALAPSARIAN SCHEME.—The first suppose that in a rational mind, that which is *ultimate* as end, is first in design; and that, in the process of planning, the mind passes from the end to the means, travelling as it were backwards. Hence, God first designed His own glory by the salvation of a definite number of men conceived as yet only as *in posse*, and the reprobation of another definite number; that then He purposed their creation, then the permission of their fall, and then the other parts of the plan of redemption for the elect. I do not mean to represent that they impute to God an actual succession of *time* as to the rise of the parts of the decree in His eternal mind, but that these divines represent God as planning man's creation and fall, as a means for carrying out His predestination, instead of planning his election as a means for repairing his fall.

SUBLAPSARIAN SCHEME.—The Sublapsarian assigns the opposite order; that God determined to create man in His own image, to place him under a covenant of works, to permit his fall and with reference to the fallen and guilty state thus produced, to elect in sovereign mercy some to be saved, passing by the rest in righteous judgment upon their sins, and that He further decreed to send Jesus Christ to redeem the elect. This milder scheme the Supralapsarians assert to be attended with the vice of the Arminian, in making the decree conditional; in that God's decree of predestination is made dependent on man's use of his free will under the covenant of works. They also assert that their scheme is the symmetrical one, in that it assigns the rational order which exists between ultimate end and intermediate means.

BOTH ERRONEOUS.—In my opinion this is a question which *never ought to have been raised.* Both schemes are illogical and contradictory to the true state of facts. But the Sublapsarian is far *more* Scriptural in its tendencies, and its general spirit far more honourable to God. The Supralapsarian, under a pretense of greater symmetry, is in reality the more illogical of the two, and misrepresents the divine character and the facts of Scripture in an odious and repulsive manner. The view from which it starts, that the ultimate end must be first in design, and then the intermediate means, is of force *only with reference to a finite mind.* God's decree has no succession; and to Him no successive order of parts; because it is a cotemporaneous unit, comprehended all together, by one infinite intuition. In this thing, the statements of both parties are untrue to God's thought. The true statement of the matter is, that in this co-etaneous unit plan, one part of the plan is devised by God with reference to a state of facts which He intended to result from another part of the plan; but all parts equally present, and all equally primary to His mind. As to the decree to create man, to permit his fall, to elect some to life; *neither part preceded any other part with God.* But His purpose to elect had reference to a state of facts which was to result from His purpose to create, and permit the fall. It does not seem to me that the Sublapsarian scheme makes the decree conditional. True, one result decreed is dependent on another result decreed; but this is totally another thing. No scheme can avoid this, not even the Supralapsarian, unless it does away with all agency except God's direct, and makes Him the direct author of sin.

OBJECTIONS TO THE SUPRALAPSARIAN.—But we object more particularly to the Supralapsarian scheme.

a.) That it is an absurbity, in representing God as having before His mind, as the objects of predestination, men conceived *in posse* only; and in making creation a *means* of their salvation or damnation. Whereas, an object must be conceived as *existing*, in order to have its destiny given to it. And creation can with no propriety be called a means for effectuating a decree of predestination as to creatures. It is rather a pre-requisite of such decree.

b.) It contradicts Scripture, which teaches us that God chose His elect "out of the world," Jno. xv: 19, and out of the "same lump" with the vessels of dishonour, Rom. ix: 21. They were then regarded as being, along with the non-elect, in the common state of sin and misery.

c.) Our election is in Christ our Redeemer, Eph. i: 4; iii: 11, which clearly shows that we are conceived as being fallen, and in need of a Redeemer, in this act. And, moreover, our election is an election to the exercise of saving graces to be wrought in us by Christ, 1 Pet. i: 2; 2 Thess. ii: 13.

d.) Election is declared to be an act of *mercy*: Rom. ix: 15, 16; xi: 5, 6, and reprobation is an act of *justice*, Rom. ix: 22. Now as mercy and goodness imply an apprehension of guilt and misery in their object, so justice implies ill-desert. This shows that man is predestinated *as fallen*; and is not permitted to fall because predestinated. I will conclude this part, by repeating the language of Turrettin, L. 4, que. 18, § 5.

1. "By this hypothesis, the first act of God's will towards some of His creatures is conceived to be an act of hatred, in so far as He willed to demonstrate His righteouseess in their damnation, and indeed before they were considered as in sin, and consequently before they were deserving of hatred; nay, while the were conceived as still innocent, and so rather the objects of love. This does not seem compatible with God's ineffable goodness.

It is likewise harsh that, according to this scheme, God is supposed to have imparted to them far the greatest effects of love, out of a principle of hatred, in that He determines to create them in a state of integrity to this end, that He may illustrate His righteousness in their damnation. This seems to express Him neither as supremely good nor as supremely wise and just.

3. It is erroneously supposed that God exercised an act of mercy and justice towards His creatures in His foreordination of their salvation and destruction, in that they are conceived as neither wretched, nor even existing as yet. But since those virtues (mercy and justice) are *relative*, they pre-suppose their object, do not make it.

4. It is also asserted without warrant, that creation and the fall are *means* of election and reprobation, since they are antecedent to them: else sin would be on account of damnation, whereas damnation is on account of sin; and God would be said to have created men that He might destroy them.

LECTURE XX.

SYLLABUS.

PREDESTINATION (Concluded.)

1. State the doctrine as taught by the Hypothetic Universalists, Amyraut and Camero.
   Turrettin, Loc. iv, ques. 17th and 18th, § 13–20. Watson's Theol. Inst., chap. xxviii, §1, 2. Richard Baxter's "Universal Redemption."
2. State and refute the Arminian scheme of predestination.
   Turrett., Loc. iv, ques. 10th, 11th, 12th and 17th. Hill, Div., Bk. iv, ch. vii, § 2 and 4. Dick, Lect. 35. Watson's *ubi supra*.
3. What is God's decree of *reprobation*, as to those finally lost? What its ground? How proved? And how does God harden such?
   Turrett., Loc. iv, ques. 14th, 15th. Hill, as above. Dick, Lect. 36. Wesley's Sermons.
4. Is predestinantion consistent with God's justice? With His holiness? With His benevolence and sincerity in the offer of mercy to all?
   Calvin's Inst., Bk. iii, ch. 23; Hill as above. Dick, Lect. 36. Jno. Howe. Letter to Ro. Boyle. Turrett., *Fontes Sol.* Loc. iv, que. 17
5. What should be the mode of preaching and practical effect of the doctrine of predestination on the Christian life?
   Turrett. Loc. iv, que. 6. Dick, Lect. 36. Conf. of Faith, ch. iii.

Hypothetic scheme.—I. The French Presbyterian Divines of Saumur about 1630–50 devised still another scheme of relations between the parts of the decree, representing God as first (in order, not in time) purposing to create man; second, to place him under a covenant of works, and to permit his fall; third, to send Christ to provide and offer an atonement for all, out of His general compassion for all the fallen; but fourth, foreseeing that all would surely reject it because of their total depravity, to select out of the rebellious mass, some, in His sovereign mercy, to whom He would give effectual calling. They supposed that this theory would remove the difficulties concerning the extent of the atonement, and also reconcile the passages of Scripture which declare God's universal compassion for sinners, with His reprobation of the non-elect.

Wherein untenable.—This scheme is free from many of the objections which lie against the Arminian; it holds fast to the truth of original sin, and it avoids the absurdity of conditioning God's decree of election on a foresight of the saints' faith and repentance. But in two respects it is untenable. If the idea of a real succession *in time* between the parts of the divine decree be relinquished, as it must be, then this scheme is perfectly illusory, in representing God as decreeing to send Christ to provide a redemption to be offered to all, on condition of faith and this out of His general compassion. For if He foresees the certain rejection of all at the time, and at the same time purposes sovereignly to withhold the grace which would work faith in the soul from some, this scheme of election really makes Christ to be related, in God's purpose, to the non-elect, no more closely nor beneficially than the stricter Calvinistic scheme. But second and chiefly, it represents Christ as not purchasing for His people the grace of effectual calling, by which they are persuaded and enabled to embrace redemption.

But God's purpose to confer this is represented as disconnected with Christ and His purchase, and subsequent, in order, to His work, and the foresight of its rejection by sinners. Whereas Scripture represents that this gift, along with all other graces of redemption, is given us in Christ, having been purchased for His people by Him. Eph. i: 3; Phil. i: 29; Heb. xii: 2.

II. Arminian Scheme.—I have postponed to the last, the fourth scheme for arranging the order of the parts of the decree, which is the Arminian. Unwilling to rob God openly of His infinite perfection, as is done by the Socinians, they admit that He has some means of foreseeing the contingent acts of free-agent, although He neither can nor does consistently with their free-agency, exercise any direct foreordination over those acts. Such contingent acts, they say, would be unknowable to a finite mind; but this does not prove that God may not have some mode of certainly foreknowing them which implies no foreordination, and which is inscrutable to us. This foresight combines with His eternal purpose in the following order. 1st. God decreed to create man holy and happy, and to place him under a covenant of works. 2nd. God, foreseeing man's fall into a state of total depravity and condemnation, decreed to send Jesus Christ to provide redemption for all. (This redemption included the purchase of common sufficient grace for all sinners.) And God also, in this connexion, determined the general principle that *faith* should be the condition of an actual interest in this redemption. 3d. Next He foresaw that some would so improve their common grace as to come to Christ, turn from sin and persevere in holiness to the end of life. *These* He *eternally* purposed to save. Others, He foresaw, would neglect their privileges, so as to reject, or after embracing, to forsake Christ; and *these* He eternally purposed to leave in their guilt and ruin. Thus His purpose as to individuals, while eternal, is conditioned wholly on the conduct foreseen in them.

Objections. 1. That the decree cannot be conditional.—This plausible scheme seems to be, at the first glance, attended with several advantages for reconciling God's goodness and sincerity with the sinner's damnation. But the advantages are only seeming For 1. The scheme is overthrown by all the reasons which showed generally that God's decrees cannot be conditional; and especially by these. a.) That every one of the creature acts is also foreordained, on which a part of the decree is supposed to be conditioned. b.) That all the future events into which these contingent acts enter, directly or indirectly, as causes, must be also contingent: which would cast a quality of uncertainty and possible failure over God's whole plan of redemption and moral government, and much of His other providence. c.) And that God would no longer be absolute sovereign; for, instead of the creatures depending on Him alone, He would depend on the creature.

2. That Paul does not reply thus to cavils.—One can scarcely believe that Paul would have answered the objections usually raised against God's sovereign decree as He does in Rom. ix, had He inculcated this Arminian view of it. In verses 14 and 19, he anticipates those objections; 1st that God would be unjust; 2d that He would destroy man's free agency, and He deigns no other answer than to reaffirm the absolute sovereignty of God in the matter, and to repudiate the objections as sinful cavils. How different this from the answer of

the Arminian to these cavils; he always politely evades them by saying that all God's dealings with men are suspended on the improvement they choose to make of His common mercy offered to them. This contrast leads us to believe that St. Paul was not an Arminian.

3. Faith, &c., consequences of electing grace.—The believer's faith, penitence, and perseverance in holiness could never be so foreseen by God, as to be the condition moving him to determine to bestow salvation on him, because no child of Adam ever has any true faith, &c, except as *fruits* of God's grace bestowed in election. This is evinced in manifold ways throughout Scripture. a.) Man is too depraved ever to exercise these graces, except as moved thereto by God, Rom. viii: 7; 2 Cor. iii: 5; Rom. vii: 18; Gen. vi: 5. b.) The elect are declared to be chosen *to* the enjoyment of these graces, not *on account* of the exercise of them, Rom. viii: 29; 2 Thess. ii: 13, 14; Eph. i: 4; ii: 10. c.) The very faith, penitence and perseverance in holiness which Arminians represent as conditions moving God to elect man, the Scripture represents as *gifts* of God's grace inwrought by Him in the elect, as consequences of his election, Eph. ii: 8; Acts v: 31; 2 Tim. ii: 25; Phil. i: 6; 2 Pet. i: 3. d.) All the elect believe on Christ, Jno. x: 16, 27 to 29; vi: 37, 39; xvii: 2, 9, 24, and none others do, Jno. x: 26; Acts xiii: 48; 2: 47. Couple these two facts together and they furnish a strong evidence that faith is the consequence (therefore not the cause) of election.

4. Express texts.—The Scriptures in the most express and emphatic terms declare that it was no goodness in the elect which caused God to choose them; that his electing love found them lying in the same mass of corruption and wrath with the reprobate, every way deserving the same fate, and chose them out of it for reasons commending themselves to His own good pleasure, and in sovereign benevolence. This was seen in Jacob and Esau, Rom. ix: 11–13, as to Israel: Ezek. xvi: 3–6. As to all sinners, Rom. ix: 16; xv: 18, 21; Rom. xi: 4–7; viii: 28. (Here the Arminians claim that God's foreknowledge precedes and prompts His foreordination. But we have shown that this foreknowledge implies *selection.*) 2 Tim. i: 9; Matt. xi: 26: Jno. xv: 16–19.

III. Reprobation.—The word *reprobate* (adokimos) is not, so far as I know, applied in the Scriptures to the subject of predestination. Its etymology and usage would suggest the meaning of something rejected upon undergoing a test or trial, and hence, something condemned or rejected. Thus Rom. i: 28, adokimon noun, a mind given over to condemnation and desertion, in consequence of great sin, 2 Tim. iii: 8. Sectaries, adokimoi peri ten pistin, finally condemned and given over to apostasy concerning the Christian system. 1 Cor. ix: 27, "Lest after I have preached to others, I myself should be adokimos," rejected at the final test. i. e., Judgment Day. Hence the more general sense of "worthless," Tit. i: 16; Heb. vi: 8.

The word ill-chosen.—The application of this word to the negative part of the decree of predestination has doubtless prejudiced our cause. It is calculated to misrepresent and mislead, because it suggests too much the idea of a comparative judicial result. For then the query arises, if the non-elect and elect have been tested as to their deserts, in the divine mind, how comes it that the elect are acquitted when they are as guilty, and the non-elect condemned when they are no worse? Is not this partiality? But the fact is, that in election God acted as a *sovereign*, as well as a judge; and that the elect are not taken because they are less guilty upon trial, but because God had other secret, though sufficient reasons. If the negative part of the decree of predestination then must be spoken of as a *decree of reprobation*, it must be understood in a modified sense.

Does it include preterition and predamnation.—The theologians, while admitting the strict unity of God's decree, divide reprobation into two elements, as apprehended by us, preterition and pre-damnation. I would rather say, that it consists simply of a sovereign yet righteous purpose to leave out the non-elect, which preterition was foreseen and intended to result in their final righteous condemnation. The decree of reprobation is then, in its essence, a *simple preterition*. It is indeed intelligent and intentional in God. He leaves them out of His efficacious plan and purpose of mercy, not out of a general inattention or overlooking of them, but knowingly and sovereignly. Yet objectively this act is only negative, because God does nothing to those thus passed by, to make their case any worse, or to give any additional *momentum* to their downward course. *He leaves them as they are.* Yea, incidentally, He does them many kindnesses, extends to multitudes of them the calls of His words, and even the remonstrances of His spirit, preventing them from becoming as wicked as they would otherwise have done. But the practical or efficacious part of His decree is, simply that He will *not* "make them willing in the day of His power."

Preterition proved.—When we thus explain it, there is abundant evidence of a decree of preterition. It is inevitably implied in the decree of election, coupled with the fact that all are neither elected nor saved. If salvation is of God; if God is a Being of infinite intelligence, and if He has eternally purposed to save some; then He has *ipso facto* equally purposed from eternity to leave the others in their ruin. And to this agree the Scriptures, Rom. ix: 13, 17, 18, 21 and 22; Matt. xi: 25; Rom. xi: 7; 2 Tim. ii: 20; Jude. iv: 1 Pet. ii: 8.

Objections. Answers.—This is a part of God's word which has ever been assailed with the fiercest cavils. It has been represented as as picturing a God who created a number of unfortunate immortals, and endued them with capacities for sinning and suffering, only in order that He might damn them forever; and to this wretched fate they are inexorably shut up, by the iron decree, no matter what penitent efforts or what cries for mercy and escape they may put forth; while the equally or more guilty objects of the divine caprice and favouritism are admitted to a Heaven which they cannot forfeit, no matter how vilely they behave. There is no wonder that a Wesley should denounce the doctrine thus misrepresented, as worthy only of Satan. There is, indeed, enough in the *truth* of this subject, to fill every thoughtful mind with solemn awe and holy fear of that God, who holds the issues of our redemption in His sovereign hand. But how differently does His dealing appear when we remember that He created all His creatures at first in holiness and happiness; that He gave them an adequate chance to stand;

that He has done nothing to make the case of the non-elect worse than their own choice makes it, but on the contrary sincerely and mercifully warns them by conscience and His word against that wicked choice; that it is all a monstrous dream to fancy one of these non-elect seeking Heaven by true penitence, and excluded by the inexorable decree, because they all surely yet voluntarily prefer their impenitence, so that God is but leaving them to their preferred ways; and that the only way He ensures the elect from the destruction due their sins, is by ensuring their repentance, faith, and diligent strivings to the end in a holy life.

Is PRETERITION GROUNDED ON THE SIN OF THOSE PASSED BY?—Yet it must be confessed that some of the odiousness of the doctrine is in part due to the unwise views of it presented by the Orthodox sometimes, going beyond all that God's majesty, sovereignty and word require, out of a love of hypothesis. Thus, it is disputed what is the *ground* of this righteous preterition of the non-elect. The honest reader of his Bible would suppose that it was, of course, their guilt and wickedness foreseen by God, and, for wise reasons, permissively decreed by Him. This we saw, all but the supralapsarian admitted in substance. God's election is everywhere represented in Scripture, as an act of *mercy*, and His preterition as an act of righteous anger against sin. The elect are vessels of *mercy*, the non-elect of *wrath*. (God does not show anger at any thing but sin) as in Rom. ix: 22. Everywhere it is *sin* which excludes from His favour, and sin alone.

But it is urged, with an affected over-refinement, the sin of the non-elect cannot be the ground of God's preterition, because all Adam's seed being viewed as equally depraved, had this been the ground, all would have been passed by. I reply, yes; if this had been the only consideration, *pro* or *con*, present in God's mind. The ill-desert of all was in itself a sufficient ground for God to pass by all. But when His sovereign wisdom suggested some reason, unconnected with the relative desert or ill-desert of sinners, which was a good and sufficient ground for God's choosing a part; this only left the *same* original ground, ill-desert, operating on His mind as to the remainder. It is perfectly true that God's sovereignty concerns itself with the preterition as well as the election, for the separate reason which grounded the latter is sovereign. But with what propriety can it be said that this secret sovereign reason is the *ground* of his preterition, when the very "*git*" of the case was that it was a reason which *did not apply* to the non-elect, but only to the elect. As to the elect, it *overruled* the ground for their preterition which would otherwise have been found, in their common ill-desert. As to the non-elect, it did not apply, and thus left the original ground, their ill-deserts in full force.

It is said again, that if we make their sin the ground of their rejection, then by parity of reasoning, we must make the foreseen piety of the other class the ground of their election; and thus return to the Arminian doctrine of conditional decrees. [As perverse a sophism as though it were inferred that because a surfeit of stewed eels killed King John of England, therefore abstinence from them should make other men immortal.] The four heads of argument which I gave against the Arminian's conditional decree, contain substantially all that can be urged on that point. And the key of them all is, that foreseen piety could not have been the ground moving God to decree men's salvation:

because no men will have any piety to foresee, save as it is the *result* of God's grace bestowed from election. But is it so with men's sin? Just the opposite. Sin is the very condition in which God foresees all men as standing, for all except Supralapsarians admit that God in predestination regards man as fallen. Man's foreseen sin may be the ground of God preterition, because it is not the *effect* of that preterition, but of another part of His eternal purpose, viz: that to permit the fall. And, as again and again taught, while *the decree* is absolute the *results decreed* are conditioned; and we cannot but conceive God as predicating one part of his eternal purpose on a state of facts which was destined to proceed out of another part thereof.

Again: it is said, Scriptures teach, that the sin of the non-elect was not the ground of their preterition. "In Jno. x: 26, continued unbelief is the consequence, and therefore not the ground of the Pharisees' preterition." Matt. xi: 25; Rom. ix: 11, 18. "God's will," they say, "and not the non-elect's sin, is the ground of His purpose to harden." And "Esau was rejected as much without regard to his evil, as Jacob was elected without regard to his good deeds." To the first, I reply, that the withholding of God's grace is the negative cause of sinner's unbelief, just as the absence of a physician is a negative cause of the sick man's death. Yet, positively, it is only the disease which kills him. To the second, God's will decides; but it is a will guided by righteousness. Nothing but sin moves a righteous will to punish. To the third, I reply, just as Turrettin does to the Supralapsarian, that it is only a *relative* guilt and innocence between Esau and Jacob, which the Apostle asserts. In fact, both "were by nature children of wrath, even as others."

God's hardening what?—When it is said that God *hardens* the non-elect, it is not, and cannot be intended that he exerts positive influences upon them to make them worse. The proof of this was given under the question, whether God can be the author of sin. See especially Jas. i: 13. God is only the negative cause of hardening—the positive depravation comes only from the sinner's own voluntary feelings and acts. And the mode in which God gives place to, or *permits* this self-inflicted work, is by righteously withholding His restraining word and spirit; and second by surrounding the sinner (through His permissive providence) with such occasions and opportunities as the guilty man's perverse will will voluntarily abuse to increase his guilt and obduracy. This dealing, though wrong in men, is righteous in God; because He alone is the *appointed Retributor*, and revenger of sin in this universe, Rom. xii: 19.

IV. Is predestination unjustly partial.—To notice briefly the standing objections: The doctrine of predestination as we have defined it, is not inconsistent with the justice and impartiality of God. His agency in the fall of angels and men was only permissive—the act and choice were theirs. They having broken God's law and depraved themselves, it would have been just in God to leave them all under condemnation. How then can it be more than just when he punishes only a part? The charge of partiality has been absurdly brought here, as though there could be partiality where there are no rights at all, in any creature on the mercy of God; and Acts x: 34; Levit. xix: 15; Deut. i: 17; 2 Sam. xiv: 14, have been quoted against us. As Calvin very acutely remarks on the first of these, one's *persona*, PROSPON, in the sense of these passages means, not his moral character, as judicially well or ill-deserving, but his accidental position in society, as Jew or Gentile, rich or poor, plebeian or nobleman. And in this sense it is literally true of election, that in it God respects no man's *persona*, but takes them, irrespective of all these factitious advantages and disadvantages. To this foolish charge, Matt. xx: 15 is sufficient answer. God's sovereignty ought undoubtedly to come in as a reply. *Within the bounds* of His other perfections of righteousness, truth and benevolence, God is entitled to make what disposal of His own He is pleased, and men are his property—Rom. ix: 20, 21. Paul does not imply here that God is capable of doing injustice to an innocent creature, in order to illustrate His sovereignty; but that in such a case as this of predestination, where the condemnation of all would have been no more than they deserved. He can exercise His sovereignty, in sparing and punishing just such as He pleases, without a particle of injustice.

IS IT UNHOLY?—2. It is objected, that God's holiness would forbid such a predestination. How, it is said, can it be compatible with the fact that God hates sin, for Him to construct an arrangement, *He having full power to effectuate a different one*, by which He voluntarily and intentionally leaves multitudes of His creatures in increasing and everlasting wickedness? And the same objection is raised against it from His benevolence. The answer is, that this is but the same difficulty presented by the origin of evil; and it presses on the Calvinist with no more force than on the Arminian, or even on the Socinian. Allow to God a universal, perfect foreknowledge, as the Arminian does, and the very same difficulty is presented. How an almighty God should have knowingly adopted a system for the universe, which would embody such results. For even if the grossest Pelagian view be adopted, that God is literally *unable* certainly to prevent the wicked acts of man's free will, and yet leave him a free agent, it would certainly have been in his power to let alone creating those who He foresaw would make a miserable immortality for themselves, in spite of His grace. The Arminian is obliged to say: "There are doubtless inscrutable reasons, unknown to us, but seen by God to be sufficient, why He should permit it?" The same appeal to our ignorance is just as available for the Calvinist. And if the lowest Socinian ground is taken, which denies to God a universal foreknowledge of the volitions of free agents, still we must suppose one of two things. He must either have less wisdom than many of His creatures, or else, he made these men and angels, knowing in the general, that large immortal misery would result. So that there is no evasion of this difficulty, except by so robbing God of His perfections as practically to dethrone Him It is not Calvinism which creates it; but the simple *existence* of sin and misery, destined never to be wholly extinguished, in the government of an almighty and omniscient God. He who thinks thinks he can master it by his theory, is a fool.

HOW RECONCILED WITH GOSPEL OFFERS TO ALL?—3. It is objected that God's goodness and sincerity in the offer of the Gospel *to all* is inconsistent with predestination. It is urged: God says He "hath no pleasure in the death of him that dieth;" that He would have all men to be saved; and that Christ declared His wish to save reprobate Jerusalem.

Now, how can these things, and His universal offer: "Whosoever will, let him come," consist with the fixed determination that the non-elect shall never be saved? I reply, that this difficulty (which cannot be wholly solved) is not generated by predestination, but lies equally against any other theory which leaves God His divine attributes. Let one take this set of facts. Here is a company of sinners, God could convert all by the same powers by which he converts one. He offers His salvation to all, and assures them of His general benevolence. He knows perfectly that some will neglect the offer; and yet, so knowing, He intentionally *refrains* from exerting those powers to overrule their reluctance, *which He is able to exert if He chose.* This is but a statement of stubborn *facts*; it cannot be evaded without impugning the omniscience, or omnipotence of God, or both. Yet, see if the whole difficulty is not involved in it. Every evangelical Christian, therefore, is just as much interested in seeking the solution of this difficulty as the Calvinist. And it is to be sought in the following brief suggestions. God's concern in trangression and impenitence of those whom He suffers to neglect His warnings and invitations, is only permissive. He merely leaves men to their own sinful choice. His invitations are *always* impliedly, or explicitly *conditional*; suspended on the sinner's turning. He has never said that He desires the salvation of a sinner *as impenitent*; He only says, *if the sinner* will turn he is welcome to salvation. And this is always literally true; were it in the line of possibilities that one non-elect should turn, He would find it true in his case. All, therefore, that we have to reconcile is these *three facts*; that God should see a reason why it is not proper, in certain cases, to put forth His almighty grace to overcome a sinner's reluctance; and yet that He should be able to do it if he chose; and yet should be benevolent and pitiful towards all His creatures. Now God says in His Word that He *does* compassionate lost sinners. He says that He could save if He pleased. His word and providence both show us that some are permitted to be lost. In a wise and good *man*, we can easily understand how a power to pardon, a sincere compassion for a guilty criminal, and yet a fixed purpose to punish, could co-exist; the power and compassion being overruled by His wisdom. Why may not something analogous take place in God, according to His immutable nature? Is it said: such an explanation implies a *struggle* in the breast between competing considerations, inconsistent with God's calm blessedness? I reply, God's revelations of His wrath, love, pity, repentance, &c., are all anthropopathic, and the difficulty is no greater here, than in all these cases. Or is it said, that there *can* be nothing except a lack of will, or a lack of power to make the sinner both holy and happy? I answer; it is exceeding presumption to suppose that because we do not see such a cause, none can be known to God!

V How to be taught, and its results.—"The doctrine of this high mystery of predestination is to be handled with special prudence and care." In preaching it, that proportion should be observed, which obtains in the Bible; and no polemical zeal against the impugners of the doctrine ought to tempt the minister to obtrude it more often. To press it prominently on anxious inquirers, or on those already confused by cavils of heretics or satanic suggestions, or to urge it upon one inclined to skepticism, or one devoid of sufficient Christian knowledge, experience and humility, is unsuitable and imprudent. And when taught, it should be in the mode which usually prevails in Scripture, viz: *a posteriori*, as inferred from its result, effectual calling.

But when thus taught, the doctrine of predestination is full of edification. It gives ground for humility, because it leaves man no ground for claiming any of the credit of either originating or carrying on his salvation. It lays a foundation for confident *hope*; because it shows that "the gifts and calling of God are without repentance." It should open the fountains of love and gratitude, because it shows the undeserved and eternal love of God for the undeserving. We should learn to teach and to view the doctrine, not from an exclusive, but from an *inclusive* point of view. It is *sin* which shuts out from the favour of God, and which ruins. It is God's decree which calls back, and repairs and saves all who are saved. Whatever of sin, of guilt, of misery, of despair the universe exhibits, arises wholly out of man's and Satan's transgression. Whatever of redemption, of hope, of comfort, of holiness and of bliss alleviates this sad *panorama*, all this proceeds from the decree of God. The decree is the fountain of universal benevolence, voluntary sin is the fountain of woe. Shall the fountain of mercy be maligned because, although it emits all the happiness in the universe, it has a limit to its streams?

LECTURE XXI.

SYLLABUS.

CREATION.

1. What is the usage and meaning of the word *create* in Scripture?
   Turrettin, Loc. v., que. 1. Lexicons. Dick, Lect. 37.
2. How else have philosphers accounted for the existence of the universe, except by a creation out of nothing?
   Turrettin, ubi supra. Dick as above. Brucher's Hist. of Phil. British Encyclopaedia, articles "Atomic Philosophy," and "Platonism."
3. Prove that God created the world out of nothing; first from Scripture, and second, from Reason and the objections to the eternity of the Universe and matter.
   Turrettin, Loc. v., que. 3. Dr. S. Clarke, Discourses of Being, &c., of God. Dick, as above.
4. Can a creature receive the power of creating, by delegation from God?
   Turrettin, Loc. v, que. 2.
5. What was each day's work of creation, in the Mosaic week? Genesis, ch. i.
   Turrettin, Loc. v, ques. 5, 6. On this and the previous questions see Knapp's Chr. Theol., Art. v, sections xlv to l.
6. What are the theories of modern Geologists concerning the age of the earth? Their grounds, and the several modes proposed for reconciling them with the Mosaic history?
   Hitchcock's Relig. and Geology. Univ. Lectures, Dr. Lewis Green. Hugh Miller, Testimony of the Rocks. Tayler Lewis' Symbol. Days. David N. Lord on Geol. Sir Charles Lyell's System of Geol. &c.

1. Terms defined.—The words rendered to create, cannot be considered, in their etymology and usage, very distinctive of the nature of

the act. The authorities make BARA means "to cut or carve," primarily, (from the idea of splitting off parts, or separation) hence "to fashion," then to "create;" and thence the more derivative sense of producing or generating, regenerating the heart, &c. The verb ASAH carries, according to the authorities, more of the sense of the Greek verb POIEO—"to do or make;" and is used for fashioning, manufacturing, doing (as a function or business), acquiring property &c. The verb YATSAR seems to me to carry more distinctively the idea fashioning out of pre-existent materials, as a potter (YOTSER) out of clay, &c. And it will be observed that wherever it is applied to making man or animals in Gen. the *material out of which*, is mentioned or implied as ii: 7. God fashioned man (VAIGITSER) out of the dust of the earth. The word usually employed from Greek in Septuagent and New Testament to express the idea of creating, as distinguished from begetting or generating is KTIDZO. This, authorities say, means primarily to "found," or "build," and hence, "to make," "create."

2. CREATION WAS OUT OF NOTHING.—It will be clearly seen hence' that the nature of the creative act is but faintly defined by the mere force of the words. Yet Scripture does not lack passages which explicitly teach, that God produced the whole Universe out of nothing by His almighty power; i. e.,that His first work of creation did not consist merely of fashioning materials already existent, but of bringing all substance, except His own, out of non-existence into existence. How impossible this seemed to the ancient mind appears from this fact, that the opposite was regarded as an axiom (*ex nihilo nihil fit*) and lay as such at the basis of every system of human device. So that it was froman accurate knowledge of the bounds of human knowledge, that the author of Hebrews says (xi: 3,) that the true doctrine of creation was purely one of faith. And this is our most emphatic proof text. We may add to it Rom. iv: 17; perhaps 1 Cor. i: 28; 2 Cor. iv: 6; Acts xvii: 28; Col. i: 17. The same meaning may be fairly argued for the word BARA, Gen. i: 1,from the fact that its sense there is absolutely unqualified or limited by any previous proposition, or reference to any material, and also from the second verse. The work of the first verse expressed by BARA, left the earth a *chaos*. Therefore it connot contain the idea of *fashioning*, so that if you refuse to it the sense of an absolute production out of nothing, you seem to leave it no meaning whatever. This truth also appears very strongly, from the contrast which is so often run by Scripture between God's eternity, and the temporal nature of the creation. See Ps. xc: 2; Matt. xxv: 34; 2 Tim i: 9; Rev. i: 11; and especially Prov. viii: 23–26, "nor the highest part of the dust of the world." It is hard to see how it could be most strongly asserted that not only was the organization, but the very material of the world as yet all non-existent.

THIS INSCRUTABLE, BUT NOT IMPOSSIBLE.—*How* almighty power brings substance into existence from absolute non-entity, our minds may not be able to conceive. Like so many other questions of ontology, it is too impalpable for the grasp of our understandings. As we have seen, the mind neither sees nor conceives *substance*, not even material; but only its attributes; only, it is intuitively impelled to refer those attributes (of which alone it is cognizant) to some *substratum* as the *substance* in which they inhere. The entity itself being incomprehensible, it need not surprise us to find that its rise out of non-entity is so. The ancients, in this case, clearly confounded impossibility with incomprehensibility.

There are three other schemes which offer us an alternative to this of an absolute creation; that of the atomic philosophers, that of the Platonists, and that of the Pantheists.

Atomic theory. Refutation.—The Atomic theory of the Universe advanced by Democritus and Leucippus, adopted by Epicurus and greatly opposed by Socrates and the Platonists, might be so stated, if freed from the mechanical technicalities of the Greeks, as to embrace as few absurdities as perhaps any possible anti-Christian system. That is, it has the merit of atheism, of making two or three gigantic falsehoods, assumed at the outset, supersede a whole train of minor absurdities. Grant, say the atomists, the eternal existence of matter, in the state of ultimate atoms, endued by the necessity of nature, with these three eternal attributes, motion, a perpetual appetency to aggregation, and diversity of ultimate *form*, and you have all that is necessary, to account for universal organization. Now, without dwelling on the metaphysical objection (whose soundness is questionable,) that necessary existence is inconsistent with diversity of form, these obvious reasons show that the postulates are not only unproved (*proof* I have never seen attempted) but impossible. First: *motion* is not a necessary attribute of matter; but on the contrary, it is indifferent to a state of rest or motion, requiring *power* to cause it to pass out of either state into the opposite. Second: Intelligent contrivance could never be generated by mere necessary, mechanical aggregations of material atoms; but remains still an effect without a cause. Third: the materialistic account of human and other spirits, which this theory gives, is impossible.

Platonic scheme. Refutation.—The Pantheistic theory has been already refuted, as space would allow, in Lecture II, which see. The Platonic is certainly attended with fewest absurdities, and best satisfied the demands of thinking minds not possessed of Revelation. Starting with the maxim *ex nihilo nihil fit*, it supposes two eternal substances, the sources of all that exists; the spiritual God, and chaotic matter; the spirits of demi-gods, and men being emanations of the former, and the material universe having been fashioned out of the latter, in time, through the agency of the nous or demiourgos. The usual arguments against the eternity of the unorganized matter of the universe, have been weighed in the Second Lecture, and many of them found wanting, (which see). I now aim only to add to what is there said, such considerations as human reason seems able to advance solidly against this doctrine. You will remember that I there argued, 1st. From the testimony of the human race itself, and 2d, from the recency of population, history, traditions, arts, &c., on the earth, against the eternity of its *organized state*. To these we may add: 3d. If matter unorganized was eternal, it must have been self-existent, and hence, whatever attributes it had from eternity must have been absolutely necessary. Hence there was a necessary limitation on the power of God, in working with such a material; and it may be that He did not make what He would have preferred to make, but only *did the best He could* under the circumstances. (Indeed the Platonist, knowing nothing of the doctrine of a *fall*, accounted for all the imperfections of the Universe by the refractory nature of matter.) But God assures us that He is sovereign and absolute, and that all creatures are absolutely dependent on His will. 4th. The elementary properties of matter, which on this theory, must have been eternal and necessary, have an *adaptation* to God's purposes in creation, that displays intelligent contrivance just as clearly as any organized thing can. But matter is unintelligent; this design must have had a cause. 5th. The production of spiritual substance out of nothing is, we presume, just as hard to account for as material substance. Hence, if an instance of the former is presented, the doctrine of the eternity of the Universe may as well be surrendered. But *our souls* each present such an instance. No particle of evidence exists from consciousness or recollection, that they pre-existed, and everything is against the notion that they are scintillations of God's substance. They *began to exist*: at least man has no knowledge whatever of any other origin; and by the rule: *De ignotis idem quasi de non existentibus*, any other origin is out of the debate. They were produced out of nothing. In conclusion, it may be said that, if the idea of the production of something out of nothing is found to be not impossible, as we think; when we have supposed an Almighty Creator, we have cause enough to account for everything, and it is unecessary to suppose another.

No creature can be enabled to create.—3. The question whether a creature *can* receive, if God choose, delegated power to create, has been agitated between the Orthodox and some of the Romanists, (who would fain introduce a plea for the making of a Saviour by the priest, in the pretended miracle of the mass) and the old Arians and Socinians, who would thus evade the argument for Christ's proper divinity, from the evident ascription to Him of works of creation. We believe, not only that the noblest of finite creatures is incapable of exercising creative power proper, of his own motion; but of receiving it by delegation from God, so that the latter is one of those natural impossibles which it would argue imperfection in omnipotence to be capable of doing.

a.) God, in a multitude of places, claims creation as His characteristic work, by which His Godhead is manifested, and His superiority shown to all false gods and idols; Is. xl: 12; xliv: 7, 24; xl: 12, 13, 18, 28; Job ix: 8; Jer. x: 11, 12; Is. xxxvii: 16; Ps. xcvi: 5. Thus *Creator* comes to be one of God's names.

b.) To bring any thing, however small, out of non-existence is so far above man's capabilities, that he cannot even *conceive* how it can be done. In order that a work may be conceivable or feasible for us, it must have *subject* and *agent*. Man has no faculty which can be directed upon nonentity, in any way, to bring anything out of it. Indeed, however small the thing thus produced out of nothing, there is an exertion of infinite power. The distance to be passed over between the two is a fathomless gulf to every finite mind.

c.) To make any *one* thing, however limited, might require infinite powers of understanding. For however simple, a number of the laws of nature would be involved in its structure; and the successful construction would demand a perfect acquaintance with those laws, at least, in their infinite particularity, and in all their possible combinations, and with the substance as well as attributes. Consider any of the constructions of man's shaping and joining materials God has given him, and this will be found true. The working of miracles by prophets, apostles, &c., offer no instance to the contrary, because it is really God who works the miracle, and the human agent only announces, and appeals to the interposition of divine power. See Acts iii : 12.

THE CREATIVE WEEK.—5. If we suppose that Gen. i : 1, describes a previous production in a time left indefinite, of the heavens and the *matter* of the earth, then the work of the first of the six days will be the production of *light*. It may seem unreasonable at the first glance, that light should be created, and should make three days before the sun, its great fountain at present, was formed. But all the researches of modern optics go more and more to overthrow the belief that light is a literal emanation from the sun. What it is, whether a substance, or an affection of other substance, is still unknown. Hence it cannot be held unreasonable, that it should have existed before the sun; nor that God should have regulated it in alternations of day and night. On the second day the atmosphere seems to have been created, (the expanse) or else disengaged from chaos, and assigned its place around the surface of the earth. This, by sustaining the clouds, separated the waters from the waters. The work of the third day was to separate the terrestial waters from the dry ground, to assign each their bounds, and to stock the vegetable kingdom with its *genera* of trees and plants. The fourth day was occupied with the creation, or else the assignment to their present functions, of sun, moon and stars. And henceforth these became the chief depositories, or else propagators of natural light. The fifth day witnessed the creation of all oviparous animals, including the three classes of fishes, reptiles and birds. The sixth day God created the terrestial animals of the higher orders, now known as mammalia, and man, His crowning work.

6. THE VIEW OF MODERN GEOLOGY EXPLAINED.—For about the last sixty years, as you are aware, modern geologists have taught, with great unanimity, that the state of the structures which compose the earth's crust show it to be vastly more than 6,000 years old. To explain this supposed evidence to you. I may take for granted your acquaintance with the *classes* into which they distribute the rocks and soils that form the earth, so far as man has pierced it. Lowest in order and earliest in age, are the primary rocks, all *azoic*. Second come the secondary rocks, containing remains of life *palaeozoic* and *meiocene*. Third come the tertiary rocks and clays, containing the *pleiocene* fossils. Fourth come the *alluvia*, containing the latest, and the existing genera of life. Now the theory of the geologists is, that only the primary azoic rocks are original; the rest are all results of natural causes of disintegration, and deposition, since God's creation. And *hence:* that creation must have been thousands of ages before Adam.

a.) Because the primary rocks are all very hard, were once liquid from heat, and evidently resulted from gradual cooling.

b.) The average thickness of the *made* rocks and earths they estimate from six to ten miles; whence vast ages were required to disintegrate so much material from rocks so hard.

c.) The positions of these *made strata*, or layers, indicate long series of changes since they were deposited, as upheavals, dislocations, depressions, subsequent re-dissolvings.

d.) They contain 30,000 *species* and more of fossils remains of life, vegetable and animals: of which, not only are whole *genera* now extinct, but were wholly extinct ages before another cluster of *genera* were first created; which are now extinct also. And the vast quantities of these fossils, as shells in some limestone, remains of vegetation in vast coal beds, &c., &c., point to a long time, for their gradual accumulation.

f.) There are no human fossils found with these remains of earlier life, whence they were pre-Adamite.

Last, Since the last great geologic changes in the strata of the made rocks, changes have been produced in them by natural and gradual causes, which could not have been made in 6,000 years, as whole *deltas* of alluvial mud deposited, e. g., Louisiana, deep channels dug out by rivers, as Niagara from Lake Ontario to the falls, water worn caves in the coast lines, and former coast lines of countries, e. g., Great Britian, which are rock-bound.

Attempts to reconcile this with Moses. 1. Chalmers' scheme.—Modern divines, too facile as I conceive, usually yield this as a demonstration; and offer one of two solutions to rescue Moses from the appearance of mistake. 1. Drs. Chalmers, Hitchcock, Hodge, &c., suppose Gen. i: 1 and 2, 1st clause, to describe God's primeval creative act; which may have been separated by thousands of ages from Adam's day: and in that vast interval, occurred all those successive changes, which geologists describe as pre-Adamite, and then lived and died all those extinct *genera* of animals and vegetables. The scene had been closed, perhaps ages before, by changes which left the earth's surface void, formless and dark. But all this Moses passes over with only one word; because the objects of a religious revelation to man were not concerned with it. The second verse only describes how God took the earth in hand, at this stage, and in six days gave it the order, the *genera* of plants and animals, and last, the human race, which now possess it. The geological objections which Hugh Miller, its ablest Christian assailant, brings may be all summed up in this: That the fossils show there was not such a clean *cutting off* of all the *genera* of plants and animals at the close of the pre-Adamite period, and re-stocking of the earth with the existing *genera*; because many of the existing co-exist with the prevalent *pleiocene genera*, in the tertiary rocks, and many of those again, with the older *genera*, in the palaeozoic rocks. This does not seem at all conclusive, because it may have suited God, at the close of the pre-Adamite period, to suffer the extinction of all, and then to create, along with the totally different new *genera*, some bearing so close a likeness to some extinct *genera*, as to be indistinguishable by their fossils.

Exegetical difficulties.—The exegetical objections are chiefly these. 1. That the sun, moon and light were only created at the Adamic period. Without these there could have been neither vegetable nor animal life before. 2. We seem to learn from Gen. i: 31: ii: 17–19; Rom. v: 12; viii: 19–22, that all animal suffering and death came upon our earth as a punishment for man's sin; which our conceptions of the justice and benevolence of God seem to confirm. To the 1st the common answer is, that the chaotic condition into which the earth had *fallen* just before the Adamic period, had probably shut out all influ nces of the Heavenly bodies; and that the making of sun, moon, &c., and ordaining them for lights, &c., probably only means their apparent creation; i. e., their re-introduction to the earth. To the 2d it is replied, that the proper application of the texts attributing all terr estrial disorder and suffering to man's fall, is only to the earth as cot emporary with man; and that we are too ignorant of God's plan, and of what sin of rational free agents may, or may not have occurred on the pre-Adamite earth to dogmatize about it. These replies seem plausible, and may possibly be tenable. This mode of reconciling geology to Moses, is certainly the least objectionable and most respectable.

THE THEORY OF SIX SYMBOLIC DAYS.—The second mode of reconciliation, now made most fashionable by H. Miller, Tayler Lewis, &c., supposes that the word YOM, day, in the account of creation, does not mean a natural day of 24 hours, but is symbolical of a vast period; during which God was, *by natural laws*, carrying on changes in the earth's surface and its inhabitants. And they regard the passage as an account of a sort of symbolic vision, in which God gave Moses a picture, in six *tableaux*, of these six vast series of geologic and creative changes: so that the language is, to use Dr. Kurtz' (of Dorpat) fantastic idea, a sort of *prophecy of the past*, and is to be understood according to the laws of prophetic symbols. This they confirm by saying that Moses makes three days before he has any sun or moon to make them; that in Gen. ii: 4, the word is used for something other than a naturul day; and that it is often used in Hebrew as a general and undefined term for season or period. Miller also argues, that geology reveals the same succession of fossils which Moses describes; first plants, then monstrous fishes and reptiles and birds, (all oviparous), then quadrupeds and mammalia, and last, man.

OBJECTIONS.—The insuperable objections to this scheme are; that some of the best informed geologists deny that succession of fossils which Miller asserts; declaring that plants *do not* predominate in the palaeozoic fossils; but crustaceous animals. Unless Gen. 1 is a *plain narrative*, there can be no faith put in Scripture language, and there is no solid system of exegesis. The word YOM must mean natural day, because it is composed of evening and morning. No other meaning gives sense and consistency to the *reason* assigned from the six days work, for the Sabath institution, Gen. ii: 2, 3; Exod. xx: 11. (The latter surely, is not a symbolic tableau, representing a *pre*diction of a past event?) Last, The attributing of the changes ascribed to each day by Moses, to the slow operation of natural causes, as Miller's theory does, tramples upon the proper scope of the passage, and the meaning of the word "create;" which teach us this very truth especially; that these things were *not* brought about by natural law at all, but by a supernatural divine exertion, directly opposed thereto. See Gen. ii: 5. If Moses does not here mean to teach us that in the time named by the six "days" (whatever it may be), God was employed in miracuously creating and not naturally "growing" a world, I see not how language can be construed. This decisive difficulty is wholly separate from the questions about the much debated word, "day," in this passage.

APPENDIX.

Without presuming to teach technical geology (for which I profess no qualification; and which lies, as I conceive, wholly outside the functions of the Church teacher), I wish, in dismissing this subject, to give you some cautions and instructions touching its relations with our revealed science.

THIS SUBJECT MUST CONCERN THEOLOGIANS.—1. There must always be a legitimate reason for church teachers adverting to this subject: because geology is virtually a theory of *cosmogony*, and cosmogony is but the *doctrine* of creation, which is one of the modes by which God reveals Himself to man, and one of the prime articles of every revealed theology. Were not all the ancient cosmogonies but natural theologies? Not a few modern geologists resent the animadversions of theologians, as of an incompetent class, impertinent and ignorant. Now I very freely grant that it is a very naughty thing for a parson, *or a geologist*, to profess to know what he does not know. But all logic is but logic; and after the experts in a special science have explained their premises in their chosen way, it is simply absurd to forbid any other class of educated men to understand and judge their deductions. What else was the object of their publications? Or do they intend to practise that simple dogmatism, which in us religious teacher they would so spurn? Surely when geologists currently teach their systems to *boys* in colleges, it is too late for them to refuse the inspection of an educated class of *men*! When Mr. Hugh Miller undertook, by one night's lecture, to convince a crowd of London Mechanics of his pet theory of the seven geologic ages, it is too late to refuse the criticism of theologians trained in philosophy?

2. WESTMINSTER CONFESSION INCONSISTENT WITH IT.—I would beg you to notice how distinctly either of the current theories *contradicts* the standards of our Church. See Conf. of Faith, ch. iv, §1. Larger Cat., que. 15, 120. If your minds are *made up* to adopt either of these theories, then it seems to me that common honesty requires of you two things: to advertise ycur presbyteries, when you apply for license and ordination, of your disbelief of these articles: that they may judge whether they are essential to our system of doctine; and second; to use your legitimate influences, as soon as you become church rulers, to have these articles expunged from our standards as false.

3. DELIBERATION ENJOINED.—Let me urge upon you a wiser attitude and temper towards the new science than many have shown, among the ministry. Some have shown a jealousy and uneasiness, unworthy of the stable dignity of the cause of inspiration. These apparent difficulties of geology are just such as science has often paraded against the Bible; but God's word has stood firm, and every true advance of science has only redounded to its honour. Christians, therefore, can afford to bear these seeming assaults with *exceeding coolness*. Other pretended theologians have been seen advancing, and then as easily retracting new-fangled schemes of *exegesis*, to suit new geologic hypotheses. The Bible has often had cause here to cry, "Save me from my friends." Scarcely has the theologian announced himself as sure of his discovery that *this* is the correct way to adjust Revelation to the prevalent hypotheses of the geologists, when these mutable gentlemen chang

their hypothesis totally. The obsequious divine exclaims: "Well I was in error then; but now I have certainly the right exposition to reconcile Moses to the geologists." And again the fickle science changes its ground. What can be more degrading to the authority of Revelation! As remarked in a previous lecture, unless the Bible has *its own* ascertainable and certain law of exposition, it cannot be a rule of faith; our religion is but rationalism. I repeat, if any part of the Bible must wait to have its real meaning *imposed upon it* by another, and a human science, that part is at least meaningless and worthless to our souls. It must expound itself independently; making other sciences ancillary, and not dominant over it.

4. Popular terms to be expected; in Bible, Reasons. But not applicable to cosmogony.—It should be freely conceded that it was not God's purpose in giving the Bible to foreshadow the scientific *rationale* of natural *phenomena.* Its object is theological. And the Bible is, in this respect, a strictly practical book. Hence, it properly speaks of those *phenomena as they appear*, and uses the popular phrases, "sun rises," "sun sets," "sun stood still," &c., just as any other than a pedantic astronomer would when not expressly teaching astronomy. Hence, we admit, that the attempt made by Rome and the Reformers to array the Bible against the Copernican System was simply foolish. The Bible only professed to speak of the apparent phase of the facts; the theory of the astronomer professed to give the non-apparent, scientific mechanism of the facts. So far as geology does the analogous thing, we should have no quarrel with it. But how far does this concession go? When Moses seems to say that God created the world and its inhabitants out of nothing about six thousand years ago, in six natural days, are we at liberty to treat him as we do Joshua when he speaks of the sun as standing still? I think not. First; Moses' reference to the facts of creation is not, like Joshua's reference to the astronomical event, merely incidental to a narrative of human history, but is a statement of what is as much a theological doctrine as a natural fact, introduced by him for its own theological purpose. Second; Joshua's language is defended as being true to the apparent phase of the event. But creation had no apparent phase; for the simple reason that it had no human spectators. There is no popular language about world-making, conformed to the seeming *phenomenon*, as we have about the moving and setting suns which we daily seem to behold; for none of us, of any generation, have witnessed the exterior appearances of world-making. Hence, I must believe that we are not authorized to class the declarations of Moses here, with those of these oft cited passages.

5. Burden of Proof rests on Geologists.—It is an all-important point that, if debate arises between a geologic hypothesis, and the fair and natural meaning of the Bible touching cosmogony, *the geologist must bear the burden of proof.* We are entitled to claim this, because the inspiration of the Scriptures is in prior possession of the field, in virtue of its own independent historical, prophetic, internal and spiritual evidences, and of the immense and irreparable stake which every awakened soul has in its truth. Hence, the geologist does not dislodge the Bible, until he has constructed his own independent, and exclusive,

and demonstrative evidence that his hypothesis *must be* the true one, and the only true one. Has the science ever done this? *This logical obligation geologists perpetually forget.* They perpetually substitute a "*may be*" for a "*must be.*" As soon as they hit upon a hypothesis which, it appears, may satisfy the known facts, they leap to the conclusion that it is the obviously, the only true one. But now, our position is not approached until such a complete, and exclusive demonstration is made. We are under no obligation, in order to defend ourselves, to substantiate another hypothesis by geologic reasoning; our defence is complete, when we show by such argument that their hypothesis comes short of an exclusive and perfect demonstration. It requires, as yet, little knowledge to show this; when the leading geologists are still differing between themselves, touching the igneous, the aqueous, the gradual, and the sudden systems; when effects are so hastily and confidently ascribed to one species of natural agency, which may, very possibly, have been effected by it, *or by one of several other* possible agencies; when we see the greatest names assuming as premises for important deductions, statements which are corrected by the practical observation of plain men; from the oversight of important questions as to the consistency and feasibility of their theories of cosmogony, with observed facts; and last, from the well known fact that the most truly scientific are most cautious in asserting any such scheme with confidence.

6. Usual inference of cause from observed resemblances.—I have reserved the most vital point to the last. It is this: How far must the admitted fact of a *creation* by God supercede the logical value of inferences from natural appearances? Geologists infer thus: "I see a given natural force producing a given structure.. I find a similar structure existing from before the times of human observation. But *I infer* that this natural force must have produced this too, in the same way." Now, I assert, that this is exactly, for any one save an Atheist, one of those inductions "*per enumerationem simplicem,*" as Lord Bacon terms them, which it was one of his esspecial glories to explode as utterly inadequate for any demonstration. He proves that it can never raise more than a meagre *probability* of truth, in the absence of a better canon of induction. To explain: Shallow observers had been saying, "I see the effect B produced a number of times by the cause A, as far as is apparent. Hence, I conclude, that in every other case where B appears, A was its cause." Now, as Bacon and all other sensible writers on the inductrve logic, teach us, the inference is worthless, until it is proved (in some other way) that no other cause capable of producing B was present in any case, save A. What can be plainer to common sense? Now, no man who is unwilling to take the blank, Atheistic ground, can deny that in the cases in hand, another adequate cause may have been present, as soon as we go back prior to historical testimony, namely: *almighty, creative power.* How on earth can the inference described prove anything as to the absence of that power, when the inference is worthless until after that question is settled by other authorities?

This invalid as against a Creator.—To apply this: Our modern geologists find that wherever stratified rocks are formed, since the era of human observation, the case is *sedimentary action.* They jump to the conclusion that therefore the same natural cause produced all the sedimentary rocks, no matter how much older than Adam. I reply: "Yes, provided it is proved beforehand, that *no other adequate cause was present.*" Unless you are an Atheist, you must admit that another cause, *creative power*, may have been present; *and present anywhere prior to the ages of authentic historical testimony.* Thus, the admission of the theistic scheme absolutely cuts across and supersedes all these supposed natural arguments for the origin and age of these structures.

Because, no creation could be devoid of seeming marks of nature.—I pray you to consider how perfect is my proof of the invalidity, the worthlessness of this sort of arguing. If its principle is valid, then it is impossible that any mind, in any possible circumstances could admit a proof of a Creator. For it is impossible to suppose any natural work of a Creator's hand, which would not seem to contain just the grounds of this pretended geologic argument for denying God's agency in it. For if God produced by a creation, a structure designed to be subjected after its creation to a natural law, *would He not have produced it natural?* Of course. Suppose, for instance, the first oak tree, parent of all subsequent generations of that species; the first horse, progenitor of all subsequent generations of horses. That first oak, first horse, must have had the whole nature of its progeny. Else, how could it become the natural head of its species? What is the scientific definition of specific unity? The properties which constitute these species are just those which descend by propagation. It is, therefore, a demonstration strictly scientific, that this first created supernatural head of the species *must* have been created strictly natural, endued with a full specific unity with its natural progeny. But, if the geologic argument were worth anything, it would prove from that very specific natural unity, that this created first head of the species could not have been created, but must have *grown* like all the later of its species. I repeat, unless you are an Atheist my argument must be conclusive to your mind.

Illustration from Paradise, &c.—As it is most important, let us illustrate it. Suppose, for argument's sake, that the popular understanding of the creation of Adam's body and of the trees of paradise is true. But now a naturalist of our modern school investigates affairs. He finds towering oaks, with acorns on them! Acorns do not form by nature in a day; some oaks require two summers to mature them. But worse than this: his Natural History has taught him that one summer forms but one ring in the grain of a tree's stock. He cuts down one of the spreading monarchs of the garden, and counts a hundred rings. So he concludes the garden and the tree must be a hundred years old, and that Adam told a monstrous fib, in stating that they were made last week. Yet Adam was right; for the creative act explained all. After nine hundred and thirty years, he visits the venerable tomb of the Father of all the living, and learns from his heir, Seth, how that his father sprang, at the bidding of God, out of the dust, an adult, fully formed man. The naturalists takes up a leg-bone of Adam's skeleton: he finds that its size, density and solidity show an adult growth. He saws off a section. He subjects a portion to his chemical solvents, and polishes down another to a translucent film, and subject it to his microscope. He says: "I perceive here the cellular structure of geletin, which once formed the incipient bone of the *foetus*, and these cells I now find filled with the deposite of *proto-phosphate of lime*, giving to it its stony strength and hardness. But I know that nature only introduces this earth gradually, as the person grows from *foetus* to adult. Whence, I learn that this specimen, like his children, grew during a period of twenty years; and the myth of his son, Seth, concerning his instantaneous arrival at an adult age, is wholly unphilosophical." Yet, Seth was right and the naturalist wrong. For, to say nothing of the inspired testimony, if this natural argument proves that Adam was once an infant, and had a father, it would equally prove the same of him, and of his father. So that we should have an infinite series of human fathers, extending back to all eternity. But such a series philosophy herself shows, is impossible.

NATURALNESS IN CREATED THINGS NECESSARY TO ADAPT THEM TO NATURAL LAW.—To pass to the inanimate creation, it is equally reasonable to say that, manifestly, a wise God, creating its structures (if there is any creator) with the purpose of subjecting them to the influence and development of natural law, would create them natural. For otherwise, they would not be adapted to their end. If they had no traits of the natural, as they came from God's hand, they would be incapable of becoming parts of a system under natural law. I repeat then, that the admission of the possibility of a creation destroys the value of every analogy to prove the date and mode of the production. The creative act (which, if it ever occurred, may have occurred at any date, when once we get back of historical testimony) has utterly superseded and cut across all such inferences.

ARGUMENT JUST, AS AGAINST EXCLUSION OF CREATOR.—This argument is usually dismissed by Geologists with a sort of summary contempt, or with a grand outcry of opposition. It does indeed cut deep into the seductive pride of their science, sweeping off at one blow that most fascinating region, the infinite past. It is urged, for instance, that my argument would subvert the foundations of all natural science. They exclaim, that to concede this would be to surrender the whole *organon* of scientific discovery. I answer, no. Within the domain of time, the known past of human history, where its testimony proves the absence of the supernatural, the analogical induction is perfectly valid. And *there* is the proper domain of natural science. In that field, their mothed of reasoning is a useful *organon*, and a legitimate; let them use it there, to the full, for the good of man. But in the unknown eternity of the past, prior to human history, it has no place; it is like the mariner's compass carried into the stellar spaces. That compass has a known attraction for the poles of this globe; and therefore *on this globe*, it is a valued guide. But away in the region of *Sirius*, where we know not whether the spheres have poles, or whether they are magnetic, it is naught. He who should follow it would be a madman.

OBJECTION FROM FOSSILS ANSWERED.—Another objection, supposed to be very strong, is drawn from the fossil remains of life. The geologists say triumphantly, that however one might admit my view as to the mere *strata*, it would be preposterous when applied to the remains of plants and animals buried in these *strata*, evidently alive thousands of ages ago. The reply to this is very plain, in two ways. First: How is it proved that it was thousands of ages ago that these fossil creatures, now buried in the *strata*, were alive? Only by assuming the gradual, sedimentary origin of all the *strata!* So that the reasoning runs in a circle. Second: Concede once (I care not where in the unknown past) *an almighty Creator of infinite understanding*, (as you must if you are not as Atheist,) and then both *power* and *motive* for the production of these living structures at and after a supernatural creation become infinitely possible. It would be an insane pride of mind, which should conclude that, because it could not comprehend the motive for the production, death, and entombment of all these creatures under such circumstances, therefore it cannot be reasonable for the *Infinite Mind* to see such a motive. So that my same *formula* applies here also. Once concede an Infinite Creator, and all inferences as to the necessarily natural origin of all the structures seen, are fatally sundered.

TENDENCIES OF GEOLOGISTS ATHEISTIC.—Again; why should the Theistic philosopher desire to push back the creative act of God to the remotest possible age, and reduce His agency to the least possible *minimum*, as is continually done in these speculations? What is gained by it? Instead of granting tha God created a KOSMOS, a world, they strive continually to show that He created only the rude germs of a world, ascribing as little as possible to God, and as much as possible to *natural law*. *Cui bono;* if you are not *hankering* after Atheism? Is a completed result any harder for *infinite* powers than a germinal one? What is *natural law;* and what its source? It originated in the creative power, and is maintained, energized, and regulated by the perpetual providence of God. Do you crave to push God away, as far as possible? It does'nt help you to say, natural law directed the formation of this mass of marble, instead of supernatural creation; for God is as near and as infinite in His common natural, as in His first supernatural working.

ILLUSTRATED BY NEBULAR HYPOTHESIS.—But if you must persist in recognizing nothing but natural forces, wherever you see a natural analogy, I will show you that it will land you, if you are consistent, no where short of absolute atheism. Suppose that *nebular* theory of the origin of the solar system were true, (which the anti-Christian, *La Place*, is said to have suggested as possible, and which so many of our nominal Christians have adopted, without proof, as certain; after Lord Rosse's telescope had desolved the only shadow of a probability for it, in resolving the larger *nebulae*.) An observer from some other system, fully imbued with the principles of modern science comes to inspect, at the stage that he finds only a vast mass of incandescent vapor, rotating from west to east around an *axis* of motion. If he uses the confident logic of our geologists, he must reason thus: "Matter is naturally inert: *momentum* must come from impact; therefore, this rotary motion which I now behold *must be* the result of some *prior force*, either mechanical, electrical, or some other. And again, I see only vapor. Vapor implies evaporation; and sensible heat suggests latent heat, rendered sensible either by electrical or chemical action, or compression. There *must*, therefore, have been a previous, different, and natural condition of this matter now votilized, heated, and rotating The geologists of the 19th century, therefore, will be mistaken in calling this the *primitive* condition of the system." Before each first, then, there must still be another first. This is, therefore, the *eternity of Naturalism*—it is *Atheism.* And such is the perpetual *animus* of material science, especially in our day.

Creation had a moral end.—In fine, if that account of the origin of the universe, which theology gives us, is to be heeded at all, the following appears the most philosphical conception of a creation: That God, in producing a world which His purposes required to pass under the immediate domain of natural laws, would produce it with just the properties which those laws perpetuate and develope. And here appears a consideration which brings theology and cosmogony into unison. What was God's true end in the creation of a material world? Reason and Scripture answer: To furnish a stage for the existence and action of a moral and rational creature. The earth was made for *man* to inhabit. As the light would be but darkness, were there no *Eye* to see, so the moral design of the world would be futile without a human mind to comprehend it, and praise its Maker. Now, such being God's end in creation, it seems much more reasonable to suppose that He would produce at once the world which He needed for His purpose, rather than spend hundreds of thousands of years in growing it.

LECTURE XXII.

SYLLABUS.

ANGELS.

1. Prove the existence and personality of Angels; and show the probable time of their creation.
   Turrettin, Loc. vii, ques. 2, 3, 5, 6, 7. Calvin's Inst., Bk. I, ch. xiv. Dick, Lect. 38. Knapp, sect. lviii, lix.
2. What is revealed of their *numbers, nature, powers* and *ranks*?
   Turrett. as above. Dick and Calv. as above. Knapp as above and sect. lxi.
3. In what moral state were they created, and under what covenant were they placed? How did this probation result?
   Turrettin, Loc. vii, que. 4. Loc. ix, que. 5. Loc. iv. que. 8, § 1-8. Dick, Lect. 39. Calv. as above.
4. What are the offices of the good angels? Have the saints individual guardian angels?
   Turrett, Loc. vii, que. 8. Dick, Lect. 38. Calv. as above. Knapp, Lect. lx.
5. Prove the personality and headships of Satan, and the personal existence of his angels.
   Calvin as above. Dick as above. Knapp, Lect. lxii, lxiii.

6. What do the Scriptures teach as to the powers of evil angels over natural elements and animal bodies; over the minds and hearts of men; in demoniacal possessions of ancient and modern times; in witchcraft and magic, and of the grade of guilt of wizards, &c.

Turrett. Loc. vii, que. 5. Loc. ix, que. 5. Loc. iv, que. 8, § 18. Calv. Inst., Bk. I, ch. xiv, § 13-20. Ridgeley, que. 19. Knapp, Lect. lxiv to lxvi. Commentaries.

7. What personal Christian duties result from this exposure to the assaults of evil angels?

I. Personality of Angels.—Against ancient Saducees, who taught neither resurrection, angel nor spirit, (Acts xxiii: 8) and made the angels only good thoughts and motions visiting human breasts; and our modern Saducees, among Rationalists, Socinians and Universalists, who teach that they are *impersonations* of divine energies, or of good and bad principles, or of diseases and natural influences; we prove the *real, personal existence* of angels thus: The Scriptures speak of them as having *all the acts* and *properties*, which can characterize real persons. They were *created* by God, through the agency of the Son, Col. i: 16; Gen. ii: 1; Exod. xx: 11. Have a nature, for Christ did not assume it, Heb. ii: 16. Are *holy* or unholy, Rev. xiv: 10. *Love* and *rejoice*, Luke xv: 10. *Desire*, 1 Pet. i: 12. *Contend*, Rev. xii: 7. *Worship*, Heb. i: 6. *Go and come*, Gen. xix: 1; Luke ix: 26. *Talk*, Zech. i: 9; Luke i: 13 Have *knowledge* and *wisdom*, (finite) 2 Sam. xiv: 20; Matt. xxiv: 36. Minister in various acts, Matt. xiii: 29, 49; Luke xvi: 22; Acts v: 19. Dwell with saints, who resemble them, in Heaven, Matt. xxii; 30, &c. If all this language was not intended to assure us of their personal existence, then there is no dependence to be placed on the word of God, or the laws of its interpretation.

The name angel (messenger) is indeed applied to ordinary messengers, Job i: 14; Luke vii: 24; to prophets, Is. xlii: 19; Mal. iii: 1; to priests, Mal. ii: 7; to ministers of the Church, Rev. i; 20, and to the Messiah, Mal. iii: 1; Is. lxiii: 9, &c., &c. But the other sense of personal and spiritual existences, is none the less perspicuous. They are called angels generally because they fulfill missions for God.

Spiritual creatures possible.—The invisible and spiritual nature of these beings is no objection to the credibility of their existence to any except Atheists and materialists. True, we have no sensible experience of their existence. Neither have we, directly, of our own souls, nor of God. If the existence of pure finite spirits is impossible, then man cannot be immortal; but the death of the body is the death of the being. Indeed, analogy would rather lead us to infer the existence of angels, from the almost numberless gradations of beings below man. Is all the vast gap between him and God a blank?

Date unknown.—To fix the *date* of the creation of angels is more difficult. The old opinion of orthodox reformers was, that their creation was a part of the first day's work. a.) Because they, being inhabitants, or hosts (see Ps. ciii: 21; cxlviii: 2) of heaven, were created when the heavens were. But see Gen. i: 1; ii: 1; Exod. xx; 11. b.) Because Scripture seems to speak of all the past eternity "before the foundation of the world" as an unbroken infinity, in which nothing existed except the uncreated; so that to speak of a Being as existing before that, is in their language, to represent Him as uncreated. See Prov. viii: 22; Ps. xc: 2; Jno. i: 1. Now I concede that the including of the angels with the heavens, under the term hosts of them, is correct. But first, the angels were certainly already in existence when this earth was begun. See Job xxxviii: 7. Second: the "*beginning*" in which God made the heavens and the earth, Gen. i: 1, is by no means necessarily the first of the six creative days. Nor does Gen. ii: 1, ("*Thus* were finished," is an unnecessarily strong rendering of WAY'CHULLU,) prove it. Hence, third, it may be granted that the beginning of the creation of God's created universe may mark the dividing point between unsuccessive eternity, and successive time, and between the existence of the uncreated alone, and of the creature; and yet it does not follow that this point was the first of the Mosaic days. Hence, it is best to say, with Calvin, that the age of the angels is unrevealed, except that they are older than the world and man.

II. QUALITIES OF THE ANGELS; INCORPOREAL? WHENCE THE FORMS OF THEIR APPARITIONS?—The angels are exceedingly numerous. Gen. xxxii: 2; Dan. vii: 10; Luke ii: 13; viii: 30; Matt. xxvi: 53; Heb. xii: 22. Their nature is undoubtedly spiritual, belonging *generally* to that class of substances to which man's rational soul belongs. They are called PNEUMATA. Heb. i: 13, 14, 7; Luke xx: 30; xxiv: 39; Col. i: 16. This also follows from what we learn of their *traits*, as *intelligent* and *voluntary* beings, as *invisible*, except when they *assume* bodies temporarily, as inexpressibly quick in motion; and as *penetrable*, so that they occupy the same space with matter, without displacing or being displaced by it. Several supposed objections to their mere spirituality have been mooted. One is, that they have, as we shall see, so much physical power. The answer is, that the ultimate source of all force is in *spirits*: our limbs only have it, as moved by our spirit's volitions. Another is, that if pure spirits they would be ubiquitous, because to suppose any substance possessed of locality must imply that it is defined by extension and local limits. But extension cannot be an attribute of spirit. I reply, that it must be possible for a spirit to have locality "definitely," though not "circumscriptively," because our consciousness assures us that our spirits are within the superficies of our body, in some true sense in which they are not elsewhere; yet it is equally impossible for us to attribute dimension, either to our spirits or their thoughts. And just as really as our spirits pass through space, when our bodies move, so really angels change their locality, though far more swiftly, by an actual motion, through extension; though not implying extension in the thing moved. Again, it is objected: Angels are spoken of as having wings, figure, and often, human shape, in which they were sometimes, not merely visible, but *tangible*, and performed the characteristic material acts of eating and drinking. See Gen. xviii: 2, 5, 8; xix: 10, 16. On this it may be remarked that Scripture expressly assigns wings to no orders but cherubim and seraphim. We see Dan. ix: 21, and Rev. xiv: 6, speaking of angels, not cherubin and seraphim, as "flying." But this may be in the general sense of rapid motion; not motion with wings. The purpose of these appearances is obvious, to bring the presence and functions of the angelic visitant under the scope of the *senses* of God's servants, for some particular purpose of mercy. Angelic apparations seem to have appeared under three circumstances—in dreams, in states of inspired exstacy, and when the observer was in the usual exercise of his senses. Only the latter need any explanation; for the former cases are accounted for by the ideal impression made on the *conception* of the dreaming or exstatic mind by God. But in such cases as that of Gen. xviii and xix, we are bound to believe that these heavenly spirits occupied for the time, real, material bodies. Any other opinion does violence at once to the laws of exegesis of Scripture language, and to the validity of our senses as inlets of certain and truthful perceptions. Whence then, those bodies? Say some, they were the actual bodies of living men, which the angels occupied, suppressing, for the nonce, the consciousness and personality of the human soul to which the body belonged. Some, that they are material, but glorified substances, kept in Heaven, ready for the occasional occupancy of angels on their missions; as we keep a Sunday coat in our wardrobes. Some, that they were aerial bodies, composed of compacted atmosphere, formed thus for their temporary occupancy, by divine power, and then dissolved into air again. And still others that they were created by God for them, out of matter, as Adam's body was, and then laid aside. Where God has not seen fit to inform us, I think it best to have no opinion on this mysterious subject. The Scriptures plainly show us, that this incorporation is *temporary*.

The Angels intelligent agents.—The angels are intelligent and voluntary beings, as is most manifest, from their functions of praising, worshipping, teaching the prophets, and ministering to saints, and from their very spirituality: for *thought* is the characteristic attribute of Spirit. We naturally infer that as angels are incorporeal, they have neither senses, nor sensation, nor literal language. Since our senses are the inlets of all our objective knowledge, and the *occasional* causes of all mental action, we have no experience nor conception of a knowledge without senses. But it does not seem unreasonable to believe that our bodies *obstruct* the cognitions of our souls, somewhat as imprisoning one within solid walls does his communication with others; that our five senses are the windows, pierced through this barrier, to let in partial perceptions; and that consequently, the disembodied soul perceives and knows somehow, with vastly greater freedom and fulness, by direct spiritual apprehension. Yet *all* of the knowledge of angels is not direct intuition. No doubt much of it is mediate and deductive, as is so much of ours; for the opposite form of cognition can only be universal, in an infinite understanding. It is very clear also, that the knowledge of angels is finite and susceptible of increase. Marc. xiii: 32: Eph. iii: 10; 1 Pet. i: 12; Dan. viii: 16. Turrettin's four classes of angelic knowledge—*natural, experimental, supernatural*, and *revealed*—might, I think, be better arranged as their concreated, their acquired, and their revealed knowledge. It is, in fine, clear that their knowledge and wisdom are great. They appear, Dan. and Rev., as man's teachers, they are glorious and splendid creatures, and they enjoy more favour and communion from God. See also 2 Sam. xiv: 20.

Powerful.—They are also beings of great power; passing over vast spaces with almost incredible speed. Dan. ix: 23, exercising portentous physical powers, 2 Kings xix; 35: Zech. xii: 8; Acts xii: 7,

10: Matt. xxviii: 2, and they are often spoken of as mighty beings, Ps. ciii: 20; Rev. x: 1, v: 2, and are spoken of as DUNAMEIS, principalities, &c., Eph. vi: 12; 2 Thes. i: 7. This power is undoubtedly always within God's control, and *never truly supernatural*, although superhuman. It seems to have extended at times, by God's permission, to men's bodies, to diseases, to the atmostphere, and other elements.

THEIR ORDERS.—The romantic distribution of the angels into a hierarchy of three classes, and nine orders, borrowed by the Pseudo Dyonisius from the Platonizing Jews, need not be refuted here. It is supposed by many Protestants, that there are differences of grade among angels, (though what, we know not,) from the fact—a.) That Paul uses several terms to describe them, Col. i: 16; b.) That there is at least one superior angel among the evil angels; c.) That we hear of an archangel, Michael; d.) That God's terrestrial works exhibit every where, gradations.

MICHAEL NOT ANGEL OF COVENANT.—If, as some suppose, Michael is identical with the Angel of the Covenant, the third of these considerations is removed. Their reasons are, that he is called *the* Archangel, and is the only one to whom the title is given; that he is called the Prince, and great Prince, who stood for Israel, (Dan. x: 31; xii: 1,) and that he is seen, (Rev. xii: 7,) heading the heavenly war against Satan and his kingdom; a function suited to none so well as to the Messiah. But it is objected, with entire justice, that his name (Who is as God?) is not any more significant of the Messiah than that of Michaiah, and is several times the name of a man—that he is one, "*one* of the chief princes." Dan. x: 13. That in Jude, he was under authority in his dispute over Moses' body, and that he is plainly distinguished from Christ, (1 Thess. iv: 16,) where Christ descends from heaven *with the voice* of the archangel, and trump of God.

CHERUBIM. WHAT?—A more difficult question is, what were the cherubim mentioned, Gen. iii: 24; Exod. xxv: 18; 1 Kings vi: xxiii: Ps. xviii: 10; and most probably, under the name of seraphim, in Is. vi: 2; Ezek. x: 5, 7, &c. It is very evident, also, that the "living creatures, described in Ezekiel's vision, ch. i: 5, as accompanying the wheels, and sustaining the divine throne, were the same. Dr. Fairbairn, the most quoted of modern interpreters of types and symbols, teaches that the cherubim are not existences at all, but mere *ideal symbols, representing humanity redeemed and glorified*. His chief argument, omitting many fanciful ones drawn from the fourfold nature, and their wings, &c., is: that they are manifestly identical with the ZOE, of Rev. iv: 6–8, which evidently symbolize, ch. v: 8–10, somehow, the ransomed church. The great objections are, that the identification is not certain, inasmuch as John's ZOE had but one face each; that there is no propriety in founding God's heavenly throne and providence on glorified humanity, as His immediate attendants; but chiefly, that while it might consist with prophetic vision to make them ideal symbols, it utterly outrages the plain *narrative* of Gen. iii: 24. And the duty of the cherubim, there described, obstructing sinful man's approach to the tree of life, with a flaming sword, the symbol of justice, is one utterly unfitted to redeemed and glorified humanity. Hence, I believe, with the current of older divines, that the cherubim are not identical with John's "living creatures," but are angels, like all the others, *real*, spiritual, intelligent beings: and that when God was pleased to appear to Isaiah and Ezekiel in prophetic vision, they received temporarily these mixed forms, to be symbolical of certain traits of obedience, intelligence, strength, and swiftness, which they show as ministers of God's providence and worshippers of His upper sanctuary. (The etymology of the word is utterly obscure.)

III. The Angel's 1st estate, their probation and issue thereof. That all these spiritual beings were created holy and happy, is evident from God's character, which is incapable of producing sin or misery; see Gen. i: 31; from the frequent use of the term *holy* angels, and from all that is revealed of their occupations and affections, which are pure, blessed and happy. The same truth is implied, in what is said, 2 Pet. ii: 4, of "angels that sinned," and so were not spared, but cast down to hell, and Jude vi, of "angels that kept not their first estate." This first estate was, no doubt, in all, an estate of holiness and happiness. As to the change which has taken place in it, we are indeed left, mainly to inference by God's word; but it is inference so well supported by His attributes, and the analogy of man's case, that I feel a good degree of confidence in drawing it. A holy, intelligent creature, would owe service to God, with love and worship, by its natural relation to Him. And while God would be under no obligations to such a creature, to preserve its being, or bestow a happy immortality, yet His own righteousness and benevolence would forbid His visiting external suffering on that creature, while holy. The *natural relation* then, between such a creature and God, would be this: God would bestow perfect happiness, just so long as the creature continued to render perfect obedience, and no longer. For both the natural and legal consequence of sin would be spiritual death. But it would seem that some of the angels are *elect*, and these are now confirmed in a state of *everlasting* holiness and bliss. For holiness is their peculiarity, their blessedness seems complete, and they are mentioned as sharing with man the heavenly mansions, whence we know glorified saints will never fall. On the other hand, another class of the angels have finally and irrevocably fallen into spiritual death. The inference from these facts would seem to be, that the angels, like the human race, have passed under the probation of a *covenant of works*. The elect kept it, the non-elect broke it; the difference between them being made, so far as God was the author of it, not by His efficacious active decree and grace, but by His permissive decree, in which both classes were wholly left to the freedom of their wills. God only determining by His Providence the circumstances surrounding them, which became the *occasional* causes of their different choices, and limiting their conduct. On those who kept their probation, through the efficacy of this permissive decree, God graciously bestowed confirmation in holiness, adoption, and inheritance in life everlasting. This, being more than a temporary obedience could *earn*, was of pure grace; yet not through a Mediator: because the angels being innocent, needed none. When this probation began, what was its particular condition, and when it ended, we know not; except that the fall of Satan, and most probably that of his angels, preceded Adam's. Nor is the nature of the sin known. Some, from Mark iii: 29, suppose it was blasphemy against the Holy Ghost. Others, from 1 Tim. iii: 6, suppose it was pride: neither conclusively. Guessing is vain, where there is no key to a solution. It may very possibly be that pride was the sin, for it is one to which Satan's spiritual nature and exalted state might be liable. The great difficulty is *how*, in a will prevalently holy, and not even swayed by innocent bodily wants and appetites, and where there was not in the whole universe a single creature to entice to sin, the first wrong volition could have place. At the proper time I will attempt to throw on this what light is in my power.

IV. Occupations of good angels.—The good angels are engaged; first, in the worship and adoration of God. Matt. xviii: 10; Rev. v: 11. Second, God employs them in administering His gracious and providential government over the world. Under this head we may notice: a.) That they aided in the giving of Revelation, as the Law: Acts vii: 53; Gal. iii: 19, and many prophetic messages and disclosures, as Dan. x. b.) They seem to have some concern in social and national events, procuring the execution of God's purposes. Dan. x: 13. c.) They are employed to punish His enemies, as instruments of His righteous vengeance. 2 Kings xix: 35; Acts xii: 23; 1 Chron. xxi: 16. d.) They are sent forth to minister to those who shall be heirs of salvation. Heb. i: 14; Acts xii: 7; Ps. xci: 10–12. e.) They guide the departing souls of Christians home to their mansions in heaven. Luke xvi: 22. Last. They are Christ's agents in the general judgment and resurrection. Matt. xiii: 39; xxiv: 31; 1 Thes. iv: 17.

How exercised?—As to the exact nature of the agencies exerted for the saints by the ministering angels, Christians are perhaps not very well instructed, nor agreed. A generation ago, it was currently believed that they communicated to their minds instructions important to their duty or welfare, by dreams, presentiments, or impressions. Of these, many Christians are now skeptical. It seems more certain that they exert an invisible superintendence over our welfare, in and under the laws of nature. Whether they influence our waking minds unconsciously by suggesting thoughts and feelings through our law of associated ideas, is much debated. I see in it nothing incredible. The pleasing and fanciful idea of guardian angels is grounded on the following scriptures: Dan. x: 13, 20; Matt. xviii: 10; Acts xii: 15. The most that these passages can prove is, that provinces and countries may have their affairs committed in some degree to the especial care of some of the higher ranks of angels: and that superstitious Jews *supposed* that Peter had his own guardian angel, who might borrow Peter's body for the purpose of an apparition. The idea has more support in New Platonism than in Scripture.

V. Satan a Person.—The personality of Satan and his angels is to be established by an argument exactly similar to that employed for the good angels. Almost every possible act and attribute of personality is ascribed to them; so that we may say, the Scripture contains scarcely more proof of the existence of a personal God, than of a Devil. He speaks, goes, comes, reasons, hates, is judged, and is punished. See for instance, such passages as Matt. iv: 1–11; Jno. viii: 44; Job i: 6 to ii: 7.

SCRIPTURES INDUCE OVER WHOLE BIBLE HISTORY THE FORM OF THE TWO RIVAL KINGDOMS.—There is no subject on which we may more properly remember that "There are more things in heaven and earth than are dreamed of in our philosophy."

It is evidently the design of the Scriptures to *make much* of Satan and his work. From first to last, the favourite representation of the world's history is, that it is the *arena* for a struggle between two kingdoms—Christ's and Satan's. Christ leads the kingdom of the good, Satan that of the evil; though with different authorities and powers. The headships of Satan over his demons is implied where they are called "his angels." He is also called Prince of Devils. Matt. xxv: 41; ix: 34. Prince of the powers of the air, and Prince of darkness. Eph. vi: 12. This pre-eminence he doubtless acquired partly by seducing them at first, and probably confirmed by his superior powers. His dominion is compacted by fear and hatred of God, and common purposes of malice. It is by their concert of action that they seem to approach so near to ubiquity in their influences. That Satan is also the tyrant and head of sinful head is equally plain. This prevalent Bible picture of the two kingdoms may be seen carried out in these particulars. a) Satan originated sin. Gen. iii: 1; Rev. xii: 9, 10; xx: 2, 10; 1 Jno. iii: 8; Jno. viii: 44; 2 Cor. xi: 3. b.) Satan remains the leader of the human and angelic hosts which he seduced into hostility, and employs them in desperate resistance to Christ and His Father. He is the "God of this world." 2 Cor. iv: 4. "The Spirit that worketh in the children of this world." Eph. ii: 2. Wicked men are his children. See above, and 2 Tim. ii: 26. He is "the Adversary" (Satan,) "the Accuser," (DIABOLOS,) "the Destroyer," (APOLLUON). c.) The progress of Christ to the final overthrow of this kingdom is the one great business of all time; the history of the conflict is the history of man and redemption. Gen. iii: 15; Jno. xii: 31; 1 Jno. iii: 8–10; 1 Pet. v: 8: Eph. vi: 11; Jno. viii: 44; Marc. iii: 23–27; Rom. xvi: 20; Acts xxvi: 18; Luke x: 18. The single fact that ungodly man, until the end of the world, compose Satan's kingdom, proves that he has, and will have some power or influence over their souls.

POWERS OF BAD ANGELS.—The powers of Satan and his angels are a.) always, and in all forms strictly under the control of God and His permissive decree and providence. b.) They are often, perhaps, superhuman, but never supernatural. If they do what man cannot, it is not by possession of omniscience or omnipotence, but by natural law: as a son of Anak could lift more than a common man, or a Davy or Brewster could control more of the powers of nature than a peasant.

There is a supposition, which seems to have plausible grounds, that as the plan of redemption advances, the scope of Satan's operations is progressively narrowed; just as the general who is defeated is cut off from one another of his resources, and hemmed in to a narrower theatre of war, until his final capture. It may be, then, that his power of afflicting human bodies, of moving the material elements, of communicating with wizards, of producing mania by his possessions, have been, or will be successively retrenched; until at last the *millennium* shall take away his remaining power of ordinary temptation. See Luke x: 18; Mark iii: 27; Rev. xx: 3. But

Over Nature—(1.)—Satan once had; and for anything that can be proved, may now have extensive powers over the atmosphere and elements. The first is proved by Job, ch. 1 and 2. From this would naturally follow influence over the bodily health of men. No one can prove that some pestilences and droughts, tempests and earthquakes are not his work now.

(2.) Over human minds.—He once had at least an occasional power of direct injection of conceptions and emotions, both independent of the *man's* senses and suggestions. See Matt. iv: 3, &c. This is the counterpart of the power of good angels, seen in Dan. ix: 22; Matt. ii: 13. It is this power which makes the crime of witchcraft possible. The wizard was a *man*, and the witch a *woman*, who was supposed to communicate with an evil angel, and receive from him, at the cost of some profane and damnable price, power to do superhuman things, or to reveal secrets beyond human ken. Its criminality was in its profanity, in the alliance with God's enemy, and its malignity in employing the arch-murderer, and always for wicked or malicious ends against others.

Witchcraft.—In Exod. xxii: 18, witchcraft is made a capital sin; and in Gal. v: 20, it is still mentioned as a "work of the flesh." Yet some suppose that the sin never could be really committed. They account for Moses' statute by supposing that the class actually existed *as imposters*, and God justly punished them for their *animus*. This, I think, is hardly tenable. Others suppose the sin was anciently actual; but that now, according to the supposition of a gradual restriction, God no longer permits it; so that all modern wizards are imposters. Doubtless there was, at all times, a large infusion of imposture. Others suppose that God still *occasionally* permits the sin, relaxing His curb on Satan in judicial anger against men, as in the age of Moses. There is nothing unscriptural in this. I do not admit the reality of any modern case of witchcraft, only because I have seen no evidence that stands a judicial examination.

(3.) Possession.—Evil spirits had power over men's bodies and souls, by usurping a violent controul over their suggestions, emotions and volitions, and thus violating their rational personality, and making the human members, for the time, their implements. This, no doubt, was attended with unutterable horror and agitation of consciousness, in the victim.

These real.—This has been a favourite topic of neologic skepticism. They urge that the Evangelists did not really mean to teach actual possession; but their object being theological, and not medical or psychological, they used the customary language of their day, not meaning thereby to endorse it, as scientific or accurate; because any other language would have been pedantic and useless. They refer to Josh. x: 12. In Matt. iv: 24, lunatics (theleniadzomenoi) are named; but we do not suppose the author meant to assert they were moonstruck. They remind us of similar cases of mania now cured by opiates or blisters. They remind us that 'possessions,' like other superstitions, are limited to the dark ages. They argue that Daemons are said, Jude 6th, to be in chains, &c.

In this case the theory is incompatible with the candour of the sacred writers. For: 1st. They distinguish between "possessions" and diseases of a physiological source, by mentioning both separately. See Mark i: 32; Luke vi: 17, 18; Matt. iv: 24, &c. 2d. The daemons, as distinct from the possessed men, speak, and are spoken to, are addressed, commanded, and rebuked by our Saviour, and deprecate His wrath. Mark i: 25, 34; ix: 25; Matt. viii: 32; xvii: 18. 3d. They have personality after they go out of men; whereas the disease has no entity apart from the body of which it was an affection. See Luke viii: 32. 4th. A definite number of daemons possessed one man, Mark v: 9, and one woman, Mark xvi: 9. 5th. Their *moral* quality is assigned. 6th. The victories of Christ and His Apostles over them, announced the triumph of a spiritual kingdom over Satan's. Mark iii: 27; Luke xi: 20.

Do "possessions" now exist? Many reply, No; some on the supposition of a progressive restriction of Satan's license; others supposing that in the age of miracles Providence made special allowance of this malice, in order to give Christ and His missionaries special opportunity to evince the power of His kingdom, and show *earnests* of its overthrow. The latter *is* one object of Christ's victories over these "possessions." See Mark iii: 27; Luke xi: 20; x: 17–20, (where we have a separate proof of the spiritual nature of these possessions, as above shown.) Whether "possessions" occur now, I do not feel qualified to affirm or deny.

4th. Temptations.—The fourth power of Satan and daemons is doubtless ordinary, and will be until the *millennium;* that of tempting to sin. This they *may* still carry on by direct injection of conceptions, or affections of the sensibility, without using the natural laws of sensibility or suggestion; and which they certainly do practice *through the* natural co-operation of those laws. Thus: A given mental state has a natural power to suggest any other with which it is associated. So that of several associated states, either one might naturally arise in the mind by the next suggestion. Now, these evil spirits seem to have the power of giving a prevalent vividness (and thus power over the attention and emotions) to that one of the associated states which best suit their malignant purposes. Here is the subtlety, and hence the danger of these practices, that they are not distinguished in our consciousness from natural suggestions, because the Satanic agency is strictly through the natural channels.

May operate through body.—The mutual influence of the physiological states of the nerves and acts of organs of sense, over the mind, and *vice versa*, is a very obscure subject. We know, at least, that there is a mass of important truth there, as yet partially explored. Many believe that a concept, for instance, actually colours the retina of the eye, as though the visual *spectrum* of the object was formed on it. All have experienced the influence of emotions over our sense-perceptions. Animal influences on the organs of sense and nerves influence both concepts and percepts. Now, if evil spirits can produce an animal effect on our functions of nervous sensibility, they have a mysterious mode of affecting our souls.

Recurring suggestions unwholesome.—We must also consider the regular psychological law, that vivid suggestions recurring too often always evokes a morbid action of the soul. The same subject of anxiety, for instance, too frequently recalled, begets an exaggerated anxiety. The "One-idea-man" is a mono-maniac. It thus becomes obvious, how Satan may now cause various grades of lunacy, and *doubtless often does.* (This is not to be confounded with actual "possessions.") Hence, in part, religious melancholies, the most frightful of mental diseases. The maniac even, has recessions of disease; or he has reasons of glee, which, if maniacal, are actual joy to his present consciousness. But the victim of religious melancholy has no respite; he is crushed by a perpetual *incubus.* You can see how Satan (especially if bodily disease co-operates) can help to propagate it by securing the too constant recurrence of subjects of spiritual doubt or anxiety. You will see also, that the only successful mode to deal with the victims of these attacks is by producing *diversion* of the habitual trains of thought and feeling.

VII. How powerful is the motive to prayer, and gratitude, for exemption from these calamitous spiritual assaults, for which we have no adequate defence in ourselves? The duty of watchfulness against temptations and their occasions, is plain. It becomes an obvious Christian duty to attempt to preserve the health of the nervous system, refraining from habits and stimulants which may have, we know not what influence on our nervous idiosyncrasy. It is also the duty of all to avoid *overcoming* and inordinate emotions about any object: and to abstain from a too constant pursuit of any carnal object, lest Satan should get his advantage of us thereby.

This discussion shows us how beneficent is the interruption of secular cares by the Sabbath's break.

LECTURE XXIII.

SYLLABUS.

PROVIDENCE.

1. Define God's *Providence.* State the other theories of His practical relations to the universe. What concern has it in physical laws and causes?
   Conf. of Faith, ch. v. Turrett., Loc. vi, que. 1, 2, 4. Dick, Lect. 41 and 42. Calv. Inst., Bk. II., ch. 1 and 2. So. Presb. Review, Art. I., Jan., 1870. Knapp, Art. viii, § 67, 69. McCosh, Div. Gov't, Bk. II, ch. 1.
2. Argue the doctrine of a *special,* from that of a *general* providence.
   Turrett., Loc. vi, que. 3. Dick and Calvin, as above.
3. Prove the doctrine of a providence, a) by God's perfections. b.) By man's moral intuitions. c.) From the observed course of nature and human history. d.) From the dependence of creatures.
   Turrett., Loc. vi, que. 1. Dick and Calvin, as above. Knapp, Art. viii, § 68.

4. Present the scriptural argument : a) From prophecy; b) from express testimonies. Answer objections.

Same authorities, and Dick, Lect. 43

5. Does God's power extend to all acts of rational free agents? What is His concern in the gracious acts of saints? What, in the evil acts of sinners? Discuss the doctrine of an immediate *concursus* in the latter.

Turrett., Loc. vi, que. 4 to 8. Dick, Lect. 42, 43. Calvin Inst., Bk. I, ch. xviii. Hill's Div., Bk. IV, ch. 9, § 3. Knapp, Art. viii, § 70 to 72. Hodge's Outlines, ch. xiii.

I & II. Definitions, and other theories.—*Providentia*, Greek, pronoia is the *execution* in successive time, of God's eternal, unsuccessive *purpose*, or prodesis. We believe the Scriptures to teach, not only that God originated the whole universe, but that He bears a perpetual, *active relation* to it; and that these works of providence are "His most holy, wise, and powerful preserving and governing all His creatures, and all their actions." It may be said that there are, besides this, three other theories concerning God's relation to the Universe; that of the Epicurean, who, though admitting an intelligent deity, supposed it inconsistent with His blessedness and perfections, to have any likings or anger, care or concern in the multiform events of the worlds; that of the Rational Deists, Socinians, and many rationalists; that God's concern with the Universe is not universal, special and perpetual, but only general, viz: by first endowing it with general laws of action, to the operation of which each individual being is then wholly left, God only exercising a general oversight of the laws, and not of specific agents; and that of the Pantheists, who identify all seeming substances with God, by making them mere modes of His self-development: so that there is no providential *relation*, but an actual identity; and all the events and acts of the Universe are simply God acting.

General Providencee unreasonable without special.—The first theory is, as we shall see, practical atheism, and is contradicted by a proper view of God's attributes. The third has been already refuted, as time and ability allowed. Against the second, or Deistical, I object that the seeming analogy by which it is suggested is a false one. That analogy is doubtless of human rulers—e. g., (a commander of an army,) who regulates general rules and important events, without being himself cognizant of special details; and of machinists, who construct a machine and start its motion, so that it performs a multitude of special evolutions, not individually directed by the maker. The vital difference is, that the human ruler employs a multitude of *intelligent* subordinates, independent of him for being, whose *intention* specifically embraces the details; whereas God directs inanimate nature, according to deists, without such intervention. The Platonist conception of a providence administered over particulars by daemons is more consistent with this analogy. And the machinist does but *adjust* some motive power which God's providence supplies (water on his wheel, the elasticity of a spring, &c.,) to move his machine in his absence; whereas God's providence itself must be the motive power of His universal machine. 2d. On this deistical scheme of providence, results must either be fortuitous to God, (and then He is no longer Sovereign nor Almighty, and we reach practical atheism,) or else their occurrence is determined by Him through the medium of causations possessed of a *physical necessity;* (and we are thus landed in stoical *fate!*) 3d. It is a mere illusion to talk of a direction of the general, which does not embrace the particulars; for a general class is nothing, when separated from the particulars which compose it, but an abstraction of the mind. Practically, the general is only produced by producing all the specials which compose it. 4th. God's providence evolves all events by using second causes according to their natures. But all events are interconnected, nearly or remotely, as causes and effects. And the most minute events often bear the connexion with the grandest; e. g., the burning of a city from a vagrant spark; the change of King Abab's dynasty by an errant arrow. Hence, according to this mode of providence, which alone we *see* God usually employs, unless His care extended to *every* event specially, it could not effectuate *any*, certainly. To exercise a general providence without a special, is as though a man should form a *chain* without forming its *links.*

The definition of Providence, which we adopted from the Catechism, divides it into two works—*sustentation* and *government.*

Providential Sustentation What? Scholastic conception of it.—According to the Augustinian scholastics, the Cartesians, and many of the stricter Calvinistic Reformers, this sustentation of creatures in being is effected by a perpetual, active efflux or *concursus* of divine power at every successive instant, identical with that act of will and power by which they were brought out of *nihil* into *esse;* and they conceive that on the cessation of this act of God, for one instant, towards any creature whatsoever, it would return incontinently to non-existence. So that it is no figure of speech with them to say, "Sustentation is a perpetual re-creation." Their arguments are, that God alone is self-existent; hence those things which have a dependent existence cannot have the ground of the continuance of their existence in themselves—that all creatures exist *in successive time:* but the instants of successive time have no substantive tie between them by which one *produces* the next; but they only follow each other, whence it results that successive existence is momentarily returning to *nihil,* and is only kept out of it by a perpetual re-creation. And 3d. They quote Scriptures, as Neh. ix: 6; Job x: 12; Ps. civ: 27–30; Acts xvii: 28; Heb. i: 3; Col. i: 17.

This not proved.—This speculation has always seemed to me without basis, and its demonstration, to say the least, impossible for the human understanding. But let me distinctly premise, that both the existence and essence, or the being and properties of every created thing, originated out of nothing, in the mere will and power of God; that they are absolutely subject, at every instant of their successive existence, to His sovereign power; that their *action* is all regulated by His special providence, and that He could reduce them to nothing as easily as He created them. Yet, when I am required to believe that their sustentation is a literal, continuous re-production by God's special act out of nihil, I cannot but remember that, after all, the human mind has no cognition of substance itself, except as the unknown *substratum* of properties, and no insight into the manner in which it subsists. Hence we are not qualified to judge, whether its subsistence is maintained in this way. The arguments seem to me invalid. When we deny self-existence to creatures, we deny that the cause which *originates* their existence can be in them; but this is far from proving that God, in originating their existence, may not have conferred it as a permanent gift, continuing itself so long as He permits it. e. g., Motion is never assumed by matter of itself; but when impressed from without, it is never self-arrested. To say that finite creatures exist *in* successive time, or have their existence measured by it, is wholly another thing from showing that this succession *constitutes* their existence. What is *time*, but an abstract idea of *our* minds, which we project upon the finite existence which we think of or observe? Let any man analyse his own conception, and he will find that the existence *is* conceived of as possessing a *true continuity;* it is the time by which his mind measures it, that lacks the continuity. Last. These general statements of Scripture only assert the practical and entire dependence of creatures; no doubt their authors would be very much surprised to hear them interpreted into these metaphysical subtilties.

MONADS NOT DEPENDENT IN SAME WAY AS ORGANISMS.—You will observe that the class of ideas which leads to this idea of a perpetual efflux of divine power, in recreation, are usually borrowed from *organized material bodies.* Men forget that the existence of organisms may be, and probably is, dependent, in a very different sense, from that of *simple* existence, such as a material ultimate atom, or a pure spirit. For the existence of an organized body is nothing but the continuance of its organization, i. e., of the aggregation of its parts in certain modes. This, in turn, is the effect of *natural causes;* but these causes operate under the perpetual active superintendence of God. So that it is literally true, the existence of a compounded organism, like the human body, is the result of God's perpetual, providential activity; and the *mere cessation* of this would be the end of the organism. But the same fact is not proved of simple, monadic substances.

WHAT IS SECOND CAUSE?—But *what are natural causes and laws?* This question enters intimately into our views of providence, inasmuch as they are the *means* with which providence works. The much-abused phrase, *law of nature*, has been vaguely used in various senses. Sometimes men seem to mean by it, a class of similar facts in nature generalized; sometimes it is used as the name for some recurring cause: but properly it means that it is *the observed regular mode or rule, according to which a given cause, or class of causes operates under given conditions.* This definition of itself will show us the absurdity of offering a law of nature to account for the existence of anything. For nature is but an abstraction, and the law is but the regular mode of acting of a cause; so that instead of accounting for, it needs to be accounted for itself. The fact that a *phenomenon* is produced again and again regularly, does not account for its productions! The true question which lies at the root of the matter is, concerning the real power which is present in natural causes. We say that they are those things which, under certain conditions, have *power* to produce certain effects. What, then, is the *power?* It is answered that the power resides in some *property* of the thing we call cause, when that property is brought into certain relations with the properties of some other thing. But still, the question recurs: Is the power, the activity, a true property of the thing which acts as cause, or is the power truly God's force, and the occurrence of the relation between the properties of cause and effect merely the appointed *occasion* of its exertion? This is the question. Let me premise, before stating the answers given, that the question should be limited to the laws of *material* nature, and to physical causes. All sound philosophy now regards intelligent spirits as themselves proper fountains of causation, because possessed of a true spontaneity and self-determination, not indeed emancipated from God's sovereign control, yet real and intrinsically active, as permitted and regulated by Him.

Some admit no natural force but God.—But, as to physical causes, orthodox divines and philosophers give different answers. Say the one class, as Dick, matter is only passive. The coming of the properties of the cause into the suitable relation to the effect is only the *occasion;* the true agency is but God's immediately. All physical *power* is God directly exerting Himself through passive matter: and the law of the cause is but the regular mode which He proposes to Himself for such exertions of His power. Hence, the true difference between natural power and miraculous, would only be, that the former is customary under certain conditions, the latter, under those conditions, unusual. When a man feels his weary limbs drawn towards the earth, by what men call gravity, it is in fact as really God drawing them, as when, against gravity, the body of Elijah or Christ was miraculously borne on high. And the reason they assign is: that matter is negative and inert; and can only be the recipient of power: and that it is incapable of that intelligence, recollection, and volition, implied in obedience to a regular law.

Theory of McCosh Defective.—Others, as McCosh, Hodge, &c., would say, that to deny all properties of action to material things, is to reduce them to practical nonentity; leaving God the only agent and the only true existence, in the material universe. Their view is that God, in creating and organizing material bodies, endued them with certain *properties.* These properties He sustains in them by that perpetual support and superintendence He exerts. And these properties *are* specific powers of acting or being acted on, when brought into suitable relations with the properties of other bodies. Hence, while power is really in the physical cause, it originated in, and is sustained by, God's power. The question then arises: If this be so, if the power is intrinsically in the physical cause, wherein does God exert any special providence in each case of causation? Is not His providential control banished from the domain of these natural laws, and limited to His act of creation, which endued physical causes with their power? The answer which McCosh makes to this question is: that nothing is a cause by itself; nor does a mere capacity for producing a given effect make a thing a cause; unless it be placed in a given relation with a suitable property of some other thing. And here, says he, is God's special, present providence; in constituting those suitable relations for inter action, by His superintendence. The obvious objection to this answer seems to have been overlooked; that these juxta-positions, or relations, are themselves always brought about by God (except where free agents are employed) by *natural causes.* Hence, the view of God's diately or remotely. Prophecy, threats, promises, and the duty of prayer prove it, (see on Decrees,) and Scripture expressly asserts it. Prov. xvi: 9; xx: 24, xxi: 1; Jer. x: 23; Ps. xxxiii: 14, 15; Gen. xlviii: 8, &c.; Exod. xii: 36; 1 Ps. xxiv; 9–15; Phil. ii: 13; Acts ii: 23; 2 Sam. xvi: 10; xxiv: 1; Ps. lxxvi: 10; Rom. xi: 32; Acts iv: 28; Rom. ix: 18; 2 Sam. xii: 11; 1 Kings xxii: 23; Ps. cv: 25.

Objections.—The objections against the Bible doctrines may all be reduced to these heads:

1. Epicurean: that God would be *fatigued* from so many *cares*.

2. That it is derogatory to His dignity to be concerned with trivialities.

3. The disorders existing in material nature, and in the course of human affairs, would be inconsistent with His benevolence and righteousness.

4. The doctrine infringes the efficacy of second causes, and the free-agency of intelligent creatures.

5. Last: It makes God the author of sin.

For answers, see above and below; and Dick, Lect. 43.

V. In proceeding to speak of the control of Providence over the acts of intelligent free agents, we must bear in mind the essential difference between them and physical bodies. A *body* is not *intrinsically a cause*. Causation only takes place when a certain *relation* between given *properties* of *two* bodies, is established by God's providence. (See § 1.) But a *soul* is a fountain of spontaneity; it is capable of will, in itself, and is self-determined to will, by its own prevalent dispositions. Soul *is* a cause.

God's Agency in Man's spiritual acts.—Now, the Bible attributes all the spiritually good acts of man to God. Rom. vii: 18; Phil. ii: 13; iv: 13; 2 Cor. xii: 9, 10; Eph. ii: 10; Gal. v: 22–25. God's concern in such acts may be explained as composed of three elements. a.) He perpetually protects and preserves the human person with the capacities which He gave to it naturally. b.) He graciously renews the dispositions by his immediate, almighty will, so as to incline them, and keep them inclined by the Holy Ghost, to the spiritually good. c.) He providentially disposes the objects and truths before the soul thus renewed, so that they become the occasional causes of holy volitions freely put forth by the sanctified will. Thus God is, in an efficient sense, the intentional author of the holy acts, and of the holiness of the acts, of his saints.

God's agency in Man's sins. Is there a concursus.—But, the question of His concern in the evil acts of free agents (and the naturally indifferent,) is more difficult. The Dominican Scholastics, or Thomists, followed by some Calvinistic Reformers, felt themselves constrained, in order to uphold the efficiency and certainty of God's control over the evil acts of His creatures, to teach their doctrine of the *physical concursus* of God in all such acts, (as well as in all good acts, and physical causes.) This is not merely God's sustentation of the being and capacities of creatures; not merely a moral influence by truths or motives providentially set before them; not merely an infusion of a general power of acting to which the creature gives the specific direction, by his choice alone, in each individual act; but in addition to all this, a direct, immediate physical energizing of the active power of creature, disposing and predetermining it efficaciously to the specific act, and also enabling it thereto, and so passing over with the agency of the creature, into the action. Thus, it is an immediate, physical, predisposing, specific and concurrent influence to act. Their various arguments may be summed up in these three: that the Scripture, e. g., Gen. xlv: 7; Is. x: 15, &c.; Acts xvii: 28; Phil. ii: 13; Col. i: 13, demand the *concursus* of God to satisfy their full meaning: that as man's *esse* is dependent on the perpetual recreative efflux of God's power, so his acting must perpetually depend on His *concursus*, because the creature must act according to his being, and that without this *concursus*. God's concern in all human acts could not be as efficacious and sovereign as Scripture asserts, and as is shown by His claim to be universl first cause, by His eternal purpose, by His predictions, &c., &c.

Turrettin obviously implies, in his argument, that the rational creature's will, like a second cause in matter, is indeterminate to any specific effect. For he argues that a cause thus indeterminate or indifferent must receive its determination to a specific effect, from some cause out of, and above itself, which must be *active*, and determinating to the specific effect. (Qu. 5, § 8, &c.)

Now, on this I remark, *see here* the great importance of the distinction I made (in last lecture, and on the difference of permissive and efficacious decrees) between material and rational second causes.

Again: Consider if Turrettin does not here surrender a vital point of his own doctrine concerning the will. That point is, that the rational will is not *in equilibrio*; that volitions are not contingent *phenomena*, but regular *effects*. Effects of what? Sound metaphysics says, of subjective motive. *The soul* (not the faculty of choice itself,) is *self-determining*—i. e., spontaneous. But this according to *a law*, its subjective law.

IT IS NOT REVEALED BY CONSCIOUSNESS.—Now, to this I reply farther, (a. The doctrine that God's sustentation is by a perpetual active efflux of creative power, we found to be *improved* as to spirits, which unlike bodies, possess the properties of true being, absolute unity and simplicity. That doctrine is only true, in any sense, of organized bodies; which are not proper beings, but rather organized collections of a multitude of separate beings, or atoms. My consciousness tells me that *I have* a power of acting (according to the laws of my nature) dependent indeed, and controlled always by God, yet which is personally my own. It *originates* in the spring of my own spontaneity. As to the relation between personal power in us, and the power of the first cause, we know nothing; for neither He, nor consciousness, tells us anything.

NOT REQUIRED BY GOD'S SOVEREIGNTY.—b.) Surely the meaning of all such Scriptures as those referred to, is sufficiently satisfied, as well as the demands of God's attributes and government, by securing these two points. First, God is not the author of sin; Second, His control over all the acts of all His creatures is *certain*, *sovereign* and *efficacious;* and such as to have been determined from eternity. If a way can be shown, in which God *thus controls* these sinful acts, without this physi-

§ 17,) admits himself to be constrained by it to hold, that no moral act has *intrinsic* moral quality per se. He even quibbles, that the hatred of God felt by a sinner is not evil by its intrinsic nature as simple act of will; but only by its adjuncts. Ans. The act, apart from its adjuncts, is either no act at all, or a different act intrinsically. There is false analysis here. Turrettin (again) is misled by instances such as these admitted ones. All killing is not murder. All smiting is not malice. All taking is not theft, &c., &c. The sophism is here, that these are *outward* acts: effectuated through bodily members. As to the mere physical *phenomenon* of volitions moving bodily members, we admitted, and argued that, abstracted from its physical antecedents and adjuncts, it has no moral quality. Proof is easy. But, in strictness of speech, the physical execution of the volition in the act of striking, &c., is *not the act of soul*—only the outward result thereof. The act of soul is the *intent* of will. In this, the right or wrong moral relation *is* intrinsic. Now, would not Turrettin say, that the *concursus* he teaches incites and directs the *act of soul*, and not that of the body merely? Certainly. Thus it appears that his distinction and evasion are inadequate.

Or thus: No Calvinist will deny that the morality of an act is determined by its *intention*. But intention is *action* of soul, as truly as volition. And if a physical *concursus* is necessary to all action, it is so to intention. Thus God's action would be determinative of the morality of the act.

LECTURE XXIV.

SYLLABUS.

MANS'S ESTATE OF INNOCENCE AND THE COVENANT OF WORKS.

[Genesis, Ch. I to III. Con. of Faith, Ch. IV and VI.]

1. In what consisted the *image* of God, in which man was created? Was he constituted of spirit and body? Wherein consisted his original righteousness?
   Turrett., Loc. V. Qu. 10. Dick, Lect. 40. Watson's Theo. Inst., Ch. 18. Knapp., Art. VI, Sect. LI to LIII.
2. Was Adam's original righteousness concreated, or acquired by acting? State the theories of Calvinists and Pelagians, and establish the true one.
   Turrett., Loc. V., Qu. 9, 11. Loc. VIII, Qu. 1, 2. Loc. IX, Qu. 2. Hill, Bk. IV, Ch. 1, § 2. Dick., Lect. 40. Knapp., Lect. LIV. Watson, Theo. Inst., Ch. 18, § I. (II.)
3. What was Adam's *natural* relation to God's law?
   Turrett., Loc. V., Qu. 12. Dick, Lect. 44. Watson as above, § I.
4. Did God place man under a *covenant of works?* And did Adam therein represent his posterity?
   Turrett., Loc. VIII, Qu. 3 and 6. Hill, Bk. IV, Ch. 1, § I, II. Dick, Lect. 44 and 45. Watson, Theo. Inst. Ch. 18, § III.
5. What was the 'condition,' and what the 'seal' of that Covenant?
   Turrett., Loc. VIII, Qu. 4, 5, 7. Dick and Hill, as above.

I. Man's Origin from One Pair.—The first three chapters of Genesis present a *desideratum* wholly unsupplied by any human writing, in a simple, natural, and yet authentic account of man's origin. The statement that his body was created out of pre-existent matter, and his soul communicated to that body by God, solves a thousand inquiries which mythology and philosophy are alike incompetent to meet. And from this first father, together with the helpmeet formed for him, of the opposite sex, from his side, have proceeded the whole human race, by successive generation. The unity of race in the human family has been much mooted by half-scholars in natural science of our day, and triumphantly defended. I must remit you wholly for the discussion to the books written by Christian scholars on that subject, of which I may mention, as accessible and popular, Cabell, the University Lectures, and the work of Dr. Bachman, of Charleston. I would merely point out, in passing, the theological importance of this natural fact. If there are any *men* on earth not descended from Adam's race, then their federal connexion with him is broken. But more, their inheritance in the *protevangelium*, that the "seed of the woman shall bruise the serpent's head," is also interrupted. The warrant of the Church to carry the gospel to that people is lacking; and indeed all the relations of man to man are interrupted as to them. Lastly, the integrity of the Bible as the Word of God is fatally affected; for the unity of the race is implied in all its system, in the whole account of God's dealings with it, in all its histories, and asserted in express terms. Acts xvii: 26. See Breckinridge's Theol., vol. I, ch. 3, i. For additional Scriptures Gen. 3:30, 7:23, 9:1, 19, 10:32. Unity of race is necessary to relation to the Redeemer.

Man, Body and Spirit.—But a yet more precious part of this passage of Scripture is the explanation it gives of the state of universal sin, self-condemnation, and vanity, in which we now find man; which is so hard to reconcile with God's attributes. The simple, but far-reaching solution is, that man is not in the state in which he was made by his Creator. The record tells us that God "formed man of the dust of the ground, and breathed into his nostrils the breath of life, and man became a living soul." Here, in the simple language of a primeval people, the two-fold nature of man, as matter and spirit, is asserted. As the popular terms of every people have selected *breath*, RUACH PNEUMA, SPIRITUS, to signify this inscrutable substance, thinking spirit. The narrative describes the communication of the soul to the body by the act of breathing. And, it may be added, the view to which reason led us, as to the spirituality of man's thinking part, is confirmed by all Scripture. Here, Gen. 2:7. The body is *first* formed from one source, and then the spirit is communicated to it from a different one. God is thus the Father of our spirits. Heb. xii: 9. At death, the two substances separate, and meet different fates. Eccl. xii: 7; 2 Cor. v: 1–8; Phil. i: 22, 23. The body and soul are in many ways distinguished as different substances, and capable of existing separately. Matt. x; 28; Luke viii: 55. The terms body, soul, and spirit, are twice used as exhaustive enumerations of the whole man. 1 Thess. v. 23; Heb. 4:12.

Image of God what.—Next, we learn that man, unlike all lower creatures, was formed in the "*image of God*"—"after His likeness." The general idea here is obviously, that there is a *resemblance* of man to God. It is not in sameness of *essence*, for God is incommunicable; nor in corporeal shape, for God is immense, and modified by figure. It was obviously in these particulars, that man is a spiritual, thinking, and immortal being—that he is God's ruler over inferior creatures, and the earth; and chiefly that he was created intelligent and *holy*. The old Pelagians and Socinians attempted to limit man's possession of God's image to the second particular, in order to gain countenance for their vain theories of the nature of sin, and denial of original sin, as we shall see. But we substantiate against them the definition of God's image; as to its first particular, by Gen. ix: 6, where we learn that the crime of murder owes its enormity chiefly to this, that it destroys God's image. See also, Jas. iii: 9. But since the fall, man has lost his original righteousness, and his likeness to God consists only in his possession of an intelligent spiritual nature. Dominion over the earth and its animals was plainly conferred, Gen. i: 26, 27; Ps. 8, and it is implied that this feature made man, in an humble sense, a representative of God on the earth, in Gen. i: 26, 27, from the connexion in which the two things are mentioned, and in 1 Cor. xi: 7, from the idea there implied, that the authority given him by God over the other sex makes him God's representative. But the likeness consists chiefly in man's *original moral perfection*, the intelligence and rectitude of his conscience. This is argued from the fact that the first man, like all the other works of creation, was "very good." Gen. i: 31. This "goodness" must, in fairness, be understood thus, that each created thing had in perfection those properties which adapted it to its designed relations. Man is an intelligent being, and was created to know, enjoy and glorify God as such; hence his moral state must have been perfect. See also, Eccl. vii: 29. And that this was the most important feature of God's likeness, is evident; because it is that likeness which man regains by the *new* creation. See Rom. xii: 2; Col. iii: 10; Eph. iv: 24. This also, is the likeness which saints aspire after, which they hope to attain when they regain Adam's original perfection. Ps. xvii: 15; 1 Jno. iii: 2.

ADAM'S NATURAL RIGHTEOUSNESS DEFINED.—If we attempt to *define* the original righteousness of man's nature, we must say that, first, it *implies* the possession of those capacities of understanding and conscience, and that knowledge which were necessary for the correct comprehension of all his own moral relations. This equality excludes the extravagant notion, that he was endued by nature with all the knowledge ever acquired by all his descendants; and its opposite, that his soul commenced its existence in an infantile state. Second. Man's righteousness *consisted* in the perfectly harmonious concurrence of all the dispositions of his soul, and consequently of all his volitions prompted thereby, with the decisions of his conscience, which in its turn was correctly directed by God's holy will. His righteousness, was then, a natural and entire *conformity*, in principle and volition, with God's law. Adam was doubtless possessed of *free will*, (Confession, ch. iv, § 2, ix, § 2,) in the sense which we saw, was *alone* appropriate to any rational free agent; that in all his responsible, moral acts, his soul was self-determined in its volitions—i. e., he chose according to his own understanding and dispositions, free from co-action. But his *will* was no more self-determining, or *in equilibrio*, than man's will now. (We saw that such a state would be neither free, rational, nor moral.) Just as man's dispositions now *decisively* incline his will, in a state of nature, to ungodliness, so they then inclined it to holiness. This inclination was prevalent, and complete for the time, yet not immutable, as the event proved. But this mutability of will did not imply any infirmity of moral nature peculiar to man, as compared with angels. The fate of the non-elect angels shows that it is the inevitable result of man's being *finite*. Impeccability is the property of none but the Infinite, and those to whom He communicates it by His indwelling wisdom and grace. *How* a creature soul could be prevalently and completely holy in its dispositions, and yet mutable, is a most obstruse problem, to which we will return in due place.

II. Adam's Righteousness concreated.—Was Adam's righteousness, in his estate of blessedness, *native* or *acquired?* The Calvinist answers, it was native; it was conferred upon him as the original habitus of his will by the creative act which made him an intelligent creature. And the exercise of holy volitions was the natural effect of the principles which God gave him. This is the obvious and simple meaning of our doctrine; not that righteousness was so an essential attribute of man's nature, that the loss of it would make him no longer a human being proper.

View of Pelagians and Socinians.—The Pelagians of the 5th century, followed by modern Socinians, and many of the New England school, assert that Adam could only have received from his Maker a negative innocency; and that a positive righteousness could only be the result of his own voluntary acts of choice. Their fundamental dogma is, that nothing has moral quality except that which is *voluntary* (meaning by this, the result of an *act* of choosing). Hence, they infer, nothing is sin, or holiness, but *acts* of volition. Hence, a con-created rectitude of will would be no righteousness, and have no merit, because not the result of the person's own act of choice. Hence, also, they say *a priori* dispositions have no moral quality, *except* where they are *acquired habitudes* of disposition resulting from voluntary acts. Of this kind was Adam's holy character, they say. And so, in the work of conversion, it is all nonsense to talk of being *made* righteous, or of *receiving* a holy heart: man must *act* righteousness, and make by *choosing* a holy heart.

Intermediate Romish Ground.—This is the most important point in the whole subject of man's original state and relation to God's law. Before proceeding, however, to its discussion, it may be well to state the evasive ground assumed by the Romish Church between the two. In order to gain a semi-Pelagian position, without avowing the above odious principles, they teach that the first man was created holy, but that original righteousness was not a natural habitus of his own will, but a supernatural grace, communicated to him temporarily by God. According to Rome, concupiscence is not sin, and it existed in holy Adam; but it has a perpetual tendency to override the limits of conscience, and thus become sin. So long as the supernatural grace of original righteousness was communicated to Adam, he stood; the moment God saw fit to withdraw it, natural concupiscence became inordinate, sin was born, and man fell. The refutation of this view of man's original rectitude will be found below, in the proof that concupiscence *is* sin, and that man was made by *nature* holy. We understand that it is implied, if man had not sinned, he would have transmitted that holy nature to his posterity: surely supernatural grace does not "run in the blood"? The idea is also derogatory to God's wisdom and holiness, that He should make a creature, and endue it with such a nature as was of itself inadequate to fulfil the end of its existence as a moral being, and so construct its propensities that sin would be the normal, certain and immediate result of their unrestricted action! It represents God as *creating* imperfection.

Proof of our view. Pelagian argument ambiguous.—We assert against the Pelagians, that man was positively holy by nature, as he came from God's hand; because the plea that nothing can have moral quality which is involuntary, is ambiguous and sophistical. That which occurs or exists *against* a man's positive volition can be to him neither praise nor blame. This is the proposition to which common sense testifies. It is a very different proposition to say that there cannot be moral desert, because no positive volition was exercised about it. (The Pelagian's proposition.) For then there could be no sins of omission, where the ill-desert depended on the very fact that the man wholly failed to choose when he should have chosen. The truth is, man's original dispositions are *spontaneous;* they subsist and operate in him freely, without co-action; and only because of their own motion. This is enough to show them responsible, and blame, or praiseworthy. A man always feels good or ill desert according as his spontaneous feelings *are* in a right or wrong state, not according to the mode or process by which they *came* into that state.

Scripture teaches our view.—b.) We have already seen, from Gen. i: 26, 27; i: 31; Eccles. vii: 29, that man was *made* in the image of God, and that this image was most essentially his original righteousness. God's word, therefore, sustains our view. The same thing is seen in the language of Scripture concerning the new creation, regeneration. This, the Bible expressly affirms, is a "creation *unto* righteousness." Eph. iv; 24; ii; 10; Rom. viii: 29; Eph. i: 4. It is a supernatural change of disposition, wrought not merely through motive, but by almighty power. Eph. i: 19, 20; ii: 1–5. It determines not only the acts, but the will. Ps cx: 3; Phil. ii: 13. And God has Himself suggested the analogy on which our argument proceeds by choosing the term "new creation," to describe it. Hence, as the new-born soul is *made* holy, and does not merely act a holiness, the first man was made righteous. Let me remark here, that ancient and modern Pelagians virtually admit the justice of this, by denying the possibility of a regeneration by grace; and on the same grounds, that a state of holiness not primarily chosen by the will, could not be meritorious. On their theory the human soul of Christ would not have had a positive righteousness by nature. But see Luke i: 35.

No natural neutrality possible.—c.) Their theory is contradicted by common sense in this: that a moral neutrality, in a being who had the rational faculties and the data for comprehending the moral relations in a given case, is impossible; and if possible, would be criminal. It is the very nature of conscience, that when the moral relations of a given case are comprehended, her *dictum* is immediate, inevitable and categorical. The dispositions also must either be *disposed* actively, one way or the other, or they are not dispositions at all.

They cannot be *in equilibrio*, any more than motion can be quiescent. And does not every sane conscience decide that if Adam, on comprehending his moral relations to his infinitely good, kind, glorious and holy Father, had simply *failed* to choose His love and service instantly; if he had been *capable of hesitation* for one moment, that would itself have constituted a moral defect, a sin?

NO PRINCIPLE OF RIGHT CHOICE WOULD HAVE BEEN PRESENT.—d.) Had Adam's will been in the state of *equilibrium* described, and his moral character initially negative, then there would have been in him nothing to prompt a holy choice; and the choice which he might have made for that which is formally right would have had nothing in it morally good. For the intention determining the volition gives all its moral quality. Thus he could never have chosen or acted a righteousness, nor initiated a moral habitude, his initial motive being *non-moral*.

CORRUPTION OF INFANTS REFUTES PELAGIANISM.—e.) These false principles must lead, as Pelagians freely avow, to the denial of original depravity in infants. That which does not result from an act of intelligent choice, say they, cannot have moral quality; so, there can be no *sin* of nature, any more than a natural righteousness. But that man *has* a sin of nature, is proved by common experience, asserted by Scripture, and demonstrated by the fact that all are "by nature the children of wrath," and even from infancy suffer and die under God's hand.

f.) If the doctrine be held that a being cannot be *created* righteous without choice, then those that die in infancy cannot be redeemed. For they cannot exercise as yet intelligent acts of moral choice, and thus convert themselves by choosing God's service. The Pelagian does indeed virtually represent the infant as needing no redemption, having no sin of nature. But the Bible and experience prove that he does need redemption: whence, on Pelagian principles, the damnation of all who die in infancy is inevitable.

THEIR THEORY HAS NO FACTS.—Last, the theory of the Pelagian is utterly unphilosophical in this, that it has no experimental basis. It is a mere *hypothesis*. No human being has ever existed consciously in the state of moral indifference which they assume; or been conscious of that initial act of choice which generated his moral character. Surely all scientific propositions ought to have some basis of experimental proof! Ethics should be an inductive science.

III. NATURAL RELATION OF CREATURE TO GOD'S WILL.—Any intelligent moral creature of God is naturally bound to love Him with all his heart, and serve him with all his strength. i. e., this obligation is not created by positive precept only, but arises out of the very perfections of God, and the relations of the creature, as His property, and deriving all his being and capacities from God's hands. Doubtless Adam's holy soul recognized joyfully this obligation. And doubtless his understanding was endowed with the sufficient knowledge of so much of God's will as related to his duties at that time. It may be very hard for us to say how much this was. Now, it is common for divines to say, that a creature *cannot merit* anything of God. This has struck many minds as doubtful and unfair, whence it is important that we should properly distinguish. In denying that a creature of God can *merit any* thing, it is by no means meant that the holy obedience of a creature is before God devoid of good moral character. It possesses praiseworthiness, if holy, and undoubtedly receives that credit at God's hands. The fact that it is naturally due to God does not at all deprive it of its good quality. But the question remains: What is that quality? Obviously, it is that the natural connexion between holiness and happiness shall not be severed, as long as the holiness continues; that, as the obedience rendered is that evoked by the natural relation to the Creator's will; so the desert acquired is of that natural well-being appropriate to the creature's capacities. The guarantee to the creature for this, in the absence of any positive covenant from God, is simply the divine goodness and righteousness, which render God incapable of treating a holy being worse than this. The creature is God's *property*.

The Creature Cannot Merit.—But it is equally obvious that such obedience on the creature's part cannot bring God in his debt, to condescend to him in any way, to communicate Himself as a source of supernatural blessedness, or stability in holiness, or to secure his natural well-being longer than his voluntary and mutable obedience is continued. And the reasons are, simply that none of the creature's obedience *can* be supererogatory, he owing his utmost at any rate; and that all his being and capacities were *given by God*, and are His property. I cannot bring my benefactor in *my* debt by giving him something which he himself lent to me; I am but restoring his own. This is what is intended by the Confession of Faith, Ch. vii, § 1. The Scriptures clearly support it. Ps. xvi: 2; Job. xxxv: 7, 8; Acts. xvii: 24, 25; Ps. l: 9–12; Luke xvii: 7–10.

But, Death would not have Entered without Sin.—But it is equally clear that mortality and the connected ills of life could not have been the natural lot of man irrespective of his sin and fall, as the Pelagians and Socinians pretend. Their motive in assuming this repulsive tenet, is, to get rid of the argument for original sin presented by the sufferings and death of infants who have committed no overt sin. The assertion is abhorrent to the justice and goodness of God. Physical evil is the appointed consequence of moral evil, and the sanction threatened for the breach of God's will. To suppose it appointed to an obedient moral being, irrespective of any guilt, overthrows either God's moral attributes, or His providence, and confounds heaven with earth. Second: It is inconsistent with that image of God, and that natural perfection, in which man was created. The workmanship was declared to be very good; and this doubtless excluded the seeds of its own destruction. It was in the image of God; and this included immortality. But last, the Scriptures imply that man would neither have suffered nor died if he had not sinned, by appointing death as the threat against transgression. And this, while it meant more than bodily death, certainly included this, as is evident from Gen. ii: 17–19. See, then, Gen. ii: 17; Rom. v: 12; vi: 23; Matt. xix: 17; Gal. iii: 12. These last evidently have reference to the covenant of works made with Adam: and they explicitly say, that if a perfect obedience were possible, (as it was with Adam before he fell,) it would secure eternal life.

Covenant of Works Gracious.—God's act in entering into a covenant with Adam, if it be substantiated, will be found to be one of pure grace and condescension. He might justly have held him always under his natural relationship; and Adam's obedience, however long continued, would not have brought God into his debt for the future. Thus, his holiness being mutable, his blessedness would always have hung in suspense. God, therefore, moved by pure grace, condescended to establish a covenant with His holy creature, in virtue of which a temporary obedience might be graciously accepted as a ground for God's communicating Himself to him, and assuring him ever after of holiness, happiness, and communion with God. Here then is the point of osculation between the covenant of works, and the covenant of grace, the law and the gospel. Both offer a plan of free *justification*, by which a righteousness should be accepted, in covenant, to acquire for the creature more than he could strictly claim of God; and thus gain him everlasting life. In the covenant of grace, all is "ordained in the hand of a mediator," because man's sin had else excluded him from access to God's holiness. In the covenant of works, no mediator was required, because man was innocent, and God's purity did not forbid him to condescend to him. But in both, there was free grace; in both a justification unto life; in both a gracious bestowal of more than man had earned.

IV. Covenant of Works, What? Proof of its Institution.—The evidences that God placed Adam under a covenant of Works are well stated by the standard authors. A covenant, in its more technical sense, according to Turrettin, implies: 1. Two equal parties. 2. Liberty to do or not do the covenanted things before the covenant is formed. In this sense there could be no covenant between God and man. But in the more general sense of a *conditional promise*, such a transaction was evidently effected between God and Adam, and is recorded in Gen. ii: 16, 17. There are—1st, the two parties. *God* proposing a certain blessing and penalty on certain conditions, and *man* coming under those conditions. It has been objected that it was no covenant because man's accession to it was not optional with him: God's terms were not a proposal made him, but a command laid upon him. I reply, if he did not have an option to accede or not, he was yet voluntary in doing so; for no doubt his holy will joyfully concurred in the gracious plan. And such compacts between governors and governed are by no means unusual or unnatural. Witness all rewards promised by masters and teachers, for the performance of tasks, on certain conditions. 2. There was a condition: the keeping of God's command. 3d. There was a conditional promise and threat: life for obedience, and death for disobedience. That the promise of life was clearly implied is shown by the very fact that life is the correlative of the death threatened to disobedience—that the *tree of life* was the symbol of the blessing secured by keeping the covenant, and from many passages of Scripture which, in expounding the nature of this covenant, expressly say that life would have been the reward of a perfect obedience. Levit. xviii: 5; Deut. xxvii: 26; Ezek. xx: 11; Matt. xix: 17; Gal. iii: 12. The fact that in some of these places the offer of life through the covenant of works was only made in order to apply an argument *ad hominem* to the self-righteous Jews, does not weaken this evidence. For the reason life cannot, in fact, be gained through that covenant is not that it was not truly promised to man in it, and in good faith; but that man has now become through the fall, morally incapable of keeping the condition. Last, the transaction is pretty clearly called a Covenant in Hos. vi: 7.

ADAM A REPRESENTATIVE.—In this transaction Adam represented his posterity as well as himself. This appears from 1. The parallel which is drawn between Christ and Adam. Rom. v: 12–19: 1 Cor. xv: 22, 47. In almost every thing they are contrasted, yet Christ is the second Adam. The only parallelism is in the fact that they were both representative persons. 2. The fact proves it, that the penalty denounced on Adam has actually taken effect on every one of his posterity. See Gen. v: 3. 3. The Bible declares that sin, death, and all penal evil came into the world through Adam. Rom. v: 12; 1 Cor. xv: 22. 4. Although the various other communications of the first three chapters of Genesis are apparently addressed to Adam singly, we know that they applied equally to his posterity, as the permission to eat of all the fruits of the earth; the command to multiply and replenish the earth; the threatened pains of child-bearing; the curse of the ground, and the doom of labor, &c.

V. CONDITION AND SEAL OF COVENANT.—The condition of the covenant was "perfect conformity of heart, and perfect obedience in act, to the whole will of God as far as revealed." The command to abstain from eating the forbidden fruit was only made a special and decisive test of that general obedience. "As the matter forbidden was morally indifferent in itself, the command was admirably adapted to be a clear and absolute test of submission to God's naked will as such." (Hodge.)

The seal of the covenant is usually understood to be the *tree of life*, whose excellent fruit did not, indeed, medically work immortality in Adam's frame, but was appointed as a symbol and pledge, or seal of it. Hence, when he had forfeited the promise, he was debarred from the sign. The words of Gen. iii: 22 are to be understood sacramentally.

THE PROBATION TEMPORARY.—Why is it supposed that an obedience for a limited time would have concluded the Covenant transaction? The answer is, that such a covenant, with an indefinite probation, would have been no covenant of life at all. The creature's estate would have been still forever mutable, and in no respect different from that in which creation itself placed him, under the first natural obligation to his Maker. Nay, in that case, man's estate would be rightly called desperate; because, he being mutable and finite, and still held forever under the curse of a law which he was, any day, liable to break, the probability that he would *some day* break it would in the infinite future mount up to a moral certainty. The Redeemer clearly implies that the probation was to be temporary, in saying to the young Ruler: "If thou wilt *enter* into life, keep the commandments." If the probation had no limits, his keeping them could never make him enter in.

LECTURE XXV.

SYLLABUS.

THE FALL, AND ORIGINAL SIN.

1. What is *Sin?* Is guilt its essence, or adjunct?
Conf. of Faith, ch. VI. Cat. que. 14. Turrettin, Loc. IX, que. 1 and 3. Knapp, Art. IX, Lect. LXXIII.

2. What was Adam's first sin? How did it affect his own relations to God and moral state? How could a will prevalently holy form its first unholy volition?
Turrett., que. 6, 7, and 8. Hill, bk. IV, ch. 1. Dick, Lect. 46. Knapp, Lect. LXXXV. Watson, ch. 18, § II.

3. Who was the tempter? What the sentence on him?
Turrett., que. 7, §9, &c. Hill, as above. Dick, Lect. 44. Watson, as above.

4. What were the effects of the Fall on Adam's posterity, a) according to the Pelagian theory; b) the lower Arminian theory, as of Whitby; c) the Wesleyan; and d) the Calvinistic?
St. Augustine, vol. 2, ep. 899, c.: vol. 7, De Natura et Gratia, and Libri duo adv. Pelag. & Cælest. Hill, as above. Turrett., que. 9 and 10. Dick, Lect. 46, 47. Whitby's Five Points. Knapp, Lect. LXXIX. Watson's Theo. Inst., ch. 18, § III and IV.

5. Are the souls of Adam's created, or generated, and how is original sin propagated in them?
Turrett., que. 12, and Loc V, que. 13. Baird's Elohim Revealed, ch. 11th. Sampson on Hebr., XII. 9. Literary and Evangel. Mag. of Dr. Rice, vol. 4, p. 285. Watson, ch. 18, §4. Augustine, De Origine Animarum.

We have now reached, in our inquiries, the disastrous place where Sin first entered our race. It is therefore proper that we pause, and ascertain clearly what is its nature.

Sin, What?—The Hebrew word most commonly used for it is HATAH, which is supposed to carry the idea of a missing of the aim. The Greek HAMARTIA is strikingly similar, expressing the same idea: while the Latin, *peccatum*, is by some supposed to be equivalent to *pecuatum*—bestiality. The abstract idea of sin, then, is of a negative: a lack of conformity to a standard. Sins, in the concrete, are, indeed, positive acts or states: their positive quality arises from the agent, their sinfulness is still a privative quality. To this agrees strikingly the definition of 1 John iii: 4: HE HAMARTIA ESTI ANOMIA (*scil*, NOMOU THEOU). Some have supposed that the distinction of sins of omission from sins of commission, which is obviously just, is inconsistent with the assertion that sinfulness is always in its nature privative. But this is not so. The basis of that distinction is in the character of the commands to which the sins are related: sins of commission being breaches of prohibitory, and sins of omission of affirmative precepts. The essential idea is still, in both cases (if I may coin a word), *disconformity* to the precept. It is objected, sins of commission consist in doing something, whereas sins of omission are refusing to do. I answer, the sinfulness is in the motive; and this is, in either case, *active*, and its sinfulness is ANOMIA.

Concupiscence is Sin.—This raises again the oft mooted inquiry, whether *inclinations* to do evil, not yet assented to by volition, are sinful. The Catechism, as vehemently assailed herein by modern Pelagians as ever Augustine was by the ancient, says: "Sin is any want of conformity unto, or transgression of, the law of God." The ethical argument on this point was presented in this course Lect. 9, § 3. I now merely add a summary of the scriptural. The Scriptures many times apply moral terms to the abiding habitudes of the soul, and these not only acquired but native. Ps. li : 5, lviii : 3 ; Matt. xii : 35, vii : 17, xii : 33. Jas. i : 15 says : "Then when EPITHUMEIA hath conceived it bringth forth sin," &c. The relationship is so near, that mother and daughter must be expected to have one character. But most conclusively, see Rom. vii : 7. Concupiscence was the very sin which convicted him.

GUILT, WHAT?—What Turrettin calls *potential guilt* is the intrinsic moral ill-desert of an act or state. This is of the essence of the sin : it is indeed an insperable part of its sinfulness. Actual guilt is *obligation to punishment*. This is the established technical sense of the word among theologians. Guilt, thus defined, is obviously not of the essence of sin ; but is a relation, viz., to the penal sanction of law. For if we suppose no penal sanction attached to the disregard of moral relations, guilt would not exist, though there were sin. This distinction will be found important.

II. MAN'S FIRST SIN.—The first sin of our first father is found described in Gen. iii : 1–7, in words which are familiar to every one. This narrative has evidently some of that picturesque character appropriate to the primeval age, and caused by the scarcity of abstract and definite terms in their language. But it is an obvious abuse to treat it as a mere allegory, representing under a figure man's self-depravation and gradual change : for the passages preceding and following it are evidently plain narrative, as is proved by a hundred references. Moreover, the transactions of this very pas-age are twice referred to as literal (2 Cor. xi : 3 ; 1 Tim. ii : 14), and the eventsare given as the explanation of the peculiar chastisement allotted to the daughters of Eve.

UNBELIEF ITS FIRST ELEMENT.—The sin of Adam consisted essentially, not in his bodily act, of course ; but in his intentions. Popish theologians usually say that the first element of the sin of his heart was *pride*, as being awakened by the taunting reference of the Serpent to his dependence and subjection, and as being unnatural in so exalted a being. The Protestants, with Turrettin, usually say it was *unbelief;* because pride could not be naturally suggested to the creature's soul, unless unbelief had gone before to obliterate his recollection of his proper relations to an infinite God ; because belief of the mind usually dictates feeling and action in the will ; because the temptation seems first aimed (Gen. iii : 1) to produce unbelief, through the creature's heedlessness ; and because the initial element of error must have been in the understanding, the will being hitherto holy.

IF VOLITIONS ARE CERTAINLY DETERMINED, HOW COULD A HOLY BEING HAVE HIS FIRST WRONG VOLITION?—How a holy will could come to have an unholy volition at first, is a most difficult inquiry. And it is much harder as to the first sin of Satan than of Adam, because the angel, hitherto perfect, had no tempter to mislead him, and had not even the bodily appetites for natural good which in Adam were so easily perverted into concupiscence. Concupiscence cannot be supposed to have been the cause, pre-existing before sin ; because concupiscence *is sin*, and needs itself to be accounted for in a holy heart, Man's, or Satan's, *mutability* cannot be the efficient cause, being only a condition *sine qua non*. Nor is it any solution to say with Turrettin. the proper cause was a free will perverted voluntarily. True; but how came a right will to pervert itself while yet right? And here, let me say, is far the most plausible objection against the *certainty of the will*, which Arminians, &c., might urge far more cunningly than (to my surprise) they do. If the evil dispositions of a fallen sinner so determine his volitions as to ensure that he will not choose spiritual good, why did not the holy dispositions of Adam and Satan ensure that they would never have a volition spiritually evil? And if they somehow chose sin, contrary to their prevalent bent, why may not depraved man sometime choose good?

Answer.—The mystery cannot be fully solved how the first evil choice could voluntarily arise in a holy soul; but we can clearly prove that it is no sound reasoning from the certainty of a depraved will to that of a holy finite will. First: a finite creature can only be indefectible through the perpetual indwelling and superintendence of infinite wisdom and grace, guarding the finite and fallible attention of the soul against sin. This was righteously withheld from Satan and Adam. Second: while righteousness is a positive attribute, incipient sin is a negative one of human conduct. The mere *absence* of an element of active regard for God's will, constitutes a disposition or volition wrong. Now, while the positive requires a positive cause, it is not therefore inferrible that the negative equally demands a positive cause. To make a candle *burn*, it must be *lighted;* to make it *go out*, it need only be *let alone*. Now, the most probable account of the way sin entered a holy breast first, is this: An object was apprehended as in its mere nature *desirable;* not yet as unlawful. So far there is no sin. But as the soul, finite and fallible in its attention, permitted an overweening apprehension and desire of its *natural* adaptation to confer pleasure, to override the feeling of its unlawfulness, concupiscence was developed. And the element which first caused the mere innocent sense of the natural goodness of the object to pass into evil concupiscence, was negative, viz., the *failure* to consider and prefer God's will as the superior good to mere natural good. Thus natural desire passed into sinful selfishness, which is the root of all evil. So that we have only the negative element to account for. When we assert the certainty of ungodly choice in an evil will, we only assert that a state of volition whose moral quality is a *defect*, a negation, cannot become the cause of a positive righteousness. When we assert the mutability of a holy will in a finite creature, we only say that the positive element of righteousness of disposition may, in the shape of defect, *admit* the negative, not being infinite. So that the cases are not parallel: and the result, though mysterious, is not impossible. To make a candle positively give light, it must be lighted; to cause it to sink into darkness, it is only necessary to let it alone: its length being limited, it burns out.

Effects of Sin in Adam—Self-Depravation.—Adam's fall resulted in two changes, *moral* and *physical*. The latter was brought on him by God's providence, cursing the earth for his sake, and thus entailing on him a life of toil and infirmities, ending in bodily death. The former was more immediately the natural and necessary result of his own conduct; because we *can* conceive of God as interposing actively to punish sin, but we cannot conceive of Him as interposing to produce it. It has been supposed very unreasonable that *one act*, momentary, the breach of an unimportant, positive precept, should thus revolutionize a man's moral habitudes and principles, destroying his original righteousness, and making him a depraved being. One act, they say, cannot form a habit. We will not answer this, by saying, with Turrettin, that the act virtually broke each precept of the decalogue; or that it was a "universal sin:" nor even by pleading that it was an aggravated and great sin. Doubtless it *was* a great sin; because it violated the divine authority most distinctly and pointedly declared; because it did it for small temptation; because it was a sin against great motives, privileges, and restraints. There is also much justice in Turrettin's other remarks, that by this clear, fully declared sin, the *chief end* of the creature was changed from God to self; and the *chief end* controls the whole stream of moral action directed to it; that the authority on which all godliness reposes, was broken in breaking this one command; that shame and remorse were inevitably born in the soul; that communion with God was severed. But this terrible fact, that any sin is *mortal* to the spiritual life of the soul, may profitably be farther illustrated.

HOW ACCOUNTED FOR BY ONE SIN?—Note, that God's perfections necessitate that He shall be the righteous enemy and punisher of transgression. Man, as a moral and intelligent being, must have conscience and moral emotions. One inevitable effect of the first sin, then, must be that God is made righteously angry, and will feel the prompting to just punishment. (Else not a holy ruler!) Hence, He must at once withdraw His favour and communion (there being no Mediator to satisfy His justice.) Another inevitable effect must be, the birth of remorse in the creature. The hitherto healthy action of conscience must ensure this. This remorse must be attended with an apprehension of God's anger, and fear of His punishment. But human nature always reciprocates by a sort of sympathy the hostility of which it knows itself the object. How many a man has learned to hate an inoffensive neighbour because he knows that he has given that neighbour good cause to hate him? But this hostility is hostility to God for doing *what He ought*; it is *hostility to righteousness!* So that, in the first clearly pronounced sin, these elements of corruption and separation from God are necessarily contained in germ. But God is the model of excellence, and fountain of grace. See how fully these results are illustrated in Adam and Eve. Gen. iii: 8, &c. Next: every moral act has some tendency to foster the propensity which it indulges. Do you say it must be a very slight strength produced by one act; a very light bond of habit, consisting of one strand! Not always. But the scale, if slightly turned, *is turned;* the downhill career is begun, by at least one step, and the increase of *momentum* will surely occur, though gradually. Inordinate self-love has now become a principle of action, and it will go on to assert its dominion. Last, we must consider the effects of physical evil on a heart thus in incipient perversion; for God's justice must prompt Him to inflict the bodily evils due to the sin. Desire of happiness is instinctive; when the joys of innocence are lost, an indemnification and substitute will be sought in carnal pleasures. Misery developes the malignant passions of envy, petulance, impatience, selfishness, revenge. And nothing is more depraving than despair. See Jer. ii: 25, xviii: 12.

What a terrible evil, then, is Sin! Thus the sentence, "In the day thou eatest thereof, thou shalt surely die," carried its own execution. Sin, of itself, kills the spiritual life of the soul.

III. Satan the Tempter.—The true tempter of Adam and Eve was undoubtedly the evil angel Satan, although it is not expressly said so in the narrative. A serpent has no speech, still less has it understanding to comprehend man's moral relations and interests, and that refined spiritual malice which would plan the ruin of the soul. It is said, "the serpent was more subtle than any beast of the field," as though this natural superiority of animal instincts were what enabled it to do the work. A moment's thought, however, must convince us that there is a deeper meaning. Moses, speaking for the time as the mere historian, describes events as they *appeared* to Eve. The well known cunning of the serpent adapted it better for Satan's use, and enabled him to conceal himself under it with less chance of detection. The grounds for regarding Satan as the true agent are the obvious allusions of Scripture. See Jno. viii: 44; 2 Cor. xi: 3; 1 Thess. iii: 5; 1 Jno. iii: 8; Rev. xii: 9, and xx: 2. The doom of the serpent is also allusively applied to Christ's triumph over Satan. Col. ii: 15; Rom. xvi: 20; Heb. ii: 14; Is. lxv: 25. It is also stated in confirmation, by Dr. Hill, that this was the traditionary interpretation of the Jews, as is indicated, for instance, in Wis. ii: 23, 24; Ecclus. xxv: 24, and the Chaldee paraphrast on Job xx: 4, 6. Turrettin supposes that God's providence permitted the employment of an animal as the instrument of Satan's temptation in order that mankind might have before them a visible commemoration of their sin and fall.

IV. Effect of Adam's Sin on His Posterity—Pelagian Theory. I propose to state the Pelagian theory with some degree of fulness, and more methodically than it would perhaps be found stated in the writings of its own early advocates, in order to unfold to the student the *nexus* between original sin and the whole plan of redemption. The Pelagian believes that Adam's fall did not directly affect his posterity at all. Infants are born in the same state in which Adam was created, one of innocence, but not of positive righteousness. There was no federal transaction, and no imputation, which is, in every case, incompatible with justice. There is no propagation of hereditary depravity, which would imply the generation of souls *ex traduce*, which they reject. Man's will is not only free from coaction, but from moral certainty; i. e., his volitions are not only free, but *not decisively caused*, otherwise he would not be a free agent.

b.) If this is so, whence the universal actual transgression of adult man? Pelagianism answers, from *concupiscence*, which exists in all, as in Adam before his sin, and is not sin of itself, and from general *evil example*.

c.) If man has no moral character, and no guilt prior to intelligent choice, whence death and suffering among those who have not sinned? They are obliged to answer: These natural evils are not penal, and would have befallen Adam any how. They are the natural limitations of humanity, just as irrationality is of beasts, and no more imply guilt as their necessary cause.

d.) Those, then, who die in infancy, have nothing from which they need to be redeemed. Why then baptized? Pelagianism answered, those who die in infancy *are redeemed from nothing*. If they die unbaptized, they would go to a state called Paradise, the state of natural good, proceeding from natural innocence, to which innocent Pagans go. But baptism would interest them in Christ's gracious purchase, and thus they would inherit, should they die in infancy, a more positive and assured state of blessedness, called the Kingdom of Heaven.

e.) All men being born innocent, and with *equilibrium* of will, it is both physically and morally possible that any man might act a holy character, and attain Paradise, or "eternal life," without any gospel grace whatever. The chances may be bad, on account of unfavourable example, and temptation, amidst which the experiment has to be made. But there *have been* cases, both under the revealed law, as Enoch, Job, Abel, Noah (who had no *protevangelium*); and among Pagans, as Numa, Aristides, Socrates; and there may be such cases again. Nor would God be just to punish man for coming short of perfection unless this were so.

f.) Now, as to the theory of redemption: As there can be no imputation of Adam's guilt to his people, so neither could there be of Christ's people's guilt to Him, or of His righteousness to them. But sins are forgiven by the mercy of God in Christ (without penal satisfaction for them), on the condition of trust, repentance, and reformation. The title of the believer to a complete justification must then be *his own obedience*, and that a sinless one. But this is not so exalted an attainment as Calvinists now regard it. Concupiscence is not sin. Moral quality attaches only to actual volitions, not to states of feeling prompting thereto; and hence, if an act be formally right, it is wholly right; nor does a mixture of selfish and unselfish motives in it make it *imperfectly* moral; for volition is necessarily a thing decisive and entire. Hence, a prevalent, uniform obedience is a perfect one; and none less will justify, because justification is by works, and the law is perfect. But as *equilibrium* of will is essential to responsibility, any shortcoming which is morally necessitated, by infirmity of nature, or ignorance, thoughtlessness, or overwhelming gust of temptation, contrary to the soul's prevalent bent, is no sin at all. See here, the nest-egg of the Wesleyan's doctrine of sinless perfection, and of the Jesuit theory of morals.

Since a concreated righteousness would be no righteousness, not being *chosen* at first, so neither would a righteousness wrought by a supernatural regeneration. The only gracious influences possible are those of co-operative grace, or moral suasion. Man's regeneration is simply *his own change of purpose*, as to sin and holiness, influenced by motives. Hence, faith and repentance are both natural exercises.

g.) The continuance of a soul in a state of justification is of course contingent. A grace which would morally necessitate the will to continued holy choices, would deprive it of its free agency.

h.) God's purpose of election, therefore, while from eternity, as is shown by His infinite and immutable wisdom, knowledge and power, is conditioned on His foresight of the way men would improve their free will. He elected those He foresaw would persevere in good.

The whole is a consistent and well knit system of error, proceeding from its PROTON PSEUDOS.

ARMINIAN THEORIES. 1. LOWER.—Among those who pass under the general term, Arminians, two different schemes have been advanced; one represented by Whitby, the other by Wesley and his Church. *The former* admit that Adam and his race were both much injured by the fall. He has not indeed lost his *equilibrium* of will for spiritual good, but he has become greatly alienated from God, has fallen under the penal curse of physical evil and death, has become more *animal*, so that concupiscence is greatly exasperated, and is more prone to break out into actual transgression. This is greatly increased by the miseries, fear, remorse, and vexation of his mortal state, which tend to drive him away from God, and to whet the envious, sensual, and discontented emotions. These influences, together with constant evil example, are the solution of the fact, that all men become practically sinners. This is the state to which Adam reduced himself; and his posterity share it, not in virtue of any federal relation, or imputation of Adam's guilt, but of that universal, physical law, that like must generate like. In that sense, man is born a ruined creature.

2. WESLEYAN.—The Wesleyans, however, begin by admitting all that a Moderate Calvinist would ask, as to Adam's loss of original righteousness in the Fall, bondage under evil desires, and total depravity. While they misinterpret, and then reject the *term* imputation of Adam's guilt, they retain the idea, admitting that the legal consequences of Adam's act are visited on his descendants along with himself. But then, they say, the objections of severity and unrighteousness urged against this plan could not be met, unless it be considered as *one whole*, embracing man's gracious connexion with the second Adam. By the Covenant of grace in Him, the self-determining power of the will, and ability of will are purchased back for *every member* of the human family, and actually communicated, by *common sufficient grace*, to all, so far repairing the effects of the fall, that man has moral ability for spiritual good, if he chooses to employ it. Thus, while they give us the true doctrine with one hand, they take it back with the other, and reach a Semi-Pelagian result. The obvious objection to this scheme is, that if the effects of Adam's fall on his posterity are such, that they would have been unjust, if not repaired by a redeeming plan which was to follow it, as a part of the same system, then God's act in giving a Redeemer was not one of pure grace (as Scripture everywhere says,) but He was under obligations to do some such thing.

CALVINISTIC THEORY.—The view of the Calvinists I purpose now to state in that comprehensive and natural mode, in which all sound Calvinists would concur. Looking into the Bible and the actual world, we find that, whereas Adam was created righteous, and with full ability of will for all good, and was in a state of actual blessedness, ever since his fall, his posterity *begin their existence* in a far different state. They all show, *universal ungodliness*, clearly proving a native, prevalent, and universal tendency thereto. They are *born* spiritually dead, as Adam *made* himself. And they are obviously, *natural heirs* of the physical evils and death pronounced on him for his sin. Such are the grand facts. Now Calvinists consider that it is no unauthorized hypothesis, but merely a connected statement, and inevitable interpretation of the facts to say: that we see in them this arrangement: God was pleased, for wise, gracious, and righteous reasons, to connect the destiny of Adam's posterity with his probationary acts, so making him their representative, *that whatever moral, and whatever legal condition he procured for himself by his conduct under probation; in that same moral and that same legal conditon his posterity should begin to exist.* And this, we say, is no more than the explanation necessarily implied in the facts themselves.

V. Origin of Souls. History of opinions.—But before we proceed to the detailed discussion of this, an inquiry, a subject of the greatest intricacy and interest arises as a preliminary: How is this connexion transmitted; what is the actual tie of nature between parents and children, as to their more essential part, the soul? Are human souls generated by their parents naturally? Or are they created directly by God, and sent into connexion with the young body at the time it acquires its separate vitality? The former has been called the theory of Traducianism; (*ex traduce*,) the latter, of creation. After Origen's doctrine of pre-existent human souls had been generally surrendered as heretical (from the times of Chrysostom, say 403,) the question was studied with much interest in the early church. Tertullian, who seems first to have formally stated Adam's federal headship, was also the inventor of the *ex traduce* theory. But it found few advocates among the Fathers, and was especially opposed by those who had strong tendencies to what was afterwards called Pelagianism, as favouring original sin. Gregory of Nyssa seems to have been almost alone among the prominent Greek Fathers, who held it. So perhaps did Ambrose among tne Latins; but when Jerome asserts that the *ex traduce* view prevailed *generally* among the Western Christians, he was probably in error. Augustine, the great establisher of Original Sin, professed himself undecided about it, to the end. It may be said however, in general, that in history, the *ex traduce* theory has been thought more favourable to original sin, and has been usually connected with it till modern times; while Creationism was strenuously advocated by Pelagians. If the Traducian theory can be substantiated, it most obviously presents the best explanation of the propagation of sin.

I shall state the usual arguments, *pro* and *con*, indicating as I go along my judgment of their force.

Arguments of Traducianists—From Scripture.—1. The Traducianists assert that by some inexplicable law of generation, though a true and proper one, parents propagate souls, as truly as bodies; and are thus the proper parents of the whole persons of their children. They argue, from Scripture, that Gen ii: 2 states, "on the seventh day God *ended* the work which He had made, and He *rested* on the seventh day from all His work," &c. Hence, they infer, God performs since no proper work of immediate creation in this earth. This seems hardly valid; for the sense of the text might seem satisfied by the idea that God now creates nothing new as to species. With a great deal more force, it is argued that in Gen. i: 25–28, God creates man in His own image, after His own likeness, which image is proved to be not corporeal at all, but in man's spirituality, intelligence, immortality, and righteousness. In Gen. v: 3, "Adam begat a son in his own likeness, after his image." How could this be, if Adam's parental agency did not produce the soul, in which alone this image inheres? Surely the image and likeness is in the same aspects. See also Ps. li: 5: Job xiv: 4; Jno. iii: 6, &c. The purity or impurity spoken of in all these passages is of the soul, and they must therefore imply the propagation of souls, when so expressly stating the propagation of impurity of soul.

From Experience and from Imputation.—They also argue that popular opinion and common sense clearly regard the parents as parents of the whole person. The same thing is shown by the inheritance of mental peculiarities and family traits, which are often as marked as bodily. And this cannot be accounted for by education, because often seen where the parents did not live to rear the child; nor by the fact that the body with its animal appetites, in which the soul is encased, may be the true cause of the apparent hereditary likeness of souls; for the just theory is that souls influence bodies in these things, not bodies souls; and besides, the traits of resemblance are often not only passional, but intellectual. Instances of *congenital lunacy*: Lunacy is plausibly explained as a loss of *balance* of soul, through the undue predominance of some one trait. Now, these cases of congenital lunacy are most frequently found in the offspring of cousins. The resemblance of traits in the parents being already great, "breeding in and in" makes the family trait too strong, and hence derangement. But the chief arguments from reason are: if God creates souls, as immediately as He created Adam's or Gabriel, then they must have come from His hand morally pure, for God *cannot create wickedness*. How, then, can depravity be propagated? The Bible would be contradicted, which so clearly speaks of it as *propagated*; and reason, which says that the attachment of a holy soul to a body cannot defile it, because a mere body has no moral character. Creationists answer: the federal relation instituted between Adam and the race, justifies God in ordaining it so that the connexion of the young immortal spirit with the body, and thus with a depraved race, shall be the occasion for its depravation, in consequence of imputed sin. But the reply is, first, it is impossible to explain the federal relation, if the soul of each child (the soul alone is the true moral agent), had an antecedent holy existence, independent of a human father. Why is not that soul as independent of Adam's fall, thus far, as Gabriel was; and why is not the arrangements which implicates him in it just as arbitrary as though Gabriel were tied to Adam's fate? Moreover, if *God's* act in plunging this pure spirit into an impure body is the immediate occasion of its becoming depraved, it comes very near to making God the author of its fall. Last: a mere body has no moral character, and to suppose it taints the soul is mere Gnosticism. Hence, it must be that the souls of children are the offsprings of their parents. The mode of that propagation is inscrutable; but this constitutes no disproof, because a hundred other indisputable operations of natural law are equally inscrutable; and especially in this case of spirits, where the nature of the substance is inscrutable, we should expect the manner of its production to be so.

Arguments of Creationists.—2. On the other hand, the advocates of creation of souls argue from such texts as Eccl. xii: 7; Is. lvii: 16;

Zech. xii: 1; Heb. xii: 9, where our souls are spoken of as the special work of God. It is replied, and the reply seems to me sufficient, that the language of these passages is sufficiently met, by recognizing the fact that God's power at first produced man's soul immediately out of nothing, and in His own image; that the continued propagation of these souls is under laws which His Providence sustains and directs; and that this agency of God is claimed as an especial honour, (e. g. in Is. lvii: 16,) because human souls are the most noble part of God's earthly kingdom, being intelligent, moral, and capable of apprehending His glory. That this is the true sense of Eccl. xii: 7, and that it should not be strained any higher, appears thus: if the language proves that the soul of a man of our generation came immediately from God's hand, like Adam's, the antithesis would equally prove that our bodies came equally from the dust, as immediately as Adam's. To all such passages as Is. lvii: 16; Zech. xii: 1, the above general considerations apply, and in addition, these facts: Our parents are often spoken of in Scripture as authors of our existence likewise; and that in general terms, inclusive of the spirit. Gen. xlvi: 26, 27; Prov. xvii: 21; xxiii: 24; Is. xlv: 10. Surely, if one of these classes of texts may be so strained, the other may equally, and then we have texts directly contradicting texts. Again, God is called the Creator of the animals, Ps. civ: 30, and the adorner of the lilies, Matt. vi: 30; which are notoriously produced by propagation. In Heb. xii: 9, the pronoun in "Father of *our* spirits," is unauthorized. The meaning is simply the contrast between the general ideas of "earthly fathers," and "heavenly father." For if you make the latter clause, "Father of spirits" mean Creator of our souls, then, by antithesis, the former should be read, fathers of our *bodies*; but this neither the apostle's scope permits, nor the word Sarx, which never means, in his language, our bodies as opposed to our souls; but our *natural*, as opposed to our *gracious* condition of soul.

Again: Turrettin objects, that if Adam's soul was created, and our's propagated, we do not properly bear his image, 1 Cor. xv: 47–8, nor are of his species. The obvious answer is, that by the same argument we could not be of the same corporeal species at all! Further, the very idea of species is a *propagated identity of nature.* But the strongest rational objections are, that a generative process implies the separation of parts of the parent substances, and their aggregation into a new organism: whereas the souls of the parents, and that of the offspring are alike monads, indiscerptible, and uncompounded. Traducianism is therefore vehemently accused of materialist tendencies. It seems to me that all this is but an *argumentum ad ignorantiam.* Of course, *spirits* cannot be generated by separation of substance and new compoundings. But whether processes of propagation may not be possible for spiritual substance which involve none of this, is the very question, which can be neither proved nor disproved by us, because we do not comprehend the true substance of spirit.

Gravest objection against Traducianism.—The opponents might have advanced a more formidable objection against Traducianism; and *this* is the true difficulty of the theory. In every case of the generation of *organisms*, there is no production of any really *new substance* by the creature-parents, but only a re-organizing of pre-existent particles. But we believe a soul is a spiritual atom, and is brought into existence out of non-existence. Have human parents this highest creative power? With such difficulties besetting both sides, it will be best perhaps, to leave the subject as an insoluble mystery. What an *opprobrium* to the pride of human philosophy, that it should be unable to answer the very first and nearest question as to its own origin!

The humble mind may perhaps find its satisfaction in this Bible truth: That whatever may be the adjustment adopted for the respective *shares* of agency which the First Cause, and second causes have in the origin of an immortal human soul; this fact is certain (however unexplained) that parents and children *are* somehow united into one federal body by a true tie of *race:* that the tie does include the spiritual as well as the bodily substances: that it is *bona fide*, and not fictitious or suppositious. See Confession of Faith, Ch. 6, § 3. "Root of all mankind." Now since we have no real cognition by perception, of spiritual substance, but only know its acts and effects, we should not be surprised at our ignorance of the precise agency of its production; and the way that agency acts. It may not be explained; and yet it may be true, that divine power, (in bringing substance out of *nihil* into *esse*) and human causation may both act, in originating the being and properties of the infant's soul.

May not the fact that souls *can* generate souls, inscrutably, throw some light on the generation of Christ? But analogy must be imperfect; for in the case of the second person, there are not two substances.

LECTURE XXVI.

SYLLABUS.

ORIGINAL SIN. (Continued.)

6. What is Original Sin? What is meant by *total* depravity? and does it affect the whole man in all faculties and capacities?

Conf. of Faith, Ch. vi, § 3. Cat. Qu. 18. Turrett. Qu. 8, 10, and 11. Dick, Lect. 46, 47. Hill, Bk. IV, Ch. 1. Watson, as above.

7. How is the existence of this total depravity proved; a.) From facts. b.) From Scripture? Are any secular virtues of the unrenewed genuine?

Turrett. Qu. 10. Dick and Hill, as above. Edwards on Original Sin, Pt. I, Ch. 1, and 2; Pt. II, Ch. 2, 3; Pt. III, Ch. 1 and 2.

8. *Define and prove* the imputation of the guilt of Adam's first sin to his posterity.

Turrett. Qu. 9, 12, and 15. Dick and Hill, as above. Edwards on Original Sin, Pt. II, Ch. 1 and 4; Pt. III, Ch. 1 and 2. Boardman on Original Sin, Wines' "Adam and Christ." Knapp, Sect. LXXVI. Watson, Ch. 18, § III.

VI. "The sinfulness of that estate whereinto man fell, consists of the guilt of Adam's first sin, the want of original righteousness, and the corruption of his whole nature, which is commonly called *original sin*; together with all actual transgressions which proceed from it."

Here, as in the Larger Catechism, Original Sin (so called because *native*, and because the fountain of all other sin) is the general term, expressing both elements, of imputed guilt, and total depravity. By many theologians it is often used for the latter specially. I discuss the latter first.

ORIGINAL SIN A POSITIVE BENT TO WRONG.—Turrettin asserts that this total depravity is not merely or negatively a *carentia justitiæ originalis* but positively, an active principle of evil. But this does not contradict the definition which represented the essence of sin as *disconformity* to law. The essential nature of virtue is, that it positively, or affirmatively *requires* something; or makes a given state or act positively obligatory on the human heart. It admits no moral neutrality: so that the simply *not* being, or not doing what God requires, is Sin. But the soul is essentially active. Hence it follows, that in a sinful state or act, the action or positivity of the sin is from the essential nature of the soul, its wrongness is from the mere absence of conformity to law. Depravity, as Prest. Edwards says, is a defective or privative quality; yet it assumes a positive form. I would prefer to say that depravity is *active* as opposed to simple negation. That it is active, is proved by Turrettin from those texts which attribute *effects* to it, as binding, deceiving, and laying, &c. Yet it is also important to distinguish that it is, in its origin, privative, and not the infusion of some positive quality of evil into the soul; in order to acquit God of the charge of being author of sin.

BUT NOT A CORRUPTION OF THE SOUL'S SUBSTANCE.—The same reason compels us to believe that native depravity is not a substantial corruption of the soul: i. e., does not change or destroy any part of its substance. For souls are, as to their *substance*, what God made them; and His perfections ensure His not making anything that was not good. Nor is there any loss of any of the capacities or faculties, which make up the *essentia* of the soul. Man is, in these respects, essentially what his Creator made him. Hence depravity is, in the language of metaphysics, not an attribute, but an *accident* of the human soul now. This is further proved by the fact that Jesus Christ assumed our very nature, at His incarnation, without which He would not be *our* Mediator. But surely, He did not assume moral corruption! Last: Scripture clearly distinguishes between sin and the soul, when they speak of it as defiling the soul, as easily besetting; Heb. xii: 1, 2, &c. If it be asked, *what* then, is native depravity: if it be neither a faculty, nor the privation of one, nor of the man's essence, nor a change of substance? I reply, it is a vicious *habitude of acting*, which qualifies man's active powers, i. e. his capacities of feeling and will. Although we may not be able to fully describe, yet we all know this idea of habitudes, which naturally qualify the powers of action, in all things.

DEPRAVITY TOTAL.—The Cofession states that the first man "became wholly defiled, in *all the faculties and parts of soul and body*." The seat of this vicious moral habitude is, of course, strictly speaking, in the moral propensities. But since these give active direction to all the faculties and parts of soul and body, in actions that have any moral quality, it may be said that, by accommodation of language, they are all morally defiled. The conscience (the highest department of rational intuitions) is not indeed destroyed; but its accuracy of verdict is greatly disturbed by evil desire, and the instinctive moral emotions which should accompany those verdicts, are so seared by neglect as to seem practically feeble, or dead, for the time. The views of the understanding concerning all moral subjects are perverted by the wrong propensions of the heart, so as to call good evil, and evll good. Thus "blindness of mind" on all moral subjects results. The memory becomes a store of corrupt images and recollections, and thus furnishes material for the imagination; defiling both. The corporeal appetites, being stimulated by the lusts of the soul, by a defiled memory and imagination, and by unbridled indulgence, become tyrannical and inordinate. And the bodily limbs and organs of sense are made servants of unrighteousness. Thus, what cannot be literally unholy is put to unholy uses.

In what sense total? And are all natural virtues spurious?—By saying that man's native depravity is *total*, we do not by any means intend that conscience is destroyed, for the man's guilt is evinced by this very thing, that his heart prefers what conscience condemns. Nor do we mean that all men are alike bad, and all as bad as they can be. Nor do we mean to impugn the genuineness and disinterestedness of the social virtues and charities in the ungodly. Far be it from us to assert that all the civic rectitude of an Aristides or Fabricin, all the charities of domestic love, all the nobleness of disinterested friendship among the worldly, are selfishness in disguise. But if it be allowed that many of these acts are of the true nature of virtue, how can man be called totally depraved? But we mean, first, that as to the chief responsibility of the soul, *to love God*, every soul is totally recreant. No natural man has *any* true love for God as a spiritual, holy, true, good, and righteous Sovereign. But this being the preeminent duty over all others in the aggregate, utter dereliction here, throws all smaller, partial virtues wholly into the shade. Second; while there is something of true virtue in many secular acts and feelings of the unrenewed, which *deserves* the sincere approval and gratitude of fellow-men to them, as between man and man, there is in those same acts and feelings a fatal defect as to God, which places them on the wrong side of the moral dividing line. That defect is, that they are not prompted by any moral regard for God's will requiring them. (Illustrate.) "God is not in all their thoughts." Ps. x: 4. Let any worldly man analyzes his motives, and he will find that this is true of his best secular acts. But the supreme regard ought to be, in every act, the desire to please God. Hence, although these secular virtues are much *less wrong* than their opposite vices, they are still, in God's sight, *short of right*, and that in the most important particular. Third; native depravity is total, because it sets man on the descending scale, from which there is no adequate recuperative power in him. His inevitable tendency is to progressive, and at last, to utter depravity. He is spiritually dead—the corpse may be little emaciated, it may be still warm, still supple, may still have colour on its cheek, and a smile on its lips—but it is a corpse: and will putrefy in due time.

VII. The proofs of a total native depravity are, unfortunately, so numerous, that little more can be attempted in one Lecture than a statement of their heads. They may be grouped under the two heads of *experience* and *Scripture* statements and facts.

1. Depravity of the Race proved, 1st, by law of reproduction.—Adam's sin reduced him to a total depravity, as has been shown in a previous Lecture. But the great law, which seems to reign throughout the vegetable and sentient universe, wherever a law of reproduction reigns, is that like shall beget like. And this appears to be confirmed by Gen. v: 3; Job. xiv: 4. Whence Adam's ruin would be *à priori*, a ground for expecting his posterity to be born depraved. There are indeed some, as Dr. Thornwell, Review of Breckinridge, January, 1858, who deny that this law would *naturally* apply here, and attribute the result of Adam's producing a sinful posterity, exclusively to the positive federal connexion appointed for them. They urge, that the thing propagated by this natural law is the attributes of the specses, not its accidents; that by this cause any other progenitor between us and our first father would be as much the source of our depravity as he; and that if the accident of Adam's fall is propagated, so ought to be the regenerate nature produced in him, and in other progenitors, by grace. This is clearly against the Confession, ch. 6, § 3, and, it seems to me, against the texts quoted. It confounds *accidents* in the popular sense with accidents in the sense of the Logician. Very true; a man who loses an arm by accident, does not propagate one-armed children. But in the other sense of the word, it will hardly be asserted that the red colour of Devon cattle are attributes and not accidents of horned cattle, and the more refractory and savage temper of the wild boar attributes of the species swine; yet both are propagated by this law of generation. As I have before said, the properties which define a species, whether attributes or accidents, are just those which are propagated in it; this is the very *idea* of species. Regenerate character does not define the species man, as a species; and hence, is not propagated, especially as it is a character only incipient in the parents in this life. Chiefly, regenerate character is not propagated by parents, because it is *not a natural, but a supernatural* property.

2. By Universal Sin.—We argue native depravity from the universal sinfulness of man, as exhibited in fact. Premise, that the strength of this argument ought to be judged according to the tendencies which this prevalent ungodliness would exert, not as it is in fact, but as it would be, *if unrestrained by the grace and providence of God.* What then is the fact? We see all men, under all circumstances, do much that is wrong. We see the world full of wickedness, much of it enormous. We behold parents, masters, magistrates and teachers busy with multitudes of rules and laws, and a vast apparatus of prisons, police, armies, and penalties, striving with very indifferent success, to repress wickedness. It is no alleviation to this picture to say, that there are also many virtues in the world, and more correct people who leave no history, *because* they quietly pursue a virtuous life, than of those who make a noise in the world by sin. For the majority of men are *relatively wicked*, taking the world over; and a truly honourable secular character, even, is the exception. Again: as we have seen, all these virtues contain a fatal defect, that of not being performed for God's honour and pleasure; a defect so vital, that it throws any element of

goodness as to man wholly into the shade. Take the standard: "Thou shalt love the Lord thy God with all thy heart," and it will be seen that the best natural man in the world never comes up to it in *any one* act. How then can he claim any good acts to balance against his bad ones, when there are none at all wholly in the right scale? None that are in the right scale as to the most weighty particular.

BY EARLY APOSTASY OF CHILDREN FROM THE RIGHT.—Again: the universal result of the growth of human beings is, that as soon as they are old enough to exhibit any moral qualities in intelligent action, they exhibit some wrong ones. And thenceforward, their doing some wrong things is a *constant* occurrence, not an occasional accident. Yea, more: infants, before they are old enough to understand their own evil tempers, show wicked tempers, selfishness, anger, spite, revenge. So testifies Scripture. Ps. lviii: 3; Gen. viii: 21.

BY OPPOSITION TO GOD AND REDEMPTION.—Once more, we find universally, a most obdurate blindness, stupidity, and opposition concerning the things of God. Rom. viii: 7. So averse are men to the spiritual service of God, that they *all*, if left to themselves, postpone and refuse it, against the dictates of reason and conscience, which they partially obey in other things, against motives absolutely infinite; and, such is the portentous power of this opposition, it overrides these motives and influences usually without a seeming struggle. This universal prevalence of sin has appeared in man's history, in spite of great means for its prevention: not only by the legislation, &c., mentioned; but by chastisements, the Flood, religious dispensations, miracles, theophanies, prophecies, and the incarnation of Christ Himself.

BY SCRIPTURE.—Such is a fair and moderate picture of human experience. Scripture confirms it, asserting the universal and prevalent sinfulness of man. Gen. vi: 5; 1 Kings viii: 46; Eccl. vii: 20; Ps. cxliii: 2; Gal. iii: 22; Rom. iii: 10–18; Jas. iii: 1, 2; Eccl. ix: 3, &c., &c.; Ps. xiv: 2, 3; Jer. xvii: 9.

UNIVERSAL EFFECTS REQUIRE A CAUSE.—Now an *effect* requires a *cause*. Here is an effect, occurring under every variety of outward condition and influences, universal, constantly recurring, appearing immediately the time arrives in the human being's life which permits it. There must be a universal cause, and that, within the human being himself. We may not be able to comprehend exactly how a moral habitude subsists in an *undeveloped* reason and conscience; but we are just as *sure*, that there is an innate germinal *cause*, in the human being's moral nature, for all these moral results, as we are that there is, in young *apes*, an innate cause why no nurture or outward circumstances will ever by any possibility develope one of them into a Newton. This intuition is confirmed by Scripture. Luke vi: 43–45, &c.; Ps. lviii: 3, with verse 4.

3. ARGUMENT AND PREVALENCE OF THE CURSE.—The universal prevalence of bodily death, with its premonitory ills, of bodily infirmity, a cursed ground, toil and hardship, show that man's depravity is total and native. These ills are a part of the great threatening made against Adam, and when inflicted on him, it was in immediate connexion with spiritual death. Why suppose them severed, in any other case? It is vain to say that these things are not now the curse of sin, but a wholesome chastisement and restraint, and thus a blessing in disguise;

for if man were not depraved, he would not need such a lesson. Why does not God see that Paradise is still man's most wholesome state, as it was Adam's? But from Gen. ii: 17, onward, death is always spoken of as a punishment *for sin*. Then, where death goes, sin must have gone. Rom. v: 12; 1 Cor. xv: 22. Especially the death of infants proves it; because they cannot understand the disciplinary effects of suffering and death. See especially the cases of the infants of Sodom, of Canaan, of Jerusalem, in Ezek. ix: 6. Nor can it be said that infants die only by the imputed guilt of Adam's sin; for imputed guilt and actual depravity are never found separated in the natural man.

4. From need of Redemption.—The fact that all need, and some of all classes are interested in the *redemption* of Jesus Christ, proves that all have a sin of nature. For if they were not sinners, they would not be susceptible of redemption. Among the Redeemed are "elect infants dying in infancy," as is proved by Luke xviii: 16; Matt. xxi: 16. But infants have no actual transgressions to be redeemed from! Socinians and Pelagians talk of a redemption in their case, which consists neither in an actual regeneration nor atonement; but in their resurrection, and their being endued with a gracious and assured blessedness. But this is a mere abuse of Scripture to speak of such a process as the redeeming work of Christ for any human being. For His very *name* and *mission* were from the fact that He was to save His people *from their sins.* Matt. i: 21; 1 Tim. i: 15; Mark ii: 17; Gal. ii: 21; iii: 21. Christ was sent to save men from *perishing*. Jno. iii: 16. His redemption is always *by blood*, because this typifies the atonement for sin. Sin is therefore coextensive with redemption.

From Regeneration.—Again; the application of this redemption in effectual calling is evidence of native depravity. In order that Christ may become ours, it is most repeatedly declared, that we must be born again. This regeneration is a radical moral change, being not merely a change of purpose of life made by a volition, but a revolution of the *propensities which prompt* our purposes. This is proved by the names used to describe the change, a new birth, a new creation, a quickening from death, a resurrection, and from the *Agent*, which is not the truth, or motive, but almighty God. See Jno. iii: 5; Eph. i: 19 to ii: 10. Now, if man needs this moral renovation of nature, he must be naturally sinful. We find our Saviour Himself, Jno. iii: 5, 6, stating this very argument. The context shows that Christ assigns the sixth verse as a ground or reason for the fifth, and not as an explanation of the difficulty suggested by Nicodemus in the fourth. Moreover, the word sarx means, by established Scripture usage, not the body, nor the natural human constitution considered merely as a nature, but man's nature as depraved morally. Compare Rom. vii: 14, 18; viii: 4, 7, 8, 9; Col. ii: 18; Gal. v: 16–24; Gen. vi: 3.

To this we may add, one of the meanings of circumcision and baptism was to symbolise this regeneration, (another, to represent cleansing from *guilt* by atonement.) Hence, sin is recognized in all to whom these sacraments are applied by divine command. And as both were given to infants, who had no intelligent acts of sin, it can only be explained by their having a sin of nature.

5. Scripture proofs.—We have seen how the Bible asserts a uni-

versal sinfulness in practice, and how it sustained us in tracing that universal sin up to its source in a sin of nature. We close with a few specimens of other texts, which expressly assert original sin. Job xiv: 4; xv: 14–16; Prov. xxii: 15; Ps. li: 5; Eph. ii: 3.

The evasions to which the deniers of Original Sin are forced to resort, to escape these categorical assertions, are too numerous and contradictory to be recited or answered here. Let these texts be carefully studied in their scope and connexion.

One of these I will notice: It has been Objected; that the innocence of children seems to be asserted in such places as Ps. cvi: 38; Jonah iv: 11; Jno. ix: 3; Rom. ix: 11. I explain, that this is only a relative innocence. The sacred writers here recognize their freedom from the guilt of all actual transgression, and their harmlessness towards their fellow men, during this helpless age. This, together with their engaging simplicity, dependence, and infantile graces, has made them *types* of innocence in all languages. And this is all the Scriptures mean.

VIII. Imputation defined.—The Hebrew word hashab, and the Greek, logidzomai, both mean primarily to *think*, then to *deem* or *judge*, then to impute or attribute. In this sense the former occurs in Ps. xxxii: 2, and the latter in Rom. iv: 6–8, as its translation. See also 2 Sam. xix: 19; 2 Cor. v: 19; Gal. iii: 6; Jas. ii: 23. Without going at this time into the vexed question, whether anything is ever said in Scripture to be imputed to any other than its own agent. I would define, that it is not Adam's sin which is imputed to us, but the *guilt* (obligation to punishment) of his first sin. This much misunderstood doctrine does not teach that Adam's act was actually made ours. This consciousness repudiates. We know that we personally did not will it. Nor does it mean that we are to feel personally defiled and blameworthy, with the vileness and demerit of Adam's sin. For us to undertake to repent of it in this sense, would be as preposterous as for us to feel self-complacency for the excellence of Christ's righteousness imputed to us. But we are so associated with Adam in the *legal consequences* of the sin which closed his probation, and ours in his, that we are treated as he is, on account of his act. The grounds of this legal union we hold to be two: 1st the natural union with him as the *root* of all mankind; 2nd the federal relation instituted in him, by God's covenant with him. Now, we do not say that the Scriptures anywhere use the particular phrase, the guilt of Adam's sin was imputed to us; but we claim that the truth is clearly implied in the transactions as they actually occurred, and is substantially taught in other parts of Scripture.

Imputation proved.—1. If Adam came under the covenant of works as a *public* person, and acted there, not for himself alone, but for his posterity federally, this implies the imputation of the legal consequences of his act to them. The proof that Adam was a federal head, in all these acts, is clear as can be, from so compendious a narrative. See Gen. i: 22, 28; xxvi: 29; iii: 15 to 19. In the dominion assigned man over the beasts, in the injunction to multiply, in the privilege of eating the fruits of the earth, in the hallowing of the Sabbath, God spoke seemingly only to the first pair; but His words indisputably applied as well to their posterity. So we infer, they are included in the threat of death for disobedience, and the implied promise of ii : 17. To see the force of this inference, remember that it is the established style of Genesis. See ix : 25 to 27 ; xv : 7 ; xvi : 12 ; xvii : 20 ; in each case the patriarch stands for himself and his posterity, in the meaning of the promise. But this is more manifest in Gen. iii : 15–19, where God proceeds to pass sentence according to the threat of the broken Covenant. The serpent is to be at war with the woman's *seed*. The ground is cursed for Adam's sin. Does not this curse affect his posterity, just as it did him? See Gen. v : 29. He is to eat his bread in the sweat of his face. Does not this pass over to his posterity? The woman has her peculiar punishment, shared equally by all her daughters. And in the closing sentence, death to death, we all read the doom of our mortality. So plain is all this, that even Pelagians have allowed that God acted here *judicially*. But Adam's posterity is included in the judgment. No better description of imputation need be required.

IMPUTATION CONFIRMED BY EXPERIENCE.—2. A presumption in favour of this solution is raised by a number of facts in God's providence. He usually connects the people and their head, the children and parents, in the consequences of the representative's conduct. Wherever there is such a political union, this follows. Nor is the consent of the persons represented always obtained, to justify the proceeding. Instances may be found in the decalogue, Exod. xx : 5, the deliverance of Rahab's house by her faith, Josh. vi : 25 ; the destruction of Achan's by his sin, Josh. vii : 24, 25 ; of the posterity of Amalek for the sins of their forefathers, 1 Sam. xv : 2. Of Saul's descendants for his breach of covenant with the Gibeonites, 2 Sam. xxi ; of the house of Jeroboam, 1 Kings xiv : 9, 10 ; and of the generation of Jews cotemporary with Christ, Matt. xxiii : 35. So, nations are chastised with their rulers, children with their parents. It is not asserted that the case of Adam and his posterity is exactly similar ; but cases bearing some resemblance to its principles show that it is not unreasonable ; and since God actually orders a multitude of such cases, and yet cannot do wrong, they cannot contain the natural injustice which has been charged upon Adam's case.

3. IMPUTATION IMPLIED IN MAN'S STATE.—The explanation presented by the doctrine of imputation is demanded by the mere facts of the case, as they are admitted by all except Pelagians and Socinians. Man's *is* a spiritually dead and a condemned race. See Eph. ii : 1–5, *et passim*. He is obviously under a curse for something, *from the beginning* of his life. Witness the native depravity of infants, and their inheritance of woe and death. Now either man was tried and fell in Adam, *or he has been condemned without a trial*. He is either under the curse, [as it rests on him at the beginning of his existence] for Adam's guilt, or for no guilt at all. Judge which is most honorable to God, a doctrine which, although a profound mystery, represents Him as giving man an equitable and most favourable probation in His federal head ; or that which makes God condemn him untried, and even before he exists.

NOT TO BE ACCOUNTED FOR BY MERE LAW OF REPRODUCTION.—Note here, that the Arminian view, in making man's fallen state by nature a mere result of the law: "Like must beget like," does not relieve the case. For who ordained that law? Who placed the human race under it, as to their spirits as well as their body? Was not God *able* to endue a race with a law of generation which should be different in this particular, or to continue the race of man by some other plan, as successive creations? The very act of God, in ordaining this law for *man whom He purposed to permit to fall*, was virtually to ordain a federal connexion between Adam and his race, and to decide beforehand the virtual imputation of his guilt to them. For note: the consequences inherited by this law are the very ones which are the retributions of guilt, in all God's dealings of man. If then, the arrangement was not a righteous judicial one, based on the guilt of Adam, it was an arbitrary one having no foundation in justice.

Argument of Rom 5th and 1 Cor. 15th.—4. But the great Bible argument for the imputation of Adam's sin, is the parallel drawn between Adam and Christ, in 1 Cor. xv: 21, 22, 45-49, and Rom. v: 12-19. The latter of these passages especially, has been the peculiar subject of exegetical tortures. See, for scheme of immediate imputationists, Hodge on Rom.; of moderate Calvinists, Baird, Elohim Rev. Chap. xiv. I shall not go over the expository arguments, for time forbids; and they are rather the appropriate business of another department; but shall content myself with stating the doctrinal results, which, as I conceive, are clearly established. In 1 Cor. xv: Adam and Christ are compared, as the first and the second Adam. In almost every thing they are contrasted; the one earthy, the other heavenly; the one source of death, the other of life; yet they have something in common. What can this be, except their representative characters? In verse 22, Adam is somehow connected with the death of his confederated body; and Christ is *similarly* (hosper . . . houto) connected with the life of his. But Christ redeems His people by the imputation to them of His righteousness. Must not Adam have ruined his, by the imputation to them of his guilt?

Exposition of Rom. 5th.—In Rom. v: 12-19, it is agreed by all Calvinistic interpreters, that the thing illustrated is justification through faith, which is the great doctrine of the Epistle to Romans, denied at that time by Jews. The thing used *for illustration* is Adam's federal headship, and our sin and death in him, more generally admitted by Jews. The passage is founded on the idea of verse 14, that Adam is the *figure* (tupos) of Christ. And obviously, a comparison is begun in verse 12, which is suspended by parenthetic matter until verse 18, and there resumed and completed. The amount of this comparison is indisputably this: that *like as we fell in Adam, we are justified in Christ. Hence our general argument* for imputation of Adam's sin; because justification is notoriously by imputation.

2. It is asserted, verse 12, and proved, vs. 13, 14, that all men sinned and were condemned in Adam; death, the established penalty of sin, passing upon them *through his sin*, as is proved, verse 14, by the death of those who had no actual transgression of their own.

3. The very exceptions of vs. 15-17, where the points are stated in which the resemblance does *not* hold, show that Adam's sin is imputed. Our federal union with Adam, says the Apostle, resulted in condemna-

tion and death with Christ in abounding grace. In the former case, *one sin condemned* all; in the latter, one man's righteousness justifies all. The very exceptions show that men are condemned for Adam's sin.

4. In vs. 18, 19, the comparison is resumed and completed; and it is most emphatically stated that, as in Christ many are constituted righteous, so in Adam many were constituted sinners. Scriptural usage of the phrase KATHISTENAI DIKAIOI, and what is taught of the nature of our justification in Christ, together with the usage of the phrase DIKAIOSIN DZOES, verse 18, by which it is defined, prove that it is a forensic change which is implied. Then it follows that likewise our legal relations were determined by Adam. *This is imputation.*

LECTURE XXVII.

SYLLABUS.

ORIGINAL SIN—(Concluded.)

9. Refute the *evasions* of Pelagians, &c., from the argument for native depravity.

Turrett., Loc. IX, Qu. 10. Edwards on Orig. Sin, Pt. I, ch. 1, § 9.

10. Answer the objections to imputation a). From Scriptures as Deut. xxiv: 16; Ezek. xviii: 20, b). From the absence of *consent* by us to the representative union, c). From its supposed injustice, d). From God's goodness.

Turrett. Qu. 9. Edwards, Pt. IV. Knapp, Sect. LXXVI.

11. Explain the theories of *Mediate*, and *Immediate* imputation, and show the correct view.

Turrett. Qu. 9. Edwards, Pt. IV, ch. 3. Stapfer, Polemic Theol., Vol. I, ch. 3, § 856-7. Vol. IV, ch. 16, § 47-49. Breckinridge's Theol., Vol. 1, ch. 32, with Thornwell's Review, as above. Chalmer's Theo. Institutes. Princeton Review, 1830, p. 481-503.

12. What the importance of the doctrine of original sin, from its connexions with the other doctrines of Redemption?

IX, We now group together the usual objections advanced by opponents against our argument for native depravity.

1. OBJECTIONS. ADAM SINNED; BUT WAS NOT ORIGINALLY CORRUPT. It is urged, if the sinning of men now proves they have native depravity, Adam's sinning would prove that he had, since the generality of an effect does not alter its nature. I reply, the sophism is in veiling Adam's continued and habitual sinning after he fell, with the first sin, by which he fell. Did we only observe Adam's habit of sinning, without having known him from his origin, the natural and reasonable induction, so far as human reason could go, would be, that he *was* originally depraved. But the proof would be incomplete, because our observation did not trace this habit up, as we do in the case of infants

to the origin of his existence. It is *revelation* which informs us how Adam became a habitual sinner, not inference. But if Adam's first sin be compared with his descendant's perpetual sins, the difference is, that an occasional effect requires an occasional cause; but a constant effect requires a constant cause.

2. Some Pelagins say, a self-determined, contingent will, is enough to account for all men's sinning. We reply: how comes a contingent force to produce always uniform effects? If a die, when thrown, falls in various ways, its falling is contingent. But if it *always* falls the same way, every gambler knows it is loaded.

3. EXAMPLE. MAY IT ACCOUNT FOR II?—Pelagians offer the general power of an evil example, as the sufficient explanation why all men grow up sinners. Calvinists answer, a). How comes it that the example *is* universally evil? This itself is the effect to be accounted for, b). If there were no innate tendency to evil, a bad example would *usually* repell and disgust the holy soul. c). All young immortals have not been subjected to an equally bad example; witness the godly families of Adam, Seth, Noah, Abraham, and the pious now, and above all, the spotless example of Jesus Christ. If the power of example were the decisive cause, these good examples (not perfect, but,) approximating thereto, would sometimes have produced an efficient upward tendency in some families.

MAY INFLUENCE OF SENSE ACCOUNT FOR SIN?—4. Some say: Sense developes before reason; and thus the child is betrayed under the power of appetite, before its moral faculties are strong enough to guide. I answer, mere animal appetite, without moral element, has no moral quality; it is the heart which gives the evil element to bodily appetite, not *vice versa*. But chiefly; we show that the result is uniform and certain: whence it is the efficient result of *God's* natural law; which makes it more obnoxious to the charge of making God the author of sin, than the Calvinistic theory.

X. OBJECTIONS TO IMPUTATION.—Against the other element of original sin, the imputed guilt of Adam's first sin, it is also objected, that it cannot be true: for then God will appear to have acted with equal severity against poor helpless babes, who, on the Calvinist's theory, have no guilt except total depravity never yet expressed in a single overt act against His law; and against Adam, the voluntary sinner: and Satan and his angels. We reply No. All infinites are not equal. Paschal and Sir Isaac Newton have shown that of two true infinites one may be infinitely larger than another. If the infant, Adam, and Satan, be all punished eternally, they will not be punished equally. Further; has it been proved that any infants who die in infancy, (without overt sin,) are eternally lost? The question however is: are infants depraved by nature? And is this tendency of will to evil morally evil? Then God is entitled to punish it *as it deserves*.

OBJECTIONS FROM SCRIPTURE.—A scriptural objection is raised, from such passages as Deut. xxiv: 16. It is urged with great confidence, that here, the principle on which Calvinists represent God as acting, [God the pure and good Father in Heaven,] is seen to be so utterly wicked, that imperfect human magistrates are forbidden to practise on it. I reply; it is by no means true that an act would be wicked in

God, because it would be wicked in man. E. G. Man may not kill, God righteonsly kills millions every year. But second: the object of civil government is very different from that of God's government. The civil Magistrate does not punish sin in order to requite absolutely its ill-desert. (This is the function of God alone,) but to preserve the public order and well-being, by making an example of criminals. Now, of *that element* of *guilt against society*, the children of the murderer or thief are clear; for the magistrate to shed their blood for this, would be to shed innocent blood: i. e. innocent as to that element of guilt which it is the civil magistrate's business to punish. Here, let it be noted, the punishment of Achan's, Saul's, &c., children, for their fathers, was the act of God, not the Magistrate. The cases were exceptional.

OBJECTION FROM EZEK. XVIII: 1–23 ANSWERED.—Again: it is urged with much clamour, that in Ezek. xviii: 1–23, God expressly repudiates the scheme of imputation of father's sins to their posterity, *for Himself*, as well as for magistrates; and declares this as the great law of His kingdom: "The soul that sinneth, *it* shall die." We reply: He does not mean to disclaim the imputation of Adam's sin to the human race. For first: He does not mean here, to disclaim all principles of imputation in His Povidence even as to parents and posterity subsequent to Adam. If you force this sense on His words, all you get by it is an irreconcilable collision between this passage and Exod. xx: 5, and obvious facts in His providence. Second, if it were true universally of human parents subsequent to Adam, it would not follow as to Adam's first sin. For there is a clear distinction between that act of Adam, and all the sins of other parents. He alone was a federal head in a Covenant of works. The moment he fell, by that act, the race fell in him, and its apostasy was effected; the thing was done; and could not be done over. From that hour, a Covenant of works became inapplicable to man, and neither parents nor chiidren, for themselves, nor for each other, have had any probation under it. So that the case *is* widely different, between Adam in his first sin, and all other parents in their sin. Third; the Covenant in which this whole passage has reference was, not the old Covenant of works, whose probation was forever past, but the political, theocatic Covenant between God and Israel. Israel, as a commonwealth, was now suffering under providential penalties, for the breach of that political covenant exactly according to the terms of the threatenings. (See Deut. 28.) But although that was indisputable, the banished Jews still consoled their pride by saying, that it was their fathers' breach of the national Covenant for which they were suffering. In this plea God meets them; and tells them it was false; for the terms of the theocracy were such, that the covenant breaking of the father would never be visited on the Son who thoroughly disapproved of it, and acted in the opposite way. How far is this, from touching the subject of Original Sin? But last: we might grant that the passage did refer to original sin; and still refute the objector thus, God says the son who truly disapproves of and reverses his Fathers' practices, shall live. Show us now a child of Adam who fulfills this condition, in his own strength, and we will allow that the guilt of Adam's sin has not affected him.

ADAM'S REPRESENTATION A HUMANE ARRANGEMENT.—In defending the federal relationship instituted between Adam and his posterity against the charge of *cruelty*, let it be distinctly understood, that we do not aim to justify the *equity* of the arrangement merely by the plea that it was a benevolent one, and calculated to promote the creature's advantage. For if it were an arrangement intrinsically unrighteous, it would be no sufficient answer to say, that it was politic and kindly. God does not "do evil, that good may come;" nor hold that "the end sanctifies the means." But still, we claim that, as the separate charge of cruelty, or harshness, is urged against this federal arrangement, we can triumphantly meet it, and show that the arrangement was eminently *benevolent;* thus reconciling it to the divine attribute of goodness so far as that is concerned in it. And further: while the benevolence of an arrangement may not be a sufficient justification of its righteousness, yet it evidently helps to palliate the charge of injustice, and to raise a presumption in favor of the equity of the proceeding. If there were *injustice* in such a transaction, one element of it must be that it was mischievous to the happiness of the parties.

ITS BENEVOLENCE PROVED BY COMPARISON.—This federal relation then, was consistent with God's goodness. Let the student remember what was established concerning the natural rights and relations of a holy creature towards his Creator. The former could never *earn* a claim, by natural justice, to any more than this: to be well treated to the extent of his natural well-being merely, *as long as he behaved himself perfectly*, or until God should see fit to annihilate him. If God condescended to any fuller communications of happiness, or to give any promise of eternal life, it must be by an act of free grace. And the covenant of works *was* such an act of grace. Now, a race of men being created, holy and happy, there were, as far as the human mind can imagine, but four plans possible for them. One was, to be left under their natural relation to God forever. The second was, to have the gracious offer of a covenant of works, under which each one should stand for himself, and a successful probation of some limited period, (suppose 70 years,) be kindly accepted by God for his justification, and adoption into eternal life. The third was, for God to enter into such a covenant of works, for a limited period, with the head of the race federally, for himself and his race, so that if he stood the limited probation, justification and adoption should be graciously bestowed on him, and in him, on all the race; and if he failed, all should be condemned in him. The third was the plan actually chosen: Let us compare them, and see if it is not far the most benevolent of the three.

The first plan, I assert, would have resulted, sooner or later, in the sin and fall of every member of the race, and that with a moral certainty. (This may be the reason that God has condescended to a Covenant with each order of rational creatures after creating them.) For creatures, no matter how holy, are finite, in all their faculties and habitudes. But, in an existence under law, i. e. under duty, requiring perpetual and perfect obedience, and protracted to immortality, the number and variety of exigencies or moral trials, would become infinite; and therefore the chance of error, in the passage of a finite holiness through them, would become ultimately a most violent probability, mounting nearer and nearer to a moral certainty. Whenever sin occurred, the mere natural relation of the soul to God would require Him to avenge it. Thus, one after another would stumble, till ultimately all were lost. This would be the least benevolent plan.

But suppose each man allowed the privilege of a Covenant of works, for some limited time, to win the grace of adoption unto life by a perfect obedience for, say, 70 years, and beginning his probation with a perfectly innocent nature. How would that work? Why; have we not here, the *very* state of the case which Socinians and Pelagians say, actually prevails? Let man's experience then, even as interpreted by these heretics, give the answer how it works. Do they not admit that, by virtue of evil example, nearly all fall? Can they deny that the earth is full of misery and wickedness; and that none remain absolutely innocent? If then, our present state were consistently interpreted as a probation under a Covenant of works, in which *any sin* forfeits the prize; if Pelagians would be consistent, and not introduce the preposterous idea of *pardon* under such a plan, where it has no business; even they would be compelled to admit that this second scheme does actually result in a total failure. Under it, all are destroyed. It too then, has as little beneficence as the first. This, I grant, is an *argumentum ad hominem:* but it is a just one. But we might leave the Pelagian's premises, and still reason, that the second scheme would only result in death. The actual failure of the first man's probation settles the question as to him. The next would have had the same chances of fall, aggravated by the evil example and enticements of the first; and pretty soon, the current of evil would have become so general, that all would go with it.

Advantages of Covenant of Works, with a Representative.—Let us come to the third plan. Is it said, that practically, all *have* died under that also, so that it is just on a par with the other two? I answer, no; because the probabilities of a favourable issue were as great as could well be imagined, compatibly with leaving the creature mutable at all. For, instead of having a risque repeated millions of times, under circumstances increasingly untoward, only one risque was permitted. And this was under the most favorable possible conditions. The probationer had no human bad company: he was in the maturity of his powers and knowledge, whereas his posterity would have had to begin their trial in their inexperienced boyhood. He had the noblest motives to stand, imaginable. Had the probation resulted favourably, so that we had all entered existence assured against sin and misery, and the adopted heirs of eternal life, how would we have magnified the *goodness* of God in the dispensation! The grace bestowed through the first Adam, would have been only second in its glory, to that we now adore in the second! Now, the failure was not God's fault; His goodness is just the same in the plan, as though it had eventuated well. It is no objection to say, that God foreknew, all the while, how unfortunately it would eventuate, and even determined to permit it. For this objection is no other than the one against the permission of evil: which no one can solve. It is but to restate the question: Why did not God just communicate Himself at once to every reasonable creature, so as to absolutely confirm His will against sin, without proposing any covenant, or probation at all? There is no answer, but Matt. xi: 26. This plan, the fourth and only other, being excluded, as stubborn fact proves it was, the federal arrangement made with Adam for his posterity, was the most liberal one.

Objection against justice of imputation.—But the grand objection of all Pelagians and skeptics, is still repeated: How can it be *justice*, for me, who gave no consent to the federal arrangement, for me, who was not present when Adam sinned, and took no share in it, save in a sense purely fictitious and imaginary, to be so terribly punished for another man's deed. This is nothing else than the intrinsic injustice of punishing an innocent man for the fault of the guilty. As well might God have gotten up a legal fiction of a federal relation between Gabriel and Satan, and when the latter sinned, dragged Gabriel down, innocent, and even ignorant of any crime, to hell. Against such a plan, the moral instincts of man rebel. It is simply impossible that they should accept it as righteous.

The several answers 1. The Wesleyan, is inadequate.—I have thus stated this objection in its full force. So far as I am aware, there have been five several expedients proposed for meeting it. 1. The Wesleyan says: the injustice would appear, if it were not remedied in the second Adam, in whom the imputation of Adam's guilt and original sin are so far repaired, as to give common sufficient grace to every child of Adam. So that the two dispensations ought to be viewed together; and what is harsh in one will be compensated in the other. This is inadmissible for many reasons chiefly because there is no common sufficient grace: and because if this solution be adopted, then the gospel will be of debt, and not of grace.

2. President Edwards also inadequate.—We find President Edwards endeavoring to evade the objection, by asserting that our federal oneness with Adam is no more arbitrary, in that it was constituted by God's *fiat*, than our own personal identity; for that also is constituted only by God's institution. If it be asked why is it just that I should be punished to-day, for a sin committed last year, our moral instincts answer: Because I am the *same person* whô sinned. But the Pelagian objection urges that we are not one with Adam in any real sense, and therefore cannot be justly made guilty for Adam's sin. But, says Edwards: "What is personal identity: and is it any less arbitrary than our federal identity with Adam?" He answers: "in no wise. Because our existence is dependent and successive. Its sustentation is a perpetual recreation. Its succession is a series of moments, of which one moment's existence does not cause or produce a succeeding moment's, not being coexistent with it, as cause and effect must always be. Hence, our continued identity is nothing else than a result of the will of God, sovereignly ordaining to restore our existence out of *nihil*, by a perpetual recreation, at the beginning of each new moment, and to cause in us a consciousness which seems to give sameness." I will venture the opinion that no man, not Edwards himself, ever satisfied himself, by this argument, that his being had not a true, intrinsic continuity, and a real necessary identity in itself. And it may usually be concluded that when any scientific conclusion conflicts thus with universal common sense, it is sophistical. In this case, a more correct Metaphysics has justified common sense Our belief in our own identity is not derived from our remembered consciousness, but implied in it. Belief in identity is an *á priori*, and necessary conception. If it be not accepted as valid, there is no valid law of thought at all. When I speak of the I, a true and intrinsic continuity of being is necessarily implied. Nor is it true that because the moments of successive time are not connected, therefore the existence which we necessarily con-

ceive of as flowing on in time, is disconnected in its *momenta*. We have seen that the notion of a perpetual recreation in the providential support of dependent being is improved. Hence we repudiate this Edwardean speculation as worthless, and contradicted by our own intuitions.

Dr. S. J. Baird's unsound.—3. Another attempt is made to establish a real identity of Adam's posterity with him, so as to lay a seeming basis for the imputation, by a class of theologians represented by Dr. S. J. Baird's "Elohim Revealed," who claim St. Augustine, as of their party. They say, we are made guilty of Adam's sin, because "we sinned in him and fell with him," not merely in a putative and federal sense, but really and truly. Thus we are involved in a true and proper responsibility for the sin of Adam, because we were actually in him seminally, as our root, They teach that we become sinners in him, because *the nature* sinned in him, and became guilty in him, as well as depraved; and this nature we have. Our nature they define to be that aggregate of forces, or attributes which constitute the human race what it is; and this, they hold, is not an abstraction when regarded distinctly from all individual men, but an objective reality, not indeed a substance, yet an entity. This nature, which thus sinned, and became guilty and depraved in Adam's act, is transferred as a real germ, to every human being from him; and hence depravity and guilt go along. This theory, while not exactly mediaeval Realism, is certainly something near akin to it; and the objections are of the same kind. That the phrase, human nature, expresses anything more than a complex conception of our thought, when abstracted from any one and every one human person, is untrue. This nature, they say, is the aggregate of all the forces which characterize man as man. But have those forces, each one, separate existence, as abstracted from all the individual men whom they characterize? Has the attribute of visibility, e. g. separate existence from each and every visible being? Obviously not. How then can the aggregate of these attributes? Again: we cannot attach the idea of sin, morality, responsibility, and guilt to anything but a *personal being*. If the nature, along with which the depravity and responsibility are transmitted, has not personality, the theory does not help us at all. But if you give it personality, have you not gotten back to the *common soul* of Averroes, the half-way house of Pantheism? Third; if the imputation of Adam's guilt is grounded solely on the fact that the nature we bear sinned and was corrupted in him, must it not follow that Christ's human nature is also corrupt, inasmuch as it was made guilty? And indeed is not our obeying and atoning in him, through the community of the nature that obeyed and atoned, precisely as real and intrinsic, as our sinning and corrupting ourselves in Adam? For these reasons, we must reject this explanation as untrue, if anything more be meant by it, than a strong way of stating the truth, that imputation is partly grounded on the fact Adam was the natural head of the race.

XI. Mediate Imputation.—The fourth solution attempted for the great objection, brings us to the 11th question: the scheme of mediate imputation. The author and history of this are sufficiently stated by Turretin. Placæus said that the imputation of Adam's sin was only mediate, and consequent upon our participation in total native depravity, which we derive by the great law, that like begets like. We, being thus depraved by nature, and, so to speak, endorsing his sin, by exhibiting the same spirit and committing similar acts, it is just in God to implicate us in the same punishments. To this view Turretin, with the stricter Calvinists, objects, that it is but mere Arminianism disguised; and that it really leaves no imputation of Adam's guilt at all. The latter charge has a certain amount of justice in it; for the scheme makes each man's own personal sin, viz., his native sin, the only virtual cause of his punishment. But it is unjust to say that it is no better than Arminianism; for it does not appear that Placæus held concupiscence to be innocent in its rise, nor that he disputed in the least the native bondage of the will to sin. The more valid objections to it are, 1st, that, like the Arminian, it offers the fact that God should have extended the law, "like begets like," to man's moral nature as an explanation of the fact. Natural laws are of God's sovereign institution, and it is His providence which sustains and regulates them. His ordaining such a natural law for the posterity of fallen Adam, would have been virtually to decide their fate by the same judicial act which decided his; and the question recurs, on what judicial basis did the sentence as to them *rest?* 2d. Placæus' scheme is false to the facts of the case, in that it speaks as though God conceived of Adam's posterity as having an antecedent depraved existence, before they passed under condemnation; whereas the Scripture shows that they are *born condemned.*

Immediate Imputation.—In opposition to this scheme, Turrettin states the view of *immediate imputation*, which has since been defined and asserted in its most rigid sharpness by the Princeton school. It boldly repudiates every sense in which we really or actually sinned in Adam, and admits no other than merely the representative sense of a positive covenant. It says that the guilt of Adam's first sin, which was personally nobody's but Adam's own, is sovereignly imputed to his posterity. Depravity of nature is a part of the *penalty* of death, due to Adam's sin, and is visited on Adam's children purely as the *penal consequence* of the putative guilt they bear. For sin may be the punishment of sin. Very true, after depravity of nature thus becomes personally theirs, it also brings an addition of personal guilt, for which they are thenceforward punished, as well as for actual transgressions. The grounds for this statement are chiefly these two: 1. That Rom. v 12–20 asserts an exact parallel between our federal relation to Adam and to Christ, so that as the imputation of Christ's righteousness to us, conceived as personally unrighteous, goes before procuring our justification, and then all sanctifying grace is bestowed working personal sanctification, as purchased by Christ's righteousness for us, so we must conceive Adam's guilt imputed to us, we being conceived as in the first instance personally guiltless, but for that guilt; and then depravity given us, working personal sin and guilt, as the mischievous purchase of Adam's federal act for us. And, as the parallel must be exact, if this view of original sin be rejected, then the view of justification must be modified "to suit;" making it consist first in an infusion of personal righteousness in the believer, and then the *consequent* accounting to us of Christ's righteousness. But that is precisely the Romish justification. 2d. Unless the justice and reasonableness of the imputation of

Adam's sin to us be admitted, we having, so far, no personal guilt, nor actual personal agency in his sin; the reasonableness of the imputation of Christ's righteousness cannot be defended, and justification is rendered impossible.

THIS THEORY DISREGARDS THE OBJECTION.—As to the great objection against our involuntary federal connexion with Adam, these divines unscrupulously impinge against it, and demand that the moral intuition on which it claims to be founded, be simply trampled down. Whether this is discreet, or true, or just, the student can easily judge for himself. Surely it is not wise so to represent God's truth, so to sharpen and exaggerate its angles, at the demand of an erroneous dialectics or overstrained exegesis, as to causelessly array against it the ineradicable intuitions of man's soul! Surely there are mysteries enough in this awful fact of original sin, to distress and awe the sensitive mind, without seeking gratuitously to exasperate them. And he who insists that the price men shall pay for admitting the orthodox theology is the surrender of their common sense, as they suppose, is practically propagating unbelief. If we are to abdicate our intuitive beliefs, we can no longer reason, nor believe anything properly. We must indeed, as we do, demand the unconditional submission of *carnal* reason, and we insist on facts which impinge against it; but not sanctified reason. One object of religion is to purify, rectify, and then *employ* this reason as necessary handmaid.

ITS SPECIAL REASONS UNSOUND.—The special reasons, on which that which is peculiar in this theory rests, are sophistical. The reasonableness of an imputation of Christ's merits to us, does *not* depend on the reasonableness of such an imputation of Adam's sin to us as they describe. The simple proof is, (it is amazing it should be overlooked;) the latter was an act of justice, of law; the former, of mercy. Surely, it does not follow, that because a gratuitous act of goodness may be reasonable and right, therefore a gratuitous act of severity is equally so! Nor is it of any avail to say, Christ was not personally an agent in our *sins*, yet the guilt of them was accounted to Him; for this also was a part of the plan of *mercy*; and *He gave His voluntary consent* beforehand. As to the first reason, drawn from Paul's parallel between Adam and Christ, it is not proved that the Apostle meant the parallel to be technically exact in every point. Such is rarely the case with illustrations; if they have analogy enough to explain, the one the other, it is enough. Does not Paul himself stop, in the midst of his illustration, even leaving his sentence suspended, to name two important respects in which the parallel was *not* exact? And is there not an inevitable difference, as he himself intimates, in the fact that the one federal arrangement was a transaction of *law*, and the other of *grace*? It was enough for his purpose to teach, what I strictly hold, that the first and second Adam were federal heads; and that as we fell in one, we are restored in the other. But, it is urged that, if immediate imputation is rejected, we are necessarily betrayed into the Popish doctrine of justification which makes inherent personal righteousness precede, and imputed follow. Let us see whether this charge may not be at least as plausibly retorted. If we are personally guiltless and sinless, till Adam's guilt is accounted to us, and then (in the order of thought) we receive *depravity* as the punishment of imputed guilt, a rigid parallelism (such as the other view demands,) must lead to this view of justification that we are personally unholy and contrasted in spiritual state with our federal Head, Christ, at the time of our justification; and afterwards, in the order of causasion, we *begin* to partake of His spiritual life and holiness, as a consequence of His imputed merit. But is *that* the Reformed doctrine of justification? Nay verily. I pray you distinguish: As to a personal *merit or righteousness procuring our acceptance with God*, we have none at all, at the time of our justification, nor ever after. But as to actual spiritual condition, we are *not* spiritually dead and depraved totally at the moment of justification. The order of sequence (not that we suppose an appreciable interval of time) is thus fixed by all the Reformed divines, so far as I know. 1. *Regeneration*, in which we begin to share the spiritual life of our head. 2. Saving faith acted by the soul, (with repentance implicitly in it.) 3. Mystical union to Christ constituted; which divides into a.) Legal union. b.) Spiritual union. So that when the soul is justified in the second Adam, it is already spiritually alive in him. We see then, that Princeton will have to relinquish the pretense of an exact parallel between our relation to the first and second Adam; or she is in danger of being driven by it into the abhorred result of mediate imputation. Do *I* then adopt the latter? No: consistency would drive Princeton to it, but not me; for I have never asserted that exact parallel. It is not to be expected, when we remember that, as to our relation to the second Adam, we each one have our own, personal, previous, existence, as depraved and guilty beings *before* we are brought into actual federal union with him. But as to the first Adam, we had no separate personal existence at all, till we *came* into existence actually and federally united to him.

IMMEDIATE IMPUTATION NOT TRUE TO FACTS.—This leads me to object, last, that this view of immediate imputation is false, in that it represents man as having a separate, indepraved, personal existence, for an instant at least, until *from innocent* it is turned into depraved, as a penal consequence of Adam's guilt imputed. Whereas, in fact, he never has any existence at all, except a depraved existence. As he *enters* being condemned, so he *enters* it depraved. This over-refinement thus leads to positive inaccuracy, as most of man's attempts to be "wise above that which is written." It sins in a similar way, with the erroneous scheme of Placæus, in the contrasted direction.

NEITHER SCHEME ADOPTED. SCRIPTURAL STATEMENT OF DOCTRINE. If you ask me then, which of the two schemes *I* hold; I answer; *neither*. I say of them, just as of the ill-starved distinction of the Supra and Infra Lapsarian, that it is a distinction which ought never to have been drawn either way; an attempt to assign an order of sequence to elements which God presents to us always united and as one cotemporaneous whole. I would prefer to represent the doctrine of Original Sin thus: (and correctly stated, it is rather a great, obvious *fact* than a hypothesis). That God, in His sovereign wisdom, righteousness, and goodness, was pleased to ordain such a natural and *federal union* between Adam and his posterity, making him their representative, that his probation should eventuate for them precisely as it did for him. That is; they are so connected with him, legally and naturally, that, into whatever moral condition, and into whatever legal *status*, Adam should *bring* himself by his act, in that moral, and in that legal condition, all his posterity should be *born*. And as in Adam, the change of condition, in both senses, was one whole connected change: so is the sin in his posterity. As in Adam, the first influx of depravity of heart was not visited on him *after* his sinful act merely, and as a *penal* consequence of it, but accompanied and prompted the act; so in Adam's posterity, the depravity of heart is as original as the guilt. In God's eyes they are condemned with their first father, as depraved with him, and they are given over to their depravity as guilty with him. And this, (in spite of Princeton,) is the view given by the current of Calvinistic divines, beginning with Calvin himself—down to Dr. Breckinridge. If a part of Edward's language could be taken, (p. 545, Note, last paragraph,) we might also include him in this list; but he has confused and marred his excellent discussion by speaking, in some places as Placæus, and by his groundless denial of an intrinsic mental identity.

Rational Objection now irrelevant.—Now, when we approach the rational difficulties of the doctrine, with this view of it, we find that they are, not indeed fully explained; (for the mystery of God's dealing in this thing, no mortal can dissipate; and least of all Pelagians and Rationalists,) but they are obviated. The charge of intrinsic injustice is removed; for the case is now so unique, so totally without parallel or illustration, that it is obviously lifted above the jurisdiction of human reason. Hence reason cannot convict the transaction of injustice, because she cannot comprehend it, nor measure it by any experimental standard. You will notice that all the illustrations of the supposed injustice of our condemnation in Adam, are cases in which the moral agent has his own, personal, separate, responsible existence, before the imputation takes place, and *that an innocent existence* so far as his personal agency went. Now such an imputation, made without his consent, would be unjust. *But such is not our case in Adam.* We never had any previous, separate, innocent personal existence of our own, constituting a legal title to immunity: which title would be violated by God's condemning us in Adam. We had no existence at all; and so, no title. For we do not represent God as visiting guilt and then depravity as its penalty, on us conceived as *á priori* personally innocent. The whole case is this: that God, in making Adam "the root of all mankind," should have ordained *the status in which our existence was to begin*, to be in all points determined by Adam's status as settled for him, by his voluntary act. It is a mighty mystery; it cannot be explained; but neither can it be convicted of any injustice. Why did God permit Sin in His Universe?

LECTURE XXVIII.

SYLLABUS.

THE LAW.

1. In what senses is the word *Law* used in the Bible?
   See Concordances and Lexicons.
2. Is the Law of God written on the natural Conscience? What the authority of this natural law? Is the decalogue of *moral*, or of *positive* obligation?
   Turrettin, Loc. XI, qu. 1, 2. Dick, Lec. 102.
3. If the Covenant of Works is now inapplicable for us, what uses has the law in a plan of Salvation by Grace?
   Turrett., qu. 22, 23. Calvin, Bk. II, ch. vii. Ridgeley, qu. 94 to 97.
4. Recite the origin of the Decalogue. How is it divided? What are the principles upon which it is to be interpreted?
   Calvin, Bk. II, ch. viii. Turrett., qu. 5 and 6. Dick, Lect. 102, 103. Ridgeley, qu. 99.
5. Is the Decalogue a perfect rule of life? Did the Saviour improve upon or abrogate any part of it?
   Turrett., qu. 3 and 4. Dick, as above. On the whole, Green's Lect. on Shorter Catechism, 34 to 36.

I. Definitions.—The word 'Law,' (torah, nomos,) is employed in the Scripture with a certain latitude of meaning, but always carrying the force of meaning contained in the general idea of a *regulative principle*. First, it sometimes expresses the whole of Revelation, as in Ps. i: 2. Second, the whole Old Testament, as in Jno. x: 34. Third, frequently the Pentateuch, as in Luke xxiv: 44. Fourth, the preceptive moral law (Prov. xxviii: 4; Rom. ii: 14. Fifth, the ceremonial code, as in Hebr. x: 1. Sixth, the decalogue, Matt. xxii: 36–40. Seventh, a ruling power in our nature, as in Rom. vii: 23. Eighth, the covenant of works, Rom. vi: 14. By the Law in the following discussions, we intend the preceptive moral law, as epitomized in the decalogue.

II. Moral Distinction Intrinsic.—The student will be prepared to expect my answer to the second point, from what has been taught of the eternity of moral distinctions. These are intrinsic in that class of acts They are not instituted solely by the positive will of God, but are enjoined by that will because His infinite mind saw them to be intrinsic and eternal. In a word: Duties are not obligatory and right solely because God has commanded them; but He has commanded them because they are right. Hence, we confidently expect to find the natural powers of reason and conscience in man impressed with the moral distinction, and pronouncing it intuitively.

a.) From the fact that the Scriptures represent God Himself, at least in one particular, as bound by this distinction of right and wrong. "God cannot lie;" that is, the eternal perfections of His own mind so regulate His own volitions that His will certainly, yet freely, refuses all error. See also 2 Tim. ii: 13.

b.) The very nature of a creature implies rightful subjection to a Creator; its denial would be utter contradiction. Thus the law of our reason teaches us, that the creature existing, these moral relations cannot but exist, whether God has published them in positive precepts, or not.

c.) If these moral distinctions owed their origin solely to God's positive will, no distinction could be drawn between *moral* and *positive* precepts. The prohibition, "Thou shalt not bear false witness," would be exactly like this: "Thou shalt not seethe a kid in its mother's milk." But there is a distinction between the two classes, recognized by God and our reason. 'Judgment, mercy, and truth,' are pronounced 'weightier matters of the law,' compared with tithing mint, annise, and cummin.

d.) If there were no cause, save God's mere will, why moral distinctions were drawn as they are, He might have made treachery a virtue, and truth a crime, &c. Against this every moral intuition revolts. Why might not God have done thus? The only answer is, that His own unchangeable moral perfections made it impossible. Just so; it is admitted that the basis of the moral distinction is *a priori* to all volition of God; which is substantially my proposition. And last, and most conclusively: If God's mere positive volition made an act of the creature morally right, then of course God must be morally right in entertaining that volition. But the moral character of volitions depends wholly on that of the principles which prompt them. So that, we see, if there were no moral distinction *a priori* to God's mere will, God could have no moral character in any acts of His will.

Consequences.—The moral distinction being then intrinsic and eternal, it follows that the intuition and feeling of its obligation must be one of the natural endowments of the rational creature made in God's image. This obligation must be recognized by man's conscience as natural and moral, and not merely positive. To this agree the Scriptures, Rom. i: 19–21, ii: 14, 15; Acts xiv: 17. And these declarations are confirmed by the *consensus populi* upon the existence of a moral obligation, and its main outlines, by a multitude of the facts of our consciousness, by the admissions of Pagans. But here, the distinction so clearly made between moral *principia* and *conclusiones*, must be noted. In some cases of moral obligation, the perception and verdict of conscience are immediate. In other cases, they are deductive. Should a creature obey its Creator? To this the sane reason answers intuitively, Yes. Should the borrower pay any hire for the use of money? To this the mind can only answer deductively; certain premises must be known to the understanding, from which the moral answer must be by deduction drawn.

If the moral distinction is thus eternal in acts, unchangeable in God, and natural in man, the preceptive law receives a new dignity, immutability, and sacredness. Then it follows, also, that the natural conscience is God's viceregent in man; and its dictates must be obeyed, or guilt arises. But when remember that the light in man's conscience is imperfect, we see that it is not true that this faculty is a sufficient rule of duty. That rule is found in God's precepts alone. The seeming paradox arising out of the dictate of an ill-informed conscience has been already considered.

III. Uses of Law under Covenant of Grace—The Law Immutable.—It has been asked, if the Law can no longer be a covenant of life to fallen sinners, what place and use can it properly have in a plan of salvation by grace? You are aware that there have been, in the Church, erroists called *Antinomians*, who, in fact, sought to exclude the law from their system, asserting that since it is no longer a term of life, since it has been fully satisfied both in its preceptive and penal demands by the believer's divine Substitute, it can have no binding force upon, and no application to him. But the view I have given of the Law, as the necessary and unchanging expression of God's rectitude, shows that its authority over moral creatures is unavoidable. If God reveals Himself to them, He cannot but reveal Himself as He is. Just these precepts are the inevitable expression of a will guided by immutable perfections. It is therefore simply impossible that any dispensation, of whatever mercy or grace, could have the effect of abrogating righteous obligation over God's saints. God's mercy through a Redeemer satisfying justice, may lift off the curse of the law for transgression; but it is impossible that it should abrogate rightful authority. The Law then must remain, under every dispensation, the authoritative declaration of God's character.

The Law convicts of our need of Christ, &c.—A second essential use of the Law under the New Covenant, is that which Gal. iii: 24 states: "The Law was our schoolmaster to bring us unto Christ." By showing us our penal debt, and the high terms of the Covenant of works, now impossible for the sinner to fulfil, it prepares his soul to submit to the righteousness of the Redeemer. A third, and equally essential use appears to the believer, after his adoption. He is "chosen in Christ that he should be holy": "redeemed from all iniquity to be Christ's peculiar people, zealous of good works." This great end, the believer's sanctification, can only be attained in practice, by giving him a holy rule of conduct. Such a rule is the Law. It is to be as assiduously observed, as the guide to that holiness which is the fruit of adoption, as though its observance could earn adoption. A fourth important purpose of the publication of the Law in the Church, appears in this: that its precepts restrain the aboundings of sin. They partially instruct the consciences even of the unrenewed. They guide secular laws, and thus lay a foundation for a wholesome civil society. And last: the publication of the Law is preparatory for that use which God will make of it in the Judgment Day, for the conviction of His enemies. He is now, in every such message, preparing to close the mouths of the disobedient in that day.

For these reasons, the preaching and expounding of the Law is to be kept up diligently, in every gospel Church.

IV. Decalogue God's Summary of Duty.—The whole decalogue is found written out in full, in two places of the Bible; beside a number of other places, where one or more of the precepts is cited. These places are Exodus xx: 2 to 17, and Deut. v: 6 to 21. It is the doctrine of Catechism, that these "Ten Words" were intended to be a summary of man's whole duty. Why, it may be asked, is so much made of them? Why not make equal account of some few verses taken from the Proverbs, or the Sermon on the Mount? We reply: the manner of their publication plainly showed, that *God intended* to give them the peculiar importance we assign them. They were uttered by Him, to His Church, in an audible voice, eis diatagas aggellon, (Acts vii: 53), with the terrible adjuncts of clouds, and thunders, and lightnings, and the sound of a trumpet. They were the only parts of Revelation thus spoken. "*These words* Jehovah spake unto all your assembly in the mount, out of the midst of the fire, of the cloud, and the thick darkness; with a great voice; *and He added no more.* Deut. v: 22. None of the ceremonial nor civic rules were thus distinguished. These ten precepts were then graven by God Himself, on two tables of stone; the imperishable material signifying the perpetuity of the Laws—and these tablets were to be kept among the most sacred things of their religion. Christ, in giving that summary of man's duty into the two precepts of love to God, and love to man, is evidently abridging the Decalogue. He says that on these two abridged commands, hang all the law and the prophets. Therefore all the Old Testament hangs on the Decalogue, of which these two are the epitome. These are the grounds, together with the obvious comprehensiveness and perfection of the ten precepts, (which will be evinced in their exposition) on which the Jewish and Christian Churches have always held this Decalogue to be designed as the epitome of the whole Law.

How Divided?—Expositors have not been entirely agreed in the division of the Decalogue. Some would have it, that five precepts belonged to the first Table, and five to the second. This opinion seems to be dictated only by a fondness for mechanical symmetry. It is now generally held, that four precepts composed the first table, and six the second. This is the natural division. Of the duties enjoined in the first four God is the direct object: of those inculcated in the last six, man is the direct object. Thus we conform our division to our Saviour's summary, love to God, and love to man. Some have supposed that they found an evidence of this division in the words of the Apostle Paul, when he calls the fifth the "first commandment with promise." It is observed that this is not the first containing a promise, if the first Table be included; whence they suppose that the Apostle calls it first, with reference to the second Table, at the head of which it stood.

Rules of Interpretation—The Precepts are Spiritual.—It remains that we settle the principles upon which the decalogue is to be interpreted and applied. If it is an epitome of duty, it contains of course more than the formal propositions in which it is verbally expressed. The first and most important of those principles is that announced by St. Paul in the 7th of Romans: 'The Law is spiritual.' It claims to regulate, not only the acts, but the desires and thoughts, the inner as well as the outer man. For farther proof, note that Christ, in His exposition (Matt. v) expressly extends the prohibitions to the secret motions of the heart towards sin. Causeless anger is declared to be the soul's sin of murder; lust is the soul's adultery; coveting, as Paul indicates, is the soul's theft. I prove the same rule from this: that Christ resolves all duties into *love*, which is an inward state of affection. And last, the same rule must follow from the spiritual nature of the God whose law it is. He claims to be 'Searcher of Hearts.' He judgeth not by the outward appearance. 'He requireth truth in the inward parts.' The law of such a Being must apply chiefly to the inward affections, as our reason approves.

The Sin or Duty Named is Representative.—Second: In each precept, the chief duty or sin is taken as representative of the various lesser duties or sins of that class; and the overt act is taken as representative of all related affections, and under it they are all enjoined or forbidden. Thus, our Saviour teaches us that under the head of murder, angry thoughts and abusive words are also forbidden. We are authorized by such examples to conclude that under the one precept, 'Thou shalt not kill,' all offences against our fellow-men's lives, safety, and personal welfare, are forbidden. So of the other commandments. This follows from the fact that the decalogue is a summary.

COMMANDMENT IMPLIED IN PROHIBITION, &c.—3. To command a given class of duties plainly implies a prohibition of the opposite class of sins, and *vice versa*. Thus: Injuries against the life and person of fellows are forbidden; this implies the obligation of active efforts to protect them, as we have opportunity. This follows from the practical scope of the law. What is the design or intent of the 6th commandment? Obviously to secure our fellows the enjoyment of life and safety. If, then, the obligation is adequate to the practical end, it must include active efforts to promote, as well as refraining from injuring, that end. This is confirmed by our Saviour's summation: 'Thou shalt love thy neighbour *as thyself*.' Hence, while the 6th commandment says, 'Thou *shalt not* kill;' it also means, 'Thou *shalt* save thy fellow from killing.'

MEANS INCLUDED IN DUTIES.—4. When anything is commanded or forbidden, the regular and necessary means and incitements thereto are also commanded or forbidden. And when any duty of one party towards another is enjoined, the relative state or duty thereto is also enjoined on the second party towards the first.

GOD BEFORE MAN: MORAL PRECEPTS BEFORE POSITIVE.—5. The precepts of the first table, containing duties towards God, are superior in obligation to the duties of the second table, towards man. See Luke xiv: 26; Matt. x: 37; Acts iv: 19; Eph. vi: 1. Whenever the authority of man clashes with that of God, the former must therefore give way. But moral duties, though they be duties of the second table, are superior to mere positive or ceremonial duties of the first table. See Matt. xii: 7; Prov. xxi: 3.

PROHIBITIONS PERPETUAL, &c.—Last. The prohibitory precepts bind us equally at all times; the mandatory only when the proper objects of the duty are present. The precept 'Thou shalt not kill,' binds at every moment; the command, 'Honour the father and mother,' only binds when we bear suitable relations to some superior.

V. THE LAW PERFECT—CHRIST MADE NO CHANGES OF SUBSTANCE, BECAUSE IMMUTABLE.—Many Socinians and Abolitionists, and some Papists, in order to support favourite prejudices, strenuously assert that the moral law, as given to the Jews, was an imperfect rule, and was completed and perfected by Jesus Christ. We grant, indeed, that Christ freed this law from the corrupt glosses of tradition, and that He showed the true extent of its application. But we deny that He made any change or substantial addition. We admit that He carried it farther in the way of detail, but we deny that He corrected anything of its principle. These errorists pretend to claim this as an honour to Jesus Christ and His mission, and as evincing His superiority over Moses. They hereby do Him dishonour. For the decalogue is as much Christ's law as the Sermon on the Mount. He was the authoritative agent for giving both. For it was "with the Angel which spake unto him in Mount Sina" (Christ, Acts vii: 38) that Moses "received these lively oracles to give unto us." Second: It would be dishonorable to a perfect God to suppose that He would reveal to His chosen people, as a rule of righteousness, a law which allowed some sin. Then, all the holiness produced under that law was spurious. Third: God forbade that the law should receive addition. Deut. iv: 2, xii: 32. Fourth: Christ honoured this law, declared it everlasting and unchangeable, and said that He came not to destroy, but to fulfil it. Fifth: Christ says that on His abridgments of this law hang all the law and the prophets. And last: St. Paul, having resolved the precepts of this decalogue into the one principle of love (Rom. xiii: 9), says: 'Love is the fulfilling of the law.' This is said by this minister of the new dispensation. And both the Old and New Testaments assert the perfection of this Old Testament law. See Ps. xix: 7; Rom. vii: 12; Ps. cxix: 96.

PRECEPTS OF NEW TESTAMENT ALSO IN OLD.—In further support of this view, I remark that the very particulars in which it is pretended Jesus amended, softened, and completed the moral law, are found stated just as distinctly, although perhaps not as forcibly in all cases, by Moses and the prophets, in their expositions of the decalogue. E. g., the love of enemies, in Matt. v: 44; see it in Exod. xxiii: 4, 5, Levit. xix: 18. The great laws of love of Matt. xxii: 37, &c.; see Deut. vi: 4, 5, Levit. xix: 18. The command of benevolence to strangers in Luke x: 36, 37; see it in Levit. xxiv: 22, xxv: 35, Deut. x: 19. The spiritual interpretation of the law, as embracing not only outward acts, but the thoughts and desires of the heart; see Levit. xix: 17, 18, Deut. xi: 13, Ps. xxiv: 4, li: 6. Christ's new commandment (Jno. xiii: 34) was only 'the old command renewed,' only a re-enactment with an additional motive: Christ's love for us. Christ, in His Sermon on the Mount, then, and other places, rebukes and corrects, not the law itself, nor the Old Testament interpretations of the law, but the erroneous and wicked corruptions foisted upon it by traditions and Pharisaic glosses. The moral law could not be completed, because it is as perfect as that of God, of whose character it is the impress and transcript. It cannot be abrogated or relaxed, because it is as immutable as He.

LECTURE XXIX.

SYLLABUS.

THE FIRST TABLE—(Commandments 1, 2, 3.)

1. What does the 1st Commandment enjoin? What does it forbid?
2. Discuss, against Romanists, the worship of *saints*, *angels*, and *relics*.
3. What does the 2nd Commandment forbid and enjoin?
4. Discuss, against Romanists, the lawfulness of Image worship.
5. What does the 3rd Commandment forbid and enjoin? Are religious vows and oaths imposed by magistrates lawful?

See on Whole: Shorter Cat., qu. 44 to 56. Larger do., qu. 100-114. Turrettin, Loc. XI, qu. 7-14 inclusive. Dick, Lect. 103, 104. Calv. Inst., Bk II, ch. 8. Dr. Green's Lect. 37 to 41 inclusive. Council of Trent Decree 25th, Rom. Cat. of Trent, Pt. III, ch. 2, qu. 4-7, and Pt. IV, ch. 6.

In the exposition of the precepts, I do not propose to detain you with those ordinary particulars, which you may find in your catechisms and text-books. I would, once for all, refer you to those authorities, especially for answers to the question, what each commandment especially enjoins and prohibits. My chief aim, in the few disjointed discussions which time will allow, is to enter into a few of the more disputed and more important questions of morals and ecclesiastical usage, which now agitate society and the Church.

SCOPE OF 1ST COMMANDMENT.—1. The affirmative and negative obligations of the 1st Commandment all depend upon the great truth of God's *exclusive unity*, which we have proved from reason and Scripture. The duty of "having Him for our God" may be said to be the summary of almost all the commands of love, reverence and obedience, which so abound in the Scriptures. But we may say that it includes especially, under the general idea of rendering Him all the affection and service which our nature, His character, and our relations to Him require; the following: The duty, a) of loving Him supremely. (See Matt. xxii: 37.) b.) Of regulating all our moral acts by His revealed will. Matt. xxviii: 20. c.) Of owning and acknowledging Him publicly. Josh. xxiv: 22. d.) Of promoting His cause and glory in all suitable ways. 1 Cor. x: 31. e.) Of rendering to Him such acts of religious worship as He may see fit to demand. Ps. xxix: 2. f.) Of thanking Him for His benefits. Ps. cvi: 1. g.) Of trusting to His promises. Is. xxvi: 4. h.) Of submitting to His chastisements. 1 Pet. v: 6. i.) Fearing His anger. Ps. lxxxvi: 11. j.) Repenting of having sinned against Him, Acts xvii: 30, and in short, k.) Chosing Him as the portion and eternal inheritance of our souls. Ps. lxxiii: 25; xvii: 15.

SIN OF IDOLATROUS AFFECTIONS.—The most current breach of this commandment in nominally christian communities, is doubtless the *sin of inordinate* affections. Scripture brands these as idolatry, or the worshipping of another than the true God, especially in the case of covetousness; (Eph. v: 5; Col. iii: 5; Job xxxi: 24-28,) and parity of reasoning extends the teaching to all other inordinate desires. We conceive formal idolatry, as that of the Hindoo, a very foolish and flagrant thing: we palliate this spiritual idolatry of passions. God classes them together, in order to show us the enormity of the latter. What then is it, that constitutes the "having of God for our God?" It includes, a) Love for Him stronger than all other affections. b.) Trusting Him, as our highest portion and source of happiness. c.) Obeying and serving Him supremely. d.) Worshipping Him as He requires. Now that *thing* to which we render these regards and services, is our God, whether it be gold, fame, power, pleasure, or friends.

II. ROMISH IDOLATRY. FOUNDED ON CREATURE MEDIATION.—Rome's worship of saints and angels is founded on her assertion of their heavenly mediation for us, which she asserts, against 1 Tim. ii: 5. You will find this error discussed and refuted in your Senior year, when we come to treat and defend the sole mediation of the Lord Jesus Christ. I shall now anticipate that conclusion, as the basis of my denial of the worship of creatures: only adding that, if you feel curiosity concerning Rome's defence of it, you may find her arguments in the places cited from the documents of the Council of Trent.

ARGUMENTS AGAINST SAINT-WORSHIP.—But as there is no heavenly mediation of angels or saints, we argue the more, that no religious worship can be paid them, without idolatry. a.) Because there are no examples nor precepts for it in the Bible. The honor due superiors is social and political; between which and religious worship, there is a fundamental difference. In all the cases cited by Rome, of the worshipping of creature-angels, there was only a hospitable and deferential obeisance to persons supposed to be dignified strangers and humans. Where there was worship proper, it was always the Angel of the Covenant, the Son of God, who was worshipped. Compare Gen. xviii: 2; xix: 1 with Gen. xviii: 23; xxxii: 26; xlviii: 16; Josh. v: 14. There is not a single example, much less one marked with the divine approval, where *religious worship* was received by any holy creature.

b.) Inspired saints and holy angels are represented in every case, as repudiating such worship, when attempted, with holy abhorrence. Acts xiv: 13–15; Rev. xix: 10; xxii: 9; Matt. iv: 10.

DOULEIA ALSO IDOLATROUS.—c.) Rome herself acknowledges, (Cat. Rom. Pt. III, Ch. 2, Qu. 4, or Pt. IV, Ch. 6, Qu. 3), it would be idolatry to worship creatures with the same sort of worship paid to God. Here then, their doctors bring in their distinction of LATREIA and DOULEIA, to justify themselves. This distinction is utterly vain and empty. Because first, the usage neither of classic nor biblical Greek justifies it; nor that of the primitive Fathers. The one word, as much as the other, is used of the worship peculiar to God Himself. See Matt. vi: 24; 1 Thess. i: 9, &c. The Galatians are rebuked for having served those who by nature are no Gods. (Ch. iv: 8), EDOULENSATE. If then the DOULEIA of the New Testament is that of Rome, the case is decided. But let us see how they distinguish their DOULEIA. Here we say, second: that it is *religious worship*. This is proved by its being rendered in Church, (God's house), at the altar, in the midst of their liturgies, on God's holy day, and mixed with God's own worship. This confusion at least is unpardonable. Third: in practice they do not limit themselves to DOULEIA, but ask of the saints, and especially of Mary, gifts most essentially divine; not intercession merely, but protection, pardon, sanctification, victory over death. Here see Romish Breviaries, *passim;* and the *Stabat Mater*. Daniel's Thesaurus Hymnolog, vol. 2, p. 133. Streitwolff, *Libri. Symbolici*, vol. 2, p. 343, &c. Fourth, even if only intercession were asked, the DOULEIA would still imply in the saints omnipresence, omniscience, infinite goodness, and such-like divine attributes. To evade this crushing objection, some Romish doctors have advanced their figment of the *Speculum Trinitatis*. They imagine that the saints blessed with the beatific vision of God, see reflected in His omniscience whatever He sees, at least of the wants and petitions of the Church. But besides the fatal lack of Scriptural warrant, this figment is absurd. For to see an overwhelming multitude of objects at once, in a mirror, reflected, will confound a finite mind as much as to see them directly. And besides, the figment contradicts Scripture, Matt. xxiv: 36; John xv: 15; 1 Cor. ii: 11.

MORAL EFFECTS OF CREATURE-WORSHIP.—Rome's saint and angel-worship is but baptized paganism, and like all other, it tends to *degrade* the worshippers. Hence, the importance of the prohibition of idolatry. Nothing but *infinite perfection* should be the object of religious worship. The reverence and admiration which worship implies invest every quality of the object worshipped with sanctity. Blemishes are always reproduced in the votaries. The worship of an imperfect object is therefore *the deification of defects.* Rom. i: 25, 26; Ps. cxv: 8. But the more the worshipper is corrupted, the more degraded will be the divinities which he will construct for himself out of his defiled heart, until the vile descent is realized which St. Paul describes in Rom. i: 22, 23.

III. Scope of Second Commandment.—As the first commandment fixes the object, so the second fixes the mode of religious worship. Under that most extreme corruption of mode which consists in image-worship, all erroneous modes of homage to the true God even, are prohibited. It may be said in general, that this commandment requires those acts and modes of worship for the true God which He hath required of us in His word, and prohibits all others. What Protestants call *will-worship* is forbidden, on these obvious grounds: God is infinite, and in large part, inscrutable to creature minds. It is His prerogative to reveal Himself to us, as He has done. If we form surmises how He is to be honoured, they will be partially erroneous; for error belongs to man. Hence (as experience too fully confirms), the offering of worship of human invention to God has always dishonoured Him, and corrupted the worshippers. Our Saviour, therefore, expressly condemns it. Matt. xv: 9.

IV. Image Worship.—The doctrine of Rome concerning the use of images in worship, with its defence, may be seen in the Rom. Cat., Pt. III, Ch. 2, Que. 9–14 inclusive. You will there remark the curious arrangement which makes our second commandment a part of, or appendix to the first, and usually prints it with small type. While this claims some little patristic countenance, its object is undoubtedly to depreciate this command. As the number of ten precepts is too well fixed to be called in question, Rome attempts to make it up by dividing the 10th, without shadow of valid reason, as we shall see.

Romish Excuses.—Rome grants (Que. 12) that the Deity should not be represented by any shape, because immense and inconceivable. To concede thus much, indeed, was unavoidable; the prohibitions are so plain. But to excuse her image-worship, Que. 13th teaches that the making of images of persons of the Trinity is no wrong, for this, when correctly understood, is no attempt to represent the Divine essence; it only expresses the property and actions which the Scripture gives the Persons. Thus, the Father is represented, in supposed imitation of Daniel vii: 9, as a hoary old man; the Son in a human figure; and the Holy Ghost, after Matt. iii: 16, as a dove. The idea of trinity in unity is usually represented as a luminous triangle.

To this evasion I reply, are not the Persons very God? Is not their essence one, and properly divine? How, then, can it be right to picture them, and wrong to picture Deity? If we may use the image of the Person, because it is designed to represent some act or property of it, why not of the Deity? Indeed, the luminous triangle is an attempt to represent the latter.

God's Example no Rule to Us.—Rome urges also that to figure or picture objects of worship cannot be wrong, because *God has done it.* He appears as a man in Gen. xviii, in Gen. xxxii: 24; as an angel in Exod. iii: 2; as a shekinah, 2 Chron. vii: 1. The Holy

Ghost appears as a dove, Matt. iii: 16. God also commanded the cherubim to be placed in the most sacred part of the oracle, at the very part towards which the High Priest directed his worship. God also directed Moses to make a brazen serpent and elevate it upon a pole. Numb. xxi: 8.

Now, the general and sufficient answer to this is, that God's doing a thing Himself is no warrant whatever for us to presume on imitating Him. May we kill people at will, because He slays some thirty millions annually? His precepts are our rule, not the acts of His own sovereignty, which His incommunicable attributes properly render unique and inimitable. The representations which God has seen fit to make of Himself to one and another prophet were temporary, not permanent, occasional—yea, rare—presented only to the prophet's own private eye, not to the Church customarily; and they were, after all, phantasmata, impressed on the prophet's imagination in exstatic vision—not actual, material constructions, like the idols of men. Chiefly, as visions, they were true, for they were to the prophets symbols of some special presence of God, and God *was* in some way specially present then and there. But these figures, when used by Papists, are symbols of no such truth; for God has not authorized them to expect any special presence where they exhibit the images. They are therefore false, while God's visions were true.

No Image-Worship in Scripture.—The carved Cherubim over the mercy-seat were not idols at all, but merely architectural ornaments, having, indeed a symbolical fitness, but no more objects of worship than the knops and lilies of the carving. The brazen serpent too, was a type, and not an object of worship. As well might the Papist bring as a plea, the fact that God has represented Christ by bread and wine. See Jno. iii: 14. Especially since the coming of the antitype, has this case not a shadow of force to excuse idolatry. That its worship was never permitted is clearly shown by 2nd Kings, xviii: 4; where we read that the good King Hezekiah, detecting the Jews in this error, had the identical serpent crushed, saying "it is brazen." ("It is but brass.") As to the picturing and worshipping of the man Jesus, the delineation of His human person has more shadow of reason, because He is incarnate. But there is no portrait or description of Christ, which is authentic. If there was, He is now, when glorified, wholly unlike it. Chiefly; an image could only represent His humanity, as distinguished from His divinity: and the former, thus abstracted, is no proper object of worship. The use of the crucifix in worship therefore, tendeth to evil.

All Idolaters profess to look above the idol.—3. The Council of Trent urges that the image is not itself regarded as divine; but only as a visible representation to assist the unlearned especially in conceiving the real presence of the invisible. To this I reply; it is just the distinction which all the pagans make, except the most besotted. Does any one suppose that the acute Hindoo is so stupid as to mistake the lump of clay or wood, which yesterday was a clod or a stick, and which he saw helpless in the hands of the mechanic, for a true God? If charged with such folly, he makes precisely the Papist's reply: that he worships the invisible God through the help of the visible representation of Him. So answered the ancient idolaters to the primitive Christians. By adopting it the Papist puts himself, where he properly

belongs, in the pagan category. And this is the very sin which the Scriptures intend to prohibit. An examination of the sin with Aaron's calf, Exod. xxxii, of Micah's idolatry, Judges xvii : 3–13, and of the sin of Jeroboam, 1 Kings xii : 28, &c., will show that in each case the criminal attempt was to worship the true Jehovah, unmistakeably recognized by His incommunicable name, through an image supposed appropriate.

This the very Definition of Idolatry in Scripture Cases. God inimitable.—4. To worship the true God by an image is, then, the very thing forbidden, because such a representation is necessarily false. For, God being a spiritual, immense, and invisible Being, to represent Him as a limited material form, is a falsehood. To clothe Him with the form of any of His creatures, angelic, human, or animal, is the most heinous insult to His majesty. God is a Spirit, cognizable by no sense. To represent Him by a material, visible and palpable image or picture is a false representation. He is omnipresent. To draw or carve Him as bounded by an outline, and contained in a local form, belies this attribute. He is self-existent, and has no beginning. To represent Him by what His puny creature made, and what yesterday was not, belies His self-existence and eternity. He declares Himself utterly unlike all creatures, and incomprehensible by them. To liken Him to any of them is both a misrepresentation and insult. Hence, a material image of the Godhead, or any Person thereof, is an utter falsehood. Papists used to be fond of saying: "Images are the books of the unlearned." We reply: they are books then, which teach lies only. The crowning argument against them, is that the Scriptures expressly forbid them; and equally plainly, base their prohibition on the fact that *no image can* correctly represent God. Deut. iv: 15, 16; Is. xl: 12–18; Acts xvii: 29. "Take ye therefore good heed unto yourselves, (*for ye saw no manner of similitude* on the day that the Lord spake unto you in Horeb, out of the midst of the fire), lest you corrupt yourselves, and make you a graven image," &c.

V. Scope of Third Commandment.—You are familiar with the answer to our last head of inquiry, which says the third Commandment requireth the holy and reverent use of God's name, tithes, attributes, ordinances, word, and works; "and forbiddeth all profaning or abusing of anything whereby God maketh Himself known." The scope of this precept is to secure a reverential treatment of God and all that suggests Him, in our speech and other *media* of communication with each other. Its practical importance is justified by what the Apostle James teaches us of the responsibility and influence of our faculty of speech. When you read His statements, and consider how fully experience justifies them; when you consider the large place which this power of communicating ideas fills in society, you will see why God has elevated the sanctification of the tongue into a place among the "ten words."

Sins forbidden in it.—Every christian is familiar with the idea that this precept is meant to prohibit sins of profane cursing and swearing in all their forms. Among these abuses may also be classed all irreverent uses of Sacred Scripture; all heartless and formal worship whether by praying or singing; all irreverence and levity in the house of God during the celebration of His worship or sacraments; all heedless ejaculations of His names and attributes; and most flagrantly, perjury. This, the crowning crime of this class, is a breach both of the third and ninth Commandments. It violates the obligations of truth; and also violates those of reverence in the most flagrant manner. An oath is an appeal to God for the sanction of the asseveration then made. It invokes all his attributes in the most formal manner, to act as umpires between the parties, and if the asseveration is falsified, to witness and avenge it. Where an oath is falsely taken, it is a heaven-daring attempt to enlist the Almighty in the sanction of the creature's lie; and is thus, either the most outrageous levity, or the most outrageous impiety, of which he can be guilty.

Lawful Oaths and Vows not Forbidden.—But we do not hold that the reverential occasional use of religious vows, or the serious taking of the oath from the civil magistrate, is a breach of this commandment. You are aware that the Quakers, and some other Christians, hold all oaths unlawful. We base our view on the following reasons:

Moses expressly commands the people to swear by the name of Jehovah, whenever they did swear. Deut. vi: 13. This surely implies that there is a right and proper time to swear. The Israelites were carefully instructed how to swear. Levit. xix: 12. Oaths were appointed to be administered by Divine authority, in certain cases. Exod. xxii: 11; Numb. v: 19. Surely God would not require His people to sin! We find that God sware; and "because He could swear by no greater, He sware by Himself." His example is worthy of mention here, although we do not presume a right to make it our rule in every case. We find that the apostles also, and especially Paul, frequently appealed to God in oaths. Rom. i: 9; 2 Cor. i: 23; Gal. i: 20. These expressions involve all the essentials of an oath. But we have a more indisputable example. Jesus Christ took an oath, when it was tendered to Him by Caiaphas the High Priest, acting as an authorized (though a wicked) magistrate of his people. Matt. xxvi: 63, 64. When the Chief Priest said; "I adjure thee [I swear Thee] by the living God," Christ, who had before refused to respond, immediately gave an affirmative answer, thereby taking the oath tendered Him. Let it be noticed, also, that in this He was acting in His human capacity. These New Testament examples also effectually estop the plea, untenable in all cases, that legislation given by Moses was corrected by Christ, so that the latter made things sins, which Moses made right. For all this was under the new dispensation, or at least after the utterance of the commands by Christ which furnish the argument of the Quakers.

Supposed Prohibition in New Testament.—Those commands are found in Matt. v: 34 and 37; Jas. v: 12. Their claim is, that these prohibitions are meant to forbid oaths under all possible circumstances; that the language is absolute, and we have no right to limit it. I reply, that if this view be pressed, all that is gained will be to represent Christ and Paul as expressly violating the new law. An understanding of the circumstances relieves the case. The Jewish elders had corrupted the third commandment by teaching that a man might interlard his common conversation with oaths, provided he did not swear falsely. They also taught that one might swear by anything else than the name of God, as his own head, or Jerusalem. Against these corruptions our Saviour's precept is aimed. In our common intercourse we are not to swear at all, because the suitable and solemn juncture is lacking. When that juncture is present, what more reasonable than the appeal to God; that God who is, by His omniscience and providence, the actual witness and umpire of all such declarations. But, in conclusion, it is a great abuse for the magistrate to multiply oaths on frivolous occasions.

LECTURE XXX.

SYLLABUS.

FIRST TABLE—(Fourth Commandment.)

1. What is required and forbidden in the Fourth Commandment? Shorter Cat., Qu. 57-62. Larger Cat., Qu. 115-121.
2. How is the Sabbath to be sanctified? Larger Cat., Qu. 117-120. Ridgeley, Qu. 117.
3. Give the practical reasons for the careful observance of the Sabbath. Largər Cat., Qu. 120, 121. Justin Edward's Sabbath Manual.
4. Is the observance of the Lord's day now binding *jure divino?*
   1. Show that the Sabbath was in force before Moses.
   2. Show that the Command is moral and perpetual, and not merely positive.
   3. Explain the teachings of the New Testament thereon.
   4. By what authority do we now substitute the first day for the seventh?
   5. Give history of opinions and usages.

   Consult on whole: Calvin Inst. Bk. II, Ch. viii, 4th Commandment, and Commentaries on Matt. xii, and Col. ii: 16, 17. Dr. Green's Lectures, 42, 43. Turrett., Loc. XI, Qu. 13, 14. Appendix to Fairbairn's Typology, 2nd edition.

Diversity Accounted for.—There is, perhaps, no subject of Christian practice on which there is, among sincere Christians, more practical diversity and laxity of conscience than the duty of Sabbath observance. We find that, in theory, almost all Protestants now profess the views once peculiar to Presbyterians and other Puritans; but, in actual life, there is, among good people, a complete jumble of usages, from a laxity which would almost have satisfied the party of Archbishop Laud, up to the sacred strictness ef the "Sabbatarians" whom he and his adherents reviled and persecuted. It is a curious question: how it has come about that the consciences of devout and sincere persons have allowed them such license of disobedience to a duty acknowledged and important; while on other points of obligation equally undisputed, the Christian world endeavors, at least, to maintain the appearance of uniform obedience. The solution is probably to be found, in part, in the historical fact of which many intelligent Christians are not aware—that the communions founded, at the Reformation, were widely and avowedly divided in opinion as to the perpetuity of the Sabbath obligation. A number of the reformation churches, including some of the purest, professed that they saw no obligation in the Scriptures to any peculiar

Sabbath observance; and the neglect of everything except attendance on the public exercises of Christianity, and that cessation of secular labor required by secular statutes was, in them, at least consistent. Now the descendants of these communions, in this mixed country, live dispersed among the descendants of Presbyterians and Puritans; and while they no longer defend the looser theory of their forefathers, they retain the traditionary practices and customs in their use of the sacred day. Thus, by example and the general intermingling of religions, a remiss usage is propagated, which is far beneath the present professed theory of Protestant Christendom. And hence, we conceive that it will be interesting and profitable to give a history of opinions on this subject, before we proceed to that full discussion of the whole grounds of our belief and practice which we shall attempt.

I. Two OPINIONS PREVALENT.—It may be stated then, in general terms, that since the primitive times of Christianity two diverse opinions have prevailed in the Christian world. The first is that adopted by the Romish, Lutheran, and most of the continental communions in Europe, including, it must be confessed, those founded by Calvin. This theory teaches that the proper sanctification of one day from every seven was a ceremonial, typical, and Jewish custom, established when the Levitical institutions were introduced; and, of course, abrogated by the better dispensation, along with the rest of the typical shadows. The Lord's day is, indeed, worthy of observance as a Christian festival, because it is the weekly memorial of the blessed resurrection, and the example of the primitive Church commends it; not because its obligation is now *jure divino.* The cessation of our worldly labors is a beneficent and commendable civil institution; and while the magistrates enjoin it, is, for this reason, of course to be practised by all good citizens. Public and associated worship is also a duty of Christians; and, in order that it may be associated, it must be upon a stated day and hour; and what day so appropriate as this, already famous for the great event of the new dispensation; and set apart by civil laws from the purposes of business. But this is all. To observe the whole day as a religious rest, under the supposition of a religious obligation, would be to *judaize*, to remand ourselves to the bondage of the old and darker dispensation.

The second opinion is that embodied in the Westminster symbols, and, to the honour of Puritanism be it said, first avowed in modern times, even among Protestants, by the Puritans of England. This is, that the setting apart of some stated portion of our time to the special and exclusive worship of God, is a duty of perpetual and moral obligation (as distinguished from positive or ceremonial), and that our Maker has, from the creation, and again on Sinai, appointed for all races and ages, that this portion shall be one day out of seven. But when the ceremonial dispensation of Levi was superadded to this and the other institutions of the original patriarchal religion, the seventh day did, in addition, become a type and a Levitical holy-day; and the theory admits that this feature has passed away with the Jewish ceremonial. After the resurrection of Christ, the perpetual Divine obligation of a religious rest was transferred to the first day of the week, and thence to the end of the world. The Lord's day is the Christian's sabbath, by Divine and apostolic appointment, and is to be observed with the same religious spirit enjoined upon the patriarchs, and the

Israelites, abating those features which proceeded from its ceremonial use among the latter, and from their theocratic government.

PAPAL OPINION.—Among the advocates of the first opinion is to be adduced first the Roman Catholic communion. This statement must, however, be made with qualification; for the "Romish Catechism" of Pope Pius V, embodying the opinions of the Council of Trent (P. III, Ch. iv), treats of the Lord's day more scripturally, in some respects, than many Protestants. But this correctness of opinion is grievously marred by the doctrine that the other Church holidays are sustained by equal authority with the Lord's day—the authoritative tradition of the Church. Bellarmine also argues, that it must be allowable to the true Church to make the observance of sacred days of human appointment binding on the conscience, because otherwise the Church would have no sacred days at all, since none whatever are enjoined in the New Testament. This reasoning obviously proceeds upon the assumption that there is no other sort of obligation for the Lord's day than for a Church festival. The well-known practice of Romish Christians, prevalent in all Popish countries, and unrebuked by the priesthood, sustains exactly that theory of Sabbath observance which we first described. After the duties of confession and hearing mass are performed in the morning, the rest of the holy-day is unhesitatingly devoted to idleness, amusements, or actual vice.

LUTHERAN OPINION.—The Lutheran communion, as ordered by Luther, Melancthon, and their coadjutors, held that it was lawful and proper for Church authorities to ordain days and rites, not contrary to the letter or spirit of Scripture, but additional to those appointed therein. It was, indeed, one of the most constant and noble parts of their testimony against Rome, that it was spiritual tyranny for any Church authority, however legitimate, to ordain anything contrary to the letter or spirit of Scripture, or to enforce any ordinance of human authority, however innocent, as binding on the Christian conscience, or as necessary to acceptance with God. But they taught that the rulers of the Church might lawfully institute rites, ordinances, and holy-days, consonant to the Word of God, though additional to those set down in it; and that they might lawfully change such ordinances, from time to time, as convenience and propriety required. But they could only invite, they could not compel the compliance of their brethren; and this compliance was to be rendered, not of necessity, but from considerations of Christian comity, peace, and convenience. When days or ordinances additional to Scripture were thus enjoined, and thus observed, it was held proper, lawful and praiseworthy, in both rulers and ruled. And the Lutheran symbols expressly assert that it was by this kind of Church authority, and not *jure divino*, that the observance of the Lord's day obtained among Christians; and that it could not be scripturally made binding on the conscience of Christians any more than the observance of Easter or Christmas, or of any other day newly instituted by a Church court, in accordance with Christian convenience and edification. They also teach that the Sabbath, with its strict and enforced observances, was purely a Levitical institution. Before proceeding to substantiate this statement from their symbols, it may be remarked, in passing, that we have here an explanation of the fact that Neander and other German antiquaries so heedlessly surrender the apostolic authority of certain Church usages, which they, in common with the Luthern Church, yet retain. The historian just mentioned says, for instance, that he finds no evidence that the baptism of infants was ever practised by the apostles. But this admission does not, to him, carry the consequences which it would involve with an Immersionist, Independent, or Presbyterian. He can still defend and practise the rite, as seemly and lawful, because he holds that Church authority. is a sufficient warrant for the observance of a rite so consonant to the spirit of the apostles. It is a pity that Immersionists do not tell this part of the story also, when they ignorantly quote his opinions concerning baptism.

But to return. In the 28th article of the Augsburg Confession, which treats of "the power of the bishops or clergy," we find the following [We will take the liberty of *italicising* those phrases which we wish to be particularly weighed]: "What, then, should be held concerning *Sunday and other similar Church ordinances* and ceremonies?" To this our party make the following reply: That the bishops or pastors may make regulations, in order that things may be carried on orderly in the Church, not in order to obtain the grace of God, nor yet in order to atone for sins, or to bind the consciences of men with them, to hold them as necessary services of God, and to regard them as if they commit sin, if they break them without offence to others. Thus St. Paul, in the Corinthians, ordains that the women in the congregation should cover their heads; 1 Cor. xi: 5. * * * * "*In like manner is the regulation concerning Sunday, concerning Easter, concerning Pentecost*, and the like holy-days and rites. Those, then, who are of opinion that the regulation of Sunday instead of the Sabbath, was established as a thing necessary, err very much. For the *Holy Scripture has abolished the Sabbath*, and it teaches that all ceremonies of the old law, since the revelation of the Gospel, may be discontinued. And yet, as it was of need to ordain a certain day, so that the people might know when they should assemble, *the Christian Church ordained Sunday* for that very purpose, and possessed rather more inclination and willingness for this alteration, in order that the people might have an example of Christian liberty, that they might know that neither the observance of the Sabbath, nor of any other day, is indispensable." Melancthon, in the 8th article of his "apology," ("*Of human ordinances in the Church*,") briefly asserts the same view "Further, the most ancient ordinances however in the church, *as the three chief festivals, Sundays, and the like*, which were established for the sake of order, union and tranquility, we observe with willingness. And with regard to these, our teachers preach to the people in the most commendatory manner; in the meantime, however, holding forth the view, that they do not justify before God." In Luther's *Shorter Catechism*, (which, singularly enough, follows the commen Popish arrangement of merging the second commandment under the first, so that the fourth becomes the third,) is the following:

THE THIRD COMMANDMENT.—Thou shalt sanctify the Sabbath day.

What does this imply?

Ans. "That we should fear and love God, so that we may not despise the preaching of the Gospel, and His word; but keep it holy; willingly hear and learn it." Here there is a marked generality of language, and evasion of everything like the injunction of a Christian Sabbath. And, in Luther's *Larger Catechism*, under the third commandment, it is said expressly: "This commandment, therefore, with respect to its outward and literal sense, does not concern us Christians; for it is wholly an external thing, like other ordinances of the Old Testament, confined to certain conditions, persons, times, and places, which are now all abrogated through Christ. But, in order that we may draw up for the uninformed, a Christian sense of what God requires of us in this commandment, it is necessary to observe that we keep the Sabbath day, not for the sake of intelligent and learned Christians—for these have no need of it—but, in the first place, on account of physical reasons and necessities, which nature teaches and requires for the common mass of people, men-servants, and maid-servants, who attend during the whole week to their labor and employments, so that they may also have a day set apart for rest and recreation; in the second, mostly for the purpose of enabling us to embrace time and opportunity on these Sabbath-days, (since we cannot otherwise embrace them,) to attend to Divine service, so that we may assemble ourselves to hear and treat of the Word of God, and afterwards to praise Him in singing and prayer."

Luther, however, adds that no one should deceive himself by supposing that the duty of associated rest and worship is fulfilled by simply leaving off labor, and presenting their bodies in the church, while, like the Papists, they indulge a stupid inattention to the service.

Such then, is the theory of the great Lutheran community, distinctly and intelligently avowed! Nor is there any reason to suppose that it is not as explicitly held at this day by many of their divines, perhaps by the bulk of them; while the almost universal laxity of Sabbath observance in Protestant Europe (continental) shows that the theory bears it legitimate fruit in practice. It was related a few years ago by an eminent American, that when visiting the pious Neander, he took the opportunity to enquire of him whether the rumour were true, which had been spread concerning Gesenius, the great Hebraist; that he was accustomed to come down from Halle to Berlin at the end of the week, in order to enjoy the Sunday night's theatricals in the Capital; which were more brilliant that night than any other of the week. Neander answered that it was true; but the offence would not strike German christians as it would Americans. For himself, he said, he would not go to theatricals on any day, because he considered them unfriendly to spirituality; but he should not scruple to do on the Lord's day, any thing which it was right for a Christian to do on any other day. And in accordance, he did actually secure the attendance of his American visitor (unawares on his part) at a sober convivial entertainment the very next Sunday afternoon!

The evangelical Christians of Germany seem now to apprehend the prime necessity of a stricter Sabbath-observance for the interests of piety; and have recently combined to promote it. But it will be vain for them to attempt to engraft such a reform on this doctrinal theory of Lutheranism. No plausible tinkering with a doctrine so fundamentally erroneous will suffice. The connection between a false theory and a vicious practice is too inevitable. If the reform is to be established successfully, its foundation must be laid in the retraction of these opinions, and the expieit adoption of the Puritan and Presbyterian theory of the Lord's day.

It may here be added, that the Mennonite Church, both in Europe and America, holds substantially the Lutheran ideas of the Sabbath, and that their practice is influenced by them in a similar way. When this communion, led by Menno Simonist, set about ridding themselves of the reproach of fanatical Anabaptism, they were careful to assume so mnch of the prevalent religion as they could consistently with their essential peculiarities, in order to substantiate their plea that they were no longer a radical political sect, but a proper, evangelical denomination. The prevalent Protestantism of those countries was Lutheran; and hence the theology of the Mennonites, and their ideas of Sabbath observance are largely Lutheran. The articles of their most current confession are silent concerning the observance of the Lord's day.

Socinian Opinion.—Next in order should be mentioned the opinions of the Socinian sect. The Racovian Catechism, the recognized Confession of this body, in the 16th century, states their erroneous belief with unmistakeable precision and brevity. Under the fourth commandment are the following questions and answers:

"What is the fourth commandment?"

"Remember the Sabbath day to keep it holy."

"What dost thou believe concerning this commandment?"

"I believe that it is removed under the new covenant, in the way in which other ceremonies, as they are called, are taken away."

"Why, then, was it inserted in the decalogue?"

"Thus, that it might be manifest the most absolute part of the Mosaic law was not perfect, and that some indication might exist of this fact, that a law was to succeed the Mosaic law, by far more perfect, the law, namely, of our Lord Jesus Christ."

"Did, or did not, Christ ordain that we should observe the day which they call *Lord's day*, in place of the Sabbath?

"Not at all; since the religion of Christ entirely removes the distinction of days, just as it does the other ceremonies, as they are called; as the Apostle clearly writes in Col. ii: 16. But since we see that the Lord's day has been celebrated from of old time by Christians, we permit the same liberty to all Christians."

A day of religious rest, then, according to Socinians is utterly abolished by Christ, just as the other Levitical ceremonies. There is no obligation whatever, but in order to avoid the odium of unnecessarily disturbing venerated customs, such Socinians as choose, *are permitted to observe* the Lord's day. It will be a harmless peculiarity! To understand the second and third answers, it should be remembered that the Socinians wholly deny that Christ did any vicarious or atoning work. Having denied this, they are of course pressed with the question: "How, then, is He more than any other eminent prophet; and why are such peculiar names and honours given Him by Scripture? Why is an importance so entirely peculiar attached by it to His mission. To find a plausible answer to this hard query; to invent a *nodus vindice dignus*, they say that one peculiarity of His mission was to reveal a code of morality greatly more pure and complete than that of Moses and the prophets. And thus they have a constant polemical interest in depreciating and misrepresenting the moral code of Moses. So, forsooth, the All-wise placed this supererogatory precept, which was of only temporary authority, in the summary of His eternal, moral law, in order to give people a standing hint of the fact that this code was far from being complete! Since the coming of Christ, men need no such hint, according to the Socinians; for one great part of Christ's mission was to tell us clearly this very thing. And before the coming of Christ, this precept could not serve that purpose; because the Old Testament contained no indication whatever, that this was not as good and *bona fide* a commandment as all the rest. One feels strongly tempted to characterize this nonsensical position, with the unsavoury phrase, which Calvin usually applied to the grosser absuridties of his opponents, as *a putidum commentum*.

Opinion of Anglican Church.—As to the ground held by the Anglican church, concerning the authority of the Lord's day, its standards are indecisive. It holds the same opinion with the Augsburg Confession, concerning the power of the church to ordain rites, ceremonies, and holy-days, additional, but not contrary to the Scriptures; but it has not observed the scriptural modesty of the Lutherans, in enforcing the uniform observance of these human appointments. While its theory on this point is not greatly more exaggerated in words than that of the Augsburg Confession, its practice has been unspeakably more tyrannical. The twentieth of the "Thirty-nine Articles," ("Of the authority of the Church,") says: "The church hath power to decree rites or ceremonies, and authority in controversies of faith; and yet it is not lawful for the church to ordain anything that is contrary to God's Word written, &c." The thirty-fourth says: "Whosoever, through his private judgment, willingly and purposely doth openly break the traditions and ceremonies of the church, which be not repugnant to the Word of God, and be ordained and approved by common authority, ought to be rebuked openly, (that other may fear to do the like,) as he that offended against the common order of the church, and hurteth the authority of the magistrate, and woundeth the consciences of the weak brethren." The articles contain no nearer reference to the Lord's day. Our purpose in quoting these words will be seen in connexion with the following from the thirteenth of the ecclesiastical canons and constitutions:

"Due celebration of Sundays and holy-days.—All manner of persons within the Church of England, shall from henceforth celebrate and keep the Lord's day, commonly called Sunday, and other holy days, according to God's holy will and pleasure, and the orders of the Church of England prescribed in that behalf," &c.

The Church of England, then, is not, by her standards, definitely committed to that loose theory which we have unfolded; but the association of Sundays and holy-days, as equal in their claims, and the nature of their authority, is significant. The Church, according to these articles, has power to ordain days, additional to those appointed in Scripture, provided they are not condemned in Scripture; and to enforce their observance by censures. And it is plainly implied that the obligation to keep a Sunday is only of the same character with the obligation to keep an Epiphany or Good Friday. Both are alike according to God's holy will; but it is God's will, not pronounced in Scripture, but through the authoritative decree of the Church. It was the primitive Church which introduced the festivals of Epiphany and others; and it was the same authority which introduced Sunday. As the thirty-fourth article claims that the same church authority which made, can unmake or alter these appointments, it would seem that even the Lord's day might be liable to change by human authority. It is not easy to see how a Protestant, who believes that the traditions and ordinances of the church are not divinely infallible, and who yet places the Lord's day and the Church holy-days on the same basis of authority, can consistently esteem the obligations of the Sabbath, as sacredly as, in our judgment, they require. Yet we doubt not that many devout and evangelical Episcopalians, both in this country and in England, do regard them as highly as the best Christians in the world. The opposite practices and feelings of many of the "high church," are well known. Their worst examplar is to be seen in Laud and his "Declaration of Sports." The Episcopalians of his party, in that day, were the most bitter enemies of those holy men, who first restored to the Protestant world the blessed doctrine that the Church of God still possessed its Sabbath by Divine authority; branding them with the names of Judaizers and Sabbatarians.

Opinion of Calvin.—We proceed now to state the opinions of Calvin, and some of the Reformed Churches. By consulting Calvin's Institutes, (B. II., chap. 8), it will be seen that his views of Sabbath-observance are substantially those of Luther. He states that, among the Israelites, there were three grounds for the observance of the seventh day; first, that it might be a type of that cessation of the works of self-righteousness which true believers practice; second, that there might be a stated day for public worship; and third, that domestic animals and servants might enjoy a merciful rest from bodily labor. Only the last two of these grounds exist, according to Calvin, under the New Testament. Hence he says (Ch. 8, Sec. 33): "We celebrate it not with scrupulous rigor, as a ceremony which we conceive to be a figure of some spiritual mystery, but only use it as a remedy necessary to the preservation of order in the Church." In the previous section he says: "*Though the Sabbath is abrogated*, yet it is still customary among us to assemble on stated days, for hearing the Word, for breaking the mystic bread, and for public prayers; and also to allow servants and laborers a remission from their labor." And in section 34: "Thus vanish all the dreams of false prophets, who in past ages have infected the people with a Jewish notion, affirming that nothing but the ceremonial part of this commandment, which, according to them, is the appointment of the seventh day, has been abrogated; but that the moral part of it, that is, the observance of one day in seven, still remains. But this is only changing the day in contempt of the Jews, while they retain the same opinion of the holiness of a day; for, on this principle, the same mysterious signification would be attributed to particular days, which formerly obtained among the Jews." And in the same tenour, he remarks upon Col. ii: 16: ("Let no man, therefore, judge you in meat or in drink, or in respect of a holy-day, or of the new moon, or of the Sabbath-days." "Such a distinction (of days) suited the Jews, to observe sacredly the appointed days, by separating them from other days. *Among Christians, such a distinction hath ceased.* But, somebody will say that we still retain some observance of days. I answer, that we by no means observe them, as if there were any religion in holy-days, or as if it were right to labor then; but the regard is paid to polity and good order, to the days." In the Genevan Catechism, written by Calvin for the urch of Geneva, and dedicated to the ministers of East Frisia in the therlands, the statements already quoted from the Institutes are so ictly reproduced, that they need not be repeated. In the Heidel-:g Catechism, the symbol of the German Reformed Church in the latinate, the opinions of Calvin are adopted, though stated with such vity, that we learn them in part by inference. The one hundred l third question and answer are:

"What doth God enjoin in the fourth commandment?"

"First: That the ministry of the Gospel, and the schools be pre-ved; and that I, with others, diligently frequent the Divine assem-es, industriously hear the Word of God, make use of the sacraments, my prayers also to the public prayers, and bestow something on the r according to my ability. Second: That in all my life I shall ab-in from wicked actions, permitting the Lord to do His work in me ough His Holy Spirit, and thus shall begin that everlasting Sabbath this life." The ideas of Calvin are here so evidently involved, and re is so studious an avoidance in the generality of the terms, of all erence to the consecration of a given day, by Divine authority, under New Testament, that we cannot be mistaken in our surmises.

Arminian Opinion.—To those who are aware of the close relation-p between Socinianism and Arminianism, it will not be surprising it the latter sect, at its birth, adopted an idea of the Lord's day only s relaxed than that of the former. It is unnecessary to multiply ations; a single passage from Limborch, one of the distinguished ds of their seminary in Amsterdam, in his commentary on Romans : 5, will be both sufficiently distinct and authoritative:

Romans xiv: 5. "Another esteemeth every day alike," viz: (explains mborch) "The converts to Christ from among the Gentiles, on whom burden of the ritual law was never imposed, did not recognize this tinction of days, but esteemed all days equal, and one no more noble in another. It is true, indeed, that the apostles and primitive Church re already accustomed to assemble in sacred meetings the first day of week; but not because they believed that day more eminent than y other, nor because they believed the rest of that day to be a part of vine worship, as the rest of the seventh day had been under the law; r that it must be observed with rigor, as formerly, under the law. no means: but because it was convenient to designate some time for red exercises; and that a man might the better be at leisure for them, st also from daily labor was required. The first day of the week, on ich the Lord rose from the dead, (which is thus called the Lord's day, v. i: 10), seemed most meet to be destined to these services; but not cause it was judged more holy, or because a rigid rest and cessation all work in observing that day was a part of Divine worship. For us, *it would have been not a taking off of the yoke, but a shifting of it.*"

Continental usage.—On the whole, it may be said that the Protest-t Churches of Continental Europe have all occupied this ground, ncerning the sanctification of the Lord's day. These Churches, prop-ly sperking, have never had the Sabbath; for it has only been to them holy-day, ranking no higher than Christmas or Easter, or a season set art by civil enactment, or a convenient arrangement for concert in public worship; and not a sacred day of Divine appointment. The manner in which it is desecrated, commonly, throughout the Protestant States of the continent is shocking to the feelings and usages of strict, American Protestants; and seems to them to approximate only too much to the license Popery. But we have now seen that this desecration is not an accidental irregularity: it is the natural and proper result of the theory in which these Churches have been educated since the reformation. That the greatest and best of the reformers should have failed to embrace the truth concerning the Lord's day, is indeed no subject of surprise. That men emerging at a bound from the meridian darkness of Popery into Gospel light should see all things correctly at first, was not to be expected. That they saw so many things "eye to eye," and erred in so few, is a wonder, only to be explained by the presence of the Spirit of all truth. It is wholesome to become acquainted with their few errors, and to explode them; for it will tend to correct that oderweening spirit of party which ever prompts Christians to call themselves by the name of men, like those who said: "I am of Paul, and I of Apollos, and I of Cephas." But it may well be inquired also, whether a part of the spiritual decline which has almost extinguished the true light in the ancient seats of Luther, Calvin, Witsius and De Moor, is not due to this misconception of Sabbath obligation, and its consequent neglect. The sacred observance of one day in seven is God's appointed means for the cultivation of piety: when piety vanishes, orthodoxy necessarily follows it in due time.

Dr. Bound.—As has been already indicated, the first successful attempt to establish the theory of *a Christian Sabbath*, since the reformation, was made among the English Puritans. About the year 1595, a dissenting minister of Suffolk, Dr. Nicholas Bound, published a book entitled "*Sabbatum Veteris et Novi Testamenti*, or, The True Doctrine of the Sabbath," in which he advocated the view afterwards adopted by the Westminster Assembly. This treatise had great currency among the devout dissenters, and evangelical churchmen, and was the beginning of a discussion which continued, under repeated attempts for its suppression by high church authorities, until the doctrines of the Puritans became those of the bulk of sincere Christians throughout Great Britain and the American colonies. Archbishop Whitgift condemned Dr. Bound's book to suppression. James I published his Declaration of Sports, encouraging the people to dancing, trials of archery, erecting May-poles, and other amusements, at any hours of the Lord's day not occupied by public worship. The flood of immoralities introduced by this measure became so odious, that the secular magistrates, at the urgent instance of the people themselves, suppressed the Sunday sports. Under Charles I, Laud invoked the aid of his clergy to re-establish them; and the strange spectacle was seen, of the laity petitioning against the profane desecration of the sacred day, and their spiritual guides compelling them to perpetrate it! (Neal, Hist. of the Puritans, Vol. I, Ch. 8; Vol. II, Ch. 2–5.)

Westminster Assembly.—The first great Synod which ever propounded, in modern ages, the true doctrine of the Lord's day, was the Westminster Assembly. Their Confession of Faith, which is now the standard of the Scotch, Irish and American Presbyterian, and of many independent churches, states the truth so luminously, (ch. xxi,

c. 7–8), that we shall repeat their words here, though familiar, as ie best statement of the proposition and text of our sebsequent disission.

Sec. 7. "As it is of the law of nature that, in general, a due proporon of time be set apart for the worship of God; so in His word, by a ositive, moral, and perpetual commandment, binding all men, in all ges, He hath particularly appointed one day in seven for a Sabbath, to e kept holy unto Him; which from the beginning of the world to the esurrection of Christ, was the last day of the week; and, from the esurrection of Christ, was changed into the first day of the week, which Scripture is called the Lord's day, and is to be continued to the end f the world as the Christian Sabbath."

Sec. 8. "This Sabbath is then kept holy unto the Lord, when men fter a due preparing of their hearts, and ordering of their common afiirs beforehand, do not only observe an holy rest all the day from their wn works, words, and thoughts, about their worldly employments and ecreations; but also are taken up the whole time in the public and rivate exercises of His worship, and in the duties of necessity and iercy."

As the doctrinal articles of the Westminster Assembly were generlly adopted by the Calvinistic dissenters of England and America, hey also embraced these views of the Sabbath. The Immersionist deominations of these countries, which arrogate to themselves the title f Baptists, came from a mixed origin. The first idea and nucleus of he sect in England were from the Anabaptism of the Netherlands and ower Germany. That continental sect was at first everywhere perseuted, and in the long and terrible oppression of Protestantism, in the Netherlands, under Charles V, and his son, Philip of Spain, they in ommon with Lutherans and Reformed, emigrated in vast numbers to very accessible place of refuge. The commercial and religious affiniies of England and the Low Countries were then very close; so that housands of the Protestant middle classes of that wretched land were oon found settled in London, Norwich and other towns. It was thus specially, that Anabaptism took root on English soil. The Baptist Churches, afterwards formed, received their other element from the Churches of the Calvinistic Independents, in which, for a considerable ime, immersion and pædobaptism were both practiced by compromise. This independent element was Calvinistic and Sabbatarian; the Anabaptist material was Arminian in doctrine, and practiced the loose views of Luther concerning the Sabbath. Hence, the Baptist Churches of England and those of this country, which are their counterparts, differed among themselves, and presented mixture and diversity of usage on both these points. The new American sect, self-styled Reformers, popularly known as Campbellite, has adopted the boldest view propounded by the Socinians; presenting here another evidence of its Socinian tendencies.

Wesleyanism is an offshoot of the Anglican Church, with the mystical Arminianism of the Moravians, and of Holland, superinduced upon it. The Lutheranism of this country claims to be a reproduction of that of Germany, only stripped of its Erastianism and doctrine of religious establishments. It takes pride in republishing the symbols of Melancthon and Luther. The Episcopacy of America strives to be a counterpart of that of England. The reader will now easily comprehend, from this historical review, what would naturally be the views of these several denominations concerning Sabbath-observance, and what is the legitimate source of that diversity, vagueness and license, which are exhibited in this country, in our Sabbath usages. To particularize further would be unnecessary, and might be supposed invidious.

II. Sabbath Command moral.—We proceed now to the attempt to give a full but summary statement of the grounds upon which Presbyterians assert the doctrine of a Christian Sabbath as it is set forth in their Confession. And *first:* it is most obvious that if the Sabbath law contained in the decalogue is "positive, moral and perpetual commandment, binding all men, in all ages," and not ceremonial and positive, like the Jewish laws of meats, new moons and sacrifices, it cannot have passed away along with the other temporary shadows of Judaism. If it was not introduced by the Levitical economy for the first time, but was in force before, and if it was binding not on Jews only, but on all men, then the abrogation of that economy cannot have abrogated that which it did not institute. The Apostle Paul justifies us here, by using an argument exactly parallel in a similar case. "The covenant that was confirmed before of God in Christ, the law which was four hundred and thirty years after cannot disannul." Gal. iii: 17. Upon the question whether the fourth commandment was of Mosaic origin, or earlier, the fathers were divided: and this fact is another among the many proofs of their slender acquaintance with the Hebrew literature and antiquities.

That it is a positive, moral, and perpetual command, we argue from the facts that there is a reason in the nature of things, making such an institution necessary to man's religious interests; and that this necessity is substantially the same in all ages and nations. That it is man's duty to worship God, none will dispute. Nor will it be denied that this worship should be in part social; because man is a being of social affections, and subject to social obligations; and because one of the great ends of worship is the display of the Divine glory before our fellow-creatures. Social worship cannot be conducted without the appointment of a stated day; and what more reasonable than that the Divine authority, who is the object of this worship, should meet this necessity, by Himself fixing the day for all mankind? And even for the cultivation of our individual devotion, a periodical season is absolutely necessary to creatures of habit and of finite capacities, like us. What is not regularly done will soon be omitted; for periodical recurrence is the very foundation of habit. Unless these spiritual thoughts and exercises were attached to some certain season, they would inevitably be pushed out of the minds of carnal and sensuous beings like man, by the cares of this world. Now, when it is our duty to perform a certain work, it is also our duty to employ all the necessary means for it. The question, whether the Sabbath command is *moral* or positive, seems, therefore, to admit of a very simple solution. Whether one day in six, or one in eight, might not have seemed to the Divine wisdom admissible for this purpose; or which day of the seven, the first or last, should be consecrated to it, or what should be the particular external ceremonies for its observance; all these things, we freely admit, are of merely positive institution, and may be changed by the Divine Legislator. But at man shall observe some stated, recurring period of religious worip, is as much a dictate of the natural reason and conscience, as imediate a result of the natural relations of man to God, as that man iall worship his God at all. And no reason can be shown why this iginal moral obligation was more or less stringent upon the Israelites the Mosaic period, than on men before or since them. If the ground the Sabbath institution, in the moral relations existing by nature, is iiversal and perpetual, is it not reasonable to expect the precept to so also?

Sabbath Command Primeval.—We argue further, that the enactent of the Sabbath-law does not date from Moses, but was coeval with ie human race. It is one of the two first institutions of paradise. he sanctification of the seventh day took place from the very end of ie week of creation. (Gen. ii: 3.) For whose observance was the iy, then, consecrated or set apart, if not for man's? Not for God's; ecause the glorious paradox is forever true of Him, that His ineffable iiet is as perpetual as His ever-active providence. Not surely for the igel's? but for Adam's. Doubtless, Eden witnessed the sacred rest of m and his consort from

> "The toil
> Of their sweet gardening labor, which sufficed
> To recommend cool zephyr, and made ease
> More easy, wholesome thirst and appetite
> More grateful."

nd from that time downward, we have indications, brief indeed, but numerous as we should expect in the brief record of Genesis and xodus, and sufficient to show that the Sabbath continued to be an instiition of the patriarchal religion. A slight probable evidence of this ay even be found in the fact, that seven has ever been a sacred and mbolical number, among Patriarchs, Israelites, and Pagans. In enesis we read of the "seven clean beasts," the "seven well-favored," id "seven lean kine," the "seven ears of corn, rank and good." Now iere is no natural phenomenon to suggest the number; for no noted eavenly body, or natural element, revolves precisely in seven hours, iys, weeks, or months. Whence the peculiar idea everywhere attached the number, if not from the institution of a week for our first paents? But to proceed to more solid facts: It is at least probable that ie "end of days," (Gen. iv: 3), rendered in our version, "process of me," at which Cain and Abel offered their sacrifices, was the end of the eek, the seventh, or Sabbath-day. In Gen. vii: 10, we find God Himelf observing the weekly interval in the preparations for the flood. We nd another clear hint of the observance of the weekly division of time y Noah and his family in their floating prison. (Gen. viii: 10–12.) he patriarch twice waited a period of seven days to send out his dove. rom Gen. xxix: 27, we learn that it was customary among the patrirchs of Mesopotamia, in the days of Laban, to continue a wedding fesval a week; and the very term of service rendered by Jacob for his wo wives, shows the use made of the number seven as the customary duition of a contract for domestic servitude. Gen. l: 10, shows us that at ie time of Jacob's death, a week was also the length of the most honorble funeral exercises. In Exod. xii: 3–20, we find the first institution the passover, when as yet there was no Mosaic institutions. This feast was also appointed to last a week. In Exodus xvi : 22–30, where we read the first account of the manna, we find the Sabbath institution already in force; and no candid mind will say that this is the history of its first enactment. It is spoken of as a rest with which the people ought to have been familiar. But the people had not yet come to Sinai, and none of its institutions had been given. Here, then, we have the Sabbath's rest enforced on Israel, before the ceremonial law was set up, and two weekly variations wrought in the standing miracle of the manna, in order to facilitate it. And when at length we come to the formal command of the decalogue, it is expressed in terms which clearly indicate that the Sabbath was an institution already known, of which the obligation was now only re-affirmed.

This proved by Decalogue.—The very fact that this precept found a place in the awful "ten words," is of itself strong evidence that it is not a positive and ceremonial, but a moral and perpetual statute. Confessedly, there is nothing else ceremonial here. An eminent distinction was given to the subjects of these ten commands, by the mode in which God delivered them. They were given first of all. They were spoken in the hearing of all the people, by God's own voice of thunder, which moulded its tremendous sounds into syllables so loud that the whole multitude around the distant base of the mount heard them break, articulate from the cloud upon its peak. "These words the Lord spake unto all your assembly in the mount, out of the midst of the fire, of the cloud, and of the thick darkness, with a great voice; *and he added no more*." (Deut. v : 22.) No other words shared the same distinction. And then they were engraven, by God's own agency, on two stone tables, whose durability was to represent the perpetual obligation of all which was written upon it. How can it be believed that this one ceremonial precept has been thrust in here, where all else is of obligation as old, and as universal as the race? This is strengthened also by the reflection that the ground first assigned in Genesis, and here repeated for its enactment, is in no sense Jewish or national. God's work of creation in six days, and His rest the seventh, have just as much relation to one tribe of Adam's descendants as to another. Note the contrast: that, in many cases, when ceremonial and Jewish commands are given, like the passover, a national or Jewish event is assigned as its ground, like the exodus from Egypt.

Proved by Tradition.—The assertion that the Sabbath was coeval with the human race, and was intended for the observation of all, receives collateral confirmation also from the early traditions concerning it, which pervade the first Pagan literature. It can hardly be supposed that Homer and Hesiod borrowed from the books of Moses, sabbatical allusions, which would have been to their hearers unintelligible. They must be the remnants of those primeval traditions of patriarchal religion, which had been transferred by the descendants of Japheth, to the isles of Chittim. The early allusions to a sacred seventh day may be sufficiently exhibited by citing a collection of them from Eusebius' *Preparatio Evangelica*, (L. xiii, Sec. 13), which he quotes from the Stromata of Clement of Alexandria. The latter father is represented as saying: "That the seventh day is sacred, not the Hebrews only, but the Gentiles also acknowledge, according to which the whole unise of animals and vegetables revolves." Hesiod, for instance, thus s concerning it:

' The first, the fourth also, and the seventh is a sacred day." (IERON MAR. DIERUM, line 6.

And again: "The seventh day once more, the splendid dawn of the ."

And Homer: "The seventh then arrived, the sacred day."

Again: "The seventh was sacred."

' The seventh dawn was at hand, and with this all the series is comted."

And once more: "On the seventh day, we left the stream of Ache- ."

And thus also writes Callimachus the poet: "It was now the Sabbath : and with this all was accomplished."

Again: "The seventh day is among the fortunate; yea, the seven is parent-day."

Again: "The seventh day is first, and the seventh day is the complent."

And: "All things in the starry sky are found in sevens; and shine their ordained cycles."

' And this day, the elegies of Solon also proclaim as more sacred, in onderful mode."

us far Clement and Eusebius. Josephus, in his last book against ion, affirms that "there could be found no city, either of the Greeks or Barbarians, who owned not a seventh day's rest from labour." is of course is exaggerated. Philo, cotemporary with Josephus, calls Sabbath EORTE PANDEMOS.

BECAUSE ENFORCED ON FOREIGNERS.—We argue once more, that the bbath never was a Levitical institution, because God commanded its servance both by Jews and Gentiles, in the very laws of Moses. "In thou shalt not do any work, thou, nor thy son, nor thy daughter, thy n-servant, nor thy maid-servant, nor thy cattle, *nor thy stranger that within thy gates.*" To see the force of the argument from this fact, reader must contrast the jealous care with which "the stranger," pagan foreigner residing in an Israelitish community, was prohibitfrom all share in their ritual services. No foreigner could partake the passover—it was sacrilege. He was not even permitted to enter court of the temple where the sacrifices were offered, at the peril of life. Now, when the foreigner is commanded to share the Sabbath st, along with the Israelite, does not this prove that rest to be no ceremonial, no type, like the passover and the altar, but a universal moral stitution, designed for Jew and Gentile alike?

CONCLUSION.—We have thus established this assertion on an impregble basis, because the argument from it is direct and conclusive. If e Sabbath command was in full force before Moses, the passing away Moses' law does not remove it. If it always was binding, on grounds general as the human race, on all tribes of mankind, the dissolution God's special covenant with the family of Jacob did not repeal it. its nature is moral and practical, the substitution of the substance r the types does not supplant it. The reason that the ceremonial ws were temporary was that the necessity for them was temporary. ey were abrogated because they were no longer needed. But the practical need for a Sabbath is the same in all ages. When it is made to appear that this day is the bulwark of practical religion in the world, that its proper observance everywhere goes hand in hand with piety and the true worship of God; that where there is no Sabbath there is no Christianity, it becomes an impossible supposition that God would make the institution temporary. The necessity for the Sabbath has not ceased, therefore it is not abrogated. In its nature, as well as its necessity, it is a permanent, moral command. All such laws are as incapable of change as the God in whose character they are founded. Unlike mere positive or ceremonial ordinances, the authority of which ceases as soon as God sees fit to repeal the command for them, moral precepts can never be repealed; because the purpose to repeal them would imply a change in the unchangeable, and a depravation in the perfect character of God.

New Testament does not Abrogate.—2. We will now proceed, in the second place, to consider the passages of the New Testament from which the abrogation of the Sabbath obligations has been argued, together with some considerations growing out of them. In attempting to refute the exposition and arguments of those who advocate the repeal of those obligations, we shall not pause to attribute each gloss which we reject to its especial author, or load our page with citations of learned names. It may be remarked once for all in the outset, that the erroneous expositions of Calvin are far the least objectionable, and, at the same time, the most subtle and acute; and that those of Neander are in full contrast with his in both these respects.

Matt. xii: 1–8; Mark ii: 23–28; Luke vi: 1–5.—The first passage is that contained, with some variation, in Matt. xii: 1–8; Mark ii: 23–28; Luke vi: 1–5. The reader, on examining these places in connexion, and supplying from the second or third evangelist what is omitted by the first, will find that our Lord advances five ideas distinguishable from each other. His hungry and wearied disciples, passing with Him through the fields of ripe corn, had availed themselves of the permission of Deut. xxiii: 25, to pluck, rub out, and eat some grains of wheat, as a slight refreshment. The Pharisees seize the occasion to cavil that He had thus permitted them to break the Sabbath law, by engaging in the preparation of their food in sacred time; objecting thus against the trivial task of rubbing out, and winnowing from the chaff a few heads of wheat as they walked along. Our Saviour defends them and Himself by saying, in the first place, that the necessity created by their hunger justified the departure from the letter of the law, as did David's necessity, when fleeing for his life he employed the shew-bread (and innocently) to relieve his hunger; second, that the example of the priests, who performed necessary manual labour without blame about the temple on the Sabbath, justified what His disciples had done; third, that God preferred the compliance with the spirit of His law, which enjoins humanity and mercy, over a mere compliance with its outward rites; for, in the fourth place God's design in instituting the Sabbath had been purely a humane one, seeing He had intended it, not as a burdensome ceremonial to gall the necks of men to no benevolent purpose, but as a means of promoting the true welfare of the human race; and last, that He Himself, as the Messiah, was the Divine and Supreme authority in maintaining the Sabbath law, as well as all others—so that it was enough for Him to pronounce that His disciples had made no infraction of it.

Our Saviour here defines Jewish Sabbath.—The first general view presented hereupon by the anti-Sabbatarians is, that Christ here, for the first time, introduces the freer, more lenient law of the new dispensation, by His Messianic authority, as a substitute for the stricter Mosaic law. The simple and short answer is, that it is the Sabbath *as it ought to be observed by Jews*, under the Mosaic laws, which our Saviour is here expounding. The new dispensation had not yet come; and was not to begin till Pentecost. After all this discussion, Christ complied with all the requisitions of the Levitical institutions up to His death. If, then, any thing is relaxed, it is the Mosaic Sabbath, as Jews should keep it, which is the subject of the alteration. But we wish the reader to bear in mind, as a point important here and hereafter, that our Saviour does not claim any relaxation at all for His disciples. The whole drift of His argument is to show that when the Mosaic law of the Sabbath is properly understood, (as Jews should practice it,) His disciples have not broken it at all. They have complied with it; and need no lowering of its sense in order to escape its condemnation. Bearing this in mind, we proceed to the second erroneous inference. This is, that our Saviour illustrates and expounds the Sabbath law by two cases of other laws merely ceremonial, the disposition of the old shew-bread and the Sabbath sacrifices. Hence the inference, that the Sabbath also is but a ceremonial law. But to those who will notice how entirely the Jewish Scriptures ignore, in their practical recitals and discussions of religious duties, the distinction which we make between the "moral" and the "positive," this inference will be seen to be utterly worthless. The Jewish mind never paused to express the distinction, in its practical views of duty. See how Moses jumbles together, in Exodus, prohibitions against idolatry, or hewing the stones of which the altar was made: against eating flesh torn of beasts in the field, and bearing false witness. See how Ezekiel (ch. xviii.) conjoins eating upon the mountains and taking usury on a loan, with idolatry and oppression, in his descriptions of the sins of his cotemporaries. But again: It has been admitted that the external and formal details of Sabbath observance may be of only positive obligation, while the obligation to keep religiously a stated season is moral. It does not, then, at all imply that the substantial observance of such a stated day is not of moral and perpetual obligation, because any of those details concerning the labours of necessity or mercy which are wholly compatible with such observance, are illustrated by comparison with other ceremonial precepts. It is argued again, that "our Saviour, in His third point, implies that Sabbath observance is but ceremonial, while the duty of mercy is of moral obligation, when He indicates that, if the two clash, the Sabbath observance is to give way. The positive gives way to the moral." The force of this is entirely removed by recalling the fact that it is not a failure of Sabbath observance, which He excuses by the argument that the positive should give place to the moral; but it is an incidental labour of necessity wholly compatible with Sabbath observance. There had been no failure. Nor is it true that when we are commanded to let one given duty give place to the higher demands of another, the former is therefore, only positive, while the latter is moral. There is a natural, moral, and perpetual obligation to worship God; and yet it might be our duty to suspend any act of worship, time and again, to almost any number, in order to meet the demands of urgent cases of necessity calling for our compassion. The wise man expresses precisely the sense of our Saviour's argument when he says: "To do justice and judgment is more acceptable to the Lord than sacrifice." (Prov. xxi: 3.) And the meaning is, that the formal acts of religious worship, though in general demanded by nature and reason, are less important in God's eyes than the direct acts which express the true spirit of holiness in which religion consists. "Sacrifice," both here, and in our Saviour's citation from Samuel, represents the whole general idea of outward religious worship. It is not because "sacrifice" is merely ceremonial, that it is postponed in importance, to mercy and justice, but because it is external, and may be merely formal. Religious worship, here intended by the more special term "sacrifice," is surely not a duty merely ceremonial and positive in its obligation, though external. Our Saviour, then, does not imply that the Sabbath is an institution merely ceremonial, by comparing it to sacrifice.

The perverted gloss of the fourth idea: "The Sabbath is made for man," is almost too shallow to need exposure. It has been used as though it sanctioned the notion, that man was not intended to be cramped by the Sabbath, but, on the contrary, it was intended to yield to his convenience and gratification. But since the object of the Sabbath is here stated to be a humane one, namely, the promotion of man's true welfare, it must be settled what that true welfare is, and how it may be best promoted, before we are authorized to conclude that we may do what we please with the holy-day. If it should appear that man's true welfare imperatively demands a Sabbath-day, strictly observed and fenced in with Divine authority, the humanity of the Divine motive in giving a Sabbath would argue any thing else than the license inferred from it.

Christ does not Remit.—The concluding words of the passage, in Matthew, have suggested an argument which is at least more plausible. Calvin paraphrases them thus: "The Son of man, agreeably to His authority, is able to relax the Sabbath-day just as the other legal ceremonies." And just before: "Here He saith that power is given to Him to release His people from the necessity of observing the Sabbath." The inference is obvious, that if this is His scope in these words, then the Sabbath must be admitted by us to be only a ceremonial institution; for we have ourselves argued that moral laws are founded on the unchangeable nature of God himself, and will never be changed, because God cannot change. But this is clearly a mistaken exposition. It may be noted that the conjunction which is rendered by Calvin and the English version, "the Son of man is Lord *even* (or also) of the Sabbath-day," is unanimously rejected by modern editors of the text. Calvin, of course, makes this conjunction regard the ceremonials just mentioned: "The Son of Man is Lord of the Sabbath also," (as well as of matters of shew-bread and sacrifice). But we should almost certainly read the clause without the conjunction: "If ye had known what this means, 'I prefer mercy rather than sacrifice,' ye would not have condemned the innocent. *For* the Son of Man is *Lord* of the Sabbath." What force shall we assign to the illative 'for,' wholly neglected by

Calvin? There is no reasonable explanation of it, but that which makes it introduce the ground on which the innocence of the disciples is asserted. "These men, blamed by you, are innocent; it is enough that I defend them: *for I* am Lord of the Sabbath. This law is my law. Mine is the authority which enacts it, and if am satisfied, that itself is innocence in my subjects." But this is comparatively unimportant. The evident reason which shows Calvin's paraphrase to be entirely a misconception, is this: As we have said, the whole drift of our Saviour's argument is not to excuse his disciples, but to defend them. He does not claim that the Sabbath law, as enacted for Jews, must needs be relaxed, in order to admit the conduct of the disciples; but that this law justified their conduct. He concludes his defence by telling their accusers, "you have condemned *the innocent.*" Now, to represent Him as shielding them by asserting a right in Himself to relax the Sabbath law for them, makes Him adopt in the end a ground of defence contradictory to the former. The last argument would stultify all the previous one. The logical absurdity would be exactly of the same kind with that contained in the trite story of the school-boy, who, when charged with striking his school-mate, answered: "I did not strike him at all; but if I did, he struck me first." And, as a question of fact, is it true that Christ did, at this time, exercise His divine authority to relax any Mosaic institution in favour of His disciples? Is it not notorious, on the contrary, that He taught them to give an exemplary compliance in every respect, until the time was fully come after His resurrection?

But to conclude. It is most obvious that, whatever is our exposition of the particular parts, our Saviour's drift is to unfold the true nature of the *Mosaic Sabbath*, as then obligatory on Jews still obedient to the ceremonial law, as He admitted Himself and His disciples to be; and not the nature of the Christian Sabbath. The latter was not to be introduced until many months after, as our opponents themselves admit. And this short view is a sufficient refutation in itself.

Is Jewish Strictness Still Required?—It may be as well to notice here a supposed difficulty attending our argument. It is said: "If you deny that Christ promises any relaxation of the stringency of the Levitical Sabbath, as of a ceremonial yoke, then you ought in consistency to exact of Christians now as punctilous an observance as was demanded of the old Jews, in every respect. You should refuse to make a fire in your dwellings on the Sabbath. You should seek to reenact the terrible law of Numb. xvi, which punished a wretch with death for gathering a few sticks."

This is only skilful sophistry. We have not asserted that all the details of the Sabbath laws, in the books of Moses, were of perpetual moral obligation. We have not denied that some of them were ceremonial. The two instances mentioned, which are the only plausible ones which can be presented against us, are not taken from the decalogue, but from subsequent parts of the ceremonial books. We expressly contrasted the Sabbath precept as it stands in the "ten words" with all the rest, with reference to its perpetual, moral nature. The precept there contains only two points—rest from secular labour, and the sanctification of the day, which means in our view its appropriation to sacred services. The matter which is of perpetual moral obligation in the Sabbath law, is only this, that a finite, sensuous, and social being like man, shall have some periodical season statedly consecrated to religious services, (such season as God shall see fit to appoint.) And all matters of detail and form which do not clash with this great end, are matters of mere positive enactment, which may be changed or repealed by Him who enacted them. But we can present several very consistent and sufficient reasons why the ceremonial details added to the great moral law of the decalogue, by the subsequent and ritual part of the Levitical legislation, should be more stringent and enforced by heavier penalties than among us. First: the Sabbath became to the Israelite not only a religious institution of moral obligation, but a type. It took rank with his new-moon, and his passover. Of this, more hereafter. But the very nature and design of a symbolical ritual demand that it shall be observed with technical accuracy. Next, the government was a theocracy, and no line whatever separated the secular and sacred statutes from each other. Hence, it is natural that offences should deserve very different penalties under such a government, and especially an offence aimed so especially against the Divine Chief Magistrate, as Sabbath labour. Third: The Hebrews' houses had no hearths, nor chimneys, except for cooking; so that in that warm climate a prohibition to light fire on the Sabbath is exactly equivalent to a prohibition to cook on the holy-day. Even if this prohibition were a part of the decalogue, it would be a ridiculous sacrifice of its spirit to its letter, to compel us, in our wintry climate, to forego the fire which is hourly necessary to health and comfort. But as the prohibition signifies in its spirit, we freely admit that with us, as with the Jews, all culinary labours should be intermitted, except such as are demanded by necessity and mercy, or by the different nature of a part of the food on which civilized nations now subsist. For us to allow ourselves further license would be to palter with that which we have so carefully pointed out as the essential and perpetual substance of the Sabbath law—the cessation of labour, and the appropriation to religious pursuits of one day (not one fragment of a day) in seven. When the Confession of Faith says that we are commanded to rest "all the day" from our own employments and amusements, and to "take up the whole time" in religious exercises, it only assumes that "a day" means, in the decalogue, a day.

The second group of passages which are used against our theory of Sabbath obligation are, Rom. xiv: 5–6; Gal. iv: 9–11; Col. ii: 16–17. To save the reader trouble, we will copy them:

Rom. xiv: 5, 6; Gal. iv: 9–11; Col. ii: 16, 17.—"One man esteemeth one day above another; another esteemeth every day alike. Let every man be fully persuaded in his own mind. He that regardeth the day, regardeth it unto the Lord: and he that regardeth not the day, to the Lord he doth not regard it. He that eateth, eateth to the Lord, for he giveth God thanks; and he that eateth not, to the Lord he eateth not, and giveth God thanks."

"But now, after that ye have known God, or rather are known of God, how turn ye again to the weak and beggarly elements, whereunto ye desire again to be in bondage? Ye observe days, and months, and times, and years. I am afraid of you, lest I have bestowed upon you labour in vain."

"Let no man therefore judge you in meat, or in drink, or in respect of an holy-day, or of the new-moon, or of the Sabbath-days: Which are a shadow of things to come; but the body is of Christ."

The facts in which all are agreed, which explain the Apostle's meaning in these passages, are these: After the establishment of the new dispensation, the Christians converted from among the Jews had generally combined the practice of Judaism with the forms of Christianity. They observed the Lord's day, baptism, and the Lord's supper; but they also continued to keep the seventh day, the passover, and circumcision. At first it was proposed by them to enforce this double system on all Gentile Christians; but this project was rebuked by the meeting of apostles and elders at Jerusalem, recorded in Acts xv. A large part, however, of the Jewish Christians, out of whom ultimately grew the Ebionite sect, continued to observe the forms of both dispensations; and restless spirits among the mixed churches of Jewish and Gentile converts planted by Paul, continued to attempt their enforcement on Gentiles also; some of them conjoining with this Ebionite theory the graver heresy of a justification by ritual observances. Thus, at this day, this spectacle was exhibited. In the mixed churches of Asia Minor and the West, some brethren went to the synagogue on Saturday, and to the church-meeting on Sunday, keeping both days religiously; while some kept only Sunday. Some felt bound to keep all the Jewish festivals and fasts, while others paid them no regard. And those who had not Christian light to apprehend these Jewish observances as non-essentials, found their consciences grievously burdened or offended by the diversity. It was to quiet this trouble that the apostle wrote these passages. Thus far we agree.

We, however, further assert, that by the beggarly elements of "days," "months," "times," "years," "holy-days," "new-moons," "Sabbath-days," the apostle means Jewish festivals, and those alone. The Christian's festival, Sunday, is not here in question; because about the observance of this there was no dispute nor diversity in the Christian churches. Jewish and Gentile Christians alike consented universally in its sanctification. When Paul asserts that the regarding of a day, or the not regarding it, is a non-essential, like the eating or not eating of meats, the natural and fair interpretation is, that he means those days which were in debate, and no others. When he implies that some innocently "regarded every day alike," we should understand, *every one of those days which were subjects of diversity*—not the Christians' Sunday, about which there was no dispute.

Anti-Sabatarian View—Reply.—But the other party give to Paul's words a far more sweeping sense. They suppose him to assert 'that the new dispensation has detached the service of God from all connexion with stated seasons whatever; so that in its view, all days, Sabbath or Sunday, passover or easter, should be alike to the Christian spirit. He who ceased to observe the Jewish days, in order to transfer his sabbatical observances, his stated devotions and special religious rest to the Christian days, was still in substance a Judaizer. He was retaining the Jewish bondage of spirit under a new form. The true liberty which Paul would teach was this: To regard no day whatever as more related to the Christian consciousness than any other day, and to make every day a rest from sin, pervading all with a sacred spirit by performing all its labours to the glory of God. This is the true, thorough, and high ground, which the apostle called them to occupy with him. But opposition to Judaism, and reverence for Christ in His resurrection had led the Christians to hold their public meetings on Sunday instead of Saturday; and some little allowance of set days (including Easter and Whitsuntide) had been granted to the weakness of the Christian life, which, in the common average of Christians, had not yet risen to that level which would enable them, like Paul, to make every day equally a Lord's day. This concession had been possibly established with Paul's connivance, certainly very early in the history of the Church; and, on the whole, was a very convenient and useful human appointment.' See this view in Neander, Hist., vol. I, sec. 3, sec. II, 3; and Planting and Training, vol. I, bk. 3, ch. v, sec. 2. The chief argument by which he supports his view is a perversion of the figurative and glowing language found in the few and not very perspicuous writings of the Christians immediately next to the apostles, where they speak affectionately of the Christian's whole life as belonging to God by the purchase of redemption, and of the duties of every day as an oblation to His honour. The thankful spirit of the new dispensation, urges Neander, unlike the Jewish, felt itself constrained by gratitude for redemption to consecrate its whole life to God. Whatever the Christian's occupation, whether secular or religious, all was alike done to the glory of God. Hence, all was consecrated; every day was a holy day, for the whole life was holy; every Christian was a perpetual priest. Hence, there was no room for the idea of a Sabbath at all. Strange that the learned and amiable antiquary should have forgotten that all this was just as true of pious Hebrews before, as of Christians after Christ—of Isaiah as of Paul. Isaiah, if redeemed at all, was redeemed by the same blood with Paul, owed substantially the same debt of gratitude, and would feel, as a true saint, the same self-consecration. The spirit of the precept, "Do all to the glory of God," actuates the pious Israelite exactly as it did the pious Christian. Let the reader compare Deut. vi: 4, 5, with Matt. xxii: 37, so that the refined argument of the learned German proves that there ought to be no room for a sabbatical distinction of days under the old dispensation, just as under the new. Unluckily, the explicit language of the books of Moses is rather damaging to the validity of the inference.

Let us also notice, just here, the consequences of the ground on which Neander places those festival observances of the early Christians on stated days, of which he could not dispute the occurrence. He represents that Paul invited and exhorted them to ascend at once to his high, spiritual ground, discarding all reference to stated days whatever, and making the whole life a Sabbath. But the average standard of spirituality was not yet high enough to make this practicable for all; and so the partial observance of stated days, Sundays, Easter, and Whitsuntide, was allowed by a sort of ecclesiastical precedent. Now, we remark, first, that this represents the Spirit of Inspiration as setting up an impracticable standard. If the average of spirituality was not high enough in the days of inspiration to make it practicable actually to discard all relation of the acts of Christian devotion to stated days, may we rationally expect that it will ever be high enough while Christians are in the flesh? In other words: Is there not an implied admission here, that there is an innate necessity in the character of human beings that they should have a sabbatical institution of some sort? The assertion of such an universal necessity is one of the corner-stones of our argument. Second: The idea reveals an unworthy and false conception of Paul's inspiration. Paul, forsooth, proposes a certain mode and standard of Christian devotion, but it is found necessary in practice to correct it by the wiser guidance of Church precedent, almost under Paul's nose! This representation of the whole matter could never have proceeded from any other than the transcendental theory of inspiration, which regards it as merely a higher mode of the natural and normal exercise of the man's own consciousness, at a more exalted level than that attained by other men. Let those American Christians who indulge their prurient literary vanity by bespattering Neander with their unintelligent praise, remember that this is the conception of inspiration to which they commit themselves in commending him.

Is the Sabbath a Type?—In our remaining discussion of the passages cited from the epistles, we may confine our remarks to Col. ii: 16–17. For it contains all the apparent difficulties for the Sabbatarian, and all the supposed arguments for his opponent, in the strongest form. The point made by Calvin upon the words, "Sabbath-days, ... are a shadow of things to come, but the body is of Christ," is far the most plausible, and indeed the only one of serious difficulty. It is in substance this: That if it be admitted that the Lord's day was never included by the earlier Christians in the term Sabbata—and the apostle is here condemning the Jewish holy-days only—still the fact will remain, that the Jewish Sabbath was a shadow. That is, it was a typical, and not a perpetual moral institution, so that it must go by the board along with all the other types, after the substance comes, unless some positive New Testament precept re-enact it. But there is no such precept. To this we answer, that the Sabbath was to the Jews both a perpetual, moral institution, and a type. That it was the former, we have proved in the first general branch of our discussion. It was as old as the race of man, was given to all the race, was given upon an assigned motive of universal application, and to satisfy a necessity common to the whole race, was founded on man's natural relations to his Maker, was observed before the typical dispensation came among all tribes, was re-enacted in the decalogue where all the precepts are perpetual, and was enjoined on foreigners as well as Jews in the Holy Land: while from all types foreigners were expressly excluded. That it was to the Jews also a type, we admit. Like the new-moons, it was marked by an additional number of sacrifices. It was to the Israelites a memorial of their exodus from Egypt, and their covenant of obedience to God. Deut. v: 15, Exod. xxxi: 13, Ezek. xx: 12. It was for a time, at least, a foreshadowing of the rest of Canaan. Hebr. iv: 4–11. It was to them, as it is to us, a shadow of the rest in heaven. Hebr. iv: 9. Calvin adds, (Bk. II. Institutes, Ch. 8, Sec. 29) that its most important typical use was to represent the cessation of the efforts of self-righteousness in us, that we may repose in the justifying and sanctifying grace of Christ. For this his proofs seem to us very slender. When the Epistle to the Colossians says that Sabbaths, along with holy days and new-moons, are a shadow, it seems to us much the most simple explanation to say that it is the sacrificial aspect of those days, or (to employ other words) their use as especial days of sacrifice, in which they together constituted a shadow. They were a shadow in this: that the sacrifices, which constituted so prominent a part of their Levitical observance, pointed to Christ the body. This is exactly accordant with the whole tenour of the Epistles.

The seventh day had been, then, to the Jews, both a moral institution and a ritual type. In its latter use, the coming of Christ had of course abrogated it. In its former use, its whole duties and obligations had lately been transferred to the Lord's day. So that *the seventh day*, as distinguished from *Sunday*, along with the new-moons, was now nothing but a type, and that an effete one. In this aspect, the apostle might well argue that its observance then indicated a Judaizing tendency.

THE "DAYS" EXCLUDED ARE JEWISH.—We fortify our position farther by re-asserting that the fair exposition of all these passages should lead us to understand by the phrases, "days," "times," "holy-days," only those days or times which were then subjects of diversity among the Christians to whom the apostle was writing. When he implies that some innocently "regarded every day alike," we ought in fairness to understand by "every day," each of those days which were then in dispute. But we know historically that there was no diversity among these Christians concerning the observance of the Lord's day. All practised it. If we uncritically persist in taking the phrase "every day" in a sense absolutely universal, we shall place the teachings and usages of the apostle in a self-contradictory light. We make him tell his converts that *the Lord's day* may be regarded as just like any other day; when we know that, in fact, neither the apostle nor any of his converts regarded it so. They all observed it as a religious festival, and as we shall show, with the clear sanction of inspired example. Again: it must be distinctly remembered that the word Sabbath was never applied, in New Testament language, to the Lord's day, but was always used for the seventh day, and other Jewish festivals, as distinguished from the Christian's Sunday. We have the authority of Suidas, Theophylact and Cæsarius, and Levit. xxiii: 24, that the "Jews called any of their stated religious festivals SABBATON. We might then argue, perhaps, that there is no evidence that the seventh day is intended in this place of Colossians at all; but only the Jewish feasts. But we waive this, as too near to special pleading. With far more confidence we argue, that since all parties have claimed the parellelism of three passages in Romans, Galatians and Colossians, as to their occasion and doctrine, we are entitled to assume that the passage in Colossians, the most explicit of the three, is to be taken as explicative of the other two. And we assert that, according to well known usage of the word SABBATA at that time, the Sundays were *definitely excluded* from the apostle's assertion. When he says here, "holy-days, new-moons, and Sabbath-days," he explicitly excludes the Lord's days. We are entitled to assume, therefore, that they are excluded when he says in the parellel passage of Romans, "every day," and in Galatians, "days, and months, and times, and years." That the Lord's days were sacred was not in debate; this is set aside as a matter known to all, consented unto by all. It is the Jewish holy-days, from the observance of which the Christian conscience is exempted.

Without Sabbath, the New Dispensation would be the Worse. Let us recur to that view of the necessity of a Sabbatical institution in some form. It is not a temporary orceremonial need, but one founded on man's very nature and relations to his God. If there is no stated sacred day, tnere will be no religion. Now shall we so interpret the apostle's words as to leave the New Testament church no Sabbath at all in any shape? After the experience of all ages had shown that a Sabbath rest was the natural and necessary means essential to religious welfare, was the New Testament church stripped more bare, left more poor than all preceding dispensations? Paradise had enjoyed its Sabbath, though needing it less. The patriarchal saints enjoyed it. Abraham enjoyed it. Israel, under the burdensome tutelage of the law, enjoyed it. But now that the last, the fullest, the most gracious and blessed dispensation of all has come, this one of the two institutions of Eden is taken away! We cannot accept such an exposition of the apostle's meaning. We must conclude that when he seems to release his converts from all obligations of days, the Lord's day is tacitly understood as reserved, as not here in question; because about this all parties had been agreed.

Neander Inconsistent.—Let us notice here how inconsistent and un-protestant is Neander's position. He asserts that it is inconsistent with the free and spiritual nature of Christianity that God should give any stated day, by His express ordinance, a closer relation to the Christian consciousness than any other day. Is it not equally inconsistent that He should give any particular place, and forms of worship a peculiar relation to the Christian consciousness? But, under the New Testament, He has done this very thing; commanding us to worship in concert at the place or building appropriated by our brethren for this purpose, and to do so with prayers, hymns, and the sacraments. It is admitted again, that after all the Church has found that practically there is a necessity, founded in man's universal nature and relations to God, which compels us to take some stated day into a peculiar relation to the Christian consciousness, to some extent at least. Sunday *is* a Christian festival, and a memorial of the resurrection—says the Lutheran—made so with sufficient validity, by a Church precedent. But is it not far more consistent with Protestantism, which teaches that nothing but God's revealed will is its religion, to find this validity, if it finds it at all, in His law, rather than a church tradition? We seek an express precept for the mode of our worship, the number and forms of our sacraments; and teach that any element of service which is not thus enjoined, is will-worship. Should we not find a Divine precept for the season of our worship also? And if we find none, does not Protestant consistency require us to say that Sunday, not being enjoined by express Divine command, is literally no more to Christians than any other day, which they agree, for conscience' sake, to appoint for a week-day, prayer-meeting, or Bible Society address, and may be changed with as little scruple? As to the motive that it is commemorative of Christ's resurrection, why will not one Sunday a year answer just as well for this, as one Good Friday a year does to commemorate the passover of our Lord? The Lutheran or Episcopalian, in enforcing a partial observance of Sunday, is indeed consistent with himself; for he believes that ecclesiastical authority is sufficient to do this, if not contrary to the Scriptures; but he is not consistent with the Word of God, which teaches, as we understand it, that nothing is to be enjoined as a stated part of His worship, except what he has expressly enjoined. "The Bible alone is the religion of Protestants."

LORD'S DAY IS CHRISTIAN SABBATH.—3. We shall now, in the third branch of our discussion, attempt to show the ground on which we assert that the Sabbath, "from the resurrection of Christ, was changed into the first day of the week, which in Scripture is called the Lord's day, and is to be continued to the end of the world as the Christian Sabbath." This proof is chiefly historical, and divides itself into two branches; first, that drawn from the inspired history of the New Testament; and second, that found in the authentic but uninspired testimony of primitive Christians. The latter, which might have been thought to demand a place in our review of the history of Sabbath opinions has been reserved for this place, because it forms an interesting part of our ground of argument. But let us here say, once for all, that we invoke this patriotic testimony, in no popish or prelatic spirit of dependence on it. In our view, all the uninspired church testimony in the world, however venerable, would never make it our duty to keep Sunday as a Sabbath. We use these fathers simply as historical witnesses; and their evidence derives its whole value in our eyes from its relevancy to this point; *whether or not the apostles left a custom of observing Sunday, instead of the Sabbaths established by their example in the Churches.* When the fathers say: "We as fathers, as bishops, as Church rulers, tell you to observe Sunday;" we reject the warrant as nothing worth. But if they are able to say: "We, as honest and well informed witnesses, tell you that *the apostolic age left us the example and warrant* for observing Sunday," we accept the testimony as of some value. Prelatists are fond of shutting their eyes to this plain distinction, in order to claim that we must either surrender all the early historic light of uninspired literature, or else adopt their semi-popish theory of tradition. We trust the distinction is so stated here, once for all, that all will see it, (except those who do not wish to see it), and will bear it in mind.

INFERRED FROM ABROGATION OF SEVENTH DAY.—Our first, or preliminary argument for the observance of Sunday as the Sabbath, is that implied in the second Scripture reference subjoined by our Confession to the sentence we have just quoted from it. If we have been successful in proving that the Sabbath is a perpetual institution, the evidence will appear perfect. The perpetaul law of the decalogue has commanded all men, in all time, to keep a Sabbath-day; and "till heaven and earth pass, one jot or one tittle shall not pass from the law of God till all be fulfilled." The Apostle, in Col. ii: 16, 17, clearly tells us that the seventh day is no longer our Sabbath. What day, then, is it? Some day must have been substituted; and what one so likely to be the true substitute as the Lord's day? The law is not repealed; it cannot be. But Paul has shown that it is changed. To what day is the Sabbath changed, if not to the first? No other day in the week has a shadow of a claim. It must be this, or none; but it cannot be none: therefore it must be this.

Proved by Precedent.—The other main argument consists in the fact that disciples, inspired apostles, and their Christian associates, did observe the Lord's day as a religious festival. And this fact must be viewed, to see its full force, in connexion with the first argument. When we find them at once beginning, and uniformly continuing the observance of the Lord's day, while they avow that they are no longer bound to observe the seventh day, and when we couple with this the knowledge of the truth that they, like all the rest of the world, were still commanded by God to keep His Sabbath, we see that the inference is overwhelming, that the authority by which they observed the Lord's day was from God, although they do not say so. That which is inferred from Scripture, "by good and necessary consequence," is valid; as well as that which is set down expressly in it." Examination shows us, then, that the disciples commenced the observance of the Lord's day by social worship the very next week after the resurrection. From John xx: 19, we learn that the very day of the resurrection, at evening, the disciples were assembled with closed doors, with the exception of Thomas Didymus. Can we doubt that they had met for worship? In chap. v: 26, we learn: "And after eight days again His disciples were within, and Thomas with them: then came Jesus, the doors being shut, and stood in the midst, and said, Peace be unto you." None will doubt but that this was also a meeting for worship, and the phraseology implies that it was their second meeting. In Jewish language, and estimates of time, the days at which the counts begin and end are always included in the counts; so that "after eight days," here indisputably means just a full week. Let the reader compare, for instance, Leviticus xiii: 4, with xiv: 10. "The priest shall shut up him that hath the plague seven days." "And on the eighth day he shall take two he lambs without blemish," &c. So the new-born child must be circumcised the eighth; but it is well known that the number eight is made up by counting the day of the birth and the day of the circumcision. A full week from the disciples' first meeting brings us again to the first day of the week. Until Pentecost we are left uninformed whether they continued to observe the first day, but the presumption is wholly that they did.

Pentecost was on First Day.—By consulting Leviticus xxiii: 15-16; Deut. xvi: 9, you will see that the day of Pentecost was fixed in this way. On the morrow after that Sabbath (seventh day) which was included within the passover week, a sheaf of the earliest ripe corn was cut, brought fresh into the sanctuary, and presented as a thank-offering to God. The day of this ceremonial was always the first day of the week, or our Sunday, which was, to the Israelites, a working day. From this day they were to count seven weeks complete, and the fiftieth day was Pentecost day, or the feast of ingathering. Remember that the Israelites always included in their count the day from which, and the day to which they counted; and taking his almanac he will find on actual experiment, that the fiftieth day will bring him to Sunday again, the first day of the week. The gospels tell us most explicitly that the year Christ died and rose again, the passover feast began Thursday evening; the day of unleavened bread (in the afternoon of which the Saviour died) was our Friday, the day His body lay in the grave, was our Saturday, or the Jewish Sabbath, and the day He rose was the first day, our Sunday. This last was also the day when the Jews offered their first sheaf. So that Pentecost day must also fall (as indeed it did every year) on a Sunday. Thus we reach the interesting fact that the day selected by God for the pentecostal outpouring, and the inauguration of the Gospel dispensation, was the Lord's day—a significant and splendid testimony to the importance and honour it was intended to have in the Christian world. But we read in Acts i: 14, and ii: 1, that this day also was observed by the disciples as a day for social worship. Thus the first day of the week received a second, sacred and august witness, as the weekly solemnity of our religion, not only in its observance by the whole body of the new church, but by the baptism of fire, and the Holy Ghost—a witness only second to that of Christ's victory over death and hell. Then the first public proclamation of the Gospel under the new dispensation began; and surely, when every step, every act of the Divine Providence was formative and fundamental, it was not without meaning that God selected the first day of the week as the chosen day.

Acts 20: 7. Lord's Day at Troas.—It is most evident from the New Testament history, that the Apostles and early church uniformly celebrated their worship on the first day of the week. The hints are not numerous; but they are sufficiently distinct. The next clear instance is in Acts xx: 7. The Apostle was now returning from his famous mission to Macedonia and Achaia, in full prospect of captivity at Jerusalem. He stops at the little church of Troas, to spend a season with his converts there: "And upon the first day of the week when the disciples came together to break bread, Paul preached unto them, (ready to depart on the morrow), and continued his speech until midnight." Here we have a double evidence of our point First, Paul preached unto the disciples on this day, while we see from the sixth verse, that he was a whole week in Troas, including the Jewish Sabbath. Why does he wait nearly a whole week to give these his more solemn and public instructions, unless there had been some usage? Again: the words, "when the disciples came together to break bread," clearly indicate that the first day of the week was their habitual day for celebrating the Lord's Supper. So that it is clear, this Church of Troas planted and trained by Paul, was in the habit of consecrating the first day of the week to public worship; and the inspired man here concurs in the habit. Neander does, indeed, suggest an evasion, in order to substantiate his assertion that there is no evidence the Lord's day was specially sanctified during the life-time of Paul. He says that it is so, very probable this day was selected by the brethren, because Paul could not wait any longer, (ready to depart on the morrow,") that no safe inference can be drawn for a habitual observance of the day by them or Paul! But chap. v: 6, tells us that Paul had been already waiting a whole week, and might have had choice of all the days of the week for his meeting! No other word is needed to explode this suggestion.

1 Cor. 16th: 1 and 2.—The next clear instance is in 1 Cor. xvi: 1–2. "Now concerning the collection for the saints, as I have given order to the Churches of Galatia, even so do ye. Upon the first day of the week let every one of you lay by him in store as God hath prospered him, that there be no gatherings when I come." The points here

indicated are two—that the weekly oblation of alms-giving was fixed for the Lord's day—and that this rule was enacted for the Church of Corinth, and all those of Galatia. The inference is overwhelming, that the Apostle made the usage ultimately uniform in all the churches of his training. Neander again attempts to destroy this evidence for the sanctification of Sunday, by saying that this does not prove there was any church meeting, or public worship on this day. The sum of alms was, most probably, simply laid aside at home, in an individual, private manner; and this is made more probable by the Apostle's own words: "let every one of you *lay by him* in store." But suppose this understanding of the passage is granted, against the uniform custom and tradition of the earliest Christians, which testifies with one voice, that the weekly alms-giving took place in the church meeting; Neander's point is not yet gained. Still *this alms-giving was*, in the New Testament meaning, *an act of worship*. See Phil. iv: 18. And the early tradition unanimously represents the first Christians as so regarding it. Hence, whether this alms-giving were in public or private, we have here an indisputable instance, that an act of worship was appointed, by apostolic authority, to be statedly performed on the Lord's day, throughout the Churches. This is evidence enough that the first day of the week was the day already known and selected for those forms of worship which were rather weekly than diurnal.

JOHN OBSERVES THE FIRST DAY IN PATMOS.—But we return from this digression to the New Testament allusions to the observance of the Lord's day. Only one other remains to be cited: that in Rev. i: 10. John the Apostle introduces the visions of Patmos, by saying, "I was in the spirit on the Lord's day." This is the only instance of the application of this title to the first day of the week in the sacred writings. But all expositors, ancient and modern, say unhesitatingly that Sunday is designated by it. On this point the Church has had but one understanding, from the first century down. The Apostle evidently means to inform us that on Sunday he was engaged in a spiritual frame of mind and feelings. The application of the name, Lord's day, to Sunday, by inspired authority, of itself contains almost enough of significance to establish its claims to sanctification, without another text or example. What fair sense can it bear, except that it is a day consecrated to the Lord? Compare Isaiah lviii: 13, when God calls the Sabbath, "my holy-day." If the Sabbath is *God's day*, the *Lord's day* should mean a Christian Sabbath. And the occupation of the Apostle this day, with peculiar spiritual exercises, gives additional probability to the belief that it was observed by the New Testament Christians as a day of devotion.

TRADITION OF LORD'S DAY.—We come now to the second branch of the historical argument—the testimony of the early, but uninspired Christian writers. The earliest of all cannot be called Christian. In the celebrated letter of inquiry written by Pliny the younger to the Emperor Trajan, for advice on the treatment of persons accused of Christianity, this pagan governor says, that it was the custom of these Christians, "to meet, *stato die*, before light, to sing a hymn to Christ as God, and bind each other in an oath (not to some crime) but to refrain from theft, robbery and adultery, not to break faith, and not to betray trusts." This letter was written a few years after the death of the

Apostle John. We cannot doubt that this *stated day*, discovered by Pliny, was the Lord's day. Ignatius, the celebrated martyr-bishop of Antioch, says, in his epistle to the Magnesians, written about A. D. 107 or 116, that this is "the Lord's day, the day consecrated to the resurrection, the queen and chief of all the days."

Justin Martyr, who died about A. D. 160, says that the Christians "neither celebrated the Jewish festivals, nor observed their Sabbaths, nor practised circumcision. (Dialogue with Trypho, p. 34.) In another place, he says that "they, both those who lived in the city and those who lived in the country, were all accustomed to meet on the day which is denominated Sunday, for the reading of the Scriptures, prayer, exhortation and communion. The assembly met on Sunday, because this is the first day on which God having changed the darkness and the elements, created the world; and because Jesus our Lord on this day rose from the dead."

The Epistle attributed to Barnabas, though not written by this apostolic man, is undoubtedly of early origin. This unknown writer introduces the Lord, as saying: "The Sabbaths which you now keep are not acceptable to me: but those which I have made when resting from all things, I shall begin the eighth day, that is the beginning of the other world." "For which cause, we (Christians) observe the eighth day with gladness, in which Jesus rose from the dead," &c. Eph. ch. xv.

Tertullian, at the close of the second century, says: "We celebrate Sunday as a joyful day. On the Lord's day we think it wrong to *fast*, or to *kneel* in prayer."

Clement of Alexandria, cotemporary with Tertullian, says: "A true Christian, according to the commands of the Gospel, observes the Lord's day by casting out all bad thoughts, and cherishing all goodness, honouring the resurrection of the Lord, which took place on that day."

But, perhaps, the most important, because the most learned, and, at the same time, the most explicit witness, is Eusebius, the celebrated bishop of Cæsarea, who was in his literary prime about the era of the Council of Nice, A. D. 325. In his Commentary on the xcii Psalm, which the reader will remember, is entitled "a psalm or song for the Sabbath-day," he says: "The Word, (Christ), by the new covenant, translated and transferred the feast of the Sabbath to the morning light, and gave us the symbol of true rest, the saving Lord's day, the first (day) of light, in which the Saviour gained the victory over death, &c. On this day, which is the first of the Light, and the true Sun, we assemble after the interval of six days, and celebrate holy and spiritual Sabbath; even all nations redeemed by Him throughout the world assemble, and do those things according to the spiritual law, which were decreed for the priests to do on the Sabbath. All things which it was duty to do on the Sabbath, these we have transferred to the Lord's day as more appropriately belonging to it, because it has the precedence, and is first in rank, and more honorable than the Jewish Sabbath. It is delivered to us (TARADEDOTIA) that we should meet together on this day, and it is evidence that we should do these things announced in this psalm."

The first Church council which formally enjoined cessation of labour upon the Lord's day was the provincial synod of Laodicea, held a little after the middle of the fourth century. The twenty-ninth canon of this body commanded that none but necessary secular labours should be carried on upon Sunday. But Constantine the Great, when he adopted the Christian as the religion of the State, had already enacted that all the labours of courts of justice, civil and military functionaries, and handicraft trades, should be suspended on the Lord's day, and that it should be devoted to prayer and public worship. This suspension of labour was not, however, extended to agriculturists, because it was supposed that they must needs avail themselves of the propitious season to gather their harvests, or sow their seed, without regard to sacred days. But the Emperor Leo (who came to the throne A. D. 457) ultimately extended the law to all classes of persons.

Christian Nomenclature.—The Christians did not for several hundred years apply the word *Sabbath* to the first day of the week, but always used it distinctly to indicate the Jewish seventh day. Their own sacred day, the first day, was called by them the Lord's day (hemera kuriake), as they said, because it was dedicated to the honour of Christ, and because it was the head, crown, and chief of all the days. They also called it *Sunday* (*Dies solis*, a phrase frequently found among the Latin Christians), because, according to their interpretation of Gen. i: 3, the sun was created on the first day of the week; but still more, because on that day the brighter *Sun of Righteousness* arose from the dead, with healing in His beams. The objection often made by persons over puritanical, that it smacks of Pagan or Scandinavian profanity to say *Sunday*, because the word indicates a heathenish consecration of the day to the sun, is therefore more Quakerish than sensible. We are willing to confess that we always loved the good old name Sunday—name worthy of that day which should ever seem the brightest in the Christian's conceptions, of all the week, when the glorious works of the natural creation first began to display the honours of the great Creator, and when that new and more divine creation of redeeming grace was perfected by the resurrection of Jesus Christ. But, in the application of the phrase "Christian Sabbath" to the first day, the Westminster Assembly had a definite and truthful design, although the early Church had not given it this name. It was their intention to express thus that vital head of their theory; that the Old Testament institute called Sabbath, which was coeval with man, and was destined to coexist with all dispensations, was not abrogated; that it still existed substantially, and that Christians were now to find it in the Lord's day. *To the Christian the Lord's day is the Sabbath.* (Such is the significance of the name) possessing the Divine authority, and demanding in the main the sanctification which was formerly attached to the seventh day.

4. Practical Argument.—Another most interesting and practical head of the Sabbath argument remains: from its practical necessity, as a means of securing man's corporeal and mental health, his morality, his temporal success in life, and his religious interests. This is the department of the discussion which has been more particularly unfolded in the "Permanent Sabbath Documents," published under the auspices of Dr. Justin Edwards, and more recently in the remarkable essays on the Sabbath, produced by workingmen in Great Britain. It is now by so much the best understood part of the Sabbath discussion that we should not have introduced it at all except that it was one of the stones in the arch of our attempted demonstration, that there is a

natural necessity in man for a Sabbath rest. The Creator, who appointed the Sabbath, formed man's frame; and all intelligent observers are now agreed that the latter was adapted to the former. Either body or mind can do more work by resting one day in seven, than by labouring all the seven days. And neither mind nor body can enjoy health and continued activity without its appointed rest. Even the structure of the brutes exhibits the same law. Again: As a moral and social institution, a weekly rest is invaluable. It is a quiet domestic reunion for the bustling sons of toil. It ensures the necessary vacation in those earthly and turbulent anxieties and affections, which would otherwise become inordinate and morbid. It brings around a season of periodical neatness and decency, when the soil of weekly labour is laid aside, and men meet each other amidst the decencies of the sanctuary, and renew their social affections. But above all, a Sabbath is necessary for man's moral and religious interests. Even in Paradise, and in man's state of innocence, it was true that a stated season, resolutely appropriated to religious exercises, was necessary to his welfare as a religious being. A creature subject to the law of habit, of finite faculties, and required by the conditions of his existence to distribute his attention and labours between things secular and things sacred, cannot successfully accomplish this destiny without a regular distribution of his time between the two great departments. This is literally a physical necessity. And when we add the consideration that man is now a being of depraved, earthly affections, prone to avert his eyes from heaven to the earth, the necessity is still more obvious. Man does nothing regularly for which he has not a regular time. The absolute necessity of the Sabbath, as a season for the public preaching of religion and morality, as a leisure time for the domestic religious instruction of the young, as a time for private self-examination and devotion, is most clear to all who admit the importance of these duties. And now, it is most obvious to practical good sense, that if such a stated season is necessary, then it is proper that it should be ordained and marked off by Divine authority, and not by a sort of convention on man's part. To neglect the stated observance of a religious rest, is to neglect religion. And when there is so much of mundane and carnal affection—so much of craving, eager worldly bustle—to entice us to an infringement of this sacred rest, it is certain that it will be neglected unless it be defended by the highest sanction of God's own authority. Nay, do we not see that this sanction is insufficient, even among some who admit its validity? Again: If such a stated rest is necessary, then it is also necessary that its metes and bounds be defined by the same authority which enjoins the rest itself. Otherwise, the license which men will allow themselves in interpreting the duration of the season, and in deciding how much constitutes the observance of it, or how little, will effectually abrogate the rest itself. If, then, the necessities of human nature require a Sabbath, it does not appear how God could ordain less than we suppose he has done, in requiring the whole of a definite length of time to be faithfully devoted to religious exercises, and in making this command explicit and absolute.

LECTURE XXXI.

SYLLABUS.

SECOND TABLE—(Fifth and Sixth Commandments).

1. What is the general scope of the Fifth Commandment?
2. Show that under the words, Father and Mother, all superiors in family, Church, and State, are included.
3. What is the meaning of the promise attached?
4. What is required and forbidden in the Sixth Commandment?
5. Does it prohibit the slaying of animals for food?
6. Does it prohibit defensive war, or personal self-defence?
7. Are capital punishments righteous?
8. Is Duelling murder?

Shorter Catechism, que. 63-69. Larger Catechism, que. 123-136.
Calvin Inst., Bk. II, Ch. 8, § 35-40.
Turrettin, Loc. XI, que. 16 and 17.
Green's Lectures, 46 to 50.
Ridgeley's Divinity, que. 123-136.

We enter now upon the consideration of the Second Table. The immediate objects of the duties of this Table are our fellow-men. But still the breach of one of them is a sin against God also, because it is He who has enjoined them, and has placed us in those relations in which the duties arise.

I. Scope of Fifth Commandment. Parents represent all Superiors.—As the first Table began with that which is fundamental to all religion, the pointing out of the only proper Object of religious service; so the second Table begins with that duty which is fundamental to all social duties, and the most important of all; subjection to domestic authority. I must here again remind you of the rule of interpretation laid down at the outset that a whole class of duties is enjoined, and of sins forbidden, under one prominent specimen. So, we understand that here, under the example of filial duties, all the relative duties between superiors and inferiors, in the family, the church, and the commonwealth, are included. Not only the duties of children to parents, but of servants to masters, pupils to teachers, and people to rulers in Church and State, are here implied. If these, most important classes of social duties are not intended to be included in this precept, then they are nowhere in the decalogue: for there is no other precept where they can be fairly embraced. Can we believe that the summary so often omits what the subsequent Scriptures so often enforce in detail? The including of all these duties under the Fifth Commandment will seem far more natural, if we remember that the original forms of government in the old world were all patriarchal; in which the Father was the head, priest, and prince of all his descendants and servants. The family was no doubt the germ out of which civil institutions and the organized Church grew. The Jewish nation was just now passing, in part, out of this patriarchal form; and many of its features were retained in the Mosaic government. How natural then, to an ancient Israelite, to represent the general idea of civil and ecclesiastical superiors under the term Parents? Servants (who were usually slaves) were on much the same footing in ancient society with children. Kings were called Fathers, 1 Saml. xxiv: 11. Prophets were generally addressed as Fathers, by the young men entrusted to their religious instruction, who, in turn, were called "sons of the prophets," 11 Kings ii: 3 and 13.

OBLIGATIONS ARE RECIPROCAL.—Many duties are of a reciprocal nature. Obligation on one side implies a correlative obligation on the other. Thus, the duties of inferiors imply the reciprocal duties of superiors. Under this Commandment then, are included the duties of parents towards their children, masters towards servants, rulers towards subjects, church-teachers towards their charges. Thus, we find that St. Paul, in the former part of the sixth chapter of Ephesians, (which may fairly be taken as his exposition of the Fifth Commandment), begins with the duties of children towards parents, but follows it up immediately with the duties of parents towards their children; and after instructing servants, proceeds immediately to instruct their masters. We feel therefore fully justified in giving the Fifth Commandment the general scope assigned to it in the Catechism. "The general scope of the Fifth Commandment is the performance of those duties which we *mutually owe* in our several relations, as superiors, inferiors, or equals."

II. It is under this head of the decalogue, that the important Scripture doctrine of the authority of the civil magistrate, and duty of citizens, should fall, which is the subject of the 23d chapter of our Confession. But this is a subject of so much importance, that I reserve it for separate discussion in the Senior course. The details of the other duties of inferiors and superiors may be seen so fully stated in your catechisms, that it would be mere repetition to recite them here.

III. EXTENT OF THE PROMISE.—The fifth commandment is peculiar in closing with a promise to encourage to its observance, "That thy days may be long upon the land which the Lord thy God giveth thee." As a long life spent in adversity would be no boon, this promise is obviously understood as one of "long life and prosperity." We understand it to give us that encouragement which is also presented by the established connexion of causes and effects in God's providence, where the faithful and general performance of the duties of inferiors and superiors, and especially of parents and children, ensures, as far as any earthly means can, general health, peace, prosperity and temporal welfare; whereas the anarchical neglect of those duties, and especially of the parental and filial, plunges every society into violence, disease, disorder, misery, and premature death. We do not understand God's promise in this commandment as absolute and universal. To claim this would be to claim that God should work for dutiful sons a continual miracle, in suspending the mutual influences of men on each other's welfare, by which the virtuous, especially when few, share the calamities procured by the more prevalent crimes of the wicked. The promise is given to a society (as to Israel) in the aggregate. The general performance of the duty is necessary to ensure the happy result. If there is a general neglect of the duties, as in our day, it must result in calamities; and some of the most dutiful of our sons may fall, as many a virtuous Confederate soldier fell, in the prime of his days, in the general disorder.

IV. SCOPE OF SIXTH COMMANDMENT.—The sixth commandment is in these terse words: "Thou shalt not kill." Its obvious scope is the *preservation of life*. It forbids all that unrighteously assails our own and others' lives, and enjoins all suitable means for the preservation of both. This command is based upon these two great truths: that life is God's gift, and therefore to be abridged or taken away only at His command; and that life is the supreme value to every man. In robbing a man of life, you would virtually rob him of every valuable thing which life includes. We have here, then, another instance of the profoundly logical arrangement which infinite wisdom has given to the decalogue. The second table, after fixing those relative duties out of which society itself emerges, then proceeds to protect, first, that value which is transcendent with every man—his temporal existence. It then secures that which is next in order of essential importance—man's chastity, including the purity of the marital relation, the foundation of the domestic; and postpones to the last those duties of commutative righteousness, and of truth, which are the outer bonds of society.

V. Animal Life may be Taken.—But when God says, "Thou shalt not kill," what are the things whose slaying is thus inhibited? There is a small class of fanatics in Christian lands, larger in some Pagan ones, who answer, that we may kill *nothing that has animal life.* Hence the use of the flesh of quadrupeds, birds, and fishes, for food, is of course inhibited by them. This party is known in America as *Grahamites.* Their tendency is infidel; for the Bible speaks too plainly on this subject to be questioned by any devout believer. We read that God gave to Adam and his family only the vegetable world for food, assigning him the use of the animals as his servants. (Hence, the skins in which God clothed Adam and Eve after their fall must have come either from the religious sacrifices which He taught them to offer, the more probable surmise; or from beasts which died by the violence of their own kind, or by disease.) But after the flood, the fruitfulness of the earth having been probably impaired for all subsequent time, God expressly gave Noah and his family the privilege of eating the flesh of animals, only reserving the blood, with which they should "make atonement for their souls upon the altar." This permission is doubtless now valid. It was expressly continued to the Hebrews, in the distinction of the clean beasts. It is equally certain that it was not abrogated after Christ came; for we find him, even after His resurrection (Luke xxiv: 43; Jno. xxi: 9), eating the flesh of fishes, and encouraging His followers to do so.

Reason approves this. The sanctity of human life is placed, where inspiration places it (in Gen. ix: 6), in man's rational responsibility and immortality. The life of the beast, "whose spirit goeth downward," is no such inviolable boon to him. And while we admit that the duty of benevolence extends to the brutes, as does God's benevolence, we argue that the employment of animals for food has, on the whole, greatly promoted their animal well-being. For man thus has a sufficient motive for their careful nurture, whereas otherwise he would regard them as nuisances.

VI. Capital Punishments and Defensive War, &c., Not Forbidden.—Still another, and a larger class of fanatics, hold that there are no circumstances under which human life can be taken lawfully by man. Claiming the admission which we have made, that life is to man God's loan, they urge that no creature can under any circumstances assume authority to take it away from his fellow man. Hence it must follow that personal self-defence against unrighteous aggression, that the defensive wars of commonwealths, and the infliction of capital punishments upon the most enormous criminals even, are all unlawful. Here is the theory of the "non-resistance" and the "peace parties."

ARGUMENTS—MAGISTRATE SLAYS BY DELEGATED AUTHORITY.—I may make the same remark of these, that they are virtually *infidel* parties. If the authority of the Scriptures is admitted, their conclusions are obviously false. They are as obviously illogical. It is true that human life is God's loan to his creatures. No one may take it away without the authority of the Divine Giver. It is therefore simply a question of revealed testimony, whether God has, in any cases, deputized to man, or to society, the authority to take life. If he has, then it is *God's authority* which, in the appropriate case, takes away the boon; and the human agent is merely God's executioner. It is, then, simply a question of fact as to the Scriptural teachings.

SELF-DEFENCE LAWFUL.—If life is thus sacred, as God's boon, and is man's one possession of transcendent value, then to take it away without right is an enormous outrage. Suppose this outrage is obviously about to be perpetrated by an aggressor upon an innocent person. Suppose, also, that the protection of the law is absent, and cannot be successfully invoked? What shall the defendant do? Is it his duty to be passive and yield up his life; or to take the defensive, and protect it by force, even to the extent of taking the assailant's life if necessary? Human laws and conscience concur in the latter answer. Remember that the aggressor unrighteously creates the *dilemma*, making it necessary that at least one life must go. Whose had best go? Obviously the life of the criminal, rather than that of the innocent man. Again: If law subsequently has its just course, the murderer, after his guilty success, will have to die for it. The case is then still stronger: that the passive theory sacrifices two lives, one innocent; whereas the theory of self-defence saves the righteous life, and only sacrifices the guilty one. Our conclusion is also confirmed by the existence in us of the emotion of lawful resentment, the righteousness of which, within its proper bounds, the Saviour allows (Matt. v: 22; Eph. iv: 26). For if there is no forcible self-defence against wrong, there is no reasonable scope for this emotion.

The Scriptures expressly confirm us. The right of slaying the house-breaker clearly implies a right of self-defence. Exod. xxii: 2. The law of the cities of refuge contains the same right. Numb. xxxv: 22. The effect of this permission is evaded, indeed, by the pretence that Moses' legislation was imperfect and barbarous, and is corrected by the milder instructions of our Saviour. Matt. v: 39. But I have taught you the falsehood of this notion, and showed you that the Old Testament teaches precisely the same morality with the New.

CAPITAL PUNISHMENT IN SCRIPTURE.—As to the delegation of the right of capital punishment for flagrant crimes, the feeble attempt has been made to represent the injunction of Gen. ix: 6 as not a precept, but a prediction; not as God's instruction what *ought* to be done to the murderer, but His prophecy of what human vindictiveness would do. The context refutes this. Look also at the express *injunction* of capital punishments for several crimes in the Pentateuch: for murder, Num. xxxv: 31; for striking a parent, Exod. xxi: 15; for adultery, Levit. xx:

10; for religious imposture, Deut. xiii: 5, &c. In Numb. xxxv: 33, a reason is given which, on general principles, necessitates the capital punishment of murder: "For blood, it defileth a land, and the land cannot be cleansed of the blood that is shed therein, but by the blood of him that shed it. Capital punishments are also authorized in the New Testament. Rom. xiii assures us that the magistrate "beareth not the sword in vain," but in bearing it he is God's minister to execute wrath upon the evil-doer.

VII. Defensive War Lawful.—Unprovoked war is the most monstrous secular crime that can be committed: it is at once the greatest of evils, and includes the worst forms of robbery and murder. Wherever war is prompted by mere pique, or lust of aggrandisement, or ambition for fame and power, it deserves all that can be said of its mischiefs and criminality by the most zealous advocates of peace. And nothing can rescue a people waging war, from this guilt, except the fact that their appeal to arms is nesessary for the defence of just and vital rights. But while the Scriptures teach this, they give no countenance to the weak fanaticism, which commands governments to practice a passive non-resistance, in such a world as this. Nations are usually unjust and unscrupulous. The very fact that they are politically sovereign implies that there is no umpire between them, except Divine Providence. A passive attitude would usually only provoke, instead of disarming attack. Hence its only effect would be to bring all the horrors and desolations of invasion upon the innocent people, while the guilty went free. God has therefore both permitted and instructed rulers, when thus unjustly assailed, to retort these miseries upon the assailants who introduce them. The very fact that all war is so terrific a scourge, and that aggressive war is such an enormous crime, only makes it more clear that the injured party are entitled to their redress, and are justified in inflicting on the injurers such chastisement as will compel their return to justice, even including the death and ruin which they were preparing against their inoffensive neighbors.

It is perfectly clear that Sacred Scripture legalizes such defensive war. Abram, Moses, Joshua, Samuel, David, Josiah, the Maccabees, were such warriors: and they were God's chosen saints. It was "*through faith* they waxed valiant in fight, turned to flight the armies of the aliens." Heb. xi: 34. God fought for and with them by giving, in their battles, answers to their prayers, and miraculous assistance to their arms. Under the New Testnment, when Christ's forerunner was preaching the baptism of repentance, he did not enjoin on soldiers the surrender of their profession as sinful, but only the restricting of themselves to its lawful duties. The New Testament tells us of a Centurion, affectionately commended by our Redeemer as possessed of "great faith;" and of a Cornelius, who was "accepted with God, as fearing Him and working righteousness." Luke iii: 14; vii: 9; Acts x: 35. The Apostle Paul, Rom. xiii: 4, tells us that the magistrate "beareth not the sword in vain; for he is the minister of God, a revenger to execute wrath upon him that doeth evil." It would be strange indeed, if the ruler who is armed by God with the power of capital punishment against the domestic murderer, could not justly inflict the same doom on the foreign criminal, who invades our soil unprovoked, for the purpose of shedding blood. The security of life and property which the magistrate is intended to provide by his power of punishing, would be illusory indeed, if it could only be used against individual criminals, while the more mischievous and widespread crimes of organized multitudes must go unpunished. Aggressive war is wholesale murder; and when the government sends out its army to repel and chastise the invader, it does but inflict summary execution on the murderer caught in the act.

VIII. Duelling Murder.—The modern duel is a very peculiar usage, which has descended to us from a perversion of an institution of chivalry; the ordeal by battle. This was a means adopted by the ignorance of the middle ages, to appeal to God's judgment where the question of right was too obscure to be unravelled by their rude courts. It was founded on an abuse of the doctrine of Providence. Because the Scriptures teach that this providence is concerned in all events, the Middle Ages jumped to the conclusion, that this providence would so decide the issue, as to vindicate justice. It needs no argument to show you the fallacy. Since the intelligence of modern days has exploded the idea of the divine ordeal, the duel remains, a barbarous remnant of the middle ages, without even the shadow of an argument in its favor.

Arguments for it Futile.—In refuting the arguments by which the duel is defended, I shall not take the ground that the sentiment of personal honour is irrational or unchristian: I shall not assume that it is no real injury to wound it. My position is, that the duel is no proper remedy for that injury. And, first; the only lawful object, when one is wounded in his honour, is self-defence, and not revenge. The latter is expressly forbidden in every case. Now, for the defence of one's honour and good name, a duel is naught. Perhaps where malignant passions are not harboured, the challenger to a duel is most frequently actuated by this feeling; that his passive endurance of an insult will cause his fellow-men to think him a coward; and that therefore he must expose himself to the dangers of combat, in order to evince that he is not a coward; and thus retrieve his credit. Now duelling does not prove courage; for notoriously, if some brave men have fought so have many cowards. It only proves a species of moral cowardice, which shrinks from the path of rectitude, and cowers before the finger of scorn. It is yet more obvious that the issue of the duel will prove nothing as to the truth or falsehood of the charge which constituted the insult. If one calls me a liar, and I kill him therefor, this shows nothing whatever as to my truth or falsehood. The proper and reasonable remedy here, is to require the accuser to substantiate his charge, or else confess its injustice. His refusal to do either would place him so effectually in the wrong, that no other reparation would be needed.

Duels Unfair.—Another objection to the duel is, that it usually prevents, and that in the most deadly manner, that very fairness and equality which it boasts of securing. The plea is, that it puts the weak man equal to the strong one, by appealing from mere, brute muscle, to arms and skill. But according to its laws, the duel authorizes an inequality of skill far more deadly. I am ignorant of the use of the pistol. A violent and malignant man who knows himself a dead shot, so outrages me, that I am impelled under the code of honour, to challenge him. He, exercising the right of the challenged, chooses pistols. Thus he has me more completely at a disadvantage than if he were a pugilist of the first fame, and I an infant; and the result is not a parcel of bruises, but my death. The system is, when tried by its own pretences, flagrantly unfair.

Jeopardizing of the Injured Unjust.—It is also absurdly unequal in this: that if its proceedings have any justice, then it puts the righteous man and the culprit on the same footing. Unless the challenger is committing a monstrous wrong, he must hold that the challenged is a capital criminal: For does he not claim that it is right to subject him to the liability of a capital punishment? Why then should the innocent man, already so grievously wronged, when he proceeds to inflict the righteous penalty, give the culprit equal chances to inflict the same penalty on him? Shall the magistrate, in putting a condemned felon to death, courteously invite him to take his equal chances to put the magistrate to death? What more absurd? If the assailant really deserves to die, and this is duly ascertained (if it is not the challenger is guilty of murder in seeking to slay an innocent man) then by all means, let him be killed, without giving him opportunity to perpetrate another unprovoked crime. When one has to kill a mad dog, he does not feel bound to give the dog a chance to bite him!

The interested made Judge, &c.—Last, the duelling code is a monstrous one, because it makes the man who supposes himself wronged, accuser, judge, and executioner in his own cause. It is righteously then, that the statute laws of the Commonwealth treat the duellist who has slain his adversary, as a murderer with prepense malice.

Pleas Refuted.—One plea for duelling is, that it is the necessary chastisement for classes of sins, (as against one's good name, against the chastity of one's family) for which the laws afford either no remedy, or such a one as no man of delicacy can seek. The answer is: that if the facts are true, they are arguments for perfecting the penal laws, not for the iniquities of duelling. Another argument is, that nothing but the code of honour will secure chivalrous manners; which it boasts of doing through the influence of the knowledge that the man who departs from that style of manners is in danger of a challenge. The answers are two. Surely that courtesy has little claim to be chivalrous, which is only coerced by fear! And facts show that the influence of the code is not what is claimed; for the societies where it has fullest sway, are always the rudest and most debauched.

LECTURE XXXI.

SYLLABUS.

SECOND TABLE—(Seventh and Eighth Commandments.)

1. What is the scope and extent of the Seventh Commandment, and what sins are forbidden under it?
2. What the degree of guilt in adultery; and what its grounds?
3. Was polygamy ever lawful? Explain Moses' Law of Divorce.
4. Ought the duties of this Commandment to be now publicly preached?
5. What is the scope of the Eighth Commandment? And what the particular duties and sins embraced under it?
6. What is the origin of the right of private property?
7. Is usury lawful?
8. What rule should govern the Christian as to taking advantage of gain from the necessities of his neighbour?

See on the Whole.
Larger Catechism, que. 137 to 142.
Turrettin, Loc. XI, que. 18th and 19th.
Calvin's Inst., Bk. II, ch. 8, § 41-46.
Ridgeley's Divinity, que. 137-142.
Green's Lect, on Shorter Catechism, 51 to 53.

I. Scope of Seventh Commandment.—As has been already observed, the scope of the Seventh Commandment is to regulate the relations between the sexes, with all the virtues of purity connected therewith. These virtues are the basis of the domestic relations. And as the family is the foundation of human society, the importance of the class of duties involved is second only to those which preserve man's existence itself. It should be added also, that the sins against personal purity are peculiarly flagrant, because they involve in sensual bestiality the body which is the habitation of the rational, responsible soul, and the temple of the Holy Ghost. See 1 Cor. vi: 15, &c. Experience also shows that sins of unchastity have a peculiarly imbruting and degrading effect on both sexes, but especially on that which should be the purer, seducing them to hypocrisy, lying, treachery, cruelty, drunkenness, gluttony, and shamelessness. For the usual details of the sins embraced under the capital instance, *adultery*, I refer you to your catechisms.

II. Criminality of Adultery.—Adultery, in strictness of speech, is the sin of illicit cohabitation by a married person. Its eminence in criminality is due to these traits; that in addition to the uncleanness, it involves the breach of the marriage contract, and the treachery contained therein; and that by corrupting the descent of families, it uproots the whole foundation of domestic society. The marriage of one man to one woman is the foundation of society. Adultery and causeless divorce are directly antagonistic thereto. They are therefore deadly stabs against all home affections, against all training of children, against every rudiment of social order. Were all to take the license of the adulterer, men would in due time be reduced precisely to the degradation of wild beasts. The sin of the adulterer therefore, is scarcely less enormous than that of the murderer. The latter destroys man's temporal existence; the former destroys all that makes existence a boon. Let the crime of the adulterer be tried by its effects upon the family it invades. We must either suppose that the husband and wife have, or have not, the sentiments of modesty, natural jealousy, purity, and shame, usually imputed to virtuous persons. If they have not, then the lack of them implies a degradation which can only make them the parents of reprobates; and the general prevalence of such a type of character would dissolve domestic society into ultimate putrescence. If the parents have those sentiments, then the success of the seducer plunges the husband into agonies of revenge, despair and wounded affection, the guilty wife into a shame and remorse deeper than the grave, the children into privation of a mother, and all the parties into a bereavement at least as irreparable as that of a death, and far more bitter. It would have been, in some aspects, a less crime to murder the mother while innocent.

Proper Punishment of it.—The laws of Moses, therefore, very properly made adultery a capital crime; nor does our Saviour, in the incident of the woman taken in adultery, repeal that statute, or disallow its justice. The legislation of modern, nominally Christian nations, is drawn rather from the grossness of Pagan sources than from Bible principles. The common law of England, and the statutes and usages which our Commonwealth has drawn thence, present a most inconsistent state. There is no statute whatever for punishing adultery as a crime! And yet a usage, which is as fully recognized both in England and in Virginia as any common law, entitles juries to acquit the injured husband of murder who slays the violator of his bed in heat of blood. This seems to be a recognition of the capital guilt of the crime of adultery, and at the same time an allowance, in this case, of the barbarous principle of 'goelism,' which the law, in all other cases, has so stringently prohibited. But here is the monstrous inconsistency, that if the crime of the adulterer be of long standing, and gradually discovered, no matter how certain the guilt, the husband, because no longer punishing in heat of blood, is debarred from inflicting the just punishment. The only other remedy that remains at the law is an action of damages against the seducer, in which the injured husband is constrained to degrade all his wrongs to the sordid pecuniary plea of the loss of his wife's *services*, as a domestic, by this interference. And juries are instructed, after ascertaining that there has been an unjust interruption of the wife's domestic services, to appraise the compensation, not at its commercial, but at any imaginary value, which the seducer's wealth may enable him to pay. Such is the wretched fiction which the law offers to the outraged spouse as the satisfaction for his wrongs.

III. Divorce and Polygamy in Pentateuch.—It has always seemed to me that much causeless doubt and debate exist among expositors, and that many gratuitous admissions have been made by the most of them, touching the true status of polygamy and divorce in the Old Testament. But so much misapprehension exists about the two cases, that the general interests of truth prompt a little farther separate discussion ot each. The two enactments touching divorce which present the supposed contradiction in the strongest form, are those of Moses in Deut. xxiv: 1 to 4, and Matt. xix: 3 to 9. These the reader is requested to have under his eye. The form of the Pharisees' question to Christ, "Is it lawful for a man to put away his wife *for every cause?*"

concurs with the testimony of Josephus, in teaching us that a monstrous perversion of Moses' statute then prevailed. The licentious, and yet self-righteous Pharisee claimed, as one of his most unquestioned privileges, the right to repudiate a wife, after the lapse of years, and birth of children, for any caprice whatsoever. The trap which they now laid for Christ was designed to compel him either to incur the *odium* of attacking this usage, guarded by a jealous anger, or to connive at their interpretation of the statute. Manifestly Christ does not concede that they interpreted Moses rightly; but indignantly clears the legislation of that holy man from their licentious perversions, and then, because of their abuse of it, repeals it by His plenary authority. He refers to that constitution of the marriage tie which was original, which preceded Moses, and was therefore binding when Moses wrote, to show that it was impossible he could have enacted what they claimed. What, then, did Moses enact? Let us explain it. In the ancient society of the East, females being reared in comparative seclusion, and marriages negotiated by intermediaries, the bridegroom had little opportunity for a familiar acquaintance even with the person of the bride. When she was brought to him at the nuptials, if he found her disfigured with some personal deformity or disease (the undoubted meaning of the phrase "some uncleanness"), which effectually changed desire into disgust, he was likely to regard himself as swindled in the treaty, and to send the rejected bride back with indignity to her father's house. There she was reluctantly received, and in the anomalous position of one in name a wife, yet without a husband, she dragged out a wretched existence, incapable of marriage, and regarded by her parents and brothers as a disgraceful incumbrance. It was to relieve the wretched fate of such a woman that Moses' law was framed. She was empowered to exact of her proposed husband a formal annulment of the unconsummated contract, and to resume the *status* of a single woman, eligible for another marriage. It is plain that Moses' law contemplates the case, only, in which no consummation of marriage takes place. She finds *no favour* in the eyes "of the bridegroom." He is so indignant and disgusted that desire is put to flight by repugnance. The same fact appears from the condition of the law, that she shall in no case return to this man, "after she is defiled," i. e., after actual cohabitation with another man had made her unapproachable (without moral defilement) by the first. Such was the narrow extent of this law. The act for which it provided was divorce only in name, where that *consensus, qui matrimonium facit*, in the words of the law maxim, had never been perfected. The state of social usages among the Hebrews, with parental and fraternal severity towards the unfortunate daughter and sister, rendered the legislation of Moses necessary and righteous at the time; but "a greater than Moses" was now here; and he, after defending the inspired law-giver from their vile misrepresentation, proceeded to repeal the law, because it had been so perverted, and because the social changes of the age had removed its righteous grounds.

The case of the polygamist is still clearer; for we assert that the whole legislation of the Pentateuch and of all the Old Testament is only adverse to polygamy. As some Christian divines have taught otherwise, we must ask the reader's attention and patience for a brief statement. Polygamy is recorded of Abraham, Jacob, Gideon, Elkanah,

David, Solomon; but so are other sins of several of these; and, as every intelligent reader knows, the truthful narrative of holy writ as often discloses the sins of good men for our warning, as their virtues for our imitation. And he who notes how, in every Bible instance, polygamy appears as the cause of domestic feuds, sin, and disaster, will have little doubt that the Holy Spirit tacitly holds all these cases up for our caution, and not our approval. But, then, God made Adam one wife only, and taught him the great law of the perpetual unity of the twain, just as it is now expounded by Jesus Christ. (Genesis ii: 23, 24, with Matthew xix: 4 to 6.) God preserved but one wife each to Noah and his sons. In every statute and preceptive word of the Holy Spirit, it is always *wife*, and not *wives*. The prophets everywhere teach how to treat a *wife*, and not *wives*. Moses, Leviticus xviii: 18, in the code regulating marriage, expressly prohibits the marriage of a second wife in the life of the first, thus enjoining monogamy in terms as clear as Christ's. Our English version hath it: "Neither shalt thou take a wife to her sister, to vex her, to uncover her nakedness, besides the other, in her lifetime." Some have been preposterous enough to take the word *sister* here in its literal sense, and thus to force on the law the meaning that the man desiring to practice polygamy may do so provided he does not marry two daughters of the same parents; for if he did this, the two sisters sharing his bed would, like Rachel and Leah, quarrel more fiercely than two strangers. But the word "*sister*" must undoubtedly be taken in the sense of *mates, fellows*, (which it bears in a multitude of places), and this for two controlling reasons. The other sense makes Moses talk nonsense and folly, in the supposed reason for his prohibition; in that it makes him argue that two sisters sharing one man's bed will quarrel, but two women having no kindred blood will not. It is false to fact and to nature. Did Leah and Rachel show more jealousy than Sarah and Hagar, Hannah and Peninnah? But when we understand the law in its obvious sense, that the husband shall not divide his bed with a second mate, the first still living, because such a wrong ever harrows and outrages the great instincts placed in woman's heart by her Creator, we make Moses talk truth and logick worthy of a profound legislator. The other reason for this construction is, that the other sense places the 18th verse in irreconcilable contradiction to the 16th verse. This forbids the marriage of a woman to the husband of her deceased sister; while the 18th verse, with this false reading, would authorize it.

Once more: Malachi (chap. ii: 14, 15), rebuking the various corruptions of the Jews, evidently includes polygamy; for he argues in favour of monogamy (and also against causeless divorce) from the fact that God, "who had the residue of the Spirit," and could as easily have created a thousand women for each man as a single one, made the numbers of the sexes equal from the beginning. He states this as the motive, "that He might seek a godly seed;" that is to say, that the object of God in the marriage relation was the right rearing of children, which polygamy notoriously hinders. Now the commission of an Old Testament prophet was not to legislate a new dispensation, for the laws of Moses were in full force: the prophets' business was to expound them. Hence, we infer that the laws of the Mosaic dispensation on the subject of polygamy had always been such as Malachi declared them. He was but applying Moses' principles.

To the assertion that the law of the Old Testament discountenanced polygamy as really as the New Testament, it has been objected that the practice was maintained by men too pious towards God to be capable of continuing in it against express precept; as, for instance, by the "king after God's own heart," David. Did not he also commit murder and and adultery? Surely there is no question whether Moses forbids these! The history of good men, alas! shows us too plainly the power of general evil example, custom, temptation, and self-love, in blinding the honest conscience. It has been objected that polygamy was so universally practised, and so prized, that Moses would never have dared to attempt its extinction. When will men learn that the author of the Old Testament law was not Moses, but God? Is God timid? Does He fear to deal firmly with His creatures? But it is denied that there is any evidence that polygamy was greatly prevalent among the Hebrews. And nothing is easier than to show that, if it had been, Moses was a legislator bold enough to grapple with it. What more hardy than his dealing with the sabbatical year, with idolatry? It is objected that the marriage of the widow who was childless to the brother of the deceased, to raise up seed to the dead, presents a case of polygamy actually commanded. We reply, no one can show that the next of kin was permitted or required to form such marriage when he already had a wife. The celebrated J. D. Michaelis, a witness learned and not too favourable, says, in his Commentaries on the Laws of Moses, of this law, "Nor did it affect a brother having already a wife of his own." Book III, ch. vi, § 98.

It is objected that polygamy is recognized as a permitted relation in Deut. xxi: 15–17, where the husband of a polygamous marriage is forbidden to transfer the birthright from the eldest son to a younger, the child of a more favoured wife; and in Exod. xxi: 9, 10, where the husband is forbidden to deprive a less favoured wife of her marital rights and maintenance. Both these cases are explained by the admitted principle, that there may be relations which it was sin to form, and which yet it is sinful to break when formed. No one doubts whether the New Testament makes polygamy unlawful; yet it seems very clear that the apostles gave the same instructions to the husbands of a plurality of wives entering the Christian Church. There appears, then, no evidence that polygamy was allowed in the laws of Moses.

Sins against Seventh Commandment to be Rebuked with Sanctity.—A supposed obligation of propriety and delicacy has usually kept our pulpits silent concerning the sins of unchastity; and hence, no doubt, in large part, the shocking callousness and unsoundness of public opinion concerning the sins of its breach. It is my opinion that *this omission should be corrected* by the pastors. When I say this, I would not by any means be understood as encouraging ministers to disregard any sentiment of delicacy or propriety which may exist. On the contrary, all such sentiments, where not positively false, are to be honoured by him; and he should be, in all his intercourse, the model of delicacy. But there is a guarded and holy way of discussing such subjects, which clearly reveals chastity, and not pruriency as its temper, and purity as its object. This is the style in which the pastor should speak on these difficult subjects.

V. Scope of Eighth Commandment.—In discussing the Eighth

Commandment, we proceed from the duties of chastity to those of commutative justice. The scope of the command is to protect the rights of property. Under the simple head of "stealing" it "forbids whatsoever doth or may unjustly hinder our own, or our neighbour's wealth and outward estate;" and "requireth the lawful procuring and furthering of the wealth of ourselves and others." This exposition implies that there is a sense in which a man may steal from himself. While there is a sense in which our property belongs to us, and not to our neighbour, and his to him, and not to us; yet we are all stewards of God, and in the higher sense, all property belongs to Him. Obviously then, God's property right may be as much outraged by our misuse of what is lawfully in our stewardship, as by interfering with another's trust. The forms in which the worldly estate of our neighbour may be wronged,are innumerable. The essence of theft is in the violation of the *golden Rule* as to our neighbor's property. The essence of stealing is the obtaining our neighbour's goods without his intentional consent and without fair market value returned. However it may be done, whenever we get from our neighbour *something for nothing*, without his consent, there is theft.

Special Sins and Duties under it.—This Commandment requires us, as to our own worldly estate, to practice such *industry* as will provide for ourselves and those dependent on us a decent subsistence—to eschew *idleness*, which is a species of robbery practiced on the common hive by the drone; to avoid *prodigality;* and to appropriate our own goods in due proportion to their proper uses. The Commandment, as it applies to our neighbour's wealth, forbids *robbery*, or forcible taking, theft, or taking by stealth, all *swindling* and getting of property by false pretences; *forestalling and regrating* in times of scarcity; *wastefulness*, tending to the greed for other's wealth. *extortion*, *embezzlement* of public wealth, *false measures and weights*, *contracting debts* beyond the known ability to pay, *eating usury*, *gambling*, *infidelity in working* for wages, or in the *quality* of things manufactured for sale, *availing onesself of legal adcantages* for evading obligations morally binding, &c., &c.

VI. Right of Possession Whence.—But what is the origin of the *moral right of possession?* The sense of *meum* and *tunim* is one of the earliest rational ideas developed, and continues to be one of the strongest. But its ethical origin has been much debated. Some have reasoned that in a state of nature, it arose out of *first possession*. But is not priority in finding and possessing a natural object, a mere accident? And if men are naturally equal in rights, as these persons always assume, can it be that a *mere accident* determines the moral right? Some, therefore, desert this theory, and suppose that the right of possession in a state of nature, arises out of the expenditure of some labour on the object possessed. This theory again, fails to account for many cases, where *no labour* is bestowed, and yet the right is perfect; and it is moreover, unreasonable. These futile surmises illustrate the folly and defect of a philosophy which insists on proceeding upon mere naturalistic grounds. These men leave out God, the most essential, and in a true sense, the most *natural* member of the theorem; and they assume a 'state of nature,' in which no creature ever rightfully existed. No wonder, therefore, that their solution is abortive. Now, the truth is, that there is but one source for a right of property, *creation out of nothing;* and consequently, but one natural proprietor, *God the Maker.* The only rational solution of the existence of a right of property in man is also the scriptural one, that contained in the second and ninth chapters of Genesis, God's gift of the world and its contents to man, as His tenant. Our individual interests in the gift are, then, based on the *golden Rule*, and properly regulated in detail by the laws of civil society.

VII. Usury, not Unlawful if Moderate.—The question whether all usury, or hire for the use of money is not unrighteous, was much debated by mediaeval moralists. The usual argument against it was, that money, coin, had in it no power of increase. A box of coin, said these Scholastics, is not like a measure of corn, capable of germination and increase; it is as barren, if left to itself, as the gravel of the Sahara. It is labour only (or nature) which multiplies values. Hence to exact hire for money is taking something for nothing—essential theft. And the legislation of Moses, which prohibited the taking of any usury from brother Hebrews, was misunderstood and then cited, to confirm their conclusion.

If their premises were true, their conclusion would be valid. Money is not, in fact, fruitless, and utterly devoid of a power of reproduction. It is a mere illusion to compare the box of coin to a box of barren gravel. For money is the *representative of values;* it is its *purchasing power*, and not its metallic constitution as simple matter, which makes it money. Now *values are reproductive.* Capital has a true power of increase. The multiplication of values is by the combination of capital and labour. If labour fecundates capital, it is equally true, that capital arms labour for success. Hence, it is just as fair that capital loaned should receive its just hire, as that labour should.

It is interesting to notice that the Bible never commits itself to any erroneous philosophy, no matter how current among men. The Hebrew laws, properly understood, do not condemn all usury as sinful. They permit taking reasonable usury from Gentiles, forbid it from their brethren. Nor was this permission as to Gentiles an expression of *hostility* towards them. The system of Moses harboured no such spirit; but taught the Hebrews to regard Gentiles (except the Amorites, &c.) as neighbours. On the contrary, the taking of a fair line for money lent, lawful and reasonable in itself, was only forbidden as to their Hebrew brethren, as one instance of that special fraternity, and mutual help, which God enjoined on them as pensioners upon his land. The case stands on the same footing with the prohibition to glean the fields, to beat the olive groves, or to take up the sheaf casually dropped from the road. These things were exacted, as special contributions to their more needy brethren. The law of the case may be seen in Exod. xxii: 25; Levit. xxv: 36, 37; Deut. xxiii: 19, 20; Nehem. v: 8, &c.; Matt. xxv: 27.

VIII. Buying and Selling under the Law of Charity.—When we take advantage of the urgent necessities of our neighbour, in buying or selling, we sin against both honesty and charity. If your neighbour is compelled by his wants to sell some commodity, for whatever he can get, that fact does not make that commodity worth less than the market price to *you* who buy it. If he is compelled to have some commodity instantly, whatever it may cost him, that fact does not make it worth *more* than the market price to you who *sell* it to him. If therefore, you take advantage of his necessity, to force him to sell you his goods for a less price than you yourself would give, if you could not take this advantage, you rob him of the difference. And it is fraud committed under peculiarly base circumstances. For his necessity, instead of arousing your cupidity, ought to excite compassion. Instead of taking advantage of his necessities, you should charitably aid in relieving them. Such measures are excused, I know, by saying that he makes the bargain voluntarily, or that his necessity makes the price which you give him, actually *worth* to him individually, in his circumstances, what he gave in exchange for it. To these heartless excuses there is one answer, which at a touch, exposes their worthlessness, "Do unto others as ye would have they should do unto you." How would you like to have *your* necessity thus abused? And yet, how many men are there who watch, like harpies, for these opportunities to make what they call a good bargain.

LECTURE XXXII.

SYLLABUS.

SECOND TABLE—(Ninth and Tenth Commandments).

1. What is the general scope of the Ninth Commandment, and what the duties required, and sins forbidden under it?
2. What is the ground of the duty of speaking truth, and how does its practical importance appear?
3. Define the sin of speaking evil of one's neighbour, and argue.
4. Is it ever lawful to deceive?
5. What is the scope and meaning of the Tenth Commandment, and what are the duties required, and sins forbidden under it?
6. What evidence of the divine mission of Moses, in the character of the Decalogue?
7. What doth every sin demand at the hands of God?

   See on whole, Larger Catechism, que. 143–152.
   Ridgeley's Divinity, que. 143–152.
   Turrettin, Loc. XI, que. 20 to 23, and 26.
   Green's Lectures, 54 to 58.
   Calvin Inst., Bk. II, Ch. 8, § 47–51.

I. Scope of Ninth Commandment.—We hold that the general scope of the Ninth Commandment is to enjoin the virtue of *Truth*. This precept "requireth the maintaining and promoting of truth between man and man, and of our own and our neighbour's good name, especially in witness-bearing." It "forbiddeth whatsoever is prejudicial to truth, or injurious to our own or our neighbour's good name."

II. Grounds of Duty of Veracity.—The duty of veracity is founded on the nature and importance of God's will enjoining truth. Truth may be said to be the using of signs by which we express or assert anything, conformably to our belief of the real state of the thing spoken of.

Only Real Communications Useful.—All the practical concerns of man's life are with the real state of things. Fictitious informations are, to us, naught, or worse than naught. They may fatally betray us into mistake; they cannot be the grounds of any beneficial or successful action. On the real state of the markets depends the merchant's profits. On the real power of the medicine depends the physician's success and the sick man's restoration. On the real nature of vegetable laws depends the reward of the farmer's toil. In every conceivable concern of man it is truth, the communication which is in accordance with reality, that is useful. Accordingly our Maker has endued us with a mental appetite of which truth is the natural food. The statement on which we cannot rely gives no pleasure. True, another faculty than the understanding, the fancy, finds its appropriate pleasure in fiction. But here also a tribute is paid to the truth; for in order that the fictitious may give any pleasure to the fancy, even, it must be *truth-like*.

Knowledge chiefly Derived.—Now veracity is the observance of truth in our communications. Its importance appears from the fact that almost all man knows is derived from communication. The whole value of the statements we receive is in their truth. If they are false they are naught, or worse than naught. The usefulness of communicated knowledge to us, depends, therefore, wholly on our confidence in its truth. Every lie helps to destroy that confidence. Just so far as we perceive lies prevail, so far the value of communicated knowledge to us is destroyed. Should we reach that state when no trust could be put in the veracity of any fellow-man, all such knowledge would, to us, virtually, cease to exist. But to what a state would this reduce us? We proudly call the brutes *dumb;* indicating that it is man's gift of speech mainly, which separates us from beasts. It is this which enables us to receive facts and ideas besides our own. The wise teach the ignorant. The skill of each generation does not die with it; but is communicated to the next. Knowledge is handed down, until our generation finds itself endowed with the accumulated experience of all previous ones. It is this which makes our civilization. But if all reliance upon communicated knowledge is destroyed, we are reduced to a state of savage ignorance, but little above that of the higher animals. We should know nothing but what we had ourselves seen and experienced; because we could trust nothing else. Education would be impossible; for how can knowledge be communicated when truth is banished? We must continue to exist in that infantile ignorance in which the child begins life, except so far as our own unaided efforts might instruct us, at the cost of suffering and perhaps of destruction. The advance which each individual made in such a condition, would wholly die with him; his son must begin life as he did, an ignorant savage, and run the same contracted round of puny, misdirected progress, and in his turn die, carrying all his knowledge to the grave with him. The latest generation would live in the same savage ignorance with the earliest. Religion would be as impossible as education; and all its blessings and consolations equally unknown; for religion cannot exist without trust. Each one of you would be an insulated, helpless, wretch, more completely deprived of society than the gregarious herds. He who deals in falsehood does what in him lies to bring his race to this degraded and miserable state. If all men should be false like him, and in all their communications, this state would be actually reached.

LIES DESTROY CONFIDENCE.—It may be shown in another light that the liar is the enemy of God and man by considering the effect of his vice on our mutual confidence. The intercourse of human business is but a countless series of implied engagements. Unless we can trust the fidelity of those whom we must employ, co-operation is at an end. If you cannot trust the postman who contracts to carry your letters, the conductor who guides the vehicle in which you ride, the pilot who steers your ship, the agent who transacts your business, the cook who engages to dress your food, you can neither write, nor ride, nor sail, nor eat, nor conduct any trade. Government would be at an end, because the ruler could not trust his agents and officers, and his power would be limited to his own presence. In short, if confidence is destroyed then all the bands which unite man with his fellow are loosed: each man must struggle on unaided by his fellows, as though he were the sole forlorn remnant of a perishing race. Confidence is as essential also, to all the social affections which shed happiness on the heart, as to the utilities of our outer life. It is the basis of friendship and love. To mistrust is to despise. To trust, to be trusted with unshaken faith, is the charm of domestic love.

FALSEHOOD UPTURNS AFFECTION.—Were there *no truth* then, every fellow-man would be your enemy; you would be insulated from your kind; every social affection would take its flight from the earth. Man would be reduced to a solitary miserable savage, "whose hand would be against every man and every man's hand against him." Even the animals must, in a certain sense, keep faith with each other, in order to make their gregariousness possible. Even savages must cultivate fidelity to truth within some narrow limits; or else the extermination of their scanty existence would speedily follow.

Indeed the conditions of savage society are sufficient illustrations of my conclusions: for when you examine into the causes of its barbarism, when you detect why savages are, compared with civilized states, few, poor, wretched, insecure and unfurnished with all the blessings which ameliorate life, you perceive that it is because falsehood and unrighteousness have made trust, mutual aid, and instruction almost impossible among them. They remain such, only because they cannot trust each other. *Savagery is simply sin;* and most notably, the sin of lying.

TRUTH IN ORDER TO ALL MORALITY.—Not only is veracity a virtue, but truth is, in a certain sense, the condition of all other virtues. Hence it is that in many places of the Bible truth is almost synonymous with righteousness. The "man that *doeth* truth" is the man that does his duty. The godly man is "he that speaketh the truth in his heart." To "execute the judgment of truth" is to execute righteous judgment. This language is profoundly accurate. The motive of every act which has moral quality must be a reasonable one; and truth, as we know, is the appointed light of the understanding. I mean that no man does a truly virtuous act unless he has an intelligent reason for doing it. But how can the mind see a reason unless it finds it in some truth? Consider, farther, that all the inducements to right actions are in the truth; but all the inducements to wrong acts are false. Error and sin are kindred evils, as truth and holiness are handmaid and mistress. Truth is the instrument by which the Holy Ghost sanctifies the soul. John xvii : 17. Thus we find its most exalted value in this, that it is the means of redemption for a ruined world. It is as beneficent as falsehood is mischievous. The one is our guide to heaven; the other leads to hell.

There is a world just such as the liar would make this: where falsehood reigns and where confidence is unknown. There, in its fiery lake, all liars have their part. The ruler of this world is he who "was a liar from the beginning and the Father of it." There to deceive and be deceived is the universal rule, and therefore mistrust sits brooding over every heart, and scowls in every look. Each one beholds in every other an object of fear and scorn, and feels an equal scorn for himself, because he knows himself as false as they. In the midst of myriads each suffering heart is alone, for it finds no other breast on which it can repose. Hostility and solitude separate each wretch from his fellows, and the only society is the reciprocations of reproaches and injuries. Hell is but the complete and universal reign of falsehood, and the tendency of every lie is to reduce our world to it. (Truth the foundation of rectitude, &c., Jas. 3 : 2.)

God's Perfection and Command the Ground of Duty.—But do not suppose that I leave the obligation of veracity resting only on utility. It has a broader and deeper foundation in the nature and will of that God who cannot lie. He is "the Lord God of truth." See Ps. c : 5. Every "liar is abomination in His sight." He requires us to honour Him by the truth, and teaches us that this virtue makes us His children.

III. Evil Speaking, What?—The sin of slander, or backbiting, where the assertions of evil in our neighbour are false, is understood. Its malignity is great, as it assails him in a point very dear to him—his good name—and is usually attended with vile adjuncts of secresy and treachery. Jas. iii : 6, 7. But it is not so well understood that it is often a sin of evil speaking to repeat true accusations against our neighbour. There are times when the cause of virtue demands that ill-conduct shall be denounced. And when such occasions arise, the virtuous man will not be afraid to speak out. But it is a sin against our erring neighbour to give unnecessary currency to his faults. "Charity rejoiceth not in iniquity." The fact that our neighbour has truly sinned does not place him outside the pale of charity, nor does it entitle us to inflict on him any unnecessary injury or pain. Moreover, the recital of evil, true or false, has a natural tendency to familiarize the soul with it, to defile the memory and imagination, and to habituate the mind and conscience to wrong. It is, especially to the young, a real misfortune to have to hear of that which is morally foul. This mischief should never be causelessly wrought by detailing sins, no matter how true, without necessity.

IV. Are all Deceptions Lies? Negative Argument.—Many Christian moralists have held that there are intentional deceptions which are not breaches of the ninth commandment, and are innocent in God's sight. They describe these, as the cases where the person deceived had no right to know; and where the result of the deception was righteous and beneficial; as when a robber or murderer is misled away from his victim by an innocent deception; or where a defensive army deceives an invader by strategems. Their arguments arc chiefly these: that the parties deceived, in such cases, being engaged in a wicked design, have no right to the benefits of veracity as between man and man: That the best men, as Joshua, Washington, &c., when commanders of armies, made adroit use of stratagems; and the common conscience of mankind approves, and would count it morbid conscience and insane quixotry to refuse such means of defence: That many instances are recorded, of Bible saints as Abraham, Moses, Joshua, &c., who prosperously employed concealments and stratagems, (see for instance, Joshua, viii: 3, &c.,) and that there are even cases in which God or Christ seems to do the same, as in the assumption of a human body, Gen. xviii: 2, in the walk to Emmaus, Luke xxiv: 28. They add, also, that the consistent enforcement of the opposite doctrine would many times be suicidal and preposterous.

Affirmative Argument.—There are however, those who hold that absolutely "*no lie* is of the truth." They admit, indeed, that it is a man's privilege, where no right exists, to demand information of him, to keep silence, or use concealment. But they assert that, if he employs any signs by which it is usually understood information is conveyed, he must employ them absolutely according to reality; and that in no case can he intentionally produce a deception, without the sin of lying. They argue, in general, that the opposite license proceeds upon a utilitarian theory of obligation. But this theory is false, and as no finite mind can correctly judge the whole utility or hurtfulness of a given declaration in its ulterior consequences, no practical basis or rule of obligation would be left at all. To the instances of deception in war, by great patriots, and their approval by the world, they reply, that good men are imperfect, and commit errors; and that the public conscience is unhealthy. To the instances of Bible-saints, they say, with justice, that often the errors of good men are recorded for our instruction, when they are by no means *sanctioned*. As to the instances claimed, from the acts of the Messiah, *concealment* is not *deception*; His appearance in human form, without at first disclosing His divinity, was not a *suggestio falsi*, but only a concealment of His nature until the suitable time. So, His seeming to design a journey farther than Emmaus was a mere question propounded to the two disciples. As to the inconveniences of absolute truth, sometimes extreme, they point to the obligations laid upon the martyrs, and remind us, that it is no rare thing for Christ to require of us *obedience rather than life*. In fine, they urge that, on any other ground than theirs, no tenable or consistent rule remains; and we have a mere 'point of honour' requiring us to speak truth under certain contingencies, instead of a fixed rule of moral obligation.

Solution.—It must be confessed, that the reasons of the latter party are more honorable to the divine authority, and more elevating and safe, than those of the former. Yet, I would modestly suggest, in dismissing this difficult question, that there may be a partial reconciliation of the difficulties here: Are there not extreme forms of aggression, aiming expressly at the destruction of the innocent object, and so clearly unprovoked, as to put the assailant, for the time being, out of the pale of human rights? Such is the case in those assaults where the right of self-defence emerges, and the innocent man righteously kills the assailant. It may be asked with much force: has this outlaw for the time being, a right to truth, after he has forfeited the right to existence? Does not the greater forfeiture include the less? Is he not, *pro tempore*, in the category of a beast of prey? But the moment he is disabled from aggression or turns to a better mind, his rights to truth revive, as do his claims on our charity and forbearance. Hence, while the good man will righteously deceive his invading enemy with stratagems, the moment a flag of truce appears, or his enemy is disabled and captured, he is bound to act with as perfect sincerity as towards his bosom friend. I would add, in guarding this concession, that if an innocent man makes a vow, promise, or engagement to his unrighteous assailant, under whatever violent threat, or other inducement, he is bound to the faithful performance of that engagement, unless the thing promised is sin *per se*. For the engagement was voluntary; he had the option of choosing to make it or endure the threatened evil. The good man is one who "sweareth to his own hurt, and changeth not." Ps. xv: 4.

V. Popish Division of 10th Commandment.—Rome, as we saw, having suppressed the 2nd Commandment, divides the 10th in order to make out the requisite number. Her 9th Commandment is, "Thou shalt not covet thy neighbor's house;" and her 10th, "Neither shalt thou desire his wife," &c. Her plea is, that houses are typical of property; and wives of those things which excite sensual desire. The 9th Commandment, therefore forbids covetousness; the 10th, lust and appetite. But unfortunately, the "ox and ass," obvious "property" are in the latter part; and in Deut. v: 21, where Moses recites the Decalogue literally, he puts the wife first, and the property second. The general unity of the subject, besides, proves that it was one command.

Its Scope.—It may be said, in brief, that this command finds the keynote of its exposition in the text: "Keep thy heart with all diligence; for out of it are the issues of life." The five commands of the second table cut off the streams of transgression; this deals with the fountain head. The others forbid wrong volitions; this forbids *concupiscence*, as tending thereto. In the 10th Commandment, then, we have the crowning spirituality of the Law; thus making it complete, and every way worthy of God, and adapted to man as a rational free agent.

VI. Decalogue only from God.—In closing this subject I would offer two remarks. The first is upon the admirable comprehension, wisdom, and method of the Decalogue. We have here ten simple and brief precepts, each one commending itself to the natural conscience of the most unlearned, simple in word, few in number, unostentatious in arrangement. When we first look at them, we are inclined to think that, while they are very true and good, there is nothing very wonderful; that they are obvious things which any good man might utter, and to a much greater number than ten. But when we examine them in detail, we find that they are the heads of *all* the branches of man's duty, arranged with the most logical order, presenting nothing superfluous, and yet, with all their brevity, omitting nothing of all the vast circle of human duty! How clear their purity and justice! How amazing their comprehension! What completeness! Let human ingenuity hunt out some branch of human duty which is omitted. It cannot. In these ten words, we have a system of morality more wise and complete than human wisdom ever devised. Now, we ask, whence did Moses get these ten words? A man of an unlearned and pastoral race, educated in the learned follies of Egypt, whose theology and morals, as they are revealed to us by Herodotus and the modern decypherers of their monuments, show an impurity and puerility utterly opposite to the Bible, goes into a waste desert, and after forty years, comes forth with this strangely wise and perfect law! Whence did he get it? There is but one rational account—that given by the Bible—that it was written for him by the finger of God. Unless Moses was an inspired man, then he has produced a miracle of wisdom more incredible than all the difficulties of inspiration.

VII. What does every Sin Deserve.—Our Catechism, while recognizing the greater gravity of some sins than others, by reason of their aggravations, teaches us that, "Every sin deserveth God's wrath and curse, both in this life and that which is to come." The exceeding demerit of sin, and its desert of eternal and grievous punishment is a doctrine which meets with obstinate resistance from sinners. It is urged that to make the desert of any sin such is to revive the old Stoic absurdity, of the equality of all sins, for if the lesser sin is punished eternally, and so infinitely, the greater cannot be punished more. The answer is, that infinities are by no means all equal; as we have shown.

To clear this awful truth of the desert of sin, from the cavils of unbelief, I would observe, first, that sinful men are in a most unlikely attitude to judge correctly between themselves and God, in this matter. They naturally *desire* to break the law. Our emotions always blind the judgment to the objects which are opposed to their current. They are condemned by the law of God, which fact produces a natural jealousy of it. They have their moral judgments brutified by the universal habitude and example of sinning, amidst which they live. It would be almost a miracle, if there were not, under these circumstances, a perversion of the moral judgments here.

Grounds.—But affirmatively the ill-desert of sin is infinite, because of the *excellence*, *universality*, and practical value of the law broken by it. Because of the *natural mischievousness* of sin to the sinner himself; as was illustrated when I spoke of Adam's first transgression. Because of the Majesty and perfections of the Law-giver assailed by transgression. Because sin is committed against mercies and blessings so great. Because it violates so perfect a title to our services, that of creation out of nothing. And last, because it is so continually multiplied by transgressors.

PART II.

LECTURE XXXV.

SYLLABUS.

THE COVENANT OF GRACE.

What the use of the words, BIRITH and DIATHEKE? The meaning of Terms "Covenant of Grace," "Covenant of Redemption?" How related to the Gospel?

Conf. of Faith, Ch. vii. Lexicon's *sub voc.* Sampson on Hebrews, ix: 15, 16. Hill's Div., Bk. v, Ch. v, § 1. Turrettin Loc. xii, Que. 1. Dick. Lect. 48.

2. Prove the existence of a *Covenant of Redemption.* How related to the *Covenant of Grace*, and DIATHEKAI?

Turrettin, Que. 2, § 13, 14, Dick. Lect. 48. Scriptures, e. g., Ps. ii: 6, 7. Isaiah, xlii: 6, xlix: 6, liii: 10. John x: 18, iii: 16, xvii: 4-6. Eph. i: 4. Heb. x: 5.

3. Who are the original parties? Explain in what sense, and for whom Christ acts as surety. What the motives of the parties?

Turrettin, as above, § 9-12. Dick. Lect. 48. Turrettin, as above, § 6 and 16.

4. What the conditions bargained between the parties? Is any condition enjoined on man? If so, what? Faith? Repentance?

Turrettin, as above, § 17-20. Dick. Lect. 48. Turrettin, Que. 3.

5. What the date and duration of the Covenant of Redemption? Explain, then, the terms, "New" and "Old" in Heb. viii: 8, or xii: 24.

Turrettin, Que. 2, § 15. Hodge on 1 Cor., xv: 24-28. Dick., as above.

1. COVENANT OF GRACE GOD'S REMEDY.—God having created man upright, and he having sought out many inventions, and thus fallen into sin; our next inquiry must be into the remedy which God's love and mercy found for this fall. This remedy, in its exhibition, was of course subsequent to the ruin; but when we consider it in its inception in the Divine mind, we must go back into the recesses of a past eternity. God ever foreknew all things; and all His works, unto the end, are according to His original, eternal plan. Conceiving of God's eternal decree then *in parts*, (the only mode of conception of it competent to our finite minds,) we must consider that part of His plan formed from eternity, which was implied in that other part of the same plan whereby He purposed to permit man's fall and ruin. *This remedial part of God's decree is the thing which the more recent Calvinistic divines term the* COVENANT OF GRACE—e. g., Dick.

IDENTICAL WITH DECREE.—When it is thus considered, as a part of the Decree, we are enabled to condense much of the discussion and proof concerning it, given by the theologians; and to say in brief: that being such, the Covenant of Grace must of course possess those general properties which we asserted of the Decree; and for the same reasons, viz., *eternity*, *immutability*, *wisdom*, *freeness*, *absoluteness*, *graciousness*.

2. In what respects a Covenant.—If there is any gospel remedy for sin, then there must have been, from eternity, such a remedial plan in the Divine mind. But the question is, was this part of the eternal decree, in any proper sense a *covenant?* Has it properly the form of an eternal compact between persons of the trinity? This is purely a question of Revelation, to be decided not so much by finding the words, covenant, compact, agreement, applied to it in Scripture, as the substance of the thing asserted. Calvinists hold that in the one, eternal decree of the Trinity, which is one in essence and attributes, and harmonious in will and thought, this remedial purpose (or part of the plan) has from eternity held the form of a *concert* or *agreement* between the Father and the Son, for the redemption of believers. But here we must carefully avoid confusing the subject, by giving to this immanent transaction of the Trinity all the technical features of a "covenant." Thus many divines have erred, especially of the *Cocceian* school. Obviously, we must not conceive of it, as though the one party produced in the other a willingness to do what he had not previously purposed, by exhibiting a certain reward or compensation, not before exhibited. Nor must we conceive that the second party produces, by his fulfilment of the conditions, a fixed purpose to bestow the given compensation, the purpose to do so having been hitherto uncertain. Nor, in a word, that there is any contingency on either hand, holding the purposes of either party suspended in doubt on the promisings or doings of the other party. But it has always been certain from eternity, that the conditions *would* be performed; and the consequent reward *would* be bestowed, because there has always been an ineffable and perfect accord in the persons of the Trinity, on those points; an accord possessing all the absoluteness of the other parts of the decree. Our limited understandings, of course, cannot fully understand the *actings* of the divine, triune spirit; seeing its *constitution* is inscrutable to us. This is perhaps as near as we can come to the conception designed to be given us.

Scriptural Proofs of a Covenant of Redemption.—The Scriptural proof of such an immanent, eternal transaction between the Father and Son, is the following: *First.* Inferentially, Eternal life was not only purposed to be bestowed, but, "promised, before the world began"—Tit. i: 2. To whom? for man did not yet exist? To Christ, for believers. Compare Eph. i: 4. Again: Christ is clearly implied to bear a federal relationship; as in 1 Cor. xv. 22, 47, 45. Our first federal head entered into covenant on our behalf; we infer that our second has; he would else not fulfil the idea of a federal person at all. Again: Christ is expressly called the *Surety* of a diatheke. Heb. vii: 22. But a surety is one who voluntarily enters under the obligations of a compact on behalf of another. Many other passages would ground a similar inference; the student has now had sufficient examples how to use them. Note all *conditional promises:* To believers, to Christ. *These* are of nature of covenants.

Second. Many express passages describe (not always in the use of word *covenant et similia*, but in substance) such an eternal agreement. See Is. xlii: 6, xlix: 8; Mal. iii: 1; especially Ps. xl: 7, 8, as quoted by Heb. x: 5. This Covenant of Christ is unfolded by other Scriptures under the specific heads of his three offices—e. g., Prophetic. Is. lxi: 1, 2. Priestly. Isaiah, liii: 10, 11; Ps. cx: 4; John, x: 17, 18. Kingly. Ps. ii: 7, 8, cx: 6; Luke, xxii: 29, &c.

3. Scripture use of Terms.—Such are the evidences on which we assert this secret of the eternal mind! When we come to the Scriptures, we find a frequent use of the words rendered in our English version, 'Covenant,' 'Testament,' applied to transactions of God *with men*, through their Surety, Jesus Christ; whence another group of proofs. Before we can proceed farther in the connected evolution of the subject, the proper meaning of these terms must be examined; BIRITH DIATHEKE. The former of these words, both by its etymology and usage, is shown to mean 'covenant,' or 'agreement;' being often used to express theologically, God's covenants with man, and naturally, compacts between individuals. There are also cases in which it means an arrangement or disposition of matters determined on. Exod. xxxiv: 28. Jer. xxxiii: 20. It must be remarked, that the word currently used by the Sept. to render this, is DIATHEKE. This fact would naturally lead us to attribute to it in the New Testament, the same meaning of disposition or covenant. It is admitted that the meaning so often given to it by our English version of 'testament,' (will,) is the primary etymological meaning in classic Greek. But there is only one case, (Heb. ix: 16,) where that meaning is supportable. Thus, when Christ is said by the English version to be "a surety of a better testament," (Heb. vii: 22,) there is an obvious incongruity between the office and the document. Wills do not have sureties. When the same version says, (1 Cor. xi: 25,) "This is my blood of the New Testament," the words KAMES DIATHEKE imply the Old, to which the character of a testament is inappropriate. But in Heb. ix: 16, 17, the meaning of 'Testament' is to be retained, (against McKnight, Hill and others.) For, if their rendering be attempted, making the passage allusive to a *covenant* ratified by an animal sacrifice, three insuperable critical difficulties arise, that if DIATHEKE means covenant, DIATHEMINON should mean the "covenanter," i. e., God the Father, (Christ being the ratifying sacrifice.) But the Father did not die; that NEKROS cannot be properly used to describe dead animals sacrificed: and that the passage would then be made to assert too much; for it is not universally true, that compacts were only of force anciently, after the death of a sacrifice to solemnize them. (See Sampson's Com. *in loco.*) Hence we assert that the statement of our Confession of Faith is substantially correct, that the Scripture does set forth the dispensation of God's grace to man under the idea of "a testament;" though perhaps not "often," as is said there. Their assertion refers to the English version.

The terms are used then, in their general or theological sense. 1st, by Theologians, and probably by Scripture, (Hos. vi: 7,) for the Covenant of works with Adam. 2nd, for the Abrahamic dispensation. 3rd, for the Mosaic dispensation. 4th, for the new or Christian dispensation. (Not *covenants*, but *dispensations;* for we shall show that there is only *one covenant*, besides that of works.)

4. Dispensations, how Related to the Covenant.—The relation between these DIATHEKAI, and the eternal Covenant of Redemption between the Father and the Son, may, we flatter ourselves, be now

made intelligible. This is, substantially and efficaciously, the covenant transaction, the forming of it bearing no relation to time; those are the exhibitions of the transaction, through the Surety, to the human beings interested in it, made with successive degrees of clearness, in time. The transaction, as it is between the Trinity, is one and eternal; its exhibitions to man have been in time and successive, and have varied in their accessaries. It must be remarked, that the Confession of Faith, and the older divines, such as Turrettin, apply the words "Covenant of Grace" to the *dispensations of promise* made by God *to man*, in and through the agreement of the Father and Son. Such an application is proper and necessary; for the fact is, that God has proposed to His people in all ages, a covenant of promise, under different dispensations, in which *He transacts with men*, through a Mediator indeed, yet with men, as parties. This different use of the phrase, however, implies no difference of view. Doubtless Turrettin and the Westminster Assembly would assent to the substance of all which Dick has said, in applying the phrase to the original compact of Father and Son. This distinction between the original compact and its dispensations to men, is useful and proper, as giving greater comprehension and clearness.

Is the Covenant of Redemption to be distinguished from the Covenant of Grace?—If, now, the question be raised whether there is a Covenant of Redemption with the Mediator, distinguishable from the Covenant of Grace with man, the answer will be plain. There is no such covenant distinguishable from the Covenant of Grace, in the sense of being two independent transactions. The latter is but the exhibition to man of the former. In the gospel dispensations, God only covenants with men in and through the Mediator, as their federal head; and in the sole terms of the original compact made with Him. But there is a difference, as the publication of the offers of grace to Christ's people differs from the original purpose of grace through Christ. When the Confession speaks of the Covenant of Grace, it is in the latter aspect. We shall be compelled to use the term thus also—*.

Refuse the distinction, as Dick does, and you run into contradictions. Is the Covenant conditioned, or unconditioned? It is impossible for Dick to answer this question truly, unless he resorts to the distinction which he has repudiated. If you speak of the Covenant of Redemption, the answer is, *yes*; if of the Covenant of Grace, the answer is, *no*. In the former, Christ fulfils the efficacious condition; in the latter, man fulfils an instrumental condition only.

5. Original Parties to the Covenant.—The original parties to the Covenant of Redemption are the Father and the Son. It is plausibly urged by Dick, that in this transaction, the Father acted not only for himself, as *one* person of the Trinity, but for the whole Godhead as representative of the offended majesty of the three persons equally His reason is, that all the persons being similar in attributes and dignity, must be conceived of as all alike offended by man's sin and guilt and alike demanding the reconciling intervention of a Daysman: the Holy Ghost as much as the Father. It must be confessed that Dick

*See lucid remarks of Turrettin. Ques. 2, § 12.

cannot present any scriptural, direct proof of this view; but it seems reasonable. The Father on the one part, then, acts as the representative of the Godhead; Christ as the representative of the elect. The question is raised by Dick: Is Christ surety for man to God only, or for God also to believers? He answers, *not* for God to believers; because this is derogatory to God, as implying that his fidelity and mercy need or admit of any higher warrant than his own word. (But see Turrettin, Loc. cit. § 16.) Does not God make known his fidelity as a promiser of pardon and life, and his mercy, precisely through this surety, as the *prophet* of the Covenant? Would man be any otherwise warranted to hope for any mercy? Further, the fact that God's goodness to us needs and admits of any certifying by a surety, results from nothing discreditable to God, but from something discreditable to us—our guilty mistrust. That God, who deserves to be trusted on his mere word, should condescend to give us warranty of his fidelity in the messages, death and sacraments of his Son; this is his amazing grace and goodness. (See 1 Tim. i: 16.) And are not the sacraments *seals?* Does not Christ in them act as surety for God to us?

To the question whether *believers* are also parties in the Covenant of Grace, no better answer can be given than that of Turrettin, § 12. In the eternal sense of the Covenant, they were not parties; in the sense of its exhibitions in time, they are parties; i. e., in their surety.

6. The Covenant Eternal.—The Covenant of Redemption being, as regards the Father and the Son, but a part of the single Decree, must be as *eternal* as that Decree. It began in the counsels of a past eternity: and in one sense, its administration will extend (if not in the mediatorial offices of the Surety, at least in the communications of grace,) to a future eternity. In proof of its eternity, see Heb. xiii: 20; 1 Pet. i: 20. Hence the Covenant can only be *one;* and therefore it can only be spoken of as "first," "second" (e. g., Heb. viii: 7,) or "old," "new," (as Heb. viii: 8; xii: 24,) with reference to its forms of manifestation.

7. Motives of God to the Covenant. The Father not persuaded by the Son to it.—Having considered the Godhead (represented in the Father,) and Christ, as the original *parties* to this covenant, the question naturally arises: What motive prompted them to this dispensation of amazing love and mercy? The only consistent answer is: their own will, moved by their own intrinsic benevolence, compassion, and other attributes. To this agree all the passages of Scripture which describe God's electing love as free and unprocured, by any thing in man; (Rom ix: 11, 16,) because our election is but the embracing of us in the Covenant of Grace. Eph. i: 4. This is equally substantiated by the argument that God could not be moved by foreseen good in us, to embrace us in this covenant; because the only foreseen good in us was that which was to result from the administration of the grace of that very covenant. It cannot be said that man's *misery* was more than the *occasion* of God's purpose in forming this Covenant of Grace; for if we supposed it the procuring, or efficient cause, the misery of non-elect men and angels ought equally to have procured a Covenant of Grace towards them also.

Some have misrepresented the truth hereupon by teaching that

Christ's undertaking to satisfy the law in man's stead is the *procuring cause* of God's purpose of mercy towards man. The error of this view is evident from this consideration that then, Christ would be originally more benevolent and merciful than the Father. But they are equal and harmonious originally, in this, as in all other excellencies. The true statement is, that Christ's promise of a vicarious atonement was necessary to enable the Father's purpose of mercy to be effectuated consistently with other attributes—that purpose being precisely as original and uncaused in the Father as in the Son.

8. Conditions pledged by Christ—just what man owed. 1st. Obedience.—Dick (Lec. 49,) has very happily simplified the question, "What were the conditions bargained by the Son to the Godhead, on behalf of His people?" by considering Him as placed precisely in His people's room and stead. He bargained to do precisely what they should have done, to supply precisely "their lack of service." The intrinsic righteousness of the rules imposed on man in the Covenant of Works, as being precisely what they ought to have been; and the immutability of God's nature, show that whoever came forward to be their surety, must expect to have to undertake precisely what was incumbent on them in that covenant. The first part of this obligation was to a life of perfect obedience. This life Christ rendered. (See e. g. Matt. xvii: 5.) A class of theologians has rejected the idea that Christ's active obedience was vicarious, and is imputed to His people. While this question will come up more naturally when we discuss the subjects of *Atonement* and *Justification*, we may briefly remark of it now, that the consideration above offered is obviously in favour of the Calvinistic view. Besides; when the Messiah is represented as saying, "A body hast thou prepared me," &c., (Ps. xl: 6, 8, quoted; Heb. x: 5, 10,) it is surely a very contracted and perverse interpretation, to suppose that He was clothed with humanity only with reference to one and the last act of His humanity; and that the general phrase, "I come to do Thy will," is to be understood only of the single act of of offering His flesh. (See also Gal. iv: 4 and 5.

2nd. Penalty.—But man, while still bound to perpetual obedience, has already come under penalty, by failing to render it. Hence, our Surety bargained to *bear* that penalty in His people's stead. This cannot be more clearly stated than in the language of Is. liii: 5, 6; 2 Cor. v: 21. Some have supposed that there is an incompatibility between the first and second condition: that if the penalty for a neglected obedience is paid, law has no longer any claim for that obedience. This represents the relation between the law and penalty, erroneously. God does not accept the penalty as an *equivalent* for obedience, in the sense that either the one or the other satisfies the demands of the Law and of his nature alike well. Look at this! His relation to His rational creatures demand of them, by an inevitable and perpetual demand, perfect obedience; and if that fails, penalty also. But waiving this, does not the believer (having paid for his past delinquency by his surety,) owe a perpetual and perfect obedience *for the future?* And can he render it in the flesh? Hence his surety must render it for him, as well as pay the penalty.

3d. The Offices of Mediator.—In the third place, we may say

scripturally, that Christ bargained, among all other compliances with His Father's will, to do as Mediator, all those things pertaining to His prophetic and kingly offices, necessary on His part, to the salvation of the elect. He undertook their instruction, guidance, protection and conquest to Himself. Weigh John xvii: 12-14, for instance, where our Saviour speaks of His agency in instructing and guiding His disciples as of a fulfilled compact. (See also, Ps. xxii: 22.)

Conditions pledged by the Father.—Passing now to the other side of the compact, we may say that the Godhead, represented in the Father, engaged on His side, to the Son, to clothe Him with humanity for the fulfilment of His task, (Ps. xl: 6,) and to endue Christ plenteously with gifts and graces therefor, (Is. xlix: 2; lxi: 2,) to uphold Him under His heavy task, (Is. xlii: 1, 5,) to give Him an elect seed as the sure reward of His labours, (Is. xlix: 6; liii: 10,) and to bestow His royal exaltation, with all its features of glory. (Ps. ii: 6; Phil. ii: 9, 10.) As there is a secondary sense, in which God, in unfolding His eternal Covenant of Grace, bargains with man, so there is a sense in which there are conditions proposed between God and believers also. It may be remarked in general, that there is a sense in which a part of the benefits promised to Christ are promised through Him also to His people; and a part of the blessings covenanted to them, are honours and rewards to Him. Thus His mediatorial graces are their gain: and their redemption is His glory. Hence, this division between benefits covenanted to His people, and those covenanted to Christ, cannot be sharply carried out.

9. Instrumental Condition Required of Men.—When we consider the covenant as between God and believers, however, it is evident that there are conditions bargained between them. These conditions may be found briefly expressed in the words so often repeated, and obviously intended to be so significant in scriptures; Gen. xvii: 7; Jer. xxxi: 33; Rev. xxi: 3; "I will be their God, and they shall be My people." In this covenant God briefly bargains, on His part, to be reconciled to believers, and to communicate Himself to them as their guide, light, consolation, and chief good. They, on their part, are held bound to the correlative reconciliation, grounding their weapons of rebellion and exercising the spirit of adoption, to a life of self-consecration and obedience, to separation from the world of His enemies, and conformity of heart and life to God's will. It is true that the transaction of Gen. 17th is rather ecclesiastical than spiritual; but the spiritual is always included and represented in the outward.

Faith the only Condition.—The question then arises, whether all the graces and duties of the Christian life may be accounted as *conditions of* the Covenant of Grace. If so, is it not reduced again to another Covenant of Works? The answer is, that it is only in a very slight, and improper sense, the Christian's holy life can be called a condition of his share in grace—only as in the order of sequence it is true that a holy life on earth must precede a complete redemption in heaven. So far is it from being true that this holy life is in any sense a meritorious condition of receiving grace, or a procuring cause, it is itself the fruit and result of grace. But when we examine more minutely the account of that gracious transaction in the Scriptures shadowed forth in the ecclesiastical transaction of Gen. 17th, and stated first more simply in Gen. 15th, we find that Abraham's *faith* only was imputed to him for righteousness. Gen. xv: 6; Rom. iv: 9, 10, &c. This effectually explains the matter. The argument in favour of the position we have assumed, is sufficiently strengthened by adding that all graces and holy living are everywhere spoken of by God, and sought by Bible saints in prayer, as *God's gifts* bestowed as the fruit of the Covenant of Grace. Citations are needless.

May Faith be properly called a condition.—The question has been keenly agitated between Calvinists, whether Faith itself should be spoken of as *a condition* of the covenant. One party has denied it, because they supposed that the language which represented man as performing a *condition* of his own salvation would make an inlet for human merit. But it is most manifest that there is a sense in which Faith is the condition in all such passages as John iii: 16; Acts viii: 37; John xi: 26; Mark xvi: 16. No human wit can evade the fact that here God proposes to man a something for him to do, which, if done, will secure redemption; if neglected, will ensure damnation—and that something is in one sense *a condition*. But *of what kind?* Paul everywhere contrasts the condition of works, and the condition of faith. This contrast will be sufficiently established, and all danger of human merits being intruded will be obviated, if it be observed that Faith is only the *appointed instrument* for receiving free grace purchased by our Surety. It owes its organic virtue as such, to God's mere appointment, not to the virtue of its own nature. In the Covenant of Works, the fulfilment of the condition on man's part earned the result, justification by its proper moral merit. In the Covenant of Grace, the condition has no moral merit to earn the promised grace, being merely an act of receptivity. In the Covenant of Works, man was required to fulfil the condition in his own strength. In the Covenant of Grace, strength is given to him to believe, from God.

No other Condition. Evasions.—The question now remains, whether, in this instrumental sense, any thing else besides faith is a condition of the Covenant of Grace. (See Cat. Ques. 33.) "Received by faith alone." There are two evasions: one that which makes Repentance a condition along with faith. Luke xiii: 3; Acts ii: 38, &c. Contrast with Jno. iii: 16–18; Acts xvi: 30, 31. The other is the one common to Papists, (meritum congruum of fides formata,) some classes of New English Divines (justification by faith apprehended as the generative principle of holiness, and inclusive thereof,) and the Campbellites, (justification by the "obedience of faith," viz: immersion.) Here is a subtile inlet for *works*. These perversions have all this common mark, that they desert the scriptural doctrine, which makes faith the instrument of justification solely through its receptive agency, and they claim for faith a purchasing power, or merit of the result.

LECTURE XXXVI.

SYLLABUS.

COVENANT OF GRACE.

1. Has God ever had more than one covenant with man since the fall? What the opinion of Socinians hereon? Of Anabaptists? Of Remonstrants?
   Turrettin, Loc. xii, Que. 5, § 1, 2, 4. Racorian C t.
2. Prove that the covenant of the Old Testament was substantially that of the New Testament.
   Turrettin, Que. 5, §. 5-23; Witsius de Œcon. Foed.
3. Under how many dispensations has the covenant been administered; and why so many?
   Turrettin, Que. 7, § 1-6, Ridgely, Que. 30, 33.
4. How much of the covenant was revealed to the Antediluvians? A mediator? Sacrificial types? Prove that Gen. iii: 15 *is a protevangel?*
   Turrettin, Que. 7, § 11-17, Heb. xi: 4. Dick, Lect. 50th. Knapp, § 89, 90, 91. Ridgeley, Que. 34.
5. What additional revelations from Abraham to Moses? Prove that Abraham's was also the Covenant of Grace. Does the Pentateuch reveal a promise of eternal life?
   Turrettin, Que. 7, § 18-23. Warburton's Divine Legation. Calvin's Institutes, bk. ii., ch. 10. Knaap and Ridgeley, as above. Compare Gen. xvii. 7, with Exod. xx. 2, Deut. ii. 5, 6, Jer. xxiv. 7, Zech. xiii. 9, Heb. viii. 10, quoted from Jer. xxxi. 33, Rev. xxi. 3.

FORMS IN WHICH GOD HAS ADMINISTERED THE COVENANT OF GRACE.

DEVELOPMENT OF GRACE TO BE TRACED.—Inasmuch as the plan of our Seminary directs the teacher of Systematic Theology to give special prominence to the successive developments of revealed truth, found as we proceed, from the Patriarchial to the Mosaic, and thence to the Christian ages, we devote other exercises to the subject above announced. In discussing it briefly, the order of topics indicated in the syllabus of questions will be pursued.

THE COVENANT ONE IN ALL AGES. OPPOSING VIEWS.—Has God ever had more than one Covenant of Grace with man since the fall? And is the covenant made with the Patriarchs and with Israel substantially the same spiritual covenant with that of the New Testament? The Socinians and Anabaptists gave a negative answer to this question, relying on the passages of Scripture represented by Jno. i: 17. They say that the covenant with Abraham and Israel was only national and temporal; that it promised only material good; that those of the Old Testament who were saved, were saved without a revealed promise, in virtue of that common natural religion, known, as they suppose, to good Pagans alike; by which men are taught to hope in the mercy and benevolence of a universal Father. To these views the European Arminians partly assented, teaching that the Gospel through the mediator is only involved implicitly and generally in the Old Testament, and that no special promise through a Christ is there.

MOTIVE OF THE SOCINIANS. OF THE ANABAPTISTS.—The motive of the Socinians is two fold; that they may escape this insuperable difficulty; if Christ's redeeming work (in the New Testament) is only what they teach that of a prophet and exemplar, and not vicarious, there is of sense in which He can have redeemed Old Testament saints, and 2nd, that by making the difference of light and grace between the Old Testament, and the New, as wide as possible, they may plausibly represent Christ as having something to do in the New Testament, *dignum vindice modum,* without any atoning work. The Anabaptists, whose Socinian affinities were originally strong, take the same view of the Old Testament in order to get rid of the doctrine that *a gospel Church* substantially identical with that of the New Testament existed in the Old Testament *with its infant church members.*

Unity of the Covenant appears a priori.—As to the unity of the Covenant, we have already argued this *à priori,* from its eternity. We may pursue this argument thus: If man's fall laid him necessarily obnoxious to certain immutable attributes of God, if man's sin necessarily and everywhere raises a certain definite difficulty between him and redemption in consequence of those inevitable attributes of God, we may fairly conclude that whatever plan (if there can be any) is adopted by God to reconcile a sinner, that same plan substantially must be adopted to reconcile all other sinners of Adam's race everywhere and always. To the Socinian indeed, this *à priori* consideration carries no weight; because he does not believe in God's essential, retributive justice, &c. Let us then see from the more sure word of Scripture whether the covenant of grace set forth in the Old Testament is not *substantially identical with that in the New, in the things promised, the parties, the conditions, and the mediator; while a difference of clearness and mode is admitted.*

Unity of the Covenant argued Scripturally.—This Scriptural argument cannot be better collected than under the heads given by Turrettin, (Que. v, § 7–23.)

a.) From direct testimonies.—The identity of the Covenant is substantially asserted in general terms—e. g., in Luke i: 68–72; Acts ii: 16, with v. 38, 39; iii: 25; John viii: 56; Rom. iv: 16; Gal. iii: 8, 16, 17; especially the last. Remark here, that the very words in which the Covenant was formed with the seed of Abraham, Gen. xvii: 7; and which are so formally repeated in subsequent parts of the Old Testament are the very terms of the compact in the new dispensation, repeated as such with emphasis. See Jer. xxxi: 33; 2 Cor. vi: 16; Rev. xxi: 3.

b.) From sameness of Mediator.—The Mediator is the same. 1 Tim. ii: 5, 6: Gal. iii: 16; Mal. iii: 1; Acts iv: 12, x: 43, xv: 10, 11; Luke xxiv: 27; 1 Pet. i: 9–12; Rom. iii: 25; Heb. ix: 15; with many passages already cited. We need not depend on such passages as Heb. xiii: 8; Rev. xiii: 8; for although their application to prove the mediatorial office of Christ under the Old Testament is probably just, plausible evasions exist.

c.) From its condition.—The condition assigned to man is the same in both—e. g., *faith.* And it is useless for the Socinians, &c., to say, that the faith of the Old Testament was not the specific faith in *the Son, the Messiah,* set forth in the New, but only a general trust in

God as the Universal Father. For their assertion is not true; and if true, it would still remain that the faith of the Old Testament and that of the New, include the same substantial features. Look at the fact that Heb. xi goes for its illustrations of faith, (surely it was inculcating the *Christian* faith,) exclusively to the Old Testament! See, also, Gen. xv: 6, with Rom. iv: 3; Ps. ii: 12. (Is not this specifically faith in the Son?) Acts x: 43; Ps. xxxii: 10, *et passim*.

d.) From its promise.—In the fourth place, it may be asserted that to this *faith* of the Old Testament saints, *redemption* in the true New Testament sense was held forth, with all its several parts; of justification, Ps. xxxii; Is. i: 18; Regeneration, Deut. xxx: 6; Ps. li: 10; Spiritual gifts, *passim*—e. g., Joel ii: 28, 32, as expounded by Peter, Acts ii; Isaiah xl: 31; eternal life: (as we shall more fully argue under a subsequent head, now only noticing.) Heb. iv: 9, xi: 10; Exod. iii: 6, as expounded by Christ; Matt. xxii: 31, 32, and this eternal life including even the resurrection of the body. Ps. xvi: 10, 11, applied in Acts xiii: 32; Job xix: 25; Dan. xii: 1, 2. In view of this array of proofs, how weak appears the idea, that nothing more than the Land of Canaan and its material joys was proposed to Israel's faith? But of this more anon.

e.) From the types.—An argument for our proposition may be constructed out of all those *types* under the old dispensation, which can be proved to have had an evangelical meaning. The promised land itself, the deliverance from Egypt, with its significant incidents; circumcision and the passover, ("seals of the rightness of faith,") with the whole tabernacle ritual, are proved by several parts of the New Testament to have had this evangelical meaning. The argument is too wide to be briefly stated; but every intelligent Bible reader is familiar with its materials. In its very wideness is its strength. As one specimen of it, take the Epistle of Hebrews itself. The Apostle, in interpreting the Levitical ritual, there shows that all prefigured the gospel, and the New Testament, Messiah and redemption. During the Old Testament times, therefore, it was but a dispensation of this same Covenant of Grace.

And in general, all the gospel features sown so thickly over the Old Testament, especially over the books of Psalms and Isaiah, prove our point.

Of such passages as Rom. xvi: 25; Gal. iv: 24; 1 Pet. i: 12, &c., we are well aware. We shall show their compatibility with the proposition above demonstrated, when we come to unfold the resemblances and differences of the two dispensations.

Two Dispensations only. Objection answered.—We conceive the familiar and established division to be correct, which makes two dispensations only, the Old Testament and the New. There seems no adequate reason for regarding the patriarchal age, from Adam to Moses, as essentially a different dispensation from that of Moses. Certainly that representation is incorrect which makes the former a free and gracious dispensation, while the latter only was burdened with the condemning weight of the moral and ritual law. For the moral law (not indeed the wording of the Decalogue) was already in force from

Adam to Moses. Sacrifices already smoked on altars, and the knife descended in symbol of wrath, on innocent victims. And gracious promises are, at least, as thickly strown over the Scriptures of the Mosaic period, as of the patriarchal. We hardly need cite cases. There are passages, such as Gal. iii: 17; Deut. v: 2, 3, which speak of a ritual burden, and law which could minister only condemnation as superadded at the Mosaic era. But we shall find that the elements of a moral law impossible for *the depraved* to fulfil, and of a ritual which typified only wrath to him who persisted in ignoring the Mediator and the Covenant of Grace, were also present in the patriarchal religion. The history of Cain too clearly establishes these traits of the patriarchal age. These elements were only re-affirmed by Moses. If it be said that they were then brought forward with far greater prominence and distinctness. I answer, so were the gospel elements brought forward, to true believers, at the same time, with increased distinctness. When the Apostles bring out so prominently this condemning burden of the Mosaic law, they are dealing, for the time, with only one side of the subject. *Because*, they are dealing with Jews who persisted in looking for justification to this law, which apart from Christ, is only a ministry of cordemnation; who persisted in stickling for *Moses*, MOSES, as their authority for their self-righteous perversions of the law and gospel. In dealing with this subject, theologians perpetually forget how necessarily the Apostles had to use the *argumentum ad hominem* against these Jews. That the patriarchial and Mosaic form properly but one dispensation appears from this. Both exhibit the great, prevalent characteristic of types: both were prefigurative instead of being; like the New Testament commemorative; both had sacrifice, circumcision, priests. The difference between them is only one of *degree*, and not of contrast. But when we come to the New Testament, there is a real contrast. Human priests, sacrifices and circumcision end. Types give place to antitypes; prefiguring to commemorative ordinances.

WHY TWO DISPENSATIONS OF THE SAME COVENANT? ANS.—To the question why God has administered the Covenant of Grace under two different dispensations, no complete answer can be rendered, except that of Matt. xi: 26. The true difficulty of the question lies chiefly back in this prior question: Why did God see fit to postpone the incarnation of the mediator so long after the fall? For, supposing this question settled, we can see some reasons why, if the effectuating of the terms of the Covenant of Grace, was to be postponed thus, its declarations to man must be by a different dispensation before and after the surety came. Before, all was *prospective*. Every promise must, in the nature of things, be a prediction also; and prediction, prior to its fulfilment, must needs be to finite minds, less plain than experience and history after the occurrence. Every symbolical ordinance (both dispensations for good reasons have such) must needs be a *type; foreshadowing*. Afterwards it is a commemoration looking backward. May it not be, that the greater variety and number of the symbolical ordinances under the Old Testament were due to the very fact that they must needs be less distinct? God sought to make up in number what was lacking in distinctness. But to the question: why the mission of Christ was postponed nearly 4000 years, there is no adequate answer. The circumstances which made that era "the fullness of time" have been pointed out by the Church Historians. But the relations of influence and causation in human affairs are too intricate and numerous for man to speculate here.

The causes assigned by Turrettin (Que. 7, § 2-6) do indeed indicate the existence of an analogy with God's other working herein. God performs all his grand results by gradations. Childhood and pupilage go before manhood and independence. So majestic a luminary as the Sun of Righteousness may be expected to rise gradually, and send His twilight before Him! True; but these are only paliations, not answers to the difficulty.

3. THE GOSPEL WAS PREACHED TO ADAM.—To appreciate correctly the amount of Gospel light possessed in the patriarchal, and even in the Mosaic ages, we must bear in mind a thing often overlooked that the human race had just enjoyed, in Adam, personal communication with God, in fullest theophanies, which Adam by the faculties of his perfect manhood, and other patriarchs, through their longevity, were admirably qualified to transmit well. Adam was cotemporary with Methuselah 243 years, Methuselah with Noah 600 years (dying the year of the flood,) and Noah with Abram 58 years. Thus Abraham received the revelations of paradise through only *two* transmissions! We must not suppose that this traditionary knowledge of God was scanty, because the hints of it given in earlier revelations are scanty; because the *purposes* of revelation do not require that we should be fully informed thereon; and the Holy Ghost never wanders from his point. But we have two unmistakeable items of a revelation unfolding the covenant of grace after the fall. The first is Gen. iii: 15. Proved to be a proper Protevangelism by the considerations that if the *serpent* represents Satan, then of course He who is to bruise his head must be more than man, already conquered by Satan; and by John xii: 31, Luke x: 19, 20, Rom. xvi: 20, Heb. ii: 14, Rev. xii: 8, 9. One thing we know, that the very earliest patriarchs had a gospel promise, because they had faith. Heb. xi: 4-7. The second item is the existence of sacrifices from the first. We conclude that these were of divine appointment from three things; that *reason* would hardily indicate their propriety, from the comparison of Gen. iii: 21 with Gen. ix: 3, 4, and from Heb. xi: 4. No doubt the Sabbath was observed from the days of Eden. (See Lecture on the Sabbath, Decalogue.)

ADDED LIGHT GIVEN TO ABRAHAM.—At the epoch of Abraham, the declaration of the Covenant of Grace was farther developed. The Sabbath, the sacrifices and the promise, subsisted as before. The *additions* were, the calling of Abraham, the formation of an ecclesiastical covesant with him and his, (*now made necessary* in order to separate a visible Church *because* of the uniform and ineradicable tendency of the bulk of the race to rebellion,) and the institution of circumcision. The new feature of a limitation of the Covenant to one race, now arises also; but this is only a result of that necessity just indicated, that there should be a *visible Church separation from the world*. In that age, the patriarchal form was superinduced on *all* organized bodies. Abraham and his seed did indeed receive a temporal promise of Canaan; but that there was a spiritual and gospel feature implied in Gen. xii: 3, xv:

5, xvii: 7, is abundantly proved by Gal. iii: 16, and by all which the New Testament says of Abraham's *faith*.

FORMULA OF THE COVENANT IN ALL DISPENSATIONS THE SAME.—That the formulary, "I will be a God to them," &c., is an application of the Covenant of Grace has already been shown, and evinced especially from Jer. xxxi: 33, Rev. xxi: 3, &c. A comparison of these and the other passages referred to, will show that the words, "I will be to them a God, and they shall be my people," are an intentional formula, by which the Covenant of Grace in all its dispensations, expresses summarily, the blessings stipulated to believers in Christ. Not only do we hear them in Genesis xvii, when God formed his Church covenant with Abraham and his seed. They recur in the most evangelical promises of the Psalms and the prophets, and always in the most cardinal declarations of God's grace. In the New Testament, the same *formula* reappears like a grand chorus. It is repeated in the Epistles; and when descriptive prophecy in the book of Revelation shows us the ransomed Church finally united to her Divine Head, in the actual fruition of grace, we hear still the same "*refrain*," "They shall be His people, and God Himself shall be their God."

ETERNAL LIFE WAS REVEALED TO THE PATRIARCHS.—And here we must pause a moment, to consider the question famously debated in the negative, for instance, by Warburton's Divine Legat. of Moses: "Whether the patriarchal ages had any revealed promise of future eternal life?" I would premise that the scantiness of the teachings on this point will not surprise us, if we remember that this fundamental truth is rather *assumed* than taught. It has been well remarked that the Bible no where sets itself deliberately *to teach* the existence of God! We may well suppose the traditionary religion received from Adam made the immortality of the soul, and future rewards, so clear that little was then needed to be said about it. But let us see if this doctrine was not plainly *implied* to the patriarchs. (Accutely argued, Calv. Institutes, L. 2, Ch. 10.) a.) They had *promises*. The New Testament expressly declares these promises were *the gospel*. Rom. iii: 21; Luke i: 69–73. But the gospel relates to spiritual and everlasting good. b) The patriarchs embraced the promises they had with faith; but faith is the principle of everlasting life. Hab. ii: 4; Heb. x: 38. c.) The Covenant with Abraham, Gen. xvii: 7, plainly implies an *everlasting* relation to Him, and therefore, eternal life. See Ps. xvi: 5, and end; xlviii: 14; Deut. xxxiii: 27. d.) The extension of God's promise to their *seed* implies the patriarchs' immortality; for if they were annihilated, what privilege would it be to them then? See also Exod. iii: 6, as expounded by Christ; Matt. xxii: 32–34. e.) If the promise to the patriarchs was only of temporal good, it was false; for they were "strangers and pilgrims in the earth," e. g., Abraham, Jacob. Last. Their dying exercises pointed to an immortality. See Heb. xi: 9, &c.; Gen. xlix: 18; Num. xxiii: 10; Gen. xlix: 33. In the subsequent Old Testament Scriptures, after the Pentateuch, the doctrine is full.

LECTURE XXXVII.

SYLLABUS.

COVENANT OF GRACE. (Concluded.)

6. What farther developments of the Covenant of Grace were made by the Mosaic Economy?

Turrettin, Loc. xii, Que. 7, § 24-26. Ridgeley, Que. 33, 34, § 1. Knapp, § 90, 91.

7. What was the true nature of the Covenant made by God through Moses at Sinai?

Turrettin, Que. 12. Calv. Inst., Bk. ii, Ch. 7. Ridgeley, a above. Turrettin, Que. 7, § 28-31.

8. How do the old and new Dispensations differ, *inter se?*

Turrettin, as above, and Que. 8, § 18-25. Calvin's Inst. Bk. ii, Ch. 11. Ridgeley, as above. Calvin Com. Gal. 4th.

9. Did the Old Testament saints enjoy actual redemption, and from their deaths glorification: or was the application of Redemption to them, postponed to Christ's resurrection?

Turrettin, Que. 9, § 1-11, and Que. 10. Knapp, § 150.

10. Do the Scriptures teach a *Limbus Patrum?*

Turrettin, Que. 11. Catechism, Rom. Pt. i, Ch. vi, Que. 1 to 6, inclusive. Knapp, § 96.

6, 7. Additions at Sinai.—Coming now to the last stage of the old dispensation, the Covenant of Sinai, we find several marked and impressive additions to the former revelations. But they will all be found rather developments of existing features of the gospel, than new elements. These traits were, chiefly, the republication of the moral Law with every adjunct of majesty and authority, the establishment of a Theocratic State-Church, in place of simpler patriarchal forms, with fully detailed civic institutions, the Passover a new sacrament; and the great development of the sacrificial ritual.

The Covenant of Sinai not a Covenant of Works.—The Covenant of Sinai has seemed to many to wear such an aspect of *legality*, that they have supposed themselves constrained to regard it as a species of covenant of works; and, therefore, a recession from the Abrahamic Covenant, which, we are expressly told, (John viii: 56; Gal. iii: 8,) contained the gospel. Now, one objection to this view, making two distinct dispensations between Adam and Christ, and the first a dispensation of the Covenant of Grace, and the one which came after, of the Covenant of Works, is *à priori*, unreasonable. For, it is unreasonable in this: that it is a recession, instead of a progress; whereas every consistent idea of the plan of Revelation makes it progressive. It is unreasonable; because both the Old and New Testaments represent the Sinai Covenant as a signal honour and privilege to Israel. But they also represent the Covenant of Works as inevitably a covenant of death to man after the Fall; so that had the transactions of Sinai been a regression from the "Gospel preached before unto Abraham," to a Covenant of Works, it would have been a most signal curse poured out on the chosen people. The attempt is made to evade this, by saying that, while eternal life to the Hebrews was now suspended on a covenant of works, they were ritual works only, in which an exact formal compliance was all that was required. This is untenable; because it is inconsistent with God's spiritual and unchangeable character, and with His honour; and because the Mosaic Scriptures are as plain as the New Testament in disclaiming the sufficiency of an exact ritual righteousness, as the term of eternal life, and in requiring a perfect, spiritual obedience. If a ritual obedience was accepted instead of a spiritual one, *that* was an act of grace—a remission of the claims of laws—so that the Mosaic turns out a dispensation of grace, after all. But grace was preached to Abel, Noah, Abraham, in a prior dispensation, through a Mediator to come. Now, through what *medium* was this gracious remission of law given to Israel, at Sinai? The answer we give is so consistent, that it appears self-evident, almost: That it was through the same Christ to come, already preached to the Patriarchs, and now typified in the Levitical sacrifices. So that the theory I combat resolves itself, in spite of itself, as it were, into the correct theory, viz: That the promise contained in the Covenant of Sinai was through the Mediator, typified in the Levitical sacrifices; and that the *term* for enjoying that promise was not legal, not an exact ritual obedience, but gospel, faith in the antitype.

Additions at Sinai.—But let us proceed to a more exact examination. We find that the transactions at Sinai included the following: a.) A republication of the Moral Law, with greatest majesty and authority. b.) An expansion of the Ritual of the typical service, with the addition of a second sacrament, the passover. c.) The change of the visible Church instituted in Gen. 17th, into a theocratic commonwealth-church—both in one. d.) The legal conditions of outward good-standing were made more burdensome and exacting, than they had been before. This last feature was not a novelty, (See Gen. xvii: 14,) but it was made more stringent.

Their Designs.—Can the designs of these modifications be explained consistently with our view? Yes. As to the theocratic state, this was necessitated by the numbers of the Church, which had outgrown the family state—and needed temporal institutions capable of still larger growth, even into a grand nation. The amplified ritual was designed to foreshadow the approaching Christ, and the promises of the Covenant more fully. Next: The legal conditions for retaining outward ecclesiastical privilege were made more stringent, in order to enable the Law to fulfil more energetically the purpose for which St. Paul says it was added, to be a pædagogue to lead to Christ. (See Gal. iii: 19, 22.) For this stringency was designed to be, to the Israelite, a perpetual reminder of the law which was to Adam the condition of life, *now broken*, and its wrath already incurred, thus to hedge up the awakened conscience to Christ. This greater urgency was made necessary by the sinfulness of the Church, and its tendencies to apostasy, with the seductions of Paganism now general in the rest of mankind.

Scripture proofs of the identity of Moses' Covenant with Abraham's.—We can farther demonstrate, now, that the Sinai Covenant was not a new one, nor was it substantially different from Abraham's. For a.) (See Gal. iii: 17,) fidelity to the bond already entered into with Abraham *and his seed* excluded such action. b.) The law, both moral and ritual, was in force under Abraham. (Rom. v: 13, 14; Gen. xvii: 14.) But if we find the very feature in the Abrahamic age, which is supposed to characterize the arrangements of Sinai, it is most evident that this feature cannot prove them different. c.) Both the moral and a (less burdensome) ritual law are still binding in the same sense, under the New Testament dispensation. (See Matt. v: 17; Jno. iii: 5; Mark xvi: 16.) Surely the New Testament is not, therefore, a Covenant of Works! Last, Christ expressly says, that Moses taught of Him. (Luke xxiv: 27; Jno. v: 46.) If Moses taught of Christ, it can hardly be, that he also taught a system so antagonistic to the Christian, as a Covenant of salvation by works.

8. Differences of Old Dispensation from New.—A correct view of the nature of that display made of the Covenant of Grace in the Old Dispensation, will be gained by comparing it with the New. All orthodox writers agree that there is both law and gospel in the Old Testament Scriptures. If, by the *Old Testament Covenant*, is understood only that legal covenant of moral and ceremonial works, then there will indeed be ground for all the strong contrast, when it is compared with the Gospel in the New Testament, which some writers draw between the severity and terror of the one, and the grace of the other. But in our comparison, we shall be understood as comparing the *Old Dispensation* with the *New*, taken with all their features, as two wholes. We find Turrettin (Ques. 8, § 18, 25), makes them differ in their *date or time*, in their *clearness*, in their *facility of observance*, in their *mildness*, in their *perfection*, in their *liberty*, in their *amplitude*, and in their *perpetuity*. Calvin (B. 2, Ch. 11,) finds five differences: that the Old Testament *promises eternal life typically* under figures of Canaan, that the Old Testament is *mainly typical*, that it is *liberal*; while the New Testament is spiritual, that it *gendered to bondage*, and that it *limited its benefits to one nation*.

The Old too much Depreciated.—I am persuaded that the strong representations which these writers (and most others following them,) and yet more, the Cocceian school, give of the bondage, terror, literalness, and intolerable weight of the institutions under which Old Testament saints lived, will strike the attentive reader as incorrect. The *experience*, as recorded of those saints, does not answer to this theory; but shows them in the enjoyment of a dispensation free, spiritual, gracious, consoling, as *truly* as our's is. I ask emphatically: does not the New Testament Christian of all ages, go to the recorded experiences of those very Old Testament saints, for the most happy and glowing expressions in which to utter his hope, gratitude, spiritual joy? Is it said? that these are the experiences of *eminent* saints, who had this full joy (even as compared to New Testament saints,) not because the published truth was equal to that now given; but because they had higher spiritual discernment. Ans. By *nature* they were just like "us, sinners of the gentiles;" so that if they had more spiritual discernment, it must be because there was a freer and fuller dispensation of the Holy Ghost to them than to us. (*Much fuller!* to repair all defect of means, and more than bring them to a level.) But this overthrows Calvin's idea of the dispensation as a less liberal one. Or, is it pleaded? These are only the inspired, and therefore exceptional cases of the Old Testament

Church. Ans. Did not God give the inspired experiences as *appropriate models* for those of their brethren? These distorted representations have been produced by the seeming force of such passages as Jno. i: 17; 2 Cor. iii: 6, 7; Gal. iii: 19, 23; iv: 1, 4 and 24–26; Heb. viii: 8; Acts xv: 10. But the scope and circumstances of the Apostles, in making such statements, are greatly overlooked. They were arguing, *for* the gospel plan, *against* self-righteous Jews, who had perversely cast away the gospel significance out of the Mosaic institutions to which they clung, and who retained only the condemning features of those institutions; vainly hoping to make a righteousness out of compliance with a law, whose very intent was to remind men that they could make *no* righteousness for themselves. Hence we must always remember that the Apostles are using, to a certain extent, an *argumentum ad hominem:* they are speaking of the Mosaic institutions under the Jewish view of them. They are treating of that *side* or aspect, which alone the perverse Jew retained of them. *Here is the key.*

The New Testament Language as to it Explained. New Testament also a Dispensation of Bondage to Ritualist.—The truth is, both dispensations are precisely alike, *in having two sides to them:* a *law* which condemns those who will persist in self-righteous plans; and a gospel which rescues the humble believer from that condemnation. The obligation of Works, (conditions of which were reënacted in the Decalogue,) *perpetual*, being founded on the very relations between man and God, on all except those who are exempted from it by the substitutionary righteousness of the Mediator. It is of force now, on all others. It thunders just as it did in Eden and on Sinai. Nor, I beg you to note, is the Old Testament singular, in enjoining a *ritual* law, which is also "the letter that killeth," a "carnal ordinance," a "ministration of death," to those who perversely refuse to be pointed by it to the Messiah, and who try to make a self-righteousness out of the ritual. The New Testament also has its sacraments; all are commanded to partake, yet he that eateth and drinketh, not discerning the Lord's body, "eateth and drinketh damnation to himself;" and he that takes the water of Baptism self-righteously, only sees therein a terrible symbol of his need of a cleansing which he *does not receive.* Let an evangelical Christian imagine himself instructing and refuting a modern Ritualist of the School of Rome or the Tractarians. He would find himself necessarily employing an *argumentum ad hominem* precisely like that of Paul against the Pharisees. The evangelical believer would be forced to distinguish between the legal or condemning, and the gospel side of our own sacraments; and he would proceed to show, that by attempting to make a self-righteousness out of those sacraments, the modern Pharisee was going back under a dispensation of condemnation and bondage; that he was throwing away 'the spirit which giveth life,' and retaining only the 'letter that killeth.'

The New Testament has also its *sacrifice;* the one sacrifice of Christ; and to him who rejects the pardon which it purchased, it is a ministry of damnation, more emphatic than all the blood of beasts could utter. Both dispensations have their "letter that killeth," as well as their "spirit that giveth life," their Sinai as well as their Zion. And in the very place alluded to, it is the killing letter of *the New Testament* of which Paul speaks, 2 Cor. iii: 6. Besides in the Old Testament no part of the ritual could be more crushing than the moral commandment "exceeding broad," is to the unrenewed. But see Matt. v: 17-20.

Again. The Old Testament distinguished both as to its word, and its ordinances, between this letter that killeth and this spirit that giveth life. Deut. x: 12; Ps. l: 16, 17, 22; Prov. xxi: 3; 1 Samuel xv: 22; Ps. li: 16, 17; Isa. i: 13-20, &c.

Now just as the Christian minister would argue with a nominal Christian who persisted in making a righteousness out of the sacraments, so the Apostles argued with the Jews, who persisted in making a righteousness out of their ritual. Thus abused, the ritual of the Old Testament *and of the New* loses its gracious side and only retains its condemning. Peter says, Acts xv: 10, the ritual was a yoke which neither Jews nor their fathers were able to bear. Did God signalize His favour to His chosen people by imposing an *intolerable* ritual? Is it true that well-disposed Jews *could* not bear it? See Luke i: 6; Phil. iii: 6. No, Peter has in view the ritual *used in that self-righteous sense*, in which the Judaizing Christians regarded it while desiring to impose it on Gentiles. As a rule of justification it would be intolerable. The decalogue (2 Cor. iii: 7) would be a ministration of death to him who persisted to use it as these Jews did. But Moses gave it as only *one side*, one member of his dispensation, "to be a schoolmaster to lead us to Christ." Gal. iii: 16 speaks of *a law* given 430 years after the Covenant of Grace, and seeming to be contrasted. But it "could not disannul it." Did not Abraham's Covenant of Grace *survive* this law, as much in the ante-Christian, as in the post-Christian times?

Gal. 3d and 4th Explained.—Calvin says, as I conceive, perverting the sense of Gal. 4th, that the time of *bondage*, in which "the heir differed nothing from the slave," was the time of the Jewish dispensation, while the time of liberation was the time of the Christian dispensation. Not so. As to the visible Church collectively, and its outward or ecclesiastical privilege, this was true; but not as to individual believers in the Church. And this distinction satisfies the Apostle's *scope* in Gal. 3d and 4th, and Heb. viii: 7, 8, and reconciles with passages about to be quoted. [cf. Turrettin on Heb. ix: 8, Que. 11, § 14.] Was David still in bondage, "differing nothing from that of a slave," when he sung Ps. xxxii: 1, 2; cxvi: 16? The time of tutelage was, *to each soul*, the time of his self-righteous, unbelieving, convicted, but unhumbled struggles. The time of the liberty is, when he has flown to Christ. This, whether he was Israelite or Christian. Isaac, says another, symbolized the gospel believer, Ishmael, the Hebrew. Were not Isaac and Ishmael *cotemporary?* Interpret the allegory consistently. And was it not Isaac, who was, not allegorically, but literally, and actually, the Hebrew, the subject of an Old Testament dispensation, a ritual dispensation, a typical one, only differing from the Mosaic in details? This would be to represent the Apostle, as making a bungling allegory, indeed, to choose the man who was actually under the dispensation of bondage, as the type of the liberty, had St. Paul intended to prove that the Old Dispensation was a bondage. And it would be bungling logic, again, to represent the spiritual liberty, to which he wished to lead his hearers, by *sonship to Abraham*, if Abraham were the very head, with whom the dispensation of bondage was formed! St. Paul warns the foolish Galatians who "desired to be under the Law." "Do ye not hear the Law?" (Gal. iv: 21.) The thing which the law says to such self-righteous fools, is read in Gal. iii: 10. "As many as are of the works of the law are under the curse," &c. St. Paul's allegory says, that Ishmael's mother (the type of the soul in bondage) represents Sinai, and Sinai again, "the Jerusalem which now is." Sarah, then, represents what? "The Jerusalem which is above, and is free." Which of these answereth to King David's Zion, "the city of the great King, in whose palaces God is known as a Refuge?" (Ps. xlviii: 3, 4.) Obviously, Sarah and her children. But the Pharisees of the Apostle's day claimed to be the heirs of that very Zion, and did literally and geographically inhabit it! How is this? They were in form the free-woman's heirs—in fact, bastards. And they had disinherited themselves, by casting away the gospel, and selecting the legal significance of the transactions of Sinai. The Sinai which now answereth to the bond-woman is not the Sinai of Moses, of Jehovah, and of Abraham; but the Sinai of the legalist, the Sinai which the Pharisee insisted on having.

Yet the Old Necessarily Inferior.—You will not understand me as asserting that the Old Testament dispensation was as well adapted to the purposes of redemption as the New. This would be in the teeth of Heb. viii: 7, &c. The inferior clearness, fulness, and liberality result necessarily from the fact that it preceded Christ's coming in the the flesh. The visible Church, in its collective capacity, was, as to its outward means and privileges, in a state of minority and pupillage. But every true believer in it looked forward by faith, through that very condition of inferiority, to the blessings covenanted to him in the coming Messiah; so that his soul, individually, was not in a state of minority or bondage; but in a state of full adoption and freedom. This state of the visible Church, however, as contrasted with that which the Church now enjoys, is illustrative of the contrast between the spiritual state of the elect soul, before conversion, while convicted and self-righteous, and after conversion while rejoicing in hope. This remark may serve to explain the language of Galatians 3d and 4th.

Real Points of Difference.—I would discard, then, those representations of the intolerable harshness, bondage, literalness, absence of spiritual blessing, in the old dispensation, and give the following modified statement:

a.) The old dispensation preceded the actual transacting of Christ's vicarious work. The new dispensation succeeds it.

b.) Hence, the ritual teachings, (not all the teachings) of the old dispensation were *typical*; those of the New Testament are *commemorative* symbols. A type is a *symbolic prediction*; and for the same reason that prophecy is less intelligible before the event, than history of it afterwards, there was less clearness and fulness of disclosure. (See 1 Pet. i: 12.) Again, because under the Old Testament the Divine sacrifice by which guilt was to be removed, was still *to be* made the sacrificial types, (those very types which foreshadowed the pardoning grace as well as the condemning justice,) made a more prominent and repeated exhibition of guilt than now, under the gospel, when the sacrifice is completed; (Heb. x: 3,) because it was harder to look to the atonement in the future, than it is now in the past, the voice of the law, the pædagogue who directed men's eyes to Christ was graciously rendered louder and more frequent than it is now.

c.) Perspicuity in commemorating, being easier than in predicting, the ritual teachings of the previous dispensation were more numerous, varied and laborious.

d.) God, in His inscrutable wisdom, saw fit to limit the old dispensation to one nation, so far at least, as to require that any sinner embracing it should become an Israelite; and to make the necessary ritual territorial and local. Under the New Testament all nations are received alike.

e.) The previous dispensation was temporary, the New Testament will last till the consummation of all things.

9 & 10. Old Testament Saints redeemed at death.—With reference to the state of the Old Testament saints in the other world, we discard the whole fable of the Papists concerning a *limbus patrum*, and the postponement of the application of redemption to them—till Christ's death. Christ's suretyship is such, that His undertaking the believer's work, releases the believer as soon as the condition is fulfilled. He is not merely *Fide jussor*, but *ex promissor* (Turrettin), Christ being an immutable, almighty and faithful surety, when he *undertook* to make satisfaction to the law, it was, in the eye of that God to whom a thousand years are but as one day, *as good as done.* (Here, by the way, is some evidence that the chief necessity of atonement was not to make a govermental display, but to satisfy God's own attributes.) See Rom. iii: 25; Heb. ix: 15; Ps. xxxii: 1, 2; li: 2, 10-13; ciii: 12; Is. xliv: 22; Luke xvi: 22; 23 with Matt. viii: 11; Luke ix: 31; Ps. lxxiii: 24; 1 Pet. iii: 19, Heb. ix: 8.

These texts seems to me to prove, beyond all doubt, that Christ's sacrifice was for the guilt of Old Testament believers, as well as those under the New Testament; that the anticipative satisfaction was imputed to the old saints when they believed, and that at their deaths, they went to the place of glory in God's presence. What else can we make of the translations of Enoch and Elijah, and the appearance of Moses in glory, before Christ's death?

No Limbus Patrum.—The strength of the Papists' scriptural argument is in the last two of the texts cited by me. I may add, also, Rev. xiv: 13, which the Papists would have us understand, as though the *terminus a quo* of the blessedness of the believing dead were from the date of that oracle; implying that hitherto those dying in the Lord had not been immediately blessed. It is a flagrant objection to this exposition, that the Apocalypse was a whole generation after Christ's resurrection, when, according to Papists, the dying saints began to go to heaven. The *terminus* is, evidently, the date of each saint's death. The testimony from Heb. ix: 8, you have seen answered, by your textbook, Turrettin. The Apostle's scope here shows that his words are not to be wrested to prove that there was no application of redemption until after Christ died. The author is attempting to show that the Levitical temple and ritual *were designed to be superceded.* This he argues, with admirable address, from the nature of the services themselves: The priests offered continually, and the High Priest every year, by the direction of the Holy Ghost; by which God showed that that ritual was not to be permanent; for if it had been adequate, it would have done its work and ceased. Its repetition showed that the work of redemption was not done; and never would be, until another dispensation came, more efficacious than it. Such is the scope. Now, the words, "the way into the sanctuary was not yet manifested," in such a connexion, are far short of an assertion, that no believing soul could, at death, be admitted to heaven. Is not the meaning rather, that until Christ finished His sacrifice, the human priest still stood between men and the mercy-seat?

ESPECIALLY, NOT IN I. PET. I: 19, &c.—But the *locus palmarius* of the Papists for a Limbus Patrum, is 1 Pet. iii; 19, &c. On this obscure text you may consult, besides commentaries, (among whom see Calvin *in loco*,) Knapp, Chr. Theol., § 96; Turrettin, Loc. xii, Que. 11, § 15; Loc. xiii, Que. 15, § 12. Here, again, our safest guide is the Apostle's scope, which is this: *Christ is our Exemplar in submitting patiently to undeserved suffering*. For Him his own people slew the very Saviour who, so far from deserving ill at their hands, had in all ages been offering gospel mercy to them and their fathers, even to those most reprobate of all the Antediluvians. But the same Divine Nature in which Christ had been so mercifully carrying a slighted gospel to that ancient generation, (now, for their unbelief, shut up in the prison of hell,) gloriously raised Him from the dead, after their equally reprobate posterity had unjustly slain Him. Here is our encouragement while we suffer innocently after the example of our Head. For this resurrection, which glorified Him over all His ancient and recent enemies, will save us. Then we, redeemed by that grace which was symbolized to the ancient believers by the type of the ark, and to modern, by the sacrament of baptism, will emerge triumphantly from an opposing and persecuting world, as Christ's little Church, (consisting then of a number contemptible in unbeliever's eyes,) in Noah's day came out from the world of unbelievers.

With this simple and consistent view of the Apostle's drift, the whole dream of a descent into Hades, and a release of the souls of the patriarchs from their *limbus*, is superfluous, and therefore unreasonable.

LECTURE XXXVIII.

SYLLABUS.

MEDIATOR OF THE COVENANT OF GRACE.

1. What the meaning of the word, Mediator? Whence the necessity for one in the Covenant of Grace?

   Turrettin, Loc. xiii, Que. 3, § 3-18. Dick. Lect. 51. Lexicons.

2. Is Jesus of Nazareth the promised Mediator of the Covenant of Gracee? (Against Jews.)

   Turrettin, Que. 2, § 3-21, and Que. 1. Horne's Introduct., vol. i. Appendix, No. vi, Ch. 1.

3. What is the constitution of Christ's person? Doctrine of Gnostics, Eutychians, Nestorians, and Orthodox hereon? What the effects of this "hypostatic union" on the Mediatorial person and acts?

Hill, Bk. iii, Ch. 8. Turrettin, Loc. xiii, Que. 6, 7, 8. Church Histories, especially *Gieseler*, vol. i, § 42–45, and 86–88. Dick., Con'. of Faith, Ch. viii, especially § 1–4. Ridgeley, Que. xxxvii.

4. Does Christ perform His Mediatorial offices in both natures? And why is each necessary?

Turrettin, Loc. xiv, Que. 2, § 1–12. Loc. xiii, Que. 3, § 19–22. Calvin, Inst., Bk. ii, Ch. 12. Dick, Lect. 51 and 53. Turrettin, Loc. xiii, Que. 9. Ridgeley, Que. 38–40.

5. What the Socinian view of the necessity of Christ's prophetic work? Answer?

Turrettin, Loc. i, § 4. Stapfer, Ch. xii, § 18–25, and 122, &c.

Mediator of the Covenant of Grace.

1. Mediator what?—The *word* mediator is in the New Testament mesites middle man. The phrase does not occur in the Old Testament, except in the Sept. translation of Job ix: 33, (Engl. v. "daysman,") and then, with thes ense of *umpire*, not of mediator. Its idea in New Testament is evidently one who intervenes to act between parties, who cannot, for some reason, act with each other directly. Thus, Moses was (Gal. iii: 19) the mediator of the Theocratic covenant. But in this, he was no more than *internuncius*. Christ's mediation included far more, as will appear when we prove His three offices of *prophet, priest and king*; which are here resumed.

Why needed in Covenant of Grace.—No mediator was necessary in the Covenant of Works between God and angels, or God and Adam; because in unfallen creatures there was nothing to bar direct intercourse between them and God. Hence the Scripture presents no evidence of Christ's performing any mediatorial function for them. On the contrary the Bible implies always, that Christ's offices were undertaken, because men were *sinners*. Matt. i: 21, Is. liii, Jno. iii: 16. But, man being fallen, the necessity of His mediation appears from all the moral attributes of God's nature; His *truth*, (pledged to punish sin,) His *justice*, (righteously and necessarily bound to requite it,) His *goodness*, (concerned in the wholesome order of His kingdom,) and His *holiness*, (intrinsically repellent of sinners.) So also, *man's* enmity, evil conscience and guilty fear, awakened by sin, call, though not so necessarily, for a mediator. See also Jno. iii: 21.

It has been objected that this argument represents God's will as under a constraint; for else what hindered His saving man by His mere will? And that it dishonours His wisdom by making Him go a roundabout way to His end, subjecting His Son to many humiliations and pangs. The answer is; the necessity was a moral one, proceeding out of God's own voluntary perfections. Note. To sustain our argument we must assert that God's *mere will* is not the sole origin of moral distinctions. See Lect. viii on that point.

2. Christ the Mediator of the Old Testament.—Against the Jews we assert that Jesus of Nazareth is the Messiah and Mediator of this Covenant. Of an argument so comprehensive and containing so many details, only the general structure can be indicated. In this argument the standard of authoritative reference assumed is the Old

Testament, which the orthodox Jew admits to be inspired. (As for the Rationalistic, they must first be dealt with as other skeptics.) Second. In this argument no other authority is claimed for the New Testament in advance, than that it is an *authentic narrative*. As such, it is substantiated by the profane and Jewish history. We then make two heads:

a.) BECAUSE THE TIME IS PASSED.—The promised Mediator of the Old Testament must be already come. For the time has passed. (See Gen. xlix: 10; Dan. ix: 24–27.) He was to come while the second temple was standing. (Hag. ii: 6–9; Mal. iii: 1–3.) He was to come while the Jewish polity subsisted; (Gen. xlix: 10,) and while Jerusalem was still the capital of that theocracy. (Hag. ii: 6–9; Is. ii: 3; lxii: 1, &c.) This polity and city have now been overwhelmed for nearly 1,800 years; so that the very ability to give genealogical evidence of the birth of Christ from David's stock, is now utterly gone! The Messiah's coming was to be signalized by the cessation of types. (Dan. ix: 27.) Last; the Messiah's coming was to be marked by the accession of multitudes of Gentiles to the religion of the Old Testament. (See Is. ii: 3; xlii: 1–6; xlix: 6; lx: 3, &c.)

b.) BECAUSE HE HAS THE APPOINTED TRAITS.—Jesus of Nazareth, is the Person; because all the qualities and incidents foretold in the Old Testament, wonderfully tally with Him and His life. (See Acts iii: 18.) The strength of the argument is in the completeness of this correspondence. In fairly estimating this proof, reference must be made to the doctrines of probabilities. The occurrence of *one* predicted trait in a person would prove nothing. The concurrence of two would not be a demonstration; because that concurrence might be fortuitous. But, when three independent and predicted traits concurred, the proof would greatly strengthen; because the likelihood that chance could account for all three, is diminished, in a multiplying ratio. So, as the number of coincident, predicted traits increases, the evidence mounts up, by a multiplying ratio, towards absolute certainty. Jesus, then, answers the prophetic description in *the time* of His birth. (See above.) In the *place;* Micah. v: 2. In His *nativity* of a virgin; Is. vii: 14. In His *forerunner;* Mal. iii: 1, &c. In His *lineage;* Gen. iii: 15, xviii: 18, xlix: 10; Is. xi: 1; Ps. cxxxii: 11; Is. ix: 7, &c. In His *preaching;* Is. lxi: 1–3. In His *miracles;* Is. xxxv: 5–6. In His *tenderness* and meekness; Is. xlii: 3. In the *circumstances of His end*, viz., His *entry* into Jerusalem; Zech. ix: 9. *Betrayal;* Zech. xi: 12, 13. *Rejection* and contempt; Is. liii: 3. *Death;* liii: 8. *Mockings* therein; Ps. xxii: 8. *Vinegar;* Ps. lxix. 21. *Piercing;* Zech. xii: 10. Yet *no bones broken;* Ps. xxxiv: 20. *Death with malefactors;* Is. liii: 9. Honourable *burial;* Is. liii: 9. *Resurrection;* Ps. xvi: 9, 10, lxviii: 18. *Spiritual effusions;* Joel. ii: 28. Again: the Messiah of the Old Testament was to have a wondrous union of natures, offices and destinies, which was mysterious to the Old Testament saints, and absurd to modern Jews; yet was wonderfully realized in Jesus. He was to be God, (Ps. ii: 7; Is. ix: 6); yet *man*, (Is. ix: 6.) The history of Jesus, taken with His words, shows Him both human and divine. The Messiah was to be both priest and victim. (Ps. cx; Is. liii.) He was to be an outcast, (Is. liii,) and a king, (Ps. ii.) So was Jesus. He was to conquer all people, (Ps. xlv: 72,

110;) yet, without violence. (Is. xlii: 3; Ps. xlv: 4.) He was to combine the greatest contrasts of humiliation and glory. These contrasts are so hard to satisfy in *one Person* (to all unbelieving Israel it looks impossible,) that when we find them meeting in Jesus, it causes a very strong evidence to arise, that He is the Mediator.

3. Hypostatic Union.—The doctrine of the constitution of Christ's person, is purely one of Revelation, and involves a mystery (1 Tim. iii: 16,) as great, perhaps, as that of the Trinity itself But though inexplicable, it is not incredible. The nature of the scriptural argument by which this twofold nature in one person is established, is analogous to that establishing a Trinity in unity. The text nowhere defines the doctrine in one passage, as we assert it. But our doctrine is a necessary deduction from *three sets* of Scriptural assertions. *First.* Jesus Christ was properly and literally *a man.* (See, e. g., Jno. i: 14; Gal. iv: 4; Jno. i: 51; Is. ix: 6; Heb. ii: 17; Matt. iv: 2; Luke ii: 40, 52; Matt. viii: 24; Mark xiii: 32; Jno. xi: 35; Matt. xxvi: 37, &c.) *Second.* Christ is also literally and properly *divine.* (See e. g., Jno. i: 1; Rom. ix: 5; 1 John v; 20; Is. ix: 6, Phil. ii: 6; Col. ii: 9; Heb. i: 3; 1 Tim. iii: 16, &c.) *Third.* Yet this Man-God is one and the same; in proof of which we need only allude to the fact, that in every text speaking of Him, oneness of person, and personal attributes, are either asserted or implied of Him. In many passages the same proposition asserts both natures in one person, (e. g., Jno. iii: 13; 1 Tim. iii: 16.)

To Socinians, and other errorists, theses passages seem contradictory, because being unwilling to admit the "incarnate mystery," they insist on explaining away one class of them. The true explanation is, that both are true, because of the hypostatic union. By these means such seeming paradoxes are to be explained, as those in Mark xiii; 32, compared with John v: 20; Matt. xi: 27, &c. The first of these verses asserts that even the Son does not know the day and hour when the earth and heavens shall pass away. The others ascribe omniscience to Him. The explanation (and the only one) is that Christ in His human nature has a limited knowledge, and in His divine nature, an infinite knowledge. The opinions of Gnostics are sufficiently asserted by Hill, (*loc. cit.*)

Gnostic Theory of Christ's Person.—As they have no currency in modern times, I will content myself with briefly reminding you of the distinction between the other Gnostics, and those called Docetai. Both parties concurred in regarding *matter* as the source of all moral evil. Hence, they could not consistently admit the resurrection and glorifiaation, either of the saints or of Jesus' body. The Docetai, therefore, taught that Christ never had a literal human body; but only a phantasm of one, on which the malice of His persecutors was spent in vain. The others taught that the *Aion*, who they supposed constituted Christ's superior nature, only inhabited temporarily in the man Jesus, a holy Jew constituted precisely as other human beings are; and that, at the crucifixion, this *Aion* flew away to heaven, leaving the man Jesus to suffer alone.

The Nestorian view.—The historical events attending the Nestorian controversy, and the personal merits of Nestorius, I shall not discuss. The system aftewards known as Nestorianism was apprehended by the Catholic Christians, as by no means a trivial one, or a mere logomachy about the THEOTOKOS. The true teacher of the doctrinal system was rather Theodore of Mopuestia, (a teacher of Nestorius,) than the latter prelate. In his hands, it appears to be a development of Pelagianism, which it succeeded in date, and an application to the constitution of Christ's person of the erroneous doctrines of man's native innocence. Theodoret set out from opposition to Apollinaris, who taught that the divine Reason in Christ substituted a rational human nature, leaving Christ only a material and animal nature on the human side. According to Theodore, Christ is a sort of impersonated symbol of mankind, first as striving successfully against trial, and second, as rewarded with glory for this struggle. He supposed Christ the Man to exercise a self-determining power of will, which, he taught, is necessary to moral merit in any man. Christ, the man, then, began His human career, with the Word associated, and strengthening His human nature. As Christ the man resisted trial, and exhibited His devotion to duty in the exercise of His self-determination, He was rewarded by more full and intimate communications of divine indwelling, until His final act of devotion was rewarded with an ascension, and full communication of the Godhead. The process in each gracious soul offers an humble parallel. The indwelling of God the Word in Jesus, is not generically unlike that of the Holy Ghost in a saint: but only closer and stronger in degree. There are, indeed, three *grades* of this one *kind* of union, first, that of the Holy Ghost, in sanctification; second, that of the same person, in inspiration; third, that of the Word in Christ. And the Nestonians preferred rather to speakof the last, as a SUNAPHEIA, than a ENOSIS—the preferred term of Cyril.

DOCTRINAL CONSEQUENCES.—This view seemed to involve two Pelagian errors; first, that grace is bestowed as the reward of man's right exercise of moral powers, (in his own self-determined will,) instead of being the gratuitous cause thereof; and second, that inasmuch as the human purity of the man Jesus went before, and procured the divine indwelling, it is naturally possible for any other man to be perfect in advance of grace. Again, from the separation of the nexus between the two natures in Christ, there seemed to the Catholics to be a necessary obscuring of the communication of attributes; so that Christ's sacrifice would no longer be *divine* and meritorious enough to cover infinite guilt. And thus would be lost the fundamental ground of His substitution for us. The whole scheme goes rather to make Christ incarnate rather a symbolical exemplar of the work of God in a believer, than the proper redeeming purchase and Agent thereof. Its tendencies, then, are Socinian.

EUTYCHIAN VIEW.—The Alexandrine theologians generally leaned the other way. Cyril was fond of quoting from the great Athanasius; that while "he allowed Christ was son of God, and God, according to the spirit, but son of man, according to the flesh; but *not two natures and* one son; the one to be worshipped and the other not: but *one nature of God the Word incarnated,* and to be worshipped by single worship along with His flesh." They loved to assert the ENOSIS, (unification) of the natures, rather than the SUNAPHEIA (or conjunction,) of

Theodore. They preferred to conceive of Christ as so clothing Himself with human nature, as to assimilate it, by a species of subusmption, with His divinity. Hence the error of Eutyches was prepared; that while the mediatorial person was constituted from two natures, it existed only in one, the divine. This error is as fatal to a proper conception of Christ's mediatorial work, as the Nestorian. By really destroying the humanity in Christ, from the moment of His birth, it gives us a Redeemer who has no true community of nature with us; and so does not render a human obedience, nor pay the human penalty in our room and stead. The creed of Chalcedon, intermediate between these two extremes, is undoubtedly the scriptural one, as it has been adopted by all orthodox churches, ancient and modern, and is the basis of the propositions of the Westminster Assembly on this point. You have these symbols within your reach; and I shall not here repeat them.

Orthodox Views.—For Orthodox creed of Chalcedon, see Mosheim, vol. i, p. 366. For *our own*, see Confession of Faith, ch. 8, § 2. This doctrine, however inexplicable, is not incredible; because it is no more mysterious than the union of two substances, spirit and body, into one human person, in ourselves. Yet, who is not *conscious* of his own personality? That the infinite Creator should assume a particular relation to one special part of His creation, the man Jesus is not impossible, seeing He bears intimate relations (e. g., as providential upholder,) to all the rest. That an *infinite* spirit should enter into personal union with a man, is surely *less* mysterious than that a *finite* spirit should constitute a personal union with a body; because the infinite and almighty possesses, so to speak, more *flexibility* to enter into such union; and because the intimate union of spirit to spirit, is less mysterious than that of spirit with body. (A perfect analogy is not asserted.)

Hypostatic Union ground of the Efficacy of Christ's work. Socinian objection quashed.—This Hypostatic union is the *cornerstone* of our redemption. The whole adaptation of the Mediatorial person to its work depends on it, as will be shown in the discussson of heads 5th, 6th. The general result of the Hypostatic union is stated well in the Confession of Faith, Ch. 8, § 7, last part. This is that koinonia idiomaton which we hold, in common with the early Fathers, repudiating the Lutheran idea of the attributes of Divinity being literally conferred on the humanity; which is absurd and impossible. Apt instances of this koinonia may be seen in John iii: 13: Acts xx. 28, xvii: 31; Mark ii: 10; Gal. iv: 4; and Rom. i: 17, or iii 21; 1 Cor. ii: 8. Hence, it is, that Mediatorial acts, performed in virtue of either nature, have all the dignity or worth, belonging to the Mediatorial person as made up of both natures. Socinians do, indeed, object: that inasmuch as only the *creature* could, in the nature of things, be subjected to the law, and to penalty, the active and passive obedience of Christ have, after all, only a *creature worth;* and it is a mere legal fiction, to consider them as possessed of the infinite worth of a divine nature, since the divine nature did not especially render them. The answer is; The *person* possessed of a divine nature, rendered them. If the Socinian would honestly admit the *personal union* as a thing which (though inscrutable) is real and literal, his objection would be relinquished. For then, many analogies of human persons (not perfect indeed, but applicable fairly) would show that this KOINONIA is not unnatural even. We shall see that the common sense and conscience of men always estimate the acts and sufferings of a compounded person (constituted of two natures) according to the dignity of the higher nature, to whichever of them those acts or sufferings may specially belong; e. g. There are many *bodily* affections, as appetite, pain, which we characterize as distinctively *corporeal;* and yet, had not our bodies souls in them, these affections could have no place. Why then is it incredible, that the divine substance in the Medatorial person should be the ground of a peculiar value in the human sufferings of that person; though in strictness of speech, the divine could not be the *seat* of the suffering? Again, corporeal sufferings of martyrs have a moral value, which can only be attributed to the fact that those suffering men were not brutes, but spiritual and moral beings; while yet the *soul* may have been unconscious of the pangs, through spiritual joy, or other cause. I argue, also, from the fact, that moral character is given to merely physical acts of men, because of the character of the *volition* prompting those acts. Now, I pray, did not the *will* of the Logos prompt all the acts of active and passive obedience performed by the human nature? If when my bones and muscles in my arm go through identically the same functions, with the same stick, to beat a dangerous dog, and to beat my friend, one physical act has the spiritual character of *lawfulness*, and the other physically identical act has the spiritual character of *sinfulness*, because of the concern of my *volition* in them, why should it be thought a thing increbible, that the human sufferings of Christ should have a divine character, when prompted by the volition of the divine nature in His person? And is not the *bodily* pain of a man more important than that of a dog? It is enough, however, to show that the infinite dignity of Christ's divine nature is, in Scripture, given as the ground of the infinite value of that work. See Heb. ix: 13. 14, vii: 16, 24; John iii: 16; 1 Pet. i: 18, 19; Ps. xl: 6; Heb. x: 5–14.

4. DOES CHRIST MEDIATE IN BOTH NATURES?—The question, whether Christ performs the functions of Mediator in both natures is fundamental. Romanists limit them to the human nature, in order to make more plausible room for human mediators. They plead such passages as Phil. ii: 7, 8: 1 Tim. ii: 5, and the dialectical argument, that the divinity being the offended party, it is absurd to conceive of it as mediating between the offender and itself.

Now, it must be distinguished, that ever since the incarnation, the *Logos* may perform functions of incommunicable divinity, inalienable to Him as immutable; such as sitting on the throne of the universe and possessing incommunicable attributes; in which the humanity can no more have part, than in that creative work, which Christ performed before His incarnation. So, likewise, the humanity performed functions, in which it is not necessary to suppose the LOGOS had any other concern than a general providential one; such as eating, sleeping, drinking. But *these were not a part of the Mediatorship.* We assert that, in all the Mediatoral acts proper, both natures To PROSOPON THEANTHROPON act concurrently, according to their peculiar properties. This we prove, 1st, by the fact, that in Christ's *priestly work*, the divine nature operated and still operates, as well as the human. See 1 Cor. ii: 8: Heb. ix: 14; John x: 18. Even in this work of suffering and dying, see how essential the concurrent actions of the divine nature were! Else, there would have been none of the *autocracy* as to His own life, necessary for His vicarious work; nor would there have been strength to bear an infinite penalty in one day. Only the Omniscient can intercede for all. Hence, we argue *à fortiori*, that if His divinity concurred in His *priestly* work, the part usually supposed most irrelevant to deity, much more does it concur in His prophetic and kingly. See Matt. xi: 27, xxviii: 18. 2d. If Christ does not perform His Mediatorial work in His divine nature as well as His human, He could not have been in any sense the Mediator of Old Testament saints; because their redemption was completed before He was incarnate. Did Romanists attend to the fact, that it is the very design and result of the Covenant of Grace, that the persons of the trinity should act "economically," in their several offices of redemption, they would not have raised the inconsistent objection about the Godhead's propitiating the Godhead. The Son, having become man's Surety, now acts economically and officially for him, in his stead propitiating the Father, who officially represents the majesty of the offended trinity. Besides, unless the Romanists will assert not only two wills, but these two in opposition, in the Mediatorial person, the divine will of God the Son must, on their scheme, have concerned itself with propitiating God; the same difficulty!

One remark applies to all His mediatorial functions also; that the will of both natures concurred in them.

Why must the Mediator be Man?—The demands of Christ's mediatorial work required that Christ should be proper and very man. Mankind had fallen, and was conscience-struck, hostile, and fearful towards God. Hence it was desirable that the Daysman should appear in his nature as his brother, in order to encourage confidence, to allure to a familiar approach, and quiet guilty fears. To such a being as sinful man, personal intercourse with God would have been intolerably dreadful; (Gen. iii: 8; Ex. xx: 19,) and even an angel would have appeared too terrible to his fears.

Again. The Bible assures us that one object gained by the incarnation of Christ, was fuller assurance of His sympathy, by His experimental acquaintance with all the woes of our fallen condition. (Heb. ii: 17, 18; iv: 15 to v: 2.) The experience of every Christian under trial of affliction, testifies to the strength of this reasoning by the consolation which Christ's true humanity gives Him. It is very true that the Son, as omniscient God, can and does figure to Himself conceptions of all possible human trials, just as accurate as experience itself; but His having experienced them in human nature *enables our weak faith to grasp the consolation better*.

Another purpose of God, in clothing our Redeemer with human nature, was to leave us a perfect human example. The importance and efficacy of teaching by example, need not be unfolded here. (See 1 Pet. ii: 21; Heb. xii: 2, &c.)

In the fourth place, Christ's incarnation was necessary, in order to establish a proper basis for that legal union between Him and His elect, which should make Him bearer of their imputed guilt, and them partakers of His imputed righteousness, and of His exaltation. (See 1 Cor. xv: 21.) It was necessary that man's sin should be punished *in the nature of man*, in order to render the substitution more natural and proper. (Rom. viii: 3.) Had the deity been united with some angelic, or other creature, the imputation of man's sin to that Person, and its punishment in that foreign nature would have appeared less reasonable. (See Heb. ii: 14–16.) So, likewise, the obedience rendered in another nature than man's, would not have been so reasonable a ground for raising *man's* race to a share in the Mediator's blessedness.

And this leads us to add, last, that a *created nature* was absolutely essential to the Mediator's two works, of obeying in man's stead, and suffering for his guilt. For the obedience, no other nature would have been so appropriate as man's. And none but a *creature* could come under law, assume a subject position, and work out an active righteousness. God is above law, being Himself the great law-giver. For the other vicarious work, suffering a penalty, not only a created, but a corporeal nature is necessary. Angels cannot feel bodily death, and brutes could not experience spiritual; but both are parts of the penalty of sin. The divine nature is impassible, and unchangeable in its blessedness. Hence, Heb. x: 5; ix: 22, &c.

5. Why the Mediator must be God.—It is of the highest importance to prove that the mediatorial offices could not be performed without the divine nature. (See Is. xlv: 22, Jer. xvii: 5-7, xxiii: 6.) Because this is one of the most overwhelming arguments against Arians and Socinians. We assert that a purpose to save elect men being supposed in God by a mediatorial plan, the very necessities of the case required that this mediator should be very and proper God. But as this was substantially argued in Lect. xvi, when proving the divinity of the Holy Ghost and the Son, the student is referred to that place.

Is Christ's Prophetic work essential, or, as Socinians say, only useful?—But the fifth question of our Syllabus raises a point in this direction, which requires fuller explanation. The scope of the Socinian system is to find *a common religion*, including the fewest possible essential elements. Hence, they like to represent that virtuous Pagans may belong to this common religion, holding the doctrines of Natural Theology. The consequence is, that the Socinians, while speaking many handsome things of Jesus Christ as a messenger from God, still concur with other Deists and infidels, in depreciating the necessity of Revelation. They say that the Scriptures are valuable, but not essential. We are thus led again to the old question of the *necessity of revelation*.

Partial grounds of argument corrected.—Let us not assert this on the usual partial grounds. The case is too often put by our friends as though the fall alone necessitated a revelation; the effects of *sin* in blinding the mind and conscience are too exclusively mentioned. Thus, there is an implied admission that a revelation is, in man's case, an exceptional expedient, caused by the failure of his general plan. Thus, the objection is suggested, which Socinians, and other enemies of inspiration have not failed to put in form; and which many of us are inclined perhaps to feel, as though the idea of a revelation were unnatural, and hence not probable. The cavil is, that the analogy of all creation discloses this plan: Our wise and good God, in creating each order of sentient beings, surrounded them with all the appointed conditions for their well-being, by the established course of nature. Having made fishes for the water, he made water for the fishes; the grass is for oxen, and the oxen for grass; the birds for the air, and the air for the birds. Every order, by living within the natural conditions provided for it secures its appropriate end. But according to the Orthodox, man, the noblest, the rational creature, cannot fulfil the ends of his being, immortal blessedness, by his natural means. A supernatural expedient must be found against the general analogy; or else man's existence is a frightful failure. This, they urge, is unnatural, discreditable to God, and improbable.

Revelation necessary to Holy Creatures.—Now I meet it by asserting that, to make a rational creature dependent on a revelation of God for his spiritual welfare, is not unnatural, or extraordinary; but for all spiritual creatures the universal, and strictly natural condition. It does not arise out of man's sin only; the truth holds as well of angels, and all other rational creatures, if there are others. We must remember that none originally had God in their debt, to assure their holiness and bliss; but were naturally under this relation, bound to obey Him perpetually; free from evil as long as they did so; but subject to His wrath whenever they sinned. Now holy creatures were not infallible, nor omniscient. Their wills were right and free, but not indefectible. Bound to an unending career of perfect obedience, they would have been to all eternity liable to mistake and sin and death. Now, when a finite wisdom and rectitude are matched against an infinite series of duties to be done, of choices to be made, each naturally implying some possibility of a wrong choice, that possibility finally mounts up from a probability to a moral certainty, that all would some day fail. How, then, could an angel, or holy Adam, inherit immutable blessedness forever? Only by drawing direct guidance from the infallible, infinite Mind. Thus we see that the enjoyment of its appropriate *revelation* by each order, is the necessary condition of its well-being; a condition as natural, original, and universal as its own moral nature and obligations. If Gabriel had not his revelation he would not be an 'elect angel.' Do I mean a *written* document? Do I speak of parchment and ink? No; but of that which is the essence of a *Revelation*, a direct communication from the infinite Mind, to instruct the finite.

Revelation not Anomalous.—Thus we may, if we choose, admit the analogy which the Socinian claims, and find it wholly against him. Our Bible is not an exceptional providence; it is in strict accordance with God's method towards all reasonable creatures. If our race had none, this would be the fatal anomaly against us.

LECTURE XXXIX.

SYLLABUS.

THE MEDIATOR. (Continued.)

5. Is there any other Mediator between God and man, than Jesus Christ? (Against Papists.)
   For Popish views, see Council of Trent, Decrteum 25th. Cat. Rom., Pt. 3, Ch. 2, Que. 4-7, Pt 4. Ch. 6. Turrettin, Loc. xiv, Que. 4. Ridgeley, Qu. xxxvi. For Refutation, Essays on Romanism, Ch. 15. Turrettin, as above. Calvin and Dick.
6. How was Christ inducted in to His office?
   Dick, Lect. 54. Turrettin, Loc. xiii, Que. 12, Loc. xiv, Que. 6. Ridgeley, Que. xli, xlii.
7. How many offices does Christ fulfil as Mediator, and why these?
   Turrettin, Loc, xiv, Que. 5. Dick, Lect. 54. Calvin's Inst., Bk. ii, Ch. 15. Conf. of Faith, ch. viii, § 5 to end. Ridgeley, Que. xliii.

5. Christ only Mediator. Rome's Argument for Contrary.—The Apostle Paul teaches us, (1 Tim. ii: 5,) that as there is but one God, there is only "one mediator between God and man, the man Christ Jesus." Rome seeks to evade this and similar testimonies, by speaking of a primary, and a secondary mediation, reserving the second exclusively to Christ. The activity of angels and dead saints as secondary mediators, Rome argues, first, from the benevolence and affection of these pure spirits. This kindness we daily experience at the hands of the saints while alive; and the Saviour (Luke xv: 7,) seems to ascribe similar feelings to the angels. The Church believes that the dead saints retain a local interest in the places and people which they loved while living; and she thinks that Dan. x: 13, teaches the angels, as ministers of God's providence, have their districts, and even their individuals, (Matt. xviii: 10,) whom they serve and watch: Second. Rome urges that numerous cases exist in which the mediatorial intervention of one saint for another occurs, in the Bible. Of this the most obvious instance is the requesting of the brethren's prayers (e. g., 1 Thess. v: 25; 2d Thess. iii: 1,) and this case alone, Rome thinks, would be enough to rebut the Protestant objections that such intercession interferes with the mediatorial honors of Christ. But, say they, there are numerous instances of more definite intervention, where the *merit* of a saint availed for other men expressly; or where, (better still,) the pardon of men was suspended on the efforts of some eminently meritorious saint in their behalf. (See Gen. xx: 7; xxvi: 5; 1 Kgs. xi: 12, *et passim*; Job xlii: 8; Luke vii: 3–6. And they assert the actual intercession of angels in heaven is taught. (Gen. xlviii: 16; Rev. v: 8, or viii: 3.)

Rome argues also, reciprocally, that the worship of saints and angels implies their mediation; because the only thing for which we can petition them, consistently with theism, is their intercession. Hence all the rational and scriptural arguments in favour of saint-worship, are by inference, arguments in favour of their mediation. See, then, such considerations, and such texts as these: God commands an appropriate reverence of teachers, magistrates, parents, kings. Can we believe that

He intends no proportionable honor of these more beneficent and majestic beings? Can it be wrong to ask their aid with Christ, when we should esteem it pious to ask the aid of Christian friends on earth? Surely these glorified creatures have not become less benevolent towards us, or less acceptable to Christ, by reaching heaven? Then see scriptural instances; (Gen. xviii: 2, 23; xix: 1; xxxii: 26; Josh. v: 14.

The closing argument of Rome is from tradition, and the Apocryphan.

Replies.—Now, the reply is, first, that all such appeal to the mediation of the saints in heaven, or of angels, is *superstition*. The Scriptures uniformly represent, that the dead are severed from all earthly relations, and are done with all earthly interests, even pious ones. The simple idea of asking their prayers for us, if we had any access to them, (which we know we have not,) would not be worse than idle superstition. But, second, the wish to appeal to them reveals always a tendency which is derogatory to Christ's priestly work. Witness the perpetual inclination of Romanists, to shove Christ into the back ground, and pray to their tutelar saints rather than Him. Third, the idea that their mediatory access is *founded on their merits*, without which dogmo, Rome's whole scheme here would be naught, is expressly injurious to Christ, utterly false, and indeed, impious. No one who comprehended the rudiments of either the Covenant of Works, or of that of Grace, would ever dream of making the supererogatory merit of an unfallen, much less of a fallen creature, a basis for an imputed righteousness. In that sense, the *creature cannot merit*. Take the case of Abraham, Gen. xx: 7. The Romish argument is ruined by the fact that Absaham was himself "justified by faith. If he was himself a sinner, accepted in the righteousness of Another, how could he have supererogatory merit to spare for a fellow-sinner? Job is mentioned, xlii: 8, as sacrificing for his erring friends; because he was righteous. But see the 6th verse, where Job avows his utter sinfulness. Surely, then, he was not righteous in such a sense as to be a meritorious mediator. Job was directed to *sacrifice* for his friends. What? Himself? No; but bullocks and rams typical of the "Lamb of God that taketh away the sin of the world." This tells the whole story: that his intervention was ministerial, and not mediatorial. As to King David, 1 Kings xi: 12, compare David's own language, Ps. xxx*ii*: 1, 2. It is God's regard for His own gracious covenant with David, and His own fidelity, which leads Him to favour Solomon. David himself, although comparatively a faithful ruler, was indebted to God's mercy both in his personal and official capacities, for escaping condemnation.

Chiefly, the Doctrine of Rome Idolatrous.—But, fourth, this appeal to saintly or angelic mediation is idolatrous, and a robbery of God. To suppose that these creatures in heaven can hear and answer is a practical ascription to them of God's peculiar attributes. Especially is this true of the more popular gods and goddesses in the Popish pantheon, the Virgin, Peter, Gabriel, &c.; to whom Romanists generally pray, the world over. They must have *omnipresence*, to be with their various votaries in different lands; *omniscence*, to discriminate, understand, and judge wisely of the multiplied requests; *omnipotence*, to bear the burden of care laid upon them; *infinite benevolence*, to be willing to care for others to so boundless a degree ; and *immutability*, to be a secure reliance, especially for the wants of a priceless soul.

No Created Angel Mediated.—The question of angelic mediation may be easily disposed of. The only instances in which an angel is worshipped, are those of the worship of the Angel of the Covenant, the eternal Word. Let the student examine all the cases of angel-worship claimed by the Romanists, and he will find that each one is a worship of that Divine Person. We are referred to Rev. v: 8, and viii: 3, for instances of angelic mediation. In the first, the odours presented by the four living creatures, and the four and twenty elders, are *their own*. They both, beyond doubt, symbolize the ransomed Church ; and the prayers they present are simply their own. In Rev. viii: 3, we assert that the great Angel, who takes the golden censer, and offers the incense, is Christ; the Angel of the Covenant again. It is objected that the Redeemer has already appeared in the scene, as "the Lamb in the midst of the throne." This is no valid objection to our exposition. The natures and functions of Christ are so glorious and full, that one symbol fails to exhaust them. Hence the multiplication of symbols for the same Divine Figure, even in the same scene, is not unusual in the prophets. The symbol of the Lamb represents Christ's humanity, the victim of justice, while that of the Angel conveys to us Christ the prophet, and intercessor, and king; a priest upon his throne. There is, then, no exegetical difficulty in receiving this angel as a symbol of Christ; and the coherency of this view, with the whole passage, and the whole Scripture, every way recommends it.

In conclusion, the powerful demonstration which the Scripture gives us against creature worship, is the strongest proof against creature mediation; for if they mediated, they must be worshipped. And the whole tenor of Scripture is, to represent Christ's tenderness as so great, and His priestly work as so efficacious, that there is neither need nor room, for any heavenly Meditator after Him. "We are complete in Him, which is the head of all principality and power." (Col. ii: 10.) Let the student study the inspired argument of that Epistle.

6. Christ's Anointing. When?—The words Messiah, Christ, mean "Anointed," in allusion to the spiritual unction bestowed on Christ. This was appropriate to all His offices; witness the anointing of Aaron, Saul, David, Solomon, Elisha. The thing typified by the oil, was spiritual endowment; and this was bestowed without measure on Christ. (See Ps. xlv: 2; Is. xi: 2; xlii: 1; lxi: 1, &c; Matt. iii: 16; Jno. iii: 34; Acts x: 38, &c.) The *reasons* of this anointing were, not a journey into heaven during the forty days' temptation; a notion unknown to Scripture, and moreover refuted by Luke ii: 46, 47; but His birth and baptism especially. The immediase seat of these spiritual influences was His humanity. His divinity was already infinite, perfect, and immutable. He is Himself a source of the Holy Ghost, as God. The consequence was, to make Him, not infinite as to His humanity, nor incapable of progress; but perfectly holy, and wise, pure zealous, faithful, &c., above all others. All forms of graces appropriate to a perfect man acted in Him, in such manners as were suitable to His Person.

7. CHRIST'S OFFICES THREE, AND WHY?—That Christ fulfils, as Mediator, the three offices of *Prophet*, *Priest*, and *King*, is proved by this argument. We find these three offices predicated of Him in Scripture in a specific and pointed manner, while all other terms of function or service applied to Him as "Servant," "Elect," "Messenger," &c., are rather to be regarded as general appelatives. For the prophetic office, see Heb. i: 1; Is. xi: 2, xlii: 1, 2, lxi: 1; Deut. xviii: 15, with Acts iii: 22–26; Is. lix: 12; John iv: 25. For the priestly, see Ps. cx: 4; Heb. viii: 1, &c., *passim;* 1 John ii: 1. Kingly, Ps. ii: 6; Is. ix: 6, 7; Ps. cx: 1; Zech. vi: 12–14, &c.; 1 Cor. i. 30.

That the offices of Christ are these three, we prove again by showing in detail, that all His mediatorial works can be refered to one or more of these three classes. All is either instructing, or atoning, or interceding, or conquering and ruling, or several of them together. The necessity for these offices, (which we show,) also proves it. Man lay under three evils—ignorance, guilt, rebellion. And Redemption consists of three parts—*announcing*, *purchasing*, and *applying* salvation.

LECTURE XL.

SYLLABUS.

MEDIATORIAL OFFICES.

8. Prove that Christ is a Prophet. Under how many periods and modes did He fulfil this office? In what points was He superior to other prophets?

Turrettin, Loc. xiv, Que. 7, § 3, 4, and 12. Dick, Lect. 54th and 55th. Ridgeley, Que. xliii.

9. Prove that Christ is truly a Priest. What the several parts of the priet's functions. What the peculiarities of Christ's priesthood.

Turrettin, Loc. xiv, Que. 89. Dick, Lect. 56. Ridgeley, Que. xliv, § i and ii.

10. Prove, against Socinians, &c., *the necessity* of an atonement.

Turrettin, Loc. xiv, Que. 10. § 16–23. Dick, Lect. 56. Hill, Bk. iv, ch. 3, § 1, Turrettin, Loc. iii, Que. 19. Ridgeley, Que xliv, § iii. Magee on Atonement. A. A. Hodge on Atonement, chs. 5th and 6th. Watson's Theo. Institutes, ch. xix.

8. The proof has already been presented, that Christ performs the office of a Prophet.

CHRIST'S PROPHETIC WORK. ITS TRUE STAGES.—The Phrophet is God's *Spokesman*, NABI, either to enforce, reveal, or predict, Christ, in the highest sense, did all. For definition of His prophetic work, see Cat., Que. 24. This work of our Saviour had three different stages.

1st, from the fall to His baptism by John; 2d, during His personal ministry until His ascension; 3d, thence to the final consummation. During *all* these stages, He has carried on His prophetic work, by these agencies common to the three; His Revelation given to us by the hand of prophets and apostles; His Spirit applying that revelation, and giving understanding and love; His providence, directing our conduct and the events happening us, including a constant, universal, and particular control of our mental laws and states, as well as physical. (This trenches on His Kingly powers.) But, during the first stage, Christ acted as prophet, in addition, by His theophanies, for which see Hengstenberg's Christol, vol. i, pp. 164–170, and His prophets, see 1 Pet. i: 10, 11.

During the second stage, Christ literally fulfilled the work of a prophet in His own person, by inculcating truths known, revealing truths, and predicting future events. During the last stage, He gave His Holy Ghost to Apostles and Evangelists, thus enduing their teachings with His own authority. See John xvi: 12–15; Eph. iv: 12.

WHEREIN SUPERIOR TO HUMAN PROPHETS.—Dick contrasts Christ's prophetic work with that of all other prophets, in its fullness, its perspicuity, (arising from His fuller endowments and knowledge, as well as from a clearer dispensation,) realities instead of tyyes, its authority, arising from His divinity, and its efficacy, arising from His divine power to send forth Spiritual influences along with His word. But when we say, Christ was *fuller* as a revealer, let us not fall into Socinian error, who, to make a *notus vindice dignus*, while they deny Christ's vicarious work, teach that Christ not only developed, but made substantial additions to and alterations in the Old Testament. A perfect and holy God could not reveal a faulty code. See also Matt. v: 17; Mark xii: 31; Rom. xiii: 9. And if the pretended cases of alteration be examinee, they will be found supported by the teachings of the Old Testament.

9. CHRIST THE TRUE PRIEST.—The proof that Christ is a true and real Priest, would begin with texts such as Ps. cx: 4; Heb. v: 5, viii: 1, *et passim*, (whose trick is to confine Christ's priestly work to heaven. for, no suffering is there—*ergo*, He *can't* be a suffering Atoner) But as the Socinians evade these, by saying that so Peter, (1 Eph. ii: 9,) Rev. i: 6, &c, call Christians *quasi* priests, because they present to God the oblation of a holy life; we must substantiate the reality of Christ's priestly work, by proceeding to prove that He literally performs the two functions thereof, *sacrifice* and *intercession*. This course of argument leads us to anticipate, of course, those proofs by which the reality of a vicarious atonement, and intercession founded thereon, are evinced. We now, therefore, merely name them. Christ is called and appointed Priest, with peculiar emphasis. Heb. vii: 20. He is the antitype of a long line of unquestioned priests. Heb. viii: 4, 5, ix: 11. Surely it is not unreasonable to expect at least as much substantial reality in the body, as in the shadow it casts before! Again: the typical sacrifices of the law contained the true vicairous idea; but they represented Christ's. Last: it is expressly said He made His *soul a sacrifice for sin* by dying. Christians are only said to make their *lives* an oblation of gratitude, *they still living*. See Rom. xii: 1.

The peculiarities of Christ's priesthood are; 1. The dignity of His person; 2, the solemnity of His appointment, by an oath; 3. His combining royalty and priesthood like Melchisedec; 4. His having, like him, neither predecessor, nor successor; because, 5. His oblation had such infinite value and complete efficacy, that, 6. It grounded at once an everlasting and all prevalent intercession; and that, 7. Not only for one man, or race, but for all the Elect.

10. Necessity of Satisfaction argued from God's perfections.—The argument for the necessity of an atonement proceeds chiefly on the question, whether distributive justice is an *essential* moral attribute of God; or whether, as Socinians assert, there is nothing in His nature which renders it less natural and proper for Him to remit guilt without satisfaction, than to create, or leave uncreated a given thing. The Socinians, as we have seen, in order to evade the doctrine of a vacarious atonement, deny both the necessity of it, and the essential justice of God.

Bear in mind, then, that in this whole argument we attribute to God all the perfections which make Him an immutable and infinite Being. We shall not pause to argue these against Socinians, but refer you to your previous course of theology.

Holiness, Justice, and Truth.—a.) The Scriptures ascribe to God holiness, righteousness, and justice, in a sense which shows them to be *essential attributes*. See Is. vi: 3; Ps. lxxxix: 14, v: 4; Gen. xviii: 25; Exod. xxxiv: 7; Hab. i: 13; Rom. i: 18, 32, ii: 6–11, iii: 6, &c., &c. Some of these passager bring to view His *justitia universalis*, or the general rectitude of His nature; and some His administrative justice, as dealing with His moral creatures. Now, we argue from the former, that since God is immutable, and this perfection is essential, He will not, and by a moral necessity *cannot*, be affected by moral evil as He is by good. It is impossible that His feeling and will can confound the two, can fail to be opposed to sin, and favourable to rectitude. But God, while His will *is* governed by His own perfections, is absolutely free; so that no doubt His conduct will follow His will. God's distributive justice we naturally conceive as prompting Him to give every one his due. As naturally as well being is the just equivalent of obedience, just so naturally is suffering the equivalent of sin; and justice as much requires the punishment of sin, as the reward of merit. To fail in apportioning its desert to either, is real injustice. Now, does not God assert that His ways are equal? Shall not the like rule guide Him which He imposes on us? See, then, Prov. xvii: 15; Rom. ii: 6–11.

The necessity not physical.—But the necessity which we assert for God's punishing guilt is only moral. It is not a physical necessity like that which ensures that fire will burn, supposing the presence of fuel, and that water will wet, supposing its application. Here, then, falls the cavil of Socinus, that if retributive justice be made an essential attribute of God, its exercise must be conceived of as inevitable in every case, because of God's immutability, (as we call it,) so that mercy in every case would be impossible. Divine immutability does not imply that God must ever act in modes mechanically identical; but that His actings must always be consistent with the same set of essential attributes. As circumstances change, His very immutability requires a change of outward actings. Again; for God to effectuate a given part of His decrees of mercy, when, *in time*, the conditions of that execution are first in existence, is no change of purpose in Him. When God passes from wrath to reconciliation, as to a given sinner, it is no change in Him. The change is in the sinner. The same attributes which demanded wrath before, now demand peace: because the sinner's guilt is gone. The proper view of God's immutable perfections, therefore, leads us to conclude, that without an atonement they would render pardon of sin absolutely and universally impossible; but that, an atonement being provided, they offer no obstacle to pardon. Since God has seen fit to pledge His *truth* to the execution of penal sanctions, this attribute also necessitates their execution. He has threatened. See Num. xxiii: 19. Now He cannot truthfully retract. This is enhanced by the repetitions, energy, and oaths with which He has said and sworn that the wicked shall not enter into His rest.

God's Glory His own properest End.—b.) We shall not say, as Hill incautiously does in one place, that the fact God is *a Lawgiver* is the first principle on which the doctrine of the atonement rests; although we shall, in its proper place, assign it due importance. The importance of God's justice being protected, does not arise only or chiefly from the fact that the order of His universal Empire is concerned therein. God Himself, and not His creature's well-being, is the proper ultimate end of His own actings, as well as of our deeds of piety; a doctrine repugnant indeed to all Socinian and rational theories, but founded in reason and Scripture. If the perfections and rights of God are such that it is proper all other beings should love and serve Him supremely, by what argument can it be proved that He should not do so likewise? Again: He being before all things, and having all the motives and purposes for making all things from eternity, while as yet nothing was, must have found those motives only in Himself. He being the only Thing existent, there was no where else to find them. Third: If creatures *ought to render* the supreme homage of their powers and being to God, *ought not* He to *receive it?* 1 Cor. x: 31. Last, to make any thing else the ultimate End of the Universe, deposes God, and exalts that something to the true post of deity; to which God is made to play the part of an almighty convenience. Let human pride be pulled down. As for Scriptures, see Prov. xvi: 4: Is. lxi: 3; Rom. xi: 36.

Satisfying His own Justice therefore His chief Motive.—God *ought*, therefore, to regard transgression, which outrages His holy attributes, and excites His wrath, in a very different way from that proper for us *creatures, sinners ourselves*, when our fellow-sinners offend us. It may be very true that it is good, magnanimous, for one of us to forgive injury without satisfaction, and to extirpate our indignation for the sake of rescuring our fellow-creature from suffering the punishment; but the reasoning does not hold, when applied to the Supreme. The executing of His good pleasure, the illustration of His perfections are, for Him, more proper ends than the continued well-being of any or all sinful worlds, bestowed at the expense of His attributes. It is a more proper and noble thing that God should please Himself in the acting out of His own infinitely holy and excellent attributes, than that He should please His whole creation by bestowing impunity on guilty creatures. And, therefore, not only do reasons which arise out of God's moral relations to His creatures as their Ruler, but yet more reasons arising directly out of His own supremacy and righteousness, require Him to punish guilt without fail.

Socinian Obcections. Ans. by 4 Distinctions.—Socinians clamorously object, that we who teach the necessity of an atonement, strip God of those qualities which in all others would be most noble, generous and admirable; a willingness to overlook His own resentment, and magnanimously forgive without payment of the injury, where penitence was expressed. That we represent God as an odious and cruel Being, who would rather see His erring creatures damned, no matter how penitent, than sacrifice His own pique; and who is determined to pour out His revenge *somewhere*, if not on the sinner, or his substitute, before He will be satisfied. These cavils are already answered by the above view. For a private *man* to act thus would be unamiable; he is himself a sinner. God has told him, "Vengeance is Mine;" and the supreme rule of the man's life is, that he shall do every thing, forgiving injuries among the rest, for *God's* pleasure and honour. But God is Himself the *supreme End* of all His doings, as well as Chief Magistrate of the universe. Turrettin, Hill, &c., also appeal to other distinctions, to rebut these objections. Four things may be conssdered in a transgression, viewed as against a human ruler. The *debt* contracted thereby, the wrath or indignation excited, the moral defilement contracted by the transgressor in the eyes of the injured party, and the *guilt*, or obligation to legal penalty, incurred. Now, the plausibility of the Socinian cavil arises wholly from regarding the first three elements of sin, and studiously averting the eyes from the fourth. So far as the injury done me, as a magistrate, was a *personal debt* of wrong, humanity might prompt me to release it without satisfaction rendered; for that element of debt being personal, I have a personal right to surrender it if I choose. So far as I have had a personal sense of indignation and resentment excited by the wrong, that also it might be generous and right in me to smother, without satisfaction, in compassion to the wrong doer. I conceive that a certain element of moral defilement has come on him by his evil act, which constitutes a reason for punishing. If he amends that moral defilement by sincere penitence and reform, that obstacle to an unbought pardon is also removed. But it is far otherwise with the debt of *guilt to law*, of which I am the guardian. That is not a debt personal to me; and therefore I, as lawgiver, may not remit it without satisfaction. If I do, I violate my trust as guardian of the laws. Such is their arguing, and it is just. But it applies to God, as against sinning creatures, far more than to human lawgivers. And the same reasonings which show that the human ruler ought to surmount the first, second, and third elements of offence, in order to pardon, *do not* apply to God. The human lawgiver is but a man, and the transgressor is also a man, his brother, and nearly his equal in God's eye. In the other case, the offended party is infinite, and the offender His puny, absolute property, whom God may and ought to dispose of for the sovereign gratification of His own admirable and excellent perfections.

Satisfaction does not compel God.—Again; it is an utter perversion to carry the idea of pecuniary debt so far, in our conceptions of guilt, as to conceive of a vicarious atonement as a *legal tender*. When a security comes forward, and offers to pay the whole debt of the poor insolvent in jail, with principal and interest, cost and charges; the creditor *must* accept this legal tender; if he does not, he cannot claim payment afterwards. And the insolvent demands his release as of right. Now, *guilt* is not a mere debt, in this sense. It is a personal obligation to penalty; because the responsibility violated was strictly personal; and strict justice would entitle the ruler to hold the guilty party to endure that penalty in himself. Therefore, when the personal relation to law is waived by the ruler, and a substitute accepted, there is an acs of grace, of mercy. This is the answer to the objection, that "if the necessity of the atonement be asserted, God the Father performs no act of grace, and deserves no thanks for letting the transgressor go free. He has exacted the last penny, and the release is a mere act of jurtice." To our our Surety it is; but not to us. Besides, was there no grace in *giving* us the surety to pay for us?

The Law requires Satisfaction.—c.) Both the moral and ceremonial law show that God's justice is essential, and therefore an atonement necessary. The former is a transcript of His own essential perfections: the precepts are of necessary and perpetual obligation, and in sundry cases, the threatening of penalty is a part thereof, e. g., in the 3d Com. The ceremonial law typifies everywhere the necessity of satisfaction. Heb. ix: 22. And the evangelical interpretation of Heb. x: 4, makes this even clearer; because if God's primitive justice might have been waived without any satisfaction, of course it might have been, *with* that of animal blood. This, however impotent to atone, did not damage the sinner's case, at least.

Else God's requirement of us unfair.—The whole of the above argument may be put in a very practical light—thus: Is not judicial impartiality with God "a matter of principle?" The upright human judge, who was entreated by the convicted man, or by his counsel, to act as the Socinian expects God to act in pardoning, would be insulted! Now, how does God require us to act, in matters of principle? He literally requires us to die rather than compromit our principles. He requires us to meet martyrdom, rathea than yield them. Now, does God first command us to seek our complete rectitude in the *imitation of Himself*, and then act oppositely to His injuction to us? Surely not. In representing the necessity of satisfaction as so high, as to call for the infinite satisfaction of Christ's death in order to make sin pardonable, we conform precisely to the system of morals which the Scriptures commend to us, for ourselves. The tendency of Calvinism is wholesome herein.

Plainly, Socinianizing theologians will never produce genuine martyrs, as history shows. *You cannot make men more virtuous then their God.* If they are taught to believe that He takes liberties with His principles, they will infallibly take more. One need never expect true, sturdy integrity, where the "New Theology" prevails. The father says to his sons: "I shall put my principles in my pocket, when I am inclined; but if you do, I will whip you to death. Such a father can rear only sneaks.

GENTILE FEARS AND SACRIFICES.—d) Reason and natural conscience admit the necessity of satisfaction to divine justice. Witness the common consent of mankind in their *fears* and *bloody* sacrifices. Says Ovid, *Timor fecit Deos.* I ask, *Quis fecit timorem?* An intuitive apprehension of God as existing, and as just, must have preceded the fear. The universal attempt of man to appease God's justice, is man's testimony to its necessity. Whence is conscience, if not from God?

ARGUMENT FROM NATURAL CONSCIENCE.—Human conscience has ever recognized the principle that natural evil is the penal consequence of moral evil. So, Rom. v: 12, vi: 23, &c. God's providence is *special and almighty;* whence we conclude that wherever there is suffering under it, there is guilt. Suffering is the fair equivalent of guilt, as happiness is of good-desert. Now, the Socinian's conception of God's justice is, that penal inflictions and rewards are merely a politic means of repression for sin, and encouragement for holiness. Not so the Bible and conscience. In addition to those reasons, God rewards or punishes, because there is an intrinsic merit of reward in the good, and of suffering in the bad conduct, so that, abstract justice forbids their final severance. For, if God's rewarding and punishing is *only* a *policy,* His benevolence can never be cleared consistently with His omnipotence. Why did He not repress sin in some more efficient and benevolent way? He had all power. He must have foreknown that this plan would secure only partial well-being to creation. On this scheme of ethicks, so called, *eternal* future punishments could never be justified, consistently with God's omniscience and omnipotence. For there the reformatory policy is wholly deserted. Hence, every Socinianizing man *tends* to Universalism.

Nor, indeed, can any temporary punishment imposed by God, consist with His infinite benevolence and infinite knowledge and power. Again; man's natural conscience repels the doctrine, that punishment originates in mere policy. For then, if it could be shown that the guilty person would be more effectually deterred from sin by punishing some beloved relative than by punishing him, it would be more *just* to punish that innocent relative! Again; since *happiness for good merit* is the exact correlative of suffering for demerit, if suffering for demerit is mere policy, so is the former—i. e., the innocent has no more *moral title* to his impunity than the guilty to his penalty. So that it might be as *right* in God to separate reward from good desert for policy's sake, as to separate punishment from ill-desert—i. e., to pardon without satisfaction. How like you this, "Mr. Legality?" See 2 Thes. i: 6; Heb. ii: 2, *et sim. passim.*

ARGUMENT FROM GOD'S RECTORAL JUSTICE.—e.) Moreover; does not God bear moral relations to His creatures, as well as they to Him? Ps. cxliv: 17. Surely. As Ruler, and especially, as almighty Ruler, with nothing to hinder Him from doing His will, He is bound to His own perfections to rule them aright, as truly as they are bound to Him, to serve aright. This being so, retributive justice will be seen to flow as a necessity from the holiness and righteousness of God. By these attributes God necessarily and intrinsically approves and delights in all right things. Wrong is the *antithesis* of right. A moral *tertium quid* is an impossibility; as the mere absence of light is darkness. There is no moral neutrality. Hence, it results, that God must hate the wrong by the very reason He approves the right; e. g., if a man feels moral complacency at filial affection, will he not, *ipso facto*, be certain to feel repugnance at ingratitude? I see not how God would be holy at all, unless His justice is necessary.

Again; were it not so, God would be *unjust* to His innocent creatures. Sin is injurious; to all but infallible Being, contagious, and universally mischievous. God has been pleased to adopt a plan of moral sanctions, to protect the universe from sin. Those beings who kept their covenant with God, have a right on Him, which He, in infinite condescension, gave them, to be protected efficiently. Hence, His righteousness must lead Him to inflict penal sanctions with exactness. For it is well known that uncertainty in this encourages transgression, confounds moral distinctions, and relaxes government. Should God do thus, He would be sacrificing the well-being and rights of those who deserved well at His hands, to a weak compassion for those who deserved nothing. God's essential justice is the foundation of the rights, and order of the universe. Unless its actings are certain and regular, we are all at the mercy of an unprincipled Omnipotence. Even the damned have no interest in making God's justice uncertain; because it is the only guarantee that they shall not be punished more than they deserve. And the wider God's dominions, the greater strength have all these arguments, forcible as they are even in the narrow domain of the family, school, or State.

Pardons by magistrates no precedents.—The parellel drawn from acts of pardon without atonement, safely and beneficially indulged in by human rulers, is deceptive; because they have not the divine perfections of omnipotence, unchangeableness, and omniscience. It might be no dishonour to a human magistrate to modify his purposes; he never professed to be either perfectly wise or immutable. Cases may arise of conviction, where the evidence of guilt is uncertain, or the criminal intention doubtful. In these cases, (and these alone,) the pardoning power may find a wholesome exercise. Such cases have no existence in the administration of an omniscient God. Once more; the power and authority of human rulers is limited. They must govern as they can, sometimes, not as they would; God can do all things.

In a word, God's moral government, in its ultimate conclusion, must be as absolute and perfect as His own nature. For, being supreme and almighty, He is irresponsible save to His own perfections. Therefore, if He is a Being of infinite perfections, His government must be one of absolutely righteous, final results. It will be an exact representation of Himself; for He makes it just what He pleases. If there is moral defect in the final adjustment, it can only be accounted for by defect in God. It must be an absolute result, because the free act of an infinite Being.

f.) The death of Christ argues the necessity of satisfaction. For Socinus admits, that He was an innocent Man, God's adopted Son. Surely God would not have made Him suffer under imputed guilt, (He had none of His own,) unless it had been morally necessary. In this view, we see that the atonement, instead of obscuring, greatly exalts God's love and mercy; that though He knew the price of pardon must be the blood of His own Son, His pity did not fail.

ARGUMENT FROM SACRIFICES.—g.) The necessity of atonement is taught in all the Old Testament sacrifices (as the gentile sacrifices are the testimony of man's conscience to the same truth.) The Apostle Paul, as already intimated, makes a grand induction of the ritual facts of the Old Testament, in Heb. ix: 22. "And without shedding of blood was no remission." It is literally true, that the ceremonial law remitted no trespass, sin, or uncleanness, without a substitutionary animal death. Search and see. The theological principle thus set forth is just my thesis; the necessity of satisfaction in order to pardon. Now, there is no idea which is inculcated, in the whole of Revelation, so constantly, so early, so carefully. It was the first truth, in the religion of redemption, taught to Adam's family. The awful, bloody symbol of it was *ever present*, in all the worship of the Old Testament Church. With God's mind, it is ever the first and strongest thought. With man's unbelieving mind, it is the last, and least. Indeed, the contrast here is amazing; and the stupidity of the human mind in apprehending this first rudiment, is one of the strongest proofs of its natural deadness in sin. God's example, in perpetually obtruding on sinners, the impressive sacrificial symbol of this truth, should be instructive to pastors. They must constantly urge the necessity of satisfaction.

TACIT ADMISSION OF ADVERSARIES.—h.) Last; it is tacitly implied in the admissions of Socinians themselves, that God could not consistently pardon without the repentance and reform of the sinner. For this gives up the point that, in some sort, a satisfaction to the divine honour must be excated. But, repentance and reform are not satisfactions. Second, we shall prove that repentance is the consequence and result of pardon; so that it cannot be its procuring cause. An injured man, we admitted, might regard repentance as obviating the third element of transgression, the subjective moral turpitude. But, in God's case, it may not: because God must bestow the repentance, as truly as the pardon; and as a consequence of the pardon. See Acts v: 31; Jer. xxxi: 18, 19.

We will close with these general Bible testimonies to the necessity of satisfaction: Heb. vii: 27; viii: 3; ix: 7, 12, 22, 23, 28; x: 9, 10, 26, 27 to 29; ii: 10, 14, 17.

LECTURE XLI.

SYLLABUS.

NATURE OF THE ATONEMENT.

1. What analogies in the course of nature and providence for an atonement? And why is not vicarious punishment more admitted among men?

Butler's Analogy, pt. ii, ch. 5. Hill, Bk. iv, ch. 3, § 1. Watson's Theol. Inst., ch. xx, § 8.

2. What the usage and meaning of the words rendered "atonement," in the Scripture; and of its kindred terms?

Symington on "Necessity of Atonement." Lexicons. Hodge on the Atonement, ch. iii. Knapp, § 110.

3. Give the direct refutation of the Socinian theory of the atonement; and of that which makes it only a governmental display.

Turrettin, Loc. xiv, que. 11. Hill, Bk. iv, ch. 2, § 1, 2. Hodge's (Ch.) Review of Beman. Dick, Lect. 57. A. A. Hodge on Atonement, ch. 21.

4. Prove Christ's proper substitution and vicarious sacrifice. a.) From the phraseology of Scripture. b.) From His personal innocency. c.) From the import of Gentile sacrifices. d.) From the import of Levitical sacrifices typical of Christ. e.) From the Bible terms describing Christ's death.

Turrettin, Loc. xiv, que. 11. Hill, Bk. iv, ch. 3, § 2, 3, 5. Dick, Lect. 57, 58. Hodge on Atonement, chs. 8 to 12. Ridgeley, que. xliv, § 4 and 5. Watson's Theol. Inst., ch. xx. Knapp, § 111.

5. On what features do the value and efficacy of Christ's work depend?

Symington on Atonement, § 2. Hill, Bk. iv, ch. 3, § 1.

1. Atonement foreshadowed by course of Providence.—To the question: How shall man be just with God, Natural Theology gives no certain answer. It seems, if we do not deceive ourselves by attributing to its light, discoveries borrowed really from Revelation, to inform us very clearly, that God is just, and man, therefore, condemned. Having thus shut us up under wrath, its light deserts us, leaving only an uncertain twilight shining towards the gate of mercy and hope. When Reason looks into the analogies presented by that "Course of Nature," as unbelief calls it, which is in truth the *course of Providence*, she sees that there are certain evils consequent upon certain faults—e. g., sickness on intemperance, want on idleness, bodily death on reckless imprudence; but she also sees that there are certain remedial provisions made in nature, by availing themselves of which men may sever the connexion between the fault and the natural penalty. This fact would seem to *hint* that in God's eternal government there may be a way of mercy provided. But then the analogical evidence is made very faint by this fact: that these natural reliefs for the natural evils incurred here by our misconduct, are rather postponements than acquittals. After all, inexorable death comes to sinful man, in spite of all expedients.

Intervention usually costs a penalty.—But the most interesting fact to be noticed in this feeble analogy is, that these partial releases from the natural consequences of our faults, are most often received through a *mediatorial* agency, and that this agency is usually exerted for us by our friends at some *cost to themselves;* often at the cost of suffering the whole or a part of the very evils our faults naturally incurred. A man is guilty of intemperance; its natural consequence is sickness and death; and without Mediatorial intervention, this consequence would become certain; for the foolish wretch is too sick to minister to himself. But Providence permits a faithful wife, or parent, or friend, to intervene with those remedies and cares which save his life. Now, at what *cost* does this friendly mediator save it? Obviously, at the cost of many of the very pains which the sick man had brought upon himself, the confinement, the watching, the loss of time, the anxieties of the sick room. Or, a prodigal wastes his substance, and the result is want; a result, so far as his means are concerned, inevitable. But his friend steps in with his wealth, pays his bebts and relieves his necessities. Yet the cost at which he does it is in part the very same incurred by the guilty man's prodigality: decrease of his substance and consequent want. We may say, yet more generally, that the larger part of all the reliefs which Providence administers to the miseries of man's sinful condition, from the cradle to the grave, from the maternal love which shields and blesses his infancy, down to the friendship which receives his dying sighs, are administered through *others;* and that at the cost of *sacrifice or effort* on their part for him. Here, then, we have a general analogy pointing to a *vicarious method* of rescuing man from his guilt, and to atonement by a Mediator for him. We have called the evils adverted to in our illustrations, *natural consequences* of our faults; but they are not therefore any the less ordained of God, and penal; for what is the course of nature, but God ordering? and does not our natural conscience show that suffering can only occur under the almighty providence of a just and good God as the *penal* consequences of ill-desert?

The revealed idea of an *atonement*, or vicarious arrangement to deliver man from guilt, has been made the butt of rationalistic objections. The value of this analogy is to silence these objections, by showing that the idea, however mysterious, is not unnatural.

SUBSITUTION UNUSUAL IN CIVIL LAW, FOR REASONS.—It has been objected by rationalists that vicarious atonements are not admitted in the penal legislation of just and civilized *men;* and if introduced, would strike our moral judgments as wrong and unreasonable. It may be remarked, that among the ancients these arrangements frequently appeared, in the cases of hostages, and ANTIPSUCHOI. In modern legislation they appear at least in the case of suretyships for debt. But there are four very good reasons which distinguish between human governments and God's.

BECAUSE GOD IS A SOVEREIGN LEGISLATOR.—1st. It is in my view, unreasonable and mischievous, to reply to objections against the morality of a substitution (Christ's or Adam's) by such a reference to God's sovereignty, as should represent it as irresponsible, not only to man's imperfect conceptions of rectitude, but to the intrinsic principles thereof. What is this but saying that because God is omnipotent owner, therefore He may properly be unjust. Does might make right?

But it is a very different (and proper) thing to say that, while God, as Sovereign, regulates His every act by *the same* general principles of rectitude, which He enjoins on His creatures, yet He very justly exercises a width of discretion, for Himsulf, in His application of those principles, which He does not allow to human magistrates, in delegating them a little portion of His power. Deut. xxiv: 16. This is made proper by His *sovereignty* (I may righteously do with *my* horse, what would be cruel in him to whom I had hired him, for a day's ordinary journey—e. g., ride him to extremity, or even to death, to rescue the life of my child.) And by God's infinite knowledge and wisdom, judging the whole results of a substitution as a creature cannot. Hence, the impropriety of vicarious arrangements among men may be compatible with their admission between God and man; and yet no contrariety of moral principles in the two governments, is involved; e. g. I delegate to a teacher, at a distance, a portion of my parental power over my child.

I tell him he is to consider himself, as to this extent, *in loco parentis*, and govern my boy on *strictly parental principles;* yet he would be very unreasonable if he assumed power to exercise every kind of discretion as to him, which I might properly exercise.

His object in punishing vindicatory.—2d. When men inflict penalties less than capital, one object of the infliction is the reform of the offender; for which a personal endurance of the pain is necessary. But when God inflicts the eternal penalty of sin, He has no intention of reforming the sufferer thereby.

No substitute among men, sui juris.—3d. In those cases where human tribunals punish by the loss of life or liberty, the vicarious arrangement cannot be adopted, because no one can be found who is owner of his own life and well-being. But he cannot pay away, in ransom of another, what he has no right to part with.

Civil Magistrate cannot sanctify.—4th. We found that one of the elements of offence contracted by wrong-doing was the moral turpitude; and that the removal of this by genuine repentance is one of the necessary conditions for pardoning the wrong-doer. Now, a vicarious atonement is inapplicable in human governments, because the human magistrate would have no means to work genuine repentance in the criminal, though an atonement were offered. But without such repentance, guilt could not be properly pardoned, by God or man, however adequate the atonement, as a satisfaction to justice. Now, God *can* work and insure genuine repentance in His pardoned criminals, through the Holy Ghost. See Acts v: 31. Hence, He can properly avail Himself of the principle of vicarious atonement. Even supposing a *man* could be found who had autocracy of his own life, time, and social relations, and who was willing to die for a murderer. When slain, he could not rise again: he would be a final loss to society, and society would gain, in exchange, the life of the murderer, now penitent and reformed, (supposing the magistrate, like God, had regenerating power over him.) So, all the result would be, that society would lose a citizen who always had been good, and gain one who was about to become good. The magistrate would not feel himself justified in admitting the substitution, for such results, however it might be generous in the friend to propose it.

IV. Definition.—Word *Atonement* is used often in the Old Testament, once in the New, Rom. v: 11. The Hebrew is usualay copher, literally, "covering," because that which atones is conceived as covering guilt from the eye of justice. The Greek is katallage,—reconciliation, as it and its cognates are elsewhere translated. It is plausibly supposed that "atonement" is "*at-one-ment*,"—i. e., reconciliation. These words, then, are generic, and not specific of the particular means of reconciliation, according to etymology. The word which I should prefer to use, is one sanctioned by the constant usage of the Reformed theologians, *Satisfaction*. This expresses truly and specifically, what Christ did for believers. It points explicitly to the divine law and perfections, whose demand for satisfaction constitute the great obstacles to pardon. It includes, also, Christ's preceptive, as well as His penal compensation for our debt. But the other terms applied to our Saviour's work de fine it. That work is called APOLUTROSIS, (ransoming,) and He is called LUTRON, (ransom price.) Again, He is said to be our propitiation, HILASTERION EXILASMOS, i. e., that which makes God, before offended, to be propitious. These terms applied to Christ's suffering work, justify us in describing His *atonement, as His vicarious suffering of the penalties due our sins, to satisfy God's justice and thus reconcile Him to us.*

III. SOCINIAN THEORY STATED.—Before proceeding to refute the Socinian theory of the atonement, let us briefly re-state it. The sufferings of Jesus, they suppose, were not penal; but only natural, such as would have been incurred by Adam in Paradise, had he not fallen. Yet God permitted and ordained them, 1st. As an *example* to teach us patience, fortitude, and submission. 2d. As an attestation of the honesty and truth of His teachings concerning the way of life through imitation of Him. 3d. To make Him a compassionate Teacher, Friend, and Patron to His brethren. 4th. To make way for His *resurrection;* which was the all-important evidence and warrant to us, that eternal life may be hoped for, through repentance and reform. Thus, He died, suffered *for us*—i. e., *pro bono nostrum*—in a general sense. Thus, He is the Saviour and Redeemer of men—i. e., the Agent of their salvation in a sense. But He made no penal satisfaction for sin.

Now, an overwhelming indirect refutation of this theory has already been given, in our argument for the necessity of a proper vicarious atonement. Another will be presented under the succeeding head, when we prove that Christ's sufferings were vicarious. But for direct refutation, note:

THEORY INCONSISTENT. 1. BECAUSE A GUILTLESS SUFFERER SUGGESTS AN UNJUST GOD.—There can be little reasonable encouragement in the example of one, who suffered so bitterly without deserving any thing. Such a spectacle, instead of shedding light, hope and patience on the sorrows of believers, could only deepen the darkness and anguish; for it could only suggest difficulties concerning the justice and benevolence of God, and raise the torturing doubt, "Can any one be secure of blessedness, any angel or saint in heaven, or is there any justice and benevolence in God, in which I may hope for release from present sufferings; seeing a creature so holy as Jesus suffered thus? He was enabled to triumph over them at last? Yea, but why did God make Him suffer at all, when He was entirely innocent? I, who am not innocent, may not be thus released after suffering!

MARTYTDOM ONLY DEMONSTRATES MARTYR'S SINCERETY.—2. To represent His death as of such importance as the attestation of the honesty and truthfulness of His teachings, contradicts good sense and Scripture. All that the death of a martyr can prove is, that he sincerely believes the creed for which He dies. False creeds have had their martyrs. The Scriptures no where refer to Christ's death as the evidence of His truth; but uniformly to His works. See John xiv: 11, v: 36, x: 25-38, xv: 24, &c.

CHRIST'S DEATH PURCHASES SALVATION, NOT HIS RESURRECTION.—3 The Socinian scheme gives the chief importance to Christ's resurrection, rather than His death, as the means whereby "life and immortality were brought to light." His death was then rather the necessary preliminary step, to make His resurrection possible; that the latter might be, to our faith, the splendid and crowning evidence of a future life for us. Did God, then, kill Jesus to have the opportunity of raising Him? Since a resurrection is but the repairing of a death, it seems to me that the whole transaction inspires at least as much terror as hope. He ordained the death of Him who *deserved to live;* so there is an instance of severity, if not injustice, fully offsetting the instance of goodness in raising Him. Again; the Scriptures do not agree to the Socinian view; for they everywhere represent the benefit we derive from Christ as chiefly flowing from Christ's *death*. Heb. ii: 14. His resurrection was indeed a glorious attestation; but it was an attestation of the sufficiency of that death, as a satisfaction to law, and an adequate purchase of our relief.

He pre-existent.—Again; the whole plausibility of the Socinian's account of Christ's death and resurrection is ruined by the fact of His preëxistence. For a mere man to rise again after dying, like Lazarus, is an encouraging instance; but the rising again of a Being who possessed a previous and glorious life besides that of His humanity, presents no analogy to encourage mortal man to hope for a resurrection. The answer is too obvious: that the strange anomaly of a resurrection in Jesus' case was most probably the result of His glorious, pre-existent nature. Man has no such nature, and therefore should not expect, from such an instance, to imitate Him. As well might a log of wood infer that, because a living creature is seen to rise erect when laid on its back, therefore logs of wood may hope to rise, when laid on their backs. 4. The Socinian scheme utterly fails to account for Christ's royal *exaltation*. We do not allude now to the fact that those regal functions (Matt. xxviii: 18, xxv: 31, 32; Eph. i: 22) could only be fulfilled by proper divinity. On the Socinian scheme, He ought not to have any regal functions. He has not earned them. He does not need them. Sinners regenerate themselves; and their own repentance and reform are their righteousness, so that the tasks of the royal priest, interceding and ruling on His throne, are useless and groundless.

Christ, on this scheme, did not redeem Old Testament saints.—5. Last; on the Socinian theory, Christ could not have been in any sense the Mediator or Redeemer of Old Testament saints. Their sins could not have been remitted on the ground of Christ's prospective satisfaction for sin; for, according to Socinians, there was none in prospect. Those saints could not have profitted by Christ's example, teachings, and resurrection; because they were in heaven long before Christ existed. But see Heb. ix: 15; Rom iii: 25; Jno. viii: 56, &c.

The middle Scheme.—Against the scheme of Dr. Price, called by Hill, the Middle Scheme, (see Hill, p. 422,) these objections obviously lie: that it represents Christ as acquiring His title to forgive sin only by His death. But Matt. ix: 6, says that the Son of Man had power on earth to forgive sins before. It speaks splendidly of Christ's *suffering* in order to acquire this title to pardon; but it gives no intelligible account of *how* these sufferings acquired that title. It is in this, as vague as Socinianism.

Governmental Influence Scheme.—The scheme of atonement with which we have now most concern, as defenders of truth, is that usually known as the governmental scheme—i. e., that which resolves the sufferings and death of Christ into a mere moral expedient of God, to connect such a display of His justice and hatred of sin, with His acts of pardon, as will prevent bad effects from the failure to punish strictly according to law. This view proceeds from that theory of ethics which resolves all virtue into *benevolence*, teaching that an act is *right* or virtuous only because it tends on the whole most to promote the welfare of Beings; (and the contrary.) (We cannot pause here to debate this theory, but only note how intimately ethics and metaphysics affect Theology.) Hence, these divines hold, God has no intrinsic, essential justice, other than His benevolence—i. e., that the whole amount of His motive for punishing sin is, to preserve His moral empire from the mischiefs which sin unchecked would produce. Hence, the only *necessity* for an atonement which they recognize, is the necessity of repairing that defence against disorder in God's government, which the dispensing with the penalty would break down. They, consequently, deny that Christ was properly substituted under the believer's guilt, that He bore any imputation, that He made a real satisfaction to God's justice, and that the justifying virtue of His righteousness is imputed to men. The author of this system in New England seems to have been the younger Pres. Edwards, son of Jonathan, and its great propagator, Dr. Taylor, of New Haven. This is the system known as the New School, in the North, and advocated by Barnes and Beman on the atonement. It is a striking matter of history, that nearly all the arguments by which Edwards, Jr., sought to remove the old Calvinistic theory, to substitute his, were unconsciously Socinian.

Refutation.—If the *necessity of satisfaction* is proved from God's essential justice, as we have attempted, this view of the atonement is proved false. Again: if we shall succeed in proving that Christ's *was* a proper, vicarious sacrifice, this, also, overthrows it. Third; we have seen that this New England plan rests on this proposition; that a governmental policy of repressing sin, is the only ground of God's justice; resolving all *right* into mere utility. The abominable consequences of this ethical principle have been shown: they are such that the principle cannot be true. We might add that man's intuitive moral judgments pronounce that sin is wrong, *not* merely because it tends to injure well-being, but wrong in itself; and that the very wording of such a statement, implies a standard of wrong and right other than that of mere utility. This ethical principle being untrue, the plan falls with it.

It gives us no righteousness imputed.—But further, for direct refutations: This plan of atonement lands us practically on Socinian ground as to man's justifying righteousness. If imputation is denied, and if Christ wrought out no proper satisfaction to justice for the believer's sin, to be set over to the believer's account for his justification, there is no alternative left; the advocates of this plan are shut up to the semi-Pelagian definition of justification, as an imputing of the believer's own faith (along with the repentance and holy living flowing therefrom) as the ground of the sinner's repentance; as his righteousness. Accordingly, Messrs. Barnes, &c., do explicitly accept this.

But we shall show, in the proper place, that such a justification is unscriptural. Justification is no longer properly through Christ, saving faith would no longer be such a coming to Christ directly, as the Scriptures describe it; and the whole tenour of Bible language concerning His divine righteousness, concerning His being the immediate object of faith, &c., &c , would be violated.

It is false on its own showing.—Last; the overwhelming objection to this plan is, that according to its definition, the sufferings of Christ would be no governmental display whatever, of the evils of sin, or of God's determination to punish. These divines avow that Christ is a Person possessed of a pre-existent, divine, holy, and supreme nature, not only guiltless, but above law; and of a pure and sinless humanity, the voluntary assumption of which only placed Him, by His own consent, under law, for a particular atoning purpose. His mediatorial person stood forth as the Exemplar of sinless purity and perfection, to all creatures, in both its natures; and in every relation; attested by holy writ, by the voice of God speaking His divine approval from heaven in tones of thunder, by the reluctant tribute of His enemies, by the haughty Pagan who condemned Him, by the very traitor who betrayed Him, as He appears scathed with the fires of his own remorse, before his plunge into hell, and confesses that he had "betrayed the innocent blood." All heaven and all earth testified to the Son of Man, that He was "holy, harmless, undefiled, and separate from sinners;" testified to the universe. And yet, the universe is invited to come and behold this Being, the only innocent Man who had appeared since Adam, delivered to torments more cruel than any of Adam's guilty sons had ever endured, "delivered by the determinite counsel" of His Father, while without guilt, either personal or imputed! Is this a glorious display of justice? Does this illustrate the evil of sin, and the inexorable connexion which God's benevolence requires Him to maintain between sin and punishment? Does it not rather confound all moral distinctions, and illustrates the evils of holiness, the cruelty and injustice of the Hand that rules the world? There is no explanation of Christ's suffering innocence, which does not involve an insuperable contradiction, except the orthodox; and that, we admit, involves a great mystery.

Orthodox view includes all the others.—Each of the false schemes attempts to express *what is true*. But ours really includes all that theirs claim, while it embraces the vital element which they omit, vicarious penal satisfaction. And *note*: It is only by predicating the latter, that the moral influences claimed by the inadequate schemes really have place. Says the Socinian, Christ's suffering work is not vicarious, but only exemplary, instructive, and confirmatory. Says the modern "Liberal Christian:" it was intended only for that, and to present a spectacle of infinite tenderness and mercy, to melt the hearts of transgressors. Says the New Haven doctor: It was intended for those ends, and also to make a dramatic display of God's opposition to sin, and of its evils. But we reply; If it was not a vicarious satisfaction for imputed guilt, then it was not consistently either of the others. But if it was a vicarious satisfaction for guilt, then it also subserves, and admirably subserves, all these minor ends.

IV. Bible proofs of true theory.—We now proceed to the centre of the subject, to establish what has been several times anticipated—*Christ's proper vicarious suffering far imputed guilt.*

1. From various sets of Bible phrases, exceedingly numerous and varied, of which we only present specimens. Thus:

Christ died for us, &c.—He is said to have suffered and died "*for us,*" "*for* the ungodly." Rom. v: 6, 8; and "for our sins." 1 Pet. iii: 18. Peri hamartion. Socinians say: "True; He died in a general sense for us, inasmuch as His death is a part of the agency for our rescue; He did die to do us good, not for Himself only." The answer is, that in nearly every case, the context proves it *a vicarious dying,* for our guilt. Rom. v: "We are justified by His blood." 1 Pet. iii: 18. "The just for the unjust." (Huper adikon.) Then, also, He is said to be a lutron anti pollon. Matt. xx: 28. This proposition properly signifies substitution. See Matt. ii: 22 for instance.

Christ bore our sins, &c.—Again: He is said to *bear* our sins, and equivalent expressions. 1. Pet. ii: 24; Heb. ix: 28; Is. liii: 6. And these words are abundantly defined in our sense by Old Testament usage. cf.) Num. ix: 13. An evasion is again attempted, by pointing to Matt. viii: 17, and saying that there, this bearing of man's sorrows was not an enduring of them in His person, but a bearing of them away, a removal of them. We reply, the Evangelist refers to Is. liii: 4, not to liii: 6. And Peter says: "He bore our sins *in His body on the tree.*" The language is unique.

Christ made sin for us.—Another unmistakable class of texts, is those in which He is said to be made sin for us; while we are made righteousness in Him. See 1 Cor. i: 30; 2 Cor. v: 21. A still more indisputable place is where He is said to be made a curse for us. Gal. iii: 13. The orthodox meaning, considering the context, is unavoidable.

Christ our Ransom.—Again; He is said in many places to be our Redeemer—i. e., Ransomer—and His death, or He, is *our Ransom.* Matt. xx: 28; 1 Pet. i: 19; 1 Cor. vi: 20. It is vain to reply that God is said to redeem His people in many places, when the only meaning is, that He delivered them; and that Moses is called the redeemer of Israel out of Egypt, who certainly did not do this by a vicarious atonement. Christ's death is a proper ransom, because the very *price* is mentioned.

2. Christ bore imputed guilt because personally innocent.—Christ's work is shown to be properly vicarious, from His personal innocence. This argument has been anticipated. We shall, therefore, only tarry to clear it from the Pelagian evasion, and to carry it further. Pelagians, seeing that Christ, an innocent being, must have suffered vicarious punishment, if He suffered any punishment, deny that the providential evils of life are penal at all; and assert that they are only natural, so that Adam would have borne them in Paradise; the innocent Christ bore them as a natural matter of course. But what is the course of nature, except the will of God? Reason says that if God is good and just, he will only impose *suffering* where there is *guilt.* And this is the scriptural account: "*death by sin.*"

Further. Christ suffered far otherwise than is *natural* to good men. We do not allude so much to the peculiar severity of that combination of poverty, malice, treachery, destitution, slander, reproach and murder, visited on Christ; but to the sense of *spiritual death*, the horror, the fear, the pressure of God's wrath and desertion, and the satanic buffetings let loose against him. (Luke xxii: 53; Matt. xxvi: 38: xxvii: 46.) See how manfully Christ approaches His martyrdom; and how sadly He sinks under it when it comes! Had He borne nothing more than natural evil, He would have been inferior to other merely human heroes; and instead of recognizing the exclamation of Rousseau as just: "Socrates died like a philosopher; but Jesus Christ as a God," we must give the palm of superior fortitude to the Grecian sage. Christ's crushing agonies must be accounted for by His bearing the wrath of God for the sins of the world.

3. Christ a Sacrifice. Pagan sense of word.—Another just argument for Christ's proper vicarious sacrifice is brought from the acknowledged belief of the whole Pagan world, at the Christian era especially, concerning the meaning and intent of their bloody sacrifices. No one doubts that, however mistaken the Pagans are, they have always regarded their bloody sacrifices as proper *offerings for guilt*. Now, we use this fact in two ways. First. Here is the great testimony of man's universal conscience to the necessity of satisfaction for human guilt. Second. The sacred writers knew that this was what the whole world understood by "*sacrifice*." Why, then, did they call Jesus Christ, in so many phrases, a sacrifice? Did they wish to deceive?

4. Jewish Sense.—We find another powerful Bible proof in the import of the Levitical sacrifices. This argument is contained in two propositions. First. The theological idea designed to be symbolized in the Levitical sacrifices, was a *substitution of a victim*, and the vicarious suffering of it in the room of the offerer, for his guilt. (See Levit. xvii: 11; Levit. i: 4, *et passim;* xvi: 21.) Second. Christ is the antitype, of which all these ceremonies were shadows. (See Jno. i: 29; 1 Cor. xv: 3; 2 Cor. v: 21; Heb. viii: 3; ix: 11–14, &c., &c.) Now, surely the great idea and meaning of the types is not lacking in the antitype! Surely the *body* is not more unsubstantial than the shadow! This important argument may seem elaborated with great learning and justice, in the standard works on Theology, as Dick or Ridgeley, in works on Atonement, such, especially, as Magee; and in works on the sacred archeology of the Hebrews, such as Dutram, Fairbairn, &c. Hence few words about it.

V. Conditions of efficacy of Christian Atonement.—The value of Christ's work may be said to depend on the following circumstances:

The infinite dignity of His person. (See Lect iv.)

The possession of the nature of His redeemed people.

His freedom from all prior personal obligation to obey and suffer.

His authority over His own life, to lay it down as He pleased.

His voluntariness in undertaking the task.

His explicit acceptance by the Father as our Priest.

[These have been already expounded.]

His union with His people.

LECTURE XLII.

SYLLABUS.

NATURE OF THE ATONEMENT. (Continued.)

1. Refute the Socinian and semi-Pelagian objections to the doctrine of vicarious satis action; viz:

a.) That to demand satisfaction takes away the grace of salvation and represents the Father as vindictive. b.) That the only thanks would then be due to Christ. c.) That either Christ's divine nature must have suffered, or else the human must have suffered eternally. d.) That imputation is immoral, and a legal fiction.

Turrettin, Loc. xiv, que. xi. (Font. Sol.) Disputations 20, 21, de Satisfac. Chr. Hodge on Atonement, ch. 20. Dick, Lect. 58. C. Hodge, Rev. of Beman. Ridgeley, que. xliv, § v. Watson's Theol. Inst., ch. xx, § iv, v.

2. What are the design and extent of the Atonement? State hereupon, a.) The Pelagian. b.) The Arminian. c.) The Hypothetic Universalist, or Amyraut; and d.) The strict Calvinist view.

Turrettin, Loc. xiv, que. 14. Hodge on Atonement, pt. ii. Hill, Bk. iv, ch. 6. Dick, Appendix, Ch. Hodge on Beman, End. Whitby, V. Points, Watson Theo. Inst., ch. xxv to xxviii.

I. Objections.—Objections to our view of vicarious Atonement are chiefly of Socinian and Pelagian origin. 1. It is objected that we represent the Father in an odious light, as refusing to remit anything till His vindictiveness is satiated, and that to suppose full satisfaction made to the penal demands of law, leaves no *grace* in the remission of sin. It is not of grace, but of debt.

Satisfaction consistent with grace in remission.—The answer to the former part of this objection is suggested in the lecture on Necessity of Atonement. Add that Christ's atoning work did not dispose the Father to be merciful; but the Father sent Him to make it, *because He was eternally disposed* to be merciful. The objection is Tritheistic. There is no mercifulness in the Son, that was not equally in the Father.

To the latter part of the objection the answer is plain: Satisfaction to Law is not incompatible with gracious remission; unless the *same person* pays the debt, who receives the grace. Does the Socinian rejoin: that still, *the debt is paid*, (we Calvinists say, fully,) and no matter by whom *paid*, it can not be *remitted?* The answer is three-fold: a.) There *is* grace on the Father's part, because He *mercifully sent His Son* to make the Satisfaction. b.) *Satisfaction* is not the *very thing owed*, but *something else*, which the Creditor designs to take in its stead. We do not hold the *Quid-pro-quo* theory of Christ's sufferings. We do not view the atoning value of Christ's sacrifice, as a quality, to be divided out by pound's weight, like some material commodity. We do not hold that there must be an arithmetical relation between the quantity of sacrifice, and the number and size of the sins to be satisfied for; nor do we admit that, had the sins of the whole body of elect believers been greater, the sufferings of the substitute must also have been increased; as when the merchant buys more pounds of the commodity, he must pay more money for his purchase. The compensation made to justice is not commercial, but moral. A piece of *money* in the hand of a king is worth no more than in the hands of a servant; but the penal sufferings of a king are. One king captive would exchange for many captive soldiers. Hence, Christ paid, not the *very total* of sufferings we owed, but *like* sufferings, not of infinite *amount*, but of infinite *dignity*. The Father's mercy appears in accepting them as a substitute, when not identical. c.) In a pecuniary debt, the claim of the Creditor is on the *thing* owed. The moral personal ill-desert is not the thing pursued in the suit. Hence, when the *thing owed* is paid, (by no matter who,) the claim is extinguished. In penal obligation for moral wrong, the claim is on the *person* owing; because moral ill-desert is personal. Hence, if the penal obligation be paid by a substitute, the claim is not distinguished; it is matter of grace with the Creditor, whether he will relinquish the debtor's person.

In fine: *The Father's grace* on our scheme is infinitely higher than on Socinian or semi-Pelagian. According to them: redemption only *opens the door for the sinner to work out his own salvation*. He may thank God and Christ somewhat, for being so kind as to open the door; and himself more, for doing the work! But on our scheme, God moved *à priori* by His own infinite mercy, gives us Christ, to reconcile vicariously the divine attributes with our pardon: and *gives us in Him, a complete* justification, new heart, sanctification, perseverance, resurrection, and eternal life.

2. Father's Grace to be Praised.—The Socinians object, that on our scheme, since Christ fully pays the Father, and He remits nothing, the redeemed have *only Christ to thank*. The answer to this is contained in the preceding.

3. Does Christ placate Himself?—It is a favourite objection of the Socinians, that if Christ is God, we Calvinists represent Him as placating Himself, by His own vicarious offering; which involves the absurdity of supposing Him so angry as to demand penalty, and so merciful as to pay it, all in one breath. The answer is; a.) This difficulty concerning God's wrath only exists, when we view it *anthropopathically*. b.) Such a state of mind, though contradictory in a private person, who had nothing but personal considerations to govern him, is not inconsistent in a public Person, who has government interests to reconcile in pardoning. c.) It is His humanity which suffers the penal satisfaction, His divinity which demands it. d.) The objection is an argument *ab ignorantia*. We do not know all the mystery of the persons in the trinity, but have good reason to believe that the Son acts economically in the Covenant of Grace, as man's representative, and the Father as that of all three persons.

4. Socinians object, that since an infinite number of sins are to be atoned, Christ must have paid an infinite penalty; and therefore you must either make His humanity suffer forever, or else make His proper divinity suffer. If the latter alternative is taken, there are two absurdities. God is impassible. But 2d, if he can suffer at all, one single pang of pain was of infinite value (according to Calvinistic principles,) and hence all the rest was superfluous cruelty in God.

How could temporal suffering satisfy for infinite guilt.—The answers are: First. Infinite guilt demands an infinite punishment, but not therefore an everlasting one; provided the sufferer could suffer an infinite one in a limited time. Christ's sufferings were vast; and the capacity for feeling and enduring conferred on His humanity by the united divinity, enabled Him to bear, in one life-time, great wrath. Second. It is the great doctrine of hypostatical union, according to Heb. ix: 14, which grounds the infinite value of Christ's sufferings. (See that doctrine, Lect. iv.) As the infinite nature of the God, against whom sin is committed, makes it an infinite evil, although the act of a finite creature, so the acts of Christ's human nature in suffering, have infinite value, because of the dignity of His person. As to the latter part of the Socinian objection, the answer is, that one pang, or one drop of blood, would not suffice; because the law demanded a penalty of similar kind to that incurred by man; a bodily death, and a spiritual death.

Imputation not unjust.—The 5th, and most radical objection is, that imputation is at best a legal fiction; and vicarious punishment intrinsically immoral. They say, God has pronounced it so; (Deut. xxiv: 16; Ezek. xviii: 4, 20,) and the moral sense of civilized commonwealths, banishing laws about hostages. Antipsuchoi, &c. They argue that the immorality of the act is nothing but that of the agent; that desert of punishment is nothing but this intuitive judgment of immorality in the agent, when brought into relation with *law;* and therefore when penalty is separated from personal immorality, it loses its moral propriety wholly. Hence guilt must be as untransferrible as immorality.

God not to be measured here by men.—To the scriptural arguments, we answer: God forbids imputation of capital guilt by human magistrates; or on special occasion (Ezek. 18th,) foregoes the exercise of it for a time Himself; but that He *customarily* claims the exercise of it in His own government. (See Josh. vii: 15; Matt. xxiii: 35.) The differences between God's government and man's, fully explain this. Human magistrates are themselves *under* law, in common with those they rule; God above law, and His will is law. They short-sighted; He infinitely wise. They cannot find one who is *entitled* to offer his life for his neighbor, it is not his property; God's substitute could dispose of His own life. (Jno. x: 18.) They if the antipsuchos found, could not ensure repentance and reform of released criminal; without which his enlargement is improper; God does. (Acts v: 31.) The human antipsuchos, having sacrificed his life, could never resume it, and his loss to the community would be irreparable; so that the transaction would give to society an injurious member, at the expense of taking from it a righteous and useful one. But Christ resumes the life laid down, and His useful position in the universe. For such reasons as these, it may be improper to have substitutes for capital guilt in man's government; and yet very proper in God's.

This, of course, implies that it is only made with the free consent of the substitute. This Christ gave.

If the objection be true, then pardon is immoral.—To the rational argument I reply:

a.) It proves too much, viz: that there can be no remission in God's government at all. For, when pardon is asserted on the general plan of the Socinian and rationalist, the elements of guilt and immorality are distinguished and separated. i. e., The *guilt* is alienated from the sinning agent, while the *bad character* remains his, so far as the pardoning act is concerned. Is not his own compunction the same as before? Hence His repentance; and the human reason apprehends that no state of soul is so appropriate to the pardoned man, as one that abounds in the heartfelt confessions of his ill desert. But we have proved irrefragably that God's rectoral justice includes the disposition to give appropriate penalty to sin, as truly, and in the same way, as His disposition to bestow appropriate reward on obedience. The two are correlative. If the one sort of legal sanction is not righteously separable from the personal attribute of the agent, even with his own consent, then the other sort (the penal) is not. But when God treats the holy Surety as guilty, (not immoral,) He makes the same separation of elements, which is made, if He should, (without vicarious satisfaction, as the rationalists say He does,) treat the guilty sinner as guiltless (not holy) by remitting a penalty of which he continues to confess himself personally deserving, (as God knows very well he is.)

b.) If imputation of guilt (without personally immorality) to Christ is unjust, even with His own consent; then, *à fortiori*, laying of sufferings upon Him without even imputed guilt, is still more unjust. This for the Socinian.

c.) Penal consequences transferred by Providence and Society.—God, in His providential rule over mankind, often makes this separation between the personal bad character, and penal consequences; for the punishments incurred in the course of nature by vice, descend to posterity; while so far is He from imputing the personal unworthiness always along with the penalty, the patient and holy enduring of it is counted by Him an excellent virtue. So, too, the whole law of sympathy, (Rom. xii: 15; Gal. vi: 2,) makes the sympathizer suffer the penalty along with the sufferer, and yet, so far from treating him as personally defiled with him, regards it as an excellent virtue.

d.) Man's own practical judgment habitually makes the separation of elements, which the Rationalistic objection declares impossible; and we feel that the separation is right. Thus, when the voluntary security relieves the bankrupt debtor, it is only at the cost of what is to him a *true mulct*, (precisely the penalty of the debtor's prodigality,) and we feel the security is rightly made to pay; but so far is this from being due to his *personal demerit* in the transaction, we feel that he is acting generously and nobly. So: we feel that we justly insist on maintaining certain social disabilities against children, incurred by parents' crimes, at the very time we approve the former, as personally, deserving people.

Thus, by indirect refutation, we prove that the objection of the Rationalist, to imputation, and the analysis on which he founds it, cannot be true, whether we are able to specify its error or not.

e.) Potential and actual Guilt.—But I think we can specify it. It is in ignoring the broad distinction, which Divines make, *between potential and actual guilt*—i. e., between the quality of ill-desert, and the obligation to punishment. Consider the objector's process, (fairly stated above,) and it will be seen that it is this: Because the judgment we have of the *ill-desert* of the bad agent is nothing else than the judgment we had of his badness, viewed in its relation to law, therefore his guilt (obligation to penalty) is as personal and inseparable to him, as his quality of badness. This is sophism. The true analysis is this.

The badness of the act is nothing else than the badness of the agent: and is his personal quality or attribute. The judgment of ill-desert arises immediately therefrom, when his quality is viewed in relation to law. True. But what is law? Religion's law is nothing else than God's will, which is its source and measure. So that, as our judgment of the attribute of badness takes the form of a judgment of ill-desert, it passes into a judgment of relation—i. e., between *two persons*, the sinner and God. So that even potential guilt is rather a relation than an attribute. But when we pass to actual guilt, (which is merely obligation to penalty, a moral obligation, as I grant, and not one of force only,) this is not the sinner's attribute at all: but *purely a relation.* And although its rise was mediated by the personal attribute of badness, expressed in the guilty acts, it is not a relation of that attribute, abstracted, to something else, but of his person to the will of God—i. e., to God willing. And in this obligation to penalty, this sovereign will is obligator. It is God's sovereignty, which, though moral, is absolute, that imposes it. Now, without teaching that God's will is the sole source of moral distinctions, or retracting anything I have said against that error, I remark, that far too little weight is attached, in the objection, to this great fact, that this obligation to penalty, which we denominate guilt, is one imposed by the sovereign and omnipotent will of our Maker and Proprietor. Let the mind take in this fact properly, and it will appear how rash is the assertion that even *He* may not, without immorality, separate from the person qualified by the attribute of badness, this relation to penalty, which His own holy will imposes, even though the party to whom the guilt is transferred freely assents; and the divine ends in the transaction are those of beneficence!

But to return: It appears that the agent's badness is his *attribute*, his guilt is his *relation;* and that, a relation to another Person and will. The two elements belong to different categories in logic! But did any sound mind ever admit this as a universal and *necessary* law of logic, (which it must be, to make the objection conclusive,) that relations are as untransferrible as attributes; as inseparable from the things related? Is it so in geometry? But it is better to show, in analogous cases, that it is not so in metaphysics; e. g., A expresses, by acts of beneficence towards me, his quality of benevolence, which institutes between us, as persons, the *relation* of an *obligation to gratitude* from me to him. A is succeeded by his son; and this obligation, in some degree, transfers itself and attaches itself to that son, irrespective of, and in advance of, his exhibiting the quality of *benevolence for me*, in his own personal acts. I present another illustration which is also an argument, because it presents an exact analogy—the *obligation to recompense*—resting on me by reason of A's benefactions to me. I say we have here a true, complete analogy; because this title to recompense from the object of beneficent acts is a fair counterpart to the obligation to bear a penalty from the ruler, who is the object (or injured party) of the bad act. Now, I ask—e. g.: In 2 Sam. xix: 31–38, was it incompetent for Barzillai, the Gileadite, to ask the transfer of King David's obligation to recompense to his son Chimham, on the ground of his own loyalty? Did not David's conscience recognize his moral right to make the transfer? But it is made irrespective of the transfer of Barzillai's *attribute of loyalty* to his son, which, indeed, was out of the question. Here, then, is the very separation which I claim, as made, in the case of imputation, between the sinner's personal attribute, (badness,) and his personal relation to God's sovereign will, arising upon his badness, (guilt.)

This discussion is of fundamental importance also, in the doctrines of original sin, and justification.

2. THEORIES OF EXTENT OF THE ATONEMENT.—The question of the *extent of the atonement* is one of the most difficult in the whole range of Calvinistic Theology. That man who should profess to see no force in the objections to our views, would only betray the shallowness of his mind and knowledge. There are three grades of opinion on this subject.

1. SEMI-PELAGIAN. REFUTED.—The theory of the Semi-Pelagian denies any proper imputation of any one's sins to Christ, makes His suffering a mere general exhibition of God's wrath against sin, having no relation to one person's sin in particular: and of course it consistently makes the atonement perfectly general and indefinite.

The refutation of this view is found in the facts already argued; that there was a substitution, a vicarious suffering of penalty, and a purchasing of the gracious gifts for the redeemed which make up the *application* of redemption.

2. ARMINIAN.—The Arminian view is, that there was a substitution and an imputation; and that Christ *provided* a penal satisfaction for every individual of the human race, making His sins remissible, provided he believes in Christ; and that He also purchased for every man the remission of original sin, and the gift of *common grace*, which confers a self-determining power of will, and enables any one to believe and repent, provided he chooses to use the free-will thus graciously repaired aright; God's purpose of election being conditioned on His foresight of how each sinner would improve it.

The fatal objections to this scheme are, particularly, that it is utterly overthrown by unconditional election, which we have proved, and that the Scriptures and experience both contradict this common grace. But of this, more hereafter.

3. AMYRAUT'S.—The view of the Hypothetical Universalists was professedly Calvinistic, and *was* doubtless, and *is*, sincerely held by many honest and intelligent Calvinists, (e. g., R. Hall, Bellamy,) although Turrettin and Dr. Hodge condemn it as no better than Arminianism in disguise. It presents the divine plan in redemption thus: God decreed from eternity, to create the human race, to permit the fall; then in His infinite compassion, to send Christ to atone for every human being's sin, (conditioned on his believing); but also foreseeing that all, in consequence of total depravity and the bondage of their will, would inevitably reject this mercy if left to themselves, He selected out of the whole a definite number of elect, to whom He also gave, in His sovereign love, grace to "make them willing in the day of His power." The non-elect, never enjoying this persuasive grace, infal-

libly choose to reject the provided atonement; and so, as its application is suspended on faith, they fail to receive the benefit of it, and perish.

Refuted.—This theory, if amended so as to say that God sent His Son to provide a vicarious satisfaction for the sin of all whom His Providence intended to place under the Gospel offers, would be liable to less objection than the others. Yet, one fatal objection lies particularly against it, to mention no others. It does not account for the elects receiving the graces of effectual calling, which make, according to the theory, all the difference, practically, while the non-elect do not receive them. This theory is compelled to deny that those graces are a part of Christ's *purchase* for sinners; and to assert that they are the direct gift of electing love, not mediated to us by Christ. But see Eph. i: 3; Titus ii: 14; Rom. viii: 32; 2 Tim. i: 9.

4. Strict Calvinistic.—The view of the strict Calvinist is as follows: God decreed to create the race, to permit the fall, and then, in His infinite compassion, He elected out of the fallen an innumerable multitude, chosen in Christ, to be delivered from this ruin; and *for them* Christ was sent, to make full penal satisfaction for their unrighteousness, and purchase for them all graces of effectual calling and spiritual life and bodily resurrection, which make up a complete redemption by His righteousness and intercession founded thereon. It represents the Atonement as limited only by the secret intention of God as to its application, and not in its own sufficiency for, or suitability to all. Symmetrical theory, but attended with some difficulties.

Inconclusive Proofs.—In proof of the general correctness of this theory of the extent of the Atonement, we should attach but partial force to some of the arguments advanced by Symington and others, or even by Turrettin. e. g. That Christ says, He died "for His sheep," for "His church," for "His friends," &c., is not of itself conclusive. The proof of a proposition does not disprove its converse. All the force which we could properly attach to this class of passages is the probability arising from the frequent and emphatic repetition of this affirmative statement as to a definite object. Nor would we attach *any* force to the argument, that if Christ made penal satisfaction for the sins of all, *justice* would forbid any to be punished. To urge this argument surrenders virtually the *very ground* on which the first Socinian objection was refuted, and is incompatible with the facts that God chastises justified believers, and holds elect unbelievers subject to wrath till they believe. Christ's satisfaction is *not* a pecuniary equivalent; but only such a one as enables the Father, consistententtly with His attributes, to pardon, if in His mercy He sees fit. The whole avails of the satisfaction to a given man is suspended on his belief. There would be no injustice *to the man*, if he, remaining an unbeliever, his guilt was punished twice over, first in his Saviour, and then in Him. See Hodge on Atonement, page 369.

Real Proofs of Calvinistic Theory.—But the irrefragable grounds on which we prove that the redemption is particular are these:

a.) From Decree.—From the doctrines of unconditional election, and the Covenant of Grace. (Argument is one, for Covenant of Grace is but one aspect of election.) The Scriptures tell us that those who are to be saved in Christ are a number definitely elected and given to

Him from eternity, to be redeemed by His mediation. How can anything be plainer from this than that there was a *purpose* in God's atonement, as to them, other than that it had as to the rest of mankind? See Scriptures.

b.) FROM GOD'S IMMUTABILITY AND POWER.—The immutality of God's purposes. (Is. lvi; 10: 2 Tim. ii: 19.) If God ever intended to save any soul in Christ, [and He has a definite intention to save or not to save towards every soul], that soul will certainly be saved. Jno. xx: 27, 28; vi: 37–40. Hence, all whom God ever intended to save in Christ will be saved. But some souls will never be saved; therefore some souls God never intended to be saved by Christ's atonement. Strength of this argument can scarcely be overrated. Here it is seen that a limit as to the intention of the atonement *must be* asserted to rescue God's power, purpose and wisdom.

c.) CHRIST'S INTERCESSION LIMITED.—The same fact is proved by this, that Christ's intercession is limited. (See Jno xvii: 9, 20.) We know that Christ's intercession is always prevalent. (Rom. viii: 34.) If He interceded for all, all would be saved. But all will not be saved. Hence there are some for whom He does not plead the merit of His atonement. But He is the "same yesterday, to-day and forever." Hence there were some for whom, when He made atonement, He did not intend to plead it.

d.) FROM FACTS.—Some sinners (i. e., elect,) receive from God gifts of conviction, regeneration, faith, persuading and enabling them to embrace Christ, and thus make His atonement effectual to themselves; while other sinners do not. But these graces are a part of the purchased redemption, and bestowed through Christ. Hence His redemption was intended to affect some as it did not others. (See above.)

e.) Experience proves the same. A large part of the human race were already in hell before the atonement was made. Another large part never hear of it. But "faith cometh by hearing." (Rom. x); and faith is the condition of its application. Since their condition is determined intentionally by God's providence it could not be His intention that the atonement should avail for them equally with those who hear and believe. This view is destructive, particularly, of the Arminian scheme.

In a word, Christ's work for the elect does not merely put them in a *salvable state;* but purchases for them a complete and assured salvation. To him who knows the depravity and bondage of his own heart, any less redemption than this, would bring no comfort.

BUT THE SUBJECT DIFFICULT. a.) FROM UNIVERSAL OFFER OF ATONEMENT.—But the difficulties which beset the subject are great; and unless you differ from me, you will feel that the manner in which they are dealt with by the current of Calvinistic writers, is unsatisfactory. The objections are of two classes: From the universal offer of atonement through Christ, and from Scripture. The fact that God makes this offer literally universal, cannot be doubted, nor must we venture to insinuate that He is not sincere therein. (Matt. xxviii: 19; Mark xvi: 16, 17.) The usual answer given by Calvinists of the rigid school to this objection is, that God may sincerely offer this salvation to every creature, because, although not designed for all, it is in its nature *adapted to*, and *sufficient for all.* Arminians rejoin, that this implies an adoption of their conception of the nature of the atonement, as a general satisfaction for human guilt as a mass and whole; that the punishment of gospel-hardened sinners for *unbelief* (which we admit will occur,) would be unjust on our scheme, since by it they would be punished for not beliving what would not be true, if they had believed it; and that since, on our scheme the believing of a non-elect sinner is not naturally, but only morally impossible, it is a supposable case for argument's sake, and this case supposed, God could not be sincere, unless such a sinner should be saved in Christ, *supposing He came.* The honest mind will feel these objections to be attended with real difficulty. Thus, in defining the *nature* of Christ's vicarious work, Calvinists assert a proper substitution and imputation of individuals' sins. On the strict view, the sins of the non-elect were *never* imputed to Christ. The fact, then, that an infinite satisfaction was made for imputed guilt, does not seem to be a sufficient ground for offering the benefits thereof to those whose sins were never imputed.

b.) FROM TEXTS TEACHING A SEEMING UNIVERSALITY.—The other class of objections is from the Bible; e. g.: Those which speak of Christ as having compassion for, or dying for, "the whole world," "all," "all men," "every man," &c. Jno. i: 29. Jno. iii: 16; iv: 42; vi: 51; 2 Cor. v. 19; 1 Jno. ii: 1, 2: Jno. xii: 32; 1 Cor. xv: 22; 2 Cor. v: 14, 15; 1 Tim. iv: 10; Heb. ii: 9, &c. The usual explanation, offered by the strict Calvinists, of these texts is this; that terms seemingly universal often have to be limited to a universality within certain bounds, by the context, as in Matt. iii: 5, that in New Testament times, especially when the gospel was receiving its grand extension from one little nation to all nations, it is easonable to expect that strong affirmatives would be used as to its extent, which yet should be strained to mean nothing more than this; that *persons* of every nation in the world were given to Christ. Hence, "the world," "all the world," should be taken to mean no more than *people of every nation in the world, without distinction*, &c. There is a certain amount of justice in these views; and many of these passages, as 1 Cor. xv: 22; Jno. i: 29, and xii: 32, may be adequately explained by them. The explanation is also greatly strengthened by this fact, too little pressed by Calvinists, that ultimately, the vast majority of the whole mass of humanity, including all generations, will be actually redeemed by Christ. There is to be a time, blessed be God, when literally *all* the then world will be saved by Christ, when the world will be finally, completely, and wholly lifted by Christ out of the gulf, and sink no more. So that there is a sense, most legitimate, in which Christ is the prospective *Saviour of the world.*

But there are others of these passages to which, I think, the candid mind will admit, this sort of explanation is inapplicable. In Jno. iii: 16, make "the world" which Christ loved, to mean "the elect world;" and we reach the absurdity, that some of the elect may not believe, and perish. In 2 Cor. v: 15, if we make the *all* for whom Christ died, mean only the all who live unto Him—i. e., the elect—it would seem to be implied that of those elect for whom Christ died, only a part will live to Christ. In 1 Jno. ii: 2, it will not do to interpret "the whole world" to mean only the elect world s distinguished from Jews: because John is not speaking particularly to Jews, and because of the strengthening word, *whole*.

From texts cautioning against a fall.—The other class of texts is those in which it seems to be implied that some for whom Christ died, may be damned; e. g., Rom. xiv: 15; Heb. x: 29; 2 Pet. ii: 1. For a good and consistent explanation of this class, see Sampson on Hebrews, x: 29. This discriminating divine there advances the following view: The addressing of hypothetical warnings of apostacy or destruction to believers is wholly compatible with the efficacy of Christ's work, and the immutability of God's counsel for them. For that counsel is executed in them, by moral and rational means, among which the force of truth holds the prime place. And among these truths, the fact that if they are not watchful and obedient, professed believer's may fall, is most reasonably calculated to produce watchfulness. But naturally speaking, they may fall; for the impossibility of destroying the elect is only moral, proceeding from the secret purpose of God. See Hodge on Atonement, p. 428, &c.

Conclusion.—This seems, then, to be the candid conclusion: that there is no passage in the Bible which asserts an *intention to apply redemption* to any others than the elect, on the part of God and Christ; but that there are passages which imply that Christ died for, and that He in some sense pitied, all sinners. But the arguments which we adduced on the affirmative side of the question demonstrate that Christ's redeeming work was limited in intention to the elect. The Arminian dogma that He did the same redeeming work in every respect for all, is preposterous and unscriptural. But at the same time, if the Calvinistic scheme be strained as high as some are inclined, a certain amount of justice will be found against them in the Arminian objections. Therefore, *In mediis tutissime ibis*. The well known Calvinistic formula, that "*Christ died sufficiently for all, efficaciously, for the Elect,*" must be taken in a sense consistent with all the passages of Scripture which are cited above.

The Difficulty the same as in the Decree, to be resolved in the same Way.—The difficulty which besets this solemn subject is no doubt in part insuperable for finite minds. Indeed, it is the *same difficulty* which besets the relation of God's election to man's free agency, (and not a new one), re-appearing in a new phase; for the Atonement is *limited precisely by the decree*, and by nothing else. We shall approximate a solution as nearly as is perhaps practicable for man, by considering the same truths to which we resort in the seeming paradox arising from election. There are in the Bible two classes of truths; those which are the practical rule of exertion for man in his own free agency; and those which are the recondite and non-practical explanations of God's action towards us; e. g., in Jno. v: 40 is the one; in Jno. vi: 44 is the other. In Jno. 3: 36 is one; in 2 Thess. ii: 13 is the other. In Rev. xxii: 17 is one; in Rom. ix: 16 is the other. These classes of truths, when drawn face to face, often seem paradoxical; but when we remember that God's sovereignty is no revealed rule for our action, and that our inability to do our duty without sovereign grace arises only from our voluntary depravity, we see that there is no real collision.

In like manner, much as the old distinction between God's revealed and secret will has been ridiculed (till many Calvinists have surrendered it) *there is a sense* in which God pities, by the general benevolence of His nature, the non-elect, while yet He only forms definite purposes of compassion to the elect. See Ps. lxxxi: 13; Ezek. xviii: 32; Luke xix: 41. In the face of these sweet assertions, it is vain to ask, with the Hyper Calvinist or Arminian, "Is God divided and vaccillating painfully in His own feelings? Is He not almighty, to do what He desires?"* We cannot find out the Almighty unto perfection. But, blessed be His name, we know that those statements are true; and we also know that He surely accomplishes all His explicit purposes of mercy. In the case of *man* we can comprehend how a wise and good ruler shall have full power to do an act to which he is truly inclined by the sincere compassions of his nature, and *yet not do it*, and most spontaneously conclude not to do it; because he is guided by other moral motives. Why not God too? There is then a sense in which God's general benevolence desires the rescue of every sinner. But there is a more definite sense in which His love and pity [being limited thereto by wise reasons known fully only to Him] explicitly and efficaciously purpose the rescue only of the elect. Christ's work has alternative purposes. See Jno. iii: 16 to 19. Apply this distinction to the purpose of the atonement. It was in one sense an expression of a general benevolence to "the world," "the whole world." In one sense, Christ's efficacious purpose was to apply its benefits only to "whosoever believe." The tendency of His general benevolence was to save; but man's obdurate rebellion and rejection [which, in His secret purpose, He never intended to remove by His effectual calling], circumvented this merciful purpose as to all but the elect, so that what was meant primarily for mercy eventuates in the display of God's righteous judgment in their deeper ruin. Compare Jno. iii: 17 and 19.

This precious passage clearly teaches an *alternative* of objects before the Divine Mind; one of compassion to *all*, the other of judicial rejection to unbelievers, with sovereign grace to His elect, in which God's *sincerity* in His universal pity; and God's immutable election of only a part, must be held, however mysterious, as both true and compatible.

I am thus compelled, by Scripture, to think that Christ's sacrifice was a genuine manifestation of divine pity to the whole world; and especially to every sinner who ever enjoys the gospel offer, including those whom He foresaw as rejectors, and purposed to leave so. (Matt. xxii: 4, 5.) At the same time, His unchangeable purpose of election made this as to His elect, a complete and efficacious purchase of redemption. All that obdurate gospel sinners can claim of God's sincerity, is, that He has truly made a provision for removing all the obstacles to eternal life, growing out of the demands of the Law, excepting those which exist in the sinner's depraved will itself.

Amayraut misrepresents the Decree. Caution to the Orthodox.—You have seen how the party of Amyraut attempted to fix an order for the parts of the decree, making the sovereign purpose to bestow effectual calling on the elect, subsequent to the purpose to make satisfaction through Christ for man's guilt. The strict Calvinists, we also saw, assigned the reversed order to the two parts. It will be well for you to remember the remarks made by me on the comparison of *supra*, and *infra* lapsarianism. In God's mind the decree is one thought, having no *succession* of parts. We saw that the proper statement was: That the Infinite, all-comprehending Mind has respect in one part of His purpose, to a state of facts designed to proceed out of another part of His purpose; yet the purpose is one, and coetaneous. The statement of the rigid Calvinist is, practically, more correct in its *animus;* because Christ is sent to purchase for the elect, the complete redemption designed for them. Yet it would not be safe to say that Christ is sent only in consequence of that election; for we know not what *other* purposes His mission was intended to fulfill.

CHRIST'S SATISFACTION NOT COMMERCIAL.—Now Christ is a true substitute. His sufferings were penal and vicarious, and made a true satisfaction for all those who actually embrace them by faith. But the Hyper Calvinist conception seems to be, as though Christ's atonement were a web of the garment of righteousness, to be cut into definite pieces, and distributed out, so much to each person of the elect; whence, of course, it must have a definite aggregate length, and had God seen fit to add any to the number of elect, He must have had an additional extent of web woven. This is all incorrect. The atonement was Christ's indivisible act, and inseparable vicarious merit, infinite in moral value, *the whole* in its unity and completeness, imputed to every believing elect man, without numerical division, subtraction or exhaustion. Had there been but one elect man, his vicarious satisfaction had been just what it is in its essential nature. Had God elected all sinners, there would have been no necessity to make Christ's atoning sufferings essentially different. Remember, the limitation is precisely in the decree, and *no where else*. Hence, to my mind, the expression, "limited atonement," "particular atonement," are not exact. It is not *the atonement* which is *limited;* but God's eternal purpose as to its effectual application. I believe in *limited redemption*, and in *particular redemption*. The other phrases are unhappy, because inexact.

HYPER-CALVINIST OBJECTIONS SOLVED.—Now, I am well aware that there are strict Calvinists who would urge hot objections to such views; from their over love for over refined symmetry of dogma.

1. They would urge, that if there was any sense whatever, in which Christ's sacrifice was related to the non-elect, as an expression of God's pity towards their penal miseries, they must inevitably be released; because *justice* would forbid the exacting of the penal debt twice over. Ans. This forsakes the old Calvinistic view of atonement, by which alone Socinian and Popish cavils can be refuted, as not a legal tender. See explanations already given. To my mind, it is not the least inconsistent to represent God as offering to sinners an adequate satisfaction actually provided, *on terms of faith;* and then, when that faith is contumaciously refused, holding the guilty man to pay the same debt, himself; with the aggravated guilt of having, by his obstinacy, disappointed, and—so to speak—baulked so glorious a provision, and caused it to remain forever suspended.

2. That if Christ's sacrifice was in any sense an expression of pity to non-elect sinners, it must have purchased for them the gift of effectual calling; on the principle of the greater's including the less; as in Rom. viii: 32. Ans. This is but asserting that God *could* not pity

at all, those whom He did not elect. But this a direct contradiction of Jno. iii: 16, 17; Ezek. xviii: 32, &c. (See above.) Had He or Christ had the *purpose to apply* redemption to these non-elect, then the greater would have included the less; and the purchase of remission would have involved the purchase of effectual calling, &c. But He did not. He had only that inscrutable (but real) compassion expressed in the above texts.

3. It would be urged by high Calvinists: *cui bono?* What does this atoning pity, which does not *elect*, come to? Wherein is it not a mere mockery and *nil?* Ans. It purchases for non-elect sinners, suspension of doom and natural mercies, during this life, according to 1 Tim. iv: 10. Had Adam's fallen race not been placed under a gospel arrangement, would not their doom have followed their sin, as Satan's? This, then, evinces, beyond a peradventure, a relation of the Mediator's pity and sacrifice to all sinners. Second; it purchases a *sincere* offer of salvation, which is, in itself, a true and inestimable good; for if sincere, it implies that it is not its own defect, but the sinner's folly, which prevents its proving an actual, infinite good. Third; it was God's plan, as to all sinners who perish under the gospel: that *all the obstacles* to their deliverance, external to their own perverse wills should be removed. And this in order to evince to the universe His divine compassion, the true malignity and obstinacy of sin, and His equity in punishing forever.

III. The atonement, then, gains these ends, as to world of non-elect. Besides this, and the actual deliverance of elect, it subserves several important ends: 1. Illustrating Divine attributes;

a.) Love and benevolence. How?

b.) Truth. How?

c.) Determination to punish. How?

d.) Wisdom.

e.) Justice, even more highly than the punishment of the elect.

LECTURE XLIII.

SYLLABUS.

PURGATORY.

1. What results are produced by the atonement. a.) As to God's glory, and b.) As to the world of non-elect?

Symington on Atonement, § 4. Hodge on Atonement. Hill, Bk. iv, ch. 6.

2. Is Christ's satisfaction so complete as to leave no room for the doctrines of Penance and Purgatory? State the Romish doctrines, with their arguments, a.) from Scripture, and b.) from Reason. Refute them.

Council of Trent. Session xxv. *Bellarmine Controversia.*, vol. ii, p. 285, &c. Turrettin, Loc. xiv, que. 12. Calvin's Inst., Bk. iii, ch. 5. Dick, Lect. 81. "Essay on Romanism," xix. Mosheim Com. de Rebus ante Const., vol. ii, p. 38. Neander, Ch. Hist., vol. i, p. 217, &c., ii, p. 675.

1. Results of Redemption to others.—Before I proceed to that

which is to be the chief topic of this lecture, the exclusion of the whole doctrine of penance and purgatory by the completeness of Christ's satisfaction, let us advert for a moment to the point raised at the close of the last lecture. This was concerning the effects on the atonement on the glory of God, and creatures other than the elect.

ANGELS NOT REDEEMED BY CHRIST, BUT INSTRUCTED AND CHEERED.—The Scriptures tell us that Christ "took not on Him the nature of angels." This, with kindred declarations, assures us that He is not the Mediator of angels; as they need no express mediation. Yet many passages show that they have a certain interest in the work of Christ. Examine 1 Pet. i: 12: Eph. i; 10; Col. i: 20; Eph. iii: 10; Phil. ii: 10: Heb. i: 6. Now, we should greatly err, if, for instance, we understood such a passage as Col. i: 20, as teaching that the Messiah has "reconciled" any angels to God by suffering penal satisfaction, and making intercession for them. For the elect angels never had any sins to suffer for; and we are assured that Satan and his angels will never be reconciled to God. What, then, is the concern of the heavenly orders, with Christ's meadiatorial work?

GOD'S CONDESCENSION SEEN AND FELT BY ANGELS.—First, the scriptures abundantly teach us that this work enhances the declarative glory of God. The Mediator is proposed to us and to all creatures likewise, as 'the image of the invisible God,' 'the brightness of His glory and the express image of His person.' But Christ's mission and character are those of ineffable benevolence, pity, love, and tenderness; as well as of purity, devotion, magnanimity, and righteousness. Hence, all creatures receive, in His incarnation and work, a revelation of God's character peculiarly dear to them; to the holy, as truly as the unholy. The holy angels now know, love, trust, and serve their Jehovah, as they would not have done, had they not learned better these lovely perfections, in the person and work of Christ. God, in taking on Him the nature of one creature, man, has come nearer to all creatures, and opened up new channels of communion with them. All the creatures had important things in common, a dependent nature, intellect, conscience and will, responsibility, and an immortal destiny to win or lose. God, in uniting Himself to one nature, has, in a certain sense, united Himself to the whole class; the condscension does not avail man alone, but brings God nearer to all orders. Thus, humanity appears to be a kind of *nexus*, or point of contact between God, and all the holy creatures. And thus, it appears that the extent and grandeur of the beneficent results of the incarnation are not to be measured by the comparative smallness of the earth and man amidst the other parts of creation. It appears how it may be most worthy of God, to have selected the most insignificant of His rational creatures, as well as the ones who were guilty, for this hypostatic union with Himself; because thereby the designed condescension to, and unification of all creatures, in heavenly communion and love, would be more complete and glorious. The lowest nature best answered the purposes.

GOD GLORIFIED IN ALL HIS ATTRIBUTES.—But God not only enhances the manifestation of His attributes of benevolence, by the incarnation of the Son. All His other moral perfections and His wisdom are equally exalted. His justice, impartiality, holiness, and determination to punish guilt, appear far more in Christ's penal sufferings, than in the damnation of Satan, and of wicked men. For they, being His mere creatures, easily replaced by His creative power, insignificant to His well being, and personally injurious to His rights and character, it was easy and natural to punish them as they deserve. Cavilling spirits might say, with a show of plausibility, that resentment alone, rather than pure justice and holiness, may have prompted Him to their doom. But when the Father proceeds, with equal inflexibility, to exact the penalty of His own Son, a being infinitely glorious, united by identity of nature and eternal love to the Judge, characterized personally by infinite moral loveliness, only the more lovely by this act of splendid devotion, and only concerned by voluntary substitution with the guilt of sinners; *there* is an exhibition of unquestionable and pure justice, impossible to be carried further. So the faithfulness of God to His covenants is displayed in the most wondrous and exalted degree. When God's truth finds such a manifestation in His threats, it appears as the equally infallible ground of our trust, in His promises. Now, as these qualities are the basis of the hope of the ransomed sinners, so they are the source of the trust and confidence of all the heavenly orders. Their bliss is not *purchased* by the Cross; but it reposes on the divine perfections which are displayed on the Cross.

Unbelievers receive temporal good through Christ.—Non-elect sinners also derive great and actual benefits from the vicarious work of Christ. The kind and sincere offers of salvation, extended to them in Christ, are a real benefit. For it is not any limitation or hindrance interposed by God to rebuff them if they would come, which renders the invitation futile; it is only their own obduracy. But it appears that all the temporal good which sinners enjoy, is also procured by Christ's atonement. We sinned in Adam, and fell with him. Why did not the summary doom and punishment of the race follow in that case, as in the case of the evil angels? No other answer can be found than that the mercy of God in Christ postponed the infliction of the curse, and bestowed on us the many temporal goods which lead us towards repentance, in order to give opportunity for the gospel offer. It cannot be said that these temporal blessings are no true good, because in the case of the reprobate they turn out to the enhancement of wrath, being abused. For it is their perversity which abuses them, and perverts them from their benevolent intent. Their becoming elements of condemnation is but the fulfilment of an *alternative purpose*. Thus it appears that Christ's substitution procures for non-elect men, these temporal blessings. But as they refuse to fulfil that instrumental condition (sincere penitent faith,) on which God has sovereignly suspended the full benefit of atonement, the blessings are, after a time, withdrawn, and such sinners meet their own full personal deserts.

2. Purgatorial ideas common to all false religions.—The general idea of a *Purgatory*, that is, of temporary penal and purging pains beyond the grave, to be followed by eternal blessedness, is the common characteristic of all false religions. It seems to be adopted in some form, by all minds not corrected by revelation; by Pythagoreans, Platonists, the Jewish Mishnical doctors, (ii Mac. ii: 12; Josephus and Philo,) by the Latins from the Greeks, (Virgil Æneid 6th,

Ergo exercentur poenis, veterumque malorum supplicia expendunt,) by the Mohammedans, the Brahmins, &c. There are two very strong and natural sources for this tendency, first the prompting of our affections to follow our dead friends with labours for their benefit, and hope; and second, the obstinate reluctance of a heart at once guilty and in love with sin to be shut up between the sharp alternatives of present repentance, or final damnation. The idea of a purgatory offers a third alternative by which the deceitful heart may for a time solace itself in sin.

HOW INTRODUCED INTO THE EARLY CHURCH.—The idea came early into the Christian Church, through two channels; a Jewish, through their perversion of the doctrine of Hades, and a Platonic, through Origen's restorationism. The extension of a final restoration to all the wicked, and even to Satan, was, however, regarded by the bulk of the Church as an extravagance of Origen. Thus, we are told, prayers for the dead appêar in the earliest liturgies, as Basil's, and in the current of the Father's, from the "Apostolic constitutions," so called, and the Pseudo Dyonisius, downward. When the priestly conception of the Christian ministry was intruded (which may be traced as early as A. D. 200,) the sacrament of the mass began to be regarded as a sacrifice, which is evinced by their giving it to infants; and soon the idea was borrowed, that it availed for the dead. Thus, says Calvin, in his Institutes, the custom of praying for the dead had prevailed almost universally in the Latin Church for 1300 years before his time. Augustine, even, tolerated it. *Aerius*, the so-called Heretic, seems to have been the only noted disentient in the early ages. But prayers for the dead imply that their state is not yet fixed, nor yet perfectly blessed, and that it may be amended. The fully developed doctrine was embodied in the Romish creed, by the Councils of Florence and Lyons, 2nd.

DOCTRINE STATED, PURGATORY THE COMPLEMENT OF PENANCE.—The student may find a very express and full statement of the Roman doctrine, in the 25th Session of the Council of Trent. To understand it, and the distinction of the *Reatus poenae*, and *Reatus Culpae*, on which it is founded, its development out of the simple usages of the primitive Church about penitents must be explained. When a Church-member had scandalized the Church, especially if it was by idolatry, he was required, after his repentance, to undergo a strict penance. This was considered as satisfaction made to the wounded credit of the Brotherhood. Out of this simple idea grew the distinction between *penitential*, and *theological*, *temporal*, and *spiritual* guilt. The latter, they suppose, is atoned for by Christ's divine blood. For the former, the believer must make atonement himself, partly in the sacrament of penance, and self-mortifications, the remainder in purgatory. The two classes of punishment are, therefore, complementary to each other: the more of one is paid, the less of the other remains to be demanded. Venial sins incur only the *reatum poenae;* mortal sins carry both forms of guilt. Baptism, the Church holds, removes all previous guilt—original and actual; so that were the infant to die immediately after its baptism, it would incur neither hell, nor purgatory. All other believers, including even the highest clergy, even Popes, except the

Christian martyrs, must go to purgatory, for a time longer or shorter, to pay the *reatum poenae* of their sins after baptism. The baptism of fire, which the martyr receives is, in his case, a sufficient purgation, and substitutes the purgatorial sufferings.

Bellarmine's arguments.—The arguments of Rome on this subject may be found so fully and learnedly stated by Cardinal Bellarmine, (Controversia, vol. ii, Bk. i, de Purgatorio, p. 285, &c.,) that nothing can be added after him. He ranks his arguments under three heads—from Scriptures, from the Fathers, from Reason.

From Apocrypha and Old Testament.—From the Apocrypha is quoted 2 Mac. 12th, which states that Judas Mac. sent to Jerusalem 12,000 drachmae, to be expended in sacrifices for the dead, and adds the sentiment: "Therefore it is holy and wholesome to pray for the dead, that they may be loosed from their sins." The answer is: the book is not canonical. The same answer may be made to the citation from Tobit iv, which recommends the giving of a sepulchral feast to the pious poor, in order that they may pray for the souls of the departed. From the Scriptures, Malachi iii: 2, 3, is also quoted, and applied to Christ's second coming instead of His first. At the final day, they say, a purgatorial influence will be very briefly exerted by the final conflagration, on the souls of those then living. There, they claim, the principle of a purgatory is granted. The answer is, that the New Testament proves that this and similar passages relate to Christ's first coming. (John i: 23; Luke i: 17; iii: 4, or iii: 16.) And the trying fire is the searching and judgment of God's convincing Spirit, then peculiarly poured out. To see how hardly bested they are for Scriptural proof, you may note how they quote 1 Sam. xxxi: 13; 2 Sam. i: 12; iii: 35: Gen. l: 25: Ps. xxxviii: lxvi: 12; Is. iv: 4; ix: 18; Micah vii: 8; Zech. ix: 11. It is only by some preposterous application of the Fathers, or mistranslation of the Vulgate, that these passages seem to have any reference to purgatory.

Texts from the Gospels.—From the New Testament are quoted the following: Matt. xii: 31, 32, where, it is claimed, there is a plain implication, that some sins are forgiven in the other world. But first, the assertion of a proposition does not prove its converse. Second, if the passage implies that any sins are pardonable after death, it implies that they are such as blasphemy against the Father and the Son. But Rome herself makes these mortal sins. Third, our Saviour's words are simply an amplification of the idea that such sin "hath never forgiveness;" as in fact He expresses it in Mark iii: 12, the parellel passage.

1 Tim. iii: 10, &c., expounded.—Bellarmine also cites 1 Cor. iii: 10–15, saying, "the foundation is Christ, the founders are the apostles, the good builders are Catholic clergy, their successors; the 'gold, silver, and precious stones,' are true Catholic doctrine; the 'wood, hay, and stubble,' are erroneous, but not damnably heretical doctrines; and the inference is, that these heedless Catholic teachers shall be punished in purgatory for their careless teaching." But if clergymen need a purgatory, the principle is established. Others reach the same conclusion more directly. Now, the true exposition of this passage, very strangely overlooked by the most of the Protestants, makes the 'gold,

silver, and precious stones,' true converts or genuine Christians united to the Church, which Christ has founded; while the 'wood, hay, and stubble,' are spurious professors. The proof is in the coherency of this sense with the whole passage; in the context, v. 16, and in Is. xxviii: 16; 1 Pet. ii: 4–6. Next, "the day" which shall try every man's work, what sort it is, is evidently the judgment day. Compare 1 Cor. iv. 3. But the judgment day is subsequent to all purgatory, according to Rome herself. The fire which is to try each man's work is figurative, the divine judgment and Spirit. Compare Heb. xii: 29. And to suppose that the fire in v. 15 is purgatorial fire implies a change of sense; for the trial is not by literal fire, as the Romanists make purgatory to be, but figuratively; "HOUTOS OS."

Other Texts.—From Matt. v: 25–26, it is inferred that the debtor may pay divine justice the last farthing, and "come out." This is not implied: If the debt is 10,000 talents, and he has nothing to pay, he will never come out. See Matt. xviii: 24, 25; Matt. v: 22, is also quoted, as implying different degrees of punishment; but if all are sent together to an eternal hell, no difference can be made. We reply, this does not follow, for all infinites are not equal. Their citations of 1 Cor. xv: 29, and Phil. ii: 10, need scarcely be argued.

The opinions of the Fathers we easily set aside by denying the Church's infallibility.

Argument from Venial Sins.—Bellarmine's arguments from reason are four. First: Some sins are venial, and since they do not deserve infinite punishment, a just God must punish them temporally. The answer is, that the Bible knows no venial sins. Some are, undoubtedly, less guilty than others. But God will know how to apportion their just penalties, without a purgatory.

Argument from nature of Christ's satisfaction, and Christians' afflictions.—Second: This acute polemic argues, that the satisfaction of Christ does not take off believers all forms of the guilt and consequences of sin; for God chastises all of them by bodily death, and by more or less of affliction. Nor is it worth while for the Protestants to endeavour to evade this by saying that these chastisements are merely disciplinary. For they are of the nature of other penal evils; they are a part of the curse; they are notoriously the consequences of sins; the paternal love of God would never lead Him to use such means for promoting the glorification of sinless creatures. And that they are actually penal is proved by two cases—that of David, 2 Sam. xii: 14, where God thus explains David's bereavement of his child by Bathsheba; and that of the baptized, elect infant, suffering and dying in "infancy. For *there* is an heir of redemption; yet it suffers the curse; and the Protestant cannot explain it as merely disciplinary, because the infantile sufferer cannot understand, and therefore, cannot profit by its own pangs. And indeed, suggests Bellarmine, here is seen the folly of Protestants, in dragging in those texts into this question, which, they say, teach that Christ's atonement is an absolute satisfaction for all guilt, such as Rom. x: 4; viii: 1; Ps. ciii: 12–14; Heb. vii: 25; x: 14. For if those texts be taken in the Protestant sense, then they are incompatible with the chastisements and deaths of justified persons, which are such stubborn facts. How does the Protestant reconcile them? Why, he has to resort to that definition of vicarious satisfaction, which all sound Christians advance: (as, for instance, to solve Socinian objections,) that satisfaction is not a legal tender, but an optionary moral equivalent for the sinner's own punishment. Hence, as the Protestant himself teaches, the offering of even an adequate equivalent by Christ does not *compel* the Father to release the debtor, the condemned sinner, absolutely; as in pecuniary debts, the offer of the legal tender compels the creditor to accept it and release his debtor, or else lose his whole claim forever. The Father's sovereign *option* is still necessary to make the transaction valid; He might withhold it if He chose. Hence, Protestants themselves infer, the extent to which, and the terms on which, the vicarious satisfaction shall avail for the sinner, depend on the actual option which God the Father sees fit to exercise. Therefore, it is all folly tor Protestants to argue, that because Christ gives us a perfect vicarious righteousness, therefore, God *cannot* exact from the believing sinner any penal debt whatever; it is not theoretically true; it is not true in fact. *How much* of the penal debt God remits, and how much He still requires of the believing sinner, must be a question of revealed testimony purely. And farther: Suppose a true believer, dying before he has gotten his fair share of penance and chastisements. He cannot go to hell; he is justified. Must there not be a purgatory, where his unpaid debt of penitential guilt can be paid? Else, when his case is compared with that of the aged and ripened saint, who, with fewer venial sins, has paid a larger amount of penances and afflictions, there is flagrant partiality.

Refutation.—In refuting this adroit argument, I would expressly admit that view of vicarious satisfaction advanced, as the true one. I would expressly accept the appeal to the revealed testimony. And now, setting aside the apocrypha, and the Fathers, as of no authority, I plant myself on this fact: that the Scriptures are absolutely silent, as to any penitential guilt remaining after the *reatus culpae* is removed, and as to any purgatorial punishment. Search and see. This is the view which decided Luther, against all the prejudices of his education. Next, the chastisements of the justified are represented by God as *only disciplinary, and not punitive.* Heb. xii: 6–10. "Whom the Lord loveth." * * * "But He for our *profit.*" Nor can the case of David, or of the dying elect infant, rebut this blessed truth. All that is said by Nathan is, that one reason of God in sending the chastisement of the infant's death was, that its manner of birth had given the wicked great occasion to blaspheme. Well: this end of the bereavement is, after all, disciplinary, and not vindicatory! The case of the dying infant, plausible at the first blush, is a complete sophism. Its whole plausibility is in the false *dogma* of baptismal regeneration. To make Bellarmine's argument hold, he must be able to say that this suffering infant is not only elect, but already justified. This, he supposes, is effected in baptismal regeneration. Now, we know that this is a figment. It is not a baptism previous, which redeems this infant, but the blood and Spirit of Christ applied only *when He dies.* So that during the time of his infantile sufferings, he is yet unjustified, is still under wrath, and is suffering for his birth-guilt.

Argument from perfect satisfaction of believers at death.—Again, I say: let the statement of vicarious satisfaction as not a legal tender, be accepted. Let us to the law and the testimony, to learn whether God, in His sovereign acceptance of Christ's equivalent righteousness, reserved any form of guilt to be exacted of the justified. Let it be a question of fact. Now, I argue, that no cleansing sufferings can be exacted of believers after death, because God says that they are then pure, and have no taint of sin to purge away. See Shorter Catechism, que. 37. If God teaches that "the souls of believers are at their death made perfect in holiness," then, according to the Papist's own showing, there is no room for purgatorial cleansing. This, then, is the cardinal question. See, then, Heb. xii: 23. "To the spirits of just men *made perfect*"—i. e., to the souls of Old Testament saints, who, according to Rome, are in the *limbus patrum*, until Christ's resurrection. 1 John iii: 2. We are like Christ when we see Him as He is. Eph. v: 27. See also 2 Cor. v: 1–8, and Phil. i: 21–23, compared with Rev. xxi: 27, or Heb. xii: 14. See also Rev. xiv: 13; Is lvii: 1, 2; 2 Kings xxii: 20. And now, I return, and from this point of view claim all those precious texts which declare the completeness of Christ's justifying righteousness, as applicable. When God, after teaching us this fact of perfect sanctification of the believer at death, adds that there is *no* condemnation to the man in Christ, (Rom. viii: 1,) that His blood cleanseth from *all sin*, (1 John i: 7,) that "by one offering He hath *perfected* (them) *forever*," (Heb. x: 14,) that "He will cast all their sins into the depths of the sea, (Micah vii: 19,) the testimony is applicable, and conclusive.

Romish argument from popular consent, &c.—Before proceeding, however, with this affirmative argument, let us notice Bellarmine's 3d and 4th points. One is to argue the principle of a purgatory, as we do the existence of God, from the *consensus populorum*. The answer is, that the universal testimony for the existence of a God is given against the leanings of a guilty conscience and self-interest; and is, therefore, valuable, because disinterested. But the popularity of a purgatory among sinners is no argument in its favour, because the invention is prompted by the leanings of a guilty heart. The Romanist's fourth argument is, that there certainly is a purgatory, because several Popish Ghosts have come thence, and stated the fact! This, of course, is unanswerable!

Refutation from Bible instances.—In pursuance of the argument, I cite the case of the penitent thief, (Luke xxiii: 43,) so well argued by Turrettin. I only add, that surely, if there ever was a justified believer who needed purgatory, this man just plucked, at his dying hour, out of the foulest sins, was the one. The Romish evasion is to say, Martyrs are exempted from purgatory. Now, first, the thief was no martyr; he did not die for the truth; but died for a robbery. Second, the exemption of martyrs is unreasonable and unscriptural. Their dying pangs are often fewer and shorter than of many saints who have died in their beds; and their devotion less meritorious. Here, also, we may quote the act of Stephen, who, speaking by immediate revelation, commended his soul to Christ in glory. So St. Paul, who, according to the Romish doctrine, had every reason at the time of his speaking to suppose himself a candidate for purgatory, evidently believed the opposite; for he held that being absent from the body was to be present with the Lord.

Next: the whole idea of "satisfaction" to divine justice by temporary sufferings is unscriptural. So, the idea that penal sufferings have in themselves any sanctifying virtue, is equally unreasonable.

THE SOUL WOULD CONTRACT DEBT IN PURGATORY.—Once more: the soul in purgatory being, according to the Popish theory, still imperfect, would be still sinning; and thus, new guilt would be accruing, while it was paying for the old. It could never get out; purgatory would be merged into an endless hell. To avoid this conclusion, which Bellarmine expressly admits would otherwise follow, the Papists lay it down as a principle, that souls after death can neither merit reward nor penalty. The only show of proof for this is the perversion of such passages of Scripture as say that, at death, man's probationary state ends; as, e. g., Eccles. ix: 10; Jno. ix: 4, &c. But the statement that probation ends at death, is better satisfied by our theory, that there is no purgatory. Hence, this reasoning is a vicious circle. The idea that souls after death cease to merit, is, moreover, absurd and unscriptural. Angels can, and did, and do merit while disembodied spirits. Responsibility is directly founded on the natural relation of Creator and rational creature; it cannot end, save by the change of the creature's nature, or of God's.

The cunning of Rome is illustrated by this dogma. He may well say, "By this craft we have our wealth." It prolongs the hold of priestcraft over the guilty fears and hopes of men, which otherwise must have terminated at death, indefinitely. Men would not pay money to evade a misery which was admitted to be inevitable; the expenditure would appear useless. The cruelty of priestcraft, in thus making traffic of the remorse of immortal souls, and the dearest affections of the bereaved for their departed friends, is as impious as unfeeling.

On the other hand, how blessed is the creed of the Bible touching the believer's death. With the end of that struggle, all our trials end, and our everlasting rest begins. With the grave, and all its horrid adjuncts, the Christian really has no concern; for when the senseless body is consigned to its darkness, the soul, the true *Ego*, the only being which fears, and hopes, and rejoices and suffers, has already soared away to the bosom of its Redeemer, and the general assembly of the glorified.

LECTURE XLIV.

SYLLABUS.

CHRIST'S HUMILIATION AND EXALTATION.

1. Wherein did Christ's humiliation consist? Did it include a descent into hell?

Shorter Cat., que. 26–28. Turrettin, Loc. xiii, que. 9 and 16. Calvin's Inst., bk. ii, ch. 16, § 8–13. Knapp, § 92 and 96.

2. Wherein consisteth Christ's exaltation? What is meant by His session at His Father's right hand?

Turrettin, que. 19. Dick, Lect. 62. Knapp, § 97, 98, and 99. Ridgeley, que. 51 to 54.

3. What the necessity of Christ's resurrection to His mediatorial work?

Calv. Inst., Bk. ii, ch. 16, § 13. Jno. xvi. Dick, Lect. 61. Ridgeley, que. 52.

4. What are the grounds, objects, and mode of Christ's priestly intercession?

Turrettin, Loc. xiv, que. 15. Dick, Lect. 59.

5. How doth Christ execute the office of a King, as God, or as Theanthropos? What His kingdom? What the extent of His powers?

Conf. of Faith, ch. 25, § 1. Book of Gov., ch. ii. Turrettin, Loc., xiv, que. 16. Dick, Lec. 64. Ridgeley, que. 45. Knapp, § 98, 99.

6. What the duration of Christ's kingdom?

Turrettin, Loc. xiv, que. 17. Dick, Lec. 64. Hodge on 1 Cor. xv: 24-28.

Christ's humiliation. Did He descend into hell? Calvin's view.—1. Wherein did Christ's humiliation consist? See Catechism, que. 27. That Christ should fulfil the work of a Redeemer in both estates, was necessary for the *purchase* and the *application* of salvation, There is seeming Bible authority for the clause of the Creed, (inserted later than the body,) which says that "He went into hell." See Ps. xvi: 10, as quoted by Peter and Paul. Acts ii: and 13. The *Hades* into which Christ is there said to have gone receives four explanations. 1. The *grave*. But it was not *the grave* into which His "soul" went. 2. The *limbus patrum*, the Popish. They quote, also, 1 Pet. iii: 19, explain it of the Old Testament saints; and thus explain Matt. xxvii: 53. But we have shown that there is no *limbus patrum*. 3. The old Lutherans understood Ps. xvi: 10; 1 Pet. iii: 19, that Christ went into the hell of the damned to show them His triumph over death, and seal their fate. Thus it was a part of His exaltation. Both this and the previous notion are contradicted by Luke xxiii: 43. 4. Protestants by *hades* of Ps. xvi: 10, now understand simply the invinsible, or spirit world, to which Christ's soul went while disembodied. Calvin understands the creed to mean, by Christ's descent into hell, the torments of spiritual death, which He suffered *in dying*, not after. His idea is, that the creed meant simply to asseverate, by the words, "descended into hell," the fact that Christ actually tasted the pangs of spiritual death, in addition to bodily, and in this sense endured hell-torments for sinners, so far as they can be felt without sin. But Calvin expressly says, that the whole of that torment was tasted before the Redeemer's soul left the body. For thence it went to rest in the bosom of the Father. He even raises and answers this question: If this is the meaning of the Creed, why is the descent into hell mentioned after the death and burial; if the thing which it means really occurred before? The answer is unsatisfactory; but this at least shows that I have not misunderstood Calvin in his peculiar view. And this is all the ground which exists, for the charge so often made, by persons who professed much more acquaintance with Calvin than they possessed, that he held to Christ's actual descent into the world of damned spirits!

Exaltation.—For Christ's exaltation, see Cat., que. 28; Phil. ii: 6-11; Is. liii: 10-12: Ps. xxii, &c. In what sense was the exaltation of a *divine* Saviour possible? a.) By removing the veil thrown over

His glory by incarnation. b.) By economical reward to *Mediatorial person*, for humiliation. See Phil. ii: 10, &c. c.) By exaltation of His human nature. Matt. xvii: 2; Rev. i: 12–16. This exaltation now, doubtless, takes place, as to Christ's humanity, in a *place*, called the third heaven, to which He went by literal local motion, from our earth. Sitting at God's right hand means nothing more than the post of honour and power. God has no hand, literally, being immense spirit. The Lutheran argument for ubiquity of Christ's humanity, drawn hence, is foolish ; for in the sense in which the humanity sits at the right hand, that hand is not ubiquitous. It is sophism by conversion of terms. Of this exaltation, the Kingship is the more permanent feature.

Resurrection of Christ proved. Its importance.—3. Christ's resurrection is every where spoken of in Scripture as a hinging point of the believer's salvation and hope. See Rom. iv: 25; Jno. xiv: 19; 1 Cor. xv: 14, 17, 20, &c. Acts i: 21, 22, 1 Pet. i: 3, &c. The Apostles everywhere put it forth as the prime article of their system, and main point of their testimony. Whence this importance? Before we answer this question, it may be well to advert to the evidences upon which we are assured, that this event, equally cardinal and wonderful, really occurred. If you are required to show that the fact is authentic, you may prove it.

a.) From Old Testament predictions, such as Ps. xv: 10. This event is one of the *criteria* predicted for the Messiah. Then, if you have proved that Jesus of Nazareth is the Messiah, you may claim that a resurrection is to be expected for Him.

b.) Christ expressly predicted His own rise. Matt. xx: 19 ; John x; 18. If He is not a monstrous impostor, which His lovely character disproves, we must expect to find it true.

c.) We have the testimony of many witnesses, who saw Him after His rise, of the Eleven, of above 400 brethren, and last of Paul, witnesses *competent*, *honest*, and *credible*. They knew Christ by sight. They had everything to lose, and nothing to gain, by bearing false testimony here. On this point the convincing arguments of the Christian writers are familliar to your reading.

d.) The miracles wrought in confirmation of the fact prove it. See Heb. ii: 4. The Apostles, we read, in the act of invoking God's miraculous aid, appealed to it as proof that their testimony was true. Now, to suppose that God sanctioned such an appeal, by putting forth His own power then, would make Him an accomplice to the deception. So, the spiritual effusion of Pentecost, especially, and all the subsequent, are proofs; for they are fruits of His ascension. See Acts ii: 33; v: 32.

e.) The change of the Sabbath is a perpetual monumental evidence of the resurrection. For 4,000 years it had been observed on the 7th day of the week. It is now universally observed on the 1st day by Christians. Whence the change? The Church has constantly asserted that it was made to commemorate the rise of its Redeemer from the dead. Now a publick monumental observance cannot be propagated among men to commemorate an imaginary event. The introduction of the observance would inevitably challenge remark, and the imposture would have been instantly exposed. Americans celebrate the 4th of July. They say it is to commemorate the Declaration of Independence. Who believes that, if that event were mythical, the observance could ever have become current?

Let us now resume and answer the questions. What the importance of this cardinal fact, in the doctrine of our redemption? 1. Because it was necessary to clear His memory of the charge of religious imposture, under which He died, and to vindicate His character as God's well-approved Son. See Rom. i: 4. 2. Because it evinced the adequacy of His satisfaction for man's guilt. When our Surety comes triumphing out of prison, we know our whole debt is settled. 3. It was necessary to demonstrate His power, as the Captain of our salvation, to conquer our most dreaded enemies. Heb. ii: 14, 15. 4. The resurrection was necessary to enable Christ to be our Sanctifier, Advocate, and King. See Jno. xvi: 7; Rom. viii: 11; 1 Cor. vi: 15; 1 Thes. iv: 14. 5. The resurrection of Christ is the earnest and proof of ours. 1 Cor. xv: 20, 23: Phil. iii: 21, &c.

Christ's intercession. Its ground, &c. When does it end?—4. The *ground* of Christ's *intercession* is His vicarious righteousness, which He pleads before the Father. Is. liii: 12. The mode of His intercession is by petition; e. g., Jno. xvii. Some have supposed that this suppliant attitude implies an inferiority incompatible with the proper divinity of the Son. *To mediate* does not imply a certain *economical* inferiority of attitude; but no more. Some find in Jno. xvii: 24. "Father, I will," &c., evidence of a more authoritative intervention. It is overstrainimg the verb, Thelo. But compare Jno. v: 6, *et passim*. Yet it is certain that Christ's petitions have a more authoritative basis than ours, being urged on the ground of His covenant and perfect purchase. 1 Jno. ii: 1. A more plausible difficulty is this: "If all power is given into Christ's hands, (Matt. xxviii: 18; Eph. i: 22; Col. ii: 9, 10,) why need He intercede at all? Why not do, of Himself, without interceding, all that His people need?" The answer is, that Christ *is* a royal Priest, (Zech. vi: 13,) not Aaronic, but Melchisedekan; and His intercession is rather a perpetual holding up of His own righteousness on behalf of His people, by a perpetual pleading, in order that He may, on that ground, have this viceroyal power of succouring all their wants. And as a royal Priest, He holds up His righteousness to the Father, as a plea for admitting each one of the elect into that body, His kingdom, to which the Father has authorized Him to dispense His fulness.

Its objects.—The objects of Christ's intercession are the elect particularly. See Jno. xvii: 9. Also, His official intercession is always prevalent; if He prayed for all, all would be saved: but all are not saved. Hence, His prayer for the pardon of His murderers must be supposed as not the intercession of the Theanthropos, but the forgiveness of the man Jesus. Or else all His murderers were saved. He must have also interceded officially for the Old Testament saints, for three reasons. The Theophanies are believed to have been interventions of *the Son*. This implies that He had already sought and obtained leave to bless His people. 2d. If they had no intercessor, how could a holy and righteous God give His favour to sinners? 3d. We have a case: Zech. iii: 1–6. But while Christ's mediation is limited to the elect, there is a sense in which He intervenes for the whole race. Doubtless it is His work for man, which prevented the doom from following the fall, as promptly as Satans's, and which procures for the world all the instances of God's long-suffering.

Its duration.—The duration of Christ's intercession seems different to different minds. Some suppose that He will plead forever; and that His pleading will secure an everlasting suspension of wrath, and bestowal of ever renewed graces and gifts. They quote Heb. vii: 25. Others suppose that this is only relatively endless, compared with the brief ministry of an Aaronic priest; and that having thoroughly reconciled the whole Church to God, and re-instated them in holiness as well as favour, no farther need of His intercession will exist; but God can dispense His blessings masked by an advocate, as on the holy angels. I lean to the former part. Add; that His priesthood is spoken of as everlasting. Ps. cx; Heb. vii: 3, 24. His *sacrifice* is ended, "once for all," if His *intercession* is not eternal, in what sense does His priesthood continue? Further: He seems still to be the *Medium*, after the full glorification of the Church, through which they receive the blessings of redemption. Rev. vii: 17, &c. And this is much the most consistent and pleasing view of the relation of the glorified Church to God.

Christ's Kingdom.—See Cat. question, 26. As eternal Son, the 2d person doubtless shares forever, the natural and infinite dominion of the Godhead. But this Mediatorial kingdom is conferred and *economical*, exercised not merely in His divine nature, but by Him as Theanthropos. The Person receives this exaltation. The extent of His kingdom is universal. See texts above, and Phil. ii: 10, 11. The Church is His immediate domain: its members are His citizens; and for their benefit His powers are all wielded. But His power extends over all the human race, the angelic ranks, good and bad, and the powers of nature. This exaltation, therefore, shows our Saviour as clearly divine, for no finite wisdom or powers are at all adequate to its task. The nature of this beneign kingdom is very clearly set forth in Ps. ii: 45, and cx: 72; in Is. ix, &c., &c., and in the passages above quoted. The phrase, "Kingdom of God," of "Heaven," &c., is used in the New Testament in somewhat varying senses; but they all signify the different aspects of that one spiritual reign, called "the kingdom of Christ." a.) True religion, or the reign of Christ in the heart. Luke xii: 31; xvii: 21; Mark x: 15; xiv: 17. b.) The visible Church under the new dispensation. Matt. xiii: 40, 41; iv: 17; Mark i: 15. c.) The perfected Church in glory. Luke xiii: 29; 2 Pet. i: 11. It is a purely spiritual kingdom, as is proved by our Saviour's words, (Jno. xviii: 36,) by the nature of its objects; the redemption of souls; by the nature of its agencies, viz., truth and mercy and holiness, (see Ps. xlv: 3, 4,) by the conduct of Christ and His Apostles while on earth, in paying tribute, living subordinate to magistrates, &c. This respects its terrestial modes of administration: for as to its secret and superhuman modes, they are properly almighty, and both physical and spiritual.

Duration of Christ's Kingdom. Beginning.—6. Orthodox divines are not agreed as to the *duration* of this kingdom. If we would fix the date of its *beginning*, we must make it, in some respects, co-eval with Christ's intercession—i. e., with the *protevangelium* proclaimed to man. For it is plain, that saints before the incarnation had all the same necessities for a divine King to conquer, protect, and rule them, which we experience now: and lay under the same obstacles as to receiving these blessings from a holy God directly, who was bound by His justice and truth to punish and destroy sinners. Again; we have seen instances, the various theophanies, in which the Son, under the person of the Angel of the Covenant, busied Himself for the protection of His people. Again, Ps. ii speaks of Christ's kingdom, not only as *promised*, but as having an institution co-eval with the declaration to man of His Sonship. See best interpretation of v. 7. But yet the God-man was only inducted into His peculiar and delegated viceroyalty, after, and as a reward of His sufferings. See Phil. ii. And the "kingdom of God" is often spoken of at the time of Christ's coming, as being then *at hand*, or as a thing then coming. We must, therefore, conclude, that while the Son was permitted to intercede and rule before His incarnation, on the ground of His work to be rendered to the Father, His kingdom received a still more explicit establishment after His resurrection.

TERMINATION?—When we come to consider the other *terminus*, we are met by a still more serious difference of opinion. Some, with Turrettin, suppose that the delegated mediatorial kingdom over the Church will undergo a change in the mode of its administration at the final consummation, its relations to its enemies, as well as the nature of its own wants, being greatly modified; but that in other respects it will continue: in that the THEANTHROPOS will be the direct *medium* for the saints' guidance and government still; and this forever and ever. The arguments are, that perpetual and everlasting duration are promised to it; e. g., Ps. lxxii: 17; Is. ix: 7; Dan. vii. 14; Dan. ii: 44. Second. His people will need protection and guidance, just as they will teaching and intercession, forever. For their glorification will not render them naturally impeccable or infallible. Yea, as we have seen, when speaking of Socinianism, they must have this ruling and teaching, or some day in futurity they will go astray again. But it seems far most natural to suppose that these blessings will still be given through Christ their Head, to whom they were spiritually united at their conversion. The personal union of the divine and human will continue. But for what purpose, if the mediatorial connexion is terminated? Moreover, the Revelation seems to decide the question, showing us the Lamb, (ch. v: 6,) receiving the homage of the glorified Church, (ch. vii: 17,) leading and feeding it still, and (ch. xxi: 22, 23,) acting, after the final consummation, as the light of heaven. Third. In Rev. xix: 7, 8, the marriage of the Church to the Lamb is spoken of as then consummated, amidst the glories of the final consummation. All that was previous was but the wooing, as it were; and it seems very unnatural to conceive of the peculiar connexion as terminating with the marriage. Then it only begins properly.

1 COR XV: 24 EXPLAINED.—Others, as Dick, seem to attach so much importance and force to 1 Cor. xv: 24–28, as to suppose that it necessitates another supposition: that Christ having re-instated the Church

in holiness and the favour of God, and subdued all its enemies, there will no longer be any necessity for the peculiar mediatorial plan; but God will rule directly over saints as over the rest of His holy universe before man fell; and Christ will have no other kingdom than that which He naturally holds as of the Godhead. In answer to Turrettin's first argument, they would say that the everlasting duration promised to Christ's kingdom, is only relative to the evanescent generations of men: and means no more than that it shall outlast all generations of earth. This, they say, is even indicated in the Ps. lxxii: 17, where the "forever" is defined to mean as long as the Sun. But "the sun shall be turned into darkness before the great and terrible day of the Lord." As to the second argument, it is admitted that the saints in heaven will always need teaching and ruling; but it is supposed that they being thoroughly justified and sanctified, God may bestow these graces on them directly, as thee lect angels, without a mediatorial intervention. These views appear plausible; but they come short of a full clearing up of the subject. They leave unbroken the force of the passages cited from Revelation. The whole tenour of the Scripture seem to imply that the peculiar relationship, not only of gratitude and affection, but also of spiritual union, formed between Christ and His people, is to be everlasting. He is their "*alpha* and their *omega*." His life is the spring and warrant of their life. It is their union to Him which ensures the resurrection of their bodies, and the eternal life of both body and spirit. See Jno. xiv: 19. The change made in the method of God's governing the universe, by means of the incarnation, will continue, in some respects to all eternity, as a standing monument of Jesus Christ's victory and grace. Nor does the passage from 1 Cor. xv: 24, seem insuperable. That a striking change will then take place in the method of the mediatorial kingdom, cannot be doubted. Perhaps it will consist largely in this, that Christ's power over the universe (external to His body, the Church,) will be returned to the Godhead. But the restoration of the Church to the Father, as an accomplished enterprise, is to be received, not as implying a severance of Christ's headship, but as a surrendering of *Himself* along with it, body and head, as an aggregate. Let 1 Cor. iii: 23, be compared.

LECTURE XLV.

SYLLABUS.

EFFECTUAL CALLING.

1. How are we made partakers of the redemption purchased by Christ?
   See Confession of Faith, ch. x. Cat., que. 29.
   Whence the necessity of a call to man?
   Dick, Lect. 65. Hill, Bk. 5, ch. 1.

3. How many calls does God give to man; and what is the difference between common, and effectual calling?

Shorter Cat., que. 31. Larger Cat., que. 68. Turrettin, Loc. xv, que. 1 and 4. Hill, Bk. 5, ch. 1. Dick, Lect. 65. Ridgeley, que. 67, (beginning.) Knapp, § 129.

4. What is God's design in the "common call" of the non-elect; and how may His sincerity therein be cleared?

Turrettin Loc. xv, que. 2, § 1-13. Howe's Works; "Reconcilableness of God's prescience, &c., with the wisdom and sincerity of His Counsels," &c. Andrew Fuller's Works, "Gospel worthy of all acceptation," pt. iii. Arminian and Socinian polemics, *passim*.

1. Application of Redemption by Holy Ghost.—"We are made partakers of the redemption purchased by Christ, by the effectual application of it to us by Christ's Holy Ghost." We now come to the great branch of Theology—*The Application of Redemption*—in which the kingdom founded by Jesus Christ's humiliation is set up and carried on. In this work, His priestly office is only exercised in heaven, by His intercession. It is His prophetic and kingly which He exercises on earth. And the person of the Trinity now brought into discussion is the Holy Ghost, which proceedeth from the Father through the Son. As the doctrines of Creation, Providence the Law, chiefly concerned the Father, that of atonement and priesthood chiefly concerned the Son, so this brings into view chiefly the Holy Ghost. This would, therefore, be the most natural place to bring into view the doctrine of the Spirit's personality, nature, and agency; but as you have already attended to these, I proceed.

2. Sin necessitates the Call.—The great necessity for the effectual calling of man is in his original sin. Were he not by nature depraved, and his disposition wholly inclined to ungodliness, the mere mention of a plan, by which deliverance from guilt and unholiness was assured, would be enough; all would flock to embrace it. But such is man's depravity, that a redemption must not only be provided, but he must be effectually persuaded to embrace it. Now, as our effectual calling is the remedy for our original sin, as is our conception of the disease, such will be our conception of the remedy. Hence, in fact, all men's theology is determined hereupon, by their views of original sin. We, who believe the unconverted will be certainly determined to ungodliness, by ungodly dispositions, therefore believe in an effectual and supernatural call. Jno. iii: 5 and 6.

3. Call either common or effectual.—Calvinists admit only two kinds of call from the gospel to man—the *common* and the *effectual*. They deny that there is any natural call uttered by the voice of nature and Natural Theology; for the simple reason that whatever information it might give of the being and government of God, of His righeousness, and of His punishments for sin, it holds out no certain warrant that He will be merciful to sinners, nor of the terms whereon He can be so. Where there is no revealed gospel, there is no gospel call. And this is only to say, that Natural Theology is insufficient to salvation.

The *common call* consists of the preached word, addressed to men's ears and souls, together with (in most, at least,) the common convincing operations of the Holy Ghost. This call is made generally to the whole human race in Scripture, and specifically to each adult to whom the gospel comes. The *effectual call*, we hold, consists of these elements, and also of a work of the Holy Ghost, "whereby convincing us of our sin and misery, enlightening our minds in the knowledge of Christ, and renewing our wills, He doth persuade and enable us to embrace Jesus Christ freely offered to us in the gospel." Arminians, indeed, assert that the call is one, and the same, so far as God's dispensation towards men is concerned, to all under the gospel; and that it only differs by its results in different cases, which difference is made only by man's free will. This we shall more fully disprove when we come to show the nature of regeneration; but it may now be disproved briefly by these thoughts: a.) That a difference is asserted between the nature of God's calls; in Scripture, Matt. xx: 16; Jno. vi: 44, 45. b.) That the effectual calling is a result of election; but the event proves that all are not elect. See Rom. viii: 28; xi: 29; viii: 30; Acts xiii: 48. c.) If the call only differed in the answer made to it by man's free will; 1 Cor. iv: 7, would not remain true; nor, Rom. ix: 16.

4. Designs of God in common call. To gather Elect.—God's design in the common call of the unconverted may be said to be threefold. First, it is His appointed and proper *means* for saving from among them, the elect. And He either must have adopted this generality in the outward call; or else he must have adopted one of two expedients: He must have actually saved all, or He must have separated the non-elect wholly from the participation of the common call. Had He adopted the latter plan, surely those who now complain of partiality would then have complained far more loudly. Had he adopted the former, where would have been His manifestation of His sovereignty; and where that evidence of regular customary connexion between means and ends, conduct and destiny, on which He has seen fit to found His government?

To express His benevolence.—God's second design in making the common call universal, was the exercise of the general holiness, goodness, and compassion of His nature, (which generally regard all His creatures,) in dissuading *all* from sin and self-destruction. God's holiness, which is universally opposed to sin, makes it proper that He shall dissuade from sin, every where, and in all sinners. God's mercy and goodness, being made possible towards the human race by their being under a gospel dispensation, make it proper that He shall dissuade *all* from self-destruction. And this general mercy not only offers a benefit to sinners generally, but actually confers one—i. e., a temporary enjoyment of a dispensation of mercy, and a suspension of wrath, with all the accompanying mercies, and the offer itself of salvation. This *offer* is itself a benefit: only man's perverseness turns it into a curse. Blessed be God, His word assures us that this common call *is* an expression of *bona fide* compassion for all sinners, elect and non-elect, (a compassion whose efficient outgoing is, however, conditioned, as to all, on faith and penitence in them.) Ezek. xxxiii: 11; Ps. lxxxi: 13; 1 Tim. ii: 4.

To clear Himself.—God's third design in making the common call universal is, that when men ruin themselves, as He foresaw they would, *His* holiness, goodness, compassion and truth may be entirely cleared, in their fate, before heaven and earth. It was a part of His eternal plan, to *magnify His own Goodness*, by offering to human sinners a provision for salvation so complete, as to remove every obstacle arising out of His justice and law; so that in their final damnation, all the universe may see how lovely God is; and how desperate an evil sin is. And this is properly God's highest end.

Is THE COMMON CALL INSINCERE?—It has been often charged that, if God makes an internal difference in sinners' hearts, between the common call and the effectual, His wisdom, or His sincerity, in extending that common call to all, is tarnished.

SCRIPTURE ORDERS IT.—In reply to this, we assert, First: The Scriptures explicitly direct the common call to be extended to all; e. g., Mark xvi: 15. They assert that God does efficaciously persuade some, and not others, to embrace it: Rom. ix: 16; xi: 7. And they also say that God is both wise and sincere in His offers and dealings. Ezek. xxxiii: 11; Luke xix: 42; 2 Tim. ii: 19. Now, in any other science than theology, when facts are ascertained on valid evidence, they are *all admitted*, whether they can be reconciled or not. I remark farther: that to deny the doctrine of effectual calling does not much relieve the subject; for God's *prescience* of the actual results of His universal call, involve very much the same difficulties as to His wisdom and sincerity.

CASES ARE INDISPUTABLE.—Second: The Scriptures show us God clearly extending warnings, dissuasions from sin, and offers of mercy, to those whom He Himself declares at the time, He intends to permit to destroy themselves. See Ex. v: 1, with vii: 3, 4; Is. vi. 8–11; Ezek. iii: 7 and 11; Matt. xxiii: 33–35, with 37. So that clearly, the apparent difficulty does not arise from any Calvinistic misstatement of God's gospel plan.

PROVIDENCE INVOLVES THE SAME QUESTION.—Third: The course of God's providence in natural things, is liable to the same difficulty. He spares sinners. "He sends His rain on the just and unjust; and causeth His sun to rise on the good and evil." See Acts xiv: 17. Now Peter (2 Ep. iii: 15) tells us that the "long suffering of our God is salvation." If His admitting sinners to the gospel call, whom He yet foresees to be bent on their own destruction, is insincere; and the reality of his benefit therein is doubted, because He never efficaciously purposed to make them repent, His providential goodness also is no true goodness. But what sinner believes this?

GOD MAY COMPASSIONATE, AND YET NOT SAVE.—Fourth: The truth is, there is apprehended no inconsistency whatever, in transactions of human governors, which are analogous enough (though God's be in other respects infinitely above them) to serve for illustration. Here is a magistrate, who truly compassionates a rebel, sincerely offers terms of pardon, and sincerely desires that the rebel should accept them. Yet this co-exists with a fixed purpose not to sacrifice the magesty of law in order to pardon, and also with a secret moral certainty in the ruler's mind, arising from his knowledge of the rebel's perverseness that he is not going to submit. Is he, therefore, insincere in his overtures? Then, Why God in His? It may be said: the magistrate has no power to make the rebel willing; God has. I reply: and this brings us to the key of the whole position; while God has a natural power to do so, He has not the license of His own infinite wisdom, and other perfections, to do so. The Arminian objects, that this view, making a difference between God's conditioned will and His own efficacious, unconditioned will, represents God as imperfect, as limited, as desiring to do what He can't do, &c. I reply: it represents His *actions* as limited by His own perfections only. To deny, that God's understanding, comprehending the whole concerns of His vast empire for all time, should see reasons of which we do not dream, other than lack of power, for not persuading certain sinners to accept His calls, reasons perfectly controlling to God's wisdom, holiness, and goodness, is sheer absurdity, pride run mad. Our highest conception of created excellence and wisdom is, that it has its natural powers and propensities most completely under the control of a general comprehensive wisdom. Why should not this, exalted to perfection, be our conception of God? God has no passions. Hence the idea of a *struggle*, between His general wisdom forbidding, and His mercy desiring, to pardon all, is erroneous. His several perfections are ineffably harmonious. Hence, the difficulty of reconciling God's sincerity in the common, with the effectual call, arises very much from an assumption of our mental vanity, That assumption, in plain terms, is this: that because we don't see any reason, therefore the infinite understanding of God cannot see any sufficient reason, other than the lack of power, why He shall, on the whole, conclude that He cannot properly save certain sinners, whom His compassion truly prompts Him to save; it being understood that He has full physical power to do so. But a moment's reflection upon the many controlling considerations of policy which arise in a little human kingdom, shows that this assumption is unutterably improbable.

COMMON CALL ALWAYS CONDITIONED.—Fifth: When we assert this sincere compassion of God in His common calls to the non-elect, we do not attribute to Him anything futile, or insincere; because, in the expressions of this compassion, He always makes an implied or expressed condition: that they shall turn. He does not say any where, that He has any desire to see any one saved while continuing a rebel. Nor does He say any where, that it is His *unconditioned purpose* to compel all to turn. But He says, He would like to see *all saved provided they all turned*. So that His will in the universal call is not out of joint with His prescience. And last: God's invitations and warnings to those who He foresees will reject them, are the necessary expressions of His perfections. The circumstance that a given sin is foreseen does not rob it of its moral character; and hence should constitute no reason why a righteous God shall forbear to prohibit and warn against it. That God shall yet permit creatures to commit this *sin against His invitations*, is therefore just the old question about the *permission of evil*. Not a new one.

LECTURE XLVI.

SYLLABUS.

EFFECTUAL CALLING. (Continued.)

5. Who is the Agent, and what the customary instrument in Effectual Calling? Hill, Bk. 5, ch. 1. Dick, Lect. 65. Knapp, § 131. Turrettin, Loc. xv, que. 4, § 23, &c. Knapp, § 130.

6. Prove against Socinians and semi-Pelagians, that in the effectual call, the regeneration is not merely by *moral suasion* of truth and inducement, but by *supernatural power* of the Holy Ghost.
Turrettin, Loc. xv, que. 6, and que. 4, especially § 28 to end. Hill, as above, and Bk. 4, ch. 8. Dick, Lect. 65. Ridgeley, que. 67, 68. Knapp, § 132, 133. Watson's Theol. Inst., ch. 24. Wood's Dr. James, Old and New Theology.

7. Does the Holy Ghost in regeneration operate only mediately through the word, or also immediately?
Turrettin, Loc, xv, que. 4, § 23, to end. Alexander's Relig. Experience. Dick, Lect. 66.

5. Agent and Instrument of Regeneration.—The Scriptures always speak of the Holy Ghost as the efficacious Agent of effectual calling. "Except a man be born of water and, of the Spirit." Jno. iii: 5. "It is the Spirit that quickeneth." vi: 63. See, also, 2 Cor. iii: 16; Eph. iv: 30. But this proposition will be supported by the whole subsequent argument. It is is also very important that we assert, against Mystics and Fanatics, the counterpart truth: that His customary instrument (in all cases except the redemption of infants and idiots) is the Word. If we allow any other standard or instrumentality of regeneration than the Word, there will be no barrier to the confounding of every crude impulse of nature and Satan, with those of the Holy Ghost. The work of grace is the work of the divine Spirit. The Word is also His; and He always works His works in accordance with, and through His word, because He is a wise and unchangeable Agent. Such is the uniform teaching of Scripture, confirmed by experience. Christians are "born again, not of the corruptible seed: but of incorruptible, by the word of God, which liveth and abideth forever." 1 Pet. i: 23. The Holy Ghost renovates the mental vision; the word of God alone furnishes the luminous *medium* through which the renovated vision sees. Here is the only safe middle ground between Rationalism on the one hand, and Fanaticism on the other. To give up the first truth is to surrender the whole doctrines of grace. To forsake the second is to open the floodgates to every wild delusion.

6. Pelagian and semi-Pelagian view of Regeneration.—There are two grades of Pelagian view, as to the nature and agency of regeneration. Both regard it is *only* a change of purpose in the sinner's mind: whereas Calvinism regards it as a revolution of the moral dispositions which determine the purpose of the mind; accompanied with an enlightening of the understanding in spiritual things. The ancient, thorough Pelagian taught, a regeneration produced in the boldest sense, by mere moral suasion—i. e., by the mere force of moral in-

ducements, operating according to the laws of mind. In His mouth, *converting grace* meant nothing more than God's goodness in revealing the moral inducements of the Scriptures; in endowing man with reason and conscience, and in providentially bringing those revealed encouragements into contact with his sane understanding. See History of Doctrines. But the New England Pelagian attributes to the Holy Ghost some indirect agency in presenting moral truths with increased energy to the soul. Still, he denies a proper supernatural agency therein; teaches that the office of the Holy Ghost is only suasive through the truth, and not renovating; and makes His work the same generically, only vastly stronger in degree, with that of the minister who holds forth the gospel to His fellow men. It was said, for instance, that Dr. Duffield said: "The only reason I cannot convert a sinner with gospel truth, like the Holy Ghost, is that I am not as eloquent as He is." !*

Regeneration properly defined.—Now, if we disprove this higher theory, the lower is of course disproved along with it. But we prove that regeneration is not a mere change of the human purpose, occurring in view of motive; but a *supernatural renovation* of the *dispositions* which determine the moral purpose, and of the *understanding* in the apprehension of moral and spiritual truth; the whole resulting in a *permanent and fundamental conversion* in the actings of the whole man as to sin and holiness—the flesh and God. To such a change the human will is utterly inadequate and irrelevant; because the change *goes back of the will*. It is therefore a divine and almighty work of the Father and Son through the Holy Ghost, as Their Agent. And this conception of regeneration is in strict conformity with that view of the nature of the will, which we saw a correct psychology dictate. It distinguishes properly, between *motive* and *inducement*, the former being subjective, the latter objective; the former being the efficient, the latter only the occasion of rational volitions. So, our view recognizes the practical truth, that the subjective disposition is decisive of all rational volitions—i. e., that the free agent chooses according to his moral nature, because his own moral nature decides how he shall view inducements. And we also concur with that practical view, which regards subjective character as a permanent and uniform cause, communicating regularly its own quality to the series of moral volition. This character is, in the sinner, *carnal*. To make the conduct spiritual, the character must be renewed.

Proved. 1. By man's failures in moral revolutions.—a.) Our view is probably proved by the fact that, while man shows so much

*You will, some of you, recall the queer statement of Woods, in his "Old and New Theology," of the geometrical illustration of conversion, given by a famous theologian of the semi-Pelagian school. The cross is the centre of attraction. The sinner is moving around it in a semi-circle, during the process of conversion, under the suasive influence of gospel truth. This finds him, at first, proceeding along the downward limb of the curve, directly towards hell. Butthe inducement deflects the sinner more and more, until at that point where the first quadrant ends, the downward motion is ceased, and an upward tendency is about to begin. This point marks the stage of regeneration. As gospel inducement still continues to draw, the sinner pursues more and more of an upward course. This quadrant represents the progress of sanctification, at the end of which, the sinner flies off at a tangent to heaven!

efficiency in all his physical exploits, especially where combined power is applied, his moral enterprises are so feeble and futile. He can bridge mighty floods, navigate the trackless seas, school the elements, renovate the surface of the globe; but how little can he do to ameliorate moral evils by all his plans! Where are all his reformed drunkards, savages civilized, races elevated, without divine grace? If his external works of moral renovation are so scanty, we may expect his internal to be so.

By different effects of truth, on same subject.—b.) The different results of gospel truth on different sinners, and especially on the same person at different times, cannot be explained consistently with the axiom: "Like causes produce like effects," without supposing supernatural grace. The same gospel is preached, and "some believe the things which are spoken, and some believe not." It is substantially the same carnality in all; yet some are subdued, some resist. Is the causation the same? But more yet: this gospel is applied, from childhood up, for twenty, fifty years, to a sinner, and fails. Its failure emasculates its moral force, by well known laws of habit; and the principles of carnality are strengthened in the same way. Yet at length the gospel triumphs! Sinner turns! Suppose a strong man attempts to uproot a sapling, but lacks strength. Yet when this tree has grown strong, and this man is in the decrepitude of age, he again tries the exploit, *and succeeds!* This is something above natural strength. Or suppose an attempt to resuscitate a lifeless body with pungent medicines. While the body becomes colder, more corpselike, the drugs are becoming effete by evaporation. But at this improbable time, the dead man arises! This is something above natural agency. Nor can this conclusion be evaded by saying that the greater energy, eloquence, or skill of the address communicates the sudden efficiency to the truth, before futile. For, first, no address can be so favourable in its adjuncts as many of those maternal appeals (for instance) which this sinner resisted long ago, when his carnality was but partially grown; and, second, truths which ought to be in themselves of infinite moment cannot be sensibly increased in efficacy, by the incidental advantages of oratory or skill. Some higher cause is there.

By radical nature of depravity.—c.) Let a practical view of man's moral state by nature be established. *Carnality* is an original, fundamental disposition in him, proved to be so by its universality in all men, under all religions, by its prevalence from each man's infancy. See Gen. vi: 5; Ps. lviii: 3; Jno. iii: 6. Now, we construct on this fact a simple argument from experience, viz: that no case was ever found, in which moral suasion ever eradicated or revolutionized one of the original, fundamental propensities or capacities of the human soul. Look and see. Man's carnality ought as much to be written down in the list of such, by a correct mental-science, as his sense of *meum and tuum*, his appetites, his love of applause, his capacity of resentment. Now, if a philosophy should tell us of a moral discipline to revolutionize these, we would laugh at it; e. g., the physician may persuade us *not to eat when hungry;* if he set about persuading us *not to be hungry*, we would think him a fool. All that education does, is to school, curb, conceal, or give new channels to these original propensities. But regeneration undertakes to revolutionize them; and is satisfied with no less. Ps. li: 6, 10. The regenerate man not only foregoes, but hates, the sin which was the former object of his natural moral appetite, and not only takes, but hungers for, the sanctity which was before his bitter medicine.

By consistent view of the Will.—This is also more than an argument of experience. By all sound mental science, man's moral spontaneity, while real, puts itself forth *according to a law*. That law is found in the natural state of his dispositions: i. e., the dispositions direct the will. Man's will is free. His soul is (wherever responsible) self-determined; but it is the dispositions which determine the will. Now, it is preposterous to expect the will to renovate the original dispositions; the effect to determine its own cause. Nor can the presentation of inducement alone change those dispositions, because the influence, which external objects shall have as inducements, is itself dependent on the state of the dispositions. For illustration: What would be thought of an attempt to revolutionize the tastes of the palate for the sweet, by presenting the bitter as attractive? It is the state of that palate by nature which determines the attraction to be in the sweet, and only repulsion in the bitter. A direct physiological agent must be applied.

By Scripture figures.—d.) We argue this truth from the tenour of Scripture. First: man's natural condition is said to be one of blindness, of deadness, of impotency, of bondage, of stony-heartedness. Rev. iii: 17; Eph. ii. 1; Rom. v: 6; Acts viii: 23; Ezek. xi: 19. Now, these *are* figures; but if there is any accuracy or justice in the Bible use of figures, they must be incompatible with the idea that light alone causes vision in the blind eye, or truth and inducement alone, motion in the dead, bound, helpless soul. Next: the proper supernatural character of Regeneration is proved by the Bible accounts of the work itself. It is a new creation. Ps. li: 10; Eph. ii: 10. A new birth. Jno. iii: 5; Titus iii: 5. A resurrection from death. Eph. ii: 1, 4, 5. A giving of a fleshly in place of a stony heart. Ezek. xxxvi: 26. An opening of blind eyes. 2 Cor. iv: 6. Here again, the creature cannot create itself, the child beget itself, the dead body re-animate itself, the stony heart change itself, the darkness illuminate itself, at the prompting of inducements. An external and almighty power is requisite. Once more: it is expressly attributed to God, in language which utterly precludes the idea that He changes the heart only through the force of truth applied to it. See John i: 13; iii: 5; vi: 44, 45; Eph. i: 19, 20; ii: 8; Phil. i: 29; ii: 13; Acts xi: 18, &c. Further: Scriptural proof will appear under the next head, Prov. xvi: 1.

By consequences of the opposite.—e.) If regeneration were by moral suasion, man would be his own saviour in a sense excluded by the Scripture; as in 1 Cor. iv: 7. If it were by moral suasion, of course regenerating grace would always be vincible; and, consequently, believers would have no sufficient warrant to pray to God for salvation. There would be only a probability at best, that God *could* save them; and to the mind taking an impartial survey of the relative numbers who have ever resisted the gospel, that probability would not appear strong.

Is the operation of the Spirit mediate? Dick's view.—7. There is a sense in which the Holy Ghost is said to operate regeneration only mediately, through the truth, which is held not by Pelagians, but by Calvinists. This seems to have been the doctrine originiated in the French Presbyterian Church, of the 17th *century*, by Claude Pajon. It may be found stated perspicuously in Dick's 66th Lecture, and even partially adopted in Dr. Alexander's Religious Experience. These divines would by no means teach that regeneration is not a divine, supernatural and invincible work of grace. But they suppose that the essential change is in the illumination of the understanding, which God's Spirit indeed almightily effects; but, to effect which, nothing more is needed than to secure for the truth a true spiritual apprehension by the understanding. The truth being truly apprehended, they suppose the renovation of the will follows as a necessary result, without farther supernatural agency; because, according to our Calvinistic psychology, the soul's *emotions* are governed by its *views* of the objects thereof; and the will always follows the latest and most decisive conviction of the understanding. They claim the order of phrases in the Catechism, question 31.

Turrettin's.—Now, the justice of this reasoning is admitted; but the mistake is in the failure to go back one step farther in the analysis. We hold, on the contrary, that there is in regeneration not only a mediate, but also an immediate operation of the Holy Ghost, not only placing before the understanding truly luminous and spiritual views of the word and its motives; but immediately revolutionizing the moral dispositions, so as to incline them to love those views. We believe that in order for the actings of regenerate nature to take place, there must be both the *object* adapted to the spiritual mind—i. e., the truth; and also the spiritual subjective adaptation and capacity to embrace that truth. And this:

Arguments. a.) Power of spirit precedes.—a.) Because the Scriptures often speak of a spiritual power precedaneous to the truth on the operation of which power, the saving apprehension of truth is conditioned. See Ps. cxix: 18. The opening is the precedent cause; the beholding of wonderful things out of the law, the consequence. As the eye closed by cataract cannot be restored to vision by any pouring of beams of light on it, however pure and condensed, so the soul does not acquire spiritual vision by bringing the truth alone in any degree of spiritual contact. The surgeon's knife goes before, removing the obstruction; then, on the presentation of light, vision results. Both must concur. Let the student examine, in the same way, Luke xxiv: 45; Eph. i: 17, 18; Acts xvi: 14; 1 Cor. iii: 6, 7, 9; Jer. xxxi: 33.

The carnal mind only hates, the more clearly the light is seen.—b.) The Scriptures represent man's mind as hostile, by reason of depravity, to the pure truth of God. 1 Cor. i: 23; ii: 14; Rom. viii: 7, &c. It is not because God's truth is misapprehended by the sinner's mind, that he repels it; he is intrinsically opposed to it. The more closely and clearly it is brought home to him, the more does his opposition revive. See Rom. vii: 7, 8, 9. It is hard to see, therefore, how this instinctive hostility could be reconciled, by giving the sinner clearer understanding of that spiritual truth, whose little glimpses even fill him with enemity and rebellion. Objective inducement cannot modify the subjective state of the moral capacities to which it is addressed, because the adaptation of the external object to be a motive at all, is determined *à priori* by those subjective states. These writers, therefore, "put the cart before the horse," in the same way with the Pealgian, (not indeed intending a Pelagian result.) When pressed with this, they say: the several faculties of the soul are not different parts or members thereof, but only different modes in which the same unit, soul, acts. True: but their theory discriminates between the soul's capacity of understanding, and its capacity of feeling thereupon, just as ours does. The plea is a mere subterfuge.

Comparison with infant regeneration.—c.) Infants and idiots are, we believe, regenerated. They cannot be regenerated mediately through the truth; for their understandings, being undeveloped, are incapable of the application of means. The operation of the Holy Ghost must be, therefore, immediate. But the disease of original sin, constituting the necessity for regeneration, is in them generically the same as in us; the state of sanctification initiated is generically the same as in us; and, therefore, the process must be substantially the same. Here is a probable argument that its means are applied in the same way.

The mind judges of moral objects as the heart feels.—d.) Last: a proper analysis of the *mode* in which intellections or *mental* convictions arise on moral subjects, will prove our theory, and remove all the plausibility in the argument for the opposite. True; emotion follows mental apprehension; and the last dictate of the understanding governs the will. But *how does the mind attain its apprehensions of objects of moral volition?* Only in consequence of its moral dispositions. Saith the acute Paschal: (Pensées) "In natural things the views of the understanding determine the feelings; but in spiritual things, the feelings determine the views of the understanding;" e. g., the belief that sweetmeats are desirable may be in the child, when distinguished from the appetency following thereupon, as properly an *intellectual* state, as the belief that two and three make five. But, that belief about the sweetmeats is none the less, itself *a consequence*—i. e., of an appetite, of a state of taste in the palate. So, the belief of the understanding as to the desirableness of holiness for *me*, &c., is an intellectual state, distinguishable from the appetency for holiness consequent thereon as an emotion; but it is itself dictated by the moral state of the dispositions. A certain moral taste in the will must exist as to sin and holiness, before the understanding apprehends holiness as desirable for me. The *opinion* of the head, on all moral and spiritual choice, is but the echo of the spontaneous verdict pronounced beforehand by the heart. Now, it may be all true, that when a spiritual apprehension of Christ and holiness, as desirable for me, is secured in the head, the emotions and volitions of the heart will all come right as a natural consequence. But how is that spiritual apprehension in the understanding to be secured? Only by a revolution of the moral dispositions. The immediate operation of the Holy Ghost must precede the mediate of the word; not indeed in time, but in causative influence. See Eph. iv: 18; Luke viii: 15; Rom. x: 10. Distinguish here between *conscience* and *appetency*. Depravity consists in perversion of *latter*.

CARNAL BLINDNESS THUS SUCCESSFULLY EXPLAINED.—e.) Add, that this view gives us a consistent *rationale* of that *impotency* of the carnal mind to comprehend the things of Christ, spoken of in 1 Cor.; e. g., ii: 14. This impotency (too plainly) exists. But those who hold with Dick cannot define it. They say it consists not in the absence of any revelation which the believer has. (That would be fanaticism.) Nor in the lack of any *Faculty*, which the regenerate gain. (This would be mysticism.) Nor in the hiding of any esoteric, allegorical sense of the Scripture, to which the believer has the key. (This would be Origenism.) In what, then, does this impotency consist? They have no answer.

THE CARNAL HEART GIVES DICTA OPPOSED TO CHRIST'S.—But I, on my theory, can give a consistent answer, just that of Eph. iv: 18; Rom. viii: 7. "The blindness of the *heart* darkens the understanding." Calvinistic expositors even have been heard construing the striking words of Eph. iv: 18, thus: "Inasmuch as the head, and not the heart, is the seat of intelligence, when the Apostle speaks of 'blindness of heart,' he must be understood as using the word 'heart' comprehensively, including the intelligence, as well as the affections, and even intending the former chiefly." In this perverse way do they shut their eyes to the invaluable instruction of the text. One would think that this exegetical reason should have taught them, that when the Apostle said "heart," he did not mean "understanding," because he has the term understanding already in the sentence. What the inspired man would signify is clearly this, that *opinion* touching the objects of moral volition is the fruit of moral disposition—the head follows the heart. But the beliefs of the sinner's understanding, thus dictated by his carnal disposition, come in collision with certain propositions which are postulates or premises to the most cardinal gospel teachings. No wonder, then, the mind does not apprehend those teachings as true. For example, the sinner's real opinion (taught him by his carnal heart) is that carnality is sweet, *per se*. It is its penalty alone, which self-love apprehends as evil. No wonder, then, that his very understanding is confounded by a gospel which necessarily implies that carnality is an evil *per se*, and holds out *salvation from carnality* as a conscious good *per se*, to be desired, eagerly embraced, and devoutly celebrated with praises to God. The mother says to her little child: "Come up to me, and I will give you something good." He replies: "Mamma, you are up stairs; how shall I come?" She instructs him by what doors and turnings to reach her; and that in terms which, had he seen that the good thing which she has prepared for him was a lucious peach, would have been perspicuous enough. But just now, he spies the fact that it is a nauseous medicine she is preparing for him. Thereupon the proposal becomes quite mystifying to him; and he is arrested as a stock. No wonder!

LECTURE XLVII.

SYLLABUS.

ARMINIAN THEORY OF REDEMPTION.

1. Give a connected view of the Arminian Five Points.
   Articles of Synod of Dort. Whitby's Five Points. Hill's Divinity, Bk. iv, ch. 8. Stapfer's Pol. Theol., vol. iv, ch. 17, § 12-35.
2. Disprove the doctrine of Common Sufficient Grace.
   Turrettin, Loc. xv, que. 3. Hill, Bk. iv, ch. 9, § 1. Ridgeley, que. 44. Watson's Theol. Inst., ch. xxv.
3. Is the grace of God in regeneration invincible? And is the will of man in regeneration, active or passive?
   Turrettin, Loc. xv, que. 5 and 6. Hill, Bk. iv, ch. 9. Knapp, § 130, 132.
4. Can any Pagans be saved, without the instrumentality of the Scriptures?
   Turrettin, Loc. i, que. 4, and Loc. x, que. 5. Ridgeley, que. 60. Annual Sermon for Presb. Board For. Miss., June, 1858.

Sources of the Arminian Theology.—The subjects which are now brought under discussion introduce us to the very centre of the points which are debated between us and Arminians. I propose, therefore, for their farther illustration, and because no better occasion offers, to consider here their scheme.

The sources of Arminian Theology would be best found in the apology of Episcopius, Limborch's Christian Theology, and Knapp's Christian Theology. Among the English may be consulted, as a low Arminian, Daniel Whitby's Five Points; as high Arminians, Wesley's Doctrinal Tracts, and Watson's Theological Institutes. For refutation of Arminianism, see Stapfer, vol. 4; Turrettin; Hill, Bk. 4, ch. 9.

I. A connected view of the Arminian tenets:

Five Points of remonstrants ambiguous.—The *five points* handed in by the Arminians to the States General of Holland, in their celebrated remonstrance, were so covertly worded as scarcely to disclose their true sentiments. The assertions concerning original Sin and Free will, were seemingly such as Calvinists could accept. The doctrine of common grace was but obscurely hinted; and the perseverance of Saints was only doubted. But their system soon developed itself into semi-Pelagianism, well polished and knit together. Discarding the order of the five points, I will exhibit the theory in its logical connexions.

Logical source in doctrine of Indifferency of the Will. View of original Sin.—1. Its starting point is the doctrine of indifference of the will, and a denial of total depravity, as held by Calvinists. According to the universal consent of Pelagians and Socinians, this *equilibrium* of the will is held necessary to proper free agency and responsibility. Take Whitby as a type of the grosser Arminians. He thinks Adam was created *li ble*, but not *subject*, to bodily death, and his immunity in Paradise was secured by his access to the Tree of Life. His sin made death and its attendant pains inevitable; and this his posterity inherit, according to the natural law, that like begets like. This has produced a set of circumstances, making all men so *liable* to sin, that, practically, none escape. But this results from no moral necessity or certainty of the will. Man has natural desires for natural good, but this *concupiscentia* is not sin till formed into a positive volition. But the sense of guilt and fear drives man from God, the pressure of earthly ills tends to earthly mindedness; man's pains makes him querilous, envious, inordinate in desire; and above all, a general *evil example* misleads. So that all are, in fact, precipitated into sin, in virtue of *untoward circumstances inherited from Adam.* This is the only sense in which Adam is our *federal head.* This relation is not only illustrated by, but similar to, that which exists between a bad parent and unfortunate offspring now—*an instance of the same natural law.*

Wesleyan view of original sin.—But Wesley and Watson repudiate this, as too low; and teach a fall in Adam, prior to its reparation by common grace, going as far as moderate Calvinists. Watson, for instance, ch. 18, (vol. 2, p. 52,) while repudiating both *mediate* and *immediate* imputation of Adam's sin, (which he evidently does not understand,) says that Adam was a public person, our federal head, and that the penal consequences of his sin (not the sin itself) are imputed to us, consisting of bodily ills and death, privations of God's indwelling, resulting in positive depravation, and eternal death. He adopts, in short, the doctrine of Dr. Watts against Dr. Taylor, of Norwich. But in defending against Pelagians, &c., the *justice* of this arrangement of God, he says it must be viewed in connexion with that purpose of redemption towards the human race, which co-existed in the divine mind, by which God purposed to purchase and bestow common grace on *every* fallen man, thus repairing his loss in Adam. (The fatal objection to such a justification is, that then God would have been under obligations to provide man a Saviour: and Christ's mission would not have been of pure grace.)

Common Sufficient Grace.—2. This leads us to their next point: God having intended all along to repair the fall, and having immediately thereafter given a promise to our first parents, has ever since communicated to all mankind a *common pre-edaneous sufficient grace*, purchased for all by Christ's work. This is not sufficient to effect a complete redemption, but to enable, both naturally and morally, to *fulfil the conditions* for securing redeeming grace. This common grace consists in the indifferency of man's will remaining, notwithstanding his fall, the lights of natural conscience, good impulses enabling unregenerate men to do works of social virtue, the outward call of mercy made, as some Arminians suppose, even to heathens through reason, and some lower forms of universal spiritual influence. The essential idea and argument of the Arminian is, that God could not punish man justly for unbelief, unless He conferred on him both *natural* and moral ability to believe or not. They quote such Scripture as Ps. lxxxi: 13; Is. v: 4; Luke xix: 42; Rev. iii: 20; Rom. ii: 14; John i: 9. So here we have, by a different track, the old conclusion of the semi-Pelagian. Man, then, decides the whole remaining difference, as to believing or not believing, by his use of this precedent grace, according to his own free will. God's purpose to produce different results in different men is wholly conditioned on the use which, He foresees, they will make of their common grace. To those who improve it, God stands *pledged* to give the crowning graces of regeneration, justification, sanctification, and glorification. To the heathen, even, who use their light aright, (unfavourable circumstances may make such instances rare,) Christ will give gospel light and redeeming grace, in some inscrutable way.

GRACE IN REGENERATION VINCIBLE.—3. Hence, the operations of grace are at every stage vincible by man's will; to be otherwise, they must violate the conditions of moral agency. Even after regeneration grace may be so resisted by free will, as to be dethroned from the soul, which then again becomes unrenewed.

REDEMPTION GENERAL.—4. The redeeming work of Christ was equally for all and every man of the human race, to make his sins *pardonable* on the condition of faith, to purchase a common sufficient grace actually enjoyed by all, and the efficient graces of a complete redemption suspended on the proper improvement of common grace by free will. Christ's intention and provision are, therefore, the same to all. But as justice requires that the pardoned rebel shall believe and repent, to those who, of their own choice, refuse this, the provision remains forever ineffective.

JUSTIFICATION.—5. In the doctrine of justification, again, the lower and higher Arminians differ somewhat. Both define justification as consisting simply of pardon. According to the lower, this justification is only purchased by Christ in this, that He procured from God the admission of a lower Covenant, admitting *faith and the Evangelical* obedience flowing out of it, as a righteousness, in place of the perfect obedience of the Covenant of works. According to the higher, our faith (without the works it fruits) is imputed to us for righteousness, according, as they suppose, to Rom. iv: 5. Both deny the proper imputation of Christ's *active* (as distinguished from his passive) obedience, and deny any imputation, except of the believer's own faith; although the higher Arminians, in making this denial, seem to misunderstand imputation as a transference of moral character.

PERSONAL ELECTION CONDITIONAL.—6. Hence, it will be easily seen, that their conception of election must be the following: The only absolute and unconditional decree which God has made from eternity, concerning man's salvation, is His resolve that unbelievers shall perish. This is not a predestinating of individuals, but the fixing of a General Principle. God does, indeed, (as they explain Rom., ix–xi chapters,) providentially and sovereignly elect *races* to the enjoyment of certain privileges; but this is not an election to *salvation;* for free will may in any or each man of the race, abuse the privileges, and be lost. So far as God has an eternal purpose towards individuals, it is founded on His foresight, which He had from eternity, of the use they would make of their common grace. Some, He foresaw, would believe and repent, and therefore elected them to justification. Others, He foresaw, would not only believe and repent, but also persevere to the end; and these He elected to salvation.

A thoroughly-knit system, if its premises are granted.

II. The refutation of the Arminian theory must be deferred, on some points, till we pass to other heads of divinity, as Justification, and Final Perseverance. On the extent of the atonement enough has already been said. On the remaining points we shall now attempt to treat.

Common Sufficient Grace refuted.—In opposition to the assertion of a common sufficient grace, we remark, 1st. That there is no sufficient evidence of it in Scripture. The passages quoted above do, indeed, prove that God has done for all men under the gospel all that is needed to affect their salvation, if their own wills were not depraved. But they only express the fact that God's general benevolence would save all to whom the gospel comes, if they would repent; and that the obstacles to that salvation are now only in the sinners. But whether it is God's secret purpose to overcome that internal obstacle, in their own perverse wills, these texts do not say. It will be found, on examination, that they all refer merely to the external call, which we have proved, comes short of the effectual call: or that they are addressed to persons who, though shortcoming, or even backsliding, are regarded as God's children already. Look and see.

Doctrine false, in fact.—2. The doctrine is false in fact; for how can grace be *sufficient*, where the essential outward call, even, is lacking? Rom. x: 14. God declares, in Scripture, He has given up many to evil. Acts xiv: 16; Rom. i: 21, 28; ix: 18. Again: the doctrine is contradicted by the whole doctrine of God, concerning the final desertion of those who have grieved away the Holy Ghost. See Hos. iv: 17; Gen. vi: 3; Heb. vi: 1–6. Here is a class so deserted of grace, that their damnation becomes a certainty. Are they, therefore, no longer free, responsible, and blameable?

3. If we take the Arminian description of common sufficient grace, then many who have its elements most largely, an enlightened conscience, frequent compunctions, competent religious knowledge, amiability, and natural virtues, good impulses and resolutions, are lost; and some, who seem before to have very little of these, are saved. How is this? Again: the doctrine does not commend itself to experience; for this tells us that, among men, good intentions are *more rare* than good opportunities. We see that some men have vastly more *opportunity* vouchsafed them by God's providence than others. It would be strange if, contrary to the fact just stated, all those *who have* less opportunity should have better intentions than opportunities.

Common Grace, if sufficient, saves.—4. We have sometimes illustrated the Wesleyan doctrine of common sufficient grace thus: "All men lie in the 'slough of despond' in consequence of the fall. There is a platform, say Arminians, elevated an inch or two above the surface of this slough, but yet firm, to which men must struggle in the exercise of their common sufficient grace alone, the platform of repentance and faith. Now, it is true, that from this platform man could no more climb to heaven without divine grace, than his feet could scale the moon. But God's grace is pledged to lift up to heaven all those who will so employ their free-agency, as to climb to that platform, *and stay there.*" Now, we say, with the Arminian, that a common sufficient grace, which does not work faith and repentance, is in no sense sufficient; for until these graces are exercised, nothing is done. Heb. xi:

6; Jno. iii: 36. But he who has these graces, we farther assert, has made the whole passage from life to death. That platform *is* the platform of eternal life. The whole difference between elect and non-elect is already constituted. See John iii: 36; 1 John v: 1; Acts xiii: 48; 2 Cor. v: 17; with Eph. iii: 17. If then there is sufficient grace, it is none other than the grace which *effectuates* redemption; and the Arminian should say, not that God by it puts it in every man's free will to fulfil the conditions on which further saving communications depend; but that He puts it in every man's free will to *save .imself*.

Or else, it is either not common, or not sufficient.—5. If the doctrine is true, it is every man's own uninfluenced choice, and not the purpose of God, which determines his eternal destiny. Either the common grace effects its saving work in those who truly believe, in virtue of some essential addition made to its influences by God, or it does not. If the former, then it was not "common," nor "sufficient," in those who failed to receive that addition. If the latter, then the whole difference in its success must have been made by the man's own free will resisting less—i. e., the essential opposition to grace in some souls, differs from that in others. But see Rom. iii: 12, 27; Eccl. viii: 11; Eph. ii: 8, 9; 1 Cor. iv: 7; Rom. ix: 6; and the whole tenour of that multitude of texts, in which believers ascribe their redemption, not to their own superior docility or penitence, but to distinguishing grace.

III. Grace in Regeneration invincible.—The views of regeneration which Calvinists present, in calling the grace of God therein invincible, and in denying the Synergisne (sunergeia) of man's will there in, necessarily flow from their view of original sin. We do not deny that the common call is successfully resisted by all non-elect gospel sinners; it is because God never communicates renewing grace, as He never intended, in His secret purpose. Nor do we deny that the elect, while under preliminary conviction, struggle against grace, with as much obstinacy as they dare; this is ensured by their depraved nature. But on all those whom God purposes to save, He exerts a power, renewing and persuading the will, so as infallibly to ensure their final and voluntary submission to Christ. Hence, we prefer the word *invincible* to *irresistable*. This doctrine we prove by all those texts which speak of God's power in regeneration as a new creation, birth, resurrection; for the idea of successful resistance to these processes, on the part of the dead matter, or corpse, or *foetus*, is preposterous. *Conviction* may be resisted; *regeneration* is invincible. We prove it again from all those passages which exalt the divine and mighty power exerted in the work. See Eph. i: 19, 20; Ps. cx: 3. Another emphatic proof is found in this, that otherwise, God could not be sure of the conversion of all those He purposed to convert; yea, not of a single one of them; and Christ would have no assurance that He should ever "see of the travail of His soul" in a single case! For in order for God to be *sure* of the result, He must put forth power adequate to overcome all opposing resistances. But see all those passages, in which the security and immutability of God's purposes of grace are asserted. Rom. ix: 21, 23, Eph. i: 4; John xv: 16, &c., &c. Eph. ii: 10.

Mere foreknowledge inadequate.—Here, the Arminians rejoins, that God's *scientia media*, or foreknowledge of the contingent acts of free agents, (arising not from His purpose of control over those acts, but from His infinite insight into their character, and the way it will act under foreseen circumstances,) enables Him to foreknow certainly *who* will improve their common grace, and that *some will*. His eternal purposes are not crossed therefore, they say, because He only purposed from eternity to save those latter. The fatal answer is, that if the acts of free agents are *certainly* foreseen, even with this *scientia media*, they are no longer contingent, but certain; and worse than this: Man's will being in bondage, all the foreknowledge which God has, from His infinite insight into human character, will be only a foreknowledge of obdurate acts of resistance on man's part, as long as that will is unsubdued. God's foreknowledge, in that case, would have been a foreknowledge that *every* son of Adam would resist and be lost. The only foreknowledge God could have, of any cases of submission, was one founded on His own decisive purpose to *make some* submit, by invincible grace.

Grace does not destroy free-agency.—The Arminian objects again, that our doctrine represents man as dragged reluctating into a state of grace, like an angry wild beast into a cage; whereas, freedom of will, and hearty concurrence are essential elements of all service acceptable to God. The answer is, that the sinner's *will* is the very subject of this invincible grace. God so renews it that it neither can resist, nor longer wishes to resist. But this objection virtually reappears in the next part of the question.

The soul passive in its quickening. Proof.—Calvinists are accustomed also to say, in opposition to all Synergistic views, that the will of man is not active, but only passive in regeneration. In this proposition, it is only meant that man's will is the *subject*, and not the *agent*, nor one of the agents of the distinctive change. In that renovating touch, which revolutionizes the active powers of the soul, it is *acted on* and not *agent*. Yet, activity is the inalienable attribute of an intelligent being; and in the process of *conversion*, which begins instantaneously with regeneration, the soul is active in all its exercises towards sin, holiness, God, its Saviour, the law, &c., &c.

This doctrine is proved by the natural condition of the active powers of the soul. Man's propensities are wholly and certainly directed to some form of ungodliness, and to impenitency. How, then, can the will, prompted by these propensities, persuade itself to anything spiritually good and penitent? It is expecting a cause to operate in a direction just the opposite to its nature—as well expect gravity to *raise* masses flung into the air, when its nature is to bring them *down*. And this is agreeable to the whole Bible representation. Does the *foetus* procure its own birth? the dead body its own resurrection? the matter of creation its own organization? See especially John i: 13. Yet this will, thus renewed, chooses God, and acts holiness, freely, just as Lazarus, when resuscitated, put forth the activities of a living man.

The objections of the Arminian may all be summed up in this: that sinners are commanded, not only to put forth all the actings of the renewed nature, such as believing, turning from sin, loving God, &c.,

but are commanded to perform the very act of giving their hearts to God, which seems to contain the very article of regeneration. See Prov. xxiii: 26; Is. i: 16; Ezek. xviii: 31; Deut. x: 16.

Objection answered.—The answer is, 1st. That God's precepts are no test of the extent of our moral ability, but only of our duty. When our Creator has given to us capacities to know and love Him, and the thing which prevents is our depraved wills, this is no reason why He should or ought to cease demanding that which is His due. If the moral opposition of nature into which God's creatures may sink themselves by their own fault, were a reason why He should cease to urge His natural rights on them, He would soon have no right left. Again: the will of man, when renovated by grace, needs a *rule* by which to put forth its renewed activity, just as the eye, relieved of its darkness by the surgeon, needs light to see. Hence, we provide *light* for the renovated eye; not that light alone could make the blind eye see. And hence, God applies His precepts to the renovated will, in order that it may have a law by which to act out its newly bestowed, spiritual free-agency. But 3d, and chiefly: These objections are all removed, by making a sound distinction between regeneration and conversion. In the *latter* the soul is active; and the acts required by all the above passages, are the soul's (now regenerate) *turning* to God.

Bible promises no salvation to Heathen.—The salvability of any heathen without the gospel is introduced here, because the question illustrates these views concerning the extent of the grace of redemption, and the discussions between us and the Arminians. We must hold that Revelation gives us no evidence that Pagans can find salvation, without Scriptural means. They are sinners. The means in their reach appear to contain no salvation. a.) One argument is this: All of them are self-convicted of some sin, (against the light of nature.) "Without the shedding of blood is no remission." But the gospel is the only proposal of atonement to man. b.) Paganism provides nothing to meet the other great want of human nature, an agency for moral renovation. Is any man more spiritually minded than decent children of the Church are, because he is a Pagan? Do they need the new birth less than our own beloved offspring? Then it must be at least as true of the heathen, that except they be born again, they shall not see the kingdom. But their religions present no agencies for regeneration. They do not even know the word. So far are their theologies from any sanctifying influence, their morals are immoral, their deities criminals, and the heaven to which they aspire a *pandemonium* of sensual sin immortalized.

God no more unjust to them than to non-elect under the gospel.—Now, the Arminians reject this conclusion, thinking God cannot justly condemn any man, who is not furnished with such means of knowing and loving Him, as put His destiny in every sense within His own choice. These means the heathen do not fully possess, where their ignorance is invincible. The principle asserted is, that God cannot justly hold any man responsible, who is not blessed with both "natural and moral ability." I answer, that our doctrine concerning the heathen puts them in the same condition with those unhappy men in Christian lands, who have the outward word, but experience no effectual calling of the Spirit. God requires the latter to obey that Law and Gospel, of which they enjoy the clearer lights; and the obstacle which *ensures* their failure to obey is, indeed, not any physical constraint, but an inability of will. Of the heathen, God would require no more than perfect obedience to the light of nature; and it is the same inability of will which ensures their failure to do this. Hence, as you see, the doctrine of a common sufficient grace, and of the salvability of the heathens, are parts of the same system.

LECTURE XLVIII.

SYLLABUS.

ARMINIAN SCHEME. (Concluded.)

1. Are God's decrees of personal election conditional or unconditional? Turrettin, Loc. iv, que. 3, § 1-7. Que. 11, § 10-24. Loc. xv, que. 2, 3. Hill, Bk. iv, ch. 7, and ch. x. Dick, Lect. 35. Knapp, Chr. Theol., § 32, and Note. Watson's Theol. Inst., ch. xxvi.

2. Show the relations between the orthodox views of effectual calling and election, and the true theory of the will and free-agency. a.) That the natural will is certainly determined to carnality, and yet free-agency exists therein. b.) That the renewed will, after it is sovereignly renewed to godliness, and efficaciously preserved therein, is yet more free: And therefore, responsibility exists in both states.

See Lect. ix, pt. i. (on Will.) Turrettin, Loc. x, que. iv. Alexander's Mor. Science, ch. 16 to 18. Hill, Bk. iv, ch. ix, § 3. Edwards on Will, pt. i, ch. 3, and pt. iii. Watson's Theol. Inst., ch. xxviii, § 3.

1. Conditional Decrees are implied in Synergism.—The favourite Arminian *dogma*, that God's will concerning the salvation of individuals is conditioned on His simple foresight of their improvement of their common grace, in genuine faith, repentance, and holy obedience, is necessary to the coherency of their system. If grace is invincible, and all true faith, &c., are its fruits, then God's purpose as to working them must be absolute in this sense. If grace is only synergistic, and the sinner's free will alone decides the question of resisting it or co-operating with it, then, of course, the sovereignty of decision, in this matter, is in the creature, and not in God; and He must be guided in His purpose by what it is foreseen the creature will choose to do. Thus we reach, by a corollary from the Arminian doctrine of "Calling," that which in time is first, the nature of the Divine purpose about it. The student is here referred to the Lecture on the Decree, in Pt. I. But as the subject is so illustrative of the two theories of redemption, the Arminian and the orthodox, I shall not hesitate to discuss the same thing again, and to reproduce some of the same ideas.

THE RESULT MAY BE CONDITIONED, AND NOT THE DECREE.—And let me begin by reminding you of that plain distinction, by the ignoring of which Arminians get all the plausibility of their view. It is one thing to say that, in the Divine will, *the result purposed* is conditioned on the presence of its means; another thing to say that, *God's purpose about it* is also conditioned or dependent on the presence of its means. The former is true, the latter false. And this, because the presence of the means is itself efficaciously included in this same Divine purpose. Thus, a believer's salvation is doubtless dependent on his repentance; in the sense that, if he does not repent, he will not be saved. But God's purpose to save him is not dependent on his choosing to repent; for one of the things which God's purpose efficaciously determines is, that this believer *shall* have grace to repent. Remember, also, that when we say God's election is not dependent on the believer's foreseen faith, &c., we do not represent the Divine purpose as a *motiveless caprice.* It is a resolve founded most rationally, doubtless, on the best of reasons—only, the superior faith and penitence of that man were not, *à priori* among them; because had not God already determined, from some better reasons unknown to us, that man would never have had any faith or repentance to foresee. And this is a perfect demonstration, as well as a Scriptural one. The Arminian opinion makes an effect the cause of its own cause. And that our faith, &c., are *effects* of our calling and election, see Rom. viii: 29; Eph. i: 4, 5; 2 Thes. ii: 13; 1 Cor. iv: 7; Jno. xv: 16.

PROVIDENCE MAKES SOVEREIGN DISTINCTIONS IN MEN'S OUTWARD OPPORTUNITIES. ESPECIALLY OF INFANTS.—b.) But to this I may add the same idea in substance, which I used against Common Sufficient Grace: That, in fact, *differences are made*, in the temperaments and characters, opportunities and privileges of individuals and nations, which practically result in the death of some in sin. Thus: what practical *chance*, humanly speaking, had the man born in Tahiti, in the 18th century, for redemption through Christ? Now, the Arminian himself admits an election of races or nations to such privilege, which is sovereign. Does not this imply a similar disposal of the fate of individuals? Can an infinite understanding fail to comprehend the individuals, in disposing of the destiny of the mass? But, under this head especially, I remark: the time of every man's death is decided by a sovereign Providence. But by determining this sovereignty, God very often practically decides the man's eternal destiny. Much more obvious is this in the case of infants. According to Arminians, all that die in infancy are saved. So, then, God's purpose to end their mortal life in infancy is His purpose to save them. But this purpose cannot be formed from any foresight of their faith or repentance; because they have none to foresee, being saved without them.

IF FORESEEN, FAITH MUST BE CERTAIN.—c.) God's foresight of believers' faith and repentance implies the certainty, or "moral necessity" of these acts, just as much as a sovereign decree. For that which is certainly foreseen must be certain. The only evasion from this is the absurdity of Adam Clarke, that God chooses not to foreknow certain things, or the impiety of the Socinians, that He cannot foreknow some things. On both, we may remark, that if this faith and repentance are not actually foreknown, they cannot be the bases of any resolve on God's part.

IMMUTABLE DECREE CANNOT BE CONDITIONED ON A MUTABLE CAUSE. SCRIPTURE.—d.) That any purposes of God should depend on the acts of a creature having an intermediate, contingent will, such as the Arminian describes, is incompatible with their immutability and eternity. But all His decrees are such. See Ps. xxxiii: 11; 2 Tim. ii: 19; Eph. i: 4; Is. xlvi: 10. In a word, this doctrine places the sovereignty in the creature, instead of God, and makes Him wait on His own servant. It is disparaging to God.

Last: This very purpose of individual election to salvation is often declared to be uncaused by any foreseen good in us. See Matt. xi: 26; Rom. ix: 11, 16; xi: 5–6, &c.

TEXTS SEEMING TO EXPRESS A CONDITIONED PURPOSE.—But Arminians cite many passages, in which they assert, God's resolve as to what He shall do to men is conditioned on their good or bad conduct. They are such as 1 Sam. xiii: 13; Ps. lxxxi: 13, 14; Luke vii: 30; Ezek. xviii: 21, &c. Luke xix· 42. Our opponents here make an obvious confusion of things, which should be distinguished. When God, perceptively, reveals a connexion between two alternative lines of conduct, and their respective results, as established by His law or promise, He does not at all reveal anything thereby, as to what He purposes with reference to permitting or procuring the exercise of that conduct by man. Of course, it does not imply that His purpose on this point is contingent to Him, or that the consequent results were uncertain to Him. We have seen that many of the *results decreed* by God were dependent on means which man employed; but that God's resolve was not dependent, because it secretly embraced their performance of those instrumental acts also. But the proof that the Arminians misconstrue those Scripture instances, is this: That the Bible itself contains many instances of these conditional threats and promises, and expressions of compassion, where yet the result of them is expressly foretold. If expressly predicted, they must have been predetermined. See, then, Is. i: 19, 20, compared with vii: 17–20. And more striking yet: Acts xxvii. 23–25, with v: 31.

EVASION ATTEMPTED FROM ROM., CH. IX: 11.—Rom. ix: 11–18, is absolutely conclusive against conditional election. The only evasion by which the Arminian can escape its force, is that this passage represents only a national election of Israel and Edom, represented in their patriarchs, Jacob, and Esau, to the outward privileges of the gospel. We reply, as in Part I, That Jacob and Esau certainly *represented themselves also*, so that here are two cases of unconditional predestination. But Paul's scope shows that the idea is false; for that scope is to explain, how, on his doctrine of justification by grace, many members of Israel were lost, notwithstanding equal outward privileges. And in answering this question, the Apostle evidently dismisses the corporate, or collective, in order to consider the individual relation to God's plan and purpose. See the verses 8, 15, 24. That the election was not merely to privilege, is clearly proved by the illusion of v. 8, compared with verses 4, 21 to 24.

CALVINISTIC VIEW AGREEABLE TO THE TRUE NATURE OF THE WILL. —2. I am now to show that the Calvinistic scheme is consistent, and the Arminian inconsistent with the philosophical theory of the will and free-agency. Let me here refer you to Part I, Lecture IX, where the true doctrine of the will is stated and defended, and request you, if your mastery of the views there given is not perfect, to return and make it so, before proceeding. While I shall not repeat the arguments, the definition of the true doctrine is so important (and has so often been imperfectly made by Calvinists) that I shall take the liberty to restate it.

True theory of the Will stated.—The Arminian says that free-agency consists in the self-determining power of the will, as a distinct faculty in the soul. The Calvinists says, it consists in the self-determining power of the soul. The Arminian says an agent is only free, when he has power to choose as the will may determine itself either way, irrespective of the stronger motive The Calvinists says that an agent is free, when he has *power to act as his own will chooses.* The Arminian says that in order to be free, the agent must be exempt from the efficient influence of his own motives; the Calvinist, that he must be exempt from co-action, or external constraint. The Arminian says, that in order to be free, the agent must always be capable of having a volition uncaused. The Calvinist says that if an agent has a volition uncaused, he cannot possibly be free therein, because that volition would be wholly irrational; the agent would therein be simply a brute. Every free, rational, responsible volition is such, precisely because it is caused; the rational agent is morally judged for his volitions according to their motives, or causes.

Motive What?—But when we ask: What is the *motive* of a rational volition, we must make that distinction which all Arminians, and many Calvinists heedlessly overlook, between motive and inducement. The object offered to the soul as an inducement to choose is not the cause, the *motive* of the choice; but only the occasion. The true, efficient cause is something of the soul's own, something subjective; namely, the soul's own *habitus*, or prevalent subjective disposition. The volition is not efficaciously caused by the inducement, or object which appeals, but by the disposition which is appealed to. Thus, the causative spring of a free agent's action is within, not without him; according to the testimony of our consciousness. (The theory which makes the objective inducement the true cause of volition, is from that old, mischievous, sensualistic psychology, which has always been such a curse to theology.) But then, this inward or subjective spring of action is not lawless; it is not indeterminate; if it were, the agent would neither have rationality nor character; and its action would be absolutely blind and brutish. This subjective spring has a law of its own activity—that is to say, its self-action is of a determinate character, (of one sort, or another.) And that character is what is meant by the radical *habitus*, or *natural disposition* of the agent. And this subjective disposition is what gives uniform quality to that series of acts, by which common sense estimates the *character* of an agent. (And this, as we saw, was a sufficient proof of our doctrine; that otherwise, the exhibition of determinate character by a free agent, would be inpossible.) God is an excellent Agent, because He has holy original disposition. Satan is a wicked agent, because he has an unholy disposition, &c.

DISPOSITION WHAT?—Now, this *habitus* or disposition of soul is not by any means always absolutely simple: it is a complex of certain active principles, with mental habitudes proceeding therefrom, and modified by outward circumstances. With reference to some sorts of outward inducements, these active principles may act with less uniformity and determinateness; with reference to others, with more. Here, modifying outward influences may change the direction of the principles. The avaricious man is sometimes prompted to generous volitions, for instance. But our common sense recognizes this truth: that the more original and primary of those active principles, constituting a being's disposition or *habitus*, are perfectly determinate and uniform in their action. For instance: no being, when happiness and suffering are the alternatives, is ever prompted by his own disposition, to choose the suffering for its own sake; no being is ever prompted, applause or reproach being equally in its reach, to prefer the reproach to the applause for its own sake. And last: this disposition, while never the effect of specific acts of volition, (being always *à priori* thereto, and cause of them) is spontaneous: that is, in exercising the disposition, both in consideration and choice, the being is *self-prompted*.

THIS THEORY OBVIOUS. CALVINISM IN HARMONY WITH IT.—Is not this now the psychology of common sense and consciousness? Its mere statement is sufficiently evincive of its truth. But you have seen a number of arguments by which it is demonstrated, and the rival theory reduced to absurdity. Now, our assertion is, that the Calvinistic doctrine of effectual calling is agreeable to these facts of our free-agency, and the Arminian inconsistent with them.

GRACE CANNOT PRODUCE AN EQUILIBRIUM BETWEEN HOLINESS AND SIN.—a.) First, the *equilibrium* of will, to which Arminians suppose the gospel restores all sinners, through common sufficient grace, would be an unnatural and absurd state of soul, if it existed. You will remember that the Wesleyans (the Arminian school which we meet) admit that man lost *equilibrium of will* in the fall; but say that it is restored through Christ; and that this state is necessary to make man truly free and responsible in choosing the Saviour. But we have shown that such a state is impossible for an active agent, and irrational. So far as it existed, it would only show the creature's action irrational, like that of the beasts. Hence, the evangelical choice arising in such a state would be as motiveless, as reasonless, and therefore, as devoid of right moral character, as the act of a man walking in his sleep. And, to retort the Arminian's favourite conclusion, all the so-called gracious states of penitence, &c., growing out of that choice, must be devoid of right moral quality. How can those exercises of soul have that quality? Only as they are voluntary, and prompted by right moral motives. But as we have seen, motive is subjective; so that the action of soul cannot acquire right moral quality until it is prompted by right moral disposition. Hence, if that common sufficient grace were anything at all, it would be the grace of moral renovation; all who had it would be regenerate.

THE NATURAL WILL DECISIVELY BENT TO CARNALITY.—b.) Second: we have seen that the notion of a moral agent without determinate, subjective moral character, of some sort, is absurd. The radical, ruling *habitus* has some decisive bent of its own, some way or other.

Is not this simply to say that *disposition is disposed?* The question of fact then arises, which is the bent or determinate direction, which man's natural disposition has, touching spiritual things? Is it for, or against? Or, as a question of fact, is the disposition of mankind naturally, and uniformly, either way? Or, are some men one way disposed by nature, and some the other, as to this object? The answer is, that they are all naturally disposed, in the main, the same way, and that, against the spiritual claims of Christ and God. What are these claims? That the sinner shall choose the holy will of God over his own, and His favour over sensual, earthly, and sinful joys in all their forms. Nothing less than this is evangelical repentance and obedience. Now note, we do not say that no men ever choose any formal act of obedience by nature. Nor, that no man ever desires (what he conceives to be) future blessedness by nature. Nor, that every natural man is as much bent on all forms of rebellion, as every other. But we assert, as a matter of fact, that all naturally prefer self-will to God's holy will, and earthly, sensual, and sinful joys (in some forms) to God's favour and communion; that this is the original, fundamental, spontaneous disposition of all; and that in all essential alternatives between self and God, the disposition is, in the natural man, absolutely determinate and certain. If this is true, then the unconverted man without sovereign grace is equally certain to choose carnally, and equally a free agent in choosing so.

Proved by consciousness and experience.—But that such is the determinate disposition of every natural man, is obvious both from experience and from Scripture. Every renewed man, in reviewing his own purposes, is conscious that, before regeneration, self-will was, as against God, absolutely dominant in all his feelings and purposes; of which no stronger test can be imagined than this conscious fact; that the very best religious impulses to which his soul could be spurred by remorse or alarm were but modifications of self-will, (self-righteousness.) Every true Christian looks back to the time when he was absolutely incompetent to find, or even to imagine any spontaneous good or joy in anything except carnality; and the only apprehension it was possible for him to have of God's service, in looking forward to the time when, he supposed, the fear of hell would compel him to undertake it, was of a constraint and a sacrifice. So, when we look without, while we see a good many in the state of nature, partially practising many secular virtues, and even rendering to God some self-righteous regards, we see none preferring God's will and favour to self-will and earth. All regard such a choice as an evil *per se;* all shrink from it obstinately; all do so under inducements to embrace it which reasonably ought to be immense and overwhelming. The experimental evidence that this carnality is the original and determinate law of their disposition is as complete as that which shows that desire of happiness is a law of their disposition. And all this remains true of sinners under the gospel, of sinners enlightened, of sinners convicted and awakened by the Holy Ghost in His common operations; which is a complete practical proof that there is not any such sufficient grace, common to all, as brings their wills into *equilibrium* about evangelical good. For those are just the elements which the Arminians name, as making up that grace: and we see that where they are, still there is no *equilibrium*, but the old, spontaneous, native bent obstinately dominant still.

Proved by Scripture—The decisiveness of that disposition is also asserted in Scripture in the strongest possible terms. All men are the "servants of sin." Jno. viii: 34; Rom. vi: 12; 2 Pet. ii: 19. They are "sold under sin." Rom. vii: 14. They are "in the bond of iniquity." Acts viii: 23. They are "dead in sins." Eph. ii: 1. They are "blind;" yea, "blindness" itself. Eph. iv: 18. Their "hearts are stony." Ezek. xxxvi: 26. They are "impotent" for evangelical good. Jno. xv: 5; Rom. v: 6; Matt. vii: 18; xii: 34; Jno. vi: 44. "The carnal mind is enmity, and cannot be subject to the law of God." 2 Co. iii: 5. Surely these, with the multitude of similar testimonies, are enough to prove against all ingenious glosses, that our view of man's disposition is true. But if man's free-agency is misdirected by such active principles as these, original, uniform, absolutely decisive, it is folly to suppose that the mighty revolution to holiness can originate in that free-agency; it must originate without, in almighty grace.

Inability does not supercede Responsibility.—Nor is it hard for the mind which has comprehended this philosophy of common sense and experience, to solve the current Arminian objection: that the being in such a state of will cannot be responsible or blameworthy for his continued impenitency. This "inability of will" does not supercede either free-agency or responsibility.

Inability defined.—There is here an obvious distinction from that external coaction, which the reason and conscience of every man recognizes as a different state, which would supercede responsibility. The Calvinists of the school of Jonathan Edwards make frequent use of the terms, "moral inability," "natural inability," to express that plain old distinction. Turrettin teaches us that they are not new. In his Locus, x, que. 4, § 39, 40, you will find some very sensible remarks, which show that this pair of terms is utterly ambiguous and inappropriate, however good the meaning of the Calvinists who used them. I never employ them. That state which they attempt to describe as "moral inability," our Confession more accurately calls, loss of all "ability of will." (Ch. ix, § 3.) It should be remarked here, that in this phrase, and in many similar ones of our Confession, the word "will" is used in a sense more comprehensive than the specific faculty of choosing. It means the "conative powers," (so called by Hamilton,) including with that specific function, the whole active power of soul. The "inability," then, which we impute to the natural man, and which does not supercede responsibility, while it does make his voluntary continuance in impenitence absolutely certain, and his turning of himself to true holiness impossible, is a very distinct thing from that physical coaction, and that natural lack of essential faculties, either of which would be inconsistent with moral obligation. It is thus defined in Hodge's outlines: "Ability consists in the power of the agent to change his own subjective state, to make himself prefer what he does not prefer, and to act in a given case in opposition to the co-existent desires and preferences of the agent's own heart." I will close with a statement of the distinction, which I uttered under very responsible circumstances. "All intelligent Calvinists understand very well, that "inability" consists not in the extinction of any of the powers which constituted man the creature he was before Adam's fall, and which made his essence as a religious being; but in the *thorough moral perversion of them all*. The soul's essence is not destroyed by the fall; if it were, in any part, man's responsibility would be to that extent modified. But all his faculties and susceptibilities now have a decisive and uniform, a native and universal, a perpetual and total moral perversion, by reason of the utter revolt of his will from God and holiness, to self-will and sin; such that it is impossible for him, in his own free will, to choose spiritual good for its own sake."

Regeneration does not violate, but perfects Free-agency.—c.) Regeneration, correspondingly, does not constrain a man to will against his dispositions; but it renews the dispositions themselves. It reverses the morbid and perverse *bias* of the will. It rectifies the action of all faculties and affections, previously perverted by that *bias*. God's people are "willing in the day of His power." Ps. cx: 3. "He worketh in them both to will and to do of His good pleasure." Phil. ii: 13. In that believers now form holy volitions at the prompting of their own subjective principles, unconstrained by force, they are precisely as free as when, before, they spontaneously formed sinful volitions at the prompting of their opposite evil principles. But in that the action of intellect and desire and conscience is now rectified, purified, ennobled, by the divine renovation, the believer is more free than he was before. "He cannot sin, because the living and incorruptible seed" of which he is born again "liveth and abideth in him." Thus, regenenation, though almighty, does not infringe free-agency, but perfects it.

Objection solved.—The standing Arminian objection is, that man cannot be praise, or blame-worthy for what does not proceed from his own free-will. Hence, if he does not primarily choose a new heart, but it is wrought in him by another, he has no more moral credit, either for the change or its consequences, than for the native colour of his hair. This objection is, as you have seen, of a Pelagian source. By the same argument Adam could have had no concreated righteousness; but we saw that the denial of it to him was absurd. By the same reasoning God Himself could have no moral credit for His holy volitions; for He never chose a righteousness, having been eternally and necessarily righteous. We might reply, also, that the new and holy state is chosen by the regenerate man, for his will is as free and self-moved, when renovated, in preferring his own renovation, as it ever was in sinning.

This because the Spirit moulds Disposition a priori to the Will.—To sum up, then: The quickening touch of the Holy Ghost operates, not to contravene any of the free actings of the will; but to mould dispositions which lie back of it. Second: all the subsequent right volitions of the regenerate soul are in view of inducements rationally presented to it. The Spirit acts, not across man's nature, but according to its better law. Third: the propensities by which the renewed volitions are determined are now noble, not ignoble, harmonious, not confused and hostile, and rational, not unreasonable. Man is most truly free when he has his soul most freely subjected to God's holy will. See those illustrious passages in John viii: 36; 2 Cor. iii: 17; Rom. viii: 21.

LECTURE XLIX.

SYLLABUS.

FAITH.

1. How many kinds of faith are mentioned in the Bible? Show that temporary and saving faith differ in nature.
   See, on whole, Conf. of Faith, ch. xvi. Shorter Cat., que. 86. Larger Cat., que. 72. Turrettin, Loc. xv, que. 7, que. 15, § 1-10. Ridgeley, que. 72. Dick, Lect. 68. Knapp, § 123.
2. What is the immediate object of saving faith?
   Turrettin, Loc. xv, que. 12, § 7-11. Dick, as above. Hill, Bk. v, ch. 1, near the end. Knapp, § 123.
3. Is faith implicit, or intelligent?
   Turrettin, que. 9, § 1-10. Knapp, § 122. Hill, Bk. v, ch. 1.
4. What are the elements which make up saving Faith? Is it a duty and unbelief a sin? Does faith precede regeneration?
   Turrettin, Loc. xv, que. 8. Hill, as above. A. Fuller, "Strictures on Sandeman," Letters 2, 3, 7. Alexander's Relig. Experience, ch. 6. Chalmer's Inst. of Theol., vol. ii, ch. 6. Ridgeley, que. 72, 73. Watson's Theol. Inst., ch. xxiii. § 3. Knapp, § 122.
5. Is Christian love the formal principle of faith?
   Council of Trent, Sesson vi, ch. 7. Calvin, Inst., Bk. iii, ch. 2, § 8 to 10. Turrettin, que. 13.
6. Is assurance of belief, or assurance of hope, either, or both, of the essence of saving faith?
   Council of Trent; Can, de Justif., 12 to 16. Calvin, as above, § 7 to 14. Dick, as above. Turrettin, que. 17. Conf. of Faith, ch. 18. Ridgeley, que. 72, 73. Watson's Theo. Inst. ch. xxiv, § ii.
7. Why is this faith suitable to be the instrument of justification?
   Ridgeley, que.73.

I. Faith of four kinds. Temporary Faith not of the kind of Saving.—After noting those cases, as 1 Tim. i: 19, where Faith is evidently used for its object, we may say that the Scriptures evidently mention four kinds—historical, temporary, saving, and miraculous. As the only difference among theologians in this list respects the question, whether temporary and saving faith are generically different, we shall only enlarge on this. Arminians regard them as the same, in all except their issue. This we deny. Because: a.) The efficient cause of saving faith is effectual calling, proceeding from God's immutable election. Titus i: 1; Acts xiii: 48: that of temporary faith is the common call. b.) The subject of saving faith is a "good heart;" a regenerate soul: that of temporary faith is a stony soul. See Matt. xiii: 5, 6, with 8; John iii: 36, or 1 John v: 1, with Acts viii: 13 and 23. c.) The firmness and substance of the two differ essentially. Matt. xiii: 21; 1 Pet. i: 23. d.) Their objects are different: saving faith embracing Christ as He is offered in the gospel, a Saviour from sin to holiness: and temporary faith embracing only the impunity and enjoyments of the Christian. e.) Their results are different: the one bearing all the fruits of sanctification, comfort, and perseverance; the other bearing no fruit unto perfection. See the parable of the sower again.

II. Christ the special Object of Faith.—The special object of saving faith is Christ the Redeemer, and the promises of grace in Him,

By this, we do not mean that any true believer will wilfully and knowingly regret any of the other propositions of God's word. For the same *habit* of faith, or disposition of holy assent and obedience to God's authority, which causes the embracing of gospel propositions, will cause the embracing of all others, as fast as their evidence becomes known. But we mean that in justifying faith, Christ and His grace is the object immediately before the believer's mind; and that if he have a saving knowledge of this, but be ignorant of all the rest of the gospel, he may still be saved by believing this. The evidences are, that *the gospel* is so often spoken of as the object of faith; [but this is about Christ;] e. g., Mark xvi: 15, 16; Eph. i: 13; Mark i: 15; Rom. i: 16, 17; *et passim* That believing *on Christ* is so often mentioned as the sole condition, and that, to men who must probably have been ignorant of many heads of divinity; e. g., Acts xvi : 31; Jno. iii: 18; vi; 40; Rom. x; 9, &c. The same thing may be argued from the experiences of Bible saints, who represent themselves as fixing their eyes specially on Christ. 1 Tim. i: 15, &c., and from the two sacraments of faith, which point immediately to Jesus Christ. Still, this special faith is in its *habitus* a principle of hearty consent to all God's holy truth as fast as it is apprehended as His. Faith embraces Christ substantially in *all His offices.* Urge, as of great practical importance, especially, as Sanctifier, as well as Reconciler. See Matt. i: 21; 1 Cor. i: 30. Cat. que., 86, ("*as He is offered* to us in the gospel.") Conf., ch. 14, § 2, near end. Hodge's Outlines, ch. 27, que. 30.

III. Faith must be explicit.—The papists represent faith as an *implicit* exercise of the mind, in which the believer accepts the doctrines, not because of his own clear understanding of their evidence, but because of the pious and submissive temper of mind towards the Church, her authority being, to Romanists, the ground of faith. Faith accordingly may be compatible with ignorance, both of the other evidence, (besides the Church's assertion,) and of the very propositions themselves; so that a man may embrace with his faith, doctrines, when he not only does not see evidence for them, but does not know what they are! Indeed, says Aquinas: Since agape is the formative principle of faith, the less a man's acceptance of the Catholic doctrine proceeds from intelligence and the more from the impulse of right dispositions, the more praiseworthy it is. This description of faith is evidently the only one consistent with a denial of private judgment.

Proofs of Romanists invalid.—Protestants, on the other hand, hold that faith must be explicit and intelligent; or it cannot be proper faith—that the propositions embraced must be *known;* and the evidence therefor *comprehended intelligently.* They grant to Aquinas, that faith derives its moral quality from the holiness of principles and voluntary moral dispositions actuating the exercise; but his conclusion in favour of an unintelligent faith is absurd, because voluntary moral dispositions can only act legitimately, through an intelligent knowledge of their objects. The right intelligence is *in order to* the right feeling. Protestants, again distinguish between a comprehension of the evidence, and a full comprehension of the proposition. The *former* is the rational ground of belief, not the latter. Many propositions, not only in theology, but in other sciences, are rationally believed, because their evidences are intelligently seen, when the propositions themselves are not fully or even at all comprehended. This distinction answers at once all the objections made by Papists to an explicit faith, from the case of the Patriarch, who believed a gospel promise only vaguely stated, and of us, who believe mysteries we cannot explain. Nor is it of any force to say, many Protestants could not give an intelligent view of any one sufficient argument for a given point in their creed. We grant that many professed Protestants have only a spurious faith. Again: an humble mind cannot always *state* in language intelligently, what he understands intelligently.

Affirmative Arguments.—For an explicit faith thus defined, we argue: 1. That it is the only sort possible, according to the laws of the mind. A man cannot believe, except by seeing evidence. As well talk of perception of objects of sight occurring in one, without using one's own eyes. But, say Papists: the Catholic's implicit faith is not thus totally blind; but rests on the *testimony of the Church.* His mind, influenced by agape, has intelligently embraced *this* as plenary and infallible. Now, may not a man have a conviction in such case, implicit even of unknown propositions? e. g., you Protestants have your authoritative rule of faith, your Scripture. Once adopt this, and you accept unknown contents as true; of which there are, to you some, until your study of Scripture exegesis is exhaustive. Ans., Very true. But the Romanist has no right to resort to this case as a parallel; because he does not permit private judgment to exercise itself in rationally weighing the proofs of *the Church's* authority, any more than of the Bible's authority. He cannot; because then, the individual must exercise his private judgment upon the Scripture; the argument for the Church's authority being dependent thereon, in essential branches. 2. The Bible agrees to this, by directing us to read and understand in order to believe, to search the Scriptures. See Jno. v: 39; Rom. x: 17; Ps. cxix: 34; Prov. xvi: 22; Acts xxviii: 27; Jno. xvii: 3; 1 Cor. xi: 29; Jno. vi: 45. 3. We are commanded to be "able to give to every man that asketh of us, *a reason* of the hope that is in us." 1 Pet. iii; 15. And faith is every where spoken of as an intelligent exescise; while religious ignorance is rebuked as sin.

IV. Is faith simple or complex?—But we now approach an inquiry concerning faith, on which our own divines are more divided. Is faith a perfectly simple exercise of the soul, by its single faculty of intellect; or is it a complex act of both intellect and active moral powers, when stripped of all antecedent or consequent elements, which do not properly belong to it? The older divines, with the Confession, evidently make it a complex act of soul, consisting of an intellectual, and a voluntary element. Turrettin, indeed, discriminates seven elements in the direct and reflex actings of faith: 1. Cognition; 2. Intellectual assent; 3. Trust; 4. Fleeing for refuge; 5. Embracing; and (reflex) 6. Self-consciousness of true actings of faith, with 7. Consolation and assurance of hope. The two latter should rather be named the ulterior consequences of saving faith, than a substansive part thereof. The first is rather a previous condition of faith, and the third, fourth, and fifth seem to me either identical, or at most phases of the different actings of the will towards gospel truth. Of the old, established definition, I have seen no sounder exponent than A. Fuller. Now, Drs. A. Alexander and Chalmers, among others, teach that saving faith is nothing but a *simple belief* of propositions; and they seem to regard it as necessary to suppose the act as capable of being analysed into a perfectly *simple* one, because it is every where spoken of in Scripture as a *single* one. Dr. Alexander also argues, with great acuteness and beauty of analysis, that since the soul is an absolute unit always, and its faculties are not *departments* of it, but only different modes it has of acting, the enlightening of the mind in regeneration and the moral renovation of will must be one simple act of the Holy Ghost and one effect, not two. And hence, there is no ground to suppose that faith, which is the first characteristic acting of the new born, and result of new birth, is complex. Moreover, he argues, since the will always follows the latest dictate of the understanding, it is unnecessary to attribute to faith any other character than a conviction of truth in the intellect, to explain its practical effects in turning the soul from sin to Christ.

THE QUESTION TO BE SETTLED BY SCRIPTURE.—Now, in examining this subject, let us remember that the resort must be to the Bible alone, to learn what *it means* by PISTIS. And this Bible was not written for metaphysicians, but for the popular mind; and its statements about exercises of the soul are not intended to be analytical, but practical. This being admitted, and Dr. Alexander's definition of the soul and its faculties being adopted as evidently the true one, it appears to me the fact, that the Scriptures every where enjoin faith as a *single act* of the soul (by the doing of which *one* exercise, without any other, the soul is brought into Christ) does not at all prove it may not be a complex act, performed by the soul through two of its modes of action. Dr. Chalmers, Dr. Alexander, and every other divine often speak of acts as single, which they yet would analyse into two elements, and those not of the same faculties; e. g., the exercise of repentance or moral approval by the soul, consisting (in some order) of a judgment and an emotion.

THE HEART GUIDES THE HEAD IN MORAL CHOICE—In explaining the defect of the other argument of Dr. Alexander, I would remind the student of the distinctions made in defending the doctrine of the *immediate* agency of the Spirit in regeneration. True, the regenerating touch which enlightens the understanding and renews the will, is one, and not two separate or successive exertions of power. True, the will does follow the last dictate of the understanding, on all subjects. But let us go one step farther back: How comes the understanding by its notions, in those cases where the subjects thereof are the *objects of its natural active propensities?* As we showed, in all these cases, the notion or opinion of the understanding is but the echo and the result of the taste or preference of the propensity. Therefore, the change of opinion can only be brought about by changing the *taste* or *preference*. Now, inasmuch as all the leading gospel truths are objects of native and immediate moral propensity, the renovation of those propensities procures the enlightening of the understanding, rather than the contrary. So in faith, the distinctive exercise of the renewed soul (renewed as *a soul*, and not only as one faculty theaeof,) it is more correct to regard the element of active moral propensity (now towards Christ and away from sin) as *sourc*, and the new state of opinion concerning gospel truth, as *result*. But now, the understanding apprehends these objects of natural moral propensity according to truth, *because* of the correct actings of the propensity towards them; and according to the soul's customary law, this apprehension according to truth, is followed by right *volitions:* the first of which, the embracing of Christ for salvation, is in the Bible—practical account of faith, included as a part of the complete act. If that which the Bible represents as a single, may yet be a complex act of the soul, exerting itself in two capacities, (which I have proved,) then it is no argument to say the embracing of Christ by the will is no part of saving faith proper, but only a consequence; because it is a natural consequence of the law that the will follows the last dictate of the mind. Grant it. Yet why may not that very act of will, thus produced, be the very thing the Bible means by saving faith? (According to the Confession.) Then, to settle this, let us resort to the Bible itself. Be it remembered that, having distinguished the two elements of belief and embracing, it is simply a *question of fact*, whether the Scriptures mean to include the latter as a *part* of that exercise, by which the sinner is justified; or a result of it. Then,

The object of Faith not an Opinion, but a Good.—1. The very object proposed to faith implies that it must be an act as well as a notion; for that object is not merely truth, but *good*, both natural and moral good. We often determine the character of the soul's actings by that of their object. Now, the exercise provoked or occasioned by an object of appetency, must be active. Here, we may remark, there is strong evidence for our view in this, that the Scriptures often speak of faith as *trust*. See Ps. ii: 12; xvii: 7; et passim; Matt. xii: 21; Eph. i: 12, &c. Chalmers most strangely remarks, that still faith does not seem to be anything more than simple belief; because when we analyse *trust* in a promise, we find it to consist of belief in a proposition followed by appetency for the good propounded; and the belief is but belief. I reply, yes; but the *trust* is not mere belief only. Our argument is in the fact that the Scriptures say faith is trust, and trust is faith. Chalmers is a strangely bald sophism?

Faith always active in Scripture.—2. The Scriptures describe faith by almost every imaginable *active* figure. It is a "looking," (Is. xlv; 22,) a "receiving," (Jno; i: 12, 13,) an "eating" of Him, (Jno. vi: 54,) a "coming," (Jno. v: 40,) an "embracing," (Heb. xi: 13,) a "fleeing unto, and laying hold of," (Heb. vi: 18,) &c. Here it may be added, that every one of the illustrations of faith in Heb. xi (whose first verse some quote as against me) come up to the Apostle's description in the 13th verse, containing an active element of trust and choice, as well as the mental one of belief.

3. The manner in which faith and repentance are coupled together in Scripture plainly shows that, as faith is implicitly present in repentance, so repentance is implicitly in faith. But if so, this gives to faith an active character. Mark i: 15: Matt. xxi: 32; 2 Tim. ii: 25.

Unbelief a sin.—4. The Scriptures represent faith, not only as a privilege, but a duty, and unbelief as a sin. 1 Jno. iii: 23; Jno. xvi: 9. Now, it seems clear that nothing is a sin, in which there is no voluntary element. The mere notion of the understanding arises upon the sight of evidence involuntary: and there is no moral desert or ill-desert about it, any more than in being hurt when hit. And the reason why we are responsible for our belief on moral subjects is, that there is always an active, or voluntary element, about such belief. The nature thereof is explained by what has been said above on the order of causation between our disposition or propensities, and our opinions concerning their objects.

Historical Faith differs how?—5. If we make faith nothing but simple belief, we are unable to give a satisfactory account of the difference between historical and saving faith. Chalmers, in the summary of his 6th chapter, as good as acknowledges this. But surely that must be a defective theory, which makes it impossible to see a difference where yet, it admits, a substantial difference exists! Some would get out of the difficulty by denying that, in strictness of speech, there is any historical faith where there is not saving faith—i. e., by denying that such persons truly believe, even with the understanding. Many candid sinners will declare that their consciousness contradicts this. Says Dr. Alexander, the historical faith does not differ in that it believes different propositions; but in that it believes them with a different and inferior grasp of conviction. I would ask, first, whether this statement does not give countenance to that radical Arminian error, which makes saving differ from temporary faith, only in degree, and not in kind? And I would remark, next: This is a singular desertion of a part of the strength of his own position, (although we believe that position includes only a part of the truth.)

It does not accept the same propositions.—It is certainly true that historical faith does not believe all the propositions embraced by saving faith, nor the most important of them. Cat. que. 86. It believes, in a sense, that Christ is a Saviour, &c., but does it believe that all its best works are sins; that it is a helpless captive to ungodliness; that sin is, at this time, a thing utterly undesirable in itself for that person; and that it is, at this moment, a thing altogether to be preferred, to be subdued unto holiness and obedience in Jesus Christ. No indeed: the true creed of historical faith is: that "I am a great sinner, but not utter: that I shall initiate a rebellion against ungodliness successfully some day, when the 'convenient season' comes, and I get my own consent. That the Christian's *impunity* and inheritance will be a capital thing, when I come to die; but that *at present*, some form of sin and worldliness is the sweeter, and the Christian's peculiar sanctity, the more repulsive thing for me." Now, the only way to revolutionize these *opinions*, is to revolutionize the active, *spiritual tastes*, of whose verdicts they are the echo—to produce, in a word, spiritual tastes equally active in the opposite direction. We have thus shown that historical faith does not embrace the same propositions as saving; and that the difference is not merely one of stronger mental conviction. But we have shown that the difference is one of contrasted moral activities, dictating opposite opinions as to present spiritual good; and thus procuring action of the will to embrace that good in Christ. See also, 2 Thes. ii: 10; Rom. x: 9 and 10.

Faith the fruit of regeneration.—It is very clear, that if this account of faith is correct, it can only be an exercise of a regenerate heart. The moral affections which dictate the opinions as to moral good and evil, according to truth, and thus procure action, are spiritual affections. To this agree the Scriptures. See Rom. viii: 7; 1 Cor. ii: 14; Eph. i: 19, 20; ii: 8; Ezek. xxxvi: 26, 27. To this representation there are three objections urged:

Objections.—1. "That of the Sandemanian, that by giving faith an active and holy character, we virtually bring back justification by human merit."

2. "That by supposing regeneration (the very git of redemption) bestowed on the sinner before justification, we make God reconciled to him before He is reconciled."

3. "That we tell the sinner to go to Christ by faith in *order to be* made holy, while yet he must be made holy in order to go." *Ans.*

Answers.—The answer to the 1st, is that we define faith as a holy exercise of the soul; but we do not attribute its instrumentality to justify, to its holiness, but to the fact that it embraces Christ's justifying righteousness. *Scholastice;* Fides sancta est; sed fides non justificat *quà talis*, sed *quà receptiva.*

To the 2d, it owes its whole plausibility to assuming that we make a difference in the *order of time* between regeneration and justification by faith. But we do not. In this sense, the sinner is justified when he is regenerated, and regenerated when justified. Again, God *has* purposes of mercy towards His elect considered as unregenerate. For were they not elected *as such?* In the Covenant of Redemption, Christ's vicarious engagement for them did not persuade the Father to be merciful to them. On the contrary, it only *enabled* His original mercy, from which the gift of Christ Himself proceeded, to go forth compatibly with His holiness. Hence, at the application of Redemption, God justifies in the righteousness of Another, in order that He may consistently bless, with regeneration and all other graces, and He regenerates in order that the sinner may be enabled to embrace that righteousness. In *time* they are simultaneous; in *source*, both are gracious; but in the order of production, the sinner is enabled to believe by being regenerated, not *vice versa.*

Sinner dependent on Grace.—To the 3d, I reply, that this is but to re-affirm the sinner's inability; which is real, and is not God's fault, but His own. True; in the essential revolution from death to life, and curse to blessing, the sinner *is dependent* on Sovereign grace; (it is the virulence of *sin* that makes him so;) and there is no use in trying to blink the fact. It is every way best for the sinner to find it out: for thus the thoroughness of legal conviction is completed, and self-dependence is slain. Let not the guide of souls try to palliate the inexorable fact, by telling him that he cannot regenerate himself and so adapt himself to believe; but that he *can* use means, &c., &c. For if the awakened sinner is perspicacious, he will answer, (logically,) "Yes: and all my using means and instrumentalities, you tell me, will be adding sin to sin; for I shall use them with wholly carnal motives." If not perspicacious, he will thrust these *means* between himself and Christ; and be in imminent risk of damnation by endeavouring to *make a Saviour out of them.* No; let the preacher still only repeat, Acts xvi: 31, while he does not retract Eph. ii: 4–8. Illustrate by Matt. xii: 10–13. If the sinner recalcitrate against the gospel paradox, the triumphant answer will be: that the root of the reason why he cannot embrace Christ in his own strength, is, that *his own spontaneous* preference is for self-will and ungodliness. So that if he fails in coming to Christ, why does he whine and grumble? He has followed precisely his own secret preference, in staying away. If the minister feels responsible and anxious for the successful issue of the case entrusted thus to his tuition, let him remember: a) That after all, it is sovereign grace that must regenerate, and not the separate efficiency of any views of truth, however correct; and that he is not responsible to God for persuading the sinner to Christ, which is God's own work; and b.) That God does in fact make the "sinner's extremity his own opportunity;" and where we see Him thus *slaying* carnal self by this thorough law-work, it is *because He intends* thereby to prepare the way for His sovereign regenerating work. Let not the minister, therefore, become disbelieving, and resort to foolish, carnal expedients; let him simply repeat the gospel condition; and then "stand still and see the salvation of God"

V. Fides formata. distinction.—Rome teaches that historical faith is the *substance* of saving; (*fides informis;*) which becames true faith by receiving its form, love. (Thus *fides formata.*) Her doctrine of Justification is accordant, viz: a change of moral, as well as legal state, consisting not only in pardon and acceptance of person, but in the inworking of holy love in the character. Now, in this error, as in most michievous ones, we find a certain perverted element of truth, (without which errors would not usually have *life* enough to be current.) For faith, as an act of the soul, *has* moral character; and that character, *holy.* But the sophism of Rome is two-fold: a.) Her *fides informis,* or historical faith, is not generically the same act of the soul at all as saving faith; being an embracing of different propositions, or at least, of far different apprehesions of the gospel propositions, being the acts of different faculties of the soul; (historical faith characteristically of the head; saving faith essentially of the heart. Rom. x 10;) and being prompted by different motives, so far as the former has motive. For the former is prompted by self-love, the latter by love of holiness and hatred of sin. b.) Faith does not justify in virtue of its righteness, but in virtue of its receptivity. Whatever right moral quality it has, has no relevancy whatever to be, of itself, a justifying righteousness; and is excluded from the justifying instrumentality of faith; Rom. iv: 4, 5; xi: 6. But faith justifies by its instrumentality of laying hold of Christ's righteousness, in which aspect it does not *contribute,* but *receives,* the moral merit.

The solution of Rome's favourite proof-texts is easy; e. g., in 1 Cor. xiii: 2, the faith is that of miracles. In Gal. v: 6, faith is the instrument energizing love, and not *vice versa.* In Jas. ii: 26, works (loving ones, of course,) are not the *causes,* but *after-signs* of faith's vitality, as breath is of the body's. 1 Cor. vi: 11; Titus iii: 5; Eph. i: 13; Luc. xv: 22, &c., refer to the sanctification following upon justification.

VI. Assurance distinguished.—By *assurance of faith,* we mean the certain and undoubting conviction that Christ *is* all He professes to be, and will do all He promises. It is of the essence of saving faith, as all agree. See Heb. x: 22; xi: 6; Jas. i: 6, 7; 1 Tim. ii: 8; Jer. xxix 13. And it is evident that nothing less than full conviction of the trustworthiness of the gospel would give ground to that entire trust, or evoke the hearty pursuit of Christ, which are requisite for salvation. The *assurance of hope* is the assured conviction (with the peace and joy proceeding therefrom) that the individual believer has had his sins pardoned, and his soul saved. Rome stoutly denies that this is a part of faith, or a legitimate reflex act, or consequence thereof, (except in the case of revealed assurance.) Her motive is, to retain anxious souls under the clutch ef her priest-craft and tyranny. The Reformers generally seem to have been driven by their hatred of this odious doctrine, to the other extreme, and make assurance of hope of the essence of faith. Thus, Calvin says: My faith is a divine and spiritual belief that God has pardoned and accepted *me*." The sober view of the moderns (see Conf., ch. 18) is, that this assurance is the natural and proper reflex act, or consequence of true faith, and should usually follow, through self-examination and experience; but that is not the essence of faith. 1st. Because, then, another proposition would be the object of faith. Not *whosoever* believeth shall be saved; but "*I* am saved." The latter is a deduction, in which the former is major premiss. 2d. The humble and modest soul would be inextricably embarrassed in coming to Christ. It would say: "I must believe that *I am saved*, in order to be saved. But I *feel myself* a lost sinner, in need of salvation. 3d. God could not justly punish the non-elect for not believing what would not have been true if they had believed it. 4th. The experience of God's people in all ages contradicts it. Ps. lxxiii: 13; xxxi: 22; lxxvii: 2, 9, 10. 5th. The command to go on to the attainment of assurance, as a higher grace, addressed to believers, shows that a true believer may lack it.

VII. Faith suitable organ of justification.—God has chosen faith for the peculiar, organic function of instrumentally uniting the soul to Christ, so as to partake of His righteousness and spiritual life. Why? This question should be answered with modesty. One reason, we may suppose, is, that human glorying may be extinguished by attaching man's whole salvation to an act of the soul, whose instrumental aspect is merely receptive, and has no procuring righteousness whatever. Rom. iii: 27. Another reason is, that belief is, throughout all the acts of the soul, the preliminary and condition of acting. Every thing man does is because he believes something. Faith, in its widest sense, is the mainspring of man's whole activity. Every volition arises from a belief, and none can arise without it. Hence, in selecting faith, instead of some other gracious exercise, which may be the fruit of regeneration, as the organic instrument of justification, God has proceeded on a profound knowledge of man's nature, and in strict conformity thereto. A third reason may perhaps be found in the fact that faith works by love: that it purifies the soul; and is the victory which overcomes worldliness. See Confession of Faith, ch. xiv, § ii, especially its first propositions. Since faith is the principle of sanctification, in a sinner's heart, it was eminently worthy of a God of holiness, to select it as a term of justification.

LECTURE L.

SYLLABUS.

UNION TO CHRIST.

1. By what similitudes is the union of Christ with His people set forth in the Scripture?
2. What are the several results to believers, of this union?
3. What is the essential, and what the instrumental bond of this union?
4. Show the resemblances and differences between this union and that of the Father and the Son, between this and that of Christ's divinity and humanity; between this and that of a leader and his followers?
5. Does this union imply a literal conjunction of the substance of Christ with that of the believer's soul?
6. How does the indwelling of the Holy Ghost in this union, differ from that by which it is everywhere present?
7. Is this union indissoluble?

See on whole, Dick, Lect. 67. Ridgeley, vol. iii, que. 66. Calvin's Inst., Bk. iii, ch. 1. Hill, Bk. v, ch. 5, § 1. Conf. of Faith, ch. 26.

I. Union to Christ effectuates salvation.—It is through this union to Christ that the whole application of redemption is effectuated on the sinner's soul. Although all the fullness of the Godhead dwelleth bodily in Him since His glorification, yet until the union of Christ is effected, the believer partakes of none of its completeness. When made one with His Redeeming Head, then all the communicable graces of that Head begin to transfer themselves to Him. Thus we find that each kind of benefit which makes up redemption is, in different parts of the Scripture, deduced from this union as their source; justification, spiritual strength, life, resurrection of the body, good works, prayer and praise, sanctification, perseverance, &c., &c. Eph. i: 4, 66, 11, 13; Col. i: 24; Rom. vi: 3, 4, 5, 6, 8; Col. ii: 10; Gal. ii: 20; Phil. iii: 9; Jno. xv: 1–5.

Described by images.—The nature of this union is to be deduced from a full comparison of all the similitudes by which the Word illustrates it. In one place it is described by the union of a vine with its branches; and in another, of the stock of an olive tree with its limbs. Jno. xv; 1–5; Rom. xi: 16–24. The stock is Christ, diffusing life and fructifying sap through all the branches. Second: Our Saviour briefly likens this union to that between Himself and His Father. Jno. xvii: 20, 21. Grace will bring the whole body of the elect into a sweet accord with Christ and each other, and harmony of interest and volition, bearing some small relation to that of the Father and the Son. Third: We find the union compared by Paul to that between the head and the members in the body; the head, Christ, being the seat and source of vitality and volition, as well as of sense and intelligence; the members being united to it by a common set of nerves, and community of feeling, and life, and motion. Eph. iv: 15, 16. Fourth: We find the union likened to that between husband and wife: where by the indissoluble and sacred tie, they are constituted one legal person, the husband being the ruler, but both united by a tender affection and complete community of interest. Eph. v: 31, 32; Ps. xlv: 9. Fifth: It is illustrated by the union of the stones in a house to their foundation corner-stone, where the latter sustains all the rest, and they are cemented to it and to each other, forming one whole. But stones are inanimate; and therefore the sacred writer indicates that the simile is, in its nature, inadequate to express the whole truth, by describing the corner-stone as a living thing, and the other stones as living things together compsoing a spiritual temple. See 1 Cor. iii: 11–16; 1 Pet. ii: 4–6.

Now, these are all professed similes or metaphors; yet they must indicate, when reduced to literal language, an exceedingly close and important union. It is hard to see how human language could be more completely exhausted, to express this idea, without running it into identity of substance or person. Its nature may be best unfolded by looking successively at its results, conditions, &c. Let it be again noted, that our union to Christ bears to all the several benefits which effectuate our redemption, the relation of whole to its parts.

II. Why called Mystical? Three results.—The results of this union may be said to be threefold; or, in different language, it may be said that the union exists in three forms. 1st. A Legal union, in virtue of which Christ's righteousneas is made ours, and we "are accepted in the beloved." See Rom. viii: 1; Phil. iii: 9. This is justification. 2d. A Spiritual, or mystical union, by which we participate in spiritual influences and qualities of our Head, Jesus Christ; and have wrought in us, by the indwelling of the Holy Ghost, which was given to Him without measure, spiritual life, with all its resultant qualities and actings. See Jno. v: 25, 26; xv: 2–5; Eph. ii: 5; Rom. vi: 11; 2 Cor. v: 17; Gal. ii: 20. This union the orthodox divines have called *mystical*, (MYSTIKA,) borrowing the expression, most likely, from Eph. v: 32. They did not mean thereby, that in their views of this union spiritual, they adopted the views held by the ancient and mediaeval Mystics, who taught an *essential* oneness of the human intelligence with the substance of the Logos, to be developed by quietism and ascetism. Orthodox divines have rather meant thereby, what is the proper, scriptural idea of the word MYSTERION, (RAUO,) something hidden and secret; not something incomprehensible and incapable of being intelligibly stated. The spiritual union is indeed mysterious in that sense; but not otherwise than regeneration is mysterious. The incomprehensible feature is not only similar, but identical; it is one and the same mystery. But the tie is called mystical, because it is invisible to human eyes; it is not identical with that outward or professed union, instituted by the sacraments; it is a secret kept between the soul and its Redeemer, save as it is manifested by its fruits. The third result of the union, is the communion of saints. As the stones of the wall, overlapping the corner-stone, also overlap each other, and are cemented all into one mess; so, every soul that is united truly tc Christ, is united to his brethren. Hence, follows an identity of spirit and principle, a community of aimes, and a oneness of affection and sympathy.

III. Its instumental and essential bond.—The essential bond of of this union is the indwelling of influence of the Holy Ghost. This

Spirit is indeed immense and omnipresent; nor is His providential agency dead or inoperative in any creature of God. But in the souls of believers, He puts forth a different agency, viz., the same which He exerts in the man, Jesus Christ, by which He fills Him with all the fullness of the Godhead. Thus the bond of union is formed. The vegetative influences of the sun are on the whole surface of the earth. In many plants those influences produce a growth, wild or useless, or noxious; but in every cultivated field, they exhibit themselves in the vegetation of the sweet and wholsome corn which is planted there. In proof of this bond, see 1 Cor. iii: 16; vi: 17; xii: 13; 1 Jno. iii: 24: iv: 13. To return to the Bible figure of a vine or tree, the sap which is in the branches was first in the stock; and proceeded thence to the branches. It has in them the same chemical and vital characters; and produces every where the same fruit. The sense and feeling of every limb are the common sense and feeling of the head. Hence, we are entitled to take this pleasing view of all genuine spiritual affections in the members of Christ, each one is in its humble measure, the counterpart of similar spiritual affections in Christ. There are indeed some affections; e. g., those of penitence, which Christ cannot explicitly share, because He is sinless; but even here the tide of holy affection, of enmity to all moral impurity, and love for holiness, wells from the Saviour's bosom; in passing through the believer's sinful bosom it assumes the form of penitence, because modified by his personal sense of sin. Each gracious affection is a feeble reflex of the same affection, existing, in its glorious perfection, in our Redeemer's heart. As when we see a mimic sun in the pool of water on the earth's surface, we know that it is only there, because the sun shineth in his strength in the heavens. How inexpressible the comfort and encouragement arising from this identity of affection and principle! Especially is it consoling in the assurance which it give us of the answer to all our prayers which are conceived in the Holy Ghost. Does the believer have, for instance, a genuine and spiritual aspiration for the growth of Zion? Let him take courage, that desire was only born in his breast because it before existed in the breast of his Head, that Mediator whom the Father heareth always.

The instrumental bond of the union is evidently *faith*—i. e., when the believer exercises faith, the union begins; and by the exercise of faith it is on his part perpetuated, See Eph. iii: 17; Jno. xiv: 23; Gal. iii; 26, 27, 28. First: God embraces us with His electing and renewing love; and we then embrace Him by the actings of our faith, so that the union is consummated on both sides. One of the results, or, if you please, *forms*, of the union is justification. Of this, faith is the instrument; for Christ "purifies our hearts by faith."

IV. The Union illustrated.—Christ compares the spiritual union of His people, to Himself, with tnat of Himself to His Father. The resemblance must be in the community of graces, of affections, and of volitions; and not in the identity of snbstance and nature. Our conciousness assures us that our *personality* and separate free-agency are as complete after as before the union; and that our being is no how merged in the substance of Christ. To this agree all the texts which address the believer as still a separate person, a responsible free agent, and a *man*, not a God. The idea of a personal or substantial union would imply the *deification* of man, which is profane and unmeaning. But when we consider Christ's relation as *Mediatorial person* (and not merely as Logos) to God the Father, we have a more apt representation of His union to His people. For this union is maintained by a spiritual indwelling in Him. The union between Christ's divinity and humanity, as conceived by the Nestorians, (see Lecture xxxvii of Part ii,) would afford also a more apt representation of the believer's union. The Nestonians represented it as a SYNAPHCIA, not a HENOSIS, and expressly asserted it to be generically the same, with, and only higher in degree than, the mystical union of the Godhead with believers. But then they were understood as making of Christ two *Persons*. We who hold with the Council of Ephesus cannot use the union of the two natures of the person of Christ, to illustrate the believer's union to Him; because we have shown that it does not result in a proper oneness of person. The Church with its Head is only a spiritual corporation, and not a literal person.

NOT THAT OF MERE LEADER.—But on the other hand, to represent Christ's union as only that of a mere Leader and His followers, a union of sentiment, interests and affections, would be entirely too feeble. In the case of the Leader admired and devotedly followed, there is only an emission of moral suasion and example, producing these results. In the case of Christ and His people, there is far more: there is the emission of a Divine and vital Substance, the Holy Ghost, who literally unites Christ and His people, by dwelling and operating identically (though far different in degree) in both; and who establishes and maintains in the creature, by supernatural power, the same peculiar condition, called spiritual life, which exists in the Head. In a word, there is truly a sap, a cement, which unites the two, that is *a thing*, and not mere an influence, a divine, living, and Almighty Thing, viz., Holy Ghost.

V. NOT A PARTAKING OF THE SUBSTANCE OF THE GODHEAD.—Yet, while we thus assert a proper and true indwelling of the Holy Ghost with the believer's soul, (and thus mediately of the soul and Christ,) we see nothing in the Bible to warrant the belief of a literal conjunction of the substance of the Godhead in Christ, with the substance of the believer's soul; much less of a literal local conjunction of the whole mediatorial person, including the humanity, with the soul. "Christ does *dwell in* our hearts by faith." "It is He that *liveth in us;*" but it is in a multitude of other places explained to mean the indwelling of His Holy Ghost.

DETERMINES OUR VIEW OF LORD'S SUPPERR—Now, I cannot but believe that the gross and extreme views of a real presence and *opus operatum*, in the Lord's supper, which prevailed in the Church from the patristic ages throughout the mediaeval, and which infect the minds of many Protestants now, arise from an erroneous and overstrained view of the mystical union. This union effectuates redemption. We all agree that the sacraments are its signs and seals. (See 1 Cor. xii: 13; 1 Cor. x: 17, *et passim.*) Now, the Fathers seem to have imagined that spiritual life must result from a literal and substantive intromission of Christ's person into our souls, just as corporeal nutrition can only result when the food is taken substantially into the stomach, and assimilated with our corporeal substance. In this sense they seem to have understood the eating of Jno. vi: 51, &c., (which was currently misapplied to the Lord's supper.) Hence, how natural that in the Lord's supper, the sacramental sign and seal of the vitalizing union, they should imagine a real presence, not only of the Godhead naturally, and of the Holy Spirit in His sanctifying influences, but of the whole Mediatorial person; and a literal feeding thereon. Hence, afterward, the fooleries of transubstantiation and consubstantiation, and the more refind, though equally impossible theory of Calvin, of a literal, and yet only spiritual feeding on the whole person. Let us disembarras our views of the mystical union; and these unscriptural perversions of the sacraments will fall away of themselves. We shall make them what the Word makes them—commemorative signs, and divinely appointed seals of covenant blessings; all of which blessings are summed up in our legal and spiritual union to Jesus Christ; and this union constituted solely by the blessed and ineffable indwelling of Christ's Holy Spirit in our souls, as a principle of faith and sanctification. There is, then, no other feeding on Christ's person but the actings of the soul's faith responsive to the vital motion of the Holy Ghost, embracing the benefits of Christ's redeeming work.

VI. The Union indissoluble.—To one who apprehends the dignity and intimacy of this union aright, there will appear a strong *à priori* probability that it will be indissoluble. The efficient parties to it are Christ and the Holy Ghost; parties divine, omniscient, immutable. The immediate effect on man's soul is the entrance of supernatural life, and the beginning of the exercise of new and characteristic and spiritual acts. One would hardly expect to find that these Divine and Almighty Agents intended any such child's play, as the production of a temporary faith and grace, in such transactions! When we discuss the doctrine of the perseverance of the saints, we shall find this *à priori* evidence confirmed. Our purpose now is not to anticipate that argument; but to suggest at this place, the presumption.

LECTURE LI.

SYLLABUS.

JUSTIFICATION.

1. What is the importance of correct views on this doctrine?
   Dick, Lect. 69. Turrettin, Loc. xv, que. 1. Owen on Justification, (Assembly's Edit.,) p. 76–82.

2. What is the scriptural idea or meaning of God's acts of justification? State and refute Popish view, and establish the true view.

Turrettin, Loc. xv, que. 1. Owen, ch. iv. Dick, Lect. 69. Hill, Bk. v. ch. 2. Ridgeley, que. 70. Knapp, § 109. Watson, Theo. Inst., ch. xxiii, § 1. Bellarmine Controversia. Liber de Justifictione. Council of Trent, Ses. 6, ch. 7. Calvin's Inst., Bk. iii, ch. 11.

3. Does the inherent grace wrought by God in the believer's soul or good works proceeding therefrom, merit anything towards justification?

Calvin's Inst., Bk. iii, chs. 15 and 17. Turrettin, que. 2. Owen, ch. v. Council of Trent, Ses. 6, ch. 7 to 10, and Canons 11, &c., de Justifi. Bellarmine, as above. Dr. A. Alexander, Tract on Justifiation.

4. Is justification mere remission of sins; or does it inclnde the bestowal of a title to favour and reward? And is Christ's active, as well as His passive obedience, imputed to believers therefor?

Tur.ettin, que. iv. Owen, ch. xii. Dick, Lect. 69. Hill, as above. Knapp, § 115. Watson, as above, § 2. Dr. A. Alexander, as above.

5. What is adoption?

Turrettin, Loc. xvi, que. 6· Dick, Lect. 73. Ridgeley, que. 74. See on whole, Conf. of Faith, ch. 11; and Catechisms·

I. Its importance.—It is obvious to the first glance, that it is a question of the first importance to sinners. "How shall man be just with God?" The doctrine of justification was the radical principle, as we have seen, out of which grew the Reformation from Popery. It was by adopting this, that the Reformers were led out of darkness into light. Indeed, when we consider how many of the fundamental points of theology are connected with justification, we can hardly assign it too important a place. Our view of this doctrine must determine or be determined by our view of atonement; and this, again, carries along with it the whols doctrine concerning the natures and person of Christ. And if the proper deity of Him be denied, that of the Holy Ghost will very certainly fall along with it; so that the very doctrine of the Trinity is destroyed by extreme views concerning justification. Again: "It is God that justifieth." How evident, then, that our views of justification will involve those of God's law and moral attributes? The doctrine of of original sin is also brought in question, when we assert the impossibility of man's so keeping the law of God, as to justify himself. It is a more familiar remark, that the introduction of the true doctrine of justification excludes that whole brood of Popish inventions, purgatory and penance, works of supererogation, indulgences, sacrifice of the mass, and merit of congruity acquired by alms and mortifications.

Justification as its Ground.—Not to go again into these subjects at large, which are illustrated in your history of the Reformation, it may be briefly repeated, that as is our conception of the meritorious ground of justification, such will be our conception of its nature. if its *ground* is absolute, complete and infinite, the righteousness of Jesus Christ, it also will be an act complete, final, and absolute, equal in all justified persons, admitting no increment, and neither leaving need nor room for any sacramental merit, or penitential atonement. Once more: The blessed doctrine of *an assurance of hope* is intimately dependent on justification. If the latter is grounded on infused grace, and admits of loss and increment, the Christian's opinion concerning the certainty of his own justification can never become an assurance, this side the grave; for the very sufficient reason, that the *fact* itself is still suspended. If he were assured of it, he would believe an untruth; for the thing itself is not yet sure. Hence, the propriety of Luther's decision, when, taught by his personal, as well as his theological experience, he declared justification to be the cardinal doctrine of the Church's creed.

II. Etymology of term.—The question concerning the true nature of justification should be strictly one of *exegesis*. All are agreed that it is God's act. Hence, the opinions of men, or the human meanings of words by which men have expressed God's descriptions of it in Scripture, are not worth one particle, in determining its nature. It may, however, be remarked, that all English theologians have adopted the Latin word *justify* (justifico) from the *Vetus Itala*, Latin Fathers and Latin Vulgate, an *unclassical* word, which would mean, etymologically, *to make righteous*. I may also remind you, that Augustine, and a few of the other fathers, misled by this etymology, and their ignorance of Greek, conceived and spoke of justification as a change of moral state, as well as of legal condition. Here is the poisonous germ of the erroneous doctrine of the Scholastics and of Trent concerning it; a striking illustration of the high necessity of Hebrew and Greek literature, in the teachers of the Church.

Bible terms. Romish definition. Our definition.—When we pass to the original Scriptures, we find the act of justification described by a Hebrew and a Greek verb, hitsdik, (hiphil) and dikaioo, with their derivatives. Now, the Romish Church asserts, that the Scriptural idea of the act is not only God's accounting, but also *making* the sinner righteous, by both infusing the divine righteousness, and declaring it acceptable, in the sinner. We believe that the true meaning is not to *make* righteous, but only to *declare* righteous; and that the act of justification does not change the moral state, but only declares, in the *forum* of heaven, the legal state of the sinner. The soundest reasons for this, we shall give, without any claim whatever to originality, merely aiming to present them in a brief, lucid, and logical order. The Holy Ghost, then, by justification, intends a *forensic act*, and not a *moral change*.

Proofs—a.) Because, in a number of cases, they express a justification of objects incapable of being made righteous by a moral change, by the justifying agents, in the given cases. Thus, Wisdom: Matt. xi: 19. God: Ps. liv: 4; Job. xxxii: 2; Luke vii: 29.

b.) Because, in a multitude of cases, to justify is the contrast of condemning; e. g., Job ix: 20; Deut. xxv: 1; Rom. viii: 33, 34, &c. Now, to condemn does not change, but only declares the culprit's moral condition; it merely fixes or apportions the legal consequence of his faults. Therefore, to justify does not make holy, but only announces and determines the legal relation.

c.) In some places, the act of a magistrate in justifying the wicked is pronounced very sinful. Prov. xvii: 15; Is. v: 23. Now, if to justify were to make righteous, to justify the wicked would be a most praiseworthy and benevolent act on the magistrate's part. From this very argument, indeed, some have raised a captious objection; saying, if it is so iniquitous in the human magistrate to pronounce righteous him who is personally unrighteous, it must be wrong for God to justify in this (Calvinistic) sense, the sinner. The answer is, that God, unlike the magistrate, is able to impute to the justified ungodly, a vicarious satisfaction for his guilt, and to accompany this justification with sanctifying grace, ensuring his future obedience.

d.) The *adjuncts* of the act of justification are all such as would indicate a forensic character for it. Rom. iii: 19, 20: the objects of the act are men who are HUPODIKOI. See also Job ix: 2, 3; Ps. cxliii: 2. There is *a bar* at which the act is performed. Luke xvi: 15; Rom. iv: 2; Is. xliii: 26. There is an advocate, pleading our cause. 1 Jno. ii: 1.

e.) Finally, the equivalent expressions all point to a forensic act. Thus, in Rom. iv: 4–6, justification is explained by the *forgiveness* of iniquity, and *covering* of sin. In Rom. v: 9, we are justified by His *blood* and saved from wrath through Him; and v: 10, it is farther explained by *reconciliation.* In Jno. iii: 18; v: 24, &c., it is being *not condemned*, and *passing from death to life.* In a word, the only sense of the word which makes Paul's argument in Romans, ch. ii–v, intelligible, is the forensic sense; for the whole question there is concerning the *way of acquittal* for a sinner before God.

Popish objections.—Papists, therefore, admit that the original words often carry a forensic sense, even an exclusive one; and that in the justification of the sinner the forensic idea is also present; but they claim that, in addition, a production of inherent righteousness in the justified person is intended by the word; so that the believer is *accounted, because made personally*, righteous in justification. And in support of this, they quote Is. liii: 11; Dan. xii: 3, from the Old Testament, and in the New, Rom. iii: 24; iv: 22; vi: 4, 5; viii: 10, 30; 1 Cor. vi: 11; Heb. xi: 4; Titus iii: 5–7; Rev. xxii: 11. Of the first two texts it is enough to say, that the forensic sense of the verb is perfectly tenable, when we assign only an instrumental agency to the gospel, or minister mentioned; and that sort of agency the Papist himself is compelled to give them. Of 1 Cor. vi: 11, it should be said that it is a case of introverted parallelism, in which the "washing" is general; and the sanctifying and justifying the two branches thereof. *Can* they be identical: tautological? "Ye are sanctified by the Spirit of our God, and justified in the name of Christ." Rev. xxii: 11, only has a seeming relation to the subject, in consequence of the Vulgate's mistranslation from an erroneous reading. The other passages scarcely require notice.

III. Protestant Definition.—The Protestant view of justification as to its nature, and meritorious cause may be seen in Shorter Catechism, que. 33.

Justification according to Rome.—The doctrine of Rome is a masterpiece of cunning and plausible error. According to this doctrine, justification is rather to be conceived of as a *process*, than an absolute and complete *act.* The *imitation* of this process is due to the gracious operation of the Holy Ghost, (bestowed first in Baptism,) infusing and inworking a *fides formata* in the soul. Free will is by itself inadequate for such an exercise, but yet neither doth the Holy Ghost produce it, without the concurrence of the contingent will of the believer. So that Rome's doctrine hereon is *synergistic.* Moreover, the meritorious cause which purchases for the believer, this grace of a *fides formata*, is Christ's righteousness and intercession. But now, the AGAPE, with resultant good works, thus inwrought by grace, is the righteousness which is imputed to the believer, for his complete justification—i. e., to entitle him to life and adoption; so that the work of justification not only accounts, but *makes* the sinner personally righteous. It will be seen how cunningly this doctrine, by mixing justification with sanctification, avails itself of the seeming support of such passages as Rom. iv: 22–24; x: 10; Acts x: 35; Gal. v: 6; Jas. ii: 26, how plausibly it evades those peculiar texts, as Rom. i: 17; Phil. iii: 9, which say that the righteousness which justifies us is God's; and how "it keeps the word of promise to the ear, and breaks it to the sense," in seeming to ascribe something to the merit of Christ, while yet it is *practically* justification by works.

CAUSES OF JUSTIFICATION ACCORDING TO ROME.—According to the Council of Trent then, the *final cause* of justification is (correctly,) God's glory in the bestowal of eternal life. The *efficient cause*, God's grace; the *meritorious cause*, the righteousness of Jesus Christ; (i. e., of His passion); the *instrumental* cause, baptism; the *formal cause*, the infused righteousness of God, dwelling in the believer. Justification will consequently be, imperfect in all, different in degree in different ones, capable of increment and diminution, and liable to entire loss, in case of backsliding; nor can its continuance unto glory be certainly ascertained by the believer, (except in case of inspiration) inasmuch as its continuance is not itself certain.

JUSTIFICATION NOT BY INHERENT GRACE AND ITS WORKS.—Now all sound Protestants assert, on the contrary, that there is no other justification than that which Romanists describe as the initiation thereof, which is a complete and absolute act; done for the believer once for all, perfect and complete in all, needing and admitting no increment; and above all, that God is not moved in any sort, to bestow this grace of justification by the congruous merit of our inwrought holiness; but that this latter is, on the contrary, one of the *fruits* of our justification. We utterly exclude our own inherent holiness.

ARGUMENTS.—a.) Because, however gracious, it is always imperfect. But the Law of God (Gal. iii: 10; Jas. ii: 10,) can accept nothing but a perfect righteousness. Nor is it worth the Papist's while to say, that the believer's holiness is perfect *in habitu*, but imperfect *in actu*. Imperfection of act is sure evidence of imperfection of principle; and see Matt. xii: 37.

EVASION OF ROM. III: 20, &c.—b.) The Apostle sternly excludes works from the ground of justification. Rom. iii: 20, 28, &c., &c. And it is no adequate answer to say: he means only to exclude *ceremonial works*. For besides that, it is improbable the apostle would ever have thought it worth his while to argue against a justification by ceremonial works *alone*, inasmuch as we have no proof any Jew of that day held such a theory; we know that the Hebrew mind was not accustomed to make the distinction between ceremonial and moral, positive and natural precepts. Moreover, the *law* whose works are excluded is, evidently from the context, the law whose works might prompt boasting, the law which was over Jew and Gentile alike, the law which was the term of the Covenant of works, and from whose curse Christ delivers us. Gal. iii: 12.

ANOTHER EVASION.—Another evasion is attempted, by saying the Apostle only excludes the works of the unrenewed heart. We reply: Was it worth his while to argue their exclusion, when nobody was so impudent as to assert their value? Again, his language is general. He excludes all works which stand opposed to *faith;* but there is as much contrast between *working* and *believing* after as before conversion. Then, the illustrations which the Apostle uses, are David and Abraham, all of whose works he excludes from their justification. Surely the Hebrew would not naturally refer to their good works, as those of an unsanctified man! In fine, the manner in which, in Rom. vi, the Apostle answers the charge of "making void the law through faith," proves that he meant to exclude *all* works.

c.) Our justification is asserted, in many forms, to be all of grace, to exclude boasting, to be by Christ's righteousness, as contrasted with ours. We assert that the freedom of grace, and the honour of Christ in our salvation are grievously marred by the Popish doctrine. Human merit is foisted in.

d.) No holy exercises, nor gracious acts, whatever their source, have any relevancy to atone for past guilt. But remission of this is the more essential (if possible) part of the justification.

e.) When once the righteousness of Christ, which the Council of Trent allows to be the meritorious cause for initiating a justified state, is applied, we assert that the whole change of legal attitude is effected; and nothing remains that can be done more. The man "*is passed* from death unto life," and "*hath* eternal life." Jno. v; 24; iii: 36. There is no condemnation to him. Rom. viii: 1. He "hath peace" with God." Rom. v: 1. He "is reconciled," v: 10, and has acquired a vicarious merit, which *à fortiori* assures all subsequent gifts of grace without any additional purchase. He is adopted. Jno. i: 12. In a word, the righteousness imputed being infinite, the justification grounded on it is at once complete, if it exists at all.

f.) The Popish idea that justification can be matured and carried on by inherent grace is inconsistent with God's nature and law. Suppose the believer re-instated in acceptance, and left to continue and complete it by his imperfect graces; why should not his first shortcoming hurl him down into a state of condemnation and spiritual death, just as Adam's first did him? Then his justification would have to be initiated over again. The only thing which prevents this, is the perpetual presentation of Christ's merit on the believer's behalf. So that there is no room for the operation of inherent grace.

IV. JUSTIFICATION IS BOTH PARDON AND ADOPTION.—The Catechism defines justification as *a pardoning of all our sins, and an acceptance of us as righteous in God's sight.* It is more than remission, bestowing also a title to God's favour, and adoption to that grace and glory which would have been won had we perfectly kept the Covenant of Works. On the contrary, the Arminian declares justification to be nothing but simple forgiveness, asserting that, as absence of life is death, cessation of motion is rest, so absence of guilt is justification. The Scriptural ground on which they rely is that class of passages represented by Rom. iv: 4–8, where Paul defines, for instance, justification as that pardon of iniquities and covering of sin which David sung in Ps. xxxii. See also Acts v: 31; Eph. i: 7; Rom. v: 16, &c. We reply: We admit that forgiveness is the first element, and a very important element of justification; and that wherever bestowed, it always infallibly draws after it the whole act and grace. In passages where it was not the immediate scope of the sacred writer, therefore, to define the whole extent of justification, what more natural than that it should be denominated by this characteristic element, in which a guilty conscience will naturally feel itself more immediately interested? Surely, if in other places we find the act described as containing more, we should complete our definition of it by taking in all the elements which are embraced in all the places. We argue, then:

a.) That the use of the words and their meaning would indicate that remission is not the whole idea of justification. Surely, *to declare righteous* is another thing than a mere declaration of exemption from penalty, even as *righteousness* is another state than that of mere exemption from suffering. This leads us to remark,

Righteousness more than guiltlessness.—b.) That the law contains a two-fold sanction. If its terms be perfectly kept, the reward will be eternal life; if they be broken in any respect, the punishment will be death. Pardon alone would release from the punishment of its breach, but would not entitle to the reward of its performance. In other words, he who broke it, and has suffered the penalty, therefore, does not stand on the same platform with him who has kept it. Suppose, for instance, I promise to my servants a reward for keeping my commands, and threaten punishment for breaking them. At the end of the appointed time, one of them has kept them, and receives the reward. A second one has broken them, and is chastised. Suppose this second should then arise and claim his reward also, on the ground that suffering the full penalty of the breach was an entire equivalent for perfect obedience? Common sense would pronounce it absurd. Hence, the Arminian logic, that remission *is* justification, is seen to be erroneous. Since Christ steps into the sinner's stead, to fulfil in his place the whole Covenant of Works, He must, in order to procure to us full salvation, both purchase pardon for guilt, and a positive title to favour and life. The sinner needs both. Arminians have sometimes argued that the one necessarily implies the latter; because a moral *tertum quid* is inconceivable; there is no place between heaven and hell, to which this person, guiltless and yet not righteous, could be consigned. We reply, the two elements are indeed practically inseparable; but yet they are distinguishable. And, while there can be no moral neutrality, yet, in the sense of this argument, guiltlessness is not equal to righteousness; e. g., Adam, the moment he entered into the Covenant of Works, was guiltless, (and in one sense righteous.) God could not justly have visited him with inflictions, nor taken away from his present natural happiness. But did Adam, therefore, have a title to that assured eternal life, including all the blessings of perseverance, infallible rectitude, and sustaining grace, which was held out in the Covenant, as the reward *to* BE *earned* by obedience? Surely not. Now, this is what the sinner needs, to make a complete justification—what Christ gives therein.

Scriptures.—c.) To this agree the Scriptures. Zech. iii: 4, 5, justification is not only the stripping off of the filthy garment, but the putting on of the fair mitre and clean robe. Acts xxvi: 18, faith obtains forgiveness of sins, and inheritance among the saints. Rom. v: 1, 2, justification by faith brings us not only peace with God, but access to a state of grace, and joy and glory. Gal. iv: 5, Christ's coming under the curse for us, results in a redemption, which includes adoption. Jno. i: 12, believing is the immediate instrument of adoption, &c., &c.

2. Christ's active obedience imputed.—*Second:* Those who admit this definition of justification, will, of course, admit that the righteousness by which the sinner is justified must include a full obedience to the preceptive, as well as the penal part of the law. And as that righteousnes, (to anticipate a point of future discussion) is Christ's, hence, the merit of His obedience to the precepts, as well as of His atoning sufferings, must be imputed to us, for justification. [It is common for theologians to say: "both His active and passive obedience" are imputed. The phrase is clumsy. In truth, Christ's *sufferings* contained an active obedience; and it is this which made them a righteousness: for mere pain, irrespective of the motive of *voluntary* endurance, is not meritorious. And Christ's obedience to precepts was accompanied with endurance.]

Arguments.—a.) All the arguments then, by which the last head was supported, also go to prove that both parts of Christ's righteousness are imputed for justification, (if either is.) He undertook to stand in our law-stead; and do for us, what the Covenant of works demanded of us for our eternal life. We have seen that after we sinned, it required an obedience penal and preceptive.

b.) It is most scriptural to suppose that *all* Christ did as a mediatorial person, was for us, and in our stead. Did Christ then, obey the preceptive law, as one of His official functions? The answer is, there was no other reason why He should do it—of which more anon. See Matt. iii: 15; v: 17.

c.) In many places, Christ's bearing the preceptive law is clearly implied to be for our redemption. See, for instance, Gal. iv: 4. By what fair interpretation can it be shown that the law under which He was made, to redeem us, included nothing but the penal threatenings? "To redeem us who were under the law." Were we under no part of it but the threats? See, also, Rom. v: 18, 19. "By *the obedience* of Christ, many are made righteous." The antithesis and whole context show that obedience to precepts is meant. Rom. viii: 3, 4. What the law failed to do, through our moral impotency, that Christ has done for us. What was that? Rather our obedience than our suffering. See, also, Heb. x: 5–7.

Osiander's view.—In the days of the Reformation, Andr. Osiander vitiated the doctrine of justification by urging, that if Christ was under a moral obligation to keep the preceptive law, (as who can doubt?) then He owed all the obedience of which He was capable on His own account, and therefore could not render it as our surety. Hence H supposed that the righteousness imputed to us is not that of the God.

man on earth, but the inherent or natural righteousness of the Deity. The Socinians and others have adopted this cavil, making it the staple of one of their objections to imputation. The answer is threefold. 1st. Christ did, indeed, owe complete obedience to law, after assuming His vicarious task. But *for what purpose* was the obligation assumed? For what purpose was the very humanity assumed, by which He came under the obligation? To redeem man. The argument is, therefore, as preposterous as though, when a surety comes forward, and gives his own bond, to release his bankrupt friend, the creditor should refuse to cancel the bankrupt man's bond, saying to the surety: "Now, *you* owe me the money for yourself, for I hold *your* bond!" But second: Christ, as God-man, was not obliged to render any obedience to the law, to secure the justification of His own mediatorial person: because He was personally accepted and justified from the beginning. See Matt. iii: 17; Heb. i: 6. *For* whom then, was this obedience rendered, if not for His people? And third: The obedience, though rendered in the human nature, was the obedience of the *divine person*. That person, as divine, could not be subject, on His own personal behalf, to law, being the sovereign. Hence, it must be vicarious obedience, and being of infinite dignity, is sufficient to justify not one believer only, but all.

V. ADOPTION. WHAT?—*Adoption* cannot be said to be a different act or grace from justification. Turrettin devotes only a brief separate discussion to it, and introduces it in the thesis in which He proves that justification is both pardon and acceptance. Owen says that adoption is but a presentation of the blessings bestowed in justification in new phases and relations. And this is evidently correct; because adoption performs the same act for us, in Bible representations, which justification does: translates us from under God's curse into His fatherly favour. Because its instrument is the same . faith. Gal. iii: 26, with iv: 6, 7; Titus iii: 7; Heb. xi: 7; Jno. i: 12. And because the meritorious ground of adoption is the same with that of justification, viz; the righteousness of Christ. See Heb. xi: 7; Eph. i: 6; and texts above. The chief doctrinal importance of this idea then is, that we have here, the strongest proof of the correctness of our definition of justification, and of the imputed righteousness upon which it is based, in the fact that it is both a pardon and an adoption.

The representation of our adoption given in Scripture, with its glorious privileges, is full of consoling and encouraging practical instructions. The student may see these well set forth in Dick's 73d Lecture.

LECTURE LI.

SYLLABUS.

JUSTIFICATION. (Continued.)

6. State the general argument, (against Moralists, Socinians, Pelagians, &c.,) to prove that works cannot justify.

Turrettin, Loc. xvi, que. 2. Owen, chs. 10 and 14. Dick, Lect. 69 and 70. Hill, Bk. v, ch. 2. Dr. A. Alexander, Tract.

7. How then reconcile James and Paul, Rom., ch. iii and iv; and James, ch. ii?

Owen, ch. 20. Turrettin, que. 8. Dick, Lect. 71. Watson's Theol. Inst., ch. xxiii, § iv.

8. Refute the lower Arminian scheme: that Christ only purchased for us a milder law, which accepts penitence and evangelical obedience, instead of perfect obedience.

Owen, ch. 11. Dick, Lect. 70. Watson, Theol. Inst., as above, and § iii.

9. State and refute the Wesleyan, (or higher Arminian theory,) that faith is imputed as our righteousness.

Turrettin, que. 7, § 1-14. Owen, ch. 3. Dick, Lect. 71. Watson, Theol. Inst., ch. xxii, § ii.

10. Complete, then, the argument of our 4th question, by showing what is the meritorious ground of justification.

See Owen, chs. 16 and 17. Turrettin, que. 3, § 11-21. Hill, Dick, Alexander, as above.

VI. Justification not by works. Evasions of Scripture.—The particular phase in which the Romish Church foists the merit of works into justification has been considered, in discussing its nature. But now that we approach the subject of *its grounds*, it is necessary that we study the general reasons for the exclusion of works, in more comprehensive views. We find the Apostle, Rom. iii: 20, declaring: "Therefore, by the deeds of the Law, there shall no flesh be justified in His sight; for by the law is the knowledge of sin."

1. To this agree the views expressed by all the sacred writers of the Old and New Testaments. See Ps. cxxx: 3, 4; lxxi: 16; cxliii: 2; Dan. ix: 18; Job xl: 4. These instances are peculiarly instructive, as showing that Paul broaches no new doctrine; and especially as excluding the Romish pretext, that only works of the carnal nature are excluded; because the Psalmist and Job are the very men who, in other places, make most earnest protestations of their sincerity and piety. Then our Saviour teaches the same doctrine. Luke xvii: 10; xviii: 14. And the Epistles likewise. Rom. iii: 28; iv: 6; xi: 6; Gal. ii: 11; Eph. ii: 8, 9, &c., &c.

Because the law convicts.—2. Justification cannot be by the law, "because by the law is the knowledge of sin." That law which has already condemned cannot be the means of our acquittal. See Eph. ii: 3. The battle is already hopelessly lost, the die *cast*, and cast against us, on this scheme. If it is to be retrieved, some other method must be found for doing it.

Because the law is absolute.—3. The law of God is *absolute;* as the transcript of God's moral perfections, and the rule of a perfectly holy God, who cannot favour any sin, it requires a perfect, universal, and perpetual obedience during the time of the probation. See Matt. xxii: 38, &c.; James ii: 10; Gal. iii: 10. Every precept applicable to our condition must be kept; they must be kept all the time; and must all be always kept with perfectly proper motives or intentions! There is not a man upon the earth who, when his conscience was convinced of sin by the Holy Ghost, and enlightened to apprehend the majesty and purity of his Judge, would be willing to risk his acquital on the best act he ever performed in his life. But see 1 Jno. iii: 20.

Because our only works fruits of Justification.—4. While sincerely good works are an all-important part of our salvation, they cannot be the ground of our justifiction, because they are a result thereof. It is by coming into a state of favour with God, that we acquire from His grace spiritual strength to do anything truly good. See Jno. xv: 1-5; Rom. v: 1–2; vi: 3, 4, 6; Gal. ii: 20. All other works which man does are carnal, selfish, or slavish, and wholly unmeritorious before a perfect God. Hence, it is preposterous to attribute to our works any procuring influence as to our justification.

Fair view from apostle's standpoint.—Indeed, the exclusion of works by Paul is so emphatic, that there must be some evasion adopted, to limit his meaning in order to leave a loophole for doubt. Those evasions we have discussed in detail. We would remark generally, in closing this topic, that the fair way to judge what Paul meant by "works of law," is to find out what an intelligent Pharisee (he was reared one, and was now debating with them,) would mean by "the Law," when named without qualification. The answer is plain; the Torah, the whole Law of the Pentateuch, moral, civic, and ceremonial. And this law was conceived of, not merely as a set of carnal ordinances, or dry forms, but as a rule spiritually holy and good. See Ps. xix: 7; i: 2. Nor are we to conceive that the intelligent Jew thought of an obedience to this law merely unspiritual, slavish and carnal. They comprehended such precepts as Deut. vi: 4, 5; Ps. li: 6, to be an important part of the Law: and the evidence is, in such passages as Mark xii: 28–33; x: 19, 20. This certainly is the sense in which St. Paul employed the phrase, *works of the Law*, when he excludes them from justification, in his epistles. See Rom. iii: 20, with vii: 1–12; viii: 3, 4; ix: 31; x: 3.

VII. James ii: 12–26.—The Scripture which has been supposed to offer the greatest difficulty against Paul's view, is Jas. ii: 12 to end. On this it may be remarked, for introduction: that if there is a real contradiction, both Epistles cannot be regarded as canonical; our alternative is to reject Paul or James, or else to show their difference only seeming. Further: when one writer treats a given topic formally and professedly, (as Paul obviously does justification in Rom.,) and another only incidentally, it is out of all reason to force the seeming sense of the latter on the former.

James' scope and terminology different.—It is well remarked by Owen, that James' *scope* is totally different from Paul's. James' is, to defend justification by faith from an Antinomian perversion. (See ver. 14.) Paul's is, to prove, against Legalists, what is the meritorious ground of justification. Rom. i: 17. Again: the faith of which James speaks, is a dead faith: such a faith as Paul himself would decree non-justifying; that of which Paul speaks, when he makes it the sole instrument of justificatian, is a living faith, infallibly productive of good works. See Rom. vi. And third: the justification of which James speaks, presents a different phase from Paul's, namely: not God's secret and sovereign judicial act, transferring the sinner from a state of condemnation at the time of his conversion, but that act declaratively manifested at any and every subsequent time, especially at the day of judgment. That this is James's meaning, is argued by Owen irrefragably from vv. 21–23. The apostle says, Abram's justification by works, when he proposed to sacrifice Isaac, was a fulfilling of that Scripture, (Gen. xv: 6,) which says: "He believed God, and it was imputed to him for righteousness. For that justification by faith was notoriously, some thirty years before the offering of Isaac. The latter transaction must therefore be, the fulfilling of the former statement, in the sense, that Abraham's justification was then not *originated*, but *evinced*. See close of ver. 23. These three remarks do sufficiently show, that James ought not to be held as contradicting Paul, when their scope and use of terms are so very different.

WORK ESSENTIAL AS SIGN OF JUSTIFICATION, WORTHLESS AS CAUSE.—But a juster view of the matter will be gained by connecting our view of James ii: 14–26, with the other passages, where a similar seeming difference is presented—e. g., Ps. xv: 1, 2; xxiv; 3, 4; Matt. xxv: 34, 35, 41, 42; Jno. xv: 8, 14; Acts x: 35; 1 Jno. iii: 7. The amount of all these texts is, that *a just life* is the *test* of a *justified state;* and the general remark is obviously true, that this is a very different thing from asserting that the former is the procuring cause of the latter. Fruit is the *test* of healthy life in a fruit tree: not therefore the cause of that life. These simple ideas go far to explain the seeming contrariety of these texts to former citations. But perhaps the application of such an explanation to Jas. ii: 14–26, will be attended in the student's mind, with some difficulty just here. Are we dealing fairly with the text, to suppose that James does indeed use the word justify, a word of meaning so exact, definite and thoroughly established in Bible usage, in a *new sense*, without giving us any notice thereof? The exegetical evidence that *he does*, is well stated by Owen, (above.) And the view is greatly strengthened by observing that the difference of meaning is in fact not so great. What is the transaction described, for instance, in Matt. xxv: 34, 35, and how does it differ from the act described in Rom. iii: 28? The latter describes the sinner's justification *to* God; the former the sinner's justification *to* God's intelligent creatures, (a more correct statement than Owen's, that it describes his justification *by* man.) Each is a declaratory, and forensic act; but the one is secret as yet to God and the justified soul; the other is a proclamation of the same declaration to other fellow-creatures. And it is most proper that the latter should be based on the personal possession of a righteous character: in order that the universe may see and applaud the correspondence between God's justifying grace and His sanctifying grace; and thus the divine holiness may be duly magnified.

VIII. CHRIST DID NOT LOWER THE LAW.—A scheme of justification has been advanced by many of the lower Armenians, which is, in its practical results, not very far removed from the Popish. It represents that the purpose of Christ's work for man was not to procure a righteousness to be imputed to any individual believers; but to offer to God such a mediatorial work, as would procure for believers in general the repeal of the old, absolute and unbending law as a rule of justification, and the substitution of a *milder* law, one which demands only sincere evangelical obedience. The thing then, which is imputed for the sinner's justification, is the whole merit of his sincere faith, humble penitence, and strivings to do his duty; which God is pleased, for Christ's sake, to accept in lieu of a perfect righteousness. These theologians would say, with the Romanists, and higher Arminians, that our "faith is accounted as our righteousness;" but they would define justifying faith as a seminal principle of good works, and inclusive of all the obedience which was to flow from it. The point of inosculation of this, and the Popish theory (determining them to be *the same* in essential character) is here. They both conceive Christ as having procured for *man* (in general) *a new probation*, evangelical indeed, instead of absolute; but in which the sinner still has *his own* proximate merit of justification to work out, by something *he* does. Whereas, the Bible conception is, that the second Adam perfected, for his people, the line of probation dropped by Adam, by purchasing for them a title to *eternal life*, and covering also, all guilt of the breaches of the first covenant.

On this theory, I would remark, at the outset, that it comes with a very poor grace from the men who object to the imputation of Christ's righteousness to us, because it was not literally and personally wrought by us. It seems they consider that it is more consistent in God to account a believer's righteousness to him as that which it *is not*, thus basing his justification on a falsehood, than to account the legal benefits of Christ's righteousness to him for *what it truly is*—i. e., a perfect righteousness! But:

PROOFS. 1. THE LAW UNCHANGEABLE AS GOD.—1. The source and basis of God's moral law is His own moral character; which is necessary and immutable. Supposing creatures to exist, there are certain relations between them and God which cannot be other than they are, God continuing what He is. Among these must obviously be the essential moral relations of the law. These flow, not from any positive institution of God alone, but also from the very relations of creatures and the attributes of God. And if any moral relations are necessary, the requirement of a universal obedience is clearly so; because our Saviour represents the obligation to love God with *all* the mind, soul, heart, and strength, and our neighbour as ourself, as the very essence of that law. Hence, the idea that God *can* substitute an imperfect law for one perfect, is a derogation to His perfection. Either the former standard required more than was right, or the new one requires less than is right; and in either case God would be unrighteous. That Christ should perform all His work as an inducement to His Father to perform such unrighteousness, would be derogatory to Him. Hence, we find that He expressly repudiates such a design. Matt. v: 17. And here we may add, that the Bible nowhere indicates such a relaxation of the believer's law of living. David, a justified person, represents the rule by which he regulated himself, as "perfect," "pure," and "right," and "very righteous." Ps. xix: 7, 8; cxix: 140; Jas. i: 25; ii: 10. Everywhere, the law which we are still required to obey, is the same law which by its perfectness condemned us. Practically, the allowance of an imperfect standard of obedience would be ruinous; because man ever falls below his standard.

ASSERTED CHANGES OF LAW EXPLAINED.—It is objected again: God *has* changed His law, substituting certain simpler and easier precepts, in place of old ones; as in abrogating the burdensome ritual of Moses, and giving in its place the easy yoke of the New Testament ceremonial. We reply: those were only positive, not eternal and natural precepts of morality; the obligation to keep them only arose from God's command to do so; and hence, when the command was retracted, there was no longer any sin in their omission. To retract such commands is far different from making that no longer sin, which is in its nature sin. Again, it has been objected, that God's permission has been given, in some cases, to do what without such permission would have been *in its nature sin*; as when Abraham was directed to slay Isaac, and Israel the Canaanites. It seems to me surprising that these cases should be advanced with any confidence in this argument, or that they should be supposed by any to prove that the intrinsic relations of morality are alterable by God's mere positive precepts; or that so acute a writer as Mansel, in his "Limits of Religious Thought," should feel occasion to take refuge from the exigencies of the case in the inability of human reason to conceive the infinite and absolute Being fully. The truth is, that in those cases there is no alteration whatever of any principle of natural morality by which God has ever regulated Himself, or His human subjects. It always has been right for God to slay any of His rebel creatures, whom He pleases; He kills some thirty millions of them each year, by various means, And *whenever* God appoints man to slay it is no sin for him to do so, be it in the case of magistrates, self-defence, or defensive war. So that God's appointment of a man to take a given life renders it perfectly moral to take it. An instance of such an appointment is therefore no instance at all, of a conversion of what is naturally sinful into right. As fairly might one say, that when the master tells his servants that the unauthorized use of his substance is theft, and afterwards directs one of them to go to take and consume some fruit of his field, he has undertaken to alter the fundamental relations of morality! We repeat: there is, and can be no case, in which God has made that which is *naturally* wrong to be right.

SAINTS STRIVE TO KEEP THE PERFECT LAW.—2. Scripture represents the Bible saints as repudiating all their own works, even while they protest their affectionate sincerity in them. See Job xl: 4, &c. Moreover, their consciences rebuke them for every shortcoming from perfect love and holiness. Surely that which cannot justify us to our own consciences, will hardly answer with God! We appeal to each man's conscience: when it is enlightened by the Holy Ghost, does not it bear out this experience of Bible saints?

THE LAW WOULD NOT BE MAGNIFIED.—3. By such a scheme of justification Christ's work, instead of resulting in a complete harmonizing of God's absolute holiness and perfect Law, in the sinner's acceptance, would leave the law forever ruptured and dislocated. We are taught in Scripture that Christ was to "magnify the Law, and make it honourable;" "that mercy and truth were to meet together, and righteousness and peace kiss each other;" that He "came not to destroy the Law, but to fulfil." Now, if He has procured the abrogation of that perfect law, during each believer's Christian life, there is a demand of the law which remains unmet; and that forever. The doctrine makes a piece of patchwork; men do not sew new cloth on an old garment.

IX. Wesleyan view. Imputation of Faith for Justification.—The higher Arminians, of the school of Wesley, now teach that faith is imputed as the believer's righteousness, on account of which he is justified. They define justification to be only mere pardon; and affirm, in many phrases, that this pardon is unbought, and for Christ's sake. So that it is hard to understand what office they assign to faith in justification, unless it be the true one of the instrument. Yet they persist in repudiating the Calvinistic doctrine of the imputation of the merit of Christ's righteousness, and in equally repudiating the lower view discussed by us above; so that the ground on which they stand seems to me wholly intangible and vague: unless it is, that in consequence of Christ's work and mediation, God is pleased to accept our faith as an equivalent, or substitution for righteousness.

Makes Faith a Work.—In this view, the doctrine is open to all the objections urged against the one just refuted above, and in greater force; for it represents God's imputation as a most glaring violation of truth, in accounting, not the imperfect duties of a Christian life, but *one imperfect act*, as a complete obedience! And while it seems to repudiate works, and establish faith, it really foists in again the doctrine of human merit and works; for faith is also an act, an act of obedience to law, (Jno. vi: 29; 1 Jno. iii: 23,) and if rendered as a matter of a righteousness before God, or, indeed, for anything except the mere instrument of accepting Christ, it is *a work*. But faith and works should be opposed.

Faith only receives.—Again: the idea that faith is accounted to us as our justifying righteousness, contradicts in two ways, that nature which Scripture attributes to it. It is said in many places, that righteousness is *by* faith. (Rom. i: 17, &c., &c.) Now, then, it cannot be identical with it. Moreover, faith is defined as an act purely receptive, and receptive of Christ our righteousness. Jno. i: 12. Now, that it should *be* a righteousness when its very nature is to *embrace* a righteousness, is as contradictory as that the beggar's confessions of destitution can constitute a *price* to purchase relief.

The righteousness imputed is God's.—And last: the whole question is decisively settled against this theory, as well as against the Popish, and all other false ones, which make the procuring cause of our justifiation to be, either in whole or in part, anything wrought by us, or wrought in us, in all those passages which declare that we are justified on account of *God's* righteousness, and sometimes it is God's righteousness as contrasted with ours. See Rom. i: 17; iii: 22; Phil. iii: 9. How can these expressions be evaded? The righteousness by which we are justified is not ours, but God's—therefore not constituted of any acts or graces of ours.

Wesleyan proof-texts considered.—But, says the Arminian, it is vain to speculate against the express words of Scripture; and here we have it, four times over, Gen. xv: 6; Rom. iv: 3, 5, 24. We reply, that they clearly overstrain and force the text. It is true, that in Gen. xv: 6, the construction is, "His faith was accounted righteousness," (no Preposition.) Now, suppose that in the other three cases in the New Testament, the construction were even as difficult as they suppose in this: would not a fair criticism say that these somewhat peculiar statements should not be strained into a sense contradictory to the current of plainer expressions elsewhere, which always say we obtain righteousness *by* our faith! And as Calvin well argues, on Gen. xv: 6, when the very context clearly shows that the whole amount of Abraham's faith in this case was *to embrace a set of promises* tendered to Him, since it did not bring anything on its own part to the transaction, but merely received what God brought, in His promise, the sense must not, and cannot be strained, to make the receptive act the meritorious cause of the bestowal which itself merely accepted. There is obviously just such an embracing of the result in the instrument, as occurs in Jno. xii: 50; xvii: 3. But our case is far stronger than even this. The Septuagint and Paul, an inspired interpreter, uniformly gives the sense, Pistis logidzetai eis dikaiosunen. This all these Arminian interpreters, with a perverse inattention or ignorance, persist in translating "faith is accounted *as* righteousness;" the English ones being probably misled by the occasional use of our preposition, "*for*" in the sense of "*as*;" (e. g., "I reckon him for a valuable citizen.") But the Greek preposition, eis, with the accusative, very rarely carries that sense: no good grammarian allows it; and its obvious force in this passage is, that of *designed result.* "His faith is imputed in order to the attaining of righteousness"—i. e., Christ's This gives faith its proper instrumental office. Compare Rom. x: 10. Pisteuei eis dikaios. Consult Harrison's Greek Prep., and Cases, p. 226. I am aware of but one case in the Scripture where this locution bears the sense imputed to it by the Wesleyans, in the texts under debate.

All locutions of Scripture prove faith instrumental.—In conclusion of this head, the Scriptures clearly assign that office, on the whole, to faith. This appears, first, from its nature, as *receptive of a promise.* The matter embraced must of course be contributed by the promiser. The act of the receiver is not procuring, but only instrumental. Second, all the locutions in which faith is connected with justification express the instrumental idea by their fair grammatical force. Thus, the current expressions are, justified Pistei (Ablative), diapisteos, ek pisteos. *Never once* are we said to be justified dia pistin, the construction which is commonly used to express the relation of Christ's righteousness, or blood, to our justification.

X. Proof of the Doctrine from Scripture.—We have now passed in review all the prominent theories which deny the truth. By precluding one, and then another, we have shut the inquirer up to the Bible doctrine, that the sinner is justified "only for the righteousness of Christ imputed to us." The remaining affirmative argument for this proposition is therefore very short and simple: it will consist in a grouping together of the Bible statements; so classified as to exhibit the multitude of proof-texts by a few representatives:

1. Our justification is *gratuitous*. Rom. iii: 24; Eph. ii: 5; Tit. iii: 7.

2. Christ is our *Surety*. Heb. vii: 22: and our sins are imputed to Him, that His righteousness may be imputed to us. Is. liii: 6 and 11; 2 Cor. v: 21; 1 Pet. ii: 24.

3. He is our *propitiation*. Rom. iii: 25; 1 Jno. ii: 2.

4. We are justified *through* Christ, or *for His name*, or *His sake*, or *by His blood*. Acts x: 43; xiii: 38, 39; Eph. i: 7, iv: 32; Rom. v: 9; 1 Jno. ii: 12.

5. Christ is called "*our righteousness*." Jer. xxxiii: 6; 1 Cor. i: 30; Rom. x: 4.

6. We are *justified by His obedience*, or *righteousness*. Rom. v: 18, 19.

7. The righteousness that justifies us is God's and Christ's, as opposed to ours. Rom. i: 17; iii: 22; Phil. iii: 9.

LECTURE LII.

SYLLABUS.

JUSTIFICATION. (Concluded.)

11. Define and prove the imputation of Christ's righteousness; and answer objections to it. Compare the case of Adam. Rom. v.
 Turrettin, Loc. xvi, que. 3, § 1-10 especially. Owen on Justification, ch. vii and viii. Dick, Lect. 70. Dr. Alexander's Tract. Watson, Theol. Inst., ch. xxiii.

12. Is justification a single, complete, and absolute act? How is it related to sins committed after conversion, and to the final judgment?
 Turrettin, que 9 and 10. Owen, ch. vi. Hill, Bk. v, ch. 2. Knapp, § 113. Trrettin, que. 5.

13. Is *faith* the sole instrumental condition of justification; or also *repentance?*
 Turrettin, que. 3, § 10-17. Owen, ch. ii. Dick, Lect. 71.

14. How are justification and sanctification distinguish?d? Are they inseparable? Why then discriminate them?
 Turrettin, que. 1. Dick, Lect. 70. Hill, Bk. v, ch. 3.

15. What the proper place and importance of good works in the believer's salvation?
 Turrettin, Loc. xvii, que. 3. Dick, Lect. 71. Hill, as above. Knapp, § 115, 116.

16. May we then sin, "because we are not under law, but under grace?"
 Witherspoon on Justification. Owen, ch. xix. Turrettin, Loc. xvii, que. 1. Dick, Lect. 72. Watson, ch. xvii, § 3.

XI. IMPUTATION.—Our last attempt was to prove that the meritorious cause of the believer's justification is the righteousness of Christ. But how comes it that this righteousness avails for us, or that its justifying efficacy is made ours? The answer to this question leads us to the doctrine of *imputation*. The Catechism says that Christ's righteousness is *imputed to us*. This Latin word, *to reckon or account* to any one, is sometimes employed in the English Scriptures as the translation of HASHAB, LOGIDZOMAI, ELLOGEO, and correctly. Of the former we have instances in Gen. xv: 6; xxxviii: 15; 2 Sam. xix: 1-9; of the next in Mark xv: 28; Rom. ii: 26; iv: 5, &c.; Gal. iii: 6, &c.; and of the last, in Rom. v; 13; Philem. xviii.

DEFINED. OWEN CRITICISED.—It is evident that sometimes the thing imputed is what is actually done by, or belongs personally to, the person to whom it is reckoned, or set over. (This is what Turrettin calls imputation loosely so called.) Sometimes the thing imputed belonged to, or was done by another, as in Phil. xviii; Rom. iv: 6. This is the imputation which takes place in the sinner's justification. It may be said, without affecting excessive subtlety of definition, that by imputation of Christ's righteousness, we only mean that Christ's righteousness is so accounted to the sinner, as that he receives thereupon the legal consequences to which it entitles. In accordance with 2 Cor. v: 21, as well as with the dictates of sound reason, we regard it as the exact counterpart of the imputation of our sins to Christ. Owen does, indeed, deny this: asserting that the latter only produced a temporary change in Christ's legal state, and that He was able speedily to extinguish the claims of law against our guilt, and return to His glory; while the former so imputes His very righeousness as to make a final and everlasting change in our legal relations. We reply: the difference is not in the kind of imputation, but in the persons. The mediatorial Person was so divine and infinite, that temporary sufferings and obedience met and extinguished all the legal claims upon Him. Again: Owen pleads that we must suppose Christ's very righteousness, imputed to us, in another sense than our sins are to Him; because, to talk of imputing to us the legal consequences of His righteousness, such as pardon, &c., is nonsensical, pardon being the *result* of the imputation. But would not the same reasoning prove as well, that not only our guilt, but our very *sinfulness* must have been imputed to Christ; because it is nonsensical to to talk of imputing condemnation! The truth is, the thing set over to our account, in the former case, is, in strictness of speech, the *title* to the consequences, of pardon and acceptance, founded on Christ's righteousness, as in the latter case it was the guilt of our sins—i. e., the *obligation to* punishment founded on our sinfulness. All are agreed that, when the Bible says, "the iniquity of us all was laid on Christ," or that "He bare our sins," or "was made sin for us," it is only our *guilt* and not our moral attribute of sinfulness which was imputed. So it seems to me far more reasonable and scriptural to suppose that in the imputation of Christ's righteousness, it is not the attribute of righteousness in Christ, which is imputed, but that which is the exact counterpart of guilt—the *title* to acquital. Owen, in proceeding to argue against objections, strongly states that imputation does not make the sinner personally and actually righteous with Christ's righteousness as a quality. We should like, then, to know what he means, that this righteousness is really and truly imputed to us in a more literal sense than our sins were to Christ. A middle ground is to me invisible.

BASIS OF JUSTIFICATION.—The basis on which this imputation proceeds, is our union to Christ. There is, first, our natural union constituting Him a member of our race, a man as truly as we are men. But this, though an essential prerequisite, is not by itself enough; for if so, mere humanity would constiiute every sinner a sharer in His righteousness. There must be added our mystical union, in which a legal and spiritual connexion are established by God's sovereign dispensation, making Him our legal, and our spiritual Head. Thus imputation becomes proper.

IS THE IDEA IN SCRIPTURE?—When we attempt to prove this imputation, we are met with the assertion, by Arminians, and theologians of the New England School, that there is no instance in the whole Bible of anything imputed, except that which the man personally does or posseses himself; so that there is no Scriptural warrant for this idea of transferrence of righteousness as to its legal consequences. We point, in reply, to Philem. 18, and to Rom. iv: 6. If God imputeth to a man righteousness without works, and his faith cannot literally *be* this imputed righteousness, as we have abundantly proved, we should like to know where that imputed righteousness comes from. Certainly it cannot come personally from the sinner who is *without works*. The whole context shows that it is Christ's. But how sorry an artifice is it to seize on the circumstance that the word LOGIDZESTHAI happens not be immediately connected with Christ's name in the same sentence, when the *idea* is set forth in so many phrases? Moreover, as Turrettin remarks, every case of pardoned guilt is a case (see 2 Sam. xix: 19,) of this kind of imputation: for something is reckoned to the sinner—i. e., legal innocency, or *title to immunity*, which is not personally his own.

PROOFS, FARTHER.—The direct arguments for the imputation of Christ's righteousness are: 1st. The counterpart imputation of our guilt to Him. (Proved by Is. liii: 5, 6, 12; Heb. ix: 28; 1 Pet. ii: 24, &c.) For the principles involved are so obviously the same, and the one transaction so obviously the procurer of the other, that none who admit a proper imputation of human guilt to Christ, will readily deny an imputation of His righteousness to man. Indeed both are conclusively stated in 2 Cor. v: 21. The old Reformed exposition of this important passage, by some of our divines, was to read, "Christ was made *a sin-offering* for us." The objection is: that by this view no counterpart is presented in the counterpart proposition: "we are made the righteousness of God in Him." It is obvious that St. Paul uses the abstract for the concrete. Christ was *made a sinner* for us, that we might be *made righteous persons* in Him. The senses of the two members of the parallelism must correspond. There is no other tenable sense than this obvious one—that our guilt (obligation to penalty) was imputed to Christ, that His righteousness (title to reward) might be imputed to us. 2d. Christ is said to *be* our righteousness. Jer. xxiii: 6; 1 Cor. i: 30, &c., expressions which can only be honestly received, by admitting the idea of imputation. 3d. By "His obedience many are constituted righteous;" KATASTATHESONTAI. Here is imputation. So we might go through most of the passages cited to prove that we are justified on account of Christ's righteousness, and show that they all involve the idea of imputation. Indeed, how else *can* the legal consequences of His righteousness become ours? To see the force of all these, we have only to remember that all who deny imputation, also deny that Christ's righteousness is the sole meritorious ground, thus plainly implying that the latter necessarily involves the former. 4th. Imputation of Christ's righteousness to us is argued by Paul in Romans. 5th. From imputation of Adam's sin to us.

Objections solved.—Objections have been strenuously urged against this doctrine, of which the most grave is that it encourages licentiousness of living. This will be separately considered under § XV. It has again, been urged that it is impious, in representing Christ as personally the worse Being in the universe; and false to fact, in representing His act in assuming our law place as the act which drew down God's wrath on Him; whereas it was an act of lovely benevolence, according to the Calvinistic view of it; and also false, as representing the sinner as personally holy at the very time his contrition avows him to be vilest. The answer is, that all these objections mistake the nature of imputation, which is not a transfer of moral character, but of legal relation. And Christ's act in taking our law place was a lovely act. In strictness of speech, it was not this act which drew down His Father's wrath, (but His love—Jno. x: 17,) but the guilt so assumed. For the discussion of more subtile objection, that guilt must be as untransferrible as personal demerit, because it is the consequence of demerit alone,—see Lect. xlii.

XII. Justification complete.—The important principle has already been stated, that justification must be as complete as its meritorious ground. Since Faith is only the instrument of its reception, the comparative weakness or strength of faith will not determine any degrees of justification in different Christians. Feeble faith which is living truly leads to Christ, and Christ is our righteousness alone. Our justifying righteousness is *in Christ*. The office of faith is simply to be the instrument for instituting the union of the believing soul to Him; so that it may "receive of His fullness grace for grace." Suppose in men's bodies a mortal disease, of which the perfect cure was a shock of electricity, received from some exhaustless "receiver," by contact. One man, discovering his mortal taint, but yet little enfeebled, rushes to the electrical receiver and claps his hand swiftly upon it, with all the force of a violent blow. He receives his shock, and is saved. Another, almost fainting, can only creep along the floor with the greatest difficulty, and has barely strength to raise his languid hand and lay it on the "receiver." He also derives the same shock, and the same healing. The power is in the electricity, not in the impact of the two hands. Hence, also, it will follow that justification is an instantaneous act, making at once a complete change of legal condition. See Rom. iii: 22; Jno. iii: 36; v: 24; Rom. viii: 1, 34 with 32; Col. ii: 9, 10; Heb. x: 14; Micah vii: 19; Jer. l: 20; Ps. ciii: 12, &c. And this legal completeness, it is too evident to need proof, begins when the sinner believes, and at no other time.

But sense and fruits of it may grow.—But here two distinctions must be taken—one between the completeness of *title*, and completeness of *possession* as to the benefits of our justification; the other between our justification in God's breast, and our own sense and consciousness thereof. On the latter distinction, we may remark: as our faith strengthens so will the strength of our apprehension of a justified state grow with it. The former also may, to some extent, be affected by the increase of our faith. God may make that increase the occasion of *manifesting* to the soul larger measures of favour and grace. But the soul is not one whit more God's accepted child then, than when it first believed. We have seen that the thing which, strictly speaking, is imputed, is the title to all the legal consequences of Christ's righteousness—i. e., title to pardon and everlasting adoption, with all the included graces. Now, the acknowledged and legitimate son of a king is a prince, though an infant. His *status* and inheritance are royal, and sure, though he be for a time under tutors and governors, and though he may gradually be put into possession of one, and another, of his privileges, till his complete majority. So the gradual possession of the benefits of justification does not imply that our acquision of the title is gradual.

Does Justification remit sins in future?—These views may assist us in the intricate subject of the relation which justification bears to the believer's future sins. On the one hand these things are evident: that there is not a man on the earth who does not offend, (Jas. iii: 2,) that sin must always be sin in its nature, and as such abhorrent to God by whomsoever committed; and even more abhorrent in a believer, because committed against greater obligations and vows; and that sins committed after justification need an atonement just as truly as those before. On the other hand, the proofs above given clearly show that the justified believer does not pass again under condemnation when betrayed into sin. Faith is the instrument for continuing, as it was for originating our justified state. This is clear from Rom. xi: 20; Heb. x: 38, as well as from the experience of all believers, who universally apply afresh to Christ for cleansing, when their consciences are oppressed with new sin. In strictness of speech, a man's sin must be forgiven *after* it is committed. How, then, stands the sinning believer, between the time of a new sin, and his new application to Christ's cleansing blood? We reply: Justification is the act of an immutable God, determining not to impute sin through the believer's faith. This faith, though not in instant exercise at every moment, is an undying *principle* in the believer's heart, being rendered indefectible only by God's purpose of grace, and the indwelling of the Holy Ghost. So God determines, when the believer sins, not to impute guilt for Christ's sake, which determination also implies this other, to secure in the believer's heart, the unfailing actings of faith and repentance, as to all known sin. So that his justification from future sins is not so much a pardoning of them before they are committed, as an unfailing provision by God both of the meritorious and instrumental causes of their pardon *as* they are committed.

How related to Judgment-day?—There are *two* qualified senses, in which we are said to be justified at the judgment-day. See Acts iii: 19–21; Matt. xii: 36, 37. Indeed, a forensic act is implied somehow in the very notion of a judgment-day. First: Then, at length, the benefits of the believer's justification in Christ will be fully confereed, and he will, by the resurrction, be put into possession of the last of them, the redemption of his body. Second: There will be a *declaration* of the sentence of justificatian passed when each believer blieved, which God will publish to His assembled creatures, for His declarative glory, and for their instruction. See Malachi iii: 17, 18. This last declarative justification will be grounded on believers' *works*, (Matt. xxv,) and not on their faith, necessarily; because it will be addressed to the fellow-creatures of the saints, who cannot read the heart, and can only know the existence of faith by the fruits.

XIII. Faith only instrument.—That faith alone is the instrument of justification, is asserted by the Catechism, que. 33. The proof is tow-fold: First. That this is the only act of the soul which, in its character, is receptive of Christ's righteousness. Repentance and other graces are essential, and have their all important relations to other parts of our salvation; but faith alone is the embracing act, and this alone is the act which contributes nothing, which looks wholly out of self for its object and its efficacy, and thus is compatible with a righteousness without works. Second. It is said in so many forms, that righteousness is by faith; and especially is this said most frequently where the technical act of justification is formally discussed, as separated from the other parts of our salvation. Then there are passages in which this is held up singly, in answer to direct inquiries, as the sole instrumental act, which do not leave us at liberty that any other one would have been omitted, if there had been one; e. g., Jno. vi: 29; Acts xvi: 31.

Connexion of Repentance Explained.—Yet, it is strenuously objected by some, (even of sound divines,) that in many places repentance is spoken of along with faith as a term of gospel salvation, and in some cases, even to the exclusion of faith. Mark i: 15; Luke xiii: 3; Acts xx: 21; and especially, Acts ii: 38; iii: 19. The chief force is in the last two. As to the previous ones, it is very obvious that to make repentance necessary to salvation, does not prove that it performs this particular work in our salvation, the instrumental acceptance of a justifying righteousness. We might even say that repentance is a necessary *condition* of *justification*, and yet not make it the *instrument;* for there is a sense in which perseverance is such a condition. Heb x: 38. But to make it the instrument is absurd; for then no one would be justified till death. But it may be urged, in Acts ii: 38, and iii: 19, repentance is explicitly proposed as *in order to remission*, which is an element of justification itself. We reply: this is not to be pressed; for thus we should equally prove, Acts ii: 38, that *baptism* is an instrument of justification; and, Rom. x: 9, 10, that *profession* is, equally with living faith, an instrument of justification. These passages are to be reconciled to our affirmative proof-texts, by remembering that repentance is used in Scripture much more *comprehensively* than saving faith. It is the whole conversion of the *soul* to God, the general acting in which faith is implicitly involved. When the Apostle calls for repentance, he virtually calls for faith; for as the actings of faith imply a penitent frame, so the exercise of repentance includes faith. It is therefore proper, that when a comprehensive answer is demanded to the question, "What must we do?" that answer should be generally,

"Repent," and that when the instrument of justification is inquired after specially, the answer should be, "Believe."

XIV. Works do not justify, yet necessary.—The question once debated: whether *faith* or *good works* be most important to a believer? is as foolish as though one should debate, whether roots or fruits were most essential to a fruit-tree. If either be lacking, there is no fruit-tree at all. Good works, when comprehensively understood for all holy actings of heart and life, hold the place of supreme importance in our redemption, as the *ulterior end*, not indeed in any sense the *procuring cause*, but yet the grand object and purpose. And the dignity of the end is in one sense higher than that of the means.

Because they most essential to God's ultimate end.—The final cause of God, or ultimate highest end in His view in our justification, is His own glory. The chief means or *next medium* thereto, is our sanctification and good works; for God's nature is holy, and cannot be glorified by sin, except indirectly in its punishment. If we look, then, at His immutable will and glory, we find an imperative demand for holiness and works. If we look next at the interests of God's kingdom as affected by us, we find an equal necessity for our good works: for it is *sin* which originates all mischief and danger, and disorder to the subjects of God's government. And if we look, third, at our own personal interest and well-being, as promoted by our redemption, we see good works to be equally essential; because to be sinful *is* to be miserable; and true holiness alone is true happiness.

Because all the plan of Redemption incites them.—Hence, we find that God in many places mentions redemption from *corruption*, rather than redemption from *guilt*, as His prominent object in the Covenant of Grace. See Titus ii: 14; Eph. i: 4; v: 25–27; 1 Thes. iv: 3; 1 Jno. iii: 8; Matt. i: 21. And all the features of this plan of redemption, in its execution, show that God's prime object is the production of holiness—yea, of holiness in preference to present happiness, in His people. The first benefit bestowed, in our union to Christ, is a *holy heart*. The most constant and prominent gifts ministered through Christ are those of sanctification and spiritual strength to do good works. The designs of God's providence constantly postpone the believer's comfort to his sanctification by the means of afflictions. When the question is, to make one of God's children holier, at the expense of his present happiness, God never hesitates. Again, the whole gospel system is so constructed as to be not merely an *expedient* for introducing justification, but a *system* of moral motives for producing sanctification, and that of wondrous power. Let the student look up its elements. And last. This very gospel teems with most urgent injunctions on believers already justified to keep this law, in all its original strictness and spirituality. See, especially, Matt. v: 17–20; Gal. v: 13; Rom. vi; 6; vii: 6; Jno. xiii: 34; 1 Pet. i: 15, 16, &c.

The law is no longer our *rule of justification*, but it is still our *rule of life*.

XV. Is justifiction by grace licentious in tendency?—We have reserved to the close the discussion of the objection, that this doctrine of justification, by faith on Christ's righteousness, tends to loosen the bonds of the moral law. There are two parties who suggest this idea—the legalists, who urge it as an unavoidable objection to our doctrine, and the Antinomians, who accept it as a just consequence of the doctrine. Both classes may be dealt with together, except as to one point growing out of our assertion that Christ fulfilled the preceptive, as well as bore the penal law in our stead. If this be so, says the Antinomian, how can God exact obedience of the believer, as an essential of the Christian state, without committing the unrighteousness of demanding payment of the same debt twice over? I reply, that it is not a pecuniary, but a moral debt. In explaning the doctrine of substitution, I showed that God's acceptance of our Surety's work in our room was wholly an optional and gracious act with Him, because Christ's vicarious work, however well *adapted* to satisfy the law in our stead, did not necessarily and naturally extinguish the claims of the law on us; was not a "*legal tender*," in such sense that God was obliged either to take that, or lose all claims. Now, as God's accepting the substitutionary righteousness at all was an act of mere grace, the extent to which He shall accept it depends on His mere will. And it can release us no farther than He graciously pleases to allow. Hence, if He tells us, as He does, that He does not so accept it, as to release us from the law as a rule of life, there is no injustice.

We preface further, that the objection of the legalist proceeds upon the supposition, that if the motives of fear and self-interest for obeying God be removed, none will be left. But are these the only motives? God forbid.

No, BUT SANCTIFYING.—Indeed, we assert that the plan of justification by faith leaves all the motives of self-interest and fear, which could legitimately and usefully operate on a soul under the Covenant of Works, in full force; and adds others, of vast superiority. Rom. iii: 31.

ALL LEGITIMATE SELF-INTEREST REMAINS.—1. The motives of self-interest and fear remain, so far as they properly *ought* to operate on a renewed soul. a.) While "eternal life is the gift of God," the measure of its glories is our works. See Luke xix: 17–19; Matt. x: 42; 2 Cor. ix: 6. Here is a motive to do as many good works as possible. b.) Works remain, although deposed from the meritorious place as our justification of supreme importance as the object and end. Hence, c.) They are the only adequate test of a justified state, as proved above. Thus, the conscience of the backslider should be as much stimulated by the necessity of having them, as though they were to be his righteousness.

FAITH PURIFIES.—2. The gospel shows its superior efficiency over a system of legality, in producing holy living, in this respect; that its instrument in justification is a *living faith*. A dead faith does not justify. Now, it is the nature of a justifying faith to give an active response to the vitalizing energy of God's truth. It is granted that the truth, which is the immediate object of its actings unto justification, is Christ's redemption; but its nature ensures that it shall be vitally sensitive to all God's truth, as fast as apprehended. Now, the *precepts* are as really divine truth, the proper object of this vital action of a living faith as the promises. Such is the teaching of our Confession in that instructive passage, ch. xiv, § ii. "By this faith a Christian believeth to be true whatsoever is revealed in the word, for the authority of God Himself speaking therein, and acteth differently, upon that which each passage thereof containeth; yielding obedience to the commands, trembling at the threatenings, and embracing the promises of God for this life, and that which is to come. But the principle acts of saving faith are accepting, receiving, and resting upon Christ alone for justification, sanctification, and eternal life, by virtue of the Covenant of Grace." The soul is not made alive in patches. It is alive all over. That principle of faith, therefore, which actively responds to the promise, responds just so likewise to the precepts, especially as precepts and promises are so intertwined. See Ps. xxxii: 1, 2; Rom. viii: 1.

GOSPEL APPEALS TO LOVE.—b.) The gospel is efficient in producing holy living, because it gives the strongest possible picture of the *evil of sin*, of God's inflexible requisition of a perfect righteousness, and of His holiness. c.) Above all, it generates a noble, pure, and powerful motive for obedience, *love*, begotten by God's goodness in redemption. And here, the peculiar glory of the gospel, as a *religion for sinners*, appears. I believe that the justified believer should have motives to holy living, which if their whole just force were felt, would be more operative than those which Adam in innocence could have felt under the Covenant of Works. See above. But when we consider that man is no longer innocent, but naturally condemned and depraved, under wrath, and fundamentally hostile to God, we see that a Covenant of Works would now be, for him, infinitely inferior in its sanctifying influences. For the only obedience it could evoke from such a heart, would be one slavish, selfish, and calculated—i. e., no true heart obedience at all—but a mere trafficking with God for self-interest. Now, contrast with this an obedience of love, and of gratitude, which expects to *purchase* nothing thereby from God, because all is already given, freely, graciously, and therefore obeys with ingenuous love and thankfulness. How much more pleasing to God! And last: Love is a principle of action as permanent and energetic as it is pure. Witness even the human examples of it. When we look to those social affections, which have retained their disinterestedness (towards man) through the corruptions of our fall, we see there the most influential, as well as the purest principles of human action, the springs of all that is most energetic, and persevering, as well as most generous.

LOVE, THE MOST OPERATIVE.—We sometimes hear the legalists, of various schools, say: "a correct knowledge of human nature will warn us, that if the principles of fear and self-interest are removed from man's religious obedience, he will render none; for these are the main springs of human action." We do not represent the gospel scheme as rejecting the legitimate action of those springs. But their view of human nature is false; fear and self-interest are not its most energetic principles. Many a virtuous son and daughter render to an infirm parent, who has no ability or will to punish, and no means of rewarding save with his blessing, a service more devoted, painful, and continued, than the rod ever exacted from a slave. Indeed, slavery itself showed by the occasional instances of tyranny, which occurred, that fear was an inadequate principle; the rod by itself never secured industry and prosperity on a plantation; but the best examples of success were always those where kindness was chiefly relied on, (with a just and firm authority,) to awaken in the slaves affection and cheerful devotion. The sick husband receives from his wife, without wages, nursing more assiduous than any hire can extort from the mercenary professional nurse. And, above all, does the infant, helpless to reward or punish, exact from the mother's love and pity, a service more punctilious and toilsome, than was ever rendered to an eastern sultan by the slave with the scimetar over his head.

Suppose, then, that the all-powerful Spirit of God, employing the delightful truths of gospel grace as His instrument, produces in believers a love and gratitude as genuine as these instinctive affections, and more sacred and strong as directed towards a nobler object, has He not here a spring of obedience as much more efficacious as it is more generous than the legalists?

> "Talk they of morals? O Thou bleeding Love,
> The great morality is love to Thee!"

When, therefore, these heretics object, that justification by free grace will have licentious results; God's answer is, that He will provide against that, by making the faith which justifies also a principle of life, which "works by love."

LECTURE LIII.

SYLLABUS.

REPENTANCE.

1. What two kinds of repentance are distinguished in Scripture, and by what words? Are they ever used interchangeably?
   Conf. of Faith, ch. xv. Sampson on Hebrews, 12, 17. Hill, Bk. v, ch. 4, § 1. Calvin, Inst., Bk. iii, ch. 3. Knapp, § 126. Watson, ch. xxiv, § 1.
2. What do divines mean by legal, and what by evangelical repentance?
   Ridgeley, que. 76. Calvin, as above.
3. Of what should we repent?
4. Who is the author of repentance; and does it precede or follow regeneration?
   Calvin, as above. Ridgeley, as above. Watson's Inst., ch. xxiv.
5. What are the relations between Faith and Repentance, and which is prior in the order of production?
   Calvin, as above, § 1, 2. Fuller on Sandeman, Letter v. Watson, as above.
6. Is repentance atoning?
   Calvin, Bk. iii, ch. 4. Knapp, § 128. Watson, as above, and ch. xix.
7. What are the proper fruits of repentance?
   See Ridgeley and Calvin, as above.

I. "Repentance unto Life is an evangelical grace, the doctrine whereof is to be preached by every minister of the gospel, as well as that of faith in Christ." Conf. xv, 1. The brevity, and in some cases neglect, with which this prominent subject is treated by many systems, is surprising and reprehensible.

Definition of terms.—In the New Testament there are two classes of words, used for two exercises, both of which, in the English version are called "repentance," "repent." One class is METAMELOMAI, METAMELEIA, the other, METANOEO, METANOIA. The one means etymologically, *after regret*, a merely natural feeling; the other, *change of mind* after conduct. And the two classes are used in the New Testament with general, or, as I would assert, universal discrimination. (The only alleged cases of confusion are Matt. xxi: 32; Luke xvii: 3, 4; Heb. xii: 17. In the first, the verb is METEMELETHETE, with accurate and proper reference to the relation between carnal conviction and sorrow, and turning to Christ, as a preparation for the result. Those expositors who will have METAMELOMAI used here for evangelical repentance, urge, that this alone is vitally connected with saving faith. The chief priests "repented not that they might believe." But give the verb its ordinary meaning: Christ charges on them such obduracy, and self-sufficiency, that they felt not even that carnal sorrow, which is the preliminary step towards true repentance, faith, and conversion. Thus, so far is the ordinary sense from being difficult here, it adds great force to our Saviour's meaning. So in the next case. Luke xvii: 3, 4. In this METANOIA is used for the professed repentance of an erring, and even a very unstable brother, to show that his *profession*, so long as it is not absolutely discredited by his bad conduct, is to be taken by the judgment of charity, (1 Cor. xiii: 7,) as evidence of genuine, Christian sorrow, so far as to secure forgiveness. A profession of mere carnal sorrow would not entitle to it. In the third, the best commentators are agreed that TOPON METANOIAS refers to a change in Isaac, which the historian indicates, *must* have been (whatever profane Esau may have hoped) Christian conviction of, and sorrow for error; (otherwise he would not have changed his prophecy.) Now, when we see that METANOEO is used in the New Testament 34, and METANOIA 24 times=58, and METAMELOMAI, and family, 7 times, the demarcation made by the sacred writers is very broad.

See this distinction carried out with instructive accuracy in 2 Cor. vii: 8–10, (original.)

In the Old Testament two families of words are used for those acts promiscuously expressed in our English version by *Repent;* SHOOBH, and its derivatives, and NACHAM, with its derivatives. The *latter* is used to express both *regret* and *repentance* proper, (variously translated by Sept.;) the former, I believe, in its theological uses, always expresses true repentance.

The Latin Vulgate has lent us a mischievous legacy, in giving us the word "repent" as the rendering of METANOEIN. "Repentance" is from *poenitet*, *poena;* and that from the Greek word POINE. Its English progeny is seen in the word *pain;* and its original idea is *penalty.* See the use of POINA; *Iphigenia in aulide*, for *expiatory penalty.* No wonder the Latin Church, in the dark ages, slid into the error of regarding *penance*, as a satisfaction for the guilt of sin; when it had been taught to call METANOIA by such a misnomer as *poenitentia*. *Lactantius*, (the most elegant in his Latinity, of the Christian fathers,) proposes to render it by *Resipiscentia*, (from re-sapio.) "Ideo que

Graeci melius et significantius METANOIAN dicunt, quam nos possumus resipiscentiam dicere."

I wish that the English tongue had enabled our version to distinguish the two exercises uniformly by two distinct words.

METAMELEIA is the natural pain consequent on sin, arising in the *carnal mind*, either with or without the common convincing influences of the Holy Ghost, and contains two elements, fear and dread of the danger incurred, and remorse or involuntary self-condemnation of conscience denouncing the sin. It is a purely selfish emotion; but it is still the emotion of a moral *nature*, and implies a conscience; though compatible with an entire *preference of will* for sin.

METANOIA is: (See Shorter Cat., que. 87. Quote ans. 87. Conf., xv, § 2.) It involves the two elements of the former; but it includes *chiefly* another; viz: "a sight and sense of the filthiness and odiousness of his sins, as *contrary to the holy nature, and righteous law of God.*" There is not only that painful sense of wrong doing inflicted by conscience on the sinner; conscience, which a depraved will, although fully set on transgression, cannot corrupt nor wholly silence. But there is the pain arising from a true hatred of sin now existing *in the will*, as a moral disposition and principle, and from the preference for, and love of conformity to God, arising out of a thorough approval of, and complacency in His moral perfection. Of course, this hatred of sinfulness and appetency of holiness, are not two principles, but *one*, expressing its spontaneous nature as to two opposite objects—sin and righteousness. And last, that view of the odiousness of sin, and attractiveness of godliness proceeds chiefly in the believer's experiences, *from the cross;* from the exhibitions of mercy, purity, goodness, and hope there made. True repentance may be defined as *the moral emotion and act of the regenerate nature towards its personal sinfulness, and towards godliness*, especially as the two are exhibited in the Cross.

II. LEGAL REPENTANCE WHAT?—The terms *Legal* and *Evangelical* Repentance have been used by divines with a mischievous uncertainty. By some, legal repentance is defined as though dentical with METAMELEIA. If this were really the distinction, the terms would be unnecessary. Paul gives us better ones in 2 Cor. vii: 10: The "sorrow of the world," and "Godly sorrow." But other divines, perceiving a truer and more accurate distinction in the actings of Godly sorrow itself, have employed the phrases in a useful sense. These, by *legal* repentance, mean a genuine sorrow for sin, including both fear of its dangers, and conscience of its wrongness, *and also* loathing of its odiousness, with a thorough justifying and approving of God's holy law; a sorrow wrought by the Holy Ghost, but wrought by Him only through the instrumentality of the convincing *Law*, and unaccompanied with conscious hopes of mercy in Christ. By Evangelical Repentance they mean that godly sorrow for sin, which is wrought by the renewing Spirit, *including* the above actings, but also, and chiefly, the tender sorrow combined with hopes of mercy proceeding from appropriating faith, when the believer "looks on Him whom he hath pierced," and sees there at once a blessed way of deliverance, and a new illustration of God's love, and his own aggravated vileness. This, in a word, is the repentance of the Catechism, que. 87.

III. Do we repent of Original Sin?—In completing our view of the nature of repentance, the question presents itself: *Of what* should man repent? The general answer, of course, must be: Of all sin. Is it man's duty, then, to repent of original sin? If we say, no, the Arminian will press us with this consequence: "If it is not your personal duty to repent of it, you imply that you are not in earnest in saying that it is truly and properly sin." Yet, how can a man feel *personally blameworthy* (an essential element of repentance) for an act committed by another, without his consent, and before he was born? "The sinfulness of that estate into which man fell. consists in the guilt of Adam's first sin, the want of original righteousness, and the corruption of his whole nature, which is commonly called original sin." The Christian will, of course, *regret* the guilt of Adam's first sin, but not repent of it. But of the corruption of nature, of the concupiscence and inordinate desire of our hearts, it is our duty to *repent*, to feel blameworthy for them, to sorrow for, and to strive against them, just as of actual transgression; for this is not only our guilt, (imputed,) but our proper sin.

Of particular Sins?—Again, Conf., xv, § 5, men ought not only to repent of their sinfulness, both of heart and life, as a general quality, but also of particular sins, so far as they are known, with a particular repentance. Repentance is the medium of *sanctification*, and sin is only conquered by us *in detail*. There is no other way for a finite creature to fight the good fight of faith. Hence, it is obvious, every conscious, and especially every known recent transgression should be made the subject of particular repentance. The impenitent man cannot be forgiven. What, then, shall we answer concerning those unconscious and forgotten transgressions (probably the "secret sins" of Ps. xix: 12,) to which the attention and recollection of even the honest penitent never advert, in consequence of the limitation of his faculties and powers? We answer, that each Christian is aware of his guilt of these forgotten faults, and grieves over the *general fact* that he *has* them. And this general repentance is accepted; so that the atonement of Christ blots them out of God's book of remembrance.

After this definition of Repentance, it need hardly be added, that it is not only an act, to be performed at the beginning of conversion, and then to be dismissed as complete, but also a life long work, proceeding from an abiding temper of soul. The saint is a penitent, until he reaches heaven.

IV. Repentance fruit of New Birth.—If we confound worldly with godly sorrow, or if we take a Pelagian view of human nature, we may indeed ascribe true repentance to the unaided workings of the natural heart. But if repentance is understood as above, we shall see that while it is a duty for man to exercise, it is still one to which he must be moved by the supernatural grace of God. Hence, the Scriptures always represent it as God's gift or work. See New Testament first, as plainest: Acts v: 31; xi: 18; 2 Tim. ii: 25. In Old Testament: Ps. lxxx: 3, 7, 19; lxxxv: 4; Jer. xxxi: 18; Ezek. xi: 19. Nor can these texts be evaded by saying, that God is the Author of repentance only mediately, by teaching that gospel which inculcates and prompts repentance. In several of them, those who are already possessed of the gospel means pray to God to work repentance in them; and in 2 Tim. ii: 25, there is a "peradventure" whether God will give a heart to repent, to those to whom Timothy was to give the light: showing that the grace of repentance is a separate and divine gift.

But let any one look at the Scriptural definition of Repentance, and he will be convinced that none but a regenerate heart is competent to the exercise. The true penitent not only feels the danger of his sins, and the involuntary sting of a conscience which he would disarm if he could, but an ingenuous sorrow for the sinfulness of his sin, and a sincere desire for godliness. Can any one feel this but a regenerate soul? Can he who hates God thus grieve for having wounded His holy law; can he who loves sin as the native food of his soul, thus loathe it for its own sake? No one feels godly sorrow, but he who is passed from death unto life.

Arminian objections to this. Answer.—But the Arminians, while avowing that repentance is the work of the Holy Ghost, assert that it must be held to begin before regeneration in the order of production, as they also hold concerning faith and justification. Their reasons are two. First: we are taught, (e. g., Ps. li: 10,) to pray for regeneration. But prayer, to be acceptable, must be sincere; and a sincere request for a holy heart implies, or presupposes, repentance for ungodliness. And second: repentance must be presupposed in faith, because to fly to Christ as a refuge from sin presupposes a sense of sin. But justification, secured by faith, must precede regeneration; because God cannot be supposed to bestow the beginning of communion in the Holy Ghost, and what is substantially *eternal life*, on a rebel *before* he is reconciled to Him. Thus, they suppose Rom. vii to describe repentance; Rom. vii: 24, 25, the dawnings of saving faith; Rom. viii: 1, first clause, the justification consequent thereon; and viii: 1, last clause, the beginning of spiritual life. Now, to both objections, we reply that their plausibility is chiefly due to the oversight of this fact, that the priority of one over another of these several steps is only one of production, or causation, *and not of time.* Practically, every one who is regenerate is *then* in principle, penitent, and believing, and justified. And since all parts are of God's grace, is it not foolish to say that His righteousness or His wrath forbids Him to bestow *this* before *that*, seeing His grace permits neither to precede in time, and none to be lacking? But on the first objection we remark, farther, if we must needs rationalize about it, it is at least as great an anomaly that a man should feel a sincere desire for godliness, while his nature remained prevalently ungodly, as it is that an ungodly prayer for a new heart should be answered by the heart-searching God. The objection derives its seeming force from a synergistic theory of Regeneration. But, in truth, no true spiritual desire can exist till God has actually renewed the will. God must do the work, not man. And God must savingly begin it, *unasked* by man. This is sovereign grace. That a man should hold this theory, and yet pray for a new heart, is no greater paradox than that the hope our sins *are pardoned* should encourage us to pray for pardon. The truth is, the instincts of a pre-existent spiritual life find their natural expression in a breathing after spiritual life. To the second objection, we reply: if it seems anomalous that God should anticipate His reconciliation to the condemned sinner, by bestowing that gift of a new heart, which virtually constitutes eternal life, it would be equally anomalous that He should anticipate the bestowal of peace, by bestowing those essential gifts of faith and repentance, to which eternal blessedness is inevitably tied by the gospel. Must not the Arminian, just as much as the Calvinist, fall back, for his solution of these difficulties, upon the glorious fact, that Christ hath deserved *all* these saving gifts for His people? To him who believes an unconditional election, there is no difficulty here; because he believes that these saving gifts are all pledged to the believing sinner, not only before he fulfils any instrumental conditions, but before he is born. There is no difficulty in it all to God; because *all is of grace.*

V. WHICH PRECEDES; FAITH OR REPENTANCE?—The relations of faith and repentance *inter se*, as to the order of production, are important to an understanding of conversion. Both these graces are the exercises of a regenerate heart alone; they presuppose the new birth. Now, Calvin, with perhaps the current of Calvinistic divines, says, that "repentance not only immediately follows faith, but is produced by it." Again: "When we speak of faith as the origin of repentance, we dream not of any space of time which it employs in producing it; but we intend to signify that a man cannot truly devote himself to repentance, unless he knows himself to be of God." And this, he adds, only becomes known by appropriating faith. The view usually urged is, that the convicted sinner cannot exercise that tender and affectionate sorrow for sin, which involves a true love to God, until he entertains some hope that God loves him, in Christ. They quote such passages as Ps. cxxx: 4; 1 Jno. iv: 19. Before hope of mercy dawns, they argue, there can be nothing but stubborn remorse and despair, after the example of Jer. xviii: 12. Now, there is a fair sense in which all this is true; and that no doubt the sense in which it commended itself to the minds of these great aud good men. But there is also a great danger of holding it in an erroneous and mischievous sense. In what we have to say, guarding these views, let us premise that we make no priority of time in the order of repentance and faith; and no gap of duration between the birth of the one or the other. Either implies the other, in that sense. Nor do we dream of the existence of such a thing as a *penitent unbeliever*, nor suppose that there is any other *means* of producing repentance than the preaching of the gospel. Repentance can exist nowhere except where God works it. In rational adults He works it only by means, and that means is the *gospel* revelation; none other. Nor do we retract one word of what we said as to the *prime* efficiency of the doctrine of the cross, and of the hope, gratitude, love, tenderness, and humiliation, which faith draws therefrom, as means for cultivating repentance. But in our view it is erroneous to represent faith as existing irrespective of penitence, in its very first acting, and as begetting penitence through the medium of hope. On the contrary, we believe that the very first acting of faith *implies* some repentance, as the prompter thereof. True, the two twin graces ever after stimulate each other reciprocally: the man begins to believe because he has also begun to repent.

ARGUMENT.—The reasons are: first, that the other view gives a degrading and mercenary character to repentance: as though the sinner selfishly conditioned his willingness to feel aright concerning his sin, on the previous assurance of impunity. It is as though the condemned felon should say: "Let me go free, and I will sincerely avow that I have done very wrong. But if I am to swing for it, I will neither acknowledge guilt, nor say, God, bless my country." Is this ingenuous repentance? Is this the experience of the contrite heart? No; its language always is: (Ps. li, pt. 1 v. 5:)

> "Should sudden vengeance seize my breath,
> I must pronounce Thee just in death;
> And if my soul is sent to hell,
> Thy righteous law approves it well."

Second: Godly sorrow for sin must be presupposed or implied in the first actings of faith, because faith embraces Christ as a Saviour *from sin.* See Cat., que. 86, last clause especially. Surely the Scriptures do not present Christ to our faith only, or even mainly, as a *way of impunity.* See Matt. i: 21; Acts iii: 26; Titus ii: 14. As we have pointed out the most characteristic defect of a dead faith, is, that it would quite heartily embrace Christ as God's provision for *immunity* in sin: but God offers Him to faith for a very different purpose, viz: for restoration to holiness, including immunity from wrath as *one* of the secondary consequences thereof. (Hence, we must demur at Owen's declaration, that the special object of saving faith is only Christ in His priestly, and not in His kingly and prophetic offices.) But now, a man does not flee from an evil, except as a consequence of feeling it an evil. Hence, there can be no embracing of Christ with the heart, as a whole present Saviour, unless sin be felt to be in itself a present evil; and there be a genuine desire to avoid *it* as well as its penalty. But does not such a desire imply a renewal of the will? This view has appeared so unavoidable to many who go with Calvin, that they have admitted, "Legal repentance precedes, but Evangelical repentance follows faith and hope." (See above, p. 146, bottom.) But does not such a legal repentance imply the new birth? Does any man thus justify and revere the very law which condemns him, and regard the Divine character, while devoid as he supposes of hope in its favour, with new and adoring approbation, while yet his carnal mind is enmity against God? Surely not. The error of their argument is in supposing that this legal repentance was the exercise of an unrenewed heart.

Third: Some passages of Scripture imply the order I have assigned; and I am not aware of any which contradict it. See Mark i: 15; Acts ii: 38; v: 31; xx: 21; 2 Tim. ii: 25, especially the last.

They are twin graces.—In a word, Repentance and Faith are twin graces, both *implicitly* contained in the gift of the new heart; and they cannot but co-exist. Repentance is the right sense and volition which the renewed heart has of its sin; faith is the turning of that heart from its sin to Christ. Repentance feels the disease, faith embraces the remedy. But when we inquire for the first *conscious acting* of faith or repentance after the instant of the new birth, the result is decided by the object to which the soul happens to be first directed. If the object of its first regenerate *look* be its own ungodliness, the first *conscious* exercise will be one of repentance; but just so surely as the volition is, potentially, in the preponderating motive, so surely does that soul look from its ungodliness to Christ, the remedy of it; it may be unconsciously at first, but in due time consciously. Or if Christ be the first object to which the new-born soul looks, its first act may be one of trust and joy in Him. Yet that trust implies a sense of the evil of sin, as the thing for deliverance from which Christ is trusted.

VI. Repentance not atoning.—The exercise of repentance, while absolutely necessary in all who are saved, creates no atoning merit; and constitutes no ground whatever in justice, why the penitent should have remission of his sins. See Conf., xv, 3. The carnal mind here labours under an obstinate delusion; and how often are pastors told, even by those who desire to profess themselves Christians, "that they hope their sins are pardoned, *because they have repented?*" Hence, importance.

Argument.—A moral fitness which demands that no impenitent person shall be pardoned, is here mistaken for another thing. Now, the ground of that moral fitness is this: that pardon having otherwise been made just, God's holiness and majesty may have some practical assurance, in the state of the sinner's own feelings, against his repetition of his sins. But this end does not express the whole intent of God's law; if it did, the law would be a mere expediency, unworthy of God. Its true object is, to express and sustain His immutable holiness. It demands perfect and perpetual obedience. Repentance is not obedience. This leads,

Second, to the remark, that repentance is no reparation whatever for past obedience. It cannot place the sinner, in the eye of the law, in the position of Him who has never sinned. It has in itself no relevancy to repairing the mischiefs the sin has inflicted. Thus men judge. To the man who had injured you, you would say: Your repentance is very proper; but it cannot recall the past, or undo that which is done.

Third: Indeed, what is a repentance but a feeling of ill-desert, and consequent guilt? Confession is its language. Now, can a man *pay* a just debt by his acknowledgments of its justice? It is a contradiction, which would lead us to this absurdity, that the more thoroughly unworthy a man felt, the more worthy he would thereby become.

Fourth: Repentance after transgression is *a work*. Acts xvii: 30. So that justification by repentance would be a justification by works, and all the principles of Luke xvii: 10; Rom. iii: 28, apply to it.

But last: Repentance is much a *gift of God* (Acts v: 31,) as the remission which it is supposed to purchase. This settles the matter. While, therefore, the impenitent cannot be justified, yet the sole ground of justification is the righteousness of Christ imputed to us, and received by faith alone.

VII. Fruits meet for Repentance.—The Scriptures command us to "bring forth fruits meet for repentance." These fruits will, in general, include all holy living; for repentance is a "turning unto God from sin, with full purpose of, and endeavour after new obedience." But there are certain acts which are essentially dictated by repentance and which proceed immediately from the attitude of penitence.

1. Sincere penitence must lead to confession. "Out of the abundance of the heart the mouth speaketh." See Prov. xxviii: 13. The

highest form of this duty is the confession of all our sins to God, in secret prayer. True repentance will always thus *utter itself* to Him. Then, if our sins have scandalized the Church, we must also make public confession of the particular sins which have produced this result. Again, if our sin is immediately aimed at our fellow-man, and known to him, repentance must lead to confession to him.

2. The next consequence of repentance will be, to prompt us to make reparation of our sin, wherever it is practicable. He who truly repents, *wishes his sin undone.* But if he truly wishes it undone, he will, of course, *undo it*, if in his power.

3. The next fruit of repentance must be holy watchfulness against its recurrence. This is too obvious to need proof. See 2 Cor. vii : 11, as admirably expounded by Calvin, Institutes, Bk. 3, ch. 3, § 15.

The worthless distinction of Rome between attrition and contrition, and the assigning of a religious value to the former, are sufficiently refuted by what precedes. Nor does the duty of auricular confession, so called, find any Scriptural support plausible enough to demand discussion. As to her ascetical exercises of penitence, they are the inventions of fanaticism and spiritual pride. The mortification which Scripture enjoins, is that of the *sins*, and not of the unreasoning members.

LECTURE LIV.

SYLLABUS.

SANCTIFICATION AND GOOD WORKS.

1. State the usages and meanings of the original words rendered "*sanctify*," and the nature and extent of sanctification.

   Sh. Cat., que. 35. Conf. of Faith, chs. xiii and xvi. Lexicons. Turrettin, Loc. xvii, que. 1. Dick, Lect. 74.

2. How is sanctification distinguished from, and how related to, justification and regeneration?

   Turrettin, que. 1, § 9, to end. Dick, as above. Hill, Bk. v, ch. 4, § 2. Knapp, § 126, 116. Ridgeley, que. 78.

3. Who is the Agent, and what the means of sanctification?

   Dick, Lect. 75. Ridgeley, que. 75.

4. Is sanctification ever perfect in this life? Consider the views of Pelagians, Socinians, and Wesleyans.

   Turrettin, que. 2. Dick, Lect. 74. Hill, Bk. v, ch. 4, § 3. Ridgeley, que. 78. Watson's Theol. Inst., ch. 29.

I. Sanctify. Definition of.—In discussing this subject, we turn again to Scripture to settle the meaning of the word. In the Old Testament we find the word KADASH used in the piel and hiphil, to express sanctification. In its lowest sense, it seems to mean simply separation to a particular purpose, and that purpose not sacred, as Jer. xxii: 7. More frequently it is used in the sense of consecrate, or dedicate as priests, utensils, the Sabbath day, where the idea is that of *setting apart to a holy use.* See Exod. xxviii: 41; xxix: 36; Deut. v: 12. But in its proper sense, it means to cleanse away ceremonial, and especially, moral pollution. 2 Sam. xi: 4; Num. xv: 40. Kindred to this is the sense where God is said to sanctify Himself, or to be sanctified by His people—i. e., declaratively. Ezek. xxxviii: 23.

USE OF WORD IN NEW TESTAMENT.—In the Greek Scriptures HAGIADZO is used clearly in all the above senses, to separate, to consecrate, to purify morally, and to declare God's holiness. There is a use of this verb, of which the clearest instances are seen in the Epistle to the Hebrews, especially ii: 11; x: 10, 14; xiii. 12, compared with i: 3. Dr. Sampson here renders the word popularly by "redeem." Sin carries two consequences—guilt and pollution—(nearly associated in the mind of a Hebrew.) From the former, Christ's blood cleanses, from the latter, His Spirit. When Christ is said to "sanctify" us by His blood, His sacrifice, &c., it is the former element, cleansing away of guilt, which is intended prominently. This is evident from the fact that the verb is used by the Septuagint as the rendering for KIPPER; which is strengthened by the fact that the kindred word KATHARIDZO is used for propitiation; e. g., 1 Jno. i: 7. See Sampson on Hebrews, i: 3; and ii: 11.

SANCTIFICATION IS OF THE SOUL. PROOFS.—Sanctification, in the gospel sense, means then, not only cleansing from guilt, though it presupposes this, nor only consecration, though it includes this, nor only reformation of morals and life, though it produces this; but, essentially, *the moral purification of the soul.* This is the great idea to which all the ceremonial sanctity of the typical dispensation pointed; (see Ps. li: 6, 7; xxiv: 4, &c.,) and it is yet more emphatically and prominently expressed in the New Testament word HAGIADZO. In our discussions with Pelagians, we have already shown that their idea is erroneous, viz: that holiness can only be *acted* by man. We have proved that there must be a previous spring in the principles of the soul, and the dispositions which dictate volitions; otherwise volitions formally right can have no true holiness. Outward reformation cannot, then, be sanctification, because the former can only be the consequence thereof; as is well stated in Turrettin, and is clearly implied by Matt. xii: 33, 34, &c. This important practical truth may be farther supported by considering, b.) that holiness in man must be conceived as the counterpart of sin. (The Pelagian admits this.) But sin is both original and actual. Sin of heart is the fountain of the sin of life. Hence, it is fair to infer, as our Saviour does, in fact, in the places cited, that sanctification has its seat in the heart. c.) This appears also by the fact, which none will deny, that infants may be subjects of sanctification. They cannot *act* a sanctification. d.) Again, the synonymous phrases all speak of "a clean heart," of "circumcising the *heart*," &c. And last, the Scriptures are emphatic in their assertions. 1 Thess. v: 23; Eph. iv: 23, 24; Gal. v: 24; Titus iii: 5; Luke xvii: 21; Rom. xiv: 17.

SANCTIFICATION IS OF THE WHOLE PERSON. IN WHAT SENSE OF OTHER PARTS THAN THE HEART?—When we inquire after the extent of sanctification, or the *parts* of the human person affected by it, the Catechism answers, that we are renewed "in the *whole man*." In 1 Thess. v: 23, the Apostle expresses the same idea of completeness, by employing the three comprehensive terms of the Platonic psychology current in his day, (not meaning to endorse that scheme.) Now, when we analyse that element of human character and of human action, in which moral quality resides, we are compelled to say that, strictly speaking, it is only in the state and actings of man's active powers. If there is neither emotional activity nor choice involved in any human act, that act has no moral character. Hence, in strictness of speech, the true seat of sanctification is *the will:* the human soul in that class of its actings expressed in Scripture by the word *heart*. But the Apostle is writing popularly, and not scientifically. The emotional and voluntary capacity of the soul is not a different member, or department of it, from the intellectual. It is the one indivisible unit, acting in different modes.

The Soul has no parts.—It is the *soul* which is sanctified, and not a faculty thereof. True, that sanctification is only a moral change of the soul, in its essence; but in its results, it modifies every acting of the soul, whether through intellect, appetite, or corporeal volition. Every one would consider that he was speaking with sufficient accuracy in using the words "a wicked thought." Now, in the same sense in which a thought can be wicked, in that sense the *power of thinking* can be *sanctified*. What is that sense? A thought is wicked, not because the faculty of thinking, or pure intellection, is the seat of moral quality, abstractly considered; but because the *soul* that thinks, gives to that thought, by the *concurrence* of its active or emotional, or voluntary power, a complex character, in which complex there is a wrong moral element. To sanctify the intellect, then, is to sanctify the *soul* in such way that in its complex acts, the moral element shall be right instead of wrong. So we speak, with entire propriety of "a *wicked blow*." The bones, skin, and muscles, which corporeally inflicted it, are the unreasoning and passive implement of the soul that emitted the volition to strike. But our members are sanctified, when the volitions which move them are holy; and when the impressions, or sense and appetite, of which they are the inlets, become the occasions of no wrong feelings or volitions.

Sanctification of the body not Asceticism.—The sanctification of our bodies consists, therefore, not in the ascetic mortification of our nerves, muscles, glands, &c., but in the employment of the members as the implements of none but holy volitions, and in such management and regulations of the *senses*, that they shall be the inlets of no objective, or occasional causes of wrong feeling. This will imply, of course, strict temperance, continence, and avoidance of temptation to the sinful awakening of appetite, as well as the preservation of muscular vigour, and healthy activity, by self-denial and bodily hardihood. See 1 Cor. ix: 27; 2 Pet. ii: 14; Jas. iii: 2. But the whole theory of asceticism is refuted by the simple fact, that the soul is the seat of holiness; and that the body is only indirectly holy or unholy, as it is the tool of the soul. The whole delusion, so far as it has sought a Scriptural support, rests on the mistake of the meaning of the word "flesh," "*caro*," "SARX," which the sacred writers use to mean depraved human nature; not the body. What those fleshly members are, which sanctification mortifies, may be seen in Col. iii: 5.

II. RELATION OF SANCTIFICATION TO NEW BIRTH AND JUSTIFICATION—Sanctification only matures what regeneration began. The latter sprouted the seed of grace, the former continues its growth, until there appears first the blade, then the ear, and then the full corn in the ear. The agent and influences are therefore the same.

In the order of production, justification precedes sanctification; for one of the benefits received by the justified believer, in virtue of his acceptance, is sanctifying grace.* While the two graces are practically inseparable, still their discrimination is of the highest importance; for it is by confounding the two that Rome has re-introduced her theory of justification, by self-righteousness. Hence, let the student remember, that the results of the two graces are different. Justification removes the guilt of sin, sanctification its pollution. Justification changes only our legal relations, sanctification our actual moral condition. Justification is an act, sanctification is a process; the one is instantaneous and complete in all,thne other is imperfect in its degree in all, unequal in different Christia s, and is increased throughout life. Justification takes place in God's court, sanctification in the sinner's own breast.

SANCTIFICATION ESSENTIAL TO SALVATION.—The necessary and uniform connexion between the two has been argued substantially in the last lecture on Justification, and to that the student is referred. But the proposition is of such prime importance that it will not be amiss, in closing this head, to state the points of our argument in somewhat different order.

a.) The Covenant of Grace embraces both. Jer. xxxi: 33; Rom. viii: 30.

b.) The sanctity of the divine nature requires it. 1 Pet. i: 15, 16.

c.) The connexion appears inevitable from the offices of Christ; for He is King, as well as Priest, to all His people. Rom. viii: 29; vi: 11; Titus ii: 14; Rom. viii: 1, 2.

d.) The office of the Holy Ghost shows this connexion; for His influences are a part of Christ's purchase. But He is the Spirit of holiness. Rom. viii: 9.

e.) The sacraments symbolize cleansing from pollution as well as from guilt. Col. ii: 11, 12; Titus iii: 5.

f.) Redemption would be a mockery without sanctification; for sin itself, and not the external wrath of God, is the cause of misery here, and eternal death hereafter. Hence, to deliver the fallen son of Adam, from his guilt, and leave him under the power of corruption, would be no salvation.

Last: the chief ultimate end of redemption, which is God's glory, (Rom. xi: 36; Is. lxi: 3; Eph. i: 6,) would be utterly disappointed, were believers not required to depart from all sin. For God's holiness, His consummate attribute, would be tarnished by taking to His favour polluted creatures. This point suggests, also, the second, where God points to His own perfect holiness as the reason for the purification of His people. No argument could be plainer. An unholy creature has no place in the favour and bosom of a holy God.

Faith embraces Christ in all His offices.—To return a moment to the third point, I would add on it a remark which I omitted in order to avoid interrupting the outline. The selfishness and guilty conscience of man prompt him powerfully to look to the Saviour exclusively as a remedy for guilt, even when awakened by the Spirit. The first and most urgent want of the soul, convicted of its guilt and danger, is impunity. Hence, the undue prevalence, even in preaching, of that view of Christ, which holds Him up as Atonement only. We have seen that even an Owen could be guilty of what I regard as the dangerous statement, that the true believer, in embracing Christ, first received Him only in His priestly office! The faith which does no more than this, is but partial, and can bear but spurious fruits. Is not this the explanation of much of that defective and spurious religion with which the Church is cursed? The man who is savingly wrought upon by the Holy Ghost, is made to feel that his bondage under corruption is an evil as inexorable and dreadful as the penal curse of the law. He needs and desires Christ in His prophetic and kingly offices, as much as in His priestly. His faith "receives Him as He is offered to us in the gospel;" that is, as a "Saviour of His people from their sins."

III. Agent of sanctification in one sense the Father, and the Son, but specially the Spirit.—The Scriptures attribute sanctification so often to God, as in 1 Thess. v: 23, that it is hardly necessary to set about collecting proofs. The *sense* in which He is the Author of the grace has been indicated, when we said that sanctification is but the continuance of the process of which regeneration is the initiation. If regeneration is supernatural, and by a mysterious, but real and almighty operation, more than the moral suasion of the truth, then sanctification is the result of the same kind of agency. The proper and immediate Agent is the Holy Ghost, as appears from Ps. li: 11; Jno. xvi: 8, 9; 2 Thess. ii: 13, &c., &c. This work is also attributed to the Son, in 1 Cor. i: 30, &c.; and this not merely in the sense of the Epistle to the Hebrews, (hagiadzo,) because His righteousness is there mentioned distinctly. Now, Christ is our Sanctifier, because He procures the benefit for us by His justifying righteousness; because He is now the God of Providence, and Dispenser of *means* to His people; and because, by His perpetual intercession, He procures and dispenses the influences of the Holy Ghost to us, who proceedeth from the Father and the Son. The Father is also spoken of as our Sanctifier; e. g., Jno. xvii: 17, because He stands in the Covenant of Grace as the Representative of the whole Trinity, and is the Devisor of the whole gracious means, and the Sender of the Son and Holy Ghost.

The means three.—While the agency in sanctification is supernatural, and the inscrutable indwelling and operation of the Holy Ghost are required, not only to initiate, but to continue growth in grace, yet He operates *through means* usually. And these means may be said comprehensively to be God's truth, His ordinances, and His providence. Such passages as Ps. xix: 1–7, plainly show that not only God's revealed word, but His truth seen through the works of nature, may sanctify the believer. But there is no reason to suppose that these truths of Natural Theology have any sanctifying agency, where they are not confirmed and enlarged by revelation. While truth has no adequate efficiency to sanctify by itself; yet it has a natural adaptation to be the means of sanctification in the hand of the Holy Ghost. For it is religious truth which presents all the *objective causes* of holy exercises and acts. That man's active powers may be holily exercised, an object of acting is needed, as well as a power of acting. Thus in natural vision. Now, religious truth presents that whole body of theological facts, of examples, of inducements, of external motives, by which the soul is incited to act. By the ordinances, we mean God's worship and sacraments; for the preaching of the word comes more properly under the former head. Worship is a sanctifying means, because the petitions there offered are the appointed medium for receiving grace; and because all the parts of worship give expression and exercise, and thus growth to holy principles. The sacraments are means whereby God symbolizes and seals to us the same truths expressed verbally in Revelation. They are, therefore, a kind of *acted* instead of spoken word, bringing to the soul, in a still more lively manner, those views of truth, which the Holy Ghost makes the occasion, or objective cause of holy exercises.

Last, God's providences, both prosperous and adverse, are powerful means of sanctification, because they *impress* religious truth, and force it home, by operating, with the word and Holy Ghost, on our natural emotions. See Ps. cxix: 71; Heb. xii: 10; Rom. ii: 4. But it should be remarked, that two things must concur for the sanctifying effect of Providences—the light of the *word* on the Providences to interpret them and give them their meaning, and the agency of the Holy Ghost inclining the heart to embrace the truths they serve to impress. *Mere suffering* has no holiness in it.

But the Word is the means in the other instruments—Looking back, we now see that there is a sense in which the *Revealed Word* is the uniform means of sanctification. It gives fulness and authority to Natural Theology. It guides, authorizes, and instructs our worship. It is symbolized in the sacraments. And it shines through the Providences, which do but illustrate it. So that the *Word* is the means, after all, in all other means. Jno. xvii: 17. Where the Word is not, there is no holiness.

Repentance and Faith mother graces.—Now, there are two graces, by whose intervention the efficacy of all these means of sanctification is always mediated to the soul. In other words, these two graces are the *media* through which all other means come in efficacious contact with the soul. They may therefore be called the *mother graces* of all the others. They are Repentance and Faith. It is only when an objective motive is apprehended by a full and active *belief*, that it becomes the occasional cause of any act of the soul. A hundred illustrations are at hand which show that this is universally true, and as true in man's carnal as in his spirtual life. *Belief* is the instigator of *action*. But in order that belief may instigate action, the object believed must be so related to the affections of the mind that there shall be appetency and repulsion. In the case of saving faith, that relation is *repentance*—i. e., the active affections of the regenerate soul as to holiness and sin, and the means for attaining the one and shunning the other. The student may now understand why God gives these graces such prominence in practical religion. They are the *media* for the exercise of all others. It follows, obviously, that repentance and faith must be in perpetual exercise during the whole progress of sanctification.

IV. Wesleyan Doctrine of Sinless perfection.—It has been a question long mooted between Evangelical Christians, and Pelagians, Socinians, Jesuits, and Wesleyans, whether sanctification is ever perfect in this life. The Pelagians and Socinians had an interest to assert that it may be; because such an opinion is necessary to establish their doctrine of justification by works; the Jesuits, in order to uphold the possibility of "merits of supererogation;" and the Wesleyans, to sustain the mystico-fanatical type of religion which they foster. As we have, practically, most to do with Wesleyans, on this point, and they reproduce the arguments of the others, let us address ourselves to their views. They assert that it is scriptural to expect some cases of perfect sanctification in this life; because, 1. The means provided by God are confessedly adequate to this complete result, should He please to bless them; and that it seems derogatory to His holy character when He assures us that "this is the will of God, even our sanctification," to suppose He will not hear and answer prayers for a blessing on those means, to *any extent* to which the faith of His children may urge those prayers. And 2. He has actually commanded us to pray for entire sanctification. Ps. cxix: 5, 6. Surely, He does not cause the seed of Jacob to seek Him in vain? 3. Not only has He thus encouraged, but commanded us to seek perfection. See Matt. v: 48. Unless obedience were possible, the command would be unjust. And 4. Perfect sanctification is nowhere connected with the death of the body by explicit texts. Indeed, the opinion that it must be, smacks of gnosticism, by representing that the seat of ungodliness is in the corporeal part, whereas, we know that the body is but the passive tool of the responsible spirit. As to the involuntary imperfections which every man not insanely vain must acknowledge, they are not properly sin; for God does not hold man guilty for those infirmities which are the inevitable results of his feeble and limited nature. Here the Wesleyan very manifestly implies a resort to the two Pelagian principles: that man is not responsible for his volitions unless they are free not only from co-action, but from certainty; and that moral quality resides only in acts of choice, so that a volition which is prevalently good is wholly good. Hence, those imperfections in saints, into which they fall through mere inattention, or sudden gust of temptation, contrary to their sincere bent and preference, incur no guilt whatever. Last: They claim actual cases in Scripture, as of Noah, Gen. vi: 9; Ps. cxix: 1; Job i: 1; David; Ps. xxxvii: 37; Zechariah; Luke i: 6; 1 Jno. iii: 9.

No Bible Saint perfect.—We reply: Perfection is only predicated of these saints, to show that they had Christian sincerity; that they had *all* the graces essential to the Christian character in actual exercise. As if to refute the idea of their sinless perfection, Scripture in every case records of them some fault, drunkenness of Noah, lying of Abraham, adultery and murder of David, unbelief of Zechariah, while Job concludes by saying, "I abhor myself, and repent in dust and ashes."

PELAGIAN FEATURES.—The most objectionable trait about this theory of perfect sanctification, is its affinities to Jesuitism and Pelagianism. These are several ways manifest. We saw that the old Pelagians, admitting that a complete obedience is requisite for a justification by works, claimed that the obedience which is formally in strict accordance with the statute, and prevalently right in purpose, is perfectly right. We saw, also, how they defended this view in consistency with their false ethicks. For they place the moral quality of acts in the volition, denying any certain efficiency to subjective (as to objective) motive. Now, volition is, of course, an entire and single act. The motives of a single volition may be complex; but the volition has a perfect unicity. Hence, if the morality of the act is wholly in the volition, and not in those complex motives, if the purpose is right, it is wholly right. But say, with us, that the volition derives its moral quality from the subjective motives, (which is the doctrine of common sense and the Bible,) and it follows that a volition may have a complex moral character; it may be prevalently right, and yet not perfectly right. And such is, obviously, the true character of the obedience of the regenerate. Now, note how the Wesleyans reproduce this Pelagian result, in their definition of what their perfect sanctification is. So, their reduction of those transgressions, to which the saint is hurried by sudden temptation, against his prevalent purpose, to the rank of mere infirmities, is sheer Pelagianism again.

There is also a dangerous affinity between these principles, and those horrible deductions from Pelagianism, made by the Jesuits, under the name of the art of "directing the attention," and venial sins. The origin is in the same speculations of those early heretics. The student may see an account and refutation in the unrivalled Provincial Letters of *Blaise Pascal.* It is not charged that the Wesleyans countenance any of these immoral and loathesome conclusions; but their premises are dangerous, as appears from these results.

REFUTATION.—To proceed: it is true that the Bible does not say, in so many words, that the soul's connexion with the present body is what makes sanctification necessarily incomplete. But it asserts the equivalent truth; as when it teaches us, that at death the saints are made perfect in holiness. It is no Gnosticism, but Scripture and common sense, to attribute some obstacles to entire sanctification to the continuance of the animal appetites in man. While God's omnipotence could overcome those obstacles, yet it is according to His manner of working, that He has seen fit to connect the final completeness of His work of grace in the soul, with this last change. Hence, when the Scripture shows that this is His plan, we are prepared to believe it so.

COMMAND NOT THE MEASURE OF ABILITY.—God commands us, says the Wesleyan, to "be perfect, even as our Father in heaven is perfect," whence its possibility must follow. I reply, True; God cannot require of us a physical impossibility. But our inability to keep God's whole law perfectly is not physical. It began in man's sin. By that sin we lost none of those faculties which, when Adam's will was right, enabled him to keep God's commands without sin. Our impotency is an "inability of will." Hence, it ought not to alter the demands of God's justice on His creatures. It is right in God to require perfection of us, and instruct us to seek it, because His own perfect nature can accept no less. Did God allow an inability of will to reduce His just claims on the creature, then the more sinful he became, the less guilt would attach to his shortcomings. A creature need only render himself *utterly* depraved to become completely irresponsible!

None sinless. Proofs.—But we argue, affirmatively, that sanctification is never complete in this life: a.) Because the Scripture says expressly that remains of sin exists in all living men. See, for instance, 1 Jno. i: 8; Jas. iii: 2; 1 Kings viii: 46; Prov. xx: 9. How can such assertions be evaded?

b.) I argue it, also, from the perpetual warfare, which the Scriptures say is going on between the flesh and the Spirit. See Rom. vii: 10, to end; Gal. v: 17, &c. This warfare, says the Bible, constitutes the Christian life. And it is of no avail for the Wesleyan to attempt evading this picture of Rom. vii, as the language of Paul convicted but not yet converted; for other similar passages remain, as Rom. viii: 7; Gal. v: 17; Phil. iii: 13; 1 Tim. vi: 12, &c., &c. Now, as long as the contest lasts, there must be an enemy. c.) The impossibility of a perfect obedience by ransomed men is clearly asserted in Scripture. Ps. cxix: 96; Acts xv: 10. It is true, that in the latter place the ceremonial law is more immediately in Peter's view; but the whole law is included, as is obvious from his scope; and if either could be perfectly kept, surely the ceremonial would be the easier. Last: The Lord's Prayer teaches all Christians to pray for the pardon of sin; a command which would not be universally appropriate if this doctrine were true. And if human experience can settle such a point, it is wholy on our side; for those who are obviously most advanced in sanctification, both among inspired and uninspired saints, are most emphatic in their confessions of shortcoming; while those who arrogantly claim perfect sanctification, usually discredit their pretentions sooner or later, by shameful falls. It is well that the Arminians have coupled the doctrine of falling from grace with this. Otherwise their own professors of complete sanctification would have refuted it with a regularity that would have been almost a fatality.

Now, the Almighty Spirit could subdue all sin, in a living saint, if He chose. Bible truths certainly present sufficient inducements to act as the angels, were our wills completely rectified. Why God does not choose, in any case, to work this complete result in this life, we cannot tell. "Even so, Father; for so it seemed good in Thy sight."

Tendencies of two theories compared.—The Wesleyans are accustomed to claim a more stimulating influence towards the pursuit of holiness, for their doctrine, and to reproach ours with paralysing results. They say, that with a rational agent, hope is a necessary element in the incentives to exertion; and that it is unnatural and impossible a man should attempt, in good earnest, what he thinks impossible to be achieved. But tell him that success, though arduous, is possible, and he will strain every nerve, and at least make great progress. They say, that Calvinists practically teach their converts not to aim high, and to make up their minds to low attainments in holiness. And hence the feeble and crippled character of the most of the religion exhibted in their Churches. We reply, that this calculation misrepresents the facts, and leaves out one of the most important of them. We do not forbid hope. We teach our people to hope for constant advances in holiness, by which they approach perfection continually, without actually reaching it in this life. The essential fact left out of the estimate is the invincible opposition of the new nature to all sin. The man renewed by God is incapable of contenting himself with any degree of sin. Here is the safeguard against the cessation of the struggle under the discouraging belief that the victory is only after death. If the indwelling enemy is thus as long-lived as the body, and immortal as long as the body lives, yet truce is impossible, because the hostility of the new-born soul to it is unquenchable. Does it follow from this view, that the life must be a life-long battle? I reply, even so; this is just what the Bible represents it to be.

We can retort on the Wesleyan, a juster objection to the working of his theory. By giving a false definition of what perfection is, it seems a much greater risk of inciting false pride, and dragging the conscience into a tolerance of what it calls guiltless, or venial infirmities.

LECTURE LV.

SYLLABUS.

SANCTIFICATION AND GOOD WORKS. (Continued.)

5. What constitutes an evangelical good work? Are any of the natural virtues of the unregenerate truly good works?
   Turrettin, que. 4. Dick, Lect. 76. Hill, Bk. v, ch. 4.
6. What the teaching of Scripture concerning human merit? What that of Rome concerning congruous and condign merit?
   Turrettin, que. 5. Hill, as above, § 2. Knapp, § 108, 125.
7. State and refute the Popish doctrine of *concilia* and works of supererogation.
   Th. Aquinas. Pars primna Secandae, que. 108. Sup., que. 13. Turrettin, Loc. xi, que. 4. Knapp, § 125. Hill, Bk. v, ch. 4, § 2.
8. What is the standard set up for the Christian's sanctification? Show the relation of Christ's example thereto.
   Dick, Lect. 75. Knapp, § 117. Chalmers' Theol. Inst., vol. ii, ch. 10.

V. A GOOD WORK, WHAT?—There is a gospel sense, in which the Scriptures speak of the acts and affections of Christians as *good works.* By this, it is not meant that they are perfect, that they could stand the strictness of the divine judgment, or that they are such as would receive the reward of eternal life under the Covenant of Works. Yet they are essentially different in moral quality from the actions of the unrenewed; and they do express a new and holy nature, as the principle from which they spring. There is also a certain sense in which

God approves and rewards them. How are these evangelical actions of the soul defined? We conceive that the Scripture characterizes them thus: 1. They must be the actions of a regenerate soul; because no other can have the dispositions to prompt such actions, and feel such motives as must concur. See Matt. xii: 33, or vii: 17, 18. 2. The action must be, in form, regulated by the revealed will of God; for He allows no other rule of right and wrong for the creature. No act of obedience to rules of mere human or ecclesiastical device can claim to be a good work; it is more probably an offence unto God. See Deut. iv: 2; Is. i: 12; xxix: 13; Matt. xv: 9. As God's will is to us practically the fountain of authority and obligation, it is obviously unreasonable that the debtor should decide for the creditor how much or what the former sees fit to pay. And moreover, such is the distance between God and man, and the darkness of the sinful mind of man, we are no suitable judges of what service is proper to render God. Man's duty is simply *what God requires of him.* Can we err in defining good works as the right performance of duty? 3. In order for that performance to be a good work, its prevalent motive or motives must be holy; and among these, especially, must be a respectful, righteous, and filial regard, either habitual or express, to the will of God commanding the act. See 1 Cor. x: 31; Rom. xi: 36, and xii: 1. No principle of common sense is plainer, than that the quality of the act depends on the quality of the intention. An act not intended to please God is, of course, not pleasing in His sight, no matter how conformed in outward shape, to His precepts.

A WORK NOT PERFECTLY HOLY MAY BE PREVALENTLY SO.—Such works are not perfectly, but prevalently holy. I have more than once remarked, that the motive of most of our volitions is a *complex* of several appetencies. Now, this habitual, or present filial regard to God's authority may be the prevalent motive of a given act; and yet it may be short of that fulness and strength which the perfect rectitude and goodness of the heavenly Father deserve. It may also be associated with other lower motives. Of these, some may be personal, and yet legitimate; as a reasonable subordinate regard to our own proper welfare. (The presence of such a motive in the *complex* would not make the volition sinful.) But other motives may, and nearly always do, mix with our regard for God, which are not only personal, but sinful: either because inordinate, or impure, as a craving for applause, or a desire to gratify a spiteful emulation. Remembering the views established in the last lecture, you will perceive that in such a case, the volition would be on the whole, right and pious, and still short of perfect rightness, or even involving, with its holiness, a taint of sin.

NO TRUE GOOD WORKS DONE BY UNCONVERTED OR HEATHEN.—But the best natural virtues of the heathen, and of all unconverted persons, come short of being gospel good works. See, for instance, Gen. vi: 5, and Rom. viii: 8. This truth recalls the assertion made of the total depravity of the race, and its grounds. It will be remembered that we did not deny the secular sincerity of the social virtues which many pagans and unrenewed men possess. Nor did we represent that their virtues were equal to the vices of the wicked. But what we mean is, that while nearer right than the open vices, they are still short of right; because they lack the essential motive, regard to God's revealed will and the claims of His love. "God is not in all their thoughts." Now, as our relation to God is the nearest and most supreme, an act which ignores this, however right it may be in other motives, still remains prevalently wrong in the sight of God. It does not reach the level of Bible holiness at all, though it may rise much nearer towards it than the sins of the reprobate. We do not, then, represent God as judging the amiable and decent transgressor equal to a monster of crime, nor condemning all secular virtues as spurious and worthless between man and man.

VI. MERIT. ROME'S DISTINCTION INTO CONGRUOUS AND CONDIGN.—The proposition, that even the good works of believers do not earn eternal life by their intrinsic merit, has been found very repugnant to human pride. Rome consequently seeks to evade the omission of it, by her distinction of *congruous* and *condign* merit. (*Meritum de congruo de condigno.*) The former she makes only a qualified kind of merit. It is that favourable quality which attaches to the good works done by the unrenewed man before conversion, which properly moves God to bestow on him the help of His grace. The condign merit is that which attaches to evangelical good works done after conversion, by the help of grace, which, by its proper value and force, entitles the believer to eternal life. True, Bellarmine and the Council of Trent, with the most of Romanists, say that eternal life comes to the obedient believer partly by the merit of his own works, and partly by virtue of Christ's promise and purchase; so that, were there no Saviour, human merit would come short of earning heaven. But they hold this essentially erroneous idea, that in the gracious works of the justified man there is a real and intrinsic merit of reward.

MERIT, STRICTLY. WHAT?—To clear up this matter, let us observe that the word *merit* is used in two senses, the one strict or proper, the other loose. Strictly speaking, a meritorious work is that to which, on account of its own intrinsic value and dignity, the reward is justly due. But when men use the word loosely, they include works deserving of approval, and works to which a reward is anyhow attached as a consequence. Now, in these latter senses, no one denies that the works of the regenerate are meritorious. They are praiseworthy, in a sense. They are followed by a recompense. But in the strict sense, of righteously bringing God in the doer's debt, by their own intrinsic moral value, no human works are meritorious.

HYPOTHETICAL MERIT.—Note further, that it is wholly another thing to do works which may fall within the terms of some covenant of promise, which God may have graciously bestowed. If the king is pleased, in his undeserved kindness, to promise the inheritance for the doing of some little service utterly inadequate to the reward, and if any creature complies with the terms exactly, then the king is, of course, bound to give what he has engaged. But he is bound by fidelity to himself, not by justice to the service rendered; for that, intrinsically, is inadequate.

STRICTLY, NO CREATURE CAN MERIT.—In the strict sense, then, no work of man brings God in the doer's debt, to reward him. The work which is worthy of this must have the following traits: It must be one which was not already owed to God. See Luke xvii: 10. It must be done in the man's own strength; for if he only does it by the strength of Christ, he cannot take to himself the credit of it. "It is not he that liveth, but Christ that liveth in him." It must be perfectly and completely right; for if stained with defect, it cannot merit. Last, it must be of sufficient importance to bear some equitable ratio to the amount of reward. One would not expect a large sum of money as wages for the momentary act of handing a draught of water, however cheerfully done. Now, it is plain at the first glance, that no work of man to God can bring Him, by its own intrinsic merit, under an obligation to reward. All our works are owed to God; if all were done, we should only "have done what was our duty to do." No right work is done in our own mere strength. None are perfect. There is no equality between the service of a fleeting life and an inheritance of eternal glory.

Natural works have no merit of congruity.—We may argue, farther, that the congruous merit of the Papist is imaginary, because nothing the unbeliever does can please God: "Without faith it is impossible to please Him." And if grace were the rewards of works done without it, then it would be no more grace. The whole Scripture holds forth the truth that Christ bestows that grace, not because of any merit, but in spite of utter unworthiness. "When we were *without strength*, in due time Christ died *for the ungodly*."

Our works under grace have no merit of condignity.—So, the merit of condignity claimed for good works done after conversion is shown to be groundless by what has been already said. Had Adam or Gabriel rendered, in his own strength, perfect works to God, apart from a covenant of promise, he could not have merited eternal life by temporary obedience. How much less can the Christian, when his works are not perfect, and are only rendered in a strength not his own? To this agree all the Scriptures. Rom. vi: 23; v: 15–18; Eph. ii: 8; 2 Tim. i: 9; Tit. iii: 5, *et passim*. Turrettin sustains this view farther, by showing that the gracious acts, for which Romanists claim merit of condignity, and the eternal life attached to them, are always spoken of as the Father's gifts; that they are always spoken of as the Redeemer's purchase; that the Christians who do them are represented in the Bible as acknowledging themselves "unprofitable servants;" and that they always confess the unworthiness of their best works, especially in view of the everlasting reward. The Scriptures which might be collected under these heads would present an overwhelming array of proof.

It does not follow that because Sin merits, our Works do.—But carnal men strongly resent this conclusion; and urge, as though it were a self-evident refutation, that as sin and good works are in antithesis, we cannot hold that man's sin carries a true and essential desert of punishment, and deny that his good work carries an equal desert of reward. To affix the one and refuse the other, they exclaim, would be a flagrant injustice. I reply: Between human rulers and ruled, it would. But they forget here the prime fact, that God is the Maker and sovereign Proprietor of men. The property may be delinquent towards its sovereign Owner, but it cannot make the Owner delinquent to it. If it fails in due service, it injures the rights of its

Owner: if it renders the service, it only satisfies those rights; nothing more. But here a certain concession should be made. While a creature's perfect obedience is not meritorious of any claim of reward upon his Lord, in the strict sense, there is a relation of moral propriety between such obedience and reward. We saw that it appeared unreasonable to claim everlasting reward for temporal service. But does not a perfect temporal service deserve of God temporal reward? I would say, in a certain sense, Yes; supposing the creature in a state of innocency and harmony with his Lord. That is, it would be inconsistent with God's rectitude and benevolence, to begin to visit on this innocent creature the evils due to sin, before he transgressed. God would not infringe, by any suffering or wrath, that natural blessedness, with which His own holiness and goodness always leads Him to endow the state of innocency. But here the obligation is to God's own perfections, rather than to the creature's merit.

Is the Covenant of Works revoked on God's part?—We may note, in this connexion, the question whether the offer in the Covenant of Works has been retracted by God, since Adam broke it? Those who say it is retracted, rely on such statements as Heb. viii: 9; Gal. ii: 21. Those who deny, advance such words as those of Christ to the young ruler: "If thou wilt enter into life, keep the commandments." Matt. xix: 17. The debate might seem a very frivolous one, in view of the fact that no mere man is morally able to keep the commandments of God. But it suggests these remarks, which are of value to set forth these subjects. Since God was not bound to promise the additional and everlasting rewards of an adoption of life, He might retract it after the creature has failed to comply, without any injustice, (as He might, without injustice, have refrained from offering it.) But second: while the temporary obedience of a holy creature does not, of itself, earn everlasting life, it was every way worthy of God's holiness and benevolence, to promise it to Adam and the elect angels on those terms. Third: man has made himself utterly incapable of complying with the terms; yet compliance is rendered, in the person of the second Adam his Substitute: and eternal life actually earned for us in that way; so that, although man failed, the Covenant of Works, in that sense, did not. Hence, it would appear from the Scriptures, that God sees fit, for the glory of His own grace, to leave that act of His condescension unrevoked, although knowing perfectly well that no mere man would ever avail himself of it; while superadding that other act of His greater condescension and grace, the gospel.

In what sense are believer's works rewarded?—It only remains, on this head, to explain the relation between the good works of the justified believer and his heavenly reward. It is explained by the distinction between an intrinsic and original merit of reward, and the hypothetical merit granted by promise. If the slave fulfils his master's orders, he does not bring the latter in his debt. "He is an unprofitable servant; he has only done what was his duty to do." But if the master chooses, in mere generosity, to promise freedom and an inheritance of a thousand talents for some slight service, cheerfully performed, then the service must be followed by the reward. The master owes it not to the intrinsic value of the slave's acts, (the actual pecuniary addition made thereby to the master's wealth may be little or nothing,) but to his own word. Now, in this sense, the blessings of heaven bear the relation of a "free reward" to the believer's service. It contributes nothing esssential to earning the inheritance; in that point of view it is as wholly gratuitous to the believer as though he had been all the time asleep. The essential merit that earned it is Christ's. Yet it is related to the loving obedience of the believer, as appointed consequence. Thus it appears how all the defects in his evangelical obedience (defects which, were he under a legal covenant, would procure the curse, and not blessing,) are covered by the Saviour's righteousnesss; so that through Him the inadequate works receive a recompense. Moreover, it is clearly taught that God has seen fit, in apportioning degrees of blessedness to different justified persons, to measure them by the amount of their good works. See Matt. xvi: 27; 1 Cor. iii: 8, of which Turrettin remarks, that the reward is "*acccording to*," but not "*on account of*" the works. See, also, 2 Cor. ix: 6; Luke xix: 17, 18. Not only the sovereignty, but the wisdom and righteousness of a gracious God are seen in this arrangement. Thus a rational motive is applied to educe diligent obedience. Thus it is evinced that the gospel is not a ministration of indolence or disobedience; and God's verdicts in Christ not inconsistent with natural justice. It is thus, because the grace given on earth is a preparation of the soul for more grace in heaven. And, last, good works are the only practical and valid test of the genuineness of that faith by which believers receive the perfect merits of Christ. This last fact, especially, makes it proper that the "free reward" shall be bestowed "according to their works;" and explains a multitude of passages, which seem to make the reward depend on the works.

VII. Works of Supererogation. Source of heresy.—It may be said that the Romish Church is indebted to the age of Thomas Aquinas, and most probably to him, for the final theory of "works of supererogation." He found everywhere among the Fathers, the distinction between Christ's *praecepta* and *concilia.* This distinction, pretending to find its grounds in certain texts of the New Testament, more probably had its origin in a desire to imitate the exoteric and esoteric, the higher and lower morals of the New Platonists. The instances of *Concilia* usually quoted are those of Matt. xix: 12 and 21; 1 Cor. vii: 38–40; Acts xxi: 23, 24, and are usually grouped by them under the three virtues of voluntary poverty, perpetual chastity, and regular obedience. The Church had long held, that while every one must strive to obey all the precepts of Christ, on pain of damnation, he is not expressly bound to comply with the "councils of perfection." If he sees fit to omit them, he incurs no wrath. They are but recommendations. Yet, if his devoted spirit impels him to keep them for the glory of God, he thereby earns supererogatory merit, superfluous to his own justification. Aquinas now proceeds to build on this foundation thus: One man can work a righteousness, either penal or supererogatory, so that its imputation to his brother may take place. What else, he urges, is the meaning of Gal. vi: 2: "Bear ye one anothers' burdens," &c? And among men, one man's generous efforts are permitted in a thousand ways to avail for another, as in suretyships. "But with God, love avails for more than with men." Yea, a less penance is a satisfaction for a brother's guilt than would be requisite for one's own, in the case of an equal sin. Because the purer disinterestedness displayed in atoning for the penitential guilt of a brother renders it more amiable in the sight of God, and so, more expiatory. If a sinning believer hits himself twenty blows with his whip on his bare shoulders, it may be that a selfish fear of purgatory is a large part of his motive; and God will subtract from the merit of the act accordingly. But when he does it for his brother's sin, it is pure, disinterested love and zeal for God's honour, the twenty blows will count for more.

IMPUTATION OF SUPEROGATORY MERIT, AND INDULGENCE THEREBY, OF PENITENTIAL GUILT.—The philosopher then resorts to the doctrine of the unity of the Church, and the communion of saints in each other's graces and sufferings, to show that the merit of these supererogatory services and sufferings is imputed to others. There is, in the holy Catholic Church then, a treasury to which all this spare merit flows. As the priesthood holds the power of the keys, they of course are the proper persons to dispense and apply it. But as the unity of the Church is especially represented in its earthly head, the Pope, he especially is the proper person to have charge of the treasury. And this is the way *indulgentia* is procured; the Pope imputes some of this supererogatory merit of works and penance out of the Church-treasure, whence the remission to the culprit of the penitential and purgatorial satisfaction due from him for sin. But his confession, absolution, and contrition are necessary; otherwise indulgence does no good; because without these exercises the man's own personal penance would have done no good. Last, this indulgence may properly be given by the Church, in return for money, provided it be directed to a holy use, as repairing churches, building monasteries, &c. (He forgot our Saviour's words: "Freely ye have received, freely give.")

DISTINCTION OF COUNSELS OF PERFECTION REFUTED.—The overthrow of all this artificial structure is very easy for the Protestant. We utterly deny the distinction of the pretended "councils of perfection," from the precepts, as wicked and senseless. It is impossible that it can hold; because we are told that the precepts go to this extent, viz: requiring us to love God with all the soul, and heart, and mind, strength. If, then, any Christian has indeed found out that his circumstances are such, the refraining from a given act, before and elsewhere indifferent, has become necessary to Christ's highest glory: then for Him, it is obligatory, and no longer optional. "To him that knoweth to do good, and doeth it not, to him it is sin." Again: how can he have superfluity who lacks enough for himself? But all lack righteousness for their own justification; for "in many things we offend all." So, the Scriptures utterly repudiate the notion that the righteousness of one man is imputable to another. Christian fellowship carries no such result. It was necessary (for reasons unfolded in the discussion of the Mediator), that God should effectuate the miracle of the hypostatic union, in order to make a Person, whose merit was imputable. "None of them can by any means redeem his brother, or give to God a ransom for him." Nor does the Protestant recognize the existence of that penitential guilt, which is professed to be remitted by the indulgence."

VIII. Standard of Sanctification, Law, and Jesus' Example.—The standard set for the believer's sanctification is the character of God as expressed in His preceptive law. This rule is perfect, and should be sufficient for our guidance. But God, in condescension to our weak and corporeal nature, has also given us an example, in the life of the Redeemer. And this was a subsidiary, yet important object of His mission. See 1 Pet. ii: 21. (We recognize in its proper place, this prophetic function of the Mediator, which the Socinian makes the sole one.) The advantage of having the holy law teaching by example is obvious. Man is notoriously an imitative creature. God would fain avail Himself of this powerful lever of education for his moral culture. Example is also superior in perspicuity and interest, possessing all the advantage over precept, which illustration has over abstract statement. If we inspect the example of Christ, we shall find that it has been adjusted to its purpose with a skill and wisdom only inferior to that displayed in His atoning offices. Examining first the conditions of an effective example, we find that they all concur in Christ. It is desirable that our exemplar be human; for though holiness in God and in angels is, in principle, identical with man's; yet in detail it is too different to be a guide. Yet, while it is so desirable that the example be human, it must be perfect; for fallible man would be too sure to imitate defects, on an exaggerated scale. Man is naturally out of harmony with holiness, too far to be allured by its example; he would rather be alienated and angered by it. Hence, the exemplar must begin by putting forth a regenerating and reconciling agency. Last: it is exceedingly desirous that the exemplar should also be an object of warm affection; because we notice that the imitative instinct always acts far most strongly towards one beloved. But Christ is made by His work the prime object of the believer's love.

Value of Christ's Example.—The value of Christ's example may be also illustrated in the following particulars: It verifies for us the conception of holiness, as generally displayed in God. That conception must lack definiteness, until we see it embodied in this "Image of the invisible God," who is "the brightness of His glory, and the express image of His person." Next, Christ has illustrated the duties of all ages and stations; for the divine wisdom collected into His brief life all grades, making Him show us a perfect child, youth, man, son, friend, teacher, subject, ruler, king, hero, and sufferer. Again, Christ teaches us how common duties are exalted, when performed from an elevated motive; for He was earning for His Church infinite blessedness, and for His Father eternal glory, when fulfilling the humble tasks of a peasant and mechanic. And last, in His death especially, He illustrated those duties which are at once hardest and most essential, because attaching to the most critical emergencies of our being, the duties of forgiveness under wrong, patience and fortitude under anguish, and faith and courage in the hour of death.

LECTURE LVI.

SYLLABUS.

PERSEVERANCE OF SAINTS.

1. State the doctrine of Pelagians, Papists, Arminians, and Calvinists hereupon.
Conf. of Faith, ch. xvii. Turrettin, Loc. xv, que. 61, § 1-8.
2. Prove the doctrine. 1. From God's election. 2. From the Covenant of Grace. 3. From the believer's union to Christ and participation in His merit and intercession. 4. From the indwelling of the seed and Spirit.
Turrettin, as above, § 8 to 28. Dick. Lect. 79. Ridgeley, que. 79.
3. Present any other direct Scripture proofs in your power.
Ridgeley, que. 79. Bible.
4. Reconcile objections; and especially those founded on Scripture passages, as Ezek. xviii: 24; Heb. vi. 4, &c.; x: 29 and 38; iii: 12; 1 Cor. ix: 27; 2 Pet. ii: 20; Rom. xiv: 15, &c.
Turrettin, as above, § 29 to end. Dick, Lect. 79. Ridgeley, que. 79, § iv. Sampson on Hebrews. Watson's Theol. Institutes, ch. xxv.
5. What is the moral tendency of the doctrine?
Same authorities.

This Doctrine encouraging to preacher.—Scripture and experience concur in imputing to man, in his natural state, an obduracy and deadness of heart, which would leave the preacher of the gospel to labour in despair, were it not for his dependence in the sovereign grace of God. But when he believes firmly in the eternal covenant of grace, whereby God has promised His Son a chosen seed, not for any merit which He sees in sinners, and to call and perfect this seed by His efficacious grace, there is ground laid for cheerful exertions. The laborious Christian then looks upon his own efforts for sinners, as one of the preordained steps in this plan of mercy, upon his prayers as taught him by the Holy Ghost, and therefore surely destined to an answer; and upon the visible success of his labours, as the evidence that that God, whose plans are immutable, and who always perfects what He undertakes, is working. He is joyfully hopeful concerning the final triumph of those who are born unto God by His instrumentality, because He sees an eternal purpose and unchangeable love engaged for their upholding. He can cheerfully leave them, though surrounded with the snares of the world; because He leaves the Chief Shepherd with them, who will easily raise up other instruments and provide other means for their guidance.

St. Paul found it so.—In this spirit the Apostle says, Phil. i: 6, that from the first day of their conversion till now, his prayers for his Philippian converts had always been offered in joy, because he was confident that the Redeemer, who had begun the blessed work in them, by their regeneration, faith, and repentance, would continue that work of sanctification, till it was perfected at the second coming of Jesus Christ, in the resurrection of their bodies and their complete glorification. This work was begun in them by God, not by their own free choice, independent of grace; for that choice always would have been, most freely and heartily, to choose sin. It must have been begun by

God from deliberate design; for God worketh all things after the council of His own will. That design and purpose of mercy was not founded on any thing good in them, but on God's unchangeable mercy; and therefore it would not be changed by any of their faults, but the unchanging God would carry it out to perfection.

Doctrine to be discussed fairly.—We have here the Apostle's plain expression of his belief in the perseverance of the truly regenerate, in a state of repentance, unto the end. In attempting the discussion of this doctrine, let us exercise the spirit of humility and candour, laying aside prejudice, avoiding all abuses or perversions of God's truth, and striving to apprehend it just as He has presented it. I would at the outset guard the truth from abuse, and from opposition by defining:

Perseverance defined.—That this perseverance in a state of grace is not innate and necessary, with the new-born nature, but gracious. It does not proceed from anything in the interior state of the regenerate soul, but wholly from God's purpose of mercy towards that soul. Security from fall is the attribute of none but God. Adam in Paradise was capable of apostasy. Holy angels were capable of apostasy; for many of them fell; and doubtless the angels and glorified saints in heaven owe their infallibility, not to their own strength, but to God's unchanging grace working in them. Much more would the Christian, in his imperfection, be liable to fall.

Not compatible with sin.—This perseverance does not imply that a man may be living in habitual and purposed sin, and yet be in a justified state. because he who is once justified cannot come into condemnation. We heartily join in everything which can be said against so odious a doctrine. It is impossible, because the living in such a state of sin proves that the man never was, and is not now, in a justified state, whatever may be his names and boasts.

Our doctrine does not teach that mary will not be finally lost, who are connected with the visible Church outwardly, and whom the Scriptures may call believers in a certain sense, because they have a temporary or historical faith, like that of Simon Magus. But those who have once had in them the true principle of spiritual life, never lose it.

Nor do we teach that all Christians have equal spiritual vitality at all times; but they may fall into partial errors of doctrine, coldness and sin, which may for a time wholly interrupt their comfort in religion, and overcloud their evidences of a gracious state. Yet is the root of the matter there.

Definition of Westminster Assembly.—It is simply this: that "They whom God hath accepted in His Beloved, and effectually called and sanctified by His Spirit, can neither totally nor finally fall away from the state of grace; but shall certainly persevere therein to the end, and be eternally saved."

As I have taken the definition of the doctrine from the Confession of Faith. I cannot do better than to take my method of discussion from the same source. Under each head many Scriptures will come in, more naturally and easily, so that the support they give to the doctrine will be more manifest, and more clearly understood.

I. Argued from Election.—"The perseverance of the saints depends upon *the immutability of the decree of election.*" When any one is born again of the Holy Ghost and justified in Christ, it is because God had formed, from eternity, the unchangeable purpose to save that soul. The work of grace in it is the mere carrying out of that unchangeable purpose. As the plan is unchangeable, so must be its execution, when that execution is in the hands of the Almighty. How can argument be more direct? Heb. vi: 17, 18. God, willing more abundantly to shew unto the heirs of promise the *immutability of His counsel,* confirmed it by an oath, &c. See also Matt. xxiv: 24; 2 Tim. ii: 19; Rom. viii: 29; viii: 33, &c.

Might be argued from certain Foreknowledge.—And even though this unchangeable election were conditional, and made in foresight of the believer's faith and obedience, yet if it has any *certainty* it must imply that the believer shall *certainly* be kept from finally falling away. If it even rose no higher than simple foreknowledge, yet a foreknowledge which means anything, must be certain. If God does not *certainly* know whether a given event shall take place or not, then He does not foreknow it at all. But if He certainly knows that it shall occur, the occurrence of that event must be without failure: otherwise God's foreknowledge would be false! So that unless we impiously strip God of His foreknowledge, (to say nothing of His having an all-wise, almighty, and immutable *plan,*) we must suppose that the perseverance in a gracious state, of all those whom He *foresees* will be finally saved, is so far necessary that they cannot finally fall away.

II. Argued from Freedom of Electing Love. No unforeseen provocation of God arises.—"The perseverance of believers follows from the free and unchangeable love of God the Father," which was the ground of their being chosen unto salvation. The Scriptures make it plain that the reason why God ever determined to save any man was not His seeing in him anything good, attractive or extenuating, but something without, known to His wisdom, which was to God a good and wise reason to bestow His eternal love on that particular sinner. Rom. ix: 11 and 16. This sovereign and unmerited love is the cause of the believer's effectual calling. Jer. xxxi: 3; Rom. viii: 30. Now, as the cause is unchangeable, the effect will be unchangeable. That effect is, the constant communication of grace to the believer in whom God hath begun a good work. God was not induced to bestow His renewing grace in the first instance, by anything which He saw, meritorious or attractive, in the repenting sinner; and therefore the subsequent absence of everything good in him would be no new motive to God for withdrawing His grace. When He first bestowed that grace, He knew that the sinner on whom He bestowed it was totally depraved, and wholly and only hateful in himself to the divine holiness; and therefore no new instance of ingratitude or unfaithfulness, of which the sinner may become guilty after his conversion, can be any provocation to God, to change His mind, and wholly withdraw His sustaining grace. God knew all this ingratitude before. He will chastise it, by temporarily withdrawing His Holy Ghost, or His providential mercies; but if He has not intended from the first to bear with it, and to forgive it in Christ, He would not have called the sinner by His grace at first. In a word, the causes for which God determined to bestow His electing love on the sinner are *wholly* in God, and not at all in the believer; and hence, nothing in the believer's heart or conduct can finally change that purpose of love. Is. liv: 10; Rom. xi: 29. Compare carefully Rom. v: 8–10; viii: 32, with whole scope of Rom. viii: 28–end. This illustrious passage is but an argument for our proposition: "What shall separate us from the love of Christ?"

III. Argued from Christ's merit.—This doctrine depends "upon the efficacy of the merit and intercession of Jesus Christ." As all Christians agree, the sole ground of the acceptance of believers is the justifying righteousness of Jesus Christ. The objects of God's eternal love were "chosen *in Christ,* before the foundation of the world," "accepted in the Beloved," and made the recipients of saving blessings, on accouut of what Christ does in their stead. Now, this ground of justification, this atonement for sin, this motive for the bestowal of divine love, is *perfect.* Christ's atonement surmounts the demerit of all possible sin or ingratitude. His righteousness is a complete price to purchase the sinner's pardon and acceptance. See Heb. ix: 12; x: 12 and 14; Jno. v: 24. See with what splendid assurance and boldness Paul argues from this ground. Rom. viii: 33 and 34. Can one who has been fully justified in Christ, whose sins have been all blotted out, irrespective of their heinousness, by the perfect and efficacious price paid by Jesus Christ, become again *un*justified, and fall under condemnation without a dishonour done to Christ's righteousness?

From Christ's Intercession.—So likewise the prevalent and perpetual intercession of Christ, founded on the perfect merit of His work, ensures the salvation of all for whom He has once undertaken. We are assured that the Father heareth Him always, when He speaks as the Mediator of His people. Jno. xi: 42. Now, after He has uttered for His believing people—for *all* who should believe Him through the gospel of His apostles—such prayers as those of Jno. xvii: 20, &c., 24, must not the answer of this request, or, in other words, the certain final redemption of all who ever shared His intercession, be as sure as the truth of God? But if any man is ever justified, that man has shared the intercession of Christ; for it was only through this that He was first accepted. Heb. vii: 25.

IV. Argued from the indwelling of the Holy Ghost.—The perseverance of the saints proceeds "from the abiding of the Spirit, and of the seed of God within them." Every Christian, at the hour he believes, is so united to Christ, that he partakes of His indwelling Spirit. This union is a permanent one. The moving cause for instituting it, God's free and eternal love, is a permanent and unchangeable cause. The indwelling of the Spirit promised to believers is a permanent and abiding gift. 1 Jno. ii: 27.

From the Seal and Earnest.—His regenerating operations are spoken of as a "seal," and an "earnest" of our redemption. Eph. i: 13, 14; 2 Cor. i: 22. The use of a seal is to ratify a covenant, and make the fulfilment of it certain to both parties. An "earnest" (arrhabon) is a small portion of the thing covenanted, given in advance, as a pledge of the certain intention to bestow the whole, at the promised time. Thus, he who promised to give a sum of money for some possession, at some appointed future day, gave a small sum in advance, when the covenant was formed, as a pledge for the rest. So the renewing of the Holy Ghost is, to every believer who has enjoyed it, a seal, impressing the image of Christ on the wax of his softened heart, closing and certifying the engagement of God's love, to redeem the soul. It is the earnest, or advance, made to the soul, to engage God to the final bestowal of complete holiness and glory. Unless the final perseverance of believers is certain, it could be no pledge nor seal. The inference is as simple and as strong as words can express, that he who has once enjoyed this seal and earnest is thereby certified that God will continue to give the Holy Ghost until the end.

Work of Holy Ghost not fickle.—It is a most low and unworthy estimate of the wisdom of the Holy Ghost and of His work in the heart, to suppose that He will begin the work now, and presently desert it; that the vital spark of heavenly birth is an *ignis fatuus*, burning for a short season, and then expiring in utter darkness; that the spiritual life communicated in the new birth, is a sort of spasmodic or galvanic vitality, giving the outward appearance of life in the dead soul, and then dying. Not such is the seed of God within us. Jno. v: 24. "Verily, verily I say unto you: He that heareth My word, and believeth on Him that sent Me, *hath* everlasting life." John iii: 15; vi: 54. The principle then implanted, is a never-dying principle. In every believer an *eternal* spiritual life is begun. If all did not persevere in holiness, there would be some in whom there was a true spiritual life, but not everlasting. The promise would not be true. See also 1 John iii: 9; 1 Peter i: 23.

V. Argued from the Covenant of Grace.—Our doctrine follows, also, "from the nature of the Covenant of Grace." God did, from eternity, make with His Son a gracious covenant, engaging, in return for the Son's humiliation, to give Him the souls of all who were chosen in Him before the foundation of the world, "that they should be holy and without blame before Him in love." This covenant is an everlasting one. Jer. xxxii: 40. It is an unchangeable covenant. Ps. lxxxix; 34, (spoken of the second David.) The sole condition of the covenant is Christ's work for His chosen people. Heb. x: 14. Now, the administration of such a covenant most plainly requires that there shall be no uncertainty in its results. If one of those whose sins Christ bore, ever fell into final condemnation, the contract would be proved temporary, changeable, and false.

This Covenant pledges grace to persevere.—On the eternal certainty of this covenant is founded the faithfulness of the gospel offer, *pledging God* to every sinner who believes and repents, that he shall through Christ receive saving grace; *and among those gracious influences thus pledged with eternal truth to the believer, from the moment he truly believes, is persevering grace.* Jer. xxxii: 40; (proved to be the gospel pledge by Heb. viii: 10;) Is. liv: 10; Hos. ii: 19 and 20; 1 Thess. v: 23, 24; Jno. x: 27; 1 Pet. i: 5; Rom, viii: end. These are a few from the multitude of promises, assuring us of our final safety from every possible influence, when once we are truly *in Christ.*

Evasions.—I am well aware that the force of these and all similar passages has been met, by asserting that in all gospel promises there is a condition implied, viz: That they shall be fulfilled, *provided the be-*

liever does not backslide, on his part, from his gospel privileges. But is this *all* which these seemingly precious words mean? Then they mean *nothing.* To him who knows his own heart, what is that promise of security worth, which offers him no certainty to secure him against his own weakness? All "his sufficiency is of God." Rom. vii: 21. If his enjoyment of the promised grace is suspended upon his own perseverance in cleaving to it, then his apostasy is not a thing possible, or probable, but *certain.* There is no hope in the gospel. And when such a condition is thrust into such a promise as that of Jno. x: 27: "None shall pluck them out of My hand," provided they do not *choose* to let themselves be plucked away; are we to suppose that Christ did not know that common Bible truth, that the only way any spiritual danger can assail any soul successfully, is by *persuasion* : that unless the adversary can get the consent of the believer's free will, he cannot harm him? Was it not thus that Adam was ruined? Is there any other way by which a soul *can* be plucked away from his God? Surely Jesus knew this; and if this supposed condition is to be understood, then this precious promise would be but a worthless and pompous truism. "Your souls shall never be destroyed, unless in a given way," and that way the only and the common way in which souls are ever destroyed. "You shall never fall, as long as you stand up."

Jer. xxxii: 40 conclusive.—But to thoroughly close the whole argument, we have only to remark, that the promise in Jer. xxxii: 40, which is most absolutely proved by Heb. viii: 10, &c., to be the gospel covenant, most expressly engages God to preserve believers from this very thing—their own backsliding. Not only does He engage that He will not depart from them, but "He will put His fear in their hearts, so that they shall not depart from Him."

VI. Independent arguments for perseverance.—Other arguments exist, from independent assertions of Scripture. It used to be common with the Calvinistic divines to advance the joy of the angels over repenting sinners, as a proof of their perseverance. The idea was, that if their state in grace were mutable, these wise and grand creatures would not have attached so much importance to it. To me this reasoning always appeared inconclusive. We have seen good Christians sometimes rejoicing very sincerely over what turned out to be a spurious conversion, because they supposed it to be genuine. Now, it does not appear that the angels are always infallible in their judgments of appearances, any more than we, although far wiser. Besides, if some true converts did fall from grace, the angels would still know that those who finally reach heaven must be sought among the sinners who experience conversion on earth. A much more conclusive argument may be drawn from those passages, which explain the apostasy of seeming converts, in consistency with the perseverance of true saints. One of these is found in 2 Pet. ii: 22. Here the apostate professor is an unclean animal, only outwardly cleansed; a "sow that was washed;" its nature is not turned into a lamb; and this is the explanation of its return to the mire. A still stronger one is 1 Jno. ii: 19. Here the departure of apostates is explained by the fact, that their union to Christ and His people never was real; because had it been real they "no doubt would have continued with us;" and their apostasy was permissively designed by God to "manifest" the fact that they never had been true believers.

Another proof presents itself in the parable of the sower. Matt. xiii: 6 and 21. The stony-ground-hearer withers because he "hath no root in himself." Still another may be found in 2 Tim. ii: 19. There the Apostle, referring to such temporary professors as Hymeneus and Philetus, explains that their apostasy implied no uncertainty as to the constitution of the body of Christ's redeemed, because God knew all the time who were truly His; and the foundation of His purpose concerning their salvation stood immovable amidst all the changes and apostasies which startle blind men.

Backslidings explained.—With reference to all objections founded on the cases of Solomon, David, Peter, Judas and such like, I reply briefly, that the explanation is either that of John's first Epistle 2: 19, that they never had true grace to lose, or else, the history contains proof that their apostasy was neither total nor final, though grievous. In Peter's case, Christ says, Luke xxii: 32, that "Satan desired to sift him like wheat, but He prayed for him *that his faith should not fail.*" Peter's faith, therefore, did not fail, though his duty did. So the prayer of David, Ps. li: 11, 12, shows that he was a true saint before and after his sin. That the principle of true grace can exist, and can be for a time so foully obscured, as in David's case, is indeed a startling and alarming truth. Yet does not the experience of society, and of our own hearts substantiate the view?

Texts advanced in objection.—Your commentaries and other text books will give you those detailed explanations which you need, of the texts advanced by Arminians against our doctrine. I may say that the two *loca palmaria* on which they chiefly rely are Heb. vi: 4–6, and Ezek. xviii: 24–29.

Heb. vi: 4.—Of the first we may briefly remark, that it does not appear the spiritual endowments there described of the apostate, amount to a true state of grace. A detailed criticism and comparison of the traits, being enlightened, &c., will show that according to the usage of the Scriptures they describe, not a regenerate state, but one of deep conviction and concern, great privilege, with perhaps charisms of tongues or healings. The examplars are to be found in such men as Balaam, Simon Magus, and Demas. And this is most consistent with the Apostle's scope. The terms here, if meant to describe ordinary saving conversion, would at least be most singular and unusual. They are evidently vague, and intentionally so: because God does not care to enable us to decide exactly how near we may go to the impassable line in grieving His Spirit, and yet be forgiven.

Ezek. xviii: 24, &c.—With reference to the passage from Ezekiel, it could only be claimed by Arminians, in virtue of great inattention to the prophet's object in the passage. Ezekiel's mission was to call Israel (especially the people in captivity in Mesopotamia) to repentance. He points to their calamities and the destruction of the larger part of their nation as proof of their great guilt. They attempt to evade his charge by pleading that "their teeth were set on edge, because their father's had eaten sour grapes." God answers, in the early part of the chapter, that this explanation of their calamities is untenable; because (while much of His providence over men does visit the father's sins upon sinful children) the guilt of sinful fathers is never, in His theocracy, and under according to the covenant of Horeb, visited on righteous children. He then goes farther and reminds them that not only did He always restore prosperity, in the theocracy, as soon as an obedient generation succeeded a rebellious one; but even more, as soon as a rebellious man truly repented, he was forgiven; just as when a righteous man apostatizes, he is punished. It would appear, therefore, that the thing of which the prophet is speaking is not a state of grace at all; but the outward, formal, and civic decency of a citizen of the theocracy; and that the punishments into which such a man fell on lapsing into rebellion were temporal calamities. But farther, the whole passage is hypothetical. It merely supposes a pair of cases. If the transgressor repents, he shall be forgiven. Does the prophet mean to teach that any do savingly repent, in whom God does not purpose to work repentance? Let ch. xxxvi: 26, 27, and xxxvii: 1–10, answer. So, does He mean to teach that any actually fall into rebellion, who share the grace of God? Let ch. xxxvi: 27, &c., again answer.

General answer.—There is one general element of objection in all these texts; that when God warns the righteous, the believer, &c., against the dangers of apostasy; or when He stimulates Him to zeal in holy living by the thought of those dangers, God thereby clearly implies that blievers may apostatise. The answer is: Naturally speaking, *so he may*. The certainty that he will not arises, not from the strength of a regenerated heart, but from God's secret, unchangeable *purpose* concerning the believer; which purpose He executes towards, and in him, by moral means consitent with the creature's free agency. Among these appropriate motives are these very warnings of dangers and wholesome fears about apostasy. Therefore God's application of these motives to the regenerate free agent, proves not at all that it is God's secret purpose to let him apostatise. They are a part of that plan by which God intends to ensure that he shall not. Compare carefully Acts xxvii: vs. 22, 23, 24, 25, with 31.

Practical results sanctifying.—In conclusion, we believe that all the supposed licentious results of the doctrine of perseverance, result from misapprehension; and that its true tendencies are eminently encouraging and sanctifying. a.) How can the intelligent Bible Christian be encouraged to *sin*, by a doctrine which assures him of a perseverance *in holiness*; if he is a true believer. b.) So far as a rational self-love is a proper motive for a sanctified mind, this doctrine leaves it in full force; because when the Arminian would be led by a backsliding, to fear he had fallen from grace, the Calvinist would be led, just as much, to fear he never had had any grace; a fear much more wholesome and searching than the erring Arminian's For this alarmed Calvinist would see, that, while he had been flattering himself he was advancing heavenward, he was in fact all the time in the high road to hell; and so now, if he would not be damned, he must make a new beginning, and lay *better* foundations than his old ones, (not like the alarmed Arminian, merely set about reparing the same old ones.) c.) Certainty of success, condition on honest efforts, is the very best stimulus to active exertion. Witness the skilful general encouraging his army. d.) Last

Such a gift of redemption as the Calvinist represents is far nobler and more gracious, and hence elicits more love and gratitude, which are the noblest motives, the strongest and best.

COMFORT OF THE DOCTRINE.—Just so far as the Calvinist is enabled scripturally to hope that he is now born again, he is, to that extent, entitled to hope that his triumph is sure; that death and hell are disarmed, and that his heaven is awaiting his efforts. To him who knows the weakness of the human heart, and the power of our spiritual enemies, the Arminian's adoption, beset by the constant liability to fall, would bring little consolation indeed. It is love and confidence, not selfish fear, which most effectually stimulates Christian effort. Let the student see how St. Paul puts this in 1 Cor. xv: 58.

LECTURE LVII.

SYLLABUS.

ASSURANCE OF HOPE.

1. What is the distinction usually made by Calvinists between the assurance of faith and the assurance of hope?
   Conf. of Faith, ch. xviii. Ridgeley, que. 80, § i. Turrettin, Loc. xv, que. 17, § 3.
2. State the doctrine of Rome concerning assurance, and her motives therein. Of the Reformers. Of the Westminster Assembly.
   Council of Trent, Session vi, ch. 9. Canons de Justifi. 13, 14 Turrettin, que. 17, § 1-11. Calvin's Inst., Bk. iii, ch. ii, § 7. Hill, Bk. v, ch. 2.
3. Is assurance of hope of the essence of saving faith?
   Turrettin, as above, § 8, 9. Ridgeley, que. 81. Hill, as above. Calvin, as above. Dick, Lect. 68.
4. Prove that this assurance is attainable, and should be the aim of every true believer.
   Turrettin, as above, § 12-23. Ridgeley, que. 80.
5. By what *means* is the believer to seek this assurance?
   See Rom. viii: 16, with Calvin, Scott, and Hodge, *in loco*. Watson's Theological Inst., ch. xxiv, § 2. Hill, as above. J. Newton's Sermons xx.
6. Reply to objections against the doctrine of assurance of hope, and especially to the objection that it will foster sluggishness and carnal security.
   Turrettin, as above, § 36, 37, and Loc. iv, que. 13, § 21 to 23. Ridgeley, as above. Hill, as above. Dick, Lect. 78.

I. DEFINITIONS.—The *assurance of faith* is that undoubting conviction which every justified person must have (except when buffetted by skeptical temptations) of the truth of the Gospel Proposition. The *assurance of hope* is that undoubting conviction which some attain, that *they* are true believers and penitents, and so, effectually called, elect, and infallibly destined to final salvation.

CAVILS AGAINST POSSIBILITY OF ASSURANCE.—Many quibbles have been offered by Papists and rationalists to show that neither of these (and especially not the assurance of hope) can rise so high as to deserve the name of an infallible assurance. If the latter did, it is urged, it should give a certainty of heaven equal to the certainty of our own existence, a certainty admitting of no *degrees* and no increase by additions of subsequent evidence. But what sober believer can honestly claim this? Now, the answer to all this is easily found in an appeal to common sense. What does a man mean when he says he is *sure of a thing?* Why, that he clearly sees some evidence of its truth, which mounts above even the highest probability to demonstration. Any valid portion of such evidence is proper ground of *certain conviction.* Does this imply that the evidence cannot be increased, so that the certainty shall have a wider basis? By no means. So, although it was certainty before, it now becomes a more satisfactory certainty. Again: Assurance of faith, and, still more, assurance of hope, embrace as elements of evidence, the state of the soul's own moral affections. The latter, for instance, is based upon a consciousness of the exercise of trust, love, penitence, submission, and peace. Hence, to every one who knows human nature, it is manifest that, however demonstrative may be such evidence in its very highest and purest examples, the certainty based upon it will be much more *felt* and conscious, at some times than at others, because the *actings* of those holy emotions, and the soul's attention to and consciousness of their actings, are more lively at times than at others. Why; will not the soul, after it is actually in heaven, have more lively attention to and consciousness of its present blessedness, at some times than at others? Does not the bereaved widow, who *knows* her loss only too well at all times, *feel* it far more sensibly at some times than at others? Third; it is a most incorrect analysis which either banishes the *will* from among the causes of belief, in cases of moral truths and evidences presented to the mind, or which denies that the certainty arising of such moral truths can be intellectually correct; because there is a voluntary element in it. In the case of all *moral* objects of belief, conviction is far from being a bare intellectual result; the *state of the will* powerfully modifies it. (See my analysis of Saving Faith.) So obvious is this, that *Des Cartes* actually places *belief* among the emotional states of the soul. And yet, the rectitude of the state of will which concurs in producing a given moral conviction of mind, may itself be the object of the mind's certain cognition. So that the mind, while aware that this mental conviction has been produced in part by a *state of will*, as well as by a *light of evidence*, shall also be certain that the will acted *aright* in that case; and hence, the given belief, though in part a result of *volition*, will be felt to be intellectually as valid as though it were a cold truth of abstract mathematics. If the student will remember, that the belief of this proposition, "I am now in a state of grace," or "I am not," is just one of those moral propositions concerning which the state of will is most influential, he will see the application of these principles. It will appear why the intellectual belief of such propositions should *vary* in its felt strength; viz: because the active and voluntary part of its elements vary. And it will appear that this degree of fluctuation (so to speak) is not at all incompatible with certainty, and a proper intellectual basis of evidence. To dispute this is as though one should say that, because the waters of the sea do not bear up the boat with the same immobility as a stone pedestal bears its statue, therefore the waters do not sustain the boat. The assurance of hope, in the breast of the true and eminent saint, is a certainty at its lowest ebbs; at its higher floods it is both solid and joyful.

Assurance a moral conviction, not a sense perception.—That the saint ought to know he is a saint as clearly as he knows that he breathes, is simply playing with words. Who does not know that sensational consciousness has a *palpable* element about it, which belongs to no intellectual belief, not even that of the exact sciences? The scholar *knows* that "the square of the hypothenuse is equal," &c.; but he does not *feel* it, as he feels his existence.

II. Romish doctrine touching Assurance.—Romanists deny that a certain assurance of hope can be attained, except in the case of those eminent saints and ascetics, to whom God gives it by special revelation—as to Stephen and Paul. In other cases, they judge it not attainable, not to be sought after, and not beneficial, even if attainable. Their *motive* is, obviously, to retain that power of priestcraft over souls, by which they may make gain of their absolutions, masses, indulgences, &c. The soul completely and finally justified in Christ, and assured thereof by grace, would be *independent*. 2 Cor. iii: 17.

Reformers' Doctrine.—The earlier Reformers, having learned to abhor this trafficking in the peace of immortal souls, felt impelled to teach that assurance is of the essence of saving faith, (though compelled to modify their assertion, in order to include even Bible saints.) Thus, Calvin, Institute, Bk. iii, ch. 2, § 7: "Faith is a steady and certain knowledge of the divine benevolence towards *us*," &c. Com. on Rom. viii: 16. "Stat itaque Sententia, Neminem posse nomonari filium Dei, qui non se talem agnoscat." Of this, more anon.

Arminian Doctrine.—The earlier Arminians (of Holland) taught that certain assurance of final salvation is not attainable in this life; and that to doubt thereof is salutary, and conducive to humility. So far as assurance is predicated of our *final* perseverance, and our election, the later Arminians of Wesley's school must of course concur. But they teach, as one of their most distinctive points, that an assurance of present conversion (followed by *some hope* of final salvation) is not only possible, but essential to every true believer. And this is the *immediate* teaching of the Holy Ghost to the heart, without the Word or self-examination. Yet assurance of hope is not made by them of the essence of faith. First, say they, come repentance and faith, then justification, then regeneration, then this inwrought consciousness of adoption—faith itself being defined as a believing and embracing of the gospel. Here we have the mystico-scholastic notion of a revealed and immediate witness, borrowed from Rome through a Moravian *medium* by Wesley, and asserted as the privilege and attainment of every true convert. A still more direct historical channel may be found for the transmission of this doctrine into the Wesleyan System from the scholastic theology of the Romish monks. Wesley was a great admirer of *Thomas à Kempis,* of whose work he published an edition. Here, in the experience of this mystical scholastic, the idea appears in full form.

Doctrine of Westminster Assembly.—The Calvinistic world has now generally settled down upon the doctrine of the Westminster Assembly, that assurance of hope is not of the essence of saving faith: so that many believers may be justified though not having the former: and may remain long without it; but yet an infallible assurance, founded on a comparison of their hearts and lives with Scripture, and the teaching and light of the Holy Ghost, through and in the Word, is the privilege, and should be the aim of every true believer. Yet, this assurance, while both scriptural, reasonable and spiritual, and thus solid, may be more sensibly felt at sometimes, and may even be temporarily lost through sin, according to the remarks of our section I.

III. Assurance of Hope not of the essence of Faith, proved a.) by experience.—Before proceeding to argue this, let us briefly show (see Lect. on Faith,) what we have again asserted; that assurance of hope is not of the essence of saving faith. First: not only do some, yea many, who give other excellent evidences by their fruits, in our days lack this assurance; but some Bible saints lacked it at times. See Ps. xxxi: 22: lxxvii: 2, 3; Is. l: 10, &c. These men did not therefore cease to be believers? The proof is so obvious, that Calvin is obliged to modify the assertions of which we have seen specimens, to include these cases, until he has virtually retracted his doctrine.

b.) The opposite would place another proposition as object of Faith.—Second: this doctrine really adds to the proposition which is the object of saving faith. That proposition is: "whosoever believeth shall be saved;" and according to its very nature, it must follow that the moment it is believed, the sinner is saved, whether he sees any other truth or not. To teach the view of the first reformers, instead of exalting Christ, as they, with their modern imitators boastfully claim, really calls the soul away from Christ, and bids him look at another proposition touching the state and actings of his own soul, before he is permitted to trust in Christ. Our view scripturally directs him to find his comfort by looking wholly out of himself to Christ. Indeed, if we adhere strictly to the terms of the gospel, we shall see that the exercise of such a faith as Calvin describes is an impossibility, without a new and direct revelation in every case. Thus, no man is saved in Christ till he has come to believe that Christ has saved *him*. But it is only *by believing* that he is saved in Christ; so that this definition of faith requires the effect to precede its own cause. The sinner must therefore find out "the benevolence of Christ towards himself," not from the gospel promise, but from the Holy Ghost directly, without the gospel. But are we ready for this? Do we surrender the great truth, that the *Word* is the object to which the Holy Ghost points the believing sinner's soul?

Finally lost, could not be convicted for unbelief.—Third: if faith were such an exercise as this, when once the finally impenitent reach hell, it will no longer be fair to punish them for not believing unto salvation; for it will then be manifest that had they believed in Christ's benevolence towards themselves, it would not have been true. So that in refusing to believe, they acted so far properly: the Holy Ghost never gave them a warrant to believe.

Its Advocates refuted.—The scriptural argument for this ultra view of faith amounts mainly to this: that the Apostles generally address believers and speak of them as persons assured in their hope. e. g., 2 Cor. xiii : 5 ; v : 1 ; 1 Peter i : 8 and 9 ; 1 Jno. v : 19, &c. But the first of these passages, when properly construed, only says that men are reprobates unless they *have* Christ formed in them, not unless they recognize Him in them. And to all of them, we reply, that when the sacred writers thus address a whole church of professed believers in terms appropriate only to the best, they only use the language of Christian hope, charity and courtesy. The proof is indisputable: for those very Corinthians are sharply rebuked by Paul, and exhorted to examine themselves jealously; and John says that one object he had in writing his epistle, was to enable the people to come to an assurance of hope. 2 Pet. i : 10; 1 Jno. iii : 9, 10. The *we* which these apostles use are often no others than the apostles themselves, with any Christians of like attainments. But there is also some justice in the surmise, that assurance of hope was more generally given in those primitive days, because the Church was called to testify, and to suffer more. So that if it should even appear that it was the common attainment of believers then, this would not prove it of the essence of faith.

IV. Assurance attainable.—We argue that the assurance of hope is attainable, and should be sought by all believers; first, presumptively;

Because it is our duty to be in Christ.—Because such a state of the case seems necessarily implied in the duty of seeking Christ. God makes it our duty to use means to place ourselves in union with Christ. Must there not be some way for us to know whether we have obeyed and do obey this command? It will not avail to say, that God makes it our duty to keep on striving just the same, to establish this union with Christ, to the end of life. True, He commands us to repeat our acts of faith and repentance all the time. But if we are not in Christ we have never believed aright, so that the thing we should be counselled to is, not to repeat those same abortive efforts, but to set about a new kind of efforts. See Rev. iii : 17, 18.

Promises imply it.—Second: the Scripture is full of commands, prayers, and promises for assurance of hope. 1 Cor. xi : 28 ; 2 Cor. xiii : 5 ; 1 Cor. ii : 12 ; John xiv : 20 ; Heb. vi : 18 ; 2 Pet. i : 10 ; 1 Jno. ii : 3 ; v : 13 ; iii 14, &c. ; Rev. ii : 17. It is true that God commands us to be "perfect, as He is perfect," and to pray for entire conformity to Christ: while yet Calvinists do not believe that this perfection is attainable in this life, by any. But here are commands of a more definite sort. e. g., 1 Cor. xi ; 28 ; 2 Cor. xiii : 5, commands to use an immediate means, self-examination, for the attainment of an end immediately connected therewith, namely, assurance. Here are promises given, Jno. xiv : 20, &c., of the enjoyment of assurance. These things make out a different case.

Has actually been attained.—Third: Both in Bible times and since, there have been instances of assurance actually enjoyed through God's blessing on the ordinary means of grace. Since the days of inspiration, saints of the greatest sobriety and truthfulness have professed such assurance, and have been encouraged by it to brave the most fearful trials. Such cases are widely distinguished from the multitudes of fanatical self-deceivers. In Bible days we find a number c other cases. Ps. ciii: 2; xvi: 8–10; Rom. v: 1; Gal. v: 22; 1 The. v: 9; 2 Tim. i: 12; 1 Pet. i: 8; 1 Jno. ii: 3; Phil. iv: 6, 7, &c.

To these it has been objected, that they were inspired cases. Note e. g., in 1 Pet. i: 8, the Apostle was inspired, but not the Christian to whom he wrote! Moreover, there are very few cases in Scriptu where we see any individual receive a revealed assurance directly c his own interest in redemption. An examination will impress us ho remarkably *chary* God has been of such helps; and how generally pecu liar spiritual charisms were bestowed for the benefit of the Church and not of the individual.

CONSCIOUSNESS OF GRACES SHOULD GIVE IT.—Fourth: The nature c the graces in exercise in the Christian heart would show that the tru believer ought to be able, with due care, to come to a certain know ledge whether he has them. In other things, men can usually inte pret their own consciousness with confidence; they can certainly te whether they love or hate, or believe in a fellow-man. Villair usually have a lurking consciousness that they are villains; and effor at self-deception are usually conscious. But Christian principles a described as peculiar, and as the very strongest principles of the sou Why then should not the love, joy, peace, trust, submission, penitenc of a renewed heart become palpable to it, with due self-examinatio We should remember also, that God, by His providential trials, cal to duty and sacrifice for His sake and bereavements, speedily giv most believers excellent tests of genuine religious principles. It objected, that "the heart is deceitful above all things and desperatel wicked." Who can know it? I reply, that the believer is not require to know everything about this deceitful heart, (an impossibility f him) in order to know his own conversion; but only to know son things. And moreover, in knowing these, he is promised the aids the Holy Ghost. And this leads us.

HOLY GHOST PROMISES IT BY HIS WITNESS.—Last. To argue fro the witnessing of the Holy Ghost, His testimony with our spirits promised, in various places and forms; and surely this pledges Go to make assurance a practicable attainment. See Rom. viii: 16; Ep i: 13; iv: 30; 2 Cor. i: 22; 1 Jno. ii: 27.

WE SHOULD NEVER TOLERATE ITS ABSENCE.—Comparing sections 3 a 4, we may see that although the dogma of the Reformers was erroneo their practical feeling concerning the importance of assurance w much more correct than ours. The saints of that age did not, like many now, sit year after year, in sinful indolence, complaining of t want of assurance, and yet indifferent to its cultivation. To them was as the vital breath, to be either enjoyed perpetually, or else, not enjoyed, to be sought with intense exertion. Now, we say, th while Faith may subsist without assurance of hope, every believer e and ought to attain in due time to the latter. And though it may lacking in a true Christian, yet no true Christian can be satisfied wi its absence. If he feels the reality of heaven, he will wish to *kno* whether it is to be his. If he truly believes there is a hell, he mu earnestly long to be certified that he shall avoid it. He cannot content to plod on, not knowing whether or not his feet are on t blood of the Redeemer, whom he loves, whether the viper, sin, which he hates, still enfolds his heart; whether he is to spend the approaching eternity bathing his weary soul in seas of heavenly rest, or buffeting the fiery billows of wrath. A willingness to be ignorant of these things is proof of *indifference*. The chief reason why so many live on without assurance is, that they have no true faith.

V. Means of Assurance. Self-examination, etc.—The *means* for attaining this assurance of hope are indicated by comparing the Confession, chap. xviii, § 1, 2, 3. In the first place, he who would seek it scripturally must be a true believer, (not clearly known to himself as such, for then there would be nothing farther to seek, but known as such to God.) Hence he who seeks long, without attaining, should probably do his first works again. In the next place, he should endeavor to live, in heart and life, in a consistent manner, exercising those principles and that conduct which the Scriptures ascribe to true children of God. For, in the third place, one means of assurance is the *c mparison* which the believer makes between the Bible description and his own heart and life. But the experience of Christians, I am persuaded, finds this process of self-examination and comparison rather an indirect than a direct means of assurance. For a faithful self-inspection usually reveals so much that is defective, that its first result is rather the discouragement than the encouragement of hope. But this leads the humbled Christian to look away from himself to the Redeemer; and thus assurance, which is the reflex act of faith, is strengthened by strengthening the direct actings of faith itself. Now, if there is nothing, or little, in himself which can be compared favorably, with the Bible-measuring rule, of course assurance cannot properly result. This comparison, then, is to be made in the work of self-examination, which must be honestly, thoroughly, and prayerfully performed. We say, *prayerfully*, for man's heart is deceitful: self-love, self-righteousness, spiritual pride, hope, and fear, are nearly interested in the decision, and the understanding of man is too feeble and uncertain an instrument, at best, to be trusted with the everlasting and irreparable issues of this question, when unaided.

Witness of Holy Ghost necessary. What is it?—Hence, in order to a scriptural and infallible assurance, there must be the witnessing of the Holy Ghost with our spirits. This witnessing, saith the Confession, is without extraordinary revelation. His operations here, are doubtless *what they are*, as to their degree and nature, *in His other sanctifying operations through the Word*; neither more nor less inscrutable, and just to the same extent supernatural. Thus, it is His to illuminate the soul, giving to the understanding spiritual apprehensions of Truth. It is His to shine upon His own work in our hearts, both brightening it, and aiding us in the comparison of it. It is His to quicken our righteousness, caution, and impartiality, by renewing and sanctifying the dispositions, and quickening our apprehensions of the Divine Judge, and of the stake at issue. Thus the *comparison* between our graces and the Bible standard, is made under His superintendence and light; so that while He communicates no new revealed fact, contributes nothing new, so to speak, to the *material* of the comparison, or of the measuring rule, the result of the measurement is reliable. If such a soul finds in itself the evident actings of such graces as the Bible calls for, then it has an assurance which is both scriptural, and reasonable, and spiritual. It is according to the rule of Scripture. It is reached according to the laws of the human understanding, intelligently and solidly. But best of all, it is also formed under the superintendence of the Holy Ghost, and He enables the humble, prayerful inquirer, to repose on it with "a hope inexpressible and full of glory." Such an assurance may well be called infallible. It may be *aped* indeed, so far as human judgment can distinguish, by false security; but the difference is known to God, and to the believer, conscious as He is of thorough, candour humility and submission; and the judgment day will reveal the difference.

Wesleyan Doctrine of the Witness.—Now the ideas of the Wesleyan concerning this witness of the Holy Ghost, are far different. He makes it indeed an independent revelation, by which the Holy Ghost reveals immediately to the convert's mind, without a mediate process of self-examination and comparison, that he is now reconciled. All the arguments on which they rely to establish this view, against ours, may be reduced to two: that *two* witnesses are said (Rom. viii: 16,) to concur, whereas our view seems to make no other testimony than that of our own spirits(assisted indeed by the Holy Ghost,) and that the assurance cannot proceed mediately from the believer's consciousness of Christian affections within; because those affections are only evoked by the assurance of our adoption. 1 Jno. iv: 19. To the first of these I reply, their view excludes the witnessing of the believer's spirit at least as much as our's seems to exclude that of God's.

Replies.—But, how can this concurrence of two witnesses be better described than in such a case as we have supposed? We protest that our view does most fully and fairly avow the concurrence of God's Holy Ghost in the witnessing. He witnesseth *along with* our spirits. To the second argument, we reply that it is worthless to all except a *Synergist*. It is simply absurd, in our view, to assert that the believer can never have any regenerate exercises characteristic of the new life, until after he has an assurance of his adoption: when we believe, and have proved, that faith itself is a regenerate exercise, as well as repentance. Second: it is false that the renewed soul has no regenerate exercises till they are evoked by an assurance of its acceptance. This is not the sense of Jno. iv: 19. The first love of the new-born soul is not thus mercenary: it cannot help loving, and repenting, and adoring, though unconscious of hope. And last: surely the exhibition ot the goodness, grace, truth and love of God made to all sinners in Jno. iii: 16, is enough to evoke the first actings of love on the new-born sinner's part, while he is still unconscious of a personal hope. To say that a regenerate soul could look at this lovely exhibition of God's mercy towards "whosoever will receive it," and feel no love, because forsooth not yet assured of *its own* personal interest in it, is to say that that soul is still in the gall of bitterness.

Refutation, farther.—This idea of an immediate witness we dispose, 1st, by the fact that *self-examination* is commanded, which would be superfluous to him already assured by a revelation. 2nd. Because Revelations have ceased, and Christians are now remanded to Scripture as the whole and sole source of all the religious informations needed to carry the soul to heaven. Jno. v. 39; 1 Cor. xiii: 8; 2 Tim. iii: 15-17. 3rd. It contradicts the experience of the very best converts [tried by their fruits,] who often exhibit good marks of penitence, submission, love: when their souls are so absorbed by the sense of God's holiness and majesty, and their own vileness, that they dare not rejoice in their acceptance. And it equally contradicts the experience of maturer converts, who usually have their assurance dawn slightly, and grow gradually, as their experience and graces grow. See Is. xlii: 16; Rom. v: 4. 4th. It opens the doors for untold self-deceptions, mistaking the whispers of self-love, carnal security, spiritual pride, fanaticism, or Satan, for this super scriptural witness. The most biting argument against it is in the History of Wesleyan revivals, with their spurious conversions. Jno. Wesley was himself so sensible of this objection, that he appeals to the other concurrent witnessing: that of the Christian's consciousness compared with Scripture to show him that the previous witness is the Holy Ghost, not a delusion. This virtually surrenders his dogma: for this witness of the believer's spirit, although mentioned last, is in reality precedent in order. As the ambassador's credentials must precede his recognition, so this witnessing of the conscious graces in the heart must give credence to the immediate impression!

VI. Effects of Assurance Holy.—Assurance of hope, scripturally founded, will result in advantage only. It increases spiritual joy. Thus it promotes usefulness. Nehemiah viii: 10. It unseals the heart to praise God. It stimulates evangelical labours. 1 Cor. xv: 58. It nerves us for self-denial. It lifts us above carnal temptations. Phil. iv: 7.

Some have thought the assurance of hope arrogant, as though it were modest and seemly to be in suspense concerning our salvation. I answer: If we expected to save ourselves, so it would be. To be in suspense whether *Christ* is able, and willing, and faithful, surely is no mark of our humility; but, on the contrary, it is a dishonor to Him.

The main objection, however, is, that assurance, coupled with the doctrine of perseverance of saints, will become the sure occasion of spiritual indolence and carnal security. We reply, that if an unrenewed man should persuade himself *unscripturally* that he is in Christ, this result would surely follow. But how can it follow to that man who scripturally founds his hope on the existence in himself of a disposition to flee from sin, strive after holiness, and fight the good fight of faith? He hopes he is a Christian, only because he sees reason to hope that he shall strive to the end. The perception in himself of the depraving consequence charged above, would at once vitiate the evidence that he was, or ever had been, a child of God, just in proportion as it was realized. The watchful garrison are confident that they shall not fall victims to a surprise, *because they intend to watch*. Such assurance only stimulates effort. The drunken rioters go to sleep flattering themselves they shall not be surprised; but this is presumption, not assurance. In the actual experiences of Christians, he who enjoys the grace of assurance ever walks most carefully and tenderly before his God, lest the precious elixir be lost through negligence. See Ps. cxxxix: 21, 24; 2 Cor. 5: 6-9; Heb. vi: 9-12.

LECTURE LVIII.

SYLLABUS.

PRAYER.

1. What is the definition, and what the parts of prayer?
   Conf. of Faith, ch. xxi. Sh. Cat., que. 98 to end, Directory of Worship, chs. v. and xv. Dick, Lect. 93. Ridgeley, que. 178.
2. Who is the proper object of prayer?
   Dick, Lect. 93. Ridgeley, que. 179.
3. What are the proper grounds by which the duty of prayer is sustained and enforced?
   Pictet. Bk. 8, ch. 10. Dick, Lect. 93. Hill, Bk. v., ch. v., § 3. Knapp, §133, Appendix.
4. Refute the objections to the reasonableness of prayer, drawn from God's omniscience, immutability, independence, decrees; and from the stability of Nature.
   Southern Presb. Rev., Jan. 1870, Art. I. Chalmer's Nat. Theol. Bk. v, ch. 3. Dick, Lect. 93. McCosh's Div. Gov., Bk. ii, ch. 2, § 5, 6.
5. What is the rule of prayer, and what the qualities of acceptable prayer?
   Dick, as above, and Lect. 94. Pictet, as above. Ridgeley, que. 185, 186.
6. What is the nature and extent of the warrant given us to expect answers?
   See, e. g., Matt. vii: 7, 8. Mark, xi: 24. Dick, Lect. 94. Pictet, as above. Dr. Leonard Wood's Lectures, 95–99.
7. Show that prayer should be both secret, social, ejaculatory, and stated.
   Dick, Lect. 94.
8. What model is given for our prayers? Dick, Lect. 95. See on the Whole. Magee on Atonement, dissertation 8th; and Dr. Leonard Wood's Lectures, 95 to 99.

I. Definition.—"Prayer is an offering up of our desires unto God for things agreeable to His will, in the name of Christ, with confession of our sins, and thankful acknowledgment of His mercies."

Its several parts are stated, in the Directory for Worship, to be adoration, thanksgiving, confession, petition, intercession and pleading. See Directory, Ch. v. § 2.

II. God the only proper object.—God alone is the proper object of religious worship. Matt. iv: 10. The general reason for this is, that He alone possesses the attributes which are implied in the offer of religious worship. The Being who is to be worshipped by all the Church must be *omniscient.* Otherwise our prayers would never reach His ears. And if conveyed to Him, they would utterly confound and overwhelm any finite understanding, in the attempt to distinuish, comprehend, and judge concerning them. Then, moreover, the Being to whom we resort in prayer must be *all-wise*, in order to know infallibly what is best for us, and how to procure it. Such omniscience as we have above described implies, of course, omnipresence. Second. This Lord must be *infinitely good:* otherwise we should have no sufficient warrant to carry Him our wants; and His benevolence would be overtaxed by such constant and innumerable appeals. Third. He must be *almighty;* else he is no adequate refuge and dependence for our souls, in all exigencies. Some most urgent wants and dangers might arise, which only omnipotence could meet.

PRAYER MAY BE TO THE PERSONS OF TRINITY.—For these reasons the offering of prayer is a virtual ascription of divinity to its object: and we reject all such appeals to saints and angels as idolatrous. For us *sinners*, the door of prayer is only opened by the Covenant of Grace. (Why?) Now we have seen that God the Father stands *economically* as the representative of the whole Trinity, or the part of the Godhead, as Christ the Son stands as sinner's representatives in that transaction. Hence prayer is usually addressed *to* the Father *through* the Son, and *by* the Spirit. Eph. ii: 18. But we must not imagine that one person is more properly the object of prayer than another. All are made alike objects of worship, in the apostolic benediction, 2 Cor. xiii: 14, in the formula of baptism, and in Rev. i: 4. But more: we find Jesus Christ, so to speak, the *separate* object of worship, in Gen. xviii: 23; Josh. v: 14; Acts vii: 59; Rev. i: 17; v: 8; Heb. i: 6, &c. These examples authorize us to address a distinct petition to either of the persons.

III. THE DUTY REASONABLE. A.) IT CULTIVATES PIETY.—The duty of prayer reposes immediately on God's command: who "wills that men pray every where." 1 Tim. ii: 8. But this is a precept which most eminently commends itself to every man's conscience in the sight of God, because so clearly founded in nature. That is, there are numerous and powerful reasons proceeding out of our very relations to God, for the duty of prayer. That this is true is obviously suggested by the strength of the instinct of devotion in every rational breast. The immediate prompting of the sense of want or sin, in the creature, is to make him say, "Lead me to the rock that is higher than I." Ps. lxi: 2. And *to pray* is mentioned of Saul as the characteristic evidence that he had learned to fear God. Acts ix: 11. Wherever there is religion, true or false, there is prayer. Even the speculative atheist, when pressed by danger, has been known to belie his pretended creed, by calling in anguish upon the God whom he had denied. This natural instinct of prayer reposes for its ground on God's perfections, and man's dependence and wants. And so long as these two facts remain what they are, man must be a *praying creature*. Let the student remember, also, that man, while finite and dependent, is also an essentially *active* creature. Emotion, and the expression of emotion, are the unavoidable, because natural, outgoings of his powers. He cannot but put forth his activity in *efforts* tending to the objects of his desires; he must cease first to be man: and *prayer* is the inevitable, the natural *effort* of the dependent creature, in view of exigencies above his own power. To tell him who believes in a God, not to pray, is to command him to cease to be a man.

IS GOD'S DUE.—Second: Prayer is the natural *homage* due from the creature to his heavenly Father, God being Himself all-blessed, and the sole Source and Giver of blessedness, can receive no *recompense* from any creature. But is no form of homage therefore due? To say this, would be to say that the creature *owes* God *nothing*, because God *bestows so much!* It would extirpate religion practically from the universe. Now, I assert, in opposition to the Rationalistic Deists, (Kant, Bolingbroke, &c.,) who say that the only reasonable homage is a virtuous life, and the cultivation of right emotions, that prayer also is more directly, and still more naturally, that reasonable homage. God must bestow on man all the good he receives; then man ought to ask for all that good. It is the homage to God's beneficent power, appropriate to a creatue dependent, yet intelligent and active. Man ought to thank God for all good; it is the natural homage due from receiver to giver. Man ought to confess all his sin and guilt; it is the natural homage due from sinfulness to sovereign holiness. Man ought to deprecate God's anger; it is the appropriate homage due from conscious guilt to power and righteousness. Man ought to praise God's perfections. Thus only can the moral intelligence God has created, pay to Him its tribute of intellectual service. I should like to see the reasoning analysed by which these skeptics are led to admit that the creature does owe to God the homage of a virtuous life and affections. I will pledge myself to show that the same reasoning equally proves he owes the homage of prayer. Conceive of God as bestowing all the forms of good on man which his dependent nature needs, without requiring any homage of prayer from man as the means of its bestowal; and you will immediately have, man being such as he is, (an active being,) a system of practical atheism. *Religion*, relation between man and God will be at an end. True, God would be related to man, but not man to God! Anomalous and guilty condition! No feeling of dependence, reverence, gratitude, wholesome fear, would find expression from the creature.

IS MEANS OF GRACE, PER SE.—This leads us, third, to the important remark, that prayer is the natural *means of grace* appropriate to the creature. Prayer is not intended to produce a change in God, but in us. Rev. Roland Hill to sailors: "The man in the skiff at the stern of a man-of-war, does not pull the ship to himself, in hauling at the line, but pulls the skiff to the ship. This line is prayer. Prayer does not draw God down to us, but draws us up to God, and thus establishes the connexion. Now, as we have seen, man being an essential active creature, the exercise of all those right affections which constitute gracious character necessitates their *expression*. And again, to refuse expression to an affection chokes it; to give it its appropriate expression fosters and strengthens it. See examples. We see at once, therefore, how prayer is a natural and necessary *means for all gracious growth*. Let us exemplify in detail. *Faith* is a mother grace to all others; but prayer is the natural and necessary expression of faith: it is its language, its vital breath. In *spiritual desires* the life of religion may be said to consist. Desire is implied in faith itself, for a man does not *trust* for what he does not *want*, and it is yet more manifest in *hope*. For hope is but desire, encouraged by the prospect of obtaining the desired object. Repentance includes a desire for deliverance from sin and attainment of holiness. Love of God includes a desire for communion with Him, and for His favour. So that it would not be very inaccurate to say that practical religion consists in the exercise of holy desires. But what is prayer, except "the offering up of our desires to God?" Prayer is the vital breath of religion in the soul. Again, it cultivates our sense of dependence and of God's sovereignty. By confessing our sins, the sense of sin is deepened. By rendering thanks, gratitude is enlivened. By adoring the divine perfections, we are changed into the same image, from glory to glory.

From all this it is apparent that prayer is the Christian's vital breath. If God had not required it, the Christian would be compelled to offer it by his own irrepressible promptings. If he were taught to believe that it was not only useless, but wrong, he would doubtless offer it in his heart in spite of himself, even though he were obliged to accompany it with a petition that God would forgive the offering. To have no prayer is, for man, to have no religion.

CHIEFLY; IS ORDAINED IN GOD'S PROMISES.—But last, and chiefly, prayer is a means of grace, because God has appointed it as the instrument of man's receiving His Spiritual influences. It is enough for the Christian to know that all his growth in grace is dependent, and that God hath ordained: "he that asketh receiveth."

Thus we see the high and essential grounds on which the duty of prayer rests, grounds laid in the very natures of God and of man, and in the relations between the two.

IV. REASONABLENESS OF PRAYER OBJECTED TO.—But it is from the nature of God that the rationalistic objections are drawn against the reasonableness of the duty. It is said, "Since God is omniscient, there is no meaning in our telling Him our wants, for He knows them already, better than we do. Since He is good, He already feels every proper impulse to make us happy, and to relieve our pains; and does not need any *persuading* on our part, to incline Him to mercy. And since He is immutable, and has already determined from eternity, every act of His future agency, by an unchangeable decree, to hope to change God by our importunity, is worse than useless, it is a reproach to Him. Hence there is nothing for the wise man to do, but to receive His allotments with calm submission, and to honour Him by imitating His moral perfections."

GENERAL REPLY.—We reply to him who had any reverence for the Scripture these assertions of God's wisdom and goodness would be arguments to *prove*, instead of *disproving*, the propriety of prayer. For has not this wise and good being *commanded prayer?* Has he not seen fit to appoint prayer as the instrument for receiving His purposed blessings? Then, to the humble mind, *there* is the best proof that prayer is reasonable. But farther, we have already remarked that, so far as prayer is intended to produce any *change*, it is not a change in God, but in us. He does not command it because He needs to be informed of our wants, or to be made willing to help. He commands it because He has seen fit to ordain it as the appointed means for reception of His blessings. And we have seen abundant reasons why it is a suitable means to be thus ordained: a wise means, a right means. It is a necessary and instinctive outgoing of the rightly feeling soul. It is the proper homage for man to render God. It is an influence wholesome for man's soul itself. And now, God having seen these good reasons (doubtless with others) for ordaining prayer as the means of receiving His favour, there is nothing in His wisdom, goodness, or immutability, inconsistent with his regular enforcement of the rule, "ask, and ye shall receive."

GOD'S BENEVOLENCE NO OBJECTION.—Not in His goodness: For if any one should take such a view of the Divine benevolence as to suppose that it will in every case bestow on the creature such blessings as God's nature and purpose permit, without requiring to be persuaded by the creature's use of means, the whole course of His providence would refute it. God is benevolent in bestowing on multitudes of farmers the fruits of the earth. If any one trusts to His immutable goodness, without ploughing and sowing his field, he will certainly be disappointed. The truth is just here: that God is infinitely benevolent, but still it is a benevolence exercised always in harmony with His wisdom, and with all His other attributes. The question then is: Have God's wisdom, sovereignty, and other attributes, impelled him to decide that he cannot consistently give some particular gifts except to those that ask? If so, it is vain to argue from His infinite goodness.

His Immutability No Objection.—Nor do God's decree and unchangeableness show that it is inconsistent in Him to answer prayer. His immutability does not consist in acting with a mechanical sameness, irrespective of change of circumstances. It is an immutability of principles. The sameness of principle dictates a change of conduct when outward circumstances change. To refuse to change in such cases would often be mutability. And the familiar old answer here applies, that God's decree embraces the means as much as the end. Wherever it was his eternal purpose that any creature should receive grace, it was his purpose equally that he should ask. In a word. these objections are just the same with those of the vulgar fatalist, who objects that, because what is to be will be," therefore it is of no use to make any effort. There is no difference whatever in the refinement or wisdom of the objectors. To be consistent, these rationalists who refuse to pray should also refuse to plough, to sow, to cultivate, to take medicine when sick, to watch against danger, &c.

Objection from Stability of Nature.—The difficulty, however which is now thought most formidable, and is most frequently advanced by Rationalists, is that drawn from the stability of nature. The argument of the objection is, that except where God acts supernaturally, as in regeneration and the resurrection, He acts only through second causes; that the tie between cause and effect is efficient, and the result regular; so that each effect is potentially in its antecedent cause, which is, very probably, an event that has already occurred, and is therefore irrevocable. Hence, it is impossible but that the effect must follow pray as we may against it; unless God will miraculously break the tie of natural causation; but that, we know, He will not do.

General Reply.—Now, this is either an argument *ad ignorantiam*, or it is atheistic. The simple, popular (and sufficient) view which refutes it is: That God governs this world in every natual event through His special providence; and the regular laws of nature are only the uniform mode of those second causes, which He employs to do so. Now, the objection is simply this: that God has constructed a machine, which is so perfect, and so completely His, that He cannot modify its action without breaking it! That is, His success has been so complete, in constructing this machine of nature to work His intended ends, that He has shut Himself out of His own handiwork! Such is the absurdity which the matter must wear in the hands of a theist. Nature is a machine which God made and now uses to effect a set of ends, all of which were foreseen and purposed; and among which were all the destined answers to the acceptable prayers foreseen to be uttered. Of course God has not so made it as to exclude Himself and His own purposes. *How* does H manage the machine to make it work those purposes? We may not know how; but this is no evidence that He does not. The inference from His general wisdom and promise is proof enough that He can and does. A very good illustration may be taken from a railroad train. It is propelled, not by an animal which has *senses* to hear command, but by a steam engine. The mechanical force exerted is irresistible by man. The conditions of its movement are the most rigidly methodical; only up and down one track, within certain times. But *there is a Conductor;* and his personal will can arrest it at the request of the feeblest child.

PRAYER A PART OF THE GENERAL LAW.—But to be more exact: The objector urges that the general laws of nature are stable. Grant it. What is nature? It is a universe of *matter and mind* related, and not of matter only. Now only postulate that desire, prayer, and the answers to prayer are among those general laws, which, as a complex whole, have been assigned to regulate nature, and the uniformity of nature only confirms the hope of answers to prayers. Has the philosopher explored all the ties of natural causation made by God. He does not pretend so. Then it may be that among the unexplored ties are some subtle and unexplained bonds which connect prayers with their answers as natural causes and effects. And all that we have said, in showing how natural prayer is to creatures, makes the postulate probable.

GOD RULES BY HIS LAWS OF NATURE AS HE PLEASES.—Again. Does natural law govern the universe? Or, does God govern it *by* natural law? Men perpetually cheat themselves with the idea that *law* is a *power,* whereas it is simply the method of a power. Whence the *power* of the natural second cause? Originally from God; and its working is maintained and regulated by God. Hence it is utterly improbable (whether we can comprehend or not) that God should have so arranged His own power communicated to His works as to obstruct His own personal will. Remember that God is *personal,* and not a mere *anima mundi.* He is a sovereign moral Person.

HIS PROVIDENCE IN ALL SECOND CAUSES.—Last, recurring to the views given in explanation of God's providence (Lect. XXIV, Part I), you will be reminded, that power in second causes only acts when the suitable relations are established between them and those things which are to be the recipients of the effects: that among all possible relations, many might be fruitful of no effects, and others of very different effects: That hence, there is *here,* room for the perpetual, present manipulation of the invisible Hand in providence. Thus, God always has resources to modify the acting of natural causes, they still acting according to their natures. As I remarked: *All* God's providence is *special;* and the supernatural is *always* with the natural; else the latter could not be.

V. RULE OF PRAYER.—The proper *rule of prayer* is the whole word of God. Not only are its instances of inspired devotion our exemplars, and its promises our warrant; its precepts are the measure of our petitions, and its threatenings the stimulants. There is no part of Scripture which may not minister to the guidance of the Christian's prayers. But further, the Word of God is the rule of our prayers also in this sense, that all which it does not authorize, is excluded. Prayer being a homage to God, it is for Him to say what worship He will accept; all else is not homage, but presumption. Again, both man's blindness and corruption, and God's infinitude forbid that we should undertake to devise acts of worship of our own motion. They will be too apt to partake of some of our depravity, or else to lead in some way unforseen to us, to developments of depravity. And God's nature is too inscrutable to our feeble minds, for us to undertake to infer from it, except as as we are guided by the light of the Word. Hence, the strict Protestant eschews "*will worship*," as a breach of the decalogue.

Qualities of Acceptable Prayer.—When we examine the inspired rule of prayer, we find that to be acceptable, it must be sincere and hearty; it must be addressed to God with faith in Christ; it must be for objects agreeable to God's will; it must be prompted by the Holy Ghost; it must be accompanied with genuine repentance and gratitude. See Ps. lxii: 8; Jer. xxix: 13; Jno. xiv; 6; 1 Jno. v: 15; Rom. viii: 26; Phil. ii: 6, 7; 1 Jno. iii: 22; Ps. lxvi: 18; Heb. xi: 6, &c.

The more immediate *model* which God has given for our prayer, is the Lord's prayer. That it was not intended for a liturgy to be servilely followed, our authors have shown, in their discussions of liturgies. But that it was intended both as a general guide in the structure of our own petitions, and as a form whose very words are to be employed by us on proper occasions, is manifest. c. f. Matt. vi: 9; Luke xi: 2. The most plausible objection to it, as a model for Christians is, that it contains no express reference to a Mediator, and answer through His merit and intercession. The answer is, that it is an old Testament prayer: is intended as such, because that dispensation was still standing. When it was about to close, Christ completed this feature of it, by enjoining the use of His name. See John xiv: 13; xv: 16; xvi: 23, 24.

VI. Extent of Warrant for Answer.—We apprehend that there is much vagueness in the views of Christians concerning the nature and extent of the warrant which they have to expect an answer to their prayers. Some err by defect, forming no definite view of the ground on which their faith is entitled to rest; and consequently, approaching the throne of Grace with no lively hopes whatever. Others err by excess, holding the promises in a sense God did not intend them to bear; and consequently their hopes are fanatical and superstitious. Now, in order that our faith may be firm, it must be correct and intelligent. The consequence of these erroneous views ultimately is disappointment, and hence, either self-accusation, or skepticism.

Extreme view described and refuted.—The warrant for prayer is of course to be sought, immediately, in the *promises*. Of these some seem very emphatic; e. g., Matt. vii: 7; Mark xi: 24. On promises of the latter class especially, some have built a theory of prayer, thus: that the only reason any prayer of one in a state of grace, and actuated in the main by pious motives, is not specifically and infallibly answered, is that it was not offered *in faith*, and that wherever such a saint *fully believes* that he shall receive that which he asks, he will receive it, as surely as inspiration. And such prayer it was the fashion to dignify with the title, "the prayer of faith," among some religionists. In opposition, I would urge that common sense refutes it; and shows that practically there is a limitation to these general promises of answer to prayer. Who believes that he can, provided his motives are in the main pious, pray away a spell of illness, or raise up a sick friend, or convert an individual sinner, with infallible certainty. But may they not put in a saving clause by saying: "Such prayers are dictated by the Holy Ghost? This makes all right." Ans.: The Christian has no mode of distinguishing the specific cases of spiritual impulse in his own heart; because the Holy Ghost operates in and through his natural capacities. Hence, *to the Christian*, the universal warrant is practically lacking. It is manifestly incompetent to the Christian to say, in advance of the answer: The Spirit dictates this prayer beyond doubt. Second: Scripture refutes it; for there are clear cases of petitions of Bible saints, made in faith, piety, urgency, and not specifically answered. See 2 Sam. xii; 16, 19; 2 Cor. xii: 8–10; and above all, Matt. xxvi: 39. And third: We can hardly suppose that God would abdicate His omniscience in His dealings towards the very objects of His redeeming love, and make their misguided, though pious desires the absolute rule of His conduct towards them. This would be the literal result, were He absolutely pledged to do for shortsighted Christians exactly what they, with pious motives, ask of Him. We may add here, that such an assumption is refuted by God's claim to chastise believers for their profit. They of course pray, and innocently pray for exemption. ("Remove Thy stroke from me; for I am consumed by the blow of thy hand.") If God were under bond to hear every prayer of faith, He would have to lay down the rod in each case, as soon as it was taken up.

Scriptural Limitations to Warrant.—There is then, of course, some practical limitation in these general promises. What is it? I answer, it is to be found in the whole tenour of Scripture. And generally in the language of 1 Jno. v: 14. All our prayers shall be specifically answered, in God's time and way, but with literal and absolute accuracy, if they are believing and pious prayers, and *for things according to God's will*. Now there are only two ways to find out what things are such: one is by special revelation, as in the case of the faith of miracles, and petitions for them; the other is by the Bible. Here the explanation of that erroneous view of the warrant of prayer, above described, is made easy and plain. It is said that if the Christian prays with right motives, and with an assured belief that he shall obtain, he will obtain: no matter what he asks, (unless it be something unlawful.) Yes, but *what warrant* has he for the belief that he shall obtain? Faith, without an intelligible warrant, is sheer presumption. Suppose, for instance, the object of petition is the recovery of a sick friend; where does the applicant read God's pledge of a specific answer to that prayer? Certainly not in Scripture. Does he pretend a direct spiritual communication? Hardly. He has no specific warrant at all; and if he works himself up into a notion that he is assured of the answer, it is but a baseless fantasy, rather insulting than honourable to God. I know that pious biography is full of supposed instances of this kind, as when Luther is said to have prayed for the recovery of

Melancthon. These are the follies of good men; and yet God's abounding mercy may in some cases answer prayers thus blemished.

Two classes of Good. The Warrant for first only is absolute.—We return then to Scripture, and ask again, what is the extent of the warrant there found? The answer is, that God, both by promise and example, clearly holds out two classes of objects for which Christians pray. One is the class of which an instance has just been cited—objects naturally desirable, and in themselves innocent, which yet are not essential to redemption, such as recovery from sickness, recovery of friends, good name, daily bread, deliverance from persecution, conversion of particular sinners, &c., &c. It is right to pray for such things; it is even commanded; and we have *some* ground, in the benevolence, love, and power of God, and tender sympathy of the Mediator, to hope for the specific answer. But still the truest believer will offer those prayers *with doubts* of receiving the specific answer; for the simple reason that God has nowhere specifically promised to bestow it. The enlightened believer urges such petitions, perhaps warmly; but still all are conditioned on an "if it be possible," "if it be consistent with God's secret will." And he does not know whether he shall receive or not, just because that will is still secret. But such prayers, offered with this general trust in God's power, benevolence and better wisdom, and offered in pious motives, are *accepted*, even though not *answered*. cf. 2 Cor. xii: 8, with v. 9; Matt. xxvi: 39; with Heb. v: 7. God does not give the *very thing sought*, though innocent in itself; He had never promised it; but He "makes all things work together for good to the petitioner." This should be enough to satisfy every saint.

The other class of objects of prayer is, the benefits accompanying redemption: all the gifts which make up, in the elect, growth in grace, perseverance, pardon, sanctification, complete redemption. For these we pray with full assurance of a specific answer, because God has told us, that it is His purpose specifically to bestow them in answer to all true prayer. See Ps. lxxxiv: 11; Luke xi: 13; 1 Thess. iv: 3; Luke xii: 32; John xv: 8. So, we have a warrant to pray in faith, for the grace to do the things which God's word makes it our duty to do. In all such cases, our expectation of an answer is entitled to be as definite as was that of Apostles, when inspired with the faith of miracles. God may not give it in the shape or channel we expected; He may choose to try our faith by unexpected delays, but the answer is sure, because definitely promised, in His own time and way. Here we may say, Heb. ii: 3, "For the vision *is* yet for an appointed time, but at the end it shall speak, and not lie: though it tarry, wait for it; because it will surely come, it will not tarry."

Promises Confirmed.—In addition to the promises, our expectation of an answer to prayer is strengthened by the following precious considerations. a.) When we pray for things agreeable to God's will, we virtually pray for what will promote His glory and good pleasure. We are like the industrious servant petitioning to a wise master, for a new tool or implement in order to *work better for him*. b.) Such prayers are prompted by the Holy Ghost, and therefore (Rom. viii: 27,) are surely destined to be answered, because the good and truthful

God would not evoke such desires only in order to repulse them. c.) Our union to Christ confirms this; because we know that the sap of spiritual affections circulates in us from Him our Root: so that the *way we come to have* a good desire is, by His having it first. Now, if He desires that thing too, we shall be like to get it. d.) Christ's intercession, so tender and generous, so prevalent, and perpetual, presents the most glorious ground of hope. He rejects no pious applicant. He ever liveth to intercede. The Father heareth Him always. Hence, Heb. iv: 15, 16.

VII. Prayer should be social and secret, stated and ejaculatory.—We are commanded to "pray always," "without ceasing." That is, the temper of prayer should be always prevalent: and ejaculatory prayer should be habitual, and frequent as our spiritual exigencies. But it is also our duty to pray statedly: the morning and evening, at least, being obviously proper stated seasons for secret, and the Lord's day, at least, for social and public prayer. The reason is, that man, a finite creature, controlled so greatly by habit, cannot well perform any continuous duty, without a season appropriated to it; and that, a stated season. He needs all the aids of opportunity and leisure. Nor is there any incompatibility of such stated seasons, with our dependence on the Holy Ghost for ability to offer acceptable prayer. Some Christians seem to be infected with the Quaker idea, that because all true prayer is prompted by the Spirit, it is best not to attempt the duty at the stated hour, if his *afflatuos* is not felt. The folly of this appears from our Saviour's words: "Behold I *stand* at the door and knock." The Spirit is always waiting to prompt prayer. His command is, to pray always. If, at the appointed hour, an indisposition to pray is experienced, it is our duty to regard this as a marked symptom of spiritual want; and to make it a plea for the petition, "Lord, teach us to pray."

Again: Man must join in acts of social and public worship, because he is a social being; and hence he derives important aids in the difficult work of keeping alive the spirit of prayer within him. It is also his duty to glorify God before his fellow-creatures, by these public acts of homage, and to seek to benefit his fellows by the example of them. Yet the duty of public worship does not exclude that of secret. See Matt. vi: 6. Every soul is bound to pray statedly in secret, because of the example of Christ and the saints; because the relation between God and the soul is direct and personal, admitting no daysman but Christ: because secret prayer is the best test and cultivation of the spirit of true devotion: because each soul has special sins, mercies, wants, of which he should speak confidentially to his God; and because there is in secret prayer the most childlike and unrestrained intercourse between God and the soul. So important are these facts, that we may usually say, that he who has no habit of secret prayer has no spirit of of prayer at all.

LECTURE LIX.

SYLLABUS.

THE SACRAMENTS.

1. What is a sacrament?
See Conf. of Faith, ch. xxvii, § 1. Turrettin, Loc. xix, que. 1. Hill, Bk v, ch. v, § 4. Dick, Lect. 86. Ridgeley, que. 162. Council of Trent Sess. 7. Can. 1-13, and Catechism. Rom. pt. ii, que. 2, 3.

2. Are the sacraments mere symbols or badges, as say the Socinians, or als seals of the Covenant?
Turrettin, que. 5. Hill and Ridgeley, as above.

3. What the parts of the sacrament? And what the qualities requisite in th material parts?
Turrettin, que. 3. Dick, Lect. 86. Ridgeley, que. 163. Conf. of Fait ch. xxvii, § 2.

4. What is the sacramental union between these parts?
Turrettin, que. 4. Dick, as above.

5. How many sacraments under the New Testament?
Conf. of Faith, as above, § 4. Turrettin, que. 31. Council of Trent, a above, and Rom. Catechism, pt. 2, que. 11, 12. Dick, Lect. 87. Burnet on the Thirty-nine Articles, Art. 25.

6. How many sacraments under the Mosaic dispensation: and what their re lation to those of the New?
Conf. of Faith, as above, § 5. Rom. Cat., pt. ii, que, 9. Dick, Lect. 87 Turrettin, que. 9. Calvin Institutes, B. iv, ch. 14, § 23-end.

Doctrine of Church and Sacraments Dependent.—The doctrin of the sacraments is closely dependent on that of the Church; and i treated by many authorities, as strictly consequent thereon, as by Tu rettin. It may also be remarked, that the doctrine of the Church i a head of the theology of redemption; and may be treated as such, a well as a source for practical rules of church-order. But as that doc trine is ably treated in another department of this Seminary, I sha assume its main principles, and use them as foundations for the discus sion of the sacraments, without intruding into that circle of inquir

Definition of Church and its Attributes.—Let us remembe then, that the true Church of Christ is invisible, and consists of th whole body of the effectually called: That the same name is given, b accommodation, in the Scriptures, to a visible body, consisting of a those throughout the world, who make a credible profession of th true religion, together with their children: That the essential prope ties of unity, holiness, indefectibility, catholicity, belong to the invis ble and not the visible Church: That God has defined the visib Church catholic, by giving it, in all its parts, a ministry, the Wor the sacraments and other ordinances, and some measure of His sanct fying Spirit: That this visible Church is traced back at least to th family of Abraham, where it was organized by God's own authority o a gospel and ecclesiastical covenant: That this visible Church is su stantially the same under both dispensations, retaining under the Ne the same membership and nature, though with a suitable change circumstances, which it had under the Old Dispensation; and that o of this visible Church catholic there is no ordinary possibility of salv tion. In this visible Church, the sacraments are both badges of mem bership, and sealing ordinances. They also represent, apply, and seal, the chief truths of redemption. Hence, the importance of their discussion. They will be found to bear a close relation to our whole system, both of doctrine and church-order.

I. BIBLE IDEAS OF SACRAMENT SIMPLE.—When one examines the Scriptures, and sees the brief and simple statements there given concerning the sacraments, he will be very apt to feel that the place assigned them in many Protestant and all Romish systems of divinity, is inordinately large. This is an evidence of the strong tendency of mankind to formalism. In our treatment of the subject, much of the length assigned it will arise from our attempts to rebut these formal and superstitious tendencies, and reduce the sacraments to their Scriptural simplicity.

CONSTITUTED OF FOUR THINGS.—According to the definitition of the Confession of Faith, ch. 27, § 1, 2, there are four things which concur to constitute a sacrament. a.) A sensible, material element. b.) A covenanted grace of graces, aptly symbolized and represented to the senses by the element. c.) A mutual pledge and seal of this covenant between God and the soul. d.) And an express divine institution. The usual patristic definition was, "a sacrament is a sensible sign of an invisible grace." But this is too indefinite, and leaves out the federal feature. *All ceremonies* are not sacraments because they are of divine appointment; for they may not have this material element as symbol of a spiritual grace; nor are all symbols of divine appointment therefore sacrament; because they may not be seals of a covenant.

GOD'S APPOINTMENT MOST ESSENTIAL.—One of the most important features is the express divine appointment. Sacraments are acts of worship. All worship not instituted by God is will-worship, and therefore offensive, because He is infinite and inscrutable to finite minds, as well as our absolute sovereign; so that it is presumption in man to devise ways to please Him any farther than the appointment of His word bears us out, and because the devices of depraved and short-sighted man are always liable to be depraved and depraving. These reasons of course apply in full force to sacraments of human device. But there is an additional one. A sacrament is *God's pledge* of some covenanted grace to the true participant. Now, by the same reason that nobody can put my sign and seal to my bond save myself, no other than God can institute a sacrament. It is the most aggravated form of will-worship.

ETYMOLOGY AND MEANING.—The remarks of Dick and Hill concerning the etymology and usage of the word, *sacramentum*, have been sufficient; (as meaning first, a suitor's money placed in pledge; second, a soldier's oath of enlistment; third, some holy secret, the usual vulgate translation of MUSTERION.) It has been plausibly suggested, that the latter is the sense primarily attached to it by the Latin Fathers, when they used it in our technical sense; as MUSTERION is the word usually employed therefor by the Greeks. This is reasonable: yet the other idea of oath of enlistment to Christ was, we know, early attached to it. For in the earliest literature of the martyrs, e. g., Tertullian, and thenceforward generally, we find the ideas enlarged on, that the Christian is a soldier enlisted and sworn, in the Lord's Supper, to die for Jesus.

II. Sacraments are seals, as well as signs.—Much of the remainder of this Lecture will consist of an attempt to substantiate the *parts* of our definition of a sacrament. The Socinians (and as Lutherans and Papists charged, the Zwinglians), being outraged by the unscriptural and absurd doctrine of Rome, concerning the intrinsic efficacy of sacraments, *ex opere operato*, adopted this view that a sacrament is but an *instructive* and *commemorative symbol* of certain facts and truths and badges of profession. This we hold to be true so far as it goes, but to be insufficient. They are also *pledges* and *seals* on God's part of covenanted gospel blessings, as well as pledges of service and fidelity on our part, (which is implied in their being badges of profession.) And here we oppose the Papists also, because they also repudiate the sphragistic nature of the sacraments, in making them actually confer and work, instead of signing and sealing the appropriate graces.

a.) Because circumcision was a seal.—The arguments for our view are the following: It is expressly said, Rom. iv: 11, that circumcision, one of the sacraments of the Old Testament, was to Abraham a sign and "*seal* of the righteousness of faith, which he had while yet uncircumcised." It must have been equally a *seal* to all other genuine believers of Israel; for the ground of its application to them was no other than their coming under the very covenant then instituted with Abraham, and inheriting the same promises. But Baptism is the circumcision of the New Testament, the initial sign of the same covenant and baptized believers are children of Abraham's promises by faith Matt. xxviii: 29; Acts ii: 38, 39; Rom. iv: 11, 16, &c. It seems very obvious therefore, that Baptism is as much a seal as circumcision was So the passover, at its first institution, was a *pledge* (as well as sign) o a covenanted immunity. See Exod. xii: 13, 23. When we establish a similar identity between the Passover and the Supper, the same argument will appear, that the latter also is a seal.

b.) The Sacraments confer outward privilege.—But second The pledge contained in the sacraments is plainly indicated in the outward or ecclesiastical privileges, into which they immediately induct the partaker. He who received the sign, was thereby at once *entitled* to the enjoyment of certain privileges the signs and *means* of saving graces. How can the idea of pledging be avoided here? And the sacramental union expressed in the Bible language implies the same In Gen. xvii; 10, 13, circumcision is *called* the covenant. In Jno. iii 5; Tit. iii: 5, baptism is called regeneration; and in Acts xxii: 16 remission of sins. In Exod xii, *et passim*, the lamb is called *the passover.* In 1 Cor. xi: 24, 25, the bread and wine are called the body and blood. Now, this intimate union, implied in such language, must be either *opus operatum*, (which we shall disprove,) or a sealing pledge For illustration, by what usage of human language could that symbolical act in a feudal investiture, handing to the tenant a green sod cut from the manor conveyed, be called "Livery of seizin;" unless it was understood to represent the conveying and guaranteeing of possession in the land?

A federal sign is necessarily a seal.—And third. When we remember that a sacrament symbolizes, not any kind of fact or truth but one peculiar sort, viz: a covenant, we see that in making a sacrament a symbol and badge, we make it a seal and pledge. For th latter idea is necessarily involved in a *federal symbol*, which is just the idea of the sacrament. When I shake hands as an indication only of general good will, the act may be merely symbolical; but when I *give my hand on a bargain*, the symbol inevitably conveys a sealing meaning.

III. MATTER OF THE SACRAMENT WHAT? NATURAL FOUNDATION FOR IT.—Both the Popish and Protestant Scholastics have defined the sacraments as consisting in *matter*, and *form*. This proceeds upon the Aristoteli dialectus. But here the student must note that by *form* is not meant the *shape* of a material thing, or the fomulary, or mode of observance outward; but (the idea of a sacrament being complex) that trait which, when superinduced on the transaction, distinguishes it as a sacrament. Both agree that the matter of the sacrament consists of a sensible symbol, and of a federal truth of religion symbolized. The trait of human nature to which the institution of sacraments is accommodated is evidently this: that man being a sensuous being, suggestions prompted by a *sensible object* are much more vivid and permanent than those prompted by mental conceptions merely, whether the associated suggestion be of thought, or of emotion. Society offers many illustrations of this mental law, and of useful social formalities founded on it. What else is the meaning and use of friends shaking hands? Of civic ceremonials? Of the symbolical acts in forming matrimonial vows? Of commemorative monuments, painting and statues? On this principle rest also the attractiveness of pilgrimages, the ties of all local associations, and the sacredness attached to the graves of the dust of those we love.

HENCE, A SACRAMENT HAS, FIRST, A SIGNIFICANT MATERIAL PART.—Hence, it is obvious that there will be in every sacrament, some *material* element, palpable to the senses, and especially to our eye-sight. This element should also be not merely an arbitrary, but a natural sign of the grace signified; that is, it should have some natural analogy to suggest the related grace. By arbitrary agreement, soldiers have bargained that a certain blast of the trumpet shall signify *advance:* and algebraists, that a certain mark (+) shall represent *addition*. There is no previous analogy. But in circumcision, the removal of the *preputium* aptly and naturally represents putting away carnality; and results in a hidden, yet indelible mark, graphically signifying the inward renewal of the heart. In baptism, water, which is the detergent element in nature, as aptly signifies cleansing of guilt and carnality. In the passover, the sprinkled blood represented the atonement: and the eating of the sacrificed body of the lamb, faith's receptive act, in embracing Jesus Christ for the life of the soul. In the Lord's supper, the *same symbols* almost, are retained ; i. e., eating something that nourishes; but not in this case *animal* food, because the typical nature of the passover, contained in the life which maketh atonement for our sin," had already terminated on Christ the antitype. But it must be added, that a mere natural analogy does not constitute a sacrament. The analogy must be selected, and consecrated by the express institution of God.

THE FORM WHAT?—The Protestant scholastics very properly (if the extremely artificial analysis of the Peripatetics is to be retained at all) declared that the *form* which constitutes the element and theological truth a sacrament, is the *instituted signification.* The Papists make the form of sacrament to consist in the *words of institution.* Those words are indeed, in each case, expressive of the appointed signification; whence it may be supposed, that the difference of definition is unimportant. But we shall see that the Papists are thereby smoothing the way for their idea of the sacramental union, involving an efficiency by *opus operatum* and the power of the canonical priest to constitute the ceremonial a sacrament or not, at his will.

IV. Sacramental union, what?—Our Confession declares, c. 27, § 2, that "there is, in every sacrament, a spiritual relation, or sacramental union, between the sign and the thing signified; whence it comes to pass that the names and effects of the one are attributed to the other." Instances of this sacramental language have been already given, (p. 302.) Others may be found, where the grace is named by the sign, in Matt. xxvi: 27, 28; 1 Pet. iii: 21; Rom. vi: 4; Col. ii: 11, 12, &c. This sacramental union is defined by the Confession as "a spiritual relation," and by Turrettin, as a "relative and moral union." The latter repudiates the proposition, that it is a "spiritual" union; but he repudiates it in the sense in which it is asserted by Papists, who mean by it a literal connexion of the spiritual benefit with the material element, such that it is conferred wherever the element is *ex opere operato.* Turrettin's "moral relation" means the same with our Confession's "spiritual relation." Both, of course, imply that this relation only is real in those cases in which the recipient partakes with proper state of heart. In such cases (only,) the elements are the means and channels of gracious benefits, not in virtue of a physical union of the grace to the elements, but of their adaptation and God's appointment and purpose, and the Holy Ghost's influence.

The Union not physical.—Should any one assert a different union from that of the Confession, he would be refuted by common sense, which pronounces the absurdity of the whole notion of the conveyance of spiritual benefits by a physical power through a physical union. It is nothing better than an instance of a religious jugglery He is opposed by the Old Testament, which declares its sacraments to be only signs and seals of grace embraced through faith. He is contradicted by the general tenour of the New Testament, which always conditions our participation of saving blessings on our state of heart. And he is inconsistent with himself; for if the tie connecting the grace with the element were a physical tie, the grace ought to go wherever the element goes. It is so with the tie between substance and attributes, in every other case. If it is the nature of fire to burn, then fire surely burns him whom it touches, whether it be conveyed to him by friend or foe, by design or chance, in anger or in friendship. Then, the intention of the priest, and the state of mortal sin in the recipient ought to make no difference whatever as to the gracious efficacy. In placing these limitations, the Papist has really given up his position; he has virtually admitted that the sacramental union is only a relation of *instituted moral influence.* But if it is such, then its efficacy must be tested just like other moral influence exerted by the Holy Ghost. Are any of them exerted, *can* they be exerted, any otherwise than through the intelligent embracing and acting upon the truth by the soul of the subject? The same topick will be more fully discussed when we consider the claim of *opus operatum*.

V. But two New Testament Sacraments. Rome has seven.—All Protestants are agreed that among the religious rites instituted by God for the New Testament Churches, there are but two, which meet the definition of a *sacrament*: baptism and the Lord's supper. As they obviously present all the requisites, and as there is no dispute concerning their claim, we shall not argue it, but proceed to consider the pretensions of the five other so-called sacraments of the Romish Church: confirmation, penance, orders, matrimony, and extreme unction. To prove that the sacraments are seven, the Roman Catechism seems to rely chiefly on this argument: As there are seven things in physical life which are essential to the propagation and well-being of man and of society, that men be born, grow, be nourished, be healed when sick, be strengthened when weak, have rulers to govern them, and rear children lawfully; so in the analagous life of the Spirit, there are seven essential wants, to each of which a sacrament answers. In baptism the soul is born unto Christ, by confirmation we grow, in the eucharist we are fed with heavenly nourishment, in penance the soul is medicined for the returns of the disease of sin, in extreme unction it is strengthened for its contest with the last enemy, in orders the spiritual magistracy is instituted, and in matrimony the production of legitimate offspring is secured. The answer to all this trifling is obvious, that by the same argument it would be as easy to make a dozen sacraments as seven: one to answer to man's home and shelter, one to his raiment to cover him, one to his fire to warm him, &c., &c., for these also are necessaries. But to proceed to details.

Confirmation No Sacrament.—Confirmation is not a sacrament of the New Testament, because it utterly lacks *the divine institution*. The imposition of hands practiced in Acts viii: 17, and xix: 6, and mentioned in Heb. vi: 2, was a rite intended to confer the miraculous charisms of the Holy Ghost, and therefore peculiar to the apostolic age, and purely temporary. The evidences of this fact are presented in the exposition of Acts. Let Rome or Canterbury *so* confer the Holy Ghost, by their imposition of hands, that they shall make men prophesy and speak with tongues (Acts xix: 6), and we will believe. Again: It is the sheerest blunder to pretend to find this rite of confirmation in any of those passages where apostles are said to "confirm" (Acts xiv: 22, Steridzein) the churches, or the souls of the brethren: The context, dispassionately viewed, will show that this was merely the instructions and encouragements addressed to them by the apostles' prayers and preachings. For these reasons, and because the Scriptures direct us to expect in baptism and the Lord's supper all the increments of grace which Christians receive through any sacramental channel, we do not hold modern confirmation to be a scriptural rite at all. But if it were, it could not be a sacrament, for two fatal reasons: that it has no material element (for the oil or chrism is of purely human addition, without one syllable of scriptural authority); and it has no *promise* of grace attached to it by any divine institution. It seals no pledge God has given.

Penance No Sacrament..—2. Papists profess to find the *matter* of the sacrament of penance in the penitent's three exercises, of contrition, confession, and satisfaction; and its form in the priest's absolution. Now, in the case of sins which scandalize the Church openly, a confession *to man* is required by the New Testament, and a profession of contrition. And when such profession is credible, it is proper for the minister to pronounce the acquittal of the offending brother from Church censure. And this is the *only case* in which anything like confession and absolution is enjoined as an ecclesiastical rite in the New Testament. The only plausible case cited by Rome, that of Jas. v: 16, is non-ecclesiastical, because it is *mutual confession*, and its object is *mutual prayers* for each other's forgiveness. That would be a queer sacrament in which recipient should turn the tables on administrator, giving him the elements and conferring the grace! Having limited scriptural confession and absolution to the single case defined above, we find overwhelming reasons why, in that case, they cannot compose a sacrament. There is no element to symbolize the grace promised; for by what title can a set of feelings and acts in the penitent be called a material element? If this be waved, there is no *analogy* between the pretended element, and a symbolized grace; for contrition and confession do not represent, they *are* themselves graces, if genuine. There is no divine warrant, in words of institution, authorizing the minister to announce a divine grace; for all he is authorized to announce is acquittal from Church discipline. "Who can forgive sins but God only?" And last: It is the nature of a sacrament to be pertaken by *all alike* who are within the covenant. But scriptural penance is appropriate only to the exceptional cases of those communicants who have scandalized their profession. The additions which the Papists have made, of auricular confession and satisfaction, greatly aggravate the objections.

EXTREME UNCTION NO SACRAMENT.—3. The formulary for *extreme unction* may be found described in Turrettin and others. The only places of Scripture cited in its support are Mark vi: 13, and Jas. v: 14. These cases so obviously fail to bear out the Popish sacrament that many of their own writers confess it. The objects were different: the apostles anointed to heal the bodies; the priests do it to prepare them for dying. The apostles anointed all sick persons who called on them, baptized, unbaptized, those in mortal sin; sacraments are properly only for Church members. The effect in the apostles' case was miraculous; can Rome claim this? And there can be no sacrament, because the priest has no divine institution and promise on which to proceed.

ORDERS NO SACRAMENT.—4. Orders cannot be a sacrament, although when stripped of its superstitious additions, a New Testament rite. For it has no *element*. The imposition of hands with prayer (chrism, &c., is all extra-scriptural) is but an action, not an element. It has no *saving* grace connected with it, by any promise or word of institution. As has been shown by my colleague, in his course, ordination *confers* no grace, but only recognizes its possession. According to Rome, the action which she preposterously elevates into a matter, is not uniform; but as there are seven orders of clergy, there are several different ceremonials enjoined in the different cases. And last: only one Christian out of a number is ordained to any office: whereas a sacrament is for all equally, who are in the covenant.

5. For the sacramental character of matrimony, the only showing of scriptural defence is the vulgate translation of Eph. 5: 32: "*Hoc est sacramentum magnum.*" Surely a mistranslation of a bad version is a bad foundation on which to build a Bible claim! And then, as has been well remarked, the great *mysterion*, on which Paul remarks, is not the marriage relation at all, but the mystical union of Christ to His people. In matrimony there is no sacramental element at all, no divine warrant for sacramental institution, no grace of redemption signed and sealed to the recipients. And to crown the absurdity, the rite is not limited to God's people, but is equally valid among Pagans! Indeed, marriage is a civil contract, and not an ecclesiastical one. Yet Rome has found it to her interest to lay her hand on the rite, and thus to elevate the question of divorce into an ecclesiastical one, and a *causa major*.

VI. Sacraments of Old Testament Two. Sacrifices not Sacraments, and Why.—As to the number of sacraments under the Old Testament dispensation Calvinistic divines are not agreed. Some seem inclined to regard any or every symbolical rite there found as a sacrament. Others, far more correctly, as I conceive, limit them to two: circumcision and the passover. The claim of these two to be sacraments need hardly be much argued, inasmuch as it is not disputed. They are symbols instituted by God; they have each their elements, bearing a significant relation to the grace represented: the thing represented was in each case federal, so that they not only signified, but sealed or pledged the benefits of a covenant.

But the various typical sacrifices of the Hebrews cannot be properly regarded as sacraments, for the very reason that they were mere types. (The passover also was a type, in that it was a sacrifice proper, but it was also more than a type, a commemorative and sealing ordinance.) For a type points forward to an antitype to come. A sacrament points back to a covenant already concluded. The type does not actually confer the good symbolized, but holds the soul in suspense, waiting for it. The sacrament seals a *present* possession to the worthy receiver. This was as true of the two Old Testament sacraments as of the New. See Rom. iv: 11; Exod. xii: 13. To the obedient and observant Hebrew, the passover was, on the night of its institution, the sign and seal of the remission of death, bodily and spiritual death, the proper penalty of sin, visited that night on a part of the Egyptians; and doubtless, in all subsequent ages, the truly believing Hebrew found it the consoling pledge of a present and actual (not typical) remission and spiritual life, through the merit of the "Lamb of God." Again, a sacrament is a holy ordinance, to be observed alike by all who are within the covenant. But many of the sacrifices were adapted only to exceptional cases: as the Nazarites, the trespass offering, the sacrifice for the purification of women, &c.

Sacraments of both Testaments Same in Signification.—The question whether the sacraments of the Old and New Testaments are the same substantially in their signification and efficacy will be found in the sequel one of prime importance. The grounds on which we assert their substantial identity are these:

a.) Presumptively: The covenant of grace is the same under the two Testaments, offering the same blessing, redemption; through the same agencies; justification and sanctification through the work of Christ and the Holy Ghost. Hence, it is natural to suppose that sacraments, especially when sealing the *same* covenant graces, should operate in substantially the same way. b.) The identity of the covenant, and of the means of sealing it, is strongly implied by Paul, 1 Cor. x: 1–4, when he says that there was a sense in which the Hebrew Church possessed baptism and the Lord's supper. Turrettin very strangely argues from this, and deals with objections as though he understood the Apostle to teach that the Hebrews of the Exodus had literally and formerly a real sacrament of baptism, and the supper, in the passage of the Red Sea, and the eating and drinking of the Manna and water of Massah. This seems to me to obscure the argument; and it would certainly have *this* effect: that we must teach that Israel had four sacraments instead of two. The scope of the Apostle is, to show that participation in sealing ordinances and ecclesiastical privileges does not ensure salvation. For Israel *all* shared these wondrous sealings to God, yet many of them perished. And to strengthen the analogy he compares them to the New Testament sacraments. Now, if Israel's consecration to God in this Exodus was virtually a baptizing and a Eucharist, we infer that the spirit of the Israelitish ordinances was not essentially different from that of the New Testament. c.) The supper is called by the name of the passover. 1 Cor. v: 7, 8. And the baptism is declared to be, Col. ii: 11, 12, the New Testament circumcision. d.) The supper came in the room of the passover, as is manifest from the circumstances of its institution, and the baptism came in the room of circumcision; compare Gen. xvii; 11, with Matt. xxviii: 19. See Acts ii: 38, 39. And, last, circumcision and baptism signify and seal the same graces. This will be manifest from a comparison of Gen. xvii: 13, 14, with Acts ii: 41; Deut. x: 16, or xxx: 6, with Jno. iii: 5, or with Titus iii: 5, and Eph. v: 26; Acts vii: 8, with Rom. vi: 3, 4; Rom. iv: 11, with Acts ii: 38, and xxii: 16. We here learn that each sacrament signified entrance into the visible Church, remission of sin, regeneration, and the engagement to be the Lord's. So the passover and the supper signify substantially the same. In our passover, the Lamb of God is slain, the blood is sprinkled, our souls feed on Him by faith, and the consequence is that God's wrath passeth over us, and our souls live.

LECTURE LX.

SYLLABUS.

THE SACRAMENTS. (Continued.)

7. Is the efficacy of the Sacraments dependent on the officiator's intention? Turrettin, Loc. xix. que. 7. Dick, Lect. 86, 87. Conf. of Faith, ch. xxvii. Ridgeley, que. 161. Council of Trent, Sess. vii, Canon 11.

8. Is that efficiency produced *ex opere operato*; or does it depend on the recipient's exercise of the proper frames, inwrought by the Holy Ghost through the Word of God?

Turrettin, que. 8. Calv. Inst. Bk. iv, ch. 44. Dick, Lect. 86. Ridgeley, que. 161. Rom. Catechism, pt. ii, que. 18. Council of Trent, Sess. vii, Canon, 4 to 8 inclusive.

9. Is participation in the Sacraments necessary to salvation?

Turrettin, ques. 2 and 13. Council of Trent, as above.

10. By whom should the Sacraments be administered?

Turrettin, que. 14. Rice and Campbell, Debate, Prop. iv. Calv. Inst. Bk. iv, ch. 15. § 20–end.

11. Do the rites of Baptism, Confirmation, and orders confer an indelible spiritual character?

Turrettin, que. 10. Dick, as above. Dr. Geo. Campbell, Lect. xi, on Eccles. Hist. (p. 183, &c.) Rom. Catechism, pt. ii, que. 19. Council of Trent, Sess. vii, Can. 9.

VII. Rome's Doctrine of Intention.—The Council of Trent asserts, (Sess. 7 canon 11), that the intention of doing at least what the Church proposes to do, is necessary in the administrator, to make the sacraments valid. Some popish divines are so accommodating as to teach that if this intention is habitual or virtual, though not present, because of inattention, in the mind of the administrator, at the moment of pronouncing the words of institution, it is still valid; and some even say, that though the officiating person have heretical notions of the efficacy of the Sacramant, e. g., the Presbyterian notion, and honestly intend a Sacrament, as he understands it, it is valid. Now there is obviously a sense, in which the validity of sacramental acts, depends on the *intention* of the *parties*. If for instance, a frivolous or profane clergyman should, in a moment of levity, use the proper elements, and pronounce the proper words of institution, for purposes of mockery or sinful sport, it would certainly not be a sacrament. But this is a *lack of intention*, of a far different kind from the popish. There would be neither the proper place, time, nor circumstances of a divine rite. The profanity of purpose would be *manifest and overt;* and all parties would be guilty of it. The participation, on both sides, would be a high act of profanity. But where the proper places, times and attendant circumstances exist so far as the honest worshipper can judge; and all the divine institution essential to the validity of the rite is regularly performed with an appearance of religious sincerity and solemnity, there we deny that the sincere participant can be deprived of the sacramental benefit, by the clergyman's secret lack of intention. And this: because

Refutation.—a) It is the opinion of all the Protestant divines, even including Calvin, (Inst. Bk. iv, ch. 14), that the gracious efficacy of the sacraments is generically like that of the *Word*. The sacraments are but an *acted word*, and a *promise in symbol*. They effect their gracious result through the Holy Ghost cultivating intelligent faith, &c. Now, the efficacy of the word is not dependent on the motives of him who conveys it. God sometimes saves a soul by a message delivered through a wicked man. Why may not it be thus with a sacrament?

b.) If the clergyman lack the right intention, that is simply his personal sin. It is preposterous to represent God as suspending the fate of a soul, or its edification, absolutely upon the good conduct of another fellow-sinner, whose secret fault that soul can neither prevent, nor even detect till too late. This is not Scripture. Prov. ix: 12; Rom. xiv: 4.

This objection to Rome's doctrine is peculiarly forcible against her, because she represents the valid enjoyment of sacraments, as essential to salvation: and because she herself teaches that the validity of the sacraments is not dependent on the personal character of the clergyman, not even though he be in mortal sin. Why should this one sin, which is precisely a *personal sin* of the officiator, no more, no less, be an exception?

c.) The possible consequences of the doctrine, as pointed out by Turrettin, Dick, &c., are such as amount to a *reductio ad absurdum.* If it it were true, it would bring in question the validity of any sacrament, of every priest's baptism and ordination, of the validity of the Apostolic Succession at every link, and of every mass; so that the worshipper would never know, while worshipping the wafer, whether he were guilty of idolatry or not, even on Popish principles.

MOTIVE FOR THE DOGMA.—Last. This doctrine is totally devoid of Bible support. But these tremendous difficulties have not prevented Rome from asserting the doctrine. Her purpose is to hold the laity in the most absolute and terrible dependence on the priesthood. She tells them that without valid sacraments it is impossible to be saved; and that even where they have the canonical form of a sacrament, they may utterly fail of getting the sacrament itself, through the priest's secret will; and may never find it out till they wake in hell, and find themselves damned for the want of it. What power could be more portentous?

VIII. DOCTRINE OF EFFICACY EX OPERE OPERATO.—In the scholastic jargon of Rome, means of grace naturally divide themselves into two classes—those which do good *ex opere operato*, and those which only do good *ex opere operantis.* The former do good by the simple performance of the proper ceremonial, without any act or movement of soul in the recipients, accommodating themselves intelligently to the grace signified. The latter only do good when the recipient exercises the appropriate acts of soul; and the good done is dependent on those exercises, as well as on the outward means. Of the latter kind of means is preaching, &c.; but Rome holds that the sacraments all belong to the former. Her meaning, then, is that the mere administration of the sacrament does the appointed good to the recipient, provided he is not in a state of mortal sin, whether he exercises suitable frames or not. So Council of Trent, Sess. 7, Canon, 6–8. But Romish Theologians are far from being of one mind, as to the nature of this immediate and absolute efficacy.

PHASES OF IT.—Their views may be grouped with tolerable accuracy under two classes. One class, embracing the Jesuit and more Popish Papists, regard the *opus operatum* efficacy as a proper and literal *effect* of the sacramental element and words of institution, by their own immediate causation. They do not, and cannot explain the nature of this causation, unless it be literally physical; and then it is absurd. The other class, including Jansenists, and the more spiritual, regard the sacramental efficacy as *spiritual*—i. e., as the almighty redeeming influence of Christ and the Holy Ghost, purchased for sinners by Christ; which spiritnal influence they suppose God has been pleased in His mercy to tie by a constant purpose, and gracious promise, to the sacraments of the Church canonically administered, by a tie gracious and positive, yet absolute and unconditioned, so that the sacramental efficacy goes to *every* human being to whom the elements go with the proper word of institution, whether the recipient exercise faith or not. That is, God has been pleased, in His sovereign mercy to the Church, to make her *sacraments* the essential and the unfailing channels of His spiritual grace. The opinion of the Prelate Fathers seems to have been intermediate—that no one got saving grace except through the sacramental channel, (excepting the doubtful case of the *uncovenanted mercies,*) but that in order to get grace through that channel, faith and repentance were also necessary. (See Augustine, in Calvin's *ubi supra.*) And such is probably the real opinion of high Church Episcopalians, and of Campbellites, as to the grace of remission.

Protestant view.—Now *Protestants* believe that the sacraments, under proper circumstances, are not a hollow shell, devoid of gracious efficacy. Nor is their use of that of a mere badge. But they are not the channels or vehicles for *acquiring the saving graces first;* inasmuch as the possession of those graces is a necessary *prerequisite* to proper participation in adults. The efficacy of the sacrament therefore is in no case more than to *strengthen and nourish saving graces.* And that efficacy they carry only as *moral means* of spiritual influences; so that the whole benefit depends on an intelligent, believing and penitent reception. And every *believer* has the graces of redemption in such degree as to save his soul, if a true believer, whether he has any sacraments or not. See Confession of Faith, ch. xxvii: § 3. In this sense we deny the *opus operat.*

Proved. By analogous operation of Word.—a) Because that doctrine is contradicted by the analogy of the mode in which the *Word* operates. As we have stated, Protestant divines admit no *generic difference* between the mode in which the Holy Ghost works in the Word, and in the Sacraments. The *form* of the sacraments is the *instituted significance* of it. But that significance is only learned in the Scriptures, and the word of institution is to be found, as well as its explanation, in the same place. The sacrament, without the intelligent signification, is dumb: it is naught. Scripture alone gives it its significance. Sacraments are but the word symbolized; the covenant before expressed in *promissory language,* now expressed in sphragistic symbols. But now, what is more clear, than that the word depends for its efficacy, on the believing and active reception of the sinner's soul? See 2 Cor. iii: 6; Heb. iv: 2, *et passim.* The same thing is true of the sacraments.

By Sphragistic character.—b.) The sacraments are defined in Scriptures as *signs* and *seals,* Rom. iv: 11: Gen. xvii: 10. Now to *signify* and to *promise* a thing is different from *doing* it. Where the effect is present, the sign and pledge thereof is superseded. When the money is paid, the bond that engaged for its payment is done with. To make the sacrament effect redemption *ex opere operato,* therefore destroys their sacramental nature. But more: They are seals of *a covenant.* That Covenant, as far as man is a party (and in the sacrament, the recipient *is* one party), was suspended on an instrumental condition, a penitent and obedient faith. How can the seal have a more immediate and absolute efficiency than the covenant of which it is a seal. *That covenant* gives it all its force.

BY GRACE PRESUPPOSED.—c.) The sacraments cannot confer redeeming grace *ex opere operato*, because, in every adult, proper participation *presupposes* saving grace in exercise. See Rom. iv: 11, last clause; Acts viii: 38, 36, 37; ix: 11 with 18; x: 34 with 47; Mark xvi: 16; 1 Peter iii: 21; Heb. xi: 6; 1 Cor. xi: 28, 29; v: 7, 8. Hence:

BY INSTANCES OF SALVATION WITHOUT SACRAMENTS.—d.) Several in Scripture were saved without any sacraments, as the thief on the cross. Cornelius, we have seen, and Abraham, were already in a state of redemption, before their participation in the sacraments. Now, inasmuch as we have proved that a true believer once in a state of grace can never fall totally away, we may say that Abraham and Cornelius were *already redeemed*. Jno. iii: 36; v: 24. And the overwhelming proof that the sacraments have no intrinsic efficacy, is in this glaring fact, that multitudes partake them, with what Rome calls canonical regularity, who never exhibit in their lives or deaths, one mark of Christian character. Nor will it avail for Rome to say, that they afterwards lost the grace by committing mortal sin: for the Scriptures say say that the redeemed soul *cannot* fall away into mortal sin: and multitudes exhibit their total depravity, not after a subsequent backsliding, but from the hour they leave the sacramental altar, by an unbroken life of sin.

DE ABSURDIS.—e.) The claim of uniform and absolute efficiency, in its grosser form, is absolute absurdity. How can physical, material elements, with a word of institution pronounced over them (which of itself can go no farther into the hearer, than the *tympanum* of his ear), effect a moral and spiritual change? It is vile jugglery: degrading to Christianity, and reducing the holy sacraments to a pagan incantation. But the Jesuit pleads, that we see ten thousand cases, where the external physical world produces mental and moral effects, through sensation. We reply that this is not true in the sense necessary to support their doctrine. Sensation is not the efficient, but only the occasional cause of moral feeling, volition, &c. The efficient cause is in the mind's own dispositions and free agency.

But if the other view of the *opus operatum* be urged: that the efficiency is spiritual, and results, not from the direct causation of the rite itself, but from the power of God graciously and sovereignly connected therewith: we demand the revealed warrant. Where is the promise to the Church from God, that this connexion shall be absolute? The Scriptures are silent, when properly interpreted. Indeed, in many places they explicitly declare the contrary. See Rom. ii: 25 to end; Deut. x: 16; Jer. iv: 4; Luke xiii: 26, 27; 1 Cor. xi: 29. It may be urged that several of these passages apply to the Old Testament sacraments. We have proved that they were substantially similar to the New. And the whole strain of Scripture, which declares that God's favour depends on the state of the heart, that He requireth truth in the inward parts, &c., renders the dogma incredible.

SCRIPTURES RECONCILED.—f.) But Papists and Prelatists quote a class of passages, which do seem to give an immediate efficiency to the rite itself. See Jno. iii: 5; Acts ii: 38: xxii: 16; Eph. v: 26; 1 Cor. x: 17; Rom. vi: 3; Luke xxii: 19, 20, &c. Protestants explain these passages in consistency with their views, by saying that they are all expressions based on the *sacramental union*, and to be explained in consistency with it; e. g., in Jno. iii: 5, the birth of the water means the birth by that which the water represents, the Holy Ghost, &c. The propriety of this interpretation is defended, first, by the analogous case of the hypostatic union in Christ's person, where God is in one place spoken of as having blood, and the Prince of Life as dying. Papists agree with us, that in virtue of the union of the two natures in one person, the person, even when denominated by the one nature, is represented as doing what, in strictness of speech, the other alone could do. So, in the sacraments, there are suggested two things—the *rite*, and the grace signified by the rite. How natural, then, that a Hebrew should attribute to the rite, by figure, what the answering grace really effects? In the second place, this probability is greatly strengthened by noticing the way, natural to Hebrew mind, of speaking concerning all other symbols, as types, &c. The symbol is almost uniformly said *to be* the thing symbolized; when the meaning is, that it represents it. Third: our interpretation of these passages is adopted by Scripture itself, in one of the very strongest instances, thus *authorizing our* view of the exegesis of the whole class. See 1 Pet. iii: 21. Here, first baptism is said to *save us*, as the ark saved Noah. What expression could be stronger? But yet the Apostle explains himself by saying, it is not the putting away of the filth of the flesh which effects it, but the answer (EPEROTEMA) of a good conscience towards God. These words ascribe the efficacy of the sacrament to the honesty of the participant's confession; and this whether with Turrettin and Winer we translate "request to God," or with Neander and Robinson, "Sponsio." Fourth. If men will persist in making the above Scriptures teach the *opus operatum*, the only result will be that the Scriptures will be made to contradict itself; for it is impossible to explain away all the proof-texts we have arrayed.

This difference between us and Rome is fundamental; because she teaches men to depend essentially on the wrong trust for salvation. The result *must be* union of souls.

IX. Sacraments, in what sense necessary.—The question of the necessity of the sacraments in order to salvation, is nearly connected with the previous one. This is indicated by the fact that the same persons usually hold their essential necessity, and their efficacy *ex opere operato*. And this consistently; for the sacraments have that marvellous virtue, it can hardly be supposed that man can safely lack them.

Now, there is a sense in which the neglect of the sacraments would destroy the soul. To observe them is God's command. He who willingly disobeys this command, and perseveres, will thereby destroy his soul, just for the same reason that any wilful disobedience will. But then, it is not the lack of the sacraments, but the impenitent state of the soul, which is the true cause of ruin. Turrettin: "*Eorum non privatio, sed contemptus damnat.*" The command to observe them is not of perpetual, and original, but only of *positive* institution; and owes its force over our consciences to the mere precept of God. Hence they should be regarded from the same general point of view with other positive rights. We sustain this:

Arguments. a). By reference to the free and spiritual character of the gospel plan as indicated throughout Scripture. God has not tied

His grace to forms, places, or sacerdotal orders. All men alike have access to his redeeming mercy, provided their hearts desire it, and under all outward circumstances. Jno. iv: 21, 23; Luke xviii: 14, &c.

b.) We infer the same thing from the numerous and exceedingly explicit passages which promise the immediate bestowal of redeeming grace, and mention no other term than believing. Some of them do it in terms which hardly admit of evasion. E. g., Jno. v: 24; 6: 29. Does not this seem to say that believing alone puts the soul in possession of redemption? True, the Papist may say that one passage of Scripture should be completed by another; and that in other places (e. g., Jno. iii: 5; Mark xvi: 16) the observance of the sacrament is coupled with the believing grace, as a term of salvation. But when those passages are well understood, it is seen that the importance of the outward sacrament depends wholly on the sacramental union. We repeat, that the places in which *faith alone* is mentioned as the instrumental condition, are so numerous, so explicit, and some of them professed answers to questions so distinct as (Acts xvi: 31) that it is simply incredible the Holy Ghost would have so omitted the mention of the sacraments if they were essential.

c). But their *nature* shows they are not. They are sensible signs of an inward grace. The reception of them therefore implies the possession of grace; a sufficient proof it does not originate it.

d.) This leads us to add, that many have actually been saved without any sacraments. Abraham and Cornelius were both in a state of grace before they partook of any sacrament. The penitent thief went to paradise without ever partaking. Circumcision could not be administered till the eighth day of the Hebrew infant's life; and doubtless many died uncircumcised in the first week of their life. Were these all lost? This Popish doctrine gives a frightful view of the condition of the infants of pagans: that, forsooth, because they are debarred from the sacrament of baptism, among the millions who die without actual transgression, there is not one elect infant! Are all these lost?

Last, the Scriptures everywhere hold out the truth, that the *Word* is the great means of redemption; and it is plainly indicated that it is the *only* essential means. See Rom. x: 14; 2 Tim. iii: 15.

X. Sacraments should be Administered only by Ministers.—The traditions and usages of the Church as to lay administration of sacraments have been in the main very uniform. It has always been condemned. The inordinate importance attached to baptism did indeed lead the Romish Church, (and after her, the English,) to decide that the baptism of a layman, and even of a woman, was valid, though irregular, if the child was *in extremis*, and no priest at hand. Even this, most Presbyterians would condemn as utterly invalid. The German antiquaries (e. g., Mosheim) sometimes assert that in the primitive Church any person who made a convert felt authorized to baptize him. This appears to me very doubtful. Ignatius, for instance, who is, if genuine, one of the earliest Apostolic Fathers, says that the Eucharist which the Bishop celebrates should alone be considered a valid one; and that no one should presume to baptize, except the Bishop, or one commissioned by him, This is certainly the language of uniform antiquity, expressed in Councils and Fathers. Nor is it merely the result of clerical ambition and exclusiveness. Since the sacraments are a solemn and formal representation of Gospel truth by symbols, a sort of pantomimic Word, it seems most reasonable that the exhibition of them should be reserved to the same class to whom is committed the authoritative preaching of the Word. And it may be urged, with yet more force, that since the presbyters, and especially the pastor of the Church, are the guardians of the sealing ordinances, responsible for their defence against abuse and profanation, it is reasonable, yea, necessary, that they should have the control of their administration. This consideration seems to me to have the force of a just and necessary inference. Again the great commission (Matt. xxviii: 19, Mark xvi: 15) seems evidently to give the duties of preaching and baptizing to the same persons. The persons primarily addressed were the apostles; but the apostles as representative of the whole Church. To deny this would be to deny to all but apostles authority to preach, and a share in the gracious promise of Christ's presence which accompanies the commission; and this again would compel us to admit that the right to preach, and the promise of Christ's blessing, have been lost to the whole Church for nearly 1800 years, or else to accept the Episcopal conclusion that the apostolic office still continues. Hence, the argument from the commission gives only probable proof. This, however, is strengthened by the fact that there is no instance in Scripture of any sacraments administered by any except men who were *ministers* of the gospel, either by charism, or by ordination. Perhaps the most practical argument against lay administration of sacraments is, from the intolerable disorders and divisions, which have always arisen, and must ever arise, from such a usage. The sacraments have this use among others, to be badges and pledges of Church-membership. The control of them cannot therefore be given to others than the appointed rulers of the Church: to do so is utter disorganization.

XI. Indelible Character Refuted.—The Council of Trent teaches that the three sacraments of baptism, confirmation, and orders, can never be repeated, because they imprint on the recipient an *indelible character*. They have not, indeed, been able to decide what this character is, nor on what part of man it is imprinted. It cannot be the graces of redemption; because Rome teaches that they may all be lost by the true believer, through backsliding, while this *character* can never be lost, to whatever apostacy the man may sink: and because she teaches that the recipient in a state of mortal sin receives no graces through the sacrament, yet he would receive the 'character.' And again, all the sacraments confer grace, whereas only these three confer '*character*' indelibly. Nor can it be any other sort of qualification for office (in ordination, for instance,) for men lose all qualification through infirmity, dotage, or heresy; yet they never lose the '*character*.' Nor can they decide *on what* it is imprinted, whether on the body, mind, conscience, or affections. This uncertainty, together with the utter silence of the Scriptures, is the sufficient refutation of the absurdity. If you seek for the *motive* of Rome in endorsing such a doctrine, you will find it in her lust of power. By every baptism she acquires a *subject* of her ghostly empire, and every ordination, while it confers on the clergyman a ghostly eminence, also binds him in the tenfold bonds of the iron despotism of the canon law. Now, it suits the grasping and despotic temper of Rome to teach that these bonds of allegiance are inexorable: that when they are once incurred, no apostacy, no act of the subject's choice or will, can ever make him less a subject, or enable him to evade the tyrannical hand of his mistress.

As to confirmation and orders, we do not feel bound to solve any questions concerning their sacramental character, because we do not believe them to be sacraments. As to baptism, we assign this reason why it is never to be repeated to the same subject like the Lord's supper: It is the initiating sacrament, like circumcision. The man who is *in* the house needs no repeated introduction into the house. It "signifies our ingrafting into Christ." He who is grafted in once is virtually united, and requires no new union to be constituted.

LECTURE LXI.

SYLLABUS.

BAPTISM.

1. Is water baptism, by God's appointment, a permanent ordinance in the Church?

Turrettin, Loc. XIX, Que. 12. Hill, Bk. V, ch. 6, § 1.

2. What are the significatien and effects of baptism? Consider the doctrine of baptismal regeneration. Does baptism represent, as Immersionists say, the burial and resurrection of Christ?

Turrettin, Que. 19, § 1–16. Armstrong on Baptism, Part II, ch. 3; Part I, ch. 8 and 9. Dick. Lect., 89.

3. What formulary of words should accompany baptism? and what their signification? Are any other formalities admissible? or sponsors?

Turrettin, Que. 17. Dick. Lect., 88 and 89. Knapp, § 139.

4. Was John's baptism the Christian sacrament of the new dispensation? For what signification was Christ baptized by him?

Turrettin, Que. 16. Armstrong, Part I, ch. 9. Dick. Lect., 88. Calvin's Inst., Bk. IV, ch. 15, § 7 and 18.

5. State the classic, and then the scriptural meanings of the words *bapto* and *baptidzo*, and their usage when applied in the Septuagint and New Testament to *Levitical washings*.

Armstrong, Part I, ch. 3, 4, 5. Rice & Campbell's Debate, Prop. Dale's Classic Bapt. Dale's Judaic Baptism. Carson on Bapt.

6. Show that a change of meaning and mode takes place in the word *baptidzo* in passing from a secular to a sacred use.

Armstrong, Part I, ch. 1, &c.

I. Water Baptism Perpetual.—The general remarks made concerning the sacraments, and applied to baptism, will not be repeated. The earlier Socinians disputed the perpetual obligation of water-baptism, as the Quakers now do of both the sacraments, and on similar grounds. They plead that the new is intended to be a spiritual dispensation; that salvation is always in the New Testament conditioned essentially on the *state of heart*: that Paul (1 Cor. i: 17) says, "Christ sent me not to baptize, but to preach the gospel:" and that the water-baptism administered by the apostles was only a temporary badge to separate the Church from Jews and Pagans at its outset. Quakers suppose that the only sacraments to be observed in our day are those of the heart, the baptism of the Holy Ghost, and the feeding on Christ by faith. The answers are: That the Old Testament, with its numerous types and two sacraments, was also a spiritual dispensation, and saving benefits were then, just as much as now, conditioned on the state of the heart; that the commission to baptize men was evidently co-extensive with that to disciple and teach them, as is proved by the accompanying promise of grace; that the commission to baptize lasts at least till all nations are converted, which is not yet accomplished; that it was *after* the most glorious experiences of the true spiritual baptism, at Pentecost, that the water-baptism was most industriously administered; and that Paul only expresses the inferior importance of baptizing to preaching, and his thankfulness at having baptized only three persons at Corinth, in view of the unpleasant fact that that Church was ranking itself in parties according to the ministers who introduced them to membership.

II. Meaning of Baptism.—The folly and falsehood of baptismal regeneration have been already pointed out in the former lecture. All the arguments there aimed against the *opus operatum* apply here. The error most probably grew as superstition increased in the primitive Church, out of the unguarded use of the sacramental language by the early fathers, whose doctrine on this point was sounder. We know that baptism, in supposed imitation of Titus iii: 5, was currently called regeneration as early as Justin Martyr and Irenæus. It is easy to see how, as men's ideas of sacred subjects became more gross, this figurative use of the word introduced the real error.

According to the Shorter Catechism (Qu. 94) baptism "doth signify and seal our ingrafting into Christ, and partaking of the benefits of the covenant of grace, and our engagements to be the Lord's." And in the Confession, chapter 28, those benefits of the covenant of grace are farther explained to be remission of sins and regeneration. Each part of this definition we can abundantly substantiate from Scripture. See Gal. iii: 27; Rom. vi: 5; Jno. iii: 5; Titus iii: 5; Col. ii: 11, 12, &c.; Acts ii: 38; Mark i: 4; Acts xxii: 16, &c.; Rom. vi: 3, 4; 1 Cor. xii: 13.

Derived from Jewish Purifications.—One of the most remarkable things about Baptism to the attentive reader of Scripture is the absence of all set explanations of its meaning in the New Testament, and at the same time, of all appearance of surprise at its novelty. Not so with the other sacrament, although that was a continuation of the familiar Passover. These things, among others, convince me that Baptism *was* no novelty to the Jews, either in its form or signification. It was the thing symbolized by the Hebrews *purifications* (katharimoi). The idea of the purification included both cleansing and consecration;

and the formalities represented both the removal of impurity from the person, in order that it might be adapted to the service of a holy God, and the consequent dedication to Him. Now, the main idea of Baptism is purification: and the element applied, the detergent element of nature, symbolizes the two-fold application of Christ's atonement (called His blood) and the Holy Ghost, cleansing from *guilt* and *depravity*, and thus also consecrating the cleansed person to the service of a holy God. Here then, we have involved, the ideas of regeneration and remission, and also of engrafting and covenanting into Christ's service. This view will be farther substantiated in treating the words BAPTISMOS, &c.

DOES BAPTISM COMMEMORATE CHRIST'S BURIAL AND RESURRECTION? Now the Immersionists, (for what purpose we shall see), have departed from the uniform faith of Christendom on this point: and while they do not wholly discard the purification, make baptism primarily symbolical of Christ's *burial and resurrection.* They teach that, as the supper commemorates His death, so baptism commemorates *His burial and rising again.* True the believer, in commemorating His death in the supper, receives also a symbol of the benefits purchased for us therein. So, in commemorating His burial and resurrection, there is a symbolizing of our burial to sin, and living again unto holiness. But the main meaning is, to set forth Christ's burial and resurrection. Only three texts can be quoted for this view. Rom. vi: 3–5; Col. ii: 12, and 1 Cor. xv: 29, and especially the first.

DISPROVED. NO SCRIPTURE PROOF.—Now our first objection to this view is its lack of all Bible support. He would be a hardy man, who would base any theory on the exposition of a passage so obscure as 1 Cor. xv: 29. We shall not discuss it, until some exposition is adduced which is at least probable. The other two passages are substantially identical: and, under the figure of a death and rising again, they obviously represent a *regeneration.* Compare especially Col. ii: 11, 12; Rom. vi: 4. So likewise the figures of circumcision, planting, and crucifixion, all represent the same, regeneration. This the immersionist himself cannot deny. The baptism here spoken of is, then, not directly a water baptism at all: but the spiritual baptism thereby represented. Col. ii: 11. It is the circumcision "made *without hands.*" Rom. vi: 3, 4. It is a baptism not into water, but into *death*, i. e., a death to carnality. Therefore it is clear the symbolism here points to the *grace of regeneration*, and not to any supposed grace in Christ's burial. His burial and resurrection are themselves used here as symbols, to represent regeneration. As justly might the immersionist say that baptism commemorates a crucifixion, a planting, a building, a change of a stone into flesh, a putting off dirty garments: because these are all Scripture figures of *regeneratibn*, of which baptism is a figure. Nor is there in these famous passages any reference to the mode of baptism, because first the Apostle's scope in Rom. vi, forbids it: and second, the same mode of interpretation would compel us to find an analogy in the mode of baptism, to a planting and a crucifixion. See Scott, *in loco.*

NO PROPER SACRAMENTAL ANALOGY.—But second: by making baptism the commemoration of Christ's burial, and resurrection, the sacramental analogy (as well as the warrant) is totally lost. This analogy is not in the *element* to the grace; for in that aspect, there can be *no resemblance.* Water is not like a tomb, nor like the Holy Ghost, nor like Christ's atoning righteousness. Nor is bread like a man's body, nor wine like his blood. The selection of the sacramental element is not founded on a *resemblance*, but on an *analogy*. Distinguish. The bread and wine are elements, not because *they* are *like* a body and blood, in their qualities: but because there is an analogy in their *uses*, to nourish and cheer. So the water is an element of a sacrament, because there is an analogy in its *uses*, to the thing symbolized. The use of water is to *cleanse.* Where now is any analogy to Christ's burial? Nor is there even a resemblance in the action, not even when the immersionist's mode is granted. Water is not like a Hebrew tomb. The temporary demission of a man into the former, to be instantly raised out of it, is not like a burial.

Christ's burial not vital.—Third: If we may judge by the two sacraments of the old dispensation, and by the supper, sacraments (always few,) are only adopted by God to be commemorative of the most *cardinal* transactions of redemption. Christ's burial was not such. Christ's burial is nowhere proposed to us an essential object of faith. His death and the Spirit's work are. His death and resurrection are; the former already commemorated in the other sacrament. And besides: it would seem strange that the essential work of the Holy Ghost should be commemorated by no sacrament, while that of Christ is commemorated by two! In the old dispensation the altar and the laver stood side by side. And here would be a two-fold covenant, with two seals to one of its promises, and none to the other!

And last: the Immersionsionist is involved by his theory in intense confusions. In the gospel history, Christ's death preceded His burial and resurrection, so the commemoration of the death ought to precede. But the Immersionist makes it *follow*, with peculiar rapidity. Again: the Supper was only practised either when the death was already accomplished, or immediately at hand; so that its commemoration intent was at once obvious. But the baptism was instituted long before the burial. Did it then point *forward* to it? Are sacraments *types?* And this difficulty presses peculiarly on the immersionist, who makes John's baptism identical with Christian. What then did John's baptism signify to Jews, before Christ was either dead or buried, and before these events were foreknown by them?

III. Baptism in Whose Name?—In Matt. xxviii: 19 the formulary of words to be employed is given by Christ explicitly, eis to onoma, &c., and this preposition is retained in every case but one. Had our Saviour said that baptism should be en to onomati (dative) &c., his meaning would have appeared to be that the *rite was applied by the authority* of that name, i. e., hebraice, of that person. The one case in which this formulary occurs (Acts x: 48) is probably to be explained in this way; but the uniform observance of the other formulary, in all the other cases (especially see 1 Cor. i: 13 and x: 3), indicates clearly that the meaning of the rite is, that it *purifies and dedicates us* unto *the Trinity*, bringing us into a covenant relation to Him. Here we see an additional argument for the definition given in § I of the meaning of baptism, and against the Immersionist idea.

Cases are not unfrequent (e. g., in Acts viii: 16, x: 48, xix: 5) in which no name is mentioned but that of Christ. But I think we are by no means to infer hence that the apostles ever omitted any of the formulary enjoined by Christ. Jews would have no objection to a baptism to God the Father. (John's was such, and exceedingly popular.) They were used to them. But Christ Jesus was the stumbling-block; and hence when the historian would indicate that a Hebrew had made a thorough submission to the new dispensation, he would think it enough to say that he had assumed Christ's name. The rest was then easy to believe and was therefore left to be inferred.

Superstitious Adjuncts.—The Church of Rome accompanied baptism with a number of superstitious rites, of which she still retains the most, and her daughter, the Church of England, a part. They were, blessing the water in the font, exorcism, renouncing the Devil, anointing in the form of a cross, anointing the eye-lids and ears with spittle, breathing on the candidate, washing the whole body *in puris naturalibus*, the baptism proper, tasting salt and honey, putting on the white robe, or at least, taking hold of a white cloth, and imposition of hands. The last, now separated from baptism, constitutes the sacrament of confirmation. We repudiate all these, for two reasons: that they are unauthorized by Scripture, and, worse than this, that their use is suggestive of positive error and superstition.

Sponsors.—The use of sponsors, who are now always other than the proper parents (when any sponsors are used), in the Episcopal and Romish churches, has grown from gradual additions. In the early Church the sponsors were *always* the natural parents of the infant, except in cases of orphanage and slavery; and then they were either the master, or some deacon or deaconess. (See Bingham, p. 523, &c.) When an adult was *in extremis*, and even speechless, or maniacal, or insensible, if it could be proved that he had desired baptism, he was permitted to receive it, and some one stood sponsor for him. If he recovered, this sponsor was expected to watch over his religious life and instruction. And in the case of Catechumens, the sponsor was at first some clergyman or deaconess, who undertook his religious guidance. It was a universal rule that no one was allowed to be sponsor unless he undertook this *bona fide*. How perverted is this usage now! Our great objection to the appearance of any one but the natural parents, where there are any, or in other cases, of him who is *in loco parentis*, as sponsors, is this: that no other human has the *right* to dedicate the child, and no other has the opportunity and authority to train it for God. To take these vows in any other sense is mockery.

Nature of John's Baptism.—The Reformers strenuously identify John's baptism with the Christian, arguing that his mission was a sort of *dawn* of the new dispensation, that it was the baptism of repentance, an evangelical grace, and that it is also stated (Luke iii: 3) to be for the remission of sins. But later Calvinists hold, against them and the Immersionists, that it was a baptism for a different purpose, and therefore not the same sacramentally, however it may have resembled as to mode, that of the Christian Church. Their reasons are, that it was not administered in the name of the Trinity, and did not bring the parties into covenant with Christ. 2nd. It was not the initiatory rite into the Church, and did not signify our ingrafting into Christ, for the old dispensation still subsisted, and those who received the rite were already in the Church of that dispensation, whereas Christ's was not yet opened, and therefore could not receive formal adherents. But, 3d, Paul seems clearly (Acts xix: 5) to have repeated Christian baptism on those who already had John's. Calvin and Turrettin indeed evade this fact by making verse 5 the words of Paul (not of Luke), reciting the fact that these brethren had already (when they heard John) received baptism. But this gloss is proved erroneous, not only by the whole drift of the passage (why had they not received charisms?), by the force of the MEN and DE, but above all by this: that if this verse 5 means John's baptism, then John baptized in the name of Jesus. But see Jno. i: 33; Matt. xi: 3. John's baptism was therefore not the sacrament of the new dispensation, but one of those purifications, preparing the way of the Messiah about to come, with which, we believe, the Jewish mind was familiar.

INTENT OF CHRIST'S BAPTISM.—The interesting question arises: With what intent and meaning did Christ submit to it? He could not repent, and needed no remission. We think it clear He could not have taken it in these senses. Says Turrettin: He took it *vicariously*, doing for His people, all that any one of them owed, to fulfill the law in their stead; and He refers, for support, to the fact that He punctually conformed to all the Levitical ritual,—was circumcised, attended sacrifices, &c. But note: His circumcision is not mentioned; compare with particular recital of John's, and it will not appear to be demonstrated that Christ was indeed circumcised. But the cases are not parallel. Christ as a Jew, (according to His humanity,) would properly render obedience to all the rules of the dispensation *under which* He came vicariously: but it is not therefore proper that He should comply with the rules of a dispensation to be wholly founded *on Him* as Mediator, and which rules were all legislated *by Him*. This for those who assert that John's baptism was the *Christian Sacrament*. There is no evidence that Christ partook of His other sacrament. See Luke xxii: 17. And while His vicarious attitude would make a ceremonial purification from *guilt* appropriate, it would not make a rite significant of repentance appropriate. Christ did not *repent* for imputed guilt, which did not stain His character. Nor would the other part of the signification apply to Him: for this imputed guilt was not pardoned to Him: He paid the debt to the full.

IT WAS HIS CONSECRATION TO PRIESTHOOD.—There seems then, to be no explanation; except that Christ's baptism was His priestly inauguration. John, himself an Aaronic priest, might naturally administer it. His age confirms it; compare Luke iii: 23, with Numb iv: 3. A purification by water was a part of the original consecration of the Aaronic family. See Levit. viii: 6; or better, Exod. xxx: 17–21, &c. The unction Christ received immediately after, by the descent of the Holy Ghost. And last, John's language confirms it, together with the immediate opening of Christ's official work.

V. REAL QUESTION AS TO MODE. NEITHER ETYMOLOGY NOR SECULAR USE DEFINES IT.—We now approach the vexed question, of the *mode* of baptism. The difference between us and immersionists is only this: whether the entire immersion of the body in water is essential to valid baptism. For we admit *any* application of water, by an ordained ministry, in the name of the Trinity, to be valid baptism. The question concerning the *mode* is of course one of meaning and usage of the words descriptive of the ordinance. But this preliminary question arises: of what usage? that of the classic, or of Hellenistic Greek? We answer, chiefly the latter; for the obvious reason, that this was the idiom to which the writers of the New Testament were accustomed, especially when speaking Greek on a sacred subject. And this, enlightened immersionists scarcely dispute. Another preliminary question arises: should it be found that the usage of the words BAPTIDZO, &c., when applied to common and secular washings, gives them one uniform meaning, would that be evidence enough that its meaning was precisely the same, in passing to a sacred ritual, and assuming a technical, sacred sense? I reply, by no means. There is scarcely a word, which has been borrowed from secular into sacred language, which does not undergo a necessary modification of meaning. Is EKKLESIA the same word in the Scriptures, which it is in common secular Greek? *Presbyter* means an elderly person, an ambassador, a magistrate. Is this the precise meaning of the Church presbyter of the New Testament? He might be a young man. Above all is this change marked in the word for the other sacrament, DEIPNON. This word in secular, social use, whether in or out of Scripture, means, the evening meal; and usually a full one, often a banquet, in which the bodily appetite was liberally fed. The Lord's Supper is usually not at evening; it is not a meal; and by its design has no reference to satisfying the stomach, or nourishing the body. See 1 Cor. xi. Indeed, it is *impossible* to adopt a secular and known word, as the name of this peculiar institution, a Christian Sacrament, without, in the very act of adopting it, superinducing upon it some shade of meaning different from its secular. Even if the favorite word of the Immersionists, immersion, were adopted, as the established name in English, of the sacrament, it would *ipso facto* receive an immediate modification of meaning as a sacramental word. Not any immersion whatever would constitute a sacrament. So that this very specific word would then require some specification. Thus we see that the assertion of the Immersionist, that BAPTIDZO is a purely specific word, and, as a name of a sacrament, admits of no definition as to mode, would be untrue, even if it were perfectly specific in its common secular meaning, both in and out of Scripture. We might grant then, that BAPTIDZO, whenever non-ritual, is *nothing but plunge, dip under*, and still sustain our cause.

VI. IMMERSIONIST POSTULATE AS TO USAGE OF WORDS.—But we grant no such thing. Let it be borne in mind that the thing the Immersionist must prove is no less than this: that BAPTIDZO, &c., never can mean, in secular uses, whether in or out of the Scriptures, anything but dip under, plunge; for nothing less will prove that nothing but dipping wholly under is valid baptism. If the words mean frequently plunging, but sometimes wetting or washing without plunging, their cause is lost. For then it is no longer absolutely specific of mode. Let us then examine first the non-ritual or secular usage of the words, both in Hellenistic (Sept. Josephus) Greek and in the New Testament. We freely admit that BAPTO very often means to dip, and BAPTIDZO still more often, nay, usually, but not exclusively.

THE ROOT "BAPTO" TO BE EXAMINED.—And first, the trick of Carson is to be exposed, by which he endeavors to evade the examination of the shorter form, BAPTO, on the plea that BAPTIDZO and its derivatives are the only ones ever used in relation to the sacrament of baptism. True; but by what process shall we more properly discover the meaning of BAPTIDZO than by going to that of its root BAPTO, from which it is formed by the simple addition of IDZO, meaning *verbal activity* (the making of anything to be BAPT.) Well, we find the lexicons all defining BAPTO, dip, wash, stain. Suidas, PLUNO, to wash clothes. These definitions are sustained by the well known case, from the classics, of Homer's lake, BEBAMMENON, tinged with the blood of a dying mouse, which Carson himself gives up. But among the instances from Hellenistic Greek, the more important to our purpose, consult the following: Rev. xix: 13, a vesture stained with blood, BEBAMMENON; Luke xvi: 24; Ex. xii: 22: 1 Sam. xiv: 27; Levit. iv: 6, 7; Dan. iv: 33. So there are cases of the secular use of the word BAPTIDZO where immersion is not expressed. See the lexicons quoted by Dr. Owen and Rice, in which it is defined, not only to immerse, but also to wash, substantiated by the cases of "the blister baptized with breast milk," in classic Greek, and of the altar, wood and victim of Elijah baptized by *pouring on* water, in Origen. Hence, the common and secular usage is not uniformly in favor of dipping.

BAPTIDZO NOT ALWAYS DIP.—But if it were, the question would still be an open one; for it may well be, that when transferred to religious ritual, the word will undergo some such modification as we saw uniformly occur in all other words transferred thus. We proceed then one step nearer, and examine the meaning of the word in the Septuagint and New Testament, when applied to religious rituals, other than the Christian sacrament itself; that is, to Jewish purifications. And here we find that the specific idea of the Jewish religious baptism was not dipping, but an *act symbolical of purification*, of which the actual mode was in most cases by affusion. In 2 Kings v: 14, Naaman baptized himself (BAPTIDZO) seven times in Jordan. This may have been dipping, but taking into account the Jewish modes of purification, was more probably by affusion. In Eccl's xxxiv: 25, the Septuagint says: "He that baptizeth himself (BAPTIDZETAI) after he toucheth a dead body, if he touch it again, what availeth his washing?" How this baptism was performed, the reader may see in Numb. xxxi: 19, 24, and xix: 13–20. In Judith xii: 7, this chaste maiden is said to have baptized herself at a fountain of water by a vast camp! In Josephus Antiq. Bk. 4, ch. 4, the ashes of the red heifer used in purifying are said to be *baptized* in spring water.

NEW TESTAMENT USE OF THE VERB NOT ALWAYS DIP.—In the New Testament there are four instances where the Jewish ritual purifications are described by the term baptize; and in all four cases it was undoubtedly by affusion. Mark vii: 4; Luke xi: 38; John ii: 6; Heb. ix: 10, vi: 2. (The last may possibly be Christian baptism, though its use in the plural would rather show that it included the Jewish.) Now that *all* these purifications called here BAPTISMOI, were by affusion, we learn, 1. From the Levitical law, which describes various washings and sprinklings, but *not one immersion* of a man's person for purification. 2.

From well known antique habits still prevalent in the East, which limited the washings to the hands and feet, and performed them by affusion. Compare 2 Kings iii : 11 ; Exod. xxx : 21. 3. From comparison of the two passages, Mark vii : 4, and Luke xi : 38, with Jno. ii : 6. These water pots were too narrow at the mouth, and too small (holding about 2 bushels) to receive a person's body, and were such as were borne on the shoulders of female servants. 4. From the great improbability that Jews would usually immerse all over so often, or that they *could*. 5. From the fact that they are declared to have practised, not only these baptisms of their persons, but of their utensils and massive couches. Numb. xix : 17, 18. It is simply preposterous that these should have been immersed as often as ceremonially defiled. Last, the Levitical law, which these Jews professed to observe with such strictness, rendered an immersion impossible any where but in a deep running stream, or living pit of a fountain. For if any thing ceremonially unclean went into a *vessel* of standing water, no matter whether large or small, the water was thereby defiled, and the vessel, and all other water put into that vessel, and all persons who got into it. See Levit. xi : 32, 36.

It is true that Immersionists pretend to quote Talmudists (of whom I, and probably they, know nothing), saying that these purifications were by immersion ; and that Solomon's 'sea' was for the priests to swim in. But the Talmud is 700 years A. D., and excessively absurd.

Inference.—Now, if the religious baptisms of the Jews were not by dipping, but by affusion ; if their specific idea was that of *religious purification*, and not dipping ; and if Christian baptism is borrowed from the Jewish, and called by the same name, without explanation, can any one believe that dipping is its specific and essential form? Immersionists acknowledge the justice of our *inference* by attempting to dispute all the *premises*. Hard task !

LECTURE LXII.

SYLLABUS.

BAPTISM. (Continued.)

7. What would most probably be the mode of baptism adopted for a universal religion?

Ridgely, Qu. 166.

8. What mode is most appropriate to the symbolical meaning of baptism?

Consult Is. lii : 15 ; compare Matt. iii : 11 ; Acts i : 5, ii : 2 and 4, ii : 15-18 ii : 33, x : 44-48, xi : 16, 17. Alexander on Isaiah. Armstrong on Baptism. Review of Theodosia Ernest.

9. What mode appears most probable from the analogy of the figurative and spiritual baptisms of Matt. xx : v. 20-23 ; Mark x : 38, 39 ; Luke xii : 50 : 1 Cor. x : 2 ; 1 Pet. iii : 21 ; 1 Cor. xii ; 13 : Gal. iii : 37 · Eph. iv : 5 ; Rom. vi : 3 ; Col. ii : 12.
See Armstrong on Baptism, Pt. I, ch. 6th and 8th.
Commentaries on Scriptures cited.

10. Argue the mode from Jno. 3 : 25, 26.
Armstrong on Baptism, Pt. I, ch. 2.

11. Discuss the probable mode observed in John's baptisms in Jordan and at Ænon, the Eunuch's, Paul's, the three thousand's at Pentecost, Cornelius', the Philippian jailor's.
Armstrong, Pt. II, ch. 3, 4. Dr. Leonard Woods on Baptism. Taylor's Apostolic Baptism. Robinson's Researches in Palestine. Commentaries. Review of Theodosia Ernest.

12. What would be the ecclesiastical results of the Immersionist dogma?
Review of Theodosia Ernest.

13. What was the cuitomary mode of baptism in the early Church, subsequent to the Apostles?
Bingham's "Origines Sacræ," Art. "Bapt." Taylor's Apostolic Baptism. Church Histories. Review of Theodosia Ernest.
See on whole, Rice and Campbell's Debate. Fairchild on Baptism. Beecher on Baptism.

VII. Dipping Impracticable Sometimes.—A consideration of some probable weight may be drawn from the fact that Christianity is intended to be a universal religion. Remember that it is characterized by fewness and simplicity of rites, that it is rather spiritual than ritual, that its purpose was to make those rites the reverse of burdensome, and that the elements of the other sacraments were chosen from articles common, cheap, and near at hand. Now, in many extensive countries, water is too scarce too make it convenient to accumulate enough for an immersion; in other regions, all waters are frozen over during helf the year. In many cases infirmity of body renders immersion highly incouvenient and even dangerous. It seems not very probable that, under these circumstances, a dispensation so little formalistic as the Christian, would have made immersion *essential* to the validity of baptism, for a universal Church, amidst all climes and habits.

VIII. Grace Symbolized is Always Shed Forth.—But we derive an argument of far more importance from the obviously correct analogy between the act of affusion and the graces signified and sealed in baptism. It is this which Immersionists seek to evade when they endeavor, contrary to Scripture, to make baptism signify and commemorate primarily Christ's burial and resurrection. (Hence the importance of refuting that dream.) The student will remember that the selection of the element is founded, not upon the resemblance of its nature (for of this there can be none, between the material and spiritual), but on the *analogy of its use* to the graces symbolized. Water is the detergent element of nature. The great meaning of baptism is our cleansing from guilt by atonement (blood), and our cleansing from the depravity of heart by the Holy Ghost. Now, in all Bible language, without a single exception, atonement is symbolized as sprinkled, or affused, or put on; and the renewing Spirit, as descending, or poured, or falling. See all the Jewish usages, and the whole tenour of the promises. Levit. xiv : 4, 51, xvi : 14; Numb. viii : 7, xix : 18; Heb. ix : 19-22, especially last verse, ix : 14, x : 22; Levit. vii : 14; Exod. xxix : 16, 21, &c.; Ps. xlv : 2; Is. xliv : 3; Ps. lxxii : 6; Is. xxxii : 15; Joel ii : 28, 29, quoted in Acts ii.

Isaiah, and other Old Testament Instances.—Nor is the force of this analogy a mere surmise of ours. See Is. lii : 15, where it is declared that the Redeemer, by His mediatorial, and especially his suffering work, "shall *sprinkle* many nations." The immediate reference here doubtless is not to water baptism, but to that which it signifies. But when God chooses in His own Word to call those baptismal *graces* a sprinkling, surely it gives no little authority to the belief that water baptism is by sprinkling! Immersionists feel this so acutely that they have ever availed themselves of the infidel glosses of the German Rationalists, who, to get rid of the Messianic features of this glorious prophecy, render yazzeh 'to cause to start up,' 'to startle.' The only plea they bring for this unscrupulous departure from established usage of the word is, that in all the other places this verb has as its regimen the *element* sprinkled, and not the object. This objection Dr. J. A. Alexander pronounces frivolous, and denies any Hebrew or Arabic support to the substituted translation. Again: In Ezek. xxxvi : 25, are promises which, although addressed primarily to the Jews of the Captivity, are evidently evangelical: and there the sprinkling of clean water symbolizes the gospel blessings of regeneration, remission, and spiritual indwelling. The language is so strikingly favourable to us, that it seems hardly an overstraining of it to suppose it a prediction of the very sacrament of baptism. But this we do not claim.

New Testament Examples of Grace by Affusion.—Our argument is greatly strengthened when we proceed to the New Testament. Collate Matt. iii : 11; Acts i : 5, ii : 2-4; ii : 15-18, ii : 33, x : 44, 45, 48, xi : 16, 17. Here our argument is two-fold. First: that both John and Christ baptize *with* water, not *in* water. This language is wholly appropriate to the application of water to the person, wholly inappropriate to the application of the person to the water. No Immersionist would speak of dipping *with* water. They do indeed reclaim that the preposition is en, here translated with, and should in all fidelity be rendered *in*, according to its admitted use in the large majority of New Testament cases. This we utterly deny; first, because in the mouth of a Hebraistic Greek, en being the established equivalent and translation of by, may naturally and frequently mean *with;* but second and chiefly because the parallel locutions of Luke 3 : 16, Acts i : 5, xi : 16, Eph. v : 26; Heb. x : 22, identify the en udate, &c., with *the ablative of instrument.* And from the same passages we argue farther, that the mode of the baptism with the Holy Ghost and fire, is fixed most indisputably by the description of the event in Acts ii : 2 and 4. The long promised baptism occurred. And what was it? It was the *sitting* of tongues of fire on each Apostle, and the "descent," the fall, the "*pouring out,*" the "shedding forth," of the spiritual influences. To make the case still stronger, if possible, when the spiritual effusion on Cornelius and his house occurred, which made Peter feel that he was justified in authorizing their water-baptism, he informs his disapproving brethren in Jerusalem (Acts xi : 15, 16) that the "falling of the Holy Ghost on them as on us as at the beginning," caused him "to remember" the great promise of a baptism, not with water only, but with the Holy Ghost and with fire. If baptism is never an affusion, how could such a suggestion ever arise?

Evasions Answered.—This reasoning is so cogent that Immersionists feel the necessity of an evasion. Their Coryphæus, Carson, suggests two. No element, nor mode of applying an element, he says, can properly symbolize the essence of the Holy Ghost. It is immense, immaterial, unique. All men are at all times immersed in it. To suppose any analogy between water affused, and this infinite, spiritual essence, is gross materialism. Very true; yet here is *some* sort and sense in which a *baptism* with the Holy Ghost occurred; and if it is gross anthropo-morphism to liken His ubiquitous essence to water affused, it is equally so to liken it to water for plunging. If there is no sense in which the analogy between the baptismal element and the *influences* of the Holy Ghost can be asserted, then it is God's Word which is in fault, for He has called the outpouring of those influences a baptism. The truth is, that here, just as when God is said to come, to go, to lift up His hand, it is not the divine essence which changes its place, but its *sensible influences.*

The other evasion is, to say that because this baptism is wholly figurative, and not a proper and literal baptism at all, therefore it can contain no reference whatever to mode. We deny both premise and conclusion: the conclusion, because Immersionists infer mode, with great positiveness, from a merely figurative baptism, in Rom. vi: 4; and the premise, because the baptism of Pentecost was in the best sense real, the most real baptism that ever was in the world. It was, indeed, not material: but if its literal reality be denied, then the inspiration of the Apostles is denied, and the whole New Testament dispensation falls.

This Argument Summed Up.—Our argument, then, is summed up thus: Here was a spiritual transaction, which Christ was pleased to call *His baptism*, in the peculiar sense. In this baptism the outward element descended upon the persons of the recipients, and the influences of the Holy Ghost, symbolized thereby, are spoken of as falling. Water baatism, which is intended, like the fire, to symbolize the spiritual baptism, should therefore be also applied by affusion.

IX. Argument from Figurative Baptisms.—While we deny that these memorable events formed only a figurative baptism, yet the word baptism is used in Scripture in a sense more properly figurative and wholly non-sacramental. Immersionists profess to find in all these an allusion to dipping; but we shall show that in every case such allusion is uncertain or impossible.

Christ's Baptism in Sorrow.—The first instance is that of Christ's baptism in His sufferings at His death. Matt. xx: 20, 23: Mark x: 38, 39; Luke xii: 50. Although Luke refers to a different conversation, yet the allusion to his dying sufferings is undoubtedly the same. Now, it is common to say that these sufferings were called a baptism because Christ was to be then covered with anguish as with an overwhelming flood. Even granting this, it must be remembered the Scriptures always speak of God's wrath as being *poured out*, and however copious the shower, an effusion from above bears a very questionable resemblance to an immersion of the person into a body of liquid beneath. Some (as Dr. Armstrong) find in this figure no reference to the mode of baptism, but suppose that the idea is one of consecration simply. Christ is supposed to call his dying sufferings a baptism because by them He was inducted into His kingly office. But this is not wholly satisfactory.

The true explanation is obviously that of the Greek fathers. As is well known to students of sacred history, the martyr's sufferings were considered his baptism. And so literal was the notion expressed by this, that the Fathers gravely argue that by martyrdom the unbaptized catechumen, who witnesses a good confession, becomes a baptized Christian, and has no reason whatever to regret his lack of water baptism, supposed by them to be, in other cases, essential. To the question why martyrdom is called by them a baptism, they answer with one voice, because Christ was pleased to call His own martyrdom a baptism, and to apply the same name to the pious sufferings of James and John. And they say farther, quoting the same texts, that the reason Christ calls His dying sufferings a baptism is, *because they cleansed away sin*, as the water of baptism symbolically does. Here, then, is no reference to *mode* of water baptism, and these Greek fathers, if they in any case press the figure to a signification of mode, speak of Christ's body as baptized, or stained with His own blood, a baptism by affusion. And the baptism of martyrdom is explained as a baptism of blood and fire.

ISRAEL'S BAPTISM TO MOSES.—1 Cor. x: 2 represents the Israelites as baptized *unto Moses* in the cloud and in the sea, in passing the Red sea. Immersionists foolishly attempt to strain a reference to immersion here, by saying that the Israelites were *surrounded* with water, having the sea as a wall on the either hand, and the cloud over head. But unfortunately for this far-fetched idea, it is expressly said that Israel went over dry-shod. And the cloud was not over them, but *behind* them. Nor is there any proof that it was an aqueous cloud (it was fire by night and luminous); and the allegorizing Greek Fathers currently understand it as representing, not the water of baptism, but God's Holy Ghost. Nor have we any proof that even aqueous vapour can be substituted for the sacramental element. There was an immersion in the case, but it was that of Pharaoh and his hosts. The lost were immersed; the saved were baptized unto Moses! The sense of the passage obviously is, that by this event Israel were dedicated, separated unto that religious service of which Moses was the teacher. The word baptize here carries *no reference* to mode, but has his proper sense of *religious separation.*

BELIEVER'S BAPTISM INTO CHRIST.—The same is its meaning in 1 Cor. xii: 13; Gal. iii: 27; Eph. iv: 5, and 1 Pet. iii: 21. When the believer is said to be baptized *into* (or unto) Christ, or into His one body, and thus to have put on Christ, there can be no allusion to mode, because then it would be the preposterous idea of immersing into Christ, or into His mystical body, instead of into water. The exact idea expressed is that of *a consecrating separation.* Baptism is here conceived by the Apostle as our separation from the ruined mass of mankind and annexation to the Saviour in our mystical union. So in 1 Pet. iii: 21, baptism is called a figure like (ANTITUPOU) to the salvation of Noah's family in the ark. This saving was from water, not *by* water, and it was effected *in* the ark. Here again there is no modal reference to immersion, for the parties saved were not dipped, and all who were dipped were lost. The baptism of Noah's family was therefore their *separation* from a sinful world, effected by the waters of the flood. If baptism in its most naked, spiritual meaning, carries to Hebrews the idea of a religious separation, it is very evident what mode it would suggest, should they permit their minds to advert to mode. Their separations were by sprinklings. The remaining passage (Eph. iv : 5) could only have been supposed to teach the essential necessity of observing water baptism in only one mode, by a mind insensible to the elevation and sacredness of the passage. It is the glorious spiritual unity between Christians and their Divine Head, resulting from the separating consecration which baptism represents.

X. Baptism is Purification.—The identification of baptism with the purifications of the Jews, in Jno. iii : 26, 25, throws some light upon its mode. The question about purifying, agitated between the Jews and some of the Baptist's disciples (v. 25), is evidently the question which they propound to John himself (in v. 26), viz.: What was the meaning of *Christ's* baptizing. The whole tenour of John's answer proves this, for it is all addressed to the explanation of this point: why Christ, baptized by him, and thus seemingly his *disciple*, should administer a baptism independent of him. Any other explanation leaves an absurd chasm between verses 25 and 26. Baptism, then, is katharismos, a striking testimony to the correctness of our account of its signification, a matter which we found to bear, in so important a way, upon its mode. But farther: Let any one consider the Septuagint use of this word, and he cannot easily remain in doubt as to the mode in which a Jew would naturally administer it.

XI. Mode of New Testament Baptism.—My time will not permit me to go into a full discussion of the actual mode indicated by the sacred historian in each case of baptism in the New Testament. Such detail is, indeed, not necessary, inasmuch as you may find the work well done in several of your authors, and especially in Armstrong, Part II, ch. 3, 4. The result of a thorough examination was well stated by a divine of our Church thus: Rule three columns on your blank paper; mark the first, '*Certainly by immersion*;' the second, 'Probably by immersion;' the third, 'Certainly not by immersion.' Then, after the careful study of the Greek Testament, enter each case where it properly belongs. Under the first head there will be not a single instance; under the second, there may be a few; while the larger number will be under the third. Immersionists, when they read that John was baptizing in Jordan, and again at Ænon, "because there was much water there," conclude that he certainly immersed his penitents. But when we note that the language may as well be construed 'at' Jordan, and that the "many waters" of Ænon were only a cluster of springs; considering also the unlikeliness of one man's performing such a multitude of immersions, and the uninspired testimony of the early Church as to the method of our Saviour's baptism, the probabilities are all turned the other way. So the improbability of sufficient access to water, at Pentecost, and the impossibility of twelve men's immersing three thousand in one afternoon, make the immersion of the Pentecostal converts out of the question. This is the conclusion of the learned Dr. Edward Robinson, after an inquiry on the spot. In like manner, the Eunuch's baptism may possibly have been by dipping, but was more probably by affusion; while the cases of Paul, Cornelius, and the jailer, were certainly in the latter mode.

XII. See T. Earnest, p. 137.

XIII. Patristic Testimony as to Mode discussed.—Your acquaintance with Church history has taught you the tenour of the usual represen tations of the antiquaries touching the mode of baptism in the patristi churches. The usual version is, that in the second and third centurie the usual mode of baptism was by a trine immersion, accompanied wit a number of superstitious rites, of crossing, anointing, laying on hands tasting honey and salt, clothing in a white garment, exorcism, &c. Ther are several reasons why we do not consider this testimony of any im portance.

First, the New Testament mode was evidently different, in mos cases at least; and we do not feel bound by mere human authority (even though within a hundred and fifty years of the Apostles, a laps of time within which great apostacies have often been matured.) Sec ond, we do not see how Immersionists can consistently claim this pa tristic precedent for dipping as of authority, and refuse authority t all their other precedents for the human fooleries which so uniforml attended their baptisms. And farther, the many other corruptions o doctrine and government which were at the same time spread in th Church, prove the fathers to be wretched examples for the New Testa ment religion. Third, the usage was *not* as uniformly by immersion as the antiquaries usually say. Thus, Cyprian teaches us, (amon many others,) that clinic baptism was usually by pouring or sprinkling in the third century; yet it was never regarded as therefore less valid and that father speaks, with a tone nigh akin to contempt, of the notio that its virtue was any less, because less water was used. Again, Dr Robinson teaches us that the early baptisms could not have uniforml been by immersion; because some baptismal urns of stone are stil preserved, entirely too small to receive the applicant's whole person And several monumental remains of great authenticity and antiquit show us baptisms actually by affusion, as that of the Emperor Con stantine. Again, Mr. Taylor, in his Apostolic Baptism, shows us ver strong reasons to believe that the immersion of the whole body wa not the sacrament of baptism, but a human addition and preliminar thereto. For instance, the connexion of deaconesses with the baptiz ing of women, mentioned by not a few, is thus explained: That a immersion and actual washing *in puris naturalibus*, being supposed es sential before baptism, the young women to be baptized were take into the part of the baptistery where the pool was, and there, wit closed doors, washed by the deaconesses; for no male clergyman coul assist here, compatibly with decency. And that after this, the candi dates being dressed in their white garments, were presented to the pres byter, at the door of the Church, and received the actual baptism, b affusion from him. This view of the distinction between the washin and the sacrament is also supported by what modern travellers observe concerning the rite among some of the old, petrified, Oriental Churches

These remarks are designed not for a full discussion: but to sugges the topics for your examination.

Recapitulation.—In conclusion of the subject of the Mode of Bap tism let us review the positions successively established in a somewha complicated discussion.

I. Having pointed out the superior importance of Hebraistic Gree usage, over the Classic in determining this question, we separate th usage of the family of words expressing baptism into two questions their meaning when expressive of common, secular washings, in either Classic or Hebraistic Greek, and their meaning when expressive of religious, or ritual washings.

II. We show that all common words applied to describe religious rituals, *ipso facto*, undergo some modification of signification. And hence, even if it could be shown that the family of words always mean nothing but dip, in common secular washings, it would not be therefore proved of baptism. But

III. The family of words do not always mean exclusive dipping, either in Classic or Hebraistic Greek, when expressive of common washings.

IV. Nor do they mean exclusive dipping, when applied to describe religious rituals other than the Sacrament of Baptism, either in the Old Testament Greek, or in Josephus, or in the New Testament.

V. Nor, to come still nearer, is its proper sacramental meaning in the New Testament exclusive dipping, as we prove, by its symbolical meaning: From the analogy of figurative baptisms; From the actual attendant circumstances of the instances of the sacrament in the New Testament; And from the absurd consequences of the dogma. I commend Fairchild on Baptism, as a manual of this discussion remarkably compact, perspicuous, and comprehensive. I regard it as eminently adapted to circulation among our pastoral charges.

LECTURE LXIII.

SYLLABUS.

SUBJECTS OF BAPTISM.

1. Who are proper subjects of Christian Baptism, and on what terms?
John Edwards. Qualific. for Communion. Mason on the Church, Essay I. Neander. Ch. Hist. on the Novation and Donatist Schisms.

2. Meet the objection, that the nature of Baptism renders it necessarily inappropriate to infants, because they cannot believe. Review of Th. Ernest.
Dr. L. Woods' Lect. 111, and 117, or Woods on Infant Baptism. Fairchild on Baptism. Armstrong on do. Pt. III, ch. 3. Ridgeley. Qu. 165. Note. Calv. B. IV, c. 16.

3. Argue infant-baptism from infant church-membership.
Mason on the Church. Essays 2-4. Woods' Lect. 111, 112. Armstrong, Pt. III, ch. 4, 5. Calvin, Bk. IV, ch. 16. Turrettin, Loc. xix, Qu. 20. Ridgeley, Qu. 166.

4. What would have been the natural objections raised by the Jews, to Christianity, had it excluded infants?
Mason on the Church. Essay V.

5. State the argument for infant-baptism from the Great Commission. Matt. xxviii: 19, 20; Mark xvi: 15, 16; Luke xxiv: 47, &c.
Armstrong, Pt. III, ch. 2, and 6. Woods' Lect. 113, &c.

I. Believing Adults to be baptized.—All adults who make an intelligent and *credible* profession of faith on Jesus Christ are to be baptized on their own application; and no other adults. The evidence of the last assertion is in Acts ii: 41, 47; x: 47, with xi: 15, 16, and viii: 12 and 37. The genuineness of the last text is indeed grievously questioned by the critical editors, except Knapp; but even if spurious, its early and general introduction gives us an information of the clear conviction of the Church on this subject. Last: the truths signified by baptism, are such that it is obviously inappropriate to all adults but those who are true believers, in the judgment of charity.

What children may be baptized?—We add that baptism is also to be administered to "the infants of one or both believing parents." (Conf. 28, § 4.) The great question here raised will be the main subject of this and a subsequent lecture. But a related question is still agitated among Pædobaptists themselves, whether one or both of the parents must be *believers*, or only decent baptized members of the Church. Papists baptize the children of all baptized persons, and Episcopalians, Methodists, and not a few of the Presbyterian family of Churches, baptize those of all decent baptized persons. They plead the Church-membership of the parents, the example of the Jewish Church as to circumcision, and a kindly, liberal policy as to parents and infants. *We object;* first the express language of our Standards, Confession of Faith xxviii: 4; Larger Catechism, question 166. "Infants of one or both believing parents," "professing faith in Christ, and obedience to Him." Second: The language of 1 Cor. i: 14, where it is not the baptized, but the "*believing*" parent, who sanctifies the unbelieving. Third: Those baptized, but unbelieving parents are Church-members, subject to its guardianship and discipline; but they are not full members. They are ecclesiastical minors, cut off by their own guilty lack of spiritual qualification from all the spiritual privileges, and sealing ordinances. Fourth: Chiefly because it is preposterous that those who make no consecration of their own souls to Christ, and do not pretend to govern themselves by His laws, should profess to consecrate the souls of their children, and rear them to God. If then, it be urged that the children ought not to be deprived of their ecclesiastical privilege, because of the impenitence of the parents; I reply. Perfectly true: There is a great and cruel wrong committed on the little ones. But it is their own parents who commit it: not the Church authorities. *They* cannot repair that wrong, by giving them the shell of a sacrament which their parent's unbelief makes perfectly empty. This is no remedy; and it only violates Scripture, and introduces disorder. This will be greatly strengthened, when we show that Infant Baptism is a sacrament to the parents also.

Under the old Covenant the children of all circumcised persons were circumcised? True. But St. Paul has changed it; because, as we surmise, ours is a more spiritual dispensation, no state-Church separation exists from the world; and all unbelievers are spiritually "aliens."

Under the Jewish Church the children of mixed marriages were out of the Church, until they came in through the gate of proselytism Neh. xiii: 23–28. But under the New Testament, if one parent is a credible believer, the child is within the Covenant. Our grounds are

1 Cor. vii : 14, and the circumcision and baptism of Timothy. Acts xvi : 3.

II. IMMERSIONISTS OBJECT; INFANTS CANNOT BELIEVE.—Before we proceed to the main point of debate, it will be well to remove out of the way the objection on which Immersionists place the main reliance. They urge that since infants cannot exercise the graces signified and sealed in baptism, (see Catechism, question 94), it is useless and preposterous to administer it to babes. Take, say they, Mark xvi · 15, 16, as a specimen of the many passages in which it is categorically said, or clearly implied, that one *must believe*, before it is proper to baptize him. Hence the administration of the rite to infants is a practical falsehood, and if unauthorized by God, even profane. What, they ask, can all your inferential arguments for infant Church-membership be worth, when the express words of Scripture prove that infants cannot have the necessary qualifications for baptism?

ANSWERS.—We reply, this plausible statement proceeds on the usual fallacy of taking the speaker's words in a sense in which he did not mean them to be applied. In Mark xvi : 16, for instance, Christ was not speaking either of the terms of *infant* salvation, or of the terms on which they could become Church members. Let the reader remember that the temporary commission to the apostles and seventy (Matt. x : 5) had already made them familiar with the fact that Christ's dispensation was to be preached to Jews. But now, in Mark xvi : 15, it is extended to "all the world," and to "every creature." These were the features of the new commission prominent to our Saviour's mind, and the disciples' attention. The terms on which Jewish families should be admitted were already familiar. The question was, how shall those be admitted who are now aliens? Why, on their faith. The evidence that infants were not here intended to be excluded from baptism by our Saviour's scope is absolutely demonstrative; for the immersionist interpretation would equally make the passage prove that infants can neither be baptized, nor be saved, because they are incapable of faith; and it would equally make it prove that the salvation of infants is dependent on their baptism! We may find many other illustrations of the absurdity of such interpretations; as, for instance, in 2 Thess: iii : 10: "If any one (EI TIS) will not work, neither shall he eat." A similar reasoning would prove that infants should be starved.

INFANTS CAN BE IN THE COVENANT, SO MAY HAVE ITS SEALS.—Further: it does not follow that because infants cannot exercise intelligent graces, therefore there is no sense nor reason in administering to them sacraments significant thereof. Infants are capable of redemption. Glorious truth! Why, then, should it appear a thing incredible that they should partake of the sacraments of redemption? Baptism signifies God's covenant with souls, as well as their covenant with Him. Can there be no meaning in a pledge of God's covenant favour applied to an infant, because the infant does not yet apprehend it? No sense at all; because it has no sense to him? Strange reasoning! But human suppositions are a bad test of what God may or may not think reasonable. To the Word and the Testimony! There we find two cases in which religious ordinances were applied to "unconscious babes." In Matt. xix : 14, Mark x : 14, Luke xviii : 16, our Saviour took up little children (BREPHE) into His arms, and blessed them, *be-*

cause they were Church members. Did they comprehend the blessing? The other case is that of circumcision, and it is peculiarly strong, because it was emblematic of the same spiritual exercises and graces now signified by baptism. See Rom. ii: 28, 29, iv: 11; Col. ii: 11; Deut. xxx: 6, x: 16; Phil. iii: 3. Yet circumcision was, by God's command, applied to all the infant males of God's people! Let the immersionist, therefore, go and turn all the confident denunciation and fiery invective against "baby sprinkling," against this parallel ordinance of God. We entrench ourselves behind it.

The Sacrament Embraces the Parents.—Once more: So far as the child himself is concerned, there is no absurdity in giving him the seal in advance of his fulfilment of the conditions. Are not seals often appended to *promissory* covenants? Yea, every covenant is in its nature promissory, including something *to be done*, as a condition of the bestowment. This is so of adult baptism. But, they say, the adult can be *a party;* infants not. Answer: *parents* are, and the efficacy of the parental relation, properly sanctified, is regular enough to justify this arrangement. Where, then, is the practical objection, so far as the infant's own subsequent edification is concerned, of his receiving the seal beforehand, so that he may ever after have the knowledge of that fact, with all its solemn meaning, and see it re-enacted in every infant baptism he afterward witnesses? But, above all, remember that the infant is not the only party, on man's side, to the sacrament. Infant baptism is a sacrament *to the parent*, as well as the child. It consecrates the *relation* of filiation, or parentage, and thus touches *both the parties* to that relation equally. The parent has momentous duties to perform, for God's glory; and momentous religious responsibilities, as to the soul of the child, which duties are also represented and pledged in this sacrament, as well as God's promised aid and blessing in their performance. Infant baptism is a sacrament to the parent as much as to the child. Now, whatever of warning, instruction, comfort, edification, the sacrament was intended to convey to the parent, to fit him better for his charge as the educator of the child for eternity: when should the parent receive that equipment? When does the moral education of the infant's soul begin? It begins just so soon as the formation of *habit* begins; so soon as petulance, anger, selfishness, can be exhibited by an infant; so soon as it can apprehend the light of a mother's smile beaming upon it as it hangs upon her breast: as soon as it can know to tremble at her frown. Here, then, is the great practical reason, which makes God's wisdom clear even to man's reason, in instituting the seal of Church-membership at the dawn of life.

III. Argument from Infant Membership in Old Testament and New—Major Premise.—We proceed now to advance the positive evidences for infant baptism. Of these, the most solid and comprehensive is that from infant Church-membership in the New Testament Church. The *major* premise of our argument is, that baptism is, in all cases, the proper rite by which to recognize membership in the visible Church. The *minor* premise is, the infants of believing parents are members of the visible Church of Christ. Hence, the conclusion: such infants are proper subjects of baptism.

On the major premise there will probably be little dispute between tts and immersionists. In the great commission, we are taught that discipleship is formally constituted by baptism (Matt. xxviii : 19). In Acts ii : 41, language is used which plainly shows that the baptism of the three thousand was equivalent to their being added to the Church. In 1 Cor. xii : 13, the spiritual engrafting of true believers by the Holy Ghost into the spiritual body of Christ, the invisible Church, is called a baptism; in evident allusion to the effect of that rite in introducing to the visible Church.

MINOR PREMISE. CHURCH FORMED UNDER ABRAHAM.—The minor premise leads us to consider the origin and constitution of the Church. Having formed in the Old Testament a visible Church state, called *Kahal*, and *Heydah*, and characterized by every mark of a Church, we trace that society up the stream of sacred history, until we find its institution (or re-institution) in the family of Abraham, and in that gospel and ecclesiastical covenant ratified with him in Genesis, ch. xvii. The patriarchal form was most naturally superinduced on this Church then, because it was the only organized form, with which man had hitherto been familiar, and the one best suited to that state of the world. The society there organized was set apart to the service and worship of God. It was organized under ecclesiastical rulers. It had the Word and gospel of God. It had its sacrament and other sacred rites. No one will dispute the continuity of this society under Moses and his successors; for the covenant of Horeb manifestly developed, it did not destroy, the body.

THE SAME UNDER NEW TESTAMENT.—But can the same thing be said of the visible Church catholic which has existed since Christ, under the organization given it by the Apostles? The Reformed Churches answer, Yes. This is substantially the same with the Church of the Old Testament. The change of dispensation is the change of outward form, not of its substance or nature. This is proved, a.) By the fact that the repeal of God's Church-covenant with Abraham and his family is nowhere stated. The abrogation of the Mosaic economy does not destroy the old body, because that economy did not introduce it. The law, which was four hundred and thirty years after, could not disannull the covenant made with Abraham. Gal. iii; 17.

APOSTLES DEVELOPE, NOT DESTROY IT.—a.) The Apostles and Christ, by their acts and sayings, recognize the existence of a visible Church, which they do not abolish, but reform, and increase. Observe in how many instances particular churches were but synagogues Christianized. Consider also, how those traits of order and ritual which are distinctive of the new dispensation, were made to overlap those which marked the old. The substitution of the former for the latter was gradual. St. Paul observed the passover after he began to keep the Lord's supper; he circumcised Timothy after he began to baptize gentiles. There is no sudden cutting off of the old, but a gradual "splicing" of the new on it.

GENTILES FORMED IT.—b.) The Apostle expressly teaches that Gentile converts, coming to Christ by faith, are under the terms of the Abrahamic covenant. Therefore that covenant is not abolished. They are "the seed;" they are "children of Abraham." They are "the true Israel." Rom. iv: 12—17; Matt. iii: 9; Gal. iii: 7. Indeed, the "seed," to whom the promises were made, never was, at any tim strictly coincident with the lineal descendants of Abraham. Ishmae Keturah's children, Esau, though circumcised, were no part of i Every heathen proselyte was. See Gen. xvii: 12, 13; Exod. xii: 48 Deut. xxiii: 8. Gentiles were always, as truly (not as numerously) now, a part of this seed.

PROMISES TO IT ONLY FULFILLED UNDER NEW TESTAMENT.—c.) Th correlative promises that "all nations should be blessed in Abrahan and that he should be "Father of many nations," were only fulfilled the gentiles were made members of the Abrahamic body. See Ro iv: 16, 17. It cannot be said that Abraham's paternity of the twelv tribes exhausted that promise, for Israel was but *one nation*. If, the the Abrahamic Church expired before the gentiles were brought i this promise was never fulfilled. It will not help the cause to say th Abraham was father of these believers, in the sense of being their *fir exemplar*. He was not. Noah, Enoch, Abel, probably Adam, we before him. The relationship is that of the head and founder of a organization, to the subsequent members of it. Nor will it be sai that the gentiles becoming 'Abraham's seed' only means their admi sion into the invisible Church, into which Abraham's faith admitte him. This is, indeed, a higher sequel to the privilege, as to all tru believers, but not the whole of it. We have proved that the Covenar was not purely spiritual, but also an ecclesiastical, visible Church co enant: Therefore the seed, or children of the covenant (see Acts ii 25) are also thereby brought into the visible Church relationship.

d.) The number of Old Testament promises to the visible Churc some of which were unfulfilled at the end of the old dispensation, mu imply that the community is still in existence to receive their fulfi ment. Otherwise God has failed. See, then, Isa. ii: 2, 3, liv: 1– xlix: 14–23; Ps. ii: 6, 8. It cannot be said that the invisible Chur is the sole object of these promises.

ROM. XI: 17, &c.—e.) Last. The figure of Rom. xi: 17 to 24 plainly implies that the Old Testament visible Church is continued u der the new dispensation. The good olive tree is not uprooted, b pruned, and new branches grafted in. And at last, the excind branches are to be regrafted "into their own olive tree." The arg ment is too clear and strong to need many words.

INFERENCE. CONFIRMED BY ALL PROVIDENCES.—Thus, our min premise is established. The ecclesiastical covenant made with Abr ham still subsists unrepealed, and all Christians are brought under As children were members of that covenant, the inference is irresistib that they are members still, unless their positive exclusion can pointed out in the New Testament. This inference is also greatly fo tified, by showing that all God's general dispensations towards the h man family have embraced the children along with the parents. In t Covenant of works with Adam: In the curse for its breach: In t covenant with Noah: In the curse on Sodom: In the doom of the C naanites, and Amalekites: In the constitution of society and course Providence in all ages; In the political commonwealths ordained Him: In all these, the infant children go with the parents. Were t visible Church different, it would be a strange anomaly.

Again: Malachi tells us (ii: 15) that God's object in constituting the marriage relation and family as it is, was "to seek a godly seed;" i. e., to provide for the Christian rearing of the offspring. Now, this is the Church's object. Would it not be strange if the visible Church failed to embrace and consecrate the family institutions as a subdivision of itself? Third: The affection, authority, and influence of parents are so unique, that when we properly consider them, it seems incredible God would have omitted them as parts of His Church instrumentalities, subject to the sanctifying rules of His house. Parental love is the strongest of the instinctive affections, and the most God-like in its permanence, forbearance, and disinterestedness. Parental authority is the most remarkable and absolute one delegated by God to man over his fellow man. Consider: it authorizes the parent to govern the child for a fourth of his life as a slave; to decide virtually his intelligence, culture, and social destiny, and even to elect for him a character and religious creed: thus seeming almost to infringe the inalienable responsibilities and liberties of the immortal soul! And last: the parental influence is so efficacious, especially in things moral and religious, that it does more than all others to decide the child's everlasting fate. Can it be that God would omit such a lever as this, in constructing His Church, as the organism for man's moral and religious welfare. Fourth: The Church-membership of children seems to be implied in that duty which all right-minded Christians instinctively exercise, of caring for the welfare and salvation of the children of the brotherhood. Fifth: It follows from the declared identity of circumcision and baptism, and from many express Scriptures. See Col. ii: 11, 12, 13; Matt. xix: 13–15; Acts ii: 38, 39; 1 Cor. vii; 14. The Church membership of infants having been thus established, the propriety of their baptism follows. Indeed, immersionists virtually admit that if the second premise is true, the conclusion must follow, by denying the Church-membership of infants under the New Testament.

Visible Church in Old Testament denied by Immersionists. Answer.—Many evasions of this argument are attempted. Immersionists deny that there was any visible Church Sate appointed for saints in the Old Testament! This is a striking, and at once a mournful proof of the stringency of my argument, that a body of evangelical Christians, claiming especial scripturalness and orthodoxy, should be forced, in resisting it, to adopt one of the most monstrous assertions of those flagrant heretics and fanatics, the Anabaptists. You have only to notice how expressly it contradicts the Scriptures, Acts vii: 38, Rom. xi: 24, Heb. iii: 5, 6: How it defies the plainest facts of the Old Testament history, which shows us God giving His people every possible feature of a visible Church state; gospel, ministry, sacraments, other ordinances, Sabbath, discipline, sanctuaries, &c.: How utterly it confounds all relations between the old and new dispensations: And how preposterously it represents Christ's own personal life, observances, and obedience, including especially His baptism by John, an Old Testament prophet, administering his rite in this Old Testament No-church, which rite is, according to immersionists, still the Christian sacrament!

Objected that the Argument proves too much—Answer.—Some of them assert that the argument, if good for anything, would equally make all adult unbelieving children of believing parents, and all unbelieving domestic slaves, Church members. Is no force to be allowed to the passing away of the patriarchal state, with the almost absolute authority of the father? None to the growing spirituality of the New Covenant? None to the express change in these features by apostolic authority, as is manifested in their precedents? Still, all that could be made of this argument would be to prove, not that the reasoning of Pædobaptists is unsound, but that their conduct may be inconsistent.

Sometimes it is objected that if infants were really made members of the visible Church, then, as they grow up, they must be admitted, without question, to all the privileges of membership, to suffrage, to office, to the Lord's supper. I reply that there is no commonwealth on earth, where mere citizenship entitles to all the higher franchises. In the State, all citizens are entitled to protection, and subject to jurisdiction. But all cannot vote and bear office. Christ's ecclesiastical commonwealth is *a school*, a place for teaching and training. To be a member of the school does not at once imply that one must share all its powers and privileges. The scholars are promoted according to their qualifications.

Peter, &c., "Chosen out of the World."—It is objected by some: If Peter and his brethren were in the visible Church, how comes it that Christ says to them: "I have chosen you out of the world?" Jno. xv: 19. I answer: Cannot that which is worldly, in the true sense, be in the visible Church? The objection begs the question. The very point in debate is, whether the Anabaptist definition of the visible Church, as a body containing only regenerate persons, is true. The Bible says that it is not: that Peter was yet worldly, while regularly in the visible Church, and was, out of that state chosen by Christ to the apostleship, and to effectual calling.

Why were Jews baptized if in the Church?—One more objection may be noted: If the visible Church of the Old and New Testaments is one, then circumcision and baptism are alike the initiatory rites. How came it then, that Jews, already regularly in it, were readmitted by baptism? I reply first. It is not so certain that they were. Note that we do not believe John's baptism to have been the Christian sacrament. But who can prove that the Twelve, and the Seventy were ever baptized again? As for the Jews after Pentecost, who certainly did receive Christian baptism, they were now, (after Christ's definite rejection, crucifixion, and ascension) "broken off for their unbelief;" and needed readmittance on their repentance. But second, where is the anomaly of re-administering the initiatory rite to members already in the Society, at the season of the marked change of outward form, when it was receiving a large class of new members. I see nothing strange in the fact, that the old citizens took their oath of allegiance over again, along with the new.

IV. No New Testament Warrant required.—Immersionists delight to urge, that as baptism is a positive institution, no Protestant should administer it to infants, because the New Testament contains no explicit warrant for doing so. I shall show that the tables can be turned on this point.

BURDEN OF DISPROOF ON THE IMMERSIONISTS.—When a society undergoes important modifications, its substantial identity yet remaining, the fair presumption is that all those things are intended to remain unchanged, about the change of which nothing is said. We may illustrate from citizenship in a Commonwealth changing its constitution. So, if there were not one word in all the New Testament, indicating the continuance of infant Church-membership, the silence of Scripture constitutes no disproof; and the burden of proof would rest on the Immersionist. And this burden he would have to assume against every antecedent probability. True, the cessation of the Mosaic dispensation was accompanied with great changes; but infant membership and circumcision never were merely Mosaic. We may say of them, as of the Covenant to which they belonged, as St. Paul says in Gal. iii: 17. All that was typical passed away, because of the coming of the Antitype: circumcision and infant membership never were types. Again, infant membership was esteemed by Jews a privilege. We understand that the new dispensation is an *extension* of the old one, more liberal in its provisions, and its grace: and embracing the whole human family. It would be a strange thing indeed, if this era of new liberality and breadth were the occasion for a new and vast restriction, excluding a large class of the human family, in whom the pious heart is most tenderly interested. Consider this in the light of the Apostle's language: E. G., in Rom. xi: 20; Acts iii: 23. In these and similar passages, the Jews are warned that unbelief of Christ, the great closing Prophet of the line, (like resistance of previous Theoratic Messengers,) will be accompanied with loss of their church membership. According to Immersionists, the meaning of this warning would be: "Oh, Jew; if you believe not on Jesus Christ, you (and your children) forfeit your much valued visible Church membership. But if you believe on Him, then your innocent children shall be *punished* for *your obedience*, by losing their privileges!"

WHAT NEW TESTAMENT WARRANT FOR CLOSE COMMUNION, &c.—Further, no immersionist is consistent, in demanding an express New Testament warrant in words, for all his ordinances. There is not an intelligent Protestant in the world, who does not hold that what follows from the express Word "by good and necessary consequence," is binding, as well as the Word itself. What other warrant have Immersionists for observing the Lord's day as a Christian Sabbath, and neglecting the seventh day? What warrant for admitting females to the Lord's table? What warrant for their favourite usage of strict communion? This, pre-eminently, is only a deduction.

NO CLAMOUR, SUCH AS MUST HAVE ARISEN AT EXCLUSION OF INFANTS. The presumption against the Immersionist is greatly strengthened again, in my view, by the extreme improbability that the sweeping revolution against infant Church membership could have been established by the Apostles, without some such clamour as would have been mentioned in the New Testament. We must remember that all Hebrews greatly prized their ecclesiastical birth. See Matt. iii: 9; John viii: 33. To be cut off from among his People, was to the Jew, a shameful and dreaded degradation. The uncircumcised was a Dog to him, unclean and despised. We have evidence enough that the believing Hebrews shared these feelings. Hence, when we see that even believers among them were so suspicious, and the unbelievers full of rampant jealousy, and eager to object and revile the Nazarenes, how is it possible that this great abrogation of privilege could be established, while we hear none of that clamour which, the New Testament tells us, was provoked by the cessation of sacrifice, purifications, and circumcision?

THAT NO SUCH CLAMOR ARGUED.—But the Immersionist may rejoin: such a clamour may have existed, and it may be omitted in the sacred history; because the history is brief, and the purposes of inspiration may not have required its notice. One is not entitled to argue from the absence of proof. *De omni ignoto quasi de non ex istentibus.*

I reply: we are not arguing herein from the mere absence of proof; for we give high probable evidence to show that if the fact had ever occurred, the traces of it *must* have been preserved. First: Not only is there a dead silence in the brief narrative of Scripture concerning any objection of Jews, such as *must* have been made had infant membership been abrogated; but there seems to be an equal silence in the Rabbinical literature against Christianity, and in the voluminous polemical works, from the days of Justin Martyn Adversus, Tryphonom, down. Second: The objections, restiveness, and attacks growing out of the revolutionizing of other things, less important than infant membership, required and received full notice in the New Testament. Look for instance, at the Epistle to the Hebrews, written practically with this main object; to obviate the restiveness and tendency to revolt produced among Jewish Christians, by the abrogation of cherished customs. The main line of argument is to show that these innovations are justifiable, and scriptural: yet there is not one word to excuse this momentous innovation against infant membership! Third: The sacred narrative, in Acts 15th, approaches so near the topic of this innovation, that it is simply incredible an allusion to it should have been avoided, had the revolution been attempted. The question which agitated the whole Christian community to its core was: shall Gentile converts entering the Church under the new dispensation be required to be circumcised, and keep the ceremonial law? The very arguments by which this question was debated are given. Now how inevitable would it have been, had the change in membership been made, which the Immersionist supposes, to say: "Whether you circumcise *adult* Gentile converts, or not; you cannot circumcise their children: because Jewish children and Gentile, are no longer admitted with their parents. But there is no whisper of this point raised. I cannot believe the innovation had been attempted. But if it had not been made at that stage, it was never made at all by divine authority; for the Immersionist professes to find it in Christ's commission at his ascension.

V. GREAT COMMISSION IMPLIES PÆDO-BAPTISM.—Paidobaptist writers are accustomed to attach importance to that great Commission. See Matt. xxviii: 19, 20; Mark xvi: 15, 16; Luke xxiv: 47–49. As we have already considered the supposed evidence for exclusive believer's baptism in Mark xvi: 16, we may take the language of Matthew as most explicit and full, of the three places. We consider that the Apostles would naturally have understood such a commission to include infants, for the following reasons:

The first thing told them is to go, and "teach" more properly, "disciple" (MATHETEUSATE) all nations. Here, says the Immersionist, is strong evidence that only believer's baptism is enjoined, because they are to be *taught* first, and then baptized; whereas infants cannot be taught. The argument is unfortunately founded only on a failure to examine the original. For this turns it against the Immersionist. The term "*disciple*," is eminently appropriate to the conception of a *school of Christ*, which is one of the Bible conceptions of the Church. See Gen. xviii: 19; Deut. vi: 7; Is. ii: 3, &c. The young child is *entered* or enrolled at this school, before his religious education begins, in order that he may learn afterwards. Matt. xxviii: 20.

Second: what would a mind free from immersionist preconceptions naturally understand by the command to "disciple *all nations?*" Does not this include the infant children, as a part thereof? But we must remember that the minds of the disciples were not only free from these prejudices, but accustomed to the Church membership of infants. They had known nothing else but a church state in which the children went along with their parents. It seems then, that they would almost inevitably understand such a command, as including the authority to baptize infants, unless instructed to the contrary. Nor is this all: these disciples were accustomed to see cases of discipleship to Judaism occurring from time to time. Proselytes were not unusual. See Matt. xxiii: 15; Acts vi: 5; ii: 10; xiii: 43, and the uniform custom was to circumcise the children and receive them into the Jewish community, on the profession of the father. So that, if we set aside for the present, the question whether proselyte baptism was as yet practiced, it is clear the Apostles must be led by all they had been accustomed to witness, to suppose that *their* converts were to bring in their children along with them; unless the notion were contradicted by Christ. Where is the contradiction of it?

LECTURE LXIV.

SYLLABUS.

SUBJECTS OF BAPTISM—(Concluded.)

6. What weight is to be attached to the prevalence of Proselyte Baptism among the Jews, as evidence for infant baptism?
   See Dr. L. Woods' Lectures, 112. Knapp's Christian Theol. § 138. Wall's Hist. Infant Bapt. Jahn's Archæology, § 325.
7. State the argument for infant baptism from the baptism of *houses*.
   Armstrong, Pt. III, Ch. 8. Dr. Woods' Lect. 114. Taylor's Apostol. Bapt. pp. 28 to 68.
8. Argue infant baptism from the titles and treatment addressed to Christian children in the New Testament.

See Armstrong, Pt. III, Ch. 7. Woods' Lect. 115, Pt. 1. Taylor, Apo Bapt. p. 100–112.

9. What historical evidence can be given for the prevalence of infant bapti from the Apostles' days downward?

Woods' Lect. 116. Coleman, Ancient Christianity Exemplified, Ch. § 6. Bingham's Origines Sacræ. Wall's Hist. Inf. Bapt.

10. Refute the objection that infant baptism corrupts the spirituality of Church by introducing unsanctified members.

Woods' Lectures, 117. Mason on the Church, Essays 6 and 7.

11. What are the relations of baptized children to the Church, and what practical benefits thereof?

Drs. Woods and Mason, as above.

VI. Argument from Proselyte Baptism of Jews.—It has be fashionable of late years for learned Pædobaptists (e. g., Dr. J. Alexander) to doubt whether the Jews practised proselyte family ba tism as early as the Christian era; because, they say, it was first serted in the Talmud (of 6th century), and these writers are unscrup lous. I see not why we may not in this case believe, because they supported thus: (see Dr. Woods.) They uniformly assert the an quity of the usage. Usage is naturally deducible from Levitical pu fications. It accounts for John's baptism being received with such cility, while neither in the New Testament, nor in Josephus, is a surprise expressed at his baptizing as a novelty. Jews certainly practise proselyte baptism at a later day, and it can hardly be su posed that they borrowed it from the hated Christians. If they ev did, it proves a prevalence of usage before they borrowed. Last: does not seem very likely that such a pretence, if first *invented* in Talmud, would have escaped denial by some earlier Christian or Je ish Christian.

Now, if apostles were accustomed to see families baptized into Ju ism, it was very likely that they would understand the command to and proselyte all peoples to Christianity and baptize them, as inclu ing whole families.

VII. Argument from Baptism of Houses.—Had the English v sion been *accurate* in the employment of the words house (οικο household (οικια), our argument on this point would appear in it m just. According to the definition of Aristotle, and well-defined clas and Hebraistic usage, the word οικος means literally the apartme inhabited by the parents and children, and οικια literally the cur lage. Figuratively, the former, *the family;* the latter, *the househo* And the idea which constitutes the former a house is *lineage.* It is birth of infants the house is built up; so that the word may more na rally mean young children distinguished from parents than *vice ver* A *house* is a cluster of *one lineage*, receiving accretion by birth a growth of children. So that when it is said in the New Testam that the οικος was baptized (never the οκια), the presence of child is forcibly implied. This distinction in usage is *always* carefully served in the New Testament as to the figurative sense of the t words, *often* as to the literal. E. g., Acts xvi: 31–34 (Greek); 1 C i: 16, with xvi: 15; Phil. iv: 22. The argument is miserably scured in the English version. Now, while some eight Christian *hou* are spoken of in the New Testament (who presumably were bapti houses), four such are explicitly mentioned as baptized. Corneli Acts x: 2, 44, 48; Lydia's, xvi: 15; the Philippian jailor's, xvi:

Stephanas', 1 Cor. i: 16. Now, on the fact that among the very few *separate* individual baptisms mentioned in the New Testament four were of *families*, is ground of two-fold probability: 1, that there were young children in *some* of them, who were baptized on their parents' faith, that this sacramental recognition of the parental and family relation *looks like Pœdobaptism* amazingly. Immersionists *don't use such language;* so that even if it could be proved there probably were *no* young unconverted children, the argument remains.

These Houses Included Children.—They say they can prove in each case there were none: Cornelius' by verses 2, 44. But see Gen. xviii: 19; 2 Chron. xx: 13; Ezra viii: 21; Matt. xxi: 16, 15. That Lydia's house were all believing adult children, or servants, or apprentices, they argue from Acts xvi: 40, "brethren." But see verses 14, 15, nobody's faith is mentioned but Lydia's; and doubtless Paul had made other converts out of Lydia's house. The proof is, that the whole context shows the meeting in verse 40 was a public one, not a family one; and the Philippian church, a flourishing body, was now planted.

That the jailor's family all believed is argued from verse 34. But the original places the panoiki, with rejoiced. That Stephanas' family were all baptized and believers, is argued from 1 Cor. xvi: 15. Answer: It was his oikia, not his oikos, which engaged in ministrations of Christian hospitality.

VIII. Infants are Addressed as Church-Members.—An argument of equal, or perhaps greater importance is to be derived from the addressing of the titles of Church-members to little children in the New Testament. That the words Hagioi, Pistos or Pisteuon, and Adelphos, are the current words employed to denote *professed Christians*, will not be denied. "Christians" is only used two or three times. The address of epistles to these titles is equivalent to their address to professed Church-members. Now, in three cases we find children addressed in the epistles. Eph. vi: 1–4; Col. iii: 20; 1 John ii: 12, 13, teknia, paidia. First, these were *not adult* children, because yet to be reared. Nor in 1 Jno. ii: 12, spiritual children, for then we must make only spiritual fathers and young men. Now, when, in an epistle addressed to the Church we find certain Christian duties enjoined on young children, we infer they are *of the Church*, just as much as the parents, husbands, servants, masters, exhorted in the context. See 1 Cor. v: 12.

The Bishop's children must be members.—Further, in Titus i: 6, they are expressly called Tekna pista. Compare for illustration, in 1 Tim. vi: 2, Pistous Despotas, and 1 Tim. iii: 4, parallel passage, where the Bishop's children being pista and upotekna, is equivalent to being well ruled, and in subjection. If the alternative be taken, that Titus' Tekna Pista mean adult children who are professors on their own behalf, of godliness, we are led into absurdities: for what must be decided of the man whose children are yet small; and who being therefore in the prime of manhood, is fit to serve the Church? Shall he wait, though otherwise fit, till it be seen whether his children will be converted? Or if the children be already come to ages of intelligence, and not converted, in spite of the Father's good rearing, must he be refused ordination? This would have excluded L. Richmond, Dr. Gar. Spring, &c., &c. The obvious sense is, the bishop's children must be consecrated and reared accordingly.

IX. AUTHORITIES ON PATRISTIC BAPTISM. REMARKS. 1. INFANT BAPTISM EARLY MENTIONED.—As the historical evidence for the early and constant prevalence of infant baptism is so well unfolded in Coleman, Woods, Bingham and Wall, and as your Church History enters fully into it, I shall not again detail the witnesses; but add some remarks to sum up. And 1st, Bingham and Wall between them mention nine fathers, of the first and second centuries, who seem pretty clearly to allude to infant baptism; some briefly and singly, others clearly and more than once. Now Mosheim's list of the genuine Fathers who wrote before A. D. 200, is only about 12 (Clement, Ignatius, Polycarp, Pseudo Barnabas, Pastor Hermae, Ep. to Diognetus, (probably Justin's,) Justin Martyr, Irenaeus, Athenagoras, Theophylus of Antioch, Clem. Alexandrinus, Tertullian,) if we omit about 12 or 15 more, whose names and works are only made known to us by other Fathers who speak of them. And his list is nearly exhaustive. Now seeing that few of these works are voluminous, and that some are mere fragments: and seeing that if our theory of pædo-baptism is correct, it was a subject which did not *need* much agitation, as being undisputed and of ancient establishment; here is fully as much notice of it as was reasonably to be expected. After A. D. 200, the notices are abundant.

DENIAL OF IT NOT MENTIONED OF ANY HERETICS.—2. The enumerations of heresies, and refutations of them drawn up by Irenaeus, Epiphanius, Philastrius, Augustine, Theodoret, (Epiphanius for instance against 80 heresies,) contain no reference to any heretics who denied infant baptism, except those (as some Gnostic sects) who denied all baptism. And *Peter de Bruys* is said to be the first sectary who ever denied it.

NOT REFUSED EVEN BY PELAGIANS, UNDER THE STRONGEST INDUCEMENT.—3. In the controversy between Augustine and Pelagius, the latter were much pressed with the argument. If infants have neither depravity nor guilt, why baptize them? Their answer was, to gain for them *heaven*, instead of eternal life. They would have gladly given the more satisfactory answer, if it had been true, that infant baptism was an innovation. But they do not. Celestius, it is stated, repudiated the insinuation that his doctrine would lead to the denial of infant baptism, saying, he had never known any sect wicked enough for this. He and Pelagius were learned and travelled.

EVIDENCE IN THE CATACOMBS.—4. In the Roman Catacombs, among the many interesting remains, are inscriptions over the graves of infants and young children, who are said to be baptized, and called "faithful," "believers," "brothers," while they are said to be of ages varying from 18 months to 12 years.

5. INFANT COMMUNION.—Infant communion, which immersionists love to class as an equal and similar superstition to infant baptism, is a clear proof of the earlier prevalence of the latter. For the primitive Church never gave the Lord's supper *before* baptism.

BUT TRADITION NO AUTHORITY TO US.—But we do not rely on the patristic testimony as our decisive argument, but on Scripture. The

Church *early* became superstitious; and many of their superstitions, as baptismal regeneration and infant communion, they profess to base on Scripture. But where they do so, we can usually trace and expose their misunderstanding of it. This current and early testimony is relied on, not as proving by itself that we are warranted to baptize infants, but as raising a strong probability that it was an apostolic usage, and thus supporting our Scriptural argument.

X. Does Infant Baptism Corrupt the Church?—Immersionists object vehemently to infant baptism and membership that it overflows the spirituality of Christ's Church with a multitude of worldly, nominal Christians. One of them has written a book on "the *evils* of infant baptism." They point to the lamentable state of religion in Europe, in the Papacy, and in the Oriental Churches, as the legitimate results. They urge: If our Confession and Government are correct in saying, 'all baptized persons are members of the Church,' &c., (Bk. Disc. Ch. I, § 6,) consistency would lead us, of course, to admit them, without saving change, to suffrage, to office, and to sealing ordinances; we should baptize their children in turn (as Methodists, Episcopalians, Papists, do), and thus the whole world would be brought unsanctified into the Church, obliterating its spirituality. But Christ intended it to be composed only of His converted followers. The only reason why Presbyterian, and other Churches in America, do not exhibit these abominable results is that they do not act out their creeds, and practically regard the unconverted baptized as *no members*." I reply:

Mixture in the Church Foreseen by Christ.—1. The notion that Christ would organize His religious kingdom on earth in contrast to human society, admitting none but pure members, is plausible and pretty. Yea, the unthinking may reason, that as He is autocrat, heart-searching, almighty, His voluntary embracing of any impure material would look like a voluntary connivance at sin, and indifference to that sanctity which the Church was formed to promote. But it is a utopian and unscriptural dream. See Matt. xiii: 24 and 47. Christ has not even formed the hearts of His own people thus; but permits evil to mix with them. A Church to be administered by human hands *must* be mixed; anything else is but a dishonest pretense, even among immersionists. Christ permits a mixed body not because He *likes* it, but because His wisdom sees it best under the circumstances.

Mediaeval Churches Corrupted Ohterwise.—2. It is not fair to argue from the abuse, but from proper use of an institution. Note: God's arrangement under the old dispensation was liable to the same evils, for infant Church-membership abused certainly led there to horrid corruptions. The wide corruptions of Popish and other European Churches are not traceable to proper use of infant baptism, but to other manifest causes: *neglect* of youthful training, State establishments, Paganism infused, hierarchical institutions, &c. If infant membership were the great corruptor, and its absence the great safeguard, immersed churches ought to be uniformly pure. How is this? It is an invidious task to make the inquiry; but it is their own game. Look, then, at Ironsides, Dunkers, Mormons, African Churches in America. We shall not be so uncharitable as to charge all this on immersion.

Safeguards.—3. Enough for us to answer for our own principles, not those of Papists, Episcopalians, Methodists. We have stated our limitations on infant baptism. Where they are observed, and the duties pledged in the sacrament are tolerably performed, it results in high benefit. When we teach that all baptized persons "*should perform* all the duties of Church-members," it is not meant with unconverted hearts. The Church states the great Bible doctrine that in baptism renewing graces are promised and sealed; and if the adult does not get them, it is *his fault.* Our doctrine does not break down the distinction made between spiritual and carnal by sealing ordinances one whit, or give to the baptized member one particle of power to corrupt the suffrage or government of the Church.

XI. The remaining cavils are best answered by stating the Scriptural view of the relation of unregenerate baptized children to the Church, and the benefits thence enuring:

Baptized Members in What Sense?—Illustrated by Minors in Commonwealth.—When our standards say, "All baptized persons are members of the Church," this by no means implies their title to all sealing ordinances, suffrage, and office. They are minor citizens in the ecclesiastical commonwealth, under tutelage, training, and instruction, and government; heirs, if they will exercise the graces obligatory on them, of all the ultimate franchises of the Church, but not allowed to enjoy them until qualified. Yet they are justly under ecclesiastical government. The reasonableness of this position is well illustrated by that of minors under the civil commonwealth. These owe allegiance and obedience, and are under the government: they are made to pay taxes, to testify in courts, and, after a time, even to do military service and labour on the highway. They can be tried for crimes, and even capitally punished. But they may neither sit as judges in a jury, bear office, nor vote for officers, until a full age is supposed to confer the suitable qualification. Such must be the regulations of any organized society which embraces (on any theory) families within it. And if the family is conceived as the *integer* of which the society is constituted, this *status* of minor members of families is yet more proper, yea, unavoidable. But such is precisely the conception of the Scriptures, concerning the integers of which both the State and the Church are constituted. Now, the visible Church is an organized human society, constituted of Christian families as integers, for spiritual ends—religious instruction, sanctification, holy living and glorification of its members. Hence, it seems most reasonable that unregenerate members of those families shall be, on the one hand, included under its government; and, on the other, not endowed with its higher franchises. The State, whose purposes are secular, fixes the young citizen's majority when, by full age, he is presumed to have that bodily and mental growth of the adult which fits him for its duties. The Church recognizes the majority of its minor citizens when they show that spiritual qualification—a new heart—necessary for handling its spiritual concernments. The Church visible is also a school of Christ. Schools, notoriously, must include untaught children. That is what they exist for. But they do not allow these children to teach and govern; they are there to be taught and restrained. The analogy is most instructive.

THIS RELATION NATURAL.—The Immersionist says that our communion is only saved from utter corruption by our own inconsistency; that while our constitution calls our children Church members, we fortunately treat them, as they do, as not Church members. Whereas the immersionist charges us with a wicked inconsistency, I will retort upon him the charge of a pious one: Those of them who are truly good people, while they say their children are not Church members, fortunately treat them as though they were. They diligently bring them under the instructions, restraints, and prayers of the Church and pastor. Happily, the instincts and influences of the Christian family are so deeply founded and so powerful that a perverse and unscriptural theory cannot arrest them. These Christians discard the Bible conception of the visible Church, as an organized body whose integers are Christian "*houses*," and adopt the unscriptural and impracticable theory of a visible Church organized of regenerate individuals. But, blessed be God! the light and love of a sanctified parent's heart are too strong to be wholly perverted by this theory; they still bring the family, as a whole, virtually within the Church. And this is the reason that true religion is perpetuated among them.

DISCIPLINE CONSISTS IN INSTRUCTION AND RESTRAINT.—But a more definite answer may be desired to the inquiry, What are the precise shape and extent of this instruction and government which constitute the Church's "discipline" over its unregenerate members? To give a clearer answer, let us distinguish the instruction from the restraint; the two together make up the idea of discipline. As to the former, the teaching of church-presbyters and catechists is by no means to supercede that of the parents, but only to assist and re-enforce it. Into the sacred relation of parent and child no other human authority, not even that which Christ Himself has appointed in His Church, may intrude. None can sufficiently replace it. But all these baptized members are the "charge" of the pastor and session; and it is the duty of these "overseers" to provide for them, and to see that they enjoy the publick and social instructions of the gospel. And pastors and elders should, moreover, extend to them that advice in temptation, and those efforts to comfort them in affliction, and to secure the sanctification of their trials, which they extend to communing members.

RESTRAINT APPLIED, FIRST, THROUGH PARENTS. THE RULE OF LIVING.—As to the ecclesiastical control or restraint over these unregenerate members. I remark, first, that the rule of morals should be the same as that imposed on communicating members, save that the former are not to be forced, nor even permitted, without spiritual qualification, to take part in sealing ordinances, and church-powers. [But as to their neglect of these, they should be constantly taught that their disqualification is their fault, and not their misfortune merely; a sinful exercise of their free-agency, a subject for personal and present repentance; a voluntary neglect and rejection of saving graces, the sincere offer whereof was sealed to them in their baptism. And for this their sin of heart, the Church utters a continuous, a sad and affectionate, yet a righteous censure, *in keeping them in the state of minor members.*] The propriety of exacting the same rule of living, in other respects, appears thus: Christ has but one law for man; these baptized members are consecrated and separated to Christ's service in the Church as truly as the communicating members; they owe the same debt of devotion for the mercies of redemption, which are their offered heritage. Hence, it should be constantly taught them that questionable worldly amusements, for instance, are as inconsistent in them as in other Church members. In a word, the end of this Church authority, under which Providence has placed them, is *to constrain them to live Christian lives, in order that thereby they may come unto the Christian graces in the heart.*

Second, as to the means of enforcement of that rule: I would answer, that in the case of all baptized members of immature age, and especially of such as are still in the houses, and under the government of parents, the Church-session ought mainly to restrain them through their parents. That is, the authority of these rulers should be applied to the parents, to cause them, by their domestic authority, to lead outward Christian lives, and attend upon the means of grace. And the refusal or neglect of parents to do this duty, may doubtless subject them to just church-censure. Perhaps we may safely say, that the session should reach this class of baptized members only through their parents, except in the case where the parents themselves refer the child's contumacy to the eldership. In this case the eldership may undoubtedly proceed to censure the recusant child. See an analogous case in the theocracy, Deut. xxi. 18, &c.

If adult, the Restraint is Direct. It may Proceed to Excommunicate.—If these baptized unregenerate members are fully adult, and passed from parental control, then the church-session must apply their restraint directly to them. The mere continuance of their unregeneracy, unfitting them for communion, will of course be no suitable ground for judicial prosecution. For the Church is already uttering her standing censure against this, in their exclusion from the Lord's table. If they become wayward in outward conduct, then the session, in addition to their constant and affectionate admonitions against their impenitence, should administer paternal cautions, advice, and entreaty, looking towards a reformation. But if they persist in flagrant and indecent sins, such as the persistent neglect of all ordinances, sensuality, blasphemy, or dishonesty, (such sins as would bring on a communing member excommunication,) then nothing remains but that the Session shall proceed, by judicial prosecution, to cut the reprobate member off from the Church.

Some Fair Way Must Be Provided to Cut Off the Reprobate. Not only the Scriptures, but common sense, justify this view. Are they "members of the Church?" (in the minor sense.) Then natural justice teaches that they cannot be stripped of the privileges of that membership, be they what they may, without a fair opportunity for defence, and confronting the accusing witnesses. To judge a man without formal hearing is iniquity. On the other hand, are they, in any sense, "members of the Church"? Then, to that degree, the Church is responsible for their discredit, and subject to the scandal of their irregularities. Common sense says, then, that there must be a fair way for the Church to obtain a formal severance of the membership, and publicly cleanse herself of the scandal of this contumacious member. That way can be none other than judicial prosecutions. Finally, when a member is so thoroughly reprobate that, to human apprehension, there is no chance of his receiving any of the ends of a Church connexion, there ought to be a way to terminate it; it has become objectless.

Our Usage Delinquent.—On this statement of the matter, it is obvious that the usage in our churches has fallen exceedingly far from the Bible rule, and that the taunts of the immersionists are to a great degree well founded; that we are not consistent in our pædobaptism. And it may be that the leavening of men's minds, in this country, with the unscriptural ideas of the immersionists may have produced a license of feeling among youths which greatly increases the difficulty of Church Sessions doing their whole duty. It may, indeed, be almost impossible for any single Session to do it among us in the face of this unfortunate corruption of society, and of the obstinate neglect of all sister Church Sessions around them. But the question for the honest mind is, Should a corrupt practice continue to preclude a right principle? Or should the correct principle amend the vicious practice? And the happy example of many of the Reformed churches teaches us that this discipline of baptized members is feasible, reasonable, and most profitable. The Presbyterian Church of Holland, for instance, in its better days; and the Evangelical Church of Holland now, uniformly governs their children on the Scriptural principles above described.

Benefits of the Bible Plan—Children of the Church its Hope. The benefits of infant baptism, and of this form of membership for the children of God's believing people, are great. Some of them are very forcibly set forth by Dr. John M. Mason, in his invaluable treatise on the Church. Borrowing in part from him, I would remark that this relation to the Church, and this discipline, are, first, in exact harmony with the great fact of experience that the children of God's people are the great hope of the Church's increase. This being a fact, it is obviously wisdom to organize the Church with reference to it, so as to provide every proper means of training for working up this the most hopeful material for Zion's increase. To neglect this obvious policy seems, indeed, little short of madness. As we have seen, immersionists' communions only enjoy true prosperity in virtue of their virtual employment of the principle of infant Church-membership; grace and love being in them, fortunately, stronger than a bad theory.

The Bible Plan Agrees with Nature and Grace—Prov. xxii: 6. Second: This Bible plan is in strict conformity with those doctrines of grace and principles of human nature which God employs for the sanctification of His people. Our theory assumes that God's covenant is with His people *and their seed.* (Acts ii: 29.) That their seed are heirs of the promises made to the fathers (Acts iii: 25); that the cause which excludes any such from saving interest in redemption is voluntary and criminal, viz., unbelief and impenitence—a cause which they are all bound to correct at once, if they are arrived at years of discretion; that the continuance of this cause, however just a reason for the eldership's excluding them from certain privileges and functions, is no justification whatever for their neglecting them. And, above all, does our plan found itself on the great rule of experience, common sense, and Scripture, that if you would form a soul to the hearty embracing of right principles, you must *make him observe the conduct* which that principle dictates. Every faithful parent in the world acts on that rule in rearing his children. If the child is untruthful, unsympathizing, unforgiving, indolent, he compels him, while young, to observe a course of truth, charity, forgiveness, and industry. Why? Because the parent considers that the outward observance of these virtues will be either permanent or praiseworthy if, when the child becomes a man, he only observes them from fear or hypocrisy? Not at all; but because the parent knows that human nature is moulded by habits; that the practice of a principle always strengthens it; that this use of his parental authority is the most natural and hopeful means to teach the child heartily to prefer and adopt the right principle, when he becomes his own man; that it would be the merest folly to pretend didactically to teach the child the right, and leave all-powerful HABIT to teach him the wrong, and to let the child spend his youth in rivetting the bonds of bad habit, which, if he is ever to adopt and love the right principle, he must break. Will not our heavenly Father act on the same rule of good sense toward His children? Is not the professed principle of the immersionist just the folly we have described? Happily, Scripture agrees with all experience and practical wisdom in saying that if you wish a child to adopt and love the principles of a Church-member when he is grown, you must make him behave as a Church-member while he is growing.

COLLATERAL ADVANTAGES.—Third: Many collateral advantages are gained by this minor citizenship of the baptized in the Church. They are retained under wholesome restraints. Their carnal opposition to the truth is greatly disarmed by early association. The numerical and pecuniary basis of the Church's operations is widened. And where the sealing ordinances are properly guarded, these advantages are gained without any compromise of the Church's spirituality. Pædobaptist communities which are scripturally conducted present as high a grade of purity, even including their baptized members, as any others. For on this corrupt earth, the best communion is far from being what it ought to be. Where the duties represented in the sacrament of baptism are properly followed up, the actual regeneration of children is the ordinary result.

LECTURE LXV.

SYLLABUS.

THE LORD'S SUPPER.

See Confession of Faith, Ch. XXIX, with Catechisms.

1. Give a definition of this sacrament, with the Scriptural account of its *institution*, *names*, and *ceremonial*.
   See Matt. xxvi: 26-29. Mark xiv: 22-26. Luke xxii: 15 to 21. 1 Cor. x: 16, 17, xi: 17 to end. Dick, Lect. 92. Turrettin, Loc. XIX, que. 21.
2. What are the elements, in what manner to be prepared and set apart, and what their sacramental significance?
   Turrettin, que. 22, 23, 24. Hill, Bk. V, Ch. 7. Dick, Lect. 92.
3. State and refute the doctrine of the real presence by a *Transubstantiation*, with the elevation and worship of the host.
   Council of Trent, Sess. 13, especially Ch. 4. Turrett., que. 26 and 27. Calvin's Inst., Bk. IV, Ch. 18. Hill, as above. Archbishop Tillottson and Bishop Stillingfleet against Transubstantiation. Dick, Lect. 90.
4. State and refute the doctrine of *Consubstantiation*.
   Turrett., que. 26 and 28. Augsb. Confession, and other Lutheran symbols. Hill, as above. Dick, Lect. 91.

I. Scriptural Names.—The only other sacrament which Protestants recognize, besides baptism, is that called by them, in imitation of Paul (1 Cor. xi: 20), "*The Lord's Supper*" (Deipnon Kyriacon). The only other Scriptural names which seem clearly established are the breaking of bread (klasis artou, Acts ii: 46, xx: 7), and possibly koinonia (1 Cor. x: 16). The cup is called poterion eulogias (1 Cor. x: 16), but this is evidently not a *name* for the whole ordinance. And in verse 21, communicating is called partaking of the Lord's *Table* (trapedza). This hardly amounts to a calling of the ordinance by the name of '*table;*' but it is instructive, as showing no favour whatever to the notion of altars and sacrifice, as connected with the Lord's supper.

Patristic Names.—Among the fathers it was called often eucharistia, sometimes synaxis or leitourgia, more often thusia, or mysterion; or, among the Latins, *missa*. The use of the word thusia was at first only rhetorical and figurative; and thus the error of considering the Lord's supper an actual sacrifice had its way prepared. While the Romanists sometimes endeavor to trace the word *missa* to other etynoms (as to mas, tribute; misteth, banquet; or to muesis, initiation), its derivation is undoubtedly from the formulary with which the spectators and catechumens were dismissed before the celebration of the Lord's supper: *Missa est* (viz., congregatio).

Definition and Nature.—The definition which Presbyterians hold, is that of our Catechisms, e. g., Shorter, Qu. 96: "The Lord's supper is a sacrament wherein, by giving and receiving bread and wine, according to Christ's appointment, His death is showed forth; and the worthy receivers are not after a corporal and carnal manner, but by faith made partakers of His body and blood, with all His benefits, to their spiritual nourishment and growth in grace." This is obviously no more than a correct digest of the views stated or implied in the sundry passages where the ordinance is described. Its institution was evidently simple and free from mystery; and had not the strange career of superstition been run on this subject by the Christian Church, the dispassionate reader would have derived no conceptions from the sacred narrative but the simple ones of a commemorative seal. And these natural, popular views of the sacrament are doubtless best adapted for edification.

HISTORY OF INSTITUTION.—I hold that our Saviour undoubtedly held His last passover on the regular passover evening, and that this ordinance, intended by Him to supersede and replace the passover (1 Cor. v: 7), was very quietly introduced at its close. To do this, He took up the bread (doubtless the unleavened bread of the occasion), and the cup of wine (after Jewish fashion mingled with water) provided for the occasion, and intruduced them to their new use by an act of solemn thanksgiving to God. Then He brake the bread and distributed it, and, after the bread, the wine—partaking of neither Himself—saying: "This do in remembrance of Me; eat, drink ye all of it, to show forth the Lord's death till He come." These mandatory words were accompanied also with certain explicatory words, conveying the nature of the symbol and pledge; stating that the bread represented His body, and the cup the covenant made in His blood—the body lacerated and killed, and the blood shed, for redemption. The sacramental *acts*, therefore, warranted by Christ are, the taking, breaking, and distributing the elements, on the administrator's part, and their manual reception, and eating or drinking, on the recipient's part. The sacramental *words* are the thanksgiving, the explicatory and promissory, and the mandatory. The whole is then appropriately concluded with another act of praise (not sacramental, but an appendage thereto), either by praying, or singing, or both. And to add any thing else is superstition.

II. ELEMENTS.—To continue this subject: The *elements* are bread and wine. The Greek Church says the bread must be leavened, the Latin unleavened; making this a point of serious importance. We believe that the bread used was paschal. But it was not Christ's intention to give a paschal character to the new sacrament; and bread is employed as the material element of nutrition, the one most familiar and universal. Hence, we regard all the disputes as to leaven, and the other *minutiæ* made essential by the Romish Rubrick (wheaten, mingled with proper water, not worm-eaten, &c.,) as non-essential. Probably the wine was also mingled with water on the first occasion; but, on the same grounds, we regard it as selected simply as the most common and familiar refreshment of the human race, and the presence of water is therefore non-essential. Indeed, modern chemistry has shown that in all wine water is the solvent, and the largest constituent.

THEIR CONSECRATION WHAT?—According to all Christians, these elements are conceived as undergoing some kind of consecration. Rome places this in the pronunciation of the words of institution, "This is My body," and teaches that it results in a total change of the substance of the bread and wine into the body and blood of Christ. But the only change which Protestants admit in a consecration of the elements is the simple change of their *use*, from a common to a sacred and sacramental one. And this consecration we believe to be wrought, not by pronouncing the words, "This is My body," but by the eucharistic act of worship which introduces the sacrament. For the natural language of consecration is that of worship; not that of a didactic and promissory sentence. Witness the cases of grace over our food, and all the consecrations of the Old Testament, e. g., Deut. xxvi: 5–10. When Christ says "This *is* My body," were the consecration what Papists suppose, these words would imply that it is already made. And last, the words, supposed by them to be words of consecration, are too variant in the different histories of the Sacrament in Sacred Scripture.

Breaking of the Bread significant.—The breaking of the bread is plainly one of the sacramental acts, and should never be done beforehand, by others, nor omitted by the minister. The words heis artos (1 Cor. x: 17) are not correctly represented in the English version. The proper force of the word, as may be seen in Jno. vi: 9, is loaf, or more properly, *cake;* and the Apostle's idea is, that the oneness of the mass of bread, and of the cup, partaken by all, signifies their unity in one spiritual body. It would be better that the bread should be taken by the officiator in one mass, and broken before the people, after the prayer. The proper significancy of the sacrament requires it; for the Christ we commemorate is the Christ lacerated and slain. Further; Christ brake the bread, in distributing it; and commanded us to imitate Him, saying: "This do," &c. Third; the Apostles undoubtedly made the breaking one of the sacramental acts; for Paul says, 1 Cor. x: 16, "The bread which *we break*," &c. Last, when the sacrament itself is more often called "the breaking of bread," than by any other one name, it can hardly be supposed that the breaking is not a proper part of the ceremonial.

Pouring of the Wine, after the Bread, Significant.—There is also a significancy in the taking of the wine *after* the bread, in a distinct act of reception; because it is the blood as separated from the body by death, that we commemorate. Hence the soaking of the bread in the cup is improper, as well as the plea by which Rome justifies communion in one kind; that as the blood is in the body, the bread conveys alone a complete sacrament. As we should commemorate it, the blood is not in the body, but poured out.

Significant Acts of Communicants.—The acts on the Communicant's part also, are sacramental and significant, viz: the taking and eating. These acts symbolize generally, *Faith*, as the soul's receptive act; just as the elements distributed by God's institution signify that which is the object of faith, Christ slain for our redemption. But the Confession 29, § 1, states, in greater detail, and with strict scriptural propriety, that these acts commemorate Christ's death, constitute a profession and engagement to serve Him, show the reception of a covenanted redemption thus sealed to us, and indicate our communion with each other and Christ, our Head, in one spiritual body. The first idea is plainly set forth in 1 Cor. 11: 24, last clause, as well as parallel passages, and in verses 25 and 26. The second is implied in the first, in the individual character of the act, in 1 Cor. xi: 25, "covenant," and in the nature of faith, which embraces Christ as our Saviour from sin unto holiness. The third idea is plainly implied in the significancy of the elements themselves, which are the materials of nutrition and refreshment; as well as in Jno. vi: 50–55. For though we strenuously dispute, against Rome, that the language of this passage is descriptive of the Lord's Supper, it is manifest that the supper was afterwards devised upon the analogy which furnished the metaphor of the passage. And the didactic and promissory language, "This is My body," "This is My blood," sacramentally understood, obviously convey the idea of nutrition offered to the soul. The last idea is very clearly set forth in 1 Cor x: 16, 17. And this is the feature of the sacrament from which it has received its popular name, of *Communion* of the Lord's Supper.

WHO MAY PARTAKE?—The parties who may properly partake of the Lord's Supper are so clearly defined, 1 Cor. xi: 27–30, as to leave no room for debate. It is those who have examined themselves successfully of their knowledge to discern the Lord's body and faith to feed on Him repentance, love, and new obedience." Shorter Catechism, question 97 See also, Larger Catechism, question 171–175. That this sacrament is to be given only to credible professors, does not indeed follow necessarily from the fact that it symbolizes saving graces; for baptism does this; but from this express limitation of Paul, and from the different graces symbolized. Baptism symbolizes those graces which *initiate* the Christian life: The Supper, those also which continue it. Hence while the former is once applied to infants born within the covenant, to ratify their outward membership, in the dependence on the gracious promise that they shall be brought to commence the Christian life afterwards, it would be wrong to grant the second sacrament to any who have not given some indication of an actual progress in spiritual life.

III. THE SUPPER SOON PERVERTED BY TWO ERRORS.—Thus far, all has been intelligible, reasonable, and adapted to nourish and comfort the faith of the plain believer. But the well-informed are aware that this ordinance, so quietly and simply introduced by our Saviour, and so simply explained, has met the strange fortune of becoming the especial subject of superstitious amplification; until in the Romish Church it has become nearly the whole of worship. It would be interesting to trace the history of this growth; but time only allows us to remark, that *two* unscriptural ideas became early associated with it; in consequence of a pagan grossness of perception, and a false exposition of Scripture One of these was that of a literal or real corporeal presence; the other that of a true sacrifice for sin. Still, those more superstitious Christians who held these two ideas, did not, for a long time, define the manner in which they were supposed to be true. At length two theories developed themselves, that of Paschasius Radbert, *transubstantiation* and that of Berengar, *consubstantiation*. The former of these triumphed in the Lateran Council 1215; the latter was condemned as heretical till Luther revived it, though stripped of the sacrificial feature.

TRANSUBSTANTIATION.—According to Rome, when the Priest canonically, and with proper intention, pronounces the words in the mass "*Hoc est corpus naeum*," the bread and wine are changed into the very body and blood of the living Christ, including of course, His soul and divinity; which mediatorial person, the Priest does then truly and literally break and offer again, as a proper sacrifice for the sins of the living and the dead; and he and the people eat Him. True; the accidents, or material qualities of bread and wine remain, but in and under them, the *substance* of bread is *gone*, and the substance really existing is Christ's person. But in this condition of things, it exists without the customary material attributes of locality, extension, and divisibility; for He is none the less in heaven, and in all the hosts, all ove the world at once; and into however small parts they may be divided, each is a perfect Christ! Hence, to elevate, and carry this host in procession, and to worship it with *Latria* is perfectly proper. Whether such a batch of absurdities is really believed by any reflecting mind, it is not for us to decide.

SCRIPTURAL ARGUMENTS FOR.—The scriptural basis for this monstrous superstructure is very narrow, while the patristic is wide enough. Rome depends chiefly in Scripture on the language of Jno. vi: 50, &c., and on the assertion of the absolutely literal interpretation of the words of institution in the parallel passages cited by us at the beginning. We easily set aside the argument from Jno. vi: 50, &c., by the remark, that it applies not to the Lord's Supper, but to the spiritual actings of faith on Christ figuratively described. For the Lord's Supper was not yet instituted; and it is absurd to suppose that our Saviour would use language necessarily unintelligible to all His followers, the subject never having been divulged to them. On the contrary, in verse 35, we find that the coming and eating is defined as the actings of *faith*. If the chapter be forced into an application to the Supper, then verses 53 and 54 explicitly teach that every one who eats the supper goes to heaven, and that no one who fails to eat it does; neither of which Rome admits: And in verse 63, our Saviour fixes a figurative and spiritual interpretation of His words, beyond all question.

WORDS OF INSTITUTION PROPERLY EXPLAINED.—When we proceed to the words of institution, we assert that the obvious meaning is tropical; and is equivalent to "This *represents* my body." The evidences of this are manifold. First, we cite the frequency of similar locutions in Hebrew, and Hebraistic Greek. Consult Gen. xli: 26, 27; Ezek. xxxvii: 11; Dan. vii: 24; Exod. xii: 11; Matt. xiii: 38, 39; Rev. i: 20; xvii: 9, 12, 18, *et passim*. Yea, we find Christ saying *of Himself*: "I am the way, the truth, the life," Jno. xiv: 6; "the vine," Jno. xv: 1; "the door," Jno. x: 9. Why is a tropical exposition more reasonable or necessary here? Yet, without it we make absolute nonsense.

TRUE MEANING OF PROSS.—But even if we had no usage to illustrate our Saviour's sense, it would be manifest from the text and context alone, that His sense is tropical. The TOUTO must be demonstrative of bread, and equivalent to, *this bread* (is my body); because bread is the nearest antecedent, the whole series of the narrative shows it; in the parallel case of the wine the *cup* is, in one narrative, expressed: and the allusion of Paul, 1 Cor. x: 16, "The bread which we break," shows it. So, the SOMA means evidently the body *dead*, (corpse,) as is proved by the expression "broken for you," and by the fact that the blood is separated from it: as well as by current usage of narratives. Now paraphrase the sentence: "This bread is my dead body," and any other than a tropical sense is impossible. For a.) The predication is self-contradictory; if it is bread, it is not body; if body, it is not bread. Subject or predicate is out of joint. b.) The body was not yet dead, by many hours. c.) Incompaticables cannot be predicated of each other. A given substance A. cannot be changed into a substance B. which was pre-existent before the change; because the change must *bring B. into existence.*

SO THE DISCIPLES MUST HAVE APPREHENDED IT.—Again: all will admit that the proper sense is that in which the disciples comprehended the words as first spoken. It is impossible that they should have understood the bread as truly the body: because they saw the body handling the bread! The body would have been wholly in its own hand!

Scripture calls it bread still after it is said, by Papists, to be transubstantiated. 1 Cor. x: 17. "All partakers of that one bread." See also, 1 Cor. xi: 26, 27, 28.

There are variations of language which are utterly incompatible with a strictly literal sense. In the gospels it is said: "He took the *cup* . . . and said This is my blood," &c. There must be here a metonymy of the cup for that which it contains—at least. But in 1 Cor. xi: 25, the words are "This cup is the new covenant in my blood," &c., where, if literalness is retained, we get the impossible and most unpopish idea, that the cup was the covenant.

TRANSUBSTANTIATION ABSURD. a.) BECAUSE IT VIOLATES OUR SENSES. But passing from the exegetical, to the general argument, a literal transubstantiation is impossible, because it violates our *senses*. They all tell us it is still bread and wine, by touch, taste, smell, sight. The senses are the only inlets of information as to external facts; if we may not believe their deliberate testimony, there is an end of all acquired knowledge. This may be fairly stated in a stronger form: it is *impossible* that my mind can be validly taught the fact of such a transubstantiation; for the only channel by which I can be taught it is the senses; and transubstantiation, if true, would teach me that my senses do not convey truth. It is just as likely that I do not hear Rome saying, "Transubstantiation is true," when I seem to hear her, as that I do not see a wafer, but a Christ, when I seem to see it. Nor is it any answer to say: the senses deceive us. This is only when hurried; and the sensible *medium* imperfect, or senses diseased. Here all the four senses of *all* men, in health, unanimously perceive only bread and wine.

b.) IT VIOLATES REASON. NO PLEA TO CALL IT A MIRACLE.—In the second place, it is impossible to be true; because it violates our understanding. Our mental intuitions *compel* us to recognize substance by its sensible attributes. Those attributes inhere only in the substance, and can only be present by its presence. It is impossible to avoid this reference. An attribute or accident is relative to its substance; to attempt to conceive of it as separate destroys it. Again: it is impossible for us to abstract from *matter*, the attributes of locality, dimension, and devisibility. But transubstantiation requires us to conceive of Christ's body without all these. Again: it is impossible for matter to be ubiquitous; but Christ's body must be so, if this doctrine is true. And it is vain to attempt an evasion of these two arguments from sense and reason, by pleading a great and mysterious *miracle*. For God's omnipotence does not work the impossible and the natural contradiction. And, whatever miracle has ever taken place, has necessarily been just as dependent on human *senses*, for man's cognizance of its occurrence, as any common event. So that if the fundamental law of the senses is outraged, man is as incapable of knowing a miracle as any other thing.

c.) IT VIOLATES THE ANALOGY OF FAITH.—Once more, the doctrine of transubstantiation contradicts the analogy of faith. It is incompatible with our Saviour's professed attitude and intention, which was then to institute a *sacrament*. But Rome herself defines a sacrament as an outward sign of an invisible grace. Hence, Christ's attitude and intention naturally lead us to regard the elements as only *signs*. This is true of all the sacraments of Old and New Testaments, unless this be an exception: and especially of the passover, on which the supper was engrafted.

Transubstantiation would utterly destroy the nature of a sacrament; because, if the symbols are changed into the Christ, there is no sign.

It contradicts also the doctrine of Christ's ascension and second advent. For these teach us, that He is at the Father's right hand now, and will only come thence at the final consummation.

It contradicts the doctrine of atonement, substituting a loathsome form of sacred (literal) cannibalism, for that *faith of the soul*, which receives the *legal effects* of Christ's atoning sufferings as its justification.

THEREFORE, HOST NOT TO BE WORSHIPPED.—Transubstantiation being disproved, all elevation and worship of the host, as well as kneeling at the sacrament, are disproved. The Episcopal reasons for the latter are, that while no change of the bread and wine is admitted, and no worship of *them* designed, yet the reverence, contrition and homage of the believer for his crucified Saviour prompt him to kneel to Christ. We reply, that the worship of Christ is of course proper at all proper times. But the attitude of worship is not proper at the moment when Christ expressly commands us to do something else than kneel. Had the paralytic, for instance, of Matt. ix: 5, 6, when he received the order, "Arise, take up thy bed and go," insisted on kneeling just then, it would have been disobedience, and not reverence. So, when Christ calls us to a communion in eating together His sacramental supper, the propor posture is that of a guest, for the time. If any Christian desires to show his homage by coming to the table from his knees, and returning from it to them, very well. But let him not kneel, in the very act in which Christ commands him to feast.

IV. CONSUBSTANTIATION EQUALLY ERRONEOUS, BUT NOT SO IMPIOUS. *Consubstantiation* teaches that there is no literal change of the elements, but that they remain simple bread and wine. Yet, in a mysterious and miraculous manner, there is a real presence, in, under, and along with them, of the person of Christ, which is literally, though invisibly, eaten along with them. Unworthy communicants also receive it, to their own damnation. While this doctrine is not attended with the impious results of transubstantiation, it is liable to nearly all the exegetical, sensible, rational, and doctrinal objections. Indeed, in one sense, the exegetical objections are stronger; because if *literalness* must needs be retained in the words of institution, it is a less violation of language to make them mean the bread is the body, than that the bread accompanies the body. The Lutheran exegesis, while boasting of its faithful preservation of our Saviour's language, really neither makes it literal, nor interprets it by any allowable trope. It does not outrage the understanding so much, by requiring us to believe that substance can be separate from all its accidents; for it professes to leave the substance of the bread untouched. Nor is it so obnoxious to the last head of objections raised against transubstantiation, in that it does not destroy the sacramental sign. But the rest of my arguments apply against it, and need not be recapitulated.

LECTURE LXVI.

SYLLABUS.

THE LORD'S SUPPER, *(concluded.)*

5. In what sense did Calvin hold a real presence? What was the doctrine of Zwinglius concerning it, and what that of the Presbyterian Church?
   Calvin's Inst. Bk. IV. Ch. 17, § 1--11. Zwinglii Ratio Fidei. § 8. Conf. of Faith Ch. xxix. Dick and Hill as above. Turrettin, Loc. xix. Qu. 28. Hill and Dick, as above.
6. Is the Lord's Suppèr a sacrifice?
   See Council of Trent, Sess. 13. Ch. 2. Catechismus Rom. Pt. II. Ch. IV. Qu. 53. Turettin, Qu 29. Dick, Lect. 91.
7. Are private communions admissible?
   Catechismus Rom. as above. Dick, Lect. 92.
8. Defend the propriety of communion in both kinds.
   Catechismus Rom. as above, Qu. 50, &c. Calvin Inst. Bk. IV. Ch. 17. Turrettin, Qu. 25.
9. Who should administer the Lord's Supper?
   Ridgeley, Qu. 168 to 170, § II.
10. What is the nature of the efficiency of the sacrament to worthy communicants, and of the sin of its abuse by the unworthy?
   Calv. Inst. Bk. IV. Ch. 14, especially, § 17. Hill and Dick as above. Knapp, § 145. See also on whole, Knapp, § 144 and 146.

PROTESTANT VIEW OF REAL PRESENCE.—V. There is a sense, in which all evangelical christians would admit a real presence in the Lord's Supper. The second Person of the Trinity being very God, immense and ubiquitous, is of course present wherever the bread and wine are distributed. Likewise, his operations are present, through the power of the Holy Ghost employing the elements as means of grace, with all true believers communicating. (Matt. 18:20.) But this is the only sort of presence admitted by us.

ZWINGLIAN VIEW OF SUPPER.—*Zwinglius*, seemingly the most emancipated of all the reformers from superstition and prejudice, taught that the sacrament is only a *commemorative seal*, and that the human part of Christ's person is not present in the sacrament, except to the faith of the intelligent believer. This he sustains irrefragably by the many passages in which we are taught that Christ's humanity is ascended into the heavens, thence to return no more till the end of all things. That this humanity, however glorified, has its *ubi*, just as strictly as any human body; that if there is any literal humanity fed upon for redemption by the believing communicant, it must be his passible and suffering humanity, while Christ's proper humanity is now glorified; (which would necessitate giving Christ a double humanity;) and that the sacramental language is tropical, as is evinced by a sound exegesis and the testimony of the better Fathers. The defect of the Zwinglian view is, that while it *hints*, it does not distinctly enough *assert*, the sealing nature of the sacraments.

CALVIN'S VIEW.—PROPERLY GROUNDED ON VITAL UNION TO CHRIST YET OVERSTRAINS IT.—Both Romanist and Lutheran minds, accustomed to regard the Eucharist from points of view intensely mystical, received the Zwinglian with loud clamour, as being odiously bald and rationalistic. Calvin, therefore, being perhaps somewhat influenced by personal attachments to Melanchthon, and by a desire to heal the lamentable dissensions of Reformed and Lutherans, propounded [in his Inst. and elsewhere] an intermediate view. This is, that the humanity, as well as the divinity of Christ, in a word, his whole person, is spiritually, yet really present, not to the bodily mouth, but to the souls of true communicants, so that though the humanity be in heaven only, it is still *fed on* in some ineffable, yet real and literal way, by the souls of believers. The ingenious and acute defence of this strange opinion, contained in the Inst. Bk. IV. Ch. 17, proceeds upon this postulate, which I regard as correct, and as eminently illustrative of the true nature of the sacramental efficiency; that *the Lord's Supper represents and applies the vital, mystical union of the Lord with believers.* Such therefore as the vital union is, such must be our view of the sacrament of the Supper. Is the vital union then, only a secret relationship between Christ and the soul instituted when faith is first exercised, and *constituted* by the indwelling and operation of the Holy Ghost: Or, is it a mysterious, yet *substantial conjunction*, of the spiritual *substance*, soul, to the whole substance of the mediatorial Person, including especially the humanity? In a word, does the spiritual vitality propagate itself in a mode strictly analogous to that, in which vegetable vitality is propagated from the stock into the graft, by actual conjunction of substance? Now Calvin answers, emphatically: the union is of the latter kind. His view seems to be, that not only the mediatorial Person, but especially the *corporeal* part thereof has been established by the incarnation, as a sort of *duct* through which the inherent spiritual life of God, the fountain, is transmitted to believers, through the mystical union. His arguments are, that the *body* of Christ is asserted to be our life, in places so numerous and emphatic (Jno. 1:4 14, 6:26, 33; 51-59, Eph. 5:30; I. Cor. 6:15; Eph. 4:16) that exegetical fidelity requires of us to understand by it more than a participation in spiritual indwelling and influences purchased for believers by his death; that the incomprehensibility of a spiritual, though true and literal, substantial conjunction of our souls with Christ's flesh in heaven, should not lead us to reject the word of our God; and that faith cannot be the whole amount of the vital union of believers to Christ, inasmuch as it is said to be by *faith*. The union must be more than the means which constitutes it.

IS CALVIN'S THE WESTMINSTER DOCTRINE.—Now, it is this view of Calvin, which we find Hill asserting and Dick denying, as the established doctrine of the Anglican and Scotch Churches, and of the Westminster Ass.. A careful examination of Ch. 29:§7, the decisive passage of our Confession will show, I think, that it was the intention of the Westminster Ass., while not repudiating Calvin's views or phraseology in a marked and individual manner, yet to modify all that was untenable and unscriptural in it. It is declared that worthy communicants "do really and indeed, yet not carnally and corporeally, but spiritually, receive and feed upon Christ crucified and all the benefits of his death: the body and blood of Christ being then not corporeally or carnally in, with, or under the bread and wine; yet as really, but spiritually, *present to the faith* of believers," as the elements themselves to their senses. Note first: that they say believers receive and feed spiritually upon *Christ crucified* and the benefits of his death; not with Calvin, on his literal flesh and blood. Next, the *presence* which grounds this receiving, is only a *presence to our faith*, of Christ's body and blood! Hence we construe the confession we think fairly, to mean by the receiving and feeding, precisely the spiritual actings of faith in Christ as our Redeemer, and on his body slain, and blood poured out, as the steps of his atoning work; so that the thing which the soul actually embraces, is not the corporeal substance of his slain body and shed blood, but their *Redeeming virtue.* The discriminating remarks of Turrettin, Qu. 28, (Introduc.) are doubtless correct; and are doubtless the expression of the very view the Assembly intended to embody. The person of Christ cannot be said to be present in the sense of substantive proximity or contact; but only in this sense: that we say a thing is *present*, when it is under the cognizance of the faculty naturally adapted for its apprehension. Thus, the sun is called present in day, absent at night. He is no farther *distant* in fact; but his beams do not operate on our visual organ. The blind man is said to be *without light;* although the rays may touch his sightless balls. So a mental or spiritual presence, is that which places the object before the cognizance of the appropriate mental faculty. In this sense only, the sacrament brings Christ before us; that it places him, in faith, before the cognizance of the sanctified understanding and heart.

CALVIN'S PROPOSITION IMPOSSIBLE.—We reject the view of Calvin concerning the real presence, [recognizing our obligation to meet and account for the scriptures he quotes, in a believing and not in a rationalistic spirit;] first, because it is not only incomprehensible, but *impossible.* Does it not require us to admit, in admitting the literal [though spiritual] reception of Christ's corporeal part, it in a distant heaven, and we on earth, that matter may ist without its essential attributes of locality and dimension?—ave not our souls their *ubi?* They are limited, substantively, some spot within the *superficies* of our bodies, just as really as ough they were material. Has not Christ's flesh its *ubi*, though orified, and as much more brilliant than ours, as a diamond is an carbon? To my mind, therefore, there is the same violation my intuitive reason, in this doctrine, as when transubstantiaon requires me to believe that the flesh of Christ is present, invisible and unextended, in each crumb or drop of the elements. oth are contrary to the laws of extension. And that Christ's orified body dwells on high, no more to return actually to earth ll the final consummation is asserted too plainly and frequently be disputed. (Matt. 26:11; Jno. 16:28; 17:11; 16:7; Luk. 24: l; Acts 3:21; 1:11.

IF ANY BODY PRESENT, IT IS THE BODY DEAD.—Second. The read broken and wine poured out symbolize the body broken and ain, and blood shed, by death. Now, according to Calvin, it is e mystical union which is sealed and applied in the Lord's Super, so as to propagate spiritual life; and throughout John VI, here His life-giving flesh is so much spoken of, it is not the ord's Supper, but the believers' union to Christ which is described. Vell, how unreasonable is it to suppose spiritual life communicated rough the actual, corporeal substance of Christ's body, at the ery stage at which the body is itself lifeless?

OLD TESTAMENT SAINTS COULD NOT SHARE IT.—Third. While e Old Testament believers had not the identical sacraments which e have, they had the same kind of spiritual life, nourished in the ame way (see Rom. 4:5; Heb. 11, and especially I Cor. 10:1 –4). Here the very same figure is employed—that of eating and rinking. How could this be an eating of His *flesh*, when that esh was not yet in existence?

THE CONJUNCTION IS SIMPLY BELIEVING.—Fourth. The sixth hapter of John contains many internal marks, by which the feedng on Christ is *identified with faith*, and His flesh is shown to be nly a figure for the benefits of His redemption. The *occasion*—e miracle of feeding the thousands with five loaves and *two* fishes, nd the consequent pursuit of Christ by the multitude, made it ery natural that Christ should adopt the figure of an eating of ood, to represent receiving Him. Verse 29 shows that eating is imply believing; for had Calvin's sense been true, our Saviour ould not have said so emphatically, that believing was the work f God. In verse 35, again, it is implied that the eating is but oming; i. e., believing. So, v. 40, 47 with 50. In v. 53, we ave language which is as destinctive of a spiritual feeding on the iteral body in the sacraments, as of a corporeal, for in either case t would be made to teach the unscriptural doctrine, that a soul cannot be saved without the sacraments. In v. 63, our Saviour plainly interprets his own meaning. And the whole tenor of Scripture (e. g. Matt. 15: 17, 18,) is unfavorable to the conception of the moral condition of the soul's being made dependent on a reception of corporeal substance.

CALVIN INCONSISTENT WITH RESULTS OF UNWORTHY EATING.—Last. (See I Cor. 11: 27, 29.) The destructive effects of unworthy communicating are here described in terms which plainly make this michief the *counterpart* of the benefit which the true believer derives, by proper communicating. Now, if this latter is an access of spiritual life through a substantial (though spiritual) reception of Christ's Person, the former must be a propagation of *spiritual death*, through the poisonous effects of this same Person, substantively present to the soul. But says Calvin, with obvious correctness, the unbelieving communicant does not get the Person of Christ into contact with his soul at all! The thing he guiltily does, is the keeping of Christ away from his soul totally, by his unbelief.

TRUE NATURE OF SACRAMENTAL EFFICIENCY.—Here we may appropriately answer the tenth question. We hold that the Lord's Supper is a *means of grace;* and the scriptural conception of this phrase explains the manner in which this sacrament is efficacious to worthy communicants. It sets forth the central truths of redemption, in a manner admirably adapted to our nature sanctified, and these truths, applied by the Holy Ghost, are the instruments of sanctification and spiritual life, in a manner generically the same with, though in degree more energetic, than the written and spoken word. So, the guilt of the unbelieving communicant is not one inevitably damning; but it is the *guilt of Christ's rejection;* it is the guilt of doing despight to the crucified Saviour by whom he should have been redeemed; and this, under circumstances of peculiar profanity. But the profanation varies according to the degree of conscious hypocrisy, and the motive of the act.

In conclusion of this head, I would remark that all these objections to that modified form of the real presence which Calvin held, apply *a fortiori*, to the grosser doctrines of the Lutheran and Romanist. The intelligent student can go over the application himself.

IS THE SUPPER A SACRIFICE? ROME'S ARGUMENTS.—VI. Rome asserts most emphatically that the Lord's Supper is a proper and literal sacrifice; in which the elements, having become the very body, blood, human spirit, and divinity of Christ, are again offered to God upon the altar; and the transaction is thus a repetition of the very sacrifice of the cross, and avails to atone for the sins of the living, and of the dead in purgatory. And all this is dependent on the Priest's intention. After the authority of Ch. Fathers and councils, which we set aside with a simple denial, Rome argues from Scripture that Christ was a priest after the order of Melchizedek; but he presented as priest, bread and wine as an oblation to God, and then made Abraham communicate in it: That Christ is a "priest forever," and therefore must have a perpetually recurring sacrifice to present: That Malachi (1 : 11,) predicts the continuance of a christian sacrifice among the Gentiles, under the New Testament. That the words of institution: "This is my body which is broken for you," when taken literally, as they ought to be, imply a sacrifice, because the bread, having become the veritable body, must be whatever the body is; but the body is there a sacrifice. And that Paul (I Cor. 10 : 21,) contrasts the Lord's table with that of devils (i. e. idols). But the latter was confessedly a table of sacrifice, whence the former must be so. But the true argument with Rome for teaching this doctrine, is that of Acts 19 : 25: they "know that by this craft they have their wealth." The great necessity of the human soul, awakened by remorse or by the convincing Spirit of God, is atonement. By making this horrible and impious invention, Rome has brought the guilty consciences of miserable sinners under her dominion, in order to make merchandise of their sin and fear. While nothing can transcend the unscripturalness of the doctrine of Transubstantiation, I regard this of the *sacrifice* of the Mass as the most impious and mischievous of all the heresies of Rome.

Refutation.—In answer to her pretended scriptural arguments: There is not one word of evidence that the bread and wine of Melchizedek, if even an oblation, were a sacrifice. Does Rome mean to represent the sacrament of the *Lord's Supper* as in exercise 1400 years before Christ had any body to commemorate? Christ's priesthood *is* perpetual; but it is perpetuated, according to Hebrews, in his function of *intercession*, which he continually performs in the Heavenly Sanctuary. And besides: it is a queer way to perpetuate *His* priestly functions, by having a line of *other priests* offer *him* as the victim of *their* sacrifices! Rome replies, that her Priest, in offering, acts in Christ's room, and speaks in his name. Such impiety is not strange on the part of Rome. We set aside the whole dream by demanding, where is the evidence that Christ has ever called one of his ministers a priest, or deputized to him this function? The prediction of Malachi is obviously to be explained by the remark, that he foretells the prevalence of *Christian institutions* among the Gentiles, in terms and imagery borrowed from Jewish rites. The same bungling interpretation which Rome makes here, would equally prove from Is. 2 : 1, 4, that the great annual feasts at Jerusalem are to be personally attended by all the people of Europe, Australia, America, &c.; and from Is. 56 : 7, that not only the "unbloody offering of the Mass," but literal burnt offerings shall be presented under the New Test.

by the Gentiles. By disproving the transubstantiation of the bread, we have already overthrown the argument founded on it. And last: it is evidently an overstraining of the Apostle's words, to infer from I Cor. 10: 21, that the thing literally eaten at the Lord's table must be a literal sacrifice. Since the elements eaten are the symbols of the divine sacrifice, there is in this an abundant ground for the Apostle's parallel. And moreover, when the Pagans met after the sacrifice, to eat of the body of the victim, the table was not an altar, nor was the act a sacrificial one.

HEADS OF DIRECT REFUTATION.—The direct refutation of this dogma has been so well executed by Calvin, Turretin, and other Protestants, that nothing more remains than to collect and state in their proper order the more important arguments. The *silence* of the Scripture is a just objection to it; because the burden of proof properly lies on those who assert the doctrine. The *circumstances of the first administration* of the Supper exclude all sacrificial character. No one will deny that this sacrament must bear the same meaning and character in all subsequent repetitions, which Christ gave it at first. But on that night it could not be a sacrifice, because his sacrifice was not yet made. Christ was as yet unslain. Nothing was offered to God; but on the contrary, Christ gave the elements to man: whereas, in a proper sacrifice, it is man that offers to God. *Not one of the proper traits* or characteristics of a true sacrifice is present. There is no victim, shedding his blood; and "without the shedding of blood is no remission." There is no sacrificial act whatever; and this is especially fatal to Romanists; because the only oblation to *God* which can by any pretext be found in the history of the institution in Scripture, is that of the eucharistic prayer. But, say they, the transubstantiation does not take place till *after* this, in the pronouncing of the words of institution. There is no death and consumption of a victim by fire; for the only thing like a killing is the *breaking* of the bread: but according to Romanists, this occurred in our Saviour's institution, before the transubstantiation. Again: the mere *fact that the Supper is a Sacrament* is incompatible with its being a sacrifice; for the nature of the two is dissimilar. True, the passover was both, but this was at different stages. But we object with yet more emphasis, that the doctrine is *impiously derogatory to Christ's one priesthood and sacrifice*, and to the sufficiency thereof, as asserted in Scripture. Christ is *sole* priest. (I Tim. 2 : 5; Heb. 7 : 24; 9 : 12.) and He offers one sacrifice, which neither needs, nor admits repetition. (Heb. 7 : 27, 9 : 25. and 10 : 10, 12, 14; 9 : 12, 14; 10 : 1 2, 10 : 26.)

PRIVATE COMMUNIONS REJECTED. WHY?—VII. Protestants deny the propriety of private communions, because they deny that the Supper is a sacrifice. It is a commemoration of Christ's death, and *shows forth* his death. There should therefore be fellow communicants to whom to show it forth, or at least spectators. It is a *communion*, representing our membership in the common body of Christ. Hence to celebrate it when no members are present to participate is an abuse. The motive for desiring private communions is usually superstitious, and therefore our Church does wisely in refusing it.

LAITY ENTITLED TO THE CUP.—VIII. The grounds on which Rome withholds the cup from the laity may be seen stated in the Council of Trent, and cited in Dick. They are too trivial to need refutation. It is enough to say that the assertion that the bread by itself is a whole sacrament, because the blood is in the body, is false. For it is the very nature of the Lord's Supper to signify that the blood is *not* in the body, having been poured out from it in death. We might justly ask: Why is not the bread alone sufficient for the priests also, if it is a whole sacrament? The outrage upon Christ's institute is peculiarly glaring, because the injunction to give the cup to the communicants is as clear and positive as to observe the sacrament at all. And our Saviour, as though foreseeing the abuse, in Mark 14 : 23, and Matt. 26 : 27, has emphatically declared that all who eat are also to drink. This innovation of Rome is comparatively modern; being not more against the word of God than against the voice and usage of Christian antiquity. It presents one of the strongest examples of her insolent arrogance both towards her people and God. The true motive, doubtless, is, to exalt the priesthood into a superior caste.

IX. For the answer to this, see Lectures on the Sacraments in General. Qu. 10.

LECTURE LXVII.

SYLLABUS.

DEATH OF BELIEVERS.

1. Why does death befall justified persons? Dick, Lecture 80. Knapp's Theol., § 147 to 150.
2. Review the arguments for the immortality of the soul. Dick, as above. Butler's Analogy. Pt. I. Breckinridge's Theology, Vol. I., Bk. I., Ch. 6.
3. What are the benefits which believers receive at death; and is entire sanctification one of them? Dick, Lecture 81. Knapp as above.
4. Is there any other place than heaven or hell, (such as that called Hades, *Limbus Patrum*, &c.,) where any souls are detained? Turretin, Loc. XII. Qu. 11.
5. Is the soul conscious and active between death and the resurrection? Dick, Lect. 81. See on the whole, Ridgeley, Qu. 85, 86.

1. DEATH A PENAL EVIL. WHY THEN INFLICTED ON THE JUSTIFIED? Death is undoubtedly a penal evil; and not merely a natural law, as Socinians and Pelagians teach. This we have already shown by the Bible, (Gen. 2 : 17, 3 : 17–19, 5 : 3; Rom. 5 : 12, 14,) and by the obvious reasoning that the benevolence and righteousness, with the infinite power of God, would combine to prevent any suffering to his moral creatures while free from guilt. Man *enters life* now, *subject to the whole penalty* of death, including temporal physical evils, spiritual death, and bodily death; and this is the consequence of Adam's fall through our federal connexion with him. From spiritual death, all believers are delivered at their regeneration. Physical evils and bodily death remain; and inasmuch as the latter is a most distinctive and emphatic retribution for sin, the question is, how it comes to be inflicted on those who are absolutely justified in Christ. On the one hand, bodily death is a *penal* infliction. On the other hand, we have taught that believers are justified from all guilt, and are required to render no penal satisfaction whatever. (Rom. 5 : 1; Heb. 10 : 14, &c.) Yet all believers die!

FALSE AND TRUE ANSWERS.—Now this question is very inadequately met by such views as these: That this anomaly is no greater than many others in the divine dealings; e. g., the continuance of imperfection and indwelling sin so many years in believers, or their subjection to the malice of evil men and demons. That the destruction of the body is necessary to a perfect sanctification, a thing shown to be untrue in the cases of Enoch, Elijah, the human soul of Christ, and all the believers who shall be on earth at the last consummation; or, that the natural law of mortality, and the rule of God's kingdom, that men must " walk by faith, not by sight," would both be violated, if so *visible* a difference were placed between saints and sinners as the entire exemption of the former from bodily death. These are partial explanations. The true answer is, that although believers are fully justified, yet according to that plan of grace which God has seen fit to adopt, *bodily death is a necessary and wholesome chastisement* for the good of the believer's soul. If this postulate can be shown to be correct, the occurrence of death to the justified man will fall into the *same class* with all other paternal chastisements, and will receive the same explanation.

GROUND AND NATURE OF CHASTISEMENTS.—Let us then recall some principles which were established in our defence of our view of the Atonement against Romanists, &c. First. A chastisement, while God's motive in it is only benevolent, does not cease to be, to the believer, a natural evil. We may call it a blessing in disguise; but the christian smarting under it feels that if this language means that it is not a real evil, it is a mere play upon words. The accurate statement is, that God wisely and kindly exercises in chastisements his divine prerogative of bringing good out of evil. Bodily death does not cease to be to the believer a real natural evil in itself, and to be feared and felt as such. Second. Hence chastisement is a means of spiritual benefit appropriate only to *sinning children* of God. It would not be just, for instance, that God should adopt chastisements as a means to advance Gabriel, who never had any guilt, to some higher stage of sanctified capacities and blessedness; because where there is no guilt there is no suffering. Third. Still, God's motive in chastising the believer is not at all retributive, but wholly beneficent; whereas his retributions of the guilty are intended, not primarily to benefit *them*, but to satisfy righteousness. Here then is the distinctive difference between Rome and us: that we hold, while the sufferings endured in chastisements have a *reference* to our sinful and guilty condition, in the believer's case they are neither paid by him, nor received by God, as any penal satisfaction whatever for guilt, that satisfaction is wholly paid by our surety. Heb. 12 : 6-10; Rom. 8 : 18-28; 2 Cor. 4 : 17; with Rom. 8 : 33; Ps. 103 : 12; Micah 7 : 19. Whereas Rome teaches that penitential sufferings of believers go to complete the actual penal satisfaction for the *reatum pœnæ*, left incomplete by Christ.

Fourth.—HOW COMPATIBLE WITH SATISFACTION FOR SIN.—The use of such means of sanctification is compatible with divine justice, although an infinite vicarious satisfaction is made for our guilt by our surety, because, as we saw, a vicarious satisfaction is not a commercial *equivalent* for our guilt; a *legal tender* such as brings our Divine Creditor under a righteous obligation to cancel our whole indebtedness. But his acceptance of it as a legal satisfaction was, on his part, an act of pure grace; and therefore the acceptance acquits us just so far as, and no farther than, God is pleased to allow it. And we learn from His word that he has been pleased to accept it just thus far; that the believer shall be required to pay no more penal satisfaction to the broken law; yet shall be liable to such suffering of chastisements as shall be wholesome for his own improvement, and appropriate to his sinning condition.

BODILY DEATH AN EDIFYING CHASTISEMENT.—Now then, does bodily death subserve the purposes of a wholesome and sanctifying chastisement? I answer, most eminently. The *prospect* of it serves, from the earliest day when it begins to stir the sinner's conscience to a wholesome seriousness, through all his convictions, conversion, Christian warfare, to humble the proud soul, to mortify carnality, to check pride, to foster spiritual mindedness. It is the fact that sicknesses are premonitions of death, which make *them* active means of sanctification. Bereavements through the death of friends form another valuable class of disciplinary sufferings. Now *that death may be actually in prospect, death must actually occur*. And when the closing scene approaches, no doubt in every case where the believer is conscious, the pains of its approach, the solemn thoughts and emotions it suggests are all used by the Holy Ghost as powerful means of sanctification to ripen the soul rapidly for Heaven. I doubt not, that when we take into view the whole moral influences of the life-long prospect of our own deaths, the prospect and occurrence of bereavement by death of friends, the pungent efficiency given to sickness by its connexion with death, as well as the actual influences of the closing scene, we shall see that all other chastisements put together, are far less efficacious in checking inordinate affection and sanctifying the soul: yea, that without this, there would be no efficacious chastisement at all left in the world. A race of sinners must be a race of mortals; Death is the only check (of the nature of *means*) potent enough to prevent depravity from breaking out with a power which would make the state of the world perfectly intolerable!

DEATH A MEANS OF GLORY TO SAINT, UNMIXED CURSE TO SINNER.—II. Yet, as the afflictions of the righteous differ much from the torments of the wicked, this is peculiarly true of their deaths. To the impenitent man, death is full of the sting of sin. In the case of the Saint, this sting is extracted by redemption. There may not be the abounding triumphs of spiritual joy: but if the believer is conscious, he usually enjoys a peace, which controls and calms the agitations of the natural feelings recoiling from death. In the case of the sinner, the horror of dying is made up of two sets of feelings, the instinctive love of life, with the natural affections which tie him to the earth; and evil conscience with dread of future retributions. And the latter is often predominant in the sinner's anguish. But in the case of the Saint it is removed; and death is only an evil in the apprehension of the former feelings. Second: to the sinner, death is the beginning of his utter misery; to the Saint it is the usher, (a dreaded one indeed) into his real blessedness. By it the death in sins, and bondage of depravity is fixed upon the sinner irrevocably: but the saint is delivered by it from all his indwelling sins. Death removes the sinner forever from God, from partial gospel privileges and communions. But to the Saint it is the means of breaking down the veil, and introducing him into the full fruition and vision of God.

Benefits Received by Saint at Death—1. Complete Sanctification.—See Shorter Cat. Qu. 37. Three benefits are here mentioned as received from Christ at the believers' death: forget. sanctification, immediate entrance into glory, and the prospect of a bodily resurrection.

We take up here, the first, postponing the others for separate discussion; and assuming, for the time, the implied truth of the immortality of the soul. The complete sanctification of believers at death would hardly be denied by any who admitted that their souls entered at once into the place of our Saviour's glorified residence, and of God's visible throne. It is those who teach a separate state, a transmigration, or Hades, or purgatory, or sleep in the grave, who deny the immediate sanctification of souls. For the attributes of God and heaven are such as obviously to require perfect purity from all who dwell there. Let the student bear this in mind, and have in view the truth to be hereafter established, that the souls of believers "do immediately pass into glory." The *place* is holy, and debars the approach of all moral impurity. (Rev. 21:27.) The *inhabitants*, the holy angels are pure, and could not appropriately admit the companionship of one tainted with indwelling sin. Three: they now fly forth to "minister to them who shall be the heirs of salvation;" but this is not a companionship. The *king* of that world is too pure to receive sinners to his bosom. He does indeed condescend by his Holy Ghost into the polluted breasts of sinners on earth; but this is a far different thing from a public, full and final admission of sin into the place of his holiness. See I. Pt. 1: 15, 16; Ps. 5: 4; 15: 2; Is. 6: 5. The *blessedness* of the redeemed is incompatible with any remaining imperfection (Rev. 21: 4). For wherever there is sin, there must be suffering. And *last*, this glorious truth is plainly asserted in the word of God. (Heb. 12: 23; Eph. 5: 27; I. John 3: 2.)

MADE FEASIBLE BY BODY'S DEATH.—*How* this sanctification is wrought, we may not tell. Recall the remark made when sanctification was discussed: that it is not mysticism, nor gnosticism, nor asceticism, to ascribe its completion to our release from the body, as a convenient occasion. Bodily appetites are the occasions of the larger part of most men's sins: as the bodily members are the instruments of all their overt sins. How natural, then, that when these are removed, God should finally remove sin. The agent of this work is still, no doubt, the Holy Spirit.

OLD AND NEW TESTAMENTS TEACH IMMORTALITY.—III. I have already remarked that all these views presuppose that immortality which is brought to light in the gospel. It has always seemed to me that it treats the question of man's immortality, as it does that of God's existence, assumes it as an undisputed postulate. Hence the debate urged by Warburton and his opposers, whether Moses taught a future existence, seems to me preposterous. To dispute that he did, flies into the very teeth of Scripture. (Matt. 22:32; Heb. 11:16, 26; and in Pentateuch, Deut. 18: 9-12. Gen. 5:22, 24; Gen. 37: 35, 15:15, 25: 8, 35: 29; Numb. 20: 24, 49: 33.) All religion and even all morality implies a future existence. But our Saviour, whose purpose it was to reaffirm the truths of Old Testament Revelation, and of natural Religion, which had been obscured by the perverse skepticism of men, does teach man's immortality with peculiar distinctness and fullness. The reader may consult for instance, (Matt. 10: 28; Luk. 16: 19, 20: 38; Matt. 25, end; Jno. 5: 24, 8: 51, 11, 12: 24; 2 Cor. 5: 1-10; 1 Cor. 15; &c. This may perhaps be a part of the Apostle's meaning, when he says, (2 Tim. 1: 10,) that Christ "hath brought life and immortality to light in the gospel." But it would certainly be a great abuse of his meaning, to understand from him that Christ was the first adequately to teach that there is an immortal existence. Paul speaks rather, as the contest clearly shows, ("hath abolished death,") of spiritual life, and a happy immortality, which Christianity procures. And it is the glory of the religion of the Bible to have clearly made this known to man.

WHICH IS THAT OF SOUL AND BODY.—It may be well to note, that the immortality of the Bible is that of the whole man, body and soul; and herein God's word transcends entirely all the guesses of natural reason. And this future existence implies the continuance of our consciousness, memory, mental, and personal identity; of the same soul in the same body, (after the resurrection). There must be also the essential and characteristic exercises of our reasonable and moral nature, with an unbroken continuity. For if the being who is to live, and be affected with weal or woe by my conduct here, is not the *I*, who now act, and hope, and fear, that future existence is of small moment to me.

RATIONAL ARGUMENTS REVIEWED.—It may not be amiss here, to review the amount of light which natural reason has been able to collect concerning man's future existence. Since the resurrection of the body is purely a doctrine of revelation, of which reason could not have any surmise (witness the Pagan philosophies,) the question must be discussed rationally as a question concerning the immortality of the soul only. All that natural experience ever sees of the body is its death, dissolution, and seemingly irreparable destruction. But since the soul is the true seat of sensation, knowledge, emotion, merit, and will, the assertion of its immortality is far the most important part of the doctrine of man's future existence. The various opinions of men on this subject, who had no revelation, may be seen stated in Knapp's Theol. § 149, viz: materialism (Epicurus,) transmigrations. (Brahmin's Pythagoras and some Jews,) re-absorption into the H. d. v. (Stoic Pantheists,) and separate disembodied immortality (Plato, &c.). Among the many reasonings advanced by ancients and moderns, these following seem to me to have probable weight.

(a.) The *consensus Populorum*, especially when we consider how naturally man's sensuous nature and evil conscience might incline him to neglect the truth.

(b.) The analogy of the fact that man and all other living things obviously experience several stages, first the *fœtus*, then infant, then adult. It is natural to expect other stages. (Butler.)

(c.) A present existence raises a presumption of continued existence, (as the sun's rising, that it will rise again) unless there is something in the body's dissolution to destroy the probability. But is there? No. For body sleeps while soul wakes. Body may waste, fatten, be amputated, undergo flux of particles, loss of sensible organs, while soul remains identical. In sensation, the soul only *uses* the organs of sense, as one might feel with a stick, or see through a glass. The more essential operations of spirit, conception, memory, comparison, reasoning, &c., are carried on wholly independent of the body, whence we conclude that the essential subsistence of the soul is independent of the body.—(Butler.)

(d.) The soul is simple, a *monad*, as is proved by consciousness. But there is not a particle of analogy, in the universe, to show that it is probable God will annihilate any substance he has created. The only instances of destruction we see, are those of disorganization of the complex. (Butler; Brown.)

(e.) The soul has higher powers than any of God's terrestrial works, strange that the brute earth, and even elephants, eagles, and geese should be more long-lived! It has a capacity for mental and moral development beyond any which it attains in this life. God has ordained that all things else should fulfill the ends of their existence. It can know and glorify God: Strange that God, making all things for his own glory, should make his rational servants such that the honour derived from them must utterly terminate.

(f.) Conscience points direct to a superior moral Ruler, and a future existence, with its retributions.

(g.) The unequal distribution of retributions here on earth, coupled with our confidence in the righteousness of God, compel a belief in a future existence, where all shall be equalized.

IS THERE AN INTERMEDIATE STATE.—IV. We have asserted it, as the doctrine of the Bible, that the souls of believers do *pass immediately into glory*. In opposition to this, there are some, among the professed believers in the Bible, who hold some kind of intermediate state, in which the souls of all, saints and sinners, are detained. The opinions of this kind may be ranked under three heads: 1. That of the Romish Purgatory, which has been already discussed. 2. That of the Jewish Hades, held by some Rabbins; and 3d. That of the ancient Socinians and modern Thomasites, who hold that the soul will sleep unconscious until the body's resurrection. The second of these opinions will be the subject of the present section and the third, of the fifth and last.

JEWISH DOCTRINE.—The Jewish doctrine seems to have been, that the souls of departed men do not pass at once into their ultimate abode; but into the invisible world, *Hades*, SHEOL, where they await their final doom, until the final consummation, in a state of partial and negative blessedness and misery, respectively. This Hades has two departments, that of the blessed, Paradise, or the Bosom of Abraham, and that of the lost, Tartarus. But this Paradise is far short of the heavens proper in blessedness, as well as different in locality, and this Tartarus far less intolerable than Gehenna, or hell proper. The following passages were supposed by them to favor this opinion: Gen. 37 : 35, 42 : 38, "Go *down* to Hades;" 1 Samuel 28 : 11, 14 and 19, "An old man *cometh up*," "Be *with me* to-morrow;" Zech. 9 : 11, where it is supposed the souls are in a place like a dry pit; Psalms 6 : 5, 88 : 10, 115 : 17, 143 : 3, where the state of the dead is described seemingly as a senseless and negative one. And some Papists have supposed that their kindred notion of a *Limbus patrum* found support in Luke 16 : 23 end.

DISPROVED.—No better disproof of this doctrine of a Hades need be sought than that of Luke 16 : 22, 23. It is manifest that being in Abraham's bosom *is* being in Heaven. Compare Matt. 8 : 11. Then, rewards and punishments are already begun; and the torments of Dives are as characteristic of Hell proper ("tormented in this flame") as any others described in Scripture.

Second. The history of the transfiguration proves that Moses and Elijah are in glory. It may be said that these are peculiar cases, and especially the latter, who is still in the body; but here we have the principle stated, that some redeemed souls have passed immediately into glory. And the revelations made to John in the Apocalypse ground a similar argument; because the souls of the redeemed are there represented as before the throne; and however figurative such language may be, it surely means something corresponding to the figure.

Third. We argue from the case of the penitent thief. Christ promises: This day shalt thou be with me in Paradise. This means Heaven proper. Cf. 2 Cor. 12 : 2-4; Rev. 2 : 7.

Once more: In the language of Paul, to be unclothed is equivalent to being clothed upon with our heavenly house, 2 Cor. 5 : 4, and to be absent from the flesh is to be present with the Lord, 2 Cor. 5 : 8.

THE SOUL CONSCIOUS AND ACTIVE DURING THE BODY'S SLEEP.—V. The last of the three opinions may be refuted by the same arguments just used upon the IVth. It only remains to add the following from the language of Stephen, Acts 7 : 59, and of Paul, Phil. 1 : 23.

The true *ego*, the soul has no concern with the grave. Here is inexpressible consolation.

LECTURE LXVIII.

SYLLABUS.

THE RESURRECTION.

1. What were the opinions of the ancient Heathens, and what of the Jews, on this subject? Does nature furnish any analogy in favor of it? Dr. Christian Knapp, §151. Dick, Lect. 82.
2. State the precise meaning of the Scripture doctrine. What will be the qualities of our resurrection bodies? Turretin Loc. xx., Qu. 1, 2 and 9. Knapp, § 152, 153. Dick, Lect. 82.
3. Will the resurrection bodies be the same which men have now? In what sense the same? Discuss objections. Turretin, Qu. 2. Dick, Lect. 82. Watson's Theo. Inst., chap. XXIX.
4. Prove the doctrine of the Resurrection, from the Old Testament; from the New. Turretin, Qu. 1; Dick, Lect. 82.
5. How is the resurrection of the Saints, and how is that of sinners, related to the resurrection of Christ? Dick, Lect. 82. Breckinridge Theol., Vol. 1, as above.
6. What will be the time? Will there be a double resurrection? Turretin, Qu. 3. Dick, Lect. 82. Scott, Com. on Rev., ch. 20th. Brown's Second Advent.

   See on whole, Ridgeley, Qu. 87; Geo. Bush on the Resurrection; Davies' Sermons; Young's Last Day.

Pagan Theories embrace no Resurrection.—I. The definite philosophic speculations among the ancient Heathen all discarded the doctrine of a proper resurrection; so that the Bible stands alone in acknowledging the share of the body in man's immortality. It is true that the poets (Hesiod, Homer, Virgil) expressing the popular and traditionary belief, in this case, as in that of the soul's immortality, less incorrect than the philosopher's speculations, speak of the future life as a bodily one, of members, food, labours, &c., in Tartarus and Elysium. But it is difficult to say how far these sensuous representations of the future existence were due to mere inaccuracy and grossness of conception, or how far to perspicuous ideas of a bodily existence conjoined with the spiritual. The Brahmins speak of many transmigrations and incarnations, of their deified men; but none of them are resurrections proper. The Pythagoreans and Platonists dreamed of an *ochema*, an ethereal, semi-spiritual investment, which the glorified spirit, after its metempsychosis are finished, develops for itself. The pantheistic sects, whether Budhists or Stoics, of course utterly rejected the idea of a bodily existence after death, when they denied even a personal existence of the soul.

What Jews believed it.—But the Jews, with the exception of the Saducees and Essenes, seem to have held firmly to the doctrine. Nor can I see any evidence, except the prejudice of hypothesis and fancy, for the notion of Knapp, and many Germans, that their belief in this doctrine dated only from the time of the Babylonish captivity. There is no historical evidence. If the proof-texts of the earlier Hebrew Scriptures are perversely explained away, and those of the Maccabees, &c., admitted, there is some show of plausibility. But it is far better reasoning to say that this unquestioning belief in the doctrine by the Jews, is evidence that they understood their earlier as well as their later Scriptures to teach it. The evidence of the state of opinion among them, and especially among the Pharisees, is found in their uninspired writings: 2 Mac. 7 : 9, &c., 12 : 43, 45; Josephus and Philo, and in New Testament allusions to their ideas. See Matt. 22, Luke 20, John 11 : 24, Acts 23 : 6, 8, Heb. 11 : 35. But the doctrine was a subject of mocking skepticism to most of the speculative Pagans; as the interlocutor in Minutius Felix, Octavius, Pliny, jr., Lucian, Celsus, &c. See Acts 17 : 32; 26 : 6-8; 23 : 24.

No Natural Proofs of it.—Hence, we may infer, that the doctrine of the resurrection is purely one of revelation. Analogies and probable arguments have been sought in favor of it, as by the early Fathers, and later writers; but while some rise in dignity above the fable of the Phœnix, none of them can claim to be demonstrations. The fact that all nature moves in cycles, restoring a state of things again which had passed away; that the trees bud after the sterility and mimic death of winter; that moons wax again after they have waned; that sun and stars, after setting in the west, rise again in the east; that seeds germinate and reproduce their kind; can scarcely be called a proper analogy; for in all these cases there is no proper destruction, by a disorganization of atoms, but a mere return of the same complex body, without a moment's breach of its organic unity, into the same state in which it had previously been. If we were perfectly honest, we should rather admit that the proper analogies of nature are against the doctrine: for when a seed germinates, *that* particular seed is produced no more; there is, in what comes from it, only a generic, not a numerical identity. When the tree really perishes, its mould and moisture and gases are never reconstructed into that same tree, but pass irrevocably into other vegetable forms. Dick supposes that the argument said to have been stated B. C. 450, by Phocylides, the Milesian, is more plausible: that inasmuch as God's wisdom led him to introduce a *genus* of rational beings, of body and spirit combined, the same wisdom will always lead him to perpetuate that kind. But if, after the soul's departure, the body were never reanimated, man would become simply an inferior angel, and the *genus* would be obliterated. To this, also, we may reply: that this argument is not valid until it is also shown that the wisdom which called this *genus* of complex beings into existence will not be satisfied by its temporary continuance as a separate genus. But this we can never prove by mere reason. For instance: the same reasoning would prove equally well, both an immortality and a bodily resurrection, for any of the *genera* of brutes! Another argument is presented by Turrettin from the justice of God, which, if possessed of feeble weight by itself, at least has the advantage of harmonizing with Bible representations. It is, that the justice of God is more appropriately satisfied, by punishing and rewarding souls in the very bodies, and with the whole personal identity, with which they sinned (Comp. 2 Cor. 5 : 10) or obeyed.

TRUE MEANING OF RESURRECTION.—II. In Scripture the image of a *resurrection, Anastasis*, is undoubtedly used sometimes in a figurative sense, to describe regeneration, (John. 5 : 25 ; Eph. 5 : 6,) and sometimes, restoration from calamity and captivity to prosperity and joy. (Ezek. 37 : 12 ; Is. 26 : 19.) But it is equally certain that the words are intended to be used in a literal sense, of *the restoration of the same body that dies* to life, by its reunion to the soul. This then is the doctrine. For when the resurrection of the dead (*nekrown*) of those that are in their graves, of those that sleep in the dust of the earth, is declared, the sense is unequivocal. Without at this time particularizing Scripture proofs, we assert that they mean to describe a bodily existence as literally as when they speak of man's soul in this life, as residing in a body; and this, though wonderfully changed in qualities, the *same* body, in the proper, honest sense of the word *same*, which the soul laid down at death. This resurrection will embrace all the individuals of the human race, good and bad, except those whose bodies have already passed into heaven, and those of the last generation, who will be alive on the earth at the last trump. But on the bodies of these the resurrection change will pass, though they do not die. The signal of this resurrection is to be the "last trump," an expression probably taken from the transactions at Sinai: (Exod. 19 : 16, 19 ; Cf. Heb. 12 : 26,) which may very possibly be, some literal audible summons, sounded through the whole atmosphere of the world. But the *agent* will be Christ, by his direct and almighty power with the Holy Ghost.

QUALITIES OF RESURRECTION BODIES.—The qualities of the resurrection bodies of the Saints are described in I Cor. 15 : 42, 50, with as much particularity, probably, as we can comprehend. Whereas the body is buried in a state of dissolution; it is raised indissoluble, no longer liable to disorganization, by separation of particles, either because protected therefrom by the special power of God, or by the absence of assailing chemical forces. It is buried, disfigured and loathsome. It will be raised beautiful. Since it is a literal material body that is raised, it is far the most natural to suppose that the glory predicated of it, is literal, material beauty. As to its kind, see Matt. 13 : 43 ; Phil. 3 : 21, with

Rev. 1 : 13, 14. Some may think that it is unworthy of God's redemption to suppose it conferring an advantage so trivial and sensuous as personal beauty. But is not this a remnant of that Gnostic or Neo Platonic asceticism, which cast off the body itself as too worthless to be an object of redeeming power? We know that sanctified affections now always beautify and ennoble the countenance. See Exod. 34 : 29, 30. And if God did not deem it too trivial for his attention, to clothe the landscape with verdure, to cast every form of nature in lines of grace, to dye the skies with purest azure, and to paint the sun and stars with splendour, in order to gratify the eyes of his children here, we may assume that he will condescend to beautify even the bodies of his Saints, in that world where all is made perfect. Next, the body is buried in weakness; it has just given the crowning evidence of feebleness, by yielding to death. It will be raised in immortal vigour, so as to perform its functions with perfect facility, and without fatigue.

"Natural Body" and "Spiritual Body;" What?—And last; it is buried an *animal* body; i. e., this is the character it has hitherto had. The *Soma Psuchikon* is unfortunately translated "natural body" in the English version. The Apostle here evidently avails himself of the popular Greek distinction, growing out of the currency of Pythagorean and Platonic philosophy, to express his distinction, without meaning to endorse their psychology. The *Soma Pneumatikon* is evidently the body as characterized chiefly by its *animal functions.* What these are, there can be little doubt, if we keep in mind the established Greek sense of the *Psuche,* viz: the functions of the appetite and sense. Then the *Soma Pneumatikon* must mean not a *body now material,* as the Swedenborgians, &c., claim (a positive contradiction and impossibility), but a body actuated only by processes of intellection and moral affection; for these, Paul's readers supposed, were the proper processes of the *Pneuma,* or *Nous.* But the Apostle, v. v. 44, 50, defines his own meaning. To show that "there is an animal body, and a spiritual body;" that it is no fancy nor impossibility, he points to the fact that such have already existed, in the case of Adam and his natural seed, and of Christ. And as we were federally connected, first with Adam, and then with Christ, we bear first the animal body, (Adam's) and then the spiritual (Christ's). And Christ's humanity also, during his humiliation, passed through that first stage, to the second; because he assumed all the innocent weaknesses and affections of a literal man. Our *Soma Pneumatikon* then, is defined to be what Christ's glorified body now in Heaven is. Complete this definition by what we find in Matt. 22: 30. The spiritual body then, is one occupied and actuated only by the spiritual processes of a sanctified soul; but which neither smarts with pain, nor feels fatigue, nor has appetites, nor takes any literal, material supplies therefor.

Resurrection Bodies of Sinners.—It seems every way reasonable to suppose that while the bodies of the wicked will be raised without the glory or splendour of the Saints, they also will be no longer animal bodies, and will be endued with immortal vigour to endure.

Identity of the Bodies Raised Proofs.—III. The Scriptures plainly teach that our resurrection bodies will be *the bodies* we now have, only modified; that is, that they will be substantially identical. This follows from the divine justice, so far as it prompts God to work a resurrection. For if we have not the very body in which we sinned, when called to judgment, that "every man may receive the things done in the body," there will be no *relevancy* in the punishment, so far as it falls on the body. The same truth follows from the believer's union to Christ. If he redeemed our bodies, must they not be the very ones we have here? (I Cor. 3 : 16; 6 : 15). It appears evidently from Christ's resurrection, which is the earnest, exemplar, and pledge of ours. For in his case, the body that was raised was the very one that died and was buried. But if, in our case, the body that dies is finally dissipated, and another is reconstructed, there is small resemblance indeed to our Saviour's resurrection. This leads us to remark, fourth, that the very words *Anistemi*, *Anastasis* plainly imply the rearing of *the same thing* that fell; otherwise there is an abuse of language in applying them to a proper creation. Last, the language of Scripture in Dan. 12 : 2; John 5 : 28, 29; I Cor. 15 : 21, 53, 54 : I Thess. 4 : 16; it is that which is "in the dust of the earth," "in the *Mnemeia*," the *Nekroi*, corpses, which is raised. It is "*this mortal*" which "puts on immortality." From the days of the Latin Fathers, and their speculative Pagan opposers, certain objections have been pompously raised against such a resurrection, as though it were intrinsically absurd. They may be found reproduced by Geo. Bush on the Resurrection.

Objection from Wonderfulness, Answered.—The general objection is from the incredible greatness of the work; that since the particles that composed human bodies are scattered asunder by almost every conceivable agency, fire, winds, waters, birds and beasts of prey, mingled with the soil of the fields, and dissolved in the waters of the ocean, it is unreasonable to expect they will be assembled again. We reply, (reserving the question whether a proper corporeal identity implies the presence of all the constituent particles, of which more anon), that this objection is founded only on a denial of God's omnipotence, omniscience, and almighty power. The work of the resurrection does indeed present a most wondrous and glorious display of divine power. But to God all things are easy. We may briefly reply, that to all who believe in a special Providence, there is a standing and triumphant answer visible to our eyes. It is in the existence of our present bodies. Are they not formed *by God?* Are they not also formed from "the dust of the earth?" And it is not *any* one hundred and fifty pounds of earth, which God moulds into a body of that weight; but there is a most wonderful, extensive, and nice selection of *particles*, where a million of atoms are assorted over and rejected, for one that is selected; and that from thousands of miles. In my body there are atoms, probably, that came from Java (in coffee), and from Cuba or Manilla (in sugar), and from the western prairies (in pork), and from the Savannahs of Carolina (in rice), and from the green hills of Western Virginia (in beef and butter), and from our own fields (in fruits). Do you say, the selection and aggregation have been accomplished gradually, by sundry natural laws of vegetation and nutrition? Yea, but what are natural laws? Only regular modes of God's working through matter which he has in his wisdom proposed to himself. If God actually *does* this thing now, why may he not do another thing just like it, only more quickly?

PHYSICAL OBJECTION ANSWERED.—But an objection supposed to be still more formidable, is derived from the supposed flux of particles in the human body, and the cases in which particles which belonged to one man at his death, become parts of the structure of another man's body, through cannibalism, or the derivation by beasts from the mould enriched with human dust, which beasts are in turn consumed by men, &c., &c. Now, since one material atom cannot be in two places at the same time, the resurrection of the same bodies, say they, is a physical impossibility. And if the flux of particles be admitted, *which* shall the man claim, as composing his bodily identity; those he had first, or those he had last: or all he ever had? To the first of these questions, we reply, that there is no *evidence* that a particle of matter composing a portion of a human corpse, has ever been assimilated by another human body. It is only assumed that it *may* be so. But now, inasmuch as the truth of Scripture has been demonstrated by an independent course of moral evidences, and it asserts the *same* body shall be raised, if there is, indeed, any difficulty about this question of the *atoms*, the burden of proof lies upon the objector; and he must *demonstrate* that the difficulty exists, and is insuperable. It is not sufficient merely to *surmise* that it may exist. Now, I repeat, a surmise is good enough to meet a surmise. Let me assume this hypothesis, that it may be a physiological law, that a molecule, once assimilated and vitalized by a man (or other animal), undergoes an influence which renders it afterwards incapable of assimilation by another being of the same species. This, indeed, is not without plausible evidence from analogy, witness, for instance: the fertility of a soil to another crop, when a proper rotation is pursued, which had become barren as to the first crop too long repeated. But, if there is any such law, the case supposed by the objector against the resurrection, never occurs. But, second: in answer to both objections, it can never be shown that the numerical identity of all the constituent atoms is necessary to that *bodily sameness*, which is asserted by the Bible of our resurrection bodies. We are under no forensic obligation whatever, to define precisely in what that sameness consists, but take our stand here, that the Bible, being written in popular language, when it says our resurrection bodies will be *the same*, it means precisely what popular consciousness and common language apprehend, when it is said my body at forty is the same body grown stronger, which I had at fifteen. Let that meaning be whatever it may be, if this doctrine of the *flux of particles*, and this possibility of a particle that once belonged to one man becoming a part of another, prove that our resurrection bodies cannot be the same that died, they equally prove that my body cannot now be the body I had some years ago, for that flux, if there is any truth in it, has already occurred; and there is just as much probability that I have been nourished with a few particles from a potatoe, manured with the hair of some man who is still living, as that two men will both claim the same particles at the resurrection. But my consciousness tells me [the most demonstrative of all proof], that I have had the *same body* all the time, so that, if these famous objections disprove a resurrection, they equally contradict consciousness. You will notice that I propound no theory as to what constitutes precisely our consciousness of bodily identity, as it is wholly unnecessary to our argument that I should; and that I do not undertake to define precisely how the resurrection body will be constituted in this particular; and this is most proper for me, because the Bible propounds no theory on this point.

Bodily Identity During Life, What?—But if curiosity leads you to inquire, I answer that it appears to me our consciousness of bodily identity [as to a limb, or member, or organ of sense, for instance,] does not include an apprehension of the numerical identity of all the constituent atoms all the while, but that it consists of an apprehension of a continued *relation* of the *organism* of the limb or organ *to our mental consciousness* all the time, implying also that there is no sudden change of a majority, or even any large fraction of the constituent atoms thereof at any one time.

Proofs that Bodies will Rise.—IV. In presenting the Bible-proof, nothing more will be done, than to cite the passages, with such word of explanation as may be necessary to show their application. If we believe our Saviour, implications of this doctrine appear at a very early stage of the Old Testament Scriptures; for indeed the sort of immortality implied all along, is the immortality of man, body and soul. (See then Exod. 3: 6, as explained in Matt. 22:31, 32; Mark 12: 26, 27.) The next passage is Job 19: 25, which I claim *quicunque vult*, as containing a clear assertion of a resurrection. Ps. 26: 9, 11, (expounded acts 2: 29, 32, 13:36, 37.) David is made by the Holy Ghost to foretell Christ's resurrection. Doubtless, the Psalmist, if he distinctly knew that he was personating Christ in this language, apprehended his own resurrection as a corallary of Christ's, (Ps. 17:15,) probably alludes also to a resurrection in the phrase: "awake in thy likeness;" for what awakes, except the body? Nothing else sleeps. (Is. 25: 8, interpreted in I. Cor. 15: 54; Daniel 12: 2.)

In the new Testament the passages are far more numerous and plain, the principal being John 5: 21, 29, 6: 39, 40: 11, 24; Matt. 22, 23, &c. I. Cor. 15; Acts 24:14, 15; I. Theso. 4 13; Phil. 3: 21; Hebr. 6: 2 and 11: 35; 2 Tim. 2: 8, &c.

The resurrection of Christ is both example and proof of ours. (I. Pet. 1: 3; I Cor. 15: 20.)

The Covenant of Grace, as expounded by Christ. (Matt. 22.)

The inhabitation of our bodies, by the Holy Ghost.

The justice of God, all as expounded by Turrettin.

Reprobate not raised in Christ, but by Christ.—V. Some divines, as e. g. Breckinridge, say that the resurrection of both Saints and sinners is of Christ's purchase, quoting I. Cor. 15: 22, making the "*all*" mean the whole human race. But we teach, that while Christ, as King in Zion, commands the resurrection of both, it is in different relations. The resurrection of *his people* being a gift of his purchase, effectuated in them by their *union* to him, and one result of the indwelling of the Holy Ghost. The resurrection of the evil is an act of pure dominion, effected in them by his avenging sovereignty. The other idea would represent the wicked also, as vitally connected with Christ, by a mystical union. But if so, why does not that union sanctify and save? Are we authorized to say that, had Christ not come, there would have been no resurrection unto damnation for Adam's fallen race at all? Moreover, that opinion puts an unauthorized and dangerous sense upon I. Cor. 15: 22, *et sim.*

Scheme of Pre-Adventists.—VI. Millenarianism has received in our day a great revival; and its advocates claim especial fidelity to the language of Scripture, and to principle. The scheme is a pre-millenial literal advent of Christ, destruction (not conversion) of unbelieving world, literal resurrection of martyrs and apostles, &c., theocratic reign of Christ in person on earth 1,000 years, (or sycle represented by this symbol) a partial falling away; and then the final end, with the second resurrection, and general judgment. Such is the outline of the scheme of the second Adventists, or modern Millennarians; but there are many diversities in their manner of representing the details; and indeed, no little disagreement among themselves.

This subject, which is now exciting a great deal of attention, is too large for the end of a lecture, which you will probably consider as already too much protracted. I can attempt no more than to set down for you a few leading remarks.

THEIR SCHEME HETERODOX BY CONFESSION.—Of these the first is: that though it is now the passion for these pre-Adventists to claim the special honours of orthodoxy, their system is distinctly against that of the Westminster Confession. Not only does that standard ignore it totally; it expressly asserts the contrary: Ch. VIII, § 4. "Christ *shall return* to judge men and angels *at the end of the world.*" (Ch. XXXII. § 2.) "At the last day,...... *all the dead* shall be raised up." (Chap. XXXIII, § 3.) "So will He have that day unknown to men," &c. (Larger Cat. Qu. 56.) "Christ shall come again *at the last day,*" &c. Qu. 86, 87. "The members of the invisible Church......wait for the full redemption of their bodies....till *at the last day* they be again united to their souls." "We are to believe that *at the last day* there shall be a general resurrection of the dead, both of the just and unjust." If these gentlemen who are Presbyterians intend to be candid then, they should openly move for a revision of our standards, in this.

COLLIDES WITH SCRIPTURAL FACTS.—Their scheme is obnoxious to fatal scriptural objections: That Christ comes but twice, to atone, and to judge; (Heb. 9: 28.) That the heavens must receive Christ until the times of the restitution of all things: (Acts 3: 21.) That the blessedness of the Saints is always placed by Scripture in "those new heavens and new earth," which succeed the judgment. That on this scheme the date of the world's end will be known long before it comes; whereas the Scripture represents it as wholly unexpected to all when it comes: That only one resurrection is anywhere mentioned in the most express didactic passages; so that it behooves us to explain the symbolical passage in Rev. 20th, 4 to 6, in consistency with them: That the Scriptures say, (E. G. I. Cor. 15: 23; 2 Thess. 1: 10; I Thess. 3: 13,) that the whole Church will be complete at Christ's next coming: And that then the sacraments, and other "means of grace," will cease finally. The opinion is also beset by insuperable difficulties, such as these: whether these resurrected martyrs will die again; whether they will enjoy innocent corporeal pleasures; whether (if the affirmative be taken) their children will be born with original sin; if not, whence those apostate men are to come, who make the final brief falling away just before the second resurrection, &c. On all these points the pre-Adventists make the wildest and most contradictory surmises.

THE SCHEME SUGGESTED BY MISTRUST.—To me it appears that the temper which secretly prompts this scheme is one of unbelief. Overweening and egotistical hopes of the early evangelizing of the whole world, fostered by partial considerations, meet with disappointment. Hence results a feeling of skepticism; and they are heard pronouncing the present agencies committed to the Church, as manifestly inadequate. But the temper which Christ enjoins on us is one of humble, faithful, believing diligence in the use of those agencies, relying on his faithfulness and power to make them do their glorious work. He commands us also to remember how much they have already accomplished, when energized by his grace, and to take courage. The tendencies of the pre-Advent-scheme are unwholesome, though it has been held by some spiritually minded men.

THEIR EXEGESIS NO MORE FAITHFUL.—Its advocates boast that they alone interpret the symbols of prophecy faithfully. But when we examine, we find that they make no nearer approach to an exact system of exposition; and that they can take as wild figurative licenses when it suits their purposes, as any others. The new interpretations are usually but violations of the familiar and well-established canon, that the prophets represent the evangelical blessings under the tropes of the Jewish usages known to themselves.

LECTURE LXIX.

SYLLABUS.

THE GENERAL JUDGMENT, AND ETERNAL LIFE.

See confession of Faith, Ch. XXXIII. Matt. Ch. 25th; Jno. Ch. 5th; 2 Thess. 1: 7, 10; Rev. 20: 12 to end.

1. What are God's purposes in holding a final universal Judgment? And what the proofs that it will occur?
   Turrettin, Loc. XX. Qu. 6. Ridgeley, Qu. 88. Davies' Sermon on Judgment. Gerhard *Loci Theologici*.
2. What will be the time, place, and accessory circumstances?
   Dick, Lect. 83; Knapp, § 155, and above authorities.
3. Who will be the Judge? In what sense will the Saints be his assessors?
   Ridgeley, as above.
4. Who will be judged? And for what?
   Ridgely and Turrettin, as above.
5. By what Rule? What the respective Sentences?
   See same authorities.
6. What will be the nature of the reward of the Righteous?
   Same authorities, especially Dick, Lect. 83; Turrettin, Qu. 8, 10, 11, 12, 13; Knapp, § 159, 160. Young's Last Day. Hill, Bk. V. Ch. 8.

Objects of General Judgment.—I. It might seem that the purposes of God's righteousness and government might, at first view, be sufficiently satisfied by a final distribution of rewards and punishments, to men, as they successively passed out of this life.—But his *declarative glory* requires not only this, but a more *formal, forensic act*, by which his righteous, holy, and merciful dealing shall be collectively displayed before the Universe. For his creatures, both angels and men, are finite, and would remain forever in ignorance of a great part of His righteous dispensations, unless they received this formal publication. By bringing all his subjects (at least of this province of his Universe) together and displaying to all, the conduct and doom of all, he will silence every cavil, and compel every one to justify Him in all his dealings.

It Stimulates Conscience.—But more than this: man is, during all his probationary state, a sensuous being. So that he certainly, if not angels, is powerfully actuated by many motives arising out of a judgment to shun sin, and seek after righteousness. The strict account, the prompt and irrevocable sentence pronounced upon it, the publication of his sins, secret and open, to all the world, the accessories of grandeur and awe which will attend the last award all, appeal to his nature, as a social and corporeal creature, arousing conscience, fear, hope, shame of exposure, affection for fellow-men, and giving substance and reality to the doctrine of future rewards, in a way which could not be felt, if there were no judgment day. But, as was remarked concerning the death of the Saints; if any benefit is to be realized from the certain prospect of an event, the event would be certain.

RATIONAL ARGUMENTS INVALID, THOUGH PROBABLE.—Several arguments have been announced by theologians to show that reason might anticipate a general judgment. (a.) From the necessity of some means to readjust the inequalities between men's fates in this life and their merits; (b.) From the terrors of man's own guilty conscience; (c.) From the pagan myths concerning future Judges, *Rhamnusia, Eacus, Minos, Rhadamanthus.* But these are rather evidences of future rewards and punishments, than of their distribution in the particular forensic form of a general judgment. Reason can offer no more than a *probable* evidence of the latter; and this evidence is best seen from the *objects* which God secures by a judgment when considered in the light of these convictions. So far as God himself is concerned in the satisfaction of the attributes of justice in his own breast, it would be enough that He should see for himself, each man's whole conduct and merits, and assign each one, at such time and place as he please, the adequate rewards. But reason and conscience make a judgment probable, because they obviously indicate the above valuable ends to be subserved by it. For it enables God, not only to right all the inequalities of his temporal providence, and to sanction the verdicts of man's conscience, but to show all this to his kingdom, to the glory of his grace and holiness; to unmask secret sin when he punishes it; to stop the mouths of the accusers of his people while he reveals and rewards their secret graces and virtues; and to apply to the soul, while on earth, the most pungent *stimuli* to obedience.

REVELATION TEACHES IT.—But this is more clearly the doctrine of Revelation. It would indeed be inaccurate to apply to a general judgment every thing which is said in the Bible about God's judgment, as is done to too great an extent by some writers. For this word is sometimes used for God's government in general (John 5 : 22) for a command or precept, (Ps. 19 : 9;) sometimes for God's chastisements, (1 Pet. 4 : 17;) sometimes for his vengeance, (Ps. 149 : 9;) sometimes for the attribute of righteousness, (Ps. 72 : 2, 89, 14;) sometimes for a special sentence pronounced. But the following passages may be said to have more or less of a proper application to the general judgment, and from them it will be learned that this has been the doctrine of the church from the earliest ages, viz.: Jude 14; Eccles. 12 : 14; Ps. 50 : 3–6, 21; possibly Ps. 96 : 13; Dan. 7 : 10; Matt. 12 : 36; 13 : 41; 16 : 27, and most notably, 25 : 31–46; Acts 17 : 31; 2 Cor. 5 : 10; 2 Thess. 1 : 7–10; 2 Tim. 4 : 1; 1 Thess. 4 : 16; Rev. 20 : 11. Other passages which will be quoted to show who are the Judge, and parties judged, and what the subjects of judgment, also apply fairly to this point. They need not be anticipated here.

THE JUDGMENT NOT MERELY METAPHORICAL.—Some laxer theologians, especially of the German school, have taught that all these passages do not teach a literal, universal, forensic act, but merely a state, to which God will successively bring all his creatures according to their respective merits; in short that the whole representation is merely figurative of certain *principles of retribution.* The answer is, to point to the previous arguments, which show that not only equal retributions, but a public formal declaration thereof, are called for by the purposes of God's government, and the system of doctrines; and to show that the strong terms of the Scriptures cannot be satisfied by such an explanation. There are figures; but those figures must be literalized according to fair exegetical laws; and they plainly describe the judgment as something that *precedes* the execution of the retribution.

TIME OF THE JUDGMENT.—DID APOSTLES MISCALCULATE?—II. The *time* of this great transaction, absolutely speaking, is, and is intended to be utterly unknown to the whole human race, in order that its uncertainty may cause all to fear; 1 Thes. 5 : 2; 2 Pet. 3 : 10; Matt. 24 : 36, &c. Hence we may see the unscripturalness of those who endeavor to fix approximately a day, which God intends to conceal, by their interpretations of unfulfilled prophecy. If the beginning of the *millenium* can be definitely fixed by an event so marked as the personal advent of Christ; if its continuance can be marked off by one thousand literal solar years; and if the short apostacy which is to follow is to last only a few years, then God's people will foreknow pretty accurately when to expect the last day. Again: the Jewish Christians, among many vague expectations concerning Christ's kingdom, evidently expected that the final consummation would come at the end of one generation from Christ's ascension. This erroneous idea was a very natural deduction from the Jewish belief that their temple and ritual was to subsist till the final consummation, when coupled with Christ's declaration, in Matt. 24, that Jerusalem should be destroyed in the day of some then living. See this misconception betrayed, Matt. 24 : 3, Acts 1 : 7. So they doubtless misunderstood Matt. 16 : 28. Now, it has ever been a favorite charge against the inspiration of the Apostles, in the mouths of infidels, that they evidently shared in this mistake. E. G. in James 5 : 8; 2 Peter 3 : 12; Phil. 4 : 5, &c. But this charge is founded only in the ignorance of the apostles' various meanings when they speak of the "coming," or "presence," of Christ. Oftentimes they mean the believers death; for that is practically His coming and the end of the world, to that believer; and the space between that and the general judgment is to him *no space practically;* because nothing can be done in it to redeem the soul. Their misunderstanding is clearly enough evinced by Paul in 2 Thess. 2 : 1-3,

&c., with I Thess. 4 : 15, 17. For the latter place contains language than which none would be more liable to these skeptical perversions. Yet in the former citation we see Paul explicitly correcting the mistake. See also 2 Cor. 4 : 14.

IT FOLLOWS RESURRECTION.—HOW LONG PROTRACTED?—But while, absolutely, the time of the judgment is unknown, relatively it is distinctly fixed. It will be immediately after the general resurrection, and just coincident with, or just after the final destruction of the globe by fire. The good and evil men do live after them. Hence, that measure of merit and demerit, which is taken from *consequences*, is not completely visible to creatures until time is completed. St. Paul is still doing good: Simon Magus is still doing mischief. "They, being dead, yet speak;" 2 Thess. 2 : 3–13; Rev. 12 : 18; 20 : 10–end, &c. The duration of the judgment is commonly called *a day;* Acts 17 : 31. Some, conceiving that the work of the judgment will include the intelligible revealing of the whole secret life of every creature, to every other creature, suppose that the period will vastly exceed one solar day in length, stretching possibly to thousands of years. If all this is to be done, they may well suppose the time will be long. But to me, it seems far from certain that this universal revealing of every creature to every other, is either possible or necessary. Can any but an infinite mind comprehend all this immense number of particulars? Is it necessary, in order that any one creature may have all defective and erroneous ideas about God's government corrected, which he has contracted in this life, to be introduced to the knowledge of parts of his dealings utterly unknown to and unconnected with him? Hence I would say, that of the actual duration of the august scene, we know nothing. But we are told that its accessories will be vast and majestic. The terrors of the resurrection will have just occurred, the earth will be just consigned to destruction. Jesus Christ will appear on the scene with ineffable pomp, attended with all the Redeemed and the angels; Acts 1 : 11. The souls of the blessed will be reunited to their bodies, and then they will be assorted out from the risen crowd of humanity, and their acquittal and glorification declared to the whole assemblage; while the unbelievers will receive their sentence of eternal condemnation.

PLACE.—The *place* of this transaction has also been subject of inquiry. To me it appears indubitable that it will occupy a *place* in the literal sense of the word. To say nothing of the fact that disembodied *souls* are not ubiquitous, the actors in this transaction will be, many of them, clothed with literal bodies, which, although glorified or damned, will occupy space just as really as here on earth. All that Scripture says about the place is, 1 Thess. 4 : 17, that we "shall be caught up . . . . into the clouds, to meet the Lord *in the air*." Some, as Davies, have supposed that the upper regions of our atmosphere will be the place where the vast assembly will be held; while they will behold the world beneath them, either just before, or during the grand assize, wrapped in the universal fires. But see 2 Peter 3 : 10. It would seem most obvious from our notions of combustion, as well as from this passage, that however that conflagration may be produced, our atmosphere, the great supporter of combustion, will be involved in it. This may serve as a specimen of the ill-success which usually meets us when we attempt to be "wise above that which is written" on these high subjects. The place is not revealed to, and cannot be surmised by us.

THE JUDGE CHRIST. WHY?—III. The Judge will unquestionably be Jesus Christ, in his mediatorial person. See Matt. 25: 31, 32; 28: 18; John 5: 27; Acts 10: 42; 17: 31; Rom. 14: 10; I Cor. 15: 25; Phil. 2: 10; 2 Tim. 4: 1. These passages are indisputable. Nor have the Scriptures left us ignorant entirely, of the grounds of this arrangement. The honor and prerogative of judging "the quick and the dead," is plainly declared, in Phil. 2: 9, 10, to be a part of Christ's mediatorial exaltation, and a just consequence of his humiliation. It was *right* that when the Lord of all condescended, in his unspeakable mercy, to assume the form of a servant, and endure the extremest indignities of his enemies, he should enjoy this highest triumph over them, in the very form and nature of his humiliation. Indeed, in this aspect, his judging the world is but the crowning honor of his kingship; so that whatever views explain his kingly office, explain this function of it. But more than this: his saints have an interest in it. Then only is their redemption completed, justification pronounced finally, and the last consequences of sin obliterated. By the same reason that it was necessary they should have a "merciful and faithful High Priest," in all the previous exigencies of their redemption, it is desirable that they should have their Mediator for their judge in this last crisis. Otherwise they would sink in despair before the terrible bar. They would be unable to answer a word to the accuser of the brethren, or to present any excuse for their sins But when they see their Almighty Friend in the judgment seat, their souls are re-assured. This may be the meaning of the words "because He is the son of man." John 5: 27.

THE SAINTS ASSESSORS.—There seems to be a sense, in which the Saints will sit and judge with Christ. Ps. 149: 6–9; I Cor. 6: 2, 3; Rev. 20: 4. We suppose no one will understand from these passages, that Christians can, or will, exercise those incommunicable functions of searching hearts, apportioning infinite penalties to infinite demerits, and executing the sentence with almighty power. There are two lower meanings in which it may be said that saints shall jude sinners. Thus, in Matt. 12: 41, 42, I. E. the contrast of the Christian's faith and penitence is a sort of practical rebuke and condemnation to those who persisted in the opposite conduct. But this does not express the whole truth. The saints are adopted sons of God: "heirs of God, and *joint heirs with Christ*; if so be we suffer with him, that we may be also *glorified together*." Rom. 8: 17. They also are "kings and priests unto God." In this sense, they share, by a sort of reflected dignity, the exaltation of their elder brother; and in this, the culminating point of his mediatorial royalty, they are graciously exalted to share with him, according to their lower measure. Having had their own acquittal and adoption first declared, they are placed in the post of honour, represented as Christ's right hand, and there concur as assessors with Christ, in the remainder of the transaction.

WHO WILL BE JUDGED?—IV. The persons to be judged will embrace all wicked angels and all the race of man. The evidence of the former part of this proposition is explicit. See Matt. 8: 29, 1 Cor. 6:3; 2 Pet. 2: 4; Jude. 6.) (And that every individual of the human race will be present is evident from Eccles. 12: 14; Ps. 50:4; 2 Cor. 5: 10; Rom. 14: 10; Matt. 12: 36, 37, 25: 32; Rev. 20: 12.

Some have endeavored to limit this judgment, (as the Pelagians), to those men who have enjoyed gospel privileges alone. But if there are any principles in God's government, calling for a general judgment of those subject to it, and if pagans are subject to it, then they also should be judged. And if the passages above cited do not assert an actual universality of the judgment, it is hard to see how any language could. It will be noticed that men will be judged, and doubtless, the wicked angels likewise, for all their thoughts, words and deeds. This is obviously just, and is called for by the purposes of a judgment. For if there was any class of moral acts which had not this prospect of a judgment awaiting them, men would think they could indulge in these with impunity. Upon the question whether the sins of the righteous, already pardoned in Christ, will receive publicity in that day, Dick states the respective arguments. To me it appears that we must admit they will be, unless we can prove that the places where men are warned that they must be judged "for every idle word," for "every secret thing," were not addressed to christians at all, but only to sinners. The disposition to deny that pardoned sins will be published in the day of judgment, doubtless arises from the feeling that it would produce a shame and compunction incompatible with the blessedness of their state. But will the saints not publish their sins themselves, in their confessions? And is it not the sweetest type of spiritual joy, that which proceeds from contrition for sin?

WILL ELECT ANGELS BE JUDGED?—It may be further noticed, that the Scriptures are utterly silent as to the judging of the holy angels. It is therefore our duty to refrain from asserting anything about it. Some have surmised that though they are not mentioned, they will be judged, because they have some connection through their ministry of love, with the men who will be judged. But, on the other hand, it may be remarked, that there is significance in the fact that all the creatures spoken of as standing at Christ's judgment are sinful ones. The holy angels never sinned; they have been long ago justified through a method totally inapplicable to fallen beings, the covenant of works, and this may constitute a valid reason why they should not bear a share in this judgment of sinning beings, who are either justified by free grace or condemned.

THE SPECTATORS.—So far as the judgment is a display of God's attributes to the creature, it is doubtless to those creatures who are conversant with this scene of earthly struggle. The holy angels are concerned in it as interested and loving spectators; the wicked angels as causes and promoters of all the mischief; man, as the victim and agent of earthly sin. If God has other orders of intelligent creatures, connected with the countless worlds of which astronomy professes to inform us, who are not included in these three classes; it is not necessary to suppose that they will share in this scene, because we have no evidence that they are cognizant of the sins and grace which lead to it. But here all is only dim surmise.

THE RULE.—V. The *rule* by which sinners and saints will be judged, will be the will of God made known to them. The Gentiles will be judged by that natural law written on their hearts; the Jews of the Old Testament by that, and the Old Testament alone; but those who have enjoyed the Gospel in addition to the others, shall be judged by all three. (See Rom. 2: 12; Jno. 12: 4, 8; Luke 12: 4, 7; John 15: 22.) God will judge justly, and render to every man his due. In Dan. 7: 10; Rev. 20: 12; the same phrase is employed: "The judgment was set, and the books opened." Perhaps the mode of understanding this, most accordant with the mind of the Spirit, would be to attempt to apply the phrase *book* to nothing in particular, in the judgments of man; but to regard it as a mere carrying out of the august figure: a grand judicial trial. But if a more particular explanation must be had, we may perhaps concur in the belief, that one of these books is the Word of God, which is the statute-book, under which the cases must be decided; another, the book of God's remembrance, from which the evidence of conduct will be read; and still another, the book of God's decrees, where the names of men were recorded before the foundation of the world.

RELATION OF WORKS OF CHARITY TO JUDGMENT.—In Matt. 25th, the reprobate are condemned because they have *not* performed to God's suffering children acts of beneficence and charity, and the righteous acquitted because they have. It may be briefly remarked here, that while sinners will be condemned strictly *on the merit* of their own conduct, saints will be acquitted solely on the merit of Christ. They are rewarded according to, not because of, the deeds done in the flesh. The evidence of this may be seen, where we refuted the doctrine of justification by works, and these very passages were brought into review. But the purpose of God in the judgment is to evince the holiness, justice, love, and mercy of his dealings to all his subjects. But as they cannot read the secret faith, love and penitence of the heart, the sentence must be regulated *according to* some external and visible conduct, which is cognizable by creatures, and is a proper test of regenerate character. It is very noticeable that not all righteous conduct, but only *one* kind, is mentioned as the test; these works of charity. And this is most appropriate, not only because they are accurate *tests* of true holiness, but because it was most proper that, in a judgment where the acquittal can in no case occur, except through divine grace and pardon, a disposition to mercy should be required of those who hope for acceptance. (See Jas. 2: 13; Matt. 18: 28, end; Matt. 6: 12.

THE SENTENCES.—VI. The sentence of the righteous is everlasting blessedness; that of the wicked, everlasting misery. The discussion of the latter must be the subject of another lecture.—The nature of eternal life I shall now endeavour to state. Far be it from us, to presume to be wise above that which is written: let us modestly collect those traits of the saint's everlasting rest, which the Bible, in its great reserve on this subject, has seen fit to reveal.

THE PLACE OF REWARD.—The *place* of this eternal life is usually called heaven. It is undoubtedly a place proper, and not merely a state. For there are *now*, the material bodies of Christ, and of Enoch and Elijah, if not of others. There will be a multitude of bodies. The finite glorified spirits there also have a *ubi*. It is vain for us to surmise, in what part of the Universe Christ's glorified humanity now holds its court. The phrases "up," "above," "ascend," &c., teach nothing; for what is above to us, is beneath to our *antipodes*, in whose places we shall be in twelve hours. A comparison of 2 Pet. 3: 13, with Rev. 21: 1–10 suggests that after the judgment, *this earth*, purified and reconstructed, will be the abode of the saints and their incarnate Redeemer. It seems not unworthy of Him, to make this rebel province, reconquered from its usurper, Satan, the final seat of his triumph in his ransomed Church. The place will doubtless have all the material beauty, commodiousness, and glory, which can please the sanctified eye and taste. If one should be inclined to deem material splendour too trivial for God to provide for the redeemed, I would point him to the material beauties of the present universe, even that part marred by sin.

THE SAINTS' BLESSEDNESS.—(A.) IN EXEMPTION.—(B.) IN HOLINESS.—But it is not place, but character, which confers essential happiness. We are taught indeed that occasion for this spiritual blessedness will be secured to the Saints by their perfect exemption from all natural evils, such as unsatisfied wants, pain, grief, sickness, violence, and death. (See Job 3:7; Is. 25:8; Rev. 7:16, 17; 21:4. But the most important fact is, that the blessedness of the life everlasting is simply the perfection of that state which is begun here by the new birth and sanctification. As saith M. Henry, "Grace is glory begun, and glory is but grace consummated." (See Jno. 5:24; 6:47; Gal. 6:7). On entering heaven the soul is made perfectly holy; and thus every root of misery is removed. When we inquire for the objective sources of the saints' bliss, we find them subordinately in the society of fellow-saints, but chiefly in God himself, and especially in the Redeemer. (Psalm 73:25; Rev. 21:23). That the Saints' happiness will be social, is plain from the Bible representations; and I believe that those who have known and loved each other here, will recognize each other there. (See I Thess. 2:19, 2; Sam. 12:23). And it appears very unreasonable that the love, and other social graces which are there perfected in their glorified humanity should then have no objects. But the Holy Trinity will ever be the central and chief object, from which the believer's bliss will be derived.

ELEMENTS OF THIS HAPPINESS INTELLECTIVE.—This happiness will consist in the satisfaction of both mind and heart. Curiosity is one of the keenest and most uncloying sources of interest and pleasure to the healthy mind. Then "we shall know even as we are known;" and our minds will find perpetual delight in learning the things of God and his providence. Here will be matter of study ample enough to fill eternity.

MORAL.—Again: To love is to be happy, saith the apostle John. "He that dwelleth in love, dwelleth in God, and God in him." Our terrestrial objects of affection have taught us, that if the heart could always be exercising its affection towards some worthy object, this would constitute happiness. But the object being earthly, we are constantly liable to be separated from it by distance, or to have it torn from us by death, when our affection becomes our torment. Or, being imperfect, it may wound us by infidelity or injustice. Or else corporeal wants drive us from it to labour. But now let us suppose the soul, endowed with an object of love wholly worthy and suitable, never separated by distance, nor torn away by death, incapable of infidelity, or unkindness, is it not plain that in the possession and love of this object, there would be perpetual blessedness, external evils being fenced off? Such an object is God, and such is the blessedness of heaven, springing from the perpetual indulgence of a love that never cloys, that is never interrupted, and never wounded, and that expresses its happiness in untiring praises.

LECTURE LXX.

SYLLABUS.

NATURE AND DURATION OF HELL-TORMENTS.

1. In what will the torments of the wicked consist?
Turrettin, Loc. XX, Qu. 7; Ridgeley, Qu. 89; Knapp, § 156.

2. State the various opinions which have prevailed as to the duration of these pains. Which now most prevalent among Universalists?
Turrettin, as above; Knapp, § 156 to 158. Debate between Rice and Pingree.

3. State and refute the usual objections against everlasting punishments, from God's wisdom, mercy, benevolence, &c.
Knapp, as above. Rice and Pingree.

4. What is the proper force in the Scriptures of the original words which state the duration of these torments?
Knapp, § 157. De Quincey's Essays.

5. Prove the everlasting duration of these torments from the sinner's perpetual sinfulness; from the Scriptural terms, Redemption, pardon, salvation, &c.; from Universal relation in Providence between conduct and destiny; from the existence of condemned angels; from the Resurrection; from temporal judgments of God on the wicked as Sodom, &c.; from the justice of God and the unequal distribution of rewards here.
Same authorities.

NATURAL PENALTIES.—I. The just reward of ill-desert is suffering. The Judgment results in a curse upon the impenitent, which dooms them, as none doubt, to some form of suffering. Theologians divide the pains which are thus adjudged to the condemned, into natural, and positive. The former are those which proceed from the natural working of their own evil principles, of themselves, and according to natural law; such pains as are foreshadowed in Isaiah 3:11; Gal. 6:8; Jas. 1:15. These natural penalties consist of the loss or privation of eternal happiness, which only faith, repentance, and holiness can procure; of the remorse, self-accusation, and despair, which the soul will inflict on itself for its own folly and sin; of all the disorders, inward and social, of inordinate and malignant emotions; and as is most probable, at least, of the stings of carnal, sensual and sinful desires deprived of all their earthly *pabulum*. As to this last, it appears most consistent to limit what is said, (I Cor. 15:45—end) of the spirituality and blessedness of the resurrection body, to the Saints. The reprobate will rise again; but as they never were savingly united to Christ, they never will "bear the image of the heavenly" Adam. Hence, we naturally and reasonably anticipate, that their bodies, while immortal, will not share the glory and purification of the bodies of the Redeemed, but will still be animal bodies, having the appetites and wants of such. But earthly supplies therefor will be forever lacking. Hence, they will be a prey to perpetual cravings unsatisfied.

POSITIVE PENALTIES.—The positive penalties of sin will be such as God will Himself add, by new dispensations of his power, to inflict anguish on his enemies. The Scriptures always represent Him as arising to avenge himself, as "pouring out his wrath" upon his enemies; and in such like, and a multitude of other expressions, whatever may be their figurative character, we cannot fail to see this truth, that God *puts forth new and direct power*, to inflict pain. The stupidity and obstinacy of many sinners, obviously, would be restrained by nothing less than the fear of these positive penalties. The mere natural penalties would appear to them wholly illusory, or trivial. Indeed, most sinners are so well pleased with their carnal affections, that they would rather declare themselves glad to accept, and even cherish, their merely natural fruits.

WILL THEY AFFLICT THE BODY?—These positive penalties undoubtedly will include, when the body is raised, some corporeal pains, and perhaps consist chiefly in them; else, why need the body be raised? And there is too obvious a propriety in God's punishing sinners through those members which they have perverted into "members of unrighteousness," for us to imagine for a moment, that He will omit it. Once more; the imagery by which the punishments of the wicked are represented, however interpreted, is so uniform, as to make it impossible to suppose the bodies of the wicked are exempted. But whether their bodies will be burned with literal fire and sulphur, does not appear so certain. In Matt. 25th, the fire into which they depart is said to have been prepared from the foundation of the world, for the Devil and his angels. They are, and will always remain, incorporeal beings; and it does not seem probable that literal fire is the instrument which God has devised expressly for their torment. Some weight may also be given to this thought; that other adjuncts, as the darkness, the gnawing worm, the brimstone, the smoke, &c., seem to be images adopted from human tortures and earthly scenes of anguish. Hence the conclusion to which Turrettin comes; that this is all imagery. But, however that may be, the images must be interpreted according to plain rules of right rhetoric. Interpret it as we may, we cannot get anything less from it than this: that sin will be punished with extreme and terrible bodily torments, as well as with natural pains.

ETERNAL PUNISHMENTS DENIED. 1. BY ANNIHILATIONISTS. 2. RESTORATIONISTS. 3. UNIVERSALISTS.—II. Those who deny the eternity of future punishments may be divided into three classes. First are those who resolve the punishment of the wicked into annihilation. They believe, accordingly, that only the redeemed enjoy a resurrection. Second are the ancient and modern Restorationists, who hold to future punishments, longer or shorter, according to men's guilt; but who suppose that each man's repentance will be accepted after his penal debt is paid; so that at length, perhaps after a long interval, all will be saved. It is said that the Originists believed that Satan and his angels would also be at last saved. The third opinion is that which is now chiefly prevalent among modern Universalists. This supposes, that the external and internal sufferings which each soul experiences during this life, and *in articulo mortis*, will satisfy all the essential demands of the divine justice against its sins: and that there will, accordingly, be no future punishments. At death, they suppose, those not already penitent and holy, will be summarily sanctified by God, in his universal mercy through Christ, and at once received into Heaven forever. The inventor, or at least, chief propagator, of this phase was a Massachusetts man, *Hosea Ballon*, whose sect now embraces all the Universalists known to me, in America. It is, therefore, with this theory that we chiefly have to do.

First Class Refuted.—To clear the way, the Annihilationist may be easily refuted, by all those passages which speak of future punishment, even though we grant it not eternal. Such are Mark 9 : 44, 46; Matt. 25th, &c. The resurrection extends to the wicked, as well as the righteous (Dan. 12 : 2; John 9 : 28, 29). Nor does the quibble avail, that the phrase, "everlasting destruction," or such-like, implies annihilation. If this consisted in reducing the sinner forever to nothing, it would be instant destruction, not everlasting. How can punishment continue, when the subject of it has ceased to exist?

God's Love Consists with Eternal Punishments.—III. But it may be well to clear away obstructions, by refuting the general grounds on which the eternity of future punishments is denied. The most common of these is that construction of the text, "God is Love," which makes Him pure benevolence, denying to Him all other moral attributes, and resolving them into phases of benevolence. But we reply; other texts say, "God is Light;" "Our God is a Consuming Fire." Is he nothing but pure intelligence? Is He nothing but primitive justice? We see the absurd contradictions into which such a mode of interpretation would lead us. Infinite benevolence, intelligence, justice, and truth are co-ordinate and consistent attributes, acting harmoniously. That God is not benevolent in such a sense as to exclude primitive justice, is proved thus: "It is a fearful thing to fall into hands of the Living God" (Heb. 10 : 31. See also, 2 Cor. 5 : 11; Ps. 66; 5). Again; God is not too benevolent to punish devils, once his holy children, eternally (see Rev. 20 : 10). Nor can this ruinous fact be evaded by denying the personality of the devils; the usual resort of the Universalists. The marks of the real personality of devils are as clear as for Judas Iscariot's.

God not to be Measured by Men.—It is equally vain to appeal to the paternal benevolence of a father, claiming that God is more tender, and to ask whether any earthly parent is capable of tormenting his own child, however erring, with endless fire.

The answer is in such passages as Ps. 50 : 21. "Thou thoughtest that I was altogether such an one as thyself, but I will rebuke thee," (Is. 55 : 8,) and by the stubborn fact that this 'God of Love' does punish a sinful world, under our eyes, with continual woes, many of them gigantic. How are these dealings to be reconciled with God's benevolence? By the sufferer's guilt. Then, if the guilt of any is endless, the benevolence of God may permit them to suffer endlessly. Even if we accept the erroneous parallel to a human parent as exact, we may ask: Would a benevolent, wise, and just parent so spare an incorrigibly wicked son, as to sacrifice the order of his house, and the rights of the good children to his impunity? This argument is sometimes put in this form: "We are commanded to be like God. We are also commanded to forgive and love our enemies. But if we were like the Calvinists' God, we must hate and damn our enemies." The replies are, that God is also a magistrate; and that human magistrates are strictly required to condemn the wicked: that we are under no circumstances required to pardon and love enemies, at the expense of justice and truth; that we are only required to restore the injurious enemy to our confidence and esteem, when he repents; that one great reason why we are enjoined not to revenge ourselves, is that "vengeance is God's; He will repay;" and that God *does* exhibit an infinite forbearance towards His enemies, by giving His own son to die for their reconciliation on the terms of faith and repentance; the only terms consistent with His perfections.

God's Wisdom Consists with Eternal Punishments.—The attempt to argue, that God's wisdom would forbid him to create immortal beings, and then permit them to forfeit the ends of their existence, is exceedingly weak and presumptuous. Before the argument can apply, it must be determined what is God's secret purpose as to the ultimate end of their existence. He must suppose himself omniscient, who imagines himself competent to decide.

Scriptural Terms Considered.—IV. One would think that the declarations of the Scriptures about eternal punishments were clear enough to decide the debate. But you are aware that the words used in the Scriptures for everlasting, eternal, &c., are said to mean also an "age," a "dispensation," a finite duration; and that we hear of the everlasting hills, and the covenant with David's house as eternal as the sun; whereas we are told elsewhere that the hills shall melt, and the sun be darkened, as David's dynasty has perished.

But these words are as strong as any the Greek language affords. (Aristotle, *iownios* from *aiei own.*) They are the same words which are used to express the eternity of God. If they have a secondary and limited meaning in some applications, the subject and context should be appealed to, in order to settle the sense.

Now, when these words are used to describe a state, they always express one as long as the nature of the subject to which they are applied can permit. When, e. g., the hills are called everlasting, it is evidently meant, that they will endure as long as the earth on which they rest. Now if "everlasting torment" is said to be the state of a sinful soul, those who believe the soul immortal are bound to understand by it a duration of the punishment coevil with that of the sufferer's being. See thus Rev. 14 : 11, 20 : 10, with 22 : 5, 2 Thess. 1 : 9, Mark 3 : 29, Matt. 18 : 8. The conclusive fact is, that in Matt. 25 : 46, the same word describes the duration of the saint's bliss and the sinner's penalty. If the latter is not properly unending, the former is not.

ETERNAL TORMENTS TAUGHT IN OTHER TERMS.—But more than this: Many texts convey the idea that the torments of sinners will never end, in terms and modes to which this quibble cannot attach. Thus, the state of men after death is *changeless;* and when the state of it is fixed at death, nothing more can be done to modify it; Eccles. 9 : 10; John 9 : 4; Eccles. 11 : 3. Then it is asserted that "their worm dieth not." "The fire is not quenched." Mark 9 : 43–47, John 3 : 3 and 36, Luke 16 : 26, Rev. 21 : 8. Compared with verses 1 and 4, Rev. 22 : 11, 12.

UNIVERSALISTS CONTRADICT WHOLE SCRIPTURE; AS SATAN'S PERSONALITY.—MAN'S PROBATION.—V. But the strength of our argument is, that to teach the limited duration of the punishment of sin, Universalists and Restorationists have to contradict nearly every fact and doctrine of the Bible. We have seen how they are compelled by their dogma to deny the personality of Satan. The Scriptures bear upon their very face this truth, that man must fulfil some condition in order to secure his destiny. Let that faith on which salvation turns be what it may, it is a something the doing or not doing of which decides the soul's state in different ways. See e. g., Mark 16 : 16, as one of a thousand places. But if the Universalist is true, he who believes and he who believes not, will fare precisely alike. And here I may add that powerful analogical argument: that under the observed course of God's providence, men are never treated alike irrespective of their doings and exertions: conduct always influences destiny. But if the Universalist is true, the other world will be in contradiction to this.

THERE IS NO PARDON, &C., NOR SATISFACTION BY CHRIST.—Again: if either the Universalist or Restorationist is true, there is no grace, no pardon, no redemption, and no salvation. For according to both, all the guilt men contract is paid for; according to the one party, in temporal sufferings on earth; according to the other, in temporary sufferings beyond the grave. Now that which is paid for by the sinner himself is not remitted to him. There is no pardon or mercy. Nor can it be said that there is any salvation. For the only evils to which the sinner is at any time liable, he meets and endures to the full. None are escaped; there is no deliverance; no salvation. So we may charge, that their doctrines are inconsistent with that of Christ's satisfaction or atonement. For of course, if each sinner bears his own guilt, there is no need of a substitute to bear it. Hence we find the advocates of these schemes explaining away the vicarious satisfaction of Christ.

UNIVERSALISTS SKEPTICAL.—Indeed, it may justly be added, that the tendency of their system is to depreciate the authority of the Word, to deny its plenary inspiration, to question its teachings with irreverent license, and to disclose much closer affinities with infidelity than with humble faith. This charge is fully sustained by the history of Universalist churches (so called) and of their teachers and councils. Finally, passing over for the time, the unanswerable argument, that sin has infinite ill desert, as committed against an excellent, perfect and universal law, and an infinite lawgiver, I may argue that even though the desert of a temporary season of sinning were only temporary penalties, yet if man continues in hell to sin forever, he will continue to suffer forever. While he was paying off a previous debt of guilt he would contract an additional one, and so be forever subject to penalty.

THEIR PROOF-TEXTS CONSIDERED.—An attempt is made to argue universal salvation from a few passages represented by Rom. 5:18, and 1 Cor. 15 : 22, in which the word "*all*," is used. I reply, 1st, that those who use this argument do not believe that "all," or any "come into condemnation" by Adam's sin, or "die in Adam;" and they have no right to argue thence that they will be saved in Christ. They cannot contradict me when I charge them with flatly denying the imputation of Adam's guilt to any of his posterity. I reply, 2d, that the word "*all*" is, notoriously, used in the Scripture when it often does not mean actual universality; but only all of a certain class; Matt. 3 : 5, Mark 1 : 37. So, in these texts, the meaning obviously is, that as in Adam all are condemned, all die, who are federally connected with him, so, in Christ, all savingly connected with him are made alive. See the context. The very chapter which says, "The free gift came upon all," &c., begins by saying that being "justified by faith," we have peace with God. It must be then that the free gift comes upon "all" that believe. So 1 Cor. 15 : 22, is immediately followed by these words: "But every man in his own order, Christ the first fruits: afterwards they that are Christ's at his coming." Obviously, it is "all" who are Christ's, who are made alive in him. But let the Scripture tell us who are Christ's. "If any man have not the spirit of Christ; he is none of his." There is this answer also, to the Universalist quoting 1 Cor. 15 : 22, that, apply it to whom we will, it teaches after all, not future blessedness, but the resurrection of the body.

THE DOCTRINE OF TWO RESURRECTIONS.—This doctrine of the Resurrection also suggests an argument against Universalism, because it is most clearly taught that there are two resurrections; one for the just and one for the unjust; one desirable, and one dreadful; one for which holy men of old strove, and one which they shunned. But if all at the resurrection were renewed and saved, there would be but one resurrection. The passage quoted from Jno. 5th, 29th, settles that point. For it cannot be evaded by the figment of a metaphorical resurrection, i. e., a conversion in this life, because of this Christ had thus been speaking in verses 25th to 27th. It is in contrast with this, that he then sets the real, material resurrection before us in verses 28th, &c. Moreover, if the resurrection be made a metaphorical one, then in verse 29th, we should have the good, in common with the wicked, coming out of that state of depravity and ruin, represented by the "graves" of V. 25, C. 6. (See also, Phil. 3: 11; Heb. 11:35.)

DEATH WOULD NOT BE A JUDGMENT TO SINNERS.—If the modern Universalist scheme is true, then the only thing which prevents this life from being an unmingled curse, and death a natural good, is the pain of parting and dissolution. If these were evaded by a quick and easy death, it would be an immeasurable benefit; a step to an assured blissful state, from one both sinful and unhappy.—The most fortunate life here is almost worthless, compared with heaven. Hence, when one is suddenly taken from this life, it is not a penalty, but a favour. We must contradict all that the Scriptures teach, of sudden deaths being a judgment of God against sinners. The antediluvians were gloriously distinguished from Noah, by being illustriously rewarded for their sins by a sudden and summary introduction to holiness and happiness; while he was punished for his piety by being condemned to many hundreds of years of suffering, including all the horrors of his watery imprisonment. So the Sodomites were rewarded for their sins, while Lot was punished by his piety. The cruel Egyptians were swept into glory on the waters of the Red Sea, while Moses was punished for his obedience by a tiresome pilgrimage of forty years.

SINS ARE NOT ADEQUATELY REQUITED HERE.—Again: the assertion that each man's temporal sufferings in this life, and in *articule mortis*, are a just recompense for his sins, is false. Scripture and observation deny it; the former in Ps. 73: 2, 14; Luk. 16: 25, and similar passages; the latter in the numerous instances seen by every experienced person, where the humble, pure, retired, prayerful christian spends years in pain, sickness, and poverty, while the sturdy rake or covetous man revels in the sensual joys or gains which he prefers, and then dies a painless and sudden death. In short, the facts are so plainly against this theory, that the notorious inequality of deserts and rewards in this life has furnished to every reflecting mind, both pagan and christian, one of the strongest evidences in favour of future reward and punishments.

God would Therefore be Partial.—In this connexion I would argue also, that on the modern Universal scheme, God would often be odiously unjust. But see Ps. 89: 14; Gen. 18: 25; Rom. 2: 6, &c. Now our adversaries stoutly deny that any guilt is imputed to Christ and punished in him. Hence, the flagrant inequality remains, according to them, forever uncompensated. The vilest and the purest would receive the same rewards, nay, in many cases, the advantage would be against the good; Providence would often reward vice and punish virtue. For, if the monster of sin is at death renewed and carried immediately to heaven, just as is the Saint, thenceforward they are equal; but before, the sinner had the advantage. While holy Paul was wearing out a painful life in efforts to do good, many a sensualist, like his persecutor Nero, was floating in his preferred enjoyments.—Both died violent and sudden deaths; and then, as they met in the world of spirits, the monster receives the same destiny with the Saint. So every one of even a short experience, can recall instances somewhat similar, which have fallen under his own observation.

Instances.—I can recall a pair of such persons, whose history may illustrate both my last arguments. Their lives and deaths were nearly cotemporary, and I was acquainted with the history of both. The one was a christian female, in whom a refined and noble disposition, sanctified by grace, presented one of the most beautiful examples of virtue which this world can often see. She united early and long-tried piety, moral courage, generosity, self-devotion, with the most feminine refinement of tastes, charity and tenderness. There was a high frame of devotion without a shade of austerity; there was the courage of a martyr, without a tinge of harshness. She united the most rigid economy towards herself with the most liberal benefactions. For many years, she denied herself the indulgence of her elegant tastes, except such as nature offered without expense in the beauties of flower, and forest, and landscape, in order that she might husband the proceeds of a moderate competency for the needy, for the suffering, and for God Her days were passed in a pure retirement, far from the strifes and corruptions of the world. Her house was the unfailing refuge of the sick and the unfortunate among her kindred and the poor; her life was little else than a long and painful ministration to their calamities; and more than once she had flown, with a moral heroism which astonished her friends, into the midst of pestilence, to be the ministering angel at the solitary couch of her suffering relatives. Never did neglect cause her devotion to flag, and never did reproach or injury wring from her a word or deed of retaliation, although she received not a little of both, even from those whom she strove to bless. Such was her life to the last.

And now let us look at her earthly reward. Her whole life was spent in uncertain, or in feeble health. It was often her lot to have her kindness misunderstood, and her sensitive affecti ons lacerated. She scarcely tasted earthly luxuries or ease; for she lived for others. At length, three years before her death, she was overtaken by that most agonizing and incurable of all the scourges which afflict humanity, cancer. For three long years her sufferings grew, and with them, her patience. The most painful remedies were endured in vain. The last weeks of her life were spent in utter prostration, and unceasing agony, so strong that her nurses declared themselves amazed and affrighted to see a nature so frail as man's, bearing such a load of anguish. A peculiarity of constitution deprived her even of that poor resource of suffering, the insensibility of opiates. Up to the very hour of death, there was no respite; without one moment of relaxation in the agony, to commend her soul to her Saviour; maddened by unbearable pangs; crying like her dying Redeemer, "My God, my God, why hast thou forsaken me," she approached the river of death, and its waters were not assuaged to ease her passage.

Now for the contrast. During nearly the same period, and in an adjoining county, there lived a man, who embodied as many repulsive qualities as it has ever been my lot to see in one human breast. His dark, suspicious eye, and malignant countenance gave fit expression to the soul within. Licentious, a drunkard, devoid of natural affection, dishonest, quarrelsome, litigious, a terror to his neighbors, he was soiled with dark suspicion of murder. He revelled in robust health; and, as far as human eye could see, his soul was steeped in ignorance and sensuality, and his conscience seared as with heated iron. He was successful in escaping the clutches of the law, and seemed to live in the enjoyment of his preferred indulgences. At length this man, at the monthly court of his county, retired to a chamber in the second story of the tavern, drunk, as was his wont, and lay down to sleep. The next morning, he was found under the window, stone dead, and with a broken neck. Whether he had walked in his sleep, or the hand of revenge had thrust him out, was never known. In all probability he never knew what killed him, and went into the other world without tasting a single pang, either in body or soul, of the sorrows of dissolution.

Can Justice make These Equal?—Now let us suppose that these two persons, appearing so nearly at the same time in the presence of God, were together introduced into the same heaven. Where is the equality between their deserts and their rewards? On the whole, the providential difference was in favor of the most guilty. If this is God's justice, then is he more fearful than blind chance, than the Prince of Darkness himself. To believe our everlasting destiny is in the hand of such unprincipled omnipotence, is more horrible than to dwell on the deceitful crust of a volcano. And if heaven consists in dwelling in his presence, it can have no attractions for the righteous soul.

Universalism has no Motive for Propagating it.—In conclusion; whether Universalism be true or false, it is absurdity to teach it. If it turns out true, no one will have lost his soul for not learning it. If it turns out false, every one who has embraced it thereby will incur an immense and irreparable evil. Hence, though the probabilities of its truth were as a million to one, it would be madness and cruelty to teach it.

But, apart from all argument, what should a right-minded man infer from the fact, that of all intelligent and honest students of the Scriptures, scarcely one in a million has found the doctrine of universal salvation in them.

Its Chief Pretext is Insensibility of Believers.—The chief practical argument in favor of Universalism is, doubtless, the sinful callousness of christians towards this tremendous destiny of their sinful fellow-creatures. Can we contemplate the exposure of our friends, neighbours, and children to a fate so terrible, and feel so little sensibility, and make efforts so few and weak for their deliverance! And yet, we profess to have faith! How can our unbelieving friends be made to credit the sincerity of our convictions? Here, doubtless, is the best argument of Satan, for their skepticism. And the best refutation of this heresy is the exhibition by God's people of a holy, tender, humble, yet burning zeal to pluck men as brands from the burning.

LECTURE LXXI.

SYLLABUS.

THE CIVIL MAGISTRATE.

1. State the two theories of the origin of civil government out of a "social contract," and out of the ordinance of God. Establish the true one.
2. What is civil liberty? What its limits?
3. What are the proper *objects* of the powers of the Civil Magistrate? What their limits? What the limits to the obedience of a christian man to the Civil Magistrate? When and how far is the christian entitled to plead a 'higher law?'
4. Is the citizen bound always to passive obedience? If not, when does the right of forcible resistance to an unjust government begin?

See Confession of Faith, Chap. XXIII. Blackstone's Com. B. I. Ch. 2. Paley's Moral, Phil. B. VI, ch. 1-5, Montesquieu Esprit des Loix, B. I. Ch. XI. Burlemaqui, Vol. IV, Pt. I. Locke's Treatise of Civil Gov. Bk. 2. Princeton Review, Jan, 1851. Bledsoe on Liberty and Slavery, Ch. I. So. Rev. Art. 'Civil Liberty.' Defence of Virginia and the South, Ch. VII, § 3.

Examined in its Christian Aspects only.—The duty of the christian citizen to civil society is so extensive, and important, and so many questions arise, as to its limits and nature, the propriety of holding office, the powers exercised by the magistrate, &c., that the teacher of the Church should be well grounded in the true doctrine of the nature of the commonwealth. Hence, our Confession has very properly placed this doctrine in its 23d chapter. It is emphatically a doctrine of Scripture.

Theories of Government Origin.—I. Three opposing theories have prevailed, among nominally christian philosophers, as to the origin and extent of the Civil Magistrate's powers. The one traces them to a supposed *social contract*. Men are to be at first apprehended, they say, as insulated individuals, separate human integers, all naturally equal, and each by nature absolutely free, having a natural liberty to exercise his whole will, as a "Lord of Creation." But the experience of the exposure, inconveniences, and mutual violences of so many independent wills, led them, in time, to be willing to surrender a part of their independence, in order to *secure* the enjoyment of the rest of their rights. To do this, they are supposed to have conferred, and to have entered into a compact with each other, binding themselves to each other to submit to certain rules and restraints upon their natural rights, and to obey certain ones selected to rule, in order that the power thus delegated to their hands might be used for the protection of the remaining rights of all. Subsequent citizens entering the society, by birth or immigration, are supposed to have given an assent, express or implied, to this compact. The terms of it form the organic law, or constitution of the commonwealth. And the reason why men are bound to obey the legitimate commands of the magistrate is, that they have thus *bargained* with their fellow-citizens to obey, for the sake of mutual benefits.

SOCIAL CONTRACT THEORY MODIFIED.—Many writers, as Blackstone, and Burlemaqui, are too sensible not to see that this theory is false to the facts of the case; but they still urge, that although individual men never existed, in fact, in the insulated state supposed, and did not actually pass out of that state into a commonwealth state, by a formal *social contract;* yet such a contract must be assumed as implied, and as offering the virtual source of political power and obligation. To us it appears, that if the compact never occurred in fact, but is only a suppositious one, a legal fiction, it is no basis for any theory, and no source for practical rights and duties.

CHRISTIAN THEORY.—The other theory may be called the *Christian.* It traces civil goverment to the will and providence of God, who, from the first, created man with social instincts and placed him under social relations (when men were few, the patriarchal; as they increased, the commonwealth). It teaches that some form of social goverment is as original as man itself. If asked, whence the obligation to obey the civil magistrate, it answers: *from the will of God,* which is the great source of all obligation. The fact that such obedience is greatly promotive of human convenience, well-being and order, confirms and illustrates the obligation, but did not originate it. Hence, civil government is an ordinance of God; magistrates rule by his providence and by his command, and are his agents or ministers. Obedience to them, in the Lord, is a religious duty, and rebellion against them is not only injustice towards our fellow-men, but disobedience to God. This is the theory plainly asserted by Paul, Rom. 13: 1–7, and I Peter, 2: 13–18 may be illustrated by the parental state.

THEORY OF DIVINE RIGHT.—This account of the matter has been also pushed to a most vicious extreme, by the party known as Legitimatists, or advocates of the divine right of royalty. The Bible here teaches us, they assert, that the power the civil magistrate holds, is in no sense delegated from the people, but wholly from God; that the people have no option to select or change their form of government any more than a child has to choose its parent, or a soul the deity it will worship; that no matter how oppressive or unjust the government may be, the citizen has no duty nor right but passive submission, and that the divinely selected form is *hereditary* monarchy—the form first instituted in the hand of Adam, continued in the patriarchal institution, re-affirmed in the New Testament, and never departed from except by heaven-defying republicans, &c.

REFUTATION.—This servile theory we easily refute by many facts. Men in society do not bear to rulers the relation of children to parents, either in their greater weakness, inferiority of knowledge or virtue, or in the natural affection felt for them, but are in the general the natural equals of their rulers. Hence, the argument from the family to the commonwealth to prove that it is monarchial, utterly fails. 2d. The chosen form given by God to the Hebrew Commonwealth was not monarchial, but republican. And when he reluctantly gave them a king, the succession was not hereditary, but virtually elective, as witness the cases of David, Jeroboam, Jehu, &c. 3. The New Testament does not limit its teachings to the religious obligation to obey *kings*, but says generally: "the Powers that be are ordained of God:" "There is no power but of God," thus giving the religious source, equally to the authority of kings and constables, and giving it to any form of government which providentially existed *de facto*. The thing then which God ordains is not a particular form of government, but that men shall maintain some form of government. Last, it is peculiarly fatal to the Legitimatist theory that the actual government of Rome, which the New Testament immediately enjoined christians to obey, was not a legitimate nor a hereditary monarchy, but one very lately formed in the usurpation of Octavius Cæsar, and not in a single instance transmitted by descent, so far as Paul's day.

THE RULER FOR THE PEOPLE.—On the contrary, while we emphatically ascribe the *fact* of civil government and the obligation to obey it, to the will of God, we also assert that in the secondary sense, the government is potentially the people. The original source of the power, the authority and the obligation to obey it, is God; the human source is not an irresponsible Ruler, but the body of the ruled themselves, that is, the sovereignty, so far as it is human, resides in the people, and is held by the rulers, by *delegation from them*. It is, indeed, the ordinance of the supreme God, *that such delegation should be made*, and the power so delegated be obeyed, by each individual; but still the power, so far as it is human, is the people's power, and not the ruler's. This is proved by two facts. All the citizens have a *general native equality*; they possess a common title, in the general, to the benefits of existence, as being all human beings and children of a common creator. They are all alike under the *golden rule*, which is God's great charter of a general equality. Hence the second fact, that the government is for the *governed*, not for the especial benefit of the *governors*. The object of the institution, which God had in view, was the good of the community. The people are not for the rulers, but the rulers for the people. This is expressly stated by Paul, Rom. 13: 3–4. Now, as before stated, the rulers have no monopoly of sense, virtue, experience, natural right, over their fellow-citizens; and hence the power of selecting rulers should be in the citizens.

SOCIAL CONTRACT REFUTED.—1. NOT FOUNDED ON FACTS.—Having thus cleared the Scriptural theory from the odious perversions of the advocates of "legitimacy," I proceed to affirm it against the vain dream of a social contract, and the theory of obligation based upon it. 1st. It is notoriously false to the actual facts. Civil government is not only a theory, but *a fact;* the origin of it can therefore be only found in a fact, not in a legal fiction. The fact is, that men never rightfully existed for one moment in the state of independent insulation, out of which they are supposed to have passed, by their own option, into a state of society. God never gave them such independency. Their responsibility to Him, and their civic relations to fellow-men, as ordained by God, are as *native* as their existence is. They do not *choose* their civic obligations, but are *born* under them; just as a child is born to his filial obligations. And the simple, practical proof is, that if one man were now to *claim this option* to assume civic relations and obligations, or to decline them, and so forego the advantages of civic life, any civilized government on earth would laugh his claim to scorn, and would immediately *compel* his allegiance by force. The mere assumption of such an attitude as that imagined for the normal one of man, and of the act in which it is supposed government legitimately originates, would constitute him an *outlaw;* a being whom every civil society claims *a natural right to destroy, the right of self-preservation.*

ATHEISTIC.—2d. The theory is atheistic, utterly ignoring man's relation to his Creator, the right of that Creator to determine under what obligations man shall live; and the great Bible fact, that God *has* determined he shall live under civic obligations.

NOT INDUCTIVE.—3d. It is utterly unphilosophical in that, while the ethics of government should be an inductive science, this theory is, and by its very nature must be, utterly devoid of experimental evidence! Hence it has no claims to be even entertained for discussion, *in foro scientiae.*

INCONSISTENT.—4th. If the authority of laws and constitutions and magistrates originates in the social contract, then certain most inconvenient and preposterous consequences would logically follow. One is, that however inconvenient and even ruinous, the institutions of the country might become, by reason of the changes of time and circumstance, no majority could ever righteously change them, against the will of any minority; for the reason that the inconveniences of a bargain which a man has voluntarily made, are no justification for his breaking it. The righteous man must not change, though he has "sworn to his own heart."—Another inconvenience would be, that it could never be settled what were the terms agreed upon in the original social contract; and what part of the existing laws were the accretions of time and of unwarranted power, save where the original constitution was in writing. A worse consequence would be, that if the compact originated the obligation to obey the civil magistrate, then any one unconstitutional or unjust act of the ruler would break that compact. But when broken by one side, it is broken for both, and allegiance would be wholly voided.

Last: The civil magistrate is armed with some powers, which could not have been created by a social contract alone, because they did not belong to the contracting parties, viz: individual men to give, for instance, the right of life and death. No man's life belongs to him, but to God alone. He cannot transfer what does not belong to him; nor will it do to say, that although the individual may not have the right to delegate away a power over his own life which he does not possess, yet the community may be justified in assuming it, by the law of self-preservation. For *there is no community* as yet, until this theory of its derivation from a social contract is established. There is only a number of individual, unrelated, independent men.

Natural Liberty what?—Civil Liberty how differing?—II. To elucidate and establish these ideas farther, let us inquire what is the true difference between man's natural liberty and his civil liberty. The advocates of the theory of a social compact seem to consider, as indeed some of them define, men's natural liberty to be *a freedom to do what they please.* They all say that Government limits or restrains it somewhat, the individual surrendering a part in order to have the rest better protected. Hence it follows, that all government, even the republican, being of the nature of restraint, is in itself a natural evil, and a natural infringement on right, to be endured only as an expedient for avoiding the greater evil of anarchy! Well might such theorists deduce the consequence that there is no *ethical* ground for obedience to government, except the implied assent of the individual; the question would be, whether it is not a surrender of duty to come under such an obligation? They also, of course, confound a man's *natural rights* and *natural liberties* together; they would be still more consistent, if, with their great inventor, Hobbes, they denied that there was any such thing as *rights,* distinct from might, until they were factitiously created by the restraints of civil government.

Radical Theory false.—True stated.—This view I consider, although embraced in part by the current of christian moralists, is only worthy of an atheist, who denies the existence of any original relations between the Creator and creature, and of any original moral distinctions. It ignores the great fact, that man's will never was his proper law; it simply passes over, in the insane pride of human perfectionism, the great fact of original sin, by which every man's will is more or less inclined to do unrighteousness. It falsely supposes a state of nature, in which man's might makes his right; whereas no man is righteously entitled to exist in that state for one instant. But if you would see how simple and impregnable is the Bible theory of natural and civil liberty, take these facts, undisputed by any christian. The rule of action is moral: moral obligations are *as original* (as natural) as man himself. The practical source and measure of them is God's will. That will, *ab initio*, binds upon man certain relations and duties which he owes to God and to his fellow man; and also defines his rights, i. e., those things which it is the duty of other beings to allow him to have and do. Man *enters* existence with those moral relations resting, by God's will, upon him. And a part of that will, as taught by His law and providence, is, that man shall be a member of and obey civil government. Hence, *government is as natural as man is.* What then is a man's natural liberty? I answer: it is *freedom to do whatever he has a moral right to do.* Freedom to do whatever a man is physically able to do, is not a liberty of nature or law, but a natural license, a *natural iniquity.* What is civil liberty then? I reply still, it is (under a *just* government) freedom to do whatever a man has a moral right to do. Perhaps no government is perfectly just. Some withhold more, some fewer of the citizens moral rights: more withhold them all. Under all governments there are some rights left; and so some liberty. A fair and just government would be one that would leave to each subject of it, in the general, (excepting exceptional cases of incidental hardship,) freedom to do whatever he had a moral right to do, and take away all other, so far as secular and civic acts are concerned. Such a government then would not restrain the natural liberty of the citizens at all. Their natural would be identical with their civic liberty. Government then does not originate our *rights,* neither can it take them away. Good government does originate our *liberty* in a practical sense, i. e., it secures the exercise of it to us.

NO NATURAL RIGHT SACRIFICED TO JUST GOVERNMENT.—The instance most commonly cited, as one of a natural right surrendered to civil society, is the right of self-defence. We accept the instance, and assert that it fully confirms our view. For if it means the liberty of forcible defence at the time the unprovoked aggression is made, that is not surrendered; it is allowed under all enlightened governments fully. If it mean the privilege of a savage's retaliation, I deny that any human ever had such a right by nature. "Vengeance is mine, saith the Lord." If it mean the privilege to attach the righteous temporal penalty, and execute it ourselves, on the aggressor, so as to deter him and others from similar assaults, I deny that this is naturally a *personal* right; for nothing is more *unnatural* than for a man to be judge in his own case. Other instances of supposed loss of natural rights are alleged with more plausibility: as when a citizen is restrained by law from selling his corn out of the country, (a thing naturally moral *per se*) from some economic motive of public good; and yet the righteous citizen feels bound to obey. I reply: if the restriction of the government is not unjust, then there exists such a state of circumstances among the fellow citizens that the sale of the corn out of the county *under those circumstances*, would have been a *natural* breach of the law of righteousness and love towards them. So that, under the particular state of the case, the man's natural right to sell his corn had terminated. *Natural rights may change with circumstances.*

NATURAL EQUALITY WHAT?—GOLDEN RULE.—Here we may understand, in what sense "all men are by nature *free and equal.*" Obviously no man is by nature free, in the sense of being born in possession of that vile license to do whatever he has will and physical ability to do, which the infidel moralists understand by the sacred name of *liberty*. For every man is *born* under obligation to God, to his parents, and to such form of government as may providentially be over his parents. (I may add, the obligation to ecclesiastical government is also native.) But all men have a native title to that liberty which I have defined, viz: *freedom to do what they have a moral right to do*. But as rights differ, the amount of this freedom to which given men have a natural title, varies in different cases. But all men are alike in this; that they all have the same general right by nature, to enjoy their own natural *quantum* of freedom, be it what it may. Again: are all men naturally equal in strength, in virtue, in capacity, or in rights? The thought is preposterous. The same man does not even continue to have the same natural rights all the time. The female child is *born* with a different set of rights in part, from the male child of the same parents; because born to different native capacities and natural relations and duties. In what then are men naturally *equal?* I answer, first: in their common title to the several *quantums* of liberty appropriate to each, differing as they do in different men; second, they are equal in their common humanity, and their common share in the obligations and benefits of the *golden rule*. All men are reciprocally bound to love their neighbors as themselves; and to do unto others, as they would that others should do to them. Here is the great charter of Bible republicanism. Men have by nature, a general equality in this; not a specific one. Hence, the *general* equality of nature will by no means produce a literal and universal equality of civil condition; for the simple reason that the different classes of citizens have very different specific rights; and this grows out of their differences of sex, virtue, intelligence, civilization, &c., and the demands of the common welfare. Thus, if the low grade of intelligence, virtue and civilization of the African in America, disqualify him for being his own guardian, and if his own true welfare (taking the 'general run' of cases) and that of the community, would be plainly marred by this freedom; then the law decides *correctly*, that the African here has *no natural right* to his self-control, as to his own labour and locomotion. Hence, his natural liberty is only that which remains after that privilege is retrenched. Still he *has* natural rights, (to marriage, to a livelihood from his own labour, to the Sabbath, and to the service of God, and immortality, &c., &c). Freedom to enjoy all these, constitutes *his natural liberty*, and if the laws violate any of it *causelessly*, they are unjust.

PROPER SPHERE OF CIVIL GOVERNMENT.—III. The two remaining questions are more practical, and may be discussed more briefly. We *discard* the theocratic conception of civil government. The proper object of it is, in general, to secure to man his life, liberty, and property, i. e. his *secular* rights. Man's intellectual and spiritual concerns belong to different jurisdictions; the parental and the ecclesiastical. The evidence is, that the parental, and the ecclesiastical departments of duty and right are separately recognized by Scripture and distinctly fenced off, as independent circles. (See also Jno. 18: 35, 36; Luk. 12: 14; 2 Cor. 10: 4; Matt. 22: 21). The powers of the civil magistrate then, are limited by righteousness, (not always by facts) to these general functions, *regulating and adjudicating all secular rights, and protecting all members of civil society in their enjoyment of their several proper shares thereof.* This general function *implies* a number of others; prominently, these three: taxation, punishment, including *capital* for capital crimes, and defensive war. For the first, (see Matt. 22: 21; Rom. 13: 6, 7;) for the second, (see Gen. 9: 5, 6; Numb. 35: 33: Rom. 13: 1-5;) for the third, (Ex. 17: 9 and *passim* in Old Testament; Luke 3: 14, 15; Acts 10· 1,2.) The same thing follows from the power of capital punishment. Aggressive war is wholesale murder. The magistrate who is charged with the sword, to avenge and prevent domestic murder, is *a fortiori* charged to punish and prevent the foreign murderer.

DUTY OF CHRISTIANS TO UNJUST CIVIL GOVERNMENT.—But, few governments are strictly just; and the inquiry therefore arises: How shall the christian citizen act, under an oppressive command of the civil magistrate? I reply, if the act which he requires is not positively a *sin per se*, it must be obeyed, although in obeying we surrender a clear, moral right of our own. The proof is the example of the Bible Saints—the fact that the very government to which Paul and Peter challenged obedience as a christian duty, was far from being an equitable one; and the truth that a harsh and unjust government is a far less evil than the absence of all government. The duty of obedience, does not, as we have seen, spring out of our assent, nor from the government's being the one of our choice, but from the providence of God which placed us under it, coupled with the fact that government is His ordinance. If the thing commanded by the civil magistrate is positively sinful, then the christian citizen must refuse obedience, but yield submission to the penalty therefor. Of course, he is entitled, while submitting either in this or the former case, to seek the peaceable repeal of the sinful law or command; but that he is bound to disobey it in the latter case, is clear from the example of the apostles and martyrs; Acts 4: 19; 5: 29; and from the obvious consideration, that since the civil magistrate is but God's minister, it is preposterous God's power committed to him should be used to pull down God's authority. But does not the *duty* of disobeying imply that there ought to be an immunity from penalty for so doing? I reply, of course, in strict justice, there ought; but this is one of those rights which the private christian may not defend by violence against the civil magistrate. The magistrate is magistrate still, and his authority in all things, not carrying necessary guilt in the compliance, is still binding, notwithstanding his unrighteous command. To *suffer* is not *sin per se:* hence, although when he commanded you to sin, you refused, when he commands you to suffer for that refusal, you acquiesce. It should be again remembered, that an unjust government is far better than none at all. It is God's will that such a government, even, should be obeyed by individuals, rather than have anarchy. If a man holds office under a government, and the official function enjoined upon him is positive sin, it is his duty to resign, giving up his office and its emoluments along with its responsibilities, and then he has no more concern with the unrighteous law, than any other private citizen. That concern is simply to seek its repeal by constitutional means. If the majority, or other controlling force in the constitution make that appeal unattainable for him, then the private citizen is clear of the sin, and has no concern with the sinful law. He is neither bound, nor permitted to resist it by force. But for an official of government to hold office, promise official obedience, and draw his compensation therefor, and yet undertake to refuse to perform the official duties of his place, on the ground that his conscience tells him the acts are morally wrong; this is but a disgusting compound of pharisaism, avarice and perjury. Thus we have, in a nutsholl, the true doctrine of a "higher law," as distinguished from the spurious.

RIGHT OF PRIVATE JUDGMENT ASSERTED.—One more question remains: Who is to be the judge *when* the act required of the citizen by law is morally wrong? I reply, the citizen himself, in the last resort. This is the great Protestant and Scriptural *doctrine of private judgment.* We sustain it by the obvious fact, that when the issue is thus made between the government and its citizen, if that is to be absolute judge in its own case, there is an end of personal independence and liberty. But the government's judgment being thus set aside, there remains no other human umpire. 2d. Every intelligent being lies under moral relations to God, which are *immediate* and inevitable. No creature in the universe can answer for him, in a case of conscience, or step between him and his guilt. Hence, it is the most monstrous and unnatural injustice that any power should dictate to his conscience, except his divine Judge. See Prov. 9: 12; Rom. 14: 4. The clear example of Bible saints sustains this, as cited above; for while they clearly recognized the legitimacy of the magistrate's authority, they claim the privilege of private judgment in disobeying their commands to sin. If it be said that this doctrine is in danger of introducing disorder and insubordination, I answer, no; not under any government that at all desires to stand; for when the right of private judgment is thus exercised, as an appeal to God's judgment, and with the fact before our faces, that if we feel bound to disobey the law, we shall be still bound to submit meekly to the penalty, none of us will be apt to exercise the privilege too lightly.

RIGHT OF REVOLUTION DISCUSSED.—IV. Thus far, we have considered the individual action of the citizen towards an unrighteous government, and have shown that, even when constrained to disobey an unrighteous law, he must submit to the penalty. Do we then inculcate the slavish doctrine of *passive obedience*, which asserts the divine and irresponsible right of kings, so that even though they so abuse their powers that the proper ends of government are lost, God forbids resistance? By no means. To Americans, whose national existence and glory are all founded on the "right of revolution," slight arguments would probably be needed to support it. But, it is the duty of thinking men to have some better support for their opinions, than the popularity of them.

ARGUMENT FOR PASSIVE OBEDIENCE REFUTED.—The argument for passive obedience, from Romans 13th, is, at first view, plausible, but will not bear inquiry. Note that the thing which is there declared to be of divine authority, is not a particular form of government, but submission to the government, whatever it is. God has not ordained *what* government mankind shall live under, but only that they shall live under *a* government. The *end* of government is not the gratification of the rulers, but the good of the ruled. When a form of government entirely ceases, as a whole, to subserve its proper end, is it still to subsist forever? This is preposterous. Who then is to change it? The submissionists say, Providence alone. But Providence works by means. Shall those means be external force or internal force? These are the only alternatives; for of course corrupt abuses will not correct themselves, when their whole interest is to be perpetuated. External force is unauthorized; for nothing is clearer than that a nation should not interfere, uncalled, in the affairs of another. Again: we have seen that the sovereignty is in the people rather than the rulers; and that the power the rulers hold is delegated. May the people never resume their own, when it is wholly abused to their injury? There may be obviously a point then where "resistance to tyrants is obedience to God." The meaning of the apostle is, that this resistance must be the act, not of the individual, but of the people. The insubordination which he condemns, is that which arrays against a government, bad like that of the Cæsars perhaps, the worse anarchy of the individual will. But the body of the citizens *is* the commonwealth; and when the commonwealth arises and supercedes the abused authority of her public servants, the allegiance of the individual is due to her, just as before to her servants. But it may be asked, How can the commonwealth move to do this, except by the personal movement of individuals against the "powers that be?" I answer, (and this explains the true nature of the right of revolution:) true: but if the individual moves, when he is not inspired by the movement of the popular heart; when his motion is not the exponent, as well as the occasion, of theirs, he has made a mistake—he has done wrong—he must bear his guilt. It is usually said, as by Paley, that a revolution is only justifiable when the evils of the government are worse than the probable evils of the convulsive change; and when there is a reasonable prospect of success. The latter point is doubtful. Some of the noblest revolutions, as that of Tell, were rather the result of indignation at intolerable wrong, and a generous despair, than of this calculation of chances of success.

LECTURE LXXII.

SYLLABUS.

RELIGIOUS LIBERTY.

1. Establish the doctrine of Religious Liberty and the right of Private Judgment.
2. Discuss and refute the theory of Church Establishments held by Prelatists, and that of Chalmers.
3. What are the proper relations between State and Church? And what the powers and duties of the civil magistrate over ecclesiastical persons and property?
   Conf. of Faith, chap. xx. and chap. xxiii., § 3. Locke's first Letter on Toleration. Milton's Areopagitica, or Plea for the Liberty of Unlicensed Printing. Vattel, Law of Nature and Nations; book I., chap. 12. Montesquieu Esprit des Loix, book xxv. Chalmers on Church Establishments. Gladstone's Church and State. Review of Gladstone, by Lord Macaulay.

THE QUESTION NOT OBSOLETE.—I. You may suppose it superflous to lecture on a subject so well understood, and universally admitted, as this is among us; but you will be mistaken. Our ancestors understood it because they had studied it, with all the earnestness of persecuted men, who had to contend with sword and pen. We hold their correct theory; but, it is to be feared, only by prescription and prejudice. Consequence: that when temptation comes, and the theory of religious liberty seems awkward just at a particular juncture, we shall be carried about with any wind of doctrine. This is ever the course; for fundamental truths to be practically learned by one generation, handed down to the next, held by prejudice for a few generations, [the words used and sense dropped] and at last lost in practice.

Again, many, even of statesmen, do not defend Religious Liberty on sound and rational grounds. Even Brougham and Macaulay (see his History of England) seem not to have found out that the proposition, "man is not responsible for his belief," is not the same with that of Religious Liberty.

AUGUSTINE FIRST ADVOCATE OF PERSECUTION.—The arguments by which Augustine induced persecution of the Donatists have ever been the staple ones of the Roman Church, for intolerance. They are so wretched and flimsy, as to be unworthy of a separate discussion. Their answer will be apparent in the sequel. But it should be observed, that the doctrines of intolerance *are consistent*, with the claims of the Romish Church to infallibility, and supremacy. A man ought not to have liberty to destroy his own soul by refusing the infallible teachings of God, on earth. This claim of infallibility puts the relations between the unbeliever and Church, on the same footing as those between the unbeliever and his God. To both he is guilty. But is the claim of infallibility to be implicitly admitted? The answer to this question shows that a denial of the right of private judgment, is essential to the Romanists' intolerance. For if the infallibility is to be brought into question, then the basis of the right to enforce absolute conformity is melted away.

HERESY IS CRIMINAL.—A far more plausible argument for the right to enforce religious conformity has been glanced at by later Romish writers. Hard to answer by many a Protestant, who inconsiderately holds to Religious Liberty, "man *is* responsible for his belief. His religious error is not simply his misfortune, but his crime. *Bad volitions* are at the bottom. Truth *is* discoverable, certain. This crime has a very certain, though indirect evil influence; this not only on men's religious, but secular conducts and interests. The heretic injures the public morals, health, order, wealth, the value of real estate, &c., &c. He may be doing mischief on a far larger scale than the bandit. Now, if his religious belief is of a *moral* quality, voluntary and criminal; and is also mischievous—highly so; and that to the interests both Church and State protect, why not punishable? Why does it claim to be exempted from the list of offences amenable to law? The cruel abuses of the power of punishing heretics, by ignorant or savage rulers, are no argument against its use, any more than the Draconian penalties, against moderate power in the magistrate, of repressing secular crimes." Ans.

BUT FORCE NOT THE REMEDY.—Every thing which is *moral* evil, and is detrimental to the interests of society, is not, therefore, properly punishable by society (e. g. prodigality, indolence, gluttony, drunkenness). The thing must be, moreover, shown to be brought within the scope of the penalties, by the objects and purposes of Government; and the relevancy of corporeal pains and penalties to be a useful corrective; and the directness of the concern of society in its bad consequences. Society may not infringe *directly* a natural right of one of its members, to protect itself from an indirect injury which may or may not occur. It only has a right to stand on the defensive, and wait for the overt aggression. It is not the business of society to keep a man from injuring himself, but from injuring others. As to his personal interests, he is his own master. Now that religious error, though moral evil, voluntary and guilty, does not come within the above conditions, we will show, and at the same time will adduce arguments of a *positive* weight.

STATE AND CHURCH HAVE DIFFERENT OBJECTS.—1. Premise. Church and State are distinct institutions, since theocratic institutions are done away; have *distinct objects.* The Church is to teach men the way to Heaven, and to help them thither. The State is to protect each citizen in the enjoyment of temporal rights. The Church has no civil pains and penalties at command; because Christ has given her none; and because they have no relevancy whatever to produce her object—the hearty belief of saving truth (see John 18 : 36; 2 Cor. 10 : 4, &c.). The main weapon of the Civil Government *is civil pains and penalties* (Rom. 13 : 4).

STATE HAS ONLY DELEGATED POWERS.—2. Premise. In the State, the good of the governed being the object, (in temporal interests) the governed are the earthly sources of sovereignty. Rulers have only a delegated power, and are the agents of the community, who depute to them, for the general good, so much of power as is necessary.

SPIRITUAL JUDGE HAS NO CIVIL PENALTIES.—Now, for the direct argument, observe: The Church's bearing penal power, and being armed with civil pains, is utterly inconsistent with her spiritual character, her objects, and the laws of Christ. Rome herself did not claim it. When the Church persecutes, it is *through the commonwealth.* This lends its corporeal power to the Church. When Romish Priests persecute, they bear twofold capacity, magisterial and clerical.

MAGISTRATE HAS NO SPIRITUAL JURISDICTION.—I. But, by what power shall the magistrate persecute his own Sovereign? Whence delegated? All the power he has is delegated. Now a citizen cannot delegate to another the right of judging for him *what is right,* because to do so is a self-contradiction, and unutterable absurdity; and because, to do so would be a crime. For the merit of all my religious belief and acting depends on my free conscientious convictions; and God has made *me* responsible for them, so that I cannot give away the responsibility.

NOR RIGHT TO ARREST MY PRIVATE JUDGMENT.—II. By the same general fact, it appears that when intolerance commands me to surrender my private judgment in religion, it is to the *Magistrate* I surrender it; i. e., a man not sacred, nor even clerical, an officer purely secular; and even upon Romish teachings, no more entitled than me, to judge in religion. But, it is said, "the Magistrate persecutes not *for himself*, but on behalf of *a Church* infallible and divinely authorized, to which he has dutifully bowed, and lent his secular power, as he ought; so that it is to this infallible Church we are compelled by the Magistrate's sword to surrender our private judgment." No; how did the Magistrate find out that this Church is infallible? Suppose I, the subject, choose to dispute it? who shall decide between us? Not the *Church in question*; because the very question in debate between us is, whether the Church ought to be allowed a supreme authority over my, or his conscience. It is to the civil *Magistrate's* judgment, after all, that I am compelled to yield my private judgment, and that in a thing purely religious.

MAGISTRATES NOT EVEN CHRISTIANS.—3. The civil authority of the magistrate is not due to his christianity, but to his official character. This follows from the entire distinctness of the church and state in their objects and characters. Proved by Scripture asserting the civil authority of *Pagan* magistrates; Matt. 22 : 21, Rom. 13, 1 Peter 2 : 13. If we were citizens of a Mahommedan or pagan country we should owe obedience to their civil rulers in things temporal. And this shows that the authority is not dependent on the magistrate's christianity, even where he happens to be a christian. Now what an absurdity is it for that which is not christian at all to choose my christianity for me? To see this, only suppose a case where the magistrate is actually infidel. The Greeks and Protestants in Constantinople struggle with each other. The Turk, more sensible than intolerant christians, merely stands by and derides both. But suppose one of them should manage to get Him on their side, and use his temporal power to persecute their bretheren? Can a Turkish infidel, who has nothing to do with christianity, confer on one sect a power to persecute another? Confer what he has not? Outrageous. But the reason of the thing is the same in any other country; because the civil authority of the magistrate is no more due to his christianity than that of the Grand Turk in Turkey, who has no christianity.

WHICH RELIGION SHALL COERCE?—4. But suppose the persecuting church repudiates the aid of the magistrate, and claims that she herself, as a spiritual power, is entitled to wield both swords, temporal and spiritual, for suppression of error, *in person*, as Rome does in some of her more imperious moods. Then all the absurdities are incurred which arise from confounding the two opposite societies of church and state and their objects; and all the Scriptures above quoted must be defied. But other arguments still more unanswerable apply. Among competing religious communions, which shall have the right to coerce the others? Of course, the orthodox one. This is ever the ground of the claim. "I am *right* and you are *wrong:* therefore I must compel you to think as I do." But each communion is orthodox in its own eyes. Every one is erroneous to its rivals. If Rome says, there are evidences of our being the apostolic infallible church, so clear, that no one can resist them without obstinate guilt, Geneva says to Rome just the same. Whatsoever any church believes, it believes to be true. There is no umpire under God; shall the magistrate decide? He has no right. He is not religious. There is no umpire. Each one's claim to persecute is equally good. The strongest rules. Might makes right.

COERCION NOT A MEANS TO FAITH.—5. But again: The church cannot use persecution to gain her end, which is the belief of religious truth; because penalties have no relevancy whatever to beget belief. *Evidence* begets conviction; not fear and pain. While we do not think that belief or unbelief of moral truth is *of no moral character*, with Brougham, we do know that it must be the voluntary, spontaneous result of evidence, and that it must be rational. That a spiritual society, whose object is to produce moral beliefs and acts determined thereby, should do it by civil pains, is an infinite absurdity. This is enhanced by the other fact: that the virtue and efficacy of religious belief and acts before God depend wholly on their heartiness and sincerity. Feigned belief, unwilling service, are no graces, but sins. Do not save, but damn. ...... Nor do persecutions have any preparing effect to open the mind to the rational and moral means which the church is afterwards to use. This the Augustinian plea. To punish, imprison, impoverish, torment, burn a man, because he does not see your arguments as strong as you think them, is surely a strange way of making him favorable thereto! To give him the strongest cause to hate the reasoner, is a strange way to make him like the reasonings! The most likely possible way is taken to give him an ill opinion of that communion he is wished to join. These measures have some natural tendency, on weak natures, to make hypocrites; but none to make sincere believers.

PERSECUTION PREJUDICES TRUTH.—Under this head, too, notice the outrageous impolicy of persecuting measures. Supposing the doctrines persecuted to be erroneous, the very way is taken to make them popular, by arraying on their side the sentiments of injured right, virtuous indignation, sympathy with the oppressed, and in general, all the noblest principles, and to make the opposing truth unpopular, by associating it with high handed oppression, cruelty, &c. The history is, that no communion ever persecuted which did not cut its own throat thereby, unless it persecuted so as to crush and brutify wholly, and trample out all active religious life *pro* or *con* to itself. The persecuting communion dies, either by the hand of the outraged and irresistible reaction it produces; or if the persecution is thorough, by the *syncope* and atrophy of a spiritual stagnation, that leaves it a *religious* communion only in name. Of the former, the examples are the Episcopacy of Laud, in Scotland and England, Colonial Church of Virginia against Baptists, &c. Of the latter, the Popish Church of France, Spain, Italy. "The blood of the martyrs is the seed of the Church."

INTRUDES INTO GOD'S PROVINCE.—6. *All* acts of religious intolerance are inconsistent with the relations which God has established between Himself and rational souls. Here is the main point. God holds every soul directly responsible to Himself. That responsibility necessarily implies that no one shall step in between him and his God. No one can relieve him of his responsibility, answer for him to God, and bear his punishment, if he has betrayed his duty. Therefore no one should interfere to hinder his judging for himself. "What hast thou to do, to judge another man's servant?" Here it is plain how essential the claim of infallibility is to a plausible theory of persecution. For a man who acknowledges himself fallible, to intrude his leadership by force on his fellow-man, who is no more fallible than himself, when it is possible he may thereby ruin his soul, is a position as satanic as impudent. But where the persecutor can say, "I know infallibly that my way is right, and if he will come into it he will *certainly* be saved," there is a little plausibility. But if infallibility is disproved, that little is gone. And more: Each man is directly bound to his God to render a belief and service *hearty;* proceeding *primarily* from a regard to *God's* will, not man's. Else it is sin. Now how impious is he, who, professing to contend for God, thus thrusts himself between God and His creature? Substitutes fear of him for fear of God! Thrusts himself into God's place? He that does it is an anti-Christ. Man's belief is a thing sacred, inviolable.

7. Let it be added, also, that persecutions ruin that cause which they profess to promote, the cause of God, by demoralizing the persecuting community. They tend to confound and corrupt all moral ideas in the populace, who see moral, merciful, peaceful men punished with the pains due to the most atrocious crimes, because they do not take certain arguments in a certain way. They beget on the one hand subserviency, hypocrisy, cunning, falsehood and

deceit, the weapons of oppressed weakness; and on the other, cruelty, unmercifulness, rapacity, injustice. Ages of persecution have always been ages of deep moral corruption; aud where persecution has been successful, it has plunged the nations into an abyss of vice and relaxed morals.

PERSECTION AGGRAVATES DIVISIONS.—8. Again: we have hinted at the tendency of intolerance to disappoint its own ends. All history is a commentary on this. More persecution, the more sects, (except where it is so extreme as to produce a religious paralysis, and there there are no sects, because there is no belief, but only stupid apathy or secret atheism). Rome tried it to the full. And under her *regime*, christendom was more and more full of sectaries, who increased till the freedom of the Reformation extinguished them. Waldenses, Albigenses, Cathari, Paulicians, Beghards, Fratricelli, Turlupins, Brethren of Free Spirit, Wickliffeites, Hussites, &c., &c. There have always been wider divergences of doctrinal opinion, within the bosom of the Romish Church itself, than there are now, between all the evangelical branches of the Protestant family, with all their freedom. And the effect of the Reformation, (most in freest countries,) has been to kill off, or render perfectly impotent, all more extravagant and hurtful sects. Where are any *Turlupins*, or mystical Pantheists like those of Germany of the 14th Century? Where any *Schwestriones? Manichaeans?*

9. Religious sects are nearly harmless to the State, when they are no longer persecuted. It is wholly to their oppression that their supposed factiousness is due; cease to oppress, and they become mild and loyal. This is just the absurd and treacherous trick of persecutors, to say, "conventicles are *secret*," when it is their oppression which makes them secret. They would gladly be open, if they might have leave. "Conventicles are factious;" it is injustice which makes them factious. Let the State treat all sectaries justly and mildly, and they at once have the strongest motive to be true to the State; indeed, the same which the majority has; that of strongest self-interest.

COERCION HYPOCRITICAL.—10. Persecution for conscience' sake is always supremely false and hypocritical, as appears by this fact. The motive assigned by persecuting religionists is, that the souls of men may be saved from the ruinous effects of error; of the heretic himself, if he can be reclaimed; of others whom he might corrupt, at any rate. But while they have been imprisoning, tormenting, burning men of innocent morals, because they held some forbidden tenets, have they not always tolerated the grossest vices in those who would submit to the Church? Adultery, profanity, violence, ignorance, drunkenness, gluttony? Was it not so during all the Inquisition in Spain and Italy, Laud's persecutions in England, James' in Scotland? But a *bad life* is the worst heresy. Surely *this* destroys souls and corrupts communities. Why do not these men then, who so vehemently love the souls of their neighbours, that they must burn their bodies to ashes, love the vicious enough to restrain their vices? Persecution for opinion's sake is wholly a political measure cloaked under religion. Its true object always is, to *secure domination*, not to save souls.

CONCLUSION.—This, therefore, is the only safe theory. The ends of the State are for time and earth; those of the Church are for eternity. The weapon of the State is corporeal, that of the Church is spiritual. The two cannot be combined, without confounding heaven and earth. The only means that can be used to produce religious belief are moral. No man is to be visited with any civil penalty for his belief, as long as he does not directly infringe upon the purpose of the government, which is the protection of the temporal rights of his fellow-citizens. The State is bound to see that every man enjoys his religious freedom untouched, because the right to this religious freedom is a secular, or political right.

The doctrine of religious liberty was not evolved at the Reformation. Protestants held it a right and duty to persecute heretics. "Rome's guilt was that she persecuted those nearer right than herself, and did it cruelly and unjustly." The first treatise taking the true ground, as far as I know, was written by Brown (founder of sect of Brownists). Dr. Jno. Owen wrote for the same cause. Dr. Jeremy Taylor wrote his plea for liberty of prophesying.—Milton and Locke are well known. Roger Williams, of Rhode Island, perhaps deserves the credit of being the first *Ruler* in the world, who granted absolute freedom to all sects, having power to do otherwise.

CHURCH AND STATE.—THE PROTESTANT CHURCHES ALL ESTABLISHED.—II. The separation and independence of Church and State was not only not the doctrine of the Reformation. No christian nation holds it to this day, except ours. In 17th and 18th centuries some Independents and others in England, and Seceders in Scotland, advocated such separation, but were branded as outrageous radicals. All the Reformation Churches, Lutheran and Reformed, held it as an axiom, that the State had, under God, the supreme care of religion. Dissenters of England now usually hold our views, (as well as Seceders in Scotland), called there *voluntaryism*. The Free Church at the head of whom was Dr. Chalmers, held to establshments. Ours is the first fair trial.

ESTABLISHMENTS JUSTIFIED BY TWO THEORIES.—THE PRELATIC.—Two theories of Church establishments prevail among nominal Protestants. The higher is that squinted at briefly in Vattel, Bk. I. Ch. 12, § 129, and more fully developed by Gladstone, Church and State, Chap. 2. That the government is instituted for the highest good of the whole in every concern, and is bound to do all it has in its reach for this object in *every* department. That a commonwealth is a *moral person*, having a personality, judgment, conscience, responsibility, and is therefore bound, *as a body*, to recognize and obey the true religion. Hence the *State* must have its religion, *as a State*. This a necessary duty of its corporate or individual nature. Hence it must profess this, by *State acts*. It must of course have a religious *test* for office, because otherwise the religious character of the State would be lost; and it must use its *State power* to propagate this State religion.

Let us discuss the abstract grounds of this theory first; then take up the second, or freer theory of Church establishments, and conclude with some *general* historical views applicable to both theories.

VATTEL'S VIEW.—1. Says Vattel: "If all men are bound to serve God, the entire nation in her national capacity is doubtless bound to serve and honour Him. This is based on a general principle: that all men are *everywhere* bound by laws of nature; and therefore the entire nation, whose common will is but the united wills of all the members, must be bound by these natural laws; because the accident of *association* cannot release men from bonds that are *universal*." (See § 5.) This is true in *a sense*, but not *the* sense necessary to prove a state religion obligatory. So far as any acts of any associated body of men have any moral or religious character, they should conform to the same moral and religious rules, by which the individuals are bound. But (a.) the obligation is nothing else but the individual obligation of all the members, and nothing more is needed to defend or sanction it than their individual morality and religiousness. And (b) there are associations whose objects are not directly religious, but secular. How can they appropriately have a *corporate* religious character, when their corporate character has no direct reference to religion.

GLADSTONE'S VIEW.—Gladstone puts the same argument substantially, calling it his *ethical* argument. "A State is a corporation. It has personality, judgment, reason, foresight. Its acts have moral character. The only safe and sufficient basis of morals is christianity; therefore they should have christian character. All things we do have religious relations and responsibilities; therefore the acts of rulers as such, should have a christian character. In a word, a State is a *moral person*, corporately regarded, and like any other person, must have its personal christian character. Else it is antichristian, and atheistic." Mr. Macaulay, (Ed. Review, 1839,) so terribly damaged this argument, by pointing out that, by this reasoning, it was made the duty of armies, Banking, Insurance, Gas, Railroad, Stage Coach companies, Art Unions, incorporate clubs, &c., &c., to have a corporate religion (consider the absurdities,) that in his second edition, the author modified and fortified it. "*These* corporations are trivial, partial. Everybody not bound to belong to one; their operations not far reaching, not of divine appointment, temporary. But there are *two* natural associations of men, alike in these three fundamental traits. They are of divine appointment; they are perpetual; they embrace everybody, i. e., every human being is bound to belong to them; they are the *family* and the *State*. All good men admit that the family ought to have a family religion. The State, a similar institution, a larger family, ought to have a State-religion."

This is the only ingenious and plausible thing in his book. The nature of the reasoning compels us to discuss the fundamental questions as to the constitution and objects of civil society. For our answer must take this shape. *The family association is wholly dissimilar from the commonwealth; because its direct objects are not the same. The source and nature of the authority are not the same. There is not the same inferiority in the governed to the governors; and there is not the same affection and interest.*

(Remember, however, the fact that *all* men are bound to be members of some family and State, has no relevancy to prove that these associations must have religious corporate character, unlike all other partial societies. Nor does the fact that they are not voluntary, but of divine appointment; because under certain circumstances, it may be of divine appointment that men should belong to an army; and this does not prove that an army ought to profess a religion as such).

State and Church have Different Ends.—The object of the family as to children, is to promote their *whole welfare*. The object of civil government is simply *the protection of temporal rights* against aggression, foreign or domestic. But this is just the view which all claimants for high powers in governments deny. Like Mr. Gladstone, they claim that the proper view of government is, that it is an association intended to take in hand *all* the interests and welfare of human beings, of every kind; everything in which man is interested, and in which *combination* can aid in success, is the proper *end* of human government. It is το παν? The total human association. Now, the plain answers to this are three: the Bible says the contrary. Rom. 13:4. It is utterly impracticable; for, by the necessary imperfection of human nature, an agency which is best adapted to one function must be worst adapted to others; and an association which should do every thing, would be sure to do all in the worst possible manner. But last, and chiefly; if this is true, then there cannot be any other association of human beings, except as it is a *part* and *creature* of the State. There is no Church. The State *is* the Church, and ecclesiastical persons and assemblies are but *magistrates* engaged in one part of their functions. There is no such thing as the family, an independent, original institution of divine appointment. The parent is but the delegate of the government, and when he applies the birch to the child, it is in fact, by State authority! All combinations, to trade, to do banking business, to teach, to preach, to navigate, to buy pictures, to nurse the sick, to mine, &c., &c., are parts and creatures of the State! Or if it be said that the State, though it has the right to do every thing, is not bound to do every thing, unless she finds it convenient and advantageous, then the ethical argument is relinquished; and the ground of *expediency* assumed, on which we will remark presently. But the ethical argument fails, also.

(a.) In this: That it makes it the right and duty of the Sultan to establish Mohammedanism; the King of Spain, Popery; Queen Victoria, Prelacy; the Emperor of China, Boodhism, &c. Julian was right in ousting Christians, Theodosius, Platonists, Constantius, Athanasians; Jovian, Arians. For if the State is a moral person, bound to have and promote its religion, the Sovereign must choose his religion conscientiously. The one *he* believes right, he must enforce. This is admitted by the advocates. Now, of all the potentates on earth, there is but *one*, that would conscientiously advocate what these men think the right religion—Prelacy. How sensible is that theory which, in the present state of the world, would ensure the teaching of errors, by all the authority of the governments over all the world, except in one kingdom?

HENCE, AGENCIES OF ONE UNFIT FOR OTHER.—(b.) If strictly carried out, it would ensure the worst governing, and the worst preaching, possible. An organization intended for a particular end, should choose agents best adapted to subserve *that end*, irrespective of other things. Otherwise, it will be miserably inefficient. And if it is best organized for that end, it must, for that very reason, be ill adapted to a different end. Hence, there should be no jumbling of functions; but each institution should be left to subserve its own objects. Suppose the British Government act out this theory. It must say to the skillful and honest financier: "You shall not help in my treasury, because you do not believe in Apostolic Succession;" to the Presbyterian General: "I will have none of your courage and skill to release my armies from probable destruction, because you listen to a preacher who never had a Prelate's hands on his head;" to the faithful pilot: "You shall not steer one of my ships off a lee shore, because you take the communion sitting," &c. How absurd; and how utter the failure of a government thus conducted!

(c.) By the same reason that it is the duty of the State to use a part of its power to propagate its religion, it is its duty to use all; and the doctrine of persecution for opinion's sake is necessary inference. For the State has power to fine, imprison, kill.

No Church Established to Control Clergy.—II. (Before we proceed to the more plausible and liberal theory advanced by Vattel, Warburton, Chalmers, &c., let us notice a point urged by the first mentioned, in § 139, &c.: That there must be à connexion between Church and State, in order that the Sovereign may have control over ecclesiastics and religion. If men wielding such immense spiritual influences, are not held in official subordination to the Chief Ruler, he cannot govern the country. It would be a sufficient reply to say that Vattel knew Church officers, chiefly as Papists. Take away their power of the keys, their exemption from civil jurisdiction, and their ecclesiastical dependence on a foreign Pope, and the difficulty is gone. The minister of religion should be a *citzen*, subject to all laws, liable to be punished for any *overt* crime committed or prompted by him. This is subordination enough. As for the power still left him to inculcate doctrines of dangerous *tendency*, unchecked by the State, the proper defence is free discussion. The medicine of error is not violent repression, but *light*. Let the Ruler content himself with protecting and diffusing free discussion. And again, Vattel's argument may, with equal justice, be extended to political teachers; and then the freedom of the press and of speech is gone).

Chalmer's View.—But we come now to what we may call the Chalmerian theory. "The proper object of civil government is man's secular well-being. But the right to prosecute this, implies the right to perform all those functions which are essential to the main end—yea, the duty. Public *morals* are essential to the public welfare. The only source of public morals is Christianity. Christianity will not be sufficiently diffused, unless the State lends its aid and means to do it. Therefore it is right, yea, binding, that the State shall enter into an alliance with Christianity (in that *form* or *forms* best adapted to the end), to teach its citizens religion and morals, as a necessary means for the public good. To fail to do so, is for the State to betray its charge."

The contested point here, is in these propositions: That "voluntaryism" will usually fail to diffuse a sufficient degree of public morals; and that a State-endowed Church, or churches, of good character and spiritual independence will do it far better. And on this point, all the *divisions* of "Dissent," splitting up of small communities until the congregations are all too small to sustain themselves, the insufficiency of funds furnished by voluntary contribution, are urged, &c., &c.

Voluntaryism most Efficient.—Now, here we join issue, and assert; in the first place, that an endowed Church, on this plan, will usually effect less for true religion and public morals, than voluntary Churches, notwithstanding these difficulties. For remember that the State is, in fact, and *must* usually be, *non-religious;* i. e., the Rulers themselves will usually have a personal character irreligious, carnal, anti-evangelical. What is the *fact?* How is the composition of governments determined? By the sword, or by intrigue, by party tactics, by political and forensic skill, by the demands of secular interests and measures, by bribery, by riches and family, by everything else than grace. It *must* be so; for the assumed necessity for a State endowment and alliance is in the fact that the community is yet prevalently irreligious, and needs to be made religious. Now, all just government is representative. It must reflect the national character. To disfranchise, and shut out of office, citizens, because carnally minded, would be an absurd and impracticable injustice in the present state of communities. Now remember (Rom. 8:7): This enmity is innate, instinctive, spontaneous. If the *State* selects preachers, some individual officers of the State selects them; and the least evangelical will most frequently be selected. Natural affinities of feeling will operate. Here, then, is one usual result of a Church establishment; that of the men who are nominal members of the Church endowed, the least evangelical and useful will receive the best share of all that influence, power and money which the State bestows. Exceptions; this is the general rule. What says History? Arians under Roman Empire; under Leuton Princes, High Church Arminians; worldly men; semi-Papists in England; Arminians in Holland; Moderates in Scotland.

Clergy tempted by Ease.—Again: The pecuniary support will be liberal and certain. Its tenure will be the favor of the Rulers; not of God's people. Hence carnally minded men will infallibly be attracted into the ministry by mercenary motives; and *the most mercenary will be the most pushing*. Hence progressive deterioration of the endowed ministry, as in English and all Popish and Lutheran churches. Shall we be pointed to large infusion of excellent men in English and Scotch establishments? We answer, that their continuance is mainly due to the wholesome competition of Dissent. (Just the contrary of the plea, that the Establishment is worth its cost, by its wholesome influence in stimulating dissent.) And the proof is, that wherever dissent has been thoroughly extinguished, the leaden weight of State patronage has in every case, brought down the endowed clergy to the basest depths of mercenary character, and most utter inefficiency for all good. E. G., Spain, France, Italy, Austria, Russia.

Endowment Unfair and Oppressive.—Again: Just as soon as any Church is endowed, it is put in an oppressive attitude towards all that part of the community who do not belong to it, so that prejudice will prevent much of usefulness in its ministrations to them, and perpetually stimulate secession. That I should be taxed to pay for the preaching of doctrines which I do not believe or approve, is of the nature of an oppression. That my minister should have no lot nor part in the manse and salary provided at the common expense, but monopolized by another man who is willing to endorse some doctrine which I think erroneous, is an odious distinction. Indeed, it might be urged, as an independent argument against the mildest form of Church Establishment, that it implies *some* degree of oppression for opinion's sake; it makes the State a judge, when it has no business to judge, and exercises partiality, where there should be equality. Nor will it at all answer to attempt to elude this difficulty, as in the colonial government of Massachusetts; because this would enlist the State in the diffusion of error and truth alike, a thing wicked; and it gives to the worst forms of nominal christianity a strength they would not otherwise have, because all the "Nothingarians," being compelled to support some Church, elect the one that has least religion.

And once more: The only fair experiment of full religious liberty, without Church and State, that of our country, proves, so far, that the voluntary system is more efficient than the endowed, in adequately supplying the growing wants of a nation. Let all denominations enjoy complete freedom and equality, and their differences become practically less, they approximate to a virtual unity and peace on an evangelic ground, and their emulation and zeal do far more than the State could do. The fact is, that this day, notwithstanding our heterogeneous people, and immense growth, we have more gospel, in proportion to our wants, than any except Scotland. And in England and Scotland almost all the enterprise, which has kept up with growth and evangelized new districts, has been either dissenting, or a sort of voluntaryism among Established Church people; as in getting up the *Quoad Sacra* chapels in Scotland. *Our success* is the grand argument against State churches.

THE ENDOWED CLERGY MUST BE RESPONSIBLE TO THE STATE.—But, second, and more conclusive. This union, on this theory, between Church and State, necessitates the surrender of the Church's spiritual independence. It can no longer preserve its allegiance to Jesus Christ perfect. The necessity of this allegiance we will not stop to prove. If the State employs a denomination to teach its subjects religion and morals, it is bound to have them well taught. The magistrate owes it to his constituents to see that the public money is well spent in teaching what shall be for the public good. And whether the doctrine taught is so or not, the magistrate must be the sovereign judge under God. In other words, the preachers of this State Church are, in their ministerial functions, State officials, and, of course, should be subordinate, as to those functions, to the State. Responsibility must bind back to the source whence the office comes. But now where is this minister's allegiance to Christ? Whenever it happens that the magistrate differs from *his* conscience, he can only retain his fidelity to his Master by dissolving his State connexion.

INSTANCE IN FREE CHURCH OF SCOTLAND.—This was completely verified in the disruption of the Scotch Establishment. The British government claimed jurisdiction over spiritual affairs, which they supported by their salaries. The faithful men of the Free Church found that the only way to retain their allegiance to Christ was to relinquish their connexion with the State. When the secession churches now exclaimed: "Here is an illustration of the incompatibility of spiritual independence and church establishments." The Free Church men answered, "No. We admit that the jurisdiction of the State and its courts is just as to the temporal emoluments of a parish, but deny it as to the care of souls, or fitness for that care." But does not a suit about *pay* for value received necessarily bring into court the nature of the value received? Must not the magistrate who decides on the *quid* decide on the *pro quo?* The right of the State is, to present to the Parish, and not to the salary of the Parish, only. The State has the same right to see the parochial duties performed by whom she pleases, as the salary enjoyed by whom she pleases.

CHRISTIAN STATE NO THEOCRACY.—3. In the incipiency of the English Establishment, the grand appeal of its advocates was to the example of the Israelitish kingdom, where State and Church were united so intimately. Hence were drawn all the arguments nearly for the King's headship over the Church. Hence Calvin's idea of State and Church. Nor is the argument yet given up. But the answer is, that a theocratic State is no rule for a State not theocratic. When a State can be shown, where there is but one denomination to choose, and that immediately organized by God himself just then: where there is an assurance of a succession of inspired prophets to keep this denomination on the right track; where the king who is to be at the head of this State Church is supernaturally nominated by God, and guided in his action by an oracle, then we will admit the application of the case.

In conclusion: The application for such an alliance does not always come from the side of the Church. Commonwealths have sometimes been fonder of leaning on the Church than the Church on commonwealths. Do not suppose that this question will never again be practical.

CPSIA information can be obtained
at www.ICGtesting.com
Printed in the USA
LVHW041947130323
741532LV00001B/290

9 783382 117443